ELVES

Long have the elves defended the world against the depredations of Chaos. From their island home of Ulthuan, far to the west of the Old World, the high elves control a terrible magic vortex that drain the power of the Dark Gods from the world, keeping it safe for all life. And from the restless forest of Athel Loren, the wood elves and their forest spirit allies keep a watch on the lands of men, ruthlessly attacking wherever the taint of the Ruinous Powers is found.

Defenders of Ulthuan – An alliance between the dark elves of Naggaroth, sundered kin of the proud high elves, and the dread powers of Chaos brings war to the island kingdom of Ulthuan itself. As phalanxes of dark elf warriors and hordes of savage northmen swarm across the land, the fate of all the elves – and the world itself – may lie in the hands of two brothers, separated by fate, treachery and their love for the same woman.

Sons of Ellyrion – Ulthuan is a land at the verge of destruction. As a fell army marches against the elven defenders, two brothers fight for forgiveness. But as the scale of the dark elves' plan becomes clear – to destroy the magical vortex that holds the power of Chaos at bay – the pair must set their differences aside and unite to save not only Ulthuan, but the entire world from the machinations of the Ruinous Powers.

Guardians of the Forest – A human knight is plunged into a strange, mystic realm when he joins forces with wood elves who are fighting to defend their forest home from marauding beastmen. As the forces of magic run wild, can elves and humans put aside their differences for long enough to defeat the forces of Chaos?

This omnibus also contains the short stories 'Kinstrife', 'Deathmasque' and 'Freedom's Home or Glory's Grave'.

A WARHAMMER OMNIBUS

ELVES

GRAHAM MCNEILL

BLACK LIBRARY

A Black Library Publication

Kinstrife first published in *The Cold Hand of Betrayal*,
copyright © 2006, Games Workshop Ltd.
Defenders of Ulthuan copyright © 2007, Games Workshop Ltd.
Sons of Ellyrion copyright © 2011, Games Workshop Ltd.
Deathmasque first published in *Black Library Live 2011 Chapbook*,
copyright © 2011, Games Workshop Ltd.
Guardians of the Forest copyright © 2005, Games Workshop
Freedom's Home or Glory's Grave first published in *Tales of the Old World*,
copyright © 2007, Games Workshop
All rights reserved.

This omnibus edition published in Great Britain in 2013 by
Black Library,
Games Workshop Ltd.,
Willow Road,
Nottingham, NG7 2WS, UK.

10 9 8 7 6 5 4 3 2 1

Cover illustration by Daren Horley

Maps by Nuala Kinrade and Karl Kopinski

© Games Workshop Limited 2013. All rights reserved.

A CIP record for this book is available from the British Library.

UK ISBN13: 978 1 84970 320 8
US ISBN13: 978 1 84970 321 5

See Black Library on the internet at

www.blacklibrary.com

Find out more about Games Workshop
and the world of Warhammer at

www.games-workshop.com

Printed and bound by CPI Group (UK) Ltd, Croydon, CR0 4YY

An ancient and proud race, the high elves hail from Ulthuan, a mystical island of rolling plains, rugged mountains and glittering cities.

Ruled over by the noble Phoenix King, Finubar, and the Everqueen, Alarielle, Ulthuan is a land steeped in magic, renowned for its mages and fraught with blighted history. Great seafarers, artisans and warriors the high elves protect their ancestral homeland from enemies near and far. None more so than from their wicked kin, the dark elves, against whom they are locked in a bitter war that has lasted for centuries.

In the haunted forest of Athel Loren, the wood elves live in uneasy accord with the spites, dryads and tree-kin that inhabit the deepest groves. Ruled by the demigods Orion and Isha – fusions of elf and forest spirit whose very existence holds their fragile alliance together – the wood elves and their sylvan allies defend their realm from encroachment by outsiders through subtle magic and brutal warfare.

Few who enter the trackless depths of Athel Loren ever emerge, and none of those who do survive unchanged.

CONTENTS

INTRODUCTION

What is it about elves that keeps writers coming back to them? Is it their beauty and sheer otherworldliness or the fact that their skills are so far beyond anything a human could manage? Is it the fact that they possess knowledge spanning millennia? Or is it just that they look cool with a bow and arrow? For me, it was all those things. Elves have been a staple of fantasy fiction for many years now, even before Professor Tolkien more or less defined them for the modern readership of fantasy fiction.

Of course elves have existed in various forms in fiction throughout the history of storytelling, from the elves of Lord Dunsanay, through various Celtic incarnations of the Sidhe and Germanic mythology all the way back to the Old Norse tradition of the Eddur. They've been an enduring element of fantasy for decades and have changed many times from supernatural creatures of, more or less, positive aspect to troublesome beings of malicious pranks and mischief-making and back again. I think this is what makes elves so interesting to write, as they have a rich pedigree of mythology to draw upon. Tolkien's work set the template for elves for a long time, and casts a large shadow under which elves in fantasy fiction can either bask or be rendered down to cheap imitations.

What I love about Warhammer elves is that they draw from all these varied aspects of elf mythology. They have their cake and eat it in many respects. Favoured children of the gods, they have the knowledge and poise of divine beings, but are wilful, capricious and capable of dark and bloody acts of violence. And that's just the ones we think of as the 'good' elves.

In the years before I came to write *Guardians of the Forest*, I'd had no interest in writing about them. They didn't interest me as a race and their background didn't have the jagged edges that attracted me to other races of the Warhammer World. That all changed when the Design Studio started work on the new wood elf book and I saw what the guys next to me were doing with the artwork, background and models. I was hooked by the darker imagery, the spikier personality of the elves and the more threatening vibe they had. The more I heard and saw of this emerging book, the more I saw the wood elves taking on the darker quality of old elves, I knew I wanted to tell a story of them.

Guardians of the Forest is a book that shows the magical nature of the elves, but to really highlight that aspect, it needed a human viewpoint character to experience that, hence the inclusion of the Bretonnian knight, Leofric Carrard. He would be the reader's eyes and ears in this place of wondrous magic and sudden cruelty, where an intruder's life hung on a slender thread of life or death. I always intended to go back and tell more stories of the inhabitants of Athel Loren, but never quite got round to it (though I did tell a tale of Leofric's further adventures in *Freedom's Home or Glory's Grave*). Instead, I turned to the high elves, thinking that, if I could be surprised and reawakened to the potential for cool stories about the wood elves, then surely the same would be true of the high elves.

I didn't much like the high elves either, as they seemed to be without the grittiness of the revitalised wood elves, but when I re-read their original background I saw a culture that was deeply divided and tragically flawed; fertile ground for exciting tales. The first piece I wrote was *Kinstrife*, a short story for *The Cold Hand of Betrayal* anthology. Like a lot of my stories, it was planned as a one-off, but as it told itself, it became clear there was great milage to be had with Caelir, Eldain and Rhianna. From the seeds sown in that story came the plot of *Defenders of Ulthuan* and *Sons of Ellyrion*, a two-parter that describes a terrifying invasion of Ulthuan by the dark elves of Naggaroth.

Defenders came out several years before I got the chance to write *Sons*, but it took no time at all to get back into the mindset of the two brothers and the war their conflict had helped unleash. I think writing *Sons of Ellyrion* was the most fun I've ever had with a novel, as it had a scope and scale that shifted from the mighty events shaping the future of Ulthuan to the intimate events between two brothers with a gulf of betrayal between them. And given that it deals with a massive invasion of dark elves, it allowed me to play with some of the mightiest elven heroes; Tyrion, Teclis, the Everqueen, Finubar and, most fun of all – Eltharion the Grim.

Eltharion quickly emerged as my favourite of the high elf characters to write. So much so that I decided to tell a story for the 2011 Black Library

Live chapbook about him. That story, *Deathmasque*, is one that explores a moment in Eltharion's life where he sees that there's a choice between remaining mired in despair or embracing the possibility of hope. What choice he makes will, I hope, be a story for a future time.

Of course, there's one glaring omission from this omnibus of elves, and that's a novel about the dark elves. Now, I absolutely love the dark elf background, the horror, the bloody intrigue and their scheming, murderous evil, so why didn't I write a book about them? Two words. Malus Darkblade. Dan Abnett and Mike Lee did such a great job with those stories, that I didn't feel there was a need to write more about them.

But there's been a few years since those books were written.

Maybe there's room for me to tell stories of the druchii and their bleak homeland after all...

Graham McNeill
January 2013

Naggaroth

Blighted Isle

Shrine of Khaine

Chrace

Phoenix
Gate

Anlec

Dragon Gate

Unicorn Gate

Griffon Gate

Ellyrion

Eagle Gate

Gaen
Vale

Tor Elyr

Sea of Dusk

The Inner Sea

Tor Anroc

The Sunken City

The Sunken Lands

Tiranoc

Shrine of
Asuryan

The Dragon Spire

150 Miles

Vaul's
Anvil

Ulthuan

The Isles

Cothique

Tor Achare

Forests of Cothique

Forests of Avelorn

Avelorn

The Shifting Isles

Yvresse

Finuval
Plain

Tor Yvresse

The Isle of
the Dead

Sea of Dreams

Saphery

Tower of
Hoeth

Lothern

KINSTRIFE

I

NAGGAROTH

The sleek, eagle-prowed vessel travelled along the river without a sound, slicing the dark water as the high elf crew rowed with smooth, rhythmic sweeps of their oars. The silver hull barely reflected on the slate-coloured water and an acrid sulphurous stench was carried on the yellow fog that hugged its black surface.

The vessel's sails were folded away and the mast lowered to avoid the dark, clawing branches of the trees that pressed in on either side of the river, and even though the orb of the sun had yet to reach its zenith, the weak light it cast over the Land of Chill barely penetrated the thick, jagged canopy.

Standing at the prow of the vessel, a tall, long-limbed elf with silver-gold hair bound by a bronze circlet watched the route ahead as the river turned in a lazy bend. In one hand he carried a long, gracefully curved bow inlaid with gold and looped with silver wire, while his other gripped the hilt of a slender, leaf-bladed sword. He wore a sky blue tunic embroidered with a golden horse, beneath which was a glimmering shirt of ithilmar mail. His features were smooth and his face oval, his eyes dark and hooded – almost without whites.

The elf leaned over the side of the boat, trying to see the riverbed through the swirling black water, but he quickly gave up.

'What depth do we have?' he asked, without turning.

'Perhaps three fathoms, Lord Eldain, maybe less,' replied one of the vessel's crew, who knelt a respectful distance behind the tall elf, a weighted sounding line playing out into the water. 'I do not believe we will reach much further up the river than this. I would humbly suggest that we tie up at the bank soon.'

Eldain nodded, turning and marching back down the deck of the shallow-bottomed ship, before nodding to the steersman at the stern to make for the shore. He heard the rush of water as the ship altered course and stared into the ghostly, dark trees that loomed over the river, wondering what catastrophe had befallen this realm to transform it into this bleak, dead landscape.

The ship drew near the bank, and Eldain switched his gaze from the haunted forest to the obsidian surface of the water and the rippling wake that spread in a 'V' from the ship's stern. A dozen more vessels, high prowed and graceful as swans, with hulls of silver and white followed his own, arcing gracefully towards the northern riverbank. Riding high on the prow of the following boat was the imposing figure of Caelir, clad in an exquisitely tailored tunic of scarlet and vermillion, the subtleties of the different colours almost indistinguishable. Trust his brother to wear something best suited to the court of Lothern while hundreds of miles from home on a desperately dangerous raid into the realm of the druchii.

Sensing his brother's scrutiny, Caelir drew his sword and held it above his head, but Eldain did not return the gesture, instead turning to face the approaching bank. Thick bracken and tangled roots reached into the water, and as the ship drew near he leapt gracefully onto the black soil of Naggaroth.

Even through his fine, hand-made boots, Eldain could feel the icy cold of this land, a chill that was not simply of the climate, but of the soul. The evil that had been plotted on this dark land arose from the earth, as though the land sought to expel it... or spread its taint yet further.

Eldain shivered and nocked an arrow to his bow as his vessel's crew swiftly began disembarking and tying up the ship. He scanned the darkened undergrowth and the dead forest for enemies, but there was nothing, no shred of movement nor breath of life.

Dank mist coiled at the base of wretched, black trees that crowded his vision in all directions, and the ashen ground was strewn with jagged rocks and thorny brush that gathered in vile clumps across this blasted forest landscape. Truly this place was a vision of utter desolation. To an elf of Ellyrion, one of the Inner Kingdoms of Ulthuan blessed with bountiful forests brimming with life and magical fecundity, this dismal place was anathema.

Elven Shadow Warriors, grey-clad scouts who moved like ghosts, slipped past him, fanning out into the black forest with swords or bows at the ready. He relaxed his own bowstring and slipped the arrow back in his quiver, satisfied that nothing could now approach their landing place without the scouts knowing about it.

'It is a grand adventure we are on, is it not, brother?' asked a young and energised voice behind him, and he turned to face Caelir. His younger brother was roguishly handsome, with boyish good looks and a mischievous, infectious grin that had seen him out of more scrapes than his considerable skill with a blade.

'The land of the druchii is not one of adventure, brother,' cautioned Eldain, though he knew it would do nothing to dampen Caelir's spirits. 'Not since Eltharion have high elves raided Naggaroth and returned alive. It is a land of death, torment and suffering.'

Caelir smiled and said, 'It is that, but soon it will be so for our enemies, yes?'

'If all goes to plan and we don't end up like Eltharion; tortured, blinded and driven to madness in the dungeons of the Witch King.'

'Ah, but it is *your* plan, brother,' laughed Caelir, 'and I have faith in you. You were always better at planning things than I.'

Eldain bit back an angry retort and moved further down the riverbank where the ships' masters were efficiently and, more importantly, quietly disembarking their passengers. High elf Ellyrian Reavers, resplendent in light mail shirts and cream tunics, swiftly formed a perimeter around the ships as the crews led their magnificent elven steeds onto dry land. The steeds could also sense the darkness in this place, and their high whinnies spoke to him of their unease at being here.

He felt his brother join him, and his irritation rose as Caelir ran forward to vault onto the back of Aedaris, a grey mare he had raised from a foal. The steed reared and kicked the air, glad to have its companion upon its back after the long sea journey from Ulthuan.

Despite himself, Eldain smiled as he saw an elven crewman lead Lotharin down the carved gangplank, patting the black stallion's muscled flanks as the animal tossed its mane in displeasure.

'I know, I know,' whispered Eldain. 'I too wish nothing more than to be away from this dark place, but we are here and we have a mission to fulfil.'

Like Caelir, Eldain had nurtured his steed from a newborn and raised it as his faithful companion. Where the barbarous humans would beat a horse and break its spirit in order to ride it, the elves of the kingdom of Ellyrion devoted their lives to building a bond of trust between rider and steed. To do any less was unthinkable.

Of all the Inner Kingdoms of Ulthuan, Ellyrion was the most beautiful. Of course Eldain knew that an elf from Caledor or Avelorn would say the same thing, but they had not lived their lives in balmy eternal summers, nor ridden a fine Ellyrion steed the length and breadth of the land with the cool wind in their hair. They had not climbed the high, marble peaks of the Annulii, nor galloped along the spine of mountains while chasing a shining storm of raw magic.

The smile faded from Eldain's lips as he glanced over at his brother

– who laughed and joked with the other warriors – and tried to recall the last time he had done such things. He pushed the thought from his mind as he checked his steed for any signs of ill effects from the journey, but the ship's crew had taken great care to ensure that the horses arrived in Naggaroth able to do all that would be asked of them.

Eldain swung onto the back of Lotharin, relishing being on horseback after so long at sea. To ride a creature such as this was an honour, and though black steeds were often seen as beasts of ill-omen amongst the high elves, Eldain would sooner cut off his own arm than choose another mount.

Caelir rode alongside him as the remainder of their force mounted up, a hundred warriors in all, lightly armoured for speed, and armed with bows and light throwing spears.

'Well, brother are we ready?' asked Caelir, and Eldain could hear the anticipation in his brother's voice.

'We will know soon enough,' said Eldain, as one of the Shadow Warriors slid from the mists enveloping the dark trunks of the black forest.

Eldain considered himself an agile figure, having attended some of the most elaborate masquerades and balls Tor Elyr and Lothern had to offer, performing graceful dances beyond the ability of elves a century younger than he, but this warrior moved as though his feet did not so much touch the ground as float above it. His grey cloak was the colour of woven mist, its fabric shimmering in the pale light and the hood drawn up over his face to shroud his features in darkness.

'The way ahead is clear, Lord Eldain,' said the scout.

'Good,' nodded Eldain. 'Three of your warriors will guide us towards Clar Karond, while the rest will remain here to guard our ships.'

'Very good, my lord.'

'The warriors who will accompany us,' said Eldain, 'can they keep up with us on foot or will they require mounts?'

The scout nodded slowly and said, 'They can keep up with you on foot, my lord.' Eldain thought he detected a hint of amusement in the scout's tone. The warrior turned away, and at some unseen signal, the remainder of the scouts emerged soundlessly from the cover of the trees.

'It has been too long since you rode to battle, brother,' said Caelir, leaning close and whispering so that none but Eldain could hear his words.

'What do you mean?' asked Eldain.

'The Shadow Warriors,' said Caelir. 'I'd wager they could reach Clar Karond and be back at our ships before we were even halfway there.'

'Yes, you are probably right,' agreed Eldain, thinking how foolish a question it had been. 'Still, it does no harm to check these things. One must never assume anything, especially in war, doubly so when the battle is against the druchii.'

'You forget, brother, you and father are not the only warriors of our family to have fought the druchii,' said Caelir, holding up his burned hand. 'I too have spilled their blood, remember?'

Eldain remembered all too well. The memory, and the sight of Rhianna's silver pledge ring on Caelir's scarred finger, brought a sour taste to his throat.

II

ULTHUAN – One year ago

'Sit high in the saddle,' said Caelir. 'Let her enjoy the ride too. You're not trying to master her, you're trying to share the experience with her.'

'I'm trying, but she wants to run too fast,' said Rhianna. 'I am afraid I'll fall.'

Caelir smiled as Aedaris cantered in a circle around him, knowing the horse was just playing with the elf-maid who rode upon her back.

'She would never allow you to fall,' said Caelir as Aedaris picked up the pace, and Rhianna let out a squeal of delicious fear and excitement. The mare ran with her head held proudly, and Caelir knew she was showing off to Rhianna's own steed, a fine, silver gelding from Saphery, named Orsien. The gelding's dappled flanks glittered and he had a haughty gleam of intelligence in his pale green eyes, but Aedaris was easily the more powerful animal.

'Are you sure?' asked Rhianna, and Caelir laughed as he saw her relax into the horse's motion, moving in time with her rhythm and getting the measure of her temperament.

'Very sure,' nodded Caelir. 'She likes you, I can tell.'

'Then I truly know I am welcome in the kingdom of Ellyrion if their horses accept me.'

Caelir smiled, but said nothing, content to watch Rhianna circling him on the back of Aedaris and enjoying the sight of two beautiful creatures revelling in the bright afternoon sunshine. Rhianna's long golden hair fanned out behind her as she rode, a stream of honey in the air, and her white gown rippled like the tall banners of the silver helms.

Her features were delicate, but had great strength in them, her almond shaped eyes like dark pools with a hint of gold. She was beautiful, and Caelir longed to touch her, to feel the softness of her hair and the marble smoothness of her skin against his own. He kept such thoughts to himself, for Rhianna was not his woman to have such desires about.

The households of Caelir and Rhianna had been close allies for centuries, and both their fathers had fought alongside the Phoenix King in his wars with the druchii, the dark kin of the elves. Rhianna's father was a mage of great power who lived in a floating citadel in Saphery, a wondrous palace bedecked in luscious flora from all across the Old World. Caelir's own sire was one of the mightiest horselords of Ellyrion, riders and warriors without compare, but a year ago, a druchii assassin's envenomed blade had put paid to his lordship's rule over his domain, leaving him paralysed and in constant pain. While the poison ravaged him, Caelir's brother, Eldain, had taken up the mantle of protecting their lands.

Rhianna laughed as the steed slowed its gallop and began to thread a nimble-footed path through the rocks, once more showing off its skill. Caelir walked towards them, enjoying the sound of her laugher. It had been too long since the halls of his family's villa in Tor Elyr had echoed to such a sound. The summer sunshine did not fill the wide, terrazzo halls for the discomfort it would cause his father, and the happy sound of song and dance no longer drew revellers from nearby villas for feasts and merrymaking.

'Is something wrong?' asked Rhianna.

'No,' said Caelir. 'Why do you ask?'

'A shadow passed across your face.'

Caelir shook his head and let Aedaris nuzzle him. Reaching up to rub behind the horse's ears, he whispered, 'You are a princess amongst steeds, my friend, but you don't need to show off for my benefit.'

The steed whinnied and tossed her mane, pleased to have made her friend proud, and Rhianna dismounted and ran her hands through her golden hair. Caelir patted his horse's neck, watching as the magnificent steed cantered towards Rhianna's gelding. Truly it was a good day to be alive, thought Caelir, tilting his head back and letting the morning sunshine bathe him in warmth.

The heat reflected from the white rocks of the Annulii Mountains, powdered fragments of quartz glittering and making the high peaks shine with a dazzling light. Whipping vortices of magical light were tantalisingly visible through the passes, and this high in the mountains, Caelir could feel the power of that magic as a pounding heat in his veins.

Rhianna reached up and placed her palm against his cheek, and he blushed at the feelings it stirred within him.

'Are you sure nothing troubles you?' she asked.

'Yes,' nodded Caelir, turning away. 'I'm fine. Don't worry.'

'You looked very serious there,' said Rhianna, 'like your brother.'

Caelir felt his jaw clench, uncomfortable with the mention of Eldain. Though his brother had made no betrothal pledge to Rhianna, and her father had offered no dowry, it was widely accepted by the nobles of Ulthuan that Eldain would wed her within the decade.

In an attempt to change the subject, he said, 'I was just thinking of my father and the revenge I will take on the druchii.'

'I see,' said Rhianna. 'He is no better? I had hoped my father's magic would have helped clear his veins of the venom.'

'No, and he grows weaker every day. The assassins of the dark ones brew potent poisons,' said Caelir, moving away from her to sit on the edge of the rocks and stare out over the expanse of Ulthuan laid before him.

From this vantage point, high in the mountains, the rolling grasslands of Ellyrion were a vast, unbroken sward of green far below, and the sight of his homeland calmed Caelir's volatile spirits, as always. Home to the horselords of Ulthuan, great herds of elven steeds roamed the sweeping plains of Ellyrion, and the silver ribbon of the River Elyr snaked across the landscape towards the beautiful city of Tor Elyr before emptying into the bay of the Sea of Dusk.

Built atop a series of verdant islands and sculpted from the living rock, Tor Elyr was a magnificent sight. There were a multitude of sweeping thoroughfares, and the villas and palaces were capped with tall towers of silver and gold. Colourful banners snapped in the breeze, and streamers of magic sparkled and foamed from the garrets of the city's wizards.

Connecting the islands of these magnificent structures was a web of curving bridges that spanned the expanse of emerald green waters with great beauty and an easy grace.

To look upon the realm of Ellyrion was to behold beauty, and Caelir felt his angry heart quelled. Rhianna moved to sit beside him and placed her hand on his arm. His blood quickened at her touch, and when she smiled at him, it filled him with yearning to see such beauty and know that it was not his to have.

'If the physicians cannot cure him, can they at least make him more comfortable?' asked Rhianna.

Caelir shook his head. 'They fuss and mutter and speak of new poultices or magical brews, but they are powerless to stop the poison eating him away from inside.'

'My father will do what he can, but...'

'I know he will,' nodded Caelir, taking her hand. 'He is a good and true friend. As are you.'

'I remember when my father first brought us to Tor Elyr,' smiled Rhianna. 'You were but a youth, full of fire and passion. I watched you showing off on your horse and thought that you looked very fine.'

'I remember that day still,' nodded Caelir. 'You wore a gown of azure silk, blue, like the summer sky. And I remember thinking that you were the most beautiful woman I had ever seen.'

Rhianna laughed and said, 'Now you are making fun of me.'

'No,' said Caelir. 'I think I have loved you since first we met.'

'Hush!' whispered Rhianna, though there was no one to hear their words, and Caelir saw the beginnings of a smile crease the corners of her mouth. 'It is not seemly for you to speak of such things while we are without a chaperone.'

'I am your chaperone,' said Caelir. 'Was it not my brother himself who asked me to take you riding and show you the ways of an Ellyrion horseman?'

'Your brother trusts your honour.'

Caelir laughed. 'And he of all people should know better than to trust *me* with such a beauty as you. Anyway, if he was so concerned, why does he not take you riding himself?'

'Your brother bears a heavy burden, maintaining your family lands,' said Rhianna. 'It is a noble thing he does, and takes much of his energies. He has not the time to spend with me in more... frivolous pursuits.'

Caelir's eyes narrowed, hearing the sadness in Rhianna's voice. And though he knew it was wrong, he felt the stirrings of opportunity. With their father incapacitated, Eldain had become dour and uncommunicative, spending all his time seeing to the myriad tasks that the master of a household must deal with every day.

Caelir had not been asked to help, nor had he offered aid to his brother, preferring the thrill of venturing into the Annulii Mountains to the drudgery of work. To hunt the fabled white lions, fearsome predators whose snowy pelts were worn by the guards of the Phoenix King himself, was the life for Caelir!

Where was the joy to be had in the running of a household? What honour or glory was there in dull lists and suchlike? No, far better that he roam the mountains as the hunter, or ride the plains as a bold adventurer.

Seeing Caelir's expression, Rhianna said, 'Eldain has a good heart,' but Caelir could see that she was defending his brother because it was the right thing to do, not because she truly believed what she said.

'He does,' agreed Caelir, 'but he is foolish indeed to let a flower as beautiful as you go unplucked. I would never allow myself to be distracted from your happiness.'

Rhianna slipped her hand from his and looked out over the wondrous expanse of Ellyrion, her brows knit in consternation. Behind them, Orsien gave a high whinny of alarm, and both elves turned in surprise.

Caelir could see nothing that might cause the horse to sound a warning, but it was a steed of Saphery and had senses beyond his. He leapt to his feet and offered his hand to Rhianna.

'What is it?' she asked, taking his hand and rising to stand next to him. 'What's the matter?'

'I don't know yet,' he answered, turning and running for his horse. Orsien reared and kicked the air, his neighs of alarm growing more strident. Caelir reached Aedaris and drew his sword, scanning the horizon for any sign of mountain predators.

Rhianna ran to her horse and unsheathed her bow, a fine longbow inset with mother-of-pearl, that exuded the taste of Vaul's magic.

'I don't see anything,' said Rhianna, nocking an arrow to her bowstring.

'Nor I,' said Caelir, 'but this may be no ordinary predator. This close to the magical vortex that circles the Annulii, there's every chance that whatever Orsien has sensed may be something drawn here by the magic. Perhaps a chimera or a hydra. Or worse.'

'Then we should go,' said Rhianna. 'Now.'

Caelir shook his head. 'No, not yet. I want to see what it is. Imagine the creatures brought here by the magic! Don't you want to see what such power can create?'

'No, I do not,' said Rhianna. 'If they are as dangerous as you say, then I very much wish to avoid encountering such a beast. And so should you.'

Caelir scanned the rocks above, catching sight of a slipping shadow where none ought to be.

Something was moving up there... something that did not want to be seen.

He felt the hairs on the back of his neck prickle, and a hot sensation of fear settled in his belly as he realised that this was neither mountain predator nor monster conjured from the mountain's magic. This was something far worse.

'Rhianna,' he said urgently, 'get on your horse and ride for Tor Elyr.'

'What is it?'

'Do it!' he hissed. 'Now. It is the druchii.'

No sooner had the words left his throat than a trio of iron crossbow bolts slashed through the air from the rocks above. Caelir twisted his body, bringing his sword up in a desperate arc to cleave the first pair of bolts in two. He heard Rhianna cry out and risked a glance behind him to see that the third quarrel was lodged in her shoulder. Blood soaked her dress and Caelir cried out in anger as three dark cloaked warriors emerged from their hiding places in the rocks above.

'Rhianna!' he shouted as she slumped against the flanks of her steed.

'Is that her name?' called out the lead druchii warrior. 'It will make torturing her all the sweeter when I whisper her name as she begs for mercy.'

Caelir turned to face the warrior, a sharp-featured elf with pallid, ivory skin and a hawk-like nose. Like his companions, his head was shaven, with a single, dark topknot dangling from the back of his skull. The druchii wore light tunics of dark cloth that seemed to swallow the day's light, and held their deadly repeater crossbows aimed unwaveringly at Caelir's heart. Each weapon bore an ebony store of bolts on its upper surface, allowing it to fire a hail of bolts rather than a single shot. The range of such weapons was much reduced, as was their stopping power, but Caelir knew that at this range and without any armour, he would be just as dead if pierced by them.

'You will not touch her,' swore Caelir, moving to stand between the druchii and Rhianna.

'And you think you can stop us?' laughed the warrior. 'I am Koradris and I have taken many heads in battle. Yours will simply be one more.'

'I will die before I let you take her.'

'So be it,' said Koradris and pulled the trigger.

But before the firing mechanisms could loose the bolts, the weapons burst into flame. Sparkling magical fire leapt from weapon to weapon, and the druchii cried out in surprise and pain as they dropped them. Caelir felt the surge of magic from behind him and heard Rhianna fall to the ground, this magical gift to him draining the last of her strength.

Without giving the druchii warriors time to recover from their surprise, Caelir leapt forwards, his sword cleaving through the nearest enemy's chest with the speed of a striking snake. The warrior collapsed, choking on his own blood, and Caelir gave an ululating yell as he attacked the others.

Koradris easily parried his blow, sending a lightning riposte to his belly. Caelir only just managed to block the cut, rolling his sword around his opponent's weapon and slashing for his head. The druchii ducked and batted aside Caelir's return stroke as the second warrior circled to his left.

Koradris lunged and the second druchii warrior attacked at the same moment. Caelir deflected the attack, and, like quicksilver, turned to parry a downward cut from the side, launching an attack of his own.

The druchii parried another strike and launched a deadly thrust to Caelir's chest, but his blow was deflected, and Caelir spun on his heel, slashing his sword at the warrior's head.

His opponent swayed aside, but the tip of Caelir's blade sliced the skin just above his temple and blood flowed from the cut. Koradris moved to encircle his prey. Caelir knew that unless he evened the odds, a duel like this could have only one outcome. Koradris and the other druchii circled him from either side, leering anticipation writ large upon their features.

'You will pay for killing Vranek,' hissed Koradris. 'He was kin to me.'

'I thought the druchii paid no mind to kith and kin,' answered Caelir.

'True enough,' agreed Koradris, charging in once more, 'but he owed me money.'

The blades met with an almighty clang, but Caelir had anticipated this. He leapt back from Koradris and spun, thrusting his sword at the other druchii who sought to slay him from behind. The blade plunged deep into his neck and the druchii's eyes bulged as he toppled to the ground, blood jetting from his torn throat.

Caelir felt the burning kiss of steel across his back as the short blade of Koradris slashed through his jerkin and bit a finger's breadth into his flesh. He cried out in pain, dropping his sword and falling to his knees as Koradris closed in for the kill. Caelir threw himself flat on his belly and rolled as the druchii's blade slashed and stabbed for him.

He needed a weapon, and cried out in agony as he rolled over something hot.

Koradris stood above him, his sword dripping blood and his mouth curled in a sneer of contempt.

'The lords of Naggaroth fill our heads with the might of the Phoenix King's warriors, but you are a pitiful specimen indeed. Tell me, youngling, do you hear the wail of Morai-Heg? She will be coming for you soon.'

Caelir fumbled beneath him and felt the burning touch of seared wood and metal. He gripped a smooth wooden stock, gritting his teeth against the pain.

'If you hear the banshee's wail, it is you she is coming for!' shouted Caelir, swinging round one of the scorched repeater crossbows and pulling the trigger. For the only time in his life, Caelir was grateful for the craftsmanship of the druchii, as the scorched weapon loosed a flurry of iron bolts.

He kept pulling the trigger until the ebony store on the weapon's top was exhausted, heedless of the stench of blistered flesh where the residue of the magical fire still burned him. Koradris looked down at the four bolts embedded in his chest and stomach, and seemed more surprised than in pain.

The sword slid from his fingers and he fell to the ground as blood began to seep into his dark tunic. Even as his lifeblood poured from him, he sneered at Caelir.

'You think you have won?' he gasped.

'You will die before me,' said Caelir, struggling to his feet.

'You have slain me, youngling, but the dark riders are but moments behind me,' hissed Koradris with his last breath. 'You are still going to die...'

Caelir turned from the dead druchii, retrieved his sword, and limped towards Rhianna. She lay beside her horse, the steed nuzzling her in fear and concern. The druchii bolt had pierced her shoulder, but had ricocheted upwards on her collarbone and the barbed tip protruded from the skin. He could feel the shaft of the bolt just beneath her skin.

'I have never seen the like... you were magnificent...' she whispered, her eyelids fluttering and her skin ashen. 'Like the Sword Masters of Hoeth.'

'Hold still,' said Caelir, 'this is going to hurt.'

Rhianna nodded and closed her eyes as Caelir sliced the blade of his sword along the line of the bolt and slid it from her body. She screamed, and Caelir held her tight, wishing he could take away her pain.

Caelir and Rhianna struggled to their feet, and Caelir fashioned make-shift bandages from the cloaks of the dead druchii to bind their wounds with.

'We don't have much time,' he said once he was finished. 'There will be more of them and they won't be far behind.'

'We must warn Tor Elyr that the druchii are here in force.'

Caelir nodded and cupped his hands to help Rhianna onto her horse. Before mounting, she leaned in close and put her palm against his cheek.

'You saved my life, Caelir, and I will never forget this,' she said, and kissed him on the lips.

'Anything for you, my lady,' he replied, the pain of his wound quite forgotten.

III

NAGGAROTH

Eldain reined in his steed as he saw the Shadow Warrior emerge from behind the thick bole of a black-barked tree, and raised his hand in a fist to halt his troop of Ellyrian Reavers.

The hooded scout bowed before Eldain and said, 'Clar Karond is beyond the rise, my lord. Where the trees thin out, the land drops away and the towers of the druchii can be clearly seen.'

Eldain sensed the scout's loathing for the druchii in every word, and felt a similar stirring in his breast at the thought of taking the fight to those who had slain his father. He stared over the scout's shoulder, seeing the light from beyond the trees.

'Well done,' he told the scout. 'Where are the rest of your warriors?'

The scout waved his hand and the other two warriors emerged from the shadows. Eldain had not noticed either of the scouts, and though it was their forte to avoid being seen, it still irked him that he had not sensed so much as a hint of them.

'Why do we stop?' asked Caelir, riding alongside.

'The trees thin out ahead,' explained Eldain. 'We are close to Clar Karond.'

'At last,' said Caelir. 'I grow weary of this forest. It weighs heavily on the soul.'

'Indeed,' said Eldain, turning away. 'Stay here, I will scout ahead with the Shadow Warriors.'

Without waiting for Caelir to complain about being left behind, Eldain dismounted and lifted his bow from the oiled, leather case slung from Lotharin's saddle. He nodded to the scout and followed him as he slipped into the forest ahead.

The scout moved effortlessly ahead of him, and Eldain felt as clumsy as a human as he attempted to match his stealth. But it seemed that every brittle branch and leaf deliberately wormed its way beneath the soles of his boots.

Slowly, they crept forwards, and though the light of the afternoon was a welcome sight after five days of travelling through the dense, dark forests of Naggaroth, it was scant comfort to an elf raised on Ulthuan.

Each day had been more grim than the previous, though the warriors made no complaint – as was only proper. Each of them was well used to spending many weeks, or longer, in the wilds as part of their training, but the bleak forests of the Land of Chill were something else altogether.

Though days and nights came and went, the sun neither warmed the skin nor refreshed the soul, instead leeching the life from the world and casting a pall of fear and doubt over their band. As dreary as the days were, the nights were a thousand times worse, with the darkness of Naggaroth unbroken by torch or moonlight. The blackness shrouded them in silence such that each warrior feared to break it with so much as a single word.

Night was a time to fear, doubly so in Naggaroth, as strange sounds echoed in the depths of the forest around them and in the sky above them. Rustling branches, crackling leaves and the drifting echoes of what sounded like the screaming laughter of lunatic children.

Each night as they made cold camp, Eldain would picture Rhianna and his fears would ease a little, though each time a shard of ice would enter his heart when his treacherous memories would unfold to include Caelir.

Eldain shook off such thoughts as the ground began to rise and he felt a pressure on his shoulder. He looked up into the hooded face of the Shadow Warrior. The scout nodded slowly and gestured to a thorny patch of briars that clung to the edge of the rise like barbed tangleweed.

The scout dropped to his belly and began crawling towards the briars, and Eldain followed him, conscious that he would need to dispose of this tunic after the mission. A saying of the reavers was that survival never took second place to dignity in the field, but that was all very well when you hadn't had the finest tailors and seamstresses in Lothern fashion your garments.

At last he reached the briar patch and parted the thorny brush to see the vast city of Clar Karond in all its hateful glory.

Three black towers the colour of bloody iron rose from the centre of the city, with tall jagged-roofed temples jockeying for position around them. A high wall, topped with blades and spikes, surrounded the centre of the city, and even from here, Eldain could see the sunlight glinting from the speartips of the city's guards. Beyond this high wall sprawled the peripherals of a city such as could be seen around many other cities: markets, temples, dwellings of the common folk and barracks of the city's soldiery.

But for all the trappings of civilisation, a vile darkness hung over its cobbled streets and black roofs – a sense of violence about to be unleashed, of blood about to be spilled. It chilled Eldain's soul to see such a place, a place of evil that festered beneath a brooding sun, and a place whose inhabitants plotted the destruction of his homeland.

Scattered around the city were tracts of elaborate vineyards, choked with grapes of deepest crimson, and Eldain's lip curled as he realised that these were harvested for the druchii's blood wine. Wretched human slaves tended to the vines, guarded by cruel warriors on horseback who emphasised their commands with blade and whip.

Between the vineyards, and stretching all the way up to their vantage point, the land was scarred by devastation. Shorn tree stumps bore grim testimony to the massive logging operations of the druchii that provided timber for the new war vessels of their raiding fleets. Thousands of trees must have been felled here, and the day echoed still with the distant sound of chopping axe blades and the rasp of saws. More slaves toiled in huge work gangs to the east, felling trees by the dozen and dragging them back towards the desolate city.

'Look to the north-east, my lord,' whispered the scout.

Eldain's eyes travelled to where the scout had indicated and saw their prize, the docks and shipyards for which Clar Karond was justly infamous. Ships filled the dark waters of the rocky bay that slowly widened until it emptied into the Sea of Malice. A warren of interlinked jetties and quays spread out into the water from the shoreline, each with great reaper bolt throwers on the seaward side, mighty war-machines capable of launching huge iron bolts that could pierce the hull of even the mightiest ship.

'What do you see?' asked the scout.

'Reavers mostly,' said Eldain. 'Some sloops of war, a few reaper-ships and… and there's something beyond that mountain spur, but I can't quite see it.'

'Look again, my lord,' said the scout. 'That's no mountain.'

Eldain looked closer, and the breath caught in his throat as he saw that what he had at first mistaken for a mountain spur of the bay was something else entirely.

'Asuryan's mercy!' he hissed as he saw that the scout spoke true.

This was no mountain… this colossus was one of the dreaded black arks.

A mountainous castle set adrift on the sea and held together by the most powerful enchantments, the black ark was a sinister floating fortress, tower upon tower, spire upon spire of living rock sundered from the isle of Ulthuan over five thousand years ago.

Crewed by an entire army, and dismal home to thousands of slaves, the black arks were the most feared and mightiest sea-going vessels in the world. Some said that the bulk they displayed above the surface of the water was but a fraction of their true size, with great vaulted caverns below the waterline that were home to terrible monsters, slaves and all manner of foul witchcraft. The truth of such things was beyond Eldain; all he knew was that the arks brought with them terror and death on a scale undreamt of.

Great chains, each link thicker than the trunk of a tree, looped from a cluster of towers at the prow of the black ark, curving down towards the impossibly huge draconic head of some monstrous and terrible sea beast that lay, half-submerged, in the dark waters of the harbour. Even from here, Eldain could sense the powerful magic keeping the colossal beast docile while the black ark was berthed at Clar Karond.

Eldain heard someone behind him and turned to see Caelir low-crawling towards the lip of the ridge. His brother had almost reached Eldain before he had become aware of his presence, and he masked his jealousy of Caelir's talents with anger at his disobeying orders.

'Blood of Khaine!' swore Caelir. 'Is that a black ark?'

'What are you doing here, Caelir?' asked Eldain, ignoring his brother's question. 'I told you to wait with the rest of the warriors.'

Caelir waved his scarred hand dismissively. 'Our warriors do not need me to tell them how to prepare for battle. I wish to see the enemy for myself.'

'You will see them soon enough,' replied Eldain. 'And be careful what you wish for.'

'It will be good to avenge father,' said Caelir, staring fixedly at the spires of Clar Karond and the black ark. 'I have great vengeance to wreak upon them.'

'We both do,' said Eldain.

'Nothing is forgotten. Nothing is forgiven,' whispered Caelir, and Eldain recognised the words as those of Alith Anar, the Shadow King of the shattered kingdom of Nagarythe, a brutal ruler who had led the Shadow Warriors in the years following the Sundering.

'How will we come at them?' asked Caelir.

'From the north-east,' replied Eldain, pointing to the logging works. 'The Shadow Warriors will lead us around to the forested hills above where those slaves are working, and under cover of darkness we shall ride into the harbour, fire as many ships as we can and cause bloody mayhem before pulling back.'

'The druchii will pay in blood for what they have taken from me,' said Caelir, and Eldain saw that his brother unconsciously rubbed his scarred hand as he spoke.

Looking at the burned flesh of his brother's hand, Eldain remembered the day Caelir and Rhianna had ridden breathlessly through the portal of the family villa on the eastern slopes of the Annullii. Both had been badly hurt, but Caelir had seen them to safety, and delivered his warning of the druchii raiders, before collapsing.

The tale of how he had heroically defended Rhianna from the dark kin had spread quickly through the courts of Tor Elyr, and Caelir's reputation as a dashing hero was established.

No one thought to mention that it had been foolish of him to take Rhianna so high into the mountains and so close to the Eagle Gate. No, thought Eldain bitterly, to do so would have been to tarnish the heroic tale of Caelir the Protector. In the weeks that followed, he had watched as Caelir and Rhianna grew closer, powerless to prevent his brother from bewitching the woman he loved with his wayward charms.

'Come, brother,' snapped Eldain, turning and preparing to rejoin the rest of the warriors. 'We should get back. If we are to reach the north-eastern slopes before nightfall, we must be away soon.'

Caelir simply nodded and crawled back with him, vaulting to his feet when they were safely out of sight below the ridge. Back with the rest of the high elven warriors, Eldain felt his spirits lift once more as he saw, by their proud and elegant features, that they were ready for battle. To have penetrated so far into the realm of the druchii was accomplishment enough, but they would achieve something that would show the dark kin what it was to live in fear of raiders from across the sea.

He issued his orders quickly and efficiently, and within minutes the band of warriors was on the move once more, stealthily riding around the eastern fringes of Clar Karond.

As the day wore on and the sun sank lower in the sky, Eldain thought of the coming raid and his brother's caution that it had been too long since he had fought in battle. True, it had been many years since he had wielded a blade, but the finest tutors had taught him, and he knew that when the blood was flowing and the thrill of battle was upon him, he would be as deadly as he had ever been.

A bruised dusk was drawing in as the scouts once again halted their progress and informed him that they were in position. He dismounted and drew his sword, dropping to his knees and reciting the vow of the Sword Masters.

> *'From the darkness I cry for you.*
> *The tears you shed for us*
> *are the blood of the elven kind.*
> *O Isha,*
> *here I stand*
> *on the last shore,*
> *a sword in my hand.*
> *Ulthuan shall never fall.'*

Though he was not one of the legendary warriors of the White Tower of Hoeth, mystic guardians of knowledge and wisdom who were masters of the martial arts, the words gave him comfort and focused his concentration on the death yet to be dealt.

The sun continued to fall until the fearful darkness of Naggaroth began to encroach upon the world, and Eldain knew that it was time. The warriors around him began their preparations for battle, weaving iron cords into their long hair – symbolic of strength, power and nobility, the mark of a true warrior – to ensure that an enemy's blade would not cut it in the heat of battle.

Eldain prayed to the Emperor of the Heavens to guide his blade and watch over him this night, and though he knew there was soon to be blood on his hands, he asked forgiveness from the elven gods. His prayers went unanswered in the darkness, but he felt at peace and knew that his soul was ready for battle. His senses spread out and he could feel the breathing of his men, the harsh whinnies of their steeds and the tense anticipation that gripped them all.

No... not all. Around Caelir was nothing but a thirst for vengeance that burned brightly in the night. Eldain was not gifted with wizard sight, but even he could feel Caelir's aggressive soul. The spirit of Kurnous burned in his brother's breast, the elven god of the wild hunt, of untamed forests, wild animals and the trackless wilderness. Many in Ellyrion venerated Kurnous, as did their rustic kin across the ocean who dwelt beneath the boughs of Athel Loren, but the fire of the hunt was stronger in his brother than he could ever remember sensing in anyone before.

But beyond even his brother's desire for vengeance, he sensed something else. Something crude to be sure, but something with a spirit burning brightly with fear and desperation.

And it was coming straight towards them.

From the primal vulgarity of the spirit, Eldain knew it must be of the race of man. He leapt to his feet, his spirit sight fading as the Shadow Warriors slid from their vantage points to intercept the threat.

Eldain sprinted towards his men and ordered them, with a gesture, to silently scatter. The Ellyrian Reavers vanished into the forest, as Eldain crouched beside a tall, claw-branched tree and risked a glance through the dark forest. His elf-sight easily pierced the gloom and he saw a group of six naked and skeletally thin men running towards the forest, their flesh bruised and scarred from months in captivity.

Behind them, Eldain saw a host of armoured druchii riders on dark steeds, in pursuit of the escaped slaves. One loosed a flurry of bolts from a repeater crossbow and slew one of the escapees. The slaves were almost at the trees, but Eldain knew they would never reach them before the dark riders overtook them.

He saw the leader of the Shadow Warriors raise his bow and aim at the druchii who had fired his crossbow.

'No,' he whispered. 'Stay your hand. If we are discovered now, then all we have achieved so far is for nothing.'

The Shadow Warrior nodded and relaxed his bowstring, commanding his scouts to do the same with some unseen and unheard signal.

Eldain watched dispassionately as the druchii quickly surrounded the escaped slaves and, rather than herd them back to their work gangs, slaughtered them where they stood. Cruel laughter drifted from the scene of butchery as the druchii killed their prey and took their heads to mount upon their saddle horns.

Within moments it was over, and the druchii warriors were riding back towards their dark city with their bloody trophies. Eldain let out his breath, relieved the druchii had been too intent on bloodshed to notice the raiders not a hundred yards from them.

As the druchii departed, Caelir approached him and said, 'that was too close.'

'Indeed,' replied Eldain.

'We should have helped them.'

'Helped them?' asked Eldain. 'To what end? Would you take them back to Tor Elyr and have them for your servants? No, to die like that was probably easier for them than to go on living.'

'Perhaps,' said Caelir, 'but it sits ill with me that we just let them die.'

'They were only humans, Caelir,' said Eldain. 'Do not trouble yourself with them. Now get some rest, we move out within the hour.'

Caelir nodded and returned to his steed, and Eldain lay back against the tree, watching him go. Emotions warred within him and to calm himself before going into battle, he closed his eyes and thought of the last time he had spoken with Rhianna.

IV

ULTHUAN – *Two Months Ago*

Lothern. Most magnificent city of all Ulthuan.

Situated in the midst of the Straits of Lothern, it guarded the approaches to the Inner Sea of Ulthuan. Men who saw the city described it to their companions back home as one of the wonders of the world, and such a title was richly deserved. Principal city of the Kingdom of Eataine, Lothern was a sprawling city-state, the lands around it dotted with vineyards, villas and summer estates to which the noble families of the city retired. The centre of power of Eataine, it was rightly said that no one who ever laid eyes upon it would ever forget it.

Set around a glittering lagoon, the tall spires of Lothern ringed the coastline, sublime palaces and elegant villas fanning upwards from the coast, their white towers climbing gracefully into the foothills of the distant mountains.

But Lothern was not simply built around the lagoon; hundreds of artificial islands had been raised within its waters and on these isles rested great palaces, temples and storehouses, forming an intricate network of canals. Statues of the great elven gods ringed the lagoon: Asuryan, Lileath, Kurnous, Isha and many others, but all these creations were dwarfed by the colossi that towered above the city and faced one another across the mouth of the bay. Statues of the Phoenix King and the Everqueen – twin rulers of Ulthuan – two-hundred feet high and carved from the marble of the mountainside by the power of the elven mages, dominated the southern skyline before the Sapphire Gate. Sailors from around the world spoke of their size, and were each story to be believed, then the statues must surely have climbed all the way to heaven.

Thousands of vessels filled the harbour, bobbing gently in the swell. Trading ships of the elven merchants, pleasure barges, and the sleek and deadly eagle-prowed warships of Lord Aislinn's battlefleet.

Dotted amongst the elven ships were vessels from all across the Old World. Since Finubar the Seafarer had persuaded Bel-Hathor to raise the interdict that forbade humans from setting foot on Ulthuan, almost four hundred years ago, trade had flowed into Lothern like never before. Dhows from Araby were tied up next to groaning merchantmen and galleons from Marienburg, who shared berths with clippers from Magritta and longships from the Norse, who, after the defeat of Erik Redaxe's fleet, realised that there was more to be gained by trading with the elves of Ulthuan than by trying to raid them.

A thriving city of culture, arts, poetry and trade, Lothern was the cosmopolitan heart of Ulthuan, and home to those elves who considered themselves part of the world rather than those who would see Ulthuan remain in splendid isolation.

Eldain and Caelir walked along the Boulevard of the Phoenix, so named for the current Phoenix King of Ulthuan who hailed from Eataine. They had set sail from Tor Elyr a week ago and passed through the gate of ruby and gold that separated the Inner Sea from Lothern only three days ago. Although both had visited the city before, its glory never failed to stir their hearts.

The boulevard ran the length of the mercantile district of the city and bustled with the activity of traders and shopkeepers, busy haggling with customers in the spirit of good natured banter. Swarthy skinned merchants in elaborate, brightly coloured robes and feathered headdresses waved their arms expansively as they held out bolts of fine silk, and incense sellers wafted their wares into the faces of passers-by.

Food sellers and wine merchants offered delicacies from all across the Old World, promising epicurean delights to satisfy even the most demanding palate.

Caelir stopped to purchase some wine and joked with the merchant that it was the finest wine he had tasted that afternoon. Eldain scowled at his brother when he had done with the merchant and said, 'It is serious business we are on, brother. We have not time to dally.'

'There's always time to enjoy a fine wine, Eldain.'

'And was that fine wine?' asked Eldain.

'No,' admitted Caelir. 'It was Tilean vinegar, but it never hurts to try new things. They say that the wines from the New World are exquisite. I met a trader, recently arrived from the Citadel of Dusk, who promised me a bottle of Lustrian venom wine.'

'Venom wine?' asked Eldain, appalled. 'That sounds utterly vile.'

'I know, but he swears it has a flavour to make the finest Avelorn vintage taste like swill.'

'And you believe him?'

'Of course not, but with a boast like that I simply have to taste it,' laughed Caelir.

Eldain shook his head and said, 'Caelir, I swear you would make a warrior of Tiranoc forget his chariot with your inane babble. Have you forgotten why we are here?'

Caelir shrugged. 'No, I haven't, brother, but we do not set sail for Naggaroth for another three weeks. We have time to enjoy the city a little, do we not?'

'Perhaps,' allowed Eldain, 'but I wish to ensure our expedition has all the supplies it needs before then. There is much that still needs to be done. Food and water to be provisioned, and weapons, armour and arrows need to be bought and stowed aboard our ships. I also need to take father's will to the counting house of Cerion to release the funds we will need. All this takes time and who is going to take responsibility, you?'

Caelir raised his hands before him in mock surrender and said, 'Very well, we'll do it your way, brother. Might we be better splitting up, then, and seeing to separate tasks?'

Eldain knew that Caelir was simply looking to get away from him and he found himself not averse to the idea. His brother was already irritating him and they had only been in Lothern for a few days.

'So be it,' he said. 'Take these promissory notes against father's estate and secure us feed for the horses; enough to see us to Naggaroth and back, with two weeks' worth for when we are on land.'

'Feed for the horses,' sighed Caelir. 'Such a glorious task.'

'A necessary one,' reminded Eldain. 'Now be off with you, and I do not want to see you until you have the feed. And get a good price, our funds are not limitless.'

'I know, I know,' said Caelir. 'I'm not a fool, Eldain.'

Eldain struggled to hold his temper at his brother's petulance and simply said, 'Then I will see you back at our lodgings at sunset, yes?'

Caelir did not answer, stalking off through the crowds of traders, and Eldain let out a long, calming breath. He knew all too well that at least one of the promissory notes he had given Caelir would be spent in a wine shop or tailor's boutique, but was too glad of the peace that Caelir's departure brought him to care overmuch.

He closed his eyes and let the bustle of Lothern soothe his spirit, though he knew he must be attracting his fair share of odd looks – standing with his eyes closed in the middle of a busy thoroughfare.

'Eldain?' asked a sweet, female voice. 'Eldain is that you?'

He opened his eyes and his heart lurched to see Rhianna standing before him, a linen covered basket held in the crook of her arm. She wore a simple, high-necked dress of emerald green with golden thread woven in curling patterns at the hem and cuffs, and was as beautiful as he remembered. Unconsciously, his eyes darted to her shoulder where she had been wounded, but the skin was hidden below the fabric of her dress.

Caelir had told Eldain that the fashion this season in Lothern was for risqué dresses that exposed the shoulders and a sizeable amount of decolletage, but Rhianna's dress exposed not one inch of skin more than was necessary.

Sensing his scrutiny of her old wound, Rhianna said, 'It still pains me now and then.'

'I'm sorry, Rhianna,' said Eldain, 'I did not mean to–'

'Don't worry,' she said smoothly. 'Caelir removed the bolt swiftly, but the druchii left me an ugly scar and I do not like to display it.'

Taking a moment to recover his composure, Eldain said, 'It is good to see you again, my lady. It has been too long since you visited us in Tor Elyr.'

'I know,' she said. 'I wanted to come for your father's funeral, but, well...'

'I understand,' said Eldain. 'Your father brought us your condolences. They were most welcome.'

An awkward silence descended upon the pair until Rhianna asked, 'Have you eaten yet?'

'Eaten? No, I have not,' said Eldain. 'I have had much to do today and have not had the time.'

'Nor have I. Will you join me in some food and wine? You are right, it has been too long since we talked.'

Eldain was about to refuse when he thought back to Caelir's advice that there was always time for a fine wine – especially with a beautiful woman – and said, 'I would be honoured to join you, my lady.'

Smiling, she accepted his offered support and the two of them strolled down the Boulevard of the Phoenix arm in arm, looking for all the world like two lovers out for an afternoon constitutional. Just being near Rhianna made Eldain feel more at peace than he had done in a long time, and as they walked, he cast sly glances at her face, remembering touching her skin and whispering promises of love in her gently tapered ear... what seemed like an age ago.

They walked in a companionable silence, turning into a narrow side street with many brightly coloured awnings providing cool shade for the patrons of the eating-houses and wineries that filled the street. Rhianna led him towards a shop with a glittering front, fashioned from coloured chips of polished glass to depict a pastoral landscape of great beauty.

'I know the owner of this establishment,' explained Rhianna. 'He sells only the finest honeycakes and freshest sweetmeats. And he has a friend that brings him bottles of Avelorn dreamwine...'

'Dreamwine,' said Eldain. 'I have not tasted it before, but am told it is fine indeed.'

'Then we shall each have a glass,' stated Rhianna. 'Take a seat and I will see to our order.'

As a proud male, Eldain knew he should see to their food and drink, but as an elf obviously not from Lothern, he knew that he would seem like a bumpkin to the vendors of the city. He found an unoccupied table near the wall and examined the mosaic on the shopfront in more detail. It truly was magnificent and it struck him as unnecessarily ostentatious for something so mundane as a shop, but then what did he know of city ways?

Rhianna soon returned, bearing a silver tray laden with succulent cakes that smelled of sweet honey and roasted cinnamon, and two tall, slender necked flutes filled with shimmering wine.

'Dreamwine?' he asked.

'Dreamwine,' agreed Rhianna. 'Fermented from the waking dreams of the handmaidens of Avelorn and sung into liquid form by the magic of

Everqueen. Be careful though, be sure to only take a small amount at a time.'

Eldain nodded and lifted the flute from the tray, taking a delicate sniff of the ethereal wine. It seemed to run like liquid smoke in his glass and its bouquet was that of a wild forest of ancient glamours where creatures of legend still roamed free. Rhianna smiled and they both took a small sip of the wine.

It was sweet, almost unbearably so, and Eldain replaced the flute on the table as he saw visions of fabulous gardens of oak and suntree tended by the ancient treemen of the forest, sun-dappled glades of unicorn and great eagles nesting in the enchanted forest's rolling hills. The image of the shopfront blurred and swam, the green of its landscape becoming incredibly rich in detail, and Eldain had the sensation that he could reach into it. Indeed, he could smell the scent of honeysuckle and jasmine, taste the salt of sea spray and feel the soft wind blowing across the hills on his face.

Rhianna said, 'It's good, yes?'

He smiled in contentment and said, 'Yes... it's very good. I can see why you are only supposed to take small sips at a time.'

The wine also had the effect of reminding him of his hunger and he devoured two honeycakes in quick succession before taking another sip of wine. More prepared for what wonders it might bring, he was nevertheless intoxicated by their splendour.

He saw beautiful elves with golden skin dancing in leafy bowers, silken pavilions of myriad colours like a great carnival, and darting faeries that lit everything with their silver laughter and sparkling light. Amidst the gaiety, Eldain saw a woman of heartbreaking beauty, with the grace and wisdom of Isha in her eyes, and knew her to be Alarielle, the Everqueen of Avelorn and consort of the Phoenix King. Her flowing hair was like a golden cloud, and graceful birds of purest white attended her as she moved effortlessly through her adoring subjects.

Tears gathered in his eyes as the face of the Everqueen faded, only to be replaced by that of Rhianna, and he pushed the flute with the rest of his dreamwine away, spilling it across the table where it instantly evaporated like mist.

'Eldain? What's the matter?' asked Rhianna, reaching out to touch his hand.

'Nothing,' he said, pulling his arm back. 'This was a mistake.'

'A mistake?' asked Rhianna. 'What was a mistake?'

'Coming here,' said Eldain, pushing his chair back. 'It has reopened old wounds that would be better left alone.'

'No, Eldain, stay. Please,' urged Rhianna. 'We should talk. We *have* to talk.'

'Why?'

Startled by the boldness of the question, Rhianna hesitated before saying, 'Because there are things that must be said between us before you set sail for Naggaroth.'

'You know of our journey?'

Rhianna nodded and said, 'Caelir sent word to my home of the blood oath you swore against the druchii upon your father's coffin. He told me you would be travelling to Lothern and asked me to come.'

'Caelir asked you to come to Lothern, why? He said nothing to me.'

'I met with him yesterday morning and...' began Rhianna, extending her hand across the table towards him. He swallowed hard as he saw a silver ring engraved with two entwined hearts shining upon her middle finger. He couldn't believe that he had not noticed it earlier.

'A pledge ring,' he said. 'Caelir gave you that?'

'He did,' confirmed Rhianna. 'We have exchanged pledge rings, and upon his return from Naggaroth he will plight his troth to me. I will make the pilgrimage to the Gaean Vale, and we shall be wed in Tor Elyr the following year.'

'Wed? You will be wed to Caelir?' laughed Eldain, though there was no humour to it.

'Yes, I love him. I am sorry that I hurt you, but I cannot change what I feel.'

'You don't love Caelir!' snapped Eldain. 'You are infatuated with him. He saved your life and you feel you ought to fall in love with him. Your heart has been clouded by his charms and his brashness. Listen to your head instead.'

'Perhaps you are right,' said Rhianna archly, 'but it does not matter now what my head tells me, my heart speaks with a louder voice.'

Eldain sat back in his chair and felt the bitterness that had festered within him since his father's poisoning, well up within him. He wanted to lash out, to hurt her, to make her feel something of the pain he now felt, but his iron control reasserted itself before he said something he knew he would later regret. He had sacrificed everything, his own happiness and the woman he loved, to protect his domain and his kin, and this was his reward?

But he could not hurt her... to do so would demean him.

'I loved you, Rhianna,' he said at last.

'I know you did, and I will always love you too, Eldain, but I am to be Caelir's upon his return from the land of the druchii,' said Rhianna. 'If things had been different I know you would have been a good husband to me and I a good wife to you, but life often takes turns we do not expect. I am sorry, but please... for my sake, do not hate Caelir for this.'

Eldain nodded and stood, scattering a handful of coins upon the table.

He bowed stiffly to Rhianna and said, 'I love you, and while I live I will love no other.'

As he walked away, Rhianna said, 'Eldain, wait...'

But he did not turn around.

* * *

V

NAGGAROTH

The night pressed in around them, and though the horses picked a silent path through the tall vines, Eldain felt sure they would be unmasked any second. Sounds of weeping men and women drifted on the cold night air, and slaves left to lie where they had fallen in exhaustion curled in terror as they passed, too brutalised by their captors to tell the difference between high elf and druchii.

They were elves, and that was enough to send those slaves who could still move crawling into the undergrowth in terror. The stench of the blood grapes was almost intolerable, and Eldain pulled his scarf tighter about his face to block out the acrid aroma.

As they drew nearer to their goal, Eldain saw occasional druchii corpses lying amid the vines, throats slit by the Shadow Warriors who ranged ahead of the hundred riders making their way to the docks of Clar Karond. The ride from the trees had been fraught with danger, each passing second bringing them closer to their goal, but also closer to being discovered. But now they were within the concealing vineyards, and Eldain could see through the vines that the entrance to the shipyards was less than a hundred yards away.

The ground was ravaged, but relatively flat, ground into channels by the passage of countless logs dragged from the hills above Clar Karond and brought within the docks for sawing and shaping. Hundreds of slaves – humans and dwarfs mostly – slept in huddled groups, no fire to warm them or blankets to cover them, and Eldain knew that these pitiful creatures were the key to them getting into the shipyards. Beyond the slaves, an open gateway was set within a timber palisade of sharpened logs with tall, spiked towers to either side.

Eldain twisted in the saddle to ensure his warriors were ready, that arrows were nocked and swords were bared. He had personally handed each warrior three of the copper coloured arrows, etched with the rune of Saroir, that Rhianna's father had presented them with on the dockside of Lothern the day they had set sail for this accursed land. Vaul's magic was upon them, and he had made sure to impress upon each warrior that these arrows must not be wasted.

'Are we ready?' asked Caelir, his bow held loosely in his left hand. The longbow was inset with mother-of-pearl, and radiated powerful magic. Eldain recognised it as Rhianna's bow and felt his jaw clench at the sight of it.

'Yes, we are,' he said.

'Good luck, brother,' said Caelir and extended his hand.

Eldain looked down at his brother's palm, the skin rough and scarred where the druchii's red-hot crossbow had burned it, and the silver pledge ring bright in the darkness.

'And to you too,' he said, taking Caelir's hand.

Caelir nodded and said, 'Then give the word, brother.'

Eldain drew his own sword and shouted a command at Lotharin, who leapt from the concealment of the vines and bore his rider towards the shivering slaves. The hundred Ellyrian Reavers followed him, screaming at the top of their lungs and riding for the heart of the slave encampment.

The ground shook with the thunder of hooves as the high elves rode towards the log palisade. Shaken from their nightmares by the noise, the slaves awoke in panic, screaming in terror at the sight of a hundred horsemen bearing down upon them. Some curled into weeping foetal balls, while others ran towards them with arms outstretched, thinking them rescuers.

But as Eldain had planned, the majority fled in blind terror away from them, towards the gateway of Clar Karond's shipyards. Within moments of their appearance, torch-wielding druchii with whips emerged from behind the walls, demanding to know what in the name of Khaine was going on.

They died without knowing what danger came their way, the arrows of the Shadow Warriors piercing their throats or slicing through their eye sockets. More druchii emerged from the shipyards, and Eldain saw that these were the feared druchii corsairs, warrior knights with tall helmets, shrouded in scaled cloaks, who bore long spears and cruelly serrated swords. The mad press of slaves desperate to find shelter beyond the palisade prevented them from mustering a cohesive defence, so they stabbed their spear points through the bodies of slaves as they fought to discover the source of the alarm.

Eldain loosed a blue-fletched arrow and felled a corsair as a flurry of arrows slashed from the charging Ellyrian Reavers. Another volley cut down yet more of the druchii, and then they were amongst them.

Elven blades rose and fell, killing many druchii in the chaos and panic of the fleeing slaves. Blood and screams filled the night air as confusion spread from the gateway, and the slaves took advantage of their captors' disarray to have their revenge. A rampaging mob of slaves spread rapidly through the shipyards, yelling and toppling whatever they could.

He heard cries of alarm from druchii who recognised them as high elves, but as each shout was raised, an elven arrow quickly silenced it.

An alarm bell began chiming. Eldain shouted, 'With me!' and rode swiftly through the mad, swirling melee. The elven riders obeyed his shouted order with a discipline and speed that made him proud as they rode onwards through the screaming slaves. In a sweeping mass, they charged through wide streets lined with huge piles of lumber, long saws and chained axes. Along each thoroughfare were bloody altars to Khaine, headsmans' blocks, and cauldrons brimming with red fluid. Whether wine or blood, Eldain had no wish to know, but each sat beneath the mutilated body of a slave nailed to a crude cross.

The stench of stagnant sea air was pungent, and Eldain rode towards
the source of the rank odour, guiding Lotharin with his knees while loosing shaft after shaft into any druchii who dared come between him and
his goal. Caelir rode alongside him, dropping the warriors of the dark
kin with a speed and ease that was astonishing, the magic of the bow he
used finding the weakness in every druchii's armour.

Their course carried them past great, vaulted structures stacked high
with timber planks, shaped and treated for use in ships' hulls, and Eldain
plucked one of the copper Saroir arrows from his doeskin quiver. He
loosed the arrow into the midst of the timber, the head thudding into
the heart of the stored planks.

No sooner had the arrow struck the wood than it erupted into a mass
of searing fire, bright orange flames spreading swiftly from the point
of impact. Within moments, the entirety of the timber was ablaze, and
flames raced through the chamber as thick pillars of black smoke curled
skywards.

'Not a bad wedding present, eh?' shouted Caelir, and Eldain had to
admit that the fire enchantment placed upon the magic arrows was powerful indeed.

Within minutes, the sky was lit with a dreadful orange glow as more
of the druchii timber stores went up in flames, years' worth of materials
destroyed in moments. A wild exultation gripped Eldain as he shot yet
more druchii, but the strategist in him saw that they would not be able
to keep this momentum going for much longer. Soon, the druchii would
organise themselves, and if he and his warriors were trapped within the
shipyards, it would only be a matter of time before they were hunted
down and killed.

The rank odour of the Sea of Malice grew strong in his nostrils, and the
cobbled street opened onto a great granite quay laden with crates, barrels
and coils of hemp rope. Hundreds of ships at anchor wallowed in the
dark waters, their sleek and deadly hulls festooned with jagged blades,
icons of Khaine and the rune of the Witch King, Malekith himself.

Riders galloped out onto the quayside, and Eldain saw that they had
not penetrated this far into the shipyards of Clar Karond without loss. A
dozen or more steeds were without riders, and many of the warriors who
still fought were bloodied. He saw that Caelir was still alive, blood running from a shallow cut on his leg, but otherwise unharmed.

'Spread out!' yelled Eldain, unslinging an Ellyrion hunting horn from
his saddle and holding it high. 'Use the Saroir arrows and burn as many
ships as you can. When you hear me blow the signal to retreat get out
immediately, no hesitation. We will rally at the top of the ridge where we
began this glorious work! Now go!'

Whooping and yelling, the Ellyrian Reavers spread through the quay,
galloping along the warren of jetties and piers that connected the berthed
ships. Eldain, Caelir and ten warriors charged along a wide, tar-stained

jetty to their left, riding parallel to the bloated, mountainous form of the black ark. Arrows slashed through the night to slay druchii crewmen who peered out over the gunwales, and flames leapt skyward as the high elves made good use of their magic arrows. Eldain knew that, no matter what happened now, their mission to Naggaroth would be seen as a triumph.

He fired a Saroir arrow into a heavy Reaper ship, laughing in released tension as the arrow exploded with flames and the tarred planks instantly caught light. More and more ships burned as the high elves rampaged through the maze of jetties. Burning Corsairs leapt from their blazing vessels into the water, but Eldain felt no pity, only a thirst to kill more of the evil druchii.

Ahead, a group of corsairs charged from their doomed ship, bearing long spears and swords. Behind them, a group of druchii crossbowmen lining the gunwale shot a volley of lethal bolts towards them. Eldain cried out as a bolt sliced through the flesh of his bicep, but the wound was not deep and the bolt passed onwards without lodging.

Six of his warriors were not so lucky and tumbled from their saddles, pierced through by the deadly iron bolts. The druchii shouted something, but Eldain could not hear it over the roar of flames and the thunder of hooves on timber. Another volley slashed out, another three reavers fell, and Eldain felt his fury grow hotter than the flames billowing around him.

Twin streaks of copper flashed from Caelir's bow, and Eldain saw two of the Saroir arrows slam into the vessel. An enormous explosion of fire mushroomed from the deck of the ship as the magical flames exploded outwards, hurling the crossbowmen through the air and breaking the ship in two. The corsairs were hurled to the ground by the force of the blast, and the high elves gave them no chance to recover their wits, charging home and slaying them without mercy.

Eldain and Caelir rode amidst the corsairs, their swords flashing in the firelight as they killed the druchii. Caelir's face was lit with savage joy as he fought, and Eldain had a fleeting vision of his brother atop a great white steed, wearing the *Ithiltaen* of the Silver Helms.

A druchii Corsair stabbed up at him, and Eldain desperately twisted his steed around, but the spear penetrated his thigh and he screamed in pain as blood streamed down his leg. He fought to turn and bring his sword to bear, but the howling druchii was quicker and the spear lanced towards his heart.

A slashing sword split the spear apart in a shower of splinters, and Caelir's reverse stroke beheaded the Corsair as he rode between Eldain and his attacker.

'Come on, brother!' shouted Caelir, turning his steed and riding further out along the wide jetty. 'This way! Hurry!'

Eldain watched as blood fountained from the druchii's neck and the corpse toppled from the jetty into the water. His breath came in great, sucking lungfuls as he realised how close he had come to death. They had pushed their luck far enough, hundreds of ships were ablaze, and even though his warriors had surely loosed every one of the Saroir arrows, the wind was certain to fan the flames to those vessels that had thus far escaped.

Yes, it was time to go.

Eldain lifted the hunting horn from his saddle and blew three rising notes followed by one low, mournful one, the eerie sound carrying all across the harbour – even over the roar of flames, the crack of splitting timbers and the screams of the dying.

Even now, his warriors would be retreating and making their way back to safety.

'My lord?' shouted the last of his warriors over the din. 'Your brother!'

'I know,' returned Eldain. 'I will get him, you get out of here! Now!'

The warrior hesitated, torn between obeying his lord's order and his duty to protect him. Eldain saw his dilemma and said, 'you do me proud with your devotion, but I would be a poor master indeed if I let my warriors die thanks to my brother's foolishness. Now go!'

The reaver nodded and turned his horse, galloping hard for the quayside. Eldain turned and with a yell, rode after Caelir. He heard iron bolts whipping past him and glanced up to see crossbowmen lining the turrets and crags of the black ark. At such range, it was doubtful they could hit him, but such were their numbers that it would only take one lucky bolt to fell him or his horse. What in the name of Isha had driven Caelir to ride onwards? Had the spirit of Loec seized him with wild abandon?

Through the glow of the firelight, he saw Caelir ahead, battling a knot of druchii warriors in the shadow of one of the giant repeater bolt throwers. Enemy warriors pressed in around him, but Caelir fought like Tyrion himself, his sword stabbing and slashing amongst the druchii like quicksilver. The combat was over before Eldain reached his brother and shouted, 'What are you doing? Didn't you hear the signal to retreat?'

Caelir nodded, too out of breath to reply, and swiftly vaulted from the back of his horse.

'What are you doing?' repeated Eldain as more bolts from the crew of the black ark thudded into the timber of the jetty.

Caelir shouted, 'Come on, help me with this!' as he swung the massive bolt thrower around on greased runners to face the black ark. Many times larger than the Eagle's Claw bolt throwers employed by the armies of the Phoenix King, this monstrous weapon was designed for punching holes below the waterline of enemy ships.

'You have got to be joking,' said Eldain. 'That won't even scratch the side of a black ark!'

'I'm not aiming for the black ark!' shouted Caelir as he pulled the firing handle and a thick iron bolt, longer than three bowstaves, flashed through the air. Eldain watched as the bolt flew towards... not the ark, but the head of the great beast tethered by the massive chains to its front!

The bolt hammered into the great dragon's head, burying itself completely in its flesh. Purple flickers of magical light erupted around it as the powerful enchantments keeping it placid fought to contain the monster's agony. The Ark shook with the beast's pain, and its head rose from the water slightly, exposing a fiery red eye and terrifying fangs longer than a knight's lance. Heavy waves rocked the jetty as the massive form of the ark shifted in the water, and giant breakers foamed at its base as the beasts kept chained in its depths were unleashed. Eldain saw spined and sinuous forms slicing through the churning waters towards them and turned to face his brother, who struggled to load another bolt onto the firing runners.

'Come on!' shouted Caelir. 'Help me!'

Despite his better judgement, Eldain leapt from the saddle, crying out in pain as he landed on his wounded leg, and limped towards Caelir. Together they heaved the bolt into position and began furiously cranking the windlass mechanism.

'This is madness!' yelled Eldain.

'You're probably right!' answered Caelir. 'Do you have any Saroir arrows left?'

'Just one.'

'Tie it to the shaft of the bolt.'

'What?'

'Do it! Hurry!' shouted Caelir, as the firing mechanism clicked home and the weapon was ready to fire. Swiftly, Eldain pulled out his last magical arrow and snapped the bowstring from his longbow. He clambered onto the giant bolt thrower's curving front section and lashed the copper arrow to the jagged iron head of the bolt.

'Ready?' shouted Caelir.

'Done!' answered Eldain, leaping to the jetty as his brother fired the machine once more.

'Now let's get out of here,' cried Caelir, vaulting onto the back of his horse. Eldain followed suit, watching as the bolt streaked straight and true into the eye of the mighty sea dragon. The baleful red light was snuffed out and an explosion of purple light flared in the firelit darkness as the beast's agonies overcame the placating magic. Flames sheeted upwards from the dragon's head as the Saroir arrow ignited and seared a burning path through the beast's skull and into its brain.

The two brothers rode like the wind as the ark rocked in the water and huge swells broke across the bay. Splintering wood erupted behind them as the beasts unleashed from the ark smashed into the jetty, hungry for blood.

Eldain glanced behind him to see a monstrous sea creature with jaws the size of an eagle's wingspan tearing up the jetty towards them. Tarred planks flew in all directions, splintered and snapped by its weight and bulk. The great sea dragon's bellows of pain were deafening, and Eldain heard a tremendous groaning as its convulsions tore the black ark free of its moorings. Bolts hammered down around them as those druchii who still remained in the harbour sought to exact some last revenge against their attackers.

Caelir whooped and shrieked ahead of him, the adrenaline rush of what they had just done inuring him to the fear of what might yet befall them. The monster behind them drew ever closer, huge waves of water drenching them as the sea dragon's death throes rocked the waters of the bay with the force of an earthquake.

Ahead, Eldain saw Caelir reach the granite of the quayside. He heard the crack of wood from behind him and felt the rank breath of the monster from the deep on his neck.

'Jump!' shouted Caelir, and Eldain dug his heels hard into Lotharin's flanks.

The black stallion leapt towards the quayside as the sea monster's jaws slammed shut on the last of the jetty, smashing it to shards. Lotharin landed on the solid quay as the great beast slammed into it beneath the water, and Eldain let out a great, shuddering breath as his steed skidded to a halt.

A massive, groaning crack of splitting stone made both brothers look up in time to see the incredible sight of the black ark toppling into the bay, its mighty towers brought low, and hundreds of druchii falling to their deaths as the dying sea dragon thrashed in its chains. The monstrous floating fortress broke apart as it hit the water and a great tidal wave of black foam surged towards the shore of the bay.

The brothers turned their steeds and galloped back the way they had come, fighting their way through the shocked druchii towards their escape. Past blazing timber stores and ruined piles of blackened lumber, spears stabbed for them and repeater crossbow bolts slashed through the air, but their speed carried them past most of their attackers without a fight.

Eldain slashed his sword through the arm of a corsair guarding the gateway and hacked down another before riding clear. He stole a glance over his shoulder to see his brother slay a pair of druchii who sought to hamstring his horse. Caelir killed them both, but he had been slowed enough for other druchii to take aim with their crossbows, and a hail of bolts slashed towards him.

One pierced his hip and pitched him from his horse, while others hammered into his steed's chest and flanks. The horse collapsed, blood frothing from its mouth and its legs thrashing in agony.

Caelir picked himself up and ran as fast as he could towards the gateway. More bolts flashed through the air, another burying itself in his shoulder. He stumbled, but kept running.

'Brother!' he yelled, holding out his hand towards Eldain.

Eldain watched Caelir run, silhouetted in the firelight from the blazing wreckage of Clar Karond, and his vision narrowed as he focussed on Caelir's outstretched hand.

He saw the callused burns of his brother's wounded hand, Rhianna's silver pledge ring shining brightly in the flames.

Eldain said, 'Goodbye, Caelir.' He turned his horse towards the hills and rode away.

He did not look back, but pushed his steed hard through the vineyards towards the survivors of the attack. He heard shouts and screams and the clash of blades behind him, but paid them no heed as he galloped onwards.

As he crested the rise and entered the dark forest, he rode for some minutes before reaching his warriors. Bloody and exhausted, they were nevertheless magnificent, and he felt a strange freedom in his soul as he thought of all that had been achieved this night.

'My lord?' asked the leader of the Shadow Warriors. 'Where is Caelir?'

'He is dead,' replied Eldain sadly.

'Dead? Isha's mercy, no!'

'The druchii killed him,' said Eldain. 'He fought bravely, but there was nothing I could do to save him.'

'Our swords are yours!' promised the Shadow Warrior. 'We will avenge him!'

Eldain could see the same resolve in the face of every one of his warriors and said, 'We have won a great victory here, but we must return to our homeland now. The druchii will not remain in disarray for long and we have many days travel ahead of us before we may count ourselves safe. My brother *will* be avenged, but not this day.'

He turned his horse towards home and shouted, 'We ride for Ulthuan!'

VI

ULTHUAN – *One Month Ago*

The omens were good, thought Eldain as the ships pulled smoothly away from the Lothern quayside towards the Sapphire Gate. The morning sun was bright and a fair wind ruffled the white sails of the Eagle ships. Caelir stood at the vessel's stern, waving to Rhianna, who stood on the dockside beside her father, a tall, powerful elf in the swirling robes of an arch-mage.

The holds of each ship were laden with horses and supplies – food, grain, water and weapons, all that was necessary for an expedition to Naggaroth. Wrapped in oiled leather was a crate sealed with mystical wards, that had come from Rhianna's father, in which there were three hundred magical arrows. A sheepish Caelir had told him that they were an early wedding gift from Rhianna's father, and though it left the bitter taste of ashes in his throat to have such a reminder of her affection for his brother, Eldain knew that they would be invaluable.

The ships passed through the shadow of the mighty statues of the

Phoenix King and the Everqueen as the Sapphire Gate at the mouth of the lagoon began to open. A gate of shining silver, set with sapphires the size of a man's head, a glittering edifice that smoothly drew wider to allow their small fleet to pass through.

Beyond the Sapphire gate, an elven pilot vessel waited to guide their ships through the magically shifting sandbanks that protected the Straits of Lothern from attackers.

Eldain made his way to the vessel's prow and felt a shiver of anticipation as the gate behind them closed and they found themselves in a wide channel between sheer cliffs of white. Castles equipped with repeater bolt throwers, ramparts and seaward defences manned by ithilmar armoured warriors of the Sea Guard, protected the Straits of Lothern, and Eldain knew almost nothing could penetrate these defences.

Eventually, the channel narrowed until they reached the great fortified arch that was the Emerald Gate, foremost of the great sea gates that guarded Lothern. Two vast valves of carved bronze studded with great emeralds were set into the cliffs and, as the pilot guided them towards the gate, it swung open on mighty hinges to grant them passage to the open ocean.

The ships passed onwards, the great gate shutting soundlessly behind them as Eldain had his first sight of the Glittering Tower.

Rearing up from the sea atop a rocky isle in the mouth of the bay, the Glittering Tower was a great lighthouse filled with thousands of lamps that could never be extinguished. Mighty fortifications clustered at its base, each bastion equipped with scores of bolt throwers and hundreds of Sea Guard warriors.

Caelir joined him at the prow and said, 'It is magnificent.'

'Yes,' agreed Eldain. 'It truly is.'

'Eldain...' said Caelir hesitantly. 'I just wanted to say, well, that I am sorry I didn't tell you about Rhianna. I meant to say something to you sooner, I really did.'

'It doesn't matter any more, little brother.'

'It doesn't?' asked Caelir, the relief plain in his voice.

Eldain shook his head. 'No. It doesn't.'

Caelir let out a nervous laugh and leaned out over the vessel's side as the Glittering Tower receded into the distance and the wind filled the sails of the ship. The two brothers watched in silence as it vanished over the horizon and Caelir eventually said, 'I wonder if I will ever see Ulthuan again?'

'What do you mean?'

Caelir didn't answer for a moment, as though weighing up whether or not he should speak, but eventually he said, 'I have been having evil dreams of late, brother.'

'What kind of dreams?' asked Eldain.

'When I wake I do not remember the substance of them, but in each of them I hear the wail of Morai-heg.'

'The Keeper of Souls,' said Eldain.

Caelir nodded. 'I hear her banshees wailing in my dreams and I fear she holds my fate in her withered palm. I am afraid she has decided that it is my time to die.'

'They are just dreams, Caelir.'

'Maybe so, Eldain, but I fear them. I fear what they might mean for me in Naggaroth.'

Eldain was about to reply, but Caelir was not yet finished. 'I want you to promise me something, Eldain.'

'What would you have me promise?' he asked.

'If... if I do not return from Naggaroth, promise me that you will take care of Rhianna.'

'Rhianna?' asked Eldain, genuinely surprised.

'Yes,' said Caelir. 'I know she still cares for you, so if I die, promise me you will take care of her.'

Eldain smiled and said, 'Of course I will, brother. You can count on me.'

DEFENDERS OF ULTHUAN

BOOK ONE
NEPENTHE

CHAPTER ONE
SURVIVORS

Thunderous booms echoed from the cliffs as the surf crashed against the rock and exploded upwards in sprays of pure white. The icy, emerald sea surged through the channels between the rocky archipelagos to the east in great swells, rising and falling in foam-topped waves that finally washed onto the distant shores of a mist-shrouded island.

Amid the great green waves, a splintered shard of wreckage was carried westward towards the island, the last remnants of a ship that had fallen foul of the obscuring mists and shifting isles that protected the eastern approaches to the island. Clinging to the debris was a lone figure whose golden hair was plastered to his skull and tapered ears, and whose clothes were torn and bloodied.

He clung desperately to the wreckage, barely able to see as salt spray stung his eyes, and the hammer-blows of the waves threatened to tear him from the wood and drag him to his doom beneath the water. The flesh of his fingers and palms was torn as he gripped tightly to all that remained of the ship he had sailed in.

Clinging to the hope that the sea would bear him to the island's beaches before his strength gave out and the water claimed him for its own, he kicked feebly as he was pitched about like a rider on an unbroken colt. His every muscle burned with fire and blood streamed from a swollen gash on his forehead, the dizziness and nausea threatening to part him from the wreckage as surely as the waves. The sea was carrying him towards the island, though the glittering mists that shrouded its cliffs seemed to distort the distance between him and his salvation; one minute promising imminent landfall, the next dashing those hopes as the land appeared to recede.

Not only did the mists confound his sight, but also, it appeared, his hearing. Even amid the tumult of the waves, he fancied he could hear the slap of water on the hull of a ship behind him as it plied the treacherous channels. He turned his head this way and that, seeking the source of the sound, but he could see nothing save the endless expanse of ghostly mists that clung to the sea like a lover and the tantalising sight of the white cliffs.

He swallowed a mouthful of sea and coughed saltwater as his body shook with exhaustion and cold. A dreadful lethargy cocooned his limbs and he could feel the strength ebbing from his body as surely as if drawn by a spell. His eyelids felt as though lead weights had been attached to them, drooping over his sapphire blue eyes and promising oblivion if he would just close them and give up. He shook off the sleep he knew would kill him and ground his torn palms into the splintered edges of the wood, the pain welcome and necessary even as he threw back his head and screamed.

He screamed for pain and for loss and for an anguish he did not yet understand.

How long he had been in the water, he did not know. Nor could he remember the ship he had sailed on or what role he had fulfilled as part of its crew. His memory was as insubstantial as the mists, fragmentary images scudding across the surface of his mind without meaning, and all he could remember was the cruel sea battering him with unthinking power.

The ocean lifted him up, high atop a roaring curve of water, before slamming him back down into yet another bottle-green trough, but in the instant he had crested the wave, he spied the landscape of the island through salt-encrusted eyes once more.

Tall cliffs of pearl-white stone crowned with achingly beautiful greenery were closer than ever before, the echoes of powerful waves splintering to crystal shards at their base now deafening. Fresh hope surged in his blood as the mists parted and he saw a golden curve of beach beyond a spur of marble rock.

Hysterical laughter bubbled up inside him and he kicked desperately as he struggled against the tide to reach the soil of his home. He gritted his teeth and struggled with the last of his strength to reach the salvation of the shore. Angry at being denied its prize, the sea fought to retain him, but he plumbed the depths of his desperation and courage to break its embrace.

Slowly the bow of beach grew larger, sweeping around the edges of a rocky bay upon which numerous watchtowers and lighthouses were perched. He felt his strength fade as he passed into the more sheltered waters of the bay and pulled himself further onto the timbers of his lost ship as the currents carried him onwards.

His vision dimmed. He knew he had pushed his tortured body too far and he had nothing more to give. He lay his head down on the smooth surface of the timber and felt his limbs relax as consciousness began to fade. He smiled as he watched the coastline of his homeland draw nearer, tall poplars and hardy grasses marching down to the shoreline from the cliff tops high above.

Winged shapes pinwheeled in the sky above him and he smiled as the sea birds filled the air with their cries, as though welcoming him home once more – though he could not recall why or for how long he had been gone. His mind drifted as the current carried him towards the beach and it took him several minutes to register the soft impact of his makeshift raft against the shore.

He lifted his head to spit saltwater as his eyes filled with tears of joy at the thought that he had returned home. He wept and pulled himself from the timbers that had carried him through the cold green waters of the sea and rolled into the shallow surf.

To feel the soft sand beneath him was ecstasy and he gouged great handfuls in his bloodied fists as he clawed his way to dry land. Inch by torturous inch, he dragged his sodden frame onto the beach, each herculean effort punctuated with wracking sobs and gasps of exhaustion.

Finally, he was clear of the ocean and collapsed onto his side, the breath heaving in his lungs and his tears cutting clear paths through the grime on his face. He rolled onto his back, staring up at a heartbreakingly beautiful blue sky as his eyes fluttered shut.

'I am home,' he whispered as he drifted into darkness. 'Ulthuan…'

Ellyr-charoi, the great villa of the Éadaoin family, shone as though aflame, early afternoon sunlight reflecting dazzlingly from gemstones set within its walls and the coloured glass that filled the high windows of its many azure-capped towers. Built around a central courtyard, the villa's architecture had been designed to render it as much a part of the landscape as the natural features that surrounded it. Its builders had employed the natural topography in its design so that it appeared that the villa had arisen naturally from its surroundings, rather than having been raised by the artifice of craftsmen.

Set amid a wide stand of trees, the villa was bounded on two sides by a pair of foaming white waterfalls that had their origin high on the eastern slopes of the Annulii Mountains. The waters of both joined beyond the villa, flowing fast and cold to a wide river that glittered on the horizon. An overgrown pathway led from the gates of the villa to a sweeping bridge of arched timbers that curved over the rushing waters and followed the course of the river through the eternal summer of Ellyrion to the mighty city of Tor Elyr.

Autumn leaves lay thick and still against the smooth stone of the villa and climbing vines curled like snakes across the cracked walls, unchecked and wild. A soft breeze blew through the open gates like a sigh of regret and whistled through cracked panes of glass on the tallest towers. Where once warriors had stood sentinel by the portal that led within and surveyed Lord Éadaoin's realm from the watchtowers, all that remained now was the memory of those faithful retainers.

Within the walls of the villa, golden leaves danced in the ghostly breaths of wind that soughed through echoing and empty rooms. No water gurgled in the fountain and no laughter or warmth filled its deserted halls. The only sound to break the silence was that of hesitant footsteps as they made their way along a marble-tiled cloister towards elegantly curved stairs that led from the courtyard to the master of this villa's chambers.

Rhianna looked up from her book as Valeina emerged from the shadow of the leaf-strewn cloister and stepped down into the Summer Courtyard, though such a name seemed now to be at odds with the autumnal air that hung over the open space. The young elf maid carried a silver tray upon which sat a crystal goblet of wine and a platter of fresh fruits, bread, cheese and cold cuts of meat. Dressed in the livery of the household, Valeina had served the lords of the Éadaoin for almost a decade now and Rhianna smiled in welcome as the young girl passed the silent fountain at the courtyard's centre.

In the year and a half since she had lived in the Éadaoin villa, Rhianna had grown fond of Valeina and valued the times they were able to speak. Inwardly, she knew that she would never have considered such a friendship back in her father's estates... but a lot had happened since she had left Saphery.

'My lady,' said Valeina, setting the tray down beside her. 'Lord Éadaoin's food. You said you wished to take it to him yourself.'

'Yes, I did,' replied Rhianna. 'Thank you.'

The girl inclined her head in a gesture of respect, the boundaries between noble born elf and common citizen still strong despite their growing friendship, and Rhianna needed no mage sight to sense that it sat ill with Valeina in bringing this repast to her instead of directly to the master of the house. Etiquette demanded that no highborn elf of Ulthuan should carry out such mundane tasks as serving food, but Rhianna had politely requested that this meal be brought to her first.

'Will you be requiring anything else, my lady?' asked Valeina.

Rhianna shook her head and said, 'No, I'm fine. Won't you sit awhile?'

Valeina hesitated and Rhianna's smile faltered, knowing that she was simply using the girl as an excuse to delay taking the meal to its intended recipient.

'I know this is... unorthodox, Valeina,' said Rhianna, 'but it is something I need to do.'

'But it's not right, my lady,' said the elf maid. 'A lady of your standing doing the work of the household, I mean.'

Rhianna reasserted her smile and reached out to take Valeina's hand in hers. 'I'm just carrying some food upstairs to my husband, that's all.'

The elf maid cast a glance towards the stairs that curled upwards into the Hippocrene Tower. Once, a portion of the crashing waterfalls beyond the villa had been channelled down grooves fashioned into the sides of the tower to feed the fountain at the centre of the Summer Court-yard, but now cracked leaves filled the cascading marble and silver bowls instead of glittering crystal waters.

'How is Lord Éadaoin?' asked Valeina, clearly nervous at such an intrusive question.

Rhianna sighed and chewed her bottom lip before answering. 'He is the same as always, my dear Valeina. The death of Cae… his brother… is a splinter of ice in his heart and it cools his blood to those around him.'

'We all miss Caelir, my lady,' said Valeina, squeezing Rhianna's hand and naming the grief that had settled upon the Éadaoin household like a shroud. 'He brought this house to life.'

'He did that,' agreed Rhianna, struggling to hold back a sudden wave of sadness that threatened to overwhelm her. A strangled sob escaped her, but she angrily caged the sorrow within and reasserted control on her emotions.

'I'm sorry! I didn't mean to–'

'It's all right, my dear,' said Rhianna. 'Really.'

She knew she had not convinced the elf maid and wondered if she'd convinced herself.

Two years had passed since Caelir's death in Naggaroth and though the sadness was still a bright pain in her heart, chains of duty that were stronger than death bound her to her fate.

She remembered the day she had watched the Eagle ships returning to Lothern after the raid on the land of the dark elves, the hated druchii, the gleaming silver of the Sapphire Gate shining like fire in the setting sun behind them. No sooner had she looked into the haunted eyes of Eldain as he had stepped onto the quayside than she knew that Caelir was lost, the visions of Morai-heg that had filled her dreams with dark premonitions suddenly brought to horrid life.

The druchii had slain Caelir, explained Eldain, and the all-consuming grief he felt at his brother's loss was as hot and painful as hers. Together they had wept and held each other close, allowing their shared loss to bring them closer that they might heal themselves.

She shook off the memory of that dark day and looked down at the pledge ring on her finger, a silver band with a swirling cobalt coloured gem set amid a pair of entwined hands. Soon after, Eldain had spoken of the promise he had made to his younger brother upon their departure for the Land of Chill; a promise that he would take care of Rhianna should anything happen to Caelir.

They had been wed the following year and the elven nobility of Ulthuan all agreed that it was a good match.

As well they might, thought Rhianna, for she and Eldain had all but been betrothed to one another, before she had lost her heart to Caelir after he had saved her from death at the hands of druchii raiders a year previously.

But dreams of love were long gone and she was now the wife of Eldain, lord of the Éadaoin family and master of this villa.

Rhianna slid her hand from Valeina's and lifted the silver tray. She stood smoothly and said, 'I should take this to Eldain.'

Valeina stood with her and said, 'He has a good soul, my lady. Just give him some time.'

Rhianna nodded stiffly and turned away, making her way to the stairs and her husband who brooded alone with his grief in the tallest tower of Ellyr-charoi.

Eldain gripped the edges of the window tightly as he stood before the tall lancet that looked out over the rolling greensward of Ellyrion and listened to the voices drifting up from the Summer Courtyard. Every word was a dagger in his heart and he closed his eyes as he felt the pain of them stabbing home. He let out a deep breath and tried to calm his racing heartbeat by reciting the vow of the Sword Masters of Hoeth.

Though he had never journeyed to the White Tower, where the legendary warrior mystics trained, he still found their mantra soothed him in times of trial, the rhythmic cadences of the words sounding like music in his ears.

Eldain opened his eyes and, taking a deep, calming breath, he raised his eyes to the soaring mountains that lay to the west. The Annulii Mountains towered over the grasslands of Ellyrion, stark and white against the pale blue of the sky, their summits lost in the swirling mists of raw magic that flowed between the outer and inner kingdoms of Ulthuan. The reassuring permanence of the mountains was a balm on his soul, and his eyes roamed over their craggy peaks and tree-swathed slopes, picking out paths and sacred groves amongst the great spires of rock.

In their youth, both he and Caelir had roamed the land of Ellyrion on the backs of steeds they had raised from foals, and who had become their boon companions since first they had ridden together. But now Caelir was dead and Eldain's steps barely carried him from Ellyr-charoi.

'He has a good soul,' he had heard Valeina say, and he did not know whether to laugh or cry at the words. He turned from the window and paced the circumference of the Hippocrene Tower, his long cloak of sky-blue cloth trailing behind him as a cold wind scattered leaves and papers across an exquisitely carved desk of walnut.

The inner walls of the tower were lined with bookshelves and pierced by tall windows at each of the eight compass points, allowing the Lord of Ellyr-charoi to survey his domain and keep watch on the mighty herds of Ellyrion steeds as they thundered across the plains.

Eldain slumped behind his desk and gathered the papers the wind had scattered. Amongst the reports of Shadow Warriors from the western coasts and missives from the garrison of the Eagle Gate high in the mountains were numerous invitations to dine at the homes of nobles of Tor Elyr, entreaties to the latest spectacle of wonder of Saphery and word from his agents in the port of Lothern concerning his trade investments.

He could focus on none of it for more than a moment and he looked up to face the portrait that hung on the wall opposite his desk. For all the difference between the portrait's subject and Eldain, he might as well have been looking into a mirror and only more careful study would reveal the differences between the two.

Both wore their platinum blond hair long and confined by a golden circlet and both had the strong, handsome bone structure common to the Ellyrion nobility – a rugged windswept countenance that spoke of a lifetime spent in the open air atop the greatest steeds in Ulthuan. Their eyes were both a crisp blue, flecked with ocean grey, but where the face in the portrait displayed a well-fed, roguish insouciance, Eldain's features were gaunt and serious. The artist had captured the boyish mischief that always glimmered in his younger brother's eyes as well as the quality of dashing adventure that always seemed to surround Caelir like a mystical aura. Eldain knew well enough that he possessed none of these qualities.

His eyes locked with those of Caelir and he felt the familiar guilt stir within, welcoming it like an old friend. He knew it was perverse to keep the portrait of his dead brother – and his wife's former betrothed – hanging before him where he would be forced to see it every day, but ever since his 'triumphant' return from the land of the druchii, he had forced himself to confront the reality of what had happened on Naggaroth.

Every day it ate away at him, but he could no more deny himself the guilty torment than he could stop the beat of his heart.

Eldain looked up as he heard Rhianna's footfalls on the steps leading up to his chambers. Even had he not heard the conversation below, he would have recognised her tread. He forced a smile to his full lips as she came into view, holding a silver tray laden with sweet smelling morsels.

He took a sharp intake of breath at her beauty, each time finding some aspect of her to savour anew. Her waist length hair spilled around her shoulders like a run of honey and her delicate oval features were sculpted more perfectly than any artist could hope to capture with the finest Tiranoc marble. Her long blue dress was threaded with silver loops and spirals and her soft eyes flickered with hints of magical gold.

She was beautiful and her beauty was yet another punishment.

'You should let Valeina do this,' he said as she set the tray down before him.

'I like coming here,' said Rhianna with a smile, and he could hear the lie in her words.

'Really?'

'Really,' she said, moving towards the window and staring into the distance. 'I like the view. You can practically see all the way to the forest of Avelorn.'

Eldain tore his gaze from Rhianna and looked down at the tray of food she had brought and reluctantly lifted a piece of bread. He had no appetite and dropped it back onto the tray as Rhianna turned from the window and said, 'Why don't we go riding today, Eldain? There's still plenty of light left in the day and it's been too long since you rode Lotharin.'

The mention of his faithful steed made Eldain smile, and though the midnight-black horse roamed the plains with the wild herds that ran free throughout the kingdom of Ellyrion, the merest thought would summon him back to Ellyr-charoi at a gallop, such was the bond they shared.

He shook his head and waved his hand at the scattered papers upon the desk. 'I cannot. I have work to finish.'

Rhianna's face flushed and he could see her anger manifest itself in the soft glow that built behind her golden eyes. A daughter of Saphery, the power of magic coursed in her veins and Eldain could feel the actinic tang of it in the air.

'Please, Eldain,' said Rhianna. 'This is not healthy. You spend every day cooped up in this tower with nothing but books and papers and… Caelir for company. It is morbid.'

'Morbid? It is morbid now to remember the dead?'

'No, it is not morbid to mourn the dead, but to live life in their shadow is wrong.'

'I live in no shadow,' said Eldain, lowering his head.

'Do not lie to me, Eldain,' warned Rhianna. 'I am your wife!'

'And I am your husband!' he said, rising from behind the desk and sweeping the silver tray onto the floor. The plates clattered noisily and the crystal goblet shattered into a thousand fragments. 'I am the master of this household and I have business to attend to that does not allow me time for frivolous pursuits.'

'Frivolous pursuits…? Is that what I am to you now?'

He could see the tears gathering in her eyes and softened his tone. 'No, of course not, that's not what I meant, it's just…'

'Just what?' demanded Rhianna. 'Don't you remember how you lost me before? When the druchii almost killed me, it was Caelir that saved me because you were spending all your time locked up in this tower "attending to business".'

'Someone had to…' said Eldain. 'My father was dying, poisoned by the druchii and who was there to look after him and keep Ellyr-charoi safe? Caelir? I hardly think so.'

Rhianna stepped towards him and he felt his resolve crumbling in the face of her words. 'Caelir is dead, Eldain. But we are not and we still have lives to lead.'

She lifted a sheaf of papers from the desk and said, 'There is still a world beyond Ellyr-charoi, Eldain, a living, breathing world that we ought to be part of. But we pay no visits to our fellow nobles, nor do we dine in the halls of the great and good or dance at the masquerades of Tor Elyr...'

'Dance?' said Eldain. 'What is there to dance about, Rhianna? We are a dying people and no dance or masquerade can conceal that. You would have me plaster on a fake smile and dance at our race's funeral? The very thought sickens me to my stomach.'

The vehemence of his words surprised even him, but Rhianna shook her head, moving close to him and taking his hands in hers. 'Do you remember that you promised your brother you would take care of me?'

'I remember,' said Eldain, picturing the handsome Caelir as he confessed the fear he had for his survival on Naggaroth as their ship had passed the Glittering Tower at the mouth of the Straits of Lothern.

'Then take care of me, Eldain,' she said. 'Others can help look after Ellyr-charoi. Look out the window, Eldain, the world is still here and it is beautiful. Yes, the dark kin across the water prey upon us and yes, there are foul daemons that seek to destroy all that is good and wondrous, but if we live our lives in constant terror of such things then we might as well take a blade to our throats now.'

'But there are things I must do, things that–'

'They can wait,' said Rhianna, pulling his hands around her waist and drawing him close. The scent of summer orchards was in her hair and he took a breath of it, feeling his cares lighten even as he savoured the scent.

Eldain smiled and relaxed into her embrace, feeling her hands slide up his back.

He opened his eyes and stiffened as he looked into the eyes of his brother.

You killed me...

CHAPTER TWO
NEW BLOOD

A red glow lit the dusky horizon behind the three Eagle ships as they patrolled the south-western coastline of Ulthuan, their silver hulls like knife blades as they cut through the green waters. Captain Finlain of *Finubar's Pride* watched the craggy peaks of the Dragonspine Mountains and the smoke-wreathed Vaul's Anvil recede as his small flotilla made its way towards its evening berthing upon the sandy shores of Tiranoc.

The thin strip of coastline of this rugged kingdom had once reached out beyond where his ships now sailed, but ancient malice and powerful magic had destroyed this once fair realm. Monstrous tides had swept over the plains of Tiranoc in ages past, sweeping thousands to their deaths and submerging its ripened fields and glorious cities forever beneath the waves. Only the mountains and the bleak haunches of land that huddled at their feet remained above the water now and Finlain knew navigating this close to the shore was always fraught with danger.

'Sounding,' said Finlain, his voice muffled by the low mist that hugged the surface of the water and slithered over his vessel's hull.

'All's well, captain,' came the reply from Meruval, the *Pride*'s navigator. Finlain glanced over to the prow of his ship, where the mage Daelis sat in a high backed chair of ivory coloured timber, his eyes closed as he probed the waters and mists ahead with his magical sight for any dangerous rocks that might pierce the hull.

His crew were on edge and Finlain shared their unease. The red sky above Vaul's Anvil bled into the clouds like a bloodstain and the air had a foulness to it that was more than simply the sulphurous reek of the volcano.

'I'll be glad when we reach the beach for the night,' said Meruval, moving from the gunwale to stand next to his captain.

Finlain nodded, peering through the purple dusk towards the other vessels in his command. *Glory of Eataine* was riding a little low in the water and *Asuryan's Fire* lagged behind, her captain keeping a little too much distance between his ship and her sister vessels.

'Indeed,' said Finlain. 'The sea has an ill-aspect to it this evening.'

Meruval followed his captain's gaze and nodded in agreement. 'I know. I've had to steer us around rock formations I've never seen before. It's worse than sailing east of Yvresse.'

'Have you known this stretch of water to be this inconsistent before?'

'Not in my memory,' said Meruval, 'but in my grandfather's time, he spoke of Tiranoc rising to the surface with great heaves that threw up bleak islands that sank almost as soon as they breached the surface.'

'As though the land sought to return to the light.'

'Something like that, yes. He said that when Vaul was angry, he would strike his anvil and the land around would heave with fire and earthquakes.'

Finlain glanced over his shoulder at the smoking peak of Vaul's Anvil and sent a quick prayer to the smith god that he would spare them such anger this night, since the light was fading fast and a brooding fog was rapidly closing in. Strange noises and flickering lights danced at the edge of perception, and though such things were not unheard of in the magical mists that obscured the isle of Ulthuan from predatory eyes, they were still unsettling.

Only the keen hearing of his crew and the mage sight of Daelis would see them safely to the shoreline and the feeling that he could do nothing more was anathema to him.

No sooner had he thought of the mage than his sonorous voice sounded from the prow.

'Captain! Land ahead, we must slow our progress.'

'Hold us here!' ordered Finlain, gripping the smooth timbers of the gunwale as the vessel came to a smooth halt.

'Come on,' he said and set off towards the mage, not waiting to see if Meruval followed him or not. He marched down the length of the ship, passing sailors eager to be on dry land for the evening. The ship was allowing the current to carry her to the shore, the crew ready to make any adjustments necessary to keep them on course.

'Almost at the beach,' he said as he passed the crew, radiating a confidence he did not yet feel. He climbed the curved steps to the elaborate eagle prow and the mage who guided them slowly through the mist.

Daelis sat rigid on his chair, his cream and sapphire robes glittering with magical hoarfrost and a soft glow limning the edges of his eyes.

Without looking up, the mage said, 'We are close to land, captain. The shore is less than two boat lengths away.'

The mage's voice was distant, as though he spoke from within a great, echoing cave and Finlain could feel the ripple of magic work its way up his spine, a fleeting image of a dark, undersea world flickering behind his eyes.

'Two boat lengths?' said Meruval. 'Impossible. We haven't sailed far enough to be that close to land. You are mistaken.'

Daelis inclined his head towards the navigator, but did not open his eyes. 'I am not.'

'Captain,' said Meruval, indignant that his piloting skills were being called into question, 'we cannot be that close. He must be wrong.'

Finlain had sailed with both Daelis and Meruval for long enough to know that both were highly skilled at what they did and he trusted their judgment implicitly. However, in this case, one of them had to be wrong.

'I'm telling you, captain,' said Meruval. 'We can't be that close to the shore.'

'I believe you, my friend, but what if Daelis is correct also?'

'I *am* correct,' said Daelis, lifting his arm and pointing into the mist. 'Look.'

Finlain followed the mage's outstretched hand and narrowed his eyes as he sought to identify what he was being shown. Scraps of mist floated like gossamer thin cloth and at first he was inclined to agree with Meruval that the mage was mistaken, but as the wisps of fog parted for a moment, he caught sight of a towering wall of glistening black rock rearing up before his ship.

Meruval saw it too and said, 'Isha preserve me if he wasn't right after all...'

'You said it yourself, Meruval, the sea was unsettled this night.'

'You have my humble apology, captain,' said his navigator. 'As do you, Mage Daelis.'

The mage smiled and Finlain shook his head as he marched back to his crew and issued the orders that would see them sail along the cliff until they reached a bay with a beach large enough to land all three ships.

'Guide us along the coast, Meruval,' said Finlain as a sudden whipcrack sound echoed behind him, followed by a trio of rapid thuds. He turned in surprise, seeing bright red runnels of blood streaming down the white back of the mage's chair and the barbed points of three crossbow bolts of dark iron that had punched through his chest.

Daelis gurgled in pain, pinned to his prow chair by the bolts, and it took a second for Captain Finlain to realise what had happened. He looked out into the mist, knowing now that Meruval had been right after all, they hadn't been close to land, and that great black cliff was not part of Ulthuan at all... it was...

The mists parted as a great crack of groaning rock echoed from the

murky depths and the mighty cliff seemed to *twist* and rise from the
ocean. Seawater poured from fanged portals and great idols of armoured
warriors carved into the rock as they rose from the sea and a great beacon
of flame bloomed high above him.

'To arms!' shouted Finlain, as a flurry of dark crossbow bolts flashed
through the air from somewhere high above him. Screams tore the air as
many found homes in elven flesh and the stink of blood filled his senses.
He staggered as a bolt tore across the side of his calf and embedded itself
in the deck. He gritted his teeth against the pain, blood pooling in his
boot, and looked up as a great flaming missile arced from the black cliff
to engulf the *Glory of Eataine*. Her sail erupted in fire and flaming brands
scattered all across her deck.

Its deception unmasked by the attack, the tall cliff of sheer rock cast off
its mantle of poisonous mist and Finlain was rooted to the spot in terror
as he saw the monstrous, unbelievable size of their attacker.

No mere ship was this, but a mountainous castle of incredible bulk
set adrift on the sea and kept afloat by the most powerful enchantments.
One of the dreaded black arks of the dark elves, this was a sinister floating fortress, tower upon tower and spire upon spire of living rock that
had been sundered from the isle of Ulthuan over five thousand years
ago.

Crewed by an entire army of deadly corsairs and dismal home to thousands of slaves, the black arks were the most feared seagoing vessels in
the world and dwarfed even the might of Finlain's Eagle ships. Finlain
had heard it said that the bulk they displayed above the surface of the
water was but a fraction of their true size, with great vaulted caverns
below the waterline that were home to terrible monsters, slaves and all
manner of foul witchcraft.

Even as he recognised the identity of their attackers, a brazen gate of
rusted iron shrieked open in the side of the ark and a long boarding
ramp crashed down over the gunwale, jagged spikes splintering the deck
and wedging it fast into its prey.

Finlain pushed himself to his feet and swept his sword from its sheath,
a glittering silver steel blade forged by his father and enchanted by the
archmages of Hoeth.

Dark shapes gathered in the shadow of the gateway in the rock and a
volley of white-shafted arrows slashed past Finlain's head to fell them
with lethal accuracy. Another volley followed within seconds of the first
and this time it was their enemies that were screaming.

He threw a glance over his shoulder to see that Meruval had formed
several ranks of archers, their bone-white bows loosing arrow after arrow
into the dark portal.

In answer, a scything spray of crossbow bolts spat from the mouth of
the ark and Finlain heard the screams of his warriors as they died in the
fusillade. Elven archers were the best in the world, but even they could

not compete with the rate of fire the infernal weapons of their enemies could manage.

Keeping low, Finlain darted forwards as the deadly crossbow bolts thinned the defending elves long enough for the boarders to dash across the lowered ramp. Screaming druchii corsairs clad in dark robes and swathed in glittering cloaks formed from overlapping scales charged from the depths of the Ark, their twin swords gleaming red in the ruddy glow of Vaul's Anvil.

Finlain rose to meet them, his sword slashing through the first warrior's neck and pitching him into the sea. He stabbed the next enemy warrior through the groin and desperately blocked a deadly riposte to his own neck. It had been many years since Finlain had fought the dark kin of his race, slender ivory-skinned elves with long hair the colour of night. Their faces were twisted in hatred and their movements as swift and deadly as his own.

So like us… he thought sadly, as he parried another blow and despatched his foe with a roll of his wrist that plunged the tip of his blade through the corsair's eye and into his brain. Blue-fletched arrows flashed past his head and sent more druchii screaming into the sea, most passing less than a foot from Finlain's head, but he feared no injury from his own warriors.

Another blade joined his and he smiled in welcome to see Meruval, armed with his twin, moonlight-bladed swords, leap into the fray. With the aid of his faithful navigator, he was finally able to take more stock of the battle and risked glances left and right to see how the other ships in his command fared.

Glory of Eataine burned from stem to stern and Finlain knew she was lost. *Asuryan's Fire* was invisible in the dark and mist, but he feared the worst as he heard the raucous victory chants of the druchii and the screams of the dying.

Only *Finubar's Pride* fought on and he knew they had to break the hold the black ark had on them if they were to stand any chance of survival. Finlain stepped back from the desperate fighting and shouted, 'Meruval! Can you hold them?'

The navigator plunged his blades into the chest of a druchii warrior and kicked another into the sea, spinning on his heel and opening the belly of a third.

'For a time,' he said, as a pair of iron bolts smacked into the deck beside him.

Finlain nodded and limped away from the desperate fight, shouting, 'Axes! Bring up axes, we need to cut ourselves free!'

Fire erupted from nearby and his heart sank as he saw *Glory of Eataine* break apart and sink beneath the waves along with her crew.

Finlain vowed that such would not be *their* fate…

* * *

'My lady,' said the warrior in the tall helm who carried a long, leaf-bladed spear. 'It is getting late and we should be heading back to the villa.'

Kyrielle Greenkin smiled as she heard the note of exasperation in the warrior's voice and put on her best pouting expression of innocence. Her auburn hair was woven in long plaits, held tight to her skull by silver cord that framed a beautiful face with shimmering jade eyes and a full-lipped mouth that could charm even the hardest heart.

A simple warrior had no chance.

'Not yet, silly,' she said, and there was beguiling magic in her voice. 'It is in the gloaming that some of the most wondrous plants flower. You wouldn't want me to return without something wondrous to present to my father, would you?'

The warrior glanced helplessly at his comrade, pinned like a butterfly by her captivating gaze and knowing he could not deny her, even had he desired to.

'No, my lady,' he said, defeated.

It was unfair of her to use magic on the guards her father had provided her with, but she had not lied when she spoke of the beauty of the night blooming flowers; the pearl-leafed Torrelain, the singing blooms of the magical Anurion (named for her father and its creator) and the beautifully aromatic Moon Rose.

She picked her way down the cliff top path that led to the beach, one guard before her and another behind as they made their way down to the shore. Kyrielle went barefoot, her keen eyes easily picking out sharp rocks and thorny brush before they could injure her.

Her long dress was fashioned from green silk and clung seductively to her slender form, its fabric woven with looping anthemion patterns. In one hand she carried a delicate reticule of tightly woven cloth and in the other a small knife with a silver blade – for night blooms should only ever be pruned with a silver blade.

The scent of the night filled her senses and she could smell the perfumes of the local flora as well as the powerful fragrances dragged from the depths of the ocean and borne upon the air. When the shifting isles on the eastern coast of Ulthuan renewed themselves, the darkness of the deep sea was disturbed and all manner of strange plant life was washed ashore as well as unknown aromas that scented the night air – the chief reason her father had sited one of his terraced garden-villas on this largely deserted peninsula of rock on the coast of Yvresse.

The pale crescent of the rising moon bathed the beach in ghostly radiance and turned the white cliffs into softly glowing walls of light as the surf crashed against them further out to sea and the waves rolled up the sand with soft sighs.

She loved this time of night, often seeking the peace and tranquillity that the sound of the waves brought her. To be out on a night like this, with the evening blooms spreading their petals and the light of the moon caressing her skin was heaven for Kyrielle, a time where she could forget the troubles of the world around her and simply enjoy its beauty.

'Isn't this magical?' she asked as she danced onto the beach, pirouetting beneath the moon like one of the naked dancers at the court of the Everqueen. Neither of the guards answered her, both aware when her questions were rhetorical. She laughed and ran down the beach along the line of the cliffs with long, graceful strides. Even this high on the beach, the sand was wet beneath her feet and she knew that the shifting isles must have undergone a violent transformation indeed to stir the oceans this strongly.

She stopped beside a particularly vivid Moon Rose, its petals slowly uncurling to reveal its romantically dark interior. The dusky scent of the plant sent a shiver of pleasure through her and she reached down to snip one of the pollen-producing anther before placing it in her reticule.

The soft clink of metal announced the arrival of her bodyguards, their armour slowing their pace, and she laughed as she imagined their consternation as she had run down the beach and left them in her wake. She moved on, taking cuttings from a dozen different plants before she stiffened as she caught the bitter scent of something else, something that didn't belong.

'Can you smell that?' she asked, turning to her guards.

'Smell what, my lady?' replied the guard she had bewitched on the way down to the shore.

'Blood,' she said.

'Blood? Are you sure that's what you smell, my lady? Might it not be some kind of flower?'

She shook her head. 'No, silly. You're right that there are some plants that carry the scent of blood, but none that are native to Ulthuan. The druchii ferment a brew called blood wine and the vine the grapes come from is said to smell like congealed blood, but that's not what this is.'

At the mention of the druchii, both guards moved to stand beside her, their movements tense and martial as Kyrielle sampled the air once more and said, 'Yes, very definitely blood.'

Without waiting for her guards to follow her, she set off towards the shoreline where the waves tumbled to the sand in cursive lines of foam. She skipped lightly across the sand, leaving almost no marks where she trod as she followed the scent of blood across the beach.

Kyrielle halted as she saw the figure at the water's edge, lying spread-eagled on his back and looking for all the world like a corpse.

'There!' she said, pointing towards the body. 'I told you I could smell blood.'

Before she could set off once more, the nearest guard said, 'Wait here, my lady. Please.'

Reluctantly she acceded to the warrior's request. After all, there *was* a chance that this person might still be dangerous. Nevertheless, she

followed behind the two guards as they cautiously advanced towards the
body. As she drew nearer, she saw that it was a young and handsome elf
dressed in a torn tunic of the Lothern Sea Guard. Even from behind her
guards, she could see the slight rise and fall of his chest.

'He's alive,' she said, stepping towards him.

'Don't, my lady,' said one guard as the other knelt beside the figure
and checked him for weapons. She watched as he removed the figure's
cracked leather belt, upon which hung a knife sheathed in a metal
scabbard of black and gold, and passed it back to his comrade.

'He's alive, all right.'

'Well, I told you that already,' said Kyrielle, pushing past the guard
now holding the knife belt to kneel beside the unconscious elf. His
hands were torn open and there was a nasty gash on his forehead, but he
was breathing and that was something. His lips were moving as though
he muttered to himself and she lowered her head to better hear what he
was saying.

'Be careful, my lady!' said her guard.

She ignored his warning and held her ear to the young elf's mouth as
he continued to whisper faintly.

'...must... told... I need... tell... Teclis. Needs to know... Teclis!'

'Please, my lady!' said her guard. 'We don't know who he is.'

'Don't be silly,' said Kyrielle, lifting her head from the unconscious figure's fevered ramblings. 'He's clearly one of our people, isn't he? Look!'

'We don't know anything about him. Who knows where he came
from?'

Kyrielle sighed. 'Honestly! Look at his tunic. Whoever he is, he's clearly
come from Lothern. Obviously his ship sank and he was able to swim
ashore.'

'I've never heard of any Lothern ships falling foul of the Shifting Isles,'
said one guard. 'Certainly not one of Lord Aislin's.'

'Lord Aislin?' said Kyrielle. 'How do you know he is one of Lord Aislin's sailors?'

The guard pointed to the partially obscured eagle claw emblem on the
figure's tunic and said, 'That's Lord Aislin's family symbol.'

'Well that settles it then,' said Kyrielle. 'It's our duty to help him. Come
on, lift him up and carry him back to the villa. My father will be able to
help him.'

Seeing no other choice, the guards knelt beside the supine figure,
hooked his arms over their shoulders and lifted him between them.

Kyrielle followed them as they carried him from the beach, smiling
happily at this mystery that had washed up on her doorstep.

Captain Finlain and three of his crew who had loosed all their arrows
fought their way through the hail of iron bolts back towards the prow
of *Finubar's Pride*, each warrior bearing a long-hafted shore axe. Searing

tongues of magical flame streaked the dark sky, but none came near Finlain's ship, the arcing missiles all slamming into the hull of *Asuryan's Fire* and punishing her terribly.

A desperate exchange of arrows and crossbow bolts slashed back and forth between his ship and unseen enemies concealed high on the jagged, rocky battlements of the black ark, his warriors forced to conserve their arrows until their keen eyes spotted a definite kill shot. The druchii showed no such restraint and showered the deck of the *Pride* with deadly bolts at will, such that her deck and the roofs of her cabins resembled the hide of a porcupine.

The sporadically lit darkness and swirling smoke from the burning wreckage of the *Glory of Eataine* that still floated hampered the druchii marksmen and Finlain used its cover to move towards the sound of shouting and clashing blades, where Meruval fought the corsairs trying to board his ship.

Blood streamed from numerous cuts on Meruval's arms and chest and Finlain wondered how he could still be fighting, such was the amount of red on his tunic. Meruval fought with speed and grace, his pale blades killing with every stroke. Finlain wanted to shout to him, but knew that to break his concentration would be fatal. Instead, he turned to the warriors who accompanied him and said, 'That boarding ramp is embedded in the deck and gunwale, so you need to cut it free. Go, and no matter what happens, don't stop until it's done. Understood?'

Their grim expressions were all the answer he needed and Finlain simply nodded and said, 'Asuryan be with you.'

The four of them rose from their cover and charged towards Meruval, Finlain lagging behind as the wound in his calf flared painfully. One of the axemen was immediately pierced through the top of the skull by a crossbow bolt and fell to the deck, but the others reached the side of the ship and swung their axes in great overhead sweeps. Finely crafted timber splintered under their blades and Finlain winced at the damage being done to his faithful vessel, even as he knew it was necessary to save her.

Finlain swung his own blade at a corsair readying a killing blow against Meruval, but the blade slid across the warrior's scale cloak without penetrating. The druchii spun to face him and slashed with a pair of wickedly curved daggers that dripped black venom. Finlain ducked under the first dagger and blocked the second, hammering his fist into the corsair's jaw and pitching him from the ramp.

'Withdraw!' shouted Finlain and Meruval stepped back from the fight as the captain of *Finubar's Pride* took his place at the head of the ramp. More bolts thudded around him, but he paid them no mind as he raised his sword to meet a fresh wave of corsairs. Before they charged, he turned to Meruval and said, 'When the ramp is cut free, get us out of here!'

Meruval nodded, too breathless and exhausted to speak, and staggered back along the deck. Finlain returned his attention to the approaching corsairs and bellowed a cry of defiance as they came at him with their cruel eyes and deadly blades.

He fought in a trance, his sword moving as though of its own accord as it opened throats and bellies with each graceful cut. He felt blades cut his own flesh, but he felt no pain as he killed his dark kin with relentless precision.

Dimly he could hear their screams of pain and hatred, mingled with the solid chopping of axe blades, but everything felt muted, as though the battle were being fought underwater. A druchii blade seemed to float past his head as he turned it aside then brought the blade back in a decapitating sweep. From the corner of his eye, he saw a cloaked warrior thrusting with a long, dark-bladed sword, his green eyes bright with centuries of malice, and knew he would not be able to block the strike.

Even as he realised that this was the blow that would kill him, the boarding ramp lurched as his axemen finally chopped it free of the deck. The druchii on the ramp staggered and the green-eyed swordsman slipped as the ground slid out from beneath him. Finlain plunged his bloody sword between the corsair's ribs and kicked him from the ramp.

'Captain!' cried one of the axemen. 'We're free!'

Finlain took a backwards step and shouted, 'Meruval! Now!'

No sooner had the words left his mouth than *Finubar's Pride* surged back from the black ark. With nothing to support it, the boarding ramp tipped a dozen druchii corsairs into the churning sea as it fell against the side of the ark with a resounding clang of metal.

Finlain lowered his sword and placed a steadying hand on the torn sides of his ship as a wave of pain and dizziness threatened to overcome him. More of his warriors rushed to help the ship into getting as much distance between them and the black ark as possible. He let out a deep breath and turned to the breathless axemen.

'Well done,' he said, as the great, dark cliff began to recede, the Eagle ship's superior speed and manoeuvrability getting her clear with great rapidity. 'You saved the ship.'

Both warriors bowed at the captain's compliment as Meruval bellowed orders to get the sails raised.

As the mist closed in around them, Finlain knew that they were by no means out of danger. He made his way along the length of the deck, offering words of praise and congratulations to his warriors until he reached Meruval, who sat slumped beside at the stern at the tiller.

'The others?' said Meruval.

'Lost. I saw *Glory of Eataine* sink and heard nothing but slaughter from *Asuryan's Fire*. I fear that only we escaped, my friend.'

'We're not clear yet, captain,' said Meruval.

'No,' agreed Finlain. 'I know nothing of how quickly a black ark can get underway, but I do not plan on waiting to find out. Get us to Lothern by the swiftest route and then have those wounds seen to. We have to take word to Lord Aislin that a black ark sails the waters of Ulthuan.'

'How in the name of Isha did a black ark get this far south?' said Meruval.

'I don't know,' said Finlain. 'But there's only one reason for it to be here.'

'And what's that?'

Finlain gripped his sword tightly. 'Invasion.'

Ellyrion possessed some of the most beautiful countryside in Ulthuan, decided Yvraine Hawkblade as she crested a rise and looked over the wide expanse of golden plains and lush forests spread between the city of Tor Elyr and the great barrier of the Annulii Mountains. Birdsong entertained her, the sweet scent of summer was in the air – as it always was – and the midday sun warmed her pale skin.

Herds of horses dotted the plains, and here and there she could make out Ellyrion riders amongst them, looking for all the world as though they were a part of them. Perhaps they were, thought Yvraine, knowing that the bond between Ellyrian nobles and their horses was more akin to that shared by old friends than that of rider and steed. Rightly it was said that it was better to harm the brother of an Ellyrian than his horse…

She set off down a sloping path, her steps sure and measured, leaving no trace of her passing, though her head was still clouded after the journey from Saphery to Ellyrion, despite the best efforts of the shipmaster to make her journey across the inner sea as comfortable as possible. It felt good to have the sun on her face, the wind in her hair and solid ground beneath her feet. Yvraine disliked travelling by any means other than her own two feet, and though the ships of the elves rode smoothly across the seas, she had found it next to impossible to meditate during the voyage, her every attempt thwarted by the conversations of the crew or the rocking swell of the ship.

Yvraine brushed her long, cream robes and adjusted the ithilmar armour that lay beneath, the gleaming links and smooth plates contoured for her slender frame. Across her back was a huge sword, sheathed in a long scabbard of soft red velvet and fastened to her armour by a golden clasp at her breast.

She stopped and shielded her eyes from the sun as she peered into the verdant countryside, seeing the far distant gleam of sunlight on the pale stone walls of a villa at the foot of a tumble of rocks. Mitherion Silverfawn had told her that the villa of his daughter's husband nestled between two waterfalls and the sentinels at the gates of Tor Elyr had given her detailed directions on how to find the Éadaoin villa.

Sure that the villa before her was the one she sought, Yvraine lifted the sword from her back, a great, two-handed blade of exquisite workmanship and uncanny grace, as she gracefully lowered herself into a cross-legged position. She would reach her destination in the morning and desired to sweep away the lethargy of the journey before then.

And the best way to do that was to perform the cleansing ritual of the Sword Masters.

Yvraine placed the huge sword across her lap and closed her eyes, letting the natural sounds of Ellyrion ease her into her meditative trance.

Her breathing slowed and her senses spread out from her body as she slowly whispered the mantra of the Sword Masters of Hoeth, as taught to her by Master Dioneth of the White Tower. Yvraine felt the softness of the grass beneath her, the warmth and fecundity of the earth below that and the raging currents of magic that pierced the very rock and kept the island of Ulthuan from vanishing beneath the waves.

The air around her sparkled as the magic carried on the wind became attuned to her subtle vibrations and a soft glow built behind her eyelids. In one smooth motion she drew her sword and held the silver, leaf-shaped blade before her, its length enormous and its weight surely extraordinary, yet Yvraine wielded it as though it were as light as a willowy sapling.

Her pale, almost white hair reflected in the smooth sheen of the blade, the perfection of the weapon matched only by the steely concentration in her sharp, angular features. Yvraine let a breath of anticipation whisper from her lips and nodded to herself.

Her legs uncoiled like striking snakes and in the blink of an eye she was standing, the sword raised high above her and glittering in the sun. The blade spun in her hands and her grip was reversed, the sword slashing in an intricate series of manoeuvres that were almost too fast for the naked eye to follow.

Her feet were in constant motion as she lunged, parried and thrust at imaginary opponents, the mighty blade cleaving the air in an impenetrable web of ithilmar that swooped gracefully around her body. One by one, she performed the thirty basic exercises of the Sword Masters before moving onto more advanced techniques.

Once more she brought the enormous sword upwards and held it before her face, the golden quillons level with her cheeks and her breathing crisp and even. With barely a trace of visible effort, Yvraine spun the sword in a dazzling series of manoeuvres that would have made the greatest swordsman of men weep at his own lack of skill and which was beyond all but the most gifted of warriors of Ulthuan. Only through the superlative training of the Loremasters of the White Tower could a warrior transcend mere skill and become a true master of the martial arts to perform feats of swordsmanship beyond imagining.

Mind and body in total harmony, the mighty sword became part of Yvraine, her perfect physical and spiritual qualities manifesting in swordplay that was simply sublime. With a selection of the most advanced techniques performed, she moved into a more personal series of manoeuvres, where her own soul flowed into the blade and informed its every movement.

Each Sword Master had their own particular style with a blade and each warrior bared an element of their heart when they fought, an aspect of their personality that was so unique and distinct as to be unmistakable to another practitioner of the art. Yvraine's sword reached further and faster, the tip cutting the air in dizzyingly fast sweeps that would have been impossible were it not for the decades of training and her mastery of her own body.

At last the sword ceased its motion, so suddenly that an observer might have been forgiven for thinking it had never moved at all. With a whip of silver steel it was returned to its sheath and Yvraine was cross-legged once more, her breathing returning to normal as she emerged from her meditation.

She opened her eyes, calm and refreshed after her exercises, and smiled as she felt the cobwebs that had entangled her soul during the journey from Saphery fall away from her as though cut by her blade. Yvraine rose smoothly to her feet, slinging the sword around her back and buckling the belt across her armour once more.

She adjusted her cloak over the sword and set off in the direction of the distant villa.

CHAPTER THREE
CALLS

First there was light. Then came sound. He could feel the light burning through his eyelids as though someone held a bright lamp before them and kept them tightly shut as he registered more of his environment through his other senses. He lay on a soft mattress, his limbs comfortable and covered by soft bedding. The air was moist and tasted green, with an earthy scent as though he lay outdoors or within a hothouse for exotic plants.

It smelled sweet and pleasant, and he took a deep breath of the myriad scents that surrounded him. Wherever he lay, it was certainly pleasant, without any sense of danger, and he felt no need to move beyond the identification of his surroundings.

He could hear droning insects and the rustle of the leaves disturbed by a soft breeze, as well as soft puffs of what sounded like perfume dispensed from a noblewoman's atomiser. By degrees, his eyes grew more accustomed to the light, and he risked gradually opening them in stages, adjusting to each level of glare before opening them still further.

At last his eyes were fully open, though the brightness of the light still made him slightly nauseous. Above him, he could see swathes of shimmering panes that rippled like water in golden frames of wire surely too slender to support the weight of such an amount of glass.

Twisting his head, he could see that the strange ceiling stretched away to his left and right, though for how far was a mystery as it was soon obscured by the tall branches of strange trees. He now saw that his earlier suspicion that he was lying outdoors was only partially correct, for he lay within a space whose shape was formed from the trunks of the trees and rendered impermeable by the weaving of bushes and plants between them.

Through the transparent ceiling, he could see clouds chasing one another across the sky, but could feel no breath of wind where he lay. Perhaps the ceiling above him was some form of magical barrier that kept out the worst of the external environment while maintaining a constant internal temperature? As he watched, a portion of one of the shimmering panes seemed to shiver before dispensing a fine spray of water across the plants nearest it.

He tried to sit up, but pulled up short as the muscles in every one of his limbs protested and he collapsed back onto the bed with a grunt of pain. Tentatively he lifted his hands, seeing that they were bound with bandages and feeling a raw numbness in his palms.

But more surprising was the fact that he wore a silver pledge ring on his left hand.

He was married? To whom? And why did he have no memory of her?

A deep and painful ache seized his heart as he tried and failed to remember the name of the maiden that had given him this pledge ring. Was she even now searching for him, unaware that he had survived his shipwreck? He wondered if she might already be mourning him…

He had to get up and discover where he was and find some means of restoring his memory if he were to return to her. Reaching up to his forehead, he felt another bandage covering the side of his head and winced as he probed what was clearly a fresh cut.

How had he come to this place? And where in the name of Isha was it?

All he remembered was floating in the sea, clinging desperately to a fragment of wreckage; beyond that was a blank. There had been a beach and he remembered clawing handfuls of sand as he had pulled himself ashore. He realised he must have been discovered by his fellow elves and the simple fact of his survival made him want to laugh and cry.

His head had been hurt and his palms were raw, but what other wounds did he bear?

He pulled back the soft sheets that covered him and discovered that he was naked beneath them, his flesh pale and obviously starved of sunlight. Tentatively, he pushed himself upright in the bed and probed his flesh for other injuries. He found knots of scar tissue on his hip and shoulder, but they were old wounds, the skin pale and long healed. How he had come by those wounds, he could not remember, but aside from the injuries to his head and palms (and the stiffness of his muscles) he appeared to be otherwise healthy.

Marshalling his strength, he slowly eased himself into a sitting position, his every muscle aching with the effort, and swung his feet onto the floor. Standing up took an effort of will and his heart thudded against his ribs with the exertion. Suddenly very aware of his nakedness, he looked around for something to wear and saw a small table sitting behind his bed with a fresh shirt and loose leggings.

Swiftly he donned the clothes, the fabric soft and fragrant. When was the last time he had worn fresh clothing? It seemed he had forgotten the softness of silk or the comfort of clothes and, try as he might, he could still remember nothing of his life before his plight in the ocean.

Who was he and how had he come to be floating in the ocean, bloodied and near death?

These were questions he desperately needed answers to, but he had no idea how to get them. Deciding that he had better find out where he was first, he took a few hesitant steps around the verdant room, testing his strength and balance.

He was unsteady at first, but with every step, he felt stronger and more confident.

The chamber he found himself within was a long oval, its perimeter formed by the trunks of slender trees with a shimmering, oily looking bark. He reached out and pressed his fingers against the nearest tree, grimacing at the stickiness of the sap. Reaching up for a wide leaf, he wiped it from his hand, though he had to admit that the fragrance of the sap was pleasant. The more he saw, the more he felt that this place was less like Ulthuan and more like the stories he had heard of the woodland realm of Athel Loren, far to the east in the Old World.

Turning from the tree, he saw that no obvious exit presented itself, but as he approached one end of the room, the coiled vines and creepers intertwined with the trunks pulled back with a rustling hiss, like a curtain of beads parted by an invisible hand.

Startled, he hesitated before moving any closer, but peering through the gap he saw long rows of plants and seed beds stretching out before him and more of the strange, rippling ceiling above them. Cautiously he stepped through and the curtain of vines hissed closed behind him.

This space was much larger than the room he had woken in and displayed some measure of the handiwork of elves: long terraced walls and graceful columns from which hung a variety of outlandish plants – most of which he did not recognise.

The door he had passed through had brought him out midway down what appeared to be a terrace of hanging gardens built into the side of a cliff. High above him, he could just make out the outline of an imposing, plant-wreathed dwelling.

He set off down the nearest aisle of plants in search of a route upwards, the air filled with a multitude of different scents and hot with a moistness that felt good on his skin. To his left, this great garden space rose up in a series of blooming terraces to a sprawling villa, while on the right it fell away in curling paths down the cliffs. Beyond the transparent liquid wall held by the golden wire, he could see the bright light of the morning and the brilliant blue of the great ocean, its vast expanse dotted with mist-shrouded isles.

He shivered as he again felt the cold of the water's embrace and turned from the ocean.

Wandering down the aisle of strange plants, he felt the unmistakable tingle of magic washing in from the sea. That, combined with the sight of the coast and the misty isles beyond, told him that he must be in Yvresse, though what had brought him here was a mystery he hoped would be answered soon.

He paused to take a closer look at some of the plants, but he could recognise none of them, which did not surprise him, for as far as he knew he was no botanist. Some plants he approached, others he did not, as many of the larger ones had a predatory quality to them. Wide, serrated petals and thorny vines waved in the air like agile whips that appeared to be beckoning him closer.

A powerful scent suddenly filled his nostrils and he turned to see a tall plant with a collection of bright red cones set amid a thorny frill of stamen that drooped like the branches of a willow tree. Almost without conscious thought, he found himself approaching the plant, hearing a strange sound that resonated beyond the simple act of hearing, as though it reached into his mind to soothe his troubled thoughts. The scent of its bloom swelled until it was overpoweringly intoxicating, and his senses filled with its seductive promise.

His steps carried him towards the plant and he smiled dreamily as he watched the red cones slowly flare open to reveal circular mouths ringed with teeth and which leaked glistening saliva.

The sight of such an array of barbed teeth should have alarmed him, but the siren song in his mind kept such thoughts at bay and he continued to walk towards the plant. The drooping stamen slowly drew themselves erect, opening outwards as he walked willingly into their embrace.

Dimly he was aware of a shape standing at his shoulder, but he could not tear his eyes from the gaping, toothed mouths of the plant as more of the sticky saliva moistened the leaves.

Then the soothing song that filled his mind turned to a scream and he cried out as the piercing wail echoed within his skull. The haunting scent of the plant faded and was replaced with the acrid stench of burning leaves. Sparkling fire leapt from the opened mouths of the plant as they writhed in the pellucid blue flames.

Freed from the plant's bewitchment, he staggered backward, suddenly repulsed by the smell of sap and earth as he dropped to his knees and gagged on the stench. When he had recovered enough, he looked up to see a beautiful elven maid standing before the shrivelled husk of the burned plant, shimmering traces of magical flames dying at her fingertips. Auburn hair held by a woven silver cord at her temple poured across her shoulders and her piercing green eyes regarded him with an expression of faintly amused exasperation.

'Silly boy,' she said. 'Father will be most displeased.'

Eldain hurried down the stairs from the Hippocrene Tower, fastening a velvet tunic over his silk undershirt as he went. Valeina had woken him just after dawn with news that a visitor had arrived at the gates of Ellyrcharoi and was asking to speak to the master of the house.

Normally, Eldain received no visitors and would have sent such a caller on their way unsatisfied, but this was no ordinary guest. When pressed for a description of the visitor, Valeina had described a warrior clad in shining ithilmar armour, a tall plumed helmet and who bore a mighty sword.

Eldain had known immediately what manner of person had arrived at his gates.

A Sword Master, one of the warrior-mystics who travelled the length and breadth of Ulthuan, gathering news and information for the Loremasters of the Tower of Hoeth. One did not refuse the visit of such an individual, and thus he had ordered Valeina to prepare a morning meal of fresh bread and fruits while he dressed himself.

What could one of the Sword Masters want in Ellyr-charoi? Even as he framed the question in his mind, a cold dread settled upon him and his last steps into the Summer Courtyard were leaden and fearful. Rhianna was already waiting for him and he could see from her expression that she was similarly surprised at the arrival of this visitor, though her surprise was more of excitement than wariness.

'Have you seen our guest?' said Eldain without preamble.

Rhianna shook her head. 'No, she awaits in the Equerry's Hall.'

'She?'

'Yes, Valeina tells me her name is Yvraine Hawkblade.'

'Did she also tell you why a Sword Master comes to Ellyr-charoi?'

'No, but she must bring important news to have come all the way from Saphery.'

Eldain nodded and said, 'That's what worries me.'

Together they crossed the courtyard and followed the line of the walls to a tall door of carved ash with gold and silver banding carved into the form of horses. Eldain took a deep breath and pushed open the door, marching through the airy vestibule of white stone and emerging in to the Equerry's Hall, a wide, dimly lit chamber lined with trophies and wondrous paintings depicting scenes of previous lords of the Éadaoin family at hunt. A long table in the shape of an elongated oval filled the centre of the hall, where in times past the equerries of the noble house would carouse and sing and dance after a successful hunt.

Now, the hall was bare, no songs were sung and it had been decades since last the lord of the Éadaoin had hunted. Eldain and Rhianna's entrance scattered fallen leaves and as they passed through the vestibule, the chamber's occupant looked over from her scrutiny of a painting that showed a noble elf atop a steed of purest white, slaying a foul, mutated beast of the Annulii.

'Is this you?' said the Sword Master, her voice soft and melodic.

Eldain glanced at the picture and felt his heartbeat jump. 'No, it is my brother.'

'He is very like you.'

'Was,' said Eldain. 'He is dead.'

The Sword Master bowed deeply and Eldain saw the tremendous sword upon her back, the weapon surely almost as tall as its bearer. 'My apologies, Lord Éadaoin, I am sorry for your loss. And forgive my manners, I have not yet introduced myself. I am Yvraine Hawkblade, Sword Master of Hoeth.'

Yvraine Hawkblade was tall for a female elf, slender and seemingly ill-suited to the role of a Sword Master. Her features were sharper than most elves of Ulthuan and Eldain relaxed as he saw no guile in her young face.

'And I am Eldain Fleetmane,' he said. 'Lord of the Éadaoin family and master of the lands from here to the mountains. And this is my wife, Rhianna.'

Again the Sword Master bowed. 'It is an honour to meet you and may the blessings of Isha be upon you both.'

'And on you,' said Rhianna. 'You are welcome in our house. Will you join us in our morning meal?'

'Thank you, I shall,' said Yvraine. 'It has been a long and, I confess, tiring journey. I would be glad of some food and water, yes.'

Yvraine took a seat at the table and Eldain caught a shadow of faint disappointment pass across her face and he could well imagine its cause. Ever since the death of his father, the ancestral home of his family had become a place of mourning instead of a place of joy. Brooding silences and ghosts of glories past filled its halls, where once laughter and song had rung from the rafters. Death had reached into the chests of the Éadaoin and stilled the wild beat of their reaver hearts.

He and Rhianna took their seats opposite Yvraine as Valeina entered carrying a wide tray bearing bread, fruit and a crystal pitcher of cold mountain water. She placed the tray in the centre of the table and Eldain nodded in thanks.

'That will be all, Valeina,' he said, reaching out to pour Yvraine and Rhianna some water before filling his own glass. Valeina withdrew and closed the doors to the Equerry's Hall behind her, leaving the three of them sitting in silence.

Yvraine sipped her water, showing no sign yet of revealing her purpose here and Eldain could barely contain his curiosity. Oft times, Sword Masters travelled with no purpose other than the gathering of knowledge, journeying to the furthest corners of Ulthuan to quiz local nobility and warriors on recent events that they might be communicated back to the White Tower, but Eldain already knew that this was no such occasion.

Every movement of Yvraine Hawkblade told Eldain that she had come here with purpose.

'Have you travelled directly from Saphery, Mistress Hawkblade?'

'I have,' said Yvraine, helping herself to a ripened aoilym fruit.

'And to what do we owe the pleasure of your company?'

He felt the heat of Rhianna's gaze upon him, knowing he was being discourteous by being so blunt, but knowing that if this warrior brought his doom then he would sooner face it than dance around it.

Yvraine displayed no outward sign of noticing his boorish behaviour, taking a bite of the fruit and savouring its perfectly moist flesh. 'I bring a message to the daughter of Mitherion Silverfawn from her father.'

'A message for me?' said Rhianna.

Eldain's heart calmed and a beaming smile of relief spread across his face. So typical of an Archmage to resort to the pomp of sending one of the Sword Masters to deliver a message, when there were a dozen different ways to communicate by magical means.

He reached out to take a piece of fruit and said, 'Then I urge you to deliver it, Mistress Hawkblade. How fares my father-in-law?'

'Well,' said Yvraine. 'He prospers and his researches into celestial phenomena continue to meet with favour from the Loremasters. In fact his divinations are proving to be of great interest these days.'

Rhianna leaned forwards across the table. 'Please do not think me rude, but I would hear what my father has to say.'

Yvraine placed the core of the aoilym back on the platter and said, 'Of course. He simply asks that you accompany me back to the Tower of Hoeth.'

'What? To Saphery? Why?'

'I do not know,' said Yvraine and Eldain could sense that there was some other part of the message yet to be imparted. 'But it was with some urgency that I was despatched. I have taken the liberty of securing us passage on a ship from Tor Elyr and its captain has orders to await our arrival before sailing. If we leave soon, we can be in Tor Elyr before nightfall.'

'Is he ill? Is that why he sends for me?'

Yvraine shook her head, a faint smile on her lips. 'No, he is quite well, I assure you, my lady. But he was most insistent that you both accompany me back to Saphery.'

At first, Eldain thought he'd misheard, then saw the look of quiet amusement on the Sword Master's face. 'Both of us? He wants both of us to travel with you?'

'He does.'

'Without a reason?'

'I was not given a reason, simply a directive.'

'And we're supposed to pack up and go because he says so?' said Eldain.

Yvraine nodded and Eldain felt his irritation grow at her lack of elaboration. Though he held great respect for Rhianna's father, he was, like many practitioners of magic, somewhat mercurial and capricious. A trait he was more than aware existed in his daughter.

But to travel the breadth of Ulthuan with no clue as to why or what awaited them at the end of the journey seemed like an unreasonable request, even by the standards of a mage.

Rhianna seemed similarly confused by her father's request, but the prospect of visiting her father soon won out over any concern as to the reason.

'He gave no hint as to why he wants us to travel to the White Tower?' said Rhianna.

'He did not.'

'Then would you mind speculating?' said Eldain. 'You must have some idea of why he sends one of the White Tower's guardians to retrieve his daughter.'

Yvraine shook her head. 'In life, the wisest and soundest people avoid speculation.'

Wonderful, thought Eldain, a warrior *and* a philosopher...

Her name was Kyrielle Greenkin and she had saved his life.

When the pain and discomfort of the carnivorous plant's aromatic siren song had faded from his mind, she helped him to his feet and tutted as she dusted off the fresh clothes that had been laid out for him.

'Look at the state of you!' she said. 'And I went to such trouble to find one of the guards the same size as you.'

'What...' he said, gesturing feebly at the smoking remains of the plant, 'was that?'

'That? Oh, that was just one of father's more outlandish creations,' she said dismissively and waving a delicate hand. 'It was a bit of an experiment really, which, between you and I, did not work out too well, but he does love to tinker with things from beyond this world to see how they combine with our own native species.'

'Is it dead?'

'I should think so,' she said and then laughed. 'Unless my magic is becoming *very* rusty.'

'You are a mage?'

'I have a little power,' she said, 'but then who of Saphery doesn't?'

'Saphery? Is that where you are from?' he said, though he had already guessed as much.

'It is indeed.' She smiled and said, 'You are a guest of Anurion the Green, Archmage of Saphery, and this is his winter palace in Yvresse. I, on the other hand, am his daughter, Kyrielle.'

He could feel the expectant pause after she had spoken her name, but he had nothing to tell her and said, 'I am sorry, my lady, but I have no name to give you. I can remember nothing before my time adrift in the sea.'

'Nothing? Nothing at all? Well that's unfortunate,' she said in a masterful display of understatement. 'Well I can't very well speak to you if you haven't got a name. Would you mind terribly if I thought of one for you? Just until you remember your own of course!'

Her speech was so quick he had trouble following it, especially with the fog that seemed to fill his thoughts. He shook his head and said, 'No, I suppose not.'

Kyrielle's face screwed up in a manner that suggested she was thinking hard until at last she said, 'Then I will call you Daroir. Will that do?'

He smiled and said, 'The rune for remembrance and memory.'

'It seems fitting, yes?'

'Daroir,' he said, turning the name over in his mind. He had no connection to the name and instinctually knew that it was not his real name, but it would suffice until he could recall what it truly was. 'I suppose it is fitting, yes. Maybe it will help.'

'So you don't remember anything at all?' said Kyrielle. 'Not a thing?'

He shook his head. 'No. I remember almost dying in the sea and crawling up the beach. And… that's it.'

'Such a sad tale,' she said and a tear rolled down her cheek.

The suddenness of her mood swing surprised him and he said, 'With a tear in her eye and a smile on her lips…'

Even though he heard himself speak the words, they sounded unfamiliar to his ears, yet flowed naturally from his mouth.

She smiled and she said, 'You know the works of Mecelion?'

'Who?'

'Mecelion,' said Kyrielle. 'The warrior poet of Chrace. You just quoted from *Fairest Dawn of Ulthuan*.'

'I did?' said Daroir. 'I've never heard of Mecelion, much less read any of his poems.'

'Are you sure? You might be the greatest student of poetry in Ulthuan for all we know.'

'True, but what would a student of poetry be doing at sea?'

Kyrielle looked him up and down and said, 'No, you don't look much like a student, too many muscles. And how many students carry wounds like yours on their shoulder and hip? You've been a warrior in your time.'

Daroir blushed, realising that she must have seen him naked to know of the old wounds on his body. She laughed as she saw the colour rise in his cheeks.

'Did you think you got undressed all by yourself?' she said.

He didn't answer as she took his hand and led him towards a gentle arch of palm fronds that parted at her approach to reveal stairs that rose towards the villa at the top of the cliff.

So artfully were the stairs cut into the rock, that Daroir wasn't sure

that they hadn't formed naturally. Unusually for this place of wondrous
flora, the steps were completely free of any trace of growth and earth, as
though the plants knew to keep this ascent clear.

He followed her willingly as she led him up the steps. 'Where are we
going?'

'To see my father,' she said. 'He is a powerful mage and perhaps he can
restore your memory to you.'

She released his hand and began to climb the steps. Daroir felt a warm
glow envelop him at her smile, as though some strange, soothing magic
was worked within it.

He followed her up the steps.

Far, far away, in a land devoid of kind laughter or sunlight that warmed
the skin, a shrill cry that spoke of spilled blood echoed from a tower
of brazen darkness. About this highest and bleakest of towers were a
hundred others, cold and reeking with malice, and about these were
a thousand more. Black smoke coiled around the towers, which rose
above a city hunched at the foot of iron mountains and which lived in
the nightmares of the world.

For this was Naggarond, the Tower of Cold... the forsaken domain of
the Witch King, dread ruler of the dark kin of the elves of Ulthuan.

The druchii.

Black castles and turrets ringed the mighty tower at the centre of the
city, shrouded in the ashen rain of those burned upon the sacrificial fires
that smouldered, red and black, in temples that ran with blood.

Walls a hundred feet high encircled the city, and from the walls rose
an evil forest of dark and crooked towers, upon which flew the bloody
banners of the city's infernal master. An army of severed heads and a
tapestry of skins hung from the jagged battlements and the sickly ruin of
their demise dripped down the black stone of the wall.

Carrion birds circled the city in an ever present pall, their cries hungry
and impatient as they crossed the bleak and cheerless sky. The beating
of hammers and the scrape of iron rose from the city, mingling with the
cries of the anguished and the moaning of the damned into one murderous death-rattle that never ended.

The dwelling places of the dark elves: bleak and shattered ruins, windy
garrets and haunted towers filled the city, each more forlorn than the
last.

The scream that issued from the tallest tower at the centre of the city
lingered, as though savoured by the air itself, and those below gave
thanks to their gods that it was not they who suffered this day. The
screaming had been going on for days, and while screams were nothing
new in Naggarond, these spoke of a level of suffering beyond imagining.

But the cause of those screams was not one of the city's ivory-skinned
elves, but a man, though he had forsaken all bonds with his species

many years ago in the ecstasy of battle and the worship of the Dark Gods of the north.

In a shuttered room lit only by the coals of a smouldering brazier, Issyk Kul worked his dark torments upon a canvas of flesh granted to him by the Hag Sorceress. Where the youth had come from was irrelevant and what he knew was unimportant, for Kul had not begun his tortures with any purpose other than the infliction of agony. To work such wonderful ruin on a perfect body, yet keep it alive and aware of the havoc being wrought upon it, was both his art and an act of worship.

Kul was broad and muscular, his body worked into iron-hardness by the harsh northern climes of the Old World and a life of war and excess. Leather coils held a patchwork of contoured plates tight to his tanned flesh, his armour glistening and undulating like raw, pink meat and his skin gleaming with scented oils. Lustrous golden hair topped the face of a libertine, full featured and handsome to the point of beauty. But where beauty ended, cruelty began and his wide eyes knew nothing of pity or compassion, only wicked indulgence and the obsession of a fetishist.

When he was done with this plaything, he would release it, eyeless, lipless and insane into the city, to drool and plead for a death that would be too slow in coming. It would roam the streets a freak, cries of revulsion and admiration chasing it into the dark corners of the city where it would become a feast for the creatures of the night.

Kul straightened from his works, discarding the needles and selecting a blade so slender and fine that it would be quite useless for any purpose other than inflicting the most excruciating tortures on the most sensitive organs of the body.

More screams filled the chamber and Kul's joined those of his plaything, his growls of pleasure climaxing in an atavistic howl of pleasure as he completed his violation of what had once been a pale, bright-eyed messenger.

With his desires sated for the moment, Issyk Kul bent to kiss the mewling scraps of flesh and said, 'Your pain has pleased the great god, Shornaal, and for that I thank you.'

He turned to leave the chamber, pausing only long enough to retrieve a gloriously elaborate sword of sweeping curves and cruel spikes. Quillons of bone pricked the flesh of his hands and a razor worked into the handle scored his palm as he spun the blade into a rippling sheath across his back.

Beyond the confines of the room he used for worship, a stone-flagged passageway curved away to either side, following the shape of the tower, and he set off with a long, graceful stride towards the sounds of chanting and wailing.

The music of the tower was pressed into its structure, millennia of suffering and blood imprinted into its very bones. Kul could feel the anguish that had been unleashed in this place as surely as if it happened right before his eyes. Ghosts of murders past paraded before him and the torments that built this place were like wine from the sweetest blood vineyard.

At last the curve of the passageway terminated at a wide portal of bone and bronze that led within the core of the tower. Six cloaked warriors in long hauberks of black mail and tall helms of bronze guarded the portal, their great, black-bladed halberds reflecting the light of the torches that burned in sconces fashioned from skulls. Each warrior's face was branded with the mark of Khaine, the Bloody Handed God of murder, hatred and destruction, and Kul smiled to see such wanton deformation of flesh.

Though he was well known in Naggarond, their weapons still clashed together to block his passage through to the ebony stairs that led to the inner sanctum of the tower.

Kul nodded in satisfaction, knowing that had they admitted him into the presence of their lord without challenge, he would have killed them himself. More than one champion of the Dark Gods had fallen foul of the treachery of a trusted comrade and Kul had not lived for three centuries by assuming that the faith of friends was eternal.

'You do your master proud,' said Kul, 'but I am expected.'

'Expected you may be, but you do not go before Lord Malekith unescorted,' said a voice behind him and Kul smiled.

'Kouran,' he said, turning to face the commander of the Black Guard of Naggarond, the elite guard of the Witch King's city. Kouran was almost a foot shorter than Issyk Kul, but was a formidable presence nonetheless, his dark armour forged from the unbreakable metal of a fallen star and his blade ensorcelled by ancient, forgotten magic.

The elf's violet eyes met Kul's and the champion of Chaos was pleased to see a total absence of fear in his gaze.

'You do not trust me?' said Kul.

'Should I?'

'No,' he admitted. 'I have killed friends and allies before when it suited me.'

'Then we will go up together, yes?' said Kouran, leaving Kul in no doubt that it was not a request. He nodded and waved the captain of the Black Guard forward. Kouran wrapped a hand around the hilt of his sword and Kul could feel the blade's malice seep into the air like sweet incense.

The gleaming blades of the Black Guard parted and Issyk Kul and Kouran passed through the portal of bone, a hazy curtain of sweet-smelling smoke arising from the floor to surround them and bear them onwards. The chamber beyond the portal was cold, a web of frost forming a patina of white across his armour. The oil chilled on his flesh and his breath feathered the air before him as Kouran led the way through the purple mists towards a spiral staircase of stained metal from which dripped a sticky residue of old blood.

Kouran climbed the stairs and Kul followed him, his bulky frame unsuited to such a narrow stairwell. He had dreamed of walking the route to the Witch King's presence a thousand times since he had brought his army to Naggarond, and felt a delicious wave of apprehension and excitement thunder through his veins as he followed Kouran upwards. Though he had killed and tortured for hundreds of years, Kul was only too aware that the darkness he had wrought upon the world was but a fraction of the shadow cast by the Witch King.

For more than five thousand years, the Witch King had reigned over Naggaroth and all the later ages of the world had known his dread power. In Ulthuan, his name was not spoken except as a curse, while in the lands of men, his power was a terrible legend that still stalked the world and plotted to bring about its ruin. To the tribes of the north, the Witch King was just another ruler of a distant kingdom, by turns a mighty tyrant to dread or an ally to fight alongside.

A red rain of spattering blood fell from high above, rendering Kul's golden hair to lank ropes of bloody crimson and he licked the congealed droplets from his lips as they ran down his face.

The creaking, iron stairs seemed to go on for an eternity, climbing higher into the aching cold and purple smoke that surrounded him. The oil on his skin cracked and his muscles began to shiver as he drew near the throne room of Malekith.

At last they reached the summit of the tower, the pinnacle of evil in Naggarond, and Kul's every sense was alive with the living quality of hatred and bitterness that flavoured every breath with its power.

The darkness of the Witch King's throne room was a force unto itself, a presence felt as palpably as that of Kouran beside him. It coated the walls like a creeping sickness, slithering across the floor and climbing the walls in defiance of the white, soulless light that struggled through the leaded windows of the tower.

Kul began to shiver, his heavily muscled frame unused to such bitter, unnatural cold and without a shred of fat to insulate him. He could see nothing beyond the faint outline of Kouran and the all-encompassing darkness that seemed to press in on him to render him blind as surely as if a hood had been placed over his head.

No, that wasn't quite right...

Kul's senses were no longer those of a mortal, enhanced and refined by Shornaal to better savour the agonies of his victims and the ecstasies of his triumphs. Even as he concentrated, he could feel a rasping iron breath in his head, as though a great engine pulsed in the depths of the tower and the echoes of its efforts were carried up its length. He could feel a presence within his mind, a clawing, scraping thing that sifted through his memories and desires to reach the very heart of him.

He knew he was being tested and welcomed the intrusion, confident that he would be found the equal of the task he had been summoned to perform. The clammy thought-touch withdrew from his mind and he relaxed as he felt the awesome power of the Witch King recede, apparently satisfied.

The darkness of the chamber appeared to diminish and Issyk Kul saw a great obsidian throne upon which sat a mighty statue of black iron, one hand resting on a skull-topped armrest while the other clasped a colossal sword, its blade burnished silver and glittering with hoarfrost. Kul knew that the magic of his own blade was powerful, but the energies bound to this terrible weapon were an order of magnitude greater and he could feel the enchantments worked upon his armour weakening just by its presence.

A great shield, taller than Kul himself, rested against one side of the great throne and upon it burned the dread rune of Shornaal – though the druchii did not use the northern names for the gods, and named his patron as Slaanesh. A circlet of iron sat upon the horned helm of the statue and at the sight of this monstrous god of murder, Kouran dropped to his knees and began babbling in the tongue of the elves.

Kul had to fight the urge to drop to his knees alongside Kouran and give praise to this effigy of Khaine, for Shornaal was a jealous god and would surely strike him down. Even in the holiest of holy places to Shornaal, Kul had never felt such awe and sheer physical presence of his own god as he felt now. The druchii were fortunate indeed to have a god of such potent physicality.

Even as he stared in awe at the magnificent and terrible idol, he felt the approach of another presence behind him and a voice, laden with lust, said, 'Do you not pay homage to my son? Is he not worthy of your obeisance?'

Pale and slender hands slipped around his neck, the nails long and sharp. They caressed his throat and he felt himself respond to their touch, a tremor of arousal and revulsion working its way down his spine. He knew who came upon him by her touch as surely as though she had whispered in his ear.

Her hands slid over the plates of armour covering his chest, sliding down to the bare flesh of his abdomen and stroking the curve of his muscles.

'Your son?' said Kul, twisting his head to the side and catching sight of her bewitching beauty. Pale skin, dark-rimmed eyes of liquid darkness and full lips that had worked their way around his body on more than one occasion.

'Yes,' said Morathi, slipping gracefully around his body to stand before him. 'My son.'

She was exquisite, as beautiful as the day she had first wed Aenarion thousands of years ago, and draped in a long gown of purple with a slash that ran from her collar to her pelvis. An amber periapt hung between the ivory curve of her breasts and Kul had to force his gaze upwards lest he be reduced to a quivering wreck of raging desire, as had countless suitors and lovers before him.

Mother and, some said, unholy lover of the Witch King, Morathi's sensuous splendour was like nothing he had ever experienced and her epithet of the Hag Sorceress seemed like such a hideous misnomer to Kul, even though he knew the hellish reality behind her wondrous appearance.

'Lady Morathi,' said Kul, bowing extravagantly before her. 'It is a pleasure to see you again.'

'Yes it is,' she said, backing away from him and toying with her amulet.

Kul took a step forward and Kouran rose to his feet, his hand reaching for the hilt of his sword. Not only was Kouran the captain of the city guard, but also bodyguard to its rulers.

'I received your summons, Lady Morathi,' said Kul. 'Is there news from the isle of mists?'

'There is,' she said, 'but first tell me of my messenger. He was to your tastes?'

Kul laughed and said, 'He was most enjoyable, my lady. He will not be returning to you.'

'I had not thought that he would.'

Kul waited for Morathi to continue, spellbound by her monstrous beauty and already picturing the violation he would wreak on her flesh if given the chance. As he stared at the Hag Sorceress, her features rippled as though in a heat haze, and a flickering image of the passage of centuries was etched upon his eyeballs, the wreckage of age and the ruin of years heaped upon flesh unable to sustain it.

Such was the dichotomy of Morathi, her beguiling beauty and her loathsome reality, one maintained at the expense of the other by the slaughter of countless innocent lives. Kul could only admire the determination and depths Morathi had plumbed to retain her allure.

'It is time for us to make war upon the asur,' said Morathi, breaking his reverie.

'First blood has been spilled?' he said, unable to keep the relish from his voice.

'It has indeed,' said Morathi. 'The *Black Serenade* encountered a handful of their ships a few days ago. Many lives were taken and one vessel was allowed to escape to carry word back to Lothern.'

'Fear will eat at them like a plague,' said Kul. 'They will be ripe for blooding.'

'And fire will be stoked in their hearts,' said Kouran, practically spitting each word. 'The asur are proud.'

'As it should be,' said Morathi. 'Much depends on the fire of Asuryan's children being directed correctly. The thrust of our sword must draw our enemy's shield to enable the assassin's blade to strike home.'

'Then we must set sail,' said Kul, flexing his fists and running his tongue along his lips. 'I long to practise my arts on the flesh of the asur.'

'As I promised you, Issyk Kul,' said Morathi. 'We will set sail with our warriors soon enough, but there are yet offerings to be made to Khaine and sport to be had before we wet our blades.'

Kul nodded towards the great iron statue behind Morathi and snapped. 'Then make your offerings to your god and be done with it, sorceress. My blade aches for the bliss of the knife's edge, the dance of blades and the pain that brings pleasure.'

Morathi frowned, then, as realisation of Kul's meaning became clear, threw back her head and laughed, a sound that chilled the soul and reached out beyond the chamber to slay a hundred carrion birds that circled the tower. She turned to the figure of iron and spoke in the harsh, beautiful language of the druchii.

Kul took a step back, reaching over his shoulder for his sword as he saw emerald coals grow behind the thin slits of the statue's helmet and felt a horrific animation build within the terrible armour, though it moved not a single inch.

No statue of Khaine was this, he now realised, but the Witch King himself...

With a speed and grace that ought to have been impossible for such a monstrous being bound within this vast armour of iron and hate, the Witch King rose from his obsidian throne. He towered above the Chaos champion, breath hissing from beneath his helmet and the light of his evil putting the paltry debaucheries of Kul to shame with the weight of suffering he had inflicted.

The great sword of the Witch King swept up and Kul felt certain that this would be his death, such was his terror of this moment.

'Mother...' came a voice so steeped in evil that Kul felt tears of blood welling in the corners of his eyes.

'My son?' said Morathi, and to Kul's amazement, her tone was awed.

'We sail for Ulthuan,' said the Witch King. 'Now.'

CHAPTER FOUR
TRAVELLERS

Anurion the Green's villa was like nothing Daroir had ever seen before. His idea of a palace was marble walls, soaring ceilings and graceful architecture that celebrated the craftsman's art while blending sympathetically with the surrounding landscape. At least on this last count, the palace more than exceeded his expectations.

The palace was a living thing, its walls seemingly grown from the rock of the cliffs, shaped and formed according to the whims of its creator – and he was a person of many whims, Daroir was to discover. Living things grew from every nook and cranny, vines creeping across walls and columns of trees forming great vaults of leaves to create grand processionals.

Not only was the natural architecture astounding, but also confounding, for no sooner had a passageway formed than it would reshape itself or be reshaped as the palace's master wandered at random through his home and caused new blooms to arise in his wake. Every open space within Anurion's palace was a place of wonder and beauty and Daroir again imagined that this must be what Athel Loren was like.

He had thought that Kyrielle was leading him straight to her father, but Anurion the Green, it appeared, followed no one's timetable but his own, and when they had reached the palace at the top of the cliff, it had been to eat a meal of bread and fresh fruit and vegetables – many of which Daroir could not recognise or had outlandish names that were not elven or of any language he could recognise.

The next three days were spent regaining his strength and in discovery as he and Kyrielle explored her father's palace, the ever growing and changing internal plan as new to her as it was to him. Aside from Kyrielle, he saw only a very few servants and some spear-armed guards around the palace. Perhaps the full complement of Anurion's retainers remained in Saphery.

Each morning they would survey the magnificent landscape of Yvresse from the tallest tree-tower, savouring the beauty of the rugged coastline fringed with dense coniferous forests and long fjords that cut into the landscape from the ocean.

Deep, mist-shrouded valleys thrust inland and hardy evergreen forests tumbled down to the water's edge, where the ocean spread out towards the Shifting Isles and the Old World beyond. To the west, the foothills of the Annulii marched off to distant peaks towering dramatically into the clouds. The tang of magic from the raw energies contained within them set his teeth on edge.

Kyrielle pointed to the south and he saw the tips of glittering mansions and towers that were all that could be seen of Tor Yvresse, the only major city of this eastern kingdom and dwelling place of the great hero, Eltharion. Daroir had to choke back his emotions at the sight of it, such was the aching beauty of its distant spires.

He would often return to the tree-towers just to see the lights of the city, knowing that soon he would need to journey to Tor Yvresse to cross the mountains and return to the inner kingdoms of Ulthuan.

Each day was spent in flitting conversation, with Kyrielle's rapid subject changes unearthing a wealth of sophistication within him he had not known he possessed.

As they spoke it soon became apparent that knowledge of poetry was not the only artistic talent of which he had hitherto been unaware. One morning Kyrielle had presented him with a lyre and asked him to play.

'I don't know how to,' he had said.

'How do you know? Try it.'

And so he had, plucking the strings as though he had been playing since birth, producing lilting melodies and wonderful tunes with the practiced grace and élan of a bard. Each note flew from his hands, though he could feel no conscious knowledge of what he was doing and had no understanding of how he could create such beautiful music when he could remember nothing of any lessons or ability.

Each day brought fresh wonders as he discovered that as well as playing music he could also create it. Now aware he could play, an unknown muse stirred within him and he composed laments of such haunting majesty that they brought tears to the eyes of all that heard them. Each discovery brought as many questions as it did answers, and Daroir's frustration grew as he awaited an audience with his unseen host.

Each piece of the puzzle of his identity that fell into place brought him no closer to the truth, and each day he fretted over the silver ring on his finger. Every day spent without knowledge of his true identity was a day that someone mourned his loss: a friend, a brother, a father, a wife...

On the morning of the fourth day of his sojourn at Anurion's palace, Kyrielle entered the bright arbour in which he sat, and he looked up from the ghost of his memories and saw that she brought him a weapon.

Without a word she handed him a leather belt upon which hung a long-bladed dagger sheathed in a scabbard of what felt like a dense, heavy metal. The scabbard was banded with three rings of gold along its length, but was otherwise plain and unadorned.

'What's this?' he said. 'Do you want to see if I can fight?'

She shook her head. 'From the wounds you bear, I'd say that's a given. No, you were wearing this when I found you on the beach. Do you recognise it?'

'No,' he said. 'I don't remember seeing it before.'

'Not even when you were in the sea?'

'No, I was too busy trying to hold onto the wreckage to worry about what I was wearing. What *was* I wearing anyway?'

'You were dressed in the tunic of the Lothern Sea Guard. I'm told the heraldry on your arm was that of Lord Aislin.'

'The Sea Guard? I have no memory of serving aboard a ship, but then I've had no memory of lots of things I've been able to do since you took me in, haven't I? Maybe I should head to Lothern after I've spoken to your father?'

'If you like...' said Kyrielle. 'Though I hoped you would stay with us a little longer.'

He heard the beguiling tone of her voice and knew she was working her charms upon him. He pushed aside thoughts of remaining here and said, 'Kyrielle, I may very well have a wife and family. When my strength is returned I should get back to them.'

'I know, silly,' she said, 'but it has been so wonderful having you here and trying to help you regain your memory. I'll be sad to see you go.'

'And I'll be sad to leave, but I can't stay here.'

'I know,' she said. 'I will send a messenger to Lothern to take word to Lord Aislin that you are here. Perhaps he will know what ship you were on.'

He nodded and returned his attention to the dagger she had given him. Turning it over in his hands he was surprised at its weight. The workmanship was plain, though clearly of elven manufacture, for there was a sense of powerful magic to it. Though he spoke truthfully in saying that he did not recognise the blade, Daroir felt a connection to the weapon, knowing somehow that this weapon was *his*, but not how or why...

'I feel I *should* recognise this,' he said, 'but I don't. It's mine, I know that, but it doesn't mean anything to me, I don't remember it.'

Daroir grasped the hilt of the dagger and attempted to pull it from the scabbard, but the weapon remained firmly in its sheath and no matter how hard he pulled, he could not draw the blade.

'It's stuck,' he said. 'I think it's probably rusted into the scabbard.'

'An elven weapon rusted?' said Kyrielle. 'I hardly think so.'

'You try then,' he said, offering her the scabbard.

'No,' she said, shaking her head. 'I don't want to touch it again.'

'Why not?'

'I felt... wrong. I don't know, I just didn't like the feel of it in my hand.'

'The magic... is it dark?'

'I do not know. I cannot tell what kind of enchantment has been laid upon it. My father will have a better idea.'

Daroir stood and slipped the belt around his waist. One hole in the belt loop was particularly worn and he was not surprised when the buckle fit exactly within it. He adjusted the dagger on his hip so that it was within easy reach, though a dagger that could not be drawn was not much protection.

Kyrielle stood alongside him and straightened his tunic, brushing his shoulders and chest with her fingertips.

'There,' she said with a smile. 'Every inch the handsome warrior.'

He returned her smile and sensed a growing attraction for her that had nothing to do with her magical ability. She was beautiful and there was no doubt that he desired her, but he wore a pledge ring that suggested his heart belonged to another...

Though he knew that he should not feel such an attraction to Kyrielle, some deeper part of him didn't care and wanted her anyway. Was that part of who he really was? Was he a faithless husband or some reckless lothario who maintained the façade of family life while making sport with other women?

That felt like the first thing that made sense to him since he had been plucked from the ocean. The idea of betrayal stirred some deep current within him, dredging up a forgotten memory of a similar cuckolding, but was it one he had perpetrated or a wrong that had been done *to* him?

He looked into Kyrielle's eyes and felt no guilt at the feelings he had for her. Reflected in her features was the same attraction and he reached up to brush his palm against her cheek.

'You are beautiful, Kyrielle,' he said.

She blushed, but he could see his words had struck home and sensed a moment of opportunity that felt deliciously familiar. He leaned forward to kiss her, her eyes closing and her lips parting slightly.

Before their mouths touched, a rustle of leaves sounded as a wall of branches parted behind them and a tall figure swathed in green robes who muttered to himself lurched into the arbour with his arms outstretched.

A flickering ball of light floated between his hands, like a million tiny fireflies caged in an invisible globe of glass.

He turned to face them and frowned, as though not recognising them for a moment, before saying, 'Ah, there you are, my dear. Would you mind helping me with these? I created a new form of honey bee this morning, but they're rather more vicious than I intended and I rather feel I'll need your help to make sure they don't do any more damage...'

Finally, thought Daroir, Anurion the Green.

Eldain watched the city of Tor Elyr recede as Captain Bellaeir eased the Dragonkin through the sculpted rocky isles of the bay and aimed her prow, freshly adorned with the Eye of Isha, through the channels that led to the Sea of Dusk.

He stood at the side of the ship, wrapped tightly in a cloak of sapphire blue, though the temperature was balmy and the wind filling the sails was fresh.

He shivered as he remembered the last time he had left shore and travelled on a ship to a distant land. Caelir had been beside him and a seed planted that was to bear bitter fruit in the land of the dark elves. On those rare days he allowed the sun to warm his skin, he could convince himself that it had been the evil influence of the Land of Chill that had caused that seed to flower, but he knew only too well that the capacity for his actions had their roots within him all along.

It had been nearly a year since he had seen Tor Elyr, but it was as beautiful as he remembered, the crystal and white spires of its island castles rising from the peaked rocks of the water like cleft shards of a glacier. A web of silver bridges linked the castles to each other and Eldain's heart ached to see it diminish behind him.

'We'll be back soon enough,' said Rhianna, slipping her arms around him and resting her chin on his shoulder as she approached from behind.

'I know.'

'It will be good for us to travel. We've spent too long cooped up in Ellyr-charoi. I've missed the sun on my face and the sea air in my lungs. I can already feel the magic of Ulthuan growing stronger all around me.'

Eldain smiled, reminded once again that his wife was a mage of no little power.

'You're right, of course,' he said, surprised to find that he actually meant it.

Perhaps it *would* be good to travel, to see cities and places in Ulthuan he had not seen before. When this business with Rhianna's father was concluded, perhaps they might travel to Lothern and sample some of the fare from distant lands.

He turned within her grip and placed his own arms around her. 'I do love you.'

'I know you do, Eldain,' said Rhianna, and the hope in her eyes was like a ray of sunshine after a storm, full of the promise that all will be well. He held her close and together they watched the jewel of Ellyrion as it slid towards the horizon.

The journey from Ellyr-charoi had taken longer than normal, for Yvraine was not as skilled a rider as he and Rhianna. Their own steeds could carry them swift as the wind through the forests and across the plains, but Yvraine did not possess the innate skill of an Ellyrion rider. As a result, by the time they reached Tor Elyr, their progress onwards was stymied by the news that a black ark had attacked the ships of Lord Aislin as they patrolled the western coasts of Ulthuan. Only a single ship had survived the encounter but its captain had managed to bring warning of the druchii's attack, and now as many ships as could be mustered were being gathered in Lothern to mount a defence in the event of an attack.

As a consequence, the three travellers had been forced to await the arrival of a small sloop from Caledor to transport them across the Inner Sea to Saphery. This setback chafed at Yvraine, who paced like a caged Chracian lion at the enforced delay, though Eldain and Rhianna had taken the opportunity to dine in Tor Elyr's exquisite eating houses and indulge in some wild riding across the grassy steppes.

In truth, Eldain had not been displeased at the delay, now relishing his time away from the stifling confines of the Hippocrene Tower and his guilt. Just being out in the open air had improved his mood immeasurably and he had laughed for what seemed like the first time in an age when he and Rhianna had first gone riding for the sheer joy of it.

As the days passed, it quickly became apparent that Yvraine had not long been in the service of the Loremasters, the subject coming up one evening while the three of them dined atop the highest spire of Tor Elyr in a crystal-walled dining room.

Rhianna had asked of the lands Yvraine had visited in her duties, only to be met by a rather embarrassed pause before the Sword Master said, 'Merely Ellyrion.'

'Is that all?' Eldain had said. 'I though you travelled all across Ulthuan?'

'I shall when I complete this mission for Mitherion Silverfawn.'

Eldain had quickly realised what that meant and said, 'Then this is your first mission?'

'It is, everyone must begin somewhere.'

'Indeed they must,' said Rhianna. 'Even those born to be kings do not become great without taking their first humble step on a long and winding road.'

Yvraine had looked gratefully at Rhianna and Eldain was struck by the realisation that, for all her outward inscrutability, Yvraine Hawkblade was desperately afraid to fail.

Thinking of the Sword Master, Eldain watched her sitting in the bow with her sword held before her as she tried to meditate. She had spoken of the difficulties in meditating while previously aboard ship, but he could only imagine how difficult it must be to achieve any sort of silent contemplation on a vessel this small.

'She's so young,' said Eldain.

Rhianna followed his gaze and said. 'Yes, she is, but she has a good heart.'

'How do you know?'

'The Loremasters do not take just anyone into the ranks of the Sword Masters. Only those who desire wisdom ever reach the White Tower. All others find their footsteps confounded until they are back where they began.'

'Where is the wisdom in using a big sword?'

Rhianna smiled and shook her head. 'Don't mock, Eldain. For some the path of wisdom lies in the exercise of physical mastery of the ways of the warrior. Yvraine will have spent many years training at the feet of the Loremasters.'

'I know,' said Eldain, 'I'm just teasing. I'm sure she is pure of heart, but it's like she's shut part of herself off from the world around her. Surely there must be more to life than meditating and practising with a sword.'

'There is, but for each of us there is a path and if hers takes her on the road to mastery of weapons, then we are fortunate indeed to have her travel with us. She may be an inexperienced traveller, but she will be a formidable warrior, have no doubt of that.'

'We are only sailing across the Inner Sea,' said Eldain. 'What could happen to us here? We are perfectly safe.'

'As I'm sure Caledor thought, right before he was attacked by assassins on his way from Chrace to become the Phoenix King all those years ago.'

'Ah, but he *was* perfectly safe,' said Eldain, 'for the hunters of Chrace saved his life.'

She sighed indulgently and said, 'But the point remains. Better to have a Sword Master and not need her help, than to need it and not have her.'

'Very true,' he said. 'But have you actually seen her do anything with that sword?'

'No, I have not, but the exercise of her art is a private thing, Eldain.'

'Well let's just hope she knows how to use it if the need arises.'

'I don't think you need worry about that,' said Rhianna.

'Hmmm... aside from the wound to the head, there is nothing that would suggest an injury severe enough to result in the loss of one's memory,' said Anurion the Green, removing a set of silver callipers from Daroir's head. The archmage checked the readings on the measuring device and nodded to himself before frowning and placing the callipers over his own skull and comparing the results.

They sat in Anurion's study, though to call it a study gave it a degree of formality it did not possess. Formed from a hybrid of marble walls and living matter, tall trees curved overhead to form a graceful arch with trailing fronds reaching to the ground like feathered ropes. Plants and parts of plants covered every surface, hanging from baskets floating in the air or suspended by streamers of magical light that bubbled upwards from silver bowls. Budding flowers climbed the legs of the chairs and tables, each of which had been grown into its current form instead of being fashioned by the hand of a craftsman.

A dense, earthy aroma hung in the air alongside a million scents from the dizzyingly varied species of blooms that covered almost every surface in the chamber. The scents of so many living things should have been overpowering, but Daroir found it entirely pleasant, as though Anurion had somehow managed to find the exact combination to ensure that the air remained pleasingly fragrant.

Once Kyrielle and her father had contained the vicious bees, the archmage had turned to Daroir and said, 'So you're the one without his memory, yes?'

'I am, my lord,' said Daroir, for it was never a good idea to show discourtesy to a powerful archmage.

Anurion waved his hand dismissively. 'Oh, stop all this "my lord" nonsense, boy. Flattery won't help me restore your memory. I'll either be able to do it or I won't. Now come on, follow me to my study.'

Without another word, Anurion had stalked into the depths of his organic palace, leading them through great cathedrals of mighty trees and grottoes of unsurpassed beauty. With each new and magnificent vista, Daroir had to remind himself that this was one of the archmage's *lesser* palaces. Though more pressing matters occupied his thoughts as he and Kyrielle set off after her father, he hoped that one day he would be able to visit Anurion's great palace in Saphery.

It seemed to Daroir that their route took them through a number of arbours and clearings of marble and leaf they had passed before, and he wondered if even Anurion knew his way around his palace – or if such knowledge was even possible.

At last, their journey had ended in Anurion's study and both he and Kyrielle looked in wonder at the sheer diversity of life that flowered here. Plants and trees that Daroir had never seen before and had probably never existed before the tinkering of Anurion the Green surrounded them.

'Sit, sit…' Anurion had said, waving him over beside a long table strewn with ancient looking texts and a host of clear bottles containing variously coloured liquids. Daroir had been about to ask where he should sit when a twisting collection of branches erupted from the earthen floor and entwined themselves into the form of an elegant chair.

And so had begun an exhausting series of tests that Daroir could not fathom. Anurion had taken samples of his saliva and his blood before proceeding to measure his body, his height, weight and lastly the dimensions of his skull.

'Right,' said Anurion. 'I have the physical information I need, boy, but you'll need to tell me everything you remember prior to my daughter fishing you from the ocean. Omit nothing, the tiniest detail could be vital. Vital!'

'There's not much to tell,' said Daroir. 'I remember floating in the sea, holding onto a piece of wreckage... and that's it.'

'This wreckage, was it part of your ship?'

'I don't remember.'

Anurion turned to his daughter and said, 'Did your guards bring the wreckage back to the palace as well as this poor unfortunate?'

Kyrielle shook her head. 'No, we didn't think to bring it.'

'Hmmm, a shame. It could have held the key,' said Anurion. 'Still, never mind, one does what one can with the tools available, yes? Right, so we know nothing about your ship, and you say you remember nothing except being in the sea, is that correct?'

'It is. All I remember is the sea,' said Daroir.

Anurion swept up a strange, multi-pronged device that he attached to a number of coils of copper wire, which he then looped over Daroir's head, pulling the wire tight at his forehead.

'What are these for?' he said.

'Quiet, boy,' said Anurion. 'My daughter tells me that you were muttering something when she found you. What were you saying?'

'I don't know, I wish I did, but I don't,' said Daroir.

'Unfortunate,' said Anurion, adjusting the wires on his head, pulling them tight and leaving a trailing length of copper over his shoulder. 'Kyrielle, I do hope you remember what he was babbling.'

'Yes, father,' said Kyrielle. 'It was something about Teclis, about how he had to be told something. Something he needed to know.'

'And that doesn't sound familiar to you, boy?' said Anurion, turning his attention back to Daroir.

'No, not even a little.'

'Fascinating,' said Anurion. 'Frustrating, but fascinating. What information could a lowly sailor have that would be of interest to the great Loremaster of the White Tower?'

'I have no idea,' said Daroir. 'You keep asking me questions to which I have no answer.'

'Hold your ire, boy,' said Anurion. 'I am taking time from valuable research to deal with you, so spare me your biliousness and simply answer what I ask. Now... Kyrielle tells me that you possess a dagger that cannot be drawn, yes? Let me see it.'

Daroir stood from the chair of branches and unbuckled his belt, handing the scabbarded dagger to the archmage.

'Heavy,' said Anurion, closing his eyes and running his long fingers along the length of the scabbard. 'And clearly enchanted. This weapon has shed blood, a great deal of blood.'

Anurion gripped the hilt, but like Daroir, he could not force it from its sheath.

'How can it be drawn?' said Kyrielle.

'Perhaps it cannot,' said Anurion. 'At least not by us.'

'A poor kind of enchantment then,' said Daroir.

'I mean that perhaps it cannot be drawn by any other than he who crafted it or without the appropriate word of power. Only the most powerful magic can undo such enchantment.'

'More powerful than yours?' said Daroir.

'That remains to be seen,' said Anurion. 'But the question that intrigues me more is how you came to be in possession of such a weapon. You are a conundrum and no mistake, young... what was it my daughter christened you? Daroir, oh yes, how appropriate. You bear an enchanted dagger and have no memory, yet it seems you possess some knowledge that your unconscious mind deems necessary to present to Lord Teclis. Yes, most intriguing...'

Daroir felt his patience beginning to wear thin at the eccentric archmage's pronouncements and a strange heat began to build across his skull, further shortening his temper's fuse.

'Look, can you help me or not?'

'Perhaps,' said Anurion, without looking up from his desk.

'That's no answer,' said Daroir. 'Just tell me, can you restore my memory?'

'What manner of answer would you have me give, boy?' said Anurion, rounding on him and gripping his shoulders. 'You have no idea of the complexity of the living material that makes up your flesh. Even the simplest of plants is made up of millions upon millions of elements that make it a plant and allow it to function as such. Now, despite the evidence of your foolish words, your mind is infinitely more complex, so I would be obliged if you would indulge my thoroughness, as I do not want to reduce your intelligence any further by acting rashly.'

Anurion released his grip as an expression of surprise spread across his face and he once again adjusted the coils of copper wire around Daroir's head.

'What? What is it?'

'Magic...' said Anurion.

Kyrielle stood and joined her father and an expression of academic interest blossomed on her features.

Daroir frowned at their scrutiny, feeling like a butterfly pinned to the page of a collector's notebook. He glanced over at the table next to him and saw the stem and blooms of some unknown plant laid open like a corpse on an anatomist's table and felt a sudden sense of unease at whatever had piqued their sudden interest.

'What is it?' he said. 'What do you mean, "magic"?'

Anurion turned from him and lifted a golden bowl filled with a silver fluid that rippled and threw back the light like mercury. He returned to stand before Daroir and lifted the trail of copper wires that dangled at his shoulder, unravelling them and placing the ends into the golden bowl.

So faint that at first he wasn't sure what he was seeing, a nimbus of light built in the depths of the liquid, slowly intensifying until it seemed that Anurion held a miniature sun in his hands.

'I mean that whatever is causing your amnesia, it is not thanks to some blow to the head or near drowning.'

'Then what is it? What happened to my memory?'

'You have been ensorcelled, boy,' said Anurion, removing the copper wires from the bowl. 'This was done to you deliberately. Someone did not want you to remember anything before you went into the sea.'

The idea of someone tampering with his memories appalled Daroir, and the horror of such mental violation made him almost physically sick.

'Can you undo the magic?' said Kyrielle.

Anurion folded his arms and Daroir saw the reticence in his eyes.

'Please,' he said. 'You have to try. Please, I can't go on not knowing who I am or where I am from. Help me!'

'It will be dangerous,' said Anurion. 'Such magic is not employed lightly and I can offer you no guarantees that what memories you retain will survive.'

'I don't care,' he said. 'After all, what am I but the sum of my memories? Without them, I am nothing, a cipher...'

He pulled the coils of copper wire from his head and threw them onto the table, standing square before Anurion the Green.

'Do it,' he said. 'Whatever it takes, just do it. Please.'

Anurion nodded. 'As you wish. We will begin in the morning.'

CHAPTER FIVE
MEMORIES

Shimmering lights chased the *Dragonkin* as she plied the mirror smooth waters of the Inner Sea, the ship silent aside from the creak of her timbers and the occasional soft conversations of her small crew. Eldain watched these elves as they calmly went about their duties and wished a portion of their calm would pass to him. Even he could feel the magical energies of Ulthuan here, the ripple of half glimpsed shapes beneath the waves and the prickling sensation of always being watched.

Captain Bellaeir stood at the vessel's prow, standing high on the bowsprit and periodically issuing orders to his steersman.

'I am beginning to understand your reticence about travelling by ship,' he said to Yvraine as a jutting series of brightly coloured islets passed alongside.

The Sword Master looked up with a smile and he returned the gesture, glad to see a less ascetic side to her. As had become customary, she sat cross-legged on the deck with her sword across her lap as she tried to meditate.

'I am sure we are quite safe,' she said, abandoning her position and rising to her feet in a smooth motion. For all his misgivings about her youth and inexperience, Eldain could not help but be impressed by her lithe grace and poise.

'You have made this crossing once before, so do you have any idea where we are?'

'I think so,' she said, pointing to a smudge of brown and green on the northern horizon.

'What's that?' said Eldain, shielding his eyes from the sun with his hand. 'Is that the coast of Avelorn? I didn't think we would come this far north.'

'We haven't,' said Yvraine. 'That's the island of the Earth Mother.'

'The Gaen Vale?'

'Yes, a long and beautiful valley of wild flowers, apple trees and fresh mountain springs. It is a place of beauty and growth, where every elf maid is expected to visit at least once in her life.'

'Have you?'

'No,' said Yvraine. 'I have not yet had the honour of setting foot on her blessed soil, but I know that one day soon I shall visit the great cavern temple of the Mother Goddess and hear the words of her oracle.'

'It sounds like a beautiful place,'

'I am told it is, but, sadly, it is a beauty you will never know, for no males are permitted within the valley on pain of death.'

'So I have heard. Why does the Mother Goddess not allow the presence of males?'

'Birth and renewal,' said Yvraine, 'are the province of the female. The life giving cycle of the world and the rhythms of nature are secrets denied to males, whose gift to the world is destruction and death.'

'That is a harsh assessment,' said Eldain.

'Prove me wrong,' she said, and Eldain had no answer for her.

'Rhianna was to travel to the Gaen Vale,' he said, watching as the island vanished over the horizon as the captain called out more orders and the ship angled its course to starboard.

'Why did she not?'

'I would prefer not to speak of it,' said Eldain, once again picturing Caelir's face. Rhianna had planned to travel to the Gaen Vale not long after she and Caelir were to be wed, but his death had put paid to such plans. After her wedding to Eldain, the subject had never come up and he wondered why she had never again spoken of travelling to the temple of the Earth Mother.

He turned away from Yvraine, his thoughts soured, and walked towards the vessel's prow without another word. He nodded respectfully at the crew and passed the foresail, its silken fabric rippling in the fresh wind that propelled them across the sea.

Eldain watched Captain Bellaeir nod to himself as they passed the last of the rocky spikes and tiny atolls that dotted this part of the Inner Sea. Sensing his scrutiny, the captain inclined his head towards Eldain as he leapt nimbly from the bowsprit.

'How long before we reach Saphery?' said Eldain.

'Hard to say, my lord. The sea around here is unpredictable,' said Bellaeir.

'In what way?'

Bellaeir gave him a sidelong glance as though he were afraid he was being mocked, but decided he was not and said, 'We've been at sea for four days, yes?'

'Yes.'

'And, given fair seas and a trim wind, I'd expect to make Saphery in maybe another four, but out here… that's not how things work. You know that, don't you? You cannot tell me that you haven't felt the pull of the island…'

'I have felt… something, yes,' said Eldain.

'The seas have never been the same since the invasion of the fat Goblin King,' spat Bellaeir and Eldain felt his own bitterness rise at the mention of the goblin invasion that had laid waste to the eastern kingdom of Yvresse.

'Grom…'

Though Eltharion of Tor Yvresse had eventually defeated the Goblin King, a great many of the ancient watchstones that bound the mighty forces that kept Ulthuan safe had been toppled by the goblins' unthinking vandalism, and the cataclysmic forces unleashed had been felt as far away as Ellyrion.

'Indeed, though do not speak his name aloud, for the echoes of the past still cling to the ocean,' said Bellaeir. 'The Sea of Dreams is now a place of ghosts and evil memory, for the magic that once kept us safe fades and the terror of the past lives again in our dreams.'

Eldain said nothing as the captain touched the Eye of Isha pendant around his neck and made his way back to the steersman. He knew what the captain spoke of, for he too had felt the unnatural sensation of time slipping away from him, and the brooding shadow of ancient things pressing in on his thoughts.

How long they had truly been at sea and how long the remainder of their journey would take was a question not even the most experienced captain could provide an answer to. The passing of days and nights seemed to have no bearing on the senses here and it took an effort of will to even feel the motion of time, for their course was taking them close to one of the most mysterious places of Ulthuan.

The Isle of the Dead.

Eldain fought the urge to cast his gaze southwards, but the allure of the powerful magic was impossible to resist. Mist gathered at the horizon, lit from within by unearthly lights that glittered and flitted like corpse candles. Within the mist a shadow gathered, a dark outline of a forgotten land with a deathly aura that seemed to reach out and take his soul in a grip of ice.

He found his steps taking him towards the gunwale and he gripped the sides of the ship as a great weight of legend welled up within him, as though the island sought to remind him of the tragedy that had seen it sundered from the world.

In ages past, the island had been a place of great power, a lodestone of magical energies that drew the greatest mages of Ulthuan to its shores that they might bask in its power.

But at the dawning of the world, the Isle of the Dead had become much more than this: it had become a place of desperate hope, a place where the world had been saved and the fate of the elves sealed.

In the time of Aenarion, the first Phoenix King of Ulthuan, the gods of Chaos had walked the earth and fought to claim the world as their prize. Hordes of daemons and foul beasts of Chaos had destroyed all before them and the horrific followers of the Ruinous Powers had finally besieged Ulthuan. Aenarion had led his people in battle for decades to keep his lands safe, but even he could not defeat a foe that was constantly reinvigorated by the monstrously powerful magical currents surging across the face of the world from the ruptured Chaos portal in the far north. Thousands of elves died in battle, but for each twisted daemon they slew, a host of diabolical enemies arose to fight anew, and doomsayers wailed that the End Times were upon the world.

Eldain remembered his father telling him of Caledor Dragontamer, Aenarion's great companion and greatest of the high mages of old, and how he had conceived of a means by which the hordes of Chaos might be denied their power. In defiance of Aenarion's wishes, Caledor gathered a great convocation of mages upon the Isle of the Dead and a spell of great power was begun, a spell to create a mighty vortex that would drain the magic from the world. Though the mightiest daemons of Chaos sought to thwart Caledor, Aenarion fought them with the Sword of Khaine, the mightiest weapon in all the world, and held them at bay long enough for Caledor's mages to complete their spell...

Great was the destruction wrought by its completion: lands sank beneath the waves as the mages' spell took effect. Death and destruction followed in its wake, but the mages of old had triumphed, drawing the excess magic of the world to Ulthuan and denying the daemons of Chaos its sustaining power.

Like fishes stranded on dry land, the daemons were without the means to remain in the mortal world and the mortally wounded Aenarion was able to lead his warriors to victory, though he was soon to pass from the ages of the world.

Though the spell had saved Ulthuan, it was to have terrible consequences for Caledor and his mages, who were trapped forever on the Isle of the Dead.

Eldain shivered as he remembered these stories from his youth, stirring tales of sacrifice and heroism that had been told down the ages since the time of the first Phoenix Kings. None now travelled to the Isle of the Dead, for the titanic energies unleashed by Caledor had destroyed time itself there and left it adrift within the currents of the world, forever unseen and unknowable.

It was a place of ghosts and memory, legend and sorrow.

He felt a hand slide into his and he smiled as Rhianna appeared at his side, following his stare out into the haunted mists at the edges of the Isle of the Dead.

'They say that if you were able to reach the Isle of the Dead you would still see the mages of old, caught like flies in amber as they chant the ancient spells that preserve the balance of the world,' said Rhianna.

Eldain shivered at the thought, overwhelmed at the idea of elves trapped forever in time and bound by ancient duty, to eternally preserve a world of men that had no knowledge of them and no understanding of the awesome sacrifice that had been made in its name.

'Why would you ever want to go to the Isle of the Dead?'

'You wouldn't,' said Rhianna. 'I'm just saying what you would see if you did.'

'I do not like passing so close to such a place,' said Eldain. 'I feel a terrible shadow envelop my soul at the very mention of its name.'

'The most powerful magic ever conceived was unleashed here,' said Rhianna. 'The sea and the air have long memories. They know what happened and they retain the knowledge of the debt we owe to those who saved our world. You can feel it with every breath you take.'

'And you?' said Eldain, well aware that her magical senses were far superior to his.

Rhianna bowed her head and Eldain was surprised to see tears glistening on her cheeks. He released her hand and put his arm around her shoulder.

'I can still feel their presence,' she said. 'I can feel the sadness all around me. The mages knew that Caledor summoned them to their doom, but they went anyway. Even as they chanted the words of the spell to create the vortex, they could feel their deaths and knew that they would be ripped from time and trapped for all eternity. I can feel it inside me and I know that doom also.'

Eldain pulled her tight and said, 'There is no doom upon you, Rhianna. While I draw breath, I give you my oath that I will let nothing happen to you.'

'I know you won't, but some things are stronger than oaths.'

'Like what?'

'Like fate,' said Rhianna, staring into the shadow-haunted mists of the Isle of the Dead.

The rustle of the softest breeze stirred the leaves above Daroir's head, its balmy fragrances helping to soothe his fears of what was to happen here. He sat cross-legged on the warm grass, naked but for a plain loincloth and with the palms of his hands pressed to the ground. The feel of the earth beneath him and the sense of peace in this part of Anurion's palace flowed through him, as though the land of Ulthuan sought to prepare him.

He sat in the centre of a clearing (or a room, it was sometimes hard to tell the difference in Anurion's palace) that was as close to the ideal of harmony as Daroir could ever have imagined. Statues of elven gods ringed the edge of the clearing – Asuryan, Isha, Vaul, Loec, Kurnous and Morai-heg. Each was rendered in silver and gold, worked into the landscape with such skill that they appeared as hidden voyeurs rather than adornments.

Kyrielle sat next to him, her face lined with concern. She held a silver goblet worked with precious stones and a silver ewer filled with an aromatic liquid that steamed gently sat beside her.

'You are sure you want to go through with this?' she said.

'I'm sure,' he said. 'What I told your father was the truth. Without my memories I am nothing. What kind of a life is that?'

'But if something should go wrong… My father said that you might lose even the few memories you have now? Is a past life you remember nothing about worth that risk?'

'I believe it is.'

'But what if it is just pain that awaits you? What if it was *you* who used magic to bury those memories? Did you consider that?'

Daroir reached up to stroke her cheek, the silver pledge ring glinting on his finger. 'That may be the case, but if it is so, then I need to stop running and face the past. But if it was not then I need to reclaim my past to undo the wrong done to me.'

He smiled and said, 'I will be fine. I promise you.'

'And if you get your memories back… what about me? Will you forget me?'

'No, Kyrielle, I will not,' he said. 'You saved my life and no one could forget such a debt.'

She nodded and Daroir looked up as Anurion the Green entered the clearing in which they sat. The archmage was clad in a shimmering green robe tied at the waist with a golden belt and bore a sea-green pendant around his neck that shone with a magical inner light. His soft features were hardened and his hair pulled back tightly over his head. He bore a long sapling of slender, dead wood, the furthest reaches of its twig-like branches bare of leaves or growths.

The archmage approached him slowly, his eyes dancing with magic, and Daroir knew that the mage had been preparing himself for this since the previous night. A crackling nimbus of power played about Anurion's head and for the first time, Daroir felt the touch of unease flutter in his stomach.

Was he ready to risk an absence of memory? If Anurion was correct and the powers binding his recollections into an impenetrable fog were too strong, what would be left of him afterwards… a drooling simpleton? An adult with no more capacity for reason than a newborn? The thought terrified him, but then the alternative was no better and his resolve hardened once more.

'Are you ready?' said Anurion, his voice sonorous with power.

Daroir nodded.

'Say the words,' said Anurion.

'I am ready.'

'There can be no turning back once we begin,' said the mage. 'It will be painful for you and you may see things you would wish you had not, but if we are to succeed, then you must be able to bear such sights. Do you understand me?'

'I understand,' said Daroir, hoping he had the strength to see this through.

Anurion nodded and lowered himself to the ground before him. He placed the sapling between them and the earth opened up to receive it. Thin roots snaked from the base of the sapling, twisting and worming their way into the dark earth.

'Give me your hands,' said Anurion. 'And close your eyes.'

Daroir did as he was bid, placing his hands in those of the mage and pressing his eyes tightly shut. Anurion pulled his hands towards the sapling and wove both their fingers along its length.

'As the branch was once dead, so too are your memories,' said the mage. 'But as the power of creation flows through it once more, a measure of the new blooming life will pass into you, and I will use that energy for growth to bring your memories back into the light.'

Daroir nodded without opening his eyes and said, 'I understand. I am ready.'

They sat in silence for a measure of time that Daroir measured in the beats of his heart and just as he wondered when Anurion was going to begin, he felt a precious, fleeting sense of things moving at a speed almost too slow to be noticed.

The ground beneath him grew warm, as though a powerful current of energy moved through it, drawn to this place by Anurion's magic. A wondrous sense of peace reached up from the ground to envelop him and the harmonies of nature suffused his entire body, spreading calming waves of contentment through him.

Was this the power of creation at work?

He could feel the heartbeat of the world, a glacially slow pulse that began in the centre of everything and reached out to touch all living things, whether they knew it or not. Tendrils of white power reached up from the depths of somewhere incalculably old, the faintest wisps of its beauty brushing against the new-formed roots of the sapling.

Daroir wept as he saw the starved roots flourish at the touch of this bounteous, healing magic, cracked wood becoming green and vibrant, dried sap running like honey along the veins of the dead sapling.

Lines of power intersected here in this clearing and it was no accident that Anurion had sited his palace here. Daroir now felt the essence of Ulthuan, the titanic energies that sustained it and kept it safe from harm. To be near such power was intoxicating, and as it flowed into his hands sudden terror seized him at the thought of touching such colossal, elemental magic.

He wanted to pull away, but Anurion's warning that this ritual, once begun, could not be stopped returned to him and he summoned all his courage to hold on.

The energy flowed along his arms and he could feel the lethargy and aches that had plagued him since his awakening vanish, washed away in the healing balms of the world. It reached into him, filling his chest with such powerful forces that he gasped in astonishment as he struggled for breath.

'Hold true, boy!' said Anurion, his voice sounding as though it came from across an impossibly distant gulf of space and time. He struggled to retain his focus as the white light filled his body and reached up his chest, flowed into his neck and onwards into his head.

'Now we begin,' said Anurion.

Daroir gasped as the scent of the ocean filled his nostrils and his senses told him that his lungs were filling with water. He fought for calm as he saw the heaving expanse of dark, mist-shrouded water all around him.

'No!' he cried out in panic, but strong hands held him firm.

'You are safe!' said a strong voice. 'Where are you?'

'I am in the sea, I am drowning!'

'No, you are not,' said the voice, and the name Anurion leapt to the forefront of his mind as he fought down the impulse to thrash his arms and kick his legs. The scent of the trees and plants around him reasserted themselves and though he could *feel* the water around him, he knew it was not real.

He fought to control his breathing, letting the vision of his memory carry him onwards.

'I can see the ocean,' said Anurion. 'This is a memory you already have. We must go further. Think, boy! Think back!'

Daroir let the currents of his memory carry him onwards, the deepest depths of his mind dredged for meaning and recall. Images flashed across the shallows of memory, cold faces with cruel eyes shrouded in shadow, rough hands holding him fast as he wept at being hurled deliberately into the sea.

No sooner had he tried to focus on the image than it sank from sight and he cried out in frustration.

'Let the new life take root, boy,' said Anurion, the effort of holding the magic in check telling in the tremor of his voice. 'Do not force it, let it come naturally.'

As much as he tried to take heed of the mage's words, Daroir found it increasingly difficult not to struggle for meaning in the morass of images that danced just out of reach and meaning. A grey mare galloped past as the sea receded and he let out an anguished cry of recognition. He knew this horse, it… it had…

Aedaris…

He knew he should know this name, but its meaning eluded him, and as the horse galloped away he saw that it ran free and joyous across a swathe of corn-ripened fields at the foot of a great range of white mountains. He knew this land and his heart swelled with love for… his home?

He tensed as he saw a dark shadow arise to envelop the landscape, a spreading shadow from the west that slowly passed over the fields and forests, turning them to ash as it went. Ancient malice and centuries of bitterness poisoned the rivers and rendered the land barren and he could do nothing to prevent it.

'This is no memory,' said Anurion and Daroir knew he was right.

'No,' he said, 'it is a warning.'

'It is indeed, boy, but of what?'

Daroir struggled to answer, but felt his inner vision carried off once more before he could answer. The tone of this memory changed to one of agony and he twisted in Anurion's grip, a fire building in his shoulder and hip. Though he could still feel the soft ground beneath him, hot, sharp pain stabbed into him and he looked down to see the spectral outline of dark crossbow bolts protruding from his body.

Blood ran from his body and he heard a soft voice whisper in his ear…

Goodbye, Caelir…

As though a pitcher of freezing water had been upended over him, his head snapped up and his hands tore free of Anurion's with the cry of a drowning man desperate for air.

'No!' he cried, seeing a face so like his own drift before him even as it vanished into the mists of his memories.

The images of his devastated homeland and the crossbow bolts faded from his mind as the power that flowed through him from the sapling was withdrawn. He collapsed like a boneless fish, his back thumping onto the soft grass and his eyes misting with tears of anguish, betrayal and anger.

The pain of the phantom wounds was still strong and he reached down to place his hands where the bolts had pierced him. The skin there was unbroken, though his body was bathed in sweat and his flesh felt hot to the touch.

He felt a hand on his forehead and looked up to see Kyrielle's face above him, her eyes speaking eloquently of her worry. Her skin was cool and he felt his strength flood back into his body as the remembered pain of his wounds faded into memory.

'Are you all right?' she asked. 'Do you remember me?'

He nodded slowly, pushing himself upright as fresh vigour filled his limbs like the rush of having just ridden a fine Ellyrion steed across the steppes. He smiled to himself as he realised that he remembered galloping hard with a grey mare beneath him and the wind in his hair.

'Well?' said Anurion, and he looked across at the mage, not surprised to see a full-grown tree in the centre of the clearing where once had stood a dead sapling. 'Has your memory returned?'

Kyrielle's father's face was ashen, his eyes listless and hollow. The pendant that had once shone with light now lay in fragments amid the roots of the tree and the crackle of magical energy hung in the air like the aftermath of a lightning strike.

He took a deep breath and said, 'I'm not sure. I have images and parts of things that might be memory, but it's disjointed and... there are things I know are memories of mine, but I can't connect them.'

'It is as I feared,' said Anurion. 'Memory is more than simply the recall of events, it is these things connected by context and experience. Without this, they will remain like tales told to you by another. Vivid certainly, but without the connection to make them real they will never be anything more. My power has unlocked the doors to your memories, but it is not sufficient to force it open and allow that which will connect them to you to return.'

He pushed himself upright, pleased at the lithe power and youthful energy he once again felt in his limbs.

'I saw my homeland,' he said.

'As did I,' said Anurion. 'Ellyrion if I am not mistaken.'

'Yes. And I saw it destroyed,' he said. 'A creeping shadow of evil from the west swallowed it and brought about its ruin.'

'Might that be the warning you felt you had to take to Teclis?' said Kyrielle.

'I think it might be, yes.'

Anurion pulled himself to his feet, using the tree that had grown between them for support. 'Then to Teclis you must go. He is the greatest mage of Ulthuan and what I have begun, he will finish. You must journey to the White Tower of Hoeth and tell him what you have seen. An evil threat gathers against Ulthuan and we must unlock the rest of your memories to uncover the nature of that threat. Only Teclis or the Everqueen have the power to do that.'

Kyrielle reached out to help her father as he swayed unsteadily on his feet.

'Daroir,' she said. 'Help me, he's weak!'

He reached out to take hold of Anurion's arms and smiled suddenly. 'That's not my name,' he said. 'I remember now...'

'Then what is your name, boy?'

'My name is Caelir,' he said.

BOOK TWO
SAPHERY

CHAPTER SIX
THREATS

Pazhek had never put his faith in omens, but as the sun set behind him, bathing the bleached white stone of the mountains in blood, he smiled in anticipation of the kill he was soon to make. Though the sun was now gone, the sky was still too light to move, the hateful brightness of the day preventing him from departing his hiding place below a tumbled rock that formed a natural overhang.

He waited patiently for the light to drain from the great valley, allowing shadows to form and darkness to creep back into the world like a guilty secret. His fuliginous robes merged with the night until only the glint of malice in his eyes was visible.

Satisfied that it was dark enough for his purposes, he slid from his place of concealment. He slithered over the top of the rock on his belly, careful to hug the edge of the valley and keep himself pressed flat. It had been fourteen nights since he had swum ashore from the magically shrouded Raven ship, moving under cover of darkness and never allowing impatience to force his pace.

Such caution was essential. The slightest hint of his presence would spell his doom, for golden-winged eagles watched from the skies and shadow-cloaked hunters stalked the mountains. These Shadow Warriors were the descendants of the Nagarythe and scions of the deadly Alith Anar, skilled hunters – the best the enemy had – but they were not the equal of one trained at the Temple of Khaine since birth to master the art of death.

Pazhek moved with all the skill his race possessed, but even the most graceful dancer of Ulthuan had not the poise and liquid grace of the assassin. His black-clad form moved like a shadow, moving from perch to perch as though the mountains themselves reformed to match his movements and hasten him on his way.

A pair of short, stabbing swords were wrapped in cloth across his back and a curved dagger hung at his waist. These were not the assassin's only weapons, for his entire body was a weapon, fists that could seek out an enemy's vulnerable regions to incapacitate or kill with a single blow, feet that could shatter bones and an array of deadly poisons concealed within a number of small pouches on his belt.

Pazhek had killed since he had been stolen away from his crib during the insane debaucheries of Death Night, raised by the dark beauties of the temple to learn the secrets of Khaine: the martial arts, the power of poisons, how to move without sound and to slip through the night unseen. The assassins were the agents of the Witch King, heartless killers who owned the darkness and slew his enemies without mercy.

The night closed in around Pazhek and though the land of Ulthuan was alien to him and its air reeked of magic, he slipped effortlessly over the peaks towards his destination. His passage was maddeningly slow, but so skilful was it that even a scout standing within a yard of him would have been hard pressed to discover him.

The night wore on, his shadowy form slipping through the rocks and crags of the mountains, his innate sense of spatial awareness telling him that he was almost where he needed to be. If the maps he had been shown in Naggarond were correct, it would be close to dawn when he reached his target.

For another three hours, Pazhek ghosted through the high peaks of the mountains until he could see a dim glow rising behind the craggy horizon above him. He did not let the excitement of having arrived hurry his movements. Such a moment was when an inexperienced assassin could let the thrill of the moment overwhelm him into making a mistake, but Pazhek was too skilled and detached to allow himself to make such an elementary error.

With as much patience and care as he had employed since his stealthy arrival on Ulthuan, Pazhek warily moved to the edge of the ridge above and found a cleft in the rock to peer through to avoid silhouetting himself against the skyline.

A pale white glow filled a wide valley below him, the soon to rise sun already seeping over the eastern horizon with the first golden hints of its arrival. Stretching from one side of the valley to the other, a high wall of silver-white stone reared up to block the route through the mountains. High elf warriors manned the walls of this great fortress, gathering sunlight winking from hundreds of spear tips, swords and bows and glinting upon mail shirts and plates of ithilmar armour.

But the most prominent feature of this mighty fortress was the jutting head of a great stone eagle that reared from the centre of the ramparts. The arc of its spread wings was cunningly fashioned into the structure of the wall to provide artfully curved bastions and its majesty gave the fortress its name.

The Eagle Gate.

Raised in the time of Caledor, the Eagle Gate was but one of the gateway fortresses built in the Annulii Mountains to defend the passes that led to the Inner Kingdoms. In the thousands of years since, not one of Caledor's fortresses had fallen and each was garrisoned by some of the finest warriors of Ulthuan. A single gate of azure steel was the only way through the wall, but anything that dared approach this fastness would be pierced by a thousand arrows before they had covered half the distance between the turn in the road and the gate.

Sculpted towers reared from the great wall, streaming blue pennants snapping from their finials and ringed with graceful parapets upon which sat fearsome war-machines. Pazhek knew only too well the carnage these machines could wreak, having seen such weapons hurling silver bolts the length of a lance that could punch through the heart of a dragon, or sending withering hails of lighter, but no less deadly darts with terrifying rapidity.

But a fortress was more than simply weapons and warriors, it had a living, beating heart that sustained it as surely as the strength of its garrison. Tear out that heart and the fortress would die.

In the case of this fortress, Pazhek knew that the heart of the Eagle Gate was its commander, Cerion Goldwing.

Using the long shadows of the imminent dawn, Pazhek made his final approach to the fortress with murder in his heart.

The land of Yvresse was harsh and unforgiving, very different from the balmy, eternal summers of Ellyrion, though Caelir was forced to admit that the land had a rugged splendour that spoke to his adventurous soul of living in the wild and facing things head on. The folk of Yvresse were known as quiet, dignified souls touched with sadness, for their land had been ravaged by the coming of the Goblin King less than a century before.

Though the land had suffered terribly at the hands of the goblins, it was a hardy realm and its rivers now flowed clear again and new forests hugged the soaring mountain peaks once more. Only the previous day they had crossed an icy river of crystal water across a shallow ford and Kyrielle had told him that this was the Peledor Ford where elven scouts had first engaged the Goblin King's army.

The river had been choked with goblin dead, and the water polluted for years to come with their foul blood. But the land of Ulthuan was strong and sustained by powerful, cleansing magic. What had once been a tainted, evil river now flowed strong and clear to the sea, the regenerative powers of the land having washed itself free of the invaders' taint.

Here and there, they passed isolated watchtowers, but they encountered no other travellers, for Yvresse was a land of jagged rock and sheer cliffs and mist. Few dwelled here and though Kyrielle had told him that the scouts of Tor Yvresse would be abroad, he saw no sign of them.

He and Kyrielle rode on the backs of fine steeds provided from the stables of Anurion's villa, while Anurion himself rode a winged pegasus, the magnificent beast circling above them even now as it stretched its wings and Anurion surveyed the landscape ahead of them. Caelir had never seen such a magical creature, its grace, intelligence and beauty unlike anything he could have imagined. Even the famed steeds of his homeland could not compare to this exquisite mount.

In addition to Kyrielle and Anurion, a dozen hand-picked guards rode with them, their armour bright and their long lances glittering in the sun.

Kyrielle wore a long gown of pastel green, her auburn tresses unbound and falling to her waist. Caelir smiled at her and she returned the smile. He felt better than he had in days, the muscles of his limbs feeling powerful and young, the oppressive fog clouding his mind lessened now that he knew his name.

Anurion had dressed for travel, with his billowing robes substituted for a practical tunic of pale green and a long cloak that appeared to be woven of autumnal leaves. He carried a staff of slender wood, its tip crowned by intertwined thornvines.

In the time since Anurion had attempted to undo the magic that imprisoned his memory, Caelir's vigour and energy were restored, and though he could remember no more than his name and homeland, he felt that it was simply a matter of time until he was restored.

They had set off later that day, making their way southwards towards the city of Tor Yvresse and the route across the mountains.

Caelir soaked up the dramatic scenery of Yvresse, basking in its wild majesty and periodically galloping off whenever they encountered a stretch of flat ground simply for the thrill of riding hard through an unknown land. The wind in his hair, the beat of hooves on the grass and the freedom that came of being at one with a steed was as close to a homecoming as he could have wished for.

The horse he rode was a fine, snow-white beast of Saphery, its coat a shimmering dust of white and though no doubt a prince amongst steeds in its stable, it was nothing compared to the regal power, strength and agility of an Ellyrion mount.

Kyrielle and the warriors would attempt to match his incredible feats of horsemanship, but none of them had been raised in a land where the young were taught to ride as soon as they could sit in the saddle.

Whatever else he had forgotten, he had not lost his skill as a rider.

Just being on a horse again lightened Caelir's mood and he laughed as he urged his steed on to greater displays of skill.

The shadows lengthened and a sombre mood came upon the company as they drew near the ruins of an ancient citadel built into the side of the mountains. Its once slender towers were now fallen to ruin, the great mansion at its centre gutted by fire. Once impregnable walls were shattered, its stones cast down and the great basalt causeway that led to its vine-choked gateway littered with fallen rubble.

Fallen guardian statues lay toppled in the dry moat, their sightless eyes staring with forlorn anguish at what had become of their former home. Caelir thought the scene unbearably sad and felt tears prick the corners of his eyes.

He turned to Kyrielle and said, 'What is this place? Why has it been left in such ruin?'

It was Anurion who answered him, his voice heavy with emotion. 'This is Athel Tamarha, once the keep of Lord Moranion and outpost of Tor Yvresse.'

'What happened here? Was it the Goblin King?'

Anurion nodded. 'Yes. The goblins came ashore further north, at a place called Cairn Lotherl, but it did not take them long to find a target for their wrath. No one knows how the Goblin King heard of Tor Yvresse, but hear of it he did, and his army burned and destroyed all in its path as they sought to find it. Fields of magical crops unique to Yvresse were trampled beneath iron-shod feet, never to be seen again, and any settlements in the goblins' path were razed to the ground. On their way south they found Athel Tamarha and, thinking it Tor Yvresse, they attacked.'

Caelir urged his mount from the route they had been following and rode towards the cracked remains of the causeway. Understanding a measure of his sorrow, both Anurion and Kyrielle followed him, carefully directing the hooves of their steeds through the rubble.

Caelir passed beneath the broken arch of the gateway, riding into the fire-blackened courtyard where the ghosts of the Goblin King's invasion lingered. Splintered gates and doors hung on sagging hinges and everywhere he looked, Caelir could see the devastating fury of the goblin attack. Broken sword blades, snapped shafts of arrows and shattered shields lay strewn about, the detritus of war forgotten and abandoned.

'They knew not what they did,' said Anurion, surveying the wreckage from the back of his pegasus. 'When the goblins came, only boys and old men defended the walls of Athel Tamarha and they say that when Moranion saw the green horde from his tower he knew that his home was lost.'

'Where was his army?' said Caelir tearfully. 'Had he no sons to fight for him?'

'His eldest son, Eltharion, led most of his army in the north against the druchii, while his youngest studied in Tor Yvresse,' said Anurion. 'By evil fate, the goblins had attacked at the worst possible time for

Athel Tamarha and its doom was sealed.'

'Eltharion the Grim…'

'The very same,' said Anurion. 'Though he was yet to earn such a sad name.'

Caelir dismounted and picked his way across the courtyard of the keep to stand within the fallen ruins of the central mansion. The ceiling had long since collapsed and piles of broken timber and fallen stone choked the once grand halls and elegant chambers.

Kyrielle followed him inside and took his hand as he wept in the lost keep of Athel Tamarha, overcome with sorrow at seeing such a magical place destroyed. Though he had never heard of Athel Tamarha before now, he could see the savage goblins running rampant through its gilded halls, tearing priceless tapestries from the walls to use as bedding, burning irreplaceable tomes of knowledge for warmth, destroying ancient works of art for their primitive amusement and swilling wines older than many human kingdoms like water.

'A palace that had endured for two millennia was levelled in a single day by a tribe of mindless barbarians who knew not what it was they destroyed,' said Anurion, his voice little more than a whisper and redolent with the knowledge of times past.

Such barbarism was beyond Caelir's understanding and his anger towards the invaders surged hot and urgent through his veins. The battle fought here was long over, yet Caelir felt the pain of loss as surely as though he had stood upon its fallen battlements and witnessed its bloody ending. The tumbled ruins spoke to him on a level he had never before experienced, as though the memory of the violence done to it was imprinted on its very walls, the horror of its destruction passing to him and ensuring that its loss would never be forgotten.

'We should go now,' said Kyrielle, taking him gently by the arm and leading him back to his horse.

'How could anyone destroy something of such beauty?' said Caelir.

'I have no answer to give you, Caelir,' said Kyrielle, her normal sprightly vigour absent from her voice. 'The goblins are elemental creatures and live only for their own gratification.'

'I cannot understand it,' he said. 'It is just… *wrong.*'

'I know, but Moranion was avenged,' said Kyrielle. 'Eltharion's army returned from the north and led the warriors of Tor Yvresse in a great battle. You must have heard the ending of the tale?'

'I have,' said Caelir. 'Eltharion sailed his fleet into the bay and his warriors fell upon the goblins from behind. It was a slaughter.'

'Indeed it was,' said Anurion. 'But many elves fell that day and the city of Tor Yvresse was almost destroyed. The goblin shaman almost undid the magic at the heart of the Warden's tower, magic that could have destroyed our beloved land. Though Eltharion stopped him, it was only at terrible cost.'

'What cost?' said Caelir, mounting his horse once more.

Anurion said, 'No one knows, for Eltharion will not speak of it, but it has blighted his life ever since. Together with the bravest warriors of his army, he entered the Tower of the Warden and undid the fearful damage done by the Goblin King's shaman, stabilising the vortex created by the mages of Caledor. He was hailed as a hero and became the Warden of Tor Yvresse, but the cheers of the crowd moved him not. In all the days since, it is said that no beauty touches him, no tale of heroism moves him and no light dares enter his soul. From that day forth he became known as Eltharion the Grim.'

Caelir took a last look around the achingly sad ruins of Athel Tamarha and said, 'I will remember this place.'

'Good,' said Anurion. 'It is right that we remember the past, for we shall surely rue the day we forget those who came before us. Whether for good or ill, it is they who shape us, form our thoughts and send us into the future with their memories.'

Caelir nodded and said, 'And what will I leave for those who come after me? I have no memories. What will be my legacy?'

'Your legacy is what you do from here onwards,' said Anurion. 'You are on a path, Caelir, and where it leads I do not know. You are young and the impetuous fire of youth burns in your heart, but I do not believe there is evil in you. Even if Teclis is unable to restore your memory, you have the chance to make new memories. Since your rebirth in the ocean, you have been creating new memories and *that* is the legacy you will carry with you. That and the lives you touch along the way, for we are all the sum of those whose influence touches our hearts.'

Caelir smiled in thanks to the archmage of Saphery, feeling his spirits rise at his words.

They rode out through the gates of Athel Tamarha and even though the sadness of the ancient palace's destruction was still lodged in his heart like a shard, he felt better for having seen it, as though the grief was like a cooling balance to the heat of his anger.

Once again, the company set off towards the south and Tor Yvresse.

Home of Eltharion the Grim.

A bitter wind was blowing from the west and Cerion Goldwing was feeling the weight of his years as he walked the length of the Eagle Gate this cold and gloomy morning. The scent of the sea air was carried on the wind, a dark, musky aroma that sent a chill down his spine as he thought of the cold, evil land that lay beyond it.

As though to dispel such morbid thoughts, he turned and cast his gaze eastwards to the land of Ellyrion. This high in the mountains, the rolling steppe of Ellyrion was a faint golden brown haze and it warmed his heart to see such a bounteous land and know that it was kept safe by the courage and heart of his warriors.

Passing the Eagle Tower, he surveyed the mountains that towered above his command, the silver peaks of the Annulii glittering with magic like a frosting of ithilmar. The magic here was so strong that even a simple warrior like him could see it and the haze of whispering energy that hung over the mountains promised more activity for his soldiers.

'Strong today,' he said to himself, feeling the magic pulse in his veins.

When the magic blew strongly, the creatures of the mountains were drawn to the rush of powerful energy that swirled around the island of Ulthuan. Such raw magic was capable of almost anything and many of the creatures drawn to such magic were unnatural monsters of Chaos.

Tall and clad in a simple tunic the colour of an autumn meadow over a thin, yet incredibly strong coat of ithilmar mail, Cerion was a stately figure of an elf. His silver helmet was tucked into the crook of his arm and he kept another hand on the hilt of his sword, a blade hammered out on the anvil by his grand sire.

His features were drawn and had once been handsome, though the passage of years had not left him unmarked. A druchii blade had taken his left eye nearly a century ago and when the blade of another had snapped, the spinning shards had left a scar that ran across his temple and over the bridge of his nose.

As he continued his morning tour of the walls, the soldiers of the Eagle Gate smiled warmly at him, though he had made no special effort to be liked in his three decades of command. The respect his warriors showed him had been earned. He was a warrior of proven courage and strategic skill, and it had been a willingness to share in the hardships endured by those who served under him that had won their respect.

He stopped beside a warrior with jet-black hair who sat cross-legged on the battlement with an unstrung bow propped beside him on the parapet. A quiver of arrows sat next to him and he worked industriously on weaving a string for his bow.

'Good morning, Alathenar,' said Cerion. 'Something wrong with your bow?'

The warrior looked up with a smile and said, 'No, my lord, nothing wrong with it.'

'Then what are you doing?'

'Just trying something out,' said Alathenar. 'My Arenia has been growing her hair for the last few years to weave into my bowstring and now it's finally long enough. I think it might help me get an extra ten or twenty yards of range.'

Cerion knelt by the archer and watched him at work, his fingers deftly working the thin strands of hair into the length of his bowstring.

'An extra twenty yards?' he said. 'You're already able to put an arrow through a druchii's eye at three hundred yards. You really think you'll be able to coax more out of that weapon?'

Alathenar nodded and said, 'She travelled to Avelorn and had the

strands blessed by one of the handmaids of the Everqueen, so I'm hoping some of their skill and magic will have passed into it.'

Cerion smiled, remembering a misspent youth in the forests of Avelorn when he had joined the wild carousing of the Everqueen Alarielle's
court and partaken in the indulgent lifestyle practised beneath the magical boughs of her forest realm.

Consort of the Phoenix King, the Everqueen was one of the twin rulers
of Ulthuan and her court roamed like a great carnival through the forest
of Avelorn, its silken pavilions ringing with music, poetry and laughter.
He well remembered the Everqueen's handmaids, elf maids as skilled
with spear and bow as they were fair of face and lithe of body...

'Well,' he said. 'If any warrior's blessing can pass into a weapon it
would be theirs. Be sure to let me know when you have put your bow
together and we'll see how the magic of the handmaids holds up.'

'Of course, my lord. We'll have an archery contest when I'm off duty.
Maybe wager a few coins upon the outcome...'

Cerion tapped his ruined eye and said, 'I do not think you need a
blessed bow to outshoot me in an archery contest.'

'I know,' said Alathenar, 'That's why I was going to let you wager on
me.'

'You are too kind,' said Cerion, pushing himself to his feet. Alathenar
was already the best shot with a bow in the Eagle Gate's garrison, and
though Cerion doubted the addition of a maiden's hair to the bowstring
would make any tangible difference, he knew well enough that the
superstitions of soldiers were a law unto themselves.

Technically, Alathenar was on duty at the moment and, in disassem-
bling his bow, was in dereliction of that duty by not having his bow at
the ready, but Cerion was wise enough to know when to apply military
law with an iron hand and when to let it bend like a reed in the wind.
Besides, such a competition would help the morale of the garrison and
strengthen the bonds between his warriors.

If only others could appreciate such things, he thought sourly as he
saw his second in command, Glorien Truecrown, marching towards him
from the Eagle Tower. Alathenar caught his expression and looked over
to see Glorien strutting towards them.

The younger officer wore an elaborate *ithiltaen*, the tall, conical helmet
of the Silver Helms, and a magnificent suit of ithilmar plate, the armour
gleaming and polished. Glorien's noble status entitled him to wear the
ithiltaen, though most nobles considered it unseemly to wear such a helmet without first having earned it by serving in a band of Silver Helm
knights.

Cerion nodded briefly to Alathenar and went to meet Glorien, hoping
to head him off before he reached the archer and decided to discipline
him.

'Glorien,' said Cerion. 'Good morning.'

'Good morning, my lord,' said Glorien, his tones clipped and formal. 'I have transcribed the latest reports from our scouts.'

He held out a leather scroll case and Cerion took it reluctantly, already aware of what it contained, having spoken with the scouts when they had returned the previous evening.

'You know you don't have to do this, Glorien,' he said.

'But I do,' said Glorien. 'It is expected.'

Cerion sighed. 'Very well. I shall read them later this morning.'

He saw Glorien looking over his shoulder and knew exactly what he saw. As Glorien was about to speak, Cerion reached up to turn him around and march along the length of the wall with him.

'Was that Alathenar the Archer without a string to his bow?' said Glorien.

'Never mind that, Glorien,' said Cerion, leading him towards the stairs cut in the face of the mountainside that led to the Aquila Spire, a narrow projecting tower built into the southern cliff face that served as his personal sanctuary and study.

'But he is without a weapon! He has to be disciplined.'

As loyal as Cerion was to his race, he now cursed its love of intrigue and petty politicking.

Cerion knew that Glorien Truecrown had only secured his appointment to the Eagle Gate through his family connections rather than any ability as a warrior, for the Truecrown family could trace its roots to those linked with the Phoenix Kings of old. Their factional power in the court of Lothern was in the ascendant, enabling them to secure prestigious positions of authority for scions of their family members.

Glorien was simply biding his time until Cerion decided to retire and thus secure the position of Castellan of the Eagle Gate, but he knew in his heart that Glorien was simply not ready for such an important position.

'You would discipline the best archer in this fortress?'

'Of course,' said Glorien. 'No one is above the rules. Just because Alathenar can loose an arrow with some skill is no reason for him to believe he is exempt from following the rules.'

'Alathenar is more than just a skilled archer,' said Cerion. 'The warriors of this fortress respect and love him. His successes are their successes and when his name is spoken of in the barrack halls of other Guardian Gates, it reflects on them too. They look up to him, for he is a natural leader.'

'And?'

Cerion sighed. 'Discipline Alathenar and you will alienate all the warriors in this fortress. If you are one day to command the Eagle Gate, then you must learn to understand the character of those you lead in battle.'

'Command this fortress? The Eagle Gate is yours,' said Glorien, and Cerion almost laughed at his clumsy attempt at denial.

'Spare me the massage of my ego, Glorien,' said Cerion. 'I know your family tried to have me replaced in order for you to take command here. Thankfully, saner heads prevailed.'

At least Glorien had the decency to look embarrassed and Cerion felt some of his anger fade. Perhaps Glorien could yet learn how to be a soldier and a leader, though he suspected the odds were against it.

'There is more to command than simply getting warriors to follow rules and regulations,' said Cerion. 'You cannot simply apply your rules and mathematical formula to the defence of a fortress. It is in the minds of your warriors that a battle will be won or lost. Warriors will fight and die for a leader they believe in, but not for one they do not trust.'

'But discipline must be enforced.'

'Yes it must,' said Cerion. 'But not when its application would do more harm than good. Discipline Alathenar now and you risk losing the hearts of your soldiers.'

'I do not care to win the affections of the soldiery,' said Glorien.

'Nor do you need it. But without their respect, you are lost.'

Cerion glanced over his shoulder, knowing that the warriors of the Eagle Gate did not need to hear their superior officers arguing. Thankfully, the elven warriors in the courtyard were sparring with swords or practising formation spear discipline and were too intent on their labours to notice the discussion.

'I will think on what you have said,' said Glorien, but Cerion already knew that the younger elf had dismissed his words as the ramblings of an aged warrior long past his prime.

'Be sure that you do,' said Cerion, 'for if this fortress *does* become yours to command, you will be entrusted with the fate of Ulthuan. If an enemy army were to breach the walls, Ellyrion would suffer terribly before the armies of the Phoenix King could muster to fight it. Think on that before you decide to weaken the defence of this garrison by disciplining its best archer.'

Cerion brandished the scroll case Glorien had given him and said, 'Now, if you will excuse me, I think I shall retire to my chambers to read these reports.'

He had no wish to read Glorien's pedantry, but it gave him an excuse to be away from his subordinate.

'Of course, my lord,' said Glorien before saluting and turning on his heel.

Cerion watched him go and his heart sank as he pictured the Eagle Gate under his command.

In its prime, Tor Yvresse had been considered the jewel of Ulthuan, but time and invasion had taken its toll on the once great city. Built atop nine hills, the great, spired city dominated the landscape, its mighty walls high and white and carved with protective runes. Glittering gold and bright silver shone in the afternoon sun and the titanic towers of its palaces soared above the walls, linked to one another by great bridges hundreds of feet above the ground.

Since the city had come into view, Caelir had stared, open-mouthed, at the magnificent spectacle. He had vague, disconnected memories of Tor Elyr, but nothing that could compare to the sheer magnificence of Eltharion's city.

Tor Yvresse shone like a beacon against the dark rock of the landscape and the green shawl of forests draped over the mountains behind it.

'It's magnificent,' said Caelir once again and Kyrielle smiled at his awe.

'You should have seen it a century ago,' she said. 'Its amphitheatres were the envy of the world. Even the Masques of Lothern would come to play in Tor Yvresse and you know how particular they are.'

Caelir didn't, but already felt he was sounding like an uncultured fool and simply nodded in reply.

Anurion flew above them on his pegasus and only Kyrielle rode alongside him, the guards keeping a respectful distance from the two of them. He could barely contain his excitement at seeing one of the great cities of Ulthuan, though he could still feel the ache in his heart from the ruins of Athel Tamarha. Tor Yvresse had suffered terribly at the hands of the Goblin King and though it had survived thanks to the heroism and sacrifice of Eltharion, he knew it had not escaped unscathed.

'Will we get to see much of Tor Yvresse, do you think?' he said.

'That depends on father, I suppose,' said Kyrielle. 'I know he is keen to get you to the White Tower and Teclis.'

'I know, but surely we can take a day to explore?'

'I do hope so. There are many things I would like to show you. The Fountain of Mist, Dethelion's Theatre, the River of Stars...'

'Perhaps we can come back after the White Tower.'

'I'd like that,' she said. 'I'd like that a lot.'

Caelir smiled to himself and returned his attention to the city ahead, its magnificent walls looming above them as they followed the road that led to its tall gate of shimmering gold. Black banners fluttered from its towers and the spears of the warriors on its walls glittered like a thousand stars.

He looked up as he heard a beat of powerful wings and Anurion's pegasus gracefully landed behind them, its wings spread wide as it came to earth once more. The magical beast's wings folded neatly along its flanks and the archmage rode up to them without pause.

Caelir could see from his face that he bore ill-tidings and grimly awaited his pronouncement.

'Father?' said Kyrielle, also recognising the import of her father's expression.

'The currents of magic are alive with tidings and portents from all across Ulthuan,' said Anurion. 'The druchii have attacked the fleet of Lord Aislin off the coast of Tiranoc. It is said that a black ark sank two ships, though a third was able to escape.'

'The druchii...' said Caelir.

'We must make all haste in getting you to Teclis, boy,' said Anurion. 'If this is connected to the vision you saw of the darkness engulfing Ellyrion, then the attack of the dark elves may well be the opening moves in an invasion.'

Caelir nodded in agreement, all thoughts of exploring the city of Tor Yvresse with Kyrielle vanishing from his mind at Anurion's mention of Teclis. 'I think you are right.'

He kicked his heels into the flank of his steed.

'Let us hasten to Tor Yvresse.'

CHAPTER SEVEN
WARDEN

Tor Yvresse, city of Eltharion...

From his initial awe, Caelir felt a strange mix of sadness and disappointment as they drew closer to the greatest city of Yvresse. What from afar had seemed mighty and regal looked faded and neglected when seen at close range. Though the high walls were no doubt steadfast and strong, the number of warriors manning them seemed woefully few for such a vast stretch of battlements.

The road leading to Tor Yvresse was deserted and their company was the only group of travellers abroad. The golden gate of the city remained closed and Caelir could feel the suspicious glares from the soldiers on the walls as they watched them approach.

An eerie silence clung to the landscape around the city and though he had no memory of travelling to such a metropolis before, he found it strange and not a little unsettling that he could not hear the bustle and vigour of a city the size of Tor Yvresse beyond its walls.

As they drew to within a hundred yards of the walls, the gate swung smoothly open and a disciplined regiment of spearmen emerged, marching in perfect step to take position in the middle of the road. Their spear tips shivered as they halted before the gate and a line of archers appeared at the embrasures of the white wall above them.

An officer at the centre of the spearmen stepped from the front rank and raised an open palm before him.

'In the name of Eltharion, I bid you halt, and demand your business within the city of Tor Yvresse.'

Caelir was about to reply when Anurion rode forward on his pegasus, his face thunderous and crackling, flickering arcs of power rippling along his robes.

'I am Anurion the Green, Archmage of Saphery, and I need not explain myself to the likes of a common gatekeeper. I demand entry to this city.'

The officer blanched at Anurion's obvious power, but to his credit, he did not back down. Instead he simply took another step forward and said, 'I mean no disrespect, my lord, but Lord Eltharion requires us to demand the business of everyone desiring entry to our fair city.'

'My business is my own,' said Anurion, but his tone softened as he continued. 'I do however wish to speak to Lord Eltharion, so convey my request for an audience to him forthwith.'

Caelir hid a smile as the captain of the gate attempted to reassert some of his authority by straightening his uniform and saying, 'I shall convey your requests to the Warden, but must ask as to the identities of your companions. All must be made known to the city guard before being admitted to Tor Yvresse.'

'Very well,' said Anurion, turning and gesturing vaguely towards Kyrielle and Caelir. 'This is Kyrielle Greenkin, my daughter, and this is her companion, Caelir of Ellyrion. The rest of our company are my household guards. Do you require me to identify them all?'

The officer shook his head and said, 'No, my lord, that shall not be necessary.'

Anurion squared his shoulders and urged his mount onwards as the officer rejoined his men and turned them about smartly. The line of archers above vanished from sight and the spearmen marched back within the city walls.

Caelir and Kyrielle followed Anurion, their armoured guards riding alongside them.

Caelir nodded respectfully to the captain of the gate as he passed him, hoping to restore a measure of the dignity Anurion's tirade had stripped from him. The officer returned the gesture gratefully and Caelir turned from him to savour his first sight of the fabled palaces and mansions of Tor Yvresse.

The light grew as they neared the end of the tunnel through the thick walls and Caelir felt himself holding his breath as he caught sight of domed roofs, silver arches and wide, tree-lined boulevards.

At last he emerged into the thoroughfares of Tor Yvresse and any disappointment he had felt when drawing close to the city was washed away in a rush of sensation as he saw its towering majesty up close. Elegant mansions, worked with great skill from the rock of Yvresse rose up in sweeping curves, the eye drawn around the graceful colonnades and gilded beauty of the multitude of marble statues that graced each roofline.

Beautiful elves in finery that would not have looked out of place in the palaces of Lothern walked the streets, glancing up with wary interest as they emerged into the wide esplanade before the gateway. Tall and clean limbed, these elves were ruggedly handsome, the equal of their land, and – he noticed – each was armed, either with sword or bow.

For all the finery and fearsome aspect of the inhabitants of Tor Yvresse, Caelir could not help but notice that the streets were nowhere near as busy as he would have expected them to be. Their route carried them along a wide, tree-lined boulevard, the marble-fronted mansions ghostly in their emptiness and the towers that rose above him on the hills seeming to stare down at him with bleak, forlorn gazes.

'This place is empty...' he said, feeling that to raise his voice above a whisper would somehow be wrong.

'Many died fighting the Goblin King,' said Anurion, 'and Tor Yvresse wears its grief like a cloak. These deaths hang heavily and the sombre mood of Eltharion carries over into his people. The celebrations and cheers that greeted his victory are stilled and now the city knows neither joy or life.'

Now that Anurion had spoken of it, Caelir could feel the ghosts of the war against the Goblin King in his bones. The distant clash of elf-forged steel against crude blades hammered out in the depths of forgotten caves, and the anguished cries of those who saw their ancestral homes burned down around them whispered at the edge of hearing.

The sorrow he had felt in Athel Tamarha was a keen blade that pierced his heart, but this... this was a deeper ache, a constant hurt for the inhabitants of Tor Yvresse, for they had endured only to see the glory of their city fade.

Throughout the city, they saw daily life continue, but the more Caelir saw of it, the more it seemed that people were simply going through the motions. It was as though a part of them had died along with those who fell in battle and were just taking their time in lying down.

The physical splendour of the city was undimmed and much had been rebuilt, but where hands and magic had once raised architecture of sublime magnificence with joy, these new edifices were hollow replacements, more akin to monuments to the dead than celebrations of life.

Caelir found the city unbearably sad, like a weight on his soul, and he initiated no conversations with Kyrielle, nor did he answer queries put to him beyond monosyllabic answers.

Eventually Anurion called a halt to their journey through the empty city and Caelir looked up to see a great tower, mightier and higher than any other around it. The mountains reared up behind the tower, but a trick of perspective seemed to extend it far beyond the magic-wreathed peaks and Caelir found himself dizzy with vertigo as his eyes travelled its full height.

A web of light seemed to pulse within the pale blue marble of the tower, its length pierced by not so much as a single window except at its summit, where a series of grim garrets and a lonely balcony stared over the city.

At the base of the tower, a single door, plain and unadorned, led within and Caelir found himself strangely reluctant to venture within this haunted, forsaken tower. This was a tower where the blackest magic had been unleashed and a duel that had sealed the fate of its inhabitant had been fought.

As their mounts halted before the tower, the door opened and a slender warrior shrouded in a plain tunic of black and armoured in gleaming plate stepped from the interior. His hair was pale to the point of being silver and his cheeks were sunken, but it was his eyes that chilled Caelir to the very depths of his soul.

Cold, dead eyes that held a wealth of bitterness that shocked Caelir with its intensity.

The elf crossed his arms and said, 'What business brings you to Tor Yvresse?'

The edge to his voice was like the last whisper of life in the mouth of a corpse and Caelir could see that Anurion and Kyrielle were as shocked as he at the warrior's terrible appearance.

Anurion collected himself and said, 'I am Anurion the–'

'I know who you are,' said the warrior. 'That is not what I asked.'

Caelir awaited the explosion of temper from the archmage, but it never came.

'Of course,' said Anurion, 'my apologies. We seek an audience with the Warden of Tor Yvresse to request passage across the mountains to reach the Tower of Hoeth.'

'I am the Warden of Tor Yvresse,' said the warrior. 'I am Eltharion.'

The interior of the Aquila Spire was pleasantly cool, a fresh westerly breeze blowing in through the narrow window that looked out over the descending slopes of the pass that led to the plains of Ellyrion. The scent of ripened corn was on the wind and Cerion thought wistfully of the times he had ridden those plains with the Ellyrian Reavers many years ago as he tried to lift himself from his gloomy thoughts.

Glorien's reports were spread out on his desk, and Cerion had despaired as he read his subordinate's take on the information he had already heard, first-hand, from the taciturn Shadow Warriors as they had returned from patrolling the mountains.

Their leader, Alanrias, had spoken of an ill-omened aspect to the mountains, a warning which Cerion took seriously, for the Shadow Warriors of Nagarythe had a bleak kinship with the darkness that lurked in the hearts of the asur. When they spoke of such things it was with a degree of authority that could not be ignored.

No mention of this was made in Glorien's report, only the fact that the scout patrols had found no living thing in the mountains... expressed with a patronising air of superiority in the dismissal of their claims of impending threat.

He rested his elbows on the desk and rubbed the heels of his palms against his temple, hoping against hope that he could somehow circumvent Glorien's family influence to have a more suitable warrior appointed to be his second in command. The thought of retiring and leaving the Eagle Gate in Glorien's hands sent a chill down his spine.

Cerion put aside the reports, rising from behind his desk and making his way to the opposite side of the room and a fine, ellemyn-wood drinks cabinet. He opened the exquisitely crafted lattice doors and lifted out a crystal decanter of silvery Sapherian wine made from grapes grown on a strain of vine created by Anurion the Green.

Though it was still early, Cerion decided he needed the drink anyway and poured himself a stiff measure of the potent wine into a polished copper goblet. The breeze blowing in from the east was pleasant on his neck and he raised the glass to his face, enjoying the astringent scent of the wine.

As he raised the goblet to his face, the breeze behind him suddenly died and a shadow passed across the reflective surface of the wine. Cerion spun and hurled the goblet towards the narrow window, where a lithe shadow crouched on the sill.

His throw was wild and the goblet smashed into the stone of the wall, but it was enough of a distraction. The dark figure rolled into the room from the window, a dark blade flashing into its hand. Cerion's sword leapt from its sheath and he stabbed the point towards the rolling shape.

Faster than he would have believed possible, the dark warrior scissored to his feet, arching his back to avoid his thrust, and landed nimbly on his feet before him. A blade slashed towards Cerion's neck and he threw himself backwards, only just avoiding losing his head. His sword came up to block another blow, but before he could do more than bring the blade back down, his attacker had another weapon in his hand.

'Intruder!' he bellowed at the top of his voice, hoping that someone would be near the bottom of the steps to hear his cries. 'Intruder! Guards!'

'Guards won't save you, old man,' said the black-clad assassin, and Cerion was not surprised to hear the dark, sibilant tones of the druchii issue from his attacker's mouth.

'Maybe not,' he said, backing towards the door, 'but they'll see you dead with me.'

The assassin did not reply, but leapt forwards once more, the twin blades spinning in his hands as though he were a blade acrobat. Cerion blocked the first blow, but could not stop the second, and the assassin plunged the blade deep into his side, dark enchantments laid upon its edge parting the links of ithilmar as easily as an arrow parts the air.

Cerion screamed in agony as the sword tore through his lungs and heart, blood pumping enthusiastically from the gaping wound as the assassin tore the blade free. He staggered backwards, the door to the Aquila Spire slamming open as he fell against it.

The assassin bounded forward and held him upright, stabbing him again and again. The blades tore into him with agonising fire, pain filled his senses, and he stared into the cruel eyes of his killer, horrified at the hate and the pleasure the druchii was taking from inflicting such pain. He wanted to fall, the strength pouring from his limbs as surely as the blood was gushing from his ruined body. His eyes dimmed, but he could feel hands keeping him from falling.

He felt fresh air on his skin and the sensation of brightness. His feet were unsteady and gore made the stairs slippery as he was dragged into the light.

With the last of his strength Cerion opened his eyes to see the wall of the Eagle Gate spread out before him, his warriors staring in open-mouthed horror at the sight above them. An archer took aim and swordsmen sprinted along the wall towards the stairs.

'Know this, old man,' said the assassin, leaning in to whisper in his ear. 'Soon all this will be in ruins and your land will burn.'

Cerion tried to spit a last defiant oath, but his words were no more than hoarse whispers. He felt the assassin's grip shift.

Something clattered against the stonework of the tower and he saw the splintered fragments of a white shafted arrow twirl away from him.

Then the world spun about him as he was hurled from the top of the steps.

At first, Alathenar had not known what to think when he heard the cry echoing from the mountains and had looked up from his freshly stringed bow in confusion. Smoothly rising to his feet, he saw that others were similarly alarmed by the sudden cry of pain. Without thinking, he nocked an arrow to his bow and leaned through the embrasure on the wall seeking a target.

Then the cry had come again and he spun towards the Aquila Spire as his keen hearing pinpointed its source. The door to the tower slammed open and he lowered his bow as he saw Lord Goldwing framed in the gloom of the tower.

Then he saw the blood streaming from his body and the shadowy form behind him.

'Assassins!' he cried and sighted along the length of his arrow.

His arrow all but leapt from his bow as he loosed, but his target was already in motion and he cried out as the commander of the Eagle Gate was hurled down the stairs cut in the rock. The bloody body tumbled downwards, end over end, and Alathenar heard the sickening sound of bones breaking.

Lord Goldwing's attacker vanished into the Aquila Spire and Alathenar swept up his quiver before taking to his heels after him. Anger and grief lent his stride speed and he sprinted past armoured swordsmen who hurried towards the tower. They halted at the bottom of the stairs, kneeling in horror beside the broken body of their beloved commander, but Alathenar already knew there was nothing to be done for him. He vaulted the warriors at the foot of the stairs, bounding upwards towards the Aquila Spire.

He reached the top of the stairs, the upper landing slick with blood, and he dived through the door, rolling as he landed and rising with an arrow pulled taut to his cheek.

The chamber was empty, though the stink of viscera and violence was fresh in his nostrils. Quickly, Alathenar scanned the room and found it empty. He slung his bow over his back and drew his sword as he saw a dented goblet in a pool of bitter wine below the chamber's only window. Carefully he edged towards the opening, his blade extended before him.

Behind him he could hear shouting voices and he knew that the assassin was long gone from this place of murder. Swiftly he swung himself through the window and caught his breath as he found himself on a narrow stone sill, hundreds of feet above jagged rocks that would kill him as surely as the assassin's blade.

He looked above him as he heard warriors pushing into the chamber behind him, spying a scuff mark on the eaves of the tower's roof. So the assassin had come over the mountains and lowered himself inside.

'He's gone over the mountains!' he shouted into the tower, before sheathing his sword and taking a deep breath. Alathenar bunched his legs beneath him and leapt straight up, grabbing hold of the edge of the roof. He swung himself up and over in one swift motion, clambering up the ridged parapet of the conical roof.

He leaned his back against the tower's finial and lifted his bow over his head. Hooking the quiver to his belt, Alathenar spared a glance back down to the wall of the fortress, seeing shouting warriors who pointed over at the cliffs of the pass. He followed their extended arms in time to see the shadowy form of the assassin as he bounded from the rocks and made his escape.

Arrows flashed through the air, but the assassin possessed some dark sense for them and either ducked back into cover or effortlessly dodged them.

Alathenar selected the finest, truest shaft from his quiver and kissed the arrowhead before nocking it to his bow and taking careful aim.

His target was at the extreme edge of his range, but he had his new bowstring and he silently offered a prayer to the Everqueen that her handmaids did indeed possess some magic. The assassin wove a ragged pattern through the rocks and Alathenar cursed as he quickly realised that there was no way he could predict his movements to aim ahead of him.

Suddenly he smiled as he saw a narrow cleft in the rock ahead of the fleeing figure and saw that his weaving course was leading him unerringly towards it. He took a breath and held it as he gauged the range to the cleft and how quickly the weaving assassin would take to reach it.

'Kurnous guide my aim,' he said.

Alathenar let out his breath, and at the end of his exhalation loosed the arrow from his bow. He watched as the blue-fletched shaft arced into the morning sunlight, reaching the zenith of its flight before dropping in an almost leisurely arc.

'Yes!' he said as his arrow slashed down and punched through the assassin's shoulder. The dark shape stumbled and fell, but even as Alathenar watched, he picked himself up and made off once more.

Alathenar pulled another arrow from the quiver, already knowing that he could not hope to hit the assassin before he was out of sight. Sure enough, the figure disappeared from view before he could loose.

He lowered his bow and wept angry tears as he looked down to see the warriors of the Eagle Gate cover the face of Cerion Goldwing with a white cloak that slowly turned to red.

Alathenar the Archer let out a terrible cry of loss and anger.

And high above the mountains, it was heard.

From the top of the Warden's Tower it was possible to survey the entire city of Tor Yvresse and Caelir soon appreciated the scale of the destruction wrought by the invasion of the Goblin King. Despite the work of the city's inhabitants, their domain still bore the scars of war, ruined mansions, fire blackened stretches of wall and abandoned parks where nature had been left to run riot.

He watched the inhabitants of the city going about their business, guessing that the city had originally been built to house at least twice the number of folk it currently sheltered. He and Kyrielle stood on the tallest balcony that overlooked the city, higher even than the tower palaces built upon the city's nine hills. Wind whipped the sea beyond the harbour into tall, foam-topped waves of blue and snapped the mournful banners upon their flagpoles, but not a breath of it touched them in the tower.

Upon meeting Eltharion, the Warden of Tor Yvresse had bid them dismount and leave their guards before following him within his tower. Its interior was as bleak as the exterior was imposing, bare walls and simple furnishings speaking of an occupant who cared nothing for beauty or ornamentation and whose ascetic tastes would make those of a Sword Master's seem vulgar.

Eltharion had said nothing more beyond his introduction and beckoned them to follow him upstairs to his chambers. Caelir inwardly groaned at the sight of so many stairs, having seen how tall the tower was from the outside, but barely had his feet set foot on the first than it seemed he was stepping onto a landing at the very top.

Looking back down the centre of the tower, he saw the ground hundreds of feet below.

Upon reaching the top of the tower, Eltharion and Anurion had retired to speak in private while he and Kyrielle had been left to their own devices in the tower's receiving chamber. Some effort had been made to make the interior of the tower less foreboding, but it was a token effort and only made the rest of their surroundings more depressing.

Food and wine had been set out for them, and so they had sated their thirst and hunger before moving out to the balcony to admire the view and await the Warden's decision.

'This isn't what I expected at all,' said Caelir.

'Tor Yvresse?'

'Yes. I remember the tales told of the city and the return of Eltharion, but I expected a city of great heroes. I did not think to find it so... deathly.'

'As my father said, a great many elves died in the war, but our children are few and it is a sad fact that fewer and fewer of us are being born every year.'

'Why would that be?'

Kyrielle shrugged. 'I do not know. Some say that our time on this world is now a guttering flame and that soon it will be over. All things have their time in the sun. Perhaps the world is now done with our kind.'

'What? Surely you don't believe that?'

'How else would you explain our fading?'

'Perhaps the power of the elves *does* wane, but our time will come again, I know it.'

'Are you so sure? How many empires of men have risen and fallen in the turning of the world?'

'Men are fireflies, their lives flicker and burn for but a moment,' said Caelir. 'They live their lives as though in a race, never building anything of permanence. How can you compare the asur with such barbarians?'

'We are not so dissimilar, my dear Caelir. Perhaps we are on the same path, but are simply taking longer to walk it.'

Caelir turned to Kyrielle and placed his hand on her shoulder. 'This doesn't sound like you, what is the matter?'

Kyrielle said, 'Nothing is wrong with me, silly boy. I think it is just being in Tor Yvresse. There are evil ghosts of memory here and they stir the darkest thoughts in me. I will be fine.'

'I have felt them too, Kyrielle, but we cannot let the evil of the past blight our lives in the here and now. The Goblin King was defeated and Tor Yvresse saved, surely that is cause for celebration?'

'Of course it is, but with every invasion, every battle, we are lessened. Every year the druchii grow bolder and so long as the Isle of the Dead draws the magical energy of the world to Ulthuan, creatures of Chaos will forever be drawn to our fair isle. We are clinging to life by our fingernails, Caelir.'

'Maybe so,' said Caelir, 'but is that reason to give up and let go? Maybe we are a fading race, I don't know, but if that is true I will still fight to the end to hold on to what we have. I do not know what will happen in the future, but I will not meekly accept despair into my heart. So long as I draw breath I will fight to protect my home and my people.'

Kyrielle smiled at him and he felt his spirits rise until he caught sight of the pledge ring on the hand resting on her shoulder. A fleeting image of a beautiful elf maid flashed behind his eyes, her eyes sad and her hair a flowing river of gold.

'What's wrong?' said Kyrielle, seeing the shadow pass over his features.

'Nothing,' said Caelir, taking his hand from her shoulder and turning away.

He was saved from further questions when he heard footsteps approaching from the tower. Anurion the Green stood before them, his features giving nothing away as to the outcome of his discussions with Eltharion.

'Well?' said Kyrielle. 'Does he grant us leave to travel over the mountains?'

'Not yet. He wishes to speak to Caelir first.'

'Me? What for?' said Caelir, suddenly nervous about meeting such a dark yet heroic figure as Eltharion the Grim.

Anurion said, 'Because I believe he thinks you a mystery and Eltharion is not one who enjoys mysteries as much as I. He has been told all that I know of you and he wishes to speak to you himself. When he asks questions, be truthful in all things. Do you understand me, boy?'

'I understand you, yes,' said Caelir. 'I am not a fool, but I still do not see why he wishes to speak with me.'

'Listen to me, Caelir, and listen well. Eltharion is the Warden of Tor Yvresse and none pass over the mountains to the Inner Kingdoms without his leave. If he wishes to speak to you then you do not refuse him.'

Caelir nodded and made his way across the receiving chamber towards the leaf-shaped archway that led to Eltharion's private chambers. The doors were shut and he knocked softly, unwilling to simply barge in.

'Enter,' said a cold voice and an icy dread settled on him as he obeyed.

Pazhek let loose a string of the foulest curses he knew as he stumbled on yet another rock and fell to his knees. Where before the mountains had risen to meet his tread and hasten him on his way, now every rock was loose beneath him and every patch of scrub tangled his foot at every turn.

His shoulder ached abominably, the arrowhead still lodged painfully beneath his shoulder blade. He still couldn't believe that he had been hit, for he had employed all the techniques of evasion taught to the Adepts of Khaine and had been beyond the furthest extent of bowshot...

Or so he had believed.

He had bound the wound as best he was able and taken an infusion of weirdroot to dull the pain before retracing his steps through the mountains. The Shadow Warriors would even now be on his trail and he was under no illusions as to the likelihood of his escape now that he was leaving a trail of his own blood behind him. But he would lead them a merry dance through the mountains and when they came for him he would kill and maim as many as he could before they brought him down.

He had applied a coating of poison to his blades, a mixture of manbane and black lotus, a concoction that would drive its victims mad with pain and delusions of their worst nightmares.

Let them come, he thought, I will give them cause to remember the name of Pazhek.

He smiled as he thought of the death of Cerion Goldwing. Though it was not an elegant death it had been a very visible and bloody one that the garrison of the Eagle Gate would not soon forget.

A shadow flashed over the ground and he spun, swords raised before him.

He saw nothing, no sign of pursuit, but knew that such things were meaningless, for his enemies would not come upon him directly, but with guile and cunning. He turned and carried onwards, his breath heaving in his lungs, all stealth forsaken in favour of speed.

If he could somehow reach the coast and find a place of concealment then he could await the time when his people would come for him.

Another shadow crossed the ground and he stopped, breathless and desperate as he backed against the cliff. Once again he saw nothing and as a screeching cry echoed from the mountainsides, he suddenly realised his error.

Pazhek looked up in time to see a great, golden shape plunge from the skies.

Its wings extended with a boom of deceleration and hooked talons slashed towards him.

He cried out and tried to raise his blades, but the mighty eagle was faster, its extended talons snapping closed over his arms and lifting him into the air. Pazhek screamed as the ground fell away, dropping his swords as the eagle crushed the bones in his wrists.

'Assassin,' said the giant bird of prey as each beat of its wings carried them higher and higher. 'I am Elasir, Lord of the Eagles, and you have spilled the blood of a friend to my kind.'

Pazhek could not answer, the agony of the bird's razor talons grinding his bones and slicing his flesh too great to bear. He twisted in its grip, the ground spinning thousands of feet below him as he fought in vain against the strength of his captor.

'And for that you must pay,' said the eagle, releasing its grip.

* * *

Caelir pushed open the door and stepped into a vaulted chamber of cold light and distant echoes. Where the rest of the tower was bleak and displayed none of the character of he who dwelled here, this room gave dark insight into the mind of Eltharion.

Racks of weapons and framed maps of Ulthuan, Naggaroth and all the known world lined the walls. Alongside them were grim trophies set on wooden plaques and mounted around the circumference of the room, the heads of vicious monsters, orcs and men.

The golden sunlight of Ulthuan streamed in through a great aperture formed in the roof, below which an elaborate saddle-like arrangement of leather straps and buckles was hung upon a wooden frame. The illumination did not warm the chamber or reach the farthest corners, as though its occupant did not desire to feel the light on his skin.

Eltharion paced beneath the opening in the roof, the sunlight only serving to highlight the pallid cast of his flesh and the shadows beneath his cheekbones. His expression was grim, as Caelir had expected, and he turned to face him with barely a glimmer of interest in his icy, sapphire eyes.

'So you are the one washed upon the shores of my land?' said Eltharion.

'I am,' said Caelir, bowing respectfully. 'It is an honour to meet you, my lord.'

Eltharion ignored the compliment and said, 'Anurion tells me your memories have been magically locked within you. Why would someone do such a thing?'

'I have no idea, my lord. I wish I did.'

'I do not believe you,' said Eltharion and Caelir was surprised at his directness.

'It is the truth, my lord. Why would I lie about it?'

'I do not know, and that is enough to give me pause,' said Eltharion, walking towards him with his hooded eyes fixed upon him. Caelir had to fight the urge to back away from the Warden of Tor Yvresse, such was the weight of his intimidation.

'I do not like the unknown, Caelir,' said Eltharion. 'The unknown is dangerous and cloaks itself in mystery to better advance its cause. I sense a dark purpose to you, but cannot fathom what danger a callow youth such as yourself might present.'

'Callow? I am a warrior and have killed our enemies before now.'

'How do you know? You have no memory.'

'I... just know that I am no enemy of Ulthuan,' said Caelir.

'I wish I could be sure of that, but I do not trust you.'

'Then do you trust an archmage of Saphery?'

Eltharion laughed, but there was no humour to it, simply a bark of amusement that came from the exposure of another's ignorance. 'One might as well trust the sea or the faith of a woman.'

'But Anurion the Green vouches for me.'

'That he does, though even he does not fully trust you.'

'Why do you believe I am a threat?'

'It does not matter why I believe it, simply that I do. Someone went to a great deal of trouble to take away your memories and I cannot believe they did so for the benefit of Ulthuan.'

'Perhaps it was because I knew something of benefit to Ulthuan that my memories were stolen,' said Caelir.

'Then why not just kill you?'

'I do not know,' said Caelir, growing weary of having no answers to explain himself with. 'All I know is that I am a true son of Ellyrion and would rather die than harm so much as a single hair on the head of any of my kin!'

Eltharion stepped forward and placed his hands either side of Caelir's head, looking directly into his eyes with a gaze that frightened him with its intensity.

'I believe that you think you are telling the truth,' said Eltharion. 'Only time will tell if that is enough.'

'I *am* telling the truth.'

Eltharion released his grip and turned away as a mighty screech came from beyond the tower and a powerful beat of wings sent a rushing downdraught of air gusting through the chamber. Parchments fluttered like autumnal leaves scattered by the wind.

A shadow suddenly blocked the light from the aperture in the roof. Caelir looked up in amazement to see a mighty, winged creature drop through and land gracefully within the confines of the tower. Its head and forequarters were like those of a powerful eagle, its hooked beak and clawed forelegs terrifyingly muscled. Behind its feathered wings, the creature's body was furred and massively powerful, its hindquarters those of a mighty lion. Its pelt was the colour of copper, with dark stripes and spots dotting its fur like the great cats said to stalk the jungles of Lustria and the Southlands.

Caelir stared awestruck as the mighty griffon paced the breadth of the tower, its head cocked to one side as it glared angrily at him.

'Stormwing,' said Eltharion by way of introduction.

Caelir bowed to the powerful beast, the intelligence glittering in its eyes plain to see. 'It is an honour.'

Eltharion turned to lift the saddle-like arrangement from the wooden frame and Caelir now realised that it was exactly that – a saddle. The Warden of Tor Yvresse threw the saddle over the griffon's back and said, 'You are heading to the White Tower?'

'We are,' said Caelir, still awed at the magnificent creature before him.

'Then I will allow you to travel to Saphery, for I desire you out of my city. But you will not travel alone.'

'No?'

'I will send you on your way with a company of my finest rangers,' said

Eltharion. 'They will take you through the secret ways of the mountains and escort you to the White Tower.'

Caelir smiled and said, 'You have my thanks, my lord.'

As Eltharion finished buckling the complex saddle to Stormwing he said, 'I do not do this as a favour to you, I do it to ensure you go where you say you are going.'

'I still thank you for it.'

'Your thanks are irrelevant to me,' said Eltharion. 'Be at the west gate at sunset and do not return, Caelir of Ellyrion. You are not welcome in Tor Yvresse.'

CHAPTER EIGHT
SAPHERY

As the sun began to set, the mountains cast long shadows over Tor Yvresse and the city felt even more empty than it had during the day. When Caelir, Anurion and Kyrielle emerged from the tower of Eltharion, a sombre darkness, more palpable than the gloom that engulfed the city during the day, hung over its populace.

Caelir looked up as the plaintive cry of Eltharion's griffon echoed from the heights of the tower and he saw the master of the city circling high above.

'He trusts no one, does he?' said Caelir as they mounted their horses and set off towards the western gate.

'Few have given him cause to, Caelir,' said Anurion. 'When Tor Yvresse was under attack, the other cities were too wrapped up in their own affairs to send aid. By the time most realised the seriousness of what the goblin shaman was attempting it was too late. Either Eltharion would stop them or Ulthuan would fall.'

'He has allowed us to pass through the mountains,' said Kyrielle, urging her mount to catch up to Caelir. 'That must count for something…'

Behind her, the guards that had accompanied them from her father's palace rode alongside Anurion, their relief at leaving Tor Yvresse clear even in the gloom.

'Only to see us gone from his city,' said Caelir.

'Did Eltharion give you any indication of who would lead us to Saphery?' said Anurion.

'He told me his rangers would show us a secret way through the mountains.'

Anurion nodded and said, 'It is said that there are ways through the Annulii that even the wisest mages do not know, but I had never thought to travel them.'

The sound of their horses' hooves echoed in the empty streets of Tor Yvresse and it took them no time at all to reach the western wall of the city. It towered above them, its defences no less impressive on the side facing the Inner Kingdoms of Ulthuan than those facing the hostile world.

Mighty towers and colossal bastions spread out to either side of them, but Caelir could see that such defences would be of little consequence if a great horde came at them, for there was a paltry strength of warriors manning the wall.

Only now did the precarious nature of Tor Yvresse truly become apparent as he saw how few souls remained alive to defend their city. The Shifting Isles protected the eastern approaches to Ulthuan and it was clear that Eltharion relied on them to keep his city safe, for there were precious few warriors to do so.

Finally understanding a measure of the warden's hostility, Caelir looked up once more at the circling form of Eltharion and said, 'I wish you well, my lord. Isha watch over you.'

Even as the words left his mouth, a number of ghostly shapes detached from the shadows and swiftly surrounded their company. They wore conical, face-concealing helmets of burnished bronze and silver, with dark cloaks that rendered them nearly invisible in the darkening twilight.

One of the warriors swept back his cloak to reveal the natural, rugged attire of a ranger, his physique tough and wolf-lean.

'You are to follow us,' said the shadow-cloaked warrior.

'Who are you?' said Anurion.

'We are servants of the warden,' came the answer. 'That is all you need know.'

Without another word, the warrior turned and set off in the direction of the city gate, which swung open noiselessly as he approached.

Caelir leaned over to whisper in Kyrielle's ear. 'Talkative types, these rangers.'

Their leader turned to face him and said, 'We speak when we have something of worth to say. Others could learn from us.'

Both Caelir and Kyrielle started in surprise, having thought the ranger far beyond the limits of hearing. She smiled nervously and Caelir shrugged as he rode towards the ranger.

Together with their mounted guard, they passed through the gate and followed the road down one of the nine hills of Tor Yvresse in a gentle curve towards the Annulii.

'Is it wise to set off into the mountains in the dark?' said Kyrielle.

The ranger nodded and Caelir could see that he found such discussions tiresome. 'We will be your eyes and there are some paths that can only be taken in darkness.'

Caelir already knew the skill of Eltharion's rangers was second only to that of the Shadow Warriors of Nagarythe, having known they had observed their approach to Tor Yvresse without once revealing themselves. Even so, the idea of leading such a company into the mountains in darkness seemed an excessive display of hubris.

A faint glow permeated the night, the aura of raw magic sweeping through the mountains, and the further they travelled along the road, the stronger the taste of it became.

Their journey took them along twisting paths, which, though they led upwards, seemed to bring the mountains no closer. Though darkness had fallen on the world, a mist of magical energy lingered on the trees and ground like a light dusting of snow, and Caelir could feel the power that resided in every fragment of Ulthuan as though it sprang from the very rocks themselves.

Tor Yvresse receded behind them, the lights of its shuttered mansions and towers a lonely, isolated beacon of light in the darkness behind them.

'How much further must we ride?' said Anurion. 'Lord Eltharion claimed you would show us a way through the mountains.'

'And so we shall,' said the nameless ranger. 'Be patient.'

At last the rangers led them into a narrow defile between two jutting fangs of rock that wound downwards into a dark hollow in which stood a tall, glistening stone at the confluence of three gurgling streams. Spiral patterns and ancient, faded runes had been carved into the rock and Caelir could see the faint image of a carved gateway against a far cliff.

Anurion and Kyrielle gasped as they followed the rangers down into the hollow and even Caelir could sense the reservoir of magic that collected in this place.

'A watchstone...' said Anurion.

Caelir had heard of the watchstones from Kyrielle, powerful menhirs that crossed Ulthuan from shore to shore and directed the energy of the vortex contained within the Annulii ever inward towards the Isle of the Dead on lines of magical energy.

Many of the island's mages built their homes atop these lines and great barrows of the dead were erected on auspicious points where these lines intersected. The souls of the dead were thus eternally bound to Ulthuan that they might guard the land they loved and escape the terrible prospect of being devoured by the gods of Chaos.

In other kingdoms such watchstones were a common sight, crossing the landscape in a web of mystical design, but in Yvresse their location was a closely guarded secret. After the catastrophe of the Goblin King's invasion, geomancers from Saphery had divined where else the toppled stones might still be positioned to perform the task for which they had been raised, and secreted them in the hidden places where none but those who knew the secret paths could discover them.

The rangers led them to the base of the hollow, waiting until everyone had reached the bottom before kneeling at the watchstone and singing a strange, lilting melody. The words were unknown to Caelir, the mystical cadences felt in the soul as much as heard. Each word slipped through the darkness and the landscape around responded, the trees sighing and the rocks stirring themselves from their slumbers to hear such beauty.

Caelir watched the rangers with a mixture of awe and fear as he felt the world around him... *change*, as though the landscape around them shifted beneath their horses' feet in response to the song.

Looking into the night sky, he could see the stars spread out before him, their luminance rippling in the sky through the magical haze washing from the mountains.

He returned his attention to the rangers and their strange, singsong chant as a glittering mist gathered at the lip of the hollow and rolled down the slope towards them.

'Anurion?' he said. 'What's happening?'

'Be silent,' said the archmage. 'Do not disturb them. They are calling on the power of the watchstone and it would be perilous to interrupt.'

The mist now filled the hollow and Caelir felt its cold touch as it rose around them. The horses whinnied in fear as strange shapes appeared in the mist, revenants of long dead elves and fragmentary images of times and places as yet unknown to the living.

The mist gathered about them, coiling around them like a living thing, questing around their bodies and cocooning them in a moist, clammy embrace.

Caelir lost sight of his companions, his sight closed off by the thick mist. Icy fear slid through his veins and he twisted in the saddle as he suddenly felt very alone, the isolation more terrifying than the ominous shapes that drifted just beyond sight.

'Kyrielle? Anurion?'

The faint outline of something dark moved through the mist and Caelir reached for his sword as it approached, determined that no spirit of the mist would take him.

The breath rushed from him as the figure resolved from the mist and he saw that it was one of Eltharion's rangers, his eyes dark and glittering with magic.

The ranger reached up to take the reins of his horse and Caelir silently allowed the warrior to lead his horse, sensing that to speak now would be unutterably dangerous.

As the ranger led his horse towards the cliff, the foggy silence remained unbroken, even the sound of hooves on rock muffled by the smothering blanket of mist. Caelir saw the sheer cliff of white rock ahead of him, but where before it had been naught but the image of a gateway, now it yawned open, black and terrible.

Sinister moans and a breath of hot, vibrant air blew from it, rich with potent energies, and Caelir felt nothing but terror at the idea of venturing through such a dread portal.

'Where does that lead?' he said, every word an effort.

'Into the river of magic,' said the ranger.

Beyond the gateway was darkness, but not darkness empty of wonders, rather one filled with magic and miracles. No sooner had the ranger led Caelir through than his senses were assaulted by a great, terrible weight of things, monstrously powerful things, lurking just at the edge of perception.

He could see nothing, but the power lurking in this place supplied the fuel – and his imagination the tools – to render all manner of terrors and dreamscapes before him. The darkness retreated in the face of such freshly realised potential: vast expanses of dark mountains ruled over by glistening towers of red meat, marching swords and spears atop great riding beasts, powerful armies destroying one another in a verdant field of blue flowers and a thousand other such visions, each more vivid and bizarre than the last.

Of his companions he saw no sign, the steps of his horse mechanical and automatic as it walked through this nightmare realm of infinite potential. Its ears were pressed flat against its skull in fear, but whether it saw the same things as he or fashioned its own skewed reality, he could not say.

His course took him along the edge of a great river, filled not with water, but the roiling bodies of the dead. A million corpses, bloated and stinking, flowed past him, their faces at once familiar and unknown to him. Caelir recoiled as the stench of the dead assailed him, the sight of so many dead sickening and unbearable.

The river vanished as the power of the magic around him dredged the depths of his mind for yet more things to make real. A cold wind that penetrated his flesh and chilled his very bones blew through him and a cavalcade of tortures paraded before him, though these were no bloody dismemberments, but sensual pleasures designed to break the spirit from within: degradations and humiliations heaped upon one another until the soul could take no more.

Caelir closed his eyes and begged the visions conjured into his mind by the power of the magic coursing through the mountains to withdraw, but such magic was raw and elemental, devoid of conscience and mercy and the visions neither relented nor retreated.

How long he remained beneath the mountains, a moment or an eternity, he could not say. In this place of magic, there was no time, no dimensions and no sense of a place in the world. Faces appeared of elves, tall cities of white towers and a hateful dark place of great iron towers that echoed to the dreadful sounds of screams and the hammering of industry.

Fires burned in this city and something in this last vision possessed some kernel of truth the others did not, and Caelir focused his attention on the rampant flames and screeches of some great, unseen monster. He saw specks of white amid the darkness and his heart leapt to see Reavers mounted on bright Ellyrian steeds spreading destruction throughout the dark city, casting down what the evil masters of the city had built.

Was this a memory or a fantasy culled from unremembered boyhood dreams?

He fought to hold onto this last image, his attention fixed on two riders, one atop a gleaming black steed, the other atop a grey. They were achingly familiar, but before he could do more than register their presence, he felt the intensity of the visions fade and he had a powerful sensation of having emerged from the rushing waters of the most powerful river imaginable.

Caelir took a great, gulping breath as strands of raw magic slid from his mind and the darkness of the mountains reasserted itself. Reality settled upon him in the click of trace and harness, the gasps of his companions and the clatter of their horses' hooves on rock.

'No, show me...' he said, twisting in the saddle to look behind him, though on an instinctual level he knew that such a term was meaningless in this conduit of magic beneath the mountains.

'Show you what?' said Anurion, riding behind him and looking exhilarated to have touched such primal energies and lived to tell the tale.

Caelir shook his head, the significance of the vision already fading from his mind as though a smothering blanket had been pulled over it. 'I don't know. I thought I saw something familiar, but it's gone now. I don't remember it.'

He turned away from the archmage and saw that the ranger still led his horse, his guide so oblivious or inured to the nightmares they had just faced that they no longer affected him.

Their company travelled along a narrow passageway cleft in the mountainside, a warm, yellow glow coming from somewhere up ahead that blew away the last of the cobwebs that entangled Caelir's thoughts after the journey through the darkness.

The rock of the narrow passageway glistened with what he at first took to be moisture, but, when he reached out to touch it, turned out to be a dewy residue of magic. Glimmering beads of light clung to his fingers and he smiled as he realised they must be close to Saphery, the horrors unleashed within his mind only moments before now quite forgotten.

Caelir emerged into the bright sunshine, shielding his eyes as the ranger led him out onto a wide shelf of rock that jutted from the cliff of the mountains. The air smelled sweet and columns of green trees grew tall around him, stark against the summer skies above.

Kyrielle sat on her horse at the edge of the plateau, her cheeks flushed with the pleasure of seeing her homeland once more. Her father's mounted guards milled around and their faces were bright and open with anticipation, such was the power of this homecoming.

A boulder-lined path curled down the mountains, leading to a fertile land of golden fields and blue, coiling rivers. Caelir looked over his shoulder and saw the ramparts of the Annulii Mountains towering above him, their shimmering peaks wreathed in a haze of magic.

'We have crossed the mountains already?' he said, amazed that they should have covered such distance in the blink of an eye. Their journey had begun in darkness, but he judged it to be early morning here, though it felt as if only moments had passed since they had left the hollow of the watchstone.

'You have,' said the ranger who had first spoken to them in Tor Yvresse.

'How?' said Caelir. 'A journey like that should have taken us several days at least.'

'Lord Eltharion wished you to reach Saphery sooner,' said the ranger, raising his arm and pointing to Caelir's left. 'And the White Tower awaits.'

Caelir followed the ranger's pointing finger and his eyes widened as he saw the Tower of Hoeth spearing half a mile into the sky, a sharp white needle of stone thrusting upwards and surrounded by light. Though the sun had yet to reach its zenith, the brilliance of the tower outshone its radiance.

'I hope for your sake you truly are a seeker of knowledge,' said the ranger, reaching up to place a hand on Caelir's arm and looking over to the tower. Though his helmet concealed much of the ranger's face, Caelir saw that his expression of concern was sincere.

'What do you mean?'

'The White Tower is unforgiving with those who knowingly approach with deceit in their hearts or who seek power for its own sake.'

'I appreciate the warning, but I spoke the truth to Lord Eltharion.'

The ranger nodded and released his arm. 'I wish you good fortune, Caelir of Ellyrion.'

'Come on!' cried Kyrielle. 'Let's go. It won't take long to get to the tower now.'

'Yes, come on, boy,' said Anurion, the wings of his pegasus spreading wide in anticipation of taking to the air. 'No slacking off now that we're almost there.'

Caelir smiled, amused at the galvanising energy that filled the natives of Saphery now that they had returned to their homeland. Would returning to Ellyrion produce a similar rush of infectious enthusiasm in his own heart?

He hoped so.

Caelir watched Kyrielle gallop down the road and Anurion take to the air, the guards following after the archmage's daughter.

He turned to thank the ranger for bringing them here so swiftly, but his words died when he saw they had vanished and the cleft in the rock from which they had emerged had disappeared.

A cold wind blew from the high peaks and Caelir pulled his cloak tighter as he felt a stirring of ancient magic, more powerful than anything left in the world, sweep over him like the breath of a terrible, slumbering monster kept imprisoned by the forgotten glamours of a distant age.

Caelir turned from the now sinister mountain, very aware that he was alone in this strange land, and set off down the path after Kyrielle and her warrior escort.

The Tower of Hoeth loomed ahead of him, stark and cold, and Caelir wondered what destiny awaited him within its walls.

He did not look back at the mountains as he rode, anxious to be kept safe by the presence of those who called this land home.

Yes, Ulthuan was an enchanted isle, full of wonders and miracles, but every now and then it taught those who dwelt upon it that magic was the most dangerous force in the world.

It was a lesson Caelir vowed not to forget.

Cairn Auriel was the name of the harbour and Eldain could remember no finer sight as the sharp prow of the *Dragonkin* sliced the clear waters of evening towards it. Together with Rhianna, he stood at the sloop's prow as they sailed past the glowing beacon of a silver lighthouse that lit the natural harbour cut into the high cliffs on the western coast of Saphery.

Structures of grace and simplicity surrounded a naturally sheltered bay of pale sand: white towers, golden domes and columned arcades were artfully arranged in an orderly and elegant manner around the fringes of the cliffs. Laughter and music drifted through the darkness and Eldain felt his heart sing in response to the sounds of life and joy. He put his arm around Rhianna and drew her close.

'I had forgotten how much I had missed Saphery,' he said. 'It has been too long since I have travelled here.'

'We were always welcome at my father's villa,' Rhianna said.

'I know, but after the expedition to Naggaroth…'

Rhianna returned his embrace and he felt as though the great weight of guilt upon his shoulders might someday be lifted by the healing magic of Ulthuan and the love of this wonderful companion beside him.

'It will be good to set foot on dry land,' said Rhianna. 'Though I feel the magic throughout Ulthuan, I feel it most strongly in Saphery.'

Eldain smiled at the sound of her enthusiasm and turned his head to call out to Captain Bellaeir. 'My thanks, captain. You have sailed us true.'

Seated at the vessel's tiller beneath a glowing lantern, Bellaeir waved and returned to his steering of the ship.

As they drew closer, Eldain marvelled at the construction of the harbour buildings, their slender marble quays projecting into the bay and floating just above the smooth surface of the water. Now that he knew to look for it, he saw the ripple of magic around the settlement, clinging to tall watchtowers, shimmering over the placid waters and carrying the sound of its inhabitants to them.

The crew of the sloop moved to attend to the task of bringing their ship into the harbour, but their efforts were unnecessary, for magical currents drew the ship in safely and brought it to a smooth halt against one of the quays.

Laughing, the crew disembarked and tied their ship to silver bollards, though Eldain suspected that the ship would remain exactly where it was without such restraints. He turned to retrieve his belongings, watching as Yvraine rose from her position in the centre of the sloop and bowed to the captain before smoothly vaulting onto the quay, her sword impeding her not at all.

Eldain marvelled at her liquid movement, knowing that, save on the back of the horse, he could never match her preternatural grace. Ever since they had sailed past the Isle of the Dead, the Sword Master had kept her own counsel, her silences broken only by the occasional affirmation of her wellbeing.

Now that she set foot on Saphery once more, Eldain could see a lightness to her spirit he had not known she possessed in all the days he had known her.

'Someone is glad to be back,' he said to Rhianna as she joined him.

She looked up with an indulgent smile and said, 'I can understand how she feels. Imagine how *you* will feel when you return to Ellyrion.'

'True. Even though Saphery is not Ellyrion, it will be good to ride Lotharin once again. The smooth waters of the inner ocean do not compare to riding a fine Ellyrian steed.'

As he gathered up the last of his possessions, the crew lowered a ramp from the side of the *Dragonkin* to the quayside and Eldain all but bounded over to the hold where their horses had spent the bulk of the sea journey.

Lotharin cantered from the hold first, his black coat shimmering in the glow of the lighthouse, closely followed by Rhianna's horse, Orsien – a fine, silver gelding from Saphery with dappled flanks and a haughty intelligence in his pale green eyes. Behind these two magnificent steeds came Irenya, a dun mare that had belonged to one of Ellyr-charoi's retainers, but who had been left riderless when her rider had perished on the same expedition that had seen Caelir lost. Yvraine had ridden Irenya from Eldain's villa and though the Sword Master had not enjoyed the ride to Tor Elyr, the horse had rejoiced in the chance to bear a rider once more.

Eldain let his horse nuzzle him and ran his hands down its neck, whispering in its ears and speaking in a manner unknown beyond the plains of Ellyrion. The horse whinnied excitedly and Eldain laughed at its pleasure in being able to bear him onwards.

He led Lotharin and Irenya from the *Dragonkin*, glad to feel solid ground beneath him, even if it was supported by magic. Rhianna led Orsien and when their mounts and belongings were disembarked, Eldain saw Bellaeir approach from the vessel's stern.

'Lord Eldain, do you wish me to await your return?' said the captain.

'Yes,' said Eldain, 'though I cannot say how long we will remain in Saphery.'

Bellaeir shrugged. 'We can rest here in Cairn Auriel for a spell, my lord. We are not required at the muster of Lothern, for a ship the size of the *Dragonkin* would be of little use in a battle.'

'I will send word when our situation becomes clearer, captain,' said Eldain. 'In the meantime, payment will be lodged at the counting house and you may take what you are owed until we return.'

'That will be most satisfactory, my lord,' said Bellaeir with a smile. 'If you are looking for accommodation for the night, you could do worse than the Light of Korhadris. The food is plentiful and the wines are of the finest vintage known to elfkind.'

Eldain waved his thanks to the captain and turned away, following his horse as it led the way to the harbour town of Cairn Auriel. He caught up with Rhianna and Yvraine as they awaited him at the end of the quay.

With the glow of the lighthouse now behind him, he saw a distant spike of white light on the horizon.

'I thought the Tower of Hoeth was supposed to be hard to find,' said Eldain.

'You have no idea,' said Yvraine.

Captain Bellaeir's recommendation that they stay at the Light of Korhadris proved to be an inspired choice, for their welcome was hearty and the menu extensive. Set amid white cliffs, Cairn Auriel spread outwards in radiating streets from the horseshoe shaped bay, fanning upwards on the slopes of the coastline towards the land of Saphery itself.

The proprietor of the establishment was a jovial elf of advancing years who bid them welcome and immediately set about seeing to their comfort with utmost vigour. The interior of his hostelry was elegant and, though somewhat ostentatious for Eldain's tastes, apparently typical of Sapherian vernacular.

Few other patrons were present and the three of them made no effort to socialise with the well-dressed travellers they saw at other tables. Softly glowing orbs of magical energy hung in the air, casting a warm, homely light throughout the public areas and Eldain felt his skin tingle with the presence of so much magic in the air.

'Is it not a little frivolous to employ magic for such mundane things as lighting?' he asked.

Rhianna laughed. 'You are in Saphery now, Eldain. Magic is all around you.'

'I suppose,' he said. 'I had forgotten how different your land is from mine.'

'Well we're here now and it's good to be back. Don't you agree, Yvraine?'

The Sword Master sat a little way from them, close enough to be included in their company, yet far enough away to appear distant. Eldain noted Yvraine had the same revitalised look he could see in Rhianna's eyes and was not surprised to hear an edge of anticipation in her voice when she spoke.

'Yes, it is good to be home. Though I will be happier when we reach the White Tower.'

'How far is it from here?' asked Eldain.

'That depends,' said Yvraine.

'Depends? On what?'

'On whether the tower deems us worthy of approaching it.'

'I thought we were invited? By Rhianna's father.'

'We have been,' nodded Yvraine, 'but the magical wards that protect the tower will not relax its guard for something as prosaic as an invitation. Only the true seeker of knowledge can approach the tower safely.'

'These wards,' said Eldain. 'What are they?'

'Spells woven in the time of Bel-Korhadris, the builder of the tower. A maze of illusions and magical snares that entrap those who come seeking power or whose hearts are poisoned by evil.'

Eldain shifted uncomfortably in his chair and said, 'And what happens to such people?'

Yvraine shrugged. 'Some find that no matter which direction they walk, their footsteps will always carry them away from the tower.'

'And others?'

'Others are never seen again.'

'They die?'

'I do not think that even the Loremasters know for certain, but it seems likely.'

Eldain felt a tightness in his chest as he thought of Caelir, and wondered if the White Tower would find that black spot in his heart and if it would judge him harshly when the time came.

Surely the acquisition of love, no matter how it was attained, could not be held as evil? He looked over at Rhianna and smiled, enjoying the play of shadows cast by the magical lights on her beautiful features.

Sensing his scrutiny, she turned to face him and returned his smile.

He reached out and took her hand as the proprietor returned with platters of silver-skinned fish, steaming vegetables and a decanter of a robust, aromatic wine.

They smiled their thanks and ate the remainder of their meal in silence, enjoying the homely atmosphere and the sensation common to all travellers enjoying one another's company in unfamiliar, exciting locales.

At the conclusion of the meal, Yvraine excused herself and retired to meditate and complete her daily regime of martial exercises. When she had left, Eldain and Rhianna climbed a curving set of stairs to the establishment's upper mezzanine, where their own chambers were located. A perfumed breeze sighed into their room, rippling the gossamer-thin curtains and carrying the salty tang of the ocean. Together, they stepped through an archway onto an elegantly crafted balcony constructed of willowy timbers that overlooked the bay.

As they made their way to the rail, Rhianna's arm naturally slipped through Eldain's and they sipped their wine as they stared out into the peace of the ocean.

Like a great black mirror, the waters reflected the stars above and a perfect image of the heavens spread before them like a velvet cloth sprinkled with diamond dust.

A few ships plied the open waters, guide lights shimmering at their mastheads and bowsprits the only sign of their passage across the sea. The lights of Cairn Auriel linked together in a golden web, as though the streets ran with molten fire, and Eldain thought the scene unbearably beautiful.

The sense of contentment he felt while looking out over the ocean was a soothing balm on his soul and the cares he had felt loosening since their departure from Ellyr-charoi now seemed as though they belonged to someone else.

'What if we never went back?' he said suddenly.

'What? Never went back where?' said Rhianna.

'To Ellyr-charoi. You said it yourself – we've been cooped up there too long. A weight of grief hangs over it now, too much for us to bear for very much longer, I think. If we remain there we will become ghosts ourselves.'

Rhianna looked up at him and he could see the idea appealed to her.

'You really mean that? You'd leave?'

'For you I would,' he said. 'Since we left to travel to Saphery, I have felt the cares of the last few years fall away and I have realised that my grief was dragging you down with me. If we are to start living our lives then I believe it must be away from Ellyr-charoi.'

'Where would we go?'

'Anywhere you like,' promised Eldain. 'Eataine, Saphery, Avelorn… Anywhere we could start afresh, you, me and… who knows, perhaps even a family.'

'A family?' said Rhianna, tears gathering in the corners of her eyes. 'Us?'

'Yes. If Isha wills it.'

Rhianna buried her head against Eldain's shoulder and he could hear her cry softly, but unlike the tears he knew she had shed in Ellyr-charoi, these were wept in joy.

'You do not know how long I have wanted you to say these words, Eldain,' said Rhianna. 'I didn't dare hope our lives would ever be lifted from Caelir's shadow.'

He smiled and pulled her close, feeling no pain at the mention of his dead brother's name, no heartsick flinch or wave of black guilt, merely an acknowledgement that his brother was gone and that Rhianna was now his.

'I know, and for that I am truly sorry. I think a lingering taint of the Land of Chill remained in my heart ever since I returned from the raid on the druchii. It poisoned me, but it is gone now, my love. I am yours now, heart and soul.'

He leaned down to kiss Rhianna and she raised her face to his. They kissed and there was no restraint and none of the reserve that had marked their expressions of love in the few times they had shared the marriage bed.

By unspoken agreement, they drained the last of their wine and withdrew from the balcony to the bedchamber. In the pale luminescence of magical light, they undressed and slipped beneath silken sheets with the excitement of lovers on the verge of new and undiscovered pleasures.

Starlight streamed in through the archway, shimmering their skin and bathing their lovemaking in pure silver light. They explored each other's flesh as though it were an undiscovered country, learning more of each other in one night than they had in all the years since they had met.

The magic of their union poured into the air of Saphery and it in turn returned their passions, magical winds swooping and dancing around the room and the softly glowing lights that floated above the bed flaring with incandescent fire.

They laughed and cried together and Rhianna held Eldain tightly as they finally lay in one another's arms; lovers, friends and, at last, devoted husband and loving wife.

As the world turned and starlight gave way to sunlight, Eldain awoke with a smile upon his face and his body singing with the promise of great things to come.

CHAPTER NINE
TOWER

Hand in hand, Eldain and Rhianna made their way downstairs to find Yvraine waiting for them at the breakfast table. The Sword Master smiled at the sight of them and said, 'You both look... refreshed.'

'I am refreshed,' said Eldain, sitting beside Yvraine and cutting several slices of bread from a freshly baked loaf. 'I feel more alive than ever before. How are you this morning? Did you finally get to meditate properly now that you're back on dry land?'

'I did,' said Yvraine, looking over at Rhianna and blushing as she understood the nature of their newfound happiness. 'I slept very well.'

Eldain passed a plate of bread to Rhianna and wolfed down a number of honeyed oatcakes before draining a glass of fresh aoilym juice. His appetite sated, he ventured outside to the stables where their horses had spent the night, pleased to find that the ostler knew his trade and that the steeds had been well cared for. Each had been groomed and fed fine Sapherian grain imbued with the magic of the land itself. Though an Ellyrian groom would have already run the horses out before now, Eldain's mood was too light to find fault with the care the horses had received.

He thanked the ostler and walked the horses around the paddock cut into the side of the cliff, allowing them to shake out the night's torpor and prepare for the ride ahead. If what Yvraine had said was true, and he had no cause to doubt her, then it could be an indeterminate time until they reached the White Tower.

By the time the horses had thrown off the lethargy of the night and were ready for the day's exertions, he could sense the anticipation they felt at the prospect of exploring Saphery and led them around to the front of the Light of Korhadris.

The streets of Cairn Auriel were busy and a number of passers-by stopped to admire the horses. Eldain spent a pleasant few moments conversing with each person as they commented on the beauty of the Ellyrian steeds, engaging in small talk he would have found intolerable only a few short weeks ago.

Yvraine and Rhianna emerged from the hostelry looking refreshed and eager to continue on their way. They mounted their steeds and Eldain checked the work of the ostler one last time before vaulting onto Lotharin's back.

He turned to Yvraine and said, 'This is your country now, Mistress Hawkblade. Lead on.'

The Sword Master pointed to a road that climbed a steep, zigzagging route up the cliffs between tall trellises of gold and silver lined with summer blossoms.

'That way,' she said. 'Once we are at the top of the cliff, we will be able to see the White Tower. We will ride towards it and if we are welcome we should arrive there sometime this evening.'

'Then let's hope we'll be welcome,' said Eldain, urging Lotharin onwards with a gentle pressure from his knees. 'Seekers after truth, you say?'

Yvraine nodded. 'If you would be a real seeker after truth, it is necessary that at least once in your life you have experienced doubt.'

'Oh, that I have in plentiful supply,' said Eldain.

Soon the white buildings of the coastal settlement were behind them and they joined the road that climbed the sheer cliffs towards the flatlands of Saphery. Lesser steeds than those of elven stock would have balked at the climb, but to horses from Ellyrion, the climb was no more arduous than a straight road.

When he was halfway up the cliffside path, Eldain looked back down onto the settlement, relishing the dizzying sensation of height. The path was barely wide enough for his horse and a sheer drop of hundreds of feet awaited him should he fall, but Eldain had no fear of Lotharin losing his footing.

Rhianna looked comfortable enough, but Yvraine held on for dear life, her face pale and her knuckles white as she gripped Irenya's reins in terror.

'Do not hold on so tight, Mistress Hawkblade,' said Eldain. 'Let Irenya walk the path. Don't try and guide her.'

'Easier said than done,' said Yvraine, her eyes flicking back and forth from the path to the drop at her side. 'I told you, I prefer to trust my own two feet.'

'You're riding an Ellyrian steed, Mistress Hawkblade. She'd sooner let a druchii on her back than allow you to fall.'

'I will take your word for it, but I have no head for heights.'

'You will be fine,' said Eldain. 'Just don't look down.'

Yvraine's head snapped up and she glared at him for giving such elementary advice, but it kept her attention focused on him rather than the drop. The climb to the top of the cliffs took almost an hour, by which time the sun had risen and cast a long golden glow across the cliffs.

Eldain's steed crested the top of the cliffs and he ran a hand through his unbound hair as he stared in wonder at the land of Saphery. Though he had travelled here on numerous occasions, the magical wonder of this kingdom still left him speechless.

Sweeping plains, as rich and welcoming as any in Ellyrion, stretched out in undulating waves, golden and green and reaching all the way to the ring of the Annulii Mountains in the distance. A rippling haze of magic hung over the land and glorious forests dotted the landscape, alive with birdsong and the lazy droning of insects. The air was heavy with the smell of magically ripened crops, which immediately conjured images within Eldain's mind of endless summers and days spent collecting the fresh harvest.

A temple of Ladrielle, its walls fashioned from the same white stone as the cliffs, rose from the edge of a field, its tumbled walls deliberately arranged so as to resemble a noble's folly, its statues artfully arranged to give the impression that they harvested the sheaves of corn themselves.

In the far distance, the White Tower dominated the landscape, reaching into the azure skies to such a height that its construction would have been impossible without the magic of the elves to raise its magnificence towards the heavens.

'It looks as though we can just ride up to it,' said Eldain.

'And we will,' said Yvraine, riding past him, her relief at having reached the top of the cliffs apparent. 'Whether we get there or not is another matter entirely.'

'That's not very reassuring.'

'She's just teasing,' said Rhianna as she passed him.

'For all our sakes, I hope so.'

Without needing to be told, Lotharin set off after his fellow mounts and his longer strides soon caught up to Rhianna's steed.

'I still wonder why your father sent for us both,' he said as he rode alongside Rhianna.

'So do I, but I just don't know. Yvraine said it was an urgent matter.'

'Do you have any idea why he would want us to come to the White Tower instead of his villa? Perhaps his divinations have shown him that we are in danger?'

Rhianna shook her head, her eyes unconsciously darting towards the far south of Saphery, where the Silverfawn villa lay beyond an outthrust haunch of the mountains. Rhianna had grown to womanhood within its tall, fiery walls and the alliance between her family and that of Eldain's had been sealed with bonds of friendship and loyalty stronger than ithilmar.

Eldain had visited Rhianna's home with his father and brother on several occasions, but the Tower of Hoeth had never been more than a faint glow over the horizon. To now lay his eyes upon such a magnificent symbol of elven mastery over the physical world was intoxicating.

Rhianna's father was a mage of great skill and renown, famed for his mastery of the magic of fire and celestial divination, but the energies required to create such potent architecture was beyond the ability of all but the Loremasters, and Eldain doubted even they could recreate such a feat of arcane engineering.

'It is impossible to be sure with father,' said Rhianna. 'But if we were in any danger surely he would have come to us instead of asking us to travel to him.'

'Then perhaps his foretelling has revealed something.'

'Possibly, but we will have to wait and see, won't we?'

'I suppose so,' said Eldain, frowning as he caught sight of movement in the waving crops.

He looked closer, seeing a tiny, thin-limbed creature of glowing light weaving in and out of the crops, its every footstep leaving an imprint where a budding shoot of fresh corn pushed its way clear of the ground. The closer he looked, the more of the tiny creatures he saw, each one dancing to an unheard tune through the sheaves of corn.

'They are *uleishi*,' said Rhianna, guessing what he was looking at. 'Magical creatures who tend to the crops and ensure the harvest is bountiful.'

'I've never seen such a thing.'

'They mostly keep to Saphery,' said Rhianna. 'It's said that they were created as a side effect of the spells used in the creation of the White Tower. Isn't that right, Yvraine?'

Yvraine nodded and said, 'Yes, they are mostly harmless little things, but they love mischief and it is common for them to steal into a house and bang pots or mess the place up if they are not happy with the care the crops are receiving.'

'So why don't the mages get rid of them? Surely they have the power.'

'Probably,' agreed Yvraine, 'but it's said that if the *uleishi* were ever to leave Ulthuan then its fate is sealed.'

'What do they do?' asked Eldain.

'No one knows, but no one wants to take the chance of finding out what happens if they ever stop.'

Eldain watched the glowing little sprites capering through the long grasses until they were lost from sight and fresh wonders demanded his attention.

Rivers bearing water so clear it was almost invisible flowed through

Saphery and though the sun was high and cast pleasant warmth over them, shining mists occasionally rose from the ground, gathering in miniature tornadoes that swept across the landscape, leaving no damage in their wake, but a glistening trail of moisture and crystal laughter.

Herds of animals so strange he had not a name for them could be seen on the horizon with every turn of the head, creatures that must surely be of magical origin, but which attracted no undue attention from Rhianna and Yvraine. He saw more of the magical sprites, a pack of them following his course for several miles, darting between Lotharin's legs until they grew bored with the lack of sport and vanished in a cloud of giggling light.

As they crossed one of the wide, shallow rivers that wound sedately from the Annulii to the Inner Sea, Eldain caught sight of a commotion upstream and watched as a host of translucent, blue-skinned nymphs with hair of foaming spume cavorted in the water, splashing and teasing one another. Realising they were observed, the nymphs disappeared beneath the surface of the river and Eldain saw them racing downstream towards him, their giggling features alive with amorous mischief.

He urged Lotharin from the water as the nymphs passed behind him and their playful laughter carried on downriver.

'Is everything in this land magic?' he said to himself.

As though in answer to that very question, a chill wind stole upon him and he blinked as a glittering phalanx of ghostly Silver Helms rose up from the ground, sunlight reflecting blindingly from the polished plates of their *ithiltaen* helms. If Rhianna or Yvraine saw them too, they gave no sign and though these wraiths appeared to have no hostile intent, Eldain found their presence far from reassuring.

'Who are these warriors?' whispered Eldain. Each time he attempted to focus on one of the silent riders, the warrior would vanish, as ephemeral as morning mist, only to reappear moments later.

'We ride along one of the lines of power,' was Rhianna's explanation for this spectral army's presence and Eldain tried to be reassured by that. Eldain had lived all his life in Ellyrion and though it too was bathed in eternal summer and power flowed through the land, it was a power that was part of the natural cycle of things and which did not manifest itself in such overt, disturbing ways.

Well, disturbing to him at least.

At last it seemed that the route they must travel to the White Tower differed from the course of the long dead Silver Helms and they faded from sight without a sound. Though their presence had been unsettling at first, Eldain felt a strange reassurance in the knowledge of their existence. He had no doubt that should he have intended any harm to Saphery, then the wrath of these spirits would have been turned upon him without mercy.

He bade the silent warriors a wordless farewell and turned his attention to the looming shape of the White Tower ahead of them.

By the position of the sun, Eldain judged that they had been travelling for at least four hours, yet the tower appeared no nearer. In fact it seemed farther away if anything.

Perhaps the magic of Saphery was distorting his perceptions or perhaps the sheer size of the tower was creating an optical illusion of distance.

The three riders journeyed in companionable silence, allowing the quiet of Saphery to lull them into the peaceful rhythm of contented travellers. Eldain felt his eyes grow heavy and blinked rapidly as he felt the gentle brush of a presence within his mind. The touch was not invasive and, curiously, he felt no threat or alarm at its arrival.

He sensed a familiarity in the touch, as though whatever power seeped into his mind was that of a friend, an old and trusted companion with whom uncounted dangers had been faced, adventures shared and terrors overcome.

Eldain looked over to Rhianna and saw the same slack smile on her face as he was sure was upon his. Yvraine alone looked untouched by whatever was occurring, her stoic, sharp features concentrating on the tower ahead...

With a start, Eldain realised he could no longer see the tower in the distance.

He spun in the saddle, but no matter which direction he looked, all he could see were the verdant fields of Saphery, dust devils of corn ears billowing above the fields of gold. He looked up towards the sun, but it was directly above him and no shadows were cast to give him an idea of which direction they rode.

Soaring white peaks rose up on every horizon, as though they were trapped within a great plain surrounded by a ring of mountains, but a distant part of Eldain's mind knew that such a thing was impossible...

Though he could feel the reassuring sway of his horse beneath him and knew that it was as surefooted a mount as any rider could wish for, Eldain wondered where it was taking him, for he could see no landmarks and no sign of the Tower of Hoeth.

The Tower of Hoeth...

Was this the tower's defences rising up to ensnare him?

'Yvraine?' he said.

'Yes,' said Yvraine, guessing his question before it was even asked. 'The tower has sensed our desire to approach and is judging our intent.'

Panic began to rise in Eldain's chest, but even as it grew, he felt the soothing touch of the presence within his mind. Now knowing what it was, he relaxed into its embrace and allowed it to roam freely within his skull, the contentment and peace that had come to him over the last week or so of travel overshadowing all other thoughts and memories.

Eldain smiled as he felt the presence withdraw from him and his vision swam as illusions he had not previously been aware of faded from his eyes and the reality of Saphery arose once again.

Like a sleeper gradually realising that he has woken in a strange place, Eldain looked about himself as though seeing his surroundings for the first time.

The White Tower loomed large in his vision, its colossal verticality staggering now that he saw it without the camouflage of illusions. Though it was still a mile or so away, Eldain could now make out details upon its white walls: arched windows, crimson banners and golden, rune-etched carvings that wove their way up the entire length of the tower.

But something closer than the tower captured his attention more fully...

A castle of white and gold that floated in the air above them.

The most magnificent structures Caelir could remember having seen before now were the island castles of Tor Elyr and the towering statues of the Phoenix King and Everqueen in Lothern, but even their soaring majesty had paled at the sight of the home of the Loremasters. A millennium had passed between the breaking of the ground and its completion over two thousand years ago and the idea of a single structure taking so long to complete had seemed ludicrous to Caelir when he had seen the tower from the mountains.

But within moments of their arrival at the tower, he appreciated that it had in fact been a mighty achievement to raise such a heartbreakingly wondrous creation in so short a span of time. Craftsmen had laboured for centuries to create the intricate carvings that ran from the tower's base to its far distant spire and the magic employed in its creation imbued the tower with strength far greater than that of stone and mortar.

The Tower of Hoeth sat within a sweeping emerald forest, rising up from a colossal crag of shimmering black rock. Flocks of white birds circled the tower's topmost spire and countless waterfalls plunged from the black rock to foaming white pools arranged in tumbling tiers at its base.

The air was spliced with the colours of a million rainbows and Caelir could not remember a more perfect sight.

He and Kyrielle rode side by side, having delighted in the wonders of Saphery as they rode from the mountains to the tower. Over the course of their short journey through the tower's magical wards, Caelir had seen many unexpected, incredible things and many more that conformed exactly to his expectations of a land steeped in magic: a flying castle that drifted overhead, swirling troupes of wind-borne dancers and spectral dragons riding on streamers of light.

Though each sight was astonishing and filled him with wonder, he could not shake the nagging feeling that he had seen such sights before and that he had visited this land in the past.

Anurion flew high above, the outstretched wings of his pegasus throwing a cruciform shadow upon the earth, and their guards formed a ring of silver blades around them.

Through all the sights they had seen, he had expected a bewildering array of illusions and magical defences, but had seen nothing that might have led him to believe the tower was defended at all.

Kyrielle had laughed when he had told her this, reassuring him that the tower's wards had clearly judged him to be a seeker of knowledge and permitted his passage.

Caelir looked up as a shadow passed over them and Anurion's pegasus landed in a flurry of scattered leaves before the edge of the forest. A crackling nimbus of power played over the mage and his mount, rippling breaths of magic fluttering his robes and slipping through his steed's mane like an invisible hand.

Anurion spoke quickly to his warriors and dismissed them with a gesture. As one, the armoured riders dismounted and began forming an impromptu camp. Clearly they were not to accompany them towards the tower.

The archmage turned to Caelir and said, 'Loremaster Teclis is expecting us, boy. We should not keep him waiting. Hurry your pace.'

In all the times Caelir had spoken to Anurion before now, he had found the mage, by turns, bizarre and eccentric, short tempered and cantankerous, but never frightening. That now changed as the power gathered at the White Tower surged through Anurion's veins.

'Of course,' said Caelir.

Anurion turned his pegasus without another word and led them into the trees, the leaves and branches of which shivered though there was no wind to stir them. The trees pulsed with the energy of living things empowered beyond their natural growth cycles and Caelir could feel the pleasure Anurion and Kyrielle took in being surrounded by such fecundity.

A sudden caw made Caelir look up and he smiled as the birds that circled the tower now descended towards the forest in a great host. White-feathered choristers perched on every tree branch to welcome the archmage with song and gave the forest a gloriously festive aspect.

Their route climbed through the forest, passing numerous streams and wondrous groves where Sword Masters – alone and in groups – trained with their great blades, sparring, performing incredible feats of balance or meditating while spinning their swords around them with a speed Caelir could never hope to match.

Each warrior broke from his or her routine as Anurion passed, bowing in respect before acknowledging Caelir and Kyrielle's presence.

'Your father is well known here,' he said.

'He is indeed, though he does not travel to the White Tower often.'

'No? Why not?'

'You've seen his villa, remember? My father so loves to tinker and create, but there are those who think his work frivolous. Inevitably, father will get into an argument and leave, swearing never to return.'

Caelir could well imagine the temper of Anurion the Green getting the better of him, but shuddered to think of the consequences of arguments between those who wielded the awesome power of magic.

At last their course brought them to the summit of the black rock and Anurion climbed from the back of his pegasus and indicated that they do likewise. Caelir slid from the back of his horse and helped Kyrielle from hers as Anurion waited for them to join him at the base of the tower.

Caelir and Kyrielle approached the fabulous structure, their gaze inexorably drawn up the carved length of the tower. The pale stone utilised in its construction was suffused with incredible power and Caelir could feel the energies coursing beneath his feet and into the tower.

He had experienced a similar sensation at the foot of Eltharion's tower, but, as magnificent as was the warden's demesne, it could not compare to the sheer power and dominance of the Loremasters' domain.

'Come on, come on,' said Anurion, moving between them and marching them towards the tower.

'How do we get in?' asked Caelir. 'There is no door.'

'Don't be foolish, boy, of course there is.'

'Where?'

Anurion stared at him as though he had asked the most idiotic question imaginable, and Caelir braced himself for an explosion of temper from the archmage.

Instead, the mage pursed his lips and brought a hand to his own forehead as though he could not believe his own thoughtlessness.

'Of course… you are not a mage, nor are you seeking to become a Sword Master.'

'No,' said Caelir, 'I just want answers.'

'Indeed you do, boy,' said Anurion, positioning him before the base of the tower. 'In that case you will need to make your own way in.'

'How do I do that?'

'Those who come as supplicants must make their own door,' said Anurion. 'Simply speak your purpose in coming here. The tower will judge the truth of your words and thus your worthiness to enter.'

Feeling slightly foolish, Caelir squared his shoulders and faced the carved face of the tower. He was no orator, so opted for the plain, unvarnished truth.

'My name is Caelir and I come to the Tower of Hoeth to seek answers.'

No door was forthcoming and the wall remained solid before him.

'Be more specific, silly,' advised Kyrielle.

'I'm talking to a wall,' said Caelir. 'It's hard to think of what would convince it to let me pass through.'

He sighed and closed his eyes, thinking back to all he had learned in his time with Anurion and Kyrielle: the truth of his name, the dagger that could not be drawn, the threat to Ellyrion from the druchii and the black gaps in his memory he hoped Teclis could restore.

Satisfied he knew what he would say, he opened his eyes to see the wall rippling like the surface of a bowl of milk, the magic bound in its creation now fluid and malleable. As he watched, the stone of the tower faded to form a golden portal ringed with silver symbols cut directly into the rock.

'Well done, boy,' said Anurion, striding confidently through the opening and into what looked to be a great, vaulted chamber devoid of furnishings and occupants.

'But I didn't say anything,' said Caelir.

'You think in a place like this you need words?' smiled Kyrielle as she followed her father into the tower.

'Apparently not,' he said.

'Well, come on then,' said Kyrielle, beckoning him inside.

'Do we just leave the horses here?'

'Of course,' said Kyrielle, pointing over his shoulder.

A handsome Sword Master emerged from the trees and bowed to the three mounts before whispering unheard words and beckoning them to join him in the forest. Their mounts followed the warrior and Caelir smiled as he recognised the skills of one born in Ellyrion.

Satisfied the horses would be well cared for, he turned and made his way within the tower in case the door vanished as suddenly as it had appeared.

As he stepped through the portal, he felt a sudden *shift*, as though a magical current had been passed through his body. It wasn't unpleasant, but it was unexpected. He pulled up short and spun on the spot to see what had happened.

The door behind him had vanished and in its place was one of the many arched openings formed in the face of the tower. Caelir's breath caught in his throat as he looked through the opening and saw the land of Saphery spread out before him like a relief map, its landscape and rivers rendered miniscule by height.

Thousands of feet below him, Caelir saw the forest the tower had been built within and the edges of the black rock it stood upon.

With one step he had travelled the entire height of the tower and he backed away from the precipitous drop as a voice said, 'Welcome, Caelir of Ellyrion.'

He turned to see Anurion and Kyrielle beside a slightly built elf in the vestments of a Loremaster. A cerulean cloak edged in gold anthemion hung from his narrow shoulders and thin strands of dark hair spilled from beneath a golden helmet with a sculpted crescent moon upon it. A sheathed longsword hung at his waist, looking incongruous as part of the apparel of a mage, and he held a golden staff topped with an image of the goddess, Lileath in the other hand…

Caelir realised who he now stood before and dropped to his knees in awe.

He had seen magnificently lifelike paintings of Teclis and his twin brother, Prince Tyrion, before – who of the asur had not? – but none of them had come close to capturing the intensity of the Loremaster's stare. His sallow features were caustic and dark, his eyes hooded and heavy with the burden of ancient knowledge. His prudent gaze reminded Caelir of Eltharion, and he wondered if all great heroes were cursed with such pain.

But where Prince Tyrion was said to be robust, warlike and gregarious, Teclis was his dark mirror, cursed since birth with frailty that could only be kept at bay with potions and the power of the staff he bore. Where Tyrion was a warrior of epic renown, no greater mage than Teclis had ever been named Loremaster and his incredible powers were as legendary as the martial skill of his brother.

Together, they were the greatest living heroes of the asur, for they had defeated the most terrible invasion of Ulthuan since the time of Chaos and Aenarion.

And now he was Caelir's only hope.

'My lord Teclis,' he said. 'I need your help.'

The breath was stolen from Eldain's lungs as he saw the palatial castle in the sky, its white walls and tapering towers built upon an island of pink stone that drifted against the wind like a rebellious cloud. Sunlight sparkled upon speartips and helmets, and Eldain watched as a warrior leaned over the parapet and waved to him. The sheer ordinariness of the gesture flew in the face of the incredible strangeness of the moment.

'There's a castle…' he said, pointing into the sky.

Rhianna waved back at the warrior on the castle walls and said, 'Yes. That is the mansion of Hothar the Fey. He is a good friend to my father, though he can be a little… eccentric.'

'Eccentric? He lives in a floating palace,' said Eldain, aware that he sounded like a rustic woodsman from Chrace, but not caring.

'Yes, but it's not the strangest dwelling in Saphery,' pointed out Yvraine. 'It's not?'

'No,' said Yvraine and Eldain could sense the amusement of his female companions. 'The Loremasters say that when Ulvenian Minaith returned from Athel Loren he raised a magical villa of the seasons to remind him of the forest kingdom.'

'A villa of the seasons? What does that mean?'

'I have never seen it, but it is said that every so often it consumes itself and reforms from the essence of one of the seasons.'

'Really?' said Eldain, unsure whether or not he was being teased.

'Yes, but I don't think the Loremasters approved.'

'Why not?'

'I think they thought it a waste of power to create something of such rustic appearance. I once heard the Loremaster say that Ulvenian had merged his power with that of the spellsingers of Athel Loren to create his palace.'

'So what does it look like?' asked Eldain, keeping his eyes fixed on the castle above him.

'Sometimes it appears on the coast as a huge palace shaped from drifts of snow and pillars of ice,' said Rhianna. 'Other times it might be formed entirely of autumn leaves and once I heard it manifested as corn sheaves and beams of sunlight as solid as marble.'

Though it sounded ridiculous, Eldain could well believe his wife's words having now seen this castle of stone and glass floating in the air and enveloping him in its cold shadow.

The base of the great castle was easily twice as large as Ellyr-charoi, though Eldain guessed that without the constraints of the natural topography, it could be as large as its owner's magical power could support.

He watched as the aerial villa altered course and began to slide away from the Tower of Hoeth, drifting without urgency or apparent purpose. Guided as it was by the whims of a mage whose epithet was 'the Fey', he doubted there was *any* purpose to its course.

As incredible as the floating castle was, it was simply another of the many wonders Saphery had to offer. Reluctantly, he tore his eyes from the domain of Hothar the Fey and concentrated on riding towards the Tower of Hoeth.

Now that they were closer and the veiling illusions had been stripped away, Eldain could see the tower perched upon a great black rock that reared up from a sprawling forest. The trees were filled with white birds and Eldain felt a growing sense of anticipation at the thought of experiencing a measure of the wonders the Tower of Hoeth had to offer.

'How long until we reach the tower?' said Rhianna.

'Not long,' said Yvraine.

'You are looking forward to returning.'

Yvraine nodded. 'It pains me to be away. I lived and trained here for years. It is my home.'

Eldain sensed the quiet regret in her voice and said, 'Will you be able to stay long?'

'If it is the will of the Loremaster, but I do not think it likely.'

'Then where will you go next?'

'Wherever the Loremasters bid me,' said Yvraine and would be drawn no more.

No more was said, and Eldain, Rhianna and Yvraine entered the forest of the tower, each relishing the prospect of their arrival for different reasons, but all unaware that a unique destiny awaited them.

A destiny that would bind their lives to the doom or salvation of Ulthuan.

CHAPTER TEN
CHAOS

The moment stretched. Caelir looked up into the pale eyes of Teclis, seeking any indication that he would help. The Loremaster stroked his thin jaw and regarded Caelir with the same academic interest as Anurion had, as though he were a particularly complete specimen of great rarity.

'Anurion tells me that your memory has been magically locked within you. Is this true?'

'It is, my lord,' confirmed Caelir, unwilling to speak more than necessary in case he made a fool of himself before this legendary hero of Ulthuan.

Teclis approached him and a warm aura preceded him, bathing Caelir in resonant magic that seeped from the Loremaster like sweat on the skin of a human. The power inherent in Teclis, even when he conjured no spell or summoned no magic, was palpable and just being near him made every sense in Caelir's body feel sharper, more *attuned*.

'Who would do such a thing?' wondered Teclis, reaching out to touch Caelir's forehead, then thinking better of it as a frown creased his thin face. The Loremaster closed his eyes and Caelir felt a surge of magical energy pass through him.

Suddenly Teclis's eyes flew open and Caelir thought he detected the hint of a curious smile tug at the corner of his mouth.

'You are a strange one, Caelir of Ellyrion,' said Teclis. 'I sense no evil to you, but there is a part of you I cannot yet reach. Something buried deep inside and cloaked in veil upon veil of magic. Someone has gone to great

173

lengths to hide it and I would know what it was and why.'

'I would ask you to do whatever you can, my lord,' said Caelir.

'Oh, I shall,' promised Teclis. 'But you may not like what I find.'

'I don't care, I just want my memories back.'

'Memories can be painful, Caelir,' warned Teclis. 'I have travelled far in this world, from forgotten Cathay to the jungles of Lustria and even the blasted wastes of the north. And there are many sights I would gladly burn from my memories if I could. You must be sure that this is what you want, because there will be no turning back once we begin.'

'Anurion told me the same thing, my lord, and I give you the same answer. Whatever it takes and whatever befalls me, I am willing to take the risk and accept the consequences of what happens.'

Teclis gave a derisive laugh and turned away from him, making a circuit of the chamber as he spoke. 'Do not be so willing to accept consequences you know nothing about, Caelir. None of us can know what will happen when I delve within your mind, but such a dark mystery should not be left unsolved, eh?'

As Teclis walked and Caelir recovered from his awe, he took in his surroundings in more detail, seeing that the top of the tower was a spartan place of meditation and serenity. The floor was a gleaming blue marble save for a circular pattern of an eight-spoked wheel at its centre marked in a mosaic of shimmering onyx. Eight narrow windows pierced the tower at regular intervals, each at the terminus of one of the wheel's spokes, and aside from a slender silver stand upon which sat a golden ewer, the chamber was devoid of furniture.

Teclis completed his circuit of the wheel and stood at the opposite side of the circle to him. The Loremaster's expression softened and he said, 'All my life I have sought out the truth behind the world and you intrigue me, Caelir of Ellyrion. Step into the centre of the circle.'

Caelir obeyed and joined Anurion and Kyrielle within the eight-spoked wheel, feeling a tremor of magic stirring within him as he did so. Kyrielle took his hand and gave it a squeeze of reassurance as her father concentrated on Teclis.

Teclis rapped his golden staff on the marble floor and a door worked seamlessly into the wall of the chamber opened in response. A procession of robed mages entered and Caelir blinked as he realised the impossibility of such a thing.

He turned his head as he looked through each of the windows in turn, seeing only the blue of sky or the magic-wreathed peaks of the Annulii through them. He looked back at the door in amazement, for surely such a door would open into the air…

But in this most sacred place of magic, he supposed that nothing should surprise him.

Behind the mages came four Sword Masters in long, shimmering coats of ithilmar mail and tall plumed helmets. Each warrior carried an elven greatsword, bearing the lethal blade as easily as Caelir might carry the lightest of bows.

The newly arrived mages were young and wore plain, unadorned robes of blue and cream. They walked unhurriedly around the circumference of the chamber until one stood at each window. Eight of them surrounded him and he could already feel a build up of power within the chamber, as though a charge of magical energy were even now being drawn up the length of the tower, gathering strength as it went from the mystical carvings worked into the walls.

The Sword Masters took up position behind Teclis, spinning their blades as smoothly as beams of light until they rested, point down, on the floor. They clenched their fists across the pommel stones and Caelir wondered what danger might require the presence of such formidable warriors.

'I am going to help you, Caelir,' said Teclis, entering the circle as the mages at its cardinal points lowered themselves into cross-legged postures in one smooth movement. 'Together we are going to find out what you know. Are you ready?'

'I am ready,' said Caelir, and Teclis nodded.

A shimmering nimbus of light built around the crescent moon on Teclis's staff and a depthless resonance saturated his voice. To Caelir it seemed as though the Loremaster's physique had swelled, the magic flowing into his frail body only barely contained within his frame.

The mages around the circumference of the circle began to chant and Caelir recognised songs of rebirth and cantrips of restoration he had heard Kyrielle mutter during his time in her father's winter palace.

Shimmering will-o'-the-wisps reflected in the blades of the Sword Masters and Caelir swallowed as he understood the magnitude of the power being wielded here.

He held on tightly to Kyrielle's hand as he felt something stir within him, something awakened by the unique aura of the Loremaster's magic. Was this his memories struggling to the surface, unlocked by Teclis's power?

Teclis advanced towards him, the moon goddess on his staff blazing with white light, though Caelir could feel no heat from it as the Loremaster lowered it towards him. Words of power spilled from Teclis and the walls of the chamber seemed to pulse with the rhythm of a heartbeat in time with his speech.

The mages around the circle rose to their feet, their arms describing complex symbols, and Caelir felt the power of Teclis's magic reach inside him, plumbing depths to which Anurion the Green's magic had not dared descend.

But the magic employed here was an order of magnitude greater than that which Anurion could wield, for Teclis was the most powerful and learned mage in the world. Even the greatest archmages of Ulthuan counted themselves fortunate if granted the opportunity to sit at his feet and learn the mystic arts.

Like a vital tonic introduced to his blood, the magic of Teclis thundered through Caelir's body and he could feel a colossal surge of magical power build within the chamber as the barrier between Teclis and what lay within him was stripped away. He wanted to fall to the floor, but his limbs were locked rigid, his grip on Kyrielle's hand unbreakable.

He shuddered as layers were stripped away and he felt his body respond to the Loremaster's magic. Teclis loomed above him, his blazing staff and fiery eyes terrifying in their determination to uncover whatever secrets he concealed...

Caelir closed his eyes to shut out the awful hunger for knowledge he saw in Teclis's eyes, turning his gaze inwards to see what secret history was now being revealed. He heard voices raised in concern, but could make no sense of them, the words meaningless as he looked deep into the pit of his stolen memories and being.

As though he looked into the depths of a forgotten chasm, he saw a formless shape rushing towards him, all restraint and barriers to its return now stripped away by the awesome power of Teclis. Hope surged bright and hot and his eyes opened wide, pearls of light streaming down his cheeks like glittering tears of starlight.

He saw Teclis before him, crackling arcs of magic playing about his head and his robes billowing as though he stood within a mighty hurricane. The Loremaster's feet had left the floor and swirls of light and howls of wind kept him aloft as chain lightning leapt from the outstretched hands of the mages around the circle.

'It's working!' shouted Caelir. 'I can feel it!'

He turned to Kyrielle and a hot jolt of fear seized him as he saw her face twisted in an agonised grimace of pain. Anurion was screaming, but Caelir could not hear the words as Teclis brought his staff up and searing blasts of lightning erupted from the edges of the circle.

Caelir struggled to understand what was happening, suddenly aware of a monstrous power building in him that had nothing to do with that employed by Teclis.

No, this had been inside him all along, dormant, concealed and lying in wait...

The magical wards placed within him had not been entrapping his memories, but something far older and infinitely more malicious.

Too late, he recognised the danger of the trap and the ancient cunning that had gone into its concealment.

Too late, he realised that this hellish energy had been waiting within him for exactly this moment, its architects knowing that only the power of the greatest mages of Ulthuan could unlock the wards they had placed around its infernal strength.

He could see their scheming eyes: dark, violent and filled with thousands of years of hatred for him and all his kind. Monstrous, diabolical laughter bubbled inside him and dark magic surged from its living host, erupting with the force of a million thunderbolts.

Purple-edged lightning roared from his eyes and ripped into Teclis, hurling him against the chamber's wall and savaging him with forked tongues of daemonic wrath.

Raw magic, unfettered by the rigid control of a mage, exploded through the chamber in a whirlwind of howling madness, tearing open great rents in the fabric of reality. Gibbering laughter and bellows of rage-filled hunger echoed as the denizens of the nightmare realms beyond the physical sensed the breach in the walls between worlds...

Caelir screamed as the chamber exploded in a firestorm of magic.

Yvraine led the way through the forest, passing bright conversation with the Sword Masters they encountered and Eldain could hardly credit the change that had come over her. Gone was the tight-lipped ascetic who gave little of herself away in her mannerisms or words, and in her place was a warm, likeable elven maiden who spoke with wit and vitality.

He shared a look with Rhianna and said, 'Homecoming suits her.'

Rhianna smiled, then the smile vanished and she cried out, her face a clenched fist of pain.

The scream cut through the air with its primal urgency and heads everywhere turned towards her. The birds took to the air in a frantic cloud of white feathers and the forest, which had seconds ago been welcoming and abundant, was suddenly shrouded in fear.

Eldain dropped from Lotharin's back as Rhianna toppled from the saddle, her hands slack and lifeless, and runnels of blood streaking her cheeks where they seeped from her eyes. He caught her before she hit the ground and held her close as she wept terrified tears.

'Rhianna!' he cried. 'What is it? What's wrong?'

She did not answer him, her attention fixed upon some terrible sight beyond him.

He twisted to look over his shoulder and his eyes were drawn to the top of the Tower of Hoeth, where dark thunderheads of magic swirled and red lightning seethed like whips of blood.

'Isha's mercy! Rhianna, what *is* that?'

Rhianna shook in his embrace, wrapping her arms around him in fear and pain.

'Evil...' she gasped. 'Dark magic!'

Eldain looked back at the shuddering tower as Sword Masters ran towards it, their gleaming blades unsheathed. Yvraine remained at his side, staring in horror at a number of objects falling from the topmost spire of the tower.

They were little more than flaming dots at the moment, and he frowned as he tried to make sense out of what he was seeing.

'Oh no...' wept Yvraine.

Horrified, he saw that the falling objects were screaming figures.

Robed acolytes of the tower or mages, he couldn't tell, for unnatural black fire consumed them as they plunged to their deaths. Trails of smoke followed them down, alongside sparkling balls of magical light that exploded like the liquid fire some human ships were wont to use in battle.

Flames leapt into existence as one of the magical fireballs slammed into the ground before him, streamers of dirty light leaping back into the air and causing Lotharin to rear up and cleave the air with his hooves.

Eldain pulled Rhianna to her feet as the flames of magic devoured the trees and monstrous laughter, rich with spiteful glee, came from within.

'Yvraine!' cried Eldain as a darting, multi-coloured creature – part hound, part dragon – emerged from the light, as though passing through a gateway from some nightmarish realm of fire.

The Sword Master spun on the spot, her sword already in her hands as the beast leapt at Eldain, wings of magical fire spread out behind it. Its face was a fanged horror of flames and bone, its skull that of a dead thing. Talons the length of Eldain's forearms and wreathed in rainbow light slashed for Yvraine, but she somersaulted over the beast and struck downwards with her sword as she passed overhead.

The beast roared in pain, trailing scads of fire from a glittering wound in its back.

Even before she landed, Yvraine twisted in mid-air and slashed her blade across its wings.

More Sword Masters rushed to help her, but for all her youth, Yvraine displayed no fear in the face of such a terrible foe. Once again she closed with the creature of fire, rolling beneath a lethal slash of its claws and vaulting from a low branch to spin above the creature as it reared up to its full height.

Her boots slammed into its searing breast and her sword spun a silver arc as she beheaded it with a looping slash of her blade. Even as it fell, she surged backwards, twisting in mid-air to land before it once more, her sword raised before her as though she had never moved.

Eldain watched as more and more of the glittering fireballs rained down from the ruin of the tower's top and dozens of vile monsters were birthed from the protoplasmic magic. Horrors of unknown dimensions, twisted monsters and unspeakable abominations ran riot, slaughtering anything in their path as they thrashed in rage at the agony of their existence.

He longed to draw his blade and rush to fight alongside Yvraine and the Sword Masters, but he could not abandon Rhianna, her body still weak at the presence of so much dark magic.

He dragged Rhianna from the path through the trees as a fine rain of shimmering droplets fell from above and Eldain shuddered, feeling as though someone had just walked across his grave at the rawness of magic in the air.

'The magic...' said Rhianna. 'Oh no...'

'What about it?'

'The tower... it sits at a confluence of power... a focus for the magic around it, but something has broken the spells that keep it under control!'

Even as he formed the thought, he could taste a greasy, ashen taste in the air.

Not magic... but *sorcery*... the dark arts.

Screams and shouts echoed through the forest, bloodcurdling cries of pain and anger. Elven greatswords clove unnatural flesh, formed from the essence of magic, and though the Sword Masters were amongst the greatest warriors of Ulthuan, even they were only mortal.

Elven blood was being spilled.

The howling winds that engulfed the top of the tower spiralled down its length, whipping cords of lightning slamming into the ground and hurling bodies and vitrified chunks of rock high into the air with its force. Shrieking spectres of magic swooped and spun through the air like spiteful zephyrs, gathering up anyone in their path and tearing them apart with claws of glittering ice.

Eldain wrapped his arms around Rhianna as the base of the tower shuddered beneath the assault, the golden carvings worked into its structure blazing with incandescent power as they fought to contain the outpouring of uncontrolled magic.

'We have to help,' said Eldain. 'We have to do something.'

Rhianna nodded, wiping the blood from her face and said, 'If we are to get to the tower we need Yvraine. Remember what I told you on the *Dragonkin*?'

'Yes,' said Eldain, watching as Yvraine fought back to back with another Sword Master, their blows flowing like a ballet, spinning in and out of each other's killing zone as they wove a shimmering steel path towards them. To fight with such skill was unbelievable and Eldain immediately cast aside any doubts he might once have harboured to her ability.

He was a fair swordsman, but no more than that.

But this...

This was skill that bordered on the sublime, unmatched by any of the other Sword Masters that fought around them. Eldain's practiced eye could see the natural grace she possessed with the sword that elevated her skill beyond that of her brethren to another level entirely.

Eldain saw Yvraine deliver the deathblow to another creature of fire with a blindingly swift series of blows that even he could not follow. The Sword Master's eyes sought them out and he waved to her as she ran towards them.

'Are you all right?' demanded Yvraine. 'Is either of you hurt?'

'No,' said Rhianna. 'We're fine.'

Yvraine nodded in relief and Eldain could see the conflicting desires raging within her: to rush into battle beside her fellow Sword Masters or to protect those who had been entrusted to her care.

Eldain took her arm and said, 'We need you with us. I can't look after Rhianna and fight off those creatures as well. Your mission was to bring us safely to Rhianna's father and it's not finished yet.'

For a moment, he thought Yvraine was going to leave them anyway, but she nodded and said, 'You are right of course. Come on, we cannot stay here, it is too exposed.'

Between them they picked their way through the trees, flashes of magical light and spurts of fire erupting from all around them as the Sword Masters and mages of the tower fought the rampant creations of uncontrolled magic.

Eldain saw a cabal of mages hurling bolts of blue-white light at a shrieking horror of tentacles and jaws, a Sword Master beheading a hydra-like creature formed from a dizzyingly bright spectrum of light and the trees of the forest writhing with unnatural life as the magic of the earth spasmed in pain.

A mage screamed as he was torn apart by a toothed whirlwind of magic. A Sword Master was turned inside out, his organs hanging wetly from his ravaged skeleton for an agonised second before he collapsed. Everywhere was chaos... the rampant vortex of magic spawning new and ever more bizarre creatures with every cascade of power from the storm raging at the tower's top.

'What in the name of Asuryan is going on up there?' he shouted over the noise.

In the topmost chamber of the tower, Caelir screamed as the reservoir of dark magic hidden from sight and knowledge within him poured into the world. The top of the chamber was gone, blasted away by a howling geyser of dark light, and a roiling sky of unnatural clouds seethed above him. The mages that had once surrounded the circle were gone, burned and cast to their deaths far below, and only two Sword Masters had survived to protect their master against the onslaught.

Teclis's body lay in a crumpled heap beside a ruined stub of blackened stone, all that had prevented him from falling to his death. His robes were a smouldering ruin, flickering black flames guttering on his chest and arms, and his flesh seared raw. The Loremaster barely clung to consciousness, the shrieking maelstrom of unleashed magic wracking his body with paralysing agony.

Manically shrieking pillars of sinuous fire sought to devour him, but the Sword Masters fought with sweeping silver blows of their greatswords to fend them off. But for their skill, the Loremaster might even now be dead. Anurion lay pinned to the floor, his face a mask of blood and terror as he stared at Caelir in horror.

Caelir felt as though the dark power flowing through him must soon consume him and he welcomed the oblivion, knowing it would finally end this pain. His limbs were locked rigid, but even as the latest wave of pain washed over him, he could feel its power begin to ebb. He looked over at Kyrielle as he heard her shrill voice rising in panic and fear.

He sobbed as he saw the dark magic ravaging her beautiful features, invisible tendrils thrashing within her flesh and draining it of life. Her pale, alabaster skin dried like ancient parchment, fine lines around her eyes and mouth deepening to become gaping cracks that bled like tears. Kyrielle's mouth opened impossibly wide, bones cracking in her jaw as the colour drained from her lustrous auburn hair and became thin and ancient, like that of a corpse.

'No... please no...' he cried, desperately trying to release her hand.

But neither his desire to save her or any power he possessed could force his hand to loosen its grip. He wept as the magic consumed her, helpless to prevent these malignant energies from using her body until she was spent. Her skin peeled away from her face, the muscles beneath atrophying to dust and falling from her bones.

Even as he screamed her name, her bones could no longer support her wasted frame and the wondrous, beautiful girl that had been Kyrielle Greenkin was gone. At last his grip was released and she fell to the floor, a shattered husk of drained, desiccated flesh housed in a green dress.

Caelir felt control return to his limbs and dropped to the floor, hot tears of pain and grief streaming from his eyes. Pain burned within him, but at least it was physical pain and therefore finite. His body would heal and the fire in his bones would fade, but the ache in his soul... that would live with him forever.

Through tear-gummed eyes he saw the wretched bones that were all that remained of Kyrielle and he screamed her name, remembering the bright, beautiful soul who had pulled him from the ocean and saved him from her father's carnivorous plant. She was dead and he had killed her as surely as if he had strangled her with his bare hands.

He stood as he felt the agony of her death, the fear and confusion that must have been her last thoughts. Caelir looked over to where Anurion lay, rendered immobile by grief or hostile magic, and said, 'I am so sorry. I didn't know...'

Caelir turned and walked to the edge of the tower as an all-consuming sensation of loss and regret flooded him. Already the dark clouds around the top of the tower were receding as the wards worked into the fabric of the tower began to regain control of the magic.

Thousands of feet below him, Caelir could see the anarchy surrounding the tower. Spots of fire lit the forest in dozens of places and smoke rose heavenward as trees that had stood for thousands of years were burned to ashes in the magical fires. He saw knots of Sword Masters fighting a legion of glittering monsters and could practically taste the blood that had been shed in defence of the tower.

Tears burned a guilty path down his face. So much death, and all of it his fault…

He had brought this evil here and that it had been others who placed it within him mattered not at all. So consumed by his need for answers was he that he had been blinded to the evil that lurked within him. Eltharion had been right not to trust him and only Teclis's obsessive thirst for knowledge had prevented him from seeing the nature of the trap.

He heard a voice call his name and turned to see Teclis, supported by the two Sword Masters and horribly burned, struggle towards him.

Caelir turned and looked down at the distant ground.

'No!' cried Teclis, guessing his intention.

'I am sorry,' Caelir said, and stepped from the tower.

Eldain drew his sword as they finally reached the tower, its white walls blazing with inner fire and the golden carvings blinding to look upon. He, Rhianna and Yvraine had fought their way through to the tower in stuttering fits and starts, the Sword Master cutting them a path through the magical creatures with lightning quick slashes of her sword.

Rhianna had regained her composure, each step taken that brought them closer to the tower reinvigorating her with the pure magic that flowed from it. Fierce battles raged on, with the Sword Masters linking up and fighting in disciplined phalanxes instead of the isolated struggles the initial attacks had forced upon them.

Yet even with such methodical precision, more and more of the horrific creatures were emerging from the slithering pools of magical energy shed by those that were slain. For every beast killed, more would rise to fight again and slowly, step by step, the Sword Masters were being forced back against the tower.

Eldain moved to stand alongside Yvraine, prepared to fight back to back with her as he had seen other warriors do, but she waved him away.

'No, you cannot fight so close to me.'

'Why not?'

'You are not a Sword Master and are not attuned to our way of fighting. Without that knowledge, my blade would cut you down or yours would wound me. Fight alongside me, but not as my sword brother.'

Remembering how Yvraine's blade and that of her fellow Sword Master had woven around one another, Eldain nodded, now understanding what a lethal mistake it would be to fight so close to her.

He moved away from her as yet more of the Sword Masters drew back to the tower. A host of shimmering monsters, formed from every nightmare imaginable, closed in and though the elven warriors displayed no fear, it was clear they could not fight off such numbers.

A hundred blades rose in unison as the beasts of magic surged forwards and battle was joined within a sword length of the White Tower. The Sword Masters were skilled beyond mortal comprehension and their weapons moved faster than thought, dazzling light cloven asunder with each precisely aimed blow. Though the odds were against them, not a single backwards step was being taken, but every second of the battle saw another elven warrior torn apart.

Eldain fought with all the skill he could muster, his sword cleaving through the jelly-like, immaterial flesh of the monsters. He ducked a sweeping tentacle of light, hacking through the limb with an upward sweep of his blade and bringing it back in time to block a razored claw aimed at his head.

Beside him, Rhianna fought with talents of her own. While she could wield a blade with no little ability, it was in the magical arts where her true skills lay. She conjured blazing walls of blue fire within the shambling ranks of the monsters that consumed them in shrieking waves. And where such flames arose, each creature was utterly destroyed, no residue of its ending creating others in its wake. Streaking tongues of flame leapt from her outstretched hands, but Eldain could see that she could not sustain such a tremendous expenditure of power for long.

Even as he despaired of winning this fight, a cascade of magical fire rained down upon the monsters. Explosions of white light exploded with retina-searing brightness as the mages within the tower finally unleashed their own powers in defence of their home.

Eldain cried in exultation as he saw that the tide of battle had turned.

The skill and sacrifices of the Sword Masters had bought the mages time to wrestle the rampaging energies of the tower back under control and now the full might of Sapherian magic was brought to bear.

He dropped his sword and turned towards Rhianna as she sagged against the tower, drained beyond endurance by the might of the magic she had unleashed.

'It's over,' he said. 'The battle's over.'

She smiled gratefully, her flesh pale and waxen. 'Thank Isha… I have no more to give.'

'Don't worry, it was enough.'

Rhianna shivered and Eldain felt as though the sensation travelled from her and into his own flesh. Eldain looked into her eyes and a shared moment of recognition passed between them, but recognition of what he could not say.

The noise of battle receded, as though an invisible fog had descended to deaden the senses. He looked back at Rhianna and knew she was experiencing the same thing.

'What…' he began, but stopped as he saw the look of wide-eyed shock upon her face.

He followed the direction of her gaze and his heart was seized in a clammy fist.

Standing amid the dying army of magical creatures was a bewildered looking elf, his features the mirror of Eldain's own.

'It can't be...' he said.

Caelir.

Instead of thin air, his foot stepped onto solid ground.

Caelir felt the same shift in reality he'd experienced when he'd first set foot in the Tower of Hoeth, that same sense of magic changing things because it could. Once again he'd travelled the length of the tower, but this time he had not wished it to. This time he had wished for the rush of air past his falling body as everything ended peacefully.

But as the magic of Ulthuan rushed in to fill the void so recently gouged in his soul by the outpouring of dark magic hidden within him, all thoughts of oblivion fled from his mind and a wracking sob burst from his chest. He realised how close he had come to an inglorious death and the thought horrified him beyond belief.

No... if he was to atone for this monstrous debacle, then he would need to live. He would need to survive and finally discover what had been done to him and why.

Caelir stood, fresh resolve filling him as he took stock of his surroundings. He stood at the base of the Tower of Hoeth, at the edge of the charred remains of the forest he and Kyrielle had ridden through with Anurion...

Kyrielle!

He closed his eyes as the image of her terror flashed across his mind, her once perfect features melting down to the bone as the dark magic consumed her. The grief was still raw and bleeding and it took an effort of will to force it down to a level where he could still function. He would mourn her properly later, but for now he had to keep moving.

A host of armoured Sword Masters fought creatures the magic had summoned, cutting them down with deadly grace and skill. Flashing spears of fire were hurled from the tower and white flames leapt from the ground in rushing walls to burn them.

The battle for the tower was almost won, and though the shimmering army of monsters was doomed, they fought on with no regard for their ultimate fate. Caelir had little doubt as to his fate should the Sword Masters take him prisoner. Their brethren had been killed and the Loremaster wounded almost unto death, so he turned and ran for the forest.

He heard a shout behind him and saw a figure break from the ranks of the Sword Masters and come running towards him. She wore long, flowing robes and her honey gold hair trailed behind her like the banner of an Ellyrian Reaver. She was beautiful but haunted, and Caelir could not bear the pain he saw there.

He reached the forest, zigzagging between fire-blackened trees that wept sap and leaping fallen bodies. Caelir heard more shouts behind him, but paid them no heed in his desperation to escape. He skidded to a halt in a clearing that remained untouched by the fire, seeing a trio of magnificent steeds standing together by the body of a fallen Sword Master. The ground glistened with blood and the residue of magic like morning dew and Caelir instantly saw that two of the steeds were unmistakably of Ellyrian stock.

Caelir almost laughed in relief to see such a welcome sight and made his way towards them. They whinnied with pleasure to see him and the Ellyrion mounts came up and nuzzled him affectionately. The familiarity of the steeds was like a touchstone to him and he wept to see such reminders of a homeland he could not recall.

One of the steeds was jet black, normally considered unlucky to the riders of Ellyrion, but it was a fine and strong beast. Its companion was smaller and less muscled, but no less majestic. The third horse was a silver Sapherian mount and it too sought to welcome him, behaviour not normally expected from such haughty beasts.

He sensed a strange familiarity to these horses, as though he knew them from an earlier life, but there was no connection, no remembrance of their names or personalities.

'Would you bear me away from this place, friend?' said Caelir, running his hands down the flanks of the black horse.

The horse bobbed its head and Caelir said, 'Thank you.'

He vaulted onto the horse's back and gathered up its reins as he heard running footsteps drawing near to him. Through the trees he could see the maiden he had seen earlier and another pang of familiarity stabbed home. Before her ran a warrior with a bared blade, his features partially obscured by the play of shadows through the smoke and trees.

Like the elf maid there was a familiarity to them, but...

Then the light shifted and Caelir cried out as he saw that the warrior's features were his own...

'Wait!' shouted his doppelganger, but Caelir was not about to obey any such commands.

He turned the horse with the pressure of his knees and rode off for the northern horizon.

Like Anurion before him, Teclis had been unable to lift the curse of his forgotten memory, but Caelir remembered that Anurion had spoken of another powerful individual who might help him discover the truth of his life.

The Everqueen.

BOOK THREE
INVASION

CHAPTER ELEVEN
LANDING

Waves lashed the jagged, rocky coastline, relentless walls of cold black water funnelling between the broken islands that lay west of Ulthuan to hammer the sunken ruins of Tor Anroc. What had once been a glorious fastness was now little more than skeletal remains, its high towers smashed and its walls sundered by an ancient, but still bitterly remembered act of spite.

The lord of Tor Anroc and his sons were gone, lost to history and the remembrances of ancient taletellers. None now spoke of them, for their destiny was too heartbreaking to hear without one's thoughts becoming moribund.

Only broken stubs of lost towers remained, jutting from the storm-lashed waters like the fingers of a drowning victim. With each passing year more succumbed to the erosion of the sea and collapsed below the waves.

A sullen grey sky pressed down on the tower, the day almost ended and the sun descending to the far horizon as a chill disc of white. Ghostly winds blew over the watchtower of Tor Anroc, a tall spire of dark rock raised upon the ruins of the sunken city.

From the tallest peak of the watchtower, Coriael Swiftheart looked over the bleak greyness of the western horizon. A shimmering, misty haze hung over the ocean, but such sights were not uncommon around Ulthuan and did not trouble him.

His armour caught the last of the sunlight and he shivered as another gust of biting wind whipped around the heights of the tower. Coriael listened to the noise of the ocean, imagining the sound to be the forgotten roars of dragons, and he recalled tales of ages past told to him by his grandsire by the fireside of their home in Tiranoc.

He had thrilled to stories of skies thick with the sinuous bodies of dragons as the magnificent warriors of Caledor had ridden them into battle. But as the volcanic fire of the mountains had cooled and the magic of the world lessened, the dragons slumbered for longer and longer, no longer rising at the clarion call of the Dragonhorn.

Coriael wished he could have lived in those days of splendour, when Tor Anroc still stood proud and strong. He longed for the heady glory of fighting in the glittering host of Ulthuan against its many enemies instead of watching the flat emptiness of the western ocean.

He gripped the haft of his spear, standing a little taller as he imagined himself standing proud in a line of spearmen, their courage unbending and their blades gleaming in the sunlight. Such was not the case, however, and though he understood the necessity of what he and his fellow warriors did here, it did not sit well with his hunger for glory to be stranded on this desolate and forgotten island as a mere watchman.

Far below him, a hundred other warriors of Tiranoc garrisoned the watchtower, guardians of the magical beacon that would give warning of any hostile force approaching the isle of the asur. In addition to these citizen soldiers, a group of Shadow Warriors had arrived the previous evening, an occurrence greeted with some trepidation, for only rarely did these cruel guardians of Ulthuan's coast choose to fraternise with the soldiers of the Phoenix King.

Right now, Coriael would have preferred it to be even rarer, for his companion upon the ramparts of the watchtower was a cold-eyed Nagarythe named Vaulath.

The Shadow Warrior wore no woollen tunic, but seemed not to feel the cold despite having only the protection of a thin shirt of dulled mail and a grey cloak that blended with the stonework of the tower. His longbow was fashioned from a wood so dark as to be almost black, the intricate embossing worked in deeply tinted copper.

'Still dreaming of being a great hero?' said Vaulath and Coriael knew he had read his thoughts in his posture.

'No harm in dreaming is there?'

'I suppose not. So long as you realise that's all it is, a dream.'

'What do you mean?' said Coriael.

Vaulath shook his head and said, 'I can't see the likes of you fighting in a battle line.'

'Why not?'

'Too much of a daydreamer. You'll be killed in the first charge, too busy thinking of the glory you want to win to defend yourself against the first enemy that tries to gut you.'

'How do *you* know?' snapped Coriael. 'You don't even know me.'

'I don't need to. I can see it plain as day. You haven't suffered the way we Nagarythe have. You still think war is about glory and honour.'

'And so it is!'

Vaulath laughed, though the cruel edge to it robbed it of any humour. 'You are a young fool if you think that. War has nothing to do with such notions. It is all about killing and death. It is about killing your enemy before he even knows you are there. Striking him down from the shadows as quickly as possible by whatever means necessary. And once he is defeated you hang his body from the gibbet tree by his entrails so that his friends will learn not to come back!'

Coriael recoiled before Vaulath's words, shocked at the vitriol if not the sentiment, for the Nagarythe were known to be cruel warriors. But to hear such words from one of the asur was chilling, more akin to something he would have expected from the mouth of a druchii.

'You are wrong,' said Coriael. 'The great heroes of Ulthuan would never stoop to such barbarity.'

'Think you not? Where was the glory when Tethlis the Slayer's Silver Helms drove the druchii from the cliffs of the Blighted Isle to break on the rocks below? You think Tyrion allowed notions of honour to stay his hand when he slew the Witch King's assassin on the Finuval Plain? No, the Everqueen's champion slew his opponent as quickly as he was able.'

The night closed in as Vaulath's venomous words spat forth, and Coriael dearly wished he could have passed this watch with another of his fellow warriors of Tiranoc instead of this caustic Nagarythe.

Disgusted, he turned away and leaned on the parapet, seeking to find something in the darkness to distract him from Vaulath's gloomy pronouncements. The Shadow Warrior said nothing more, apparently content he had made his point and dashed Coriael's dreams of glory.

Aside from the booming crash of the water and white patches of surf, he could see little of interest, though that did not surprise him. Dark clouds loomed on the horizon, drawing nearer with every second, and a storm was likely brewing far out to sea.

A sliver of darkness shifted below him, the light of the rising moon casting long shadows over the rock, and he stared over the edge of the parapet in puzzlement.

'Did you see that?' said Vaulath, his whispered voice audible even over the crashing waves.

'I saw something,' nodded Coriael.

'Look again.'

Coriael leaned further over the parapet, squinting against the darkness in an attempt to spot the shadow once again. He heard the soft creak of Vaulath's bow being drawn and turned to ask what he saw when he heard a series of soft clicks and excruciating fire exploded in his shoulder.

He screamed in pain as Vaulath loosed a black-fletched shaft, falling to the stone floor of the tower as he heard an answering cry of pain from the base of the tower. Coriael rolled onto his back and dropped his spear, staring in shock at a pair of iron crossbow bolts jutting from his flesh. Blood streamed down his cream tunic and he felt a nauseous panic swell within him as he imagined that the barbed heads might be poisoned.

A clang of bolts smacked against the stonework of the tower and he looked up as Vaulath ducked behind a tapered merlon. Anger began to overwhelm his pain as he realised the Shadow Warrior had used him as bait to lure whoever was below into loosing and making himself a target.

'Still alive?' said Vaulath.

'No thanks to you!' spat Coriael. 'I could have been killed!'

'Maybe, but I killed the one that hit you,' replied Vaulath. 'Still think there's honour in war?'

Coriael didn't deign to answer that question and pushed himself to his knees, gritting his teeth in pain. He reached up to pluck one of the bolts from his shoulder, but Vaulath shook his head. 'Leave it. You'll bleed to death.'

He glared at the Shadow Warrior, looking over his shoulder as he saw the storm clouds he had noticed earlier drawing closer with unnatural speed.

'What's happening?' he said.

'We are under attack, what do you think is happening?' said Vaulath. 'Go below and light the beacon. If they have come with numbers then we will need help soon to live through the night.'

'Who are they?'

'Druchii. Who else?'

Coriael nodded, frightened, yet also exhilarated enough that he was now involved in a fight to protect Ulthuan that the pain of his wounds receded for a moment.

From below he heard shouts and the clash of weapons, but over and above that he heard a dreadful sound like a torn sail in the wind, a leathery ripping that set his soul to thinking of dark caves and mountain lairs filled with gnawed and bloody bones.

Vaulath heard it too and looked up as a thrashing blanket of living darkness blotted out the sky. But this darkness had little to do with the setting of the sun save that it was the shroud that hid the vile creatures within it from the sight of all that was good and pure.

With a speed that amazed Coriael, Vaulath loosed arrow after arrow into the seething cloud of flapping wings and screeching cries that filled the air.

'Go!' shouted the Shadow Warrior as he drew and loosed with terrifying speed.

A flare of purple fire from below lit up the sky and Coriael cried out as he saw thousands of hideous creatures circling in the air above the tower, their bodies a dreadful amalgam of female anatomy and that of a gro-tesque daemonic bat. In the flickering spears of purple lightning, he saw faces little better than those of wild animals, hunger-driven and horrible to look upon. Their wings were composed of an ugly stretched sinewy fabric, their claws and horns formed from diseased and yellowed bone.

Fear lent his limbs speed and he scrambled over to the stairs cut into the floor that led to the chamber of the beacon. He heard more piercing shrieks as more of Vaulath's arrows found homes in unclean flesh.

The tower shook as though from a mighty blow and Coriael gasped in pain as the impact threw him against the stonework. He dropped into the stairwell as he heard Vaulath's bow clatter to the floor, and the stink of unclean flesh filled his nostrils. The noise of the creatures' flapping wings grew as the cloud of monsters descended to the tower and engulfed its top in a flurry of screeching bodies.

Coriael looked behind him, but could no longer see the Shadow Warrior. He heard the warrior scream in hatred as his sword clove the flesh of the flying beasts. The scent of blood and howls of triumphant bloodlust tore at his senses as he pushed down the stairs that curved towards the beacon chamber. He tried not to imagine the horror of being torn to pieces by these abominable creatures.

Deafening shrieks echoed behind him, the flickering light of torches throwing the madly jerking shadows of his pursuers against the white inner walls of the stairwell. He stumbled onwards, snatching a torch from its sconce with his good arm as he reached the landing.

A white-timbered door blocked further progress and he staggered against it.

'Lady Isha, in whose grace I trust, I bid thee open!'

The timbers of the door pulsed with a soft light and he heard the click of the latch as the magic that barred the passage of enemies withdrew. He pushed open the door as a screeching cry of triumph and the clicking of bone claws scratching on stone echoed from behind him.

Coriael threw himself through the door and turned to hurl his weight against it, leaning his back against the door to push it shut. Before the door could close, a body slammed against the other side of it and he cried out as the shock jarred his injured shoulder. He pushed against the creatures on the other side of the door, the timber shuddering beneath their assault as iron-hard claws tore at the wood.

Shrieks of pain echoed in the corridor as the purity of the magic burned their flesh and he fought against the pain of his wound as he doubled his efforts to press the door shut. The glowing blue orb of the warning beacon pulsed in readiness in front of him, but while the door remained unbarred, it might as well have been on Ulthuan for all the good it did him.

A gnarled hand of hard flesh hooked around the edge of the door, the bloody claws tearing across his chest.

Coriael flinched in pain and his weight on the door eased a fraction…

Arms corded with sinewy muscle forced their way through the wider gap, and with the extra leverage the door was hurled open. Coriael sprawled on the floor, wracked with pain, but knowing he had one last duty to perform before these depraved monsters killed him.

He crawled towards the warning beacon, but even as he reached for it a heavy weight pinned him to the ground as the winged monsters landed on him.

Coriael screamed as clawed hands tore into him.

His world ended in pain as fanged mouths fastened upon his flesh.

Moonlight spilled over the peaks of the Annulii, bathing the rocky headlands and sandy bays of northern Tiranoc in silver as the fullness of night drew its veil over the world. The shimmering haze Coriael Swiftheart had seen in the twilight faded and as the sea reflected the light of the moon, a vast fleet of ships emerged from the haze.

Sleek, dark-hulled Raven ships with hooked rams and black sails carried hundreds of dark elf warriors and great wooden longships with high dragon prows bore the warriors of Issyk Kul. Hundreds of ships sailed into a sheltered bay known as Carin Anroc that thrust inland at the border between Tiranoc and the Shadowlands.

With the watchtower of Tor Anroc neutralised, stealth and cunning were sacrificed for speed. Though the warning beacon had been silenced, it would not take long for the defenders of Ulthuan to become aware of the invaders in their midst.

The first dark elf ships slid up the shingled bay and armoured warriors leapt into the shallows. They rushed ashore, blades bared and their cruel eyes eager for bloodshed. Ship after ship slid up the beach and scores of warriors assembled before the whips and shouted orders of their leaders.

Cloaked warriors led dark steeds from the holds of their vessels and rode out to watch for any enemy scouts as phalanxes of warriors clad in long mail shirts – called *dalakoi* – and golden breastplates waded through the surf. These warriors bore the feared *draich*, a mighty executioner's weapon, and a pall of dread came before them as they marched onto the beach.

Heavy-hulled ships lowered ramps of thick timber and a host of dark armoured knights rode green skinned reptilian beasts onto the beach. Far larger than the mounts of their cloaked brethren, these scaly skinned creatures were muscular and vicious and their powerful jaws were filled with jagged fangs. The knights carried barbed lances that glittered in the moonlight and the thick, growling heads of their mounts swung back and forth as they tasted the air for blood.

Disassembled machines worked from gracefully curved spars of ebony and gold were lifted from the holds of other vessels, together with barrel-loads of deadly missiles – long bolts that more resembled heavy, iron lances and hundreds of smaller, lighter darts.

A black shape wheeled in the air high above the assembling army, a beast of darkness that bore the mistress of this host through the night. Its outward form resembled a powerful winged horse, and its sleek outline was like the essence of night bound into physical shape. Its burning, predatory eyes glowed red in the darkness and a jagged thrust of bone jutted from its skull.

Morathi straddled the night-hunting pegasus with her wicked lance held high for all to see. Against the blackness of her mount, her skin was like marble, smooth and pale and beautiful. A corslet of gleaming black leather and plate protected and exposed her flesh in equal measure and she was attended by a darkly glittering host of malevolent spirits that gathered about her in a cloak of woven mist.

Pledges of lust and adoration arose from the warriors below at the sight of her, but Morathi ignored them, soaring high on the magical energies blowing from the Annulii Mountains and smiling as she contemplated the undoing of her enemies.

Issyk Kul, her ally for the time being, landed his own ships further along from those of the Hag Sorceress, marching through the waters and onto the sand with his many bladed sword raised. Behind him a naked familiar led a towering steed with red flesh and heaving flanks that glistened with blood and exposed musculature. A silver saddle was sewn onto its back and its sapphire eyes blazed with ecstasy as the saltwater bathed its exposed viscera in fire.

Morathi watched as Kul vaulted into the metal saddle of the fleshy steed and raised his sword high above his head. He threw back his head and issued a long, whooping howl as he swung his sword like a madman.

At this signal, scores of men dropped into the sea from the longboats. These were leather-tough men of the far Northern Wastes, their hard flesh sculpted by the rigours of battle and slaughter. Warriors in dark armour, furred cloaks and horned helms marched ashore, their curved swords and mighty axes hungry for slaughter and degradation in their god's name.

Beasts with shaggy, horned heads loped alongside these warriors, their anatomies hugely muscled and furred by the fusion of man and beast. Snorting monsters with curling horns sprouting from their skulls bullied smaller, red furred beasts ahead of them with bellowed grunts and thumps of spiked clubs.

Great ramps were hurled from the sides of larger vessels and a dozen warriors clambered over the sides, each group hauling a chained abomination behind them.

Howling roars echoed through the night as huge, misshapen masses of flesh were dragged onto the land, their many gnashing mouths snapping shut at anything that came close. The beasts shambled forwards on grossly swollen and twisted limbs with weeping sores clustered in pockets of flab and sinew at the joints. Their bloated bodies were thick with heavy cartilage and clawed limbs, too many for any natural creature, and none possessed any obvious head or primary means of discerning the world around them.

Whatever manner of creatures they had once been, each was now a monster spawned by the mutating power of Chaos, little more than a terrifying living engine of destruction and slaughter. Other ships began disgorging yet more of these deformed monsters, horrifyingly distorted and warped creatures that defied understanding or description. Monstrous hulks of distended flesh, their bodies were horrors of thrashing claws, fused heads, elastic limbs and spurting tentacles.

It was impossible to know whether their hideous wails were of rage or pain, but whatever the reason for their ululations, the winds blowing from the sea carried them far inland.

Issyk Kul rode his loathsome steed along the length of the beach, howling like a rabid wolf as his army came ashore. His horse reared, like a great heroic statue of pink marble come to life, and the blood that ran down Kul's arms from the barbed hilt of his sword was like oil in the moonlight.

Such silver radiance from the heavens was both a help and a hindrance, for though it made the night landing easier, it also made the many ships and hundreds of warriors easier to spot.

Time was of the essence and it was with cruel efficiency that the forces of Morathi and Issyk Kul pushed from the beaches and up the craggy slopes to the land of the elves.

The invasion of Ulthuan had begun.

This high above the Annulii, the winds were charged with magical energy, bearing the three eagles aloft with only the barest minimum of effort. Warm air from the Inner Kingdoms rose from the eastern flanks of the mountains and met the cold barrier of wind blowing inwards from the sea. Mingled with the waves of raw, powerful magic, the resultant thermals made racing through the skies an exhilarating experience, though the mighty birds of prey appeared to care little for the sensation.

The eagles flew abreast of one another, though the bird in the centre of their formation was clearly the mightiest of the three, his feathers a stunning mixture of gold and brown except for his regal head, which was covered with feathers of purest white. This was Elasir, Lord of the Eagles, and greatest of his race.

His kind had soared the magical currents of the world before the rise of the race of men, and the Phoenix King himself knew the eagle's proud countenance. Even the Loremasters of Saphery took heed when the eagles spoke.

Elasir angled his flight, dipping his left wing a fraction and descending as he followed the curve of the mountains. Together with his brothers,

Aeris and Irian, eagles as regal and proud as he, Elasir flew southwards with powerful beats of his sweeping wings, anxious to return to the eyries around the Eagle Gate as soon as possible.

After slaying the druchii assassin, Elasir had flown north to Avelorn to take counsel from the birds and beasts of the forest realm, for their knowledge of hidden things was great. Elasir had told the counsel of the death of Cerion Goldwing and the doves had promised to carry the news of his passing throughout Ulthuan. Then the ravens had spoken of grim omens and the scarlet pheasants of the Everqueen had pronounced prophecies of great doom upon Ulthuan before urging Elasir to return home with all speed.

The sadness of Cerion Goldwing's death still sat heavily upon Elasir and the slaying of his assassin had done little to ease it. Revenge was a motive beneath the lord of the eagles, but natural justice had been served by the druchii's death, and for that reason it had given him pleasure. The commander of the Eagle Gate had been a friend to his kind and had always displayed the proper respect their ancient lineage demanded.

Yes, Cerion Goldwing would be missed, for he had been a warrior of honour and humility.

A sudden shift in the currents of magic brought an acrid scent to the mighty eagle and Elasir cocked his head as he sensed a rank odour of hate carried on the wind.

Brothers, do you sense what I sense? asked Elasir, his words forming within their minds.

We do, they said in unison.

Druchii, added Aeris.

Corrupted ones, said Irian.

Elasir could taste the foulness of the air, knowing now that the birds of Avelorn had spoken true.

Come, brothers, we must know the nature of this threat and carry warning to the asur.

And kill the corrupted, said Irian.

Yes, kill them. Tear their flesh and pluck out their eyes! cried Aeris.

Elasir felt the same hatred for these terrible foes as keenly as his brothers, but could already sense that the threat below was too great for them to defeat on their own. He dipped his wings and pulled them in close to his body as he swooped down through the air and angled his course westwards.

The Eagle Gate would have to wait.

Eloien Redcloak reined in his grey mare as she tossed her mane with unease, ears pressed flat against her skull. He knew his mount well enough to know that she had senses superior to his own and that if she believed something was amiss, she was usually right.

Something was abroad this night and he raised a fist to halt his patrol of ten Ellyrian horsemen, their exquisite skill the envy of all save the knights of the Silver Helms.

Steep fangs of stone rose around them and knifeback ridges of wind-eroded rock surrounded them. The moon was almost directly overhead and few shadows were cast, which would make spotting any movement easier, though the undulating terrain made it difficult to see much beyond a hundred feet or so. With a gentle pressure of his knees, he directed his mount forwards, her hooves making no sound as they traversed the stony ground.

He did not yet know the source of his steed's unease, but lifted his bow from its leather sling and nocked an arrow to the string. His warriors followed his example and Eloien scanned the landscape around them, letting his own senses spread out into the night as he sought to pinpoint the source of his mount's unease.

Further ahead, the ground rose up in a gentle slope before falling away sharply in a great cliff that dropped to the sea and he slid silently from his saddle. Eloien slithered forward on his stomach, not wishing to silhouette himself against the skyline, and peered through the scrubby grass at the cliff's edge.

'Asuryan's fire!' he hissed, shock overcoming his natural caution.

On the beaches far below, a fleet of invasion mustered, the coast thick with boats of a shallow enough draught to be drawn up the sand. Warriors in dark armour formed up into disciplined regiments on the beach and the breath hissed from him as he saw druchii banners raised alongside those of foolish humans who gave praise to the Dark Gods.

He slipped quietly back down the slope to where his reavers awaited him, their faces tense as they sought to read his expression. Without a word, he climbed back into the saddle and settled his cloak over his horse's rump.

Fallion Truespear, his clarion and closest friend said, 'Well? What did you see?'

'Druchii,' said Eloien. 'And corrupt men.'

'Druchii?' said Fallion. 'Then let us take the fight to them, Eloien!'

He shook his head. 'No, these are no mere raiders, this is an army of invasion.'

The awful nature of the threat spread through the troop of reavers and Eloien let it sink in for a moment before saying, 'We ride for the Eagle Gate to take warning to its castellan.'

Fallion opened his mouth to reply, but before he could speak, an iron bolt flashed through the air and punched through the back of his helmet. The clarion toppled from the saddle and Eloien realised with sick horror that his mount's unease had been at something far closer than the enemy warriors on the beach.

He spun his horse as a volley of crossbow bolts slashed from the darkness and unseen shadows detached from the rocks around them.

Screams of elves and horses sounded as iron bolts hammered into them. A shaft buried itself in his horse's neck and pitched him from the saddle as her legs buckled beneath her.

He leapt free of the dying beast and landed lightly on his feet with his bow drawn and an arrow ready to loose. A druchii shadow melted from the darkness and leapt towards him, a curved blade slashing for his groin.

Eloien let fly with his arrow and the attacker fell with a goose-feathered shaft buried in his throat. He dropped to one knee and loosed another shaft at a leaping figure that sprang from the rocks. The arrow punched low into the figure's stomach and the warrior doubled up in mid-air before crashing to the ground in a tangle of limbs.

He spun, searching for fresh targets, and brought down another three of their attackers before a crossbow bolt ricocheted from the boulder beside him and slashed through his bowstring.

The clash of blades rang clear in the darkness and Eloien saw that his few remaining warriors would soon be overwhelmed. More than a dozen of the druchii – though it was hard to be sure, so seamlessly did they blend with the shades of night – still fought and at least five of his reavers were dead.

A hooded killer came at him with his blade bared and Eloien stepped to meet him, swinging the useless bowstave in a hard upward arc. The blow connected and as his attacker reeled, Eloien spun around him and drew his sword in one smooth motion. Silver ithilmar flashed and an arc of blood jetted from the druchii's opened throat.

More bolts flashed and Eloien's anger boiled within him as he heard the screams of horses. The druchii were targeting their mounts to prevent word of their landing from escaping.

Three more druchii killers ran towards him and Eloien relaxed into a fighting crouch, blade outwards and left arm cocked behind him. He swayed aside from the first attacker's blow, spinning and chopping the hard edge of his palm against the druchii's throat.

His foe collapsed, clutching his shattered windpipe as Eloien blocked the sweeping sword blade of his second attacker. A blade whistled over his head as he dropped to the ground and scythed his leg out in a wide arc.

The two druchii fell, their legs chopped out from under them. Eloien leapt forward, driving his sword through the chest of the first, but before he could turn to dispatch the second, searing pain exploded within him as a cold blade plunged into his back.

Eloien staggered and fell forward onto one knee, bright stars of pain bursting before his eyes. He turned as blood poured down his back and managed to block the druchii's next blow, but knew he could not block another. He raised his sword, the blade feeling as though weighted with iron bars. The sound of fighting diminished and he knew his warriors were dead.

Cruciform shadows flashed over the moonlit ground as he looked up into the faces of his killers. Perhaps a dozen of the cruel-eyed druchii remained standing, their blades bloody and their ivory skinned faces twisted with hatred.

He struggled to hold onto his sword as the hooded druchii that had stabbed him advanced slowly towards him, malicious intent writ large on his features.

A screeching cry ripped the darkness and to Eloien it sounded like salvation.

The druchii looked up in panic...

But before they could move, the eagles were amongst them.

Three died without knowing what had killed them, ripped in two by powerful claws or sheared to the bone by the snap of a powerful beak. Eloien laughed, despite the pain, as the great eagles tore through the druchii, killing with the swift economy of seasoned hunters.

The druchii scattered, but the eagles were too swift, tearing limbs from bodies or crushing skulls with massive beats of their wings. In the centre of the slaughter, Eloien saw a magnificent eagle with a golden-feathered body and a head of purest white.

Eloien had seen charging Silver Helms, the thunderous might of a host of Tiranoc Chariots and the glittering host of the Phoenix King's army arrayed in all its glory, but he had never seen a sight more welcome or awesome as this mighty eagle as it slew the druchii.

Even as he formed the thought, he saw the warrior that had been on the verge of killing him level his ebony crossbow at the eagle.

'No!' cried Eloien.

With the last of his strength, he hurled his sword at the druchii, the point burying itself between his shoulder blades. The druchii screamed foully and dropped to his knees, clawing at the blade jutting from his back. He toppled and Eloien slumped onto his side, relieved beyond words that he had prevented the cloaked warrior from harming the eagle.

Dimly he thought he could hear the sound of hooves on rock and through his dimming eyes he saw a host of dark riders galloping towards the battle.

He struggled to rise, but had no strength left and could only watch as the druchii riders drew near.

Then Eloien gasped as he felt strong claws grip his body and lift him upwards.

The ground fell away and cold wind rushed past his face as the angry cries of the druchii below faded with distance. Eloien looked up and saw the white-headed eagle as it bore him into the skies of Ulthuan.

Rest, warrior, said a noble voice in his head. *I have you now.*

Eloien closed his eyes as the eagles carried him to safety.

CHAPTER TWELVE
MEMORIES

In the aftermath of the battle around the Tower of Hoeth, Eldain found little time to process the fact of Caelir's survival. With the reestablishment of the binding spells that channelled the magic of Saphery through the tower and into the wards, peace had once more settled on the land of magic.

Fires still smouldered and dark scars cut through the forest where it had burned trees to the ground with its magical potency. The Sword Masters gathered the bodies of the slain and covered each warrior with their own bloodstained cloaks. Tears and songs of lament echoed through the violated forest as each new body was discovered and Eldain helped wherever he could.

He kept himself busy to avoid lingering on what he had seen, unable to believe that his younger brother was in fact alive. Together, he and Yvraine carried the body of a Sword Master towards the tower while Rhianna sat at the edge of the forest where Caelir had vanished. Her head was bowed and Eldain could not begin to imagine what she was feeling.

'You should go to her,' said Yvraine.

'And say what?' demanded Eldain.

'You do not need to say anything.'

He nodded and helped her lay the body they carried next to the others. A chill entered Eldain's soul as he appreciated the true cost of the battle. *So many dead...*

Row upon row of dead Sword Masters and mages, so many it was inconceivable. The Sword Masters were amongst the greatest warriors of Ulthuan and to see so many of them dead shocked Eldain to his very core.

'Excuse me,' he said and turned away, making his way towards Rhianna, his steps leaden.

His wife's outline seemed shrunken, as though part of her had fled on the back of Lotharin with Caelir. He wondered if Caelir's choice of steed had been deliberate or was it simply that the fates had decided to mock Eldain by having his brother escape on the back of his betrayer's horse?

He knelt beside her and put his hand on her shoulder.

'Rhianna?'

'He is alive, Eldain,' she said without turning. 'How can that be?'

'I do not know,' replied Eldain, unsure of what answer she sought.

She turned to face him and he saw tears in her eyes.

'You told me he was dead, Eldain,' she said. He searched for any accusation in her tone, but found none, simply a need for answers. Answers he could not give.

He knew he had to speak and said, 'I... I thought he was. It happened so fast. We rode out of Clar Karond and his horse was killed beneath him. I rode back for him, but he was hit by druchii crossbow bolts and he fell.'

'But did you see him die?'

Eldain shook his head and closed his eyes, reliving that bloody night as they had charged through the dockyards of Clar Karond and burned scores of druchii ships at their moorings. Flames clawed at the sky and smoke blotted out the moon as fire raced through the docks. He remembered Caelir's hand reaching up to him, the glint of firelight on the pledge ring Rhianna had given him.

'The druchii were everywhere,' he said. 'I saw Caelir fall with druchii bolts in him. I wanted to go to him, but if I had stayed they would have killed me also.'

Rhianna heard the pain in his voice and the haunted memories of that night. She reached up to take his hand in hers and the force of the guilt that rose in him made him want to snatch it away from her.

For the grief he saw in her eyes was not just for herself, it included him.

An overwhelming urge to confess his crime arose within him, but he resisted the urge to tell her the truth. As much as the guilt weighed heavily upon him, he still desired what his betrayal had won him and he hated himself for such weakness.

He had not ridden back for Caelir, but had abandoned him to the druchii...

He had as good as murdered Caelir to win back the woman he loved.

The woman his brother had stolen from him.

Such self-deceit had kept the worst of the guilt at bay, but confronted with the reality of his crime he found he could not justify what he had done, no matter how many times he told himself that he had acted out of love.

He looked up as he heard footsteps approach, half expecting to see Caelir coming towards him to claim his vengeance with a bared blade.

Instead he saw a tall mage with long golden hair bound by a silver circlet inset with a gem at the forehead. His robes were a cobalt blue and he wore a wide belt of gold and gems at his waist. Behind the mage stood Yvraine, her greatsword once again sheathed over her back.

Eldain nodded in recognition and rose to his feet before the mage.

'It gladdens my heart to see you, Eldain,' said the mage.

He bowed and said, 'You honour me, Master Silverfawn.'

The mage turned to Rhianna as she rose to her feet and fresh tears ran down her cheeks.

'Father,' said Rhianna.

Once clear of the forest, Caelir pushed hard for the north, aware that even now there might be pursuers hunting him. After the initial mad dash of escape, he had taken more care to disguise his route, but there was little need; the black steed he rode was as surefooted and eager as any he could remember riding and left virtually no sign of their passing.

His path took him through the rocky lowlands of the Annulii foothills, along narrow paths and craggy defiles shaggy with gorse and flowering plants of all colours and descriptions. This close to the mountains, even the undergrowth was ripe with magical energies and Caelir could see why Anurion was fascinated by such fecund growth.

Anurion…

Tears fell from Caelir's face once again as he thought back to the terrible, bloody events at the Tower of Hoeth.

Kyrielle Greenkin was dead and he had killed her.

If not by his own hand then by dragging her into the disaster that was his life.

The image of her melting features as the life had been sucked from her would haunt his dreams for as long as he lived and he knew he could never make amends for depriving the world of her bright spirit.

The gardens of Anurion the Green would flourish a little less brightly without her and he vowed to plant a flower in her memory when he reached his destination.

Avelorn.

The realm of the Everqueen was his only hope now, for her magic was bound up in Ulthuan's magical cycle of healing and renewal. When the Everqueen laughed, the sun shone brighter, and when she wept, thunder rolled across the heavens.

What Teclis's magic had unleashed, hers must surely undo.

Time passed, though he could not say how much, for he had no right to look up and gaze at the face of the sun. The mountains rolled past on his right and clouds gathered over the Sea of Dreams on his left and though it was surely beyond the horizon, it seemed as though he could see a thin line of emerald green forest ahead of him.

He rode as though the arrow of Morai-heg herself were aimed at his heart, wanting to put as much distance between himself and the White Tower as possible.

The carnage itself was terrible, but that had not been the worst of it.

The sight of the elf warrior who could have been his twin had shocked him to the core, for who could he have been? Was he even real? Was Caelir? Could 'Caelir' be some evil doppelganger of this brave hero who fought to defend the Loremaster's tower?

Might Caelir be some creation of magic designed to infiltrate the secret sanctums of the asur and unleash destruction? As much as the idea horrified him and the evidence bore it out, he did not think it likely, for there were too many images burned in his mind that were too real, too resonant to be anything other than genuine memories.

Who then was this warrior? His brother…?

Just thinking the thought made it seem real and the more he turned the idea over in his head, the more likely it became. Though it seemed the most likely explanation, it did not explain the terrible fear and anger that welled up within him as he thought of this warrior being his brother. Why should the thought of a brother cause such conflicting emotions within him?

And the woman…

He had no conscious knowledge of her, but he had seen her face when he had spoken to Kyrielle and felt the first stirrings of attraction towards her. He looked at the silver pledge ring that glinted on his finger. Was she the maiden who had given him this token of love?

Such thoughts were too painful and he pushed them aside as he concentrated on the ride ahead. He had a long journey ahead and still had one last obstacle to overcome before then.

The battlefield of Finuval Plain.

Mitherion Silverfawn's chambers within the Tower of Hoeth had escaped the destruction unleashed at the top of the tower. Filled with long benches strewn with astrolabes, lens grinders and all manner of instruments for celestial observation, it resembled a workshop more than a place of mystical study. Thick tomes of magic lay open, apparently at random, throughout the laboratory and a hundred or more scrolls were strewn about the room alongside dozens of inkwells.

Charts of astronomical movements and phenomena hung like war banners from the walls, each a mass of spirals and looping orbital patterns.

Though not at the summit of the tower, a great glass ceiling rippled above them like the surface of a lake. Though impressive, Eldain realised it could not possibly be a window, for it showed a star-filled night sky.

Mitherion made his way towards a long bench upon which sat a silver object that resembled a globe made from hundreds of thin loops of silver wire bound together with scores of brass-rimmed lenses. The object floated above a shallow concave disc of gold and spun gently on its axis as lenses slid through the silver wires, apparently at random.

Eldain and Rhianna followed him into the chamber, and Eldain could not help but sense a distance between them now that she knew Caelir was alive. The touch she had given him beyond the walls of the tower had not been repeated and though he ached to reach out and hold her, he suspected the gesture would not be returned.

'Father,' said Rhianna. 'What happened here?'

'I wish I knew,' said Mitherion.

'Does it have something to do with why you summoned us here?' asked Eldain, lifting a pile of books aside to find a place to sit.

Mitherion nodded as he checked the silver globe device and said, 'Perhaps. I am not sure, but your arriving here just as disaster strikes does seem rather auspicious.'

'Auspicious? We were almost killed.'

'True,' said Mitherion, wagging his finger at Eldain. 'But you are still alive. And the poor unfortunate who arrived with Anurion the Green claimed his name was Caelir. Rather a coincidence wouldn't you say? But it could not have been the Caelir that I once knew.'

Eldain stood and began to pace through the disorder of Mitherion's chambers. 'We saw him. Outside the tower. It was him.'

'Caelir Éadaoin. Your brother,' said Mitherion, glancing at his daughter. 'You are sure?'

'It was him, father,' nodded Rhianna. 'I saw him with my own eyes.'

'But how could he be alive? I understood he died on Naggaroth.'

'So did we all,' said Rhianna and Eldain winced at the unspoken, nascent accusation.

Mitherion returned his attention to the silver globe and adjusted several of the lenses before concentrating on an open book that lay beside him.

'Most curious...'

'What is?' asked Eldain.

'Caelir's appearance, if he is your brother, may indeed have something to do with our current troubles.'

'In what way?' said Rhianna, moving to stand beside her father.

'In every reading of the stars, I saw symbols that spoke of a figure without a name or a face, a phantom if you will. I did not know to whom this referred, but Caelir would seem to fit this description, arriving as he did with no memory save his name.'

'He has no memory?' said Eldain.

'So Anurion said. Apparently he attempted to restore it, but was unsuccessful. Hence why he brought him to see the Loremaster Teclis. A mistake, in retrospect...'

'And what happened?' said Rhianna. 'Did Caelir see Teclis?'

'He did,' nodded Mitherion. 'Another mistake I feel, but then the Loremaster does so love to seek answers where ignorance might be preferable. I do not know what happened between Teclis and Caelir, but whatever it was, it unleashed terrible dark magic and upset the balance of power flowing through the tower. And, well, you saw what happened...'

They let the moment hang in silence as they thought of the dead laid out below bloody cloaks at the base of the tower.

'Does this have anything to do with why you summoned us here?' said Eldain.

'It may have everything to do with that,' said Mitherion, rising and pulling yet more books from sagging shelves.

'And why was that?' said Eldain, his frustration turning to anger.

Mitherion opened the books, revealing page after page of scribbled notes, cosmological diagrams and calculations beyond understanding. 'These are divinations I took over the night skies to the far north of the Old World.'

'The Northern Wastes!' said Rhianna. 'Father, you know that is dangerous.'

'I know, but I had seen much darkness in your futures. Both of your futures and I had to know more.'

'And what did you see?' asked Eldain.

'I saw terrible danger descending on Ellyr-charoi. Death, destruction and the fire of war.'

'Then why send for us?' snapped Eldain. 'Why not warn us? If our home is in danger then we should be there to defend it.'

'Against this danger there is no defence.' said Mitherion. 'And if I had told you Ellyr-charoi was in danger what would you have done?'

'We would have stayed,' finished Rhianna.

'Exactly.'

Eldain wanted to argue, but he knew they were right.

He sighed. 'What is this danger?'

Mitherion said, 'That I do not know, but the currents of magic speak of dark times ahead, Eldain. Whatever fate is to come, both you and Rhianna are bound to it. The druchii attack our ships and the ravens of Avelorn bring news of omens seen throughout the land. Something evil is coming, of that I have no doubt.'

'You are wrong, Mitherion Silverfawn,' said a cracked voice behind them.

Eldain and Rhianna turned and gasped as they saw the terribly wounded elf borne on a litter between four Sword Masters.

The flesh of Teclis's face was raw and burned, poultice-dipped bandages wrapping his skin and covering his thin chest and neck. His robes had been burned from him and he now wore a simple gown of white.

'The evil you speak of,' said Teclis. 'It is already here.'

The conclave gathered in the ruins of the uppermost chamber of the Tower of Hoeth. The scent of discharged magic was carried on a strong wind, but the enchantments of the tower prevented its force from disturbing those who gathered to hear the Loremaster's words.

Only blackened stubs remained of the upper walls of the tower and the clouds displaced by the wind in the clear sky gave Eldain a giddy sense of flying since he was unable to see the ground.

Seated on his padded litter, Teclis convened them and was attended by his Sword Masters. The Loremaster's voice was weak and Eldain could see the effort of will it took for him to address them.

The tales spoken of Teclis told of how sickly he had been as a youth and Eldain marvelled that he was able to remain upright after the grievous hurt done to him. Dark magic had ravaged his body, melting the flesh from his bones, and he now resembled a skeleton draped in loose flesh and robed to appear in some mannish freak show.

Despite the Loremaster's terrible appearance, to stand in such illustrious company was an honour and a terror for Eldain and he kept his gaze lowered, humbled and not a little frightened at the presence of so many powerful individuals. What fate might Teclis pronounce upon him? Did he know of what Eldain had done on Naggaroth? Might this be some ritual pantomime to humiliate and punish him?

Rhianna stood on his right, a subtle distance between them, and Mitherion Silverfawn had a fatherly arm around her shoulders. Yvraine stood to his left and her robes were still smeared with the blood of her fellows.

A stooped mage in a tattered green robe stood beside Teclis and Eldain wondered what horrors he had recently endured, for his face was a mask of anguish. Other mages, whose names Eldain did not know, gathered around Teclis, though they kept a discreet distance from their green-robed fellow, as though they wished not to be associated with his sorrow.

Looking at the assembled company, Eldain could see that no one here appeared at ease, for a lingering current of dark magic still hung in the air, a greasy, ashen taste in the back of the throat that tasted like biting on metal.

Teclis rapped his staff on the ground and all eyes turned to him.

'We have suffered a grievous hurt this day,' said Teclis, in what Eldain felt was a gross understatement.

Murmurs of assent circled the room as Teclis continued. 'One thought lost to us returns, but instead of joyful reunion, he brings death and treachery. I speak of the one named Caelir and his apparent return from the dead.'

Startled gasps greeted this pronouncement, for none had considered that the dread sorcery of undeath might have played a part in today's terror.

Teclis stilled such fears. 'Be at ease, my friends. It is not of necromancy that I speak, but perhaps Lord Éadaoin would elaborate on the tale of Caelir?'

Eldain felt all heads turn towards him and looked up to see the sunken eyes of Teclis staring at him with a look of pity. His mouth felt dry and he knew he was expected to speak, but no words would form in his mind that were not those of his confession.

'Lord Éadaoin,' said Teclis, seeing his hesitation. 'If you please?'

Eldain nodded and cleared his throat, taking a deep breath before continuing. 'Yes, my lord, of course.'

He looked around the room, picturing the scene as he and Caelir had boarded the ship that was to carry them to their destiny on Naggaroth.

'We set sail from Lothern with a fair wind at our back,' said Eldain, and he went on to tell of how he and Caelir, together with a company of the finest Ellyrion Reavers, had sailed across the Great Ocean to Naggaroth to avenge the death of their father. He spoke eloquently of the chill that descended as they approached the blasted coast of the land of the druchii and the pall it cast over the company.

Eldain's voice grew stronger as he spoke of the evil, sulphurous river they had sailed along to get as close to the druchii city of Clar Karond as possible, whereupon they had continued on horseback. He spoke with pride as he told of how the skills of the Reavers had been tested to the utmost as they evaded patrols and fought the gloom of the soul that the druchii's homeland pressed upon them.

Eventually, they had reached the outskirts of Clar Karond and laid eyes upon the target of their raid, the shipyards where slaves toiled to construct the ships of the druchii fleet. No finer raiding force existed than the Ellyrion Reavers, and Eldain's voice surged as he spoke of how he and his warriors had run riot through the shipyards, burning ships with enchanted arrows provided by Mitherion Silverfawn.

Eldain vividly described how he and Caelir had toppled a mighty craft built onto the back of a great sea drake and he could feel the emotions of those around him swell with this tale of heroism and valour. So caught up was he in the telling that Eldain could almost convince himself that such had been how events had eventually played out, but his voice faltered as he described how the raiding force, having done as much damage as it could do without being overwhelmed, had ridden away.

He hesitated as he reached the crux of his tale, and he licked his lips as he pondered his next words. 'When Caelir and I rode through the gates of the shipyards, we were met by a hail of crossbow bolts. Caelir was hit and his horse was killed. He fell…'

Eldain's voice cracked as he pictured what happened next and he saw that his audience believed it to be anguish at the thought of his brother's 'death'.

'He ran to me, but… another bolt hit him and he… he went down.

I... couldn't reach him. I tried, but the druchii were all around and I...'

'You would have died trying to save him,' said Teclis.

'Yes,' nodded Eldain, tears of guilt streaming down his cheeks. The fact that they were mistaken for tears of grief made them harder to bear, but he choked back his self-loathing and continued.

'There was nothing I could do and, Isha help me, I rode away... I left him there. I thought he was dead, but...'

'It would have been better for all of us if he *had* died that day,' said the mage in the ragged green robe beside Teclis. The Loremaster reached out and placed a withered hand on the mage's arm, the sorrow etched on his gaunt face matching that of his companion.

'Anurion the Green speaks a sad truth,' said Teclis, 'for it is clear now that Caelir did not die that day, but was taken alive by the druchii. A fate none gathered here can imagine.'

'I curse the day Caelir came to my household,' wept Anurion and Eldain felt the mage's sorrow cut lines of fire across his soul. 'My dear daughter would still be alive...'

Eldain shuddered as he felt the echo of a departed soul, heard her screams and felt the agony of her final moments. He saw from the reactions of those around him that they too sensed her passing.

The sadness of her death was like a poison in the air, though none turned away from it.

No one spoke for many minutes until Rhianna said, 'How did Caelir come to reach the Tower of Hoeth? Did he escape from the dungeons of Naggaroth? Is such a thing even possible?'

Teclis shook his head. 'No, none have escaped from such captivity.'

'Then how?' said Rhianna, shaking her head.

'Anurion tells me that his daughter found Caelir washed upon the beaches of Yvresse, bereft of his memory and muttering my name.'

'How could such a thing happen?' whispered Eldain.

'I do not know,' said Teclis, 'but it seems clear that the druchii must have hurled Caelir into the ocean of the Shifting Isles, knowing the waters would bring a true son of Ulthuan home. Master Anurion's daughter, Kyrielle, discovered him and nursed him in the home of her father. Caelir returned to health, and when Anurion's magic could not unlock his memory, he was brought to me.'

Mitherion leaned in close to Eldain and whispered, 'You see? Auspicious. Two brothers, divided by loss, reunited at almost the exact moment...'

Eldain did not answer as Teclis continued. 'When Caelir stood before me I looked into his mind, but I saw no evil in him. I have given thought as to why this should be so and I believe that the goodness of his soul blinded me to the darkness placed within him.'

'Who could have placed such darkness within him?' demanded Anurion.

'There is only one amongst the druchii I know of with the power to rob someone of their memory and so cunningly conceal such a deadly trap,' said Teclis.

'The Hag Sorceress…' said Anurion, clutching at a delicate silver pendant at his breast.

Teclis nodded. 'Yes, Morathi.'

At the mention of she who had once been Aenarion's consort, a visible shudder went through the assembly, for her mastery of the black arts was the terror of those who stood against the druchii. No other being had opened the gates to the Chaos hells and emerged as powerful as she. Vile, unnatural blood rites kept her as youthful as the day she left the shores of Ulthuan over five thousand years ago, and even the strongest willed hero had been reduced to a brainless fool by her bewitching allure.

'It is my belief that Caelir was taken by the Hag Sorceress,' said Teclis, 'where his mind was broken by unnatural tortures.'

'No,' spat Anurion. 'I examined him thoroughly before I attempted to unlock his memories. I saw no evidence of torture.'

'There are other forms of torture than those that are inflicted upon the body, Anurion. The Hag Sorceress has ways of reaching into the farthest depths of a mind to wring out its worst fears, its darkest desires and its secret lusts. There are ways to break a mind that leave no mark.'

Eldain fought against fresh tears as he tried to imagine the torments Caelir must have endured at the hands of the druchii. Better that he had cut his throat in his sleep than allow him to suffer such pain.

'Morathi is unmatched in her mastery of the darkest pleasures,' said Teclis. 'There is not one amongst us who could resist her wiles, not even me. We should not hate Caelir, my friends, we must pity him and we must help him, for it is clear to me that he did not do this thing knowingly or willingly. He will be frightened and desperate for answers, but his ultimate destiny is beyond my powers to see.

'We must find him and undo what has been done to him, for I fear that he has yet a part to play in events to come. I feel the touch of the druchii somewhere upon our shores and a black ark lurks on our southern coast. The destruction unleashed here is but the first stage in a grander scheme, my friends, one that aims to destroy us all.'

'So how do we find Caelir?' asked Eldain. 'He is my brother and if anyone is to hunt him it should be me.'

'Indeed it should, Lord Éadaoin,' agreed Teclis. 'As Master Silverfawn says, it is more than coincidence that you arrive here on the same day as your brother. Fate has delivered you to us and it is clear there is a bond between you and Caelir that goes beyond that of brotherhood. But you shall not hunt alone.'

Teclis turned to Rhianna, his shadowed eyes narrowing as he spoke. 'Amongst the confusion of Caelir's mind, I saw one thing brighter than all others. I saw your face, Lady Rhianna. Clearer than any other thought in his head, though even he is not fully aware of it.'

Rhianna held her head high as she said, 'Caelir and I were once betrothed.'

Teclis nodded, as though he had expected her answer. 'Yes, and that is why you must accompany Eldain. Together you must find Caelir and save him.'

'Caelir rides an Ellyrion steed,' pointed out Eldain. 'He will leave no sign of his passing. He could be anywhere by now.'

'How will we find him?' said Rhianna. 'Can your magic locate him, my lord?'

'No,' said Teclis. 'The key to finding Caelir lies with you, Rhianna, daughter of Mitherion. I cannot probe the forbidden mysteries of a daughter of Ulthuan, but the priestess of the Mother Goddess can.

'You must travel to the shrine of the Earth Mother within the Gaen Vale. She will tell you what you need to know.'

CHAPTER THIRTEEN
ARMIES

No sunlight warmed the Finuval Plain, though it lay within the Inner Kingdoms and would normally be spared harsh winters and perpetually bathed in balmy summers. A shadow passed over Caelir's soul as he rode from the entangling forests and beheld the plain where Prince Tyrion had led the desperate armies of the asur to victory against the host of the Witch King.

Outwardly, the plain resembled the flatlands of Ellyrion or the rest of Saphery, but there was a distinct chill in the air, the memory of lives lost reaching from the past and touching the present.

Though he could have been little more than a babe in arms, Caelir still remembered the tales of this place, though, frustratingly, not the teller...

Two hundred years ago, the Witch King had led an invasion that cut a bloody swathe through Avelorn and threatened to completely overrun Ulthuan. The Everqueen had been thought lost, though Prince Tyrion had rescued her from the clutches of assassins and kept her safe while the armies of the Phoenix King fought for the survival of the asur.

This had been the darkest hour of Ulthuan since the days of Aenarion, but Tyrion had returned with the Everqueen to fight the final battle against the druchii and their infernal allies on the Finuval Plain.

The slaughter of that day still resonated across the bleak moor of Finuval, nature and history combining to create a melancholy mood that drove most right thinking people to seek other places to dwell. Civilisation had chosen not to take root here, save for wisps of smoke from the

213

occasional remote village huddled in the twisting trails of sharply rising hills or upon the high cliffs of the coastline.

The path he followed curled around rounded hills smoothed by eons of wind and water, while clouds raced across the barren hillsides, their shadows swathing vast areas of the plain in darkness before swiftly moving on. Caelir's route narrowed as the ground dropped into the Finuval Plain, becoming a long, tight valley flanked by massive crags that loomed overhead like grim sentinels.

He rode down through three squat peaks separated by rocky ravines. He splashed through water dancing over stones as it sought to find the quickest way down the mountains in impromptu waterfalls. A few hardy trees clung to the streambeds, under the cliffs or any other place even vaguely protected from the biting wind that blew off the plain.

His mood soured in sympathy with the broken terrain and the long dead spirits of the battle fought here many years ago. He shivered in the darkness of the ravine, the long shadows draining his body and spirit of any warmth.

At last the rocky shingle of the ravine gave way to earth beneath his horse's hooves and the ground began to level out as he left the crags leading down to the plain behind.

Before him, the Finuval Plain stretched out in an endless vista of broken moorland and withered heath. There would be no hiding in this place and all he could do would be to cross the ancient battlefield as quickly as he was able and hope any pursuers would be similarly discomfited by the melancholy that seeped from every square yard of this place.

He rode onwards, the black steed making good time though he had not stopped to feed or water it for some time. The horse had welcomed him as a rider, as though they shared some kinship he was not aware of, and he was grateful for such a blessing.

Though apparently deserted, it was soon clear to Caelir that others still travelled the Finuval Plain. He saw recent hoofprints and the long trails of what looked to be the wheel ruts of a caravan or wagon, though he had no idea as to who might choose to travel this way.

The morning receded into the afternoon and as the day wore on, Caelir saw more and more relics of the great battle fought here. Broken speartips and snapped sword blades jutted from the ground, and here and there he caught sight of a splintered shield. He saw no bones, for those of his people would have been gathered up and those of the druchii would have been burned.

He kept his thoughts focused on the journey ahead, letting his horse find its own path across the windswept plain, the ghosts and echoes of the battle leeching any thoughts of his own from his mind as surely as though he were drunk on dreamwine. He tried to remember the warrior he believed was his brother, but found himself becoming inexplicably angry every time he summoned his face.

Each thought of anger was dispelled as soon as he thought of the golden-haired elf maid who had accompanied him. He wished he could remember her, for she was a balm on his soul and he would often catch himself indulging in daydreams where they rode the mountains, her atop a steed with glittering silver flanks and he upon a grey mare…

He shook off such dreams, knowing they could never come to pass, miserable and angry in equal measure.

As night fell and a hunter's moon rose above the mountains, he drew near a bare, rounded hillock in the midst of the battlefield. A collection of barrow mounds had been raised around the circumference of its base and each was topped by a tapering menhir carved with spiralling, runic patterns.

Elven hands had clearly fashioned these mausoleums in ages past, for there was a grace and symmetry to each that was beyond the skill of the lesser races. Darkness framed by marble pilasters and lintels led inside, but Caelir felt no compulsion to venture within, for the echoes of the dead were strong here and they jealously guarded their final resting places.

A low mist hugged the ground and Caelir wrapped his cloak tighter about himself as he contemplated riding through the night. Though his horse had valiantly borne him from the White Tower without complaint, he knew that it would need rest soon or else he risked riding it into the ground.

He looked for somewhere to rest, but could see nowhere that would offer more shelter from the wind than the spaces between the barrows at the base of the hillock. As much as he did not relish the prospect of spending the night in such close proximity to these monuments of battle, he felt no threat from the dead gathered here, for they were defenders of Ulthuan and they watched over this land.

Caelir made a quick circuit of the round hillock before dismounting and hobbling his horse next to a mausoleum with a graceful arched entrance. A cold wind gusted from within like a sigh and he bowed respectfully before finding a patch of dry, flat earth upon which to lay his saddle blanket.

He wrapped himself tightly in his cloak and settled down to sleep.

When he awoke, he saw stars above him, but not the stars beneath which he had fallen asleep. The mist that had been gathering when he had stopped for the night was thicker than before, but only now did he see that it was no ordinary mist.

Elves moved within it, ghostly warriors in armour of times past limned in silver light who marched around the hillock in grim procession. He rose to his feet, amazed at how refreshed he felt and turned to look up at the hillock.

And gasped in horror as he saw his still sleeping form curled on the ground.

Caelir lifted his hands to his face as he saw the same spectral light that outlined the ghosts emanating from his own flesh. In panic he reached down to his body, but his fingertips simply vanished within as though he were no more than an apparition.

'Am I dead?' he asked himself, but as he saw the rhythmic rise and fall of his sleeping form, he slowly came to the realisation that he was still alive.

Caelir watched the marching warriors for a time, their ranks swelling as an endless tide of sentinels emerged from the arched entrances to the barrows. He wondered what purpose this moonlit vigil served and glanced up at the top of the hillock, where he saw a shadow where no shadow ought to be, a sliver of darkness against the moon.

A figure stood there, etched against the night as though an evil memory had been caught in time and now raged at its captivity at the hands of these ghostly warriors.

Though no more solid than smoke and memory, the shape wore the suggestion of armour, as though this were a revenant of the battle fought here long ago. It raged biliously, and Caelir took a step towards the shape, something in its armoured darkness familiar and repulsive.

It towered above the battlefield, green orbs of malice staring out from behind the cruel curves of its mighty, horned helmet and Caelir felt his legs go weak as he realised that he looked upon the black imprint on time left by the Witch King of Naggaroth.

His pulse quickened, though how such a thing could be possible in ghost form he didn't know. This figure of evil had lurked in the darkest nightmares of the asur for thousands of years, yet few had laid eyes upon him and lived to tell of it.

With sudden, awful certainty, Caelir knew that he could count himself amongst their number. Though he had no memory of the event, he knew he had stared into those eyes and had felt his soul shrivel beneath their awful gaze.

'What did you do to me?' he shouted, dropping to his knees. 'Tell me!'

The shadow at the top of the hillock did not answer him or even acknowledge his presence, for it was merely an echo, a phantom of that bloody day when the fate of Ulthuan had been decided in blood and magic upon the Finuval Plain.

Caelir lay down on the glittering grass of the hillock and wept silver tears.

And the spectral guardians continued to circle.

The Aquila Spire was now clean and pristine, the very model of a noble commander's quarters, though Glorien had taken the sensible precaution of having the Eagle Gate's mages cast a warding spell upon the open window. A precaution the late Cerion Goldwing would have been well advised to implement, he thought wryly.

The blood of his former commander had been washed away and Cerion's personal keepsakes sent back to his family in Eataine, together with a detailed letter in which Glorien had outlined the unfortunate events that had led to his death, together with several suggestions he had made previously on how such a tragedy could have been prevented.

That he had made no such suggestions was immaterial, but they would enhance his reputation as a warrior of vision and sense, and if his time at the court of Lothern had taught Glorien Truecrown anything, it was that reputation and perception was everything.

The Eagle Gate was his now and with the elderly Cerion out of the way, albeit in a bloodier way than he would have preferred, he was free to run this fortress the way it ought to be run. A neat row of bookshelves now occupied the far wall, stacked high with treatises on the art of war by great heroes of Ulthuan. Mentheus of Caledor's great texts, *Heart of Khaine* and *Honour and Duty*, sat next to *In Service of the Phoenix* and *The Way of Kurnous* by Caradryel of Yvresse. Other, lesser works, gathered over his years of advancement, had been read and devoured, each with its own specific instructions on how the military might of the asur must be properly commanded.

Heart of Khaine sat open before him and the words of General Mentheus filled him with the glories of ancient times in the long wars against the druchii. Now that this fortress was his, he would organise and run things the way the books told him they should be done, not in the slapdash, ad hoc way that Cerion had advocated with his talk of hearts and minds.

No, a garrison of high elf warriors respected discipline and he would ensure they received it in abundance. Glorien snapped shut the book and returned it to the bookshelf before turning to the armour rack beside him.

He already wore his mail shirt beneath his tunic, the assassin's attack having made him cautious if nothing else, and lifted his gleaming silver helmet. The glorious, conical helm was a masterpiece of elven craftsmanship and cost more than the combined pay of every soldier stationed at the Eagle Gate. Its ithilmar surface was decorated in embossed filigree and the edges lined with fluted gold piping. Nothing so crude as a visor would obscure his features, for how would those around him see his face?

A carved golden flame rose above the forehead of the helmet, and Glorien longed to add wings to its side, white feathered wings that would proclaim his courage to all who looked upon him. Only the High Helm of a troop of Silver Helms was permitted to adorn his helmet with such things – a petty regulation that only served those who chose a more prosaic, obvious route to glory by riding a horse straight at the enemy.

He slipped the helm over his head and checked his appearance in the full-length mirror that sat opposite his desk.

The warrior reflected in the silvered glass was every inch the perfect commander, the very image of Aenarion himself. Long hair spilled from beneath his helmet and his patrician features were exquisitely framed by the curve of his helmet's cheek plates. An elegantly cut tunic, fashioned by the most sought after tailors of Lothern perfectly fit his slender frame and he wore wyvern skin boots, crafted from the hide of a beast slain by his father's hunters.

Satisfied with his appearance, he turned as a knock came at the door to the chamber.

'Yes?' he asked.

'Lord Truecrown,' said the voice of Menethis, his adjutant. 'It is time for your dawn inspection.'

'Of course it is,' he said, straightening his tunic and opening the door.

Menethis stood to one side as Glorien emerged from the Aquila Spire to take a deep breath of crisp mountain air and survey his command.

Dawn's first light was easing over the eastern horizon and the stark whiteness of the Eagle Gate glittered with armoured warriors holding spears and bows at precisely the right angle. Bolt throwers on the parapets of the high towers were manned by crews standing to attention and blue banners fluttered in a bitingly cold wind from the west.

As much as Glorien knew this assignment to the Eagle Gate would advance his career, he looked forward to his next posting when the garrison was rotated to another command and where he would not have to suffer the chill blowing in from the ocean.

'A fine sight, eh, Menethis?' said Glorien, setting off down the steps and pulling a pair of kidskin gloves from his belt.

'Yes, my lord,' said Menethis, quickly catching up to him. 'Though if I might make an observation regarding your inspection?'

Glorien scowled and paused in his descent. As much as it chafed him to listen to the prattling of his underlings, the writings of Caradryel spoke of how a good leader should take counsel from those around him.

'Go ahead.'

'I wonder if it might improve the morale of the warriors to conduct such formal inspections with less regularity? Perhaps a weekly inspection would better serve our needs?'

'Weekly? And have the discipline of the garrison slide in between? Out of the question. Why would you even suggest such a thing?'

Menethis averted his eyes as he spoke, saying, 'It is tiring on the warriors, my lord.'

'Tiring?' snapped Glorien. 'Soldiering is *supposed* to be tiring. It's not meant to be an easy life.'

'Yes, but we have only so many warriors, and to defend the wall as fully as you deem necessary allows no rest time in between the guard rotas. Each warrior has barely enough time to sleep, let alone maintain his weapons and armour to the high standards you demand.'

'You think my standards too high, Menethis?'

'No, my lord, but perhaps some leeway–'

'Leeway? Like Cerion Goldwing permitted?' demanded Glorien. 'I think not. Look where that got him, an assassin's blade between his ribs. No, it is thanks to such lax enforcement of discipline that soldiers like Alathenar think they can get away with leaving their bows unstringed while on duty. I was lenient in simply confining him to barracks. He deserved to be sent home in disgrace.'

'Alathenar *did* wound the assassin who murdered Lord Goldwing,' pointed out Menethis. 'No one else managed that.'

'Yes, the archer may have a decent eye, but that does not give him the right to flaunt regulations. And anyway, it was that eagle that caught the assassin,' said Cerion, waving a dismissive hand as he remembered the gruesome sight of the druchii's corpse.

A magnificent white-headed eagle had flown back to the fortress and deposited the bloody remains of Cerion Goldwing's assassin upon the battlements, though quite what it had expected them to do with them, it had not said.

Before Glorien could speak to the creature, it had spread its wings and flown northwards, leaving them to deal with its kill.

Glorien understood that war was a bloody business from his books, but to see such a gory mess had been highly unsettling to an elf of his refined sensibilities.

He shook his head and set off once again. 'No, Menethis, we will continue with dawn inspections and daily drilling. I will tolerate no laxness among my command and, tired or not, I demand the highest standards of readiness and competence from every warrior. Is that understood?'

'Yes, my lord,' said Menethis.

Glorien nodded, satisfied his orders were clear, and made his way along the length of the wall. His warriors stood to attention, each one a tall, proud and noble specimen of elven soldiery. He reached the Eagle Tower at the centre of the wall and climbed the curving steps cut into the back of the carven head.

He emerged onto a recessed battlement in the neck of the great carving where sat a trio of Eagle's Claw bolt throwers. These mighty weapons were the elite of his command, powerful weapons resembling a huge bow laid upon its side and mounted upon an elegantly crafted tripod carriage. As with so many martial creations of the asur, the bolt throwers merged art and warfare, such that each weapon resembled a majestic eagle in flight, with the apex of the bow worked in gold to resemble the noble head of the birds of prey.

Each weapon could fire a single bolt capable of bringing down the most terrifying monsters or a hail of smaller shafts that would scythe through enemy warriors at a far greater speed than any group of archers could manage.

Individually, these weapons were fearsome, but grouped together they were utterly deadly. Nine more such machines were spread along the length of the wall, and Glorien nodded to himself as he saw that each weapon gleamed with fresh oil and that the golden windlass mechanisms were spotless.

The crews appeared tired but proud, and he rewarded them with a smile of appreciation. Their armour gleamed and their white tunics were crisp and pristine. Each carried a long spear, a weapon Glorien had decided was more in keeping with his idea of how such warriors should be armed.

He turned to make his way back down to the wall when one of the crewman next to him shouted in alarm, 'Target sighted!'

All three crews leapt into action, discarding their spears and seizing wooden 'combs' that contained enough bolts for several volleys. One crewman slotted the comb onto the groove rail on top of the weapon, while the other sighted it.

Glorien stood back and watched, pleased at the alacrity of the crews, but irritated that they had simply dropped their spears to the ground.

Within moments, all three weapons were ready to fire and Glorien awaited the distinctive, rippling *crack-twang* of bolts being loosed.

'Why aren't they unleashing?' he asked when the weapons didn't open up.

'There is no need,' said Menethis, pointing to the western horizon. 'Look!'

Glorien squinted into the dim light of morning and saw three shapes flying towards the Eagle Gate. At first he didn't recognise them for what they were, but when he noticed the distinctive white head on the lead bird, he saw they were eagles.

'One of them carries something,' observed Menethis.

Glorien sighed. 'Another bloody offering perhaps. I don't remember Cerion Goldwing being presented with everything these birds killed. Come on then, I suppose we ought to see what they've brought us this time.'

Menethis followed him as he made his way back down to the ramparts and the crews of the bolt throwers made their weapons safe once more.

By the time he had descended to the wall, the eagles were much closer and Glorien could see that the white-headed eagle carried another body. Exactly what it was, he couldn't yet see, but it appeared to be swaddled in a red cloak.

The warriors on the wall cheered as the eagles approached, for the sight of an eagle over a battlefield was an omen of victory and Glorien permitted them this brief moment of relaxation.

He marched to the centre of the battlements and watched as the trio of eagles circled lower and lower until they landed before him in a boom of outstretched wings. The eagle bearing the red-cloaked burden gently laid it at Glorien's feet and he saw that it was not some bloody trophy torn by claws or beak, but an elven warrior in the accoutrements of an Ellyrion Reaver.

The eagles stepped back as Menethis knelt by the warrior and unwrapped the blood-stiffened cloak from around him. Glorien's lip curled in distaste as he saw the paleness of the wounded elf's features.

'Is he alive?'

'Yes,' said Menethis, 'though he is badly hurt. We must get him to our healers if he is to live.'

The bloodied warrior's eyes flickered open at the sound of elven voices and he struggled to speak.

'What is your name, warrior?' said Glorien.

'Druchii...' hissed the warrior through bloodstained teeth, his voice barely a whisper.

'What did he say?'

'He said "druchii", my lord,' replied Menethis.

'What does he mean? Quickly, ask him!'

'He needs a healer!' protested Menethis.

'Ask him, damn you!'

Menethis turned to the wounded elf, but he spoke again without prompting. 'I... I am Eloien Redcloak of Ellyrion. My warriors... all dead. The druchii... landed at Cairn Anroc. An army of them. Druchii and corrupted men. Coming here...'

'How close are they?' demanded Glorien. 'When will they reach us?'

Eloien's eyes shut, but as he slipped into unconsciousness he said, 'By... tomorrow...'

Glorien felt a cold in his bones that had nothing to do with the winds blowing over the walls of the fortress as the bird that had borne the wounded Eloien Redcloak threw back its head and let out a deafening screech.

The druchii are coming, he thought. By tomorrow.

Isha preserve us...

CHAPTER FOURTEEN
COMPANIONS

Warm sunlight filled the pavilion, but the warrior within cared little for the delicate aromas carried on the cooling breeze. He stood naked but for a white loincloth as two of the beauteous handmaidens of the Everqueen oiled his flesh before scraping him clean with ironwood knives.

His muscles were hard as stone and perfectly sculpted, the perfection of his form marred only by the many scars that crossed his body. All these old wounds were to the fore and it was clear that this warrior had faced every enemy head on and had never once retreated from a fight.

Long blond hair streamed from his temples and the maidens bound it into braids with iron cords to prevent an enemy blade from cutting it and depriving him of his strength in the midst of war. Not that there were any skilled enough to perform such a feat, for this was Prince Tyrion of Avelorn, greatest warrior of the age.

He raised his arms and a long shirt of white was slipped over his muscled arms and shoulders, before being secured at the front with silver ties and buttons. Swiftly the handmaidens dressed Tyrion in soft leggings of pale blue before retreating to the corners of the pavilion as he sat a thin diadem of gold upon his brow.

Tyrion's face was thunderous and at odds with the sounds of music and laughter that drifted in through the rolled sides of the pavilion. A burning pain filled his thoughts and his limbs ached as though he had been fighting continuously for a week.

Though his training and practice sessions with the Everqueen's handmaidens had been as rigorous as ever he knew that this pain within him had a very different origin.

Teclis…

Ever since their youth, he and his twin brother had shared a bond that not even the wisest of the Loremasters could explain. What one felt, the other felt, and now he experienced a measure of his brother's pain as though inflicted upon his own body. Over impossible gulfs, each twin knew how fared the other and Tyrion knew some dreadful evil had befallen Teclis with every fibre of his being.

He closed his eyes and let the sound of the forest wash over him, hoping the gentle rhythms of his queen's realm would soothe the troubles and pain that weighed heavily upon him.

He opened his eyes and stared at the suit of magnificent golden armour hanging on a wooden rack across the pavilion from him. No finer suit of armour had ever been forged, by elven craft or dwarven skill, and the sunlight seemed to flicker with an inner flame within its burnished plates.

Forged within Vaul's Anvil, the Dragon Armour of Aenarion had been worn by his legendary forefather, the Phoenix King who had saved Ulthuan from the forces of Chaos in ancient times.

Tyrion's father had presented the armour to him before the great victory of Finuval Plain and he had worn it in every battle since, its siren song to war never far from his thoughts.

As wondrous as the armour was, Tyrion knew it was a relic of a time long passed, a time when the mad fury of Aenarion waxed mightily and the fiery soul of the elven race had burned brightly upon the face of the world.

Such times were lost now and each time he donned the armour, he felt that loss keenly.

'It calls to you, does it not?' said a voice behind him and he smiled at the soothing, feminine tone as the words flowed like honey into his mind.

'It does, my lady,' said Tyrion, turning and dropping to one knee before his queen. 'The curse of Aenarion lives on within his armour.'

The sun's glory flowed with her and the pavilion was filled with light that had no source yet seemed to carry all the goodness and warmth of summer. The scent of fresh blossoms came to him and Tyrion felt his pain diminish and the warlike call of the armour recede.

'It surely does,' agreed the Everqueen and warm rain pattered softly on the roof of the pavilion. 'His madness lives on and casts a shadow over us all, but please, my prince, stand. You of all people need not kneel before me.'

'I will always bend the knee to you, my lady,' said Tyrion, looking into the face of the most beautiful woman imaginable, the blessed child of Isha and most beloved scion of Ulthuan.

'And I can never disobey you,' he said with a smile, rising smoothly to his feet.

The Everqueen of Ulthuan moved without effort, her every gesture graceful beyond measure and her every word like the sound of spring's first song. Her long gown clung to her shapely form and it filled his heart with love to have her near him.

Her name was Alarielle, the Everqueen of Ulthuan, and it was said her beauty could move even the immortal gods.

Just to have her address him was the most sublime pleasure, and to be her champion was an honour for which Tyrion knew he would never be worthy. Beyond her immaculate beauty, the Everqueen was bound to the land of Ulthuan like no other elf. Where she walked, new blooms followed in her wake. Where she sang, the world was a gentler place and when she cried, the heavens wept with her.

'You would leave without saying farewell?' she said.

Tyrion bowed his head. 'War is coming, my lady. I am needed elsewhere.'

'I know,' she said and the light dimmed as she spoke. 'I too have felt the tread of those who worship the Lord of Murder upon our land. They come with the followers of the Dark Gods to wreak great wrong against us.'

'Then it is even more imperative I leave now, my lady.'

'You go to your brother?'

'I do,' said Tyrion. 'I feel his pain and I must go to him.'

'Yes,' nodded the Everqueen. 'You must, but promise me you will heed what he says, for your heart will be filled with anger and you will seek to avenge his hurt.'

'I will,' promised Tyrion as the two handmaidens lifted his armour from the rack and began buckling it to his body. Breastplate, greaves, vambrace, gorget and pauldrons; each was fitted to his form as though designed for him and him alone.

With each piece of armour placed upon his body, Tyrion felt the peace brought by the Everqueen diminish and the warlike spirit of his people surge through his veins. Lastly he lifted his mighty weapon, the rune-sword, Sunfang, a blade forged in elder days to be the bane of daemons.

Tyrion buckled on his sword belt and accepted the last piece of his armour, a fabulously ornate helm decorated with glittering gems and sweeping golden wings. He reached up and slid the helmet down over his head, feeling the fire of Aenarion's legacy overwhelm the last of his gentler qualities.

He turned to face the Everqueen and said, 'I am ready now.'

'May Asuryan watch over you, my champion,' said the Everqueen, moving aside to let him pass.

Tyrion marched from the pavilion into a clearing within the forest of his queen, a wondrous kingdom of dreams that nestled beneath a patchwork sky of deepest blue. Tall trees with great, arching canopies of emerald green surrounded him and the sound of crystal laughter drifted from beneath their enchanted boughs.

Darting sprites whipped through the undergrowth and glimmering lights ghosted in the deepest reaches of the forest. Magic was in the air, taken deep into the lungs with every breath, and Tyrion felt an ache in his heart that he must leave.

Music and song filled the air and beautiful elves of both sexes danced beneath a rain of petals, garlanded with flowers and laughing as though the cares of the world were unimportant and far distant.

For a moment Tyrion despised them. What did such revellers know of the blood he had shed and the sacrifices he had made to keep them safe? How dare they dance and sing as though the darkness of the world was not their concern?

He was gripping Sunfang's hilt when a gentle hand touched his and the rage fled from his body.

'Calm yourself, my prince,' said the Everqueen. 'Do not let the curse of your forefather lead you down the same path he once trod. You resisted the call of the Widowmaker once, you will do so again.'

Tyrion let out a deep breath and turned as he heard the whinny of horses approaching and the joyous note of a silver clarion. He saw a group of armoured knights on horseback, a silver assemblage of glorious warriors in gleaming ithilmar armour and shimmering white robes. Their silver helms were polished to a mirror sheen and they carried long white lances tipped with blades that shone like diamonds in the dappling sun.

Each rode a pale white horse, draped in cloth of blue and white and armoured in flexible ithilmar barding that caught the sunlight in a multitude of glittering sparks.

At the head of the knights rode Belarien, Tyrion's boon companion and most trusted lieutenant. Alone of the knights, his helmet was furnished with a set of feathered wings that swept back from the cheek plates, indicating that he was the leader of this warrior band.

Belarien led a magnificent white stallion sheathed in a caparison of deepest blue and armoured in a similar fashion to the other horses of the knights, though with a girth of gold and gems encircling his deep chest. But as Tyrion was above the knights, so too was his horse more magnificent than those of the Silver Helms.

This was Malhandir, a gift from the kingdom of Ellyrion and last of the bloodline of Korhandir, father of horses. No finer mount existed in the world and Tyrion felt a measure of his war-lust ease as he went to meet his steed.

Belarien handed him the reins and Tyrion climbed smoothly into the saddle as a crowd gathered to watch the knights depart. The Everqueen's handmaidens sang songs of glory and musicians played epic laments from elder days as the knights' guidon unfurled Tyrion's personal banner.

The knights cheered as the wind caught the long streamer of crimson silk, revealing an embroidered golden phoenix entwined with the Everqueen's silver dove.

Tyrion looked down from his horse and bowed his head towards the shimmering beauty of the Everqueen.

She smiled and a beam of yellow sunlight speared through the treetops to shine through the silken banner.

Tyrion felt his spirits soar, watching the phoenix ripple as though aflame.

'Knights of the Silver Helm!' he cried. 'We ride for Saphery!'

Caelir rode through the morning, pushing the black horse hard as he journeyed towards the northern horizon. Though the battle of Finuval Plain had spread throughout the northern reaches of Saphery, he had ridden through the heart of it at last and the melancholy gloom of the moor receded with each mile that passed beneath him.

He had woken upon the hillock where the Witch King himself had stood on that fateful day when Teclis had struck him down and banished him from Ulthuan once more. Whether Caelir had been in any danger from the dark shadow from the past, he did not know, but if he *had* been imperilled, the spirits of the fallen asur had recognised him as one of their own and kept him safe.

The image of the Witch King still burned in his mind, but it was a phantom, fading like a dream as he travelled onwards. The further he rode from the battlefield, the more he felt the elven land come to life, as though the magic of Saphery was only now reclaiming land tainted by the tread of its enemies.

He crossed slender rivers that flowed crystalline through the landscape and Caelir quenched his thirst in their waters, though hunger still gnawed at his belly. A night's rest had refreshed his horse, and each time they stopped to rest, it ate heartily of the verdant grasses. His steed would have no problem reaching Avelorn, but he was going to need some nourishment before then.

Caelir reckoned upon reaching the realm of the Everqueen with perhaps another few days' ride and he could just make out the bright green limits of the northern forests.

He had seen yet more signs of travellers, the trails of wagons and horsemen riding side by side across the moor now a familiar sight, and had decided to follow them in the hope of obtaining some food. He had no coin with which to buy it, but he still had the strange dagger that could not be drawn. It was of little use to anyone, but perhaps one of the travellers would find it curious enough to trade for a little sustenance.

Some hours after midday, Caelir and his mount reached a shallow ford and waded through the water. He tilted his head back, enjoying the cold, crispness of the meltwater as it splashed on the rocks marking the crossing and filled the air with refreshing spray and glittering rainbows.

On the other side of the river, he saw deep tracks in the sodden earth of the riverbank and slid from his saddle to examine them. Whatever other memories he had forgotten, he had not lost his skills as a tracker and knew this trail was no more than a few hours old.

Caelir leapt back onto his horse and rode onwards, pushing harder than he would normally dare. Darkness would be upon him soon and he had no wish to spend another night alone upon the Finuval Plain, even far out on the fringes of the battlefield.

The sun dipped into the west and the sky deepened from shimmering blue to dusky purple. He had all but despaired of catching up to the travellers before him when he saw a series of twinkling lights ahead, shining silver and gold in the gloaming.

He slowed his pace as he saw that the lights were not moving and heard voices raised in song followed by enthusiastic clapping. Music soared and he heard unabashed laughter wrung from many throats.

As Caelir drew closer, he saw three brightly painted carriages drawn up in a curved line, each decorated with gleaming lacquer that shone in the light of oil burners suspended from tall staves arranged in a circle around a colourful rug. A crowd of elves sprawled languidly on the ground before the rug, its surface decorated with twisting symbols and patterns that drew the eye in confusing spirals.

A delicate elf maid with winsome features danced in the centre of the rug, spinning and leaping with joy as music flowed through her. She danced with her eyes closed, her limbs flowing fluidly around her and her body seeming to float in the air as though held aloft by the notes.

Caelir saw the musicians at the side of the wide rug and for a fleeting second he had the distinct impression that the music was playing *them*, its desire to be heard and enjoyed using their breath and fingers as a means to manifest its bounty.

The audience watched the performance with rapturous eyes and Caelir found he could not tear his eyes from the maiden's sensuous dance. Her skin gleamed in the torchlight and the gossamer thin fabric of her slip clung to her lithe, athletic form.

The music shifted in tempo, becoming faster and faster and driving the dancing girl to incredible heights of ecstasy. The audience whooped and cried as her form became a twisting blur of radiant skin and light.

Then suddenly it was over, the music died and the dancing girl made one final leap into the air. She twisted as she descended and landed gracefully in the centre of the rug, her head thrown back and her arms outstretched.

Applause exploded from the audience and Caelir found himself joining in, desperate to show his appreciation for this incredible performance.

The sound of clapping faded as the gathering became aware of his presence and he felt himself blush as open faces turned towards him with curious expressions.

Caelir slid from the back of his horse as a tall elf with lush features and long silver hair moved from the audience and came towards him. He extended his hand to Caelir.

'Welcome, dear boy, I am Narentir,' said the elf, his voice lyrical. 'Will you join us?'

'Caelir,' he replied. 'And yes, I will join you.'

'Most excellent,' said Narentir, guiding him towards the firelight. 'I take it you liked Lilani's performance then?'

Caelir nodded and the dancing girl threw him a coquettish grin before vacating the rug as other performers took her place.

'Very much,' said Caelir as Narentir handed him a silver goblet of smoky, aromatic wine. 'I have never seen anyone move like her.'

'I shouldn't think you have, she's a rare jewel is our Lilani.'

Smiling faces surrounded him as Narentir led him into the audience gathered about the rug. They were genuinely pleased to see him and Caelir felt the tension within his chest ease at the sincerity of the welcome.

He took a drink from the goblet and gasped in pleasure as it ran like liquid smoke down his throat. The wine was sweet, almost unbearably so, and its bouquet was that of a wild forest where creatures of legend still roamed free. Caelir smiled as it conjured visions of fabulous gardens, sun-dappled glades and the scent of honeysuckle and jasmine.

'You've never had dreamwine before, have you?' said Narentir as they sat beside the rug and the musicians began to play once more.

'Yes,' said Caelir, giddy from the taste, 'but this is good. Very good.'

'Be careful, though,' said Narentir. 'You shouldn't drink too much of it.'

'I have a strong stomach.'

'It's not your stomach you need worry about,' smiled Narentir as he took another drink.

'No?'

Narentir laughed. 'Do as you will, dear Caelir. Perhaps it will help your performance.'

'My performance? What performance?'

'Everyone takes their turn upon the rug.'

'But I'm not a singer and I can't dance,' said Caelir.

Narentir smiled. 'That doesn't matter. I'm sure you'll think of something.'

Caelir opened his mouth to protest, but the elves standing on the rug began their performance and all other sounds ceased as they sang ancient songs of love and rapture. He wanted to tell Narentir that he could not entertain them, but his enjoyment of the singers drew out a remembrance of the unknown talents Kyrielle had discovered within him.

Another sip of wine relaxed him and Caelir smiled contentedly as he settled back to listen to the performance. The singers' voices were exquisite, their music and lyrics swirling around the torchlit gathering like an unexpected, but wholly welcome guest.

Tears pricked Caelir's eyes as he felt his soul take flight in time with their achingly beautiful melodies.

The ride back to Cairn Auriel was without the magic that had accompanied the ride towards the White Tower. It felt strange not to be riding Lotharin, though Irenya was a fine steed and bore him proudly on her back.

They rode in silence for much of the way, Rhianna lost in thought and Eldain unwilling to break the silence for fear of what might be said. Yvraine once again rode with them, Mitherion Silverfawn insisting that the young Sword Master accompany them, though now she rode a powerful Sapherian gelding.

After seeing her martial prowess in battle, Eldain wasn't inclined to gainsay the mage, and welcomed her presence. If war *were* coming to Ulthuan, there were worse things to have at your side than a Sword Master of Hoeth.

The land itself seemed to recognise the strained mood that had settled upon them and restrained its more outlandish excesses of enchantment. Magic still permeated every breath and whispering sprites gusted through the long grasses with wild abandon, but Eldain paid such sights no mind, too preoccupied with Caelir's survival and the absurd notion of hunting his own brother.

The subject of what would happen when they caught up with Caelir had arisen when they drew near the cliff top path that led down to Cairn Auriel.

'I wonder if he will remember us,' said Rhianna, breaking the silence of their journey.

'I don't know,' said Eldain. 'He didn't seem to back at the tower.'

'But maybe seeing us jogged his memory, brought something back.'

'Perhaps, but will it make any difference if he does remember us?'

'It will to me,' said Rhianna. 'I can't bear the thought of him forgetting us.'

'Us?'

'You. Me. His life. Can you imagine how that must feel, Eldain? Not remembering your childhood, your parents, your friends–'

'Your lovers?' interrupted Eldain and he hated the caustic tone he heard in his voice.

Rhianna sighed. 'Is that what you are afraid of? That if Caelir's memory returns and we get him back that I will leave you for him?'

'Wouldn't you? You were betrothed to him once.'

Rhianna rode close to Eldain and reached out to take his hand. 'Caelir is alive and for that I give thanks to Isha, but I have made a commitment to *you*, Eldain. You are my husband and I love you.'

Eldain felt his throat constrict and squeezed Rhianna's hand, wishing he could truly believe what she was saying. 'I'm sorry. I just… I just don't want to lose you. I lost you to him once before and… I don't think I could again.'

'You won't, Eldain,' promised Rhianna. 'I can't deny that seeing Caelir again brought back a lot of emotions, but much has changed since he and I were together. You and I are married. And there is blood on his hands.'

There is blood on his hands…

Eldain fought down the guilty nausea building in his stomach as Yvraine said, 'There is also the question of what happened to him in Naggaroth. The druchii held him in the dungeons of the Witch King for over a year. The Caelir you both knew may no longer exist.'

'What do you mean?'

'I have heard it said that the loyal slave learns to love the lash,' said the Sword Master. 'Your brother may yet be an enemy of Ulthuan.'

'What are you saying?' said Eldain, hearing a cold anger in Yvraine's voice.

'I am saying that when we find Caelir, we may have to kill him.'

'Kill him?'

Yvraine nodded. 'Who knows what else he has been sent back to do? What if the trap to catch the Loremaster was just the first of his missions of assassination?'

'I cannot kill my own brother,' said Eldain, forcing the words from his mouth when he saw Rhianna's look of horror at what Yvraine had just said.

'You may have to,' said Yvraine as she reached the cliff top path. 'But if you can't, I will.'

The Sword Master rode onto the path that led down the cliff to Cairn Auriel and Eldain and Rhianna shared a look of unease as they followed her. The idea that their hunt might end in blood had clearly not occurred to her, but in Eldain's mind it had been the only possible outcome.

As he watched Rhianna ride onto the path, cold resolve hardened in his heart and he knew he would have no hesitation in striking Caelir down should the fates decree they stand face to face once again.

He had come so far and gained so much that he could not bear the thought of losing everything again. The guilt would always be with him, but no burden was too great to keep Rhianna by his side, no deed unthinkable and no price too steep.

A small fleet of ships bobbed in the glittering blue water against the floating quays of Cairn Auriel and red tiled dwellings rose up in tiered layers from the sea. Eldain thought the scene unbearably sad, picturing druchii ships sailing into the bay and fanatical warriors of the Witch

King butchering women and children as the streets ran red with blood.

He shook off such grim images and rode onto the path. The blooms garlanded around the trellises were now white flowers of spring and the fragrances were those of the dawn.

Eldain passed beneath the flowers and picked his way carefully down to the settlement.

Captain Bellaeir was pleased to see them again, for it sat ill with him to have a crew idle when there were seas to cross and magical winds to be caught in the sails. His sailors had made friends with the other crews berthed in the harbour and news and rumours from across Ulthuan had quickly passed between them.

Yet more druchii ships had been spotted off the southern coasts of Ulthuan, but had apparently made no forays to shore. The skies above the Annulii were thick with birds crossing from one side of the island to the other and it was said that the magical currents roaring through the mountains were becoming more powerful.

More and more creatures were coming down from the mountains, drawn there by the dangerous currents of magic, and hunters from Chrace were fighting a near constant battle against unnatural monsters preying upon the inhabitants of the northern kingdoms.

Vaul's Anvil rumbled and smoked as though the smith god himself was displeased and one crew claimed to have been caught in a storm in the seas around Avelorn, a sure sign of dark times ahead. Most of the other crews had scoffed at such a tale, but upon seeing the battering the ship had taken and the blackened scars of lightning impacts, they had retreated to their own vessels to ponder this evil omen.

More worrying, however, was the news that the druchii had landed on the western coast of Ulthuan. No one seemed to know exactly where, but as Eldain recalled Mitherion Silverfawn's warning of terrible danger descending on Ellyr-charoi, he feared the druchii were even now marching upon one of the gateway fortresses that protected Ellyrion.

All across Ulthuan, citizen levies were being armed for war and portents of doom were being reported from Yvresse to Tiranoc. As they had ridden through Cairn Auriel, Eldain had felt the potent fear of its inhabitants upon the air like a contagion.

Captain Bellaeir had taken the liberty of purchasing supplies for the journey, though he had not liked the news of their destination.

'The Gaen Vale?' he said with a frown. 'Not a place for the likes of us.'

'No,' agreed Eldain, 'but we have no choice. The Loremaster himself has despatched us.'

Bellaeir nodded absently and looked out to sea. 'I have sailed the waters of the Inner Seas for many years, my lord. When Finubar the Seafarer became the Phoenix King I saw the ironwood ship carrying him to the Shrine of Asuryan and followed long enough to see the great flame.

In my youth, I sailed as close as any have dared to the Isle of the Dead and I saw the day of my own passing.

'But in all my years as a seafarer, I have never once thought to venture near the Gaen Vale. The warrior women of the Mother Goddess jealously guard its shores and no male dares to set foot on that island. Any that try are never seen again.'

'Then you and I will be sure to remain on board the *Dragonkin* while Rhianna and Yvraine go ashore,' said Eldain.

Bellaeir sighed and left Eldain standing at the quay, directing Rhianna and his crew in getting the horses on board safely. They were intelligent beasts and none of them relished the prospect of being cooped up in the cramped hold of the sloop for several days.

Eldain couldn't blame them and shrugged apologetically as Rhianna's horse caught his eye and glowered at him. He saw Yvraine standing with her arms wrapped around herself, watching the sailors leading the horses onto the ship. The wind blowing in off the sea tousled her platinum hair and she was clearly not looking forward to another sea journey.

He made his way across the quay to stand beside her and said, 'It seems you loathe travelling by sea as much as our mounts, Mistress Hawkblade.'

'Can you blame me?' she said.

'I know why the horses dislike it,' said Eldain. 'In Ellyrion they are used to the freedom of the steppes, but why do you hate it so?'

Yvraine shrugged. 'I do not like placing my fate in another's hands. I prefer to be master of my own destiny.'

'Can any of us claim that?' asked Eldain. 'Does the will of the gods not shape our future?'

'I do not know. Perhaps it does, but I make my own choices and live by my own code.'

'Does that code include killing my brother?'

Yvraine shielded her eyes from the low sun and said, 'If that is what it takes to keep Ulthuan safe. Do not think to stop me.'

'If Caelir threatens Ulthuan, I will wield the blade myself,' said Eldain, surprised at the lack of feeling such an utterance caused within him.

'Then we understand one another,' said Yvraine, returning her attention to the horses.

'It would appear so.'

An awkward silence fell until eventually Yvraine said, 'Isha willing, your horses will soon know the freedom of the steppe again.'

'You sound as though you're not sure they will.'

'Perhaps I am not,' agreed Yvraine. 'You heard what Lord Teclis said. The druchii are abroad and war is coming. None of us may see our homelands again.'

'Are you worried you might not see Saphery again?'

'No,' said Yvraine, shaking her head. 'It is the fact that I am *leaving*

Saphery when war is coming that disturbs me. I should be with my brethren defending the White Tower as I swore to do.'

Eldain smiled grimly. 'If Lord Teclis is right, then all of us will have to fight soon. I do not think it matters overmuch where we make our stand.'

'It matters to me.'

'Then for all our sakes I hope your blade fights where it is most needed,' said Eldain.

CHAPTER FIFTEEN
CONFLUENCE

The morning sun rose higher, long shadows of dawn retreating before the advancing day and illuminating the valley before the Eagle Gate. Since the eagles had brought the wounded reaver and news of the advancing enemy, Glorien Truecrown had done all his books had recommended before battle.

Three riders had set off on the fastest steeds to Tor Elyr to bear news and request reinforcement, and scouts had been despatched to watch for the arrival of the enemy. Arrows had been stockpiled on the walls and every weapon checked and rechecked. The few mages attached to the Eagle Gate had spent the night in meditation, gathering their strength and powers for the coming battle.

He had personally inspected every inch of the wall and gate for weakness and had been relieved to find nothing out of place. As sloppy as Glorien had considered Cerion Goldwing's leadership, he could find no fault with the defences.

At midmorning the Shadow Warrior, Alanrias, returned and Glorien met him at the gate.

The news was not good.

'They will be here in an hour, maybe less,' gasped the hooded scout, blood coating his grey cloak where an iron bolt had pierced him. 'We harried them from Cairn Anroc, but the druchii of the Blackspine Mountains are skilled hunters and many of us were slain. Dark riders range ahead of the army, fighting running battles with reaver bands from Ellyrion.'

'Where are these reaver bands now?' asked Glorien, seeing no horse-men behind the scout.

'Most are dead, though some will have escaped into the mountains.'

Glorien thanked Alanrias and sent him to the healers before return-ing to the walls with Menethis at his side, trying not to let the fear that threatened to overwhelm him show in his long strides and confident mien. Together, they walked the length of the wall and Glorien took heart from the steely determination he saw in every warrior's face. He dearly wished he felt the same confidence as these soldiers, for he had never yet faced an enemy in battle…

He attempted to converse with the warriors, as he had seen Cerion do on many occasions, but his words were awkward and stiff and he gave up after a few attempts. Instead, he took heart from the sheer solidity of the fortress, its sweeping white walls high and impregnable, its towers proud and inviolate. Hundreds of elven warriors manned the defences and he was as knowledgeable as any noble who had commanded its walls.

Caledor had built his fortresses well and never once had a guardian fortress fallen to an enemy. That thought alone gave Glorien hope.

That hope sank in his heart as the sun climbed higher and the enemy host came into view.

They marched along the centre of the valley, thousands of dark elf war-riors in disciplined regiments, carrying long spears and serpent banners on poles topped with silver runes. Armoured warriors with executioners' blades slung over their shoulders advanced next to them in grim silence, banners scribed with the blasted rune of Khaine held proudly before them.

A ripple of horror passed along the wall as a trio of huge, black-scaled beasts with many serpentine heads was herded onwards by sweating beastmasters armed with long-tined goads. Acrid smoke seeped from the fanged mouths of the monsters and their roars echoed from the valley sides as they snapped and strained at the chains that bound them.

Glorien's eyes widened as he saw a group of prisoners herded before the monsters, their garb and fair hair marking them as warriors of Ellyrion.

'Oh no…' he whispered as one of the prisoners stumbled and was snatched up in the jaws of one of the hydra creatures. His screams carried in the cold air and Glorien watched in horror as the beast's many heads fought over the body, ripping it to shreds in a feeding frenzy.

Already blood was being spilled and the reptilian cavalry of the druchii snorted and clawed the ground as they caught its scent. The dark nobles who rode these beasts wore elaborate armour of ebony plate and carried tall lances, the dread symbols of their houses borne proudly on kite-shaped shields.

Flocks of winged creatures wheeled above the advancing army, leath-ery fiends of repulsive feminine aspect, filling the air with loathsome screeches.

Alongside the druchii, a horde of corrupt men marched with raucous cries while beating their axes and swords upon their shields. Whipped madmen capered before the horde, deviant slaves sewn into flesh suits fashioned from flayed elven skin.

Barbaric tribesmen bellowed and shouted, their bodies glistening with oil and gleaming with plates of metal fused to their flesh by unnatural magic. As brutal as these men were, Glorien felt his blood run cold as he saw the champions who commanded them, warriors who had sworn their souls to the Dark Gods and whose runes were carved into the meat of their bodies.

Each champion was surrounded by his own bloodthirsty band of followers: muscular beasts that walked on two legs, mutant horrors of indefinable form, outcast warriors touched by the warping power of Chaos and gibbering shamen uttering forbidden doggerel.

Thousands of warriors filled the valley and Glorien watched as the terrifying host halted just outside the extreme range of his bolt throwers.

'So many...' he said, his throat dry and his stomach knotting in fear.

Menethis said nothing, but pointed a trembling finger to the centre of the enemy horde.

Two figures rode towards the Eagle Gate, one an alluring woman atop a dark steed with sinewy wings of night, and the other a monstrously powerful man riding an enormous, skinless horse with its saddle and bridle fused to its exposed musculature.

'What should we do, my lord?' asked Menethis.

Glorien licked his lips and said. 'Nothing yet. Let me think.'

The two riders stopped and Glorien knew they were well within range of every one of his archers. He knew he could order them killed, but such a dishonourable act was beneath him. Men and druchii might behave without respect for the honourable conduct of war, but Glorien Truecrown was a noble of Ulthuan.

Instead, he took a deep breath and hoped his voice would not betray his awful fear.

'These lands are the sovereign territory of Finubar, Phoenix King of Ulthuan and lord of the asur. Leave now or die!'

The silence of the valley was absolute, as though the mountains themselves awaited the response of the enemy leaders.

The druchii woman threw back her head and laughed, a bitter, dead sound, and the giant on the glistening steed shook his head, as though he could taste the fear in Glorien's voice.

Glorien flinched as the woman's dark steed spread its wings and leapt into the air, its red eyes like fiery gems and its breath a snorting cloud of evil vapours. Though she wore no saddle and held no reins, the woman showed no fear as the evil pegasus carried her through the air towards the fortress.

'Archers!' shouted Glorien. 'Stand ready!'

Six hundred bows creaked as every archer on the wall drew back his string and stood ready to loose. Glorien would not kill an enemy who came to parlay, but this reckless ride was something different altogether.

Now that she was closer, Glorien could see that this was no ordinary druchii female, but one of incredible dark beauty, her pale flesh slender and taut and her hair a thick mane of shimmering darkness. She gripped the flanks of her mount with her thighs and Glorien knew he had never seen a more powerfully erotic sight.

'My lord?' said Menethis. 'Shall I order the archers to loose?'

Glorien tried to answer, but he could not form the words, his soul ensnared by the unearthly allure of this dark femme. His lips moved, but made no sound and he was struck by the sheer absurdity of fighting this woman.

He felt a strong grip on his arm and shook it off as he continued to stare at this vision of dark beauty. Nor was he the only one so afflicted, for many of his warriors were similarly struck by the incredible power of this druchii's rapturous comeliness, easing their strings and staring in wonder at this druchii.

Druchii…

The word screamed in his mind and Glorien gasped in horror as the spell of the woman's beauty slipped from his mind.

This was no ordinary druchii…

He let out a great breath, as his body threw off the glamours of the sorceress and gripped the white stone of the merlon as his legs threatened to give out beneath him.

Glorien turned to his archers and shouted, 'Bring her down! Now!'

Barely half the archers loosed, the rest still enraptured by her evil charisma, and at such close range, Glorien would have expected every warrior to hit his target.

But as the volley of shafts flashed through the air, a crackling haze of magic bloomed around the woman and the arrows fell from the sky as withered, ashen flakes. In response, she aimed her barbed staff towards the fortress and uttered a dreadful chant in the foul language of the druchii.

Howling winds, like the freezing breath of Morai-heg, swept over the battlements and Glorien cried out as bone-numbing cold seized his limbs. The deathly chill of the utterdark burned through him and an icy mist drifted over the battlements.

He heard screams as warriors dropped to their knees in pain, and glittering webs of frost appeared on the stonework of the fortress. Slicks of dark ice formed underfoot as Glorien's every breath felt like daggers of frost in his lungs.

'I can taste your fear and it pleases me!' shrieked the druchii sorceress with malicious amusement. 'An eternity of agony in the Chaos hells awaits those who stand before my warriors. This I promise, for I am Morathi and you are all going to die!'

* * *

The warm glow of the torches surrounded him and the applause of the audience filled Caelir with confidence as he made his way to stand in the centre of the rug. Smiling faces wished him well and he dearly hoped that he would not disappoint this gathering with his performance.

Narentir had given him a silver harp and he plucked a few strings experimentally, hoping the skills he had discovered with Kyrielle had not deserted him. The thought of Anurion's daughter gave him pause, but instead of pain, the memory awakened only pleasant memories and he dearly wished she was here to see him play.

'Come along,' said Narentir, 'don't keep us waiting all night!'

Good-natured laughter washed over him and Caelir smiled as he saw Lilani lounging at the back of the audience, watching him with naked interest.

He closed his eyes and though he knew of many songs, he suddenly realised he didn't know how to play any of them. A hot jolt of fear seized him as his mind went blank.

Had his unremembered talent deserted him?

The thought of letting down his audience terrified him and though he knew it was the dreamwine talking, he felt as though it would be the greatest failure of his life were he to stand here useless and without the gift of music.

He ran his hands across the instrument once more and then, without conscious thought or effort, his fingers began to dance across the strings. Golden music leapt from the harp to fill the night and Caelir emptied his mind of fear, giving his unknown muse free rein over his hands.

Delighted laughter sparkled from the audience and they clapped in time with the melodies wrung from his instrument. Caelir laughed as the music poured from him, fuelled by the appreciation of his listeners, and he knew that he had been accepted as one of them.

Before he knew what he was doing, he began to sing, the words flowing as naturally as though taught from birth:

Isha be with thee in every forest,
Asuryan at every day revealed,
Grace be with thee through every stream
Headland, ridge and field.
Glory to thee forever,
Thou bright moon, Ladrielle;
Ever our glorious light.

Each sea and land,
Each moor and meadow,
Each lying down, each rising up,
In the trough of the waves,

On the crest of the billows,
Each step of the journey thou goest.

And then it was over, the words ended and the tune played out. He lowered the harp and let the moment hang, his breath hot in his throat and the excruciating desire to please still hammering in his chest.

Heartfelt cheers and applause greeted his song and Narentir rose from his seat at the edge of the rug. His face was smiling as he said, 'Well done, Caelir, well done,' and pulled him into an embrace.

'It was just a simple wayfarer's tune,' said Caelir, faintly embarrassed by the praise.

'True enough,' said Narentir, 'but you sang it honestly and played it well.'

Caelir smiled and felt the muse within him cry out for more, but he handed the harp back to Narentir as another performer made their way to the rug.

Hands clapped his back and kisses were planted on his cheeks as he returned to the fold of the audience. He felt their approval wash over him and smiled as he was handed yet another glass of dreamwine.

Caelir passed through the audience in a blur, painted faces and smiles and kisses passing in a whirl of excitement and the rush of performance. He drained his glass and another was immediately thrust into his hand.

He laughed with them and joined in their applause as more performers came to the rug. A hand slipped into his and he found himself face to face with Lilani, her dancer's physique pressed close to his and her wide eyes looking up into his.

'Your song was sad,' she said, and her voice was as silken as her movements.

'It wasn't meant to be.'

'I meant beneath the words,' she said, leading him beyond the torchlight towards the grassy slopes of a low hill. 'Your heart is in pain, but I know ways to heal it.'

'How?' said Caelir as her hands slipped up and around his neck. Lilani pressed the curve of her body against his and without conscious thought he leaned down to kiss her. It was instinctive, and her boldness – which did not surprise him – felt like the most natural thing in the world. She tasted of dreamwine and berries, her lips soft and her skin cool beneath his hands.

With barely a shrug her robe and his clothes were discarded and they lay down in the silvered grass together as music and song and laughter drifted on the air.

But Caelir heard none of it, for there was only Lilani and the time they shared beneath the moon.

Caelir opened his eyes and blinked rapidly in the light of the risen sun. For a moment, he wondered where he was, and then looked down to see the sleeping form of Lilani, her arm draped across his chest. Morning dew glistened on her skin and he smiled as the hazy memory of last night's pleasurable exertions returned to him.

'Ah, you're awake at last, dear boy,' said a voice, and he looked up to see Narentir holding out a plate of bread and fruit to him.

Caelir slipped from Lilani's embrace and scooped up his clothes, feeling faintly ridiculous as he pulled them on before this stranger. He remembered hugging him last night and feeling as though they were as close as brothers, but without the effects of the dreamwine, he realised that he knew almost nothing about these people beyond their names.

His stomach growled, reminding him that it had been days since he had eaten, and he gratefully took the offered plate, wolfing down great mouthfuls.

'Thank you,' he said.

'You are most welcome,' replied Narentir. 'I trust you enjoyed yourself last night?'

'I did, yes,' said Caelir between bites of fruit. 'I have never performed before an audience before.'

'Oh I know, but I meant with Lilani.'

Caelir blushed, looking back at the sleeping dancer and unsure of how to respond.

Narentir laughed at his discomfort, though there was no malice to it, and said, 'Don't give it a moment's worry, my boy. Here, we do not restrain our desires with antiquated moral codes, for we are all travellers on the road of the senses.'

'The what? I don't understand,' said Caelir.

'Really?' smiled Narentir, slipping an arm around his shoulders and leading him towards the wagons, which Caelir now saw were lacquered in a riot of colours and patterns. 'I thought from both your performances last night, you were only too well acquainted with the life of the voluptuary.'

'Wait a minute...' said Caelir, as the import of Narentir's words sank in. 'You said *both* my performances?'

'Yes,' said Narentir, gesturing towards Lilani. 'Or did you think your singing was the only thing you had an audience for?'

Caelir blushed at the thought of having been observed, but there was no judgement or lasciviousness in Narentir's comment and he felt his embarrassment fade. Instead, he smiled and said, 'Then yes, I did enjoy myself. As you said, she is a rare jewel.'

'That's more like it,' said Narentir. 'That's the kind of attitude that will get you noticed in Avelorn. Now come on, sate your appetite and we shall be on our way.'

'Wait, you are heading to Avelorn?'

'Of course. Where did you think we were going?'

'I... I hadn't given it much thought, to be honest,' said Caelir.

'Everything happened so quickly, I didn't get a chance to think about it.'

'True enough, but isn't that just the most delightful way of living life?'

Narentir climbed onto the padded seat of the lead wagon and Caelir asked. 'What takes you to Avelorn?'

'What takes anyone to Avelorn, dear Caelir? Music, dancing, magic and love.'

Caelir smiled, bemused at Narentir's carefree attitude, but as he watched the revellers of last night rouse themselves from their slumbers and ready themselves for travel, he could not fault their enthusiasm in greeting the day. The group was made up of perhaps two dozen elves, and everywhere Caelir looked, he saw smiles and genuine affection for those around them.

Laughter and yet more music filled the air and to Caelir's eyes his surroundings seemed more vital, more alive than they had before, as though the land welcomed the travellers' joy and returned it tenfold.

He smiled as elves he had met only the previous night welcomed him with kisses and the familiarity of old friends. An arm slipped around his waist and he turned to see Lilani beside him.

'Good morning,' he said.

She smiled and Caelir felt a surge of wellbeing suffuse him. Perhaps she had indeed healed his heart as she had claimed she could.

'Do you travel with us?' she asked, slipping around him and planting a kiss on his lips.

Caelir looked at the love and friendship he saw in the elves around him and felt more at home than he could ever remember.

'I think I will be, yes. At least until we reach Avelorn.'

'Good,' she said, dancing around him with teasing grace. 'Because I think I'd like you to perform for me again soon.'

The island of the Gaen Vale came into view as a beautiful swathe of green, gold and sapphire. Glittering blue cliffs, shaggy with lush forests, rose from the sea and the scent of wild flowers and flowering plants were carried from its centre. Game roamed free within the low-lying forests and Eldain could see deer and pale horses running wild through the surf that skirted the western shores of the island.

The *Dragonkin* had sailed from Cairn Auriel with the first tide and Eldain had spent much of the journey sitting alone at the tiller with Captain Bellaeir, finding him a voluble conversationalist, so long as their discussions revolved around ships and sailing. The closer they had sailed to the Gaen Vale, the more excited Rhianna and Yvraine had become, their anticipation at setting foot on the hallowed soil of the Mother Goddess passing like a magical current between them.

Neither seemed inclined to discuss the island, as though doing so with a male would somehow defile the beauty of it for them.

He and Rhianna still slept together beneath the stars, but with each mile that brought them closer to the Gaen Vale, he felt the distance between them widening. He prayed that it was simply the proximity of the island and not some deeper gulf opening between them.

On the morning of their third day of travel, Captain Bellaeir stood on the tiller step and pointed towards an outthrust spit of rock fringed with tall evergreens. As the ship swung around the peninsula, Eldain saw that it formed the edge of a natural bay and he gasped as he saw the wondrous landscape beyond.

'Lady Rhianna, yonder is the Bay of Cython!' cried Bellaeir.

Rhianna and Yvraine joined Eldain at the gunwale and linked their hands at the sight of the island's beauty.

Golden beaches and verdant forests spread out before them, with crystal waterfalls tumbling from rounded boulders into foaming pools that ran to the sea. Flocks of white birds circled overhead and the sound of silver bells sounded from somewhere out of sight. The waters of the ocean were unimaginably clear, the sandy sea bottom rippling beneath the ship like the bed of the freshest stream of Ellyrion.

Eldain thought the scene unbearably beautiful, but as he looked over at his wife, he saw that Rhianna and Yvraine were weeping openly.

'What's wrong?' he said.

Rhianna shook her head. 'You wouldn't understand.'

He shared a look with Bellaeir, but the captain simply shrugged and turned the tiller inwards towards the shoreline.

No sooner had the vessel's prow turned towards the island, than a silver shafted arrow streaked from the forest at the end of the peninsula and hammered into the mast. Eldain ducked as the arrow vibrated with the impact and Bellaeir swore, turning the *Dragonkin* away from the island.

'They're loosing arrows at us?' exclaimed Eldain, catching a glimpse of a naked archer at the edge of the trees. 'Why are they doing that?'

'It's us,' said Bellaeir. 'It's because there are males aboard. I should have realised.'

'Then how do we land?'

'You don't,' said Yvraine. 'Lady Rhianna and I will have to swim ashore.'

Eldain rounded upon the Sword Master and said, 'It's nearly half a mile.'

'The island will guide us.'

'We'll be fine, Eldain,' said Rhianna, smiling as she looked towards the island. 'Nothing bad will happen to us here.'

Captain Bellaeir weighed anchor and the two elf maids stripped down to their undergarments in preparation for their swim. Yvraine reluctantly passed her sword to Eldain and it was clear how much it pained her to venture into the unknown without her weapon.

'Be careful,' he said as Rhianna took a deep breath at the edge of the rail.

'I will be, Eldain,' she promised. 'This is a place of healing and renewal. Nothing bad can happen here.'

'I hope you are right.'

She leaned forward and gave him a soft kiss, then turned and dived into the water with the natural grace of a sea sprite. Yvraine followed her a moment later and together they swam through the clear waters of the Sea of Dusk towards the beach.

Eldain saw more of the archer women moving through the forests as they shadowed these new arrivals to their island.

He hoped that Rhianna was right.

Hopefully nothing bad could happen here.

Rhianna swam with powerful strokes, the water blessedly cool and crystalline. The waves were small and the island quickly drew closer, as though the sea itself were helping to carry them inwards. Yvraine swam ahead of her, her more powerful, warrior's physique allowing her to pull ahead more easily.

She swam onwards, feeling the cares of the world melt away with every stroke. Ahead, Yvraine splashed through the gentle surf of the beach and Rhianna felt an irrational stab of jealousy that Yvraine would set foot on the island before her.

No sooner had the thought surfaced than it instantly washed from her mind as she realised how ridiculous it was. Yvraine was also a supplicant here by the simple virtue of her sex and a fellow devotee of the Mother Goddess. Competition between them was irrelevant. Such futile strife was the preserve of the race of males.

At last Rhianna reached the shallows and began wading ashore. She felt the welcome of the island in her very bones, as though it had been waiting for her for uncounted years, and she cursed that she had waited this long to journey to it.

Yvraine was waiting for her, her sodden undergarments plastered to her body, and they hugged as the island's joy filled them with love.

The ground beneath Rhianna's feet felt charged with the magic of creation and they made their way hand in hand up the beach, the warmth of the white gold sand between their toes delicious and warm. Gentle winds carried homely scents and a life-giving breath that seemed to reach out from the trees and draw them in.

'Which way do we go?' asked Yvraine.

'Just onwards,' said Rhianna. 'The island will show us the way.'

Yvraine nodded and followed as Rhianna set off towards the edge of the forest.

As she drew near the trees, Rhianna saw a narrow path winding upwards from the beach, its boundaries marked by gleaming white stones, and immediately knew that this would lead them to where they needed to go.

The warmth of the sun penetrated the leafy canopy and spears of light waved through the shadowy trees as they followed the path up through the forest. Though the path was long and the slope steep, Rhianna found the going easy, as though the ground itself rose to meet her every footfall. It took an effort of will not to abandon all restraint and sprint to the end of the path. She could see the same excitement on Yvraine's face as they passed between the ancient trees of the island.

The forest air was a tonic in her spirit, the cares of the world far behind her and insignificant in the face of the ancient power that lay beneath the earth here. The mages of Hoeth might wield power that could destroy whole armies, but not one amongst them could create life as this sacred place could. Who amongst the warriors of the world could match the awesome power of the Mother Goddess?

'Rhianna…' whispered Yvraine.

She stopped, though her feet ached to carry her onwards.

'What is it?' she said, turning to see Yvraine kneeling to examine the edge of the path.

'Look at this,' said the Sword Master, beckoning her over.

Rhianna tore her eyes from the inviting horizon and knelt beside Yvraine as the Sword Master dug rich, black loam from around one of the smooth white marker stones. Dark earth fell away as she lifted it from the ground, and Rhianna recoiled as she saw that Yvraine held a smooth, fleshless skull.

'Isha preserve us,' she said, now realising that all the white markers were similarly gruesome artefacts. 'Skulls? But why?'

Yvraine replaced the skull in the ground and said, 'I imagine that these belong to males who could not contain their curiosity.'

Rhianna felt a chill pass down her spine and the forest, which had previously been filled with light and promise, now seemed a darker and more dangerous place. For the first time, she understood that the energy she felt here was elemental and raw, the awesome power of creation without the discipline of intellect.

Perhaps Eldain had been right to counsel caution.

'We should move on,' said Yvraine.

'Yes,' agreed Rhianna, backing away from the buried skulls and making her way uphill along the dead centre of the path.

Their route curled uphill, weaving a circuitous route through shady arbours and golden clearings until, at last, they arrived at the edge of the forest and a rippling curtain of sunlight.

Rhianna closed her eyes and walked through the light, feeling warmth caress her skin with soothing, welcoming affection.

She opened her eyes and wept at the beauty before her.

CHAPTER SIXTEEN
DUTY

Rhianna had lived amid the magical wonders of Saphery and ridden the enchanted plains of Ellyrion. She had seen the glory of Lothern and marvelled at the rugged splendour of Yvresse, but nothing could compare to the wonder of the Gaen Vale. The landscape spread out before her in a rolling patchwork of bountiful forests, fast-flowing rivers and wide groves of graceful statues and temples of purest white.

Music filled the air, but it was not the tunes of elves, but the melodies of the earth: birdsong, the rustle of wind in the branches of tall trees and the gurgle of life-giving waters as they flowed from a rocky peak at the centre of the island.

Together the sounds of the island formed a natural orchestra that played the symphony of creation in every breath. She felt Yvraine's hand take hers and she squeezed it tightly as they made their way into the depths of the island.

'I expected it to be wonderful,' she said, 'but this... this is incredible.'

'I know,' agreed Yvraine. 'I wish I had travelled here sooner.'

Rhianna nodded, only too aware that she had meant to travel here after her wedding to Caelir. She pictured Caelir's face as she had last seen it, terrified and running for his life, and a strangled sob burst from her as a host of emotions, which until now she had kept buried deep inside her, were dragged to the surface by the magic of the Gaen Vale.

Yvraine stopped and said, 'Rhianna? What is the matter?'

'Caelir,' she sobbed, sinking to her knees beside a pool of mirror-still water. 'I can't even imagine the torment he must have endured at the hands of the druchii. I thought he was dead and I married another. I should have waited… I should have waited!'

Yvraine held her tight and said, 'You were not to know, Rhianna. His own brother told you he was dead. What more could you have done?'

'I should have known,' said Rhianna. 'I should have felt he was still alive.'

More sobs shook her frame and she cried into Yvraine's shoulder.

'I had a duty to him and I failed…' she whispered.

'No, you didn't,' stated Yvraine without pity, but not unkindly. 'He was dead and you moved on. Now you have a duty to Eldain and your duty to him is to love him as you once loved Caelir.'

Rhianna looked up into Yvraine's face and felt her composure return at the Sword Master's words. She smiled through her tears and said, 'Thank you, Yvraine. I underestimated you.'

'How so?'

'I thought you just a warrior, but I see now there is more to you than that.'

Yvraine smiled. 'I learned more than how to fight from Master Dioneth: ethics, philosophy, history and many other skills. If the Sword Masters are to be the eyes and ears of the White Tower they must know how to see through deception to unearth the truth.'

'Then is there nothing you fear?'

Yvraine considered the question for a moment before saying, 'I fear to fail.'

'To fail? You?'

'Yes,' said Yvraine. 'My first mission was to bring you to Saphery, but when we reached the Tower of Hoeth and the beasts of magic attacked, I feared failing Master Silverfawn more than my own death.'

'I never knew…'

'Like you, I have a duty, but if I fail in mine, people die and that is a heavy burden for any shoulders.'

'And how do *you* cope with such a burden?'

Yvraine smiled. 'I strive to do my duty to the best of my ability and through doing so, I learn a little more about myself. All any of us can do is our best and let the gods take care of the rest.'

Rhianna found herself admiring the youthful Sword Master more and more, pleased that she had been right to defend her against Eldain's opinion that there was no wisdom in wielding a sword for the Loremasters.

She shook off her sadness and felt the healing touch of the Gaen Vale flow through her as she forgave herself for believing Caelir to be dead. A warm, golden light built behind her eyes and she said, 'Thank you.'

No sooner had the words left her than a shadow fell across them and a skyclad elf maid carrying a moon-coloured longbow emerged from the undergrowth. Yvraine's hand instinctively reached for her greatsword before she realised where she was and that her weapon was still aboard the *Dragonkin*. Rhianna rose to her feet in surprise at the maiden's sudden appearance.

The elf maid's skin was unblemished and startlingly white, her blonde hair reaching down to the backs of her knees. Her features were thin, elliptical and Rhianna thought she was perhaps the most beautiful person she had ever seen.

'The oracle consents to see you,' said the maiden. 'You must follow me.'

Alathenar drew and loosed yet another arrow as the enemy horde came at them once again. The arrow thudded home between the neck plates of a warrior armoured in heavy plates of iron and he collapsed in a heap before the charge. Alathenar loosed arrow after arrow, his fingers and forearm raw from the volume of shafts he sent slashing into the enemy ranks. The day was less than four hours old, yet the defenders of the Eagle Gate had already seen off three separate attacks.

'Don't they ever stop?' he hissed as he loosed his last arrow and snatched up a fresh quiver from the ground.

'Apparently not,' said Eloien Redcloak, his shorter bow reaping a lesser, yet no less deadly tally than Alathenar's. The magic of the Eagle Gate's mages had saved the reaver's life, but Alathenar knew he should not be fighting, for his wound was not yet fully healed.

Despite this, Eloien had immediately taken his place on the wall and refused any notion of riding to Ellyrion. This enemy had killed his warriors and he had vowed to exact a measure of retribution for their murder.

Alathenar had liked his spirit and kept a wary eye on the reaver, fighting back to back with him on several occasions. Both immediately recognised the warrior spirit in the other and Alathenar could feel bonds of friendship forming as they often did between warriors in battle.

'Be ready with that sword of yours, Redcloak,' advised Alathenar. 'We're not going to stop them before they get to the walls.'

'Have no fear of that, archer. Just be sure to leave enough for me.'

Alathenar wanted to believe the Ellyrian's words were a jest made of bravado, but saw the grim set to his jaw and knew that no levity remained within the reaver.

The welcome *crack-twang* of the bolt throwers unleashing was audible over the baying of the corrupted humans as they charged the walls of the Eagle Gate again. A score of the debased followers of the Dark Gods were mown down like wheat before the scythe as the lethal hail of darts thudded home.

The valley floor was carpeted with the dead and wounded, bodies trampled underfoot as the howling champions of Chaos drove their followers forward with whips and threats. A tide of armoured warriors surged towards the walls, armed with roped grapnels and long ladders. Their raucous war chants rang from the sides of the valley and Alathenar knew he had never heard voices so filled with hate.

Blue-white rods of molten light leapt from the walls, immolating a dozen tribal warriors in a searing explosion of winged flames, and volley after volley of deadly accurate arrows sliced through armour and flesh as the defenders sought to keep the enemy from the walls.

'Ladders!' shouted Alathenar as an iron-topped ladder thumped into the wall in front of him, sending sparks flaring from the stonework. He stepped away from the battlements as a gold banner was raised and a disciplined line of warriors armed with swords stepped forward, glittering weapon points aimed at the tapered embrasures.

A roaring warrior with a monstrous axe appeared and Alathenar sent an arrow through the eye slit of his helmet. The man screamed and toppled from the ladder, but even as he fell, another warrior clambered up and Alathenar's arrow thudded uselessly into his raised shield.

All along the length of the wall, struggling warriors in fur cloaks and dark helmets fought to gain a foothold on the ramparts and the bloodshed was horrendous. Artisan-fashioned steel met steppe-forged iron in a clash of brute strength and martial skill.

Eloien stepped in close to the parapet and stabbed his sabre through a bare-chested warrior with a skull-fronted helm. Another warrior appeared and Eloien clove his sword through his shoulder, hacking the arm from his body. The tribesman fell from sight and Eloien reared back as a monstrous creature with the head of a snarling bear hauled its bulk over the pale stone of the wall.

Alathenar loosed an arrow that ricocheted from the braying creature's skull as it reared above the ramparts and Eloien lunged forwards to stab his blade through the beast's jaws.

The monster howled and bit down, snapping the reaver's blade. Another arrow hammered home in its chest, penetrating barely a handspan before snapping against the stone of the wall.

Eloien rolled beneath a sweep of its massive clawed hand and with a muscular scramble the beast was on the ramparts. Blood drooled from its jaws and Alathenar saw that its fangs were so monstrous and distended that it could not possibly close its mouth.

Screeching wails of the winged she-creatures sounded above him, but he could only hope the great eagles who had brought warning to the fortress could defeat them. He put the aerial battle above the fort from his mind as the mighty beast unlimbered a great hammer from its back and swung it in a wide arc.

Elves were smashed asunder by the blow, broken and dead as they flew from the wall to land in the courtyard far below. Alathenar threw himself flat to avoid the huge hammer's head and Eloien pressed his back against the wall.

The reaver swept up a fallen sword and slashed it across the monster's hamstrings.

The thick sinewy cords were like wet rope and the blade scored across the backs of its legs without cutting them, but his attack had given the defenders on the wall an opening. Two warriors armed with spears charged from either side and plunged their long polearms into the beast's flanks.

It roared in pain and Alathenar rolled onto his back, holding his bow side-on and offering a prayer to Kurnous as he loosed a pair of shafts at the beast's head. Both shafts struck home and gushing blood jetted from its torn throat.

The straining spearmen used their weapons to push the monstrous beast from the wall and Alathenar rolled to his feet as the sounds of battle rushed in to fill his senses.

Desperate clashes between elves and men and creatures that defied description ran the length of the wall. Warriors with swords defended the ramparts, while archers filled the skies with shafts and brought down the disgusting winged creatures that harried the crews of the bolt throwers.

Spearmen periodically surged forward to hurl the enemy back and flames of magic leapt back and forth: the blinding white of elven magic and the dark, purple fire of druchii sorcery.

Mystic sigils of protection worked into the stone of the wall dissipated the worst of the enemy magic, but each rune smoked and hissed as the dark arts of the Hag Sorceress gradually burned through their strength.

Periodically the wall would shake as the horrifying beasts the corrupted humans had brought to the battlefield hammered the gate below. Such monstrous by-blows of the Dark Gods were virtually immune to pain and only a multitude of shafts could bring them down.

Ladders were cast down by straining warriors and magical fire, and grapnels were cut with single sword strokes, elven steel easily parting the crudely woven human ropes. Spearmen thrust forward in linked ranks, pushing the enemy back from the wall, and the battlements became slippery with the blood and viscera of the dead.

'We have them now,' said Eloien, his chest heaving with the exertion of battle. 'They're fighting to live now, not to win.'

Alathenar nodded. 'Maybe so, but it's not over yet!'

He pointed further along the wall where a tribal war leader in a suit of dark armour had formed a fighting wedge and was pushing the defenders back with wide sweeps of a mighty greatsword. Dozens of warriors waited behind him and it would only be a matter of time until the enemy swept the defenders away.

Alathenar vaulted onto the saw-toothed ramparts to get a better view and nocked another arrow to his bow. He saw crossbowmen below taking aim and knew he did not have much time.

He waited until the warrior's sword was raised above his head and whispered, 'Guide my aim, Arenia my love,' and loosed a pair of shafts, one after the other. Both sliced through the mail at the warrior's armpit to punch through his ribs and pierce his heart.

Alathenar leapt down as a flurry of crossbow bolts clattered against the wall and the war leader fell to his knees, a jet of blood pouring from beneath his helmet.

The elven warriors he had kept at bay surged forwards, their speartips stabbing and driving the remainder of the enemy from the walls. The last of the ladders was cast down and archers moved to the walls to slay as many of the enemy as possible as they fell back to their camp.

A ragged cheer chased the corrupted ones away and elven warriors sagged against the stone of the ramparts as they realised they had won another respite.

'That was an incredible piece of archery,' said Eloien, cleaning his sword on the tunic of a dead tribesman.

Alathenar said. 'I have my true love's hair woven into the string.'

'Does that help?' asked Eloien, lowering himself to the ground with a wince of pain.

'I like to think so.'

He sat on the rampart as the reserve groups of warriors made their way up from the courtyard to take the place of those who had been fighting. The bodies of fallen elves were carried away to the rear wall of the fortress while those of the foe were hurled unceremoniously over the walls. Buckets of water sluiced the worst of the blood away and stretcherbearers carried injured warriors to the infirmary and the surgeons' arts.

'Shall we get down from this wall and have some water?' said Eloien.

'That sounds good,' agreed Alathenar. 'All too soon it will be our turn to fight again.'

'And when will it be your glorious leader's turn?' asked Eloien, nodding towards the imposing crag of the tall tower at the end of the wall.

Alathenar did not reply, but privately had wondered the same thing.

When *would* Glorien Truecrown leave his precious books to come down from the Aquila Spire and fight with his warriors?

Their guide led them through the wondrous valley of the Gaen Vale and the natural beauty of the landscape enchanted Rhianna with every step she took. All Ulthuan was a marvel of nature's genius, but here it was allowed its reign unfettered by the handiwork of the elves. Wild groves of apple trees and waterfalls filled the air with pungent scents of good earth and fresh water, and the magical creatures – unicorns, pegasus and griffons – that roamed freely through the forests were unafraid of them.

The deeper they journeyed into the high-sided valley, the more of its fey inhabitants they saw, dancers and archers who practised their arts in groves so glorious Rhianna felt her heart would burst at the splendour of them.

White marble temples sat in overgrown arbours, priestesses of the Mother Goddess pouring wine and honey on the sacred places as they gave praise for the fertility of the land. Kneeling maidens of Ulthuan received instruction from the inhabitants of the island and everywhere Rhianna looked, she could see welcoming smiles of acceptance at their presence.

From somewhere she acquired a floral wreath and the sound of haunting earth music came from ahead, as if to draw them onwards, though the island had no need of such blandishments, for their approach was a willing one.

Their guide had said little since she had surprised them, though, in truth, neither she nor Yvraine had desired to talk, so caught up in the wonders of the isle were they. The elf maid's body was hard and toned through a lifetime of duty and Rhianna had to force herself to keep her eyes from lingering too long on the sway of her muscular back.

Their path led them up through an archway formed from the overhanging branches of looming trees. Through the gently waving canopy she could see the tall peak at the centre of the island, streams of mountain water pouring down its flanks like trails of tears.

A wide stream tumbled energetically over a cascade of pebbles worn smooth over thousands of years and Rhianna felt her pulse quicken as they emerged from the forest and she saw a dark cavern ahead.

The path curled up towards the flanks of the peak through a procession of votive statues and piles of offerings to the Mother Goddess. Sparkling mist clung to the rocky ground before the cavern and shimmering rainbows arced from the glistening stones.

Their guide halted while they were still a hundred yards or more from the entrance.

'I can go no further,' she said. 'You must travel on alone.'

Rhianna looked towards the cavern mouth, its yawning darkness wide and fearful now that she knew they faced it without the protection of one who dwelled amongst its wonders.

'The oracle is within?' asked Rhianna.

'She is,' confirmed the maid. 'Now go. It is perilous to waste her time.'

With that warning, the elf maid turned and vanished into the forest as effortlessly as she had appeared, leaving them alone and uncertain before the cavern temple of the Mother Goddess.

The mountain loomed over them, powerful and frightening now that they stood at its base and saw the raw, hard-edged ruggedness of it. From a distance it had appeared regal and majestic, but here, its stone was dark and threatening.

'We should move on,' said Yvraine, when Rhianna didn't move.

'Yes...' said Rhianna.

'Is something wrong?'

'I don't know... I just feel a little frightened now, but I am not sure why.'

Yvraine looked from Rhianna to the cave mouth and said, 'I understand what you mean. I thought everything on the island would be like what we've seen before, but…'

'But it's not, is it?' finished Rhianna.

'No,' agreed Yvraine. 'This is different. Dangerous. But we should have expected this.'

'How so?'

'So far we have only seen the beauty of the island, but for everything of beauty there is a balancing darkness: day and night, good and evil. For everything wondrous in nature, there is cruelty to match. Nature is a bloody world of death and rebirth. So it is here too.'

'Now I *really* don't want to go in.'

'It is perilous to waste her time,' said Yvraine, repeating the elf maid's warning. 'I do not think we have a choice.'

'No, I suppose not,' agreed Rhianna, setting off with fresh resolve towards the cave mouth.

They climbed the path and as they reached the darkness of the cave Rhianna smelled the aroma of dark, smoky wood, as though a fire smouldered deep within the mountain. She caught the aroma of white poppy, camphor and mandrake, and her vision blurred for a moment as she took a breath of the aromatic smoke deep into her lungs. Rhianna saw flickering lights ahead and as she stepped into the cave, she saw bowls of oil on the floor, blue flames dancing just above the rainbow-sheened liquid.

The cavern walls were adorned with a multitude of paintings of the moon, new-blooming roses and writhing serpents. She walked deeper into the cavern, walking with the oil bowls to either side of her. Her eyes adjusted to the gloom, but even so, there was a darkness here that her elven eyes could not penetrate. The oil lamps created no smoke, yet she felt a cloying thickness to the air as though spider webs ensnared her every step.

Momentary panic fluttered within her and she looked over her shoulder to check that Yvraine was still with her.

She was alone…

Yvraine was nowhere to be seen and even the light at the cave mouth was gone, as though a great door had come down to block off the outside world. Rhianna fought down her rising unease and forced herself to continue, following the route of the dancing blue flames as it led her deeper into the painted temple.

The deeper Rhianna went, the more she became aware of a soft tremor to the earth, like an infinitely slow heartbeat, powerful and yet impossibly distant. She could feel it in the earth and in the air, as though the pulse of the world was all around her, and its rhythmic cadence eased her spirits.

The passageway widened and Rhianna emerged into a smoky cavern, at the centre of which sat a thick stone with a carving of a knotted net across it. Pungent smoke drifted from the top of the stone, and standing behind it was a hooded figure dressed in a long white robe and who carried a staff made from the branch of a willow tree.

'Welcome, Rhianna, daughter of Saphery,' said the figure, and the voice was powerfully feminine. Rhianna tried to reply, but the thickness of the smoky air coiled in her throat and she could not form the words of a reply.

The woman beckoned her forwards and pointed to the stone. 'At the birth of the world, the Emperor of the Heavens sent a phoenix and a raven to fly across the world and meet at its centre. Upon the omphalos stone is where they met and through it, the oracles of the Mother Goddess can speak to the kingdom of heaven. Though whether they understand the reply is another matter.'

'Where is my friend?' said Rhianna, her voice muffled and weak. 'Where is Yvraine?'

'She is safe,' said the oracle. 'This is not her time to learn of the future. It is yours.'

'The future...?'

'Yes, for is that not why you journeyed here, child? To know of things hidden and things as yet unknown?'

Rhianna felt a mounting terror as her feet carried her towards the smoking stone at the centre of the cave. This wasn't what she had come for, she didn't want to know the future.

All she wanted was to find Caelir...

'They are one and the same, child,' said the oracle, her voice rising in power and authority as she spoke words of ancient power:

'The New Moon is the white goddess of birth and growth;
The Full Moon, the red goddess of love and battle;
The Old Moon, the black goddess of death and divination.'

Powerless to resist, Rhianna placed her hands upon the stone and looked into its hollow core as the darkness of the cavern rose up around her. Her spirit felt as though it was being pulled down into the smoke and the hot breath of the gods engulfed her.

She screamed a wordless cry of anguish as images thundered through her, flashing swords and howling blood-hungry warriors, Caelir, Eldain and a wondrous forest kingdom of magic and beauty – not the natural magic of the Gaen Vale, but the artful enchantments of elves...

Fire swept over her and it seemed as though the cavern filled with roaring, searing flames that burned the paintings from the walls and seared the flesh from her bones. A whirling vortex of terrifyingly powerful energies swept over her and she was aware that she was no longer alone. A circle of mages surrounded her, their hands describing complex mystical symbols in the air and chanting words of ancient power.

Their bodies were wasted and gaunt and their eyes spoke of a suffering that never ended, an enduring agony that stretched from times forgotten to times unknown.

Amid the phantom mages she saw a laughing, raven-haired druchii princess, her beauty bathed in blood and her eyes full of an age's malice. She moved through the chanting mages like a dancer, spinning and leaping with a curved dagger in each hand. With each leap, a blade swept out to cut the throat of one of the mages and as each one died, the chaos around her surged in power.

'Stop it...' she cried. 'Please stop it!'

'No, child,' said a voice that sounded as though it came from a far distant time and place. 'Like all things a woman must suffer, this cannot be stopped. Only endured.'

The image of the murderous princess faded and Rhianna wept in relief as she saw the enchanted forest once again and the shimmering form of a woman so beautiful she could only be the Everqueen of Avelorn. The bright light enveloping her was a soothing balm upon her soul and she let out a great, shuddering breath.

No sooner had her racing heartbeat calmed when a black rain began to fall and Rhianna cried out as the dark waters stained the purity of the Everqueen's robes. Her face withered as the rain melted away everything that was good and pure of her, and as Rhianna watched, a bright red spot of blood appeared at her breast.

'No, please... no!' said Rhianna as the bloodstain spread like a blossoming rose.

As the Everqueen faded, the land sickened and died, the grasses turning black and the trees cracking and wilting as the life was drained from them.

With the last of her strength, the Everqueen looked up and her eyes locked to Rhianna's.

'Come to me, my child,' she said. 'He needs your help. Save him and you will save me!'

Rhianna closed her eyes and screamed as she saw a spreading bloodstain on her own chest. She felt the pain of a wound, the same sharp, piercing agony she had felt when the druchii crossbow bolt had pierced her shoulder so long ago, and her hands flew to her breast.

As her hands left the omphalos stone the pain vanished and her sight returned to normal. She slumped to the ground, her breathing ragged and her mind filled with the residue of what the oracle had shown her.

The darkened cave snapped back into view and she saw the oracle step around the stone to stand above her. Rhianna looked up, a glimmer of light shining beneath the woman's hood, and she screamed again as she saw her face transform.

In an instant, her face changed from that of a youthful elf maid to one of full womanhood and then to that of a deathly crone, ravaged and withered by time. Even as she watched, the cycle repeated itself over and over and Rhianna scrambled away, desperately pushing herself to her feet.

She turned from the oracle and fled the cavern temple of the Mother Goddess.

Tyrion knelt by his twin's bed and held his hand, watching his thin chest rise and fall, each breath a victory for his magically ravaged body. When he and his Silver Helms had ridden into the forest surrounding the Tower of Hoeth, he had been shocked rigid by the devastation he had seen, unable to comprehend what power could unmake something so powerful as the Scholar King's tower.

He had ridden hard and without pause, but when he had seen the ruin of his brother, Tyrion wished he could have pushed Malhandir to even greater speeds. Even before his wounding, Teclis had been slight and reliant on the power of magic to sustain him, but now he was a shadow even of that.

'Do I really look so terrible? ' asked Teclis.

'No,' said Tyrion. 'I am just tired from the ride south. You are looking better.'

'Ah, Tyrion, my dear brother,' smiled Teclis. 'You have too good a heart to be much of a liar. I know how I must look and I know that it pains you that you cannot fight it.'

Mitherion Silverfawn had explained as best he could what had happened to Teclis and Tyrion had kept vigil by his twin's bed, holding his hand and praying to Isha to grant him the strength to survive.

'I will hunt down this Caelir and kill him,' promised Tyrion.

'No!' said Teclis, pushing himself onto his elbows with a grimace of pain. 'Promise me that you will do no such thing, my brother!'

'But he nearly killed you! And who knows what else the druchii will have him do?'

'He is as much a victim as I,' said Teclis. 'We must not hate Caelir for what has been done to him. I need you to promise me that you will not harm Caelir if your paths should cross.'

'I cannot do that,' said Tyrion, rising to his feet. 'He is an enemy of Ulthuan and deserves only death.'

'No,' said Teclis, reaching up to grasp his arm. 'Please, Tyrion. Listen to me. You are a great warrior and your name carries great power. In the days of blood that are coming, your presence will be needed to steel the courage of all around you. If you give yourself over to this quest for vengeance, others will look for your leadership and they will falter when you do not provide it. You have a duty to Ulthuan and that duty does not include revenge!'

Tyrion looked at the urgency in his twin brother's face and took a deep, calming breath. He sat back down next to Teclis and said, 'I promised the

Everqueen I would heed your counsel.'

'And you can never disobey her,' smiled Teclis.

'No,' said Tyrion. 'It is the curse of males to be forever in the thrall of beauty.'

'Some things are worth being in thrall to.'

'I know,' said Tyrion, his earlier anger forgotten. 'Very well, if you will not have me hunt Caelir, what would you have me do, sail to Ellyrion and lead the defenders of the Eagle Gate? Rumours from the west say that the Hag Sorceress herself leads the armies of the druchii.'

'She does,' said Teclis. 'I have felt her power on the winds of magic.'

'Then I will go to Ellyrion,' spat Tyrion, 'and cut the vile heart from her chest!'

'No, for there are warriors there with the seeds of greatness within them and Ellyrion must look to its own defence for now. The hammer of the druchii will land elsewhere, and it is there that your courage will be needed most.'

'Tell me, brother, where will this hammer strike?'

'In the south,' said Teclis. 'Upon Lothern.'

BOOK FOUR
AVELORN

CHAPTER SEVENTEEN
SEA OF BLOOD

Of all the marvels of Lothern, the Glittering Lighthouse was one of the most famed and most magnificent. Rearing up from the sea atop a rocky isle to the south of Ulthuan, it was a great beacon filled with thousands of lamps that tradition held could never be extinguished. Mighty fortresses clustered at its base, each bastion equipped with scores of bolt throwers and garrisoned by hundreds of Sea Guard warriors.

Designed to protect the Emerald Gate that led to Lothern itself, the fortifications blended seamlessly with the cliffs and rocks of the island in a manner both lethal and aesthetically pleasing. The Emerald Gate itself was a mighty arched fortress that spanned the gap between the jagged fangs of rock that formed the mouth of the Straits of Lothern. A gleaming gate barred the sea route to Lothern, though such was the skill of the gate's designers that it could be opened smoothly and quickly when the need arose.

The fleets of the asur roamed freely around the southern coasts of Ulthuan thanks to its protection, for should any vessel be threatened, it could flee to the coverage of the war machines mounted on the walls of the lighthouse and the Emerald Gate.

The first warning of the attack came as low, lightning-split thunderheads rolled in from the south and a dusky mist drew in around the lighthouse. Its dazzling halo of lanterns faded until it was visible as little more than a soft glow from the watchtowers of the Emerald Gate nearly a mile away.

A looming shape, like a mountain shorn from the land and set adrift on the sea, hove into view, the wreckage of a silver ship smashed against its flanks.

A host of smaller trumpet blasts sounded from the lighthouse and magical lights flared in the gathering night as the elven lookouts recognised the mountain as one of the feared black arks of the druchii.

Cries of alarm passed from bastion to bastion and warriors rushed to the ramparts and Eagle's Claw bolt throwers were loaded with deadly bolts. A host of enemy war machines known as Reapers, an evil corruption of the noble bolt throwers of the asur, opened up from the ark and loosed hails of barbed iron darts from on high. Hundreds of shafts slashed through the air and, without protection from above, dozens of elven warriors were skewered and half a dozen bolt throwers were smashed to splintered ruin.

Coruscating fireballs of dark magic streaked from the crooked towers of the ark and exploded against the tower of the lighthouse. Streaming like horizontal rain, the purple fire of druchii sorcerers hammered the marble bastions of the island, searing flesh from the living and melting stone like wax.

Great rents were torn open in the fortress walls of the island and many brave warriors died as they were carried to their deaths by the collapsing walls. The black ark crashed against the island of the Glittering Lighthouse with the force of continents colliding, and a host of timber boarding ramps slammed down on the rock. Hundreds of druchii warriors stormed from the interior of the colossal black fortress, their sword blades reflecting the light of the beacon above them.

Fierce battle was joined as the Sea Guard of Lord Aislin rushed to plug the gaps torn in their defences by the druchii magic. Screams and the clash of blades echoed over the sea.

For all the carnage wreaked by the druchii, the defenders of Lothern recovered quickly from their surprise and fought back with all the skill and ferocity of their race. Hundreds of war machines opened up on the black ark and druchii were swept from their rocky battlements by a rain of lethal darts.

Magical bolts of white fire conjured by the lighthouse's mages erupted across the face of the black ark and the rock vitrified into glistening glass wherever it touched. The fighting on the Glittering Lighthouse waxed fierce as Lord Aislin's soldiers fought face to face with their ancestral enemies and neither side was in the mood to offer quarter.

The Emerald Gate groaned as the huge bronze valves to either side of the huge, arched fortress began to turn and, though it seemed impossible for such immense portals to move at all, they smoothly swept open to reveal the Straits of Lothern and a shimmering fleet of ships.

The elven fleet slipped easily through the bottle green waters, surging into the open ocean to engage the enemy. Hundreds of ships sailed through the gate, white sails bright in the evening sun and decks glittering with armed warriors. Such a fleet was more than capable of destroying a black ark and the warriors of the Emerald Gate held their fire as they watched the ships of the elven fleet sail out to do battle.

But as the mist parted before the lighthouse, it soon became apparent that the black ark had not come to make war on Lothern alone.

Captain Finlain watched with trepidation as the mist parted before *Finubar's Pride* and he saw the full scale of the approaching druchii fleet. A tightening of his jaw was the only outward sign of his concern, for he did not want his unease to pass to the crew. Though it was hard to be certain, Finlain estimated that nearly three hundred ships cut through the waters towards the Emerald Gate. Raven warships armed with fearsome Reaper bolt throwers and hooked boarding ramps led the advancing fleet in a wedge formation with the point aimed straight for his ship.

Behind the leading warships came a host of wide galleys with high sides and a multitude of decks. No doubt these ships were packed with druchii warriors and Finlain longed to get in amongst these lumbering vessels, where his newly mounted Eagle's Claw would wreak fearsome havoc. But Lord Aislin's plan had another role for *Finubar's Pride*…

A host of fighting ships followed behind the druchii troop galleys in line abreast, but his lookouts high on the mainmast had already reported that too wide a gap had opened between the galleys and this last line of ships to make it a truly effective rearguard.

Thunder boomed overhead and a flash of lightning briefly painted the sky in blue. The first spots of rain fell and Finlain could feel the swell beneath his ship gathering in strength.

Finlain smiled and Meruval the navigator said, 'What can you possibly find amusing in all this?'

'The druchii are fearsome warriors, but they are no sailors,' replied Finlain.

'How so?'

'These vessels are clearly new, yes? Normally they make war upon the sea from these damned floating fortresses, but they've yet to learn how to fight properly on a ship of war.'

'And we'll teach them a lesson in how it's done, is that it?' said Meruval, angling the *Finubar's* tiller a fraction to keep her in line.

'Indeed we shall,' said Finlain.

He glanced left and right, satisfied that his fellow captains were following Lord Aislin's hastily assembled battle plan. For all its ad hoc nature, Finlain had to admire the admiral's instinctive grasp of what the druchii attempted and how it might be countered.

The elven ships sailed into the worsening weather to meet the druchii, manoeuvring perfectly into line abreast with the ships on the flanks sailing slightly ahead of the centre. As the distance closed between the two fleets, Finlain spared a glance to his left where the sounds of furious battle carried over the seas from the fighting on the slopes of the Glittering Lighthouse.

'Asuryan grant you strength, my brothers,' he whispered, knowing that, for the moment, the warriors there were on their own. Flaring explosions of magical light and the tinny shriek of swords seemed pitifully quiet for what must surely be a desperate struggle to the death.

He shook off thoughts of that battle and focused on the bloodshed and horror in which his own ship and warriors were soon to be embroiled. The decks of *Finubar's Pride* were crammed with Sea Guard in glittering hauberks of ithilmar mail and her sails snapped and billowed in the blustery winds.

'They're coming on fast,' said Meruval.

'Good,' nodded Finlain. 'Their hatred will drive them on faster than any storm wind.'

His experienced eye watched the advancing wedge of druchii ships surge forward as their crews tacked into the wind with more skill than he would have expected and he cautioned himself against underestimating the druchii sailors.

The threatening wedge of dark ships was pulling ahead of the main body of galleys, no doubt hoping to punch through the thinner line of elven ships and scatter them before turning to savage them like a pack of wolves.

You'll think you're about to get your wish, he thought as he nodded to Meruval.

Closer now, the druchii ships resembled the long, dark birds for which they were named. Their prows were hooked and a boarding ramp with heated iron spikes stood ready to hammer into the deck of its prey. The glow of the lighthouse shimmered on hundreds of blades and Finlain shuddered as he imagined these warriors penetrating the defences of Lothern.

The druchii ships were almost upon them and Finlain knew he had to judge the next moment with exacting precision. Too soon and the druchii would realise his intent, too late and they would be overwhelmed and destroyed.

White foam broke against the sleek hulls of the Raven ships, sending high sprays of dark water over their decks, and Finlain could see Reaper crews preparing to loose their deadly volleys of black darts.

He turned to Meruval and said, 'Now, my friend.'

The navigator swung the tiller around and *Finubar's Pride* heeled violently to port. Either side of her, the entire centre of the elven fleet seemed to pirouette upon the sea. Crewmen raced to haul lines and swing the sails around to catch the same winds the druchii flew upon and the deck became a flurry of activity.

Finubar's Pride plunged into a trough of green water, a rush of the sea pouring in over her deck at such a violent manoeuvre, but Finlain wasn't worried about that. Within moments, his ship was aimed straight back at the Emerald Gate, the sails booming as they filled with strong southerly winds and a hard rain began to fall.

Like colts freed from the stable, *Finubar's Pride* and a hundred other ships raced back towards Ulthuan with the Raven ships right behind them.

'Well done!' cried Finlain as he heard the ratcheting *whoosh* of the Reaper bolt throwers loosing. He looked over his shoulder and saw the long, wickedly sharp bolts arcing through the rain towards them and then splash into the sea less than a spear length behind them.

The druchii ships surged after them, hatred driving them after the fleeing elven ships.

'Well, they're definitely coming...' said Meruval.

Finubar nodded, watching with grim satisfaction as the elven ships on the flanks of what had once been their line surged forwards into the newly formed gap between the pursuing Raven ships and troop galleys that was widening by the second.

'They're reacting exactly as Lord Aislin predicted,' said Meruval.

'Let's hope they continue to do so,' said Finlain.

Avelorn. Magical kingdom of the Everqueen and most ancient of the elven realms.

Every tale Caelir could remember of the enchanted forest realm had spectacularly failed to capture the beauty and sense of wonder he felt in every breath he took of the heavenly fragrances that hung heavy in the air. Everywhere were wonders for the senses; sights to beguile, scents to savour and sounds to revel in.

Music and song followed the company through the forest, some of Caelir's own creation and some of the forest itself. An air of barely suppressed excitement had seized the group as they crossed the river at the outskirts of the forest and Caelir had felt a potent sense of the ancient magic that lurked beneath the bewitching glamours of this land.

The air gossiped with news of their passing and tales of their songs, and each time they had crested a rolling hill or entered a different season of the forest, its inhabitants were ready to greet them with wine and requests for entertainment.

The journey northwards had been one of excitement and awakening for Caelir, and he had relaxed into a routine of talking and laughing with his fellow travellers during the day then enjoying the luxury of hot food and a soft bedroll at night. The rugged splendour of the Finuval Plain had eventually given way to the forested outskirts of Avelorn and Caelir had performed for the travelling company several times upon the rug, discovering yet more talents he had not previously been aware of. He recited long forgotten epics of Aenarion, played haunting laments from the time of Morvael and sang arias from the creation operas of Tazelle with Lilani.

The presence of such beauty kept the cares of the world at bay, and the blood and death that had surrounded Caelir since his awakening seemed to recede into the hindmost part of his thoughts.

Days passed in a blur of song and wonder and each time Caelir had thought his capacity for amazement exhausted, he would see yet another marvel to render him speechless with delight. In sun-dappled glades he saw elf maids clad in shimmering gowns of mist on the backs of unicorns, great, golden feathered eagles soared above the forest canopy and as they had descended into a shadowed dell, he heard the creaking, heavy footfalls of what Lilani told him was one of the ancient forest's treemen.

The dancer was a lover of rare vigour and nor was she shy in telling others of *his* prowess. On nights when the dreamwine flowed and ardent performances fired the blood of the company, they would take other lovers in the heat of passion and petty concerns such as jealousy and morality became irrelevant when art of such beauty and meaning was in the air.

Such behaviour was at odds with the disciplined life of the asur Caelir remembered, but he could not find it in himself to think of it as wrong.

He had spoken of this as the company penetrated deeper into the Everqueen's forest, and in answer, Narentir had spoken to him of the group's philosophies. They sat together on the padded seats of one of the wagons as Lilani rode beside them on Caelir's black steed and listened with wry amusement to their conversation.

'It's really quite simple, my dear boy,' said Narentir. 'To deny yourself the pleasures of the senses is to deny your soul its nourishment. Why would the gods have given us this capacity for sensual pleasure and enjoyment if not to use it?'

'I don't know,' he said. 'I don't think I'm much of a philosopher.'

'Nonsense, dear heart,' said Narentir, putting his arm around Caelir. 'Life is hard and every year it gets harder. Norse raiders attack from the sea and every day new horrors are unleashed upon the world. But none of that concerns us.'

'It doesn't?'

'No, for we are not heroes or warriors, are we? We are dancers, poets, musicians and singers. What possible use could we be in times of crisis? Folk such as us do not fight wars. We celebrate those who do in songs and poems. Without people like us, there would be nothing worth living for. A bland and tasteless world it would be without songs and singers to give them voice. So why let the cares of the world hang from our shoulders when there are elves like that golden fellow we saw with the splendid silver knights to bear them for us?'

Caelir remembered the armoured warrior with the winged helmet as he had ridden by them several days ago, and the strange feeling of accomplishment that had swept through him when they had ridden past still lingered in his memory. Only later had he realised that the warrior had been none other than Prince Tyrion and he wished he had savoured the sight of such a legendary figure.

'But surely everyone has to contribute to the greater good,' protested Caelir, dragging his thoughts back to the present. 'The citizen levies, for example.'

Narentir shook his head. 'Dear boy, can you see me as a soldier?'

'Maybe not now, but you must have spent some time in the levy.'

'I did, I did, that is true. I spent a loathsome summer in the ranks of the Eataine Levy and I was a terrible warrior. More dangerous to my comrades than the enemy I shouldn't wonder. Each of us has a place in the world, Caelir, and to try and fit where one does not belong is wasteful. When I realised this fact, I gave myself over to absolute pleasure and gathered like-minded souls about me to seek gratification in all things.

'Of course some small-minded types disapproved of wantons such as us, declaring we were little better than the Cult of Pleasure.'

Caelir's eyes widened at the mention of the dark sect begun by the Hag Sorceress many thousands of years ago. Its devotees had indulged their every sordid whim and desire, plumbing depths of insanity never imagined, and evil stories of their excesses were still told as cautionary tales to the young.

'I see you've heard the name, dear boy, but we are nothing like those terrible monsters, merely poor players who wish to wring each moment dry of sensation and indulge in our passion for the arts. I ask you, do we look like the sort to engage in blood sacrifices?'

Caelir laughed and said, 'No, you certainly don't.'

'Thank you,' smiled Narentir. 'And since we clearly were unwanted in Lothern, we decided to make for the one place on Ulthuan I knew we would be welcome.'

'And what do you plan to do now that you are here?'

'Do, my dear Caelir?' said Narentir. 'I do not intend to *do* anything at all, I simply intend to *be*. To sing songs and tell wonderful tales, to make love beneath the stars and to become part of the Everqueen's court.'

'And become one of her consorts…' said Lilani.

Narentir laughed and said, 'Perhaps even that, my dear, perhaps even that. For this is Avelorn and who can guess what miracles are possible beneath its boughs?'

The druchii galleys were monstrous ships, high sided and dark hulled, constructed in the hellish shipyards of Clar Karond. The vessels ran low in the water, such was the weight of warriors they carried, and displayed none of the usual grace of elven hands, even druchii ones, for they had been constructed with the bloody toil of slaves. These were simply hulks, fashioned to bear troops to another land and not to bring them back.

The Eagle ships that had sailed on the flanks of the elven line were wolves in a herd of slumbering sheep, their speed and manoeuvrability enabling them to slash through the lines of ships and attack with virtual impunity. Druchii crossbowmen shot iron darts from behind shield-lined gunwales, but the Eagle ships danced across the waves beyond their range.

Heavy silver bolts from Eagle's Claw bolt throwers smashed through the timbers of the troop galleys, wreaking havoc in the decks below as they speared dozens of warriors at a time. Hails of smaller bolts swept the decks of the druchii ships and they ran red with rivers of blood.

Elven mages hurled rippling sheets of fire from the forecastles of the Eagle ships and the tarred wood of the hulks burst into flame. The gathering storm clouds reflected the light of battle as a hateful orange glow and only the rain saved many of the hulks from instant immolation. The druchii ships attempted to sail close to one another for protection, but against the speed and skill of the elven captains there was nothing they could do but suffer the hails of blue-fletched arrows and lethal bolts that punched through their hulls and slaughtered their warriors.

The Eagle ships wove between the wallowing troop galleys like predators of the wild, denying them any respite from the killing. Flames leapt from ship to ship as flaming sheets of sail were caught on hot updraughts and set light to other ships.

Timber groaned and split as a druchii hulk broke apart and spilled its complement of warriors into the sea. Druchii screamed as they fell into the dark, flame-lit waters, splashing frantically as their armour dragged them to the bottom of the ocean.

The eastern flank of Lord Aislin's fleet drove many of the ungainly transports towards the cliffs of Ulthuan, where they would be dashed to destruction against undersea rocks.

The rearguard of the druchii fleet, seeing the horrifying carnage wreaked amongst the galleys, surged forwards and suddenly the Eagle ships were faced with a foe that had teeth and could fight back.

The Raven ships were larger than those of the asur, but no less manoeuvrable, and the battle degenerated into a bloody duel of deadly missiles as the two fleets darted between burning galleys and hunted one another in billowing clouds of smoke and ocean spray.

Thus far, the Eagle ships had had the best of the battle, but the Raven ships were not the simple prey the transport galleys had been.

Druchii sorcerers froze the water around the elven ships, whereupon they were ripped apart by hails of bolts or boarded by screaming warriors. Vicious boarding actions erupted as druchii assault ramps hammered against the hulls of trapped Eagle ships, and warriors fought to the death on the heaving, blood-slick decks of their vessels.

Sorcerous fire blasted great chunks from Eagle ships and sent them to watery graves as the sea poured inside their pristine hulls. The attacking rearguard reaped a fearsome tally of Eagle ships, but they were still out-numbered and without the added strength their vanguard provided, the Eagle ships could still win the fight.

Even through the rain, Captain Finlain could see the walls of flame from behind the pursuing Raven ships. Lord Aislin's flanking ships would even now be running amok amongst the slower, heavier transport galleys and druchii warriors would be dying.

The thought made him grin.

Their feigned retreat had drawn the wedge of the druchii ships forward and he knew it was time to turn and fight. The flanking ships would need their support if this battle were to be won.

But first the druchii ships at his stern needed to be sunk.

'How many do you think?' he shouted over to Meruval.

The navigator threw a glance over his shoulder and said, 'Perhaps sixty or so.'

Finlain nodded, agreeing with Meruval's assessment. Sixty armed warships was not a force to underestimate, but he had more ships and the best mariners in the world at his command.

And soon he would have the element of surprise when they turned on their pursuers...

The rain and wind were growing in power and intensity, but he had sailed the oceans of the world for long enough to know how to make use of such things.

'Meruval, prepare to turn about!' he cried over the howling winds. 'It's our turn to earn glory and honour!'

'Glory and honour, yes sir!' returned Meruval as Finlain marched between the eager warriors lining his deck. Their tunics were plastered to their armour by the rain and their silver speartips glittered with diamonds of moisture.

He nodded to these warriors as he passed, confident that they would smash this druchii fleet and send it to the bottom of the ocean, along with every one of their crews. They were almost within range of the mighty bolt throwers on the Emerald Gate and when they were, he would turn the ships of the elven fleet to face their pursuers as swiftly as they had turned away from them.

Caught between a suddenly resurgent foe and the lethal bolts of the Emerald Gate, the destruction of the druchii would be swift and merciless.

Finlain looked up into the sky as he heard a booming crack of air and awaited the flicker of lightning a second later. The skies remained resolutely dark and his eyes narrowed in puzzlement, but he put it from his mind as Meruval shouted from the tiller. 'Captain! Come quickly!'

Hearing the alarm in Meruval's voice, Finlain sprinted across the deck and flew up the steps to the vessel's tiller. He looked over the stern of *Finubar's Pride* and saw with horror the druchii were turning to rejoin the battle raging between his flanking Eagle ships and the enemy rearguard.

'What are they doing?' he cried as the Raven ships surged away from his ships.

'Looks like they're not taking our bait,' said Meruval.

'Quick! Turn us about!' shouted Finlain.

The *Finubar's Pride* angled into the sea and her sleek prow cut through a wall of dark water as she began a sharp turn. The other captains in his line had seen the same thing he had and were also bringing their ships about.

A tail pursuit was far from the ideal way to fight a sea battle, but Finlain saw they had no choice. If the enemy vessels earmarked for destruction at his hands were able to add their strength to the battle raging further out to sea then all was lost.

Once again Finlain heard the booming crack of air above him, but as he looked up once more, he realised that this was no peal of thunder as he saw a monstrous dark shape flash through the low clouds overhead.

He ran to the side of *Finubar's Pride* as he saw the dark shape drop through the clouds upon the silver ship next to his.

A terrifying reptilian shape, massive and scaled in darkness, spread its mighty wings and seized the ship's mast in its taloned hind legs. Timber shattered with a splintering crack as the boat was wrenched upwards and its keel split apart under the strain.

Finlain's heart turned to a lump of ice as the colossal black dragon was illuminated in a flash of blue thunder. Its great horned head snapped down and a handful of flailing elves were scooped up in its fanged jaws. Blood sprayed from between its teeth as it bit down and Finlain forced himself to act.

'Ready the Eagle's Claw!' he shouted as his archers took aim at the terrifying beast that beat the air into a whirlwind with its wide wings.

A streaking bolt of violet lightning leapt from behind the dragon's colossal head and Finlain had a brief image of a giant in dark armour sitting between the spines of the roaring monster. Cold green eyes glittered behind the figure's helmet and Finlain knew there was only one denizen of Naggaroth who encapsulated such force of hate and malice.

This was no mere druchii princeling...

This was the Witch King himself.

The dragon beat its wings and flew towards another ship, mercifully not the *Finubar's Pride*, and its jaws opened wide as a streaming cloud of hissing vapours erupted from its gullet. Finlain could only watch in horror as the ship's crew fell screaming to the deck, the skin melting from their bones and their lungs burning in the dragon's corrosive breath.

Arrows slashed towards the great beast, but its dark hide was proof against such irritants, and its diabolical rider hurled deadly arcs of lightning that set ships aflame with every flick of his clawed hands. Ships burned with magical fire or were smashed to matchwood by the power of the dragon. To their credit, Finlain's crew were able to loose a silver bolt at the rampaging monster, but the unnatural power of its rider protected it and the bolt burned to ashes before it even struck home.

A few captains attempted to sail clear of the carnage and reach the flanking Eagle ships, but the dragon and its hateful rider thwarted every effort, smashing them to ruin and slaughtering their crew. Ship after ship splintered and broke apart under the assault and Finlain saw that nothing could stand against such raw, violent strength.

'We cannot fight this!' shouted Finlain. 'Meruval, get us back through the Emerald Gate.'

The Witch King and his roaring dragon made sport of Lord Aislin's fleet and the destruction they wrought on each of their victims allowed a precious few of the remaining ships to turn and sail back towards Ulthuan.

Along with a handful of Eagle ships, *Finubar's Pride* fled the slaughter that was turning the ocean red and Finlain knew that, without support, the Eagle ships still fighting further out would soon be at the bottom of the ocean.

Through the smoke and fires of battle, Finlain could hear the blood-soaked victory chants of the druchii as they fought through the fortress walls of the Glittering Lighthouse. The shimmering beacon atop the lighthouse flickered for a moment in the storm-wracked darkness, as though fighting to stay alight.

He closed his eyes in sorrow as the light guttered and died.

The *Finubar's Pride* sailed between the great arched walls of the Emerald Gate and he whispered, 'Forgive us...'

The first battle for Lothern had been lost.

CHAPTER EIGHTEEN
KINSTRIFE

The mouth of the River Arduil was a gentle bow in the coastline of Avelorn, and Eldain felt his pulse quicken as Captain Bellaeir steered them around the forested headland that separated it from the Sea of Dusk. To walk in the enchanted realm of the Everqueen would be a new experience for Eldain, but even as he felt the breath of magic from the northern kingdom, he reminded himself that they were not travelling here as pilgrims.

Then as what? Rescuers? Assassins?

Eldain didn't know and nor did he know yet which he would prefer.

He looked over his shoulder to where Rhianna and Yvraine sat huddled in conversation beside the mast and suppressed a flash of annoyance. Since swimming back to the *Dragonkin*, neither woman had elaborated as to what had happened on the island of the Gaen Vale. Rhianna had simply told Bellaeir to sail for Avelorn.

The mood of the ship had lightened the further from the Gaen Vale they travelled and Rhianna had come to him one night as they sailed beneath the starlit sky with her arms open.

'You understand I am forbidden to speak of the island,' she had said.

'I understand,' he said, though, in truth, he did not.

'Can you tell me anything at all?'

'Just that we have to go to Avelorn.'

'Is that where Caelir is?'

'It's where he is going.'

Graham McNeill

'Why? Do you know?'

She pursed her lips and shook her head. 'Not for certain, but I am beginning to think that what happened at the Tower of Hoeth was just the beginning. Whatever Caelir was sent back to do is just beginning.'

'That's a reassuring thought.'

'It's not his fault,' said Rhianna. 'You heard what the Loremaster said. Caelir is as much a victim here as anyone else.'

He nodded, but had not answered, and took her in his arms as the ship sailed onwards.

'Save him and you save me...' she whispered in the darkness.

'What's that? A quote?'

'No, something I heard. Something important.'

'What does it mean?'

'I don't know yet.'

She burrowed deeper into his embrace as a chill gust blew in off the water and a red shooting star flashed south across the blackness of the sky. They stayed that way, like a statue of embracing lovers, as night turned to day and the sea transformed from a dark mirror of the heavens to a glorious green.

Morning brought the coast of Avelorn into view and the sight of land that he could actually walk upon raised Eldain's spirits immeasurably. He made his way from the vessel's prow to the tiller, where Captain Bellaeir sat enjoying the stiff breeze blowing from the kingdom of the Everqueen.

'Captain,' he said, resting his arm on the raised gunwale.

'My lord,' nodded the ship's master. 'Isha willing, I'll have you in Avelorn in a few hours.'

'That sounds good,' said Eldain. 'I mean no disrespect when I say this, but it will be good to set foot on land once more.'

Bellaeir nodded. 'Spoken like a true Ellyrian, my lord. But you are right, it will do us all good to be off the seas for a spell.'

The sentiment surprised Eldain and he said, 'Really? I thought you would be happy to spend your whole life at sea.'

'Normally I would be,' agreed Bellaeir, 'but there are dark currents stirring in the waters and they are full of sadness. I don't know where, but somewhere elves are dying at sea.'

Eldain heard the pain in Bellaeir's voice and decided not to press the point as the captain guided them towards the river's mouth.

Towering trees rose up from the edge of the land, sprawling forests that stretched eastwards as far as the eye could see in vivid splashes of green, russets and gold. Misty with distance, the blue crags of the Annulii were a far distant smudge on the horizon, a barrier between the kingdom of the Everqueen and war-torn Chrace.

The *Dragonkin* eased past the forested headlands and Eldain narrowed his eyes as he saw a froth of white water bubbling where the placid waters of the river met the sea.

'Water sprites,' said Bellaeir as he saw Eldain's expression. 'We call them *keylpi* and they are playful things mostly, but don't get too close to them.'

As the ship drew nearer, Eldain saw the suggestion of white horses cavorting in the depths of the water and fancied he could hear their whinnying neighs of amusement in the foam that surrounded them. The sprites moved alongside the ship and Eldain saw the ghostly horses of shimmering light galloping beneath the surface, their manes flowing with the current and their tails a fan of white bubbles behind them.

The urge to ride such a beast was almost irresistible, and his Ellyrian soul ached to climb upon its back and ride the waves, but such creatures were said to be capricious entities, as likely to drag him to his death as they were to grant him an exhilarating ride.

Eldain could hear the stamping hooves of their own horses in the ship's hold and knew they must also be sensing the siren song of the magical water horses. He turned away from the *keylpi*, hearing their displeasure as a crash of water against the side of the ship. A wave splashed over the gunwale and Bellaeir laughed as Eldain was drenched in water.

'I told you not to get too close,' said Bellaeir.

Eldain shrugged and went below to change his clothes, and when he emerged the water sprites were far behind them. The *Dragonkin* had passed from the Sea of Dusk and into the River Arduil, the waterway that marked the border between Ellyrion and Avelorn.

To the west, golden plains basked beneath an indolent summer sky and a sudden stab of homesickness pierced Eldain as he pictured his home of Ellyr-charoi. He saw the white-walled villa nestling between the two waterfalls, the heights of the Hippocrene Tower, the Summer Courtyard and the sweet smelling pines that shawled the landscape around it.

He missed his home. He longed to see it once again and to share it with Rhianna before leaving it forever.

Eldain shook off these reminiscences and turned from the land of his birth to face the kingdom of Avelorn.

Shaggy with dense and sprawling forest, the sound of distant music drifted on the air and twinkling lights seemed to dance in the forest's depths. Colourful birds nested in the treetops and a sense of powerful magic threaded between the smooth trunks.

The forests of Ellyrion had a youthful splendour to them, but Avelorn was of an age beyond reckoning, its farthest depths home to creatures that had dwelled there even before the coming of the asur: eagles, treemen and slumbering things whose names had been forgotten.

The forest had an eternal quality to it, an ageless majesty that not even invasion and war could diminish. The druchii had tried to burn the old forest, setting fires amid groves that had been planted when the world was young, but even they had failed to diminish its grandeur.

Trees that had stood sentinel over the Everqueen's realm towered above them like grim watchtowers and Eldain felt a brooding hostility from the forest's edge, as though their shadows cast a grim warning to any who harboured evil thoughts in their heart.

Eldain shivered and the *Dragonkin* sailed on.

The sounds of battle echoed within the Aquila Spire and Glorien Truecrown could not shut it out no matter how hard he tried. He concentrated on his books, desperate to find some clue as to how to defeat the foe that daily hurled itself at the walls of the Eagle Gate. The bloodshed was prodigious and hundreds of the followers of the Dark Gods were dying every day, pierced by arrows, hurled from the walls or cut down by graceful blows from swords and spears.

Thus far the druchii had not attacked, save by sending in the disgusting flying creatures that filled the air with their unmusical screeches and swooped on the crews of the bolt throwers. Morathi was content to batter the humans against the wall and her monstrous ally, the great tribal warleader with the standard revering the Dark Prince, seemed eager to let her.

Screaming tribesmen erected mounds of their fallen and made sport of the flesh before burning them in great funeral pyres and conducting their filthy worship in full view of the fortress. The sight of such unclean devotions had made Glorien sick and driven him to his books, his precious books, to seek a solution.

But he had found nothing, despite days of searching, and the brawling sound of battle from beyond the locked door and shuttered windows of the tower continued unabated.

Glorien had sent desperate petitions for more warriors to Tor Elyr, but his mages reported that a terrible sea battle had been lost at the gates of Lothern and all musters of the citizen levy were being sent to Eataine. Some *were* gathering in Ellyrion, but not enough, and not with enough speed to take the pressure off the warriors fighting on the bloody ramparts.

Casualty lists spoke of a hundred dead warriors already, with almost twice that injured. Many of those would not live to fight again and those that might would not heal in time to make any difference. The healers worked day and night, but they were too few and the enemy was sending them victims too quickly.

A sharp rapping came at the tower's only door and Glorien flinched at the sound.

'My lord, I must speak with you,' said a voice he recognised as belonging to Menethis.

Glorien rose from behind the desk and said, 'Are you alone?'

'Yes, my lord. There is no one with me.'

'Very well,' said Glorien and unbarred the door.

Menethis entered with unseemly haste and Glorien caught a glimpse of the fighting behind him. Once again, a host of ladders had been thrown against the wall, a trail of dead and wounded bodies scattered over the ground before it. Arrows and bolts filled the air as flocks of winged beasts circled above the towers, and desperate combats surged and withdrew like a dark tide along the length of the ramparts.

Glorien slammed the door shut as soon as Menethis was inside, unwilling to look upon the fighting raging below.

'What is it, Menethis?' said Glorien. 'I am very busy here. I am looking for a way to win this fight and I cannot do it with constant interruptions.'

'My lord, the situation below is desperate.'

'You think I don't know that?' said Glorien, indicating the piles of books scattered on the desk. 'The answer is in here, I know it.'

'With respect, my lord, it is not,' said Menethis, taking his arm firmly and pointing at the shuttered window. 'It is out there on the walls with the warriors who are fighting and dying to defend this fortress.'

Glorien threw off his second in command's grip. 'Ah, yes... but I found a passage in the works of Aethis. Here, look, it's in *Theories of War*.' Glorien scanned down the page until he found the specific passage he was looking for and held it up before him. 'Here, listen to this. "Any competently commanded fortress can expect to withstand a siege for an indefinite period of time so long as its garrison is well supplied, courageous and the enemy has not more than a three to one superiority of numbers." So you see, Menethis, everything hinges on the courage of the warriors. Only they can let us down, since we are well supplied, yes?'

'That was written a long time ago, my lord and Aethis was no soldier, he was a poet and a singer who fancied himself as a great leader. He never fought in a single battle.'

Glorien said, 'I know all that, but he was a *thinker*, Menethis, a thinker. His ideas are astounding. I know that if I can just–'

'My lord, I beg you!' cried Menethis. 'You have to come out and fight with our warriors. Morale is practically nonexistent and it is only the likes of Alathenar and Eloien Redcloak that are holding us together. You need to be seen, my lord! You need to fight!'

'No, no...' said Glorien, returning to sit behind the desk and placing his hand upon the scattered tomes. 'My books tell me that if the commander of an army should fall, it is disastrous for morale. No, I'll not expose myself to such danger until the time is right!'

'That time is now, my lord,' said Menethis.

Soaring high above the bloody fighting on the Eagle Gate, Elasir and his two brothers swooped across the mountains as they sought out enemy warriors to attack. The skies above the fortress were clear now, for they had driven off the twisted harpy creatures, though the golden feathers of all three were bloodied and torn. Elasir himself sported a ragged scar, red and angry, across his white crown.

Though battles such as the one now being fought in the mountains were not to their liking, they had nested in the high eyries and lent what aid they could to the defenders of the Eagle Gate. As battle raged they would swoop low over the walls, tearing off heads and slashing limbs with their claws and beaks.

Druchii crossbowmen tried to bring them down, but the eagles were too swift for them to hit and the cry of the eagles soon became the terror of the Asur's enemies. At the sight of the diving eagles, men would scatter in panic and druchii would desperately try to gather enough crossbows to fill the sky with bolts.

Elasir turned and extended his wings, slowing his flight as he spied a foe worthy of their strength.

Approaching the gate, he said, bringing his wings back in and turning in a tight circle.

His brothers had also spotted the danger and angled their course to match his, tucking their wings in close to their bodies as they plummeted back down towards the valley.

Drawing close to the gate was a monstrous hydra, a many-headed monster with iridescent scales, roaring and tearing the ground as a pack of straining druchii drove it forward with barbed tridents and vile curses. Its multiple heads writhed on long, sinuous necks, and sulphurous smoke billowed from each set of snapping jaws. Long spines like blistered growths sprouted from its back and a viscous slime seeped from weeping sores along its flanks where heavy iron plates had been fastened to its body with long chains and barbed hooks.

Volleys of arrows bounced from its armour or stuck in its flesh, but the monster was impervious to such minor wounds. Shouted cries echoed from the walls as war machines were brought to bear.

The eagles dived towards the hydra as its heads snapped forwards at a shouted command enforced by a barbed goad. A tremendous stream of liquid flame erupted from every mouth and the ramparts were bathed in searing fire. Elven warriors screamed as the creature's blazing excretions set them alight and gobbets of blazing sputum drooled down the wall.

Heavy bolts from asur war machines stabbed through the air towards the beast. Some ricocheted from the armoured plates while others penetrated its massive body with spurts of black ichor.

Elasir sensed the Chaos taint within its flesh and knew the beast would not stop until every last drop of blood had been wrung from its body. He let loose a terrifying cry and opened his wings with a great boom and swung his claws around beneath his body.

Crossbow bolts slashed the air, but none came close to the diving eagles.

The hydra's nearest head twisted in the air like a snake as it heard their cry. Its jaws opened wide, but Elasir was already upon it. His iron hard claws raked across its skull, ripping through flesh and tearing into its dark, soulless eyes.

The head bucked under the assault and tore free from his claws in a wash of blood. The eagles surrounded the hydra in a flurry of beating wings and powerful claws, tearing at its heads with vicious slashes of their beaks. Flames bloomed and Elasir heard Irian cry in pain as his feathers caught light.

Druchii warriors flocked around the beast, and Elasir dropped to land on the nearest, tearing his head off with a casual flick of his beak. Blood fountained and the eagle launched himself at the others as they levelled crossbows of dark wood.

Some ran and lived. Others stood their ground and died.

Elasir leapt back into the air and with powerful beats of his wings he came upon the hydra from behind. His golden brothers still fought the madly twisting heads, two of which lay limp and dead while three others fought with manic energy and terrible fury.

The lord of the eagles lunged forwards and fastened his claws on the base of one of the necks still fighting. The hydra bucked as it felt him land on its body, but his claws were dug into its hide and it could not dislodge him. Elasir's beak slashed into the meat and bone of its neck, slicing through it with three swift blows.

Druchii warriors swarmed around the beast, but were forced to keep their distance by the madly thrashing mêlée. Bolts filled the air and Elasir felt one score across his chest. Aeris opened the throat of another head and Irian blinded the last with a vicious sweep of his razored beak.

Helpless, the creature trampled druchii and men underfoot as it thrashed in its death agonies. The beast was as good as finished, and its final, frenzied moments would see yet more of the enemy dead.

The time had come to leave.

Fly, my brothers, cried Elasir, spreading his wings and taking to the air as yet more druchii ran towards the battle with crossbows. Fast or not, the lord of the eagles knew that with so many bolts in the air, at least some were sure to hit their targets.

Leaving the dying hydra behind them, the three eagles flew to safety.

Alathenar slumped against the parapet, drawing his thighs up to his chest and resting his forehead on his knees. His body ached from exertion and a score of cuts he could not remember receiving.

The valley seemed abruptly silent now that the clamour of fighting had faded. To Alathenar's ears, days had two states: one of screaming steel and one of just screaming. As the sun dipped into the west and long shadows crept into the courtyard of the fortress, the sounds transitioned from the former to the latter as wounded warriors were carried from the walls and the routine of clearing the enemy dead began.

He was too exhausted to move and simply nodded as a wounded elf with his arm missing below the elbow handed him fresh quivers from a pannier slung around his neck.

Victual bearers made their way along the wall and Alathenar gratefully took a battered silver goblet of cool water and a hunk of waybread. Only when sluicers came to clean the wall of blood did he force his battered frame upright and make his way to the courtyard.

Eloien Redcloak was already there and arguing with the fortress's master of horses, but gave up and walked away when he saw Alathenar descending the cut stairs.

'Still alive then?' said the reaver.

'Just about,' agreed Alathenar. 'What was that about?'

'The fool wants to run the horses down to Ellyrion, but I told him we need them here.'

'For when we have to abandon this place and run,' finished Alathenar.

'Just so.'

'So you are not hopeful that we'll hold.' It wasn't a question.

'Are you?' countered Eloien.

'We may yet.'

'Don't be naïve, my friend. Look at the faces around you. The warriors are exhausted, leaderless and, worse, they have no hope.'

They walked over to a bench carved into the base of the Eagle Tower and sat in companionable silence for a few restful minutes to gather their strength. So far, the enemy had displayed an unwillingness to attack at night, content with burning corpses and chanting praises to the Dark Gods, but both warriors knew it was just a matter of time until such a ruse was attempted.

Eloien glanced up at the tall spike of the Aquila Spire. Yellow light seeped from the edges of the shuttered windows.

'Do you think he is ever going to come out of there?' asked the reaver.

'I don't know. I wish Cerion still commanded.'

'He was a good warrior?'

'One of the best,' nodded Alathenar. 'Knew when to keep to the rules and when to bend them. He had the heart of a Chracian lion, though he took a druchii blade to the face and never got his looks back.'

Alathenar jerked his thumb at the rearing length of the wall and said, 'He would have seen this rabble off in no time, but Glorien…'

'Is an idiot,' said Eloien, 'a noble born fool who wouldn't know which end of a sword to hold and will see us all dead before he comes out of that tower. We'd be better off without him. What about his second? I've seen him fighting, but what is he like as a leader?'

'Menethis? More of a follower than a leader, but his heart is good. Why?'

'No reason, I just wondered if we might not be better off with someone else in charge?'

'Someone like Menethis?'

'Maybe, but as you say, he's not really what you would call leadership material.'

'Then who were you thinking of?'

'Don't be obtuse, Alathenar,' said Eloien. 'I've seen the way the warriors look to you and take your lead in all things. I'm talking about you.'

'Me? No… I'm not a leader, don't talk nonsense.'

'Nonsense, my friend? Nonsense would be letting Glorien Truecrown's cowardice lead us to death. Nonsense would be sitting and doing nothing about it.'

'Be that as it may, Glorien is the commander of the Eagle Gate and there's nothing we can do about that.'

'Maybe, maybe not,' said Eloien nodding thoughtfully and leaning forward, resting his elbows on his knees as a warrior Alathenar had not previously noticed emerged from the shadows beside them.

From his intense features and the skilful way he had concealed himself, Alathenar knew him to be one of the Nagarythe, and a shiver of apprehension worked its way down his spine.

'This is Alanrias,' said Eloien by way of introduction.

'I know who he is,' said Alathenar as Eloien continued.

'It is time to face up to the truth of our situation, my friend. If Glorien Truecrown remains in command of the Eagle Gate, it will fall. You know that to be true, I can see it in your eyes.'

'So what are you suggesting?' asked Alathenar, his gaze shifting from Eloien to the Shadow Warrior.

'You *know* what we are suggesting,' hissed Alanrias.

'This is sedition,' said Alathenar, rising to his feet. 'I could be executed just for hearing this.'

Eloien rose with him and said. 'You know I'm right, Alathenar.'

He took a deep breath. 'I will think on what you have said.'

The coarse, braying note of a tribal horn sounded from beyond the wall, echoing from the valley sides, and warriors began hurrying to the battlements.

'Don't think for too long,' advised Eloien.

The storm had passed and the sea at the gates of Lothern was calm once more.

Smashed timbers and the dead bodies as yet untouched by sharks floated on the surface in sad bobbing clumps of defeat. Barely a handful of elven vessels had managed to escape into the sanctuary of the Straits of Lothern, the rest now little more than wreckage and grief.

The defenders of the Emerald Gate could only watch in impotent horror as the druchii fleet landed its surviving troop galleys on the island of the Glittering Lighthouse, its beacon extinguished and its walls home to the victorious warriors of Naggaroth. The Eagle ships had destroyed a great many of the troop galleys, but the returning vanguard of the druchii fleet had attacked without mercy and the slaughter had been tremendous.

Not a single Eagle ship survived the night and the druchii now had control of the ocean before the gates of Lothern. Sleek and deadly Raven ships patrolled the sea around the island of the lighthouse, alert for any counterattack and taking care to remain beyond the range of the Emerald Gate's war machines. Hulking galleys hove to alongside the island of the lighthouse in grim procession and thousands of dark-cloaked warriors marched from the packed holds with their spears glinting.

As each vessel was emptied, it would sail around the southern coast of the island to join a growing line of wide-bodied ships anchored side-by-side to form a great bridge between the island of the lighthouse and Ulthuan. Thick hawsers were lashed between the galleys and anchored to the land at either end.

Atop the ruined peak of the lighthouse, the armoured form of the Witch King sat astride his mighty dragon, Seraphon, and watched the labours below with grim satisfaction. Hundreds of warriors garrisoned the captured fortifications of the island and thousands more were disembarking from the galleys in preparation of marching on Ulthuan itself.

The Witch King knew that attacking the Emerald Gate from the sea was as close to impossible as made no difference, but if the fortresses guarding the shoulder haunches of the arching fortress could be taken…

The great, black-scaled dragon leapt from the ruined lighthouse and spread its midnight wings as it swooped down over the island with a bellowing roar of challenge.

CHAPTER NINETEEN
AWAKENINGS

Of all the music and beauty Caelir could remember, none came close to matching those of the court of the Everqueen. He reclined on soft, autumn leaves and watched Lilani dance to the music and song of Narentir. The sound of silver bells chimed in the distance and a crowd had gathered beneath colourful silken pavilions to watch Lilani's performance.

Her movements were sinuous and graceful, but Caelir saw a harsh, aggressive vigour to her movements now, the muscles bunching and swelling beneath her glittering skin. At first he had wondered why the softness had disappeared, but then saw one of the Everqueen's Handmaidens among the appreciative spectators.

Like Lilani, the Handmaiden was slender and taut, but unlike the dancer, she wore a form-fitting breastplate of gold and carried a long spear. A scarlet plume, the same colour as her cloak, swept down the back of her helmet and a bone coloured longbow was slung across her shoulder.

The Handmaidens of the Everqueen were not mere courtiers, but warriors the equal of any elven knight with bow, spear or sword. Chosen from the best dancers, singer, poets and lovers of Ulthuan, the Handmaidens epitomised the pinnacle of achievement in elven society with their mastery of both the courtly and martial arts. Caelir cast an appreciative eye over the Handmaiden, taking in her long bare legs and the moulded physique of her breastplate.

Watching Lilani dance, he now understood her reasons for seeking out the court of the Everqueen and saw they were little different from Narentir's.

He smiled to himself as he closed his eyes and let the sensations of the forest wash over him. To perform in the court of the Everqueen! Such things were the dreams of every elf of Ulthuan.

Musicians and singers trained all their life to be worthy of playing in Avelorn and the youths of Ulthuan dreamed of becoming a consort of the Everqueen while the maids aspired to become one of her Handmaidens.

Life in Avelorn was like living in an eternal festival, decided Caelir. They had been here for a few days now and, at every turn, musicians delighted audiences, dancers made play in the forest and poets recited their latest works.

The days were magical and the nights scarcely less so.

Ghostly light filled the court at night and glittering sprites darted from tree to tree to light the wondrous folk of the forest as they created art and beauty with every breath. Gaily coloured pavilions were pitched randomly through the forest and all manner of elves from all across Ulthuan came to play and make merry in the forest of the Everqueen.

Despite himself, Caelir had been caught up in the spirit of Avelorn and slipped into an easy routine of player and spectator. By day he would sing to steadily growing crowds of admirers, and by night he would walk the moonlit paths of the forest with Lilani and make love beneath the stars on a bed of golden leaves.

Thus far Caelir had seen no sign of the ruler of Avelorn, but Narentir assured him that the Everqueen rarely ventured openly among the court until she knew whom she would choose to accompany her glorious cavalcade through the forest realm.

The urgency that had driven him to seek the Everqueen had all but vanished, his anguish smothered by the healing magic of Avelorn. The imperative to see her arose powerfully with every dawn, beating its fists against the walls of his mind, but the soothing balms of the forest's music and light soon eased his troubled brow and the day would go on as before.

The sound of rapturous applause signalled the end of Lilani's dance and Caelir opened his eyes to see her perched on the low branches of a sunwood tree, her chest heaving and her hair unbound and wild.

Caelir joined in with the applause as she bowed deeply to her audience and somersaulted from the tree. The gathered elves moved on swiftly, their butterfly interest already anticipating the delights the rest of the forest had to offer. Narentir went with them, surrounded by a gaggle of admirers, and Caelir smiled to himself as Lilani danced over and lay down next to him.

'Did you see?' she asked breathlessly, draping herself across his chest. Her skin glowed golden and he leaned down to kiss her.

She tasted of wild berries and her breath was hot in his mouth.

'I did, you were exquisite as always.'

'Liar,' she said. 'You were asleep. I saw.'

'No, I was awake,' he said.

'Then why didn't you watch me?'

'You weren't performing for me,' he said. 'I saw the Handmaiden in the audience.'

'I think she was impressed. Perhaps she will speak of me to the Everqueen,' said Lilani, her words coming out in a rush. Caelir smiled at this youthful, insecure side of Lilani, finding it an entertaining change from the confident aloofness she usually affected.

Such insecurity was understandable, for, as Caelir was quickly learning, the forest of the Everqueen was a seething hotbed of ego and intrigue, where every performer vied for the favour of the Everqueen and the chance of a place at her side.

To be chosen as a consort or Handmaiden was the highest honour imaginable for a youth of Ulthuan, but those whose artistry failed to impress the fickle inhabitants of the forest soon found themselves objects of ridicule.

Only the previous day, Caelir, Lilani and Narentir had watched a pair of singers perform in a sun-dappled glade. He had thought their voices magnificent, soaring into the treetops and entwining like lovers as the notes fell back to earth in a rain of flowers. He had found himself alone in applauding them and quickly stopped as he felt disapproving stares upon him.

A tall noble in a long robe of shimmering teal had stepped from the audience and bowed to the singers. 'Congratulations,' he had said. 'The Keeper of Souls must weep to know that one of her own has fallen from the heavens to entertain us with song. Truly it is said that anything too prosaic to be said is sung instead.'

The crowd had dispersed with ringing laughter and Caelir saw the light of joy flee from the singers' eyes at the comment, though he had been mystified as to why.

'My dear boy,' explained Narentir later. 'In Avelorn excellence is the very *least* that is expected of a performer. And while the caterwauling of those two so-called singers might impress the rustics of Chrace, it was hardly of the standard required here.'

'But that noble congratulated them.'

Narentir shook his head. 'You must learn that many of the quips directed at a performer, while appearing to be congratulatory, conceal deadly barbs.'

'I don't understand.'

'That noble compared their singing to the wailing of Morai-heg's banshees,' said Lilani.

He realised he was being spoken to and shook off thoughts of the previous day.

'Can you feel that?' said Lilani. 'Something's happening...'

He looked up, seeing the same leafy canopy of brilliant green and radiant summer sky beyond it. White birds perched in the treetops and their song trilled pleasingly. Nearby performers smiled and hugged one another, their faces alight as a subtle vibration raced through the air, a burgeoning sense of anticipation and excitement left in the wake of its passing.

Caelir leaped to his feet as the vibration surged through him, inexplicably invigorated by this strange sensation sweeping the forest.

'What is this?' he cried.

His question was answered when Narentir danced back into the clearing and swept them both into a crushing embrace, his eyes bright with tears of joy. 'Do you feel it?' he wept.

'We do!' nodded Lilani.

Seeing Caelir's confusion, Narentir laughed and said, 'The Everqueen, dear boy. She walks among us at the dawn!'

Asperon Khitain drew his sword, a weapon crafted in the forges of Hag Graef and quenched in the blood of slaves. His armour was the colour of bloodwine, fresh from the vine and his long dark hair was bound in a trailing scalp lock.

His warriors formed up around him, a hundred hardened fighters in long mail coats and lacquered breastplates that gleamed like the oily waters of Clar Karond. Long, plum-coloured cloaks hung from their shoulders and those few who did not carry long, ebony hafted spears helped carry scaling ladders.

As the glorious standard of House Khitain was raised high, he felt a thrill of anticipation and knelt to take a handful of the coarse, powdery stone of the ground he stood upon.

To have sailed across the Great Ocean and set foot once more on Ulthuan...

The mountains reared up above him and the sun bathed everything in a warm glow that made his skin itch. He remembered the last time he had fought in the land of his ancestors, pillaging and killing through the green forests of northern Ulthuan, hunting down the queen witch through the blazing ruin of her realm. The invasion had stalled when her protector had rescued her and Asperon shivered as he recalled the fury of the golden armoured warrior cutting down scores of the greatest druchii warriors in their escape.

Such a blademaster came but once in an age and Asperon cut his palm open as an offering to Khaine, mixing the welling red liquid with the dust of Ulthuan. He stood and climbed onto a nearby boulder to better see the preparations for the assault on the Emerald Gate.

Thousands of druchii warriors had crossed the great bridge of galleys from the island of the lighthouse and now marched along the overgrown pathways that crisscrossed the coastline. Perhaps these had once been the route of the long dead builders of the lighthouse or a neglected patrol route, but Asperon did not care what purpose they might once have served. Now they allowed the army of the Witch King to march into the mountains and lay siege to the shoulders of the first sea gate of Lothern.

Forests of speartips and lances glittered and Asperon watched as great war machines were unloaded from the troop galleys and carried onto the mainland by sweating, straining slaves. A host was being assembled that would sweep over the Emerald Gate and allow them to push the asur back along the Straits of Lothern.

As he watched, a red banner was unfurled upon the peak of the captured lighthouse and he grinned wolfishly as he leapt down to rejoin his warriors. The signal soon passed to every warrior in the army and a predatory hunger for slaughter swept through Asperon.

'Warriors of Naggaroth!' he cried, his noble voice easily carrying across the mountains to his soldiers. 'Today we bathe our blades in the blood of the asur! We march on their fortress and we will not stop until the banner of House Khitain flies above its ruins!'

A hundred spear shafts hammered on the white rock of the mountains and Asperon took his place within the ranks of his warriors. A great chorus of horn blasts sounded from the assembled army and echoed from the mountains like the bloody fury of Khaine himself.

He raised his sword above his head and shouted, 'Onwards!'

With disciplined steps, he and his warriors set off up the slopes of the mountains, their strides long and sure. The ground was rough, but far easier than the rugged harshness of the Iron Mountains around Hag Graef where he relentlessly drilled his soldiers. Compared to the harsh climate and terrain his warriors trained on, this was easy going.

Their mile-eating stride carried them swiftly up the rocky slopes, the hard packed earth of the wide paths overgrown and partially obscured, but providing a swift route up the mountains. The occasional flurry of arrows flashed from above as cloaked scouts loosed shafts from hiding and screams of pain swiftly followed.

The shock of the lighthouse's capture and the crushing defeat of their fleet had paralysed the asur into inaction and the pathways through the mountains were only lightly defended. Small groups of their own scouts darted forwards and soon the rain of arrows halted and Asperon heard sounds of vicious struggles from above.

At last he could see the crest of the ridgeline above him and briefly halted their advance on the rocky plateau to redress the ranks that had become ragged on the climb. Ahead, a gentle slope led towards the eastern flank of the Emerald Gate and Asperon felt his blood surge as he saw what lay before them.

The thought that the Glittering Lighthouse might be captured and the

Emerald Gate be attacked from the sides had clearly never entered the thoughts of its builders, for its defences had clearly been designed to face a frontal assault from the sea.

From what Asperon could see, the defensive architecture of the fortress's flanks consisted of little more than a hastily prepared defensive ditch and a turreted blockhouse. A wall of less than a hundred paces safeguarded the route onto the arched span of the fortress, but it was low and unprotected by outworks or high towers.

Yet more druchii warriors marched onto the plateau before the fortress and Asperon laughed as he saw the panic sweeping the silver armoured elves on the wall at the sight of such a host. He could taste their panic on the air and shouted, 'You see, the Asur's complacency and arrogance will reap them bloody ruin!'

More carnyx sounded, the skirling sound heralding the death they would inflict upon their enemies. He reopened the cut on his palm and reached up to smear his blood upon the standard of his house to offer those who would fight and die beneath it to Khaine.

A rumbling tremor of weapons clashing on shields echoed from the mountains and Asperon could see the desperate scramble on the wall ahead of him as archers and spearmen rushed to fill the ramparts.

The advance began as a steady trot, the druchii walking briskly with their spears raised, then became a jog as spears lowered and ranks of crossbowmen formed up behind them.

Asperon could see faces pale with fear and drank in that fear as the wall drew nearer. His heart thudded in his breast and his fingers flexed on the wire-wound grip of his sword.

He saw a sword with a silver blade chop downwards and a singing volley of arrows arced from the wall in a white rain.

'Shields!' shouted Asperon and his warriors dropped to their knees and lifted their left arms above their heads. A whooshing *thwak* of displaced air sounded and a hundred arrows slammed into them, but most smacked harmlessly into his warriors' shields. A few screamed in pain as a lucky arrow found its mark, but most quickly rose to their feet unharmed.

Though they had sacrificed speed to stop and raise shields, he saw that they had suffered least amongst the advancing army, with many druchii corpses simply trampled by their charging comrades in their hunger to reach the wall.

Insane courage was all very well, but it was pointless if you reached the enemy with too few warriors to kill them.

A staccato ripple of crossbow strings filled the air with black bolts and Asperon laughed as he saw a dozen enemy warriors pitched from the walls. Blood stained their pristine tunics as they fell. More bolts slashed towards the blockhouse as they set off towards the ditch before the wall and gate. Blue-fletched shafts slashed down, though many fewer than before thanks to the relentless hammering of crossbows.

An arrow punched through the helm of the warrior next to him and blood spattered Asperon's face as the warrior fell. He licked the droplets from his lips as the druchii warriors ahead of his own hurled their ladders against the wall.

Swords flashed and blood was spilled as the asur fought the warriors at the tops of the ladders. Screams and ringing steel cut the air and warriors toppled from the ramparts, skulls cloven or chests sliced open. The wall was not long and Asperon halted his warriors as he scanned its length, his experienced eye seeking out the weakest section of the defences against which to lead his warriors.

Then something unbelievable happened.

The gates of the blockhouse were opening.

Had they carried the wall so swiftly that some brave warriors were even now within?

'With me!' he shouted and sprinted for the gate. His warriors followed without hesitation and Asperon screamed with inchoate elation as he pictured being the first noble of Naggaroth to plant a standard in the Emerald Gate.

His euphoria turned to horror as he saw the column of knights with tall, gleaming helmets of silver galloping from the fortress. Dust billowed at their passing and Asperon felt his innards clamp in terror as he saw the warrior in golden armour that led them. He carried a blazing sword, like a sliver of the sun bound within a length of shimmering steel, and rode a white steed adorned with glittering scales of gem-encrusted barding.

Golden wings swept back from his helm and though he had never before laid eyes upon this warrior, he instinctively knew him, for his identity was a curse and the terror of the druchii.

Tyrion, Defender of Ulthuan...

Tall banners of white streamed behind the cavalry and their silver lances lowered in unison as they charged out. Elven soldiers armed with spears and long swords spread out behind the cavalry, cutting into the disorganised ranks of the druchii as they milled at the base of the wall.

'Halt!' shouted Asperon. 'Form a shield-wall!'

Even as he gave the order, he could see it was already too late.

His warriors were spread out, scattered as they raced to the opened gate, and easy prey for mounted warriors.

He snatched a shield from the warrior next to him and raised his sword as the pounding of hooves on stone swallowed them and the charge slammed home with a deafening thunderclap of splintering lances and screams.

Blood spurted as glittering lance blades spitted their ranks and the fiery sword of Tyrion clove warriors in two with golden sweeps that melted through armour and seared flesh. The charge of the asur cavalry punched through the disordered ranks of Asperon's warriors and trampled them into the ground, leaving scores of broken bodies in their wake.

He picked himself up from the ground, blood pouring from a deep gash on his forehead and white agony flaring as splintered bone jutted from his elbow. His shield was useless and he heard the screams of warriors dying before the relentless slaughter of the asur.

An ululating note sounded from a silver trumpet and the cavalry expertly wheeled on the spot as they prepared to charge once more. The golden warrior at the head of the silver knights aimed his sword at him, and Asperon welcomed the challenge of the gesture.

If he were to die this day, then what better way to end his days than in combat with the infamous Tyrion himself?

A beam of radiant sunfire leapt from Tyrion's blade and Asperon's flesh was burned from his body in a firestorm with the power of a star dragon's breath.

Hot, sulphurous fumes clung to the rocky walls of the underground passageway like gauzy curtains and wisps of hot steam drifted lazily from vents cut into the floor. A dim red glow, like cooling lava, seemed to come from the rocks themselves, and banked braziers added their own smoke and heat.

The sound of distant song came from somewhere far below and its musical cadences were unlike anything heard elsewhere on Ulthuan. The songs sung here were ancient beyond understanding, the rhythms and harkening melodies unknown in the world above save by those who dared to venture below the mountains of Caledor and learn the songs of awakening.

The songs of the dragons…

The mists parted like a smoky yellow curtain before a warrior who delved deep into the labyrinthine passages of the mountains, the songs of valour and tales of peril echoing within his soul like a lone voice in an empty temple.

His name was Prince Imrik, and of all the waking denizens of the caverns below the Dragonspine Mountains, none carried themselves with a fraction of the martial nobility and courage as did he. His countenance was fair, his long white hair bound with iron cords and his strength of purpose was like the furnace heat that stirred below the peak of Vaul's Anvil.

The blood of Caledor Dragontamer flowed in his veins and his lineage was of the proudest noble house of Ulthuan. In him, it was said, the strength of Tethlis the Slayer was reborn and the might of his sword arm was unmatched, save perhaps by that of Prince Tyrion.

Red light shimmered like fresh blood on Imrik's armour, an engraved suit of ithilmar mail that was as light and flexible as silk, yet was impervious to sword and fire. His cloak billowed in the heat of the passageway and the swiftness of his stride, for bleak news had come from Lothern and all the might of Ulthuan was being roused to war.

The passageway widened out into an impossibly deep cavern, though it was next to impossible to gauge its exact dimensions because hot, aromatic smoke obscured its farthest reaches. A distant rumble, like the breath of the world, vibrated the air at a frequency beyond the comprehension of most mortals, but to Imrik it was as clear as a note wrung from the great dragonhorn at his side.

It was the breath of slumbering dragons.

The songs of awakening grew louder as Imrik entered, and his soul took flight as he saw the multitude of scaled, draconic forms clustered around scalding vents that plunged into the deepest heart of the volcanic mountains.

Fire roared and seethed in the air, held aloft by the songs of the fire mages who sang to the slumbering dragons. He heard the songs in his heart and cast his gaze around the chamber to see if any of the mighty creatures were close to waking.

Powerfully muscled chests rose and fell in time with the chants of the mages, but the dragons' hearts beat a slow refrain, a beat that had slowed as the molten heat of the mountains had cooled and the magic of the world diminished.

Imrik knew there had been a time when the sight of dragons riding hot thermals rising from the Dragonspine Mountains had been commonplace, but such a vision had not been seen in hundreds of years. In these threatening times, only the younger dragons commonly awoke, though even they were a shadow of the former glory of Caledor and its famed dragon riders.

Naysmiths at the court of Lothern bemoaned the slumber of the dragons as indicative of the slide into ruin of the asur, but Imrik had never surrendered to such melancholy. Long had he studied the ways of dragons and no mortal could claim to know this most ancient of species better than he.

Imrik made his way around the circumference of the cavern, careful not to disturb the rites and chants of the singing fire mages. Many of these chants would have begun months, if not years, ago and none knew better than he the folly of interrupting a dragonsong.

He made his way to the centre of the cavern where a great brazier burned with a white gold light. Mages in scarlet robes and with long hair that fell like cascades of flame from their scalps surrounded the brazier, speaking with heated voices that crackled with a fire the equal of the conflagration before them.

The debate ceased as Imrik drew near, though he could see the golden light of Aqshy smouldering in their eyes. Ever were the hearts of those who studied the fire wind bellicose.

'My friends,' said Imrik. 'The Phoenix King sends for our aid. What should I tell him?'

'The dragons still slumber, my lord,' said a mage known as Lamellan.

'How many awake?'

'None save Minaithnir, my lord,' said Lamellan. 'His soul burns brightly and the hearts of the younger dragons stir with thoughts of war, but the dreams of the great dragons are too deep to reach. We summon the heat that burns at the heart of the world with songs of legendary times and glorious deeds, but the memories are cold, my lord...'

'The fire of the dragons is gone?' said Imrik. 'Is that what you are trying to say?'

'Not gone, my lord,' said Lamellan. 'But buried deep. It will be years before the ashes are wrought into flaming life. Too late for us now.'

'You are wrong,' said Imrik, pacing around the brazier and his pale eyes reflecting the fire that burned at its heart. 'The age of glory can never be forgotten, by elf nor dragon. By such means are the dragons of Caledor roused from sleep. The druchii once more set foot on our beloved homeland and the Phoenix King has sent missives pleading for our aid. Lothern is besieged and the Hag Sorceress herself leads an army at the Eagle Gate!'

'My lord,' protested Lamellan, 'you know as well as I that to reach the heart of these noble creatures takes great time and effort.'

'Time is the one thing Ulthuan does not have, my friend,' said Imrik. 'Our fair isle would have fallen into darkness long ago without the might of the dragons. They are as much a part of Ulthuan as the asur, and I will not believe that they will fail to heed our call to arms in this time of woe.'

He could see his words were fanning the flame of Aqshy that burned in the hearts of the fire mages and stoked the warlike embers of their souls to greater effort.

'Ulthuan is under attack and requires all the martial power it can assemble. Go! Sing the songs of ancient days!

'The dragonriders of old must soar the skies again!'

CHAPTER TWENTY
ANATHEMA

The pyres burned long into the night, illuminating the battered white wall of the Eagle Gate with hellish light and thick with the aroma of roasting meat. Warriors with plates of armour fused to their flesh by magic capered around the giant bonfires, their scarred bodies jerking as though they were not theirs to command.

And perhaps they are not, thought Issyk Kul as he watched the sensuous dances and orgiastic feasting. The flesh-suited madmen capered in time to the beat of Hung drums, and chants in praise of Shornaal soared with the sparks spat from the fires.

His own body was slathered in the blood of his latest kill, and the exquisite high he had achieved with his latest partner in violation had been sublime. The elves of Ulthuan were far superior subjects to the poor specimens who dwelt in the cold wastes of the far north. To those used to a life of misery and hardship, torture meant little, but to effete souls raised in a land of plenty and who had never known the brutality of life beyond their pampered existence, it was a nightmare that enhanced Kul's pleasure tenfold.

The defenders of the wall still held, though he knew it was simply a matter of time until they broke. And when that moment came, he and what remained of his followers would debase the remainder and make bloody ruin of this isle.

He turned from the wall and made his way through the campsite towards the neat lines of the druchii camp, shaking his head at such rigidly enforced order. The camp of his warriors was a battered and broken landscape dotted with piles of shattered weapons, excrement and dead or insensible bodies. Order was anathema to Kul and he allowed, and encouraged, his warriors to indulge every sordid desire, so long as they were able to fight upon the dawn.

A bloody procession of chanting zealots, chained to one another by flesh hooks piercing the meat of their arms, danced around him. He acknowledged their devotion to the Dark Prince by gathering up the chains that bound them all and jerking them savagely, ripping the iron hooks from their flesh and drawing shrieks of bliss and blood from their lips.

Kul dropped the chains and left his torn followers behind as he approached the sentry line of druchii warriors. Morathi kept her followers carefully segregated from his own, lest the entire army devolve into a heaving, bloody mass of perversion and slaughter.

The guards recognised him and stepped aside to let him pass and Kul could taste their fear of him. Mingled with that fear was a colossal arrogance and condescension, for these were warriors of a race that looked upon humanity from the perspective of those that had almost held the world in their grasp.

He resisted the urge to draw his sword and cut them down for such presumption and naïvety. The evidence of their foolishness was clear for all to see, for was not the surface of the world crawling with the maggots of humanity? Such arrogance was misplaced when you were forced to eke out an existence in the coldest, bleakest place imaginable.

Everywhere within the druchii camp he could see ordered ranks of flimsy tents that wouldn't last a night on the steppe, yet were thought to be fit to bring on campaign.

Druchii warriors gathered around campfires and the noise of low conversations buzzed in his ears like an insect trapped in a bottle. Only recently had warriors arrived that Kul thought the equal of Morathi, a troupe of long-limbed she-elves clad in gleaming leather and fragments of flexible armour. Wild-haired and sumptuous, he had thought them dancers or courtesans until he saw them slay armed prisoners in ritual combats of spectacular violence.

Those same warrior women now stood guard around Morathi's tent, a monstrous pavilion of purple and golden silk that billowed as though it had breath. A trio of the manic she-elves paced before the pavilion's entrance, scenting the blood that dried on his skin.

As he drew near, two peeled off to the side while one remained defiantly before him. The two circled him, moving slowly, but with exquisite grace as they ran fingers over his hard muscles and scraped blood from his flesh with their fingertips.

'Are you going to get out of my way?' said Kul to the she-elf before him.

'Maybe,' said the elf woman, exposing her teeth, and Kul fought the urge to break his fist against her jaw. 'Maybe we will demand a price for your passage.'

'What price?'

The she-elf thought for a moment and said, 'Send ten of your finest warriors to us.'

'Why?'

'So we can kill them, of course.'

'And why would I do such a thing?'

'They will be honoured with bloody deaths,' said the elf. 'And it would please us.'

Kul nodded, for he knew this was no negotiation, simply a price to be paid. 'I will send them to you in the morning. Kill them and give me their hearts when you are done.'

'Very well,' said the elf. 'When we have their blood, you may have their hearts.'

Without seeming to move, the she-elf slipped aside and the three of them bowed extravagantly to him. His business with them was over and he ignored their mocking obeisances as he entered Morathi's tent.

Inside, the luxury of the Hag Sorceress's domain had been transported from Naggaroth and reassembled here. Velveteen throws were draped over an ebony chaise longue and carved busts no doubt thought exquisite stood on black marble plinths. More of the insane she-elves lounged around the perimeter of the tent, sharpening knives, turning bloody trophies over in their hands or sipping goblets of ruby liquid.

Gold brocade hung from the ceiling and a low fire burned in the centre of the pavilion.

A great black cauldron of beaten iron hung on graceful black spars over the fire, the metallic reek of blood coming from the gently steaming red liquid that filled it to the brim.

As Kul watched, a thin hand emerged from the bubbling cauldron, pale and as unblemished as virgin marble. Arms followed, sculpted and smooth, and Kul felt arousal stir at the sight of this bloody birth.

A mane of black hair plastered red with blood rose from the cauldron and a pair of wide, staring eyes wept red tears as the Hag Sorceress emerged and lifted her head. The blood in the cauldron hissed as Morathi let it soak her breasts, hips and thighs. Her flesh was white and renewed, streaked with red as thick, gooey runnels ran down her naked, ivory body.

Stripped of her robes, Morathi was the single most desirable thing Kul had ever seen, a siren of death and sensation that commanded devotion in all things. Her flesh glowed with vigour and a bloom of youth that was surely impossible for one of such unimaginable age.

Not even the most powerful shamans Kul had slain had displayed such carnal devotion to Shornaal and he longed to rip her from the cauldron and violate her in every way imaginable.

He restrained his rabid impulses, knowing that this was not the time for such loss of control. The she-elf protectors would rip him to shreds before he came within striking distance of Morathi and he had no wish to end his days as fodder for their ritual sacrifices.

In any case, the Hag Sorceress had bigger plans than simple pleasures of the flesh, plans that would see the world dragged through the gates of hell and unleash the realm of the Dark Gods upon its surface.

The restraint of his desires was painful to a devotee of Shornaal and as Kul saw the knowledge of his frustration in her eyes, he felt the killing rage rise in him once more. He closed his eyes and recited the six secret names of his patron, gripping the hilt of his sword and concentrating on the pain as the blades and spikes cut into his palm.

When he opened them again, Morathi was reclining on a chaise longue and clad in a robe of crimson doupioni, its fine weave already staining with the blood on her limbs. One of the she-elves plaited her bloody hair, pulling sodden, matted lengths into long, drooping spikes.

'Your messenger said you had news,' said Issyk Kul.

Morathi flicked her eyes towards him and nodded slowly. 'My son makes war on the asur at Lothern. His warriors lay siege to the Emerald Gate.'

'Then we must make haste to take this fortress,' said Kul.

'Must we?' said Morathi, her voice smooth and seductive, like a young maiden. 'But it seems like your warriors so enjoy to fight.'

'They relish the chance to fight and feel the bliss of pain,' agreed Kul. 'But they wish victory more. I need to know when your warriors will take to the field of battle.'

Morathi smiled and shook her head.

'My warriors will fight soon enough,' said the Hag Sorceress. 'When this dirty little siege is over. I leave such grubby battles to your northern tribes.'

'The battle would go swifter if you were to commit warriors to the fight,' pointed out Issyk Kul. 'You claimed time was of the essence.'

'And so it is, my dear Kul,' said Morathi, rising from her repose to stand before him. 'But such inelegant battles are ill-suited to our sensibilities. You knew the price for allowing you to join me was the blood of your warriors. Trust me, when the Eagle Gate is ours and Ulthuan is laid open before us, you will receive all that you desire.'

'All?'

'All,' said Morathi, allowing her robes to fall open and expose a slice of virgin skin.

Kul licked his lips as he pictured the rewards of success.

More was at stake than simply the attainment of the promise of ravaging Morathi's flesh – the fulfilment of what the weak fool, Archaon, had singularly failed to achieve.

Morathi spoke again. 'When will your warriors carry the wall?'

'Soon. Your race is a spent force in the world,' he said, enjoying the flare of anger he saw in her eyes. 'Even in the remote north, that fact is understood. I have warriors to lose by the hundred, but each enemy that falls in battle is an irreplaceable loss. We will simply batter them into defeat, for my warriors do not fear pain or death. They do.'

'Then be sure to give them what they fear,' said Morathi.

Kul smiled, exposing sharpened teeth and said, 'Never doubt it.'

Caelir had not slept at all and neither, it seemed, had any other inhabitant of Avelorn. The news that the Everqueen would walk amongst the forest had banished all thoughts of rest and imparted a manic energy to the elves that had come to pay homage and hoped to become part of her court.

Though no one had seen them come, fresh pavilions with an ethereal quality of simple grace had appeared in the midst of the forest, ones that needed no cords or poles to support them and were held aloft by the soft winds that gusted around them.

Lights flitted around these pavilions and armoured elf maids in golden armour ringed them, though the presence of such warriors did not detract from the peace and tranquillity of the scene.

Lilani held his hand and Narentir stood behind them both with a paternal hand on their shoulders. Neither could keep the joy from their faces and Caelir suspected that his face was similarly stretched with an unrestrained smile. All through the assembled elves – over a hundred estimated Caelir – he could see the same unabashed love and radiant happiness that made him proud to be part of this gathering.

His mind was a mad whirl of thoughts and emotions, a jumble of ideas vying for supremacy in his consciousness. He would see the Everqueen, the most beautiful woman in the world, and his memory could be restored. He would play for her and who knew what might transpire in the wake of such a performance?

Caelir had dressed in clothes lent to him by Narentir, an elegant tunic of silks and satins that was thin and light, yet clung warmly to his skin. He carried the harp that had won him such acclaim within the forest and wore a belt of black, upon which was hung the dagger he had carried since being washed upon the beach of Yvresse – such a long time ago it seemed.

So much had happened since then and though he knew much of it had been terrible, the magic of Avelorn prevented the true horror of it intruding into his thoughts, as though the forest could not bear the thought of its inhabitants' anguish. Dimly he realised that such denial was unhealthy, but shook off such gloomy thoughts as a pale nimbus of light built from within the Everqueen's pavilion.

'She comes...' breathed Narentir and Caelir felt the hand on his shoulder tighten.

Caelir gripped the harp and ached to play a welcoming refrain upon its strings, but restrained himself, sensing that to spoil this moment with his own selfish desires would be gross and unwelcome.

The skin of the Everqueen's tent peeled back and a bright light, like sunlight on golden fields poured from inside. Amid the wondrous halo of shimmering brilliance, the ruler of Avelorn emerged – the most beauteous elf in creation and most wondrous ruler of Ulthuan.

The assembled elves dropped to their knees, overcome by wonder and emotion. Tears of joy spilled from every eye and even the skies shone with the reflected radiance of her smile.

Caelir wanted to join them in worship of this enchanted daughter of Isha.

Instead, he found himself gripping the hilt of his dagger.

The forest of Avelorn flashed past them as they rode for the court of the Everqueen. Eldain pushed Irenya hard, digging his heels into her flanks in a way he would never normally do. He risked a glance over at Rhianna, seeing the same anxious expression that had settled on her face as soon as they had set foot on dry land at the fork of the River Arduil.

It was stupid to be riding this fast through a forest, for a moment's inattention could cost a rider dear. A low branch or rabbit hole could be the end of a rider or mount, but Rhianna had insisted that they immediately ride into the depths of the forest.

'Save him and you save me...' she had whispered, repeating the phrase she had first uttered on the *Dragonkin* as they sailed towards Avelorn as a mantra.

The implications of the phrase were not lost on Eldain and a clammy hand had taken hold of his heart despite the wondrous beauty and sun of the Everqueen's northern realm. He knew the sights and sounds of the forest should beguile him, should entrance him with their incredible splendour, but his mind endlessly turned over the dreadful possibilities of what might be about to happen.

As much as the deaths he had witnessed recently pained him and weighed guiltily upon his soul, the thought that the Everqueen herself might be in danger eclipsed them all. The idea that it was he who had led to her being placed in danger had silenced any objections to riding at speed through the forest.

Yvraine rode behind him, her aversion to travelling by means other than walking forgotten as she shared a measure of Rhianna's fear that they might already be too late.

Eldain caught sight of her greatsword and knew that if Caelir dared hurt the Everqueen, he himself would gladly wield the blade that would end his life...

The Everqueen...

Caelir's hands began to tremble as the ruler of Avelorn walked amongst her people. Though no musician played, the forest provided an accompaniment of its own for her. Birds trilled musically, streams gurgled and the wind sighed through the excited branches of trees.

The land itself welcomed her.

Behind her came a Handmaiden bearing a banner of emerald leaves plucked from the branches of trees and woven with golden hair. The light of the forest was captured in the banner, but it was a willing captive, and it bore the heart of Avelorn in its rustling, living fabric.

Caelir saw fresh white flowers spring from the ground where the Everqueen walked and her radiance caused those already in bloom to turn their faces towards her. The forest came alive at her presence and the adoration in every face was heartfelt and pure.

None averted their gaze from the Everqueen, for she desired her subjects to know beauty, and she blessed them all with the healing light of her magic.

Without knowing how, he knew the dagger he gripped was now loose in its sheath and he could feel a terrible hunger from the blade, willing him to draw it. He fought its malign touch, pressing the quillons hard against the heavy scabbard.

I have to get out of here, he thought desperately, but the haunting majesty of the Everqueen held him fast. He could feel the puzzlement of those nearby and a number of faces tore their gaze from the Everqueen and regarded him with hostility at his lack of respect.

'Caelir!' whispered Lilani. 'What are you doing?'

'I don't know...' he hissed between clenched teeth as he fought the urge to draw the dagger from its heavy black scabbard. He remembered Kyrielle telling him that she had not liked holding the blade and her father saying that it had shed a great deal of blood.

The Everqueen moved amongst the people of the forest, smiling and radiant, reaching out here and there to touch the forehead of a kneeling elf. The foremost artistes, singers, musicians, poets, artisans and mages laughed as she selected them to become part of her court and their laughter was like the chiming of the clearest golden bells.

Caelir fought to move, to turn and run from the dark emanations slithering up his arm from the dagger, but his limbs were not his to command, his grip held fast to the metal hilt. More performers were chosen, and as each rose from their knees, the Handmaidens of the Everqueen led them into the forest.

The Everqueen came closer and Caelir's limbs twitched, as though two opposing forces waged silent war for control of his body.

Then she paused as she reached towards a gifted poet and tilted her head as though listening to a faraway sound. Her posture stiffened and the sunlight fled the sky, a forlorn gloom and unknown menace descending from the forest in an instant.

Caelir heard the roaring of a storm in his head.

He wanted to scream a warning.

The Everqueen looked up.

Their eyes met and a moment of awful knowledge passed between them.

'Caelir...' she said.

At the sound of his name from her divine lips, the chains slipped from around his memory and what had been locked away now rushed to the forefront of his mind.

It all came back.

Everything...

The line of warriors emerged from the trees as though they had been part of them but a moment ago. Spears levelled, ten elf maids in golden armour and plumed helmets barred their way forward and only Eldain's superlative horsemanship saved him from running straight into a line of lethal spear points.

Rhianna and Yvraine halted with somewhat less grace, but their horses saved them from running straight into the blades of the warrior women. Without waiting for them to demand his business, Eldain cried, 'Please, we have to get to the Everqueen. She is in danger!'

A warrior with long dark hair beneath her helmet put up her spear at his words. She took a step from the ranks of her warriors and said, 'You are wrong. The Handmaidens of the Everqueen protect her within the boundaries of Avelorn. She is quite safe.'

'No,' pressed Eldain, riding towards the elf maid. He heard the creak of bowstrings being pulled taut and knew he was a hair's breadth from dying. 'You don't understand the danger she is in. We have to reach her court.'

'What manner of danger do you mean?'

Rhianna rode alongside him and said, 'There is a young elf here under an enchantment of dark magic, though he does not know it. He will seek to harm the Everqueen.'

'What is this elf's name?' said the Handmaiden. Eldain could see her scepticism and wished he could penetrate her disbelief at what he knew must seem a fantastical claim.

'Caelir,' said Eldain. 'He is my brother.'

A ripple of recognition passed through the handmaidens and Eldain felt a sick dread settle in the pit of his stomach.

Caelir was already here...

'They speak the truth,' said Yvraine. 'I speak as a Sword Master of Hoeth and emissary of the White Tower. You must let us pass.'

The Handmaiden's eyes narrowed as she took in Yvraine's sword and martial bearing and reached an uncomfortable conclusion.

'Someone of that name is known to the forest,' she said before turning on her heel and issuing curt commands to the Handmaidens accompanying her. In seconds her warriors had vanished into the forest and she turned back to Eldain.

'Quickly then,' she said. 'Follow me.'

Caelir remembered everything in the space of a heartbeat…

The dockyards of Clar Karond were aflame, the magical arrows that had been a wedding gift from Rhianna's father proving their worth as fire tore through great stockpiles of timber and ships with hungry appetite. Smoke curled from the devastated shipyards in monstrous black pillars and the screams of the druchii were music to his ears.

Aedaris bore him with the grace of Korhandir himself, galloping through the twisting, nightmare streets of the druchii's dockyards with unerring skill and speed. Ellyrion Reavers rode in ones and twos ahead of him as they made their escape and Caelir laughed with the sheer joy of what they had accomplished.

Eldain rode ahead of him, the black flanks of Lotharin heaving as his brother's stronger mount stretched the gap between them. He rode past blazing timber stores and ruined piles of blackened lumber as spears stabbed for him and crossbow bolts slashed through the air.

He crouched low over his steed's neck, speed carrying them past the stunned druchii without a fight. Ahead, Eldain slashed his sword through the arm of a warrior guarding the gateway and hacked down another before riding clear.

A pair of druchii charged him, their spears aimed for his horse's chest, but Caelir hauled back on the reins and Aedaris danced around the spear thrusts. His horse reared and its lashing hooves crushed the chest of its closest enemy and Caelir split the skull of the other with a swift blow from his sword.

The blood sang in his veins with the thrill of the fight and he turned to ride after his brother. He heard the snap of crossbow strings and cried in pain as an iron bolt slammed into his hip. Yet more bolts flashed through the air, hammering into Aederis's chest and flanks.

He felt himself falling as the horse collapsed, blood frothing from its mouth and its legs thrashing in agony. He hit the ground hard and rolled as the breath slammed from his chest. He saw druchii running towards him and scrambled to his feet, weeping tears of pain and loss as he saw that his beloved Aedaris was dead.

He ran with a stumbling gait towards his brother.

Eldain would save him!

More bolts flashed through the air, and he screamed as another missile buried itself in his shoulder. He stumbled, but kept running.

'Brother!' he yelled, holding his hand out towards Eldain.

Eldain looked at him and Caelir saw his gaze fall upon the silver pledge ring that glittered in the firelight – seeing a depth of bitterness that shocked him to the depths of his soul.

Eldain said, 'Goodbye, Caelir,' and turned his horse from him.

Caelir dropped to his knees in horror as he watched his brother ride away towards the hills, the pain of his wounds nothing compared to the ache of betrayal that stabbed his heart with the force of a lance.

He hung his head as he heard the druchii surround him, the last of his strength stolen from his body at Eldain's abandonment of him. His vision turned from grey to black and the world fled from him as he pitched forward onto his face.

Darkness.

Pain.

Sorrow.

Anger.

Hatred.

Light...

He remembered long months of black horror and longer days of cold terror. He remembered sweating agony as a nightmare figure in iron armour and with blazing green eyes had regarded him with dread fascination and words Caelir could not understand. A terrifying, sinuous woman with raven hair and the face of a seductress worked upon him day and night, subjecting him to degradations and dark pleasures that left him full of loathing and revulsion.

A dark tower of brazen iron that presided over a city of murder and death.

The screams of a city that bathed in blood and celebrated the vilest practices imaginable.

Nightly his violation continued, pleasured and tormented by the weakness of his flesh and tortures that left his body unmarked, but left nightmarish scars upon his mind. He was plunged deeper into the abyss of madness than any mortal should ever go until his sanity began to crack and buckle at the seams.

He screamed himself hoarse, forgetting his name and past, everything that made him Caelir, brother of Eldain and husband to be of Rhianna. His mind detached from his history and he was reduced to a frame of meat and bone without intellect, reason or memory as magical tendrils wormed their way into his mind to plant a seed.

Only emotion remained: anger, hatred and fear...

And when there was nothing left of him but the last fragment of his self, he was brought back, the building blocks of his psyche rebuilt enough for him to function as a sentient being. He resisted, unwilling to face the horrors he had just lived through, but he felt the touch of magic as those memories of pain, darkness and manipulation were closed off, hidden beneath enchantments of such cunning that they could only be released by secret commands or specific magic.

Dreadful nightmares plagued him as he lay weeping in his cell, but as the magic took hold within his mind, he slept more soundly, lost in the wilderness of his mind as new thoughts and talents – music, art, poetry and song – were seeded within him.

Still he was but a mass of emotion and selective memory, and only as he had been held above a heaving ocean on the deck of a black ship that pitched and rolled in a shimmering fog had the last shreds of intellect and reason been returned to him.

Then he was falling and cold liquid filled his lungs as he hit the water and *sank beneath the waves. He struggled to the surface and coughed a heaving breath of saltwater.*

A fragment of timber detritus bobbed next to him and he gratefully seized it.

Thunderous booms echoed from the cliffs as surf crashed against rock and exploded upwards in sprays of pure white. The icy, emerald sea surged through channels between rocky archipelagos in great swells, rising and falling in foam-topped waves that finally washed onto the distant shores of a mist-shrouded island...

Caelir let loose a howl of pain and betrayal as the memories buried within him surfaced in a torrential rush at the magic of the Everqueen. Time slowed and his focus narrowed as he gripped the hilt of the dagger and saw the beautiful ruler of Avelorn reach for him with outstretched arms.

He saw the pleading look in her eyes and wept bitter tears to see her so anguished.

Her very presence was anathema to the thing at his side and the heavy scabbard of black metal disintegrated in the face of Isha's power to unmake the baubles of Chaos...

Where before he had held a sheathed weapon that could not be drawn, he now held a triangular sectioned blade of crimson iron that reeked with the blood of a thousand victims and the evil bound within it.

The ground beneath him blackened and the trees around him died in the blink of an eye as the power of its evil rotted them to the core. Birds dropped dead from the trees and the elves of Avelorn cried out as they felt the diabolical presence within the blade.

Caelir fought to resist the impulse to raise the weapon, but his limb was no longer his own.

The weapon smoked, dark tendrils of magic seeping from the blade as the daemonic power within fought to resist the Everqueen's purity.

Everything around him was moving as though in a dream, with glacial slowness and terrible inevitability. A trio of riders arrived at the edge of the clearing around the Everqueen's pavilion and Caelir felt as though a blazing fist had seized his heart.

One rider he did not recognise, an elf maid with a greatsword sheathed across her back.

But the others... oh, the others...

Rhianna.

Eldain.

Hot anger surged in him and the dagger in his hand fed upon it, drawing on the well of hatred that had been stoked within him to sustain its blasted existence in this realm of healing magic.

Caelir heard someone shout his name, the sound drawn out and slow.

He saw Eldain, now knowing him as his brother and not some monstrous doppelganger.

He saw the betrayal his own flesh and blood had visited upon him.

Caelir screamed as the smoking, daemonic weapon thrust itself into the Everqueen's chest.

SONS OF ELLYRION

BOOK ONE
HEROES

CHAPTER ONE
TEARS OF ISHA

Ulthuan was weeping.

Waterfalls and wailing rivers carried its tears to the sea. The clouds gathered in solemn thunderheads and the wind howled its sorrow through the air, which hung torpid and heavy over even its most carefree inhabitants. Not since the days of the Sundering, when brother had slain brother and a race favoured by the gods turned on one another, had the realm of the elves known such grief.

The skies above the mist-shrouded island faded to black, the sun unwilling to bear witness to such horror. Only the shimmering emerald orb of the Chaos moon dared show its face on such a night, but the clouds over Ulthuan hid the torment of its inhabitants from such a leering gaze.

Ulthuan's brightest and most beauteous star had been torn from the heavens, and that grief was for her people alone.

The masked statues upon the Shrine of Asuryan wept blood from their hidden eyes, and the waters around Tor Elyr broke and seethed with anger, shattering crystal bridges that had stood for thousands of years. Roaring waves heaved the surface of the Inner Sea, capsizing the few silver-hulled ships that plied its waters and dragging sorrowful mariners down to their doom.

The lands of the Inner Kingdoms, golden realms of eternal summer, knew at last the touch of winter as cold winds blew from the north and ignoble rains battered the balmy plains. Magical sprites, capricious things of glittering mischief, transformed in an instant, their mischief turned to spite, playfulness to malice. The forests of Chrace echoed with the sound of enraged beasts, and lone hunters abroad in the shadowed depths sought the sanctuary of caves or tall trees.

Towering breakers battered the rocky coastline of Cothique as the ocean surged with fury, desperate to spill over the land. Within the Gaen Vale, the mountain of the crone maiden rumbled as though ancient geological faults tore open, and black smoke clawed from its summit. From Sapherian villas and the coastal mansions of Yvresse, to the rocky, cliff-top towers of Tiranoc and palaces of such beauty that they may only be told of in song, the land of the elves knew pain and sorrow.

The great statues of the Everqueen and the Phoenix King that stood sentinel over the mighty port of Lothern trembled upon their mighty footings. The light of a thousand torches illuminated Lothern, but the marbled Everqueen remained shrouded in the deepest shadows, and all who looked upon the regal features of the Phoenix King saw the stern and unflinching countenance crack, like the carven track of a single tear.

Ulthuan's warriors, mages, poets and peacemakers alike wept with their magical home. That shared woe passed from the elves to the land, and from the land to the air. And as Ulthuan mourned, it spread on the winds of magic throughout the world until even distant kin in ports as far away as Tor Elithis breathed in the sorrow of the Everqueen's fate.

The distant asrai of Athel Loren grieved with their long lost brothers and sisters, the slumbering Orion and fey queen Ariel dipping the branches of their forest home in shared anguish. Though the paths of the asur and asrai had taken very different turns through the ages of the world, their shared heritage was still a bright thread of connection between them.

Even the crude and unsophisticated race of man felt something amiss in the world. Children – who alone of the race of men retain their sense of wonder – woke from troubled dreams with a scream on their lips, and those forced to pass the long watches of the night in wakefulness felt the touch of the grave draw ever closer. Dramatists and dreamers felt an aspect of beauty pass from the world, while those whose lives had been touched by the asur in some way felt an unreasoning grief they could not explain when the sun's rays once again illuminated a world that seemed just a little less bright than before.

If the dwarfs of the mountain holds felt anything of these events, none could say, for elf and dwarf had long since lost any love for the other.

Only the fallen elves of Naggaroth revelled in this time of suffering. As drops of blood fell to the loamy earth of Avelorn, cold laughter echoed from the crooked towers of the druchii's accursed cities of dark iron and bloodstained stone.

Leading his army of invasion against the gates of Lothern, the Witch King himself, greatest and most hated son of Ulthuan, bellowed with laughter astride his midnight-skinned drake perched atop the Glittering Lighthouse. The ocean boomed and crashed far below him, but his mirth drowned the noise of the furious water.

In her gaudy pavilion of debaucheries before the embattled Eagle Gate, Morathi the Hag Sorceress whipped her devotees into bloody paroxysms of opiate-fuelled madness before bathing in a cauldron of their hot blood.

The myriad voices of the world spoke with a million voices in a million ears, subtly different every time, but all singing the same lament.

Alarielle, the Everqueen of Avelorn, was dead.

Eldain saw Caelir stab the Everqueen, yet still could not believe what his own eyes were telling him. He'd known his brother's purpose in coming to Avelorn, but to see it enacted was worse than he could ever have imagined. Though it was over in an instant, Eldain saw everything, from the tiniest detail to the full panorama of the murderous deed. Alone of all those in the garlanded arbour, it seemed that he must bear witness to the full horror of events as they unfolded.

Was this his punishment for being the treacherous architect of this assassination, to see every detail and feel every nuance of the bloody deed?

He saw the black sheath of Caelir's dagger crumble away, blown by perfume-scented winds like cinders from a dead fire. The blade itself, dulled by old blood and reeking of ancient murders, crossed the all too short distance between Caelir's fist and the Everqueen's chest. Yet though he had come to Avelorn on a mission of murder, Caelir's face was not the face of an assassin, but that of a horrified witness.

Eldain willed the magic of the Everqueen to turn aside the blow, hoping that some innate power possessed by the chosen of Isha to undo harm or malicious intent before it could be wreaked would save her. No such magic intervened, and the black wedge of ensorcelled iron plunged into her breast. Blood welled from the wound, each droplet that stained her gown of silk and starlight shockingly bright in the darkness that fell like the last night at the end of the world.

The Everqueen did not cry out or scream or give voice to the pain of her wounding. A single tear spilled down her cheek as her body fell like the most graceful tree in the most magical forest hewn by the axe of an unthinking dwarf. Though no living race was quicker and more agile than the asur, not one amongst those assembled before the Everqueen's gilded pavilion moved so much as a muscle to save her.

Acrobats, poets, warriors, singers, musicians and taletellers had gathered in this leafy bower of Avelorn to witness the Everqueen walking among her people, to bask in her divine radiance and feel the joy of her breath play across the sculpted lines of their perfect features. The land had welcomed her arrival, fresh blooms springing up in her footsteps, and the leafy canopy parting with every grateful sigh of the wind to allow the sunlight to caress the Everqueen's radiant skin. Those blooms now withered and died, and the treetops closed over this scene of murder with an ashamed rustle of branches. The patter of rain fell from a cloudless sky.

The Maiden Guard, resplendent in their ivory robes, bronze breastplates and long spears, could do nothing as their mistress fell. Not since the days before Finuval Plain had they lapsed in their duty of protection, and each warrior woman felt as though Caelir's blade had pierced her own heart.

Eldain saw those closest to Caelir, a soft-bodied poet and a wiry woman with the body of a dancer. The male fell to his knees, his hands clasped theatrically over his cheeks as he howled with loss. The woman's fists were clenched, the corded muscles in her arms and legs bunched in readiness to fight.

No matter where his gaze fell, Eldain's eyes were always drawn back to the Everqueen as she fell with languid grace to the soft grass. She struck the ground with a sigh of silk and a gasp of pain. Her eyes met those of Eldain, and he felt the awful weight of his betrayal in that tawny-gold gaze. She saw past the mask he presented to the world, and into the secret heart of him. In that unbreakable moment of connection, Alarielle did the one thing he could never do for himself.

She forgave him.

Her head rolled to the side and golden tresses woven from sunlight and joy fell across her face, mercifully covering her alabaster features. The moment of connection ended and Eldain's splendid isolation from the flow of the world's time was at an end.

He slid from the back of his horse as an inchoate roar of aggression sounded from a hundred throats. Though the grief was too raw and too powerful for mere words, the sentiment was clear.

Blood must answer for blood.

Caelir's hand burned from holding the dagger, his palm scarred with the imprint of its hateful grip and his soul rebelling at the memory of the thousand assassinations and uncounted lives it had ended on the sacrificial altar. He watched the Everqueen fall away from him, as though she tumbled into the deepest chasm from which there could be no escape. Her gaze did not condemn him, such eyes could hold only love, and he looked away, unable to bear the shame of her forgiveness.

Instead he looked across the twilight glade and saw an elf whose countenance was the mirror of his own. Softer and without the harsh lines of Caelir's angular cheekbones, he finally recognised his older brother, Eldain. Rhianna stood beside him, and his heart broke anew to see the matching pledge rings upon their hands. Next to them, a warrior woman in the garb of a Sword Master had her blade drawn, but Rhianna's restraining hand was on her shoulder.

Caelir knew everything now. Washed up on Ulthuan's shores without his memory, he had been a weapon primed by the Witch King and his hellish mother, and aimed at their most powerful enemies. Teclis of the White Tower had already been laid low, and now the Everqueen had fallen victim to Caelir's unwitting treacheries. Yet even as he saw his part in these attacks, he knew that none of this would have been possible but for Eldain's betrayal in Naggaroth.

'You left me to die, brother,' he said, his voice softer than a whisper, but flying like blazing arrows to Eldain's heart.

His life was forfeit. There could be no return from a deed of such unadulterated evil, and Caelir awaited the pain of a hundred arrows piercing his flesh and silver lances plunging into his body to split his worthless heart in two. Briefly he cursed the Fates that he would die without first taking his revenge, but the fading light of the Everqueen spoke of the futility of such notions. Vengeance only begat vengeance and thus was the cycle of hatred perpetuated.

Yet even as he awaited death, a voice in his head whispered his name. The sound was a zephyr of wind across the Ellyrion plains, the rumble of hoof beats from the Great Herd, and the boom of thunder from the Annulii. Soft, yet with a power stronger than the roots of the earth itself, it told him one thing, and Caelir could not disobey.

Flee, it said. *Flee and forgive...*

Rhianna saw Caelir's blow as it landed, the magic within her leaping to her fingertips as soon as she felt the weight of the hateful dagger's evil. As the Everqueen fell away from Caelir, she wanted to unleash that magic in a torrent of fire. Hotter than Vaul's forge and brighter than Asuryan's fire, it would unmake Caelir in a heartbeat.

No sooner had that intent surfaced in her mind than it was quashed.

This was the boy she had loved and had planned to wed.

Caelir was the reckless scoundrel who had taken her on wild rides across the plains of Ellyrion upon the backs of the most incredible steeds of Ulthuan. He had taken her into the Annulii, higher than anyone else would have dared, and shown her the majesty of the untamed magic that boiled within the thunder-haunted peaks. His roguish charms had won her away from Eldain, but his loss in the Land of Chill had ended their dream of a life together before it had begun.

She could not bring herself to undo the memory of that young boy. She had loved him once, and saw the same innocence behind his tortured face she had seen that day in the mountains when she had first lost her heart to him.

Those around her showed no such restraint and she saw their horror turn to anger in a heartbeat. Bows were bent and silver-bladed lances brought to shoulders, ready to spill the blood of this traitor.

Caelir stumbled away from his black deed, turning to Eldain and running towards him as though the whip of a Tiranoc charioteer was at his back. As fast as Caelir was, there was no way he could possibly reach his brother before the arrows of the Everqueen's protectors cut him down.

The dark-haired leader of the Maiden Guard that had brought them to the Everqueen's bower had her horsehair bowstring taut, an arrow fletched with feathers from a white raven aimed at Caelir's heart.

Save him and you will save me…

The words lanced into Rhianna's mind, the mantra she had kept close to her heart ever since her journey into the cave of the oracle. Though they seemed contradictory, she knew better than to doubt the words of the high priestess of the Gaen Vale.

A score of Maiden Guard bows creaked and loosed in the same instant, and each shaft arced through the air with accuracy no other race could match.

This time the magic flew from Rhianna's hands without restraint and she poured it into the towering oak beside her. Shimmering light spilled from its cracked bark, and the flurry of arrows arcing towards Caelir veered from their course like iron drawn by a navigator's lodestone to hammer the ancient wood.

Splinters of bark made her duck as a second volley was similarly torn from its natural course. Cries of anger and frustration echoed from the forested glade as the Maiden Guard cast aside their bows and took up their lances. They bounded through the crowds of panicking elves, intent on slaying the killer in their midst.

'Caelir, wait!' yelled Eldain, but his brother was in no mood to listen. He vaulted onto the back of Eldain's steed with the grace of one to whom being on horseback was as natural as breathing. Caelir settled onto the back of Irenya, the reins leaping into his hands as he turned the beast's rearing into a curving turn.

With a wild yell, Caelir leaned low over the horse's neck and it surged to a run in the time it took to take a breath. The Maiden Guard were superlative warriors, but their martial skill could not defeat the horsemanship of an Ellyrion rider. Their lances struck only empty air as Caelir twisted his mount left and right, and no arrow, no matter how skilfully loosed could find its target thanks to Rhianna's magic.

Caelir galloped into the depths of the forest, the trees closing around him as though accomplices in his escape. Groups of bronze-armoured warrior women set off after Caelir, but Rhianna knew they would not capture him. An Ellyrion horseman would only be caught if he wished to be caught. Only the forest could prevent Caelir's escape, and Rhianna had a suspicion that the ancient sentience that dwelled in the soil, air, water and wood of Avelorn had prescience beyond even the asur, and would thwart every attempt at pursuit.

Rhianna felt the magic drain from her and dropped to her knees as a keening wail of abject loss split the night with a depth of fury no mortal could know and sorrow beyond the reach of even the most broken hearted. Yvraine was at her side in a heartbeat as groups of warriors and poets gathered around the fallen Everqueen.

'What did you do?' asked the Sword Master in disbelief.

'What I had to,' said Rhianna, staring at the fallen Everqueen.

Alarielle's hair spilled around her head like a pillow of spun gold. A single droplet of blood marred the illusion that she was simply resting, and tears welled in Rhianna's eyes.

She looked up as a shadow halted before her.

Through tear-blurred vision, Rhianna saw the leader of the Maiden Guard, her dark hair wild and unbound beneath her bronze helm. Cold fury glittered in her amber eyes, and a terrible grief was held in check only by centuries of training. Her lance was aimed at Rhianna's heart, and the urge to drive it home was evident in every taut sinew and bunched muscle.

'You will come with me,' hissed the Maiden.

Ten warriors of the Maiden Guard led Eldain, Rhianna and Yvraine into a deeper part of the forest, one where what little light remained to the day was filtered through a damp mist of drizzle. Though the ride from their landing at the River Arduil had been frantic, Eldain had not been blind to the soaring magical nature of the forest, yet here its beauty was as flat and dull as any forest of the Old World. The trees here looked dead and withered, devoid of magic and light.

Eldain felt the potent anger of the Maiden Guard, the hostility that came off them in waves, but also the fear that they would be held accountable for this disaster.

'Are we prisoners?' whispered Rhianna.

Eldain shrugged, unsure of their status in Avelorn. 'I don't know, maybe.'

'But we came with a warning,' said Yvraine, chafing at the loss of her greatsword. The Maiden Guard had divested them of weapons, and to take away a Sword Master's blade was like taking a limb. 'We tried to stop this.'

'But you did *not* stop it,' said the Handmaiden with midnight tresses. She removed her helm, setting it down on a moss-covered rock carved with spiralling vines. He face was beautiful, but with its angular lines and narrowed eyes, her beauty took on a twilit aspect that chilled Eldain's blood. 'You aided the Everqueen's attacker in his escape.'

'And he's only getting farther away,' pointed out Yvraine. 'You are wasting time.'

'Your deeds are known to me, Yvraine Hawkblade,' said the Handmaiden, 'so I will not take you to task for your youthful impudence. I am Lirazel, Chief Handmaiden of Everqueen Alarielle, and I do not like others telling me my business.'

'Every moment we tarry here, Caelir slips beyond our grasp,' pressed Yvraine.

Lirazel said, 'For now he is beyond my reach,' and Eldain saw how much it hurt to say those words.

Rhianna saw it too and said, 'Then let us go. We know Caelir. We have been following him since the attack on the White Tower. I have to save him.'

'Save him?' demanded Lirazel, stepping close to Rhianna with a white-knuckled grip on her silver lance. 'After what he did? Who are you, and why would you say such a thing?'

'I am Rhianna Silverfawn, child of Saphery and daughter of Mitherion Silverfawn' said Rhianna. 'And I can say this because I once loved Caelir. We were to be wed in a gentler time I can scarce recall.'

Lirazel's eyes flicked from the pledge ring on Rhianna's hand to the matching one upon Eldain's. Her eyes narrowed as she took in the contours of his features.

'You are kin to Caelir,' she said.

'I am his brother, Eldain of House Éadaoin,' said Eldain, feeling the Handmaiden's gaze strip him bare. Lirazel had failed to protect the Everqueen from one assassin's blade, and she wasn't about to take the chance that murder ran in the family.

'You are one of the horsemasters?'

'Indeed,' agreed Eldain. 'My family has trained with the herds for a thousand years, and none know the way of the horse as we do.'

Lirazel nodded, and said, 'Do you also desire to save Caelir?'

'I do not wish him dead,' replied Eldain, hoping she believed him. In truth, Eldain wasn't sure what he desired. To see Caelir dead would allow him to live the life he had only recently won back, but the chance for redemption that had come with the reawakening of his brother's true self would die with him. The Everqueen might have forgiven him, but hers was not the forgiveness he craved.

'Tell me how you came to be in Avelorn,' said Lirazel. 'Leave nothing out.'

Eldain told how Yvraine had escorted them to the Tower of Hoeth at the behest of Rhianna's father, of how they had arrived in the midst of a terrible battle between the Sword Masters and nightmarish creations of raw magic unleashed by a trap laid in Caelir's memories by Morathi.

Rhianna took up the tale as they sailed across the Inner Sea to the Gaen Vale and travelled the hidden paths on the isle of the Mother Goddess. Her voice fell to little more than a whisper as she spoke of what happened at the island's heart, her soft tones heard only by Yvraine and Lirazel. Eldain made no attempt to hear what passed between the oracle and Rhianna, for it was clearly not meant for the male of the species.

'Save him and you save me,' said Rhianna as she concluded her tale of events on the Gaen Vale. 'I do not understand what it means, but it is all I have.'

From the island of the Mother Goddess they sailed for Avelorn and there the tale ended as Yvraine described their ride through the forest to reach the Everqueen before Caelir. When their tale reached its conclusion, Eldain saw Lirazel's suspicion ease a fraction, and let out a pent-up breath.

Lirazel planted her spear in the earth and ran her hands through her hair. Her skin was tanned from a life spent in the forest, yet her pallor was deathly, as though her wellbeing was contingent on some external factor.

Eldain realised there was one question no one had yet asked.

'What of the Everqueen?' he asked. 'Did Caelir... I mean... is she...?'

'No,' snapped Lirazel. 'And do not say the words. Her mortal flesh hangs in the balance, and the connection to the power within her remains intact only by the slenderest of threads.'

'She's alive,' breathed Rhianna.

'For now,' agreed Lirazel. 'All Ulthuan would feel it were it not so.'

'How can we help?' asked Yvraine, as one of the Maiden Guard appeared at her side bearing her sheathed greatsword. The Sword Master looped the belt around her shoulders, the soft shagreen scabbard slipping exactly into place. 'I am bound to House Éadaoin and Silverfawn by the Oath of the Sword Masters. Where they go, I go.'

'There is little that can be done,' admitted Lirazel. 'Though perhaps the soft wretches that brought Caelir within the borders of Avelorn can shed some light on how they managed to avoid the snares and delusions that should have enraptured any evildoers.'

Eldain looked over his shoulder as he heard a commotion at the edge of the trees, and saw several Handmaidens usher a group of gaudily dressed elves into the clearing. He recognised two as the poet and dancer who had been next to Caelir as he plunged the dagger...

No, don't think it!

'Please!' begged the poet, 'this is all a terrible misunderstanding. We had no inkling that Caelir was a killer. You have to believe us!'

'Shut up, Narentir,' hissed the dancer, with a venom that surprised Eldain. 'You might not have known he was a killer, but I did.'

'Sweet Lilani,' said the poet. 'You have a most delectable mouth, but please, for the love of Loec, keep it shut or you will see us all slain! And lover of new sensations though I am, the embrace of Morai-Heg is not one I am keen to experience.'

'I don't think that is up to me,' said the dancer as Lirazel plucked her spear from the earth.

'Actually it is,' said the Handmaiden.

In the spaces between life and death, magic and reality, Alarielle floated in an ocean of pain. Her lifeblood was all but spent, drawn out by the

Graham McNeill

dark magic bound to the blade of cold iron, and her spirit was adrift in a place where she was alone.

No, not alone. Alone would have been a blessing.

She heard the howls of the banshees in the distance, far away, but closing on her with all the dreadful hunger for which they were rightly feared. The hounds of Morai-Heg, their keening wail was a portent of death, and Alarielle wondered if this was to be her time to pass from the embrace of the Everqueen.

Her body lay on a bed of leaves somewhere impossibly distant, held fast to her spirit by the slenderest of silver cords wrapped around her wrist. What floated in this abyssal darkness was not the crude matter of flesh, but her ageless, immortal essence of magic. One could not exist without the other, and as one sickened so the other faded.

Alarielle felt the banshees gathering, like ocean predators with the scent of blood in the water. Their wailing laments echoed in the void, but their cries were not for her. All around the island of Ulthuan, elves were dying. War had come to her fair isle, the druchii once again bringing hate and blood to the land they had forsaken all those centuries ago.

That age was a time of legend to Alarielle, but little more than a blink of an eye to the power that dwelled within her. Chosen since before her birth to take up the mantle of Everqueen, she had studied and trained for decades before rising to become one of Ulthuan's twin rulers. She remembered the day of her coronation, the terror and awesome sense of multiple threads of fate converging upon her.

Though complex rituals of magical preparation had readied her for the moment of surrender, nothing could have prepared her for the surging torrent of power that coursed through her. The crown upon her brow was a living connection to every queen who had ruled in Avelorn, their memories were her memories, and she struggled to hold on to all that was Alarielle.

What the asur called the Everqueen rose up within her, claiming her for its own ancient purpose. The lives, loves, hopes, dreams and nightmares of all who had held the title before her filled her mind with ancient knowledge. Her mother and grandmother rose up to greet her, easing her into the embrace of the Everqueen and welcoming her to their numberless sisterhood. The line of motherhood stretched back to time immemorial, and Alarielle felt the strength of her lineage steel her to retain her own identity in the face of the vast, elemental power of the Everqueen.

That power was a distant memory, lost to her now as though carved away by a butcher's blade. She could feel it somewhere in the darkness: directionless and unfocussed without a mortal host. It was angry, though such a small word did no justice to the roiling fury that sought her in the darkness. Alarielle felt a great weariness closing in on her, and the magical cords binding her spirit and flesh loosened, unwinding from her wrist like a silken glove, and she felt herself drifting away from the earthly realms. The swirling black shapes of the banshees closed in, their faces hidden, but with gleaming fangs bared and sharpened claws uncurling from gnarled fists.

Hold fast, my daughter, your time in the realm of mortals is not yet over…

It was not one voice, but many, and she knew them all. Hundreds of voices layered into one spoke to her, and each was right to call her daughter. The banshees wailed, this time in anger as this most succulent of morsels was drawn away from them.

Alarielle gripped the silver cords tighter.

'I cannot hold on,' she whispered to the voices within her.

You can. You must. Ulthuan yet needs you…

The voices spoke with one purpose, but a hundred voices, each one subtly different and seeming to come from a multitude of places within her skull. So many voices, so many lives, she could only retain her sense of self thanks to the decades of preparation and her own mastery of the winds of magic. A lesser being would have been driven to madness the instant the crown had been placed upon their brow.

Alarielle held to the voices, letting them guide her back towards her destiny. She followed their gentle urgings, feeling her strength grow the closer she came to the colossal power that lay at the heart of Ulthuan. Leave the Phoenix King his comforting fiction of a shared rule, the power of the Everqueen dwarfed that of any male sovereign.

In her was embodied the true power of creation, what *king* could match such a gift?

At last she felt the power that made her whole, the power she had been wedded to since her birth and which had been waiting for her since before even that.

The banshees retreated, realising there would be no prize beyond the hundreds of souls being sent to them daily from the blood being spilled on Ulthuan's ancient soil. Alarielle felt the pain and suffering of her children, and surrendered herself to the gathering power of the Everqueen.

Her body was wounded unto death, but the frailties of a mortal vessel were insignificant in the face of the Everqueen's ability to heal and renew. She knew there would be pain, and braced herself for a return to the world of flesh.

With a cry of agony, Alarielle opened her eyes.

And the Everqueen looked out.

CHAPTER TWO
WAR CALLS

The blue-fletched arrow leapt from Alathenar's bow, arcing through the cold air to punch through the cheek-plate of a druchii helm. The warrior fell from the ramparts of the Eagle Gate, and Alathenar nocked another arrow to his bow. His fingers were raw and callused, his limbs weary beyond imagining. Once again he loosed, and once again a druchii warrior was pitched from the ramparts.

Beside him, the Shadow Warrior, Alanrias, loosed shafts with a speed and precision that put his own rate of fire to shame. Each black-shafted arrow thudded home in the belly or neck of an enemy fighter, hits that would take them out of the fight, but leave them writhing in agony for days.

Alanrias paused only to take a drink from a ceramic wine jug placed behind the toothed parapet.

'Thirsty work, killing druchii,' he said, as though they were shooting at targets instead of fighting for their lives.

Alathenar wasted no words on the Shadow Warrior, seeing in him a reflection of the druchii army that battered itself bloody against the mighty fortress that guarded this route through the Annulii to Ellyrion. He reached for another shaft, but his hands closed on empty air. His quiver was spent.

'Here,' said Alanrias, tossing him a full quiver of black leather.

'My thanks,' said Alathenar, drawing an arrow from the quiver. It was lighter than he was used to, fashioned from some withered tree of

Nagarythe, and the iron tip was barbed to make it next to impossible to remove. Its length was spiked with tiny thorns that would cause ghastly torment to any victim as they writhed in pain.

Alathenar said nothing, but nocked the arrow to his bow. The string was woven with strands of hair from his beloved Arenia, and her love gave his arrows an extra ten yards at least. The string slipped, as though rebelling at so vile a barb, but Alathenar whispered words of soothing magic and the bow was appeased.

He scanned the walls of the Eagle Gate, looking for a target worthy of his bow.

There were plenty to choose from.

The walls of the fortress stretched across the mountain pass, its white and blue stonework marred by weeks of war and magical attack. An unbroken line of elven warriors, wondrously arrayed in tunics of cream and gold, blue and silver, held the wall against thousands of dark-armoured druchii and human fighters in burnished plates of iron and baked leather. The defenders of the Eagle Gate were magnificent and proud, yet there was a brittle edge of desperation to their fighting.

An assassin's blade had ended the life of the Eagle Gate's commander, Cerion Goldwing, and the heart of the defenders had died with their beloved leader. Alathenar glanced towards the Aquila Spire, and a splinter of ice wormed its way into his heart. The warriors of the Eagle Gate were fighting to protect their homeland against the bitterest of foes, yet Cerion's successor had yet to wield a blade alongside them.

A flitting shadow darted overhead, and Alathenar cursed his inattention. Screeching, bat-like creatures with a repellent female aspect swooped overhead, darting down to tear at the defenders with ebony dewclaws. He sent a shaft into the breast of one of the flying creatures, sending it tumbling down to the floor of the pass, where druchii beastmasters goaded even more terrible creatures into battle.

Chained draconic things with a multitude of roaring heads sprayed the wall with caustic fire and bellowed in pain at their master's tridents. Beside them, mindless abominations with elastic limbs and forms so abhorrent they resembled no creature known to the Loremasters of Hoeth, clawed and howled as they smote the reinforced gateway. The air crackled and fizzed with unleashed magic as elven mages countered the sorceries of the druchii, and protective runes worked into the parapet blazed with powerful light.

Druchii warriors clambered up black ladders, only to be met with asur steel, and the carnage was terrible to behold. Precious elven blood made the ramparts slick, and the healers were stretched far beyond their ability to cope with the number of wounded being carried to them by stretcher bearers.

Alathenar saw Eloien Redcloak fighting at the centre of the wall, where once a mighty carven eagle head had stared into the west. His sword was a blur of silver, his cloak a darting wing of blood as he wove a path of destruction through those druchii who gained the walls. The warrior of Ellyrion was a master of war from horseback, but was just as lethal on foot.

A towering brute in crudely strapped plates of iron daubed in lurid blue rose up behind Redcloak, and Alathenar sent a borrowed arrow through the gap between his neck torque and helmet. The enemy warrior dropped and Eloien raised his sword in salute, knowing full well who had loosed the fatal shaft. Alathenar soon found other targets, a druchii climbing the face of the Aquila Spire, another poised to deliver the death-blow to a fallen asur warrior, a screeching monster that swooped down on a wounded archer. Each time his arrow slashed home with deadly accuracy, though none were killing strikes.

'Is it my imagination, or are these arrows spiteful?' he shouted to Alanrias.

The Shadow Warrior grinned. 'I crafted them from the trees upon which the blood of the druchii fell after Alith Anar nailed seven hundred of them to the walls of Griffon Pass. If there is spite within them, it is of their own making.'

'They say your people are touched by the Witch King,' said Alathenar, slotting another arrow to his bowstring. 'I can well believe it.'

'Do not presume to judge me, warrior of Eataine,' snarled the Shadow Warrior. 'Wait until your land and home is destroyed by the druchii and see how much mercy fills your heart for their worthless lives!'

Alathenar recoiled from the warrior's anger.

'I will kill them, and I will return to them the pain my people have known tenfold.'

'*Your* people?' hissed Alathenar. 'We are one people. We are the asur.'

'Think you so?' said Alanrias, nodding in the direction of the tallest tower still standing upon the Eagle Gate. 'You would count him amongst us?'

Alathenar knew exactly to whom the Shadow Warrior was referring. Within the impregnable walls of the Aquila Spire, Glorien Truecrown, the commander of the Eagle Gate was ensconced with his dusty books and ancient treatises on war. While the defenders fought and died upon the walls of the Eagle Gate, Glorien fretted over the words of long dead scholars instead of leading his warriors with the courage and nobility expected of an elven prince.

'The commander of a fortress is its heart,' said Alanrias. 'And no living thing can fight without its heart. You know this to be true, archer.'

'I know those words could see you executed,' said Alathenar.

'The warriors of this fortress look to you to lead them, not Truecrown,' replied Alanrias. 'I know what must be done to win this day, and I see from your eyes that you know it too.'

Alathenar bit back a furious retort. He wanted to chastise the Shadow

Warrior for his sedition, to reprimand him for his lack of loyalty, but he could not find the words. The realisation tasted of ashes in his mouth, and he felt the splinter of ice harden his heart.

For he knew Alanrias was right.

With every mile he rode, Caelir expected death. With every mile that passed without it, he wondered why. He had slain the Everqueen. The fact of that deed was evident in the grey sky, the weeping rain and the sagging branches of every tree. The life had bled out of the forest, the magic that had sustained it for an eternity now ended in one treacherous dagger thrust.

His clothes were plastered to his body in the rain, an impractical mix of silks and satin that looked like they belonged to some courtly noble- man, not a horseman of Ellyrion. The rush of memory was still raw and rough edged, his abused mind struggling to cope with the return of a life unremembered. He thought his skull might burst with the torrent of images, sensations and vivid recall that flooded his senses. He could remember the succulent taste of roast stag, hear a forgotten sound of crystal bells and feel the lost warmth of a mother's embrace.

Caelir fought to hold onto the present, blinking tears and raindrops away as he rode madly through the depths of Avelorn Forest. Blurred shapes passed him, oaks, ash, and willow. He heard chittering voices, capering sprites and the ancient creak and groan of creatures older than the elves as they moved unseen in the darkness. To ride like this was madness, as a hidden burrow or a concealed root could trip his horse and break its leg. This beast was no Ellyrian mount, but one of Saphery, its coat lambent and silky with magical residue. The black steed he had ridden to Avelorn...

Lotharin!

Yes, Lotharin, that was Eldain's mount. His brother had scoffed at the naysayers who said that a black horse would bring its rider ill-fortune. He remembered the vision he had experienced in Anurion the Green's overgrown villa on the coast of Yvresse, that of a dappled grey stallion galloping through the surf.

Aedaris...

On the heels of that memory came the pain of knowing that his beloved Aedaris was dead, her flanks pierced by druchii bolts in the dockyards of Clar Karond. He recognised the mount that bore him now, a powerful mare by the name of Irenya, who galloped with sure and steady grace through the haunted forest. Once she had borne a retainer of his father's villa, but that warrior had died...

More memories intruded, Rhianna, Kyrielle, Lilani and all that had hap- pened since his return to Ulthuan. Caelir wept to know that he had been used as an instrument of murder, but the guilt he felt was tempered by the knowledge that there were few alive who could have withstood the tortures and unclean magic that had been worked upon his flesh and spirit.

'You should have killed me, Eldain,' he wept. 'Better dead than left to the druchii.'

His horse flicked its ears in annoyance at the name of the dark kin from across the ocean, and Caelir rubbed its neck as it ran. Trees and lightless arbours flashed past him, and Caelir could not fathom why the forest had not killed him.

He sensed its hostility in every looming tree, every grasping branch that whipped him as he passed. Yet for all their bitter spite, they did not stop him, did not unhorse him and seemed to close up behind him as though reluctantly aiding him. The steed rode paths of the forest unknown to even the Maiden Guard, traversing the secret ways known only to the trees and denizens of Avelorn who had made their home here before the coming of the elves.

Caelir had no idea where the paths of the forest were leading him, or where his horse was taking him. In truth, he didn't care. There was nothing left to him now, no refuge, no friends and no loved ones to take him in or offer him succour. Caelir was alone in the world and every place of goodness and decency would surely reject him. In such times where could anyone go?

The first Caelir was aware of how far he had ridden was when he heard the sound of rushing water, and smelled the scent of the Inner Sea. His head came up and he saw the forest thin ahead of him, thick, ancient-bodied trees giving way to younger, more vigorous saplings hungry to break the borders forced upon them by elfkind. Though still many miles before him, the escarpment of the Annulii reared up in a towering white cliff that soared beyond the clouds. The majestic peaks of the distant mountains were shawled with tumbling streams of raw magic drawn to Ulthuan by the long lost mages of Caledor Dragontamer.

He rode from the trees, seeing a wide river before him and knowing it as the Arduil, the watercourse that marked the boundary between Avelorn and Ellyrion. A small ship rode high in the water, a mid-sized sloop with runes etched into its prow that named it *Dragonkin*.

Its crew were already aboard and the ship was ready to make sail, but its captain made no move to take her out, as though waiting for something or someone to return. Caelir rode to the edge of the river and the captain of the ship came over to the gunwale. His skin was ruddy from a life spent upon the waters, and his keen eye took in Caelir's unusual garb with a curious glance, which surprised Caelir. This was Avelorn, and this seafarer must have borne stranger travellers than he to the Everqueen's realm.

'My lord,' said the captain. 'I dreamed I would see you again. Yet I dreamed you older, not younger.'

Caelir knew in that instant how Eldain had come to Avelorn, and shook his head.

'You mistake me for another, friend captain,' said Caelir, turning his horse away. 'When you see my brother again, ask him if it was all worthwhile.'

'You are not Lord Éadaoin?'

'No, nor will I ever be,' said Caelir, riding away towards a point where Irenya could cross the river. Caelir glanced over his shoulder. The crew of the boat were watching him, and he gave the captain a wave. No such gesture was returned and Caelir guided his mount down the muddy slopes of the bank and into the river. The riverbed was barely a yard and a half below the surface, a depth that would have been impassable to any ships but those of the asur.

The water was cold, icy from its journey down the flanks of the Annulii, yet Caelir welcomed its frozen touch. He rode into the centre of the river and stopped, feeling the water churn with the agitation of nymphs beneath the surface. They called to him with tiny splashes and gurgles, capering around his horse's legs with fearful burbles.

'I have no tears left to spare,' he said, and they sped off upriver with hurt splashes.

Caelir paused a moment before resuming his crossing, bathing in the cold magical energies of Ulthuan's waters. He tipped his head back and spread his arms, letting the touch of the river wash him clean of the dark enchantments surrounding him. He closed his eyes and let loose an almighty shout, a primal scream of loss, anger and catharsis.

All that had been done to him poured out in his cries, and he yelled till he was hoarse.

When it was done, he tapped his heels to the horse's flanks and rode towards the far shore. Like Avelorn, low clouds smothered Ellyrion's beauty, the enduring summers that warmed its wide, trackless steppes and unbroken wilds banished in the face of the grief that engulfed the land of Ulthuan.

Even shrouded in sorrow, Ellyrion was a tonic for the spirit. A wind blew across its face, carrying the scent of the wild herds, the open plains and the long grass that waved in gentle breezes that caressed the skin like a lover.

Caelir rode from the cold waters and onto the soil of Ellyrion, feeling the land welcome him as a prodigal son. In the shadows of the mountains lay Ellyr-Charoi, the marble-walled villa where he had grown to manhood and learned the ways of the horse lords from his father. This was where he belonged, in a wild, untamed land where elf and steed roamed free and answerable to no one.

Ellyrion was a golden kingdom, and no sorrow could dim its radiance for long.

The clouds parted somewhere far to the south, and a single brilliant beam of sunlight broke through to shine on a distant city of crystal castles, silver bridges and fabulous, soaring towers of gold and silver.

It was the most beautiful thing Caelir had ever seen.

'I am home,' he said.

In all his long life, Prince Tyrion of Ulthuan had never known weakness like this. Though he had been wounded before, by those few foes skilled enough to penetrate his defences, the pain that was now his constant companion cut deeper than any sword thrust or axe blow.

This was a wound of the spirit.

He clung tightly to Malhandir's reins as a wave of pain washed over him, and only his superlative mastery of his own body kept him in the saddle. His aquiline features, so noble and yet so harsh, were now drained of colour and his eyes held the emptiness of a corpse long lain within its tomb.

The dusty plain before the mountain castle was thick with druchii dead, their plum-coloured cloaks stained with ignoble blood. Though this had been little more than a skirmish, a prelude to the slaughter to come, it felt good to kill again, and shed the blood of those who dared invade his homeland and strike down his loved ones.

Such terrible lust to kill was not born within Tyrion, but far to the north upon the Blighted Isle, where the ancient blade of Aenarion reared proud from its blood-soaked altar and called to the cursed descendants of that legendary hero. The pleasure Tyrion took in slaughter was the Sword of Khaine's gift to him, driving his blade home and giving him the strength he needed to slay his enemies.

In times of peace its song was a curse, in times of war a boon.

Tyrion hated that its keening wail of murder made him feel so alive, yet what other power could keep his grief and pain at bay?

Every instinct screamed at him to abandon Lothern and ride with dragonspeed to the forest realm of his beloved Alarielle. He was the Ever-queen's champion and he was far from her side at her hour of greatest need. She lay on the cusp of death, yet he could do nothing for her. So fleet was Malhandir that Tyrion could be in Avelorn by nightfall, yet his promise to Alarielle bound him to the defence of Lothern with chains of duty stronger than the finest ithilmar.

He had promised her that he would heed his brother's counsel, and Teclis had bade him fight alongside the Phoenix King's warriors in their desperate battle against the druchii invaders. King Finubar and his White Lions fought with the warriors of Eataine on the ramparts of the Emerald Gate, and he had entrusted Tyrion with securing the castles on the rocky shoulders of the mighty portal that blocked entrance to the Straits of Lothern.

'Keep my flanks secure, Tyrion,' Finubar had urged him as they parted in the shadow of the great statues that towered over the wondrous port. 'If the druchii take but one of the castles then the Emerald Gate must be yielded. I would not see it so, my friend.'

'Nor I, my king,' Tyrion had promised. 'I will hold it as long as I can.'

The memory faded and Tyrion slumped over Malhandir's neck as his strength ebbed, like the tide around the bloody, bone-choked shores of the Blighted Isle. His vision blurred and he pictured the plain of bones and the smouldering black sword of his ancestor. Even over so great a distance the Sword of Khaine called to him with promises of the power to win victories undreamed.

Tyrion shook his head, eyes closed and teeth gritted together to resist its call, for damnation and ruination would fall upon any who drew the cursed blade.

Belarien rode alongside him, his sword wet with enemy blood. They had fought as brothers since the last great invasion of the druchii, and spilled blood together on the blasted plain of Finuval. They had sailed the great oceans of the world and seen its wonders side by side. Only Teclis, it was said, was closer to Tyrion than Belarien.

'My lord,' cried Belarien as Tyrion swayed in the saddle. 'Are you wounded?'

'By this rabble?' hissed Tyrion, ramming Sunfang back in its red-gold scabbard. 'Not unless I have lost every skill I once possessed.'

The battle Tyrion and Belarien's Silver Helms had fought before the gate of the castle had been brief and bloody. The druchii had been poorly led, overconfident and scattered by their ill-disciplined charge. Easy pickings for the finest heavy cavalry in the world.

His ancient blade had drawn deep from the well of druchii blood, and reaped many souls to send to Morai-Heg. Yet no sooner had they crushed this first attack beneath the glittering hooves of their steeds than Tyrion had felt the dagger thrust as though it had plunged into his own heart.

'Lead us within the walls,' hissed Tyrion. 'Now!'

Belarien waved to the Silver Helms' clarion and a shrill note was blown from an icy trumpet that rallied the triumphant riders to their prince. Steeds of dappled grey formed up around Tyrion, their flanks gleaming with their own inner light. Tyrion spun his horse, taking up position at their head as the Silver Helms moved off. No commands, no vulgar blows from a whip or raking violence of spurs had been needed, for these steeds understood their masters' will as though rider and mount shared one mind.

Tyrion gripped tight to Malhandir. The steed felt its rider's pain and bore him with all swiftness to the safety of the castle. The gate shut behind them, and a volley of arrows hissed from the gleaming ramparts as the druchii gathered for another attack. Tyrion had seen the opportunity to ride out against the last attack, but the enemy would not be so incautious again.

A squire took Malhandir's bridle and Tyrion nodded his thanks. He slid from the saddle, and hissed with pain as the impact of his landing jarred the phantom wound in his heart. He placed his hand upon his chest. Though the golden scales of Aenarion's armour remained unbroken, Tyrion felt the cold touch of death drawing ever closer to his heart.

'My lord?' said Belarien, dismounting next to him and handing his steed's reins off to another squire. 'The pain is getting worse.'

Tyrion took a deep breath, marshalling his strength.

'No,' he said at last. 'It is the same.'

'I was not asking a question.'

'I know,' said Tyrion, accepting a goblet of water from a warrior in the livery of the Eataine citizen levy. Belarien removed his helmet, a gleaming silver artefact adorned with a host of battle honours, ribbons and eagle feathers. His thin face was etched with concern for his prince, his pale grey eyes glittering with flecks of amber. He too accepted a goblet, and drained it in one long swallow.

'Are we not friends enough that you can speak to me truthfully?' asked Belarien. 'I saw you almost fall from your saddle.'

'Malhandir would never allow it,' stated Tyrion.

'Maybe not,' agreed the High Helm of Tyrion's riders. 'But I saw what I saw.'

Tyrion saw Belarien would not be dissuaded from his questions, and sighed.

'You are my dearest friend,' said Tyrion. 'But some burdens are mine to bear alone.'

'Only because you choose to make it so,' pressed Belarien, taking Tyrion's arm. 'Remember you have friends with wide shoulders.'

Tyrion smiled and said, 'I know. Asuryan and Isha have blessed me with my companions in war and peace, but weakness is for mortals, not those upon whom the survival of their race depends.'

Belarien saw the truth of Tyrion's pain. 'You still feel the Everqueen's wound.'

'I do,' admitted Tyrion. 'It is like a slow-moving dagger pushing towards my heart. Only with Teclis do I share a closer bond, but his near death at the hands of the traitor Caelir was a swiftly forgotten ailment compared to this weakness. Until Alarielle heals I will share a measure of her pain, as she once bore a measure of mine when the forests of Avelorn burned and the assassins closed in.'

'Then is there nothing I can do?'

'I fear not. Every battle host draws its will to fight from its leader, and I must be as strong and powerful as ever to the warriors around me. More so, now that I need them to stand fast in the face of an unwinnable fight.'

'You do not believe we can hold this castle?'

On the ramparts, archers loosed volley after volley at the druchii beyond the walls. Here and there, a scream punctured the clear sky as a bolt of black iron from an enemy crossbow felled one of the defenders.

'You and I will not ride like that again, Belarien,' said Tyrion. 'The druchii leader was a glory seeker, but the next assault will be commanded by a more cautious warrior.'

'And we will hurl his rabble back too,' promised Belarien.

'Your ardour does you credit, my friend, but this castle was not built to resist anything other than skirmish troops or a probing force. No one foresaw the need for it to be stronger. It will fall eventually, that is certain.'

Belarien replaced his helm and fixed Tyrion with a determined gaze. 'Then we will make them pay for its walls in blood.'

Tyrion drew Sunfang from its sheath, and the Silver Helm mirrored his movement in one fluid unveiling of glittering silver steel.

'That we shall,' promised Tyrion, his proud voice carrying to every warrior within the castle. 'I promised the Phoenix King that I would hold this place, and no scrap of Ulthuan will be yielded without an ocean of druchii blood spilled in its name.'

He raised Sunfang high, the weak light catching the radiant blaze of its shimmering blade. For one shining moment, the grief and hideous twilight of the Everqueen's pain was banished in a burst of brilliant sunlight. The cold fire in Tyrion's chest was no less diminished, but pain was fleeting, legends would last forever.

'For the Everqueen and Ulthuan!' yelled Tyrion, leading the Silver Helms towards the ramparts. That the castle would fall was inevitable, but Tyrion would make its doom so bloody for the druchii that this battle would live in their memories for all eternity.

On the Blighted Isle, the Sword of Khaine simmered with anticipation in its dripping, reeking altar.

CHAPTER THREE
VOICES FROM ANCIENT DAYS

Birdsong had returned to Avelorn, though Eldain hardly noticed. He wandered the shadowed groves and garlanded arbours of the forest, letting its twisting paths guide his steps rather than any conscious thought of a destination. Sunlight and joy had drained from the enchanted forest, but it had not been extinguished.

The Everqueen had survived Caelir's blow, though none yet knew what damage had been done to her. Eldain knew well how the weapons of the druchii could cause such hurt as to leave the body intact but destroy the life within. His own father had fallen to such a weapon, his wasting flesh lingering long after his spirit had withered and died.

Eldain had not thought of his father in some time, and the guilt of that was another cold nail hammered into the hard muscle of his heart.

How much could any soul endure before it became too heavy a burden to bear?

Plants and trees bent their backs away from him and the path turned him around, this way and that, as he roamed at random through the leafy depths. He had no idea where he was, and that was dangerous in a place like Avelorn. No one, not even the Everqueen or her Maiden Guard, knew the full extent of what lay at the forest's heart. To stray with such lack of care in a place of magic was reckless beyond words.

Eldain looked up from the path, hearing voices raised in song. Not a lament, this was a song of love triumphant and the joyous union of souls. Notes struck from a lyre of glorious timbre drifted through the trees and where they fell, the leaves shone a vivid green, and grass once withered bloomed anew. It was music to lift the heart and refresh the soul. Anger touched Eldain. What right did anyone have to sing such songs in times of woe? The more he listened, the more the music and joyous lyrics seemed to mock him, as though chosen with deliberate irony.

His fists bunched at his sides, and he set off in the direction of the players, seeing drifting forms in gossamer-thin robes of silk through the foliage. Riotous colours fluttered in the spaces between the trees and bushes. Eldain saw elves of both sexes, none wearing the white of mourning as they danced and swayed to the wondrous tunes of the musicians.

A figure stepped from behind a tree before he could intrude on the recital, a female elf of striking appearance. Clad in a twisting weave of auburn silk and crimson damask, her body was lithe and hard with wiry cords of muscle. Her hair fell about her shoulders in golden tresses, and Eldain recognised the dancer that had stood beside Caelir and who been brought before the Maiden Guard.

'Whatever you are about to do, think again,' she said, her voice hard and pitiless.

'They mock my pain,' hissed Eldain.

'No, they celebrate the Everqueen's survival,' said the dancer. 'There's a difference.'

Eldain nodded in understanding, ashamed he had allowed music and laughter to enrage him so. He gripped the branch of a tree, feeling thorns prick his skin and the leaves shake in irritation at his touch.

'You and the forest are not friends?' asked the elf maid, seeing a drop of blood on his arm.

'I have no friends,' said Eldain. 'Least of all in Avelorn.'

'I am Lilani,' said the dancer with a seductive purr. 'I could be your friend.'

'You don't know me.'

'I knew your brother,' said Lilani. 'You look a lot like him. Sadder, though.'

'I saw you beside Caelir when the Everqueen…' began Eldain. 'How did you know him?'

'We met crossing the Finuval Plain,' she said, linking her arm with his and leading him towards the musicians and dancers within the grove. 'He and I were lovers for a time.'

Eldain was taken aback at her frank admission, but knew he shouldn't have been. Avelorn was a realm where the normal rules of conduct and etiquette were proudly flouted. What would have shocked the polite society of Lothern or Tor Elyr was a daily occurrence within the Everqueen's realm.

'I didn't know that,' he said, hating how prudish his words sounded.

'Why would you?' she said.

Eldain shrugged, trying to think of something to say that wouldn't make him sound like more of a dullard than he already felt. Lilani led him into a wide clearing, across which had been spread a riotously garish spread of blankets. Elves lay sprawled throughout the clearing, drinking dreamwine from crystal goblets that sparkled like ice in the evening twilight.

A goblet appeared in his hand, though Eldain could not recall anyone passing near enough to have given it to him. Within the goblet, the dreamwine swirled like a miniature whirlpool of glittering quartz and mist. He hesitated to taste it, remembering when he had drunk a similar vintage with Rhianna before leaving for Naggaroth.

'You've drunk dreamwine before, haven't you?' said a fluid voice before him.

Eldain looked up into the eyes of the elf poet the Maiden Guard had spoken to in the wake of Caelir's attack.

'I have,' agreed Eldain, turning his wrist and upending the goblet. 'And it didn't agree with me then either.'

'What a dreadful shame,' said the poet as the dreamwine floated away like a whispered secret. 'And a terrible waste. Good dreamwine is hard to come by, especially now. Still, I am sure the wind will enjoy it, though what the wind dreams of only fools and eagles know.'

'You are Narentir?' said Eldain.

'How wonderful to be recognised,' said the poet, clapping his hands in delight. 'You have read my work?'

'No,' said Eldain. 'I saw the Maiden Guard drag you before them.'

'Ah, yes, an unfortunate business,' said Narentir, turning away from him and threading his way through the lounging elves. Lilani followed him, taking Eldain with her, and he found himself powerless to resist. Her beauty was intoxicating, her touch magical and exhilarating.

Narentir stopped beside a brightly painted wagon and lifted out a gleaming breastplate and a sword encased in a scabbard of sapphires and rubies.

'Your brother, for I see by the proud jaw, aquiline nose and brooding eyes that you are related to our erstwhile companion, has caused us quite a considerable amount of trouble. Merely for the crime of knowing him, the members of our happy troupe were subjected to many hours of objectionable questioning by the Everqueen's protectors, though, given her current condition, I use that description laughingly.'

Eldain took his arm from Lilani and nodded. 'I am Caelir's brother, yes.'

'Well of course you are, dear boy,' said Narentir, casting his gaze up and down. 'Though I fear young Caelir alone inherited the family talent for song and rhyme.'

'He performed for you?'

'For some more than others,' grinned Narentir, with a sly look at

Lilani. The elf maid did not blush or show any sign of embarrassment at the poet's lascivious comment. Eldain ignored Narentir's unabashed tone and looked around the gathering of elves.

'How long did you travel with Caelir?' asked Eldain, as a pair of musicians again began to play their instruments. This time, the music was melancholy, bittersweet and full of regret. Eldain felt his anger at these performers abate, for what had they done except take Caelir in as a travelling companion?

With a start, Eldain realised that the clearing had begun to fill without his noticing. Dozens of elves had silently slipped through the gloaming, appearing in the gaps between the trees in greater and greater numbers until hundreds had gathered around the colourful stage of blankets.

'He came upon us at the northern extent of Finuval Plain,' said Narentir, apparently oblivious to the swelling numbers of observers. 'A curious fellow, and no mistake, but I saw the soul of a rake and a rogue in him, a fellow traveller on a whimsical road that leads everywhere and comes from nowhere.'

Narentir sighed. 'How I was mistaken, for though Caelir was all those things and more, a darkness was hidden within him and I, in my innocence, failed to see it. Woe unto the poet that he should always seek the best in others.'

A single note of music chimed, and Narentir smiled with theatrical zeal.

'But, alas, I must take a turn as a poor player before my audience, for in times such as these, what is left to us but tales of valour to rekindle hope and stir the hearts of those who will defend us?'

Eldain turned to Lilani, the poet's overblown manner beginning to irritate him. 'Do you know what he's talking about?'

She nodded and said, 'Come. Sit with me awhile and you will see.'

Narentir took centre stage on the blankets, clad in his gleaming breastplate and with his gilded scabbard belted at his side. He wore a cloak of brilliant blue, which billowed around him, though not a breath of wind stirred the leaves and grass of the clearing. A winged helm sat upon his head, such as might be worn by an elven prince of a forgotten age. The ensemble should have been ridiculous, for Narentir was clearly no warrior, but Eldain found himself picturing the poet as a great hero, a leader from distant times who none now remembered, save in song.

'Let me tell you of a time long passed, when gods walked the earth and mighty heroes were as common as gemstones upon the fingers of an Eataine princess. Let me tell you of the doom of the Ulthane and the glorious time of their rebirth. Let me tell you of ultimate evil unleashed, and the bright heroes of legend who stood against it!'

Despite himself, Eldain felt himself caught up in Narentir's words. Flitting will-o'-the-wisps bobbed through the clearing, casting a diffuse glow over the gathered elves. Eldain saw every face enraptured by the poet's presence, the cadence and rhythmic flow of his delivery perfectly capturing the spirit of the age.

Narentir prowled the stage of rugs, his arms spread wide and his head thrown back as he told the epic of Aenarion, when the land of Ulthuan had burned with the touch of daemons from beyond the great gateway. Hearts thrilled to the tales of battles fought in the shadow of impending destruction, and though all knew the outcome – for the legend of the Defender was taught to every child upon their mother's knee – tears were spilled and breath caught at each twist in the tale.

At last Narentir came to the tale of Caledor Dragontamer, Aenarion's greatest and most trusted friend and architect of the final victory against the daemons. Eldain felt Lilani press herself to him in fear as Narentir told of how the great Chaos powers laid siege to the Isle of the Dead to prevent Caledor from completing his great ritual to deny the daemons their source of power.

Eldain found himself able to picture the limitless hordes of daemons battling to overcome Aenarion's brave defenders. As Narentir leapt and spun, slashing the air with graceful sweeps of his sword, Eldain saw the epic confrontation between the mighty daemon lords and the Phoenix King. He flinched with every depiction of that incredible battle, and when the poet was done, Eldain wept as he heard of how Caledor and his fellow mages had drained the world of volatile magic, leaving the daemonic host powerless and dying, like fish stranded by the tide. The price of that success was beyond imagining, for Caledor and his fellow mages were now trapped forever in a vortex of powerful magic upon the Isle of the Dead. They now existed in a place beyond time and beyond the reach of mortals.

Eldain shivered at the mention of that accursed island. He remembered the shifting mists and bitter taste of old magic as the *Dragonkin* had sailed close to its unnatural boundaries. The sea around the Isle of the Dead was gloomy and bleak with timeless melancholy, and Eldain swallowed a sudden bilious nausea at the thought of that doomed island out of time.

He blinked, listening as Narentir recounted the last flight of the mortally wounded Indraugnir, greatest of dragons, who carried the dying Aenarion to the Blighted Isle. A respectful hush fell across the audience, and heads bowed at the memory of the fallen Phoenix King. He and Caledor had been the greatest of the asur. Their selfless deeds ensured the world would live on, though none beyond the shores of Ulthuan would ever know of their incredible sacrifice.

Yet as the tale wound to its well known conclusion, Eldain saw that Narentir was not finished. His tale had more to reveal, and like all good tales, it grew in the telling.

'Greatest master of magic though he was, not even Caledor could tame such forces as were unleashed by the first masters of the world,' sang Narentir. 'Though his great ritual drew the storms of magic to Ulthuan that they might be drained from the world, not all enchantments can be so neatly caged.'

Narentir prowled the stage, his sword now sheathed and his hands grasping the air as though struggling to contain some unseen power that flitted just beyond his grasp.

'Cracks there were in the world, for the devastation wrought in the great cataclysm that brought Chaos to the world was like nothing seen before or since. Wild magic seeps into the world through those cracks, like water through a crumbling weir. In enchanted groves, spellbound forests, mist-wreathed marshes or mystical caves, that magic lights the world around it, gives it life and fills the hearts of all those who look upon them with joy, though they know not what beguiles them. But not all such cracks are places of wonderment, some are gateways to the terrible powers that almost destroyed the world, and such places must be guarded by those with hearts as pure and strong as the first dawn.

'Such warriors were the Ulthane! Heroes cast in the image of Aenarion and Caledor combined, yet none here know their names, for they desired not fame nor riches nor glory, for they served a higher purpose. The gods had chosen them, granting them power beyond the ken of mortal and asur alike, for they stood watch on the one place Caledor's spell could not seal, a bloody isle unknown to maps or seafarers, yet which lived in the hearts of men as a dark tale of shipwrecks and lost souls.'

Narentir paused before Eldain. The poet's eyes shone with the vibrancy of his tale, as though a portion of that dark time passed from that age to this. Even the shimmering forest lights had dimmed, and the elves gathered around Narentir held their breath as they waited for him to continue. The poet knew his craft, letting the anticipation of his next words build before pressing on with his tale.

'The gods of Chaos are cunning, and, worst of all, patient. They knew that no creature of this world could fully tame the tides of magic, and they waited for their chance to strike. The Dark Powers sent their minions to that island, and laid siege to it as once they had besieged Ulthuan. With the light of Aenarion gone from the world, they knew of no enemy that could stand before their numberless hordes. Yet for all their cunning, they knew not of the Ulthane, for each among them had shed their former lives and vanished from the pages of history, becoming nameless warriors in the service of order. The Dark Gods could not see them, could not know them, and could not defeat them.

'Upon the shores of that black island, a battle to save the world was waged. A host of daemons fell from the skies, and an army of leviathans rose from the deepest ocean trenches. The very rock rebelled at their touch and writhed in new and terrible forms. And upon that once-fair isle, the blood ran in rivers, turning the waters red for leagues in all directions, yet not once did the Ulthane falter! Their swords were thunder-forged lightning, their shields ice-wrought mirrors. A hundred daemons fell with every blow, and beneath the Ulthane's red-lit eyes, no creature born of Chaos could stand but be withered and cast back to its diabolical abode.'

Eldain could dimly remember hearing legends of the Ulthane when he had been a child, but the memories were hazy and indistinct, like a fleeting dream that escapes recall upon waking. Though Narentir told his tale with vigour and charm, its details were already fading from his mind, as though the memory of the Ulthane dared not linger in the memories of those who heard of them for fear the Dark Gods of the north might learn of their existence.

'And like Aenarion before them, the Ulthane hurled back the foe, fighting a hundred battles in as many days. Though the foe attacked without mercy, neither did the Ulthane stop to lament their fallen brothers nor pause to take sustenance. Their swords smote mightily, and little by little, the attacks of the monstrous horde lessened until, at last, the Dark Powers abandoned their assault.

'The battle was won, but at a fearful cost. Barely a handful of the Ulthane remained, and all knew that there could be no return to the lives they had known. Another attack would come, from the daemons or some other foe intent on seizing the incredible power that lay at the heart of the island. The Ulthane gathered at the twisted heart of the island and swore mighty and unbreakable oaths to stand guard upon its shores forever more.

'Though ages of the world came and went, the Ulthane stood sentinel over the island, summoning up an enchanted mist to keep the island from the thoughts of lesser races and never once relaxing their penetrating gaze. And should a time come where the world needs their blades again, the Ulthane will return, thunder-forged swords and shields of mirrored ice out-thrust to whatever enemy dares to wreak harm upon the world they have sworn to defend. And such times are upon us now, dear friends. The shadow of the Witch King lies long upon the lands of Ulthuan as he and his damnable mother strike at the heart of our fair isle. In this time of woe, shall not the greatest heroes of the age rise to our salvation? Shall not every heart be filled with martial pride and towering fury to drive these invaders away? Though darkness claws at the horizon with iron nails, we must not forsake hope. Though our enemies gather like wolves around a wounded stag, we will not despair, for even the sly wolf knows the stag can fight back. Hold to hope, my friends, for Ulthuan has never yet fallen, and nor shall she fall now!'

Thunderous applause erupted from every elf in the clearing and from thousands more unseen in the forest's depths. Eldain joined in, bruising his palms with the vigour of his clapping. He surged to his feet, convinced the towering forms of the Ulthane were about to march from the trees with their thunder-forged swords held high.

Lilani uncoiled from the ground, vaulting into the air and landing on an overhanging branch. She loosed a wild shout of joy, an exultant cry that was taken up by all the gathered elves until it seemed the entire forest was yelling with one voice.

Only when three bronze-armoured Maiden Guard entered the clearing did the thunderous noise begin to diminish. All heads turned to the grim-eyed warrior maidens as they marched past the exhausted Narentir. Eldain watched them also, knowing in a heartbeat that they had come for him.

Lirazel came at their head, her silver-bladed lance held at her side as she fixed him with a steely-eyed gaze that left no doubt as to what would happen if he tried to resist. Eldain had no intention of resisting, for he knew where they would be taking him.

Lilani dropped to the leafy floor of the clearing beside him and clutched his arm tightly. She leaned in close and whispered urgently in his ear.

'Remember Narentir's words. Do not forsake hope. Never give in to despair.'

With those words she sprang away, vanishing from sight amid the gradually dispersing crowd of elves. With the taleteller done, their whims and fancies carried them away like leaves in an autumn wind.

Lirazel halted before Eldain, and her eyes held the promise of winter in their amber depths. Something awesome shimmered beneath her skin, a fragment of a presence incalculably ancient and merciless. The elemental power of Avelorn lurked within this warrior of the Maiden Guard, and Eldain felt his heart hammering in his chest at its nearness.

'I know why you are here,' he whispered. 'You will have no need of lances or bows.'

'Then let us begone from these minstrels and troubadours,' said Lirazel in a voice that echoed with the weight of ages and an unbroken line of life that stretched back to the birth of Ulthuan itself.

'For we are the Everqueen,' said Lirazel. 'And we would know the truth of you, Eldain Éadaoin.'

Dawn was creeping into the eastern horizon, bringing an end to the welcome respite from the fighting brought by darkness. Beyond the walls of the Eagle Gate, the fires of the enemy burned with queerly shimmering flames, lighting the white stone of the Annulii with writhing shadows. Menethis almost tripped on the steps leading to the Aquila Spire, exhaustion making him as clumsy as an orc.

He couldn't remember the last time he had slept in a bed.

Injured warriors brought food and water to those who defended the ramparts, and healers worked their way along the wall, using what little magic remained to them to seal sword cuts and mend broken bones. Their powers gave strength to weary limbs, but such boons came at a cost, and every one of the fortress's healers stumbled like a dreamwalker, their own reserves of energy drained by the effort of tending to so many. Though he knew little of magic, Menethis knew the healers were at the limits of their endurance.

'Much like the rest of the garrison,' he whispered, before chiding himself for the disloyal thought that came hard on its heels. He straightened his tunic and did his best to smooth down his hair. They may be under siege, but Glorien tolerated no laxness of behaviour or appearance.

He reached the top of the stairs and knocked on the reinforced door. The wood was scorched where a bolt of rogue magic had burned it. From inside the tower, Menethis heard a clatter of metal, and wondered what new foolishness Glorien was attempting.

'My lord,' he said. 'It is Menethis. May I enter?'

'Menethis! Thank Isha, yes, come in, I need you!'

Menethis pushed open the door and entered the cramped tower. Intended as a perch for the commander to watch an unfolding battle before drawing his plans, it had become Glorien's refuge from the horrors below. Stacks of books were strewn on the wide table, unrolled scrolls lay in limp piles, and balls of crumpled parchments rolled across the floor as Menethis opened the door.

Glorien Truecrown stood before a full length mirror, its edges wound in silver wire like interleaved vines. He wore his wyvern skin boots and a mail shirt, over which was a finely cut tunic of softest cream. Glorien once claimed he had hunted the wyvern himself, and Menethis had made admiring sounds, though he knew the lie for what it was.

A breastplate of ithilmar hung from Glorien's chest, its straps loose and flapping as the commander of the Eagle Gate spun around, trying in vain to buckle himself into his armour.

'It's so frustrating,' said Glorien, as Menethis entered.

'My lord?'

'This armour. Whoever designed it must have been a blind idiot. It's impossible to put on, Menethis. Is that not the most foolish thing you've ever heard? Armour that can't be worn!'

'A noble of Ulthuan should have his squires to armour him, my lord,' said Menethis. 'He would not be expected to gird himself for war alone.'

'Of course,' said Glorien, with a relieved sigh. 'Squires. Of course. I completely forgot about squires. It's this warrior's life, it drives all thoughts of civilised behaviour from your head. I required your help, so why were you not here? Remiss of you not to attend upon me, when I needed you.'

Menethis bit back a harsh retort and said, 'I was on the walls, my lord. The druchii and their barbarous allies sorely press us.'

'Fighting, yes,' said Glorien. 'And that is why I need you. If I am to fight, then I must be armoured in the proper fashion. A prince of Ulthuan must shine like the sun when he goes to war.'

Menethis forgot his anger in a heartbeat, and he took a step towards Glorien.

'You fight with us now?'

'Of course,' said Glorien. 'Whatever gave you the impression I wouldn't?'

Menethis looked at the scattered books and scrolls, the words of ancient warriors and scholars on the arts of war. For as long as the enemy had been before the walls of the Eagle Gate, Glorien had buried his head in the pages of his beloved books, seeking solace and inspiration from their inked wisdom. Until now, Menethis had thought it panic that had kept Glorien locked within the tower, but had it been prudence after all? Had Glorien found what he sought in the words of these long dead warriors?

'Nothing, my lord,' said Menethis. 'It lifts my heart to know you fight with us. Your warriors will fight like Aenarion reborn with you at their head.'

'No doubt,' said Glorien. 'Now help me into this damned armour.'

Menethis lifted the carven breastplate, a wondrously sculpted artefact with more than a hint of the enchanter's art woven into its metal. It was light, and Menethis felt the magic tingling at his fingertips as he strapped it to Glorien's body. As he added each piece of armour, Glorien at last began to resemble the noble elven warrior he needed to be.

Menethis glanced down at the scattered books.

'If I might enquire, my lord,' he said. 'Which author finally convinced you it was time to don armour and draw your sword?'

'None of them,' said Glorien with a dismissive glance towards the books that had held him prisoner within the tower. 'Last night as I slept amid these treatises on war, the truth was revealed to me in a great dream.'

Menethis had heard of the gods sending dreams to their chosen champions, but Glorien hardly seemed a likely candidate to be such a warrior. But then, the ways of the gods were mysterious, and who could say what made them chose one individual over another?

'You believe it was a true vision, my lord?'

'I do, Menethis, for I dreamed of a Phoenix King of old.'

That was certainly auspicious, for dreams of ancient kings were often heralds of great deeds. It was said that Finubar had dreamed of Caradryel the night before his coronation in the Flames of Asuryan.

'Which of the Phoenix Kings did you dream about?' asked Menethis, lifting a gleaming pauldron of silver and gold from the armour rack in the corner of the tower.

'I dreamed of Tethlis.'

'Tethlis?' said Menethis, his hand hovering over the buckle. 'The Slayer?'

'Indeed,' answered Glorien. 'In my dream I found myself upon the mist-wreathed shores of a black island, the rocks and sand awash with blood and bones. It was quite the most frightful place I have ever seen.'

'The Blighted Isle!' gasped Menethis, making a protective ward symbol over his heart.

Glorien nodded. 'I should have been deathly afraid, but I was at peace. I felt no fear as I saw a figure farther up the shore. And when he beckoned me, I felt compelled to obey.'

'And you believe this was Tethlis?'

'I know it was,' said Glorien. 'He was exactly as I remember him from the Phoenix Gallery in Lothern. I walked towards the king, and the mist parted. I saw corpses all around me, thousands of them, maybe more, but still I was not afraid. In some places the dead host lay a hundred deep. Blood streamed from their ruined bodies and into the sea, and I knew that the bloody lance in Tethlis's hand had seen every one of these warriors slain.'

'A dream of Tethlis is one of ill-omen, my lord,' breathed Menethis. 'None know for sure how he met his end on that dread island. Found dead at the foot of the Altar of Khaine, some say his own warriors cut him down, lest the Sword of Khaine twist his soul into that of a bloody-handed tyrant who would lead Ulthuan to its doom.'

Glorien shook his head. 'I have heard those tales, but I do not believe them. No elf of the asur would turn his weapon on his betters.'

'Tethlis's rages were well known, and I have heard stranger things than a leader cut down by his own warriors. Tell me, my lord, did Tethlis speak to you in this dream?'

Glorien's mouth opened, and he cocked his head to one side, as though struggling to remember an elusive fact. He started to speak, but could not find the right words. At length, he said, 'I heard no words, but the Phoenix King bade me draw my sword, for the enemy was upon us. The mist gathered around us, and within it I saw ghostly apparitions, shadowy warriors closing in on us with bared blades. Though I could not remember unsheathing it, my sword was in my hand. The Phoenix King and I were back to back as the foe let loose a terrible yell and charged towards us.'

'What were they? Druchii?' asked Menethis.

'I do not know,' said Glorien. 'I could not see them clearly. But we fought them, Tethlis and I, killing them with cut and thrust, lunge and riposte. We fought for an age, and when the foe was done, Tethlis turned to me, and his gaze bored into me with eyes of fire. His command was clear, and I knew the time had come for me to wet my sword in druchii blood in the waking world. I have studied my books long enough, Menethis, and there is little I do not know on the theory of war, but it is time to stand with the warriors of the Eagle Gate and let them see me fight alongside them.'

Glorien saw the look in Menethis's eye before he could mask his surprise and said, 'I admit I was... wary of standing in the battle line with weapon in hand, but the druchii's axes will fall on my neck whether I remain in this tower or on the walls.'

Menethis looked upon Glorien with new eyes, seeing the proudly straight back, the strength in his bearing that had always been there, but which fear had masked. Clad in his battle armour of gold and silver, and with a shimmering helm of ithilmar upon his head, he was the image of the heroes of song and verse. The transformation was nothing short of miraculous, and Menethis wondered that he had not seen the young prince's potential before now.

'Your warriors will be joyous at your presence, my lord,' said Menethis, and meant it.

Glorien smiled, and Menethis felt his heart swell with pride. He had despaired of this moment ever coming, fearing that the death of Cerion Goldwing had doomed the Eagle Gate.

But with this dream, true vision or not, perhaps they had a chance.

'Dawn is almost upon us, Menethis,' said Glorien, 'and it is time for me to take my place on the Eagle Gate as a warrior.'

'A new dawn,' said Menethis. 'A time for fresh beginnings.'

Menethis opened the door to the Aquila Spire, and Glorien stepped onto the top step. The first rays of sunlight caught the gold of his armour, glittering like the fires of the phoenix, and Menethis felt the exhaustion that hung around his neck like a tombstone fall away from him.

Glorien marched down the steps, and the faces of the asur turned towards him, recognising that something had changed, but not knowing what. Menethis saw hopeful looks passed from warrior to warrior, following each glance as the news of Glorien's arrival flew around the fortress.

This was hope reborn. This was the fire of victory lit in every heart.

But Menethis's step faltered as he saw the brooding countenance of a hooded warrior crouched in the gloom of the parapet. Alone among the garrison, this warrior's face remained impassive, and Menethis quailed at the unflinchingly hostile stare of this dark-cloaked archer.

Though he could not see the warrior's face, there was no doubt as to his identity.

Alanrias, the Shadow Warrior of Nagarythe.

Menethis thought of Glorien's dream of Tethlis and his newfound hope turned to fear.

CHAPTER FOUR
BITTER TRUTHS

Eldain had wandered aimlessly through the forest, but the Maiden Guard took a more direct path towards the Everqueen. They marched with grim purpose, and Eldain knew that whatever awaited him at the end of this journey would change his destiny forever. The gloom that had hung over the forest was now lifted, and fresh sunlight shone through the tops of tall trees that lifted their branches towards the sun once more.

New growths budded on the ends of limbs of wood, and the grass beyond the invisible paths shone with newfound lustre. Lirazel had said nothing to him after her demand that he accompany her to the Everqueen, and Eldain had not attempted to engage her in conversation.

The crowds that had gathered to listen to Narentir's tales vanished into the forest, yet he could feel them nearby, as though they watched with accusing eyes from the shadows. The forest was alive again, but it was not the life of Avelorn as it had been. It was rampant, vital and unchecked.

Wild magic seeped into the roots of Avelorn, and it was responding to that touch with unfettered growth. New blooms choked older plants, aggressive saplings fought for light and the earth churned with competing life. As unrestrained as Avelorn had seemed before, now it reminded Eldain of the tales he had heard of the wild wood of Athel Loren. The growth of the asrai's domain was kept in check by powerful waystones, but whatever power had held the full power of Avelorn in check was now absent.

Eldain heard the creak and groan of new wood, the breath of forest creatures as they stalked the undergrowth like hunters. The entire forest had turned hostile.

No, not hostile exactly, but the power that had once turned the thoughts of the creatures of Avelorn to joy and carefree abandon had become violent and predatory. Even the Maiden Guard walked warily, their bows bent and spear points aimed outwards. Not even the protectors of the Everqueen could travel these paths without caution, it seemed.

Eventually Lirazel halted before a woven archway of green wood, the sap running along newly formed shoots like glistening amber. The smell of growth and fecund life was almost overpowering, and the scent of life resurgent was a powerful taste in the back of Eldain's throat.

'You must enter,' said Lirazel.

'You are not coming in?' asked Eldain.

'We need no protection of blades,' replied Lirazel, though the voice was not her own. 'The only life at risk is your own. Enter and follow the path.'

He followed Lirazel's instruction, and stepped through the archway into a verdant grove of dazzling light. The brilliance blinded him, and his every step was taken without the knowledge of where it might lead. He walked until a powerful sensation that he had reached his destination swept over him.

The veil of light withdrew from his senses, and Eldain blinked in the sudden rush of colour. Everywhere he looked, new blooms sought to outdo one another with the brilliance of their hue. Shimmering roses of glittering ebony wove around tree trunks garlanded with flowers that Eldain had never seen before. Plants of vivid purple, gold, white and azure grew wherever they could, and the sheer mass of growth was like the grandest arboretum ever devised.

In the centre of it all sat the Everqueen.

Not Alarielle.

The Everqueen.

Eldain appreciated the difference without even realising there had been one until now.

Clad in a shimmering robe of ice and rainbows, she sat upon a throne of roots and grass that split the ground beneath her and pulsed with the magic that sustained it. Light surrounded the Queen of Avelorn, radiance that sheened the grove in warmth and breathed vitality into everything it touched.

She was simultaneously clad in her robes of light and magic, and naked. Her ivory flesh was sculpted and perfect, no trace of the wound Caelir had done her visible through the mist of glamours that surrounded her. She was just as Eldain remembered her, but so much more.

Her golden hair framed a face of such aching beauty that Eldain wanted to drop to his knees and declare his love for her. At that moment he would have cast aside everything he held dear just to be allowed to devote his life to her. With an effort of will he lifted his gaze to the Ever-queen's face, her cold and lethal face.

Though everything around her exploded with life, her eyes held only the promise of death.

Outwardly, the Everqueen was exactly as she had been before, but a force more powerful than any known to the asur beat within her breast. Eldain understood immediately that this was old magic, perhaps the oldest in the world. The first heartbeat of creation empowered her, the birth cry at the beginning of the universe sighed from her lungs, and the power to create everything that was or could be shone in the light that bathed her.

Rhianna was here too, similarly enraptured by the Everqueen's bril-liance, and it was all Eldain could do to acknowledge her. She spared him the briefest glance before returning her fervent gaze to the force at the centre of the grove.

The Everqueen shifted in her living throne of roots, raising her hand and beckoning Eldain closer. He could no more disobey that gesture than he could stop his own heart from beating.

'Eldain Éadaoin, called the Fleetmane,' said the Everqueen. Her voice was the sound of new life, and Eldain felt the years melt from him at the sound of his name on her lips.

'My lady,' said Eldain. 'How would you have me serve you?'

She smiled, but it was the smile of a cat with a helpless mouse in its claws.

'I would see your truth unveiled,' she said. 'I would see you undone and your secrets revealed before those you love.'

Eldain fell to his knees, and shooting buds of new wood erupted from the ground, writhing like fast-growing vines to wrap around his wrists and pull his arms wide. The Everqueen's throne groaned as the roots twisted and bore her towards Eldain. She reached out and cupped his chin with her glistening fingertips. Eldain's skin thrilled at her touch, even as he realised she could destroy him utterly.

Her eyes locked with his, and Eldain felt the primordial energies that danced within the frail mortal frame of the woman before him. She poured into him, and he cried out at the touch of such enormous power. It burned him, and his entire body felt afire with its surging, ancient force. It hollowed him out, scouring his body for every memory, thought and deed that made up his long life. In a heartbeat she knew him entirely, understood what he loved, hated and desired. In that one moment of connection, she knew him better than he knew himself.

'You left your brother to die,' said the Everqueen, looking up at Rhi-anna. 'For her. You told yourself it was for love, but nothing so noble turned you away from him. Jealousy, spite and hurt pride drove you. You deluded yourself that good could come from evil, but all that springs from evil is tainted by it.'

With the comforting shield of his denial stripped from him, the full force of Eldain's guilt rose up in a choking wave of horror. He saw Caelir's outstretched hand, the silver pledge ring glinting in the cold, bleached light of Naggaroth. Eldain relived that moment a thousand times in the space of a heartbeat, experiencing the shame of his betrayal over and over again.

He had told himself that the love that bloomed anew between he and Rhianna made his betrayal a small thing. Time and unconscious self-preservation had built walls around the memory of Caelir's abandonment, but the power of the Everqueen smashed them asunder and forced him to confront what he had done.

In that moment, he had hated Caelir, hated that he was more liked, more carefree, more beloved and naturally luckier. Caelir took everything that was once Eldain's, and he did it with such ease that no deed of Eldain's could ever compete. The world fell into Caelir's lap without effort, and in that glinting instant, Eldain let a lifetime's worth of bitterness spill out in one terrible mistake.

A moment of weakness, that was all it had taken to betray his life, his love and his own flesh and blood. Eldain wished he could take it back, undo the damage his actions had set in motion, but it was too late for regrets. Too late by far.

'I could have saved him,' said Eldain. 'Lotharin was strong enough to carry us both clear. Caelir ran to me. He called for me to save him, but I ignored him. Worse, I told him I was leaving him to die. I *wanted* him to know why he was going to die. Oh, Isha forgive me!'

'You left him...?' gasped Rhianna, experiencing the full weight of Eldain's betrayal as it filled her mind with the memory of that black night. 'You returned from Naggaroth and lied to me? I loved Caelir and you left him to die!'

'I loved him too,' said Eldain, but Rhianna wasn't listening. Her hands seethed with magical fire, incandescent in the presence of the Everqueen's power. Tears of grief and horror spilled down Rhianna's cheeks as the certainties of her life crumbled around her. Eldain felt the build up of killing magic, and awaited his just punishment. Rhianna would kill him, and it would be a death well deserved.

Before the fire could erupt from Rhianna's hands, the Everqueen snapped her fingers and the roots entwining Eldain's limbs withdrew into the ground like retreating snakes. Unseen hands jerked him to his feet and sheathed him in protective energies as Rhianna's magic blazed. Blue flames washed over Eldain, licking hungrily at his body. But like a Phoenix King of old, not a single hair upon his head was so much as singed by the fire.

The roaring of incredible magic burned the air around him, the air fizzing and cracking with its violence, but none of it touched him. The fire retreated, and Rhianna fell to the ground, sobbing with aching loss and sickness. Her eyes blazed hatred at him, and Eldain welcomed it.

The Everqueen rose from her throne, and Eldain said, 'Why did you save me? Let me die, please. I deserve everything Rhianna's hatred can do and more.'

'Think you that I am so limited in view as mortals?' said the Everqueen. 'There is purpose that might yet be served by my mercy.'

'There is nothing left for me,' begged Eldain. 'I beg of you, let me die.'

The Everqueen shook her head, and her spun gold tresses were like corn before the scythe. Eldain felt himself lifted from the ground by invisible winds, his body suspended before the awesome force that claimed the Everqueen's body.

'No, Eldain Éadaoin, called the Fleetmane,' said the Everqueen, and Eldain thought he heard the faintest echo of the mortal vessel that contained her power. 'You will live with the guilt, the shame and the torment all your remaining days. Now go, little elf, fly away before my forgiveness is spent.'

With a flick of her wrist, the magical winds holding Eldain aloft gusted with hurricane force, and he was hurled from the grove like a dust mote in a thunderstorm. Trees and branches and leaves whirled past him in a blur as he spun through the forest.

Cast forever from Avelorn like a banished spirit.

Cold winds blew over the Eagle Gate, carrying the smoky tang of sensual oils and gaudy incenses. Alathenar could taste the seductive promise of fleshy delights they offered in every breath, like the scent lamps in a Lothern pleasure court. The smell made him hungry and angry, for he knew it was a lie. Nothing that blew on the wind from the druchii camp could be trusted, it was an art as black as the land that birthed it.

Morathi had yet to rejoin the battle, her debaucheries within the silken pavilion leaving her no time to fight alongside her mortal allies. Any other army would have balked to have an ally take so little part in the fighting, but these northern barbarians had such a hunger for battle and bleeding that they cared little for the inequalities of blood shed to carry the fortress.

Their battle cries were vulgar obscenities as they climbed barbed ropes that sliced their palms or raced up scaling ladders of heated iron. Alathenar had emptied six quivers of arrows, and once again had taken a fresh quiver from Alanrias. The Shadow Warrior seemed always to have arrows to spare, and Alathenar hated that he relished using such spiteful shafts on the foe.

He knelt beside the splintered remains of the left wing of the eagle that had once proudly kept watch over the pass, loosing arrow after arrow into the mass of tribesmen. They were big men, brutish giants with bloated bodies of muscle and fur and iron. Iron axes and wide-bladed broadswords smashed through elven armour, and their frothing madness gave them strength enough to withstand injuries that would have slain any normal mortal twice over.

The walls were thick with fur-cloaked warriors, grappling and slashing to gain a desperate foothold on the ramparts. They bit and clawed without grace or skill, relying on strength, narcotic roots and ferocity to keep them alive long enough to win. Eloien Redcloak fought from the ramparts high on the eastern flank of the fortress, protecting the few bolt throwers left to them.

Redcloak cut down enemy warriors with darting sweeps of his curved sabre. It was a weapon designed for use on horseback, but it was a perfect weapon for slitting throats, slashing tendons and opening bellies as he danced past clumsy mortals as though borne on a fine Ellyrian steed.

In the centre of the wall stood Glorien Truecrown.

Surrounded by a dozen asur warriors, his lack of skill as a warrior was hopelessly exposed. He despatched dying humans, stabbed and flailed with his sword at foes that had been disarmed by his protectors. Alathenar saw that Glorien thought he was fighting like Tyrion himself. He yelled and whooped in delight, and the warriors assigned to protect him by Menethis had to fight twice as hard as any other. The garrison's morale had shone at the sight of Glorien on the walls, but that had soured as his lack of ability became plain.

'Truly it is like Aethis reborn,' said Alanrias, looking over Alathenar's shoulder at Glorien's wild attacks.

Alathenar started. He hadn't heard the Shadow Warrior approach. He wanted to contradict Alanrias, but the comparison was an apt one. Aethis had been Phoenix King over a thousand years ago, a poet and dreamer who had scorned the arts of war in favour of decadent plays, indulgent artwork and grand public performances.

'I'm not sure I like the comparison,' said Alathenar.

'What do you mean?'

'Aethis was slain by a trusted friend. A poisoned dagger to the heart, if I remember my history.'

'You do,' said Alanrias, loosing a shaft over Alathenar's head. It took a tribesman low in the groin, and the man fell from the wall with a squeal of pain.

'Ha! No sons to bear your name into the future!' shouted Alanrias.

Alathenar couldn't read the Shadow Warrior, and never knew if the words he spoke were intended to be laden with hidden meaning. Was his naming of Aethis simply to deride Glorien's skill or was it a further nail in the young prince's coffin?

Alathenar watched as Glorien's protectors saved him from a baying mob of tribesmen. Two fine warriors were cut down in the process, lives that might not have been lost were their efforts bent to their own battles instead of another's. Even on the walls, Glorien was costing them dearly.

A heavy metal clang shook dust and rock splinters from the parapet behind them. Alathenar spun to see a smoking ladder of hissing iron bounce from the stone. A flailing hook swung up over the battered parapet and he rolled aside as it bit where he had knelt a moment before. Callused hands appeared in the embrasure, and a muscular warrior clad in soft ermine and baked leather strips vaulted onto the rampart. He bore a short, stabbing sword in his free hand, and a long length of chain in the other.

Alanrias put an arrow in his belly, but the warrior didn't even blink. Two more fur and leather-wrapped tribesmen clambered up the ladder and onto the rampart. Alathenar dropped his bow, and his sword was in his hand a second later. Before the warriors could drop to the walls, Alathenar's sword lanced into a belly and emptied its entrails. The man shrieked as he died, but before Alathenar could turn to face the second human, a hobnailed boot slammed into the side of his head.

He dropped and rolled as stinging light flared before his eyes. He kept moving, bringing his sword up to block a killing sweep. Crude, steppe-beaten iron slammed into gleaming steel from a craftsman's forge, and Alathenar grunted at the brute strength of the blow. He went with it, letting himself roll backwards to his feet as his attacker came at him again. The human was a fang-toothed warrior with hideous brands burned into his cheeks, and his eyes blazed with drug-induced fury. Behind the tribesman, more enemy warriors had gained the ramparts, and Alanrias fought three of them as he tried to keep them from taking this part of the walls.

'We need more warriors!' shouted Alanrias.

'There are no more!' returned Alathenar. The fang-toothed warrior came at him again, but Alathenar was ready for him this time. As the tribesman swung his axe, Alathenar spun in low and rammed his sword, two-handed, into his belly. He used his forward momentum to drive the blade up into the man's heart, twisting the blade and sliding it clear in one motion.

The tribesman grunted in pain and dropped to his knees as his life-blood poured out. Alathenar was disgusted to see a look of exquisite pleasure twist the man's features as he died. Another six enemy warriors had gained the wall, and Alathenar saw it was hopeless to try and plug this breach. Alanrias bled from several wounds, and was backing steadily away from the wall. The northern barbarians could scent victory and their baying cries rose in volume.

A clear elven voice cut through their raucous bellows, like a beam of sunlight through a thundercloud.

'Get down,' it said.

Alanrias and Alathenar obeyed without hesitation as a hissing cloud of starwood bolts scythed the air above them. A dozen, then a dozen more flashed past in a blur of pale wood and glinting leaf-bladed barbs. The volley of bolts swept the walls clean of barbarian warriors, and Alathenar looked up to see Eloien Redcloak on the far side of the fortress with an

Eagle's Claw bolt thrower turned towards their struggle.

He started to wave his thanks, but stopped as he saw a look of horror on his friend's face.

Alathenar rolled to his feet as a monstrously muscular warrior clad in a patchwork of contoured plates held fast to his tanned flesh by a mass of leather coils dropped to the rampart. His armour glistened like flayed meat, branded with the rune of the Dark Prince, and his body reeked of a hundred scented oils. The warrior smiled, and Alathenar was struck by the hammer-blow of his fierce beauty. This was not the mask of a killer, this was the face of a lover, a poet and a dreamer.

Then Alathenar saw his eyes, cruel and hateful, filled from a well of hate and indulgence, seeing through the mask of beauty a moment before the glamoured warrior would have killed him. A curved and barbed sword with too many blades cut the air with a scream, and Alathenar hurled himself to the side. A hooked barb cut into his chest, slicing through his mail shirt and tearing the skin beneath. Blood flowed down his body and Alathenar fell onto his haunches, desperately scrambling backwards to escape this madman's blows.

'I am Issyk Kul!' roared the warrior. 'And this wall is mine to do with as I please!'

Half a dozen elven warriors rushed to secure the wall so recently cleared of enemy fighters, but the ferocious enemy champion cut them down in as many blows. His sword flew faster than any of the elven warriors could match. Its blade was surely woven with dark enchantments, for none in the mortal realm were swifter than the asur. Alanrias was struck, hurled down into the courtyard by a savage blow. Alathenar watched him fall, but could not see whether he yet lived.

Issyk Kul towered over Alathenar, and he heard his name shouted from behind him.

'Time to die, frail thing,' growled Issyk Kul, his voice the rasping growl of a jungle cat.

Alathenar heard a powerful *thwack* of starwood and coiled rope, and spat his defiance at the worshipper of the Dark Gods.

'For you,' he said as the single, mighty bolt of an Eagle's Claw flew straight and true.

Kul's sword swept up and the enormous bolt was smashed from the air with a single blow.

The champion grinned and looked up at the Eagle's Claw that even now was being made ready to fire once more. Kul sprang onto the broken stumps of the battlements and aimed his sword at Alathenar.

'The gods bid me spare you for a reason,' he said with a gleeful laugh.

Another bolt from the Eagle's Claw punched the air, but Kul had already slid back down the ladder, leaving Alathenar breathless on a rampart filled with the dead. He slowly picked himself up, resting on the blood-slick parapet as the enemy host withdrew once again.

Alathenar heard a wild yell of triumph, and turned to see Glorien True-crown thrust his sword towards the sky, as though this reprieve was a victory he had won single-handed.

Anger filled Alathenar, and he looked back into the courtyard as Alanrias climbed painfully from the ground, his bow arm cradled close to his chest. Alathenar's eyes locked with those of the Shadow Warrior.

He saw the question, and slowly, Alathenar nodded.

And their pact of murder was sealed.

The grove was silent, the winds that had billowed its branches and shaken the leaves from the trees now stilled. Rhianna watched Eldain snatched from sight, and hot tears spilled down her cheeks. She wept for Caelir, for herself and the world that had suddenly changed in the time it took to draw breath. Rhianna knew betrayal was in the blood of mortals, but to know that one of the asur could turn on another was like a dagger of ice to the heart. She clenched her fists as anger began to overtake horror, and coruscating sparks of fire rippled around her arms. Reflected power from the Everqueen shone in her eyes and it pulled Rhianna to her feet.

She had thought the grove silent, but now saw that wasn't true. Birds had returned to the trees and slender-limbed deer nuzzled at bushes at its edges. Doves mingled with ravens, peacocks and kingfishers. Hawks settled on the tallest branches, attended by white-plumed falcons and red-breasted warblers.

Shapes creaked within the heartwood of the trees, suggestions of faces and limbs formed by the groan of roots and branches. Darting lights spun through the foliage and giggling laughter echoed on the last breath of drifting zephyrs. They floated through the grove in hopeful loops, gathering above the Everqueen and bathing her in their dream-like radiance. Rhianna shielded her eyes as that brightness was taken into the Everqueen's body, filling her with such brilliance that it seemed a second sun had come to Avelorn.

The light spread through the forest, suffusing every living thing it touched, travelling on the wind, the earth and the water until its power was spent. Whatever the light of the Everqueen touched would never be the same, and a part of their spirit was forever filled with joy and wonder.

The effect on Rhianna was instantaneous and she felt her anger ebbing away. The wrathful magic that suffused her limbs dimmed until, finally, it was gone. She took a deep breath and wiped her eyes free from tears as the light of the Everqueen began to fade. Rhianna bowed her head as the Everqueen came towards her, gliding over the soft grasses of the grove and leaving only new life in her wake.

A slender hand, with soft fingers and delicate nails lifted her chin.

Rhianna looked into warm hazel eyes that knew no hate, no bitterness or spite.

'You are Alarielle,' said Rhianna.

'For now,' agreed the Queen of Avelorn. 'The Everqueen slumbers, regaining her strength, even as I do. Alarielle speaks to you now, but while our flesh heals, my power will wane and the Everqueen's will wax like the turning of the seasons. But the light of the forest shines once more, and the balance between us will be restored soon.'

Rhianna looked into the Everqueen's eyes

'Why did you let him live?' asked Rhianna.

Alarielle smiled. 'I would never have harmed Eldain, for all the asur are my children. I could no more strike him down than I would strike you down.'

'It looked like you were going to kill him.'

'The power of the Everqueen might have killed Eldain, but it spared him for some purpose I do not understand.'

Rhianna turned away from Alarielle. 'I wish she had killed him. He deserves to die. I hate him for what he did. To Caelir. To me... to Ulthuan. Why did he do it? You saw inside him, I know you did. Why did he leave his brother to die?'

The light of Alarielle followed her, and Rhianna felt a gossamer-thin touch upon her shoulder. Its warmth flowed into her, but she resisted it, hanging onto her anger in the face of the soothing balm of forgiveness.

'He did it for love,' said Alarielle. 'At least he once believed that was why.'

'For love?' hissed Rhianna, spinning to face Alarielle. 'What kind of love brings about such pain and suffering?'

'Mortal love,' said Alarielle. 'For it is bound by the confines of a life, and is therefore fleeting. Swords have been bloodied throughout the history of the world in the name of love, Rhianna. Love of a land, a colourful flag, an ideal. A beloved wife...'

'Eldain's betrayal had nothing to do with love,' said Rhianna, as fresh tears spilled out. 'I will hate him forever for what he did.'

The light of the grove dimmed at her words, and Alarielle's eyes shone with the light that had passed into the forest. Rhianna felt its healing properties, magic that could heal a heart broken into a thousand pieces.

'There is no hurt in the world that cannot be undone by the power that lives in me,' said Alarielle, 'but you have to let it in. The heart that does not want to heal cannot be remade.'

'Maybe some hearts should not be remade.'

'And be left only with hate to fill them? No, hate is a poison that will turn the purest soul to the blackest deeds. It is a seed that can only flower in bitter soil. Do not feed it, and it will wither away. Do not water it with your tears and it will never grow again.'

Rhianna sobbed and sank to her knees. 'How? I do not know how.'

'You will learn,' promised Alarielle. 'You must if you are to fulfil your destiny, for what you hold in your heart will shape Ulthuan for all time.

For all our sakes, do not let it be hate.'

'I don't understand,' said Rhianna.

'No, but you will.'

Alarielle closed her eyes and Rhianna saw a tremor pass through her. When next the queen looked upon her, a measure of the Everqueen had become part of her again.

'But the time for talking is over,' said the Everqueen. 'The hate of which I speak has flowered in the hearts of those who stand against the druchii in the west. All too soon it may bear bitter fruit, and we must be ready to fight.'

'You will go to war?' said Rhianna.

The Everqueen nodded, and the light inside her swelled until it seemed as though her body could no longer contain it. The warmth in her eyes became a furnace, and Rhianna thrilled to the passion of the Everqueen's emotion.

'I will summon the army of the forest,' said the Everqueen with a sound like thunder in a clear sky. 'The treemen of the deep woods, the dryads of the bracken, the great eagles, the faun, the sprites and the fair folk. All the kith and kin of magic shall heed my call. The Maiden Guard, the singers, the poets, the dancers, the warriors, the playwrights and the acrobats, all shall delight at gathering beneath my banner of ice and song. The raven shall carry my words to Chrace, the dove to Cothique. All shall heed my summons!'

Rhianna felt the elemental power of the forest pass to every creature that filled the grove. Every bird that could fly took to the air to carry the Everqueen's command. Each beast of the forest that could run took to its heels to gather its kind.

The Everqueen turned her blazing gaze upon Rhianna, and she saw the fierce exultation in those ancient eyes at the thought of gathering her magical army.

'Avelorn marches to war!' cried the Everqueen.

CHAPTER FIVE
LOST SOULS

Eldain awoke from troubled sleep by the lapping banks of a river. He felt refreshed and unhurt. He had expected neither after the Everqueen had stripped him of his armour of self-denial. Eldain had thought the light of the Everqueen would burn him to cinders in punishment for his terrible crime. He could not think of a single reason why she might spare him. A memory of fire lingered in his mind, a vast portal and a silent sentinel, but he could make no sense of it.

He pushed himself to his feet, looking around to gain a sense of where he was. Across the river was an impenetrable wall of trees, their leaves shimmering with their own inner light, a luminosity that could have but one source. Though the river was shallow here, Eldain knew it would be suicide for him to re-enter the woods of Avelorn. He had been cast from beneath its magical boughs, and to return there would be the death of him.

To the west, the Annulii scraped the clouds from the sky and gathered them like cotton haloes around their magical summits. He turned to the south, already feeling his heart lighten at the thought of what he would see.

Ellyrion.

Land of his birth, it opened out before him like a mother's embrace. Its golden fields and wild steppe spreading as far as the eye could see. The sight of so wild, so untamed, so free a land made Eldain weep. He had no right to be here. No right to see so fantastical a land and certainly no right to receive its welcome. He had betrayed one of its sons, and as he had been banished from Avelorn, so too should he be banished from every kingdom of Ulthuan.

Yet, as much as he knew he deserved to feel no sense of welcome or homecoming, its presence was as potent as any he had known. This land had been birthed in an age beyond Eldain's imagination, and would endure long after he was dust in the wind. It had no need to pass judgement upon anything as petty as the affairs of the mortal creatures that crawled upon its body like ants on a fallen tree.

Ellyrion was his home, and it welcomed him as its son.

His joy was short-lived as he thought of his likely future. Beyond Ellyrion he would receive no welcome. He would be shunned as a pariah, hated for what he had done, and a bleak mood settled upon him as he thought of how far he had fallen since the heady days before the raid to Clar Karond. He was alone, and would be alone forever.

Forever was a long time for one of the asur.

Would he be able to bear the weight of the centuries alone? Could he stand to face the long years locked behind the walls of Ellyr-Charoi, withering and diminishing with every passing century? The Everqueen had spared him, but death would have been preferable to such a grey end to a life. To lessen with the years, growing dim and haunting the ruins of his villa until it too collapsed into forgotten rubble at the foot of the mountains.

His would be a life measured by despairing centuries and spent in eternal regret.

That was to be his fate, and Eldain accepted it.

It was a long walk to Ellyr-Charoi, but no sooner had he taken his first step south, than a familiar scent came to him as the wind shifted. Eldain knew that scent better than anything, hearing the welcome sound of hoof beats on good earth. He turned to the long grass of the west in time to see a black horse galloping towards him with fierce joy in every step.

'Lotharin!' he cried, running towards the midnight steed.

The last he had seen of his faithful mount had been when Caelir had ridden him from the Tower of Hoeth. He had assumed the horse now roamed within the borders of Avelorn, but no steed of Ellyrion could be kept long from its homeland. Eldain had known Lotharin since his birth, both elf and horse growing to adulthood with a bond closer than any mortal rider could ever hope to understand.

'I have missed you, old friend,' said Eldain. The horse nuzzled him, and Eldain rubbed its neck. Lotharin's coat was freshly brushed and shone with fresh vitality.

'Time in Avelorn has done you good.'

The horse tossed its mane, and Eldain saw that no matter what he had done, Lotharin would always be with him. Nothing could break the bond between an Ellyrion horseman and his steed, and Eldain thanked

Asuryan that he had been lucky enough to be born in such a wild, passionate land.

He vaulted onto the horse's back, needing no saddle, bridle or reins.

Though he rode to his eternal doom, Eldain welcomed this last ride upon so fine a mount as Lotharin.

'Come, Lotharin,' said Eldain. 'Homewards. To Ellyr-Charoi.'

The sun felt good on his skin, and Tyrion turned his face towards it, hoping its golden rays would send him a measure of his beloved Everqueen's warmth. Druchii blood coated the golden scales of his armour, and his azure cloak was stiff with the stuff. Sunfang lay unsheathed across his lap, though not a drop stained its gleaming blade. The caged fire within its heart burned any impure blood away.

Days had passed since his arrival at the castle, and, as he had predicted, the druchii had indeed attacked with greater skill and cunning after their first, abortive, assault. He had been proved right, though he took no pleasure in that. The Naggarothi were descendants of the asur. Of course they would be skilled.

More of the dark-cloaked warriors were even now assembling beyond bowshot, together with heavy bolt throwers and monsters that roared and bellowed behind hastily thrown up walls of boulders. Soon there would be a force thrown at the castle that not even he could fight against.

Already Tyrion had given Finubar more time than could be expected. The Phoenix King had sent word that the Sea Guard and Lothern citizen levy was taking position on the Emerald Gate, but every minute Tyrion could give him was vital. It was a heavy burden Finubar had placed upon him, but such was the way of kings, to ask great things of those that served them.

'Resting when there are druchii still to slay?' said Belarien, returning from the crumbling keep with two platters of bread, cheese and fruit. He sat down beside Tyrion, and set the food down on his lap.

'I am trying to, but you are making it difficult,' answered Tyrion.

'We shall sleep when we are dead, eh?'

Tyrion tried to smile. He had said those same words before the battle at Finuval. Rescued from a mighty daemon prince of Chaos by Teclis, he had gone on to fight the Witch King's greatest assassin in single combat though his spirit had almost been lost in the abyss. Then, those words had been defiant, now they sounded hollow. Belarien saw the emptiness in Tyrion's eyes and was immediately contrite.

'Apologies, my lord. I spoke without thought.'

'No need,' said Tyrion. 'I should watch what I say in future if I cannot stand my own words quoted back at me. And you are right. I will sleep when this is done.'

'How is the pain?'

'Happily lessened,' said Tyrion. 'Alarielle yet lives, and grows stronger.

I can hear the birds of Ulthuan sing again. She will recover, and each day I feel her pain less and less.'

'Then why the grim mood?'

'We face an enemy who will soon gather enough force to overwhelm us. Is that not reason to be grim?'

'You've faced worse odds than this and prevailed,' said Belarien. 'I know, I was there for all of them and I still bear the scars.'

Tyrion said nothing. How could he tell Belarien of the dark siren song of the Widowmaker? Every time he closed his eyes, he saw the black, blood-veined altar and the smoking blade buried in its heart. The bones of the dead and the yet to be slain rattled around it, unquiet in their death and looking to him to give their deaths meaning. Every blow he struck against the druchii was a pale shadow of the destruction he could wreak with the Sword of Khaine in his hand. With its power he could end the threat of the Witch King forever, take the war across the sea and destroy their blighted homelands in one bloody sweep.

He let out a breath, knowing these were the Widowmaker's thoughts, not his own.

They were not lies, these thoughts. Lies would be easier to dismiss. The sword *would* give him all the power it promised, but it was power that could never be given back. Aenarion had learned that lesson too late, dooming his lineage to forever be bound to that black blade of murder and bloodshed.

Belarien knew the stories of Aenarion as well as any in Ulthuan, but he could never really understand the terrible attraction the Sword of Khaine had for Tyrion.

'My lord?' said Belarien.

Tyrion was saved from answering by the glorious note of a hunting horn. Cheers went up from the garrison as a group of warriors marched into the castle through the Autumn Gate in the western wall. Tyrion rose to his feet as he saw the shimmering sea-serpent banner that went before these axe-wielding killers, each one clad in tunics of sumptuous cream and embroidered with golden thread and fire-winged birds. Their helms were bronze, and about their necks were mantles of brilliant white fur, taken from the bodies of the deadly lions that hunted the mountains of Chrace.

Led by a giant with a pelt cloak so voluminous that it seemed impossible it could have come from a single beast, the White Lions escorted a singular warrior clad in scarlet dragonscale armour and a shimmering cloak of mist and shadow.

'The Phoenix King,' said Belarien.

'None other,' agreed Tyrion, pushing himself to his feet and sheathing Sunfang. As highly regarded as he was, not even Tyrion would dare stand before the Phoenix King with a bared blade. Korhil, the towering master of Finubar's bodyguard, would never allow it, and the mighty, double-bladed axe slung at his shoulder was a potent deterrent against such foolishness.

Tyrion went to meet Finubar, the Seafarer as he was known, and bowed as the White Lions parted smoothly to allow their king to meet his greatest champion.

'My king, you honour us,' said Tyrion.

'My friend, how many times do I need tell you that you should not bow to me?'

'A king must always be bowed to, or else none shall know him as a king.'

'Prince Tyrion quotes Caledor the Second,' said the broad-shouldered White Lion at Finubar's side. 'Even as he shows respect, he mocks.'

The words were said without anger, and Tyrion smiled. 'Ah, yes, I always forget that you Chracians actually know how to read and write, let alone study history.'

'Careful, Tyrion,' warned Finubar with a smile. 'Korhil's blood is still afire after he slew the champion of a druchii witch cult yesterday.'

'He is welcome to test that lumbering tree-cutter against Sunfang any time he wishes.'

'Tree-cutter?' growled Korhil. 'Chayal would find your neck before you could pull that shiny toothpick from its sheath.'

Tyrion smiled and said, 'It is good to see you, Korhil.'

The White Lion bellowed with laughter and swept Tyrion into a crushing embrace. Rightly it was said that Korhil was the strongest elf of Ulthuan, and Tyrion felt his ribs creak in the powerful embrace.

'Enough,' said Finubar. 'As much as I always enjoy your games, there is little time for them now.'

Korhil released Tyrion and stepped back behind his king. Tyrion drew in a breath and stood tall before his friend and his king. Finubar was handsome and had the look of one whose eyes were always seeking the next horizon. His blond hair was almost as pale as the cloaks of his White Lions, and the green of his eyes matched the thousands of gems set within the gate that led to the Straits of Lothern.

'How goes the fighting here, Tyrion?' asked Finubar. 'The castle on the far side of the Emerald Gate yet resists. Thanks to a few scattered survivors of the battle before the gate, no force of any significance has managed to land on the southern coast. It is here the druchii will bend their every effort.'

'Then they fare better than we do, my lord,' said Tyrion. 'Every day the druchii bring up more warriors across that damned bridge of boats. Tell Aislin to send those scattered survivors to destroy the bridge and we may hold this castle.'

Finubar sighed. 'You know Aislin, my friend. Not even the counsel of a king will sway his thoughts. He and Kithre Seablaze rally whatever ships will answer their call from the Inner Sea, thinking to sail out and win this war in the water before the Emerald Gate.'

'Then he is a fool,' snapped Tyrion.

'Choose your words with more care, Tyrion, Aislin is still a prince of Ulthuan, and Seablaze is his protégé,' warned Finubar. 'And we will need their ships if the Emerald Gate is ever yielded.'

'Which it must be if this castle falls,' said Korhil.

As if to prove the point, the hatefully discordant blare of a druchii war horn echoed from the mountainside. Its echoes faded, only to be replaced by the cold-hearted chants of advancing warriors and the bellows of blood-hungry monsters.

Tyrion smiled grimly at Korhil. 'Time to put that axe of yours to good use,' he said.

Korhil glanced at Finubar, who nodded.

'Could you use us on the walls, Prince Tyrion?' asked the Phoenix King.

'Always, my lord,' said Tyrion.

The attack was led by the beastmasters. Two iron-scaled abominations, each with a writhing mass of serpentine necks and snapping, biting heads, stalked ahead of a host of marching warriors in lacquered armour of crimson. The monsters' bodies were dark and rippling with iridescent scales, their eyes glossy and reflective. Teeth like swords of yellowed horn dripped blood and venomous saliva.

Driving the pair of monstrous beasts forwards with cruelly barbed goads, the beastmasters loosed ululating cries from strange horns and yelled jagged words that could only be commands.

'Khaine's blood,' hissed Finubar, drawing his starmetal sword. 'Hydras!'

Tyrion could not take his eyes from the king's weapon, its blade curved in the manner of southland warriors, and golden like the last arc of sunset. The blade had been a gift from one of the coastal potentates of Ind, a land of exotic spices and strange ritual. Finubar had saved the life of the king's daughter and had received this wondrous blade in return. No smith trained in the Anvil of Vaul could unlock the mysteries of its creation, but the power of the magic worked into its blade was beyond question.

'Some heavy meat for Chayal to cleave,' grunted Korhil, unfazed by the sight of so terrible a pack of monsters. His White Lions hefted their heavy axes, resting them on their shoulders with nonchalant ease.

Tyrion took a calming breath as the dark presence of the Sword of Khaine eased into his thoughts. With that blade in his grip, these beasts would be carved into bloody chunks in moments. He forced thoughts of murder from his mind and sought the peace Teclis had taught him, the state of mind that allowed him to fight unencumbered by doubt, free from anger and able to find the space to kill with complete precision.

'I am the master of my soul,' he whispered under his breath. 'Aenarion's curse is not my curse. I wield my blade in the service of my kind and my home. No thought of selfish gain, no lust to rule, no urge to slay shall guide my arm. I am Tyrion, and I am the master of my soul.'

He felt Korhil's gaze, but ignored him, feeling his heart slow and his senses sharpen to the point where he could pick out the individual faces of every single druchii warrior in the advancing army.

'They are so like us,' he said.

'They are nothing like us,' said Korhil, and Tyrion blinked, not realising he had spoken aloud. He did not allow Korhil's gruff voice to distract him from achieving oneness with his sword. Its grip grew hot in his hand, and he smiled as though welcoming a long lost friend.

'Eagle's Claws!'

At Tyrion's command, the castle's bolt throwers spoke with one voice, and three long shafts streaked towards the hydras. One plunged into the flank of the most eager hydra, yet even the power of such a weapon could only drive the point a hand span through the creature's scaled flesh. Another skidded clear and the third was snatched from the air by a darting, draconic head and bitten in two.

'They'll not be stopped by bolts,' said Korhil.

'No,' agreed Tyrion.

More bolts leapt from the war machines, swiftly followed by a volley of goose-feathered shafts from the archers leaning over the parapet. Volley after volley billowed up into the sky as archers in the courtyard loosed over their comrades' heads. These fell among the druchii warriors, but most thudded home in heavy wooden shields or bounced away from burnished helms. A hundred, two hundred, three. Enough arrows to fell these invaders thrice over hammered down, but barely a handful died. Answering flurries of repeater crossbow bolts clattered against the walls. Iron-tipped bolts shattered on the hard stone, but screams of pain told Tyrion that many were finding their mark.

Tyrion lifted a sapphire blue amulet from around his neck and kissed the smooth stone. Encased within the blue gem were woven strands of golden hair, preserved like flies in amber, and he felt it respond to his touch.

'Be with me, queen of my heart,' he said. 'Watch over me this day.'

Arrows hammered the druchii line, and more were falling as the enemy cast down their shields and heavily armoured warriors ran towards the walls bearing scaling ladders. The first hydra was limping badly, two heavy bolts jutting from the rippling swathes of muscle around its neck. The second beast was being driven at the gateway, and its heads coiled back over its shoulder.

Tyrion knew what would come next.

'Get down!' he yelled.

The many heads of the hydra shot forward with their mouths gaping wide. Ashen smoke and fire belched from the guts of the monster in a torrent of volcanic destruction. Like a frothing wave of evil red light, the fiery breath of the hydra broke against the walls of the castle. Sulphurous flames billowed over the ramparts and asur warriors screamed as their tunics caught light. Flames rippled along the wall as the first beast exhaled its volatile breath of fire and fumes.

Asur warriors dropped from the walls, blazing from head to foot as the monster's fiery breath consumed them. Tyrion coughed and spat as black smoke roiled around the parapet, instantly turning day into night. Sunfang shone brightly, a beacon in the darkness, and he vaulted to his feet as he heard the smack of wood on stone.

'To arms! The enemy is upon us!'

A druchii helmet appeared in the embrasure and Tyrion removed it with a brutal thrust of his blade. The headless body dropped from the ladder as another druchii warrior clambered up to take its place. He died screaming, and Tyrion leapt into the gap between the merlons, bringing Sunfang's blade down in a two-handed sweep.

The ladder split asunder, spilling armoured warriors into the seething haze of fire and smoke that boiled at the wall's footings. Tyrion watched the druchii die, trying to maintain his equilibrium in the face of so much death. He turned from the destruction he had wrought as yet more ladders thudded into the length of the wall. Druchii leapt over the parapet and formed fighting wedges to allow the warriors behind them to gain the walls.

Swords and axes clashed as the ancient enemies spilled bitter blood. Beside him, Belarien slew druchii with cold, economical thrusts and slashes. Without the skill of Tyrion, his friend killed the druchii with the classic sword strokes of one schooled by the best. There was no flamboyance to his killing, simply the efficient blows of a killer.

Finubar fought with his golden sword, slaying the druchii as quickly as they climbed the walls. The Phoenix King was a fine swordsman, but his talents were those of peace, not war, and the White Lions were called upon to protect their liege lord on more than one occasion.

The White Lions fought like the grim hunters they were, each hacking blow measured and merciless. Their axes clove through druchii armour with ease, and they bellowed coarse Chracian insults at their slain enemies. Korhil's axe wove a silver web of destruction around him, the twin blades crashing through armoured plates, breaking bones and slicing flesh with horrifying ease.

Even as he slew enemy warriors, Tyrion couldn't help but be impressed. Korhil was a giant, broad shouldered and more powerful than any elf Tyrion had known, and he wielded his axe with a speed that belied his massive form. A duel between them would be a dance of blades to savour.

A druchii blade scraped over Tyrion's chest, and he spun around, driving his elbow into his attacker's face. A bronze cheek-guard crumpled and the warrior staggered. Sunfang plunged through a crimson breast-plate and the warrior screamed as the weapon flared with power, burning him alive from the inside.

Tyrion kicked the charred corpse free of the blade and danced down the length of the wall, finding the spaces between the fighting to stab, cut, slash and chop as he went. He flowed into the gaps, always with enough time and space to take the killing blow. Belarien followed him, but could barely keep up with his incredible skill and speed.

The castle wall shook and the fighting stopped for the briefest second as a trio of monstrous heads on sinuous necks appeared over the battlements. One darted forward and an elven warrior was snatched up in its jaws. He screamed briefly before the teeth bit through his armour. Fire spewed from the jaws of the other heads, and an entire section of the wall was suddenly empty as Tyrion's warriors burned in the searing fire.

'With me!' shouted Tyrion, charging along the ramparts towards the beast as its forelegs, each the thickness of a tree, grasped the stone of the parapet. A dozen elven warriors followed him, readying long-bladed lances to fight this giant creature of nightmare. It hauled its bulk up and onto the walls, screeching as its masters jabbed its hide with their barbed goads. The rampart crumbled beneath its weight, cracked masonry falling to the base of the wall.

Tyrion sprang onto a piece of crumbing stone and leapt towards the nearest head.

Sunfang flared with dazzling brightness as Tyrion brought the magnificent blade around and clove through the beast's neck. The head flew clear of the stump of neck, and the monster roared in pain. Tyrion landed lightly and rolled, slashing his sword across the beast's chest. Blood frothed from the wound and the rampart split as the beast's claws tore at the walls.

Elven lances plunged into the hydra's body and drew spurts of stinking blood, yet even as the blades plunged home, wounds already inflicted stopped bleeding and the scaled hide reknit. Tyrion swayed aside as a head snapped down, bringing Sunfang down like an executioner's blade. Another head was severed, and Tyrion knew that this wound would never heal. No living thing could withstand so incredible a blade.

'Tyrion!' cried a voice amid the monster's screaming roars of pain, and he spun around as the second hydra hauled its enormous body onto the walls. Flames rippled around its body, hazing the air with the hellish heat of a forge of the damned. Finubar and Korhil appeared in the swirling morass of smoke, as a heaving breath of fire and heat erupted from the hydra's reeking jaws. Tyrion threw his arm up before him as the battlements were engulfed.

The flames roared and heaved like an ocean of fire, and Tyrion wept at the sound of elven screams as his warriors died around him. Their bodies burned like warlords of the northmen on their pyres, consumed by the monster's infernal breath. But the armour of Aenarion had been forged in the depths of Vaul's Anvil, quenched in the blood of the mightiest dragons of ancient times and shaped with hammers touched by the smith god himself. No magical by-blow's fire could defeat its protection, and Tyrion stood like an invulnerable god before its hellish breath.

Tyrion saw Finubar and Korhil further along the wall, sheltering in the lee of the sagging parapet and swathed in the Phoenix King's dragonscale cloak. Korhil rolled away from the king and beat out smouldering embers in his cloak before swinging his axe to bear once more. The hydra's heads swayed above them, hissing; jelly-like ropes of saliva drooling from its smoking jaws.

Finubar ducked a snapping bite and thrust his blade into the hydra's mouth. He uttered a word of power and molten light filled the creature's skull, streaming from its eyes in golden fire before the head exploded in a welter of boiling blood and bone. Korhil swung Chayal in a mighty, two-handed sweep, cutting another head from the hydra's body with one blow.

Tyrion turned back to the beast he had first fought, its one remaining head coiled away from him as it dragged more of its bloated body onto the wall. Cracks split the rampart and Tyrion felt the wall shift beneath him as its foundations crumbled. A mighty foreleg smashed down, but Tyrion had seen it coming and dived beneath the blow. Nimble as a cat, he sprang to his feet and thrust Sunfang up into the beast's belly, wrenching the sword to open a wide tear. Dark fluids gushed from the wound, drenching Tyrion in stinking, Chaos-touched blood that ran from his armour as water from a fowl's back.

The beast's body shuddered, yet its head remained beyond his reach. It spat a mouthful of corrosive bile at him, but Tyrion swatted it aside with his blazing sword. As the creature reared up to slash its front legs at him once more Tyrion aimed his sword at its head and felt the powerful surge of magical energy pulsing in his blood.

'In Asuryan's name!' shouted Tyrion, and a blazing spear of white light erupted from the sword blade. The hydra screeched in agony as the furnace heat burned the flesh from its skull and boiled the brain in its head. The blackened stump flopped lifeless to the wall, and its body slid from the rampart as its life was extinguished.

Without waiting to watch it fall, Tyrion turned in time to see Korhil and Finubar despatch the second hydra. The White Lion's axe was drenched with the hydra's blood and the Phoenix King's cloak smoked from the heat of the battle. Korhil bellowed a Chracian victory oath as Finubar shouted for fresh warriors to defend this portion of the castle.

The wall was a blackened ruin, stripped of merlons and embrasures by the attack of the hydras. If the druchii came at this portion of the castle again, there would be no protection for the defenders as they awaited the enemy scaling ladders. Tyrion saw Belarien driving the enemy from those sections of the wall the hydras had not demolished, and breathed a sigh of relief to know that his friend had survived this attack.

The druchii fell back from the battle, limping, bloodied and broken. They had thrown their all into this assault, but they would be back with warriors fresh and eager to swarm over the walls of the castle. Arrows punched through the backs of the fleeing druchii, but they were few and far between.

A crossbow bolt smacked into a stump of rampart, reminding Tyrion that even in victory there was danger. He darted over to Finubar and Korhil, as more elven archers took up position on the wall. Both warriors were spattered with blood, but how much of it was their own, Tyrion could not tell.

'Not so terrible now, are they?' beamed Finubar, between breaths.

'No, but there will be more of them, my king,' said Tyrion. 'And this castle is ruined.'

Finubar squared his shoulders, immediately catching Tyrion's implication. 'I will not yield, Tyrion. We fight on. We must.'

'We will not,' stated Tyrion, as the calm spaces in which he had fought faded away.

'You defy your king?' demanded Finubar.

Anger, hot and urgent and bloody filled Tyrion. 'I will not throw my warriors' lives away in a battle I cannot win.'

Before Finubar could speak again, Korhil said, 'The prince speaks the truth, my king. The walls offer no protection, the gate is burned and there are few enough left alive to fight for it.'

The Phoenix King said nothing for long moments before letting out a sorrowful breath. He nodded reluctantly as he took in the cost of repulsing this latest attack. Scores of elven warriors were dead, and many more were horribly burned. At best, a hundred warriors remained to defend the walls.

'I know,' said Finubar. 'Yet if this castle is lost, then so too is the Emerald Gate. I do not relish my legacy to be the first Phoenix King who allowed the druchii within the Straits of Lothern.'

'You have no choice,' said Tyrion, feeling the pulse of an ancient and malevolent heartbeat keeping time with his own. 'War seldom allows us the luxury of doing as we might wish. We must do whatever it takes to survive.'

'We must do more than survive, Tyrion,' said Finubar. 'We must triumph.'

The captain of the White Lions stepped between the two warriors, pulling at the fur of his cloak as he put a hand on Tyrion's shoulder. 'I think I understand what Prince Tyrion is proposing, my king. It's like when I hunted Charandis. I drew that great lion farther and farther away from the mountains for days on end until his strength was weakened and I could choke the damned life from him. So you see, my lord, we're giving

them the gate, and drawing them into the Straits of Lothern. It's a killing
ground. We draw the druchii in, and hit them from all sides. Even as they
come at the Sapphire Gate, every fortress along the length of the straits
will be hammering them with bolts and arrows and magic. And if Aislin
and Seablaze want to sail out to fight the druchii, they've got the perfect
opportunity to earn some glory. Trust me, it will be a slaughter.'

Korhil turned to Tyrion and fixed him with his cold gaze. 'Isn't that
right?'

'Yes,' said Tyrion with relish. 'That's right. A slaughter.'

CHAPTER SIX
EMBERS

No song of the elves was older than dragonsong. The red-lit caves beneath the Dragonspine Mountains echoed with the ringing chants of fire mages as they sang of ancient days, when dragons soaring over the highest peaks were as common a sight as doves in Avelorn. Hot steam and a magma glow suffused the glistening rocks of the caves, and braziers burned with aromatic oils said to be pleasing to the senses of dragons.

Ghostly figures moved through the cavern, exhausted mages whose voices were hoarse with singing the songs forgotten by all save the line of dragonriders. Hidden by the acrid smoke, vast forms of scale and claw and wing lay coiled around the hottest vents, their mighty chests rising and falling with the slow rhythms of their ancient hearts.

The dragons of Caledor slumbered on, and none could reach them.

The old songs of valour could not rouse them from their dreams, and the clarion call to wake fell upon deaf ears. As the mountains had cooled, so too had the ardour of the dragons to shake themselves from their centuries of sleep. Only the younger dragons awoke now, and even that was becoming rarer and rarer.

Prince Imrik sat cross-legged before a great split in the rock, through which hissed a curtain of sulphurous smoke and the heartbeat of creatures older than any now living could remember. His white hair hung in wet ropes around his thin face, and droplets of sweat ran down his cheeks like tears. He had sung every song of elfkind, even the secret ones taught to him by his master so long ago.

Nothing was working, and though the naysayers of Lothern woefully claimed the fire of the dragons had gone out, Imrik refused to believe that, not when so many still lived in these mountains. A species as noble and ancient did not just slip away as their hearts cooled.

He knew things these naysayers did not.

Once, as they had flown through storms raging around the Blighted Isle, Minaithnir had told him that the dragons of Ulthuan would all die together in the last battle against the Dark Gods. It had been an uncharacteristic pronouncement, one perhaps brought on by the proximity of the Widowmaker, and the dragon had made Imrik promise never to repeat his careless words.

Imrik had told no one of Minaithnir's grim prophecy, but he held to its promise of a reawakening as he gathered his strength for another song. His brazier had burned low, and he threw another handful of heartleaf into the flames. The plant burned white gold, and its light had been used in ancient times to guide dragons to their riders in times of war. As the flames took hold and the aromatic leaves filled the air with the pungent tang of sulphur and blood, Imrik felt the presence of another elf.

He looked up, seeing a fire mage in billowing robes of crimson making his way across the cavern floor towards him. His steps were uneven, like those of a drunk, and Imrik knew Lamellan had not slept in weeks.

'My friend,' said Imrik, 'What news? Have any of your brothers had their songs answered?'

Lamellan shook his head. 'No, my lord,' he said, his voice little more than a whisper. 'The great drakes do not heed our calls. One of the younger sun dragons almost rose from its slumber, but slipped back into sleep before we could renew the song of awakening.'

'We must keep at it, Lamellan,' pressed Imrik, rising smoothly to his feet. He had long ago discarded his armour as too clumsy and restricting to fully perform the dragonsongs, and was clad only in a long white robe tied at the waist with a golden belt. His features were sunken and pale, for dragonsong drew upon a warrior's heart and soul for its power.

'The dragons do not heed us,' said Lamellan. 'My brother mages are beyond the limits of their endurance, and there is little more we can do. The dragons sleep on, and they will wake or sleep in their own time.'

Imrik sighed, letting the frustration of the last few weeks pour from him.

'I refuse to accept that,' he said. 'The dragons will come! If we die, they die, and the dragons of Caledor will not be slain in their sleep by druchii invaders. I will not allow that, do you understand me?'

'I do, my lord, but I do not know what else we can do,' said Lamellan. 'We have sung all the songs we know, and they do not reach the dragons. Only the songs known by the dragons themselves will rouse them now, and none among the asur know them.'

Imrik paced the cavern floor, the red light of countless braziers and the shimmering reflections of dragonscale casting stark reflections over his noble countenance.

'That is not strictly true, my friend,' he said at last.

'What do you mean, my lord?'

'I know them,' said Imrik. 'And you are right, the dragons will not wake with the old songs of the asur, so we need to sing the songs of the dragons themselves.'

'How can you know these songs?' asked Lamellan. 'Teach us how to sing them and we will fill these caverns with our voices. With such songs, even the most ancient dragons of Ulthuan will wake!'

'I cannot teach you these songs,' said Imrik. 'Minaithnir taught them to me, but had me swear that I would never sing them in the presence of any save dragonkind.'

'Why?'

'The songs of the dragons are powerful, and not meant for the minds of mortals, even ones as long lived as the asur, for it is said these songs are powerful enough to reach the minds of even the oldest star dragons. But they hold the true names of all the dragons of Ulthuan, and such secret knowledge should never be used lightly.'

'Tell us!' demanded Lamellan, the glittering light of fire magic crackling in the hazel of his eyes. 'Ulthuan is lost without the dragons.'

Imrik placed a hand on the fire mage's shoulder and shook his head, speaking with all the calm he could muster. 'In all the years you have known me, have I ever broken an oath to a friend?'

Lamellan sagged. 'No, my lord. Never.'

'And never shall I,' said Imrik with a weary smile. 'Now gather your brothers and return to the surface. Seal the caverns behind you, and let none enter on pain of death. Ulthuan will have need of the fire mages, with or without the dragons.'

'And you will sing the songs of the dragons alone?' asked Lamellan.

'I will.'

'Then you will die. If such songs are as powerful as you say, then there will be nothing left of you by their ending.'

Imrik drew himself up to his full height and his skin shimmered with vitality, the earlier fatigue that had threatened to overwhelm him vanished. Just the thought of singing the songs of the dragons filled him with energy, as though the song itself ached to be sung.

'Have faith in me, old friend,' said Imrik. 'I will rouse the dragons, and I will lead you all in battle as we fall from the skies upon the druchii!'

Lamellan bowed and shook Imrik's outstretched hand.

'We will burn them from Ulthuan together,' said Lamellan.

'Count on it,' replied Imrik.

Powerful aromas of flesh on the fire and incense created from rendered bones filled the silken pavilion, together with the reek of human sweat.

Morathi luxuriated in the delicious scents filling her senses, letting each one linger on the tongue before savouring the next. The air had a sluggish, greasy texture in the aftermath of powerful sorcery, and she could still feel the phantom caresses of her daemon lover.

Sated bodies lay strewn around her, marbled flesh quivering and beaded with sweat and oil. Coiling wisps of smoke streamed from candles and the flames from hanging censers danced on the walls. Her flesh was newly restored, iron-hard and unblemished after the blood of a dozen captives had been drained to make it so.

She ran her fingers across her flat stomach and down her thighs, relishing the cold smoothness of her skin. Rolling onto her side, she found a ewer of spiced wine that had somehow avoided being spilled during the carnal revelry, and poured it into a goblet of ice she formed in her other hand. Fingers from beneath a wolfskin rug pawed her, but she ignored them, sliding into an upright position and taking a long draught of the wine.

It was bitter, the creature she had summoned to pleasure her having soured it, but she drank it down nonetheless. Morathi knew enough of creatures from beyond to know that it was never wise to decline their gifts, intended or otherwise. The wine tasted of blood, but that was of no consequence to her. She had tasted far worse in her thousands of years of life.

Many of her lovers tonight would not live to the dawn, their throats and bellies opened in the frenzy of coupling that had brought forth the daemon. Such was the price of approaching the flame too closely. Slaves, captives or willing participants, it made no difference to Morathi, each was a pleasure to be taken by force or by seduction.

A chill wind blew through the pavilion, snuffing out several of the candles, and she felt a wistful pang for her homeland across the sea. Immediately she corrected herself. *This* was her home, and had been for many years before she and Malekith had been cast from their rightful place as rulers of Ulthuan. The thought angered her, and she wondered if it was being back on this island that made her moods so unpredictable.

Morathi pulled a thin robe from the floor, and wrapped it around her youthful body. Lustrous dark hair spilled around her shoulders, thick and glossy and black as night. She had the body of a maiden, but the eyes of a crone. Suffering the likes of which mortals could not imagine had paraded before those eyes, and no matter how much blood she spilled to preserve her youth, nothing could wash away the weight of ages in her gaze.

She poured more wine into the crackling goblet of ice and moved to the entrance of her pavilion. Lithe elves in armour of banded leather that barely covered their flesh lounged upon velvet blankets, seemingly in repose, but poised and ready to react to danger in the blink of an eye. Servants of the witch cults, they looked up languidly before returning their gaze to the fortress wall in the east.

The Eagle Gate still barred the way to the summerlands beyond. The white of its walls was stained with blood and fire, and the eagle carved into its ramparts was barely recognisable. Its towers were ruined, and only what the defenders built up during the night served as battlements now. Torchlight and the soft hue of magical light shimmered beyond the walls, like a frozen moment of time just before the dawn. Moonlight glittered from spear points and helmets.

Wards beaten into the stone of the fortress prevented her from casting her spirit gaze beyond its walls, but she knew well enough what it protected. Lands of eternally golden summer, fecund soil and pure waters like the clearest crystal. In days past she had ridden those lands without a care, confident in the path her future would take, but those days were gone, and only bitterness remained in her heart. What Morathi could not have she would destroy.

Or if not her, then another…

Morathi remembered the last time she had seen Caledor, and the threat he had made. She wondered if he even remembered it. The magic of the vortex had all but driven him mad, and Caledor would sooner destroy this land than allow her or Malekith to claim it.

She wondered if the asur knew that.

Once she could not have allowed her thoughts to stray to Caledor and the magical vortex at the heart of Ulthuan, for fear that he would become aware of her presence. But many centuries had passed since their last meeting, and her knowledge of the arcane arts had grown immeasurably – enough that she could weave spells to hide her from the archmages' sight. Morathi was not deluded enough to believe that she was the equal of Caledor Dragontamer, but she had one advantage over the trapped mage lord.

She wasn't utterly insane.

Morathi smiled as she wondered if that were true.

Her sinuous guards uncoiled from their supine positions, long-bladed daggers appearing in each hand as a towering figure in armour like flayed skin appeared at the edge of the torchlight. Handsome to the point of ridiculousness, his body was as fine a specimen of mortal flesh as could be imagined.

'Is it safe to approach?' he enquired with a wry grin. 'Or must I again send you my best warriors to die under your knives?'

'Approach, Issyk Kul,' said Morathi. 'I am, for the moment, sated.'

The warrior emerged fully into the light, and Morathi took a moment to appreciate the sheer dynamism of his body. So raw in its muscularity and power, so blunt in its threat. So different from the slender bodies of Naggaroth.

'How goes the fighting?' she asked.

'You would know if you fought instead of rutted,' said Kul, 'though there's pleasure to be taken in both. Perhaps we should swap roles.'

Anger flared momentarily, but she quelled it, knowing the warrior of the Dark Prince was simply goading her. He relished her anger, and she was in no hurry to indulge him. Not yet.

'Why should I fight when you and your tribesmen take such pleasure in it?' she said.

'There's truth in that,' agreed Kul. 'The blood flows freely, and the asur fight well. It is a battle of blood, of pain and of exquisite wounds. The kiss of an ithilmar blade stings like no other.'

'In any case, my battle is fought in subtler ways,' said Morathi.

'I like subtle,' said Kul, and Morathi laughed.

'So I see,' she said.

Kul drew his many-bladed weapon from the sheath across his shoulder, and Morathi's witch cultists were at her side in a heartbeat. Kul grinned, exposing his tapered fangs.

'Tell your witches to beware,' he said. 'I do not wish you dead until I have taken my fill of your flesh.'

'When the war is won, you will have your prize,' said Morathi, letting her robe fall open to reveal a slice of her toned thigh. Kul's gaze lingered on her body, following its contours from her hips to her breasts to her face. His grin was one of pure lust, and it never failed to amaze Morathi how much importance mortals placed on physicality. Copulation was the least of the ways in which a soul could be pleasured, the easiest, the most direct and the most human.

Issyk Kul would never satisfy his base, animal needs with her.

He would be dead before then.

'Your son still lays siege to Lothern?' said Kul, picking up a discarded cup and holding it out to her as though she was some kind of servant girl. She bit back her anger and poured the soured wine into his cup.

Kul drank it down in one gulp. 'Pungent,' he said.

She dropped the ewer, letting its contents ooze out onto the rock of the pass.

'Malekith enjoys success at Lothern,' she said. 'The Emerald Gate is his, as are the shoulder castles on the cliffs. Every day fresh warriors cross the bridge from the Glittering Lighthouse to the mainland. It is only a matter of time until Lothern is ours.'

'From what I hear, getting to the next gate will be a fight of great magnitude.'

'It will be bloody,' admitted Morathi.

'Mayhap we will be in Lothern before your son,' suggested Kul playfully.

'Not if this fortress continues to stand.'

'It will fall soon,' promised Kul. 'It is a certainty. And it will be soon.'

'What makes you say that?'

'There is one among the elves who is touched by the Dark Gods.'

'An asur?'

'Aye. An archer, I think.'

'They are all archers, Kul,' pointed out Morathi.

Kul shrugged. 'You elves all look the same to me,' he said. 'Pale skin, strange eyes and pointed ears. I could have killed him, but I saw the touch upon him as clear as midnight. His soul is at war, and all it will take is a small push to make him ours.'

'How small a push?' asked Morathi.

'One you could easily provide,' said Kul.

Alathenar took a seat on the carved bench at the foot of the walls and let out a relieved breath. He rested his bow against the wall and placed the plate of bread and cheese beside him. He was too tired to eat, but knew it was the only chance he was likely to get to satisfy his hunger. His muscles ached abominably and the sword cut on his hip had reopened. Blood stained his leggings, and he had loaned his needle and thread to one of the healers whose magic was exhausted. He tried to remain still, knowing that the wound would seal eventually, and grateful for this chance to rest. The walk from the mess hall had all but drained him, and he knew that he could not survive much longer without rest. He leaned his head back against the wall and closed his eyes, but sleep would not come. Too many images of hacked open bodies and friends screaming in pain paraded before him to allow him to sleep.

He wondered if he would ever sleep again.

The defenders of the Eagle Gate were in a sorry state. Barely eight hundred of them remained alive, and only two-thirds of those were fit to fight. Rumours kept circulating that reinforcements were being gathered, but they had yet to see any sign of them. Stories of far off battles filled the fortress, bleak tales of war being waged at Lothern, human fleets ravaging the coasts of Cothique and Yvresse, and assassins striking at the leaders of the asur.

No one knew what to believe anymore.

Warriors gathered in small groups, talking in low voices, and he wondered if they gave voice to the same thoughts as slithered around his skull. Healers moved from group to group, using what little magic remained to them, and victual bearers brought water to parched throats.

'We are battered, but resolute,' he said. 'But for how much longer?'

'Not much longer if Glorien keeps wasting lives,' said Alanrias, walking over from the direction of the mess hall. The warrior of Nagarythe carried something beneath his cloak, but Alathenar could not tell what it was. Eloien Redcloak came with the Shadow Warrior, and though he still bore his scarlet cloak, it was torn and burned in so many places that it seemed foolish to retain it. His features, already hardened from a life in the saddle, had been hardened further by his time at the Eagle Gate.

'I was about to eat,' said Alathenar, ignoring the Shadow Warrior's obvious barb.

'A delightful feast indeed,' agreed Eloien, taking a slice of bread from

Alathenar's plate. He bit into the bread and grimaced before spitting it out. The Ellyrian wiped his lips with the back of his hand.

'You don't like the bread?' asked Alathenar.

'It is stale.'

'Stale? Elven bread does not go stale.'

'Then you had better tell the bakers,' said Eloien. 'Either this bread has been in the stores since the time of Bel Shanaar or the sorceries of the druchii have found new ways to make us miserable.'

Alathenar took a mouthful of bread and was forced to agree with Eloien. Elven bread could last for years without going hard and tasteless, but this was like stone or the bread the dwarfs were said to favour.

'It seems you are right,' he said, taking the half-chewed lump from his mouth.

'Enough prattle about bread,' hissed Alanrias. 'I saw you on the wall, we made a compact. I saw it in your eyes. Let us be about our business.'

Alathenar sighed and looked toward the Aquila Spire. Soft light emanated from the windows, where Glorien Truecrown rested in comfort.

'Yes,' he said. 'We did, but that does not mean I take pleasure in what we must do.'

'I don't care whether you take pleasure in it or not,' hissed Alanrias. 'Only that you do it.'

'Be at peace, brother,' soothed Eloien. 'Alathenar knows what must be done. It does him credit that he takes no joy in its necessity.'

The Shadow Warrior sat back and shook his head. 'We are on the brink of ruin and you dance around the issue like children. On the walls tomorrow. That is when it must be done.'

Anger flared in Alathenar's heart and he rounded on the Shadow Warrior. 'If you are so ready to spill Glorien's blood, then why not do it yourself?'

'You are the best archer in the garrison,' said Eloien. 'You are the only one who is certain not to miss.'

'You think you can move me to murder with flattery?' hissed Alathenar.

'If need be,' said Alanrias. 'You saw how many died protecting him today. How many will die tomorrow? How much longer can we bear his incompetence? Until the fortress falls and we are all dead?'

Alathenar started to reply, but before he could form the words to respond to Alanrias, he tasted a bitter metallic flavour in his mouth and a bilious wave of resentment washed over him. He wanted to tell Alanrias that he would not kill one of his own kind – murder was beneath him – but all those noble sentiments were swamped by images of the dead and maimed.

He did not like Alanrias, but could not deny the truth of his words. Glorien's foolishness had cost them all dear, had seen brave elves die and brought them to the edge of defeat. His half-hearted attempt to win back their favour by taking to the walls was an insult to the warriors who had died in his name.

This was the true face of Glorien Truecrown, a petty martinet, a strutting popinjay who saw war as a means of advancement. To have fought on the walls of the Eagle Gate would be just the posting to secure influence and prestige for his family. No matter that it would be bought with the lives of warriors who had spilled their precious elven blood under his command. Behind this tide of anger, part of Alathenar rebelled at what the dark voices were telling him, but the greater part of him embraced it.

Alathenar's expression turned to stone and he said, 'I cannot do the deed with one of my arrows. Nor even yours, Alanrias. We cannot be implicated.'

'We have thought of that,' said Alanrias.

The Shadow Warrior moved aside his cloak to reveal what he had brought to their plotting. It gleamed in the moonlight, the stock fashioned in polished ebony and the wound strings woven from a coarse horsehair. Alathenar reached out to touch it, but his fingers stopped short of the iron bolt resting in the groove of the weapon. It was a weapon of brutal yet elegant design.

A druchii hand crossbow.

Alathenar's fingers slipped around the weapon's handle. It felt natural, as though the weapon had been crafted just for him.

'Tomorrow then,' he said.

Morathi let the drained body fall from her grip, the blood dripping from her fingertips as the last of the spell faded away. It had been a tiny thing, requiring only the blood of a single sacrifice, for the daemons of hate were simple to conjure and needed little encouragement to venture into the realms of the living.

Brought forth beneath the light of the Chaos moon, and loosed on the winds of magic, it had been a matter of moments for the daemonic spirits to ease their way through the cracked and broken defences of the fortress. Wards that had kept her sorcery at bay for weeks were now virtually exhausted, simplicity itself for creatures of Chaos to overcome.

She felt the surge of hatred within the fortress and laughed.

Warriors who had been brothers moments ago now traded hurtful words, and tiny grievances now swelled to monstrous insults. It would be short lived and swiftly forgotten, but potent while it lasted.

'Is it done?' asked Kul, licking his lips with anticipation.

'It is,' confirmed Morathi. 'Though how a single moment of hatred will serve our cause is beyond me. By morning the asur will not remember their sudden anger.'

'Do not be too sure,' said Kul. 'A moment of weakness matched to an instant of hate, and the course of a life can be changed forever. My divine master is patient, and swift to snare any soul that lowers its defences, even for a second.'

'And you think this brief hatred is enough?'

'Once the dark prince has a claim on a heart, there is no escape,' hissed Kul. 'You of all people should know that. Your bloody-handed god is jealous of his followers, but Shornaal cares not from where the souls come. Only that they be ripe for corruption.'

Kul laughed and strode away from Morathi.

'Tomorrow,' he said. 'This ends tomorrow.'

CHAPTER SEVEN
BLACK SWANS

Ellyrion opened up to him, its rolling fields endless and its skies huge. The land before him was a thin strip of golden corn, the heavens an unending bowl of blue skies and streamers of silver clouds. Eldain's ride across the land of his birth was a revelation, like he was seeing it with new eyes. Eldain had believed he and Lotharin had ridden every path of Ellyrion, but his senses were alive with the pleasure of discovery.

Every hill and forest seemed new and freshly risen, each dawn as though it had been wrought just for him. Eldain had no idea why his homeland should welcome him as it did, for the kingdoms of Ulthuan kept no secrets from one another. What the land knew in Avelorn, it knew in Ellyrion and Saphery and all the other realms of the asur.

Eldain had taken an indirect route to Ellyr-Charoi, keeping clear of the main settlements and pathways. He slept by streams gurgling towards the Inner Sea, and ate plants that grew on their banks, rising each morning more refreshed than before. He had lost track of the days, but knew he could not be far from his home. His clothes were travel-stained and had begun to smell, but Eldain didn't mind. This ride was what it meant to be an Ellyrian, free from the constraints of society and its rules.

Here and there, he would see herds of wild horses grazing or drinking at a pool of crystal water. Most of these herds ignored him, but others would gallop over and ride alongside for a time, conversing with Lotharin in a series of whinnies and snorts. It felt good to be with the herds of Ellyrion, and brought back a particularly fine memory from his youth.

'You remember it too, don't you?' he said, as Lotharin tossed his mane and stamped the ground. His mount broke into a run at his words, and he laughed as the joy of that day returned with the potency only a memory of the asur could render.

He had ridden out with Caelir when they had been no more than twelve summers old, taking their still-wild steeds out into the plains to gallop alongside the Great Herd. Once every few decades, the countless wild herds of Ellyrion would gather somewhere on the plains, drawn by some nameless imperative to run together in a thousands-strong stampede of fierce exultation.

Every son of Ellyrion longed to ride with the Great Herd, to mingle with the powerful beasts as they joined together in one thunderous ride to glory. Only the best riders dared join with the herd, for these steeds were wild and cared nothing for the safety of the mortals in their midst. Many an experienced rider had been crushed to death beneath the thundering hooves of the Great Herd. Eldain and Caelir took their horses out by the light of the moon and rode north from their home to the burned copse where Laerial Sureblade had slain Gauma, the eleven-headed hydra.

Here they followed the tracks of the lowland steeds, and joined the smaller herds as they crossed a confluence of rivers that foamed white as though desperate to be part of the ride. Eldain remembered seeing hundreds of horses all around them, the numbers growing with every passing moment as the white herds of the south were joined by the dun and dappled beasts of the mountains. The greys of the north and the piebald mounts of the plains galloped in, proud and haughty, to be met by the silver herdleaders of the forests.

Here and there, a black steed galloped in splendid isolation, honoured and shunned in equal measure by its equine brothers. Soon the plains were filled with thousands of wild horses in a mighty herd that stretched from horizon to horizon, and the blood surged in Eldain's veins to be riding with such a host.

Beside him Caelir whooped and yelled, standing tall in Aedaris's stirrups and waving an arm over his head like a madman.

'Sit down!' Eldain had yelled. 'You'll be thrown and killed!'

Caelir shook his head and vaulted onto his horse's back, his limbs flowing like water as he bent and swayed to compensate for the wild ride. Dust billowed in thick clouds as the Great Herd galloped for all it was worth. The earth shook and the pounding beat of unshod hooves on the hard-packed earth was like the storms that boomed and rolled over the Annulii when the Chaos moon waxed full.

Eldain saw groups of Ellyrian horsemen riding through the herds, listening to their laughter and hearing their passionate cries. A herd of dun mares jostled him and he hauled the reins to the right, but pulled into the path of a group of pale stallions with the light of madness in their eyes. Lotharin was struck from both sides, and Eldain fought to stay on his back. Like Eldain and Caelir, their steeds were youthful and much smaller than these powerful beasts.

He felt the panic in his mount, and struggled to disentangle himself from the stallions. The horses had their head, and he was enclosed from all sides. Lotharin was tiring fast and to slow in such a desperate gallop would be suicide.

'Eldain!' shouted Caelir, and he looked over to see his brother sat astride Aedaris once more. 'Ride to me!'

Eldain pulled Lotharin through the barging, heaving mass of horses towards his brother, but Lotharin's strength was fading fast. Sweat stung Eldain's eyes and his muscles burned from the effort of keeping upright. Caelir was less than five yards to his right, but a bucking mass of wild horseflesh occupied the space between them.

'Jump!' shouted Caelir. 'Lotharin can break free if he does not need to worry about you!'

Loath as Eldain was to abandon his horse in the midst of this pandemonium, he knew Caelir was right. An Ellyrian steed would die to protect its rider, but that loyalty would see them both killed here.

Eldain kicked his boots free of the stirrups and leaned over his mount's neck.

'Run free, my friend, and I will see you after the ride is done,' he said.

Lotharin threw back his head and whinnied his assent. Eldain sprang onto Lotharin's back, the black horse a lone spot of darkness amongst the pale grey stallions. Caelir fought to hold Aedaris steady at the edge of the heaving mass, holding his hand out to Eldain.

'Jump, brother!' Caelir yelled.

Eldain swayed on Lotharin's back, gauging the right moment to leap. One misstep and he would fall through the press of horses and be crushed beneath their hammering strides. The horses were turning now, leaning into a sharp left turn. It was now or never.

Eldain jumped, hurling himself from Lotharin's back and into the air. He came down on the bouncing shoulder blades of a white stallion and sprang onwards, twisting to come down behind Caelir. His brother gripped him as he slid back and they rode clear from the crescendo of galloping horses.

Caelir rode until they were cantering on the fringes of the Great Herd, content to watch the majestic sweep of the mass of horses as they let loose their untamed hearts and shared the joy of a wild ride with their brothers and sisters. Eldain slid from Aedaris's back at the foot of a jutting scarp of rock, knowing that Caelir wasn't yet done with the Great Herd.

'Go,' he said. 'Ride with the herd. I know you want to.'

'Without you, Eldain?' laughed Caelir, though Eldain could see the fierce desire in him to ride back into the herd. 'Where would the fun be in that?'

'Don't be foolish, how often does the Great Herd gather? Go!'

Caelir loosed a wild yell and Aedaris reared up before charging head-long into the swirling mass of dust and thundering horses. Eldain watched him go, proud to have so fearless a brother and, he could now admit, a touch jealous that he would not get to spend the day amid the frantic, pulse-pounding energy of the Great Herd.

As night fell, and the Great Herd began to break up into myriad smaller groups, Caelir rode Aedaris to the rock where Eldain had watched the ebb and flow of the mad stampede. Sweat-stained and exhausted, Caelir was nevertheless exultant, his cheeks ruddy with excitement and joy. His mount's flanks were lathered with sweat, but he too was overjoyed to have been part of something so ferocious. Lotharin followed his brother's horse, similarly drained, but equally joyous.

Together they had ridden back to Ellyr-Charoi, and Eldain spent the entire journey hearing of the magnificent sights at the eye of the herd, the swirling mass of horses and the madness of the jostling, barging, crashing herds. Eldain revelled in his younger brother's tales, laughing and yelling with each telling of Caelir's reckless stunts. Dawn was lighting the eastern horizon by the time they passed through the gates and allowed the equerries to take their horses from them.

Though that ride had been many years ago, Eldain still remembered it like it was yesterday. That all too brief moment of sheer, unbridled joy as he rode with the Great Herd was like nothing he had ever experienced before or since. It was a golden memory, and he silently thanked the land for its boon. Lotharin gave a long whinny of pleasure, and they rode on in companionable silence. The horses of the wild herd that had accompanied him for many miles now turned and galloped for the mountains. Eldain waved them on their way.

'Farewell and firm earth,' he said, as the last horse vanished over an undulant hill fringed with pine. At the foot of the hill, a jutting rock carved by childish hands into the shape of a rearing horse poked from an overgrown tangle of thornspines, and Eldain smiled as he recalled carving it for Rhianna, the first summer she had come to visit from Saphery.

Time had weathered the poor carving, and obscuring plant life had grown up around it, making it look like an ambush predator was dragging the horse down. Eldain shivered at the image that conjured, and tried not to think of it as an omen.

He was close now, that carving had been made when they were little more than children and not permitted to venture far from the villa. Eldain cut south until he found a hill trail that led south, a hidden pathway that none save an Ellyrian would know. Eldain saw it had been travelled recently, the hooves of a horse not native to Ellyrion having come this way. For an hour he followed the trail, winding through the high gullies and forest lanes until he emerged onto a rolling hillside of lush green grass.

Below him lay a glittering villa set within a stand of orange-leaved trees that nestled between two waterfalls.

Ellyr-Charoi.

Home.

Light was fading from the sky by the time Eldain reached the villa, and the evening sun reflected from the many gemstones set within its walls. Azure capped towers surrounded a central courtyard, and the tinted glass of their many windows shone with a rainbow of colours. Autumnal leaves drifted on the winds around the villa, and withered vines climbed to the tiled copings of its walls.

Eldain took a deep breath and tried to feel something other than foreboding at the sight of his home. Ellyr-Charoi grew from the earth, wrought with great cunning by its builders to merge seamlessly with the landscape and become part of its surroundings. As was the fashion of Ellyrian dwellings, it was elegant and understated, without the riot of gaudy decorations common to Ulthuan's more cosmopolitan cities.

He rode slowly down the path until he reached the overgrown track of a gently arched bridge. So many memories jostled for attention. Sitting on the bridge with Rhianna and throwing in flower petals. Racing Caelir to the bridge on their new steeds. Cheering as his father rode to join a warrior host setting out for Naggaroth.

Weeping as the white-clad mourners brought his mortally wounded father home.

The gates were open, and the wind blew through like a moan of grief, whistling through cracked panes of glass on the tallest towers and filling the air with dancing leaves of gold and rust. No one challenged him as he rode into the courtyard, where once warriors had stood sentinel on the walls with bows bent and arrows nocked. Those faithful retainers were long gone, and Eldain felt the villa's abandonment settle on him like an accusing glare.

He slid from his horse's back and turned slowly, taking in the neglected villa's disrepair. Where once an autumnal air had held sway, now winter was in the ascendancy. The fountain at the heart of the Summer Courtyard was empty of water, and only dead leaves filled the pool. A marble-tiled cloister bounded the courtyard, and Eldain made his way towards the elegantly curved stairs that led from the courtyard to his chambers at the top of the Hippocrene Tower. He climbed the first step, and paused as he heard the brittle sound of fallen leaves crumbling beneath a riding boot.

Knowing what he would see, Eldain turned around.

Caelir stood by Lotharin, clad as Eldain remembered him from Avelorn. Like him, he was travel-worn and tired, but unlike Eldain, Caelir was armed. He carried a slim-bladed sword with a blue sheen to its edge. Eldain recognised it as their father's sword, the weapon he had borne to Naggaroth on the eve of his death.

'Caelir,' said Eldain. 'I hoped you would be here.'

His brother took a step towards him, and ran a hand down Lotharin's lathered flanks.

'A true horseman would see to his mount before anything else,' said Caelir. 'But then we both know you are no son of Ellyrion, don't we brother?'

By midmorning the armies of Morathi and her mortal allies had launched two major attacks upon the Eagle Gate. Both attacks had been repulsed, though the defenders had suffered heavy losses, for the Hag Sorceress had held nothing back from these assaults. Flitting she-bats swooped from the skies, bellowing hydras unleashed breaths of fire, and rock-shielded bolt throwers hurled enormous, barbed shafts at the fragmenting walls.

Morathi herself took to the air, unleashing black sorceries from the back of her midnight pegasus, and every magicker in the fortress bent their efforts to keep her at bay. Her spiteful laughter rang over the battlements, driving her warriors to ever greater heights of suicidal courage.

It sat ill with Menethis to think of the druchii as possessing so noble an attribute as courage, but there was no other word for it. The blood in their veins came from the same wellspring as did his, and for all their other hateful qualities, courage was, unfortunately, not a virtue they lacked. Yet it was not the equal of asur courage, he knew, for its origins lay not in duty, honour or notions of self-sacrifice, but in fear.

The mortal followers of the dark prince attacked with reckless disregard for their own lives, many of them seeming to welcome the stabbing blades of the elves. The towering warrior in the flayed-flesh armour bellowed his challenges from the top of each ladder he climbed, killing any who came near him with chopping blows of his many-bladed sword.

Three times he had gained the rampart, and three times he had been hurled from the walls, only to rise from the ruin of broken ladder and splintered bodies to seek a new way up. The deformed monsters dragged towards the fortress in chains battered its crumbling walls, and the musk of their excretions drifted over the battlements in nauseating waves.

Yet for all the ferocity of these attacks, Menethis sensed a growing sense of something else behind the dark helms of the attackers. He wanted to believe it was desperation, for the walls of the Eagle Gate had held far longer than he would have thought possible. Designed to be impregnable, the garrison had been steadily run down over the years until only a token force remained. The warriors fighting and dying here were now paying for that foolishness with their lives.

Perhaps our enemies know they are on borrowed time, he thought, thinking of the sealed scroll that had arrived in the hands of a rider from Tor Elyr moments before the second attack had hit the walls. Glorien had read it first, then handed it to Menethis. With every word he read, a growing sense of euphoria filled him.

'We have done it,' Glorien had said, his eyes alight with the prospect of victory. 'This will be over in days. All we have to do is hold a little longer.'

Arandir Swiftwing, the lord of Tor Elyr, was mustering an army and his foremost general, Galadrien Stormweaver, was marching to their relief. Every able-bodied warrior had been summoned to Lothern, but as more and more of the citizen levy had answered their lord's summons, another army took shape on the martial fields around Tor Elyr.

A portion of that army would reach the Eagle Gate in two days.

Perhaps that was why the three great eagles had flown from the fortress, sensing that their aid was no longer required. Some had seen it as a bad omen when the three mighty birds had flown over the northern peaks of the mountains, but the news of their relief made sense of their departure.

There had been no time to disseminate the wondrous news of Stormweaver's imminent arrival, for the enemy were attacking once more. Menethis watched the armoured host of enemy warriors marching towards the walls as a host of white-shafted arrows slashed towards them. Stocks of arrows were low, and Glorien had decreed that only the best archers be given an extra quiver. The Eagle's Claws were out of bolts and their crews stood on the walls with their fellow warriors, spears glittering in the high sun.

Menethis drew back the string of his bow, picking out a druchii warrior without a helm at the forefront of a group of ladder-bearers. The warrior's face was pale, and a glistening topknot of black hair hung down to the nape of his neck. His armour was bloodstained and carved with jagged runes. Between breaths, Menethis let fly, watching the arrow arc downwards before plunging home in the druchii's neck. The warrior fell, clutching at his throat as blood squirted from the wound.

The enemy broke on the walls with a thunderous crash of iron and wood. Ladders were thrown up and looping grapnels sailed over the makeshift battlements. Menethis leaned out over the crumbling rampart and loosed arrow after arrow into the mass of surging warriors below. Each shaft found its mark, punching through the top of a helmet or slicing home in a gap between armoured plates.

Menethis did not waste his arrows on the mortals, only druchii warranted his attention. Within moments, his quiver was emptied and he drew his sword as the enemy climbed their ladders. Hundreds of screaming warriors were coming to gain a foothold on the walls, in a mass of stabbing blades, hewing axes and streaking iron bolts.

'Steady now,' said Menethis, hearing iron-shod boots on metal rungs.

A druchii appeared at the top of the ladder. An asur spear stabbed out but was blocked, and the warrior hauled himself through the embrasure.

Menethis plunged his sword into the warrior's chest. Twisting the blade, he kicked the druchii from the wall and chopped down into the head of the enemy behind him.

'The ladder!' yelled Menethis, seeing that the iron hooks at its end had not bitten into the stonework of the parapet. 'Help me!'

He gripped the top of the ladder and heaved with all his strength. Three more elves ran to help him, but the first dropped as an iron bolt hammered into his throat. The two elves took position either side of Menethis and leaned into the task. Another druchii reared up and stabbed his blade into the warrior beside Menethis. He gave a strangled cry and dropped to his knees, but with the last of his strength he gripped his killer's blade tightly, trapping it within his flesh.

The ladder squealed with a grating scrape of iron on stone, but Menethis felt it pitch past its centre of gravity. Powerless to prevent the ladder from falling, the druchii released his sword and leapt onto the walls with a dagger aimed at Menethis's heart. A black-shafted arrow sliced out of nowhere and thudded home into the druchii's armpit. Arterial blood flooded out and the warrior fell as the ladder was cast down. Screaming druchii tumbled to the base of the wall, and Menethis sought out his rescuer.

He gave a begrudged nod of thanks as he saw it had been the Shadow Warrior, Alanrias, who had loosed the arrow. The cloaked warrior sketched a casual salute and bent his bow once more, picking off druchii warriors who were in danger of forming a fighting wedge on the ramparts. All along the length of the wall, a tidal wave of druchii and barbarians were pushing hard. The ramparts were slick with blood, and though the asur line was bending, it was holding.

In the centre of the wall, Glorien stood in the midst of the garrison's best warriors. His sword was bloody and his armour would never be the same again, but he was fighting hard. Even Menethis had to admit that Glorien's skills with a blade left much to be desired, but war forced a warrior to be a swift learner. Though there was not an elf in this fortress Glorien could best in a clash of blades, there were the makings of a fine warrior coming to the fore.

Perhaps Glorien's dream vision was just that, a dream, not some nightmare premonition of doom. Menethis had kept a wary eye on Alanrias throughout the fighting, but the Shadow Warrior had done nothing untoward, calmly and methodically killing druchii with lethally accurate arrows.

Menethis crouched behind the crumbling rampart and removed his helm, pulling his hair back and securing it in a long ponytail. He reached up to wipe a film of sweat from his brow and blinked as he saw something out of place. A stillness, amid the frenetic scrum of battle raging along the length of the wall.

A lone warrior crouched in the shadows at the base of the Aquila Spire with a druchii crossbow resting on a broken stub of rock. His eyes were cold and merciless, the eyes of a murderer. Menethis opened his mouth to shout that a druchii assassin had scaled the walls undetected, when he saw that this assassin wore a cloak of pale blue, muted in the shadows, but unmistakably of asur design.

'Here they come again!' shouted a voice, and Menethis heard the clang of iron ladders and the biting of grapnel hooks into stone. He ignored them, and ran along the wall, ducking and weaving a path through desperate combats.

'No!' he shouted, knowing where the iron bolt of the crossbow was aimed.

The assassin loosed and Menethis screamed a denial as the bolt slashed through the air and hammered through the temple of Glorien's helmet. The commander of the Eagle Gate was punched from his feet, falling against the parapet as blood poured down his stricken face.

His protectors tried to catch Glorien, but the shock of the impact stunned them to the point where not even their superlative reflexes were swift enough. Glorien toppled forwards, his body falling from the walls to land in the midst of the enemy.

A terrifying howl of triumph erupted from below, for there could be no doubt which of the asur had fallen. Glorien's armour clearly marked him as the commander of the Eagle Gate, and Menethis ran to the edge of the wall in time to see Glorien's body torn to pieces by the frenzied savages who served the barbarian warlord.

A palpable wave of grief and horror swept over the defenders of the Eagle Gate, a physical sensation of loss and despair. Few had any love for Glorien Truecrown, but seeing their commander slain so suddenly tore the heart from everyone who saw it. Even the healers and the wounded beyond the walls felt the pain of Glorien's death.

Wracked with grief, the defence faltered.

Just for a moment, just for the briefest instant, but it was enough.

Scores of ladders thudded against the fortress as Menethis and the defenders wept for their lost master. Enemy warriors hurled themselves over the ramparts, and this time, there would be no stopping them.

Menethis turned towards the Aquila Spire, the need for vengeance fanning a terrible fury in his heart. He saw the druchii weapon thrown from the wall as the assassin who had wielded it stepped from the shadows, confident that no one had seen his perfidy.

Menethis gasped as he saw who had loosed the treacherous bolt.

'Alathenar!' he screamed.

Eldain had dreaded this moment, but now that it was here, he felt strangely relieved. Ever since that fleeting moment when he had allowed hateful feelings of jealousy to overcome a lifetime of brotherly love, he had known he would have to answer for his crime. The blade in Caelir's hands would exact the price he would have to pay.

'Do you want to kill me?' he asked.

'Can you think of a single reason I shouldn't?'

'No,' said Eldain, stepping down into the Summer Courtyard. 'I deserve your hatred.'

The wind sighed through the gates, blowing the leaves from the inlaid marble flagstones into miniature whirlwinds. The last embers of sunlight shone from the colourful windows of the villa's towers and the evening-hued blade in Caelir's hands.

'Tell me why, Eldain,' demanded Caelir, and Eldain wanted to weep at the wrenching sorrow he heard in his brother's voice. 'Tell me why you left me to die. I need to know.'

Eldain shook his head. 'It will not make any difference.'

'It will make a difference to me, Eldain!' roared Caelir. 'I rode day and night from Avelorn, trying to comprehend why my own flesh and blood would betray me to the druchii, but I could think of no reason, no reason at all. So make me understand, brother. Tell me what great insult did I do to you that made you hate me so much?'

'Hate you, brother? No, never that. I loved you.'

'You loved me? You must have a strange definition of the word.'

Eldain circled the fountain, and Caelir mirrored his movements, keeping the waterless centrepiece between them.

'Perhaps you are right,' said Eldain. 'I no longer know. I loved you and was jealous of you in equal measure. Nothing I did could ever match what you would accomplish. Anything of worth I could achieve, you would outdo. Wherever I shone, you shone brighter.'

'I only sought to be like you, brother,' cried Caelir. 'You were my inspiration!'

Eldain shook his head. 'When our father died, who took care of our estates? Who kept our family name alive and dealt with the necessities of life? I did. Not you. I was the one who took care of us when father died, you ran like a spoiled child. Hunting, carousing and riding with the herds was the life you led, being the heroic warrior I had not the time to be.'

'And for that you betrayed me?'

'You stole everything of beauty that should have been mine!'

'What are you talking about?'

'You took Rhianna from me!' cried Eldain, turning and walking towards the tall building at the edge of the Summer Courtyard. He pushed open the ash doors of the Equerry's Hall, and a gust of leaves followed him inside. Within was dimly lit and smelled of neglect, though it had been only weeks since he had last set foot in this grand hall. Hunting trophies and faded portraits of former lords of the noble Éadaoin family hung from the walls, and a long oval table filled the centre of the echoing space.

Eldain sank into the high-backed chair at the end of the table as Caelir stood silhouetted in its wide doorway by the last light of day. The sword in his hand sparkled in the gloaming. Caelir shut the doors behind him and stepped inside, letting his eyes adjust to the thin light coming through the vents in the roof. In ages past, the lords of the Éadaoin would gather here to feast and sing songs of the wild hunt, but those songs were sung and no more would they lift the rafters with their wild notes.

Caelir sat at the opposite end of the table from Eldain, and laid the sword before him.

'I did take Rhianna from you,' he said at last. 'I knew it was wrong, but I did it anyway. It was that ride into the Annulii. We were attacked by the druchii and I fought them all. We should have ridden away, but I *wanted* to fight them. I wanted her to see how strong and brave I was. Foolish, I know, but back then I was a little in love with death I think.'

'She was never the same after that day,' said Eldain. 'I accused her of being infatuated with you because of your reckless bravery. I spoke harshly to her, and she did not deserve my anger. I had too long ignored her happiness, and all but forced you together.'

'I did not mean to fall in love with her, but...'

'But you did,' said Eldain. 'She is a woman impossible *not* to fall in love with.'

'And you married her,' said Caelir. 'I saw the pledge rings. You came back from Naggaroth and told her I was dead. You betrayed me and took up your life where you had left off now that the inconvenience of Caelir was removed.'

'That is true,' admitted Eldain. 'But I think that it was not hatred of you, but love of Rhianna that was my undoing.'

'Again, your definition of love is a mockery of the word.'

'Perhaps, but love is a powerful emotion, one that blinds us to many things. Love is also the gateway to other, darker, emotions: jealousy, paranoia, possessiveness and lust. I told myself I loved her, and anything that brought us together could not be altogether evil. I was wrong, I know that now. And though it can make no difference to how this must end, I ask your understanding if not your forgiveness.'

Caelir rose to his feet, his face reddening as through Eldain had slapped him. 'You speak of forgiveness? Of understanding? You left me to the druchii and told the woman I loved that I was dead. You cannot know the things the dark kin did to me, how they made me do... terrible things and cause untold harm to my own kind.'

'I know what they made you do, I understand–'

'You understand nothing!' screamed Caelir. 'Hundreds of people are dead because of me, because of what you did. Don't you understand? Kyrielle, Teclis, the Everqueen... Our enemies used me as a weapon!'

Caelir vaulted onto the table and charged along its length, scattering dusty plates and cutlery. He hurled himself at Eldain and the two brothers crashed to the floor in a tangle of flailing limbs. The sword lay forgotten on the table, as Caelir straddled Eldain's chest and wrapped his hands around his neck.

Eldain struggled in his brother's grip, holding onto Caelir's wrists and fighting to take a breath. The light of madness was in Caelir's eyes, yet behind it was an ocean of sorrow and pain and guilt. That guilt was rightfully Eldain's, that sorrow his legacy, and he knew he had more than earned Caelir's vengeance. This death was a small thing, the last gift he could give his brother in lieu of any means to make amends.

Caelir's grip tightened, and Eldain's throat buckled under the pressure. He could take no breath, and he released Caelir's wrists, letting the grey at the edges of his vision deepen to black until he could see no more.

At last, Eldain knew peace.

CHAPTER EIGHT
AMENDS

No sooner had the bolt left the druchii crossbow than Alathenar knew he had made a terrible mistake. He watched it cut the air, hoping for a freak gust of wind or a chance movement that would see it plunge home in an enemy's chest. He closed his eyes as the bolt punched through Glorien's helm, and sent a whispered prayer to Asuryan that he might, one day, be forgiven for this murder.

'What have I done…?' he said as Glorien fell from the wall.

Alathenar hurled the druchii weapon away as though it were a poisonous serpent, and took up his bow as he swiftly stepped from the shadows. He pulled his cloak tight, feeling his soul already growing heavy with the enormity of his deed. He had slain a fellow elf, one of the asur. No less a warrior than his commanding officer. He was no better than the dark-armoured warriors who threw themselves at the walls with bloody war cries.

He heard his name shouted, and saw Menethis running along the battlements. He knew immediately that Menethis had seen him loose the fateful bolt, and part of him was glad. He didn't think he could bear the weight of such a dark secret.

The defenders of the Eagle Gate were paralysed by Glorien's sudden death, as horrified by his ending as they had been by Cerion Goldwing's. Sword arms were stilled and bowstrings went slack as they watched their fallen leader's body savagely torn apart by the enemy. No matter that he had been derided for many weeks, he was a noble of Ulthuan and had finally begun to live up to that title. Only now, when it was too late to undo the deed, did Alathenar understand what Glorien might have become.

The druchii swarmed the walls, and Alathenar saw the barbarian warlord in his crimson armour scramble onto the ramparts. His sword swept out and three elves were torn apart in a spray of blood. He bellowed his triumph, keeping the defenders at bay with wide arcs of his monstrous blade. Dozens of leather and fur-clad warriors in crudely strapped armour gained the walls behind him, massing for a push outwards along the length of the rampart. Elsewhere, heavily armoured druchii with long, executioner's blades forced a path onto the wall, and more of their plate-armoured brethren came with them.

The wall was lost, any fool could see that.

Menethis slammed into him and bore him to the ground. Alathenar's sword slipped from its scabbard, and he sprang to his feet as Menethis came at him again.

'You murderer!' yelled Menethis, slashing wildly with his blade. 'I will kill you.'

Alathenar leapt away from each attack. Grief and anger had made Menethis clumsy, and he sobbed even as he fought.

'Wait!' cried Alathenar, backing away.

Glorien's lieutenant paid his words no heed and launched himself at Alathenar again. He had no choice but to block the blows with the stave of his bow, feeling every bite of the sword's edge, and mourning every splinter broken from the weapon.

'Menethis!' he shouted. 'The wall is lost, but the garrison might yet be saved!'

Another blow slashed towards his head. He ducked and spun inside Menethis's guard, hammering an elbow into his temple. Menethis was knocked from his feet and Alathenar stepped in to snatch up his fallen sword.

He knelt beside Menethis and rested the tip of the blade on his throat.

'You will kill me too?' snapped Menethis. 'How long have you been a servant of the druchii? You are a worthless traitor, and I spit on you.'

'I am no servant of the druchii,' he said. 'Suffice to say I allowed the bitterness of others to poison my thoughts and upset the moral compass of my heart. But I make no excuses. I have no defence for what I have done.'

'Because there *is* no defence! You murdered Glorien just as he was becoming the warrior he needed to be.'

'I fear you are right, but we have no time for debate or regrets.'

Menethis glanced away from the blade at his throat to the fighting on the walls. The elven line had not yet broken, but it was a matter of moments only.

'You and your plotters have condemned us all to death,' said Menethis. 'You know that?'

'No,' said Alathenar. 'For you will lead what is left of the garrison to Ellyrion. There are horses aplenty in the landward stables, enough to carry the bulk of our warriors to safety.'

'The druchii will break through and cut us down before we have a single horse saddled.'

'Not if I hold them back,' said Alathenar.

Menethis laughed, a bitter, lost sound that cut Alathenar deeply.

'You are a fool as well as a traitor,' he said.

'You'll get no argument from me on that account,' said Alathenar, standing and lifting the sword from Menethis's neck. 'But regardless of your opinion of me, you must go now if any lives are to be saved.'

He reversed the sword and held it hilt-first before him.

Menethis took the weapon, and Alathenar could see the urge to plunge the blade into his throat in his eyes. The hurt anger diminished and Menethis sheathed the weapon. He took a deep breath and turned to the steps leading down to the esplanade behind the doomed wall.

He glared back at Alathenar. 'All Ulthuan will know what you did here,' he promised.

Alathenar nodded. 'So be it. If I am to die hated, then that is all I deserve.'

Menethis gripped his sword and said, 'Your honour is lost and will never be regained, Alathenar. Your death here will not even the scales of Asuryan.'

Alathenar took up his damaged bow and said, 'When I stand before him in judgement, I will be sure to remind him of that.'

Eldain opened his eyes and found himself looking at the tapered ceiling of the Hippocrene Tower. His throat ached abominably and it was painful to draw a breath. He turned his head, seeing that he was lying on his bed, still fully clothed, and was the chamber's sole occupant.

What had happened to him?

His last memory was of Caelir throttling him and the black mist of death reaching up to drag him down. Eldain reached up and ran his fingertips along his neck, feeling the skin there swollen and bruised.

Eldain sat up, feeling every ache in his body magnified. Holding his throat he took a painful breath and swung his legs onto the floor. Everything here was just as he had left it when he and Rhianna had followed Yvraine to Saphery. It seemed like a lifetime ago that he had been called to attend upon the young Sword Master, and Eldain was reminded of how swiftly a life could change its course

He rose from the bed and stood at his walnut desk. Sheaves of curling scrolls lay strewn across its surface, along with a quill stone and inkpot. Bookshelves surrounded him, each one filled with the works of great scholars, poets, dramatists and historians.

Eldain had read every book in his library, yet their worth seemed transitory and meaningless in the face of how the world now turned. Would the druchii keep any of these books? Would they build a new library in the ruins of Lothern? Would any of the works composed over the thousands of years since asur and druchii had gone their separate ways survive this invasion?

He realised such questions were irrelevant, and moved to one of the eight windows set into the compass points of the tower's walls. Eldain leaned on the western window's stone frame and looked up at the enormous peaks of the Annulii. Their peaks were wreathed in magical storm clouds, roiling thunderheads of magical energy that spat lightning bolts of raw power into the earth. Contained within those peaks were the titanic energies bound by Caledor Dragontamer in the time of Aenarion, and it never failed to humble Eldain that a mage of Ulthuan had mustered such power.

Eldain turned from the panoramic vista and his thoughts moved to more immediate concerns. That he still lived was a surprise and a mystery.

Why had Caelir not killed him?

He more than deserved death, and his last sight had been of Caelir's grief-wracked face as he choked the life from him. There had been no mercy in those eyes, so why had his brother carried him upstairs to his chambers? Part of him wanted to remain in this tower, isolated and without the need to venture into a world that despised him.

Eldain recognised that for the cowardice it was, and opened the door.

He descended the steps that led to the Summer Courtyard, finding it deserted and echoing with the ghosts of long-passed glories. Leaves gusted around the silent fountain, and he scattered them with his boot as he walked a circuit of the courtyard. Once, this had been a place of joy, where laughter and song had breathed life and colour into the world. Ellyrians were a proud people, haughty and free-spirited, with a love of life that the people of other kingdoms saw as quick-tempered.

Yet as quick as an Ellyrian was to anger, he was just as quick to forgive.

Eldain heard the sound of horses, and knew where Caelir would be.

He swept his fingers through his platinum-blond hair and made his way towards the rear of the villa where the stables were situated. In any other kingdom, stables were simply functional structures, designed to house mounts and nothing more. Horses were equals in Ellyrian households, and a noble of this land lavished as much care and attention on the building of his stables as he did on his own quarters.

Ellyr-Charoi's stables were crafted from polished marble and roofed with clay tiles of stark blue, each stone rendered with intricate carvings and gold leaf representations of heroic steeds from family history. The starwood doors were open, and Eldain heard his brother talking to the horses in low, soothing tones.

Though elf and horse did not converse as such, there existed a bond that allowed each to sense the needs of the other. When steed and rider were together, there was no division between them, their thoughts were one and they moved and fought with perfect synchronicity. No other cavalry force in the world could boast so intuitive a connection, and rightly were the riders of Ellyrion known as the horse lords.

Eldain rounded the chamfered columns of the door, and the warm welcome he always felt in Ellyr-Charoi's stables enfolded him. A central passageway ran the length of the building, with twenty stalls to either side, though it had been many years since each one had been filled. Lotharin and Irenya were ensconced in neighbouring stalls, and Caelir fed them handfuls of good Ellyrian grain. A grain-fed horse would have stronger bones, more powerful muscles and could easily outrun a grass-fed horse.

Caelir looked up as Eldain entered.

What could he possibly say to his brother?

'Hello, Eldain,' said Caelir. 'I think we need to talk, don't you?'

'Will that talk end the way of our last?'

Caelir shook his head. 'No, brother. Not unless you desire vengeance.'

'Vengeance? No, there is no malice left in me.'

'Nor in me,' agreed Caelir.

'Why?' said Eldain, wary of opening so raw a wound, but needing to understand why he still lived.

'Why what?'

'Why did you not kill me?' asked Eldain.

'Because you are my brother,' said Caelir.

Alathenar ran to the edge of the wall, loosing shaft after shaft into the surging host of enemy warriors. Blue-cloaked elves streamed from the walls, obeying the trumpeted order to retreat even as isolated groups stood firm to deny the enemy the slaughter of pursuit. Alathenar ducked a sweeping axe blow and sent a shaft through the eye of a screaming tribesman at point blank range. Another sliced open the throat of a druchii bearing a heavy, two-handed blade, and another punched through the heart of a warrior reloading his ebony crossbow.

The hordes of the enemy strained at the few defenders remaining on the wall, yet they could not break through such determined resistance. Bound by shared guilt at Glorien's death, these were the warriors who had wished for his death, or had imagined his fall and now knew the true cost of such disloyal thoughts. Without any orders needing to be given, every warrior of the Eagle Gate knew in a heartbeat whether he should remain until the bitter end or escape the slaughter to come.

Alathenar fought like Alith Anar himself, weaving a path through the enemy warriors like a ghost. Across the rampart, he saw Eloien Redcloak, cutting enemy warriors down with graceful sweeps of his cavalry sabre. Like Alathenar, the terrible nature of what they had done was etched on his hard features, and the Ellyrian wept as he killed.

Alanrias crouched on a jutting perch of stone, sending the last of his barbed arrows into the sweating, grunting mass of enemy warriors. The savage humans could smell victory. It was just within their reach, but these last, few elves were denying them the full splendour of slaughter. Alathenar had not known whether the Shadow Warrior would remain to face the consequences of their conspiracy, but should have known better. For all his dour and bitter pronouncements, he was still one of the asur.

His quiver emptied, Alathenar broke his bow across his knee and swiftly unwound the string from the notches at either end. Woven with tresses from his beloved Arenia, he was not about to have it fall into the hands of the druchii. He wrapped the bowstring around the fingers of his right fist and swept up a fallen sword.

He looked down into the courtyard, seeing Menethis hurriedly organising the evacuation of the fortress. Hundreds of elven warriors saddled horses and prepared to ride eastward. Many of the escapees were from Ellyrion and were already riding for their homeland. The majority of what was left of the garrison would escape, but Menethis needed more time to get everyone clear.

A hellish bellow of rage echoed from the sides of the pass, and Alathenar saw Issyk Kul slay the last of the defenders holding his barbarous warriors back. A tide of unclean and perverse humans surged onto the walls, bellowing with triumph as they swept left and right along the ramparts.

'Redcloak! The stairs!' he yelled, running towards the head of the western steps. One warrior could hold the steps for a short time only, but perhaps that would be enough. Eloien Redcloak took up position at the head of the eastern steps, while Alanrias kept up a relentless stream of killing arrows. The Shadow Warrior let fly with no thought for spite in his barbed arrows. Each shaft tore out a throat, plunged through an eye socket or into a heart.

Three warriors against an army.

There could be no redemption for any of them, but at least they would die in the service of Ulthuan.

A screaming tribesman came at Alathenar, and he ducked beneath the slashing blade of a heavy broadsword. His blade lanced out, opening the man's belly and hurling him to the courtyard below. A warrior with an arm covered in weeping sores that looked like eyes leapt at him, and Alathenar hammered his sword across his neck, all but severing his head.

A hurled spear tore a gash in his hip, and Alathenar staggered as blood washed down his leg. The wound in his side reopened and he knew he had moments at best to kill as many of these dogs as he could. Three more tribesmen died by his blade, and he risked a glance over to the eastern stairs to see Redcloak bleeding from a score of wounds. His right arm hung uselessly at his side, but he fought equally well with his left.

A druchii warrior with a full-faced helm of bronze came at Alathenar with a long, hook-bladed spear. He could see the druchii grinning beneath his helm and anger flared at the relish he saw in his enemy's face.

'Come and die, dark one!' he shouted.

The druchii ignored him and thrust with his spear; Alathenar batted it aside and lunged forward. No sooner had he moved, than he realised he had been lured into the attack. The druchii stepped back and swept his spear to the side, the haft slamming into Alathenar's torso and pitching him over the edge of the steps.

Alathenar felt himself falling, and reached out to grip the spear with his free hand. The druchii warrior gave a cry of surprise as Alathenar dragged him from the top of the steps, and the two of them fell from the wall.

Alathenar slammed into the cobbled esplanade, screaming in pain as the bones of his legs shattered with the force of the impact. The druchii landed next to him, his skull smashed to splinters and blood pooling around his caved-in helm. Alathenar rolled onto his side, crying out in pain as the broken bones of his legs ground together. Enemy warriors streamed down the steps into the fortress, and Alathenar wept to see one of Caledor's great fortresses fall.

Through tear-blurred vision, he saw Eloien Redcloak cut down by the warlord of the tribal host. The champion's horrific sword opened the Ellyrian from collarbone to pelvis, and sent his ruptured body tumbling to the courtyard. An ivory figure astride a winged black horse dropped through the sky to land at the centre of the wall. Morathi's laughter rang from the sides of the pass, and Alathenar had never hated anyone with greater passion.

A flickering stream of black light erupted from her outstretched hand, and Alathenar watched in horror as the deadly fire engulfed Alanrias. His cloak ignited and the archer vanished in a pillar of searing flame that burned hotter and darker than any natural flame could possibly burn. The black fire quickly dissipated, leaving only a smeared ashen outline on the wall where the Shadow Warrior had once stood.

Alathenar tried to sit up, but the pain from his broken bones was too great. He closed his eyes and brought his hand to his mouth. He kissed the bowstring wrapped around his fingers, picturing the beautiful elf-maid who had so delicately cut strands of her hair for him.

'Forgive me, Arenia,' he whispered.

He kept the image of her perfect beauty in his mind as a talisman against the pain, wishing he could have done things differently, that he had not loosed that fatal bolt.

A shadow fell upon him and he cried out as the vision of Arenia vanished. Alathenar opened his eyes and saw the towering form of Issyk

Kul looming over him. The warlord's bulk blotted out the sun, and Alathenar saw the dark halo of the Dark Gods' favour rippling around his
cruelly beautiful features.

'I knew the gods had me spare you for a reason,' said Kul.

Alathenar tried to spit a defiant answer, but his mouth was full of
blood.

Issyk Kul knelt beside Alathenar, and pressed a broken sword into his
bloodied palm.

'No warrior should die without a blade in his hand,' said Kul. 'It is one
of the few things the worshipers of the Blood God and I agree upon.'

'Kill me,' gurgled Alathenar.

Issyk Kul smiled, exposing sharpened teeth and a glistening tongue.

'All in good time,' he said. 'All in good time.'

Eldain and Caelir spent the next hour in silence, brushing their steeds
and carefully grooming them as though they were soon to participate in
one of the grand ridings of Tor Elyr. The use of the farrier and stableman's
tools was second nature to them, and Eldain found the work cathartic
and restful. There was a rhythm and peace in caring for horses that could
be found in no other labour. Lotharin and Irenya stood proudly as the
two brothers brushed their coats, wound iron cords through their tails
and cleared their hooves of stones and earth.

At last they stood back from their mounts, satisfied their work was
done. Both brothers had worked up a powerful thirst and appetite, and
though Eldain's throat was still bruised from Caelir's earlier assault,
he was pleasantly out of breath by the time the two steeds were fully
groomed.

'I will fetch food and drink from the kitchens,' said Caelir. 'Clean up
and I will see you in the Equerry's Hall.'

Eldain nodded and watched as Caelir left the stables through a side
door. Both horses watched him go also, and Eldain stroked their necks.
Lotharin's hide gleamed like shimmering oil, while Irenya's dun flanks
were like polished mahogany.

'I do not deserve such loyalty,' he said, knowing it was true, but grateful beyond words to know that he was not yet beyond redemption. The
horses nuzzled him, and he indulged them momentarily before heading
outside. Midmorning sunlight filled the Summer Courtyard, and though
he and Caelir were alone, the villa felt more like a home than it had in
years.

Eldain made his way to a dry trough built into the eastern wall of
the villa. Diverted water from the streams on either side of Ellyr-Charoi
should be flowing through these troughs, but only dead leaves filled
them now. Eldain bent to scoop leaves from the carved horse's mouth
that channelled water out of the trough and back to the stream, then
did the same at the other end. No sooner had he scooped out the first

handful than water splashed over his hands in a gloriously refreshing spray. Icy water from the Annulii gurgled into the trough, swiftly filling it and flowing along its length.

He washed his hands and splashed water onto his face, relishing the shock of its coldness. The water tingled with the residue of magic, but what else could he expect when its source was high in a range of mountains suffused with the most elemental energies of the world?

Eldain washed in the glittering water, and by the time he was finished, his skin shone as though rejuvenated. He ran his hands through his hair, aware now of how unkempt he appeared. Riding alone with the wild herds, it was acceptable to look like a rustic, but Eldain was still a noble of Ulthuan, and Ellyr-Charoi was not the open plain.

Refreshed, Eldain climbed the steps of the Hippocrene Tower and stripped out of the clothes he had worn for days. His wardrobe still had a wide sartorial selection, and he chose a tunic of pale cream, over which he slipped a gold-edged shirt with silver embroidery at the collar. Next, he selected leggings of soft buckskin and high riding boots of tan leather with a wide heel. Finally, he snapped a black belt around his waist, and fastened it with a golden buckle worked in the form of interlocking horse heads.

With his ensemble complete, Eldain took a silver comb and ran it through his long hair until he was satisfied he had worked out the burrs and knots of the last few weeks travelling. He plaited several iron cords into his hair, and pulled it back into a loose ponytail before securing it at his temples with a circlet of polished ithilmar inset with a liquid sapphire.

Eldain looked in the mirror to check his appearance, and gave himself a curt nod, satisfied he was the equal of his position in attire. A thin smile touched the corner of his lips, as he realised that this was the first time in many a month he had been able to look in the mirror without despising the reflection.

He left his chambers and made his way back down to the Summer Courtyard.

Eldain smiled as he saw that his labours in removing the leaves from the villa's walls had brought water back to more than just the trough. The fountain in the centre of the courtyard now frothed and burbled, the pool slowly filling with cold mountain water. Leaves floated on the surface, and the wind gusted those lying within the courtyard out through the open gates.

'Ellyr-Charoi returns to life,' he said, tilting his head back and allowing the sun to warm his skin. The smell of toasting bread drew his attention to the open doors of the Equerry's Hall. It had been days since Eldain had eaten anything other than berries and leaves, and only now did he realise how famished he was.

He crossed the courtyard and entered the hall. The smell of sweet tisane and toasted bread made his mouth water. The inside of the Equerry's Hall was bright and airy, its shuttered windows now thrown open and the dust of neglect being swept away by a warm wind that blew from the high rafters with soft sighs. Platters of toasted bread and cheese, together with copper ewers, sat on the table, and Eldain saw his father's sword lay where his brother had placed it the previous evening.

Caelir stood before a tall portrait depicting a noble elf atop a pure white steed as he slew a foul, mutated beast of the Annulii. Like Eldain, he too had cleaned and washed himself. He wore earthy riding clothes of fine quality, with dark boots and a short cloak of sky blue. A leather circlet wound with bronze cord secured his hair and Eldain smiled to see his brother dressed as an Ellyrian once more.

'I didn't know I looked so heroic,' said Caelir, gesturing towards the picture with what remained of a slice of bread. 'This is me, isn't it?'

'Yes,' said Eldain. 'I had the picture commissioned for Rhianna upon my return from Naggaroth.'

'Ah,' said Caelir. 'It is a memorial.'

'It was,' agreed Eldain, helping himself to a slice of toasted bread. 'Now it is just a portrait, I suppose.'

'It is a good likeness,' said Caelir. 'Who painted it?'

'An artist of Lothern by the name of Uthien Sablehand.'

'He is talented.'

'He ought to be for the money I paid him.'

Caelir turned away from the portrait, and Eldain was struck by how his brother had aged. Though only a few years separated their births, Caelir had always possessed youthful good looks that made that gap appear much larger. Though his features still bore a roguishly handsome cast, his eyes were those of a veteran.

'Nobles of Ulthuan in all their finery,' said Caelir, taking in Eldain's fresh appearance.

'It felt right,' said Eldain.

'It should, brother,' agreed Caelir. 'We are home. Can you feel it welcoming us?'

'I can,' agreed Eldain. 'It is a good feeling and has been too long in coming.'

Caelir finished his bread and poured a goblet of warm tisane. 'Whatever happened to Valeina?' he asked. 'I saw no sign of her in the kitchens or the maids' quarters. Did you dismiss her?'

'No,' said Eldain, accepting the goblet as Caelir poured another for himself. 'When Rhianna and I left for Saphery, she was still here. Perhaps she rejoined her family in Tor Elyr when word came of the attack on the Eagle Gate.'

Caelir nodded and said, 'More than likely.'

Eldain sipped the tisane. It was sweet, but the aftertaste stung the tongue with its sharpness. Eldain recognised the blend of flavours, and was instantly transported back to when he and Caelir were little more than callow youths.

'Mother's recipe,' he said.

'Yes, it seemed appropriate,' said Caelir. 'She was always the one who brought us together after we quarrelled. Father would be content to let us squabble and bicker, but mother could never bear it when we fought.'

Eldain smiled at Caelir's reasoning and took a seat at the table. He placed the goblet before him and let the familiar smell of wild lemon and honey fill his senses.

'So what do we do now, Caelir?' he asked.

'We talk, brother,' said Caelir, taking the seat next to Eldain.

'What is there left to say that your hands on my neck did not already say?'

Caelir sipped his tisane before answering. 'Tell me all that has happened since your return from Naggaroth.'

'Why?'

'Because I wish to know.'

Eldain began haltingly, telling Caelir of how he had taken care of Rhianna upon his return from the Land of Chill, eventually taking her as his wife. Caelir's jaw tightened at this retelling, but he said nothing as Eldain went on to tell of Ellyr-Charoi's gradual decline and the arrival of Yvraine Hawkblade, the Sword Master from the Tower of Hoeth. He told of their journey across Ulthuan to Saphery, the voyage to the Gaen Vale and finally their arrival in Avelorn.

In return, Caelir told him of his return to Ulthuan, washed ashore on the coastline of Yvresse, and the beautiful girl who had found him on the beach. Caelir's eyes misted over as he told of how Kyrielle Greenkin had nursed him back to health, and Eldain remembered meeting her grieving father on the blasted summit of Bel-Korhadis's tower. Caelir spoke of his journey across the Finuval Plain and his meeting with Narentir's troupe as they made their way to the forest of the Everqueen.

Here again, their stories became intertwined as they relived the moment the dark power hidden within Caelir unleashed its darkest sorcery yet. Both brothers had been cast from the forest and ridden to the one place in Ulthuan where they knew they would find sanctuary.

Ellyr-Charoi.

Worn thin by their respective tales, Eldain and Caelir sat back, their tisanes cold and the bread forgotten. Silence fell, but it was not uncomfortable. At last, Caelir sat forward.

'I wanted to kill you, brother. And I nearly did,' he said. 'But when your eyes closed, all I could think of was a voice I heard in Avelorn.'

'What did you hear?' asked Eldain.

'I think it was the Everqueen,' said Caelir. 'I stood before her with the dagger in my hand and I heard a voice like the most beautiful sunrise of Ellyrion.'

Caelir paused, as though reliving that wondrous voice.

'What did she say?' asked Eldain.

'She told me to flee. And to forgive.'

'Do you think she was talking about me?'

'There is no one else who needs my forgiveness,' pointed out Caelir.

Eldain thought of the last time he had stood in the presence of the Queen of Avelorn. He remembered the killing light in her eyes, the ancient power that had passed from mother to daughter down the ages since the world was young. There had been little forgiveness in those eyes, yet she had not killed him. The mortal goodness of Alarielle tempered the merciless power of the Everqueen, and *that* had spared Eldain's life.

Now it had spared it again.

'You have a good soul, Caelir,' said Eldain. 'Better, I think, than most. I deserve your hatred, and to let me live speaks greatly of your heart.'

'My soul is not so pure, Eldain, you know that,' said Caelir. 'And I do not hate you. I did, but I believe that is what the Everqueen meant when she told me I had to forgive. Hatred is the root of all evil, brother. It turns good hearts bad, and sows the seeds for all that is ignoble in this world. I will not carry hate in my heart. Not any more.'

'Not even for the druchii?'

Caelir shook his head. 'Not even the druchii. Once they were like us, and perhaps they can be again.'

'The druchii will never let their hatred of us dim,' said Eldain.

'Most likely not,' said Caelir, 'but I will not hate them. Not any more.'

'The Everqueen touched you deeper than you know, brother.'

Caelir laughed, a sound Eldain had never thought to hear again. His younger brother leaned forward and said, 'You may be right, Eldain. She has power beyond anything you or I will ever understand. Something inside me has changed for the better.'

Caelir took Eldain's hand, and Eldain felt closer to his brother now than he ever had before. The connection was powerful, and Caelir's words touched him deeply.

'I was foolish, vain and selfish and cared not a whit for the wants and needs of others,' said Caelir. 'We both had a duty to Ellyr-Charoi and Ulthuan after father died, but I ignored mine. You shouldered my burden, and one soul is not meant to carry the weight of two.'

'Then are we at peace, brother?' asked Eldain.

Caelir said nothing for a few moments, looking over at his portrait.

'Not yet,' he said, 'but I believe we will be. There is still one matter to discuss.'

Eldain knew what this would be without Caelir having to voice it.

'Rhianna,' he said.

'Rhianna,' agreed Caelir. 'She is your wife.'

'Not for long, I would think,' pointed out Eldain. 'She hates me now.'

'For a while she will, but Rhianna is a better person than you or I will ever be. Hate will find no place to lodge within her.'

Eldain dearly hoped so, but knew that even if Caelir was right, he could not remain wedded to Rhianna. He had won her heart through lies, and no relationship could survive being built upon such rotten foundations. He wondered if she would become Caelir's wife, and was surprised to find the thought brought no jealousy or pain.

'So what do we do now?' asked Eldain.

'We ride for Tor Elyr,' said Caelir. 'And we make amends for the damage we have done.'

'Why Tor Elyr?'

'We are sons of Ellyrion, and our land is at war,' said Caelir. 'Where else would we go?'

CHAPTER NINE
WAR CALLS

Eldain walked Lotharin through the gates of Ellyr-Charoi, enjoying the scent of wild flowers borne on the warm summer breeze from the plains. Caelir pulled the gates of their home closed, and Eldain wondered if he would ever return here. Lotharin tossed his mane, stamping at the ground, and Eldain rubbed his neck.

'Patience, great heart,' he said. 'The plains of Ellyrion will be yours to run soon enough.'

'He is impatient,' said Caelir. 'I don't blame him.'

'No, I suppose not. It has been too long since I let him have his head on the steppe.'

Caelir checked Irenya one last time, rubbing her flank with his palm before vaulting into the saddle. For so short a ride to Tor Elyr, a saddle was not necessary, but if they were to ride to war, then it would be madness to fight without one.

'You are a fine steed, of that I have no doubt,' said Caelir, 'but I miss my Aedaris. He was wide-chested and powerful, with long strides and a heart as big as the ocean. You would have liked him.'

Irenya snorted, and Eldain grinned. 'Spoken like a true steed of Ellyrion,' he said.

Caelir had a fine double-curved bow of yew and starwood looped over his shoulder, and a host of quivers strapped to Irenya's flanks. A long, curved-bladed sword hung at his hip, for Caelir had insisted that Eldain bear their father's sword.

That blade now hung at Eldain's side, and the weight of duty and responsibility it represented was formidable. He had failed in his duty as a noble of Ulthuan, but he would not fail again. The black handle was wound with thin silver wire, and a polished onyx gleamed at the pommel. He held tight to the sword, its legacy of dutiful service tethering him to this land and his responsibilities more surely than any sworn oath.

Along with his father's sword, Eldain too was armed with a bow, and though other Ellyrians might consider him a competent archer only, that still put him head and shoulders above most others of Ulthuan. He mounted up, and settled himself onto Lotharin's back. This was where he felt most at ease, feeling the land below him through the motion of a fine steed that knew his moods, his skills and his heart better than any other.

They rode down the pathway towards the bridge, enjoying the gentle sway of their mounts and the clear air between them. As they crested the bridge, Eldain felt closer to his brother than he had his entire life.

'It feels good to be riding from Ellyr-Charoi with you, Eldain,' said Caelir. 'Even if it must be to war.'

Eldain nodded and rubbed Lotharin's neck as a shiver of prescience made him look back over his shoulder.

'I fear war is riding to us,' he said.

Caelir shielded his eyes from the sunlight reflecting on the glittering peaks of the western mountains and the sparkle of magic at their summits. He followed Eldain's gaze towards the cleft in the peaks where the Eagle Gate spanned the pass through the mountains. Thin trails of smoke marred the pale blue of the sky, but it was to the cloud of dust that his eyes were drawn.

'Riders,' said Caelir. 'How many do you think?'

'Maybe three or four hundred,' replied Eldain. 'They are not druchii.'

'No,' agreed Caelir. 'But whoever they are, they are riding at speed.'

'From the Eagle Gate, do you think?'

'They must be,' said Caelir. 'And there can be only one reason why so many horsemen would ride swiftly from Eagle Pass.'

Eldain nodded grimly, and they urged their mounts to greater speed as the pathway wound its way up the hillside towards the road to Tor Elyr. The road they followed was visible only as pale lines in the landscape; nothing so crude or mannish as stone formed the roads of Ulthuan. After an hour, the land levelled out, and Eldain saw the vast sweep of the landscape at a meeting of four roads that converged from the corners of Ellyrion. A tall waystone carved with interlocking circles and images of rearing horses rose from the confluence of the roads like an obsidian fang, and the air around it shimmered with agitation.

'The stone is troubled,' noted Caelir.

'Likely with good reason,' said Eldain, riding Lotharin in a tight circle around it.

To the east, the glittering spires of Tor Elyr were visible as a shimmer of gold and silver against the brilliant blue of the bay in which it sat. A mist from the waters rolled out over the fields and outposts before the city, while to the south, a pall of dark cloud hung low over the landscape. Dancing lights shimmered on the northern horizon, like the glow that smeared the sky when the magic contained within the Annulii surged with vitality.

The western road was known as the Aerie's Path, and Eldain halted Lotharin at its edge as he awaited the arrival of the riders from the pass. It would not be long, for he had set their pace in order to reach the way-stone just before them.

Sure enough, the vanguard of the riders from Eagle Pass emerged from a forest of mountain firs. They saw Eldain and Caelir and spurred their mounts onwards.

'Khaine's blood,' swore Caelir as the mounted warriors approached. 'They have ridden their mounts into the ground!'

Eldain felt his brother's anger and recognised it in himself. To treat a horse with such disrespect was inexcusable.

He bit back on his own anger. 'Be calm,' he said. 'Your emotions are being amplified by the waystone's magic.'

'But those horses–'

'Are not ours,' finished Eldain. 'And you do not know from what these warriors ride.'

Caelir said nothing, but urged Irenya away from the waystone, letting his emotions become less volatile. The first warrior rode towards Eldain and raised a hand in greeting.

'Are you from Arandir Swiftwing?' he demanded.

'I am not,' said Eldain. 'I am Eldain Éadaoin, lord of Ellyr-Charoi. This is my brother, Caelir.'

'You have not come from Tor Elyr?'

'No. It is to Tor Elyr that we ride. Have you come from the Eagle Gate?'

The rider nodded. 'We have,' he said breathlessly. 'Or what is left of it. The fortress is taken, and the druchii are marching on the Inner Kingdoms.'

Though Eldain had known that could be the only reason these warriors would ride with such recklessness, it was still a shock to hear that one of Caledor's great mountain fastnesses had fallen to the druchii.

'Are you the commanding officer?' he asked.

'I am now,' said the rider. 'Menethis of Lothern. Adjutant to Glorien Truecrown, who was slain by a traitor in our own ranks, a vile serpent known as Alathenar.'

'Slain by one of your own?' hissed Caelir, riding in from the shadow of the waystone.

'If you can believe such a thing,' said Menethis. 'Barely three hundred of us remain.'

'Why did you ask if we were from Arandir Swiftwing?' asked Eldain. 'You were expecting reinforcements from the lord of Tor Elyr?'

'So said the last missive we received,' agreed Menethis. 'His general, Galadrien Stormweaver, was marching to our relief.'

'We have seen nothing of any relief force,' said Eldain. 'But we have only just ridden from our villa.'

'Then join us in heading east,' implored Menethis. 'For the west is lost.'

Caelir leaned in towards Eldain. 'Most of the warriors of Ellyrion will have gone to Lothern. If Lord Swiftwing has raised an army, it will be the citizen levy only.'

'And what of it?' asked Eldain.

'They will be footsoldiers,' said Caelir. 'If we are to have an advantage in Ellyrion, they must fight on horseback.'

'There will not be enough horses left in Tor Elyr to mount enough of them to make a difference,' pointed out Eldain.

'I know, but there are more than enough on the Ellyrian steppes,' said Caelir. 'Eldain, we have to gather the Great Herd.'

'I know of this Great Herd,' said Menethis, 'but I was led to believe that no one can say for sure when it will gather, and we do not have time to wait. The druchii will be at the gates of Tor Elyr within days.'

'That is indeed true, Menethis,' said Eldain, though his heart beat faster in his chest at the idea of gathering the Great Herd. 'But this is our land and I know the steeds of Ellyrion will heed our call.'

Menethis saw the determination in their faces and said, 'Then I beg you, gather as many as you can and ride to Tor Elyr. I will see you there, and pray to Isha and Asuryan that the stories of your people are true.'

Caelir tugged at Irenya's reins and rode off to the northwest with a wild yell, and Eldain could not resist a flourish of showmanship as Lotharin reared up and pawed the air with his forelegs.

'Farewell, Menethis of Lothern!' he cried, turning his horse to ride after Caelir. 'In two days I will see you in Tor Elyr. And we will have all the herds of Ellyrion at our backs!'

The upper reaches of the Tower of Hoeth were being rebuilt. Priests of Vaul shaped stone from the Annulii, and the mages in service to Hothar the Fey lifted them into the air on magical currents. At the top of the tower they were set with such precision that none but a master mason could spot the joins between them.

Already the walls destroyed in the aftermath of Caelir's unwitting attack had been raised, and shipwrights from Cothique were singing songs to shape the heartwood beams of the roof. Teclis turned his scarred face to the circle of sky above him, letting the flavoursome tang of woodsap carried on magical currents fill his senses.

He stood with the support of his moon-topped staff, his body not yet healed from the damage done to it in the recent attack. A gift from the Everqueen, the staff was a conduit to the healing magic of Ulthuan, but Teclis had found himself relying on restorative potions brewed by the light of the moons more and more often. Healer-mages had done their best to alleviate the pain, but their power was wholly inadequate to restore him to health.

That Teclis lived at all was little short of a miracle, for the terrible energies unleashed had been at the limits of control, and only magic beyond the reach of any save the mages of old could completely undo the damage. Many others would never get the chance to heal: mages, Sword Masters and Kyrielle Greenkin, daughter of Anurion the Green. The darkness hidden within Caelir by the Hag Sorceress had consumed her utterly, using her innocence as fuel for its destruction.

'How like Morathi to twist purity into a weapon,' he whispered, as a measure of guilt for Kyrielle's death settled upon him. Her father remained at the Tower of Hoeth, channelling all his energies into aiding the priests of Vaul in their war-magic, accelerating the growth of arrow shafts that were as straight as sunlight to be fitted with enchanted arrow-heads that could pierce even the thickest armour. Anurion grew spear shafts that would seek out an enemy's flesh in forests around the tower, and shaped bowstaves of golden heartwood for the citizen militias of Saphery.

Teclis could understand such industry, knowing it was always better to avenge a loss with positive action instead of wallowing in grief. Anurion would not rest until the druchii were cast from Ulthuan, but the true measure of his character would come when the war was over. Teclis knew that vengeance was a poor motive for action, but in times such as these, it was more common than any other.

Once more he cursed his obsessive need to know everything, to understand the workings of the universe and all its complexities. Morathi had known he would not be able to resist plumbing the depths of Caelir's mind and unlocking the barriers within.

But just as Morathi knew Teclis, so too did he know her.

The Witch King would be content simply to destroy the asur, but so mundane a thing as annihilation would not satisfy Morathi. No, her ambitions went beyond simple conquest into the realms of madness.

She wanted more, and Teclis had an idea what that might be.

He drew on the power of his staff and sent his mage-sight over the landscape of Saphery, swooping low over the ravaged landscape around the tower. He rose into the sky, passing through the clouds and pulling away from the world below. Teclis found peace here, a refuge from the pain of his weakened flesh, and a measure of calm that could only be achieved without the pull of flesh to intrude.

Much of his recovery had been spent in such fugue states, his consciousness divorced from his body and roaming the land on the currents of magic that flowed around Ulthuan. He had seen the bolt that killed

Glorien Truecrown, and watched as his twin pulled the elven forces back from the shoulder fortresses at the Emerald Gate.

Druchii ships now roamed the mouth of the Straits of Lothern, but they did not yet dare to push on the Sapphire Gate. The floating mountain that housed an army of druchii lurked somewhere off the southern coast of Ulthuan, but even Teclis could not penetrate the cloaking shadows that concealed it.

An enemy army now bore down on the defenders of Ellyrion, and it was only a matter of time until the warriors at Lothern were under full attack. Teclis let the currents of magic carry him into the north, hoping to learn more of the Everqueen's plans. A wall of mist and magic shimmered at the borders of Avelorn and not even he would risk attempting to scry beyond its boundaries.

Teclis opened his eyes and let the full weight of his body return as his spirit-self settled back in his bones. Never had Ulthuan needed him more, and he was weaker than at any other time in his life.

'Why must we always face such times at our worst?' he whispered.

'Because war never comes when your enemy knows you are strong,' said the voice of Loremaster Belannaer. Teclis smiled to hear his old master.

'Always the teacher, my friend,' said Teclis.

'You may have surpassed me in ability, but you will never surpass me in age and hoary wisdom.'

Teclis turned and gave a short bow, acknowledging the venerable Loremaster's words. Swathed in a glittering robe that shimmered with captured starlight, Belannaer wore his long white hair unbound by circlet or helm, and his long face was old even among a race that lived on the edge of immortality. Belannaer had worked his enchantments when Bel-Hathor ruled the asur, and only Teclis had a greater understanding of the workings of magic.

Two other mages stood with Belannaer, Anurion the Green and Mitherion Silverfawn – father of Rhianna Silverfawn. Both were drawn and tired-looking after many weeks of imbuing weapons and armour with war-magic. Four Sword Masters accompanied them, for no mage of Saphery walked unescorted now. Their presence helped Teclis settle back into his flesh, for they were elves firmly rooted in the physical world.

'My friends,' said Teclis. 'It is good to see you.'

'And you, Teclis,' said Mitherion Silverfawn. 'You are looking better every day.'

'And you are a rogue, Master Silverfawn,' said Teclis, moving to sit on the padded litter that had been his sickbed since the attack. 'I am weary and heartsick, but I appreciate the sentiment. How does your work proceed?'

'It progresses, Warden,' said Mitherion. 'I have studied the celestial movements closely, and, well, the signs are not good.'

'Elaborate, please.'

Mitherion retrieved a series of scrolls from the Sword Master behind him and unrolled the largest on a table already piled haphazardly with heavy books, hourglasses, moonstones and empty glass vials. Teclis limped over and studied the astronomical chart, its midnight blue surface covered in arcing silver orbits, geometric patterns and intersecting lines. Teclis knew enough to know that he was looking at a map of the heavens, but so cluttered was it with Mitherion's notes, observations and postulations that it was next to impossible to read.

'Damn you, Mitherion,' said Anurion, scanning the map. 'This is unreadable.'

'There's a system, Anurion,' said Mitherion. 'You just need to know the system. It's really quite simple.'

'Then how is it that only you know it?' demanded Anurion, his tolerance for Mitherion's eccentricities wearing thin.

'Because no one else has the patience to learn it,' snapped Mitherion. 'Now, if I may continue?'

Teclis nodded and Mitherion traced a slender finger over a curving line that arced across the page to intersect with a number of other lines, some geometric, some arrow-straight and others curved.

'The stars move strangely, Warden,' said Mitherion. 'The Chaos moon passes close to our world and introduces many variables of incalculable complexity into any equation. Which means any conclusion drawn from such equations must be viewed with a degree of uncertainty.'

'In other words, nothing you say can be trusted to be accurate?' said Anurion.

'Not as such,' said Mitherion, ignoring Anurion's hostility. 'I can read the patterns of the stars and offer insight into aspects of the world. But any prediction, no matter how apparently certain it might be, is always subject to the vagaries of chance.'

'What have you learned?' asked Teclis, forestalling another comment from Anurion.

'The stars are not right,' said Mitherion.

'Not right?' asked Belannaer. 'What does that mean?'

Mitherion tapped the map and said, 'In every path of the future I have followed, the stars move out of alignment with the routes they currently trace across the sky.'

'What could cause that?' asked Anurion.

'Only one thing I can think of,' said Mitherion.

'Well don't keep us in suspense,' demanded Anurion. 'What?'

'The only way we would be seeing an effect like this would be if our world were no longer following the same course it is now,' said Mitherion. 'You must understand that even a tiny shift in this world's path would be catastrophic. Depending on whether we are carried closer or farther from the sun, our world could be doomed to an eternal ice age or every living thing might be burned from its surface.'

'What could cause the world to shift like that?' asked Belannaer.

'A vast outpouring of magic,' said Teclis.

'That is what I thought at first,' agreed Mitherion, 'but there is no magicker on this world capable of wielding such power. Not even the lizard lords in their jungle temples can cast magic that powerful. It must be something else.'

'I believe I know what is powerful enough to throw our world out of its proper place in the heavens,' said Teclis, bowing his head and sighing deeply. 'I had hoped I might be wrong, but I believe your calculations have confirmed my worst fear, Master Silverfawn.'

Belannaer moved to stand beside Teclis and put a hand on his shoulder.

'She would not dare, Teclis,' said the ancient Loremaster. 'Caledor would know of it and he will not allow his great work to be undone.'

'Perhaps so,' agreed Teclis. 'But five millennia have passed since those days. Who can say what remains of Caledor and his convocation? Morathi is cunning beyond measure, and she has had a long time to find a way to hide her presence from his mage-sight. We can afford to take nothing for granted.'

'Isha preserve us,' hissed Anurion as he grasped the horrific scale of the threat to Ulthuan and the world.

Teclis looked up and the weakness that had plagued him earlier returned with greater potency. He sagged against the table, and but for the hands of Belannaer and Mitherion, he would have fallen to the floor. They carried him to his litter and laid him upon it.

He tried to muster a smile to allay their fears, but saw they were unconvinced.

'In the days to come, the armies of the asur will have need of our powers,' he said. 'I cannot take to the field of battle, so you must lead my mages and Sword Masters to war. I regret that I must ask even you, Belannaer, to take up the blade of Bel-Korhadris one last time.'

'It will be my honour to fight for Ulthuan, Teclis,' said Belannaer. 'I always knew there would be one last challenge ahead of me before I might find my peace.'

'Lead the mages of fire and water to Lothern,' said Teclis. 'Counsel Tyrion and Finubar, for they are warriors and are ruled by the heart. They will have need of your wisdom in the dark days to come, Tyrion especially…'

Teclis turned to Anurion and Mitherion. 'My friends, you must take the mages of sky and earth to Ellyrion. Morathi herself leads a host of dark warriors from the mountains, and she must be stopped before the walls of Tor Elyr, whatever the cost may be.'

A shadow passed over Teclis's features, and his gaze fell upon the celestial map belonging to Mitherion Silverfawn. 'And I fear it will be a bitter cost to bear.'

* * *

They chased the sun as it edged across the vastness of the sky, angling their course towards the rivers that flowed from the Annulii to the Inner Sea. The herds roamed freely over the wide steppes of Ellyrion, but Eldain knew they would not stray too far from water. He rode Lotharin hard, letting the horse have its head as it stretched its muscles in a flat out run. Caelir galloped beside him, letting Irenya understand a measure of Lotharin's strength.

She was an Ellyrian steed, haughty and proud, but she quickly grasped that she was not the equal of Lotharin. It felt good to ride the steppe, letting his mount choose their path, for he was bound to this land in ways Eldain would never understand, and knew where the leaders of the herds were likely to be found.

They rode past scattered villages, all now empty of elves, and isolated woods of larch and evergreens. The landscape felt empty, and the soft light of eternal summer spread an indolent blanket over the horizon. Heat haze rippled from the undulant hills of the middle distance and the gauzy cornfields of their surroundings.

Eldain could see no horses, and his heart sank at the prospect of finding none of the herds. He had proudly boasted that they would bring the Great Herd to Tor Elyr, but Ellyrion was silent, even the capering sprites and darting creatures of magic that haunted the hidden places of magic and mystery keeping far from sight.

He halted Lotharin at the top of a rounded hill, letting his mount catch his breath as Caelir and Irenya drew alongside.

'Where are the herds?' asked Caelir.

'They feel the coming of the druchii and are keeping to their secret watering holes,' said Eldain. 'They know the dark kin will try to break them and force them to serve our enemies.'

'So how do we find them?'

Eldain considered the question. Even a warrior of Ellyrion could search the plains for a lifetime and never find the hidden ranges of the herds. Such places were known only to horsekind, and the first elves to settle in Ellyrion had always respected their privacy. It would be impossible to find the herds unless they wished to be found.

'We have to bring the herds out onto the plains,' said Eldain.

'And how do we do that, brother?'

Eldain looked out over the majestic sweep of Ellyrion, drinking in the wondrous vista before him like a tonic. His eyes lost their focus as his soul was drawn into the magnificence of this bounteous kingdom, feeling the heartbeat of its unchanging season as a slow warmth in his blood. The golden land stretched as far as the eye could see, a verdant paradise of bountiful fields, rolling plains and endless acres upon which to ride. Thick forests of evergreens shawled the foothills of the mountains to provide the herds with shade, rivers of fresh water fed their watering holes and the vast expanse of flat earth was their playground.

No finer land for horses existed in the world, as though the gods had crafted this land for the herds and not the asur.

'Brother?' said Caelir.

'The steeds of Ellyrion know this land better than the asur,' said Eldain, his voice soft and dreamlike. 'It is through the land we will reach the herds.'

'What do you mean?'

'I mean we must ride!' shouted Eldain, standing tall in his saddle and galloping down the hillside. 'Ride like the horse lords of old!'

Lotharin surged downhill, his long legs bunching and stretching as he thundered across the plains. Grassland and forest, hill and stream flashed past as he galloped faster and harder than ever before. Eldain hung on tight, letting the horse remember its heritage as a proud steed of Ellyrion.

Caelir and Irenya followed him, the mare galloping for all she was worth, and feeling the power of the land surging through her as she strove to keep up with Eldain and Lotharin. Eldain held tight to Lotharin's mane, feeling the magic of Ulthuan in every pounding hoof beat and every sway and stretch of the horse's back. This was what it meant to be an Ellyrian, to ride like the gods across the face of the world and feel the land respond.

Eldain risked a glance over at Caelir, and laughed as he saw his brother holding on for dear life, terrified and exhilarated in equal measure. No words needed to pass between them, for both understood that this was the ride of their lives. Even were they to die in the next few moments, neither would have any regrets.

Never had Eldain ridden so fast, not even when escaping the shipyards of Clar Karond. His hair whipped his face and his eyes watered in the wind as he leaned low over Lotharin's neck. He whooped and yelled with a mixture of fear and excitement, knowing that at such speed, the slightest mistake would see him hurled from the saddle. An Ellyrian steed would never normally allow its rider to fall, but even Lotharin would not be able to save him were he to lose focus for even a second.

Ellyrion whipped past in a blur. Eldain had no idea where they were; fields, forest, rivers and hills flashing by in a golden-green blur. Lotharin eased into a sweeping curve, and Irenya came alongside, her eyes wide and ears pressed flat against her skull. Ellyrion responded to their wild ride, and the earth beneath the horses released its magic in a shimmer of starfire that billowed from the ground like mist. Eldain felt the power of his homeland in every breath, like taking in a lungful of cold air on a frosty morning.

It filled him with light, and he saw the pulsing lines of magical energy running through the world, a rainbow hued storm that roared across the face of the landscape. These iridescent colours disturbed not a blade of grass or so much as a single leaf, yet they flowed through every living thing, leaving behind a measure of their essence. Eldain gathered that power within him, shaping it into a wordless cry of supplication.

He loosed that power not with words, but through the might of his steed, letting it carry his message to the Ellyrion herds through the thunder of its hooves upon the earth. Lotharin ran faster than he ever would again, blowing hard as he leapt a wide streambed. Irenya could not match his leap, and Caelir turned her towards a shingled ford as Eldain and Lotharin rode ever onwards. The river of colour faded from sight, and he let out a cry of loss as his mortal eyes lost the sight of his homeland's magic.

Yet as the blinding light of magic faded from his sight, he saw that he no longer rode alone. Dozens of horses surrounded him, duns, blacks, greys, whites, dappled and bay, piebald and silver. Herds from all across Ellyrion galloped over the plains beside him, and more were coming with every passing moment. They emerged from forest shadows, from hidden gullies and sheltered dips in the land. They answered the call of one of the sons of Ellyrion, and they came in their entirety.

Eldain watched with tears in his eyes as the Great Herd formed around him. The silver horseleaders ran with Lotharin, unspoken communication passing between them. Caelir and Irenya were behind him, galloping in the midst of a host of white-gold horses. Caelir waved at him, and Eldain's heart surged with joy to see so many had answered his call. Billowing clouds of dust hid the true numbers of the herd, but the beating war drum of their hooves and the snorting bellows of myriad herds told Eldain that more than enough had come.

At last, Lotharin could run no more, and Eldain gently eased the horse into a wide turn that bled off his speed. Lotharin's flanks heaved and bellowed, and Eldain knew his steed had run himself to the edge of destruction. Even a horse as mighty as Lotharin had his limits, and they had reached them.

The Great Herd followed his lead, slowing until Eldain and Caelir sat in the midst of a thousands-strong herd of proud steeds. His brother rode alongside him, both he and Irenya blown and exhausted. Yet the thrill of the wild ride across the face of Ellyrion had left its mark on them both. The mare's eyes shone with delight, and Caelir's face was that of an excited child.

'Brother,' gasped Caelir. 'Not even Tyrion and Malhandir could have ridden like that.'

Eldain reached out and gripped his brother's shoulder.

'The ride of our lives, eh, Caelir?' he said.

'No one has gathered a herd like this in ten lifetimes,' swore Caelir. 'Even the first Ellyrians never knew such joy.'

'We called and they came,' said Eldain. 'And now we ride for Tor Elyr.'

CHAPTER TEN
THE GLITTERING HOST

Considered by many of the asur to be the most beautiful city in Ulthuan, Tor Elyr nestled on the shores of the Sea of Dusk within a placid bay of mirror-smooth water. Glittering castles of silver rose from forested islands of smooth marble, each like sheer pinnacles of ice crafted by a master sculptor. Tapered domes of azure and gold capped these towers, and finials bearing pennants of emerald and ruby snapped in the wind blowing off the sea.

A web of crystal bridges linked the hundreds of island castles, grown from the living rock by spellsingers of old, and a handful of crimson-sailed ships plied the waters beneath them. Tendrils of mist coiled around the base of each island, and faint songs of lament echoed from the peaked castles as the mothers and wives of Tor Elyr sang to the gods to watch over those who rode to war.

High atop a carven balcony, the lord of Tor Elyr, Arandir Swiftwing, listened to the songs of his city and pondered on the vagaries of time. The asur were a long-lived race, yet their survival might yet come down to a matter of days. In the end, didn't everything depend on timing? A warrior might deflect an enemy's blow, and a heartbeat later could be struck down by another or dodge aside at the last moment.

Or a poison-tipped crossbow bolt might slay a beloved steed so swiftly that she could not prevent herself from rolling over her rider and crushing him beneath her weight…

As always when he thought of Sarothiel, Lord Swiftwing's hand strayed to his twisted and misshapen hip. Slain beneath him in a skirmish with druchii raiders seeking to plunder the northern herds of Ellyrion, his steed had rolled on top of him and smashed his pelvis. The healers had been unable to reknit the bone, and his muscles had reformed wrongly around the ossified mass.

Thirty years later, he still walked with a painful limp, and his days of riding out with his warriors were over.

He hated the Fates of Morai-Heg that she had cursed him so. A lord of Ellyrion who could not ride. It would be funny if it were not so painful to think about.

Lord Swiftwing pushed aside these bitter memories, and stared into the west. The storm-wreathed Annulii dominated the horizon, and though the mages advised it best not to stare too long into the clouds of magic, he could not tear his eyes from the seething cauldron of power that thundered between their peaks.

Morathi's army was marching on his city from those mountains.

Impossible as it was to believe, the Eagle Gate had fallen, and the three hundred survivors of that disaster painted a bleak picture of the power and size of that host. Lord Swiftwing could defend Ellyrion against Morathi's army with more warriors, but the Phoenix King had all but emptied Tor Elyr for the battle at Lothern.

He had baulked at the idea of sending the majority of his warriors to Lothern, but Finubar had assured him that none of the gateway fortresses could be taken. Tor Elyr was quite safe, Finubar had said, and Lord Swiftwing felt his lip curl in a sneer at the thought of the Phoenix King's empty promises.

'That's what you get when you choose a king who thinks only of lands far from home,' he whispered, as the light moved from afternoon to the gloaming. He disliked this time of day, for it was a shadowy cloak that concealed assassins or spies, and returned to the candlelit warmth of his chambers.

As befitted a noble of Ellyrion, his quarters were clean and sparsely decorated, with only a few trophies taken in his time as a Reaver Knight hanging on the walls. Numerous bookshelves sagged under the weight of treatises on mounted warfare, with one such essay penned by no less a figure than Aenarion himself. Admittedly, his tactical writings dealt with fighting from the back of a dragon, but the fact that the Defender's hand had touched that scroll was reason enough to treasure it. These days, warriors of Ulthuan were fortunate if they had even *seen* a dragon, let alone fought from the back of one.

He paused by a table heaped with hastily scrawled despatches and idly flicked through them, carefully reading those that caught his eye, and discarding those that did not. Much of what he read was concerned with the current muster of citizen soldiers. With the majority of his city's warriors now fighting at Lothern, Lord Swiftwing had been forced to spread the net of his levy far wider than at any other time in Ellyrion's history. He had mustered an army and sent its most experienced warriors with his best general into the west to relieve the beleaguered defenders of the Eagle Gate.

But what a difference a few days could make.

Barely had the relief force departed Tor Elyr than word had come that the fortress was lost. Galadrien Stormweaver had returned the previous evening, and Lord Swiftwing had watched the general's dejected riders climb the crystal bridge to Castle Ellyrus, the gateway to Tor Elyr. A warrior named Menethis of Lothern had brought three hundred warriors who had escaped the slaughter at the Eagle Gate to Tor Elyr this morning. It was a paltry force, but any additions to Lord Swiftwing's army were welcome, especially as they were veterans.

And Asuryan knew, he needed veterans!

Nearly eight thousand citizen soldiers were now under arms in Tor Elyr, yet Lord Swiftwing knew that number concealed the fact that many of these would normally be considered too young or too old to fight in the battle line. With nowhere near enough horses in his stables, most of these soldiers would need to fight on foot, which was anathema to warriors of Ellyrion.

A door opened, and a gust of wind blew out a handful of candles. Irritated, Lord Swiftwing glowered at the venerable elf that entered his chambers with a wooden tray bearing a steaming goblet of honeyed wine and several bottles of warmed oils.

'Casadesus, you are as clumsy as an ogre,' snapped Lord Swiftwing.

'My apologies, my lord,' said Casadesus. 'I shall endeavour to ease the winds around your tower before I enter next time.'

Casadesus had served Lord Swiftwing for the entirety of his adult life, since before the ascension of Finubar to the Phoenix Throne. He had borne Lord Swiftwing's banner when the Ellyrians rode to war, they had watched friends pass away and, as was the way of things, they had grown old together. Lord Swiftwing's wife was long dead, his daughter apprenticed to a mage at the Tower of Hoeth and his sons abroad somewhere in the Old World. Casadesus was the only family he had left, and no one got under Lord Swiftwing's skin like family.

'Whatever happened to the notion of bondsmen showing respect?' he grumbled.

'I suspect the same thing that happened to nobles having nobility.'

Lord Swiftwing grunted and said, 'You should have gone to Saphery. Or Yvresse. It's not safe in Ellyrion anymore.'

Casadesus shook his head. 'I am where I need to be, my lord.'

'I released you from your service to me a century ago, there is no need for you to stay.'

'I remain here for the same reason you do, my lord,' said Casadesus, placing the tray on the table and handing Swiftwing the goblet.

'And what reason is that?'

'Duty, my lord. You have yours and I have mine. Now, drink the wine and sit down.'

Lord Swiftwing knew better than to argue, and took a long draught of the warmed wine. It was sweet and cloying, just the way he liked it, and the medicinal powders sprinkled through it gave it a grainy texture. Immediately, he felt its soothing balm and lowered himself onto the specially carved chair that allowed him to sit with the least amount of discomfort.

Casadesus sat on a stool opposite and lifted Lord Swiftwing's leg to rest upon his knees. He grunted in pain, but knew better than to complain. Slowly and with deft finger strokes, Casadesus worked the warmed oils into the knotted muscle tissue of his leg. Alchemists and healing mages had produced a poultice that eased the pain of his wound, though it could never undo the damage. Every night, Casadesus would massage his ruined leg, and every morning he would be able to walk without pain until the effect of the poultice wore off.

'I hear Stormweaver is back,' said Casadesus, working his thumbs deep into the muscle of Lord Swiftwing's thigh.

'That he is,' agreed Lord Swiftwing.

'Then it is true? The Eagle Gate has fallen?'

'You already know the answer, so why ask the question?'

'I was taught to only trust first hand information, not rumour or hearsay.'

'Yes, the Eagle Gate has fallen, and yes, Stormweaver has returned,' snapped Lord Swiftwing. 'Anything else?'

'I wondered if you had received any responses to the messages you sent to King Finubar and the Warden of Tor Yvresse,' said Casadesus without looking up.

Lord Swiftwing sighed. 'No, there have been no responses, and nor do I expect any. Finubar has stripped my city of warriors and is not about to send them back when his own city is threatened. As to Eltharion, he broods in his miserable city of shadows and pretends the rest of the world does not exist. His land is free of invaders, yet he sends no warriors to me or to Finubar!'

Casadesus paused in his massage. 'Tor Yvresse is a city of ghosts, my lord. There are fewer warriors in Lord Eltharion's city than in Tor Elyr. If our situations were reversed and he sent *us* a request for aid, would you send him any troops?'

'With so few warriors left to defend my city? No, I would not,' said Lord Swiftwing with a wry smile. 'There you go using logic again. Did I not tell you that it is unwise to point out the flaws in a noble's reasoning?'

'You did, but I chose to view that as advice rather than an order.'

Before Lord Swiftwing could respond, a single note from an elven war horn blew from one of the northern islands. Both men looked up as other horns joined it, the glorious trumpeting growing in power until a chorus of triumphant music was blowing from every tower of Tor Elyr.

Casadesus helped Lord Swiftwing to his feet, and together they made their way out onto the balcony overlooking the city and the endless plains beyond. The pain in his leg was forgotten as Lord Swiftwing gripped the stone balustrade and his heart leapt with excitement at the sight before him.

'I don't believe it...' gasped Casadesus.

Lord Swiftwing wept tears of joy, knowing he would never see so fine a sight in all the days left to him. The wide open plains before the city were awash with horses, thousands of wild animals galloping towards the gate in a thundering herd of many colours. At their head rode two warriors, one mounted on a midnight-black steed, the other upon a dun mare.

'The Great Herd,' said Lord Swiftwing.

'How is this possible?' asked Casadesus.

'I do not know, but Asuryan has smiled on us this day.'

Though hot steam filled the air of the cavern, Prince Imrik felt a chill deep in his bones. Clad only in a loincloth, his muscular body was now thin and gaunt, like the starved prisoners he had rescued from a druchii slave ship so many years ago. He sat cross-legged, with his arms hanging at his side and his breath coming in long, soft breaths.

He had lost track of how long he had been here, for nothing ever changed in the cave of dragons. Their great, slumbering hearts beat ever on with gelid slowness, never varying their cadence or tempo. Sleep had stolen upon him in the times between songs, and his dreams had been filled with the faces of lost loved ones and never-won glories. Each time he would wake and curse the weakness that had seen him sleep. Then he would sing, filling the air with the wondrous sound of dragonsong.

Minaithnir had taught him these songs many decades ago, placing the words that were not words and the music that was not music directly into his mind. Until now, he had never heard the songs sung aloud, and he wept as he finally gave them voice. Their soft beauty was quite at odds with the creatures that created them, and Imrik dearly wished his race had known of these songs in ages past.

His eyes closed as he felt the dragonsong draw on his strength for sustenance, for such magical sounds could not be sustained simply by a mortal's voice. His breathing slowed as the song flowed from him and Imrik felt as though his mind was sinking into a forgotten trench at the bottom of the ocean, where monstrous beasts made their lairs.

The darkness was complete, yet this was as close as he had come to reaching the vast, unfathomable consciousnesses of the dragons. In this deep, dark, unreachable place, their minds roamed free, too vast and too far beyond mortal comprehension to be confined within their skulls.

In this place of emptiness, the dragons dreamed of distant stars and the myriad worlds that circled them.

The dragonsong surrounded Imrik, and he felt the steady heartbeat of something infinitely more colossal than he could ever imagine pounding in the darkness. If the heartbeat of the dragons was infinitesimally slow, this was yet slower. He had no idea to what he was listening, but no sooner had he wondered at its origin than the answer was given to him.

This was the heartbeat of the world, and Imrik at last recognised the truth of the dragons.

They were linked with the world in ways too complex to fully understand, but Imrik knew enough of dragons to know that as the world cooled, so too did their hearts. The dragons were as much a part of the world as were its rivers and forests, its mountains and deserts. As one rose, the other rose. As one declined, so too did the other.

Imrik felt the colossal presences of the dragons as their minds finally registered his intrusion into their shared dreamspace. As a man might regard a fleabite, so Imrik was to the dragons; an irritant; something so trivial and minor that he was virtually beneath their notice.

Yet they *had* noticed him.

Though he knew his body did not exist in this darkness, he sang the dragonsong with ever more passion, allowing the wordless music free rein within his flesh.

Take of me what you must, but hear me dragonkin! I am Imrik, and Ulthuan needs you!

Other minds, still immense, but smaller than the glittering, star-filled presences of the most ancient dragons, darted around him. They looked at him as a curiosity, a diversion to be toyed with and enjoyed for a brief spell while they slept away the ages. It was the tiniest connection, but it was more than he had managed in all the days he had been singing.

A yellow eye, slitted like a cat's, opened in the darkness before him. Enormous beyond words, it filled the void, a sensory organ as vast as a landscape. It regarded Imrik curiously, before deciding he was unworthy of attention. The mind's eye closed and Imrik was once again plunged into sightless oblivion. He screamed his frustration into the void as his hold on the dragonsong faltered.

No sooner had its ritual rhythms been disrupted than his connection to this dream world was ended. His spirit was hurled back to the world above, and Imrik opened his eyes with a great intake of breath and a cry of frustration bursting from his throat.

He had been so close!

Feeling as weak as a newborn foal, Imrik calmed his frayed nerves and slowed the rapid tattoo of his heart. His hands were shaking and his throat was raw with the effort of shaping songs that no mortal was ever meant to sing.

'You heard me!' he wept. 'Why do you not wake?'

He knew the answer, and his heart sank with the knowledge that he could never reach the minds of the dragons. The world was dying, and the magic of Ulthuan faded with every passing moment the druchii stood upon its soil.

The heat of the cavern enfolded him, yet Imrik felt only the cold of the grave.

Though he knew it would eventually kill him, Imrik began the dragonsong once more.

The castle at the heart of Tor Elyr had been built by the first horsemasters of Ellyrion, and was the ancestral dwelling place of the city's master. Such was its age that no difference could be seen in the stone of its walls and the rock upon which it was built. As though its alabaster walls had grown from the island, the castle soared gracefully from the water like a linked series of stalagmites carved in glistening marble and polished quartz. Its many towers were studded with windows and roofed in gold, but it was in the chamber at the castle's heart where Lord Swiftwing gathered his most trusted warriors for councils of war.

Known as the Reaver Hall, its walls were fashioned from cream marble threaded with gold veins, and its icy rafters were hung with ancient and colourful banners depicting galloping horses, proud manes and crossed lances. Many of these were from the time of Caledor the Conqueror, and one was even said to have been borne alongside Caradryel as he ordered the last retreat from the Old World.

It never failed to move Lord Swiftwing whenever he came here, for it was a potent reminder of the long and faithful service of Ellyrion to the Phoenix Throne. His own banner bore the image of a rearing silver horse upon a crimson field. That banner still had pride of place above his starwood throne, which sat at the head of a long oval table that filled the bulk of the chamber, but never more would Casadesus bear it into battle.

He smiled as his earlier reflections on the nature of time returned to him.

A lifeline had been thrown to the warriors of Tor Elyr this day.

And not just one.

Less than an hour after Lord Éadaoin and his brother had brought the Great Herd to Ellyrion, a silver-hulled vessel had emerged from the mists at the mouth of the bay and docked with the great castle at the centre of Tor Elyr. None of the sentries had spotted the vessel, but upon seeing the silvery moon emblazoned upon the vessel's sail, Lord Swiftwing understood how such a vessel could have escaped detection.

The ship had sailed from Saphery, and many of its passengers were mages of that enchanted kingdom. In the space of a single day, Tor Elyr had been blessed by the arrival of enough horses to mount whole companies of the citizen levy, and a convocation of mages powerful enough to lay waste to any enemy that dared attack the city.

Galadrien Stormweaver stood at the head of the table with his most experienced Reaver Knights close to him, as the commanders of horse he had appointed took their seats. As nobles and bringers of the Great Herd, Lord Swiftwing had graciously allowed the brothers Éadaoin to attend this meeting.

As the masters of the Sapherian mages entered the hall, Lord Swiftwing immediately knew that had been a mistake.

The mage known as Anurion the Green blanched at the sight of Caelir Éadaoin, and Lord Swiftwing felt the powerful build up of magic. Clad in an emerald robe tied at the waist with a belt of woven ferns, Anurion's eyes flashed with hostility and his hand snatched at the silver pendant around his neck.

'You!' he cried, and everyone in the hall staggered under the force of his words. Killing fire leapt to life around Anurion's hands, and the lethal taste of war-magic filled the air in the Reaver Hall with an actinic flavour like the aftermath of an Annulii lightning storm.

Lord Swiftwing's knights reached for their swords, but he stopped them with a gesture, knowing it would be suicidal to intervene when such powerful magic was involved. The other warriors in the hall rose from their seats in alarm, but took their lead from Lord Swiftwing and did not intervene.

The elf next to Anurion, a tall, distinguished mage in a cobalt blue robe, named Mitherion Silverfawn, put a hand on Anurion's shoulder, but it was angrily shrugged off.

Caelir Éadaoin stood, and Lord Swiftwing saw the terrible guilt etched on his face. The boy's brother stood, but Caelir shook his head and he sat back down.

'Anurion,' said Silverfawn. 'Control yourself.'

'He killed my daughter,' said Anurion, tears of sorrow spilling down his face.

'No,' said Mitherion. 'Not him. He was an innocent victim of the Hag Sorceress.'

'It was him,' wept Anurion. 'I saw Kyrielle die, Mitherion. I saw my daughter die.'

Caelir moved around the table, taking measured steps towards Anurion the Green, and Lord Swiftwing held his breath. The tension was almost unbearable, for the proximity of such bellicose magic surged through every warrior's veins like the first moments of battle.

'Master Anurion,' said Caelir, bowing to the powerful mage. 'You have every reason to hate me, and I would not blame you if you were to kill me. Isha knows I took your daughter from you after she was kind enough to welcome me into your home. You gave me shelter and tried to help me. I repaid you with betrayal, and for that I am truly sorry.'

Anurion took a step towards Caelir, and the deadly fire wreathing his hands shone from the marble walls of the Reaver Hall. Lord Swiftwing saw Galadrien Stormweaver ease his sword from its sheath and shook his head firmly. The sword emerged no further from the sheath, but neither was it replaced.

'She was the light of my life,' said Anurion. 'Of all the wonders in my life, none was brighter and more beautiful than her. And you ended her...'

Caelir nodded and said, 'I understand, and I share your pain. Not a day has passed since that moment I do not think of Kyrielle and the light I took from you and Ulthuan. I am truly sorry for what happened, but I swear I knew nothing of the darkness within me.'

'The boy speaks the truth, Anurion,' said Mitherion. 'You heard Teclis say the same thing.'

'When she died I swore I would destroy you,' said Anurion, placing his hand on Caelir's chest. 'I dreamed of killing you every day.'

'If that is what you wish, then I will not stop you,' said Caelir.

As though in response, the wooden floor buckled and warped as new buds sprouted from the living wood and swelled upwards with surging growth. Pulsing tendrils of sapwood writhed like kraken tentacles as they wrapped themselves around Caelir's legs. Upwards they climbed, enveloping his torso and upper body, and Lord Swiftwing knew that they could crush Caelir Éadaoin to death in an instant.

'I loved her so much,' said Anurion, as the sweet-smelling branches tightened on Caelir's body. 'You took everything she had and everything she was going to do. Ulthuan is the poorer for her absence.'

Caelir nodded and said, 'I loved her too, and could never have knowingly hurt her. But do with me as you will, Master Anurion. You deserve your vengeance.'

Anurion's fist clenched and Lord Swiftwing felt sure he would do as Caelir Éadaoin bid. Slowly his fingers uncurled, and he lowered his hand. The roots holding Caelir released their grip, the incredible growth reversing as suddenly as it had begun until no trace remained that they had existed at all.

'Kyrielle would never forgive me,' he said as the last of the magic faded. 'I know it was the crone of Naggaroth who killed my daughter, but it is painful for me to look upon your face, Caelir Éadaoin.'

'I understand,' said Caelir.

Mitherion Silverfawn eased Caelir away from the grieving mage, and led him back to where his brother sat. The mage spoke quietly to the Éadaoin brothers, and Lord Swiftwing saw there was clearly some connection between them as they embraced with the sadness of grieving relatives instead of friends.

Anurion the Green took a seat at the table and folded his arms. Lord Swiftwing let out a relieved breath and waved everyone in the hall back to their seats. He blinked the last remnants of Anurion's magic from his eyes and pushed himself to his feet. He winced in expectation of pain, but none came, and he smiled at such an unexpected boon.

'Now that we are all friends again, I suggest we turn our attention to the coming war with the druchii,' said Lord Swiftwing. 'Unless there are any more dramatic reunions to be had.'

The horseman Eldain and Caelir had met on the Aerie's Path began the council of war, telling of Morathi's host and the fall of the Eagle Gate. Eldain listened in disbelief as Menethis told of how the men in thrall to the Dark Gods had hurled themselves at the wall, letting themselves be cut down by the defenders while the druchii watched. Whether it was a lingering after-effect of Anurion's magic or simply the power of Menethis's retelling, Eldain found himself caught up in the emotion of his tale. He soared as the fortress repulsed wave after wave of attackers, and despaired as he heard again of the treachery of the vile Alathenar that saw Glorien Truecrown slain.

Lord Swiftwing's general, an angular-featured warrior known as Galadrien Stormweaver, demanded specifics on the enemy from Menethis: numbers, dispositions, weaponry, order of battle, discipline and a host of other morsels of information. Eldain took an instant dislike to Stormweaver. His manner of questioning left Eldain in no doubt that he viewed Menethis as a coward for not dying at the Eagle Gate, as though the senseless loss of elven life in so futile a gesture would have been better than their survival.

Menethis answered Stormweaver's increasingly belligerent questions in calm, measured tones that spoke of a warrior in love with the logistics of war.

In a pause between questions, Eldain leaned over the table and said, 'How many warriors do you have at Tor Elyr, General Stormweaver?'

The warrior looked over, his irritation at being interrupted plain.

'A little over eight thousand, Lord Éadaoin,' said Stormweaver, and Eldain did not miss the emphasis the warrior put on his title.

'And how many of them have seen battle?'

'Perhaps a third.'

'A third? Then it seems to me that you would do well to be less antagonistic to the warrior who commands three hundred veterans. Spreading his warriors throughout your force will help steady those that are yet to be blooded.'

Stormweaver glared at Eldain. 'You think to teach me how to wage war? I am a general in the army of Tor Elyr!'

'And I have led warriors into the heart of Naggaroth,' said Eldain. 'Have you?'

Stormweaver did not answer, and it was Lord Swiftwing who spoke next.

'Lord Éadaoin,' he said, 'I am grateful to you and your brother for bringing us the Great Herd, but had I known how volatile a presence you would prove to be, I might have thought twice before allowing you to join this council of war.'

'I apologise, my lord,' said Eldain.

'Now you, Stormweaver,' said Lord Swiftwing.

The general nodded and gave a curt bow of the head. 'I apologise, Lord Éadaoin.'

'Now is there anyone else who needs to vent before we return to the business of defending these lands? No? Good. Now, Casadesus, the map if you please.'

The robed elf who had stood silently at Lord Swiftwing's shoulder stepped forward and unrolled a long map of Ellyrion. It was a work of beauty, each river, hill, forest and village picked out with the care of an artist who knew his work would endure for centuries to come.

Eldain smiled as he saw Ellyr-Charoi rendered in loving detail, captured perfectly by someone who had clearly visited the lands around the villa. He felt a pang of homesickness at the sight of his villa as Lord Swiftwing addressed the gathered warriors and mages.

'Our enemy has the initiative for now, and that offends me,' said the lord of Tor Elyr. 'As an Ellyrian and a Reaver Knight, I understand how vital it is to keep the enemy off balance. Under normal circumstances, we would have harried the druchii all the way from Eagle Pass, but these are not normal circumstances. Stormweaver, what do your scouts tell you about the enemy's movement? How soon will they get here?'

'Tomorrow. Dusk at the earliest,' said Stormweaver.

'Then we still have time,' said Lord Swiftwing, turning to Menethis of Lothern. 'I want you to take your riders and give the druchii a bloody nose. Jab and cut them, but keep out of their reach. Stall their advance and let them know that we will give them a fight they will not soon forget.'

'My lord,' began Menethis. 'My warriors are exhausted. They need rest and–'

'Nonsense,' said Lord Swiftwing. 'They need a victory. Their spirits are stained with the loss of the Eagle Gate, and you need to wash it away in druchii blood. Restore their honour, Menethis, and they will fight all the harder when battle is joined on the fields of Tor Elyr.'

'It will be done, my lord,' Menethis assured him, and Eldain saw the great warrior Lord Swiftwing had once been as he turned his attention to the mages across the table.

'Master Silverfawn, tell me what you bring to this fight, and I warn you I have no time to indulge in any lengthy digressions. I know how you mages love the sound of your own voices, so be swift and clear in your answer.'

Mitherion Silverfawn rose and nodded to the assembled gathering.

'Loremaster Teclis sent us to you with a company of Sword Masters and forty mages,' said Mitherion. 'Mages whose specialisations are in the realms of air and earth.'

'What does that mean?' demanded Galadrien Stormweaver.

'It means that we can summon mists to conceal our attacks and confound their crossbowmen,' snapped Anurion the Green. 'It means we can bring forth walls of spikethorns to entangle their warriors as we make their flesh irresistible to every arrowhead on the battlefield. It means we can help defend this city. What more do you wish to know?'

'We can also counter the sorceries of Morathi,' cut in Mitherion smoothly. 'The Hag Sorceress possesses a mastery of the dark arts beyond any other living being. Without our help she will freeze the blood in your veins, conjure your worst fears and make them real or drag your soul screaming into the Chaos Hells.'

'Must you work together to do this, or can you spread yourselves throughout the army?' asked Lord Swiftwing.

'It will be best if we spread our presence, with each mage accompanied by his Sword Masters,' said Anurion. 'The mages of Saphery fight not with blade or spear, but the flames of Asuryan. Wherever we fight, we will rain that fire down on the druchii.'

Lord Swiftwing nodded and turned to Eldain and said, 'You say you led an expedition to Naggaroth, Lord Éadaoin?'

'I did,' confirmed Eldain without looking at Caelir. 'My brother and I led a raiding force to Clar Karond and burned the druchii shipyards to the ground. We toppled one of their floating castles and then… then we made our escape.'

'Then you will lead a detachment of my Reavers,' said Lord Swiftwing. 'I will give you command of a hundred of my bravest knights. When the druchii arrive before my city, I want you tearing at their flanks. Make them fear to take so much as a single step forward.'

'My lord, you can count on me,' said Eldain.

'And you, Caelir Éadaoin?' asked Lord Swiftwing. 'Will you fight in Tor Elyr's army?'

Caelir rose to his feet and placed a hand on his heart. 'It will be my honour.'

BOOK TWO
SACRIFICES

CHAPTER ELEVEN

BATTLELINES

The sea in the Straits of Lothern was troubled, churned to white foam at the base of the cliffs that formed its sheer sides. Captain Finlain of *Finubar's Pride* gripped the gunwale of his ship and craned his neck to look up at the escarpments either side of his vessel. The tops were lost to him, hidden by low clouds that were emptying their cargo of rain over the fleet that bobbed and jostled in the swells that made for a treacherous sea.

Finlain stared at the wreck of an elven warship near the mouth of the straits, its sunken remains hauled to the surface atop a rocky outcrop pushed up from the depths. He wondered which ship it was, and what, if any, omen could be read in why it had chosen this day to rise to the surface. The ship's prow was garlanded with seaweed, and the name carved into the hull was impossible to read, but Finlain felt a profound desire to learn its identity for fear that his own vessel might share its fate.

Twenty ships were all that remained of the once-proud asur fleet that had sailed out to meet the druchii in battle before the Emerald Gate. Spread across the straits, they formed a thin silver line of warships with the *Mist Maiden* at its centre. A navy blue sail emblazoned with a stooping hawk was furled to the mast of Lord Aislin's golden, eagle-prowed flagship, and its many banks of rowers had their oars pulled in hard to the hull.

Many of Aislin's fleet still bore the scars of battle, and *Finubar's Pride* was no different. Her silver prow was burned black in patches, and her armoured hull was splintered where scores of crossbow bolts had struck.

Finlain still had nightmares of that battle, recalling the terrible sight of Malekith himself dropping from the thunderous skies on the back of his black dragon to rip the masts from foundering vessels. Finlain took a measure of comfort in knowing that the Witch King would not dare fly his dragon within the straits. High above the warships of the asur, tier upon tier of fortifications cunningly wrought into the rock of the cliffs ran the length of the straits, making it a death trap of Eagle's Claws and archers.

Nor were these defences the only danger an attacker must face.

Sandbars rose and fell throughout the channel in unpredictable ways, tides might change in a heartbeat or winds that had been gentle could suddenly rise to become dangerously unpredictable squalls and dash a ship against the cliffs. All of which made navigation hazardous for even experienced captains. Finlain had sailed these waters for decades, but knew better than to take their good graces for granted. Many an arrogant captain had found out the hard way that the waters of Ulthuan were capricious and punished those who sailed without the proper respect for the sea.

Dark clouds massed at the mouth of the straits, and a curtain of rain obscured the ocean beyond. When the Emerald Gate had been flanked, the druchii had attacked the castles to either side, draping the corpses of those they had slain from the mighty sea gate. Despite the best efforts of Lothern's mages to protect the mechanisms controlling the gate, the sorcery of the Witch King had undone their enchantments, and the gate had swung open as dawn climbed over the Annulii.

Within the hour, Lord Aislin had mustered his surviving vessels and sailed out from the Sapphire Gate to meet the invaders. Twenty ships was not enough to defend these waters, and everyone aboard knew it. Today would see elven blood stain the sea red, and Finlain just hoped that none of it would belong to his vessel's crew.

'Not much of a fleet,' said Meruval, echoing Finlain's unspoken thoughts while shielding his eyes from the rain. 'At least *Finubar's Pride* is still sailing. That's got to count for something.'

'We may not have the numbers,' replied Finlain, 'but we have ships and crew worth ten times any druchii galley.'

'True enough,' agreed Meruval, gripping the top edge of a kite-shield slotted home in the gunwale as a vicious wave broke against the hull. Water spilled onto the deck and the spray of salt water soaked into their cloaks.

'Bad seas,' noted Meruval. 'I miss Daelis. Isha's tears, I never thought I'd say such a thing, but he knew his way around a whimsical seabed.'

Finlain smiled. Daelis had been their mage-navigator, and though he had been hard to like, he had always steered them true in dangerous waters. A druchii crossbow bolt had taken his life off the coast of Tiranoc, and *Finubar's Pride* had lost a valuable member of its crew.

'Yes, he was a prickly character, but we could use him now.'

'The water is in a foul mood,' said Meruval. 'Not the kind of sea anyone should be sailing. One of the crew told me he dreamed of the Conqueror last night. He drowned at sea, you know.'

'I know, Meruval,' said Finlain. 'It was a bad end for a great king, but neither dreams, portents nor omens will stop us from venturing out today. Lord Aislin has decreed it, and I doubt even the Phoenix King could stop him.'

Meruval leaned in close to Finlain. 'You know it is madness to sail when the sea is acting up like this. Lord Aislin might not care, but I can see you agree with me. I've served with you long enough to know your thoughts, captain.'

Finlain shook his head. 'For the sake of morale aboard ship, I am going to pretend you did not speak such seditious words, Meruval. Lord Aislin has commanded that we sail, and that is the end of the matter. The druchii are massing their ships at the mouth of the straits, and it behoves us to show them that we will not yield these waters without a fight.'

Meruval glanced over at the *Mist Maiden*, and Finlain saw that threats of disciplinary action were not going to dissuade him from speaking his mind. Under normal circumstances, Finlain valued Meruval's plain speaking, but not today.

'I understand that, captain, but look above you!' said Meruval. 'Castles, ramparts, Eagle's Claws beyond number. Archers and spearmen, mages and warriors. These waters will not be taken without a fight, but to sail into harm's way when there are such defences in place seems like recklessness, not bravery. Aislin felt the Phoenix King's wrath at the defeat before the Emerald Gate, and now he seeks to regain his honour in this desperate gamble.'

'I could dismiss you for this,' said Finlain.

'But you won't because you know I'm right.'

'No, it is because if we are to keep *Finubar's Pride* afloat, I need you at the helm,' said Finlain. 'Now be silent and listen, for your rank aboard this vessel depends upon it.'

Before Meruval could reply, Finlain took a deep breath and walked along the deck of *Finubar's Pride*. The vessel's forecastle had been repaired after the battle with the black ark, and a pair of fearsome bolt throwers had been mounted on a rotating platform at her prow.

He vaulted nimbly onto the edge of the hull, balancing on the rows of shields and gripping the sweeping bow of the nearest Eagle's Claw as he drew his sword with his free hand. The crew of his vessel gathered on the deck, each one sensing their captain's need to speak.

'Warriors of *Finubar's Pride*, listen well to me,' he cried. Lightning arced in the gloom, and Finlain pointed to the rain and darkness filling the mouth of the straits. 'The druchii are out there, ready to sail into this channel, and all that stands between them and Lothern is us.'

Thunder rolled overhead as the sea did its best to unseat Finlain from his perch. The vessel rolled to starboard, but Finlain leaned with the motion of his ship.

'Many of you are wondering why we sail out to fight the druchii at all when there are such strong defences worked into the cliffs. Why risk our lives in battle when we can fight our enemies from afar? You all know me, for I have captained *Finubar's Pride* for many years, and I know warfare as well as any and better than most. So I tell you this: if we yield the straits without a fight, we hand the initiative to the enemy. They will believe that we have no will to fight, and their warriors will be heartened by so easy a victory. When the time comes, which it will, to give battle on the Sapphire Gate, the druchii will fight all the harder, believing that we are already defeated.

'*That* is why we must give battle here! We will tell our enemies that no part of Ulthuan will be surrendered without a fight. They must learn that every yard they advance will exact a fearsome toll in blood. Yes, this will be dangerous, and yes we may see our ships sunk, but not to sail out is the most dangerous thing of all. We are *Finubar's Pride*, and does anyone fight harder than us?'

His crew yelled at the stormfront advancing through the straits, and Finlain dropped from the row of shields with their cheers ringing in his ears. The cheering was taken up by the crew of *Hammer of Vaul*, the vessel sailing alongside *Finubar's Pride*, and spread along the line of elven warships until the entire fleet was shouting its defiance.

The cheering died moments later as a lightning-shawled mountain emerged from the cloaking shadows wreathing the Emerald Gate. A rearing crag of black rock, its impossible bulk smashed the edges of the massive gate and sent its towers and ramparts tumbling downwards. Thousands of tons of rock crashed into the sea, throwing columns of water hundreds of feet into the air and sending a surging wave towards the fleet of elven warships.

Rock ground on rock as the black ark forced its way into the channel, the sound like continents colliding or a never-ending avalanche as the glittering marble of the straits was crushed to powder. Fire from infernal furnaces within the mountainous abomination burned at its spiked summit, and lit the inner faces of the straits with hellish orange light.

Though he had seen this sundered peak once before, Finlain still felt his heart clamped in the grip of icy terror. How could any fleet fight something so unimaginably vast? Like a gnarled plug of cooling magma forcing its way down the neck of a dying volcano, the black ark ground its way, inch by inch, into the straits of Lothern.

And surging from its base came a hundred raven-hulled warships.

The sun had passed its zenith as the druchii army marched into sight of Tor Elyr. It came in a cloud of dust, with the sky darkening and the land growing silent before it. The scent of freshly spilled blood was carried on the cold winds surrounding the dark host, as though a cocoon of winter shielded the warriors from the balmy climate of Ellyrion.

Ahead of the druchii came Menethis of Lothern and his Reavers. They rode hard for Korhandir's Leap, the crystal bridge to the southwest of Tor Elyr said to have been built in the first days of Ellyrion, with scattered groups of dark-cloaked riders in pursuit. Eldain's practised eye told him the druchii would not catch Menethis before he crossed the river. No sooner had Lord Swiftwing's council of war broken up than Menethis had taken his warriors west, and Eldain was pleased to see that most had returned from their reaving.

But others had not, and all of Ulthuan would grieve their loss.

The pursuing druchii gave up the chase as they came within bowshot of the River Elyras, and Eldain watched Menethis lead his Reavers over the glittering bridge with a heavy weight in his heart.

It had been Eldain's betrayal that had brought the druchii to Ellyrion, and he would bear a measure of guilt for every life that was lost in its defence. He tried to keep that thought from distracting him from his role in the coming battle, but as he looked around at the faces of elves surely too young or too old to fight, he could not help but picture them as headless corpses or rotting feasts for the carrion birds that followed any druchii host.

Menethis rode up the slope towards Eldain, his horse breathless and lathered with sweat. The warrior's face was lined with joyous exhaustion, his ivory cloak was bloodstained, and the riders who followed him were alight with exultation.

'Lord Éadaoin!' cried Menethis. 'We return triumphant!'

'You return alive,' said Eldain. 'That is what is most important to a Reaver.'

'All night we harried them,' said Menethis. 'We slew their sentries, scattered their horses and fired their tents. Perhaps three or four hundred dead, many more injured.'

'Good work, Menethis, we will make an Ellyrian out of you yet,' said Eldain. 'Now ride to the centre. General Stormweaver will have orders for you and your warriors.'

'Indeed,' said Menethis, turning his horse with a flourish and leading his riders towards the grassy flatlands that spread before the backdrop of Tor Elyr. As Eldain watched Menethis ride off, his gaze was drawn along the glittering battle line of Lord Swiftwing's army.

Arrayed in serried ranks of shimmering spear points, azure cloaks, polished helms and gleaming breastplates, the army of Tor Elyr occupied the slopes overlooking the southern banks of the river. The army had assembled as dawn's first light bathed the land in its honey gold warmth, marching from the city under Galadrien Stormweaver's direction.

This close to the sea, the river was wide and deep, yet its waters flowed languidly and without urgency. Blocks of spearmen and lines of archers held the field, with a mass of heavy horse at their centre. Beneath a banner of crimson, Stormweaver led the Silver Helms of Tor Elyr from the back of a mighty steed the colour of a winter's sky. As though carved from silver, the horsemen stood silent and unmoving, perfectly disciplined and courageous beyond mortal reckoning.

On each flank of the army, a thousand Reaver Knights strung their bows or sharpened the already keen edges of their spears. Thanks to the gathering of the Great Herd, most of Ellyrion's citizen levy was now mounted, and Eldain hoped it would be enough to tip the balance in their favour.

Scores of Eagle's Claw bolt throwers had been set up on the high ground behind the archers, and several weapons had been assembled further south upon small hillocks overlooking Korhandir's Leap and in the north on the slopes of a hill crowned by a circle of waystones. No druchii warriors would be able to cross the river without suffering beneath a relentless hail of powerfully driven arrows.

Eldain lifted a hand as he saw Caelir riding across the plain towards the left flank of Lord Swiftwing's army. His brother waved back, elated to be defending his homeland at the head of a hundred Reaver Knights.

Caelir was a war leader now, a noble of Ellyrion riding out in defence of his homeland, and Eldain felt pride that was almost paternal in its strength. Only now did he understand that the jealousy he had felt towards Caelir had been completely unnecessary. They had never been in competition, but the wild spirit of Ellyrion had driven them both to foolish acts of betrayal. They were part of a race of near immortals on the brink of extinction, and yet they could still fall prey to damaging emotions just as easily as the mortals of the Old World they looked down upon. More so, in many cases, for the pulls of the heart endured by mortals were but pale shadows of those that drove the asur. That the wounds between Eldain and Caelir were healing was his only consolation as the druchii emerged from the penumbra of shadow that swathed them like a shroud.

Rank upon rank of warriors in dark cloaks and oil-sheened armour the colour of obsidian filled the centre of the plain with the tramp of their marching feet. Blood-red cloaks billowed in the icy winds that followed them, and their black-hafted spears were tipped with bronze. Heavily armoured warriors atop snarling, snapping reptilian steeds rode in the southern wing of the army, and beastmasters goaded roaring beasts with many writhing heads towards the river.

Hideously malformed creatures of raw flesh, wailing, fang-filled mouths and unnaturally jointed limbs hauled their corrupted bulk alongside these beasts. Sweating mortals held them on chains, hard-muscled men of the north clad in furs, brazen iron and horned helms.

Though allied, Eldain saw there was clear division in how the enemy host would give battle. The druchii would attack to the south of Tor Elyr over Korhandir's Leap, while the tribal barbarians would force a crossing in the north. It seemed a foolish plan, for there was no bridge in the north, and the savage warriors of the Dark Gods would be forced to wade through the river while enduring endless volleys of arrows from the citizen levy's archers.

The bloodshed would be terrible, but from the scarred, wild and hungry look of these warriors, Eldain suspected they would welcome the pain. Certainly the mighty warrior atop a fleshy steed with a silver saddle stitched to its naked hide could barely contain his eagerness to ride into the water. A dark halo that looked like naked flames seemed to coil across the warlord's skin, and Eldain wondered if he was even aware of it.

A chill took hold of Eldain's heart as the plain across the river filled with regimented ranks of druchii and howling mobs of axe-wielding savages. He had hoped the battle before the walls of Eagle Gate might have bled this host of its power, but the army of Lord Swiftwing was still outnumbered by at least four to one.

A lone rider emerged from the ranks of the enemy army, and a fierce, ululating scream of worship and devotion was torn from every druchii throat.

She was ivory-skinned and clad in leather armour that revealed more flesh that it protected. A twisted crown of dark iron and bone encircled her brow, and she bore a dread weapon that dripped blood and made Eldain clutch his chest as though it might tear his heart from his body even from so far away. Eldain knew exactly who she was, her name was a byword for unnatural perversions, ancient hatred and endless spite.

'Morathi,' he hissed, spitting the name like poison sucked from a wound. She was the architect of Caelir's transformation from loyal son of Ellyrion into a weapon aimed at the heart of Ulthuan's best and brightest. She had tortured his brother and driven him beyond sanity with her excruciations and seductions.

Eldain gripped his sword hilt tightly, hoping that the chaos of battle would see him face to face with his brother's tormentor. As though sensing his hatred and savouring it, the Hag Sorceress turned her mount in his direction. Morathi's steed was blacker than the heart of the most merciless tyrant, its eyes a simmering furnace red, and a pair of nightmarish wings were folded in at its flanks.

Morathi raised her pale arms above her head with a crack of displaced air. The sky split with thunder and a wind straight from the Land of Chill swept across the river and into the army of the asur. Not a heart failed to miss a beat, not a sword arm did not tremble, and not one amongst the defenders of Tor Elyr failed to hear the banshee wail of Morai-Heg.

Yet not one warrior took a backwards step.

A host of discordant war-horns sounded from the enemy host, and with a clash of swords and shields, Morathi's army marched on Tor Elyr.

The order came from Lord Aislin's ship, and the asur fleet surged towards the shadow-cloaked vessels at the base of the black ark. It was a wondrously foolish charge, but the nineteen captains of the Sea Lord obeyed instantly, sailing south in the direction of the open sea. Kithre Seablaze led the western half of the fleet, Lord Aislin the east, and it was the Sea Lord's lieutenant that struck first.

Racing ahead of the rest of the ships, Seablaze ran his ships at speed towards the druchii raven ships as a mist arose from the surface of the water. No natural sea mist was this, but one conjured from the foamy wave-tops that swirled around the druchii ships like a winter's fog. It clung to their dark hulls, gathered in their sails and confounded the warriors on the prow-mounted dart throwers.

Seablaze sailed into the mist, and no sooner had his ships reached its edge than the mist sank back into the sea. Cries of alarm echoed from the decks of the raven ships as their crews saw the sleek vessels of the asur bearing down upon them. Eagle's Claws loosed withering hails of bolts into the packed ranks gathered on the decks, and fearful was the carnage. Another volley flashed, hurling scores of arrows through the druchii Corsairs. One final volley of darts was loosed before Seablaze gave the order to turn about.

Even as his ships pirouetted on the ocean, additional Eagle's Claws mounted on the quarterdeck loosed their shafts. While the enemy crews reeled from the slaughter wreaked on their decks, the Eagle's Claws let fly with heavy ithilmar-tipped bolts designed to punch through the hull of a ship. Aimed below the waterline, three druchii vessels were holed and began wallowing in the swells as their lower decks began filling with seawater.

Black bolts from the prows of the enemy ships flashed through the air, but loosed too swiftly they were poorly aimed. Yet with so many unleashed, some found their targets, and blood was spilled across the decks of the elven ships.

As Seablaze raced back to the asur fleet, a rain of arrows and bolts fell from the castles and ramparts carved into the cliffs of the straits. Hundreds slashed down onto the raven ships, punching through armour, cutting ropes and slicing sails. The heavier bolts smashed through decks to slay dozens of slave rowers or even punch through the bottom timbers of the hull.

In answer, swarms of iron crossbow bolts flew from the black ark, and the battle below was fought beneath a sky darkened with deadly projectiles. Monstrous balls of flaming pitch were hurled from the summit of the black ark, arcing through the air with languid ease to slam into the pristine walls of the defensive castles. Fires blazed across the cliff side defences and thick columns of black smoke curled skyward.

Finlain sent *Finubar's Pride* racing towards the unnamed ship wrecked upon the new island, aiming his prow for the narrow gap between it and the eastern scarp of the straits. *Hammer of Vaul* came with him, and he waved to its captain as they sailed on this gloriously mad course. Despite what he had said to his men, Finlain knew this was a desperately risky gambit. No matter how skilled a sailor, the odds of winning a victory against such numbers was practically zero, but this fight was not about victory, it was about making a statement.

In the centre of the fleet, Lord Aislin's ship rode the crest of the waves, a host of glistening, bottle-green wyrms breaking the water either side of his prow. The creatures of the far ocean had come at Aislin's command, predators of the deep with the strength and ferocity to sink even the largest ships. The Sea Lord's blue sail caught the last rays of light in the straits, and it shone like the skies at the centre of the Sea of Dusk.

More mists oozed from the sea, coiling over the gunwale as it cloaked the asur ships from the sight of the enemy. Finlain held to his course, knowing that he could afford no mistakes in his heading or else be dashed upon the rocks.

'Steady as she goes, Meruval!' he yelled, his voice deadened by the mists.

'Aye, captain,' returned his helmsman, as *Finubar's Pride* cut the waters of the straits.

'Eagle's Claws ready?'

'Ready, aye, captain,' came the shouted reply.

The wind caught the sails and *Finubar's Pride* leapt forward, keeping her prow low to the water as she cut the waves like a knife. A druchii bolt flashed overhead, grazing the mainmast, and spinning off into the mist.

'They know we're here,' said Finlain.

The rocky island of tumbled blocks and dripping seaweed emerged from the mist. Finlain saw a fallen statue of Isha lying on its side, with seawater dripping from her granite eyes like tears. Behind the statue the sagging hull of the wreck hid his ship from the druchii, and Finlain glanced over his shoulder to see that *Hammer of Vaul* was still with him. Up ahead, rising like the sheer face of a mountainside, the black ark smouldered like the sea volcanoes that rose without warning in the southern oceans. A wall of water went before the black ark like a surge tide, bearing all manner of detritus from the bottom of the ocean in its oily foam.

Light glimmered evilly from the many towers and garrets built haphazardly on the scorched flanks of the black ark, and the dull hammer of iron on iron echoed from within. Hideous screams and bloody chants to Khaine accompanied the metallic cacophony, and Finlain knew he took a terrible risk in coming this close to such an abominable creation.

Across the straits, druchii sorcery battled with asur magecraft as the mists conjured by the sea-mages of Lord Aislin were dissipated by roiling clouds of fire. Blazing ships foundered in the channel, and burning elves hurled themselves from the decks of their doomed vessels rather than be consumed by the flames.

The druchii's advantage in numbers was now paying off, as Kithre Seablaze found himself trapped against the walls of the straits. Swifter raven ships pushed north into the straits as more heavily-laden galleys engaged Seablaze's vessels. In such close confines, the deadly rams affixed to the hulls of the raven ships were next to useless, but the druchii had other means of taking the elven ships.

Corvus boarding ramps with heavy iron spikes in the shape of barbed beaks slammed down on the decks of the elven ships, shattering gunwales and embedding themselves firmly in the timbers of the deck. Corsairs in scaled cloaks charged onto the elven vessels, and the slaughter was prodigious as these merciless killers butchered the crews of the eagle ships. With nowhere to run, two elven ships were run aground, their hulls broken to splinters and their crews dashed upon the rocks by the powerful waves.

Lord Aislin's ships cut a wedge through the centre of the druchii line, Eagle's Claws sweeping the crew from the decks of raven ships with volley after volley of arrows. His sea-mages dragged two raven ships beneath the waves in a crushing, whirling vortex of water, while another was left becalmed as its crew were bewitched by the glamours of oceanid song that rose from the haunted deeps.

Fire fell from above in blazing lumps of pitch as the castles on the cliffs burned, and flames caught the sails of the close-packed druchii ships. Those that could not fight the fires were sunk by their fellows, and the sea filled with screaming Corsairs who fought to reach a spar of broken timber before the weight of their armour dragged them to their deaths.

Captain Finlain watched the battle raging across the width of the straits, and felt his heartbeat quicken. They had sunk their own number of druchii vessels at least, and many more were aflame or sinking. Yet for all that, the asur fleet now numbered only seven vessels. Even as he watched, Finlain saw Kithre Seablaze's vessel ride up onto a fang of rock at the base of the western cliff. The hull of his vessel broke apart like matchwood, and its crew spilled like seeds into the dark waters.

'Meruval!' shouted Finlain. 'On my word!'

The seas bucked and heaved at the base of the black ark, and Finlain saw its lower ramparts and donjons through the mist and sea spray. Shouting druchii warriors pointed at them as they emerged from the mist, but before they could do more than shout a warning, scores of arrows flensed the lower walls of the black ark.

'Come about!' cried Finlain. 'Now, Meruval, now!'

Finubar's Pride heeled hard to starboard, the ship leaning down into the water and exposing its silver underside to the black ark as it spun around to make a perfect course change of ninety degrees. *Hammer of Vaul* followed her round, and the two vessels surged forward into the flanks of the druchii fleet, borne aloft on the thundering bow wave driven before the sea-borne mountain. Finlain gripped the ropes tied to the mast to keep his feet as *Finubar's Pride* rode the waves faster than she had ever done before.

Crossbow bolts smacked into the deck, and Finlain looked over his shoulder to see druchii crossbowmen racing to the ramparts of the black ark.

'Keep our backside clear!' ordered Finlain, and his best archers took up position on the quarterdeck. Arrow after arrow flew from their bows, any druchii who dared show their face punched from his feet by the volley. Finlain turned and ran to where Meruval wrestled with the tiller, his face contorted with the effort of holding their course. The prow of *Finubar's Pride* was aimed towards the sea, and the power of the wave they rode was like nothing Meruval had sailed before.

Finlain threw himself at the tiller, adding his own strength as they guided their vessel into the druchii fleet.

A raven ship trading arrows with the *Mist Maiden* was the first to feel their wrath.

Finubar's Pride slammed into the druchii ship, her reinforced prow smashing through the raven ship as though it were a child's toy and not a ship of war. The vessel broke in two and the screams of its crew were short lived as the oncoming wave swallowed them.

Two more ships were smashed to pieces in this way before Finlain was forced to give the order to turn *Finubar's Pride* to the north. His archers loosed until they had no more shafts in their quivers, and his Eagle's Claws exhausted their supply of heavy bolts a moment later.

The surface of the ocean was awash with broken timber, burning ships and drowning sailors. Castles burned high on the cliffs, and savage lightning crackled from the sorcerers' towers of the black ark. A towering column of fire erupted beside *Finubar's Pride*, and Finlain watched in horror as *Hammer of Vaul* was struck dead centre by one of the giant balls of flaming pitch. Immediately, the vessel was ablaze from bow to stern, and Finlain knew there was no saving her.

'Captain!' cried Meruval. 'Help me.'

Finlain shook off his sorrow at the loss of his fellow captain's ship and bent his efforts to helping Meruval control their wild course. Iron bolts thudded into the quarterdeck and mast now that the druchii in the black ark could target them without fear of reprisals.

'Time to get out of here,' advised Meruval.

'Agreed,' said Finlain, and they hauled the tiller around until they were aimed to the north and the gleaming blue glare of the Sapphire Gate. Using the power of the wave surging ahead of the black ark, the vessel shot away from the vast mountain, passing the rocky island of the wreck.

Viewed from this angle, Finlain could see the faint outline of the runic carvings worked into this side of the newly revealed prow.

Morelion.

Finlain felt a stab of hope at the sight of the name, for it was that of the firstborn twin of Aenarion and Astarielle. In the ancient war against the Chaos powers, the daemons of the Dark Gods had fallen on Avelorn in a tide of bloody claws and slaughter. The Everqueen had been slain and Morelion and Yvraine thought lost to the daemons, but an ancient forest spirit of Avelorn had kept Aenarion's children safe and eventually returned them to their people.

Though the asur fleet was scattered and sunk, Finlain did not despair, for as Morelion had survived impossible odds to fight again, so too would *Finubar's Pride*.

'Blood of Khaine!' hissed Meruval, making Finlain flinch with the invocation.

'Watch your tongue,' said Finlain. 'I'll not have the murder god's name spoken aloud on my ship.'

'Apologies, captain,' said Meruval. 'But look!'

Finlain followed Meruval's outstretched hand, and was almost moved to give voice to the bloody-handed one's name himself.

Her navy blue sail ablaze, the *Mist Maiden* sailed into the heart of the druchii fleet with two raven ships locked alongside her, their corvus boarding bridges wedged tightly in her decks. The sea around the ships churned with blood as sea wyrms tore at hideous monsters loosed from the bowels of the black ark, and purple lightning set the water ablaze with magical fire. Elven warriors fought in the leaping shadows of the flames, and Finlain saw the magnificent form of Lord Aislin as he swept the curved blade of his ithilmar sword through the Corsairs attempting to capture his vessel.

For a brief moment, Finlain dared hope that the Sea Lord might yet break free of the druchii vessels. But as the water churned with strange lights and a groaning roar of something beneath the ocean, that hope was cruelly dashed.

Something vast and scaled broke the surface beneath *Mist Maiden*, and her keel broke like a dead sapling as she was lifted out of the water. Like a kraken of the deep, the monster had eyes the size of chariot wheels and row upon row of ivory teeth in an obsidian gash of a mouth. Its fangs closed on the *Mist Maiden*'s hull and the ship exploded in a welter of smashed timber and elven bodies.

The creature fell back into the water with a thunderous boom of crashing waves, and Finlain blinked away tears of anger and sorrow. He turned from the Sea Lord's death and let the fierce winds and pounding waves carry *Finubar's Pride* towards the postern of the glittering sea gate ahead.

'The straits are lost,' said Meruval accusingly, as though unable to believe the words.

Finlain nodded, too grief-stricken to answer.

Only the Sapphire Gate now stood between the druchii and Lothern.

CHAPTER TWELVE
FIRST BLOOD

Caelir drew in the reins of his horse at the foot of the domed hill to the north of Tor Elyr. Its summit was crowned by a ring of white stones, each taller than two elves, and cut with sigils of ancient power. In days long since passed, it was said that the mages of Ulthuan could travel to other dominions with a single step through such portals, but none now lived who were powerful enough to walk between worlds.

His Reaver Knights were eager for action, hungry to take the fight to the druchii, and Caelir liked that aggressive spirit. A Reaver Knight needed a reckless streak, yet one tempered with iron control. It was a contradiction of wildness and discipline that only a very few could understand or master. Above his warriors, a line of Eagle's Claw bolt throwers were being loaded with arrows, and Caelir waved to the warriors that crewed them.

Across the river, the enemy host milled and stamped, beating axes and swords against iron-bossed shields. It was grim theatrics, designed to intimidate, and against another army of mortals it might have worked, but directed at the asur, it was failing miserably. The braying of horns echoed over the river, and Caelir felt his pulse quicken as the enemy moved towards the water.

Though they were but mortals, the warriors across the river were powerful and wolf-lean, bred tough by a life spent on the verge of extinction. Living in the harsh tundra of the north meant that only the strongest, most ruthless survived, and only by a man's strength and power could he be measured against his foes. Clad in beaten plates of iron, wolf and bear pelts, these northern savages had a primal ferocity that could not be underestimated. Though crude, a club to the head would kill you as surely as the finest blade. They howled a guttural refrain, a deafening war-chant that was discordant, melodious, ear-splitting and hideous all at once. It spoke of delirium, the loss of control and the pleasure that could be had from surrendering all restraint.

Caelir shifted uncomfortably in his saddle, feeling the clashing sounds touching some deep part of his soul. He recognised the urge to allow desire to overrule control, and hated that he shared even this scrap of connection with the enemy. The northern warriors did not advance, content simply to bang their swords and shields, lift their bloody banners high, and hurl vile taunts across the wide river.

Instead, the beasts charged.

Terrible perversions of nature, these hybrid abominations were taller and more powerfully built than all but the mightiest tribesmen. Their bodies were covered in rank, matted fur and most carried heavy clubs or crude axes. No two were identical, but each bore the unmistakable trait of some forest beast, be it mastiff, bull, fox, bear or wolf. They walked on two legs in imitation of the noble creatures of the world, but nothing could disguise the horror of their condition. Caelir almost felt sorry for them.

The beasts plunged into the river, howling and braying as its purity burned their Chaos-tainted flesh. Where a mortal warrior would be dragged to the bottom of the river, the beasts swam with powerful strokes, and hundreds of shaggy-haired monsters drew near the gently sloping banks of the river. Archers positioned on the northern flank of the army let fly with a volley of arrows, and the river ran with blood as they slashed down into the warped flesh of the beasts.

Another volley hit home, and another, but the beasts' hides were thick and their flesh leather-tough. Some sank beneath the river, but many more pressed on through the waters to the far bank. Raucous cheers from the tribesmen drove them on, and Caelir saw that arrows alone would not stop the beasts from reaching the riverbank.

'With me!' shouted Caelir, hauling on the reins and urging Irenya to a gallop.

His knights followed instantly, riding north in a curving loop to come upon the beasts at an oblique angle. Caelir stood tall in the saddle, and craned his neck to see that numerous other Reaver bands had followed his example. Perhaps five hundred riders thundered across the plain as blocks of spearmen advanced to fill the gap they had just left.

The first of the monsters had reached the shoreline and were dragging their hulking bodies onto dry land. They shook their fur free of water and bellowed their challenges as more arrows thudded home. Caelir saw a towering monster with the head of a horned bull and a breastplate of beaten iron strapped to its body, snap a pair of arrows from its stomach and roar its hate at those whose bodies were unblemished.

The Eagle's Claws on the hill unleashed flickering volleys of arrows, and several beasts fell, pierced by a host of shafts. Scores of monsters had gained the riverbank, as Caelir raised his left fist and chopped it down to his hip.

As one, the Reaver Knights wheeled their horses, changing direction in an instant and riding towards the monsters. Caelir hauled back on his bowstring and loosed at the bull-headed monster. His arrow plunged into its side, but it seemed not to feel the impact. Arrows flashed past him as his fellow knights let fly, but only a handful of the beasts fell. Many hundreds of the terrifying monsters had assembled on the banks of the river, and were advancing towards the glittering elven lines with a bestial, loping gait.

'Fly, Irenya!' shouted Caelir. 'Ride like never before!'

Though Aedaris had been the faster horse, Irenya was still a proud steed of Ellyrion, and she rode as if all the daemons of Chaos were on her tail. The ground thundered beneath her, and Caelir loosed three more shafts before exerting pressure with his left boot and swinging his mount around.

Less than a hundred yards separated the beasts and the asur battle line, and Caelir led his Reavers into that gap. He twisted in the saddle, drawing and loosing arrow after arrow with swift economy of movement. His arrows plunged into eye sockets and open mouths, the only vulnerable areas of soft flesh on the beasts' bodies.

'Turn about!' yelled Caelir, as Irenya pirouetted and reversed her course.

The gap between the elves and beasts was shrinking rapidly, and Caelir hoped he hadn't left it too late to ride out. He looped his bow around his shoulder and flicked his spear free of the leather thong holding it to his saddle.

A wolf-headed beast leapt for him, and he rammed the spear into its throat. The beast howled and fell beneath Irenya's hooves. Shimmering speartips slashed and stabbed in a terrifying scrum of bodies. Howls and grunts filled the air as the beasts fought to drag the Reavers down, but such was the speed and agility of their steeds that not a single knight was slain. Blood sprayed and his arm ached with the effort of driving his spear into iron-hard flesh. This close to the enemy, Irenya was a weapon too, her hooves caving in skulls and chests with every stride.

Then they were clear, and Caelir whooped with the sheer bliss of riding free. His weapon and armour were drenched in bestial blood, but he was alive. They had ridden into the jaws of death and spat in the eye of Morai-Heg before riding out. His heart beat a racing tattoo within his chest, but no sooner had he brought Irenya to a canter than the charging beasts struck the elven line like a hammer-blow.

Spears shivered and snapped with the impact, and a braying, honking, roaring mass of furred flesh slammed into the silver line of lowered spears. The elven line bent back, but held. Warriors in the ranks beyond the fighting rank thrust their spears forward, driving the razor-sharp points into the unclean flesh of the beasts.

Great axes and monstrous clubs slammed into the elven warriors, hurling broken bodies through the air or pounding them into the earth. Screams carried over the clang of weapons and armour, and Caelir fought the urge to ride into the fray. With their spears lowered, the Reaver Knights would wreak fearsome harm, but getting bogged down in such a brutal fight was not where they excelled.

Instead, Caelir wheeled his horse back to the river as yet more bestial creatures forded the waters. Behind them came mortal warriors from the Old World, chanting, jeering and screaming tribesmen in leather breastplates and bronze helms. They carried fleshy banners daubed with obscenities and blasphemous runes dedicated to gods whose names should never be spoken.

Riding at the head of these brutal warriors was a towering warlord, his armour a mix of leather, bronze and iron, his helm beaten to resemble a raven with swept-back wings at the sides. Caelir felt the power and threat of this champion, knowing that this was surely the master of the mortal horde. The warrior sat astride a mountainous horse, its raw-meat bulk and saw-toothed snout marking it as an abomination of Chaos.

This warrior of the Dark Gods bore a sword with many blades, a weapon that glittered with cruel light and infinite malice. Caelir had tried to keep the memories of his many torments in the depths of Naggaroth buried in the deepest, darkest recesses of his memory, but the sight of this warrior unlocked the blackest of those horrors.

He sobbed as he remembered the many violations wreaked upon his flesh, the pain and the loathsome pleasures designed to break him down to his component parts in order to rebuild him in a manner pleasing to the Hag Sorceress. He remembered this warrior's face leering down at him, a vision of perverse beauty that repulsed and beguiled in equal measure.

'Issyk Kul,' whispered Caelir, his anger and hate rising to the surface in a bilious tide.

Between them, Kul and Morathi had tainted everything of worth in his soul, and Caelir would never forgive them for that. As the warriors of the Dark Gods approached the riverbank, Caelir waved his spear in the air and loosed an aching cry of grief and pain.

Irenya reared up, startled by his sudden outburst, and his Reaver Knights milled around in confusion. Caelir spun his spear and scanned the battle raging between the elven line and the beasts. More of the beasts were pouring into the fight, punching ragged holes in the elven host, which were swiftly filled with warriors from the rearmost ranks.

Blue-fletched shafts dropped amongst the beasts from archers behind the spears, plunging into shoulders and skulls.

A cold wind, icy and filled with the actinic tang of magic flowed across the river, and Caelir saw the surface of the water grow sluggish and gelid. Frosted patterns crazed across the river as rippled ice began to form. Ellyrion was a land that never knew the touch of winter, yet the northern stretch of the river was freezing solid.

A carnyx formed from the bones and skull of some long-dead leviathan echoed over the frozen waters, and Issyk Kul led his warriors onto the ice.

'Reavers, with me!' shouted Caelir, riding for the river.

Poets told that the goddess Ladrielle had woven Korhandir's Leap from starlight and moonbeams when the gods first shaped Ulthuan for the asur. Given to the horse lords in ancient times in gratitude for their aid during the coming of the daemons, it was a trysting place for the young of Tor Elyr, and the young bucks of the city would leap into the river from its crystal arches to impress their chosen fillies.

Now it was a killing ground.

Druchii warriors bearing kite-shaped shields emblazoned with the heraldry of their dark houses charged asur warriors positioned at the midpoint of the bridge on the crest of its grandest arch. Wide enough for only twenty warriors to stand abreast, it was a perfect choke point to stymie the druchii advance. Silver-tipped spears splintered shields and drew chill blood, as cold-forged iron hacked through mail shirts in return. Warriors heaved against one another, grunting and stabbing and cutting.

This was battle at its most primal, strength against strength, blood upon blood until one force could stand no more of the slaughter. It was the kind of war fought by savages, not the elegant, sophisticated warriors of the asur. Yet all too often, war chooses its own form, regardless of who fights it, and warriors either adapt or die.

Eldain rode Lotharin along the banks of the river, loosing shafts across the water to slay druchii warriors crouched on the opposite bank who unleashed iron-tipped crossbow bolts into the flanks of the warriors defending the bridge. His Reavers traded barbs with dark-cloaked druchii kin with ebony weapons pulled in tight to their shoulders, like the uncouth black powder weapons of the dwarfs. Loosing several bolts from top-mounted magazines with every squeeze of the firing bar, they were lethal at close quarters, but lost power swiftly at range.

Eldain's bow suffered no such loss in power and most of his shafts sent a druchii warrior tumbling into the river. The battle on the bridge was the key to the southern flank of the elven army. Hold the bridge and the druchii could not bring their superior numbers to bear. Lose the bridge and their flank would be turned.

Along the line of battle, the elven host sent arching flocks of arrows over the river, and Eldain relished the thought of the suffering the enemy would be enduring. Flickering bolts of pellucid white flames zipped across the river, answered by crackling arcs of purple lightning and cold streams of icy air as the mages sent from the White Tower did battle with the magickers of the Hag Sorceress.

Freezing fog obscured the land to the north of the battle line, and Eldain saw only the faintest outline of the hill of waystones. He could see nothing of Caelir's Reaver Knights, and whispered a short prayer to Asuryan to look kindly on his younger brother. Eldain cast his gaze over the river, watching the enemy host jostle for position as yet more blocks of infantry moved up to the river, spear-armed warriors, heavily armoured warriors with executioners' blades, screeching hydras and rank upon rank of crossbowmen crouched at the edge of the river.

Movement far to the south caught his eye, and Eldain saw numerous groups of black-cloaked horsemen apparently riding away from the battle. They were pushing their mounts hard, and though their direction made no sense, Eldain guessed their destination; a gently curved portion of the river that foamed white where buried rocks broke the surface. Eldain immediately saw the danger and turned to his lieutenant, a rider named Alysia. Her hair was crimson and gold, held in place by a silver pin shaped like a butterfly.

'The river, can it be forded there?' he demanded, pointing to the river's curve.

'When the rains are mild,' she said. 'But it is too deep for even one such as Korhil to cross.'

'But not so deep that it would trouble a lightly-laden cavalryman,' snapped Eldain, dragging Lotharin's reins around and urging him southwards. 'Ride! All of you, with me!'

Eldain's Reavers swirled around him as he rode south along the riverbank, forming a wedge of horsemen with him at its tip. The druchii riders, seeing their manoeuvre was discovered, threw off any pretence at subtlety, the disparate groups coming together and galloping for the river.

Laurena Starchaser's Reaver band joined Eldain's knights, and he waved to their flame-haired leader. He had met Starchaser the night before, her long limbs, auburn hair and strikingly angular features reminding him of a hunting bird. With both bands joined together, nearly two hundred warriors now rode to intercept the flanking riders.

The enemy had the lead on them, and reached the ford first, splashing into the river and striking for the far bank. The water reached up to their horses' necks as they crossed the ford, walking slowly but surely through the river. Eldain cursed that neither Lord Swiftwing nor Galadrien Stormweaver had thought to mention this ford. Forty riders had made the crossing already, and hundreds more were already halfway across.

Eldain nocked an arrow to his bow and let fly. The shaft pitched a druchii from his saddle, and a host of arrows flashed past Eldain to engulf the cloaked riders. Only a handful fell, for these riders were almost as nimble as his Reavers. Like the enemy warriors by the riverbank, these riders were armed with the deadly repeater crossbows, and swarms of deadly bolts were fired in return.

Eldain heard screams as his knights were struck, and loosed another shaft. His target swayed aside at the last moment, raising his crossbow and firing a pair of bolts in return. Eldain leaned low over Lotharin's neck as one bolt flew past his ear and the other ricocheted from the ithilmar boss on his mount's bridle. More of the dark-cloaked riders had gained the riverbank, enough to pose a threat, but not enough to out-number them.

Eldain slung his bow and raised both his arms, before spreading them out to the side. Both groups of Reavers split apart, Eldain's heading straight for the druchii, Starchaser's swinging around in a sweeping curve to come at them from the flank. Arrows and crossbow bolts sliced the air, and Eldain ducked and swayed in the saddle to avoid being struck.

The druchii charged out from the river, but Eldain's larger band of war-riors met them spear to spear. Warriors and horses screamed as the two hosts met in a clash of blades and flesh. The black horses of the enemy were vicious beasts, biting and butting heads with their Ellyrian cousins, but such steeds were not without their own fire. While the warriors in the saddle fought with spear and sword, the horses kicked their back legs and pawed the air with shod hooves to crush ribcages and pitch riders from their mounts.

Eldain thrust his spear into a druchii's belly, twisting the blade and pulling it clear before the suction of flesh could trap it. He slammed the haft into a screaming warrior's face, then reversed the weapon to open the throat of a crossbowman as he reloaded. His spear spun, stabbed, blocked and thrust, drawing blood, breaking bones and parrying slashing blows of swords. The noise of battle was incredible: grunting, snorting horses, shrieked calls of the murder god's name, and the shrill clash of blades and armour.

Lotharin bucked as a crossbow bolt sliced across his rump, cutting a long furrow, but not lodging. His back legs snapped out, cracking into the thigh of a druchii circling around him. The warrior howled as his femur was crushed, and he dropped the sword he had been about to plunge into Eldain's back.

'My thanks, old friend,' said Eldain, as Lotharin snorted in a way that perfectly captured an admonishment to watch his back.

Warriors swirled around each other in a chaotic, heaving mass of des-perate combat. There was little shape to the battle, simply horses and warriors weaving an intricate, formless dance around one another as they fought for a killing position. The Reavers were having the best of the fight, and many more of the black horses were without riders than the brown and silver horses of Ellyrion.

More of the dark-cloaked riders were crossing the river, but not in so great a number that gave Eldain the fear that they would be overwhelmed. His spear snapped as a druchii sword slashed down and took a chunk out of the haft. The lower half of the spear spun away, but Eldain grabbed what was left of the speartip and plunged the blade into the swordsman's heart. The broken weapon was wrenched from his hand, and he drew his sword as Starchaser's Reavers slammed into the battle.

Eldain's knights and the druchii had struck together, but Starchaser hammered into the druchii with all the power of an Ellyrian charge. Her warriors attacked with spears lowered like lances, and the druchii were skewered like meat on a spit. Picking out one horseman to strike in the midst of such a frenetic battle was a feat beyond any but the most skilled riders.

Child's play to an Ellyrian Reaver Knight.

Nearly a hundred of the druchii riders were killed in the first moments of the charge, and Eldain rode into the stunned survivors as they reeled from this sudden reversal. He killed three warriors in as many blows, and laughed with the primal ferocity of this fight as the druchii fell back in disarray towards the river. He rode after a fleeing warrior, and lanced his sword into his back. The druchii fell from the saddle, and Eldain saw the riders in mid-crossing pause as they realised the battle on the riverbank had been lost. They milled in confusion until a barking command was shouted and a hunting horn blew.

Eldain lifted his gaze to the far bank and his heart chilled as he saw the group of bolt throwers dragged there. The crews slammed home heavy magazines of bolts on the firing mechanism and worked the windlass in readiness to fire.

'Back!' shouted Eldain. 'Get back from the banks!'

The Reavers obeyed instantly, but even that was too slow, as the bolt throwers spoke with a whickering voice that filled the air with hundreds of black-fletched arrows. Elves and horses went down in the withering hail, dozens pierced by four or more shafts. Eldain turned Lotharin away, making him a smaller target. An arrow sliced over the skin of his neck and another struck him between the shoulder blades. The impact was painful, but his armour held firm and the arrow dropped free without piercing his skin.

Arrow-pierced horses flailed on the ground, screaming in pain and kicking their legs as the barbed tips of the arrows tore their flesh. Reaver Knights lay where they had fallen, many shot through the head and neck. Eldain and Lotharin galloped away from the riverbank as the bolt throwers' crew worked to unleash another volley.

Eldain saw Starchaser, her shoulder and hip streaming blood.

'We must yield the bank,' she cried.

'No,' said Eldain, riding alongside her and turning his horse. 'Enough of us remain to hold them here. We wait until the druchii gain the bank and then charge in again. They won't shoot while their own warriors are in the way. We can do this!'

'I do not doubt it, but if we do not pull back we will be cut off from the rest of the army! Look yonder to Korhandir's Leap!'

Eldain twisted in the saddle and saw the druchii warriors on the bridge fall back as bulky reptilian quadrupeds of dark scale and wide, fang-filled jaws lumbered onto Korhandir's Leap. Eldain knew of these creatures, called Cold Ones by their masters, but had never seen one in the flesh. Monstrously powerful, and ridden by tall warriors in plate of black and gold, their eyes were dull and listless, and frothed saliva drooled from between teeth like daggers. The druchii upon their backs carried long lances and their helms were fringed with flaring blade-wings.

'The warriors on the bridge will not be able to resist such a charge,' said Starchaser, and Eldain knew she was right. 'If we stay here, we will be trapped. Druchii to the left and right and the sea at our backs. Not a place any Ellyrian should find themselves.'

The idea of yielding the riverbank galled Eldain, but the idea of being trapped offended his Reaver Knight sensibilities even more.

He nodded and turned Lotharin back to Korhandir's Leap.

'Then we form a new line at the bridge,' he said.

The sounds of battle drifted over the centre of the elven line, the sounds tinny and distant, though blood was being shed and lives were being lost no more than a few hundred yards from where Menethis stood. A thick fog had gathered over the river to the north, obscuring the fighting until only the tips of the waystones atop the rounded hill could be seen.

Beyond Korhandir's Leap, a sprawling clash of horses raged, though Menethis could not tell who was in the ascendancy. He supposed the Ellyrians could, but even after his ride with them to harry the druchii vanguard, Menethis was still a foot soldier at heart. He preferred the ground beneath his feet as he fought, a longbow or sword as his weapons of choice.

Menethis stood in the front rank of the citizen levy of spear gathered by Lord Swiftwing, for the rank of sentinel had been bestowed upon him for his service at Eagle Gate. The two-hundred strong host was largely made up of warriors who had already lived a life of war and had hoped never to see another battle. Others had yet to see the ugly face of war, and it was these warriors Menethis was heartbroken to see arrayed in armour and bearing long-hafted spears. These were the young of Ulthuan, the hope for the future, the inheritors and shapers of the future.

Now there might not *be* a future for any of them.

As much as Menethis tried to remain optimistic about the coming fight, he found it difficult in the face of such a ferocious enemy that came in such numbers. To either side of his warriors were long lines of archers, resplendent in long cream robes over shirts of mail. Each archer in the front rank had emptied their quiver, placing their arrows in the ground before them, indicating that they would not run in the face of the enemy.

Their lines were thin, and would not stand long against a determined enemy charge.

Numerous spear hosts formed the centre of Lord Swiftwing's army, though the finest troops were positioned just behind the front lines. Stormweaver's Silver Helms looked magnificent in their polished ithilmar armour and gleaming helms, but there were only two hundred of them. Every warrior's helm was decorated with ribbons, gemstones or golden edging, indicating that these were the bravest of Lord Swiftwing's knights. Galadrien Stormweaver rode at their centre, his helm additionally embellished by swept-back eagle feathers of gold and white.

The enemy army was marching towards the river, and Menethis fixed his gaze on the disciplined ranks of druchii warriors directly across from him. They wore heavy hauberks of blackened iron and purple robes embroidered with fierce runic emblems of death. Bronze helms concealed their faces, and the fearsome swords resting on their shoulders marked them out as Executioners.

The weapons they carried were known as *draich*, killing blades forged in the blackest temples and blessed by priests of Khaine. Menethis had seen their skill with such executioners' swords on the walls of the Eagle Gate, and shivered at the bleak memory.

Behind these veteran warriors came something huge and crafted from bronze and jade, a towering effigy of murder and blades. A red-lit mist billowed around it, and hideous shrieks were carried on the wind alongside the bitter taste of iron. The red mist seeped out to envelop the Executioners, and their chants grew louder as they breathed in the sanguineous fog. Some drew their palms along the blades of their swords, while others reached up to touch their loathsome battle standard, a hateful icon with a grotesque mannequin chained to the upright and crossbars.

Its limbs jerked and twisted in a horrid parody of life, and Menethis turned away from the vile creation, but a broken voice called out to him from across the river. Suspecting some druchii trickery, Menethis paid the sound no mind, but it came again, and though it was the last gasp from a ruined throat there was a familiarity to the sound that was unmistakable.

He looked back at the Executioner's banner in horror as he realised it was no mannequin, but a living being nailed to timbers, one who had been horrifically disfigured through unimaginable torments only the insane could devise. His eyes had been put out, his limbs broken and every portion of his anatomy burned and flensed with skinning knives, yet this was a living being Menethis recognised.

It was Alathenar.

'Isha's mercy...' hissed Menethis.

The warriors to either side of him glanced over at his reaction, and Menethis knew he should reprimand them for such a lapse in focus, but he could not tear his eyes away from the horrors wrought upon the archer's body. How could he even know Menethis was here? Had he somehow sensed his former comrade's presence, or had he simply been repeating a familiar name ever since his capture?

The archer's lipless, toothless mouth worked up and down, crying out for Menethis, and he felt his heart moved to pity despite Alathenar's treachery. No one deserved such a fate, and Menethis pulled an arrow from his quiver and nocked it to his bow. He pulled back on the string, sighting down the length of the arrow, letting his breathing slow and imagining the path it would take. His focus shifted from the arrowhead to the mewling wreckage of the archer's body.

Menethis loosed between breaths, watching as his arrow arced out over the river. The point glittered in the weak sunlight as it slashed downwards. Alathenar turned what was left of his ravaged features to the sky, as though sensing his torment was about to end.

The arrow buried itself in Alathenar's throat, and the archer's head slumped over his chest as he died. A bawdy cheer went up from the Executioners, and Menethis hated that he had provided them any sort of pleasure.

'I give you peace, Alathenar,' Menethis said, 'but I do not forgive you.'

CHAPTER THIRTEEN

BLOOD OF ULTHUAN

The black ark filled the horizon, a shard of Ulthuan now filled with evil and twisted to serve the druchii. The castle fortresses worked into the cliffs had been abandoned as the black ark ground its way deeper into the straits, crushing them to rubble against the sea walls. Every warrior of Lothern now stood on the glittering ramparts of the Sapphire Gate, ready to face an army of druchii that drew closer with every breath.

Every day had seen the black ark draw nearer to the sea gate, but today would see it close enough for the killing to begin. Black clouds swirled in a vortex above it, spreading out over the mountains to either side like oil in water. Every now and then, Tyrion would catch fleeting glimpses of a monstrous winged form in the darkness, a figure in purple-limned armour astride its serpentine neck.

The Witch King himself had come to see Lothern humbled, and Tyrion longed for the chance to cross blades with the ancient foe of Ulthuan. The sea battered the cliffs of the black ark and crashed against its lower reaches, but what could the waves do to so towering an edifice as a mountain in so short a time? Tyrion felt the sea's anger as it sought to eject this thorn from the flesh of Ulthuan, and shared its frustration that it was powerless against it.

Powerless? No, that was not right.

He *could* have the power, but he chose not to wield it.

Tyrion gripped the hilt of Sunfang tightly, feeling the conflicting pulls on his heart as deep aches in his soul. His beloved Everqueen was beyond his sight in Avelorn, wounded and in need of his comfort, while Lothern would surely suffer greatly without his presence. Yet the greatest pull on his heart was that which turned his eyes to the north whenever his attention wandered or his focus slipped.

In those moments, he would see the storm-lashed isle in the cold, grey northern seas and feel the pull of that blood-bladed sword. Countless thousands had died over that hostile scrap of rock, their bones littering its desolate shale, their blood soaking its gritty black sand. All for possession of a weapon that could destroy the world. How ridiculous such a notion was. Why would anyone kill to possess a weapon that was doom incarnate?

Yet he *would* draw it and drive the druchii from Ulthuan if only he could be sure that he would set it back into the dripping altar as Aenarion had done. Tyrion knew he was strong, but was he strong enough to resist the lure of such a powerful weapon once it had been unsheathed? He didn't know, but the world would be a grimmer place were he to find out.

He heard someone call his name and shook off thoughts of the Blighted Isle.

'What?' he said.

'The island again?' asked Belannaer.

Tyrion nodded. 'Am I so transparent?'

'The Sword of Khaine is a mighty and terrible artefact,' said the Loremaster. 'And you are the greatest warrior of the asur. A hero of the line of Aenarion. Who else would it call to?'

Tyrion nodded towards the black ark as it ground its way along the straits of Lothern towards the Sapphire Gate.

'I fear what will happen if I do not answer its call,' said Tyrion. 'Yet my greater fear is of what will happen if I *do* answer it.'

'Then I am reassured,' said Belannaer. 'Only the foolish dream of such dangerous power, the wise know when not to meddle.'

'I am not wise, Sire Belannaer,' said Tyrion.

'You are wiser than you know, my friend.'

Tyrion shrugged, uncomfortable with such compliments, and said, 'Thank you, but I do not wish to speak of it further. Let us change the subject.'

'As you wish,' said Belannaer.

'Did my brother ask you to counsel me?'

Belannaer smiled. 'I am here to offer counsel to any who will heed it.'

'That's not an answer.'

'It is, just not the one you were looking for.'

'You mages and your secrets...'

'I keep no secrets, Tyrion,' said Belannaer. 'I am here as a representative of the White Tower. No more, no less.'

Tyrion said, 'Very well, I will press no further. But I would value any counsel you would give. Like how we will stop the druchii from sweeping over us when that rock is upon us.'

'You will stop them with heart and courage,' said Belannaer. 'Every warrior on this wall is looking to you to show them how a prince of the asur fights. Finubar may be king, but *you* are the one they would wish to be. Remember that as you fight.'

Tyrion shook his head. 'No one should wish to be me.'

'In this instance, the truth of *being* Tyrion does not matter, it is the *idea* of Tyrion that is paramount. Every warrior here knows of your exploits; the rescue of the Everqueen, the duel with Urian Poisonblade, and the battle against N'Kari. You are a hero, whether you see it or not, and you *must* live up to that ideal.'

'So the legend of Tyrion becomes more important than who I really am?'

'In this case, yes.'

Tyrion said nothing for a moment, then gave a mirthless chuckle. 'You do not offer comforting counsel, Loremaster.'

'I offer the truth,' said Belannaer, 'and that is sometimes unwelcome.'

Further discussion was prevented by the arrival of the Phoenix King and his retinue of White Lions. Korhil was easy to spot, his lion-pelted shoulders and braided hair bobbing above those of his fellow warriors. Finubar's scarlet armour shone like polished ruby, and he carried his helm in the crook of his elbow so that all might see his mane of silver-blond hair streaming in the wind coming in off the straits.

'My king,' said Tyrion with a curt bow.

'Tyrion,' said Finubar. 'And Sire Belannaer, I trust you and your mages stand ready to defend my city?'

'We do, my lord,' answered the mage, resting his hand on the pommel stone of the sword of Bel-Korhadris. 'With spell and with sword if need be.'

'Good, good,' said Finubar. 'If only all my subjects were so loyal.'

'Sire?' said Tyrion.

Finubar stood at the edge of the battlements, looking out at the dark clouds gathering above the black ark. Shards of lightning split the gathering gloom and the spread wings of a mighty dragon could clearly be seen silhouetted against the actinic light.

'We face Ulthuan's greatest foe, and yet there are those among my people who do not answer the call to fight. Prince Imrik seals himself in the volcanic caverns of the mountains and refuses to ride his dragon into battle. And messages to Eltharion are answered only by empty silence. I fear the Warden of Tor Yvresse has fallen too far into despair to lead his warriors in battle ever again.'

'I know Eltharion,' said Tyrion. 'He is a cautious warrior, it's true, but I cannot believe he will allow Ulthuan to fall without fighting in its defence.'

'Then perhaps you should go to Tor Yvresse and convince him to come,' snapped Finubar.

Tyrion shared a glance with Korhil at the Phoenix King's outburst, and the mighty White Lion gestured to the city behind the gate with his eyes. Far below, gathered in neat ranks on Lothern's quayside, a thousand grim-eyed warriors in pale white armour and cloaks of vivid scarlet edged with golden flames stood beneath a banner of a fiery phoenix.

Tyrion now understood the cause of Finubar's discomfort, for these were the Phoenix Guard, the silent guardians of the Shrine of Asuryan. It was said that within the temple was a forbidden vault known as the Chamber of Days, whereupon was inscribed the fates of every Phoenix King that had ever lived and ever would. The Phoenix Guard were privy to the secrets of time, and would arrive without warning to escort a newly-chosen Phoenix King to the fires of Asuryan.

Or carry a dead Phoenix King to his final rest.

The ice spread over the water like sickness from a wound. Issyk Kul's savage warriors charged onto the solid surface of the river, brandishing heavy axes and swords and screaming filthy chants to the Dark Gods. Their horned helms gave them the appearance of daemons, and Caelir knew that was very nearly the case. Every one of the mortals who lived in the frozen north was touched by the warping power of Chaos.

The warrior hosts of Tor Elyr fought the twisted beasts, rank upon rank of spearmen thrusting their sharpened points into the heaving mass of furred flesh over and over again. It was an unequal struggle, for their foes were many times stronger. But where the beasts fought as raging individuals, the asur host gave battle as a cohesive whole. In perfect unison, elven spears were withdrawn and then rammed forward, each time bathed in the unclean blood of the monsters.

The arrival of the tribesmen would tip the balance of this flanking battle, but Caelir would not let that happen. The ice had reached the near shore, and Caelir saw Anurion the Green and his mages fighting to hold back its spread down the length of the river. Anurion's magic caused fresh blooms of grass and flowers to rear from the water's edge as he brought forth the life-giving magic of Ulthuan, only for it to be withered by the cold and corruption of the dark magic from the tribal shamans.

This was an aspect of the battle Caelir could do nothing to affect, and he led his charging warriors onto the frozen surface of the river as powerful enchantments were woven, cast, countered and deflected. Any steeds other than Ellyrians would have slipped and fallen on the smooth ice, but there were no more sure-footed mounts in the world.

The tribal warriors saw his riders coming and loosed a wild cheer, as eager for the fight as the charging Reavers. Caelir tucked his spear into the crook of his arm and picked out the tribesman he would kill first. A barbarian wearing a bearskin cloak and a spiked helm lined with fur. His armour was crudely fashioned from lacquered leather and burned with a curving rune that brought bile to Caelir's throat.

The Reaver Knights smashed into the horde with a deafening clatter of blades. Caelir's spear punched into the tribesman's chest, tearing down through his heart and lungs before erupting from the small of his back. Caelir's spear snapped and he hurled away the broken haft. He drew his sword as Irenya smashed a path into the heaving mass of warriors. Blades flashed and blood sprayed the ice as the Reaver Knights wreaked fearsome havoc on the mortals. Armoured warriors slipped and went under the hooves of the Ellyrians, crushed against the diamond hard surface of the ice.

Irenya spun and kicked out as Caelir fought the northern tribesmen with the ferocity of a berserker. He heard elven voices calling his name, but he ignored them, driving his horse ever deeper into the sweating, stinking horde of savage mortals. Ahead, he could see Issyk Kul, his powerful form dwarfing those around him.

The warlord saw him coming and grinned with what looked like genuine pleasure, opening his arms as though welcoming home a prodigal son. Caelir screamed his hate and drove Irenya straight at the champion. Kul laughed and goaded his red-skinned beast towards Caelir. Both riders pushed their mounts hard, and as they passed, Caelir struck out with his sword, the blade slicing across the flesh of Issyk Kul. The warlord's skin was like iron, and Caelir's blade slid clear.

In return Kul's monstrous blade swept out and beheaded Irenya with a brutal overhead cut.

Caelir was hurled from the corpse of his mount as she crashed to the ice. He twisted as he fell, landing on his feet atop a fallen tribesman. Blood flooded from his headless steed, and he stared in horror at the twitching remains. Warriors surged forward, but Kul reined in his horse and waved them away. The raw-fleshed steed radiated heat, and the ice steamed with every step it took.

'You have returned to join us?' asked Kul, his voice wetly seductive, and Caelir wanted to laugh at the ridiculous question. Tears streamed from his eyes at Irenya's death, and he hurled himself at the warlord, oblivious to the swirling combats going on around him. Warriors were dying on the ice, *his* warriors, but all he could see was the gloating form of Kul as he loomed over Caelir's steed.

'You killed her!' screamed Caelir, charging at Kul.

The mounted warlord batted aside Caelir's clumsy attack and slammed an armoured boot into his face. Caelir reeled from the power of the blow as Kul dropped from his horse, the beast snarling and stamping the ground in its eagerness to trample him underfoot. Kul thrust his sword into the ice, a black malevolence radiating from the blade and into the ice.

'Why are you fighting me?' asked Kul. 'I made you what you are, little elf. Have you not realised that yet?'

Caelir spun on his heel, slashing for Kul's throat, but the blow struck the champion's armoured forearm as it came up to block. Kul's fist hammered Caelir's chest and something cracked inside. He dropped to one knee, struggling to catch a breath. Issyk Kul shook his head and reached up to remove his helm, hanging it from his saddle horn. The warlord retrieved his sword from the ice and swung it around his body, as though loosening up for a mildly diverting sparring session.

'You were nothing until we remade you,' hissed Kul, his repulsively handsome face more disappointed than angry. 'A pathetic life wasted on petty cruelties and dabblings on the fringes of true excesses. You called yourself free, but you were just as much a prisoner of the grey chains of life as the rest of your dull kind. I did you a favour, and you welcomed it.'

'No!' screamed Caelir, surging upright and stabbing his blade at Kul's groin.

Kul stepped aside and thundered his knee into Caelir's side. A right-cross slammed Caelir to the ice and his sword skittered away from him. He scrabbled across the ice to retrieve it. Kul followed him with long strides and grabbed him by the scruff of the neck.

Caelir twisted in his grip, but Kul was too strong for him.

'Pathetic,' sneered the warlord, and Caelir spat in his face.

Kul laughed and dropped him to the ice. 'That's more like it. Show me your hate and passions! Accept the ecstasies of the dark prince and you will know true freedom!'

Caelir's sword lay within his reach, and he swept it up, scissoring himself to his feet in a blur of motion. He stepped in and drove his blade into Kul's belly, but the blade snapped as though he had stabbed it into the side of a mountain.

'The dark prince protects his favoured sons,' sneered Kul at Caelir's attack. 'And if you choose to deny his seductions, then it is time to be rid of you.'

Kul's sword sang for Caelir's neck, its many blades glittering like icy shards of blood.

The chill winds blowing from the far bank carried the foul odour of the cold ones: rotting meat, stagnant water and oily, scaled bodies that shunned the light. It caught at the back of Eldain's throat and he retched at the rank, dead taste.

'Isha's mercy, how can they stand it?' he spat.

Eldain rode towards the crystal horses at the end of Korhandir's Leap in time to see the black knights thunder onto the bridge with terrifying speed as they dug razor-tipped spurs into the reptiles' flanks. The crystal bridge shook with the force of their charge, and the knights raised a crimson banner as they lowered their lances.

Arrows bounced uselessly from the scaled hides of the cold ones, spinning off into the dark waters of the river below. A shimmering skin of freezing fog crept across the water and Eldain saw that some of the arrows skittered across the surface of the river instead of sinking.

'The riders!' shouted Eldain. 'Kill the riders!'

His Reavers wheeled their mounts and stood tall in their saddles, bringing their bows to bear on these armoured knights. Flurries of arrows sped towards the black knights and a handful fell as particularly skilful or lucky archers found a gap between breastplate and helm, but it was not enough to stop the charge.

Eldain loosed a shaft at the exposed neck of a lancer. The arrow sliced deep into his flesh and the warrior toppled from the saddle. His mount snapped at the dangling corpse, biting it in two with one swipe of its jaws. Eldain sent another shaft into the knights, but this arrow ricocheted from a curved shield.

Perhaps a dozen knights were pitched from their saddles, but it was nowhere near enough to stop the charge from hitting home. The druchii heavy cavalry smashed into the bulwark of spears before them and the carnage was terrible. The sheer force of the impact obliterated the front two ranks of the asur battle line, their bodies crushed beneath the clawed feet of the reptilian monsters. Dark lances plunged home, punching screaming elves from their feet as the cold ones bit and tore at those who avoided the stabbing blades.

Eldain reined in his horse at the end of the bridge as blood-maddened cold ones rampaged amongst the dead. Despite the barbed spurs and goads of the black knights, the reptiles paused to gorge themselves on the warm meat laid before them like a feast. The bridge's defenders fell back from the slaughter, and only the shouted commands of the sentinel prevented the retreat from becoming a rout.

Though every fibre of his being wanted to ride onto the bridge, Eldain knew his lightly armed Reavers could not hope to stop the black knights. The broken ranks of infantry would need time to rally before marching back into the fray. Eldain's warriors could not give them that time, but help was coming from a different quarter.

Mitherion Silverfawn stood amid the flow of warriors from the bridge, his silver robes billowing in the cold winds coming off the river. A small band of mages and Sword Masters attended him, and even from here, Eldain saw Rhianna's father was gaunt and drawn, though the battle had only just begun. Eldain recognised one of Master Silverfawn's Sword Masters, and he nodded to Yvraine Hawkblade as she unsheathed her mighty greatsword.

Mitherion Silverfawn threw his arms out to the side before bringing his hands together in a mighty thunderclap. The booming echo of the sound was like the hammer of Vaul upon the anvil of the gods, and Eldain's heart was instantly transported to the days of heroes, when Aenarion and Caledor Dragontamer bestrode the fields of Ulthuan like gods. He hauled back on the reins as a surge of vitality and confidence pounded through his body like the war drums of ancient armies that might conquer the world. He felt as though he could slay every one of the black knights and their monstrous mounts single-handed, riding through them to Morathi herself and cleaving her fell heart in two.

Eldain reluctantly shook off the effects of Mitherion Silverfawn's magic, knowing it was too dangerous for his warriors to get drawn into such a fight. Fleetness of hoof was their greatest weapon, not charging headlong into heavily armed warriors riding killer beasts.

All around him, elven warriors who had moments ago been in full retreat now turned back to the twin piers of crystal horses at the end of the bridge. Light seemed to dance within them, like sunlight in ice, and every warrior felt their wise eyes upon him. They braced their spears and marched back onto the bridge, a cold and merciless fire burning in their eyes.

More warriors manoeuvred towards the bridge, as though drawn by the raw courage of the bridge's defenders. While the cold ones feasted on the flesh of the dead, the asur marched back onto the bridge with aching laments of Aenarion wrung from every throat.

The dark knights cursed and struck their mounts, but such tender morsels were a rare luxury to these monsters and no amount of threats could rouse them from their feast.

With a rousing war cry, the elven warriors charged into the dark knights, spears thrusting home with strength enough to penetrate mail shirts and iron plates. A score of knights died to the vengeful spears of the asur, and their reptilian mounts screeched with agony as long blades stabbed them repeatedly. The surviving knights saw the murderous determination in the eyes of their foes, and fell back before their grim resolve.

Yet even this would not be enough.

Druchii warriors, fresh to the fight, marched onto the bridge beneath a banner dripping in blood and emblazoned with the rune of Khaine. Their armour and cloaks were plum-coloured and their barbed spears were as black as their hearts. They charged past the slaughtered cold ones and fallen knights to hammer into the scattered spearmen in a clash of blades.

Centuries of bitterness gave the druchii strength, and their spears were red and bloody in moments. The enchantment of Mitherion Silverfawn was losing its power, and the magic that had steeled the hearts of the asur faded like the last rays of sunlight in winter. The fighting was desperate and bloody, shouts of anger and pain echoing from the sides of the bridge as the sundered kin of Ulthuan fought without thought of quarter or clemency.

Warriors from both sides fell to the freezing river below, and blood seeped through the bridge's rainholes as though Korhandir's Leap wept for the slaughter being performed upon its divinely crafted arches. The banner of the druchii pulsed with life, as though with a heartbeat of its own.

Eldain twisted in the saddle and sought out Mitherion Silverfawn amid the fog and marching warriors. At last he spied the mage's silver robes at the edge of the river, and he urged Lotharin through the press of bodies towards him. Silverfawn looked up as he approached and smiled weakly.

'Eldain,' he said. 'I am glad to see you alive.'

'Master Silverfawn,' said Eldain. 'Any aid you can give us would be most welcome. The bridge will not hold long, and there are druchii across the river to the south.'

'I feared as much,' said Silverfawn cryptically, but Eldain had no time to dwell on the mage's eccentricities.

'Can you help or not?'

The Sword Masters attending Silverfawn stepped forward, angered by his tone, but Yvraine held them back as the mage nodded.

'I can, Eldain,' said Silverfawn. 'But the bridge will fall, I have seen it in every reading of the stars.'

'You have seen the future?' asked Eldain.

'Parts of it, yes,' admitted Silverfawn. 'Enough to know that the bridge will fall, and that we must hold this line as long as possible. You understand, time and the future are not linear, but curved, yes? What will be has to be *made* in the present by our own deeds. We work to create the future, and thus nothing is certain.'

'I do not understand you, Master Silverfawn,' said Eldain. 'All I understand is that our people are dying here, and more will die if you do not help.'

'Not help? Of course I will help,' snapped Silverfawn, striding towards the end of the bridge with Yvraine's Sword Masters at his heels. 'As though I would not, the very idea!'

Eldain made to follow, but before he could urge Lotharin onwards, Laurena Starchaser rode next to him. Her hair was matted with dried blood and she had lost her spear somewhere along the way.

'The druchii are crossing the river in ever greater numbers,' she said. 'Heavy horse as well as the fast riders.'

Eldain swore. 'Our flank is turned.'

'The spear hosts at the southern edge of Tor Elyr are aligning to meet this new threat,' said Starchaser. 'But if the druchii take the bridge, we will have no choice but to fall back to the city itself.'

Eldain glanced at the bridge, remembering Mitherion Silverfawn's words. The bridge would fall, the mage had said, but if there was one thing Eldain had managed to take from his rambling words it was that nothing was set, nothing was ever inevitable.

'Gather thirty of your best riders and follow me, Laurena,' said Eldain.

'Where are we going?' asked Starchaser, even as she wheeled her mount.

'Onto the bridge!' cried Eldain, riding after Mitherion Silverfawn.

The Executioners crossed the river with heavy strides, though how such a thing could happen was a mystery to Menethis. In a land of endless summer, how could a river suddenly freeze? Red mist clawed up from the water's edge, and the heavily armoured warriors came up the slopes of the hills with their *draich* swinging in glittering arcs.

With the Executioners on this side of the river, Menethis finally saw the terrible effigy of bronze and jade on the opposite bank. A towering automaton of blades, it was a mechanical representation of the murder god himself, shaped by madmen and hellions with bare hands on molten metal. Blood streamed down the carven limbs and flowed in endless rivers from the serrated blades held in the statue's outstretched hands. That blood was collected in a vast bronze reservoir below, a blood-stained cauldron that hissed and spat with poisonous fumes, reeking of spoiled meat.

Chanting, slender-limbed elves with pale skin and near-naked bodies danced around the construction, and the blood of uncounted sacrifices made Menethis want to retch. The malign influence of the thing was potent, and stank of the blackest murder and sorcery.

Menethis tore his gaze from the hideous effigy as arrows slashed down upon the Executioners. Hundreds of shafts were loosed from archers positioned behind and on the flanks of the spear hosts. The red mist clung to the grim warriors, and many of the arrows were burned to ash before they struck home. Hideous beasts came behind the Executioners, draconic creatures with numerous reptilian heads atop serpentine necks, and disfigured abominations goaded by hunchbacked mortals.

Then the charge hit. A forest of stabbing spears punched through the armour of the Executioners' front rank, drawing blood and then ramming home again.

'Thrust!' cried Menethis, and the warriors behind him shouted as they drove their spears into the enemy ranks.

'Twist! Withdraw!'

Over and over Menethis shouted the mantra of thrust, twist and withdraw, but these cold-eyed killers had no fear of death. Fresh warriors stepped over the bodies of the slain, chopping spear heads from hafts or gripping the weapon that killed them with blood-slick hands and keeping it wedged in their bodies.

Grunts of pain came from the druchii, but no screams. These were tough, grim warriors who understood that pain was a warrior's lot and accepted it. Their blades hacked into the spear host, lopping heads and limbs with every stroke. The precision of their blows was extraordinary, honed over a lifetime of beheadings and executions in the name of Khaine.

Though his warriors fought magnificently, the Executioners were now living up to their name, hacking down rank after rank of Ellyrion's finest. Menethis understood the ebb and flow of a battle well enough to know when the courage of warriors was at its most brittle.

This was that moment, and there was nothing he could do to prevent it breaking.

The terror of the Executioners' blades became too much for his spear host, and they fled from their murderous strokes, breaking ranks and sprinting for the lines of archers behind them. They fled in ones and twos, all cohesion forgotten in the desperate flight for life. The Executioners cut down those not quick enough to flee, methodical to the last.

'Hold! Stand fast!' shouted Menethis, though it was far too late for mere words to keep the line from disintegrating. As his warriors fled, Menethis stood his ground before the black line of Executioners, his anger at what they had done here like a forest fire in his heart.

'You took Cerion, you took Glorien and now you come for me,' he said, calmer than he would have believed possible. His heartbeat was like thunder over the Annulii as he lifted his sword to his shoulder and charged towards the Executioners with the name of Asuryan upon his lips.

His sword slashed across an Executioner's chest, the blade sliding up under the cheek plate of the warrior's helmet to slice his face open. A flap of skin flopped down over his jaw, but still he did not scream. A sweeping two-handed blade arced towards Menethis's neck, but he leaned into the blow and rammed his sword through the eye slits of the Executioner's helm.

The warrior dropped with a strangled grunt, but another stepped over his corpse without pause and crashed the pommel of her sword into his forehead. Menethis reeled back, blood streaming down his face as the Executioner closed in for the kill.

He looked up through the visor of her helm. She had the most beautifully violet eyes.

Menethis tried to raise his sword, but the *draich* was too fast.

The thunder of his heartbeat swelled, but before the Executioner's blade parted his head from his shoulders, a silver lance punched her from her feet and lifted her high into the air. Thundering shapes of white and silver streamed past him, heavy horse armoured in ithilmar mail and caparisoned in ivory and gold.

Warriors clad in gleaming plate and high silver helms that shone like moonlight on still water rode these mighty steeds, and their lances and swords cut like lightning from the hand of Asuryan himself.

CHAPTER FOURTEEN
BREAKING POINT

Caelir had heard that at the moment of death, a person's life would flash before their eyes, but as Issyk Kul's sword swept towards him, he knew that was a lie. It was not the deeds of the life about to end that paraded through a mind, but the life unlived and the roads not taken.

He saw himself as lord of Ellyr-Charoi with Rhianna at his side, and children playing in the meadows beyond. Horses filled the stables and summer's calm lay upon the hillsides. In the space of a single heartbeat, Caelir saw the joys, the tears and the absurdities of existence that make up the rich pageant of lives intertwined. Eldain was there too, his brother sat astride Lotharin as he rode the endless plains of Ellyrion with a song in his heart.

It was fiction, a dream of a future that never was and never could be, but it gave him a moment's comfort in this last breath of life left to him. Caelir closed his eyes, but instead of death, he heard an earthy sound like a Chracian's axe biting fresh wood.

Standing before him was a glistening tree trunk, and embedded in the wood was Issyk Kul's monstrous sword. Ice and water ran from its branches, and the sweet smell of new sap filled Caelir's nostrils as it poured like amber blood from where Kul's blade had hacked into it. The ground creaked beneath Caelir, and he saw the splintered hole in the ice where the tree had burst through the ice covering the river's surface.

Kul wrenched his sword from the soft wood, and Caelir sprang away as the ice bucked and heaved beneath him. Jagged black cracks split the ice, racing away in zigzag courses from the new roots and branches pushing their way up from below. An entire forest was rising from the depths of the river, growing with incredible ferocity.

'Life magic!' hissed Kul, as though the presence of such things were anathema to him.

Caelir was astounded, and scrambled away from this burgeoning forest as the ice heaved and split apart. This was no passive greenery, but aggressive growth like the ancient forest trees said to dwell within the forgotten heart of Athel Loren. Jagged roots speared up into the tribesmen, piercing their flesh and growing up through their bodies.

He lost sight of Issyk Kul as spreading branches ensnared terrified warriors and looped around limbs to tear them off with wrenching heaves of growth. Scores of armoured tribesmen were lifted from the ground and impaled upon sharp, new-grown wood or ripped in two by spreading branches. Within moments, a thick forest of dripping trees had arisen from the river, and hundreds of torn bodies hung from their branches like corpses in gibbets.

Nor was the threat of the forest the only danger.

As roots burst the ice, a measure of the sorcery holding the water in its frozen state was unravelled, and screaming warriors dropped through into the river. In the midst of this rampant fecundity strode a mage in emerald robes that swirled in the billowing streams of magic that spiralled around him like a caged whirlwind.

'Anurion!' cried Caelir.

The mage ignored him and strode into the howling mass of tribesmen. His arms wove complex patterns, and where he gestured new life erupted from the ground to entangle, to stab and to tear. The river became a thick forest, dense with dark trees and overhanging boughs of thorny wood. So complete was Anurion's mastery of life-giving magic that it mattered not that thick sheet ice lay between him and the touch of earth.

Baying and blooded tribesmen who had escaped the slaughter of the rampaging forest threaded a path through the trees towards the mage. A throwing axe was turned aside by the swaying branches of a willow, and a hurled spear changed in flight to become a twisting sapling that spun harmlessly away. A raven-fletched arrow sliced into Anurion's thigh, and blood stained his robes with vivid scarlet.

A tribesman in a wolf-faced mask hurled himself at Anurion. The mage pointed a finger at him, and the branch of a tree lashed out to take his head off with the precision of a rapier. More closed in, and the forest defended its creator, grasping roots dragging men beneath the river and long saplings slashing like razor-edged whips to open throats and remove limbs.

Yet it had cost Anurion dear to raise a forest from the depths of the river, and already its rapid growth was slowing. Caelir took up a fallen spear from the body of a slain Reaver Knight and half ran, half slipped towards Anurion.

The mage saw him and shook his head.

A wall of thorns and thick, grasping briars arose, completely blocking Caelir's path towards Anurion.

'No!' shouted Caelir. 'Anurion! Come back!'

Caelir's voice was lost in the bellows of the mortal warriors, and tears stung his eyes at the thought of the line of Anurion the Green being ended forever. No sooner had the thought arisen, than a spectral voice sounded in his mind.

So long as one blade of grass or flower blooms in Ulthuan, I will live on.

Caelir tore at the jagged coils of briars. The thorns, recognising one of their own, turned their barbs from his skin.

'Anurion, no!' he yelled. 'Please! Come back to us!'

Make them pay, Caelir. That is all I ask, make them pay…

Caelir nodded and turned from the sheets of briars, weeping and stumbling over the disintegrating ice towards the riverbank. Reaver Knights rode back to solid ground as yet more of the ice cracked and came away from the riverbank. He leapt as the ice beneath him retuned to water, breathless and grief-struck at the loss of Anurion.

He took a heaving breath and reasserted a measure of control. Anurion was gone, and that was a grievous loss, but the battle had yet to be won. Caelir turned and ran to where his Reaver Knights awaited him. Around sixty still lived, and he vaulted onto the back of a bay mare with a silver mane and midnight black tail.

'I am Caelir Éadaoin of Ellyr-Charoi, and I grieve with you for the loss of your rider,' said Caelir, 'but if you will have me, I will be your brother in this fight. What say you?'

The mare tossed her mane and stamped the ground in assent, and Caelir rubbed a hand over her neck as a name appeared in his thoughts.

Liannar.

'I will be a loyal companion, Liannar,' he promised as his knights formed up around him.

The northern flank of Lord Swiftwing's army was still holding. Remorseless spear hosts drove the bestial monsters that had first crossed the river back to the water's edge. A combination of unending arrows dropping from above and elven stoicism had prevailed, and the beasts were being slaughtered in ever greater numbers.

The mist was clearing, and Caelir saw the summit of the rounded hill and its marble crown of waystones. As the conjured mist dissipated still further, the bolt throwers unleashed a hail of arrows into the druchii forces massing on the far bank of the river. Caelir wheeled Liannar southwards, shielding his eyes from the low sun to gauge how the rest of the army fared.

The ground to the north of Tor Elyr sloped gently down towards the bay, levelling out to a wide plain to the south, and Caelir's jaw clenched as he saw the druchii had crossed the river south of the city. The army's centre was bending back like a bowyer testing the strength of a bow stave, but Galadrien Stormweaver's Silver Helms were fighting hard to give the infantry time to rally and reform the battle line.

The Reavers around him saw what he saw, and he sensed their dismay at the ring of blades closing in on Tor Elyr like a hangman's noose. If the centre broke, then this battle was as good as over. He saw that same realisation on every face around him, and knew that the courage of his warriors hung by a thread.

Caelir rode out before the Reavers around him, and turned his horse to face them. More scattered horsemen rallied around his warriors, until hundreds were ready to listen.

'This battle is *not* lost,' he shouted. 'The druchii have crossed the river, but the centre still holds and Stormweaver's Silver Helms are fighting to keep it so. We hold the north, and Anurion the Green gave his life that we might continue to do so! The enemy will attempt another crossing, and it is up to us to stop them. Either we stop them or Tor Elyr is lost. We fight here, or we die elsewhere. It is that simple.'

He lifted his spear and Liannar reared up on her hind legs.

'We are Ellyrians, and this is our land!' yelled Caelir. 'Are you ready to fight for it?'

Hundreds of spears stabbed the air, and a wordless Ellyrian war cry echoed across the water and corpse-thronged forest to their enemies. Caelir turned Liannar back to the riverbank as the icy mist once again crept across the water to freeze its surface.

A war horn sounded from the opposite side of the river.

Far to the north a glittering curtain of light shimmered on the horizon, and a sparkling rain fell beneath a rainbow's arch like diamond tears.

'Isha be with us,' said Caelir.

Tyrion dived beneath a slashing line of iron barbs loosed from a bolt thrower situated on a craggy bluff of the black ark and rolled to his feet with Sunfang held out before him. The entire length of the Sapphire Gate was swathed in the shadow of the vast, seaborne fortress, its monstrous bulk finally wedged deep in the rocks of the straits some thirty yards from the sea portal. Heavy iron corvus ramps slammed down on the ornamented battlements, and druchii swordsmen poured from inside the hellish mountain.

Asur warriors stood frozen in death alongside him, their bodies turned to glassy ice by the bleak sorceries of the druchii magickers. One body lay shattered into crystalline fragments beneath the spiked end of a boarding ramp, like a marble statue struck by a sledgehammer. Tyrion leapt onto the iron ramp bridging the gap between the black ark and the Sapphire Gate as warriors in scaled cloaks like dragonhide charged at him with curved sabres and cutlass daggers unsheathed. Tyrion ran to meet them, his golden-bladed sword cleaving through the first three attackers in as many strokes. Crossbowmen took shots at him from rocky bluffs high above the ramp, but Tyrion was always in motion, ducking, spinning, leaping and lunging.

Many of their bolts hit their fellow druchii, sending them falling thousands of feet to the churning waters below. The ramp swayed and bounced with the weight of bodies upon it, and Tyrion used its motion to help him dodge the clumsy blows of his enemies. Yet he was only a single warrior, while the druchii were many, and time and time again, he found himself having to take a backwards step to avoid being flanked.

'Asur!' he yelled, vaulting back onto the battlements of the Sapphire Gate.

'Ho!' came the shouted reply, and a score of goose-feathered shafts sliced home into the attacking druchii. He watched as warriors were pitched from the ramp, falling like flower seeds blown from a gardener's hand. Elven warriors took up position at the end of the ramp, hacking at the stonework with heavy hammers and axes to dislodge the penetrating spikes.

Belarien was at his side a heartbeat later, a bent bow in his hand as he pulled the string taut. He loosed and another druchii was punched from the ramp.

'Must you always run off on your own?' hissed Belarien. 'It makes it much harder to keep you safe.'

Tyrion gave a wry smile. 'You must be getting old, my friend. You never had any trouble keeping up with me at Finuval.'

'I was young and foolish back then,' said Belarien. 'Now I am just foolish.'

'We are all foolish, else we would not be warriors, but poets and dreamers.'

'If only life gave us the chance, eh?'

'If only,' agreed Tyrion, as the ramp was broken loose from the ramparts. It dropped from the walls, but heavy chains looped around iron rings stopped it from falling too far. A grinding windlass mechanism within the ark started turning, and the ramp began to rise, ready for more druchii to pour across it in yet another attack. A dozen ramps disgorged hundreds of druchii onto the Sapphire Gate, and the fighting on its glittering structure was fierce indeed. Flights of arrows and swarms of bolts cut the air back and forth, and streams of magical fire lit up the unnatural darkness as Belannaer's mages burned the rock of the black ark to glass.

In return, freezing winds swept the Sapphire Gate as the Witch King's sorceries sucked the life from the elven defenders, and writhing tendrils of darkness snaked up over the walls to drag screaming warriors to their doom. The vast brazier atop the black ark bathed the battle in a hellish orange glow, and each battle was fought in its leaping shadows.

Like a single colossal siege tower, the black ark unleashed thousands of druchii onto the Sapphire Gate in an onrushing tide. Finubar's warriors had fought off every attack thus far, but all it would take was one boarding ramp to capture its part of the ramparts for the defenders to lose control of the gate.

Tyrion scanned the fighting, looking for any weaknesses the druchii could exploit.

At the meeting point of the two halves of the sea gate, he saw Finubar's crimson armour amid a brutal swirl of daggers, axes and barbed shields. Korhil fought beside the Phoenix King, his enormous axe cleaving druchii in two with every blow. Those he could not strike with his axe, he picked up and hurled from the battlements.

A pair of ramps hammered down on the ramparts to either side of the Phoenix King, and Tyrion immediately saw the danger.

'Belarien, with me!' he yelled, and ran towards the centre.

Tyrion sprinted through the morass of struggling warriors, ignoring all but the most pressing dangers. He cut and slashed as he ran, killing the enemy even as his attention was focussed on the Phoenix King. Druchii warriors poured down these new ramps, cutting the king off from his warriors.

Tyrion felt his sword grow hot in his hands and swept it around in a wide arc, holding it two-handed and unleashing a brilliant ray of fiery sunlight from its blade. It cut through the druchii, setting light to their dragonscale cloaks and melting the flesh from their bones. Burning warriors screamed in agony and hurled themselves from the sea gate to the waters below, while others sagged on heat-softened bones to fall in pools of molten skin and liquefied organs.

The screaming was terrible, and the stench even worse, but Tyrion felt nothing for the warriors he killed. They were his enemies. They had attacked his homeland and his people, and deserved no more. Tyrion ran through the flame and blackened lumps of crackling meat, Sunfang now cold in his grip. The heat of his sword's fire hazed the air, and a druchii warrior appeared before him, his skin blackened and his armour fused to his skin in glossy black runnels. Tyrion took his head off without missing a step and ran to where he heard the bellows of the White Lions.

A sharp metallic flavour bit the air, and Tyrion tasted the taint of sorcery. Heat gave way to cold in an instant, and Tyrion pulled up short at the shock of it. It billowed out like debris from a falling star, and Tyrion dropped to one knee as it blew over him. Freezing fog enveloped the centre of the sea gate, and flash-formed icicles hung like ice dragon teeth from the overhanging machicolations.

The sounds of battle faded to silence, and Tyrion forced himself to run into the icy mist. The marble flagstones were slippery with ice, and as Tyrion came upon the fighting, it was akin to entering the winter gardens of Lothern at festival time. The mages of Saphery would amaze visitors to their gardens with startlingly lifelike creations fashioned from ice that could move and interact with the patrons.

Except the figures that populated the ramparts were not simple creations of water, they were living beings.

Or they *had* been…

The White Lions stood frozen in place, layers of frost coating their thick pelts like icing on a feast cake. Their skin was translucent and ghostly, their veins vivid red and blue against the white. Frozen arcs of crimson curved from the edges of weapons and wounds spilled blood in a frozen tableau.

In the centre of the frozen scene was Finubar, the brilliant red of the Phoenix King's armour ice-dusted white and blue. Before the king, frozen in mid-leap, was Korhil, his powerful frame draped in icicles and crackling webs of frost like spider webs.

'Isha's mercy!' cried Tyrion, weaving a path through the frozen figures towards the king.

Beyond the icy figures, Tyrion saw druchii hacking a path towards the king with heavy-bladed felling axes. The targets of their axes shattered and fell to the ramparts with glassy cracks, and Tyrion felt his smouldering anger turn to incandescent rage.

A druchii axeman smashed a frozen White Lion aside, but died a heartbeat later as Tyrion buried his sword in his chest. Tyrion kicked the axeman from his blade and leapt to intercept the others. He could hear shouted voices behind him, but dared not take his eyes from the druchii warriors facing him. Cold-eyed and thin-lipped, they wielded their heavy executioner's blades as easily as a child would swing a wooden sword.

An axe swung past him, missing his ear by a hair's breadth, and he jumped back, almost losing his footing on the ice. He turned that slip into a spin, bringing Sunfang up into his attacker's midriff. The warrior grunted and dropped to his knees, his glistening entrails steaming in the cold air.

Arrows whickered through the frozen statues of the White Lions, carefully aimed and lethally accurate. Tyrion knew Belarien's warriors would no sooner hit him than they would the Phoenix King, and fought the druchii as arrows passed fingerbreadths from his body.

'Come on and die!' he yelled, when the axemen hesitated.

Tyrion saw their cruel smiles and, in that moment, knew their attack had been but a diversion. He turned and ran back towards the Phoenix King in time to see a black-cloaked figure land on the ramparts with finesse that spoke of only one possible profession.

'Assassin!' yelled Tyrion.

The hooded figure drew a black dagger from an iron sheath and ran towards the Phoenix King. Arrows sliced by him as he moved like liquid, twisting, swaying and leaping over every incoming shaft. Tyrion sprinted towards the assassin, though he was too far away to save the Phoenix King. The black dagger came up and Tyrion screamed Finubar's name.

As the weapon plunged down, another warrior leapt in front of the

Phoenix King. Mail links parted before the blade, and blood squirted as it twisted in the wound. Tyrion screamed as he saw Belarien fall at the Phoenix King's feet, his heart pierced by the assassin's dagger. The black hood fell away from the killer's face, a wholly unremarkable face that would pass unnoticed in a crowd and leave no impression upon anyone who saw him.

The assassin wrenched the dagger free of Belarien's chest and turned back to the Phoenix King. Tyrion drew back his arm, ready to hurl Sunfang in a last ditch attempt to prevent the assassin from carrying out his mission.

Before he could throw, a cracking sound like a gallery of windows breaking echoed over the gate, and a mighty, frost-hardened fist swung around to slam into the assassin's shoulder. Korhil of the White Lions shrugged off the last of the ice encasing him in an expanding mist of ice shards, his fury like that of the beast whose pelt he wore upon his shoulders. The black-cloaked killer twisted at the last moment to rob the blow of its power, and spun around Korhil. The black dagger stabbed out again, and Korhil grunted as it was withdrawn bloody.

The White Lion staggered against the parapet as the assassin moved in to finish him. Before the dagger could stab home again, Korhil surged forward and wrapped his arms around the assassin, dragging him into a crushing bear hug. The killer fought to free his arms, but the champion of the White Lions kept them pinned at his sides and exerted every ounce of his legendary strength.

Tyrion heard something give way with a sickening crack, and the assassin went limp in Korhil's arms. The White Lion released the assassin, who fell to the ground like a limp marionette. Korhil picked him up by the scruff of the neck and swung the corpse around to dangle it over the edge of the sea gate.

'You nearly made me fail,' he growled. 'And I *never* fail.'

With those words, Korhil hurled the assassin out to sea, watching as the body bounced and flopped down the craggy sides of the black ark to the hungry waters below.

Tyrion ran past Korhil, and skidded to a halt beside Belarien's limp form.

His friend was dead, of that there could be no doubt. Whatever venom had coated the assassin's blade had been deadly enough to slay him a dozen times over. Belarien's face was slack, his limbs already cold, and Tyrion felt a lifetime's rage coalesce in his heart.

A crushing hand gripped his shoulder and pulled Tyrion to his feet.

He lashed out, but a wide palm caught his fist.

'Grieve later, young prince,' said Korhil, releasing Tyrion's hand and shaking the last of the icy sorcery from his limbs. 'We have greater enemies to face now.'

Tyrion looked at the White Lion through a mask of tears. Korhil's face was ashen from the after-effects of sorcery and the assassin's venom, and how he had not succumbed to their effects was beyond Tyrion's ability to understand.

'He saved Finubar's life,' said Tyrion.

'Aye, that he did,' agreed Korhil. 'And he will be remembered for his sacrifice. But this fight isn't over yet, not by a long way. Look!'

Tyrion followed Korhil's outstretched axe, and saw the midnight black form of a mighty dragon swooping overhead. Its scaled body glistened like obsidian, and the warrior astride its neck was encased in armour of curved black plates, spines and barbed horns. Flares of dark magic slicked the air around the Witch King, and he threw searing purple lightning from his hands as he flew over the sea gate. Explosions of actinic light swept the sea gate, and elven warriors were hurled to their deaths or burned to cinders where they stood.

'Malekith,' hissed Tyrion, but Korhil gripped his arm before he could charge off to face the Witch King.

'Unhand me, Korhil,' demanded Tyrion.

'We'll get to the traitor king in good time, young prince,' said Korhil, turning him around as an adult might turn a child. 'We have other druchii to gut first.'

The druchii axemen were surging forward in the wake of the assassin's failure, hacking a path through the frozen figures of Korhil's White Lions. The sorcery that had frozen them in place was wearing off, and these warriors screamed as the axe blades cleaved them. Tyrion forced his grief at Belarien's passing aside, and distilled the fury raging within him down to a diamond-hard core of utter clarity of purpose.

He swept Sunfang up to his shoulder and nodded to Korhil.

Before they could charge to meet the axemen, a flurry of arrows arced down from the rocks on the eastern side of the gate. Each one found its mark with uncanny accuracy, dropping an axeman with a single arrow to the throat. A single volley of arrows had felled two score armoured warriors.

'Blood of Aenarion!' swore Korhil. 'Where did those arrows come from?'

Tyrion squinted through the gloom to see who had loosed these incredible arrows, but could see nothing. It was as though the cliff itself had let fly.

Then he glimpsed movement, but it was movement he saw only because the warrior making it *wanted* him to see it. Almost invisible against the rocks of the straits, Tyrion saw an archer clad in slate grey and gorse green, with a dun cloak pulled tightly around his body. He wore a conical, face-concealing helm of burnished bronze and silver, and Tyrion knew of only one group of warriors who went to war so attired.

'The rangers of Tor Yvresse!'

'But how can they be here?' said Korhil. 'Unless…'

From the darkened sky came a screeching roar, and a powerful beast with the hindquarters of a jungle cat and the upper body of a ferocious beast of prey stooped from the storm clouds wreathing the upper reaches of the black ark. Its wide wings were feathered gold and brown, and its powerful beak was the colour of ebony and mahogany. Sat in a heavy leather saddle on the griffon's back was an elven warrior clad in golden, gem-encrusted armour and a winged helm of white and blue feathers. He unsheathed a rune-encrusted longsword that broke the darkness like a fang of silver light, and even over so great a distance Tyrion could see the grim set to the warrior's features.

'Eltharion has come!' shouted Tyrion.

Korhandir's Leap was slick with blood. Druchii spearmen shouted with every thrust of their spears, pushing the bridge's defenders back with every step. Barbed spears bit flesh and tore armour, and even a touch of their blades was agony, for they snagged skin and ripped wounds wider.

A thin line of elven warriors was all that stood before the druchii, and Eldain could sense their despair as they took yet another step backwards. The rippling blood banner writhed upon its cross pole, as though feeding on the carnage being wrought in its shadow. Ghostly laughter drifted at the edge of hearing, and Eldain tasted bile in the back of his throat as he rode through the terrible sprawl of ruptured bodies.

The bodies of slain elves lay together in death, and if it were not for their armour it would have been impossible to tell asur from druchii. That thought alone made Eldain want to weep, for what had divided them all those thousands of years ago but one individual's arrogance and lust for power? Could such a sin be worth thousands of years of war and death? That his race, so proud and aloof and superior had allowed themselves to be caught up in such a terrible cycle of hatred astounded Eldain.

We make lofty claims to be an elder race, greater than any other, yet we hold to ancient wrongs like spoiled children...

Ahead, Mitherion Silverfawn strode to the centre of the bridge, streamers of raw magic feathering the air with translucent fire. The mage walked with purposeful steps, and the cloaks of the dead flapped and billowed in his wake. Eldain felt the build up of powerful magic, and urged Lotharin to greater speed.

The line of elven spearmen finally broke, and they turned to flee before the triumphant druchii. The hideous banner cackled gleefully as black-bladed spears stabbed and spilled yet more blood. A host of druchii warriors broke from the ranks and ran towards Mitherion Silverfawn, eager to claim so valuable a trophy. Yvraine's four Sword Masters stepped to meet them with their great, silver blades looping around them in shimmering arcs. Trained and schooled by the Loremasters of the White Tower, the Sword Masters fought with a grace and precision the likes of which even legendary heroes like Laerial Sureblade or Nagan of Chrace would have struggled to match.

Yvraine and her fellow warriors wove a silver path of destruction through the druchii, slaying any who came near Mitherion Silverfawn with graceful strokes of their blades. They wielded their mighty swords with an ease that only decades of training could provide, ducking, swaying and leaping over the weapons of their enemies like acrobats. In less than a minute two score druchii lay dead, cut to pieces with contemptuous ease.

Seeing that the Sword Masters would not be taken by such futile heroics, the druchii line advanced en masse with their barbed spears lowered. But the Sword Masters had no intention of fighting an entire battle line of spears. Without any command being spoken, Yvraine moved her warriors behind Mitherion Silverfawn as he unleashed the full power of his magic.

A coruscating stream of blue fire poured from his outstretched hands to engulf the druchii. Iron weapons melted, flesh boiled from bones and the screams of the enemy warriors were mercifully brief. Shrieking bodies tumbled from the bridge, blazing fireballs that not even the waters of the river could extinguish. The banner of writhing blood went up like an oil-soaked rag, an incandescent plume of fire that screamed like a child as it died.

The druchii line collapsed as the dozens of warriors disintegrated like ashen statues, and the cries of terror that came from those who saw their comrades immolated was music to Eldain's ears. The druchii reeled as the cackling blue flames danced over the crystalline structure of the bridge, and Eldain spun his spear up to point at the druchii.

'Now, Starchaser!' he yelled. 'With me! For Ulthuan and the Everqueen!'

Lotharin leapt forwards, and Eldain clung tight to the reins as his faithful mount carried him over the smouldering, blackened ruin of the druchii. Starchaser's Reavers followed him, a thundering wedge of vengeful horsemen with lowered spears. The druchii saw them coming, but their line was scattered and broken, easy meat for cavalry.

The Reavers punched into the reeling druchii, spears thrusting and swords slashing. Eldain stabbed his spear through the neck of a warrior whose armour and cloak smouldered with blue flame. Even before the druchii fell, Eldain was moving on, plunging the leaf-shaped blade into the panicked mass of enemy warriors. A sword sliced up at him, but Lotharin sidestepped and lashed out with his hooves, hurling the druchii champion from the bridge.

The druchii fled from the blades of the Reavers, but there was no mercy to be had, and no way to escape the speed of an Ellyrian steed. None survived to reach the end of the bridge. Eldain circled his horse as Mitherion Silverfawn waved to him. The mage's skin was pallid and his features drawn by the expenditure of such powerful magic. Unleashing the fiery conflagration had cost him dear.

'Eldain, you should not be here!' said Mitherion.

'And yet I am,' countered Eldain. 'You still think the bridge will fall?'

'I *know* it will,' said Mitherion in exasperation. 'Do you think something as obvious as a charge of the Reaver Knights would prevent it? Look, the druchii are already gathering crossbows and swordsmen.'

Eldain swore as he saw the truth of Mitherion's words. Hundreds of druchii were moving towards Korhandir's Leap, bearing spears, crossbows, and swords. Too many for their small Reaver band to fight.

'Our charge was glorious,' said Laurena Starchaser, riding alongside and voicing Eldain's fear, 'but we will not hold against so many without more warriors.'

Eldain turned to Mitherion Silverfawn. 'Is your magic spent?'

'Not yet, but what power I have left will not keep the druchii from crossing.'

'More warriors will come,' said Eldain. 'We will hold the druchii here until they do.'

Mitherion shook his head. 'If you stay on this bridge you will die. You must ride!'

'Retreat?' said Eldain. 'After we fought to drive the druchii away?'

'I did not say retreat,' said Mitherion. 'I said ride. Ride on, Eldain, it is the only way!'

'Ride on? Into the druchii army? Have you lost your mind?'

Mitherion gripped Eldain's hand, and he felt the coruscating heat of the magic fire within the mage. Eldain saw the desperation in Mitherion's eyes, the aching need to be believed.

'Trust me, Eldain, you must cross the river and destroy the red giant,' said Mitherion. 'It is the only way you live.'

'Red giant? What are you talking about?' said Eldain, snatching his hand back and turning Lotharin towards the druchii. At least five hundred warriors were marching towards the bridge, a force many times beyond what he would ever think of riding straight towards. He saw no red giant among them, and wondered what foolishness had taken hold of the mage.

He caught Starchaser's eye, and she gave an almost imperceptible nod of acceptance. Whatever he ordered, she and her riders would obey.

'Death surrounds us,' she said. 'One way to face it is as good as another.'

'Better to face it head on then,' said Eldain.

Ithilmar-tipped lances split the Executioners apart. Caparisoned in blue and white and gold, the Silver Helms of Galadrien Stormweaver smashed through the close packed ranks of the heavily-armoured druchii. Bravest of all the riders in Ulthuan, the Silver Helms were called headstrong by some, reckless by others, but all agreed that they were the most magnificent warriors of the land. Only the Dragon Princes of Caledor could lay claim to superiority, but such was the arrogance of those riders that their boast was largely discounted, save by those who had seen them in battle.

Stormweaver leaned hard into the stirrups and drove his lance through the breastplate of a druchii warrior. The blade tore free of his victim and he lined up another target. The druchii swept his unwieldy sword around in an effort to smash the head from Stormweaver's lance, but it was a move of desperation. He looped the lance tip around the *draich* and its tip plunged into the warrior's belly. Stormweaver lifted the screaming warrior off the ground, letting his own weight tear him from the blade, and enjoying the sound of his scream.

The Silver Helms bludgeoned their way through rank after rank of druchii, and Stormweaver saw a banner go down, trampled into the mud beneath his clarion's horse. The white mounts of the Silver Helms were bred to be stronger than almost any other horse in Ulthuan, and fought with as much pride and power as their riders.

The Executioners fought back, and Stormweaver had to grudgingly admit that they were not without skill. He saw Irindia plucked from his horse by a well-aimed strike to the belly, and Yeledra thrown to the ground as her horse was beheaded in a single stroke. These were just the last gasps of hate, not real courage, and they were far too late to alter the outcome of this charge. Scores of druchii were ground to smashed bone and ground meat beneath the hooves of the Silver Helms' mounts, and those few that remained were aghast at such swift slaughter.

Onwards the Silver Helms plunged into the druchii, killing with every yard gained from the lofty heights of their saddles. Gods of the battlefield, the Silver Helms slew and crushed all before them, revelling in their pre-eminent power and skill. The noise was incredible, like a drunken mortal hammering every plate of metal in a smith's forge with clumsy missteps.

An Executioner leapt to meet him, sword swinging low for his horse's legs. His steed leapt over the blow, lashing out with its hind legs to shatter the druchii's skull with a sharp blow from its hooves. Another cloaked druchii stabbed his murderous blade towards Stormweaver's chest, but a jink of the reins stepped him away from the blow. Too close for a lance strike, Stormweaver released the reins and drew his sword in one, fluid motion. He wheeled his horse in around the Executioner and slashed his blade down onto his neck, hacking down past the druchii's collarbone and into his lungs.

The Executioners could take no more and turned to flee from the silver horsemen in their midst. Some threw down their weapons to aid their escape, whilst others clung to them in the mistaken belief that they would live to fight with them again.

What had, moments before, been a desperate struggle of blades now became a slaughter as the Executioners fled from the storm of blades and lances. But their flight only brought more doom down upon their heads. Dozens were hacked down in the first moments of their panic, others run down beneath the heavy horses of the Silver Helms, yet more skewered on the tips of still-sharp lances.

As much as he loved the moment of the charge, this was the moment Stormweaver relished the most; riding down a defeated foe. Every horseman dreamed of the enemy broken and fleeing before him, easy prey to the glorious rider with fire in his heart. The Silver Helms ran amok, slaying and laughing and singing as they unleashed furious wrath upon their dark kin.

Stormweaver pictured his warriors pursuing the druchii all the way back to Eagle Gate and beyond. Riding over them until only a handful remained alive to reach their black ships on the coast.

'No mercy!' shouted Stormweaver. 'Drive them into the river!'

The Silver Helms followed his lead and broke apart into hunting groups as they slew the druchii with wild abandon. Stormweaver led the massacre, riding for the river and plunging his lance into unprotected backs. This was joy! This was vengeance!

He heard heavy cracks of splintering ice and splashes from up ahead, and imagined the Executioners' desperate struggles as the weight of their armour dragged them under the water. As his lance sliced clear of another dead druchii, he looked up to see how few remained.

His elation turned to horror as he saw the titanic scaled beasts climbing from the river.

'Hydra,' he said, as the nearest monster spread wide its jaws and unleashed a burning stream of volcanic ichor.

It was the last thing he ever said.

CHAPTER FIFTEEN
DESPAIR

Like a golden arrow loosed from Asuryan's silver bow, Eltharion cut through the air on Stormwing's back with his glittering runesword held before him like a lance. The Witch King had not seen him, and only when the griffon slowed its descent with a thunderous boom of spreading wings did the master of the druchii look up. Malekith hauled the chains looped around his dragon's maw and its vast form banked quicker than anything of such size should be able to move.

Yet still it was not fast enough.

Stormwing's forepaws took hold of the membranous frill where the dragon's wing met its body, and his rear claws raked the underside of its belly, drawing a wash of brackish blood. Eltharion's sword looped out and bit into the pauldrons of the Witch King's armour. The runes worked into the blade shone with trapped moonlight as the sword came free, and Eltharion twisted in his saddle to avoid a strike from Malekith's ensorcelled black blade.

The dragon bellowed and its long neck twisted around to tear at Stormwing. Ichor-dripping teeth like dagger blades snapped on empty air as the griffon pushed off the dragon's body and the aerial combatants broke apart.

Wild cheering greeted the arrival of Eltharion, but he cared nothing for their jubilation. With the element of surprise now gone, this fight had just become far more dangerous.

'Up, Stormwing!' he cried. 'Height is everything.'

The griffon beat its wings furiously, and Eltharion looked over his shoulder to see the Witch King's dragon surging towards him. Thousands of feet below, the Sapphire Gate was a thin line of white marble, blue gemstones and golden ornamentation set in the midst of pale rock. The dragon's jaws spread wide and Eltharion knew what was coming next.

He leaned left and exerted pressure with his knee, and Stormwing obeyed instantly. A seething geyser of noxious black gases vomited up from the dragon's belly. It went wide, but the caustic reek of it caught in the back of his throat. Stormwing tucked one wing into his body, twisting and stooping down onto the rising Witch King.

Eltharion looked into the shimmering emerald glow of Malekith's eyes, remembering the last time he had seen that dread iron mask. Looking upon him from a cold tower of bleak obsidian, the Witch King had prophesised an agonising death for Eltharion. Moments later, the poisoned blade of a druchii witch cut him, and he had hovered at the edge of life for days.

By rights he should have died, but the ghost of his father had called him back to fight for Ulthuan against the rampaging horde of the Goblin King. If that had been the worst the Witch King could do to him, then Eltharion welcomed this fight.

Malekith's armour was black as midnight and Eltharion's keen eyes could make out the runic script worked into the plates of star iron. The Witch King thrust a clawed gauntlet towards Eltharion and a booming voice echoed from within his horned helm. It was a single word, yet a word that should never be uttered or heard by any mortal.

Shrieking pain blitzed around Eltharion's body, and he screamed as every nerve in his body was bathed in fire. His vision greyed and he felt his heart spasm fit to burst. Blinding lights exploded before his eyes, and it was all he could do to retain a grip on his sword. Sensing his rider was incapacitated, Stormwing screeched and banked to the side as the dragon roared in to the attack. Its jaws snapped. Hind legs swung up to claw, and its enormous wings beat the air to pummel the griffon into a spin.

Stormwing twisted out of the way of the dragon's teeth and dipped his wings to avoid a lethal clawing. Buffeting turbulence spun him around, but he pulled his wings in tight and aimed himself towards the earth. The dragon followed him round, slower and less agile than the griffon, yet murderously powerful.

Eltharion gritted his teeth and fought through the pain, letting it bleed from his body as he and Stormwing plummeted back to earth. The Witch King was right behind him, and the dragon's onyx eyes glittered with terrible appetite. Its jaws drooled acidic saliva and Eltharion could see it was building another gullet of toxic breath to exhale. He jinked Stormwing left and right as the Witch King hurled crackling arcs of purple fire from his iron gauntlets. The Sapphire Gate rushed up to meet him and Eltharion pulled Stormwing left and dug his heels into his feathered flanks.

The griffon spread his wings and the force of deceleration almost tore Eltharion from the saddle. He risked a glance over his shoulder in time to see the crimson jaws of the dragon upon him. Stormwing rolled and looped around underneath the dragon as the two creatures passed within a few feet of one another. The dragon's tail slammed into the griffon, and Eltharion felt his mount's pain as he fought to right himself.

He pulled Stormwing around in a tight turn, swooping back to the fight as a black sword sang for his neck. He brought his runesword up and a blazing rain of sparks flew from the two weapons as they struck. Stormwing fought to keep out of reach of the dragon's claws as he and Malekith traded blows. With every clash of iron, Eltharion felt the destructive power of the dark sorcery worked into the Witch King's blade.

But his sword had been fashioned by the first Warden of Tor Yvresse and its enchantments were too strong to be overcome by the pretender's magic of unmaking. Time and time again their swords clashed as Stormwing and the dragon twisted and spun and climbed and dived, as though engaged in some bizarre mating dance.

Their battle was fought with blade and spell, and every blow was followed by a blast of white fire or crimson lightning. Stormwing's feathers were burned from his shoulder and portions of the dragon's neck were fused to glass by the lethal magic. Eltharion knew his magic was nowhere near as powerful as that of Malekith, and he was nearing the limit of his endurance. The Witch King's blade hammered down again, and Eltharion felt its cackling glee as it devoured a portion of the magic empowering his runesword.

Stormwing spun away from the dragon, and Eltharion fought to stay upright as his faithful griffon used every ounce of its speed and agility to outmanoeuvre the Witch King's mount. He pulled Stormwing into a tight turn, one wing stooped, the other spread wide. Malekith passed beneath him, and Eltharion slashed down with his sword. The blade bit into the Witch King's armour, but slid clear before tasting flesh. In return, Malekith's sword stabbed up into Stormwing's belly, opening a long gouge that drew a shriek of pain from the noble creature.

The two creatures spun around one another, clawing and tearing. Stormwing was the more agile of the two, twisting aside from the dragon's powerful jaws and slashing talons. Yet what the dragon lacked in speed, it made up for in sheer power. Stormwing looped over the dragon's neck and a slicing talon tore out the mighty creature's right eye. The dragon roared and thrashed its heavily muscled limbs in agony. A slicing blow from its hind legs cut deep into Stormwing's flank, gouging down to the bone. Stormwing screeched and Eltharion held on tight as the griffon bucked in pain.

In such a close quarters fight, there could be only one winner, and it would be the dragon.

'We have done all we can for now, old friend,' said Eltharion.

Stormwing folded his wings and dropped away from the dragon, diving hundreds of feet before levelling out over the walls of the sea gate. Flights of arrows flew from the defenders' bows towards the dragon. Most bounced from its thick scales, but a lucky few pieced its body where the battle with Eltharion had torn them loose. The enraged dragon turned about and was flying after him, its wings pounding the air and scattering the fighters on the wall below with the force of the downdraught. A flurry of iron bolts zipped past Eltharion and he swung his mount lower, passing within ten feet of the ramparts.

The cliff wall was fast approaching. He was running out of space.

A sibilant voice sounded in his head, and it was a voice he knew to trust implicitly.

Fly to me, Eltharion! By the western cliff!

Eltharion obeyed instantly, turning in a sharp bank and roll manoeuvre as he flew back the way he had come. The dragon matched Stormwing's turn, but Eltharion could hear his mount was blowing hard now, a sure sign of imminent exhaustion.

'Fly just a little more, brother,' said Eltharion.

The griffon extended its wings and flew westwards as the Witch King's dragon roared in anticipation of the kill. They sped over the wall, through a mist of arrows and bolts, weaving through the air and jostling for position. Eltharion scanned the walls for any sign of his friend, and spotted the star-cloaked mage exactly where he had said he would be.

Loremaster Belannaer stood swathed in a cerulean cloak of moonwrit runes and read aloud from a heavy golden book, its kidskin covers embossed with the motif of a rising phoenix. His voice was ancient beyond reckoning and the words he spoke were of Asuryan and the creation of the world.

Eltharion drew Stormwing in, and the griffon spun as the Witch King and his dragon closed. The dragon's wings boomed wide as it slowed its flight, and no sooner had Malekith reared up to strike down at Eltharion than Belannaer unleashed a coruscating vortex of pure white fire from the tip of his crescent-topped staff. The flames enveloped the Witch King and his dragon, but instead of bellows of agony, there came only gloating laughter.

The flames vanished in a heartbeat, and Eltharion saw the Witch King's shield glowing with a blistering light where it had swallowed the full force of the magical fire.

Stormwing landed on the ramparts of the sea gate, and Eltharion saw Belannaer stagger away from the wall as though struck. The Loremaster held himself upright with the aid of his golden staff and though he was greatly weakened, he kept reading from his magical tome.

'In Vaul's name, I unweave the winds of magic, their colours to be unmade, their enchantments to be undone!'

The air between Belannaer and Malekith buckled with unleashed force and the Witch King's shield shattered into a thousand fragments. The dark plates of his armour cracked, and searing lines of magical fire clawed his light-starved flesh. The Witch King roared in pain, and pulled his draconic mount away from Belannaer's magic. As the dragon pulled up and away, its long neck rippled with peristaltic motion.

Eltharion shouted a warning and Stormwing leapt into the air as a black torrent of lethal fumes and searing bile erupted from the dragon's jaws to envelop the Loremaster. Eltharion could only watch in horror as Belannaer's body erupted in incandescent flames that burned hotter than the forge of the Smith God himself until nothing remained.

The mist rolling in from the river thinned as it reached the riverbank, and Caelir saw vast blocks of marching warriors emerge from its edges. They were big men, thick of limb and wide of shoulder, each armed with a great felling axe that dripped with amber sap. The flesh of their bodies was sliced open from head to toe, and barbed thorns were snagged on their armour or embedded in the meat of their arms and thighs.

They came on in a screaming host, beneath a forest of crude banners and braying war horns. A thousand warriors, and then a thousand more emerged from the mist, a multitude of warbands, sword-packs and axe-brothers. Caelir felt his courage sink to his boots at the sight of so many warriors.

Riding tall in the centre of the host was Issyk Kul, his shoulder guards draped with a fresh cloak of torn emerald robes and pale flesh. Stretched over the warlord's spiked pauldrons, Anurion the Green's face gave voice to a silent scream, while the emptied skin of his body flapped as a grotesque rag of bloody flesh.

'Gods above!' hissed Caelir. 'Anurion...'

He fought down his rising panic as he tried to think of some way they could hold the northern flank. The Reaver bands numbered fewer than five hundred riders, and the spear hosts barely a thousand. The fighting around Korhandir's Leap had drawn in too many warriors, and the north was now dangerously exposed.

And that weakness had been exploited.

The spear hosts angled themselves to meet the oncoming horde of tribesmen as the clear notes of elven battle horns trumpeted. The sound gave Caelir hope, and he smiled wryly as he thought of the tales Narentir had told of Aenarion in the performance circles of Avelorn. The poet always sang of hope in the darkest hours, of how heroes never gave in to despair and always clung to the hope of victory. He would spin spellbinding tales of all the great heroes of Ulthuan: Aenarion, Caledor Dragontamer, the sword-mages, Firuval and Estellian, and of course Tyrion and Teclis.

One night Caelir had asked Narentir why he never told the tale of Eltharion, for it was an epic tale that surely best exemplified his belief in holding on to hope in the darkest hour.

Narentir had shaken his head and said, 'Dear boy, you are young and beautiful. Some stories should not be told too often, for the soul is heavier for hearing them.

Caelir had sensed evasion and said, 'Save your fancy words for the circles, poet. Tell me. Why do you not speak of Eltharion?'

'Because I choose not to,' said Narentir. 'He is a warrior of great sadness and anger. Not someone about whom one should speak without his leave. Dear Caelir, you met Eltharion in Tor Yvresse, and even you must have realised that about him without someone like me having to explain it to you.'

'I met him, yes,' agreed Caelir. 'He seemed sad more than angry.'

'And with good reason.'

'Have you met him?'

'Once,' said Narentir. 'And before you ask the question I sense is rushing towards those exquisite lips of yours, it is not an experience I care to relive, so do not ask.'

Caelir had cajoled him all night, but Narentir would not be drawn on the matter. Events had overtaken them, and Caelir guessed he would never get the chance to learn the reasons for the poet's reluctance to speak of Eltharion.

'You were a fool, Narentir,' whispered Caelir. 'A wonderful, brilliant fool. I wish you were here to tell me there was still hope.'

On the ride to Tor Elyr, Caelir had chided Eldain for not believing there was still hope.

How naïve he must have sounded. How childish.

The enemy had crossed the river, and there was no hope of holding them back.

Eldain and Lotharin rode onto the western bank of the river, and Starchaser's Reavers followed close behind. It was glorious madness to be on this side of the river, with enemies all around them, but where else should an Ellyrian Reaver Knight be but deep within enemy territory with the threat of death all around?

He had a handful of warriors against an army, which were the odds an Ellyrian liked.

But where to lead them?

'The red giant,' said Eldain. 'Gods, Mitherion, what in Isha's name did you mean?'

To the south, hundreds of druchii hurried to the ford, which became more passable with every moment as fell magicks were brought to bear to hold back the waters of the river. The spear hosts were already embroiled in battle, and though the line was holding, the druchii could simply hurl warriors at it until it broke. Hundreds of warrior bands of druchii were marching towards the bridge, eager to flank the elven spears, and as much as Eldain dearly wished to oppose them, he knew it was a fight his riders could not win.

Eldain could not see what was happening in the north, for a thick fog-bank obscured all but the distant hill of waystones and the Eagle's Claws upon its slopes. To left and right, druchii crossbows and bolt throwers unleashed withering hails of arrows. Small bands of crossbowmen were, even now, making their way from the riverbank to take aim. Iron-tipped bolts whickered from the undergrowth, and two of Eldain's riders were pitched from their saddles. A bolt embedded itself in the thick leather of his saddle horn, and Lotharin reared up as the tip pricked his flesh beneath.

Eldain angrily tore the bolt free and hurled it aside.

'Ride north along the riverbank!' he shouted, guiding Lotharin around with pressure on his right knee. His black steed turned on the spot and galloped away from the bridge with Starchaser's Reavers behind him. Less than a hundred yards to his left, thousands of druchii warriors marched towards the river, so close he could pick out individual faces and shield designs. It was madness to be riding so close to the front of the enemy host, but where else was there to go?

Eldain felt the snap of druchii crossbow bolts flashing past them, and heard the screams of Reavers as they were cut down. He shouted in anger and took up his bow, loosing shaft after shaft in return. He saw enemy warriors fall, but took scant comfort in their deaths. No matter if each of his riders killed a druchii with every arrow in their quivers, there would still be ten times too many for them to fight.

'Damn you, Mitherion!' shouted Eldain as he heard another of his Reavers die.

The ground became harder under Lotharin's hooves, and Eldain felt the air grow icy, like the depths of winter in Cothique. Ellyrion never knew winter's touch, and it chilled his soul like nothing else to know that his land could be so touched by the fell influence of the druchii. Cold mist oozed from the river, and Eldain heard the slap of water on ice... the tramp of booted feet on ice.

Eldain could see nothing save the grey curtain of mist before him. To ride blind was madness, but to ride slow would see them skewered on the bolts of the druchii crossbowmen.

'Ride sure, old friend,' he shouted to Lotharin.

The horse tossed its mane and plunged into the mist, the cold wetness of it soaking Eldain through in moments. He could see nothing save vague shapes, dark outlines and hazy silhouettes as Lotharin rode deeper and deeper into the mist. The sounds of hideous chanting came from all around him, mired in the muffled sound of clashing blades, screams of pain, beating war drums and wildly blowing horns.

Mired in the mist, the battle might already be won or lost for all Eldain knew.

Something vast, golden and jade loomed in the mist, the towering outline of a warrior. Taller than any elf could ever be, it was swathed in red mist that tasted of burned metal and set his nerves afire with its hateful resonances of pain, murder and fear. Vast blades descended from outstretched arms, and Eldain saw writhing forms leaping and dancing around a steaming cauldron that sopped and sloshed with blood. The taste of the air set his teeth on edge and brought tears to his eyes.

'The red giant,' said Eldain, amazed that they had come upon it in the mist.

The red mist parted and Eldain saw the lithe forms of near-naked druchii warrior women spinning around the mighty effigy of their bloody-handed god. Each was a dark beauty of sinister allure, and each carried dripping black-bladed daggers in both hands. Khaine himself leered down at the Reavers, and the ruby eyes of the statue pulsed in anticipation of bloodshed. Eldain let fly with his last arrow at one of the women, who leapt over the speeding shaft and bounded towards him like an acrobat.

Eldain was reminded of the elf-maid Lilani he had met in Avelorn, but where her grace was natural and sinuous, these druchii women had the predatory agility of stalking cats. One of the women vaulted into the air and leapt at him feet first. Lotharin reared up and flailed the air with his hooves, smashing her ribcage and hurling her back. Eldain used the respite to take up his spear as the Reavers rode into the women.

Two were killed almost instantly, crushed beneath the sheer mass of horses, and another pair were pinned to the ground by a flurry of arrows loosed by archers more skilled than Eldain. The Reavers outnumbered the dancers of Khaine, but they cared nothing for their own deaths and slew for the cruel enjoyment of the deed. Eldain felt something tear along his shoulder, and ducked over Lotharin's neck as a pair of iron razor-stars slashed by his head.

A naked elf with dark tattoos garlanding her body balanced on the edge of the slopping cauldron of blood like a witch-hag from the terror stories used to frighten children. Her hair billowed around her thorn-crowned head, and barbed torqs of thornvines wound their way along her legs and arms. Though her body was that of the fairest elf-maid, her face was a loathsome melange of youth and ancient malice.

Eldain turned Lotharin toward the witch, feeling his hatred intensify the closer he rode to the looming statue and its dripping blades. The eyes of the effigy burned with the light of a furnace, hot, raging and always in motion. Eldain's lip curled in anger as he stared at the witch-hag, letting his hate build as she sprang from the edge of the cauldron with a hateful scream that tore at his nerves. It was a name he had never heard uttered from a living being, it was the name carried in the death rattle of those with a knife in their back or a murderer's hands wrapped around their throat. It was the wordless exultation of murder.

At that moment, Eldain knew the terror of prey.

Lotharin reared in panic, and Eldain dropped his spear as the witch queen's word of power took him back to the days of darkness, when even the elves huddled close to the fire for fear of what might lurk beyond its light. He wanted to reach for his sword, but his muscles were terror-locked in paralysis. Even as she came at him with twin daggers that hissed with venom, he could not move, could do nothing save imagine the pain as she cut out his heart.

The witch sailed through the air as though in defiance of gravity and Eldain saw her face split apart with the feral grin of a savage killer. Her blades never connected, for a leaf-bladed speartip erupted from her rib-cage and plucked her from the air.

Laurena Starchaser rode past like the Huntress of Kurnous herself, her auburn hair wild and unbound and trailing behind her like a fiery comet. The witch queen slid from her spear, punctured clean through and wailing impotent curses from bleeding lips.

'Have you forgotten how to fight?' asked Starchaser, circling her horse and whipping the blood from her spear.

Eldain shook off the terror of the witch-hag's spell and said, 'No.'

'She bewitched you?'

'Maybe,' said Eldain, unwilling to dwell on the naked fear he had felt.

'This is the red giant Mitherion Silverfawn spoke of?' she asked.

'I believe so.'

'Then let's hurry up and destroy it, there are more druchii coming.'

'Any idea how?'

Starchaser slid from the saddle and waved the surviving Reaver Knights over. Eldain rode around the statue as Starchaser and another five Reavers put their shoulders to the brass cauldron and pushed. Eldain unhooked his lasso from his saddle and spun the loop once before hurling it up and over the statue's head. He wound the end of the lasso around Lotharin's saddle horn as three other Reavers followed his example. One rope snapped on the drooping blades, and Eldain felt the statue's smouldering anger as the Ellyrians worked to bring it down.

'Now, Laurena!' shouted Eldain. 'Push!'

Lotharin strained against the heavy weight of the statue, and Eldain glanced over his shoulder to see the red glow of its baleful eyes spread throughout its metal body. He heard angry shouts of druchii warriors and leaned over Lotharin's neck.

'Come greatheart, you are the strongest horse I know,' he said. 'If any can pull this damned statue down it is you.'

Lotharin's shoulders bunched and he strained at the enormous weight at his back until at last the statue's base cracked and it began to fall. Blood sloshed from the cauldron, hissing as it hit the good soil of Ellyrion and rendering it barren for years to come.

Then the statue tipped past its centre of gravity and fell without effort from the elves. Eldain's lasso unwound from the statue's neck, and he coiled it back onto his saddle as the cauldron fell from its mounting and flipped over. The bronze face of the murder god slammed into the ground as the cauldron rolled towards the mist-shrouded river.

Instead of a heavy splash, Eldain heard the booming clang of metal striking something solid. The sound continued as the cauldron vanished into the mist. Starchaser and her Reavers ran back to their horses as armoured warriors emerged from the mist around the fallen statue. Crossbow bolts flashed through the air as the Reavers took to their heels.

Eldain spun in the saddle, seeing druchii approaching from all sides.

All sides but one.

Eltharion brought Stormwing in over the centre of the sea gate. The aerial duel with the Witch King had brought the fighting to a halt as all eyes turned to watch the awesome clash of might and magic. His armour torn open and his dragon wounded, the Witch King had flown high into the boiling clouds. The sight of Eltharion's triumphant entry to the fighting galvanised the defenders to push the druchii from the walls for the time being.

Tyrion and Korhil stood to either side of Finubar as he went to greet the Warden of Tor Yvresse. The Phoenix King was still weak from the druchii sorcery that had slain his White Lions, but Tyrion knew it was more than luck that kept him alive. Finubar was the mortal vessel of Asuryan's fire, and the Creator God did not suffer weaklings to guide his chosen people.

The griffon's claws gripped the edge of the wall and he folded his wings back with regal poise. Tyrion saw the beast was lathered with sweat and its eyes filled with pain.

Tyrion and Eltharion had once been close, but ever since the Goblin King's assault on Yvresse, they had barely spoken. Tyrion had learned the particulars of the battle from those who had fought the goblins, but Eltharion had always refused to speak of it. Whatever had happened in the Warden's Tower at the height of the fighting had changed Eltharion in terrible ways. His grim demeanour was understandable. His lands had been ravaged and his family slain, but the haunted lifelessness of his eyes was hard to bear.

Tyrion's old friend now shunned company, avoided his boon companions and brooded alone in his sullen city of ghosts. As timely and welcome as his arrival had been, Tyrion found it hard to be glad that the Warden of Tor Yvresse now fought with them.

'Eltharion,' said Finubar, as the grim-eyed warden dismounted and dropped to the ramparts. 'You are a sight for sore eyes, my friend.'

Eltharion nodded curtly. 'My king was in danger. I had to come,' he said, and Tyrion heard the hollowness of the sentiment immediately.

Finubar embraced Eltharion warmly, a gesture that looked forced and awkward to Tyrion, but which was greeted with a rousing cheer from the defenders of the Sapphire Gate. As the two warriors broke the embrace, Tyrion saw the simmering anger behind Finubar's façade of camaraderie. Yes, Eltharion had come, but he had taken his sweet time about it and brought precious few warriors with him. Aside from a handful of rangers, it was clear the armies of the eastern realms remained within the walls of Tor Yvresse.

'As king of Ulthuan, I am glad to have you,' said Finubar, ever the diplomat.

'Stormwing is injured,' said Eltharion. 'I would ask your healers see to his wounds.'

'Of course,' said Finubar, waving to a nearby archer. 'Immediately.'

Tyrion stepped forward. 'Sire Belannaer?' he asked. 'I saw the dragon…'

Eltharion shook his head. 'He is dead.'

'Are you sure?' pressed Finubar.

'I am sure,' said Eltharion. 'I saw the flames consume him. He is dead.'

Tyrion wanted to strike Eltharion for announcing the death of one of the White Tower's greatest Loremasters with so little emotion. Coming so soon after Belarien's death, Tyrion's anger surged to the surface. Before he did anything rash, Korhil took hold of his arm and gave an almost imperceptible shake of his head.

The sound of hunting horns echoed from the sides of the cliffs, and shouts of warning came from the watchtowers as the iron boarding ramps cranked down from the black ark.

'Druchii!' shouted Korhil, running to the edge of the ramparts. 'Stand to! Archers!'

Finubar nodded to Eltharion and Tyrion, then drew his sword and ran to muster the defenders. Warriors flocked to the Phoenix King as arrows and bolts flew between the black ark and the Sapphire Gate once more.

Eltharion turned to follow the king, but Tyrion grabbed his arm and said, 'Why did you really come?'

'Lothern is ready to fall, where else would I be?'

'Platitudes like that may appease Finubar, but I know you better,' said Tyrion. 'Tell me.'

Hostility and aching loneliness swam in Eltharion's eyes, but it was soon replaced by cold resentment. Tyrion saw a cruelty in his old friend that he liked not at all.

'You really want to know?' asked Eltharion.

'I do.'

'I remembered something a poet once said to me.'

'What did he say?'

'Nothing I will ever tell you,' said Eltharion, pulling his arm free and walking away.

CHAPTER SIXTEEN
BATTLE'S END

Menethis watched in disbelief as the monsters destroyed the Silver Helms. Three monsters with writhing masses of heads tore them apart with snapping bites and gouts of hellish red fire vomited up from their bellies. Alongside these scaled monstrosities, deformed abominations of flesh, bone, gristle and raw meat fought with lunatic fury. Snapped chains whipped from barbed collars, and mouths opened randomly in the elastic, warping flesh of the hell-spawned beasts.

The slaughter was so swift that Menethis could scarce believe it had happened at all. One moment, Stormweaver's Silver Helms were slaughtering the Executioners, the next, monsters had emerged from the mist and destroyed their salvation. Menethis watched a hydra snatch up a horse in its jaws and bite it in two. Half the beast went down the monster's gullet, the rest spat back into the killing. A Silver Helm, unhorsed and pouring blood from where his arm had once been, staggered back from the slaughter, but one of the spawn creatures swept him up in a gelatinous tentacle and swallowed him whole.

'Isha save us, sweet mother of mercy,' said a spearman behind him.

'Be silent,' ordered Menethis.

With the timely arrival of the Silver Helms, Menethis had rejoined his spear host on the gentle slopes before Tor Elyr. Once in sight of the spires of the city, the citizen soldiers had steeled their courage and banded together around their banner. Menethis had discovered them marching back to join him, and not since he had stood on the walls of

Eagle Gate had he felt such humbling pride.

'Raise spears,' he said, knowing it was futile. If such warriors as the Silver Helms could not fight such monsters, then they had little chance. That did not matter, for they had sworn to defend this land, and nothing could be gained by running save a few wretched moments of life. That they had no chance of prevailing was immaterial.

That they stood with courage unbroken before such beasts was all that mattered.

The mist at the river began clearing and Menethis saw the full might of the druchii army across the river. Despite the numbers their host had killed, the druchii still outnumbered them. No matter that they had fought with bravery and strength beyond what anyone could have expected. They were still doomed.

The vortex of storm clouds above the black ark seethed with elemental power, swirling and gathering strength with every passing moment. Torrential rain fell in soaking sheets, washing the ramparts clean of blood, and Tyrion's robes were plastered to his skin. Sunfang hissed like an ingot fresh from the furnace in the downpour.

Deafening peals of thunder echoed from the cliffs and blinding forks of lightning burned crackling traceries across the sky. If this was to be the end of Ulthuan, then the heavens were providing a fitting accompaniment. Tyrion turned aside an overhand cut with his dagger and spun around the druchii swordsman, plunging Sunfang into his lower back. The warrior grunted in pain and fell to the blood-wet flagstones of the gate.

Two thousand elven warriors fought on the Sapphire Gate, faced with who knew how many druchii. Tens of thousands might lurk within the black ark for all Tyrion knew.

Let them come, he thought. *Let them come and I will kill them all!*

He almost smiled at the thought, welcoming the intrusion of the Sword of Khaine this time. Belarien was dead, as was Loremaster Belannaer. Who else was to die before this was over? Alarielle? Teclis? Finubar? Tyrion?

Strangely, the thought of his own death did not trouble him, but the thought of losing those closest to him filled him with such dread that he had trouble breathing.

Two dozen druchii swarmed down the boarding ramps, howling their hatred. Arrows pierced a handful and sent them plummeting to their doom, but the rest came on without pause. They hurled themselves onto the gate, only to be met by cold steel and courage. Swords clashed and armour rang with the bitter songs of battle, and for the fifth time this day, the ancestral enemies of Ulthuan and Naggaroth fought to the death.

A broad-shouldered warrior in overlapping bands of plate led these warriors, and arrows bounced from his armour. Armed with an axe-bladed polearm, he landed on the ramparts and spun his weapon around until it was aimed at Tyrion.

'The Tower of Grief will have your head!' promised the warrior, his voice muffled by the form-fitting helm of bronze he wore.

'Come and take it,' answered Tyrion in reply.

Tyrion's blade struck first, skidding from the druchii's breastplate. In reply, the polearm swept down. Tyrion raised Sunfang to block, before realising the blow was a feint. The haft of the polearm suddenly reversed and swept down to smash against the side of his knee. Tyrion leapt over the attack, ramming his dagger at the warrior's neck.

The druchii leaned into the blow and Tyrion's blade snapped on the flared metal of his helmet. Tyrion landed lightly and ducked beneath a slashing blow of the axe head. He thrust, and it was deflected. He feinted, rolled and leapt, but each time his attacks were intercepted and turned aside by the halberd, its longer reach keeping him at bay.

More druchii were gaining the walls, pushing out from the space their champion had created. The elven line was bowing and the druchii kept pouring on the pressure, sensing a chance for a breakthrough. Anger touched Tyrion. He was a prince of Ulthuan, its sworn protector, and some upstart druchii champion was fending him off?

The halberd swung at him again, but instead of parrying the blow, Tyrion stepped to meet it and hacked the blade from the haft with one blow. The druchii stared stupidly at the broken end of his weapon and Tyrion gave him no chance to recover. He pushed the broken halberd aside and rammed his sword into the champion's gut, the enchanted blade sliding between the bands of contoured plate.

Tyrion pushed the dying warrior to the edge of the wall and lifted him onto the battlements, still skewered upon Sunfang's blade like a butterfly on a collector's pin. Behind the faceplate of his helm, the druchii's violet eyes were wide with agony as the sword's caged heat boiled his innards.

'Tell Kouran I will see his tower cast down within the year!' bellowed Tyrion.

He twisted his sword blade and the champion fell from the walls, to howls of dismay from his fellow druchii. Thunder crashed across the heavens again, but something in the timbre of the sound made Tyrion look up. Nothing of the storm clouds raging above the black ark could be called natural, but this thunder was unnatural even for such a freakish phenomenon.

The Witch King dropped from the clouds of torrential rain on the back of his dragon as lightning split the sky with dazzling brightness. The dragon's left wing was torn and ragged from the battle with Eltharion and Stormwing, but Malekith's armour bore no traces of that desperate fight.

Those druchii still on the wall began falling back as though at some prearranged signal. Tyrion watched them go, but instead of elation he felt only an acute sense of danger. Instincts honed on a hundred battlefields were screaming at him that something terrible was about to happen.

Arcs of powerful lightning played across the Witch King's body, coiling around his dragon and flaring with a million hues of colour. Variegated light swirled within Tyrion's sword and armour, and he tasted the bitterly metallic flavour of powerful magic in the air. He ran along the length of the gate, keeping one eye on the motionless form of the Witch King as he drew all the lightning in the sky to him.

In the centre of the wall, Finubar and Korhil watched the unfolding drama with wary eyes. Korhil's pelt was bloodied, yet Tyrion was heartened to see that not even an assassin's venom could lessen the Chracian's strength and power. Likewise, Finubar had thrown off the worst effects of the druchii sorcery, and his golden blade was wet with blood.

'I'll wager this bodes ill,' said Korhil as Tyrion approached.

'What do you think he is doing?' asked Finubar.

'Nothing good,' said Tyrion. 'The druchii pulled back inside the ark the moment he appeared.'

'I saw that,' said Finubar, as the coruscating sphere of rampant lightning built around the Witch King until he was almost completely obscured by the whipping cords of power.

A mage in robes of cream, blue and gold stood at the edge of the walls, staring up at Malekith with frightened eyes.

Tyrion hauled him to his feet and said, 'What is happening? What sorcery is this?'

'I… I am not sure,' gabbled the mage. 'It cannot be what I think it is…'

'You are not sure? Then what use are you? Did Teclis send us fools or mages?' growled Tyrion.

'It is magic, but… but of a kind I know only from legend. It has the feel of ancient power, creation magic from when the world was made. Only fragments of it are said to remain in forgotten places lost to the races of this world.'

'Creation?' spat Tyrion. 'The Witch King knows nothing of creation, only destruction.'

'They are two faces of the same aspect,' the mage gasped. 'Creation. Destruction. You cannot have one without the other. As one thing is created, another is destroyed. It is the most dangerous kind of magic, the magic of the Old Ones. It is said its misuse caused the fall of the world in the ancient days before the rise of the elder races.'

'You speak in riddles,' hissed Tyrion, before throwing the mage back against the wall. He watched as the lightning wreathing the Witch King grew even brighter, like a newborn sun hovering in the straits. Stark shadows were cast by its radiance, but the light was without life or warmth, only raw luminous power.

'We need to get everyone off this gate,' said Tyrion as he saw the truth of Malekith's sorcery. 'Now!'

'What?' demanded Korhil. 'Madness. The druchii will simply walk onto the gate.'

'Trust me,' said Tyrion. 'In a few moments I do not think there will *be* a gate…'

'What if you are wrong?' demanded the Phoenix King.

'I will stay on the gate.'

'Alone?' said Finubar. 'You cannot hold the druchii back alone.'

'If I am right, I will not need to.'

'If you are right, you had better be a damn good swimmer,' said Korhil.

Finubar nodded and gave the order to abandon the Sapphire Gate. That order was obeyed instantly, and elven warriors ran to the cliffs, where wide steps were cut into the sides of the straits. Sprays of power blazed from the Witch King as hundreds of elves hurried down the curving steps that led down to the quays of Lothern. Korhil and Finubar went with them, and Tyrion stood at the junction of the two halves of the gate.

He watched the defenders of Lothern fall back to the quays, each sentinel of spear and bow quickly reforming their warriors alongside the unmoving ranks of the Phoenix Guard already arrayed there. The storm winds bellied their banners wide and full, and as the warriors evacuating the wall took up position around them, Tyrion saw they were perfectly placed in this newly formed battle line.

'They knew,' he said. 'They *knew* this would happen…'

Then the Witch King unleashed his new and terrible power.

A streaming fountain of black light blazed from the sphere of lightning, striking the dead centre of the Sapphire Gate. Too bright to look upon, its power did not destroy that which it touched, rather, it *unmade* it. Tyrion watched through half-closed eyes as the very fabric of the gate was unwoven. Matter was unravelled, like a loose thread in a cloak that snags on a thornbush. Ithilmar, starwood and sapphires larger than a warrior's fist came apart like snow before the spring, broken down into their constituent fractions and consumed.

Tyrion staggered as the entire gate slumped and portions of its load-bearing structure were eaten away by this dreadful power. Vast swathes of the gate dissolved into nothingness as the ball of lightning surrounding the Witch King continued to pulse with ancient magic. He ran to the cliffs, now knowing there was no need to stay. The druchii were not going to be coming over the gate, they were going through where it *used to be*.

What remained of the gate cracked, and those portions of it that still stubbornly held on to existence now began to split apart. Flagstones cracked beneath Tyrion's feet as he ran for the cliff side steps. He leapt to the battlements as the flagstones were consumed by the decay of its material form. Pieces of the gate were disappearing at random, and Tyrion leapt from solid ground to solid ground as the dissolution of the gate increased exponentially.

Fifty yards lay between him and safety, but it might as well have been five hundred.

Only fragments of the Sapphire Gate still existed, and what had taken thousands of artisans decades to construct was unmade in moments. Tyrion leapt for one of the last portions of the gate still maintaining its structural integrity, but no sooner did his feet touch the stone than its matter was unmade by the Witch King's stolen magic.

Tyrion's eyes told him there was stone there, but his feet passed through as though it were as insubstantial as the confounding mists wreathing the shifting islets to the east of Ulthuan. Panic gripped him as he tumbled downward, spinning and flailing his arms in a desperate attempt to control his descent.

Tyrion closed his eyes and let his body find its poise. He rolled and angled his descent towards the sea, but knew that falling into water from such a height was akin to landing on solid rock.

What a galling way for a prince of Ulthuan to die...

Not in battle, not at the claws of some ancient nemesis, but falling from a great height.

The ignominy of it angered Tyrion more than the thought of his own death.

'Extend your arms, Tyrion!' shouted Eltharion's voice above him.

Tyrion heard a screeching roar and felt a booming rush of air above him. He did as Eltharion commanded, and the griffon's ebon-hard claws seized his arms. His plummeting descent slowed and smoothed out as Stormwing took his weight and flew over the empty quays and the hastily assembling defenders of Lothern.

Eltharion brought Stormwing down into the port, coming in slow and allowing Tyrion to drop the last yard to the paved quay before setting the griffon down. Tyrion's heartbeat was racing at his brush with death, and he turned in gratitude to Eltharion.

'My thanks, brother,' said Tyrion.

Eltharion shrugged and said, 'It was nothing. I was there.'

Tyrion gripped Eltharion's hand. 'I owe you my life. That is not nothing. You understand?'

Eltharion shook his head, and Tyrion despaired of ever reaching his friend again. All understanding of the bonds of brotherhood engendered by decades of friendship had been scoured from his soul, and only an empty shell that wore the face of Eltharion remained.

'What happened in that tower?' whispered Tyrion. 'What price did you pay?'

'You of all people should know better than to ask such a thing,' snapped Eltharion.

'What do you mean?'

'You are of the line of Aenarion,' said Eltharion, 'accursed to the last generation by his blood and forever drawn to battle and death. Your soul is still yours for the moment, but mine is already forfeit.'

'I do not understand.'

'You will,' said Eltharion. 'And on that day you will know what it means to be cursed.'

Eltharion took to the air on Stormwing's back, but Tyrion did not watch him go.

Instead, he stared at the great gap where the Sapphire Gate had once stood and at the towering immensity of the black ark. Whatever power Malekith had used to unmake the great sea gate was spent, but its work was done, and the route into Lothern was open.

Iron portcullises at the base of the black ark clattered upwards and a crimson-sailed fleet of raven ships and troop galleys surged out towards the quays of Lothern.

Tyrion turned and ran to stand alongside his king.

Lord Swiftwing watched the battle for Tor Elyr from the spired ramparts of his castle and felt despair like the morning he had learned he would never ride again. He wore his ithilmar breastplate and carried his winged helm in the crook of his arm. His family blade was sheathed at his side in a scabbard specially modified to fit around his lopsided waist, and an azure cloak flapped in the wind that whistled around the high tower.

Casadesus stood beside him, and the mood was grim as they watched the mist lifting from the river and saw the scale of the enemy facing what remained of his army.

The southern flank was buckling under the weight of the enemy attack, and the horde of tribesmen was massing to charge the thin line of spears in the north. The noose was closing on Tor Elyr, and no amount of heroics would change the inevitable outcome of this battle.

In the centre of the army, amid a troupe of cavorting blade-maidens, was Morathi.

Seated astride her winged steed of darkness, the hag sorceress had taken no part in the fighting, which surprised Lord Swiftwing, for history told that she was a leader who relished the chance to get her hands bloody.

'Why do you not fight?' whispered Lord Swiftwing. 'What are you saving your powers for, she-witch?'

The wind blew cold, and Lord Swiftwing pulled his cloak tighter about himself.

'You should go from here, my lord,' said Casadesus. 'I have a ship waiting at the lower docks. It is fast, and the druchii will not catch it.'

'Go?' said Lord Swiftwing. 'Go where?'

'To Saphery perhaps,' said Casadesus. 'There are no reports of fighting there. You would be safe and could rally support to retake Tor Elyr.'

Lord Swiftwing shook his head. 'You would have me flee? You should know me better than that, Casadesus.'

'I would have been disappointed if you had said yes,' agreed Casadesus, 'but I had to ask.'

'I understand, old friend,' said Lord Swiftwing. 'How could I look myself in the mirror knowing I had fled my city and left my warriors to die? No, if this is to be the last day of Ellyrion, then I will die with my land. You should go, there is no reason for you to die too.'

'You tried to send me away once before, and I seem to remember telling you that I was where I needed to be, my lord.'

'Duty?'

'Duty,' said Casadesus.

'It will be the death of us all,' said Lord Swiftwing, watching as a small Reaver band rode across the frozen river with rank upon rank of druchii marching after them. Red mist trailed from their lathered horses, but how they came to be on the other side of the river was a mystery. Though if there was one thing that could always be said of Ellyrion Reaver Knights, it was that they would always cause havoc from the direction least expected.

'A river in Ellyrion turned to ice. Who would have believed such a thing was possible?' said Lord Swiftwing. 'The druchii do not fight with any notions of honour, though I should not be surprised at such a thing. It is hard to believe they were once like us.'

'They *were* us,' said Casadesus. 'But I agree, it is hard to credit.'

A shimmering light rippled the horizon to the north, and Lord Swiftwing saw the graceful arc of a glorious rainbow. A shimmering curtain of stars glittered beneath it, though he had no idea what could have caused such a wondrous display.

'What magic is this?' he wondered. 'Ours or theirs do you think?'

'Who can say?' replied Casadesus. 'Ellyrion is a land of mystery.'

'There is truth in that,' agreed Lord Swiftwing, turning away from the battle and placing a hand on the hilt of his sword. 'But that is one mystery that will need to remain so for today.'

'My lord?'

'Ready my chariot, Casadesus,' said Lord Swiftwing. 'I may not be a Reaver Knight this day, but I will take to the field of battle as my last act.'

'Will you permit me to be your spear-bearer, my lord?'

'I would be honoured,' said Lord Swiftwing.

The crystal spires of the city glittered like the icy stalactites in the Dragon Caves of the Frostback Mountains. Issyk Kul had killed a mighty creature of ancient days in those caverns, dragging its monstrous skull down onto a spike of ice and earning the favour of the dark prince in the process.

His flesh burned with the need to defile, to violate and to debase. This battle had given him precious little chance to honour his god in the proper manner, and the few tortures he had managed to inflict on the green shaman had only served to inflame his passions further.

Blood coated his chin where he had drunk the blood of a dying elf-maid, and his hands were slick to the elbow where he had reached into the chest of an injured warrior to remove his still-beating heart. Petty debaucheries in which even the lowliest devotee of Shornaal would happily indulge, but trifling and dull to him. He needed to violate something innocent, to destroy something beautiful and to corrupt something pure.

His warriors bayed for blood, for battle and for the sheer noise of it. A deafening symphony of discord arose from the horde, a wailing, braying, honking, skirling wall of sound that was music to his ears. The blaring cacophony, the smell of sweat, blood, fear and exultation were a potent mix, and the striking colours of the landscape and sky and city all combined in a scintillating chorus of sensation.

His horse pawed the earth, its flesh hot and raw and heaving with the need to trample warm bodies beneath its clawed hooves. It had feasted on elven meat and bloody saliva dripped from between its chisel-like fangs. The very air of this island was pain to its exposed flesh, but the beast welcomed it as a fellow creature of Shornaal.

The invasion of Ulthuan had been like no other campaign, for the sheer potency of war waged on a land of magic was like nothing he had experienced before. He had led the northmen's wolfships over the Sea of Claws to the Empire, but its rain-lashed shores held little appeal for him. The men that called that land home were dull, mud-caked grubbers of the earth, who knew nothing of the wonders of the true gods.

He could feel the aching need of his warriors to be unleashed, but held them in check a moment longer. The wall of spears before them was thin and fear came off the silver-armoured warriors in delicious waves. Against his horde, they would break and run at the first charge. Horsemen rode at the flanks of the battle line, and Kul licked his lips as he saw the warrior he and Morathi had broken in the haunted dungeons of Naggarond.

The young elf had been a playful pet, and had taken a long time to break, but when he had, oh… the degradations he had enjoyed, the torments he had begged for. To have endured so complete a debasement and still retain even a scrap of sanity spoke of a measure of denial or fortitude that Kul could only admire.

Caelir, that was his name, and Kul imagined skinning him alive and taking his flesh for a scabbard in which he would sheath his many-bladed weapon. A lone warrior with a horned helm and a cloak of thick bearskin broke from the horde with an ululating scream of hatred, but a white-feathered arrow punched through the visor of his helm before he had covered more than ten yards.

The elven spears trembled, and Kul let their fear grow. His anticipation built until finally he could stand it no longer.

He raised his sword and loosed a battle howl of lustful rage. It was answered by his horde, and they sprinted forwards in a mass of axes, swords, shields and clubs. Kul rode with them, keeping pace with his warriors to better savour the raging swell of emotions that surrounded them. This would be a charge like no other, a charge of blood, noise and joy. The air hazed with the sheer violence of the spectacle assaulting Kul's senses.

'Yes!' he yelled. 'Yes, Shornaal, yes!'

The sky behind the elven battle line shimmered like the lights that burned on the northern horizon when the Chaos moon waxed full. The rounded hill crowned with menhirs like the herdstones around which the forest beasts would gather was aflame with colour, and a dazzling rainbow soared from its centre. The stones raised atop the hill blazed with magic, and the runes cut upon them shone like the fires that burned in the hottest forges of the Kurgan metal-shamans.

Glittering rain fell like sparkling snow, and a rumble of thunder rolled across the plains of Ellyrion as a searing crack split the sky. It crackled and spat, like a blazing lightning bolt tapped in the moment of its birth. The charge of the horde faltered at such a sight, and Issyk Kul felt a rush of powerful magic. The crack spread wider, tearing open like a curtain at a window, and the overpowering scent of wild blossoms, new wood and fresh-grown grass gusted from beyond its light.

Shapes moved through the glow, large and small, capering and lumbering, and Issyk Kul spat a mouthful of blood as he tasted the raw power of unfettered life magic. Songs and music sounded from the hilltop, festival-wild and redolent with the promise of rebirth and the cycle of living things. It was a hatefully melodious counterpoint to the blessed din of his horde's noise, and Kul's anger grew.

The rainbow faded and the light on the horizon vanished as suddenly as it had come.

In its place was an army of magic, a host of whip-limbed dryads, capering fauns with barbed tridents and glittering carpets of sprites that covered the hillside and the land to the north. Towering over the curved waystones came trees with vestigial faces and limbs of creaking, groaning timber. These wooden giants lumbered down the hillside, followed by a glittering host of wild creatures of all shapes and sizes.

Wild boars, silver-tailed wolves and huge bears with golden fur came alongside a garishly attired host of elves armed with bows, spears and swords. Flocks of birds erupted from a sky that had been empty moments before: ravens, doves, hawks, red-breasted falcons, starlings, white-tailed jays and a host of birds of myriad species and plumage.

Soaring over the flocks were three golden-winged eagles, wide of pinion and noble in bearing. They flew like the sky was their own private kingdom, and Kul dearly wished for a horn bow like those carried by the Hung horsemasters to bring them down. An eagle with a white-plumed head soared higher than his brothers, and Kul remembered this bird killing his warriors before the walls of the Eagle Gate. Kul instantly dismissed the birds as he laid eyes upon a vision of ancient, eternally enduring perfection at the centre of the magical army.

It was an elf-maid, but an elf-maid like no other.

The purest white light streamed from her supple limbs, like sunrise on northern ice or the shimmer of gold in a streambed. Hair the colour of ripened corn fell about her shoulders like a waterfall, and her face was a vision of perfect beauty.

Eyes of hazel flecked with gold. Full lips and a smile that forgave him all his violations.

Kul hated her with a passion.

By virtue of her race, she was innately more beautiful than Kul could ever be, and the fires of his jealousy burned hotter and fiercer than ten lifetimes worth of hatred.

There could be no doubt as to her identity.

This was the Everqueen of Avelorn.

Finally, something worth defiling.

CHAPTER SEVENTEEN

BREAKING THE NOOSE

Narentir felt his stomach lurch as the magic faded, and his mouth dropped open at the sight of the enemy horde below. Thousands of savage warriors draped in animal skins, beaten pig-iron armour and horned helms advanced upon a perilously thin line of elven spearmen. Narentir had served his time in the citizen levy and was no warrior, but even he could tell that the northern tribesmen would smash through the spear hosts with one charge.

He clutched the spear Lirazel had given him as though it was a dangerous serpent that might turn on him at any moment. A heavy shirt of mail weighed on his shoulders, and how anyone expected him to fight while carrying such an extraordinary weight was quite beyond him. Narentir had explained this to Lirazel, but no amount of protest had changed her mind.

'You are one of the asur,' she had said. 'You will fight for Ulthuan. There is no other option.'

That had been the end of the discussion, and though he knew he was quite useless as a warrior, he had marched with the Everqueen's army to a long line of waystones hidden in a mist-shrouded valley deep in the heart of Avelorn. Here, the Everqueen bid her army make camp, and there they had remained for Isha knew how many days, until, as the sunlight began to fade, the same wordless summons that had awakened the denizens of her forest to her presence now brought them to battle readiness.

'Remember to point the sharp end at the enemy,' said Lilani, startling him from his memory and putting a reassuring hand on his arm. 'Stay close to me and you will live through this.'

Narentir took a deep breath and said, 'I believe you, my dear, though the gods alone know why.'

'Because you are in love with me,' she said.

'Obviously,' replied Narentir. 'But so is half of Ulthuan, and you can't be right about them all, now can you?'

'Maybe not, but you *will* live through this,' said Lilani. 'And you will tell tales of this day for hundreds of years.'

'Really?'

'Really,' she said, and Narentir took comfort from her certainty.

Cruciform shadows passed overhead as the three eagles banked low over the army of Avelorn. A chittering, cackling mass of sprites and faeries swarmed towards the tribesmen, as flocks of birds swooped down and obscured them in a mass of feathers. The elves of Avelorn followed them, all the dancers, poets and singers of the Everqueen's realm come together to fight for the land they celebrated in song and verse. Leading them was the Maiden Guard, a solid core of marble-limbed elf-maids with sculpted breastplates and long spears of bronze.

Narentir was carried along by the stream of bodies, one hand clutching his spear to his chest, the other holding on to Lilani's arm. Despite the dancer's assurance that he would live, fear took hold of him, and his mouth dried at the thought of facing one of these dreadful barbarian warriors in combat. The bloody heave of battle was for heroes and killers, and he was assuredly neither. He told tales of heroes, he was not a hero himself.

He might die on this hillside.

This could be his last day on Ulthuan.

Narentir turned to Lilani and looked deep into her eyes.

'You'll look after me, my dear, won't you?' he said, almost begging.

'Count on it, Narentir,' she replied.

Eldain led Starchaser and their Reavers around the rear of the elven army at the gallop. They had left the druchii army behind and now swung around the battered survivors of the attack over the river. The centre still held, and it was strong, but the flanks were buckling under the pressure.

The druchii stranglehold on Tor Elyr was closing ever tighter, and if this were to be the end, then he would face it by Caelir's side. He could not know for sure that his brother still lived, but the same intuitive belief that Caelir had not died on Naggaroth told him that he still fought on.

Tor Elyr rose up before him, beautiful and shimmering like a dream. How long would it take the druchii and the tribesmen of the north to bring it down? How quickly would this unthinking enemy reduce a city that had endured for centuries to ash and broken glass?

Eldain pictured its marble castles aflame, its silver towers sagging in the awful, intolerable heat of tribal revel fires. He saw its beautiful inhabitants crucified from the highest spires, their blood staining the white cliffs, and the flocks of carrion birds as they flew in lazy circles, bloated by the feast of flesh below.

Great sorrow replaced the anger in Eldain's heart at the thought of such wanton destruction and needless murder. Against such bitter hate, what chance did any of the races of the world stand? When such forces of darkness were ranged against all that was bright and pure, how could anything of goodness endure?

Yet even as despair threatened to overwhelm him, he saw the gates of Tor Elyr opening and ten warriors ride through on black steeds, each as dark as Lotharin. They were few in number, yet it was the banner they rode beneath that restored Eldain's hope that there was always reason to fight on. Shining like the last sunset, the banner flapped from the armoured prow of a chariot constructed from lacquered black starwood edged in gold, that thundered from the city in the midst of the horsemen.

Upon that banner was the rearing silver horse upon a crimson field of Lord Arandir Swiftwing.

'The lord of Tor Elyr rides with his warriors once more!' shouted Laurena Starchaser, and a chorus of skirling yells answered her. Eldain watched the crippled master of the city lift his sword high, a glittering blade of sapphire steel, and in that moment the images of Tor Elyr in flames vanished, replaced with it shining at its most glorious.

The riders and the chariot charged down the statue-lined causeway from the bastion castle at the edge of the bay, and Eldain lifted his sword in salute as Lord Swiftwing's chariot plunged into the swirling combat in the centre of the battle. To fight alongside the master of Tor Elyr would be an honour, but the northern flank was in danger of collapse and needed his warriors to keep it steady.

Bodies lay twisted on the frozen riverbank, sprawled next to monstrous beasts with the heads of wolves, bears and bulls. Everywhere Eldain looked, he saw death. The smell of blood, rotten meat and mangy fur was like a poison in the air. A raucous melange of horns, drums and beaten iron came from the mortal host of tribesmen, a sound to end worlds.

'But not this world,' swore Eldain, riding around groups of wounded elves. They cheered at the sight of Lord Swiftwing riding out, and turned their broken bodies back to the fighting ranks. Riderless horses milled around the edges of the battle, and with every passing moment, Eldain's Reaver band grew larger as these grieving mounts joined their wild ride.

He saw the horde of northern tribesmen and his stomach turned at the sight of so terrible and numerous a foe. The savage warlord sat atop his red-raw steed at the centre of the enemy line, and Eldain angled the course of his Reavers towards the edge of a thin line of spears and archers.

The archers were strung in a line two deep and loosed the last of their shafts into the onrushing horde. It wouldn't be enough to stop the charge, and Eldain knew the spearmen did not have the mass of numbers to stop them either. With perfect synchrony, the Reaver hosts parted and flowed around the flanks of the elven host. Starchaser rode along the edge of the river, while Eldain curved around the eastern end of the line in the shadow of the waystone crowned hill. A bloodied Reaver band milled at the foot of the hill and Eldain rejoiced to see his brother at its head. His brother had lost his helm and his armour bore all the hallmarks of hard fighting. Caelir saw him and raised his sword with a boyish flourish.

They shouted each other's name in unison, riding together as a burst of rainbow light blazed from the hillside above them and the warriors of Avelorn took the field. An army like nothing else on this world emerged from the shimmering curtain of light that parted the sky like a silken theatre curtain in a Lothern playhouse.

Creatures of myth and legend, even in a land such as Ulthuan, came at the behest of this army's leader, and both brothers felt the awesome light of her presence as she trod the grass of Ellyrion.

'She lives...' breathed Caelir. 'Thank all the gods!'

Eldain nodded, too dumbfounded to answer as he saw the beautiful elf at the Everqueen's side. Though outshone by the Queen of Avelorn's brilliance, she was in every way, more radiant and more precious to Eldain than any divine ruler could ever be.

'Rhianna,' he said.

On the western bank of the river, the spectacular arrival of the Everqueen's army caused a ripple of unease to pass through the ranks of the druchii warriors. Her powers were rightly feared by the denizens of Naggaroth, and their own legends were filled with terrible stories of the fey queen's ability to bewitch and unmake even the mightiest champion.

Only one amongst the druchii did not quail at her sudden appearance.

Morathi smiled as the glittering host stepped from the blazing portal opened through the waystones. It had only been a matter of time before the bitch of Avelorn intervened, and now that she had made her move, it was time for Morathi to make her own.

It had been hard to stay her hand from intervening in the battle, for her powers could easily have destroyed whole swathes of the asur, but in the battle to come she would need all her power to oppose the greatest mage the world had ever seen. No matter that he was completely insane, Caledor Dragontamer was still a force to be reckoned with. Centuries of study and disciplined training had enabled her to shield her thoughts from others, even ones as canny and watchful as Caledor.

He would not see her coming, and the threat he had made all those years ago was surely now as empty as when he had first bluffed her with it. Then she had been young and just discovering the full extent of her power. Now she was the mistress of the dark arts, a sorceress unrivalled in ability and strength. No power in the world could match her, not even the shadowy guardians who faded with Caledor on the island.

Morathi's blood sang with the prospect of her final triumph. Let Malekith tear down the gates of Lothern, and let this host topple the castles of Tor Elyr. These were mere sideshows in the great battle that had begun over five thousand years ago when the fires of Asuryan had left her beloved son a burned and wretched husk.

She could feel the titanic energies swirling around the island even from here. They were calling to her, and she would answer their siren song of salvation with one of destruction.

Morathi shrieked and jabbed her barbed spurs into Sulephet's flanks. The beast snarled in anger, spreading its wings and powering into the sky. Flocks of screeching, bat-winged harpies rose like flocks of startled carrion birds, their leathery wings flapping wildly as they struggled to keep up with her dark steed.

Morathi watched the world recede, the desperate life and death struggles playing out upon its surface now meaningless to her. Let whichever side carried the field have its moment of glory. By day's end it would be irrelevant.

The Everqueen had come to Ellyrion, but Morathi did not care.

She flew away from the battle, over the glittering spires of Tor Elyr towards the magical heart of Ulthuan.

The two hosts came together in a clash of mortal bodies and magical flesh. Birds of many colours swooped and dived, with razored beaks pecking out eyes and sharp talons raking the skin from exposed limbs. The eagles flew low over the enemy host, slashing with claws and beak as they plucked warriors from the ground and tore them apart in the air.

Elasir, the lord of the eagles, hunted the largest warriors, ripping them to pieces even as they shouted commands to their vassals and huscarls. His brothers did likewise, their ebon claws ripping armour as though it were no more substantial than silk.

Streams of liquid sprites coursed through the tribesmen, biting and tearing with glittering claws of sparkling energy. Towering figures formed from bark and centuries-aged timber and moss stomped through the swirling mêlée, arms of ash, oak and willow smashing men through the air or crushing them beneath root-formed feet. Fauns gored, wild animals snapped, arrows sliced home, and hurled spell-flames burned the northmen, but even under such fantastical assault they did not break.

These were warriors reared amid the harshest environments imaginable, where life was unimaginably brutal and only the strongest, most ruthless warriors survived. The tribes of the north lived on the very edge of the world, in the scrap of land where the division between the realms of men and daemons was at its thinnest. The touch of Chaos lay upon that land, and the things living in the northern wastes were far stranger and more dangerous than these capering sprites.

Northern axes clove the giants of wood and spears spitted the fauns and wild animals. Swords bludgeoned the birds from the air and heavy wooden shields bore the brunt of the rain of arrows. In the centre of the northmen, Issyk Kul battered a path through the raging combats to face the oncoming Queen of Avelorn, roaring his eagerness for the fight like a bellowed challenge. His warriors followed him in a swirling mass of rabid blades and clubs, all cohesion lost in the rush to destroy the incandescent elf-queen.

Eldain and Caelir rode around the edges of the tribesmen towards the lower slopes of the hill, loosing arrows into the mass of grunting warriors as they went. They rode without heed for the rest of the battle. Right now, *this* was all that mattered. Both brothers knew that they owed their lives to the Everqueen, and they rode to fight at her side. They could never repay her mercy or undo the hurt they had done, but they could offer their souls as sons of Ellyrion.

Eldain saw Lirazel lead a charge of the Maiden Guard, their shrill war cries like the wails of a thousand banshees. Their bronze spears plunged into the closest warriors, and then they were in amongst them, leaping, stabbing, kicking, punching and slashing. Elves of both sexes who had no business being warriors fought men who had spent their whole lives in battle, and Eldain wondered at the kind of devotion that could inspire such courage.

Caelir let fly with his last arrow and threw aside his bow.

'Brother!' he shouted. 'It's time!'

Eldain knew exactly what he meant and nodded. 'Into them!'

He turned Lotharin towards the tribesmen and unsheathed his sword, riding hard towards the armoured warriors. Hundreds of Reaver Knights rode with him and their charge was a thing of beauty, perfectly coordinated and smooth as glass. Four hundred horsemen smashed into the fur-clad army, trampling and spearing the mortal warriors in a stampede of shod hooves and blades.

Moving languidly, as though she ghosted down the hillside without touching the ground, the Everqueen came in a shimmering cloud of drifting flower petals and perfumed air. She brought the light with her, and where she so much as glanced, the land threw off the chill of winter and summer blooms rose from the ground. She cast no magic, content to draw the healing energies of the land within her and let it flow into the warriors around her.

At her side, Rhianna displayed no such restraint, basking in the potent wash of magical energies to empower her own spells. Searing fires leapt from her hands, dancing among the tribesmen with screeching cries of predatory birds. Her face was carved from granite, harsh and merciless as she killed, but to Eldain's eyes she was still wondrous.

Surrounded from all sides, the tribesmen responded by pulling back and bringing their shields around in perfect concert. Arrows thudded into heavy timbers and the Reaver Knights were forced to turn away from the solid barrier of spiked shields and jutting blades. Issyk Kul rode to the edge of the shield wall and raised his sword in challenge to the Everqueen.

'Face me and I shall ruin you, woman!' he shouted.

The Everqueen said nothing, but stepped down to the earth as though to answer the warlord's challenge. Though the battle continued to rage around the shield wall, it seemed to Eldain that the world around these two combatants faded to shadowy echoes. Kul burst from the shield wall on the back of his mighty steed, a monstrous sword of many blades held over his head and poised to slice the Everqueen in two.

The grass around her surged with life, the green of every shoot and leaf becoming eye-wateringly brilliant and vivid. Until now, Eldain had thought Ellyrion a land of great life and vibrancy, yet the Everqueen's touch poured the power of primordial creation into its very soul. Sweetly perfumed air spread from her, and the sunlight followed her every step as she faced a warrior who was her opposite in every way.

What she could create, he would destroy.

Where she breathed life, he carried death.

Where his dark patron corrupted, she renewed.

The Everqueen lifted a slender arm and pointed at the red-fleshed steed. Kul's charge was undone as the horse reared in agony, but it was not the pain of some magical attack that caused it to scream. The warlord leapt from the saddle, as chestnut strands of colour wound their way around the thrashing beast's legs, like thread onto a weaver's bobbin. Exposed musculature was once again clothed in flesh and skin, the colour moving upwards until the warm, mahogany coloured coat was reknitting onto the horse's back. The raw stump of its tail grew again, and a lustrous mane of long black hair sprouted from its gleaming neck.

Within moments, the horse was transformed, the hideous changes wrought upon its form now undone. The horse climbed to its feet, eyes wide and ears pressed flat against its skull as it saw the world with eyes untouched by warping powers.

The northmen shouted oaths to their Dark Gods, horrified at the ease with which their power was broken. Eldain threw off his surprise at the Everqueen's magic to see that the gap opened in the shieldwall by Kul's charge was still open. While it remained solid, a shieldwall was virtually impregnable, but once it was broken…

Lotharin saw what Eldain saw and sprang toward the gap.

'Reavers, ho!' shouted Eldain. Some of the tribesmen recognised the danger and moved to close the gap, but Eldain was quicker. Lotharin barged through, using his weight and power to smash men from their feet. More warriors saw the danger and rushed towards the incoming

Reaver Knights. Eldain wheeled Lotharin around, lancing his sword through the neck of a tribesman wearing a full-faced helm of iron.

More Reaver Knights joined Eldain and their charge split the shield-wall as a wooden wedge splits a log for the fire. Caelir kicked a warrior in the face and slashed his blade through another man's arm. Starchaser rode into the shieldwall and her Reavers tore into the northmen from within. What had once been a fortress was now a deathtrap. Hundreds of cavalry charged the disintegrating shieldwall, and the savage warriors of the north were forced to fight as individuals. Though they still outnumbered the elves, they were scattered and alone.

The northmen were doomed, and Eldain swung his horse around as Issyk Kul ran at the Everqueen with his sword swinging for her throat. Once again, she raised a hand, palm up. Kul's sword vanished into a haze of glittering sparks, as though remembering the fire from which it had been created. The warlord cast aside the hilt as it burst into flames, and screamed his hatred at the Queen of Avelorn.

'You do not hate me, Issyk Kul,' said the Everqueen. 'You love me, as I love you.'

'I... I... love no one,' hissed Kul, struggling to reach the Everqueen as though he walked through the thickest mud. 'I am to be feared, not loved.'

His every step was a battle, and sinews stood out like taut cables on his neck and chest as he fought to reach her. His hands closed around her neck and Eldain wanted to scream at such an insult.

'That is a lie,' said the Everqueen. '*She* loved you, but you offered her to the prince of pleasure for power. You gave away the most precious thing in the world, and for what? Power? You think what you have is power? Mortal power is fleeting, a blink in the eye of the cosmos. Love is eternal, and lasts all the ages of the world.'

Kul screamed and his hands dropped to his sides as he fell to his knees. Eldain saw the healing light of her magic worming its way into his flesh. Kul's body was swollen with muscle, warped to gross proportions by the Dark Powers he served. The magic of Avelorn filled him, seeking to undo the horrific changes he had willingly accepted. The Everqueen wished to destroy him, but Alarielle would not, for it was anathema to end life when she could restore it.

Eldain saw the northern warlord *diminish*, as though his entire body was being drained of the corruption that had given him such impossible strength and hatred. The face that was both beautiful and monstrous reshaped itself, losing its magnificence and becoming pugnacious and, worst of all, ordinary. His hair darkened until it was the same sandy, flaxen colour as his warriors, his flesh dirty and bruised, hard and leathery.

But the changes worked on his flesh had been at the whims of the dark prince, and such a god was a jealous master who did not willingly abandon his playthings. Even as the Everqueen remade Kul's body in its original form, so the petulant god of pleasure incarnate poured his malice, his spite and his perverse glee back into Kul. Ancient powers warred within the champion's flesh, and the effect was as horrifying as it was sudden.

Renewal and the power of unfettered excess ripped Kul apart, his body expanding and tearing with new growth. Limbs swelled and bloated as the power of the dark prince ran riot within his blood and bone. Gristled extrusions of marrow erupted from the raw flesh of the mutating champion, along with spindly growths, rubbery bladders of meat and hairless body parts that had no business being on the outside of any creature.

Within seconds, nothing that resembled a man remained, simply a mewling mass of degenerate flesh that flopped and squealed and honked its insanity through a dozen flapping mouths. A hundred eyes oozed into existence all over its warp-spawned flesh, and each one of them burned with hatred and madness. A warrior who had once been the chosen of the gods had now been abandoned, cast aside by his master like a broken toy.

Yet this broken toy was still awesomely dangerous, its lashing limbs hooked and barbed with lethal claws, its many mouths filled with swollen, broken teeth and needle-like fangs. The Everqueen's light was eclipsed by the darkness boiling from the monster's myriad eyes and it came at her with all the fury of a thing that knows only that the source of its pain is standing before it.

Then Caelir was beside the Everqueen, his borrowed sword held before him.

A bladed limb slashed for the Everqueen, but Caelir's blade was there to intercept it. He cut it away as more spined, thorny limbs lashed out like a whipping forest of razor-edged blades. He fought with the speed and skill of a Sword Master, slashing grotesque appendages from the creature spawned from Issyk Kul's remains.

As swiftly as he sliced its unclean flesh, more growths erupted from its heaving bulk. The Maiden Guard surrounded the monstrosity, plunging their spears into its gelatinous body and putting themselves between its rampage and the Everqueen. Lirazel rammed her spear into the creature's body, gouging and twisting the blade to draw forth spurts of steaming black ichor. The monster screeched and attacked with even greater fury. A slicing barb took Caelir high on the shoulder as another tore his armour just above his hip. He staggered, and a host of blackened limbs struck him with gleeful frenzy.

Eldain leapt from his saddle and cut a path towards the creature through its whipping limbs, organic debris and thrashing, frond-like tentacles. Stinking fluids gushed from each wound, and Eldain retched at the miasma as a jelly-like limb of toothed suckers wrapped itself around Caelir and lifted him into the air. A pair of mouths rippled into existence on the monster's unquiet flesh, fangs like sword blades unsheathing from drooling gums of pus-yellow meat.

Before they could bite down, Eldain slashed his sword through the side of the creature's head. A flood of stinking black blood and fatty tissue frothed from the wound. The reek was incredible, rotten meat and decaying matter that smelled as though unearthed from a freshly opened grave.

The beast hurled Caelir aside, gurgling in lunatic amusement as it sensed a more succulent morsel nearby. Eldain ran to his brother's side as Rhianna stepped before Issyk Kul's new and repulsive form. The Everqueen's light filled her, white fire shining in her eyes and blazing along her body like the magic that thundered through the Annulii.

'Are you hurt?' said Eldain.

'I'm bleeding, but nothing serious,' answered Caelir. 'Come on, we have to help her.'

'No,' said Eldain, holding Caelir back. 'This is not a fight for the likes of us, brother.'

Rhianna stood before the monster, unfazed by its expanding horror, and magical vortices of fire spun around her body in pulsing waves.

Acidic drool and hissing spittle flew from the monster's jaws as it hauled its lumpen mass towards her on twisted limbs of misshapen bone and roiling frills of undulant flesh. Faces blurred on its drum-taut skin as though a hundred bodies writhed within it, and claws, teeth and drooling orifices opened in the meat of its distended belly.

'I am a mage of Saphery,' said Rhianna, her voice resonating with wells of power no mortal ought to tap. 'And a daughter of Ulthuan. The blood of queens flows in my veins.'

Eldain and Caelir shielded their eyes as a torrent of blazing light erupted from Rhianna's body. A horizontal geyser of white fire shot from her hands and eyes.

It was killing magic. Dangerous magic. *Old* magic…

Alarielle would not destroy, but Rhianna was more than willing to do so.

The light played over Kul's transformed flesh, and where it touched, it burned like the fires of Asuryan himself. Like tallow before a flame, bloated flesh sizzled and ran like butter. Drooling ropes of it melted from grossly twisted and deformed bones that cracked in the heat with the sound of splitting wood. The creature's many mouths gave voice to one ululating shriek of pain and horror as its body was devoured by the cleansing flame of Avelorn.

Eldain tasted the ancient power of this magic. This was the energy that had brought the world into being, a fragment of the power that had shaped worlds and allowed its builders to cross from one side of the cosmos to the other in a single step. Against its awesome potency, the power of the dark prince was as a leaf in a hurricane.

Kul's body shrank before the firestorm, but whatever spark of life remained to animate his monstrous form remained alive until the last. The screaming went on until nothing remained of the creature save a molten pool of smouldering ash and liquid bone.

The spear hosts charged into the ragged horde of northmen and drove them back with disciplined thrusts of their weapons. With graceful, methodical precision, the tribesmen were either slain or driven back to the river. Caught between the precise slaughter of the spears and the crazed whirl of magical beings, spells and creatures of legend, the warriors of Issyk Kul had already held beyond the limits of human endurance.

And, without him to lead them, they broke.

Here and there, small groups banded together, but the Reavers simply circled them and sent well-aimed shafts through helmets, exposed limbs and necks until they too collapsed. Fewer than a hundred warriors survived to reach the riverbank.

The spear hosts left the final slaughter to the creatures of Avelorn, obeying the shouted commands of their sentinels to reform and march to the aid of the centre. The Everqueen moved through the wounded, spreading her healing light to those who were still beyond the reach of Morai-Heg's banshees. She would take no part in the killing, and the magical beings she had brought to Ellyrion swarmed around the edges of the spear hosts, eager to take their killing to the centre.

Beneath the ragged, battle-torn banners of Tor Elyr's citizen levy, the victorious warriors of the northern flank turned south.

CHAPTER EIGHTEEN
THE LAST HOUR

The raven ships hit the quayside first, sweeping the docks with iron bolts that killed any of the defenders not behind cover and driving the rest back. Heedless of the damage to their ships, the slave-masters of the troop galleys cracked their whips and drove their hulls straight into the sloping quays. The ugly boats cracked and disgorged scores of druchii swordsmen onto stonework that had known the tread of many races, but had never seen Naggarothi in thousands of years.

Tyrion had joined the Phoenix King and Korhil in the centre of the battle line, amid a silent, armoured host of Phoenix Guard. Tall and unmoving, silent and grim of feature, these warriors were unlike any other of Ulthuan. It seemed a lambent light glowed beneath their skin, and their eyes were dark pools that had seen too much. Even standing next to them gave Tyrion a sense of ages passed and ages yet to come.

He felt the weight of grief borne by Ulthuan, the endless cycle of battle and bloodshed waged in the name of a power struggle begun thousands of years ago. He saw the bloody Sword of Khaine above it all, revelling in the long-burning hatreds that flared anew with every generation, as mothers and fathers told their children of ancient wrongs over and over.

Truly Aenarion had saved and cursed his people by drawing the sword.

'Would you have drawn it had you *truly* known the price we would pay?' Tyrion wondered aloud. 'If you had seen the millennia of woe it would bring, would you still have drawn the sword?'

He knew the answer to that, just as he knew what his own answer would have been.

The druchii were massing beneath a relentless hail of arrows, but still the Phoenix King did not give the order to advance.

Tyrion moved along the front of their line until he stood next to Finubar. The king gave him a weak smile, and Tyrion saw the fear in his eyes. He feared to give the order, and not without good reason. The Phoenix Guard's presence was a grim omen: praetorians and pallbearers all in one.

'Sire,' said Tyrion. 'We must advance. The druchii need to be driven from the quayside.'

'I know,' said Finubar.

'Then give the order.'

'I am afraid, Tyrion,' said Finubar. 'If I order the advance, I will die. I know it.'

'You will die anyway,' said Tyrion. 'We all die sooner or later. Better on our terms than theirs, my king.'

The warrior beside Finubar nodded, and Tyrion saw the rune of Asuryan upon his brow. Clad in a shimmering hauberk of orange-tinted gold and ithilmar, he was swathed in a white cloak of mourning and carried a slender-hafted halberd with a shining silver blade. The warrior's face was full and roguish, like that of a libertine, yet his eyes were filled with the shadows of past regrets and future knowledge.

'Caradryan,' said Tyrion, recognising the famed Captain of the Phoenix Guard.

The warrior mimed drawing a sword and cocked his eyebrow.

Tyrion looked from Caradryan to Finubar and Korhil, seeing their incomprehension. It was the question only a warrior without words could ask, and Tyrion knew the answer even as the question was posed.

Yes, the Sword of Khaine would give him the power to end the druchii threat once and for all, but the price was higher than Tyrion was willing to pay. Aenarion might not have known the full truth of the damnation he laid upon his people by drawing the Widowmaker, but Tyrion knew it all too well. Power such as the sword would grant could never be given back by something so simple as driving it back into an altar. Once loosed, it was *always* loose; in the hearts of all who heard of it, and in their blood that sang of its slaughters.

Nothing could undo the damage Aenarion had done by wielding the Sword of Khaine, but Tyrion would not add to his people's woes by drawing it anew. He had the strength of his friends and courage of his own to steel him in the face of the enemy. Yes, the sword offered a chance for victory, but Tyrion would not let its temptations draw him into its web. The faces of lost loved ones paraded before him, but Tyrion welcomed them, reliving the joy he had known in their lives instead of mourning their passing.

Tyrion held himself taller than he had in a great many years as the anger he had carried for so long vanished in a heartbeat.

Tyrion smiled, and Caradryan saw the revelation within him.

'You look *different*,' said Korhil.

'I am,' agreed Tyrion.

'What has changed?' asked Finubar.

'Me,' replied Tyrion. 'I have changed.'

Korhil shrugged, dismissing the matter as irrelevant, but Finubar continued to stare at him. The Phoenix King seemed to take a measure of comfort in Tyrion's calmness and looked over to the druchii massing on the quayside. Crossbowmen were moving out with their black weapons tucked into their shoulders, and swordsmen marched behind them beneath freshly raised banners.

Above them all, the Witch King flew on the back of his dragon. The sky above Lothern was calm and peaceful, unsullied by so much as a single cloud, and Tyrion followed the Witch King as he swooped and dived over the city, unleashing bolts of purple fire from his gauntlets and noxious breaths of toxic fumes from the dragon's jaws. Flames leapt up from the stricken city, and the sight of his city burning galvanised the Phoenix King at last.

'Everyone dies,' he said at last. 'And if this is to be my time, then so be it.'

Finubar raised his sword and the fiery banner of the Phoenix Guard caught its golden edge. All along the elven battle line, swords and spears were raised in answer.

'In Asuryan's name!' shouted Finubar.

The Phoenix King charged, and the host of Lothern went with him.

Eldain and Caelir rose to their feet as Rhianna approached. The light of borrowed power still shone in her eyes, and it seemed that she did not know them for a moment. Then the light of recognition arose and her face went through a complex series of expressions ranging from relief, to anger and regret. So many emotions churned within her that Eldain had no idea how she would react to seeing him again. The last time they had stood in one another's presence, Rhianna had tried to destroy him with her magic.

Caelir took matters into his own hands and swept Rhianna into a passionate embrace. Her arms hovered for a moment before returning the embrace, and Eldain let out a relieved breath as he saw tears of happiness spill down her cheeks.

'My love,' said Caelir. 'Gods above, but I have longed for this moment.'

'Caelir,' said Rhianna. 'I thought I would never see you again.'

'I have a habit of doing what others do not expect,' he said, kissing her on the mouth.

She returned the passion of his kiss, and Eldain felt his heart break anew. He had lost Rhianna to Caelir once before and it had hurt like no other pain ever could. That wound had festered, but this one was clean.

Caelir and Rhianna belonged together. Eldain knew that now, but still it hurt.

No one could ever lose a maiden like Rhianna without pain, but this was *good* pain, as though a barb he hadn't known was lodged in his heart had suddenly been removed by a healer's magic. Guilt had been a torment he had lived with for so long, he had forgotten what it was to live free of it.

He made to turn away, but a restraining hand took him by the arm.

'Eldain,' said Rhianna. 'I do not know what to say to you.'

'You do not have to say anything,' said Eldain. 'I do not expect your forgiveness, for I did you and Caelir great wrong. He and I have made a peace of sorts, but I expect nothing of the kind from you.'

Rhianna took a deep breath. 'I can forgive you, Eldain, but first you have to forgive yourself.'

Eldain shook his head. 'Look around you. All of this is my fault. I brought this death and destruction to Ulthuan, and I can never forgive myself for that. Do not waste your forgiveness on me, Rhianna. I do not deserve it.'

'The heart that does not want to heal cannot be remade.'

'Maybe some hearts should not be remade.'

'I said the very same thing once,' said Rhianna. 'I believed it then, but I do not believe it now. Broken hearts are empty, and empty hearts soon fill with all that is dark in this world. I would not see you live so.'

Eldain said, 'It is not your choice to make, Rhianna.'

'No, it is not,' said a sad voice of radiant wonder. 'And it never will be.'

They turned to see the Everqueen standing before them in a pool of golden light. None of them had heard her approach, and Eldain fought down a rising fear as he felt the presence of the ancient power of the Everqueen lurking behind the mask of Alarielle.

Which of the Queen of Avelorn's two faces would be in the ascendancy?

'Be at peace, Eldain of Ellyr-Charoi,' said Alarielle. 'You need not fear me. Nor should you, Caelir of Ellyr-Charoi. The Everqueen spared your lives for reasons I could not fathom, but which I now understand. Ulthuan needs you like never before.'

'I am yours to command,' said Eldain, dropping to one knee.

'My life is yours,' vowed Caelir.

Warm approval greeted their pronouncements, as a black shape passed overhead, a stain on the purple sky as it passed over the face of the sinking sun. Eldain looked up and saw a black steed galloping through the air. Its sweeping midnight wings beat with powerful strokes and there could be no doubting the identity of the ivory-skinned druchii sorceress sat astride its back.

'The Hag Sorceress,' hissed Caelir. 'She flees!'

'No,' said Rhianna, with a haunted look settling upon her features. 'She does not flee.'

'Then what is she doing?' asked Eldain.

'She seeks to unmake that which she cannot possess,' said the Everqueen.

Eldain said, 'Where is she going?'

'Rhianna knows,' said Alarielle. 'Don't you?'

'Isha, no…' said Rhianna, as though reliving a dark memory or despairing foresight. 'The vision of the oracle… the druchii princess… I saw her kill them.'

'Kill who?' asked Eldain.

'The mages!' cried Rhianna. 'Without them the ritual will be undone!'

'What does that mean?' asked Caelir.

'Aenarion's bride flies to the Isle of the Dead,' said Alarielle. 'To unmake the vortex of Caledor Dragontamer.'

The song was killing him. He knew it, but kept singing it anyway.

His body was wasted, drained of energy to keep the melody alive, and his mind was lost in the darkness of ancient dreams. Prince Imrik, though the name now held little meaning for him, floated in the depths of the mountains. He had long since cast off the silver threads that bound him to his flesh in his desperation to reach the ancient minds of the slumbering dragons. Even were he to succeed, his mind would be lost forever in the spaces between thought and physicality. Unable to return to his body, his mind would wander in darkness for all eternity, or at least until his empty frame eventually succumbed to the ravages of time.

Yet it would be worth it if he could only reach the minds of the sleeping dragons.

He raged and pleaded for them to awake, but still they ignored him. He offered them riches, magic and servitude if only they would rouse themselves from their dreams. They took no heed of his blandishments, and dreamed on.

He felt them moving around him in the darkness, vast, mountainous consciousnesses that rolled and turned like vast leviathans of the deep. They took no notice of him, lost in their own dreams of glory and open skies. What lure did the world above have for such minds?

The magic of the world was in decline, drawn away by an ancient ritual, and without that magic, the world of mortals was a cold and tasteless realm. Better to live in dreams, where magic was all powerful and never faded.

Who would ever choose to leave such a place?

Why would *he*?

Imrik finally accepted the truth of the naysayers in Lothern.

The dragons were sleeping away the ages of the world, and would never reawaken.

He had avoided that conclusion for so long, but now it was inescapable. With its acceptance, Imrik felt his will to awaken the dragons erode until there was nothing left, just a broken mind bereft of a body to which he could return.

Imrik surrendered to despair, adrift on currents of ancient thought.

Lost forever in the shared dreamspace of dragonkind.

The air above the Inner Sea was cold and flecked with clouds like rumpled snow. Eldain held tight to the feathers of the eagle's neck, though he knew it would never let him fall. Primal fear of heights kept Eldain's grip firm, and though the view beneath him was spectacular, he tried to keep his eyes fixed on the creature beneath him.

Its plumage was gold, not the gold poets spoke of when describing a beautiful elf-maid's hair, but the gold that would drive a dwarf to madness with its lustre. Only the eagle's head was different, pure white and unblemished by so much as a single feather of another colour.

The bird's name was Elasir, and he was the lord of the eagles. Such a self-proclaimed title among mortals would have invited ridicule, but for Elasir it was completely appropriate, and, indeed, seemed entirely too prosaic for so magnificent a creature. Its two brothers were no less spectacular, and when they had landed behind the Everqueen, Eldain felt the need to bow to them as he had bowed to her.

'Follow Morathi,' said the Everqueen. 'Stop her.'

Simple commands, yet Eldain had not the faintest idea as to how they would obey them.

The first part had been easy. Two of the eagles stooped their wings, and Caelir and Rhianna had eagerly leapt upon their backs. Eldain had only reluctantly climbed aboard Elasir's back, for he was a rider who preferred his mounts to remain earthbound. No sooner had he settled himself on the back of the eagle than it lifted with a deafening cry, spreading its wings and powering high into the sky.

I am Elasir, Lord of the Eagles. Be calm and grip the feathers of my neck.

The voice was powerful and layered with wisdom gathered from across the world. Eldain obeyed instantly, and felt the noble bird's amusement at his nervousness.

Your companions have no fear of flying on Aeris and Irian, came the gently chiding voice of the eagle, *nor should you. I will not let you fall.*

'Rhianna is a mage of Saphery, she is used to such strangeness. And Caelir, well, he relishes this kind of thing.'

Few earthwalkers earn a chance such as this.

'Believe me, I know that, and I am grateful, but I will be glad when I am back down.'

I doubt that, said the eagle, and Eldain wondered what he meant.

The ongoing battle at Tor Elyr had faded behind them in the mist, and Eldain felt a pang of guilt at leaving before the outcome was decided.

Even with the magical forces of the Everqueen, the army of Lord Swift-wing was still in dire straits. Neither force would emerge from the battle without grievous losses, but it was clear that the outcome of the battle held little meaning for Morathi.

The Inner Sea was a churning blue shimmer of breaking waves and foaming crests. Eldain remembered crossing that sea on the *Dragonkin* and it had been like a mirror, smooth and untroubled by much in the way of waves. Captain Bellaeir had complained that the seas were troubled, and Eldain wondered what he would make of them now.

Scraps of islands passed beneath them, tiny dots in the expanse of sea that looked like shapes on a map instead of actual landscape. To the north, Eldain saw a smudge of smoke on the horizon from the ever-smouldering volcano on the Gaen Vale. Only reluctantly did he allow his eyes to be drawn to the shimmer in the air before them that masked their destination.

The Isle of the Dead.

No one with any sense sought to travel to that doomed rock, for it was a place of mist and shadow, grief and loss. Eldain forced himself to look at the seas around the island. Where the rest of the ocean was unsettled and threatening, the waters around the Isle of the Dead were calm and smooth, as though painted on the surface of the world by an ancient artist. A grey and craggy smear of land was just visible through the mists that hugged the shoreline, and Eldain was reminded of Narentir's tales of the Ulthane and the lost island they guarded.

Did anything similar protect the Isle of the Dead?

No, the island has protection of its own, came the voice of Elasir.

Eldain nodded and said, 'Yet it still needs us to fly to save it?'

I did not say those defences were on the island.

Eldain could not argue with that logic, and watched as the island grew larger on the horizon. They flew into the mist, and Eldain felt the clammy touch of it. His breathing grew shallow, for the air here was cold and without life, like a mansion left empty by the death of its owner. It tasted of abandonment, a place where nothing has stirred the air for centuries, and nothing ever would.

Even their presence left no mark.

The beating of the eagles' wings did not stir the clouds, and their cries back and forth to one another did not echo. Caelir shouted over to Eldain, but his words were swallowed in the dead space between them. Here and there, he saw glittering lights and distant glows in the mist and cloud, but no sooner were they noticed than they faded away.

'What are they?' he asked, knowing Elasir would understand.

Souls who approached too close and were trapped by Caledor's great magic. Do not look upon them too long or your heart will break with sadness.

Eldain took that advice and averted his gaze whenever he saw the flickering corpse-candles. Instead, he concentrated on the lost island that faded in and out of perception as the eagles flew ever deeper into the deathly mist. It had been thousands of years since this land had last known the tread of elves, caught forever in a timeless, deathless embrace of powerful magic.

Just thinking of the Isle of the Dead was enough to settle a lump of cold dread in his stomach, for it was a place of incredible heroism and awesome tragedy. The fate of the asur had been sealed and saved on this island, as had the lives of the mages who made the ultimate sacrifice in joining Caledor.

Elasir began to drop through the air, his wings folding back and dipping as he lost altitude and began his approach to the island. Eldain swallowed as the clouds enveloped them once more. He could see nothing but the cloying mist and the dim lanterns of the souls trapped by the island's magic. Would he be such a light for some future traveller to see? The idea terrified him, and his mouth went dry at the thought of being trapped here for all eternity.

Then they were clear of the clouds, and the Isle of the Dead spread out before him.

A bleak shoreline of tumbled boulders rose from the sea, leading to shingled beaches of polished stones and thence to forests of leafless trees. Though the sea around the island was like a polished mirror, it pounded the rocks of the island itself. Booming waves hammered the island and Eldain felt the sea's fury at being kept from these shores for so long.

Elasir brought him in low, coming in fast over the shoreline. Broken swords with black blades and skull-topped pommels drifted in the surf, and the bones of long-dead monsters lay half-buried in the sand. The eagle landed high up the beach and Eldain dropped to the black sand with a relieved sigh.

Aeris and Irian landed a moment later, and Caelir vaulted from the back of his mount, his face flushed with excitement.

'That was incredible, Aeris,' he said, running his hands along the eagle's flank as he would an Ellyrian steed. 'I don't think I've known anything like it.'

The eagle ruffled its feathers and Eldain felt its pride. Rhianna slid demurely from the back of Irian, adjusting her mage's robes as she turned to face them. She bowed to her eagle, and whatever words passed between them were for her and Irian alone.

We will take to the air now, said Elasir.

'You will not come with us?' asked Eldain.

We cannot. Mortals cursed this place, and only mortals may walk its paths.

'So how do we get back?' asked Caelir.

We will be here, replied Elasir, and Eldain caught the note of hesitation in his words.

Caelir looked around the dismal beach. Grey fingers of mist eased from the forests higher up on the scrubby bluffs overlooking the beach, and the surf spread yet more weapons and bones over the sand. Caelir picked one up, its hilt still sticky with blood and the blade razor-sharp. A skull-rune was stamped on the pommel stone and Caelir threw it away in disgust.

'I thought this place was supposed to be timeless,' he said.

'It is,' said Rhianna.

'Then why does the sea still surge and recede? Why does the mist writhe in the trees?'

'The island is cut off from the rest of the world,' said Rhianna. 'If anyone could see us, we would appear to be standing still. Time flows around us here, not with us.'

A faint tremor shook the beach and stones rattled as they were carried down to the water.

'What was that?' asked Caelir.

'Morathi,' answered Rhianna.

'We'd best get a move on,' said Eldain, setting off for the bluffs overlooking the shore.

Beyond the beach, the island was just as bleak and desolate. It had all the hallmarks of a battlefield, for the dunes were formed from piles of skulls and heaps of rotted armour. The noise of the sea receded, and the island became utterly quiet. The forest was unnaturally silent. No birds nested in the leafless trees, no burrowing animals made their lairs amid their roots, and not a breath of wind stirred the skeletal branches.

'What was this place?' asked Caelir as they followed a path that wound a serpentine route through the trees. 'I mean, I know the stories of what happened here, but what was it before then?'

'I do not know,' said Eldain, glancing nervously between the narrow trunks at the scraps of mist that seemed to be following them. 'I have only ever known it as the Isle of the Dead.'

'It was where the asur were born,' said Rhianna. 'This is where Asuryan made the first of us. It was once a place of creation, the cradle in which our race was first given form.'

'How do you know that?'

Rhianna hesitated. 'I am not sure. I feel it as though I have always known it, though the thought never occurred to me until now. It feels like… like memory.'

'We should hurry,' said Eldain, glancing over his shoulder. 'I believe we are being followed.'

Caelir drew his sword. 'By who? Morathi?'

'No,' said Eldain. 'I don't know what it is, but I can feel it drawing near.'

Eldain scanned the trees, his eyes darting from shadow to shadow as he saw the sinuous form of a slender figure ghosting between the trees. Dark of eyes, and with black fingernails and black hollows for eyes, he knew he should know this figure, but could not place its identity. He knew him, he *did* recognise him, but from where?

Eldain searched the recesses of his memory, but could not think of this figure's name. There was something dreadfully familiar to the cruel cast of his smile, the empty blackness of his gaze and the spidersilk weave of his dark robes.

'Stand forth and make yourself known!' he yelled, but the mist and the trees swallowed his words. He heard mocking laughter and spun around as it seemed to come from all around him. Only then did he notice that he was alone.

Caelir and Rhianna were nowhere to be seen.

'Who are you?' he demanded.

Eldain stood alone in the dark forest, and the mist gathered around him. The lights he had seen in the clouds were all around him, sparkling and dancing as though amused at his ire.

'They are pleased to see you,' said a voice from the trees.

A tall elf, slender and thin-limbed, walked from the trees, his robe rustling softly around him as he walked. He wore a pale ivory mask, and Eldain saw he had mistaken the features painted onto its surface as the elf's true expression. Long white hair gathered at his shoulders, and a jade amulet in the form of a black-bladed sword hung at his neck. The name of Khaine was stitched into his robes with silver thread, and Eldain saw variations on that theme in the hems and cuffs of the figure's attire.

'Why are they pleased to see me?' asked Eldain, trying not to show fear as he recognised the elf. 'They don't know me.'

'Oh, but they do,' said Death. 'They have nothing to do but watch the comings and goings of the world. You have amused them greatly, for they have seen your path lead you inexorably to this place. And they do so love to welcome new souls to their ranks.'

'New souls?' asked Eldain. 'Am I dead?'

Death cocked his head as though considering the question. 'Not in the way you would consider it, but for the purposes of our conversation you might as well be dead.'

'I think I am still alive,' he said.

'In that your heart still beats and you have breath, then I suppose you are,' conceded Death with a non-committal shrug. 'In that you are part of the world and its grand pageant, you most certainly are not.'

'Is this even real?' asked Eldain.

Death sighed. 'Another one who wants to argue about the nature of reality... what is this obsession you mortals have with reality?'

'Well? Is it real?'

'Real is such an ambiguous term, Eldain,' said Death. 'This is as *real* to you as it needs to be, but others would doubt it were you to tell them of it. Is that good enough for you?'

'Real or not, I have nothing to say to the likes of you,' said Eldain, turning away.

Death was at his side in an instant, walking beside him as though they were old friends out for a convivial stroll in the forest.

'The likes of me?' said Death, sounding almost hurt. 'That was uncalled for, especially as we have so much to talk about.'

'What could we possibly have to talk about?'

'What do you imagine Death and a mortal would talk about?' said Death, lacing his hands behind his back. Eldain saw they were beautiful hands, craftsman's hands. The nails were black, but not painted black. They were the black of the void, nails that could mould the warp and weft of reality in ways unknown to those who did not have the power of a god.

'Am I going to die?' asked Eldain.

'Of course,' answered Death. 'All living things must die.'

'Even Morathi?'

'Even Morathi,' laughed Death. 'She can avoid me for only so long. She thinks she "cheats" me every time she emerges from that tinker's cauldron, dripping with the blood of babes and innocents, but she is not immortal. Not yet. She only postpones the inevitable. Even this is just another parlour trick to delay my touch upon her flesh.'

'She is going to destroy the world,' said Eldain, feeling more at ease talking with Death, though the nature of the experience was still confusingly surreal. 'That hardly seems like a parlour trick, as you call it.'

'Exist as long as I have existed and even the mightiest deeds will seem trifling to you too.'

'Even the end of the world?'

'Even the end of *worlds*.'

Though Eldain knew this was a realm of magic and deceit, he was quick to spot the lie.

'If that were true, why are you here now? Shouldn't this bore you?'

Death shrugged and said, 'I have an affection for this world, and I have grown fond of the grand players in its performances. Some are mad, some are deluded and others are so very nearly gods that it amuses me to watch them weave their plans as though they will last forever. As to why I am here, some mortals need their endings to be witnessed. Otherwise their lives will pass unremarked, and that would be a terrible tragedy.'

'Are you speaking of me?' asked Eldain.

Death laughed. 'No, Eldain. At best, you are a minor player in this world's drama.'

The masked figure put a hand on Eldain's shoulder and said, 'Yet even the minor players may make the greatest of differences.'

'How?'

'By accepting the inevitable,' said Death. 'By knowing when to give in.'

'That sounds like grim counsel,' said Eldain.

'You *are* talking to Death, you know.'

The path they were following led out through the trees, and Eldain saw they had come to a wide plain of black sand that had turned to obsidian in the fires of some ancient cataclysm. Lightning-shot mist gathered on the plain, swirling around its perimeter in a ceaseless vortex. Crackling lines of power raged in the depths of the howling mist, and pillars of light stabbed into the sky from its centre. Eldain had the sense of unimaginable power being drawn to this place, lines of convergence that had taken a lifetime to map and devise. The air was rich with magic, and he felt his blood sing with its proximity. His flesh tingled with the desire to drink that power and reshape itself into new and ever more wondrous forms.

Only with an effort of concentration was he able to force that desire down.

Thousands of carved waystones were strewn around the exterior of the vortex, some toppled, some still standing, but all rendered glassy by whatever infernal heat had vitrified the plain.

'What is this place?' he asked.

'You know what it is,' said Death. 'Every part of your body can feel where you are.'

'This is where Caledor Dragontamer enacted his great ritual,' said Eldain. 'This is where Caledor died.'

Death laughed again, and there was real amusement in the sound.

'You are half right,' agreed Death. 'This is indeed where Caledor drained the magic from the world. But *died*? Perhaps. It is hard to tell sometimes, I have not been kind to the old elf and his mind is not what it once was. In any case, it is a moot point, for this is where I will leave you, Eldain Éadaoin. Just remember what I told you and you may yet leave this place alive.'

Eldain wanted to ask more, but the world blurred around him and Death had vanished.

In his place were Caelir and Rhianna, both with the same expression of surprise he was sure was plastered across his features. They looked into the vortex of magical energy, elated and horrified in equal measure that they had reached their destination.

'Eldain! Rhianna!' cried Caelir, sweeping them both into a powerful embrace. 'I lost you both. I was lost and alone in the forest, but then I felt someone else beside me.'

'Who was it?' asked Eldain.

'Our father,' replied Caelir, as a tear ran down his cheek. 'We rode through the woods of Ellyrion, and he told me that he loved me and was proud of me. We spoke for hours, and I said all the things I wished I had said to him while he still lived.'

'I saw an old man,' said Rhianna. 'I did not know him at first, but then I recognised him from a colour plate in one of the books my father keeps in the Tower of Hoeth.'

'Who was he?' asked Caelir.

'His name was Rhianos Silverfawn, and he lived a very long time ago.'

'He was an ancestor of yours?' said Eldain. 'How long ago did he live?'

'In the time of Caledor Dragontamer,' said Rhianna. 'He was filled with sadness to see me, but before he could say any more, he vanished and I found myself at the edge of this obsidian plain.'

'Who did you see, brother?' asked Caelir.

Before Eldain could answer, the very air rumbled and a crack split the ground. The world shuddered as a powerful earthquake shook it. The trunks of the trees split open and they toppled, disintegrating into billowing clouds of dust as they struck the ground. Flickering magical fire seethed from the cracks in the earth, like the fire at the heart of the world oozing up through wounds in its surface. Forks of lightning arced from the vortex and struck deep in the forest. Fire bloomed as tinder-dry trees caught light.

One of the towering columns of light in the centre of the plain was snuffed out, and the heaves of the ground intensified. Like the gods themselves bestrode the earth with titanic footsteps, the ground bucked with thunderous heaves.

The spiralling mist split apart as whipping tendrils of mist and light began spinning off, like debris from an apprentice potter's wheel that spun too fast. Monumental power sheared from the vortex and bled ferociously back into the world.

'What's happening?' asked Caelir.

'We are too late,' said Rhianna. 'Morathi has unmade the vortex, and everything is unravelling.'

CHAPTER NINETEEN
THE VORTEX UNDONE

No sensation in the world came close to the thrill of battle, and that thought saddened Lord Swiftwing, even as he drove his spear through the heart of another druchii warrior. Casadesus steered with great skill, wheeling and twisting the heavy chariot in exquisite arcs that carried it close enough to the enemy to strike, but fast enough that they could not board it.

Iron bolts hammered the chariot's armoured flanks, but the enchantments woven into its timbers kept it from harm. Lord Swiftwing could not draw a bow, but Casadesus passed him long javelins that he hurled with deadly accuracy. They rode away from the druchii line as the spear hosts marched forward with their blades lowered to engage the enemy.

Lord Swiftwing saw Menethis of Lothern in the front rank, his tunic bloodied and his face set with resolve. The young elf had earned great glory this day, and Lord Swiftwing only hoped he would be able to reward him properly at battle's end. Command of a squadron of Silver Helms would be good for him.

'Coming about, my lord,' said Casadesus, as he brought the horses around in a tight turn.

'Once more, dear friend,' said Lord Swiftwing, as two Reaver Knight hosts formed up on his flanks. Laurena Starchaser commanded one group, while an elf-maid with hair of crimson and gold, held in place by a butterfly pin worked in silver, led the other.

'Take us in, Casadesus!' shouted Lord Swiftwing.

Archers loosed arrows into the druchii as Mitherion Silverfawn sought to counter the druchii's sorcery with spells of his own. His Sword Masters were led by a fierce-looking elf-maid with auburn hair. A little too square-featured for Lord Swiftwing's tastes, but her prowess with the heavy broadsword she carried set his blood afire.

Cavalry skirmishes broke out on the left flank as the dark-cloaked riders who had crossed the river fought with a scattered band of Reavers. Both groups of horsemen swirled around one another, stabbing, loosing and riding in, only to break apart in dusty spirals. Each clash left elves and horses on the ground, bloodied and dead, but neither side showed any sign of breaking.

A glittering host of light and magic filled the horizon to the north, and Lord Swiftwing anxiously awaited news of what it heralded. Frantic word had come that it was the army of Avelorn, but he had received no clear confirmation as to what was happening on his right flank. Even atop his chariot, he could see little that made sense. Phantoms of light and colour shimmered on the fields he knew, and from that rainbow miasma he could hear the sounds of battle. But who was doing the majority of the dying was a mystery to him.

Salvation or doom awaited on that flank, and only when it arrived would he know which.

Lord Swiftwing led the charge in the centre, and though it was anathema to throw a chariot straight at the enemy, there was little room left for subtlety in this fight. The Reaver Knights alongside him kicked their horses to the gallop and Lord Swiftwing loosed an ancient war cry in the old tongue of Ellyrion.

The two hosts of warriors came together with a resounding clash of blades and flesh. Casadesus threw the chariot into a long skid. The spinning wheels swung around and smashed into the druchii, scattering them like children's skittles. Axle blades scythed them down in droves, and blood splashed Lord Swiftwing's armour.

The Reavers slammed into the druchii and their spears stabbed and broke as they rammed them home like lances. They switched to swords, hacking at the druchii as they turned to flee from the thundering hooves and slashing blades of the Reavers. The wedge of the charge had punched deep into the druchii, but still they held on.

The chariot bucked as enemy warriors went under the wheels, ground to red paste as Casadesus tugged the reins and pushed deeper into the mass of druchii. Lord Swiftwing threw his last javelin and drew his sword, leaning out over the edge of his chariot and stabbing down. His blade parted mail links and cut through plate with pleasing ease, and his buckler deflected the worst of the return strikes.

'I overestimated our enemies' prowess!' he yelled as the chariot rumbled onwards.

His spear hosts shouted as they drove their weapons forward, the archers raised their bows and let fly in arcing lines over the fighting ranks. He laughed as he struck left and right, letting Casadesus pick their route through the killing. A crossbow bolt struck his left shoulder and ricocheted away. Another hit him square in the chest and wedged there, the tip an inch from penetrating his heart.

The chariot circled around and carried him out of reach of the druchii, and he broke the shaft of the bolt with the hilt of his sword, angry more than shocked at so close a brush with death. Druchii milled in confusion, bodies lay broken and bloodied all around, like stalks of corn in a trampled field. Swords, bows and spears lay discarded like unwanted playthings, and the soil of Ellyrion was stained red with the blood of slaughter.

'Come, Casadesus!' he shouted. 'Into them once more!'

'As you say, my lord,' replied Casadesus, turning the chariot back to the fighting.

Once again the chariot carved a gory path through the druchii, the ithilmar axle blades cutting through greaves, meat and bone to leave only screaming cripples in their wake. Swords and axes slammed the wood and metal of his chariot, some biting deep and splintering armoured plates, others sliding clear. Lord Swiftwing lopped limbs and heads with each blow of his sword as Casadesus swung the chariot like a madman, weaving a bloody course through the druchii.

'Again, Casadesus! Again!' yelled Lord Swiftwing. 'Turn and ride them down again!'

The chariot swung around, but all thoughts of another charge were forgotten as the druchii swarmed them. A spear punched through the timber sidings of the chariot and punctured Lord Swiftwing's leg armour. He grunted and hacked the haft in two. Blood streamed down his leg, but he could barely feel it. Crossbow bolts zipped past him and he ducked.

An ear-splitting roar echoed over the field, and Lord Swiftwing saw a rearing hydra creature with a huge body and a multitude of serpentine necks. It reeked of decaying meat and soured sweat, its many mouths screaming one discordant wail of fury.

Casadesus didn't even wait for Lord Swiftwing's order, turning the chariot towards the creature. Druchii and asur alike fled from the beast's rampage as its grossly swollen tail of chitinous barbs swept warriors from their feet and fed them into gaping maws filled with grinding teeth.

Its pendulous heads turned towards Lord Swiftwing's chariot with a roar of monstrous appetite. It vomited up a host of half-digested remains and bellowed in hunger.

The chariot slashed along its flanks, the scythe blades opening up a yard long gash that sprayed foaming ichor and black blood. A rippling frond of torn muscle tangled itself around the wheel of the chariot. Such was the speed of the attack that the muscular tissue was ripped out of the hydra's body, but not before its drag slewed the chariot around and threatened to tip it over.

Lord Swiftwing gripped the edge of the chariot with his free hand and fought for balance. Casadesus braced himself against the fairings, but the horses pulling the chariot had no such luxury, and the first had its jaw broken by the sudden jerk of the bit in its mouth. The second had its back legs shattered as the yoke snapped and the entire bulk of the chariot rolled over them. The horses screamed horribly and thrashed in agony.

Casadesus leapt from the ruined chariot and lanced his sword through the throats of each stricken beast. Both were beyond help, and no horse of Ellyrion should suffer such pain. Lord Swiftwing twisted around in the specially modified seat in the chariot as the hydra hauled its body around to face him.

Asur warriors ran to his side, spears stabbing its bulk, but the beast had clearly set its sights on him. A long neck curled towards him and he hacked it away. Another swung at him and it too was despatched. Then Casadesus was at his side, keeping the beast at bay with jabs and swings of his spear.

'Still glad you stayed at my side?' said Lord Swiftwing.

'I am beginning to have second thoughts,' replied Casadesus.

The beast spat a hawking wad of burning phlegm at them, and Lord Swiftwing ducked behind the cracked fairings of the chariot. Instantly, the chariot's sides began melting, the molten heat of the venomous mucus eating through ithilmar plates with horrifying ease. Droplets had spattered his armour, and burned rivulets streaked the unblemished lustre of his breastplate.

'Damn you!' he cried. 'This was hand-crafted by the Old Man of Vaul himself!'

He reared up, though a shooting lance of white hot pain burned its way up through his twisted pelvis. His sword swung out and cut deep into the meat of the hydra's head, splitting one of its eyes open in a popping spray of white fluid. The beast shrieked, and Lord Swiftwing stepped down from the chariot, taking painful step after painful step towards it.

Its flesh melted before the enchantments woven into his blade, and each strike was hideously painful to it. Lord Swiftwing lost all sense of the battle around him, the screams of asur and druchii mingling into one constant death note. Shimmering light, like droplets of rainbows, fell around him and he heard the most wondrous music from the very air itself. It made him want to dance, and that angered Lord Swiftwing, for he never danced now.

His sword rose and fell, each time cutting deep into the muscular flesh of the hydra. Its cries were feeble now, hideous, gurgling, honking sounds of something dying. At last he halted his mechanistic swings. The monster was dead, its flesh collapsing in on itself like a deflated bladder, and its limbs snapping and twitching as the last spark of life fled its carcass.

'Asuryan and Isha preserve us,' he gasped as the world snapped back into focus around him. His armour and cloak were matted with blood and ichor and other, less identifiable, fluids. Cheering warriors surrounded him, waving bloodied spears in the air as they rejoiced at having fought alongside the master of Tor Elyr.

The surge of adrenaline that had kept him on his feet drained from him in an instant, and Lord Swiftwing gasped as the pain of his crippled leg and pelvis shot through him once again. He sagged, and a spearman caught him. Another two helped, and they carried him away from the awful stench of the hydra's body, which was already beginning to decay like a week-old cadaver.

'Casadesus? Casadesus, where are you?'

He looked into the faces around him, and knew none of them.

'Where is Casadesus?' he asked, almost blind with pain. The spearman looking at him was nonplussed. He shared a look with one of his spear-host brethren.

'I do not know who that is,' he said.

'My spear bearer,' said Lord Swiftwing. 'My chariot...'

'He's gone, my lord,' said the spearman. 'I am sorry.'

'What? No! Impossible!'

Lord Swiftwing threw off their supporting arms and searched for his chariot. There it was, listing badly where the hydra's fire had devoured the timber and supports. One wheel was little more than spokes and a slowly dissolving hub. The scythe blade drooped like a melting candle.

'Casadesus?' he said, upon seeing the slumped form of his bondsman. 'No!'

He lowered himself to the ground and placed a hand on Casadesus's chest. His face and upper body was all bloody meat and scorched bone, eaten away by the corrosive flame of the creature's breath.

'Damn you and your duty,' he snarled. 'You wouldn't listen and now look where it's got you. You glorious fool, you stupid, glorious fool...'

Lord Swiftwing wept for his lost friend and almost didn't notice the gentle hands lifting him from the ground. He felt the hard edges of the grips and looked up into faces formed from bark and moss and broken edges of timber. They were creatures of the forest, knots of wood and splinters for eyes, slender trunks for bodies and twisting root legs to bear them.

'No!' he cried. 'I will not leave him for the druchii!'

The tree creatures did not answer him, but the bark around where their mouths would have been creaked and rasped with clicking, cracking sounds. If it was language, it was no language Lord Swiftwing understood. A nimbus of radiant light shone in the heart of their bodies, and he saw they had not come alone.

Wild wolves snapped at the druchii and capering fauns with emerald skin fought them with shimmering axes of light. Gambolling sprites swirled like water around the druchii, nipping and biting and clawing. Something tall and in flames battled another many-headed hydra, its heavy limbs of bark and timber breaking necks and rupturing spines with every blow of its heavy branch limbs. Another two such creatures joined their oaken brother, a whip-limbed willow and a clawed pine.

'What is happening?' he yelled, and one of the creatures of wood turned its bole towards him. Its bark cracked into a semblance of a face and a soft voice issued from its mouth, utterly at odds with the harsh lines and earthy nature of the creature.

'I am Alarielle, and my army is here to fight alongside you.'

'The Everqueen? You are the Everqueen?'

'I am all things in Avelorn,' said the Everqueen in the guise of the wooded creature. 'I am speaking to you through this dryad, but I am close at hand.'

'Then we are victorious?' said Lord Swiftwing, hardly daring to believe it.

'No,' said the Everqueen sadly, as the dryads stood him up. They had carried him far and fast, and Lord Swiftwing found himself on the slopes of the causeway that led up to the great bastion castle of Tor Elyr, looking over the battlefield.

The centre had broken, and the warriors that had fought so valiantly alongside him were being driven back by heavily armoured blocks of druchii infantry. Mitherion Silverfawn and his Sword Masters coordinated the retreat, and their courage alone kept the retreat from becoming a rout.

The south was folding rapidly, the spear hosts and Reaver Knights falling back to the city in good order. It was clear that the Everqueen's army had indeed come from the north, and though its magnificence was wonderful and beautiful to behold, its troubadour warriors, poet archers and acrobat swordsmen were no match for Morathi's determined and ferociously disciplined army.

The noose had finally closed on Tor Elyr and his city was doomed.

'We are defeated,' said Lord Swiftwing.

'Not yet,' said the dryad with the voice of beguiling sweetness. 'Wait…'

The world exploded with light and magic.

All across Ulthuan, the magical lines of force devised by Caledor Dragontamer surged with power. Conduits of magic blazed through the landscape, like lines of mercury fire poured onto the land. Power that once drained from the world now found no outlet, and unimaginable energies spilled into its magical winds.

The Annulii screamed as the titanic power chained within their peaks surged like a molten river of light at floodtide. Streamers of fire poured down the mountainsides in glittering waterfalls, sparkling with unleashed power and uncontained magic. Where it touched would never be the same, the solid substance of matter reshaped and born anew in chaotic jumbles of random form.

The wild creatures of the mountains – the chimera, the cockatrice, the jabberwocky and other magical beasts of incredible form and myriad variety – came down from the highest peaks. Lonely hunters' cabins high in the mountains were ripped apart by voracious beasts driven to madness by the surging power boiling their brains, or destroyed in the tsunami of raging magical energy.

Nor was the devastation confined to the mountains. Earthquakes of terrifying power ripped across Ulthuan, shearing kingdoms from one another and cracking the earth like a second Sundering. The walls of Tor Yvresse broke open and whole swathes of the city were buried beneath a monstrous avalanche. Three hundred souls were lost, from a city that could ill-afford to lose any of its sad inhabitants.

In Lothern, the fighting on the quayside halted as the city threatened to tear itself apart. Grand villas of marble slid down the hillside of the lagoon as the land rumbled and heaved and shook. The towering statues of the Everqueen and Phoenix King that stood sentinel over the city cracked and swayed and the outstretched hands of the pair finally met as the Phoenix King toppled forwards and smashed into the marble face of the Everqueen.

Floodwater spilled over the docks and through the streets of the city as Ulthuan tipped and the seas roared over its coastal regions. Once again, Tiranoc knew the terror of being lost beneath the waves as seawater gushed through its fjords and spilled onto its fields. Towns and villages along the coasts of Nagarythe and Caledor sank beneath the waves, their people obliterated in a heartbeat as the pulse of magical energies threatened to break the island apart.

Throughout Ulthuan, the waystones blazed like spears of fire, desperately venting magical energies as they tried to dissipate the colossal power building within them. Some exploded as that power became too much for them to contain, others melted to liquid rock in the searing heat.

On the Gaen Vale, the smouldering volcano at the heart of the island exploded, filling the air with ash and smoke. Vast rivers of lava poured down the flanks of the volcano, boiling the waters around the island to steam.

Wherever the currents of magic met the surface of the world, they buckled and twisted like colts in heat, breaking the earth and burning the air with its power. Hundreds of the asur died in the opening moments of the cataclysm, and hundreds more were soon to follow them as the waves of destruction and unfettered magical energy spread out from the Isle of the Dead.

Piece by piece, Ulthuan was tearing itself apart.

* * *

'How does it feel, old ghost, to know that I have undone your great work?' yelled Morathi.

She shrieked to the misty air, for she stood alone on the glassy plain of basalt. Howling winds surrounded her, yet the space within the vortex was silent, an eye of a hurricane of magical energy that was unravelling before her eyes.

Crackling shapes moved in the mist, mighty figures that shimmered and faded as they endlessly described complex patterns with their hands. The motions required of the great ritual were complex and exacting, and these mages had been weaving them for thousands of years, never changing and never stopping.

Except one *had* stopped.

Morathi laughed and brandished a golden-bladed dagger of strange design above her head. Coagulating blood dripped from its edge onto the body at Morathi's feet. It decayed at a furious rate, skin and hair flaking from bone that powdered in an instant. In moments, even that was scattered by the wind until all that was left was an empty robe of silver weave.

'It took me hundreds of years to learn how to shield my thoughts from you,' she said. 'Hundreds of years, thousands of lives and an age of searching for the right weapon to slay your all-powerful mages.'

Morathi stalked the plain, shouting to the empty air, gloating, though there was no one over whom to gloat. Her body was slathered in old blood, and her black steed pawed the hard ground as though here under sufferance. It was eager to be away and its wings ruffled at its flanks.

'You scared me once, I'll admit that,' said Morathi. 'When last we spoke, I was afraid of you. I believed you when you said you would destroy this place rather than allow me to take it. What a fool I was! You had no power then, and you have none now.'

'Is that what you think…?'

Morathi spun, and there he was, just as she remembered him.

Caledor Dragontamer, if this revenant could still be called such, was ghostly pale, his skin near translucent. The meat of his muscles wriggled on his skull, and his eyes were black coal, devoid of life and sanity.

'It is what I know,' said Morathi, gesturing to the empty robes. 'One of your precious cabal is dead by my hand and your ritual is broken.'

'Always so literal, Morathi,' said Caledor. 'It is one of your greatest failings.'

Morathi scowled, knowing the old ghost was simply trying to make her angry.

'You look terrible, Caledor,' said Morathi. 'You were once a fine specimen of an elf, tall, broad-shouldered and handsome, but all that is left of you is a skeletal wreck.'

'I am reminded daily of how deathly I look,' said Caledor. 'I think it amuses him.'

'What are you talking about?' asked Morathi. 'To whom do you talk on this dead island?'

'Why, Death, naturally,' said Caledor, as though she had asked a particularly obtuse question. She smiled and threw back her head to laugh.

'I believed you mad before. Now I know it.'

'Mad? A distinct possibility,' agreed Caledor. 'Mad, but not stupid. I created the vortex, and I told you once that I would not allow you to have it.'

'I do not *want* it, I am here to destroy it.'

'Why?'

'Why not?'

Caledor laughed. 'That is your answer for destroying a world? *Why not?*'

'That you desire it saved is enough for me to want it destroyed.'

'How petty you have become, Morathi,' said Caledor, sounding more disappointed than angry. 'Death may not suit me, but immortality suits you even less. You may hide behind a fair face, but your heart is rotten to the core. I warned Aenarion about you, but he would not listen. Too wrapped in grief to see the corruption behind your mask of beauty. What would he think were he to see you now?'

'Aenarion is dead, Caledor,' snapped Morathi. 'As you should be. We are not so different you and I, for we have both cheated death.'

'Not so,' said Caledor. 'As you say, I am an old ghost, nothing more.'

'Then I am done with you,' said Morathi. 'Your vortex is coming apart and Ulthuan is doomed. My vengeance is complete knowing that you will die with it.'

Caledor shook his head. 'All those thousands of years, and you *still* do not understand...'

'Understand what?' shrieked Morathi.

'That I will never let that happen,' said Caledor.

'There is nothing you can do to stop it,' answered Morathi. 'It has already happened.'

Caledor smiled. 'One age ends, another begins. You do not realise what you have done, what you have begun.'

'And what is that?'

'A new age,' said the old ghost.

Reclined upon his padded litter atop the Tower of Hoeth, Teclis closed his eyes and ran his hands across the obsidian moonsphere. For six hours he had attempted to send his spirit eyes within its impenetrable surface. It was said the secrets of the future were locked within its impossibly dense structure, the course of every possible event encoded in the complex lattice of its formation. Most likely that was not true, but Teclis had never been one to allow the impossibility of a task deter him from trying.

Not even Bel-Korhadris had been able to unlock the secrets of the moonsphere, and generations of Loremasters had similarly failed to discover what lay within. It had been gathering dust in the archive chambers of the Tower of Hoeth for hundreds of years, forgotten by all save the most dedicated of scholars.

Teclis did not know what had compelled him to send one of the Sword Masters to fetch it, but he had little else with which to occupy his time. The potions that had kept him strong as a youth now did little to sustain him, and only sufficed to take the edge away from the constant pain that wracked his limbs. Though the healers remained optimistic, Teclis knew he was dying, his weakened frame finally succumbing to Morathi's sorcery.

He had observed the battles raging at Lothern and before the walls of Tor Elyr, lamenting every death and rejoicing in each turn in the asur's favour. He wept as the fire consumed Belannaer, then laughed as he saw the book from which the old Loremaster read. His spirit soared as he felt Tyrion's rejection of the Sword of Khaine's influence, even though he knew it was but a temporary reprieve. Such a dread shard of the murder god's power would not easily surrender its most treasured son.

That was a struggle for another time, and Teclis savoured this small victory.

His eyes snapped open a moment before the surge of magical energy roared up through the tower. Like magma boiling up from the heart of a volcano, raw power filled every stone in the White Tower and blazed from the golden finial where the Sword of Bel-Korhadris would sit in times of peace.

Teclis surged to his feet as the unbridled power of magic poured into him, reknitting torn flesh, mending ruptured blood vessels and making whole necrotic tissue in his heart and lungs. In an instant, his flesh was reborn, healed more fully than any potion could hope to cure. His body was still the frail shell of flesh it had always been, but the hurt done to him in the fires that burned the tower was undone as surely as though it had never happened.

The moonstone fell from his hands and fell to the patterned marble floor of the tower.

It cracked open in the storm of magical energy that blazed through the tower, and Teclis looked upon its internal structure with eyes that shone with titanic power. Greater than any wielder of magic in this or any other age, Teclis saw the insane geometries within the moonsphere and laughed as he saw the fate of a million futures mapped out.

Teclis spoke a word of power and his plain robe was instantly transformed into one of cobalt blue, ivory white and shimmering gold. A shining sword and moon-topped staff appeared in his hands, and upon his head, a crown of gold and sapphire glittered with lambent light.

Fire billowed around Teclis, but did not touch him.

He roared with the sheer joy and terror of commanding all the magic in the world.

Then he vanished.

Imrik was no more, and yet he could hear song.

Who could be singing in this place of dreams, where ancient minds slept away the cares of the world? He had sung songs of glory once, but no one had heard them and he had stopped when he had run out of will to give them voice. His life was a flickering ember, a dying spark lost in the darkness.

No, not darkness…

Fire, blazing fire, surrounded him. What had been a fading glow now leapt to life as a great song enfolded him. It was the greatest song in the world, yet he knew he would never be able to do it justice were he to live long enough to recount this event. It had no words, no melody and no tune, just an exultant evocation of wondrous times of glory, when Ulthuan was young and still cooling from the molten fires of creation that had shaped it.

Light pulsed from the heart of the world, billowing up in great waves that filled the air with hot thermals of the purest magic. On these winds flew the first dragons, the chosen children of the gods and the inheritors of all that magic could achieve. These were the glory days, when anything was possible, and impossible was a concept that simply did not exist.

Imrik saw all this and more.

Days of glory where cycles of the universe were but the blink of an eye. Voyages between the stars, where a dragon's wings could carry it to distant suns with a single beat. Imrik saw fierce battles fought between rival dragons that snuffed out worlds and birthed them anew in the fires of their great wars. It was an age undreamed and unknown, a secret history known only to dragonkind, and told to him now by the mightiest of dragons.

Imrik found himself face to face with a vast eye. It was the size of a star, and he a mote in its eye, yet still it saw him. All that had been lost in his endless wanderings was remade by the music of the oldest dragons. They sang songs unknown to the elves and younger dragons, and bore Imrik up through the white heat of their dreamings, where no mortal was ever meant to venture.

Imrik cried out as he opened his eyes and found himself once more in the vast cave beneath the mountains. His wasted flesh was whole once more, the effort of singing the songs of awakening undone by the magic of this last song. What the power of the elves could not achieve was child's play to the dragons.

Steam and ashen smoke filled the air and the ground shook with violent tremors.

Imrik rose to his feet as mighty shapes moved and shifted in the steam.

Dragons. Hundreds of awakened dragons.

A huge beast with a body that glittered as though constellations were captured in its scales loomed over him. Its vast head dipped, and its eyes shone with ancient fire.

We are the dragons of Ulthuan, and we come to fight!

CHAPTER TWENTY
SACRIFICES

The vortex was unravelling, and it was madness to run into its collapsing heart, but that was what they were doing. Eldain and Caelir ran side
by side, with Rhianna matching them stride for stride. Howling winds
tried to push them back and random flares of raw magic burst with
painful brightness all around them. Their skin glistened with magic, and
even their breath sparkled with the nearness of such boundless creative
energy.

Eldain's blood shone like painted rubies, and though it had long since
dried on his armour, it ran as though fresh from the vein, eager to *become*
something. The life-giving properties of the vortex tugged at their flesh,
urging it to change, to reshape itself and take advantage of this magical
boon.

What else could you be? What might you become?

The lure was strong, and colours swirled around him in washes of
brightness: reds, golds, white, orange and lilac. Colours that had no
names, and which the mages and wizards of the world had forgotten,
bled into existence, their power magnified in this place of confluence.

Rhianna staggered under the effect of so much magic, like a reveller
after too many goblets of dreamwine. The power here was intoxicating
and overwhelming. It overloaded the senses until nothing else mattered.
Caelir was lifted from his feet by the force of the magic, laughing like
a maniac as febrile energies coursed through his body. Their headlong
run into the vortex was halted in an instant, and all three came to a

dazed halt as their senses swam in the myriad complexities of the vortex's power.

Magical energy surrounded them, passing around and through them, drawn to their mortal desires and flesh by the beat of their hearts. It bathed them and filled their bodies with limitless potential. Against such power, what could three mortal elves achieve?

Eldain held out his hands.

'Hold on to me!' he yelled, the words taking shape as colour and light as soon as they left his mouth. His hair whipped around his head and he saw a thousand spinning concepts at play in the air above him. Dreams, nightmares and the amorphous things in-between. The vortex was a towering loom of potential, a thundering engine of creation that could make the impossible commonplace, the unreal solid.

He felt Caelir take his hand, his brother staggering as though bowed under a heavy load. Rhianna took his other hand, and they followed his lead as he pushed on into the vortex. There was no way to tell if he was heading in the right direction, for nothing in this swirling morass gave any clue to forwards or backwards, left or right. Such mortal constraints held no sway here and for all Eldain knew he might be walking in circles.

Caelir cried out, waving his free hand at some terror only he could see. Rhianna wept tears that flew off like tiny winged jewels, and screamed meaningless words to the howling winds. No sooner had one emotion seized them than another would replace it. They laughed, danced with joy and tried to pull away from him to chase invisible heart's desires.

Eldain dragged them after him, like a master with two recalcitrant hounds.

They screamed and raged and cried into the vortex, assailed by visions of things only they could know. Eldain wondered why he was unaffected by the power of the vortex. Were his dreams so banal and mundane that they were beneath its notice?

Perhaps it was because he had no dreams left, and wasn't that all magic was?

Wasn't that what made magic wondrous? That it could make any dream reality?

The magic of the vortex could reach deep into the furthest recesses of a heart and make real anything it desired. It was the power at the heart of creation, and there was nothing beyond its ability to conjure into being. Yet all Eldain saw was the raging heart of the disintegrating vortex, its lightning spalls, its fiery unmaking and the destruction being wrought on the landscape by its death throes.

Though every step was a battle, like walking in a dream where everything is arrayed in opposition, Eldain struggled onwards, dragging Caelir and Rhianna behind him. He bowed his head against the fierce magical winds and concentrated on simply putting one foot in front of the other. The ground beneath his feet was no longer the glassy plain, but a swirling sea of luminescent colours that was solid only because he believed it to be so. No sooner had the thought taken shape than the ground became soft and spongy.

Eldain gritted his teeth and willed the ground to solidity, and grinned as it instantly transformed into marble flagstones that ran with silver light. Understanding the potential of the magical gale buffeting him, Eldain lifted his head into the wind.

'Be still and grant me passage!'

The wind dropped immediately and the swirling colours parted before him, as though he walked through an invisible tunnel of force that bored through the maelstrom of raging magic. He knew better than to believe he was the master of this power, and hurried onwards to where he saw a pale stillness ahead. Caelir and Rhianna came with him, blinking and panting as the delusions beguiling them vanished.

'How...?' gasped Caelir.

'What did you do?' said Rhianna.

'I'm not sure,' said Eldain. 'But the way is clear.'

They moved onwards, the passage through the howling vortex sealing behind Eldain as he walked towards the eye of the hurricane. He did not ask what they had seen in the magic, for there was a haunted look on both their faces that spoke of some dreams that ought never to be dragged into the light.

At last they emerged from the swirling vortex and found themselves standing at the edge of a glassy plateau of shimmering rock. The funnel of the vortex towered above them, its top lost to sight in thundering storms of magical discharge as the power it was intended to contain flooded back into a world unready for it.

In the centre of the plain stood Morathi and another elf who looked more like a cadaver than a living being. Her back was to them, and Eldain saw the same dread weapon that had so terrified him before the battle at Tor Elyr had begun strapped to her back.

'Morathi...' hissed Caelir, drawing his sword.

She turned at the mention of her name, and smiled as though greeting a long lost friend. The gaunt elf beside her looked up into the storm raging above him, and Eldain saw his eyes were black and lifeless, his face like a skeleton with a thin layer of flesh pasted over it. He wondered who this was and what terrible fate had seen him trapped in such a place. The old elf seemed pleased to see them, and began moving his hands in esoteric patterns that left glittering trails in the air.

Rhianna gasped as she drew the unchained magic into her body, her hands crackling with power as she whispered the first syllables of a spell. Caelir went left, and Eldain went right. Morathi faced Rhianna with a withering look of contempt. She spared a glance for the old elf of no less contempt.

'This is it, Caledor? *This* is the best you can summon to your defence?'

Eldain pulled up in shock at Morathi's casual use of the name.

His eyes flicked to the old elf, now seeing him for who he truly was.

He was Caledor Dragontamer, and he was dead.

The legends spoke of a towering mage of awesome power. A giant of magic. A wielder of power like no other in the world. The greatest mage in Ulthuan's long history, he was Aenarion's boon companion, a mighty warrior-mystic who fought the daemonic horde with spell and sword. He was a hero of the ages, all powerful and all knowing.

Perhaps once, but no more.

This was Caledor…?

Yet if Eldain's passage through the vortex had taught him anything, it was that nothing was as it seemed. In life, there had been no mage as powerful and subtle as Caledor. Who knew how powerful he had become in death…?

Morathi's gaze bored into Caelir, and she threw back her head and laughed.

'My little slave,' she said, drawing her barbed weapon from over her shoulder. 'You have come back to me.'

'I am no one's slave,' said Caelir. 'I am here to kill you for what you did to me and what you have done to Ulthuan.'

'Kill me, little slave? Oh no, you won't be doing that.'

Rhianna unleashed a stream of crackling fire from her hands, but Morathi casually batted it aside. The vortex greedily sucked it in to its swirling mass, and Morathi loosed a crackling orb of purple fire from her barbed weapon. Rhianna caught it in a shimmering prism of light and crushed it between her palms.

'The she-elf has some power,' said Morathi. 'Not nearly enough though.'

Cold wind gusted from the Hag Sorceress, like a swirling tornado laid upon its side. Rhianna was swept up by the wind, and crackling webs of frost spread over her mage's robes. Caelir ran at Morathi, and Eldain followed him.

His brother's sword stabbed for Morathi's belly. She spun into the air, twisting over Caelir's head and driving her heel into the back of his neck. Caelir fell flat on his face as Eldain brought his sword around in a disembowelling sweep. Morathi blocked the blow without looking and spun around him, hammering her elbow into his cheek. Eldain staggered and brought his sword up to parry a return stroke of her rending lance. Sparks flew from the impact, blinding him, and he threw himself away from Morathi.

He heard laughter and rolled to his feet as Caelir picked himself up.

They circled Morathi, wary of her speed as she bounced on the balls of her feet with a feral gleam of malicious enjoyment. Caledor seemed content to watch the unequal contest of arms without intervening, if he even could. Eldain met Caelir's eyes and they nodded, circling in opposite directions to come at Morathi from two sides.

They attacked together. Morathi leapt towards Eldain, swaying aside from an elegantly delivered thrust and launching herself at him, feet first. Her legs scissored around his waist, and she spun around him. A slender dagger nicked the skin of his neck as she vaulted clear.

Caelir's sword stabbed past Eldain, but Morathi was long gone.

She danced from foot to foot, spinning her long-hafted weapon before her.

Eldain's vision blurred, and terrible weakness slipped along his limbs.

'Are you all right, brother?' shouted Caelir.

'No,' said Eldain, as Rhianna dropped from the storm above to land between him and Morathi. Words of mystic significance spilled from her lips and a cage of white fire sprang into being around Morathi. It burned with searing brightness and Eldain shielded his eyes.

Morathi snapped her fingers and the cage vanished, its bars of light transformed into writhing black snakes that she hurled towards Rhianna. With a gesture, they became streamers of golden mist. Silver fire erupted from the ground beneath Morathi, but the druchii sorceress leapt into the air, somersaulting over Caelir and landing in a cat's crouch on the glassy rock.

Eldain forced himself to his feet. His limbs felt like water, and a throbbing pain flared in his lower back. He took a step forward, but dropped to one knee as his legs lost their strength. He knew he had been poisoned, and the realisation that he could do nothing against it galled him. He lost his grip on his sword and it fell to the ground with a glassy clatter.

Rhianna and Morathi traded spells back and forth, each one drawing on the thundering power of the vortex to augment their attacks. Blazing tongues of white fire leapt from Rhianna's fingertips, and forking traceries of amethyst lightning arced back in answer from Morathi. Magic powerful enough to level cities and destroy armies was unleashed, all to no effect. Spell and counterspell. Killing magic and destructive power flared between them, flaring, building and bleeding off as the vortex sucked at their violence. Caelir tried to help Rhianna, but the backwash of deadly magic kept him from getting too close.

Eldain felt the world go grey around the edges of his vision and fought to stay conscious.

This was end of the world fighting, and he had to see how it ended.

Dimly, he felt a touch, and looked down. Fingers like reeds and skin like poorly made parchment rested on his shoulder. Yet for all their frailty, Eldain felt incredible power in that hand. He gasped as that power flowed through him, burning Morathi's poison from his blood.

'I may be dead,' said Caledor, 'but I am not without a few tricks of my own.'

Eldain surged to his feet. 'Then help her,' he demanded. 'Morathi is too powerful.'

'She is powerful,' agreed Caledor, the black pits of his eyes and the deathly countenance of his face twisted in what might have been a faint smile. 'But I was shaping world-changing magic before she could even master the simplest enchantment.'

Caledor lifted his hands and the vortex above bent inwards, its awesome power his to command. Morathi and Rhianna paused in their magical battle as Caledor drew the swelling power building in the world to him. The eye of the hurricane had been calm, but the power of the vortex was destabilising, drawn within itself as Caledor spoke incantations that were unknown beyond the time of Aenarion.

Eldain stepped away from the old elf as he *swelled*, his gaunt frame filling out with powerful muscle and youthful flesh. His face bloomed with vitality until he was an elf in the prime of his life. Eyes that were once black and dead were now sparkling and green, flecked with gold and silver. His lips were full and lush, his hair regrown to its youthful lustre.

This was Caledor Dragontamer, the mage who had shackled the riotous magic of the world and bound it to his will. His robes billowed in the raging winds and the storm of magic descended with booming peals and blasts of lightning.

'I warned you, Morathi,' he said with a voice that commanded respect from elf, man and dragon alike. 'I told you what would happen if you pressed me. You loosed the power of the vortex, but only I know how to harness it!'

Caledor's growth had gone beyond any simple restoration of his previous form. His body swelled to titanic proportions, twice, then three times the size of even the largest elf of Ulthuan. He towered over them, and his powers were growing by the second. Morathi quailed before him, and Eldain saw Caelir circling behind her with his sword poised to strike.

Eldain shouted a warning, but his voice was lost in the tempest of Caledor's mighty growth. Caelir hurled himself at Morathi, his sword held two-handed to plunge between her shoulder blades.

Eldain ran toward Caelir.

Time slowed, Eldain screamed.

Rhianna held out her hands.

Too late.

Morathi swayed aside from the blow. Her own rending blade came up and rammed into Caelir's chest. She wrenched the blade and a squirting arc of crimson misted the air. Caelir staggered, a look of disbelief twisting his boyish features. He collapsed into Rhianna's embrace and her arms were instantly soaked with blood.

Eldain screamed Caledor's name, but the enormous mage had concerns greater than the lives of mortals who had foolishly ventured into this place of his making. Morathi ran to her black pegasus and vaulted into the saddle. Her bladed lance dripped with Caelir's blood, and Eldain ran towards her.

Caledor said, 'You were always too arrogant to *listen*, Morathi. I told you that the destruction of the vortex would liberate an enormous amount of magical energy. And I told you I would use it for one purpose, to slay you. I gave you my word.'

'I remember, Caledor,' said Morathi, her dark mount taking to the air. Hurricane winds buffeted it, but Morathi held it steady in the storm. 'But it makes no difference now. Your great work is undone and the world is doomed.'

'Once again you underestimate me,' said Caledor. 'Now begone.'

Caledor waved a contemptuous hand, and Morathi and her mount were hurled from the vortex. They vanished into the roiling clouds of magical energy as though swatted by an enormous fist. Caledor dropped his hands to his side and the enormous growth that had propelled him to giant proportions began to reverse.

Eldain dropped his sword and ran to Caelir's side.

One look at the blood soaking his ruined chest told Eldain that the wound was mortal.

Rhianna looked up at him with tear-filled eyes.

'Eldain…' she said. 'He's dying.'

Once again the hill of waystones above Tor Elyr erupted with magical light, but instead of an entire army stepping from the glow, a lone figure emerged from the gateway. He was clad in the shimmering finery of a Loremaster of the White Tower, and all who saw him knew him in an instant.

Teclis!

A blinding corona of titanic energies surrounded him, cracking the sky with its brightness and pulsing from him in uncontrollable waves. Teclis floated over the battlefield, his body awash with magical energy like never before. His eyes burned with the fire at the heart of the world, and the druchii looked upon him and saw their doom.

The armies of Avelorn and Ellyrion gathered before the walls of Tor Elyr, but there would be no heroic last stand, no futile bravery to stem the advance of the druchii.

It would not be needed.

Crossbow bolts and powerful sorcery flew up at Teclis, and though the unmaking of the vortex had enhanced the spells of Morathi's pet magickers also, they were like children before the might of Teclis. Iron bolts were transformed into seeds that fell upon Ellyrion's soil, and spells were turned aside by the shimmering arcs of power that played about Teclis.

The Everqueen's magic flowed into the land. The icy mists smothering the summerlands of Ellyrion dissipated, and the river was returned to flowing water. The black corruption of the bloody cauldron's demise was reversed, and no trace of the spoor left by the hydras and spawn creatures was allowed to remain.

Such was the Everqueen's duty, yet Teclis was here not to heal, but to destroy.

He was the greatest practitioner of the arcane arts since Caledor Dragontamer himself, and the power he now commanded had last been wielded when the builders of this world first shaped its continents into shapes pleasing to them.

Yet with all the power of a god at his fingertips, Teclis yielded to the first inclination of mortals, and used it to kill. He swept his hands out before him, and a wall of white fire engulfed the druchii army.

Warriors and heroes, monsters and steeds all burned in the fire. It left no mark upon the ground, but no creature of darkness could be touched by the fire of Teclis and live. The screams of the druchii were terrible to behold, but no tears were shed for their death agonies.

Teclis hovered in the air above Tor Elyr and burned an army to death.

Lothern. The end.

The druchii swarmed the docks, and the battle was fought in knee-deep water. Tyrion slashed his sword through the neck of a druchii axeman, and ducked beneath an avenging blow from another cold-eyed killer. Behind him, Lothern burned in the fires of the Witch King's malice, and the citizens of the city fled to the high villas overlooking the cityport.

Perhaps some would escape, but not many.

The Witch King contented himself with watching his enemies die from above, drifting on the lazy thermals from the burning city. His dragon roared and the Witch King's hateful laughter drifted over the doomed warriors below.

'Come down here and fight, and I will choke you with that laughter,' promised Tyrion.

The Phoenix Guard fought with silent menace, their halberds cutting down any druchii who dared to come near with brutally efficient strikes. The flanks of the asur line bent back and crumbled, but the centre held strong. Korhil swept his mighty axe left and right, while Finubar fought like a berserker, all thoughts of restraint lost in the fury of battle. Caradryan of the Phoenix Guard swept his halberd in killing arcs, his blade reaping a fearsome tally in druchii dead.

Eltharion flew above Lothern, diving on Stormwing's fury to attack the druchii from the air. Brave fighters all, killing many enemy warriors, but just spots of light against the darkness. Not enough to counter the encroaching night.

Tyrion had killed two score druchii already, and the battle was still young. He had lost track of time, but the autumnal cast to the sky spoke of sunset. Appropriate, he thought, that we should face our ending as light vanishes from the world. He fought with all the skill he possessed, but could already see that it would not be enough. The druchii had limitless numbers to call on. Thousands more warriors were crossing from the black ark in yet more troop galleys. The sea was awash with black-tarred vessels bearing druchii killers.

He fought through a mass of druchii swordsmen towards the Phoenix King as the sky lit up with a dazzling eruption of light. Another earthquake ripped across the city, and a high tower of blue marble and crystal sculpture toppled into the lagoon. Pieces of the Everqueen's statue broke off and fell into the water, smashing a slender bridge of golden crystal and a handful of raven ships. A fresh wave swept into the collapsing city.

The sky to the west burned with orange light where the volcanoes of the Dragonspine had erupted. Blistering, red-lit clouds smeared the tops of the cliffs, and the sharp tang of sulphur tainted the air. Ash fell in a black rain and Tyrion felt that the world was weeping.

The fighting paused with each fresh disaster, and Tyrion splashed through the floodwater as he saw a host of warriors in black armour and scaled cloaks advance on the Phoenix King. Finubar had plunged deep into the mass of druchii and was cut off, but before the Corsairs could attack, a host of sailors bearing the blue cloaks of Lord Aislin charged into the fray. They were without armour, but took on the druchii with a fury that could only have its roots in vengeance.

Tyrion ran to join them, and cut down the last of the druchii as Finubar came to his senses and fell back to the battle line with a grateful look on his face. The sailors went with him, and Tyrion stopped one with the look of command about him.

'You are a ship's captain?' asked Tyrion.

'Aye, my lord. Captain Finlain of *Finubar's Pride*,' said the sailor.

Tyrion laughed and let him go, pleased with the aptness of the captain's ship.

He jogged back to the fighting line as the druchii regrouped and hundreds of fresh warriors disembarked from their ugly galleys onto the cracked and sunken quayside.

Korhil gave him a nod, and Finubar shot him a weak smile. Caradryan thumped the butt of his halberd against the wet cobbles in a gesture of respect between warriors.

'Ready for one last fight?' asked the Phoenix King.

'Always, my lord,' answered Tyrion.

'This will be it, Tyrion,' said Finubar. 'They will break us with the next charge. This will be my last battle. I know it.'

'Never say that,' said Tyrion. 'If there is one thing Teclis has taught me, it is that there is always hope.'

Finubar shook his head and indicated the glowering forms of Caradryan's warriors. 'The Phoenix Guard are here, and they would only have come unasked to take me to my final rest.'

Beside him, Caradryan shook his head and pointed to the two enormous statues that dominated the skyline of Lothern. The Everqueen's statue was battered and portions of it had fallen into the sea, but the

Phoenix King's statue had taken the brunt of the damage. Its colossal plinth had split, and the statue listed drunkenly at an angle, the helmeted head resting on the shoulder of the Everqueen across the bay.

Finubar and Tyrion looked at the Captain of the Phoenix Guard in confusion, and it was left to Korhil to fathom the meaning of the gesture.

'They made a mistake,' he roared.

'What are you talking about?' demanded Finubar.

'I don't know exactly what they saw in that Chamber of Days, but I am willing to bet it was something about a Phoenix King *falling*. True enough, but they got the wrong one!'

The light of understanding dawned, but the answer brought another question.

'How is it possible that any of us survive this battle?' asked Finubar as the druchii hefted their spears and axes. War horns sounded the advance.

The answer came a second later as a series of deafening roars echoed from the cliffs.

All heads turned to the sky as the red-lit clouds of the west broke apart and a host of dragon riders swooped overhead.

They came in many colours, golden, crimson, silver and white. Copper and bronze, glittering with sunlight and starlight. Ten came, then ten more, then too many to count. They swept over the mountains in their hundreds and fell upon the druchii in a tide of fang and claw that could not be resisted.

The sky was filled with dragons, and Tyrion would see no finer sight in all his days. To see one dragon upon the field of battle was an honour, but to lay eyes upon such a host was something no elf had witnessed for thousands of years.

The dragons stooped on the close-packed galleys and raven ships in the harbour, breathing great blasts of fire from their jaws. A score of ships immediately caught light, a dozen more a second later as the beating of the dragons' wings spread the fire. Astride the neck of many of the dragons were mages clad in robes edged with red-gold. They hurled streaking bolts of blue light from outstretched hands and staffs, and the druchii burned in the flames of their magic.

Leading the winged host was the Lord of Dragons himself, Prince Imrik of Caledor.

Sat astride the neck of Minaithnir, Imrik flew towards the Witch King, his lance glittering like captured starfire and his dragonhorn sounding a high note of challenge. The Witch King answered his challenge and angled his dark mount towards Imrik.

Tyrion watched the two dragons climb as they flew at each other, but it was Malekith's beast that climbed higher. His dragon drew in its wings and its long neck extended as frills of scales opened at its throat. Before the monstrous dragon could unleash its noxious breath, Imrik's horn sounded again and the Witch King's mount convulsed as though struck.

Its wing beats faltered and in that moment of pain, Imrik leaned low over his saddle to drive the shimmering point of his lance deep into its belly.

The dragon roared in agony as the starmetal of the lance pierced its scaled hide and tore into its body. Its claws raked Minaithnir's flanks, but it was an attack of flailing spite. Malekith hauled his dragon away as Imrik drew back his lance for another strike. Once again the lance stabbed home, gouging a long scar down the dragon's rump.

Malekith struck with his sword and only Imrik's superlative reflexes saved his life. The dragons broke apart, but as Imrik circled Minaithnir for another tilt at the Witch King, his opponent was already flying towards the Straits of Lothern.

Tyrion cheered as Malekith fled, willing Imrik to turn and ride him down. Younger dragons chased the Witch King, mage riders hurling shimmering fireballs of incredible power. Though wounded and defeated, their quarry was still incredibly dangerous. Just as the fire mages' magic was enhanced, so too was his. Malekith froze dragons and their riders to sculptures of ice with a glance, and sheared the wings from others with chopping gestures of his bladed gauntlets.

The pursuit of the Witch King was abandoned, and Malekith's dragon limped away to the south through the straits, its wings dipped and a drizzle of hot blood falling from its torn belly to the black ark below.

The harbour was alight from one side of the bay to the other with blazing ships, and the druchii trapped on the quayside watched with growing terror as the dragons turned towards them. Fire scoured them from the quaysides and the water boiled to steam around their legs. Some of the druchii attempted to swim to the black ark, but it was an impossible goal, and their armour dragged them to the bottom of the ocean. The defenders of Lothern cheered and embraced one another as the dragons did in moments what they could not have done in a hundred lifetimes.

'We are saved!' cried Finubar as the dragons burned the druchii from Lothern.

'We are indeed, my king,' said Tyrion, putting up his sword as Imrik flew over the burning waters of the bay with his silver lance raised in salute.

Rhianna cradled Caelir, wiping blood from his face and letting her tears fall onto his face. Eldain knelt at Caelir's side and took his hand. The wound gouged in his chest was deep, and blood flowed from between his splintered ribs. Caelir's Ellyrian armour had offered no protection against Morathi's dread lance, and his heart had been all but plucked from his chest.

His brother was dying in front of him, and there was nothing he could do.

Only one person could save Caelir now, and she was far away in Ellyrion.

'Alarielle of Avelorn!' he yelled, hoping against hope that she might somehow hear his desperate plea over the miles that lay between them. 'I beg of you, help my brother!'

Caelir groaned and his eyes fluttered open.

'Eldain?'

'I'm here, Caelir,' he said. 'Do not move. I will save you, I promise.'

'You should not make promises you can't keep, brother,' said Caelir. 'I thought you'd have known that by now.'

'I will keep this one, and you will not die. You won't dare. Not now.'

'Remember,' hissed Caelir, painfully. 'I have a habit of disappointing you.'

Eldain shook his head. 'You never disappointed me, little brother. I was so very proud of you. Always.'

Rhianna wiped Caelir's brow and wept tears like shimmering diamonds. Eldain looked into her eyes and he felt the last shreds of animosity melt away in the face of Caelir's ending. The power of her battle with Morathi still clung to her, a haze of white light that danced just beneath her skin with a luminous glow.

'Can you save him?' asked Eldain.

'I have not the power,' she said.

'Here, in this place, you do not have the power?'

'I am not the Everqueen,' said Rhianna.

A figure appeared behind them, and Eldain saw Caledor Dragontamer standing over them.

He looked down at Caelir and grimaced.

'She always did have a penchant for needless cruelty,' he said.

'You!' said Eldain, surging to his feet. 'You have the power to save my brother. Please, you have to help him.'

Caledor shook his head. 'He is beyond saving, Eldain. His hurt runs deeper than you know. His soul is torn and bleeding. Even the Everqueen could not save him.'

'I cannot accept that,' said Eldain.

'It is not up to you,' said Caledor, extending a hand towards Rhianna. 'Come, my dear. It is time for you to fulfil your destiny. The world does not have time for grief.'

'What are you doing?' said Eldain.

'What needs to be done,' said Caledor. 'I am powerful and have held the vortex from collapsing, but I cannot hold it on my own, and I do not have long before *he* returns to vex me.'

'You are not on your own,' stated Eldain, suspecting the truth of Caledor's purpose. 'You have your cabal.'

'One of them is dead. A mage named Rhianos Silverfawn. Morathi cut his throat with a dagger forged from the golden metal once used to construct the great gateway above the northern polar regions. My ritual is complex and precise. It needs all the mages to keep it in balance. One had died, and one must take his place. Who better than his descendant?'

Eldain knelt with Caelir as Rhianna stood before Caledor.

'The Everqueen spoke of this moment,' said Rhianna.

'I warned her not to,' said Caledor. 'She has a loose tongue.'

'What would you have me do?'

'Rhianna, no!' cried Eldain. 'Whatever he wants you to do, don't do it!'

'I have to, Eldain,' said Rhianna. 'You know what will happen if I do not. Ulthuan will be destroyed, and the rest of the world will soon follow. I think I have known that this moment was coming for a long time.'

'You can't do this!' shouted Eldain. 'Caledor Dragontamer would never demand such a sacrifice! He was a hero!'

Caledor's face hardened to granite. 'A hero? No, Eldain, he was a mage who sought to stop the daemons, that is all. And I *did* demand such sacrifices, Eldain. That is exactly what I did all those years ago. I told my cabal that they would never leave the Isle of the Dead, that they would be forever bound to my ritual. It was a sacrifice they all made willingly. And now Rhianna Silverfawn, daughter of Mitherion Silverfawn and descendant of Rhianos Silverfawn makes that same sacrifice.'

'No, please! You cannot take her!'

'He is not taking me, Eldain,' said Rhianna. 'I go of my own free will.'

Tears spilled down Eldain's cheeks, and he reached out to Rhianna with a bloodied hand.

'Don't leave,' he begged. 'Don't leave me alone!'

'We are all alone, Eldain,' said Caledor. 'It is the one truth I have come to realise in this place. We may gather many friends and loved ones to us throughout the long years, but we all walk alone in the end.'

'Rhianna will not walk alone,' said Caelir, grunting in pain as he pushed himself to his feet. 'I will walk with her. Until the end of time, the way it was always meant to be. The way I would have pledged to you had we been wed.'

'Caelir, what are you talking about?' cried Eldain.

Caelir coughed a wad of blood and held himself upright only with Eldain's help.

'If I return to the world beyond the vortex I will die,' he said. 'Here I will live forever.'

'You would stay here?'

'With Rhianna, brother,' said Caelir, gripping his shoulder tight. 'We will not be dead, we will be everlasting. You know it is the only way.'

Eldain bowed his head and nodded, remembering the words Death had spoken to him on their journey through the empty forest.

'By accepting the inevitable,' he said. 'By knowing when to give in.'

'This is not giving in,' hissed Caelir with the last of his strength. '*This is our victory.*'

'Come,' said Caledor. 'It happens now or it does not happen at all.'

Eldain released Caelir, and Rhianna and Caledor carried him to where a loose robe of silver weave lay discarded on the reflective ground. Eldain watched them go, Caledor's shoulders becoming more stooped the further away he went.

Rhianna and Caelir embraced, two souls entwined at last, and Eldain cried tears of sorrow and tears of joy as the light of the vortex swallowed them up. They were gone, but not dead. Trapped forever in the vortex, they would live in a perfect moment of union for all time, and Eldain envied them that eternal bliss.

Almost immediately, the raging anger of the vortex began to subside as Rhianna took up the role she had been born to play. Ancient plans and temporal designs laid down long ago finally came to fruition as the cascade of magical energy once again began to drain from the currents of the world.

Caledor turned back to Eldain, and the great hero of the asur had once again assumed his mantle of frailty. Eldain wanted to hate him, to spit curses at him for what he had lost, but the words would not come.

'You should go, Eldain,' said Caledor. 'The vortex is sealing and Lord Elasir waits to carry you back to Ulthuan. If you remain much longer, you will be trapped like me, cursed to live forever as a deathly revenant neither alive nor dead. A wraith of ancient days.'

'What is there left for me on Ulthuan?' said Eldain.

'More than you know,' said Caledor.

'Everything I love is gone.'

Caledor smiled. 'Not everything.'

EPILOGUE

Grief hung over Ulthuan for a long time after the victories of Tor Elyr and Lothern. The fire of the dragons consumed the druchii fleet in less than an hour, and as the black ark attempted to extricate itself from the Straits of Lothern, the dragons attacked it with all their fury. It could not last long against so mighty an assault, and its ramparts and crooked castles were cast down by creatures older than Ulthuan itself.

Tyrion led a host of Silver Helms into the mountains, driving the few druchii survivors back over the rocky peaks to the shoulder fortresses at the Emerald Gate. The warriors of the asur offered no mercy to their foes, and beneath a banner of the Everqueen, Tyrion charged across the pontoon bridge linking Ulthuan to the Glittering Lighthouse.

At battle's end, Eltharion took his leave of the Phoenix King and returned to Tor Yvresse to count the cost of the invasion among his own people. He said farewell to no one, and as Tyrion watched him fly away, he felt nothing but sorrow for his old friend.

In Ellyrion, the dead were gathered and mourned, every rider and citizen carried to their final rest as aching laments were given voice by the singers of Avelorn. A poet who had fought in the battle composed an epic verse as the sun rose on a new day, dedicating it to a young elf of his former acquaintance. Of the druchii who had fought at Tor Elyr, there were no traces. The fire of Teclis had been thorough, and only grief remained to speak of their invasion.

Thus were the druchii driven from Ulthuan.

The magic of the vortex pulsed through the veins of the world for many weeks, but as geomancers and mages spread through the land, toppled waystones were lifted and new ones established in freshly-mapped areas of mystical confluence. Slowly, and with great pain, the damage done to Ulthuan was healed.

The island would never be quite the same, for it was not in the power of those who lived in the world to undo every hurt done to it. Only those who had built the world were capable of such feats, and they were long gone. As with all damaged things, what could be done to keep life going was done, and the scars would simply have to be borne.

Nor were those scars confined only to the land of Ulthuan.

Too many lives had been lost for the asur to ever forget this war.

Good lives and bad had been spent in the defence of their island, miracles worked and dark wonders played out. The Eagle Gate was rebuilt and Menethis of Lothern appointed its castellan. Lord Swiftwing had offered him command of a company of Silver Helms, but Menethis had, instead, asked for Eagle Gate.

Lord Swiftwing stepped down from his role as master of Tor Elyr, and word was sent to the Old World for his sons to return home. The Great Herd returned to the wilds of Ellyrion, though many bonds of companionship had been forged in the battle, and many were the people of that land who would go on to become fine Reavers in time.

The Everqueen returned to Avelorn, and her army of fauns, dryads and treemen went with her. Her entourage of poets, dreamers and dancers went with her, and from amongst them was picked a young dancer named Lilani, who became a warrior of the Maiden Guard and one of Lirazel's most trusted captains. The revellers of Avelorn travelled north in a grand carnival of light and magic, and wherever they passed, the land bloomed in gold and green. Ellyrion was already a land of eternal summer, but the coming of the Everqueen made the sun shine a little brighter, the warm winds more welcome and the rivers just a little fresher.

Seasons passed, the world turned, and the decline of the asur continued. Nowhere was this more evident than in Ellyr-Charoi.

The leaves blew on...

Ellyrion basked in the warm, honey-gold light of a drowsy summer, but within the walls of Ellyr-Charoi, only autumn held sway. Eldain sat in the Hippocrene Tower and looked out over the endless plains as the dust gathered on his bookshelves and tables of his domain.

Golden leaves filled the summer courtyard, and the trough on the eastern wall was blocked once again. Drifts of fallen leaves were heaped at the open gates of the villa, and filled the air with playful swirls as cold winds blew down from the mountains. Leaves rested on the roof of the Equerry's Hall and tumbled from the eaves of the stables.

Dust rolled through Eldain's study, but he had neither the interest nor inclination to clear it away. Days passed without him moving from his chair, content to watch the passing of the sun and moons across the thin windows of his tower.

He ate and drank when necessary, but the actions were mechanical.

He took no joy in wine or fresh meat. The pleasures of the flesh were forgotten, and it seemed as though his heart had turned to stone.

The leaves blew on.

He entertained few visitors, for he was not viewed through the same heroic lens as others who had fought in the battles against the druchii. While other heroes were heaped with plaudits, Eldain quietly retired to Ellyr-Charoi to nurse his broken heart.

Lord Elasir had carried him back to Ulthuan. Aeris and Irian flew with their golden wings dipped in honour of those they left behind, and the mighty eagle left Eldain to his silence. Mitherion Silverfawn and Yvraine Hawkblade had journeyed to Ellyr-Charoi, seeking news of Rhianna, and Eldain told them all that had happened on the Isle of the Dead. Mitherion wept for his daughter, but was consoled by the words Caelir had spoken as he and Rhianna followed Caledor into the vortex.

Eldain did not invite them to stay, and they did not seek his hospitality.

They were gone within the day, leaving Eldain to walk the empty halls of his villa.

The leaves blew on.

Time became malleable. Eldain tried to stave off the worst of his isolation by taking long rides through Ellyrion on the back of Lotharin. The black steed shared his melancholy, galloping with less and less joy at each ride. At last, Eldain led him to the gates of Ellyr-Charoi and removed his saddle.

'Ride, my friend,' he said. 'Be free. Join the Great Herd and live your life in joy.'

Lotharin nuzzled him, and all that their friendship had meant passed between them in a single, beautiful moment of connection. The horse tossed its mane and cantered down the overgrown path to the bridge. As Lotharin crossed the gurgling stream, he reared up in salute to Eldain before trotting off into the evening's light to rejoin the wild herds of the plains.

Eldain watched him go, knowing the last shred of what held him to this land was gone.

He shut the gates of Ellyr-Charoi.

Seasons passed, though Eldain had no idea of how many.

On the rare occasions he could rouse himself from his study, he would walk the cold halls of the villa like a sleepwalker, moving from room to room as though in a trance. Though he had spent nearly all his life within its walls, the villa was lost to him now. Its rooms were unknown, and places that had once been familiar and homely were now bereft of feeling. He *knew* its halls and corridors, but he was disconnected to them, as though the villa now belonged to someone else.

He paused by an empty window as a cold wind gusted through a cracked pane of glass.

Snowflakes drifted through, dancing in the air for a moment before settling on the floor and melting to tiny spots of water. Eldain opened the window and saw the leaves that carpeted the courtyard below were now white and frosted. Snow fell in drifting clouds, lying thick and still upon the edges of the high wall surrounding the villa.

Eldain walked outside, barely feeling the cold, and wondering how snow could fall in a realm of eternal summer. He trudged through the courtyard, not knowing where his steps were carrying him, but knowing that there was somewhere he needed to be.

He entered the Equerry's Hall, shivering with cold, and looking upon the dusty emptiness within. The firelit revelries that had once filled this hall were now ghostly memories, and Eldain could barely recall them. He circled the dusty table and stood before the frosted portrait that hung on one of the long walls.

Eldain had not looked at this portrait since he and Caelir had last stood here.

Until now, he had not been able to even *think* of his brother's name.

The portrait was a good one, and he remembered the shame he had felt as Uthien Sablehand had first revealed the result of his labours. Now it was a reminder of happier times, and Eldain felt a moment of wistful pleasure at the sight of his younger brother. Yet even the thought of happiness was too much for him, and he turned away from the picture, unwilling to allow even a single ember of joy to lodge in his heart.

Winter closed a fist around Ellyr-Charoi, and the ice in Eldain's heart was no less bitter.

Now, as always, Eldain wrapped himself in furs and a heavy cloak before venturing outside. The freezing temperatures were like nothing he had known, and there was no end in sight to the winter. Snow fell every day, wreathing the villa in a chill blanket, but through the windows of his tower, Eldain could see nothing but the golden light of summer.

It seemed this winter was for him and him alone.

It was no less than he deserved.

Until, one day, a visitor came to Ellyr-Charoi.

He was a warrior, but a warrior like none Eldain had ever seen.

He arrived one morning as the snow was falling within the walls of the villa, and presented Eldain with a token of his authority: a golden phoenix set in an amulet of jade. Clad in a shimmering hauberk of orange-gold and silver, he was a head taller than Eldain, and carried a long-bladed halberd. His robes were of cream and azure, and tailored with exquisite care.

He came alone, and his forehead bore the glittering rune of Asuryan, but it was in his eyes that Eldain saw the truth of his identity. The warrior's eyes were dark pools of hurt and unasked for wisdom. They were eyes that had seen too much, but which had not shied away from that knowledge.

Eldain saw a terrible weight of sorrow in those eyes, and understood all too well what that could do to a soul. He saw the same expression every day in the mirror.

Though the warrior spoke no words, Eldain knew exactly what was required.

He dressed in simple travelling clothes and followed the warrior from Ellyr-Charoi.

He left the gates open, and together they walked east over the sunlit hills and grassy meadows of Ellyrion. Eldain turned for one last look at the villa that had been his home for so many years, and felt a sudden pang of regret as he saw the first signs of spring breaking around the snow-locked walls.

A black horse led a wildly galloping herd in the distance.

Eldain knew this was the last time he would ever see the land of his birth.

They crossed the sea in a ship named *Dragonkin*, commanded by a venerable captain named Bellaeir who welcomed Eldain with great warmth.

'I dreamed I would see you again,' said Captain Bellaeir, but Eldain did not reply.

The ship sailed east across the waters of the Inner Sea, and Eldain did not venture above deck during the journey. He felt the presence of the Isle of the Dead, but could not bring himself to look out over that mist-shrouded rock for fear of what he might see.

At last, the ship docked in an island harbour of tall pillars and masked statues.

In the centre of the island stood a vast pyramid, and the fire burning at its peak lit the waters for miles around.

The silent warrior led him into the pyramid, along high, fire-lit corridors of red marble and golden carvings of the many aspects of the Creator God. They had not spoken during the entirety of their journey from Ellyr-Charoi, and Eldain found nothing unusual in that. The temple was home to many other silent warriors, and Eldain felt a kinship with them he had not felt with any other soul in a long time.

At last his silent guide brought him to a huge chamber at the peak of the pyramid, its walls golden and lit by a thousand torches. It had the feel of a temple, and Eldain knew he was standing in one of the most sacred sites of Ulthuan. A masked statue of Asuryan sat on a glassy throne at the far end of a long processional, and a wide portal was carved into the statue's legs, tall enough for a giant to walk through.

A host of armoured warriors lined a marble-floored path towards the portal, and the warrior that had brought him from Ellyrion led him between them. Golden doors led beyond, though what lay on the other side was a mystery. Curling runes lined the coffered panels, and Eldain saw many contradictory ideas represented there. He saw *Urithair* next to *Harathoi*, *Elthrai* abutting *Quyl-Isha*, but foremost among the runic concepts was *Saroir*, the symbol representing eternity and infinity, the flame of love that burns all it touches. He blinked as the runes seemed to pulse with their own heartbeat. Eldain had the prescient notion that the runes he was seeing were different to the runes another supplicant might see.

Supplicant…?

Yes, he supposed that was exactly what he was, though he had not thought so until now.

The golden doors swung wide and warm light shone from within the chamber beyond. It grew brighter than the sun, spilling out into the temple, and Eldain looked to his guide.

The warrior nodded and gestured towards the doors.

Until this moment, Eldain had not been afraid, but as the warm light beckoned him in, he dreaded taking even a single step into the chamber at the heart of the pyramid. The warrior gestured again, and this time Eldain obeyed.

Golden light enfolded him, and he felt the warmth of a nearby flame. He entered the chamber as the great doors closed behind him with a soft brush of metal. The light dimmed to a level where he could see, and he looked around at the vast space he found himself within. It was enormous beyond imagining, surely too vast to be contained within the top of the pyramid. A vast circle of black marble filled the centre of the chamber, and a towering flame of the purest white burned at its heart.

The walls of the chamber tapered inwards and were covered from top to bottom with runic script. A thousand lifetimes worth of words were written on the walls, maybe more, and Eldain marvelled at the wealth of information inscribed here.

This was the Chamber of Days, a living record of all the Phoenix Kings who had ever lived and ever would. The walls told the story of Ulthuan as it was known, and the story of Ulthuan that was yet to be written.

Even as he understood what was chronicled here, he felt the flame at the heart of the chamber burn hotter and brighter. A chorus of song issued from the fire, and Eldain closed his eyes as the dead and unborn spoke to him with one voice, the echoes of all the Phoenix Kings of the past and the voices of those yet to be crowned.

This was history and legend combined, a tale of days that had no beginning and no ending.

The kings spoke to him of their reigns, and Eldain lived their lives in a heartbeat.

He learned of their loves, their joys, their sorrows and their great deeds. He lived the history of an entire land and its people in one bright and shining moment. Eldain felt Caelir and Rhianna within the grand sweep of the tale, and wept as he relived their final sacrifice on the Isle of the Dead. His remembrance of them had grown cold and lifeless, but in this chamber of eternal life, they burned as bright as stars.

The heart that does not want to heal cannot be remade...

Eldain finally understood those words, and with that understanding, he was made whole.

He had seen all that had ever been and all the future held; the wonders yet to come to pass, the resurgent glory of the asur and the last great battle for the fate of the world.

Eldain would be part of that, though he would never speak of it.

The temple doors opened and the Phoenix Guard awaited the return of their chosen warrior.

DEATHMASQUE

Death's messenger stalked the streets of Tor Yvresse. Clad in a fuliginous cloak that cast off light and shadow in equal measure, he ghosted towards his inevitable destination with grim strides. He wore his hood up, and the gleam of a white porcelain mask beneath reflected distant torchlight and gave the impression of features moving from youth to death in a heartbeat. A few platinum tresses were all that escaped from behind the mask, like the last wisps of hair clinging to a fleshless skull.

He could hear voices raised in song and his bloodless lip curled in disdain.

On this night of nights, they mocked him with their vibrancy and sense of hope.

This portion of the city was in darkness, the magnificent buildings to either side of him empty and abandoned. No glow of candles or softly-shimmering magic shone from their lightless windows, and only ghosts haunted their echoing vestibules and dining chambers. He liked to roam the streets here, finding comfort in the silence and absence of the living. Solitude was peace, social interaction was torture, and he relished the time he could spend in the twisting, empty streets with only the ghosts of the past for company.

He remembered a time when Tor Yvresse had bustled with life. It had been a city of grace and wonders that outshone Lothern, which had been little more than a city-port in decline until Finubar the Seafarer became Phoenix King. This street had once boasted a thriving market where the choicest sweetmeats and pastries could be purchased. An epicurean delight, the many stalls had groaned under the weight of delicacies from all across Ulthuan, food and drink to satisfy even the most demanding gastronome.

Before the coming of the goblin king, he had come here with his brother and happily whiled away the hours haggling with traders, sampling dreamwine from Avelorn, shimmer-fish caught off the coast of Cothique and lion meat hunted in the forests of Chrace. It angered him now to think of those days, how he had wasted time with frivolity when the world was just waiting to tear away the comforting illusion of peace.

He turned a corner, following a marble-flagged thoroughfare that led to a wide amphitheatre where plays commissioned in the time of Aethis had been performed. His mother had loved the theatre and had come here with his father whenever the demands of duty allowed him the time.

He walked into the centre of the amphitheatre, hearing the long-dead voices of performers as they strutted across the proscenium, delivering their lines with theatrical aplomb. Even before the beginning of the end, he had loathed the theatre, preferring the blood-thundering fury of war. Like many of the brash asur his age, he had lived life with fierce relish, taking pleasure in the arts of death over all others. As a youth he had led daring expeditions to Naggaroth, fought the druchii on the shores of Ulthuan and slain the dread beasts that ventured from their lairs in the Annulii.

His mother had chided him for being so sombre in times of peace, but as he stood in the centre of the deserted amphitheatre, he knew time had proved him right. The songs from the distant festival were louder here, the perfect acoustics throwing back random echoes of words and music. Even in this gloomy, shadow-haunted part of the city, there was no escaping the fierce sounds of life resurgent.

He knew he would need to venture out into the festival. The thought held no joy for him, but there was blood to be spilled this night. The Festival of Masques was a time for wild abandon, the pursuit of excess without consequence. For some that meant indulgence in food, others in drink or opiates. Far more indulged their hedonistic impulses, flouting all bounds of decency behind their anonymous masks and painted on identities.

For others, it allowed darker appetites to be sated.

He left the amphitheatre and made his way towards the centre of the city. At the heart of Tor Yvresse reared the gleaming tower of the Warden, and he made that his destination. The minstrel he came to find had announced he would play out his tale at Dethelion's Theatre.

That would be the perfect place to end this charade.

The song-tale the minstrel was reciting had spread throughout Yvresse, and this grand retelling would no doubt be best served with the tower as a backdrop. He had the minstrel's name, but little else to go on, but that was all he needed. In any case, a physical description would do him little good on this night. Behind their masks, the players of the city were invisible and free from repercussions.

Once again, he made his way through the empty streets. It seemed an age ago that the city had been so full that this many dwellings had been required to house its inhabitants. Since the invasion of the goblin king, the city could house many times the number of elves who called Tor Yvresse home.

The walls of the city were high and strong, made mighty by the magic woven into their construction, but there were too few warriors left to defend them. Tor Yvresse was finished as a bulwark against invasion, and the knowledge was galling. How could so formidable a city have come to such a low ebb?

The noise of the festival was getting louder, and he steeled himself for the discomfort and irritation that close proximity to others engendered. The music bounced from the walls, skirling through the streets like serpentine streamers of light. It sought to lift him, but only depressed him more. Anyone with a brain could see there was no room for songs of love and victory.

Just because elves still occupied Tor Yvresse didn't mean it wasn't already lost.

The street he was following bent to the north and a soft, flickering glow of light, both magical and natural, illuminated the road. Ahead was the River of Stars, a street of magic and light, a place of wonder and glittering enchantment. Shadows danced on the walls, a mockery of life and animation that sent a spike of anger into his heart. The minstrel's arrival had brought joy to the city, sending a spreading wave of euphoria through its inhabitants. Everyone had heard fragments of his song, but tonight would see it played out for people who had seen the events it described first hand.

The Theatre of Dethelion would play host to this rogue minstrel's dangerous work, but surely anyone who had witnessed the bloodshed of the goblin king's assault would balk at its horrors being told in song. Some things were best consigned to history – not forgotten, never that – but not celebrated. Not immortalised in song. He paused to draw a calming breath, feeling his hands bunch into fists. His was a quick temper, but he forced his anger down with a series of mental exercises taught to him by his father.

He turned into the River of Stars and let the full force of the festival wash over him.

Everywhere was light and magic. The elves of Tor Yvresse, normally so stolid and not given to gaudy behaviour, thronged the streets in their hundreds. They wore their grief like a cloak, but tonight it was cast off as costumes of all description and colour bedazzled the eye. Revellers dressed in a riot of flesh and fabrics that would make a courtesan of Lothern blush. Magical will-o'-the-wisps darted overhead, flitting to the sound of music played by unseen lyres and flutes.

Fire breathers capered in the centre of the street, and a spellsinger wove their blazing exhalations into dancing forms above the heads of the crowd. Blazing representations of colourful dragons, eagles and battling warriors burned the sky. A troupe of dancers and tumblers spun and wove through the fire, twirling in tight spirals as they performed an ancient dance from the time of Aenarion. Their robes were like wings and they moved as though in defiance of gravity.

He moved into the mass of cavorting anarchy, feeling the press of bodies around him like a physical pain. He longed for his rune-encrusted sword, but the shimmering chimera-skin sword belt lay in his bedchamber. Only a slender, leaf-bladed dagger hung at his thigh, in defiance of the joyous spirit of the festival.

The fire breathers moved on, and another band of entertainers took their place, a host of painted figures more akin to the barbarously insane wardancers of the asrai than any noble family of Ulthuan. Like the acrobats before them, they darted through the crowd, spinning swords and spears in dazzling displays of martial skill. Their oiled bodies gleamed in the torchlight, and laughing revellers pawed at them with lewd caresses.

He felt the woman's touch coming a heartbeat before she made contact with his arm.

He spun, catching her wrist as it reached out to his shoulder. Acting on instinct, he twisted the wrist and sent his free hand pistoning towards her masked face.

His fist never connected, the killing blow intercepted a hair's breadth from the bejewelled features of her mask. As he held one of her wrists, she too held one of his. They released each other in the same instant, and he stepped back as the crowd pulled away, his violent outburst a flagrant breach of festival etiquette. The woman straightened and massaged her shoulder where he had twisted it fiercely.

She took in the darkness of his robe, and the pale, lifeless white of his half-hidden mask.

'You are fast,' she said. 'As a banshee should be.'

'As are you,' he replied. 'I might have killed you.'

'But you did not. Be thankful for that, for it would have displeased my husband greatly, and he is a great hunter.'

'Really?' he said. 'And who is he, this great hunter?'

She cocked her head to the side, and he saw that her eyes were the most brilliant amber colour. Silver flecks of icy white glittered there, and he saw her great sadness, like a mother who has outlived all her children. Golden hair, like fresh-ripened corn, framed a delicate heart-shaped mask of silver with a single painted tear that curved down her cheek.

'You know it is impolite to ask for names during the Festival of Masques.'

He shrugged. 'Then do not answer. I care not.'

He turned to walk away, but the woman caught up with him.

'I will tell you if you really want to know.'

She had intrigued him at first, with her speed and secret beauty, but he was already weary of her presence and had no wish to indulge her further. He had work to do.

'His name is Kurnous,' she said, and he stopped in his tracks.

'Ah,' he said, without turning. 'You are mad.'

She danced around him, trailing her fingertips over his chest. 'If grief makes one mad, then yes, I suppose I am.'

'Your husband is dead, is he not?'

'No, not dead,' she said, looking furtively around her as though afraid of being seen talking to him. 'He is merely… elsewhere.'

He pushed on through the crowds, watching a tumbler in the guise of Loec spin and laugh through the revellers like a mischievous child. A troupe of cloaked shadows followed him, forever dancing to unheard music and never stopping. The followers of the Shadow Dancer were capricious and given to unpredictable behaviour, teasing and cajoling, stealing and giving offence in equal measure.

'I love watching their dance,' said the woman. 'It gives me hope.'

'Then you are deluded as well as mad,' he replied, increasing his pace.

'Why do you say that?'

'Because hope is a fool's refuge. Where is the hope left to this world?'

'Look around you, banshee. It is everywhere. You can see it in every smile, taste it in every tear and hear it in every tune. It is sung from the highest tower and every shadowed arbour. Even in the darkest times, there is always hope.'

He rounded on her as a carnival of sword dancers paraded down the street, their blades spinning silver webs around them, through which the followers of Loec tumbled and twisted. Wild cheers echoed from the buildings to either side of them, and the music swelled in volume as the crowd applauded their skill.

The woman gripped his arm in fear as the warriors moved past, their leader naked save for a crimson mask of Khaine.

'Their swords are bloody,' she said.

'No, it is just the firelight.'

She gripped him tighter. 'You are wrong. Khaine's swords are always bloody. Vaul's labours are never-ending, and many are the weapons of infinite cunning he crafts for the wars against the Dark Prince. And no sooner are they forged than they are bloody.'

'I see no blood,' he said. 'Only the silver-white of the finest ithilmar.'

'You do not see the blood, for you do not know grief as I know it,' she replied.

Anger touched him, and his hands bunched into fists. His heart surged with the urge to strike her, to show her just how well acquainted he was with grief. He had sacrificed all that he had in service to Ulthuan, and still that had not been enough. No one knew the terrible price he had paid to keep these lands safe, and she thought the loss of a single loved one could outweigh his pain?

'Your anger will be your undoing,' she said, and his fury ebbed to the point where he felt he could speak without violence.

'I know grief,' he said, every word forced from behind clenched teeth.

'You know mortal grief,' she said. 'When you must watch the beautiful children you love above all else wither and die throughout eternity, then you will know true anguish.'

Yvresse had more than its share of grieving widows and mothers. Goblins, druchii and men had seen to that. Every family in the city had suffered loss, and the white cloaks of mourning were more common on the city streets than the gaudy silks of Lothern's latest fashions. He remembered his own father's death, which had been swiftly followed by his brother's. He had had no time to mourn, the demands of war allowing no respite for grief.

Chains of duty held him fast, and the life he had known, where hope and the promise of a return to the Golden Times, was a distant memory. This woman was an irritating distraction, and had already wasted too much of his time. Whatever sorrow had undone her sanity was of no interest to him, and he stepped away.

'I must take my leave, madam,' he said. 'I am sorry for your loss, but I have other duties to attend to this night.'

'On festival night?' she said. 'Tor Yvresse sheds tears enough throughout the year, do not sully this one night of revelry and hope with anything as tawdry as duty. All year, these people mourn and walk through life like shadows. Allow them this one night to remember that they are alive, to act with abandon and live a few hours without fear for the future.'

'They *should* fear for the future,' he snapped, no longer caring whether he offended her with his boorish behaviour. 'The future is blood and war, death and grief. That is all there is, and all there will ever be. To believe anything else is delusional.'

He turned and moved deeper into the crowd, ignoring offers of companionship from naked elves of both sexes. Their painted bodies writhed in the magical light that bathed the city, and the tempo of the music increased the deeper into the city he went. From street corners, he heard snatches of verse, drifting echoes of the minstrel's song. His heart hardened with every fleeting glimpse of joy, every tantalising echo of the hateful ballad that told of the city's greatest battle. Everywhere he looked, he saw eyes shining with tears, yet they were not tears of sorrow and emptiness, they were shed in newfound hope and the promise of a better tomorrow.

'Fools,' he hissed, watching as couples swayed in time to the song.

'Is it foolish to believe things can get better?' said the woman, appearing at his side.

He sighed. 'Will I never be rid of you?'

'Never,' she answered with a laugh like the chiming of silver bells. 'It is my nature to be persistent, to always believe that spring's hope will follow winter's despair.'

He halted as pleasurable warmth spread through him, the restful peace of a good night's sleep. Ever since that night in the tower he had been wracked by dreadful nightmares, and had almost forgotten how it felt to be rested. He turned to face the woman, feeling her hand in his, though he had not felt her take it.

'After all, a world of winter will die, just as surely as a world of summer. Hope is the light that offers a chance for life, and without it there will only ever be darkness. Remember that before you drive that dagger home.'

He snatched his hand back as though burned. The crowd surged, and a starburst of magical fire exploded overhead to rapturous cheers. Spirals of white and gold light tumbled through the air, and a thousand songs filled the glittering heart of the city, drifting out through the empty streets, abandoned villas and deserted markets. Distant echoes seemed to answer, the memory of those beyond death roused by the potency of this night.

The sounds faded and he looked for the masked woman, but she was nowhere to be seen.

'Thank the gods for that,' he muttered, turning and following the crowd.

To Dethelion's Theatre.

The great dramatist Dethelion of Tiranoc had penned some of Ulthuan's greatest artistic works, such as *The Forest of Midnight, Aurelia and Timore*, as well as composing many of its most heart-wrenching songs of lament. His work had travelled beyond Ulthuan's shores, though little of the true power of his works survived translation into human tongues. The songs men knew of the fey folk were poor shadows compared to the originals. Dethelion had been a melancholy poet, his works inevitably ending in tragedy, with star-crossed lovers doomed never to find happiness, heroes cursed to triumph at the cost of everything that mattered to them most.

He had read all of Dethelion's compositions, and admired the long-dead poet's work greatly. Despite the grand melodrama of his epic tales, there was a commendable lack of sentimentality to his characters. Was it an affront to have this minstrel's work played out in Dethelion's theatre, or was it more apt than he cared to admit? In truth, he did not know.

The excitement of the crowd was palpable, a delicious frisson that passed from skin to skin like a charge of tingling magic. He felt it pass through his own flesh, the gestalt magical nature of his race buoying him up on a wave of shared wonderment. He viciously suppressed the feeling, knowing it would only serve him ill were he to be caught up in the tale like the rest of these fools.

These are your people, said a treacherous voice inside him.

He shook his head as the River of Stars widened into a great piazza which, to the untrained eye, appeared to be ruined. Designed by Dethelion himself, it was a recreation of one of the ancient cities of Ulthuan that now lay at the bottom of the ocean. No one now remembered the city's name, though it was said that its ruins could be seen far beneath the waters off the coast of Tiranoc when the skies were bright and the seas calm.

Fashioned from artfully sculpted stone of pale blue and green, it resembled a coral reef raised from the rock upon which Tor Yvresse was built. It had all the appearance of a labyrinth, yet no matter where a viewer was to stand, they would have a perfect view of the proscenium. Islands of tiered seats worked in fluted stone and bathed in the light of the stars gave prince and pauper an unrivalled perch from which to enjoy whatever play or drama was to be acted out before them.

Beyond the majesty of the theatre rose the Tower of the Warden.

Its blue marble was subdued, where normally a fine web of magical energies pulsed through its stonework. Its base was obscured by the ruined artifice of the theatre, yet its windowless length reared up over the skyline, dominating the fanged peaks of the Annulii in the distance. Crepuscular light glimmered weakly from the Warden's lonely windows, and a single balcony gave its solitary occupant an unrivalled view of his empty city.

Shadows danced in the window, as though a lonely figure stirred within, and he turned away from the sad tower. It was within the tower that the city had been saved, and a soul damned. He never knew how to feel whenever he saw the tower from this angle, for it was a symbol of great victory and a reminder of dreadful loss.

A figure jostled him, an elf clad in a robe and horned mask intended to render unto him the semblance of Orion, the atavistic huntsman of Athel Loren. It was a poor likeness, for the King of the Wild Wood was a fearsome avatar, a ferocious, elemental force that chilled the soul with its rapacious fury. The figure bowed to him with an ululating laugh and spun away into the crowd. The sight unsettled him, for he was seeing the faces of gods in every fleeting glimpse of a mask, every half-concealed smile. The Festival of Masques was a time of miracles and raptures, when poetic souls claimed that the gods might walk the earth, but he had never thought it to be a literal sentiment. He shook off his unease and moved on, pushing ever closer to the stage.

Never before had the theatre played host to so many. Every portion of wall and tier was occupied, all of Tor Yvresse spilling from their draughty homes to listen to this minstrel's tale of their greatest tragedy. It seemed at once abhorrent and self-flagellating to come out in such numbers to hear the tale of so terrible a battle.

He moved through the throng, making his way towards the stage, where the lilting sounds of music and voices preparing for song could he heard. He attracted no little attention as he moved with grim purpose, each masked face that turned in his direction quickly averted as the eyes behind it beheld his garb as one of Morai-heg's deathly messengers.

The dagger at his side grew warm, and he realised he was gripping its hilt tightly. He couldn't remember slipping a hand beneath his dark cloak, and it took all his self-control not to draw the weapon. He blinked away a blurred red haze from his eyes, pushing through the murmuring crowds with ever greater urgency as he felt his heartbeat pulse in time with the swelling music. The light, the noise and the heat assaulted him, and the breath caught in his throat as he felt the crowd pressing in on him, smothering him and threatening to crush him beneath their constant demands, the never-ending duty and the fear that he could never match up to their expectations. He was deep in the labyrinth of twisting walls and passageways, lost in a maze of possible routes, and his skull throbbed with pain.

He paused, releasing his grip on the dagger, and pressed his hands to his temple. The pain building behind his eyes was like a spike of hot iron driven into his skull. He threw back his head and loosed a wail of anguish and pain, the sound echoing from the walls of the theatre and bouncing back and forth across the suddenly quiet crowd.

The silence that followed his wail was like a void in the world, an emptiness of the soul, and he ran from the hostile stares and quizzical looks he was attracting. He ran past dancers, singers, musicians, spellsingers and weavers of enchantments. The beat of hammers rang from the walls, sparks flying as a blind and hooded priest of Vaul shaped swords and armour by the light of the moons.

He ran until he came to a secluded hollow behind the stage, where a trio of brightly painted wagons had been left. Each was gaudily coloured and lacquered so that their flanks shone like rainbows in the light reflected from the tower. A tall elf with lush features and silver hair stood beside the wagons, pacing back and forth and waving his arms as though debating with an army of invisible ghosts. Alone of all the people he had seen tonight, this elf wore no mask, but was clad in armour that was ludicrously impractical, and so ornamented in gold and over-elaborate fretwork that it would be impossible to wear in combat.

A long sword was belted at his waist, but it was too low to draw without effort. Whoever he was, this elf was no warrior.

The costumed elf turned and his handsome features paled at the sight of him.

'Dear boy, one does not sneak up on one of artistic temperament dressed thusly,' said the would-be warrior.

'I am sorry,' he said. 'I believe I am lost.'

'Aren't we all in the grand scheme of things?' replied the handsome elf, taking a step towards him and extending his hand.

'I am Narentir,' said the elf. 'You may have heard of me.'

Narentir's features were soft, gentle even, and his warrior's garb now seemed offensive. Only one who had faced the enemy and drawn blood had the right to dress like this. Not some poet who took the horrors of others and turned them into bloodless dramas.

'I have heard of you,' he said, feeling his heart-rate return to normal. 'In fact I have sought you all night.'

'But of course you have,' said Narentir, closing his eyes and smiling, tilting his head back to breathe in the air and listen to the murmur of the crowd from beyond. 'Everyone in Tor Yvresse has come to see me. My music and poetry fills a need in these people they did not even realise they had until tonight, an unrequited urge to relive their greatest joy and most poignant sorrow.'

'Some sorrows should be left alone,' he snarled. 'No good can come of reopening old wounds.'

'I disagree,' said Narentir, oblivious to his threatening tone. 'If we ignore such wounds they fester like the fruit left too long on the branch. No, we must embrace the glories of the past and all our memories of them. Those joyous *and* those painful, for without the bitter the sweet tastes not so sweet.'

The hilt of the dagger slipped into his hand once more, and the urge to plunge the blade into the minstrel's neck right now was almost uncontrollable.

'You speak of things you do not know,' he said. 'You sing songs of honour, hope, love and triumph, when such things are for children's stories. They are not the way of the real world.'

Narentir laughed. 'Oh, my dear fellow, how mistaken you are. You, who come dressed as a harbinger of death, have allowed the grim fatalism of Morai-heg to enter your soul, but I now see that your arrival is the very thing that will make this night complete!'

A swelling roar of applause began spontaneously as the gathered elves sensed that the grand retelling they had come to witness was about to begin. Narentir swept forward and took him by the arm, leading him up a curved flight of steps towards the marble proscenium. His heart filled with warring desires as he realised where Narentir was taking him.

'The Tale of Eltharion is nothing without the spectre of death hovering in the wings!' exclaimed Narentir. 'I am but one player, and in my time play many parts, but you will be my muse, the living promise of death's dark shadow. What say you, nameless banshee, will you strut upon this lonely stage with me, the darkness to my light?'

He hesitated, unsure of the turn this night had taken. 'I will,' he said at last, feeling a measure of the minstrel's enthusiasm pass between them.

'Wonderful,' said Narentir, striding past onto the stage as the throats of Tor Yvresse opened to welcome him. Still clutching the dagger, he followed the minstrel as he took his position and the applause began to fade. He had expected the ludicrously armoured elf to wax lyrical upon taking the stage, but he began his tale without grandiose pontificating.

Narentir spoke with the perfect pitch and timing of a professional teller of tales, a saga poet with the power to enchant an audience with words. Like all good storytellers, he set the stage upon which his tale would be told, a mordant coastline of mist and shadow amid a storm of ill-omen. From this splintered darkness came the goblins, a ragged fleet of them, drunk on slaughter and hungry to wage war on the island home of the asur.

From the wings of the stage, he felt Narentir's gaze upon him and he stepped onto the stage, letting the shadows curl around him as he prowled the edges of this retelling of his nightmares. His anger built as he heard Narentir speak of the goblin king, he who called himself Grom. Prowling the stage, Narentir's voice dropped as he spoke of how the goblins had laid waste to the land of Yvresse, burning mansions and castles that had stood for thousands of years in a single night.

The audience responded to his softly-sung tale as the music built from wistful lament to horror. Emotions filled the air, and even though he knew the truth of those days, his throat choked as Narentir retold the fall of Athel Tamarha and the death of Lord Moranion. He had not seen that beautiful castle burn, and had never visited its blackened ruins, but as Narentir spoke of Lord Moranion's selfless valour in facing the goblin king, he dearly wished he had taken one day to fly to the fallen castle and breathe in the past.

He was circling Narentir, and the audience gasped as they saw him clearly now. The dagger was unsheathed in his hand, and Narentir nodded to him as he drew closer with every circuit. He barely heard the rest of the tale, his attention fixed on the pale neck of the minstrel. A vein pulsed below the curved sweep of his jaw, an ideal place for the keen point of a blade to plunge home.

What an ending this would be. Not the terrible battle fought around the Warden's Tower, but the curtain falling on the narrator's death. No one who saw this bloody truth would fail to see the lie of hope. Without its weight, the elves of Tor Yvresse would be free to fight with the grim knowledge of their doom, for what warrior ever fought harder than the one with nothing left to lose?

The clouds parted and stars came out in droves, bathing the stage in their ancient glow. Narentir's armour shone with their light, and he now displayed not the soft features of a minstrel, but the hard, hollow-cheeked visage of a killer. So complete was the transformation that he paused in his circular path, the breath catching in his throat as Narentir sang the conclusion of his tale.

Behind him, the tower shone in the starlight, as though a willing participant in this retelling. He listened as Narentir held the audience spellbound in the palm of his hand, singing in hushed tones of Eltharion entering the tower with his closest companions and returning the following morning alone.

He felt a keening moan of sorrow begin in the back of his throat as he thought back to that terrible night. The horror and unimaginable sacrifices he had made that night were too awful to remember, and here they were being paraded for the aggrandisement of a mere bard. He took a step towards Narentir, the dagger's blade glinting in the moonlight. The crowd hushed. Not a breath of wind or a rustle of fabric disturbed the silence. He and Narentir might as well have been the only two souls left in the world.

Narentir turned to face him, and they walked towards one another slowly. He lifted the dagger until it was aimed at Narentir's throat. A chill passed through him, and he heard distant laughter, at first girlish and full of childhood mischief, then rich with age-won wisdom, finally brittle and cackling, like that of an ancient crone.

His steps faltered, and he looked out into the audience. An entire city watched him, utterly still and silent but for one figure, a woman robed in cream with a silver mask. She seemed to glide through the audience, though no one acknowledged her. Wherever she passed, he saw the faces of the elves around her bathed in light. Every one of them shone with hope and joy, their spirits soaring to hear how Eltharion had saved them all.

He saw the strength and courage that filled them. His example had lifted them to greater heights of nobility than ever they could have imagined. They loved their grim liege-lord, understanding on levels they could never articulate that he had sacrificed everything he was to save them.

Hope is the light that offers a chance for life, and without it there will only ever be darkness.

He stood face to face with Narentir. Barely a foot separated them, and the minstrel tilted his head a fraction, exposing the delicate flesh of his neck.

'Do you still desire to slay me, my lord?' he said, fear making his voice tremble.

The dagger shook in his hand. He looked out into the audience, hoping for another glimpse of the silver-masked woman. The audience waited with bated breath to see what would happen next, knowing that events of great moment were unfolding before them.

Would it be murder or salvation?

He lowered the dagger. 'You know who I am?' he asked.

'You are Eltharion, Warden of Tor Yvresse,' said Narentir. 'And you are here to kill me.'

'You knew?'

Narentir nodded. 'I knew the moment I heard your banshee wail.'

'Yet you did not flee?'

'What would have been the point?' said Narentir, his voice regaining a measure of composure. 'I could die alone begging for life, or I could die on stage, remembered forever by all who saw me struck down. Which would you choose?'

'You are braver than you look,' said Eltharion.

Narentir laughed in relief. 'I assure you I am not, my lord. If this has been my greatest performance, it is in no small measure thanks to the fear that your dagger would spill my blood across this fine stage. Dethelion would, I am sure, have approved of the suitably tragic ending for the noble minstrel.'

Eltharion took a deep breath and turned to the crowd. He reached up and tore off his mask, letting it fall to the stage. It shattered with a thwarted shriek, and Eltharion sighed to be rid of the ghastly visage.

The crowd erupted in applause, and wild cheers filled the air as Narentir took his bow. Though Narentir waved at him to do likewise, Eltharion did not follow the minstrel's example, for this night was not his. It belonged to Narentir.

'What changed your mind?' asked Narentir as he stood straight once again.

Eltharion considered the question, and the ghost of a smile split his bloodless lips.

'I met a woman,' he said.

'Ah, the fairer sex,' said Narentir with a theatrical sigh. 'Truly they tame the raging beast within us and make us yearn to be better than we are. Was she beautiful?'

Eltharion tried to picture the woman, her golden, corn-coloured hair and amber eyes, but the image was already hazy and indistinct. His gaze swept the farthest reaches of the theatre, longing for one last sight of her. He caught a flash of golden hair and a mask of purest silver at an arched entrance. Though a great distance separated them, he could see the pools of her amber eyes as though she stood right next to him. The silver that concealed her face no longer seemed like a mask, but the embodiment of her divine radiance.

A single tear rolled from her eye and a great weight lifted from Eltharion's heart. The doom he had brought upon himself on that dread night remained, as it always would, but the all-consuming despair that had almost driven him to murder was gone.

She had come to save him, when he had not even known he needed saving.

'Who was she?' asked Narentir. 'This handmaiden to whom I owe my life?'

'She was hope,' said Eltharion. 'Simply hope.'

GUARDIANS OF
THE FOREST

30 miles

the wild beach

PARRAVON

the northern sentinels

X
battle of the red harvest

tree of woe

greenskin monolith of anchiryl

halls of anaereth

mirror pools of tehoren

GREY MOUNTAINS

hills of the dead

tower of the eternal wood

glade of the lost

glade of eternal moonlight

upper gaiuralpe

deep forests of ourithu

feast halls of the wardance

waterfall palace of the naiad court

council of beasts

chasm glade of behdir seun

vales of winter

eyrie of the byorn lords

crag halls of findol

the bridge

BRETONNIA

miragliano

fool peak

quenelles

athel loren

parravon

alebort

bíln

the empire

talabheim

nord

karak norn

putrid swamp

karak izor

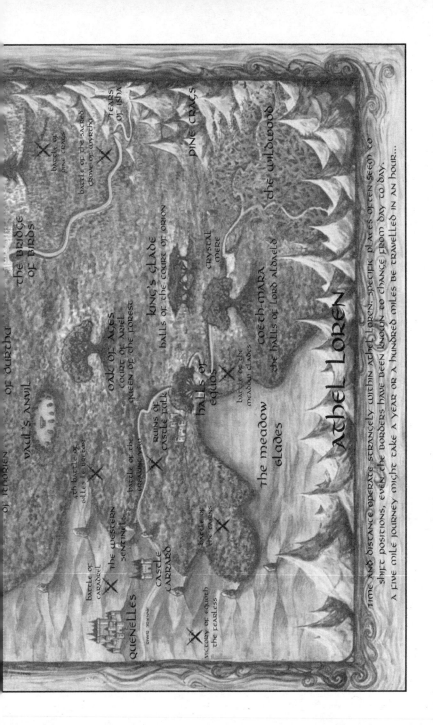

Athel Loren

time and distance operate strangely within Athel Loren. specific places often seem to
shift positions, even the borders have been known to change from day to day.
A five mile journey might take a year or a hundred miles be travelled in an hour...

'I shall wolfe your flesh and snap your bones,
Skrind your folk and burne their homes.
For mocking ked to dare my rage,
Your jibe it traps me like a cage.
The unclaimed ones must dread my kinde,
Can never squander fear behind.'

PROLOGUE
SEASON OF THE BEAST

The beast at the centre of the cave dreamed of blood, blood and war, civilisations torn down and entire populations gorged upon by the children of Chaos. Flames and the coming of the End Times consumed its every thought, order overturned and the rule of the Dark Gods absolute.

Its massive, shaggy form shifted position, its cloven hooves rippling the rock as though it sat upon glistening mud. Curling horns sprouted from its bestial skull, protruding from a ripped and stained leather mask behind which two bovine eyes glimmered with dark malice. A web of skulls was woven into the shaggy mane that ran the length of its twisted spine, the jaws opening and closing in silent screams of anguish.

The monster clutched a gnarled and twisted staff in one massive fist, its substance slithering and insubstantial, as though the beast's flesh merged with the dark wood. It traced patterns and lines in the fluid matter of the cavern floor, ever more chaotic and irregular as they overlapped and spiralled.

Clouds of stinking vapour gusted from its snorting nostrils, twisting and swirling in the air before being absorbed by the fabric of the walls. The rock glistened with a dank dew of moisture, dancing images of war and death burning in its depths, reflections of the twisted thoughts of the shaggy beast that drooled thick ropes of animal saliva.

Humans called it the Shadow-Gave, while the elves knew it as

Cyanathair, and in the dwarf tongue it was called Gor-Dunn.

The fires of war burned in its eyes and it could feel the approach of its children, the true inheritors of the world. It could sense the breath of Chaos within them, the boon of change and mutation that marked them out as the chosen of the gods. Three came, the mightiest beasts of their herds, fierce and proud, filled with power and drawn towards this dank, icy cave to seek approval from the gods that theirs was the right to rule this gathering of warherds.

It turned a rheumy eye towards the cave mouth as the weak autumn light was blocked off by the three supplicants. It saw they were tall and broad, with great, corded muscles beneath dark, matted fur, each the master of a great warherd. All three carried crude weapons: heavy iron axes or thick, blade-studded clubs, though in truth any one of them could fight as well with horn, tooth or claw. One stood on thick, goat-like legs, its shaggy head crowned with a mass of bronze-tipped antlers and a thick mane of bright orange fur. Another stamped iron-shod hooves, its rump elongated like that of a horse, though its skin was scaled and bronze. Dark spines grew from its back and an extra set of arms sprouted from beneath its armpits.

But greatest of all the Beastlords was a massive, bull-headed creature with dark, bloodstained fur, its hide scarred by decades of killing and battle. Thick, hooked chains looped across its chest and it wore spiked shoulder guards crudely fashioned from the breastplates of those it had slaughtered. It carried a massive, double-headed axe, its blades rusted, but with a potent magical aura surrounding them.

The beast in the cave let out a single bray, guttural and wet, and the three supplicants advanced towards it, their steps halting and unsure, though none wished to show weakness before the others. To do so would be to die.

The Shadow-Gave felt the breath of the gods sluicing through its body in a torrent of power and exhaled it as a noxious cloud of dark, writhing mist. The mist pulsed with the essence of the north, growing and billowing outwards to envelop the three who had come to stand in its presence.

Instantaneously, the creature with bronzed antlers collapsed, roaring in agony as its body was gifted with the power of the gods and thrashing limbs and grasping, thorned pseudopods erupted from its fluid flesh. The other two backed away from the howling creature spawned from the Shadow-Gave's gifts and awaited their fate at the hands of the magical mist.

Both were enveloped by the miasmic cloud of sorcerous power and the Shadow-Gave felt their will and ambition war with the power of change that seared through their veins. The bronze-skinned centaur creature reared up on its hind legs, the dark spines on its back mutating into rippling tentacles with snapping jaws. It lunged towards the Shadow-Gave with a shriek of bestial fury, but a massive, clawed hand dragged it back, the huge bull-headed monster slashing its axe through the writhing creature's midsection. Dark ichor sprayed from the wound, hot and stinking, and the Beastlord cried out as its matted fur burned where the blood spattered then ran in rivulets down its fanged, bovine features, scarring pale grooves in its face.

Its flesh darkened, taking on the bronze hue of the beast it had just killed and its breath smoked with the heat of a furnace. It let out a mighty bellow, the very walls of the cave cracking at its din, and the Shadow-Gave nodded in acceptance as the writhing black mist dispersed and faded from sight.

The massive beastman let out a great, snorting breath, its hide now dark and scaled, its horned head scarred and burnt, but its flickering, multi-coloured eyes shining with purpose and power. It raised its axe in a brief salute to the shaggy, horned creature at the centre of the cave and ripped one of the chains from its armour, plunging a barbed hook into the screaming flesh of the thrashing creature that had first succumbed to the Shadow-Gave's magic.

Without further ado, the Beastlord turned and marched from the darkness of the cave, leading the snapping, howling spawn by the thick chain looped around a muscled forearm. Its thoughts crystallised as it left the dank confines of the Shadow-Gave's lair, feeling the breath of cold air from the mouth of the passageway.

It stepped into the cold light of day, feeling its eyes burn with its purity, and grunted in satisfaction as it saw the gathered warherds. Hundreds of twisted bestial creatures awaited the return of their leaders, braying minotaurs, growling beastmen, stamping centaur creatures and all manner of things so blessed by the touch of the Dark Gods that any resemblance to the beasts of this world had long since vanished.

As great a herd as it was, the Beastlord knew that many of these beasts would not survive the winter, too malnourished and too weak to hunt what they needed to survive. The resurgence of the rat-things in the high peaks had driven them from their hunting grounds and down the northern flanks of the mountains.

The herds had bemoaned their fate, but the Beastlord now saw this for what it truly was – a sign from the gods.

Now it was time to descend to the lands of men and feed once more.

The Beastlord led its chained spawn towards the monstrous host, revelling in their howls and snorts of abasement – the touch of the Shadow-Gave was upon it and all the beasts could see its favour. They gathered around the Beastlord, raising their bellowing voices in praise of the Dark Gods as it marched through the herd.

Far below, the Beastlord could see a massive, sprawling expanse of forest, a patchwork of browns, greens and golds, nestling at the foot of tall, snow-capped peaks of grey rock.

With his newly enhanced flesh he could smell the rank stench of earth magic emanating from the forest and see the dimming power that radiated from its heart as winter closed in.

The Beastlord raised its axe and led the warherd towards the forest.

BOOK ONE
AUTUMN'S DYING FIRE

'The beastmen, the children of Chaos and Long Night, are our sworn enemies. They fight us for our right to exist in the woodlands and forests, and have always, and will always, seek to claim and corrupt Athel Loren for themselves. These are your enemies, child. Know them well, and keep your bow always ready.'

CHAPTER ONE

Leofric could feel the tension in the men-at-arms around him as they rode through the cold, autumn morning, sensing it in their stiff, awkward movements and strained conversation. He felt apprehension too, but hid it beneath an aloof exterior. It would not do to show nervousness to the lower orders and it would only serve to unsettle his men more were they to sense their lord's unease.

The day was cold and Leofric could feel the coming winter in the sharpness of the air and see it in the golden leaves of the few trees they had passed. The further east through the dukedom of Quenelles he and his soldiers rode, the more scattered patches of snow he saw, the little-used roadway unnaturally dotted in crisp white with drifting clouds of icy mist clinging to the muddy ground.

Thirty nervous-looking peasant men-at-arms rode behind him, their yellow surcoats bright and stark against the dreary landscape. A cold wind blew off the mountains far to the south, their soaring dark peaks cloaked in shawls of snow, and despite the thick, woollen undergarments Leofric wore and the padded jerkin beneath his magnificent plate armour, he could still feel the coming cold deep in his bones.

'How far is it to the forest now?' said a voice beside him.

Leofric reined in his tall grey gelding and twisted in the saddle to smile at his wife, Helene, who was riding side-saddle on a slender bay mare. She wore a long gown of red velvet and was wrapped in a thick cloak of bearskin from a great beast Leofric himself had slain with a single lance thrust while on the hunt. Tousled blonde hair spilled around her shoulders and despite her smile, a worry line just above the bridge of her nose spoke to Leofric of her unease.

'Not far now, my dear,' answered Leofric, raising the visor of his helmet. 'Lady willing, perhaps another mile or so.'

Helene nodded and shivered beneath her cloak.

'Are you cold?' asked Leofric, guiding his horse alongside his wife's and detaching his long wolf-pelt cloak from his carved, silver pauldrons.

'No, I'm fine,' she answered. 'It's not the cold. It's... well, you know what it is.'

Leofric nodded. He too could instinctively feel the forest's fey presence on the air, a ghostly, feathery sensation down his spine as though a thousand eyes were spying upon him. His instincts had always served him well as a warrior and he fought the urge to draw the broad-bladed sword that hung at his waist.

'Don't worry,' said Leofric, patting a canvas sack that hung from his saddle, 'once we reach the waystone, it will only be a matter of hours before we are on our way back to the castle and our son. I will have Maixent prepare a hot bath for you, and we will all eat roast venison before a roaring fire in the grand hall, then the three of us shall fall asleep together.'

'That sounds heavenly,' agreed Helene. 'I just hope little Beren isn't giving old Maixent too much trouble. You know what he's like when we're not with him.'

'If he is, he'll soon regret it,' said Leofric, remembering the punishments meted out to him at the hands of the castle's sharp-tempered chamberlain. 'It will teach him the virtue of discipline.'

'He's only three, Leofric.'

'A boy is never too young to learn the duties and responsibilities of a knight of Bretonnia,' said Leofric sternly.

Helene stood in the wide footrest of her sidesaddle to kiss her husband and said, 'You're adorable when you're being all serious.'

Leofric Carrard was a tall man, powerfully muscled from long years of wielding a long lance and wearing heavy plate armour into battle. He carried himself like the warrior he was, confident, brave and noble – every inch a knight of Bretonnia. A dark moustache and a triangular wisp of beard below his bottom lip were his only concession to vanity, and his clear green eyes were like chips of emerald set in an angular, regal face that plainly wore the cares of his twenty-five years.

Another horse drew near and a heavyset man with a long beard halted his mount in a splash of mud. He wore a yellow surcoat over a jerkin of studded leather armour, a domed sallet helmet and carried a long, iron-tipped spear. He was accompanied by a similarly dressed figure, a young boy of no more than thirteen summers who carried a tall banner pole. Atop the banner, a fringed pennant of gold depicting a scarlet unicorn rampant below a bejewelled crown snapped in the wind – the banner of Leofric Carrard, lord and master of these lands.

'My lord–' began the heavyset man, respectfully touching the brim of his helmet.

'What is it, Baudel?' said Leofric.

'Begging your pardon, my lord, but we had best not be dawdling here,' explained Baudel, Leofric's chief man-at-arms. 'Best we don't get caught out in the open this close to the forest folk's realm. This time of year it ain't good to be outside.'

'It's never a good time to be outside according to you, Baudel,' pointed out Leofric.

'Aye, nor it is, my lord,' said Baudel, nodding to the east. 'Leastwise not near Athel Loren, anyway.'

'Don't speak that name, Baudel,' chided Helene. 'They say the faerie folk can hear when mortals name their land and are much vexed by how ugly it sounds from our mouths.'

'Begging your pardon, milady,' apologised Baudel. 'I meant nothing by it.'

'You're right though, Baudel,' agreed Leofric, looking into the lifeless grey skies, 'best to be done with this and away before night falls. Prithard of Carcassonne sends word of beastman warbands in his lands – the damn things are everywhere now.'

'My lord!' scoffed Baudel. 'The Distressed is always sending word of such things. He worries when he has nothing to worry about!'

'True,' agreed Leofric, 'but this time I think he might not be crying wolf. I have had similar correspondence from Anthelme and Raynor, men not known for their scare-mongering.'

'All the more reason to be away from here sooner rather than later.'

Leofric nodded, saying, 'And I wish to be near that damned forest not one second longer than I have to be.'

'Hush, Leofric,' said Helene. 'Don't say such things.'

'I'm sorry, my love. I apologise for such language, but you know…'

'Yes,' said Helene, reaching out to lay a hand on Leofric's vambrace. 'I know.'

Leofric patted his wife's hand and gave her a forced smile before snapping down the visor of his helmet and raking back his spurs.

'Ride on!' he yelled, setting off along the road that led towards Athel Loren.

A low mist closed in around the riders, deadening sound and imparting a ghostly quality to the soldiers that followed Leofric as he rode ever eastwards. The road, which had never been more than an overgrown mud track, little travelled and little cared for, petered out to nothing more than a flattened earthen line, barely distinguishable from the rest of the landscape.

The lands of Bretonnia were rich and fertile, the soil dark and fecund, its landscape tilled by the peasants, its sweeping plains of the dukedoms open and green. Unlike the thickly forested realm of the Empire far to the north over the Grey Mountains that embraced the new sciences of alchemy, astrology and engineering, the realm of Bretonnia kept to the ancient ways of chivalric conduct. The beloved King Leoncoeur maintained the codes of behaviour set down by King Louis over a thousand years ago and held by the grail monks in the Chapel of Bastonne.

By such martial codes of honour did the knights of Bretonnia uphold their honour and defend their king's lands. To be a knight of Bretonnia was to be a warrior of great skill, noble bearing and virtuous heart, a paragon of all that was honourable.

Leofric felt his right hand slip from the emblazoned reins of his horse and grasp the hilt of his sword as he crested the misty summit of a low rise, and saw a dark line of green and gold on the horizon.

Athel Loren…

For centuries this forest had lived in the dreams and nightmares of the Bretonnian people. Even from here, Leofric could feel the power that lay within the dark depths of the forest, a drowsy, dreaming energy that clawed its way into the landscape like the roots of a tree. Dark oaks stood like sentinels at the forest edge, their branches high and leafy, a mixture of greens and russet browns.

Cold mists hugged the ground leading towards the forest, a wild, scrubby heath of unkempt grasses and thorns with stagnant pools of water and lumpen, snow-covered mounds of earth. Here and there, Leofric could see a rusted sword blade, spear point or arrowhead and the occasional bleached whiteness of bone.

No matter how many times he had come to enact the traditional family ritual, the sight of this ancient battlefield always unsettled him, as though restless spirits of the dead still haunted this bleak landscape.

'It's not like I imagined it to be,' said Helene, her voice just a little too shrill.

'No?'

'No, it's… it's, well, I don't know, but I thought it would look different. Given what you've told me I expected something more… unnatural.'

'Trust me, my dear,' said Leofric, 'there is nothing natural about this place.'

'I don't like it though,' said Helene, pulling her cloak tighter about herself. 'It feels like death here.'

'Aye,' agreed Leofric, 'it is a place of darkness.'

'What are those?' asked Helene, pointing to the raised mounds of earth and stone.

Riding alongside Leofric's wife, Baudel said, 'They say that those mounds are burial cairns, raised by the first tribes of men to come this way.'

'Really?' asked Helene, ignoring Leofric's disapproving gaze. 'What else do they say?'

'Well,' continued Baudel, warming to his theme. 'My old da used to tell us that an evil necromancer once raised the dead from their tombs and tried to destroy Athel Loren itself.'

'I know that story!' nodded Helene. 'His army entered the forest and was never seen again. Do you know what happened?'

'It was the forest, milady,' said Baudel, lowering his voice theatrically. 'My old da said that it was the forest what came alive and destroyed his skeleton army.'

'Hush, Baudel!' snapped Leofric. 'Do not be filling my wife's head with such nonsense. If this necromancer existed at all, then no doubt he was killed by the elves of the forest. That's what they are good at, killing and stealing what is not theirs!'

'Sorry, my lord,' said Baudel, suitably chastened.

'Oh, come now, husband, surely it's just a story,' said Helene.

Leofric stopped and turned his horse to face his wife, his face drawn and serious. He shook his head and said, 'Helene, I love you with all my heart, but you are from Lyonesse, not Quenelles.'

'What has that to do with anything?'

'It means you have not grown up in the shadow of the faerie forest, not had to lock and bolt your doors on certain nights to be sure that elven princelings do not come and steal away your children. You have never had to spend days with every gate and shutter drawn as the wild hunt thunders through the sky, killing everything in its path. Trust me on this, we will find no welcome here.'

Helene opened her mouth to let fly a witty riposte, but saw a familiar look she had come to know all too well in her husband's eyes, and the quip died in her throat. She nodded and said, 'Then let us be about our business.'

Leofric nodded curtly and turned his horse back towards the forest. The mist thinned as they drew near the forest's edge and he saw the familiar sight of the waystone within the passing of an hour. It reared up atop a flowering mound of grass, its smooth grey surface carved and painted with symbols and spirals, meaningless to him, but which nevertheless raised the hairs on the back of his neck.

He looked left and right, knowing that there were other stones spread evenly along the edge of the forest, but unable to see them due to the clammy mist that the sun seemed unable to burn away.

The knight guided his horse into a hollow depression in the earth with an icy pool at its base and a low cluster of rocks and bushes gathered around its ragged circumference. The top of the looming waystone was still visible, but the majority of its unsettling form was hidden from sight by the lay of the land.

'Halt!' he shouted as he reached the base of the hollow, dragging on his reins and bringing his horse to a halt. He rose in his stirrup and swung his leg over the fine saddle, its leather the colour of polished mahogany. As he dismounted, he saw that the tasselled ends of the yellow and scarlet caparison were muddy and stained, but it couldn't be helped. The gelding was named Taschen, standing seventeen hands high with wide shoulders and powerful muscles that could carry his armoured weight into battle without effort. King Leoncoeur himself had presented the magnificent animal to Leofric after he had saved the king's life during the charge against the daemon prince at Middenheim...

Leofric pushed the thought away, unwilling to relive the terrible memories of the horrific days defending the great northern city of the Empire from the traitor knight Archaon.

He handed Taschen's reins to his squire, a lad whose name he hadn't bothered to learn after his previous squire, Lauder, had died screaming with a beastman's spear in his gut.

The rest of his soldiers drew up in a circle around their lord, dismounting and walking their horses before brushing them down and loosening their girths. Compared to Leofric's steed, the men-at-arms' mounts were poor specimens indeed, and did not bear any heraldic devices or caparison, their riders' lowborn status prohibiting them from doing so.

Leofric marched over to his wife's horse, the reddish brown coat of which was silky and well cared for. He reached up and helped her dismount gracefully from the saddle, smiling as she hitched up her long red robes to avoid the worst of the autumnal mud.

'I warned you that your dress would get muddy,' he said gently.

'And I told you that I didn't care,' she said with a smile. 'I've grown tired of this gown anyway. My ladies tell me that red is very passé for this time of year and that you should be buying me something in lavender next season.'

'Oh they do, do they?' said Leofric. 'Then the peasantry must work harder next year to pay for it.'

'Indeed they shall,' said Helene and they laughed, not noticing the pained looks on the men-at-arms' faces at their overheard conversation.

Leofric turned from Helene and removed the canvas sack from his saddle, shouting orders to his men and directing them to the ice-covered pool at the base of the hollow. The men began breaking the thinner ice at the edge of the pool with the butts of their spears, taking it in turns to lead the horses to drink.

Leofric and Helene's horses drank their fill first as was only right and proper.

The knight of Quenelles moved to the far side of the icy pool as his squire struggled to lift a gilt-edged reliquary adorned with woodcuts from the back of his dray horse and carried it over towards Leofric.

'Set it down there,' ordered Leofric, pointing to a flat rock before him and drawing his sword, a magnificent blade as long as the butt of a lance and fully three fingers wide. Though it was stronger than steel, the sword weighed less than the wooden swords the peasants trained with and could cut through armour with lethal ease. Its blade was silver steel and shone as though captured starlight had somehow been trapped in its forging. The sword had been touched by the Lady of the Lake herself many centuries ago, and had been passed down the line of Carrard since time before memory. Leofric knew that it was a great honour to bear such a blessed weapon and that when he could no longer carry out his duty to defend his lands and people, he would pass it to Beren, his only son and heir.

Leofric's squire gently set down the reliquary before his master. The box was crafted from young saplings hewn from the Forest of Chalons and carved with stirring scenes that told of the heroic battles of Gilles le Breton, legendary founder of Bretonnia.

Atop the box, an image of the Lady of the Lake, goddess of the Bretonnians, was picked out in silver and rendered with swirling golden tresses. Leofric dropped to his knees as his squire closed his unworthy eyes and opened the winged doors of the reliquary.

The insides of the reliquary were painted with scenes of wondrous lakes and pools of reflective water, with the image of a breathtakingly beautiful woman rising from the depths. A deep cushion of sumptuous red velvet sat within the reliquary, together with the broken hilt of a sword and a faded scrap of cloth, its golden edges frayed and torn.

Leofric closed his eyes, feeling the peace of the Lady's presence wash over him at the sight of such holy relics: the faerie flag, a scrap of shimmering material supposedly torn from the cloak of an elven princeling by Leofric's great grandfather after he chased him from Castle Carrard, and the hilt of a Carrard sword that had cut down the orc warlord, Skargor of the Massif Orcal.

Leofric reached out and ran his gauntleted fingers along the broken hilt and folded cloth as he began his prayers to the Lady.

'Lady, bless me your humble servant, grant me the strength to confront those who ignore the wisdom and beauty of your holy light. You, whose bounty is with me all the days of my life, grant the lands I defend in your name the peace that this appeasement might bring...'

As Leofric began his prayers to the Lady, Helene sat upon a rock at the edge of the cold pool, gathering her skirts beneath her to make it marginally less uncomfortable. She felt a coldness here, and not just the coldness of the coming winter – something deeper chilled her. She looked back over her shoulder, seeing the gently swaying treetops of Athel Loren and the very tip of the tall waystone that marked the edge of the elven realm.

Strange that the forest did not grow beyond the stones. Idly, Helene wondered why, but then put the thought from her mind as Baudel approached with a pewter plate laden with cuts of cold beef, apples and a wedge of pungent cheese.

'Some lunch, milady?'

'No thank you, Baudel,' she said. 'I'm not really feeling hungry at the moment.'

'I'd ask you to reconsider, milady. It'll be a good few hours before we get back to the castle. Nice cheese, fresh beef to keep you going till then?'

'Very well, Baudel,' said Helene, accepting the plate.

Baudel turned to leave, but Helene looked over at Leofric with a concerned expression and said, 'Sit with me awhile. I want to talk.'

'Milady,' nodded the man-at-arms and sat on a nearby rock, his spear still held upright.

'Baudel, does Leofric seem different to you?'

'I'm not sure I follow, milady,' replied Baudel, guardedly.

'Yes you do,' said Helene. 'Ever since he came back from the Empire and the battles against the northern tribes I've felt a distance between us. You were there too, Baudel, does he seem changed... after the war, I mean?'

'War changes a man, milady.'

'I know that, Baudel, I'm not some milkmaid from Brionne. He's gone off to fight before, but he's never come back like this.'

'Like what?'

'Withdrawn and unwilling to talk about what happened.'

Baudel sighed and glanced over the pool at Leofric who was still kneeling before the Carrard reliquary, deep in his prayers. 'It wouldn't be right, me speaking out of turn about my lord and master, milady.'

'It's all right, I give you leave to speak your mind.'

'I appreciate that, milady, but it still wouldn't be right.'

Seeing the defensive look in the man-at-arms's eyes, Helene nodded and said, 'Very well, Baudel, your loyalty to your master is commendable.'

'Thank you, milady.'

'If you won't tell me what happened, at least tell me of Middenheim, it sounds like a magnificent place.'

'Aye,' nodded Baudel, 'it's grand all right, you've never seen nothing like it, milady, perched on top of a great big rock they call the Ulricsberg, higher than the lighthouse of l'Anguille by a long ways. To look at it you'd think nothing could take it, not man, not monster or nothing. But them northmen had wizards, dragons and other flyin' things that tore the place up with fire and magic, and they damn near won.'

'But they didn't, did they,' stated Helene.

'No, they didn't, but it was a close run thing, let me tell you,' said Baudel, darkly. 'The king himself led a hundred knights in the charge that faced a great daemon lord. Leofric rode in that charge and only the king and a handful of his knights rode out from that battle and... and you're a clever one aren't you, milady, getting me to spill my guts like that.'

Helene shrugged, realising that she would get no more from Baudel this day. She nibbled on a cut of meat and broke off a piece of cheese.

'It was devious of me wasn't it?' she admitted with a smile.

'Downright cunning,' agreed Baudel, rising from his seat.

'One last thing before you go,' said Helene.

'Yes?' asked Baudel, warily.

'Why can't I hear any birds or animals here? It's all very quiet apart from us.'

'The forest sleeps milady. It's waiting, just waiting for spring. As for the animals, well I think that perhaps they're all getting ready to sleep away the winter.'

'Yes, that must be it, Baudel. Thank you.'

'You're most welcome, milady,' said the man-at-arms, making an extravagant bow before turning and making his way back down to the pool, where the rest of the soldiers looked to their mounts or ate hunks of hard bread moistened by a thin gruel.

Helene watched him go, frowning and cursing herself for being too obvious. Baudel might be a peasant, but he was cleverer than most and had seen through her, admittedly clumsy, gambit.

She shivered again, feeling a crawling sensation up her spine and the ghostly caress of something unseen. Nothing stirred the air or broke the unnatural silence around her, save the hushed conversations of Leofric's soldiers. The cold was seeping through her furs and she wished to be away from this place, back in the castle with little Beren clutched close to her as she read him tales of heroic knights who slew evil dragons.

She missed her little boy and hoped that this strange ritual of the Carrard family would not take too long.

Helene still didn't understand the full significance of the ritual Leofric was here to perform, something to do with planting a seedling before the waystone and making an offering to the faerie folk.

Apparently, the practice had begun eighty years ago when family legend told that a much loved ancestor of Leofric's had been taken by the elves as a young boy and had never been seen again. Carrards had been coming to the edge of Athel Loren every five years since then to enact its quaint traditions.

She knew that Leofric begrudged such entreaties to the elven realm, though understood that he would never think of leaving the ritual unperformed, as such a stain upon the family honour would be unthinkable to a knight of Bretonnia.

As she watched her husband pray, she smiled, feeling the love she had for him as a contented warmth in her heart. She remembered the sun-drenched tilting fields outside Couronne where she had first met Leofric, picturing the dashing young knight errant with his scarlet unicorn pennant streaming from his lance as he unhorsed Chilfroy of Artois, a feat none of the gathered knights and dukes ever expected to see in their lifetimes.

Leofric had had the pick of the ladies that day, all wishing him to carry their favour upon his lance, but he had knelt before her, Helene du Reyne, sweat-streaked hair plastered across his forehead and a mischievous grin creasing his face.

'It would honour me greatly if you would consent to grant me your favour,' he'd said.

'Why should I do such a thing?' she had replied, straining for a regal aloofness.

'Lady, I have unhorsed my opponent in the glory of the joust!' he said. 'None other than the Duke of Artois himself. I am the greatest warrior here!'

'You are arrogant, young man, and have not the humility of a knight.'

'It is not arrogance if it is the truth,' he had pointed out.

'How do I know that for sure?'

'Tell me how I may prove it to you, my lady, for I love you and would ride to every corner of Bretonnia if you would but grant me a kiss.'

'Only the corners of Bretonnia? Is that all?'

'Not at all, I would ride to far Araby and drag back the greatest sultan were you to look favourably my way.'

'Just to Araby?' she had teased.

'Only to begin with,' he had continued with a smile. 'Then I would sail to the far jungles of Lustria and bring back the treasures of the heathen gods if you might consent to speak my name.'

'Impressive.'

'I'm only just getting started,' he said. 'I've the rest of the world to travel yet!'

Deciding she had teased him enough, Helene had laughed and handed him a silken blue scarf, edged in white lace, and said, 'Here, you may carry my favour, sir knight. Win me this tourney and I might let you attempt to make me happy...'

'I shall, my lady! I will unhorse every man here if it will make you happy!'

And he had. Leofric had defeated every knight at the tournament before courting her as diligently and as wonderfully as any young woman could want. They were wed in the grail chapel in Quenelles a year later, and ten months after that, Helene had borne Leofric a strong son, whom they had named Beren, after one of the heroic Companions of Gilles.

Beren was so like his father, proud and with the haughty arrogance of noble youth. Though since Leofric had come back from the Errantry Wars in the north, a knight errant no more, but a knight of the realm, he had lost much of his former boisterousness.

Such was only to be expected, for a knight of the realm was tempered in battle, the fiery impetuosity of a knight errant moulded into a dutiful warrior.

But there was more to it than that. Helene knew her husband well enough to know that something more terrible than a bloody charge had happened in the war that had engulfed the Empire.

What had turned her fiery husband into a melancholy warrior who saw the cloud rather than the silver lining, the rain, not the nourished crops?

She finished the last of the beef and cheese and set down the plate on the rock beside her, feeling a shiver ripple its way along her spine.

'Colder than a Mousillon night,' she whispered to herself, as the sound of a soft, mournful weeping drifted on the air from above.

Helene twisted around, wondering if she had perhaps imagined the sound when it came again... a barely audible sobbing that tugged at her maternal heart. Unbidden tears welled in the corners of her eyes as she listened to the unseen mourner, the sound reaching deep inside her, and touching something primal in her very soul as she realised that the sobs were those of a child.

She rose from the rock and turned her gaze towards the forest.

The sound of the weeping child came again, beguiling and wistful, and, without conscious thought, Helene began walking towards the edge of the hollow. She glanced over her shoulder, seeing the yellow-surcoated men-at-arms gathered at the base of the hollow while Leofric continued his prayers.

She considered bringing the unearthly sound to the attention of her husband and his soldiers, but even before the thought was fully formed it was plucked from her head and vanished like morning mist, replaced with an insistent, urgent need to find the crying child.

Helene climbed from the hollow, the full majesty of the forest stretching out before her. The thick trunks of the mighty trees seemed to lean towards her, their branches sad with leaves of autumn gold. Leaves lay thick and still about the trees' roots and blew in a soft wind that whistled between the branches like an ancient lament.

Coils of greenish mist crept from the treeline, but Helene ignored them, her attention fixed on the sight of a young girl kneeling at the edge of the woods, clad only in an ankle-length nightgown of pale cream. The girl's back was to her, and Helene's heart went out to the child, whose long black hair fell about her shoulders and reached almost to the ground.

'Oh, my dear...' wept Helene as she saw the distraught condition of the child, feet stained green with grass, and twigs and branches caught in her hair.

Was this what had happened to Leofric's ancestor? Had he been snatched as a child and left to die on this bleak moorland before the great forest of Athel Loren? Was this one of those poor unfortunate children taken by the elves, never to be seen again?

Helene took a step forward, hearing the jingle of trace and whinny of horses from behind her, and the thought of fetching help once again came to her.

The little girl let out a grief-stricken sob and all desires, except that of aiding this poor, wretched child, were banished from her thoughts.

'Hello? Child, can you hear me?' asked Helene, taking yet more steps forward, feeling a growing fear settle in her belly with each mist-wreathed footfall. Dim lights flickered at the periphery of her vision and she had the fleeting impression of haunting melodies of aching loss from far away.

The child did not reply and though Helene tried to stop herself, she felt her arm reaching towards the young girl and said, 'Please…'

Her hand closed on the girl's shoulder and Helene sobbed in terror, feeling the softness of her flesh as a mulchy wetness.

The child's dark-haired head slowly turned to face her, and Helene whimpered in terror as she saw that this was no innocent child, but a thing of horror.

In an instant, the blackness of the girl's hair thinned, becoming a whipping tangle of thorned barbs, her face a haggard crone's, full of heartless spite and wicked malice. The nightgown sloughed from the thing's body, its greenish skin transforming into lashing wood, its fingers stretching into razored talons.

The creature of the forest leapt upon Helene with snapping fangs and slashing claws that ripped and bit and tore.

Helene screamed and screamed as pain and blood filled her senses.

CHAPTER TWO

The scream tore through the morning air, its tone reaching deep inside every man gathered in the hollow. Leofric surged to his feet, spinning his sword in his grip so as to hold it before him. Instantly, he saw that Helene was not in sight and that a soft greenish mist gathered at the lip of the hollow.

'Helene!' he yelled, running for his horse.

The men-at-arms stood transfixed in fear by the green glow at the top of the hollow, coils of mist slithering down towards them. Another wailing scream, anguished and terrible, echoed from beyond the hollow and the spell was broken, soldiers running for horses and gathering their weapons.

Leofric lifted his foot into the stirrup and hauled himself into his saddle, raking his spurs viciously back and driving his mount onwards. A terrible fear gripped him, hot and urgent in his belly, as he once again shouted Helene's name. Behind him, his squire struggled to catch up, the gold and red of Leofric's banner waving crazily in the air.

The greenish mist sparkled with light and Leofric muttered a prayer of protection to the Lady as he rode Taschen into its glittering depths. Hidden, spiteful laughter whipped around him, together with something that sounded like the musical tinkling of an icy wind-chime.

'Come on, damn you!' he yelled, looking over his shoulder to ensure that his men-at-arms were following. 'Your lady is in peril! Make haste!'

His sword shone with a spectral light, its blade cutting through the mist with ease as Leofric felt the ground level out beneath his horse. Ahead, he could faintly see the dark outline of the forest's edge, the gnarled trunks of the oaks seeming to close ranks as he charged towards the source of the screams.

'Helene!' he shouted, circling his horse and riding up and down the length of the treeline. 'Helene! Can you hear me?'

Leofric heard the muffled thump of hoof beats and turned as he saw Baudel and the men-at-arms riding towards him.

'Spread out!' yelled Leofric. 'Ride along the forest's edge and do not stop until you find her!'

Baudel nodded, but before any of the soldiers could begin the search, another scream sounded, this time beyond the trees, echoing from inside the forest. Leofric turned his horse once more and felt his flesh chill as he saw a splash of fresh blood on a tree trunk.

'Oh no...' he whispered. 'The forest has her.'

'Wait, my lord!' shouted Baudel as Leofric rode his horse towards the dark, mist-wreathed trees. 'We can't go in there.'

'We have to,' cried Leofric. 'In the name of the Lady, I order you to follow me!'

The soldiers milled in fearful uncertainty, their duty to their master warring with their lifelong dread of the faerie folk's realm. Sparkling laughter, rich with the promise of dark amusement, rippled through the mist, and the horses stamped their hooves in fear, eyes wide and ears pressed flat against their skulls.

Leofric snarled in anger and jabbed his spurs into his mount's flanks, riding into Athel Loren.

Behind him he could hear Baudel shouting, 'Come on, men! Lady Carrard needs us and you're just going to let her die? Call yourselves men of Bretonnia, you're no better than bloody dogs! Move!'

Belittled into action, the majority of the men-at-arms followed Baudel as he rode after Leofric, but some did not, dragging the reins of their beasts and riding away, tears of shame and fear burning their eyes.

Leofric charged heedlessly through the forest, seeing a flash of a scarlet gown ahead, his horse plunging deeper into the forest as he cried out Helene's name once more.

'Baudel!' he shouted, pointing with his sword. 'Left! Go left!'

There was no reply and Leofric angrily twisted in his saddle, ready to berate his soldiers, but his mouth snapped shut as he saw that he was alone. Dimly, he could see the shadowy forms of horsemen riding beyond the dark lines of the trees, ghostly and indistinct. Laughter and a hissing rustle of leaves in a strong wind sounded and Leofric spun his horse searching for the source of the noise.

Again he saw the flash of scarlet and urged his mount towards it. He rode through the trees, emerging into a glade with a fallen tree at its centre, resting atop a cloven rock. The ground was churned with hoof prints and a broken spear lay in the mud.

'Helene!' shouted Leofric, once more catching sight of her red gown and pushing his mount onwards. He leapt his horse over a growth of thorns, landing on a worn path, and charged around a spur of dark evergreens before emerging into another glade, similar to the previous one.

No… not similar, he realised, seeing the same fallen tree and cloven rock, identical. How could he have circled back on himself? More hoof beats sounded and he heard a scream, a man's, then a gurgling cry of pain.

The noise of rustling leaves grew louder and louder, as though a storm whipped through the forest, but Leofric could see nothing.

'Helene! Where are you?'

His fury and fear growing by the second, Leofric rode from the glade once more, leaving by a different path, as he heard the sounds of battle from ahead. Briars snatched at him as he rode past, tearing his caparison, branches seeming to close in and block his passage, but he slashed and hacked with his sword and the way was opened.

He rode into another clearing, thankfully a different one from before, in time to see two of his men-at-arms snatched from their saddles by unseen assailants, dragged into the deep undergrowth behind them.

Leofric charged forwards, shouting, 'Come out and show yourselves, damn it! Fight with honour!'

The undergrowth shook with terrible violence and one of his men-at-arms crawled from the greenery, his face a mask of blood and terror. Something green and icy-white rose up behind the soldier and Leofric cried out as he saw the gnarled, hag's face atop a writhing branch-like form of moss, weeds and wood. Slashing fingers struck at the man, who screamed in agony as he was torn to shreds.

Leofric charged forwards, swinging his sword in a downward arc towards the hag's face. His sword struck the centre of her skull, but fast as quicksilver, the crone of wood came apart, her outline blurring as the branches and leaves reknit themselves once more.

Leofric turned to strike another blow, but something landed with a malicious cackle on the back of his horse, slashing at his armour with grasping talons. The rank stench of winter moss assailed him, the rich wetness of the cold earth. Lank hair, like that of a corpse, spattered his armour.

He gagged and hammered his elbow back, hearing the crack of splitting wood as another creature of branches and pallid green flesh erupted from the undergrowth.

His horse reared and struck out as it had been trained to do, its iron-shod hooves smashing into the creature before it with the crack of splintering wood. The creature burst apart in a flurry of leaves and mud, and the sickly smell of wood sap filled Leofric's senses.

'Get off me!' he yelled, hammering his elbow back once more and crying out as he felt razor-sharp talons slide between the gaps in his armour and pierce the mail below. Blood streamed down his leg as he reversed the grip on his sword and hammered the point backwards through the gap between his arm and body, feeling it slide into wet, mulchy flesh.

His assailant screeched in rage, tumbling from the back of his horse as he saw Baudel ride into the clearing, with his men-at-arms behind him. He could see the fear on their faces, but could not spare them any words as he wheeled his horse to face his fallen attacker.

The thing of branches sprang through the air, its haggard face full of spite, and Leofric swung his sword in a great upwards sweep that hacked it in two as it leapt. It exploded in a green mist of sap, wood and leaves, a dazzling ball of light whipping from its remains and flashing into the trees.

Leofric raised the visor of his helmet and shouted, 'Baudel! Any sign of my wife?'

'No!' called back Baudel. 'We have to get out of here. I don't know how many men we've lost already!'

'No! I won't leave without her,' roared Leofric. 'Come on, she can't be far.'

Without waiting to see if his men followed, Leofric rode off once more, desperation surging in his veins. He charged wildly into the forest's depths, the cackling laughter of the woodland hags following him at every turn. Darting lights spun and looped through the high branches of the trees and sparkling mists wove in and out of his path.

Leofric wanted to weep in frustration as the forest closed in around him. Where was she? He could no longer tell which way was which…

Again he saw a flash of red and pushed his lathered mount onwards once more. He thundered down the overgrown path, emerging into a clearing with a familiar fallen tree and boulder.

'Lady, no!' he wept. 'Please, please, no!'

He slumped over the neck of his horse, his hope that he might find Helene growing fainter by the minute. What chance did he have when the very forest conspired against him?

Angrily he pushed such despairing thoughts from his mind. Was he not a knight of Bretonnia, sworn to uphold the traditions of chivalry? A knight never gave up, never despaired and never abandoned a damsel in distress.

He straightened in the saddle as Baudel and six other riders finally caught up with him. All of them bore the scars of battle and their yellow surcoats were stained with blood and dirt. Fear was writ large on every face and their desire to flee the forest was plain. His banner still flew, but the lad who bore it wept in terror.

'Spread out into a line!' ordered Leofric. 'We'll quarter this area of the forest.'

'My lord, it's no use,' said Baudel. 'It's impossible, the trees confound us at every turn!'

'I know,' snapped Leofric, 'but what choice do we have?'

'We can live,' said Baudel, pointing to a patch of clear sunlight beyond the trees that plainly led back to the heath before the forest.

'No, we stay,' stated Leofric. 'I won't leave her.'

Baudel nodded and said, 'Then we stay too.'

Even as the words left his throat, the light of the sky was snatched away as the branches of the trees closed in. Leofric readied his sword as the cackling of the woodland creatures grew from all around them, the crack of branches weaving themselves into new and terrible forms and the frenzied rustling of leaves growing louder with every passing second.

'Ride!' shouted Leofric as the creatures attacked once more.

Monsters of branch and root rose up from the ground, weaving from the trunks of the trees with an unearthly green light. With thick, ridged skin of hardened bark and malicious black eyes, they tore at the Bretonnians with implacable fury. Leofric chopped his sword through the branch-like limb of one of the creatures, the timber cracking from its body in a spray of sweet sap.

It screamed in rage, its other arm slamming into his breastplate with a solid thump and Leofric grunted in pain, feeling as if he'd been hit by a thunderous lance impact. He reeled back in the saddle, dragging on the reins to prevent himself from being unhorsed and brought his sword back in a deadly reverse stroke that took the forest creature's head off.

He rounded on the other creatures in time to see his standard fall, the young lad lifted from his saddle with a scream of terror. Long, stabbing talons plunged into his chest, dragging his body high into the trees with a deathly wail.

Leofric rode forwards and caught the falling banner, wedging its base into the stirrup cup normally used to hold the butt of his lance.

'Carrard!' he yelled as the ground beneath him writhed with life. His horse sidestepped nimbly as roots and creepers surged upwards, grasping and clawing with thorny appendages.

Another man was dragged down, his body obscured by dancing lights that spun around him with capering laughter. Shifting forms spun through the lights: imps, daemons and tiny, ghostly knights. Baudel rode through the mass of branch creatures, stabbing with his spear and screaming obscenities at his foes.

Leofric urged his horse onwards, riding towards Baudel's aid as a whipping branch leapt at him, striking the visor of his helmet with a ringing hammer blow.

Starbursts exploded around him and he felt the banner slip from his fingers as he fought to stay conscious. His head rang with the impact and he could taste blood, but he gritted his teeth and held on. He couldn't see properly, his visor had been buckled inwards by the blow, so he snapped it upwards.

Something dropped from above him with a high, skirling laugh and he felt moist, clawed hands tearing at him. Straddling his horse's neck before him was a creature of pallid green flesh, its features running like wax, changing from a maiden of unearthly beauty to a hideous, wrinkled hag and back again in a heartbeat. She was laughing, but there was nothing but hate and bitterness in the icy sound.

Leofric slammed his helmet into the hag's face, and her laughter turned to a squeal of rage as she toppled from his horse, but by then it was already too late. Baudel fell from his horse, his belly torn open and emptying its contents across the forest floor, his eyes glazed and dead.

'No!' shouted Leofric, as slashing branches pummelled him and he felt himself pitched from his saddle, landing in an ungainly heap across the fallen tree. He cried out as he felt at least one rib crack and rolled onto the wet ground, fighting through the pain.

'Forgive me, Helene,' he hissed. 'I failed you...'

A flash of colour caught his eye and he reached out with a blood-stained gauntlet to grasp a silken scarf of blue, edged in white lace that lay on the forest floor.

'Helene...'

Leofric snarled in anger, snatching up Helene's scarf and tucking it inside his gauntlet, before pushing himself to his feet as a dozen or more of the fell forest creatures emerged from the wood, capering, malicious crones and blank-faced tree wraiths surrounded by clouds of swirling lights. His horse whinnied in fear and cantered over to him, its nostrils wide and flaring in fear.

He pushed himself painfully to his feet, hot agony flaring in his side where his ribs were cracked. Blood streamed down his leg and he felt nauseous and dizzy from his head wound.

'I am Leofric Carrard! A knight of the realm and warrior of Bretonnia!' he shouted defiantly, 'and if you damned forest creatures want me dead then you're about to find out how a knight of Bretonnia meets his end!'

He raised his sword in salute until the quillons were level with his chin and kissed the blade.

'For Quenelles, the king and the Lady!' he roared.

But before he took a single step, the forest creatures hissed and pulled back from a growing light that slipped effortlessly through the forest. Its course was towards this thrice-cursed glade and Leofric felt a surge of hope flare as he saw the faint outline of a glowing woman in the depths of the light.

Was this the Lady of the Lake come to save him?

The spiteful forest beasts retreated from the light, but as the stranger drew closer Leofric saw that this woman was not the Lady, but must surely be elfkind. She moved effortlessly through the woodland, the branches and roots of the forest parting before her and easing her passage towards him.

She wore a long robe of spun gold and elven runes, weaving streamers of pale blue and green billowing around her as though in the grip of an invisible wind. Her hair was the colour of molten copper, teased into braided tresses above her tapered ears with silver pins and woven with feathers and gemstones. She turned her large, almond-shaped eyes on Leofric and he could feel a great and terrible power in the elf witch.

She carried a long staff of woven twigs with a carven eye at its top and the creatures of the forest backed away from her. Despite the obvious power of the elf sorcerer, the forest wraiths were not cowed, their spite and anger plain at being denied their kill for now.

Behind the elf, Leofric could see the outlines of a great many figures, but each time he tried to focus on one, it blended back into the forest, leaving him unsure of what he was seeing. Was that the curve of a bow, the glint of sunlight on an arrowhead?

So that was it… they were going to kill him themselves.

Trust an elf to want to finish the job.

Though it railed against his code of chivalric conduct to attack a woman, he knew that this was no ordinary woman, this was an immortal elf with the terrible power of magic at her command. He pulled out Helene's scarf, the very same favour she had given him on the tilting fields of Couronne, and wrapped it around the hilt of his sword.

Leofric screamed in loss and rage and charged the elf woman, pain and anguish lending his limbs fresh strength. The elf didn't move, the creatures of the forest surging forwards as he charged.

Tears blurred his vision as his sword slashed towards the elf's head.

Dazzling sparks of cold fire leapt from a resounding impact and Leofric shook his head clear of the blinding light to see that his blow had been intercepted by another blade – a blade the colour of moonlight, its length curved in a long, leaf shape and etched with intricate, spiralling patterns.

His gaze travelled the length of the exquisitely crafted weapon, past the intertwined leaves of its silver quillons towards the gauntleted hand that held it.

Leofric felt a prickling sensation of magic and wrenched his eyes from the blade to the warrior who bore it, seeing a magnificent figure riding a steed with a mane the colour of fire, clad head to foot in a suit of heavy plate armour, fluted and chased in the manner of a Bretonnian knight. In his other hand, the knight carried a banner of rippling cream silk, emblazoned with a heraldic device Leofric did not recognise, a scaled dragon of pale jade set atop the image of a flowering oak.

The knight's armour was old, ancient even, and heavily damaged. A series of parallel grooves carved a path diagonally down the knight's breastplate and his vambrace and cuirass were browned as though burned by some corrosive substance. Pieces of the knight's armour were also mismatched, the helmet was a design Leofric had never seen before, and the pauldrons had clearly been repaired many times.

But for all that, there was a terrifyingly potent aura of power surrounding the knight, a faint, yet unmistakable haze of something unseen. The green eyes behind the helmet's visor blazed with some internal wychfire, and though they spoke eloquently of great power, Leofric sensed no evil in them, only an aching sadness and purity.

And what manner of knight rode a steed such as this one? The knight sat atop a destrier with a remarkable coat of purest white, but whose mane was a fiery bronze, like captured flames rippling from the wonderful beast's neck. Its limbs were elegant and muscular, sculpted as though from marble.

Leofric knew the qualities of a fine steed as well as the next knight, and while the Bretonnian warhorse was a creature of rare power and endurance, this was an elven steed, a beast of savage beauty, strength and grace.

Was this knight…? Could he be…?

A Grail Knight, one of the virtuous few who had long quested for the grail, driven ever onwards by visions of the Lady of the Lake to seek for her chalice in far-off lands, to vanquish evil, to aid the needy and forever prove his virtuous heart in the heat of battle. If this knight was such a warrior, then he had supped from the grail, blessed beyond all men and honoured with a life of service to the Lady.

A Grail Knight… A saint amongst men, a warrior beyond compare who had slain great monsters, fought in wars beyond number, vanquished the most dreaded of foes and who had been granted powers beyond the ken of mere mortals.

Leofric opened his mouth to speak, but the mounted knight shook his head.

He stumbled as a wave of dizziness threatened to overcome him and the creatures of the forest closed, scenting their prey's weakness.

Without seeming to give his mount a signal, the strangely clad knight interposed himself between Leofric and the hissing hag-creatures, and their lashing, branch-woven forms retreated before him.

Leofric supported himself on the fallen tree, watching the power and authority that the warrior commanded. It seemed to him that a shimmering golden aura surrounded the knight, but Leofric could not be sure, his vision blurring as blood loss and pain conspired to rob him of his strength.

'We are not your enemies, sir knight,' said a melodic voice at his ear and he cried out in surprise. The elf witch was at his side, a cadre of fey-featured elves behind her with long recurved bows carried lightly at their sides. Though the forest floor was thick with dry leaves, they had made no sound as they approached.

Clad in a mixture of russets and greens, their clothing was perfectly chosen to blend with the colours of the forest, and they carried scabbarded swords belted at their sides. The elves regarded him with expressions of faint disdain.

Each had feathers and braids woven into their long hair, held in place by leather circlets, and the pale skin of their heart-shaped faces was almost translucent, painted with curling tattoos.

Leofric tried to raise his sword, but its normally lightweight blade felt as though it weighed as much as a greatsword.

'No…' he whispered, dropping to his knees. 'Helene!'

The elf witch glanced over at the hulking form of the Grail Knight who said, 'We are too late again?' His voice was rich and deep, yet filled with pain.

'We are,' nodded the elf. 'But we may yet–'

'Spare me your platitudes,' said the knight, turning his horse and riding away. 'I have heard them all before.'

'When will we see you again?' the elf sorceress called after the knight's retreating form.

'You already know the answer to that, Naieth,' replied the knight, disappearing into the forest without another word.

Leofric watched the exchange with dazed incomprehension, feeling his limbs fill with a strange lethargy as the elf sorceress returned her careworn gaze upon him once more. The elven archers surrounded her, their bows drawn and grey-fletched arrows nocked to the strings.

Her voice was musical and lilting, with a haunting edge to it as she spoke to him, the words running like honey through his head.

'Leofric, I bid you welcome to the woodland realm of Athel Loren,' she said. 'My name is Naieth and I have been waiting for you for a very long time.'

CHAPTER THREE

Crystal foam sprayed the air, cascading over glistening rocks from high above, the roaring of the tumbling waterfall drowning out the cries of distant eagles and the calls of wolves as they padded through the evening. The waterfall cut a deep groove through the rocks above and fell in lazy arcs to the foaming pool in the centre of the clearing below, where two figures lay naked in each other's arms and two elven steeds roamed its edges.

Morvhen Éadaoin held her lover, Kyarno Daelanu, tightly, relishing the hard, alabaster smoothness of his skin against her own. Both elves were long limbed and graceful, with a languid suppleness to their movements as they made love by the water's edge. A mist of fine water sheened their bodies as they moved against one another until at last Kyarno gave out a long sigh and rolled from her, a contented smile creasing his boyish features.

He lay back, curling an arm behind his head as she lay close to him, enjoying the light of evening as it spilled like molten gold over the treetops. Darting lights flitted between the trees and bobbed like fireflies across the surface of the churning water, dancing in the air with gleeful abandon.

Morvhen draped an arm around Kyarno's chest and whispered, 'That was wonderful...'

'Yes,' agreed Kyarno. 'I'm no expert, but it looked like you were enjoying it.'

'Oh, I think you're an expert, my love,' smiled Morvhen, sliding on top of Kyarno to straddle him and leaning down to kiss him.

They made love once more, finally lying side-by-side as the sun dipped below the treetops and soft moonlight spilled into the glade. Distant songs could be heard from the trees, carried on warm winds from the north.

Morvhen ran her hand across Kyarno's smooth, hairless chest and teased the wet locks of his braided, chestnut hair around her fingers, leaning up to kiss his chin. His features were hard and angular, as though carved from stone, though there was a softness to his dark eyes that most folk missed, simply seeing the arrogant, troublesome youth many considered him to be. Spiralling tattoos looped across his chest and neck, winding in coiled snake patterns on the hard muscles of his shoulders.

Even in repose, she could feel the buried tension in Kyarno, a tension that nothing she could do could quite dissipate. As a lover, Kyarno was tender and giving, though she knew that there was a part of him that she still had not reached.

'So much for having me back to Coeth-Mara before nightfall...' said Morvhen.

Kyarno smiled and ran a hand through Morvhen's lustrous, dark hair, kissing the top of her head.

'Not my fault,' he protested.

'No? How so?' laughed Morvhen. 'I seem to recall it was you who wanted to stop at the Crystal Mere for "a rest".'

'True, but then I wasn't the one who suggested we go for a swim, was I?'

'Tell that to my father,' said Morvhen, instantly regretting the words as she felt him tense up beneath her fingers.

'Would he listen?' snapped Kyarno. 'Or would he send the Hound of Winter to cast me from Coeth-Mara once again?'

'I'm sorry,' said Morvhen, rising up on her elbow to look into the eyes of her lover. 'Forget I mentioned him.'

'How can I?' said Kyarno. 'His disapproval hangs over everything we have like a shadow, Morvhen. You know as well as I that he will never accept me.'

'No,' agreed Morvhen sadly. 'But things can change.'

'How?'

'I don't know, but there must always be hope. Don't judge my father too harshly, he has a duty to his kinband, and–'

'And I'm not part of that, I know,' said Kyarno bitterly. 'I am nothing but a troublemaker and that's that.'

Morvhen sighed and reached up to run her hand across Kyarno's brow, feeling the anger and bitterness he carried as a poison that ran through him as surely as the blood in his veins. She kissed the clenched line of his jaw and ran her hand through his hair, slowly easing his anger with gentle caresses and feathered kisses.

The moon rose higher in the night sky and Morvhen could feel Kyarno's anger recede, giving way to the love she knew he felt for her. Sadness touched her as she realised that he was right, her father would never accept Kyarno the way he was now – there was a reckless wildness to him that sat ill with the lord of the elven halls of Coeth-Mara. Lord Aldaeld of the Éadaoin kinband had a sacred duty to protect his people and the forest of Athel Loren, and Kyarno was not a part of that, as much as she could see he desperately wanted to be.

Darting spites flitted overhead, like laughing shooting stars against the darkness of the night sky, and the two lay in silence for a while before Kyarno broke the uncomfortable silence.

'I'm sorry,' he said at last. 'I didn't mean to get angry at you.'

'Hush…' whispered Morvhen. 'Let's not allow it to spoil this night, it's too beautiful for harsh words.'

'No, *you* are too beautiful for harsh words,' said Kyarno, cupping Morvhen's face and looking into her sapphire eyes and taking in the graceful curve of her jaw. 'I know what others think of me, and they are right to, but when I am with you… I feel a stillness, I am at peace. I want that feeling to stay.'

'I know, I know,' whispered Morvhen, holding him tightly, knowing that his wishes were as dreams, fleeting and insubstantial, though she had not the heart to tell him.

'Did you see what Naieth and the Waywatchers brought in earlier?' she asked, quickly changing the subject. 'A human.'

'Yes,' nodded Kyarno. 'Though why she brought him to Coeth-Mara is beyond me. She brings more woe upon the asrai than even I do.'

Morvhen said nothing, knowing the source of Kyarno's rancour towards Naieth.

'Why did they not just kill him and be done with it?' continued Kyarno. 'The human entered our forest and the Waywatchers should have slain him.'

'Kill him? Oh, come now… it's just one human, what possible harm could he do?'

'You don't understand,' said Kyarno. 'Where one comes, others will follow, it's their way.'

'Maybe, but this was one of the horse-warriors from the lands to the west and they don't often come this way. Just think of what far-off lands he might have travelled to, what strange things he could have seen!'

'Why do you care?' asked Kyarno. 'What is there beyond Athel Loren but enemies? No, far better that we have nothing to do with the humans.'

Morvhen sat up, stretching like a cat and running her hands through her hair, tying it back into a long ponytail with a leather cord.

'So you're not the least bit curious why she brought him back?'

Kyarno shook his head. 'No. And neither should you be. Your father won't allow you to associate with a human.'

Morvhen laughed and gave him a pointed stare, 'Just like he didn't allow me to associate with you, and we all know how much attention I paid to that.'

'That's different,' said Kyarno. 'Aldaeld doesn't like me, but he hates humans.'

Morvhen shrugged, tucking her leg beneath her body and smoothly rising to her feet. She began gathering up her long ochre dress and doe-skin boots, her body drying in the warm breeze as Kyarno collected his clothes and bow.

'Well, I for one will speak to the human, learn of his lands and his life,' said Morvhen, slipping on her dress and pulling on her boots. 'I want to hear of his adventures in far-off realms against monsters and the armies of the Dark Gods! I want to know of lands with high mountains, deep blue seas and endless deserts. Can you imagine a desert? A land-scape without trees or greenery that stretches out beyond the horizon and never ends.'

'Sounds horrible,' said Kyarno. 'Why would you ever want to go to such a place?'

'Oh, I don't want to go to a desert, but I wish to know everything about it.'

'Be careful what you wish for, Morvhen,' cautioned Kyarno, pulling on his clothes and beckoning his horse to him. He sheathed his bow in an oiled, leather case and buckled on his sword belt as his steed nuzzled him. 'You may not like what you hear.'

Morvhen laughed at Kyarno's seriousness and leapt lightly to the back of her horse, its rump painted with spiralling patterns and its tail woven with garlands of leaves.

She twisted her fingers into its silvered mane and said, 'We should get back to Coeth-Mara. The Hound of Winter will be going out of his mind looking for me before my father finds out I'm not there.'

Kyarno nodded, a gloomy expression settling on his features once more at the mention of his uncle and the prospect of return to Coeth-Mara. He vaulted onto the back of his horse, riding alongside Morvhen and leaned close to kiss her. She could feel the heat of his skin as his hand slipped around her neck, drawing her close until their lips met.

They kissed long and tenderly until Kyarno reluctantly pulled back, still with his hand resting at the nape of her neck. He rested his forehead on hers and said, 'When will I see you again?'

Morvhen started to speak, when a strident voice from the edge of the clearing shouted, 'You won't! I'll have your hide first!'

Kyarno groaned and turned to see Cairbre, the Hound of Winter and champion of Lord Aldaeld Éadaoin, ride into the glade. The warrior of the Eternal Guard wore armour of banded gold, with a grey cloak of feathers and leaves worn draped over one shoulder. His bronze helmet was conical and ridged, its sheen bright and polished.

Carried lightly in one hand was a thin-hafted spear, both ends bearing long, leaf-shaped blades of pearlescent white that were rich with etched spirals and grooves.

'Cairbre, Kyarno was just about to escort me back to Coeth-Mara,' said Morvhen, as the Hound of Winter walked his horse towards her, his face a mask of controlled anger beneath his bronze helmet.

'He shouldn't be here with you, my lady, you know that,' said Cairbre, without looking at Kyarno. 'How can I protect you if you insist on behaving like this? Your father was clear about your liaisons with my nephew. Why is he with you?'

'I am right here, uncle, you can ask me yourself,' growled Kyarno.

Cairbre's spear was a pale blur and Kyarno was pitched from the saddle as the flat of one of the blades smashed into the side of his head. He sailed through the air, twisting to land lightly on his feet with an arrow nocked to his bow and a murderous anger in his eyes.

'Kyarno, no!' shouted Morvhen, but Cairbre shook his head.

'Damn you, uncle, I'll put an arrow through your throat!' shouted Kyarno.

'Don't be foolish, boy, even you are not that stupid,' said Cairbre.

Kyarno and Cairbre locked eyes and Morvhen could easily see the familial bond in both their features. But where the Hound of Winter was tempered by battle and age, Kyarno's face still carried all the fires and foibles of youth.

'Stop this foolishness!' she cried, her voice laden with all the noble authority of her lineage. 'There will be no blood spilt this day. Cairbre, take me back to Coeth-Mara, I wish to return to the halls of my father.'

'As you wish, my lady,' nodded Cairbre, turning away from his nephew.

As Cairbre led her horse towards the edge of the glade, Kyarno lowered his bow. Morvhen saw the fire dim in his eyes, his anger replaced by sadness. She wanted to go to him, to say something hopeful, but knew that Cairbre would never allow it. The Hound of Winter may have tutored her since she was a child, but he was still her father's champion, first and foremost.

As they reached the edge of the clearing, Cairbre turned his horse and shouted back to Kyarno. 'You too should head back to Coeth-Mara, boy. Lord Aldaeld desires to speak with you.'

'He does?' replied Kyarno, warily. 'Why?'

'Don't be stupid, boy,' said Cairbre, seeing the defiance in Kyarno's eyes, 'you know better than to disobey such a command. Make your way to your lord's hall. Now.'

'And if I don't?'

'Then I'll drag you there myself,' stated Cairbre.

Kyarno swung onto the back of his horse and said, 'One day you will push me too far, old one.'

The Hound of Winter did not answer, but Morvhen saw the disappointment in his eyes as Kyarno yelled and pulled on his steed's mane, riding hard and plunging into the darkness of the forest.

The warm dusk of the forest closed in around Morvhen and Cairbre, fluttering spites in the shape of glittering butterflies lighting their way as they flew alongside the horses. A gentle breeze blew from the west, carrying smoky, aromatic scents and the sounds of life, and Morvhen felt the invigorating heartbeat of the forest in her blood as she rode once more beneath its russet canopy.

As they rode from the glade towards the settlement of Coeth-Mara, Morvhen rounded on Cairbre, her anger rising as she saw his grim exterior assert itself once more.

'Must you always be so harsh on him?' she said. 'He has gone through so much.'

'I know,' said Cairbre. 'I was there when the beasts killed his family, remember? But the boy brings trouble on his own head, my lady.'

'Do you hate Kyarno?' asked Morvhen.

'Hate him?' exclaimed Cairbre, turning to face her. 'No, of course I do not hate him. He is my kinsman and I love him, but there is a madness to him that I do not understand.'

'Have you ever *really* tried?'

'Believe me, I have, but every time we speak we argue, as though he sees my every word as an insult. As much as I wish to, I cannot reach the boy and I am too old to change my ways now.'

Seeing a rare moment of vulnerability in the warrior, Morvhen reached out and placed her hand on the metal of Cairbre's bronze vambrace and said, 'His heart is true, Hound of Winter, trust to that.'

'I know,' said Cairbre sadly, 'I see courage and the seeds of greatness within him and know that he could become a fine warrior. But he takes after his father in too many ways, and I fear that will be the undoing of him and anyone close to him.'

'Come now, Cairbre. Surely you're exaggerating?'

'You think so? What about his theft of the Laithu kinband's steeds from their stable glades? That foolishness may cost your father dear and I do not wish to see you caught up in his reckless folly.'

'He released the Laithu steeds almost as soon as he stole them,' pointed out Morvhen. 'He only took them to prove that he could.'

'That is not the point,' replied Cairbre. 'Valas Laithu is not quick to forgive an insult done to his kinband. He will demand recompense.'

Morvhen nodded, remembering the last time she had met Valas Laithu and his odious sons: a gathering of kinbands at the King's Glade sixty years ago. She had not liked him then, and had no reason to suppose he had changed any in the intervening years.

'Valas is a snake,' said Morvhen.

'Aye, he is,' agreed Cairbre, 'but a powerful one, and that is another reason why you must not remove yourself from my protection. The forest is a dangerous place at this time of year, and if something were to happen to you, Lord Aldaeld would have my life. And that of Kyarno. You know this, yet still you defy his wishes.'

'I am not a child any more, Cairbre,' said Morvhen. 'You taught me to shoot and to fight. I can take care of myself.'

Cairbre chuckled. 'Of that I have no doubt, but I have sworn to protect the Éadaoin kinband as well as Athel Loren, and the Hound of Winter does not forswear such an oath.'

Morvhen nodded, grateful to have such a faithful protector as Cairbre, and they rode on in silence through the secret paths known only to the Eternal Guard, before eventually reaching the glittering lights and warmth that were the elven halls of Coeth-Mara. Its beauty never failed to captivate Morvhen and she rode into the settlement with a light in her heart.

'Home...' she said.

Golden light like honey.

Silken voices like a symphony of maidens.

The sensation of floating, as though in a dream.

Leofric felt at peace, his limbs relaxed and lightweight, his body cured of all its hurts. He smiled dreamily to himself, the singsong voices spinning in his head like dancers, coyly flitting from understanding as he tried to concentrate on what was being said.

Flickering lights fluttered before his eyes, though he could feel they were still shut. Tiny, shrill laughter seemed to come from the lights, and slowly he opened his gummed eyes, squinting against the brightness.

A trio of hazy green lights hovered in the air above him, insubstantial wings flickering behind them and giggling faces swimming in each one's depths. The distant voices grew louder as he rose from sleep to wakefulness, their meaning still a mystery to him, but their ethereal beauty beyond question.

The green lights spun away from him, squealing in fright as his eyes opened.

Above him he could see the slender branches of several trees, their boughs curving gracefully to form a leafy, arched roof, through which he could see the cool, pale blue of the sky. He pushed himself upright on his elbows, his head still groggy as though he had drunk too much wine. He was lying on a bed of golden leaves nestled between the roots of a mighty oak. A silken sheet of golden cloth covered him and from its soft, almost liquid touch on his skin, he could feel he was naked beneath it.

A low partition of woven branches and impossibly graceful saplings offered him some privacy, though not from the laughing lights that bobbed and wove in the air above him. He heard distant music carried

on the fragrant air, its lilting melodies both beguiling and terrible, and
smelled a mouth-watering aroma of nearby cooking.

He lifted a hand to his head, trying to remember how he had come to
this place, wherever this place actually was…

Memories struggled through the cloudy mists of recall, but they
remained frustratingly out of reach. The flickering lights darted down
from the roof to hover before him again, and though he knew he should
be wary of such things, he felt nothing but a faint amusement at their
impish behaviour. One transformed into a ghostly image of a tiny knight
on horseback, another a flitting butterfly. The third swooped and dived
between them, daring them to chase it as they zipped around his head.

He laughed, the sound sending the creatures rushing back to the safety
of the roof as he saw two tall women glide into view from around the
partition of saplings. As they drew near, he saw they did not glide, but
walked with such effortless grace that it seemed they barely touched the
ground they walked upon.

Leofric felt his jaw hang open at their beauty, their forms slender and
exquisite. Clad in ankle-length, crimson dresses, the women had long,
fine-boned features with alabaster skin, pale and smooth like a doll's.
Their eyes were oval and dark, their hair bound up in coiled, leaf-bound
tresses above their gracefully curved, pointed ears.

Something in their appearance tugged at the cords of memory, but
such thoughts evaporated as they smiled hesitantly at him, and his heart
broke to see such beauty in that simple gesture.

'What…' he said. 'Where…'

His heart lurched as he realised he looked upon the features of elves,
the faerie folk, the woodland creatures. The lords and ladies of the wood.
His heart hammered in his chest, fear and dread warring with the allure
and beauty of the elven maids before him.

One carried a bowl of crystal water and a wooden platter of fruit and
bread, the second a bundle of what appeared to be neatly folded clothes.
The food was offered to him and he gratefully snatched a handful of berries, wolfing them down as he suddenly felt a fierce hunger.

He had taken several mouthfuls, the juice of the berries staining his
chin, when he noticed a tiny disdainful curl to the elf maid's mouth.

'I'm sorry,' he said, wiping the juice from his face. 'My manners have
deserted me.'

The elf maid tilted her head curiously to one side, glancing at her companion who set down the clothes beside him, clearly not understanding
his words. She spoke a few words in a language Leofric did not know, but
could have listened to for hours, such was its lyrical splendour.

The other shook her head, reaching out to pull the silken sheet from
him, and Leofric was seized by a sudden fear as she touched his skin. He
held himself immobile, trying not to imagine what manner of enchantment the touch of the fey folk might put upon him.

Her fingers were long and dexterous, questing beneath the sheet to his hip, and despite himself he could not help but be aroused by her touch. Fighting to hide his embarrassment, he reached out to remove her hand. Fast as quicksilver, her hand was withdrawn before he could touch her and she backed away from him, her umber eyes wide and fearful.

'Don't touch me,' he said, grunting in pain as he felt stitches pull tight across his hip and he shifted position to better conceal his shame. The pain cut through the fog of his awakening and his smothered memories, and he moaned in fear as he remembered the battle with the forest creatures, he and his men-at-arms blundering like blind men through the forest searching for...

'Helene!' he cried, fear and loss tearing at him as the full weight of remembrance surged into his mind. He remembered the pallid, hag-faced forest wraiths that tore his men apart and the awful screams of his squire as the tree creature had stabbed him with fingers like long daggers.

'Helene!' he said once again, pushing himself away from the fearful elf maids. They backed away, quickly disappearing from sight behind the screen of slender, curved branches.

Tears of loss streamed down his face as he realised he had lost Helene, lost her to the damned forest of dark magicks. Hot anger flared at the thought of another of the Carrard line taken by Athel Loren and he cast his eyes around this place looking for a weapon, anything with which to strike back at the evil creatures that had taken his beloved.

Leofric threw off the sheet and staggered to his feet, swaying as he realised how weak he still was. Sweet Lady, they had taken everything from him! Helene...

He dropped to his knees as grief swamped him and he wept bitter tears as the enormity of his loss threatened to crush him in its grip. Leofric howled his pain to the skies, beating his fists against the thick roots of the oak, scattering his bed of leaves and cursing all the gods of the world. The green lights that fluttered around him, dropped towards him, their giggling faces now drawn into fearful grimaces and fanged, skeletal grins.

He collapsed against the thick trunk of the great oak, his warrior's anger brimming over and submerging his grief for the moment. He turned, dizzy and weak, and batted away the lights, shouting, 'Get away from me, damn you!'

They buzzed away from him, a kaleidoscope of colours flashing through their insubstantial bodies, angrily hissing at him as they grew horns and claws of light.

He ignored them and gathered up the clothes the elf maids had left him, tugging on a pair of soft, buckskin trousers and a thin overshirt of cream silk.

Leofric wiped the tears from his eyes and ran his hands through his shoulder-length black hair, taking deep breaths and gathering his strength. He had no idea where in the forest he was, but was damned if he would meekly face whatever fate the elves had in store for him. The elf maids had long since fled and he was in no doubt as to the fact that they would even now be seeking help.

Fighting to keep his grief at bay, he moved swiftly around the saplings the elf maids had disappeared behind and found himself in a wide chamber of curved walls crafted from gently swaying branches and leaves. The floor was an elegant weave of thin branches and coloured stone that formed a graceful mosaic. Through gaps in the wall, he saw flashes of other figures and the verdant green of the forest.

The irritating floating balls of light still followed him, darting in with shrill shrieks and whipping around his head as he limped towards a leaf-shaped archway that looked as though it offered the best chance of escape.

He had taken only a few steps, keeping one hand pressed to his hip, the other batting away the troublesome spites that continued to pester him, when two warriors in segmented golden armour over rugged brown troos stepped through the arch. Both wore long grey cloaks and open helmets of fluted bronze, with elaborate patterns etched into the metal. Each bore a pair of curved daggers at his side and a quiver of arrows slung at his shoulder.

'Ah... I wondered when someone like you would show up,' grunted Leofric as they each drew one of their long, slender bladed daggers. Leofric knew full well that unarmed and unarmoured, he would be killed if he fought these elves, but his grief drove him onwards and he lunged at the nearest as they warily approached him.

The elf nimbly sidestepped his clumsy attack, moving with a liquid grace that amazed Leofric with its speed. He could see amusement on their narrow, alien faces and he furiously attacked again, launching a thunderous right hook at one of the elves. Again his blow was dodged and Leofric knew he would never be able to strike these warriors. In the King's Errantry War, he had been privileged to witness Kislevite *Droyaska* fight in battle, swordsmen who could move with incredible speed, but this was something else entirely, the elves displaying a rapidity that bordered on prescience.

'Stand still, damn you!' he roared, missing with yet another punch and feeling his already weakened constitution falter. He dropped to one knee, his breathing hoarse and ragged, blood seeping from the torn stitches on his hip.

After a pause, the two elves reached down to drag him to his feet. It was the moment Leofric had been waiting for and he snapped his head back, slamming it into the face of one of the elves as he leaned down. The elf staggered back, blood streaming from his broken nose, and Leofric spun, snatching the remaining dagger from the scabbard at his hip. He slashed at the second warrior, who leapt aside, only barely avoiding having his belly opened.

'Ha! Not so tough when your prey has a weapon, eh?'

Leofric turned to the stunned elf and kicked him between the legs, dropping him to the floor with a grunt of pain.

But before he could deliver the killing blow, a silver-white blade swept out from behind him and plucked the blade from his hand, sending it spinning across the room. Leofric turned in time to see another elf warrior, similarly attired to the others, but with a silver hound engraved upon his armour. He was older, with an implacable coldness to his eyes, and carried a spinning spear with two shimmering white blades.

The spear slashed towards his legs, its bladed edge turning at the last minute and the haft hooking his legs out from under him. Leofric crashed to the floor, the breath whooshing from his lungs as he hit the ground. He struggled to rise, but saw the elf with the cold eyes standing over him, the two-bladed spear aimed squarely at his throat.

'Do not move, human,' said the warrior, his voice redolent with age and threat. 'I am Cairbre, the Hound of Winter, and I will kill you if you so much as touch one of my warriors again.'

Leofric's eyes darted between the tip of the spear, its lethal point a hair's breadth from his Adam's apple, and the furious features of the elf. He saw an icy resolve in his face, and knew that were he to move in any way that displeased this Cairbre, the spear would be instantly rammed through his throat.

Leofric nodded, the movement almost imperceptible thanks to the blade at his neck.

'I would kill you now, but Naieth wishes you alive,' said Cairbre.

'Who?'

'The Prophetess.'

'The witch?' sneered Leofric, remembering the female elf that had appeared to him in the forest. 'What could an elf witch have to tell me that I would want to hear?'

'Your future,' said Cairbre, touching the cold blade to his neck. 'Or, more precisely, whether you have one.'

CHAPTER FOUR

Fangs snapped shut on the iron plates of the Beastlord's armour, break-ing on the thick metal as the wolf-headed monster slashed at its bronzed flanks with sharp talons. The Beastlord rolled, using its superior weight to pin its opponent, but before it could snap the neck of the challenger, the wolf-creature squirmed free of its grip and savagely tore at its flesh in a flurry of tooth and claw.

Blood the colour of liquid bronze splashed the glistening rocks and the Beastlord hammered its gauntleted fist into the challenger's face. Fangs snapped and spittle flew in the rain-lashed air as the combatants snarled and roared and pummelled one another in a frenzy of blows. The Beast-lord lowered its head and rammed a ridged horn into the wolf's belly, tearing upwards with a powerful twist of its thickly ridged neck muscles.

The wolf-monster howled and leapt back, pressing a clawed hand to its torn side, desperation clear in its wide eyes as the Beastlord's monstrous spawn slithered after it, a multitude of snapping, tentacled mouths and grasping, clawed pseudopods. The Beastlord growled, hauling on the spawn's chain and pulling it away.

It could destroy this upstart beast without the help of its ever-hungry spawn.

Howls and brays surrounded the combatants: monsters with bestial faces marked by the favour of the gods stamping in the mud washed down from the peaks. The snarling challenger howled, thick saliva spat-tering its grey, blood-spattered fur. The Beastlord answered with its own roar of challenge, hefting its massive axe and awaiting its opponent's charge.

The wolf-creature leapt towards it, clawed arms reaching for its throat, but the Beastlord sidestepped and hammered the axe into the rival beast's midriff, hacking the creature in two in a spray of dark blood. The shorn halves dropped to the rocky shale of the mountainside, the remains twitching feebly as it died, and the warherd roared its approval of the kill.

The Beastlord kicked the upper torso of the creature it had just killed over onto its back and hammered the axe into the wolf-creature's chest. It dropped to one knee, reaching down and placing its thick fingers into the great wound, then heaving the beast's chest open with a loud crack of splintering bone.

It reached into the exposed chest cavity and tore out the challenger's heart, rising to hold its axe and the gory organ high above its horned head for its followers to see. The Beastlord bellowed in triumph as the rest of the warherd saw the fate of the beast that had questioned its right to lead. It lowered the heart and swallowed the hot, dripping meat with one throaty gulp.

The meaning of the gesture was clear: defy me and die.

The nearest creatures, red-furred centaurs with long spears, backed away from the Beastlord, their heads bowed in supplication. Others let out a series of ululating cries in its honour, their loyalty assured... at least until another challenger arose.

Such challenges made no sense to the Beastlord. None could doubt the blessings the gods had bestowed upon it, nor the favour they displayed by allowing it to stand in the presence of the Master of Skulls and live. The reasons for such behaviour were a mystery, but it did not let such trivial thoughts distract it from its duty. If other challengers arose it would fight them and it would kill them.

The Beastlord turned from the carcass, allowing the scavengers to gather around the corpse and tear fresh meat from its body with great bites. Warm meat was a rarity and none were about to let such a morsel go uneaten. The weakest members of the herd had already been slaughtered for their flesh, but the Beastlord knew that he would need fresh meat if he hoped to keep the herd together, favour of the gods or not.

The mountains were becoming less steep now that they had descended from the summits, the jagged black rock of the highest peaks giving way to the mossy, scrubby shale and powdered scree of the lower slopes. Their goal was now almost within their reach. Three times had the warherd rested since the Beastlord gathered it beneath its rule, the creatures' loyalty maintained through fear and displays of sheer brutality.

Below, the forest had gone from a greenish brown stain on the landscape to an undulating swathe of greenery that offended the Beastlord's altered eyes. Tendrils of rain-soaked mist and dangerous magic snaked upwards from the vast expanse of forest below, trickling into the mountains like rivulets from a cracked dam. The Beastlord could feel the power stinging its flesh through its iron-hard hooves, though the power was weak and unfocussed. With its newly gifted senses, it could feel the glacial heartbeat of the woodland realm ahead of it, the rank purity filling its heart with the urge to destroy.

Warm rain fell in dreary sheets from the corpse-grey sky, washing down the misty mountain in foaming waterfalls of silt and dark earth. The herd followed the Beastlord, its braying filling them with purpose and power, the Children of Chaos its to command. The sacred task appointed to the Beastlord by the Master of Skulls now became clear as its gaze was drawn to a dark shape, barely visible as more than a tall, black shadow through the clammy mist.

With a clarity it should not have possessed, the Beastlord saw the task appointed to it by the gods and roared in affirmation as the herd devoured the latest challenger.

Kyarno loosed an arrow, a second nocked to his bow almost before the fletching of the first had passed his bowstave. A third followed the second and then a fourth. He pressed his left knee against Eiderath's flanks, guiding his steed a winding course through the trees as he sent arrow after arrow thumping into the bole of a long-dead ash tree.

His frustration grew with every arrow he loosed, picturing Cairbre's face on the bole until at last his doeskin quiver was empty and he halted Eiderath with a gentle pressure of his knees. He vaulted from the back of his steed, a light sweat coating his chest and a pleasant burning sensation in his arms from hours spent practising with his bow.

The bow was finely crafted from soft yew, a perfect six-foot stave offered directly from the trunk with the bark, sapwood and reddish, nut-brown heartwood intact. Kyarno had made an offering to the tree, seeking its permission to make use of its body and the tree had consented to grant him a portion of its precious wood.

Taking the stave, thick with grain lines, he had placed it in the fast-flowing and pure waters of the forest river until the sap and resin were washed out before beginning the long process of crafting such an elegant weapon. He had taken no less care with his arrows, each finely wrought and deadly, crafted with a skill that would make the finest human fletcher's work look shoddy and amateurish.

He loosened the bowstring from the end of the bow, allowing the stave to relax, and placed the weapon on an oiled leather cloth. He wiped the back of his hand across his forehead and gathered up his arrows, not one having failed to find its mark in the wood of the dead tree.

Though his anger at Cairbre was great, he knew there was no sense in angering the forest around him with his own woes. The creatures and spirits of the forest were restless and agitated, more so than was usual for this time of year, when, traditionally, the forest slowly slid into a quiet period of slumber.

As he sheathed the last arrow, he cupped his right fist in his left palm and bowed to the tree.

'Thank you, brother,' he whispered, 'for allowing me to hone my skills to better protect your living brethren and the forest that shelters me.'

He hung the quiver from a branch next to Eiderath, rubbing a hand down the magnificent animal's lathered chest. Taking out a brush, Kyarno rubbed the horse's silver flanks down and said, 'And thank you, my friend. As ever you are my companion in all things.'

Eiderath whinnied, nuzzling him gently before Kyarno moved towards the small, gurgling stream that meandered its way along the edge of the glade. Stripping off, he waded into the knee-deep stream and lay down, allowing the icy waters to cleanse the sweat from his body and massage the tension from his shoulders and arms.

As the waters rushed over his flesh, he angrily recalled his meeting with Lord Aldaeld the previous evening. Though he had travelled back through the shadow paths of the forest, it had still taken him the best part of three hours to reach the warmth and safety of Coeth-Mara.

The towering oaks that formed the great, arched processional were wreathed in the ghostly light of flitting spites, their capricious laughter echoing from the boughs high above as he made his way towards the halls of Lord Aldaeld Éadaoin.

Grey-cloaked Eternal Guard with their twin-bladed spears parted to allow him access to the great hall. Its magnificence was wasted on Kyarno, who had seen it many times, though usually only briefly before once again being banished from its glory.

The lord of the Éadaoin kinband was flanked by more of his Eternal Guard, seated before them upon a throne of pale wood sung from the roots of the hall's trees. His cloak of leaves and feathers was swept over his shoulders, revealing his bare chest, slender yet powerful and covered with looped tattoos of dragons and winged serpents.

A longsword with a flaring, leaf-shaped blade lay across his lap, its pommel glowing with a faint green light and the blade an exquisite blue steel.

Cairbre paced the hall like a caged wolf, having obviously returned some time ago via the paths known only to his warriors and the wild and dangerous wardancers.

'Kyarno,' began Aldaeld, 'Cairbre tells me you have been with my daughter once again.'

Kyarno shot a venomous look towards the Hound of Winter, but said nothing, knowing it would do no good to deny the accusation.

'Is that true?' demanded Aldaeld.

'Yes,' nodded Kyarno, defiantly meeting the lord of the Éadaoin kin-band's eyes.

'Even though I forbade you to do so?'

'Even though,' agreed Kyarno.

'You are a troublemaker, Daelanu, and you would be gone from my lands forever, but for the counsel of your uncle.'

Kyarno gave Cairbre another look, puzzled as to why he should speak on his behalf.

'I am not to be banished?'

Lord Aldaeld shook his head. 'No, though my every instinct is to hurl you to Valas Laithu and be done with you.'

'Valas Laithu is coming to Coeth-Mara?' asked Kyarno, a cold dread settling in his belly. 'Why?'

'You know fine well why,' said Aldaeld. 'He and his sons will be here for the Winter Feast, and though I do not know what season he carries in his heart, I do not think it will be summer.'

'What are you going to do?'

'I will keep my own counsel on that, stripling,' growled Aldaeld, and Kyarno bristled at being branded so. 'But your uncle seems to think that you may yet earn your place in my kinband by more than an accident of birth. It is now time for you to prove him right.'

Now Kyarno understood. Lord Aldaeld had some menial task that Cairbre had volunteered him for and he felt his resentment flare once more.

'What would you have me do?' he said at last.

'Naieth has need of you,' said Lord Aldaeld. 'She brings a human amongst us, and though he should be dead, she believes he may yet be of use to us.'

'What use could a human be to the kindreds of the forest?'

'That is for her to know,' said Aldaeld, and Kyarno caught the elven lord's irritation at his ignorance of the Prophetess's motives. 'But you will attend upon her come the morn.'

'It demeans an elf to nursemaid a human, my lord,' protested Kyarno.

Lord Aldaeld nodded. 'Indeed it does, but I do not offer this task to you as a choice, Kyarno Daelanu. You will do this duty or I will hand you over to Valas Laithu.'

Faced with such a destiny, Kyarno knew that he had no choice but to agree and bowed curtly, saying, 'Then I will do as you bid, my lord,' before striding from the hall with his head held high.

His anger had not dimmed with his distance from Coeth-Mara, rather it had swelled until he felt his hatred for this human grow like a weed within his heart. Trust his uncle to have convinced Aldaeld to curse him with such a duty. The aged warrior hated him and seemed to bend his every effort to seeing Kyarno humiliated.

As the first rays of dawn had spilled over the treetops, he had ridden hard into the forest to take out his frustrations with some archery, though, in truth, it had done little to ease his bitterness.

He leaned his head back into the stream, holding his breath and letting the water cover his face. Its chill touch numbed his skin and he surrendered to the cold, staying beneath the water until his lungs were on fire, before finally sitting bolt upright in a wash of cold water and heaving breaths.

'One of these days you'll not come up in time and I'll have to drag your body back to Coeth-Mara,' said a voice.

Kyarno shook his head free of water and smiled humourlessly at the newcomer, 'And tell me, Tarean Stormcrow, who would mourn for Kyarno Daelanu?'

'Well, no one, obviously,' said Tarean, brightly, 'after all, you're nothing but an inconvenience to us.'

'Is that so?' said Kyarno, not bothering to conceal his hostility and climbing from the stream to pull on his clothes.

'Almost certainly,' nodded Tarean, stroking Kyarno's steed's mane. 'Though Morvhen seems to like you, so perhaps you should think of her the next time you play your dangerous games.'

Kyarno shrugged on his overshirt, warily watching Tarean as he strolled around the glade, reading the tracks of where he had been training.

Tarean Stormcrow was tall and physically resembled him, in that they were the same age and shared the same lithe, supple physique common to most of the Glade Riders of the Éadaoin kinband, but his features had an easy confidence to them that Kyarno knew his did not. Tarean's golden hair was held in place by a silver circlet, upon which was set a sapphire gem and his clothes spoke of an elf not given to living alone in the forest. A long-bladed sword was buckled at his waist, and he carried a short, recurved bow slung over one shoulder.

Kyarno knew that Tarean's appearance was deceptive, for though he might look as though he were more at home in the comfortable confines of Coeth-Mara, he had fought many battles to defend Athel Loren against intruders.

'You use that bow well, Kyarno, and that steed of yours is a fine beast.'

'His name is Eiderath, and he is the finest steed I have ever ridden,' agreed Kyarno.

'Better even than those of the Laithu kinband?' laughed Tarean.

'Ah…' said Kyarno, 'then that is what this is about.'

'What?' replied Tarean. 'Can't I offer a friendly word without there being an ulterior motive?'

'You and I are not friends, Tarean,' said Kyarno, gathering up his bow and sheathing it over Eiderath's back. 'You are Lord Aldaeld's herald and kin to him.'

'And that precludes us from being friends?'

'Say what it is you are here to say and begone,' said Kyarno. 'I do not wish your company.'

Tarean sighed and said, 'Your words are needlessly barbed, Kyarno

Daelanu. I offer you friendship, but you do not see it.'

'I need no friends,' snapped Kyarno.

'You are wrong,' said Tarean, grasping Kyarno's arm. 'We all need friends, now, in these dark times more than ever.'

Kyarno shrugged off Tarean's grip and swung onto Eiderath's back. 'And you would be my friend?'

'I would, yes,' said Tarean, offering his hand with a grin, 'though Isha alone knows why, you're a hard one to like.'

'You mock me!' spat Kyarno.

'No,' said Tarean, 'I was merely making a poor jest and if I offended you, then I am sorry. If you wish me to go then I will go, but you are right, I do have a message for you.'

'What is it then?'

'Lord Aldaeld bids me command you that it is time for you to fulfil your duty to your kinband and take the human to the Crystal Mere.'

'To nanny a human,' cursed Kyarno. 'He mocks me in all things.'

Tarean shook his head. 'No, Lord Aldaeld honours you with this charge. See this duty for what it is and you will see no slight in its issue.'

'What good can it possibly do to have a human within Athel Loren? They are nothing but firestarters and fellers of trees. They are not to be trusted.'

'For what it is worth, I agree with you, my friend, but Lord Aldaeld has made his desire in this matter plain.'

'Then Kyarno the troublemaker will see it done,' said Kyarno bitterly.

Tarean shook his head and said, 'I feel sorry for you, Kyarno. You could be part of this kinband, but you won't let yourself.'

'I don't need your pity, Tarean,' said Kyarno, digging his heels into Eiderath's flanks and riding away, leaving Lord Aldaeld's herald alone in the glade.

Leofric watched the elf named Cairbre as he spoke quietly with the two who had prevented him from leaving this place. Their voices were clear and song-like, but Leofric knew not to put his faith in such false beauty. Though the words were unknown to him, it was no leap of imagination to surmise they were speaking of him and whatever terrible fate they had in mind for him.

As the adrenaline of his brief fight with the elves wore off, the pain of loss returned to him as he pictured Helene's smiling face, her laugh and her beauty. He had sat on the shaped stump of a tree and wept as the sunlight dappling in from overhead changed from the strong, clear light of dawn to the soft, warmth of midmorning.

What was left to him now that Helene was gone? Assuming he was able to escape this place, how would he tell Beren?

Leofric felt hollow, as though his spirit, so nearly crushed on the east causeway of Middenheim, had now been shattered into a thousand pieces. The dark shadow that had settled upon his soul since facing the lord of daemons and the rout at the hands of the Lord of the End Times once more threatened to swallow him completely.

He heard the sound of voices once more, the rich tones of the males accompanied by the soft, feminine lilt of a woman's voice. For the briefest moment, his soul was soothed by the sweet, musical sound, before he reminded himself that this was the beguiling voice of an elf and therefore not to be trusted.

His fists clenched as he saw the hawk-faced elf-witch who he had seen in the forest enter the chamber of branches, her movements as graceful as those of the young elf-maids that had attended him earlier. She wore the same dress of spun gold and carried her staff of intertwined branches, her hair still bound in an elaborate headpiece of leaves, pins and feathers. A faint corona of light surrounded her and Leofric could sense the unwholesome aftertaste of faerie magic.

'Good day, Leofric,' said the elf-witch. 'My name is Naieth. Do you recall me from our meeting in the forest?'

'You are a witch,' spat Leofric.

'Your kind have called me worse than that before now,' said Naieth without apparent offence. 'But that is unimportant. What *is* important is that you listen to me, Leofric.'

'Why should I? I am held prisoner while my wife may lie dead somewhere in your forest!' stormed Leofric. 'And how is it that you know my name and speak it as though we are friends?'

'The answer to that is complex, Leofric, I know a great deal about you. More than you do yourself.'

'Spare me your riddles, elf. Answer the question.'

'As you say, I am a witch and thus I know many things. Some I would wish not to know, but that is not for me to choose.'

Leofric surged to his feet, the grey-cloaked elves raising their weapons before them as he did.

'Damn you, woman, tell me where my wife is!' raged Leofric before sitting back down on the stump of wood. 'Please…'

'You will show respect, human,' said Cairbre, raising his spear towards him.

'Leofric, your wife is with the forest now,' said Naieth softly. 'I am sorry. We tried to come to your aid, but we were too late.'

'With the forest? What does that mean?' demanded Leofric, sudden hope in his heart. 'Can we get her back?'

'It means that the spirits of the forest took her,' said Naieth, drawing up her robes to sit on a delicately curved swathe of branches that curled outwards from the walls as she lowered herself to sit upon them. 'Dryads, branchwraiths and tree spirits. As winter draws in they become malicious and spiteful, taking all who cross into the forest as their victims.'

'Victims…' whispered Leofric. 'Then she is dead?'

Naieth reached out to lay a hand on his shoulder, but he pulled back, his face a mask of resentment and pain. 'I am truly sorry, Leofric, but the forest exacts its own vengeance on those who pass its borders.'

'She harmed no one!' shouted Leofric. 'She was an innocent.'

'I know, but she is at peace now,' said Naieth. 'This world is a dangerous place. Orcs and the beasts of the dark places of the world pillage and destroy, the warriors of the Dark Gods lay waste to the lands of your kind and the dead rise from their tombs to slay the living. She is spared that horror now and will live forever as part of Athel Loren. She will live on in your heart, your memories and through your bloodline.'

'But I want her back, I need her!' cried Leofric.

'I'm sorry, but it is not in my power to grant that wish.'

Leofric took a deep breath, attempting to compose himself in the face of the elves. He was a knight of Bretonnia and it did not behoove a knight of the realm to comport himself in this manner.

'She gave me her favour at the Couronne tournament,' he said slowly, 'a silken scarf of blue, edged in white lace.'

Cairbre leaned close to Naieth and she nodded as he whispered something to her.

'I am told it was wrapped around the hilt of your sword,' she said.

'It was,' agreed Leofric, 'and it is precious to me.'

'Then I will see that it is returned to you,' promised Naieth.

He straightened his back and nodded his thanks through red-rimmed eyes at the elf-witch and her guardians as another thought occurred to him.

'The knight who was with you, the one with the heraldry of a dragon, a green one I think. Who is he?' asked Leofric. 'Is he here?'

Naieth shook her head. 'No, he is not. He has travelled beyond this place.'

'Do you know his name? He is one of the holy few is he not? A knight of the grail...'

'Yes,' agreed Naieth, 'he is that. He is a friend to the asrai and that is all that need concern you of him. He is gone from Athel Loren and will not return for... some time.'

'The asrai? Who are they?'

Naieth smiled. 'It is an ancient elven word from across the seas that means "the blessed ones". It is the word we use for our race, the kin of the forest.'

'And how is it that a noble knight of the Lady rides with your people atop an elven steed and wielding an elven blade? Surely such a thing is unthinkable.'

'He has done great service for my people and I would speak no more about him, for he is a warrior of great sorrow and he would not thank me for speaking of him.'

Seeing he would get no more from Naieth about the mysterious grail knight, Leofric said, 'So be it, but if I am to be held here, then surely I deserve at least to know where I am.'

'Indeed you do,' agreed Naieth, waving her hand at the branch walls, which parted to reveal a glorious woodland landscape of golden browns and brilliant greens. Majestic trees soared upwards, their trunks thicker than a castle tower and older than the most ancient ruins Leofric had ever seen. Brilliant lights wreathed each canopy, haunting melodies and laughter weaving through the greenery like a gentle breeze.

Elves on foot and elves on horseback moved gracefully through the trees, and animals – white-furred wolves, sinuous cats and golden-feathered birds – meandered through the undergrowth or flitted between the trees without fear.

'You are within the woodland realm of Athel Loren,' said Naieth, 'a guest of Lord Aldaeld Éadaoin of the asrai in the halls of Coeth-Mara. Lord Aldaeld rules this region of the forest in the name of Isha and Kurnous, and by your way of thinking, we are in the south-eastern part of the forest, near the foot of the mountains you call the Vaults.'

'You say I am a guest,' commented Leofric. 'Does that imply I am free to leave?'

'No, I am afraid that it does not,' said Naieth reluctantly. 'Normally intruders within Athel Loren are killed without mercy. You have lived in the shadow of our forest for enough years to know this.'

'Aye,' agreed Leofric. 'So the question then becomes why am I not dead?'

'Indeed. You are alive only because I decreed it and Lord Aldaeld has consented not to slay you for the time being.'

'So my position is what might be described as "precarious",' stated Leofric.

Naieth made a sound like the opening of a song and it was several seconds before Leofric realised that she was laughing.

'Yes, Leofric, your situation is precarious… as is mine if it turns out I was wrong to save you. Your life depends now on the good graces of Lord Aldaeld, so walk warily in his realm, Leofric Carrard.'

'So why did you save my life then?'

'Not on a whim, I can assure you of that, there was method to my actions.'

'Then I ask again, why did you save my life?'

Naieth hesitated for the briefest of seconds and Leofric knew with sudden clarity that she would not tell him the truth.

At last Naieth said, 'I see many things, Leofric, and the future is not the impenetrable veil to me that it is to others. Nor is it fixed, there are many fates that await us, and not even the mightiest seers can know them all. There is a time of great moment approaching for the asrai and in many of my waking nightmares of the future, I see you. What part you have to play in the coming days of blood and war I do not yet see, but that you are there is enough for me.'

Leofric sensed that the elf-witch was holding something back, but knew better than to press her too much.

'So what happens now?' he asked. 'You keep me prisoner until this time draws near?'

'No, of course not,' smiled Naieth. 'Lord Aldaeld desires to speak with you before deciding your fate. Once he has made his decision we will resolve what is to be done with you.'

Leofric looked down at his sweat and tear streaked robes, the stain on his hip where his stitches had torn now grown into a large patch of dried blood.

'I am in no fit state to meet a lord,' he said.

'I know,' agreed Naieth. 'That is why I have arranged for someone to take you to the Crystal Mere where you will be cleansed and made presentable to Lord Aldaeld.'

'Who?'

'Don't worry,' said Naieth with a smile, though Leofric saw that it did not quite reach her eyes. 'I'm sure you and Kyarno will get along famously.'

This close to the forest of the elves, the Beastlord was cautious, having moved the herd slowly through the low, scrubby hills at the foot of the mountains. It knew full well the dangers inherent in being so near the woodland realm. Its senses were alive with the sensation of magic emanating from the trees and ground. It felt it as a sour taste in the back of its throat, a rank, bitter flavour that fuelled its urge to despoil.

A dark rain fell as the forest's edge came into sight over a cold, windswept heath of tall, yellow grasses and stagnant pools of brackish water. The Beastlord waved its thick arms and the beasts of the herd dropped to the ground, crawling and stalking their way towards the edge of the heath. Claws of mist gathered about the dark and twisted oaks of the forest, their trunks and upper branches wreathed with skulls and hides of beasts, orcs and ratkin. Waving, leafy sprouts drooped from eye sockets and a low groaning issued from the depths of the forest.

Drifting lights, sluggish and lazy, wafted between the shadowed trunks deeper in the woods, but the Beastlord paid them no heed, intent on the massive waystone that reared up from the ground at the treeline. Its surface was worn smooth by the elements, though the looping carvings and elven script that spiralled across its surface remained crisp and deep. The Beastlord felt the ancient power that saturated the waystone, reaching deep into the earth to the foundations of the world, and grunted in pleasure as it pictured the stone torn down then corrupted to become its herdstone.

It raised its axe, waving forward a group of around twenty smaller creatures with thin, reddish brown fur and elongated, bestial skulls with small, budding horns. Each beast carried a short, iron-bladed axe and cast fearful glances towards the forest, unwilling to approach it too closely.

The Beastlord sensed their fear and let loose a terrifying bellow, cowing the smaller creatures with its power. It swung its axe towards the forest once more and the beastmen loped towards the treeline, their instinctive fear of the woodland realm outweighed by the more immediate fear of the Beastlord.

Their braying cries were strangely deadened as they charged, the Beastlord watching as they reached the edge of the forest and waved their axes in the air. Some chopped at low branches with their weapons, some defecated on the trees and others skulked deeper into the forest with low growls.

The altered eyes of the Beastlord could see spiralling lines of magical energy seeping up from the ground and watched as the forest reacted to the intruders.

A beast squatting over the roots of a tree was the first to die, its head torn from its shoulders in a fountain of blood by a looping noose of razor-sharp thorns that whipped down from the tree above. Another died as the earth opened beneath it and swallowed it whole. The ground erupted in rampant growth, slashing, tearing and ripping the beasts to bloody ruin. Soon the forest's edge was a thrashing mass of screaming beasts, lashing branches and jagged bushes that tore at flesh and crushing boles that split skulls.

Snaking branches and curling thorns spiralled from the ground at the edge of the forest and the trunks of the trees, an impenetrable barrier of lethally sharp barbs. A dark hiss and rustle of angered forest life crept across the heath, the sound of screaming beasts sending a ripple of fear through the warherd.

The Beastlord nodded to itself. It had expected no less and the sacrifice of the smaller beasts had simply confirmed its suspicions. Turning from the carnage unleashed by the forest and the pitiful cries of the dying creatures, the Beastlord waved another of its herd forward, a withered, hunched figure swathed in rotted robes of patched leather and hides.

Long, curling horns sprouted from its shaggy, bear-like skull, and its hooded eyes held the spark of a dark, malicious intelligence. It carried a long staff of gnarled black wood, its substance slick and somehow alive. The breath of the gods surrounded the creature, a shaman whose powers not even the Beastlord could match.

The shaman looked upon the tall stone that marked the boundary of the forest and nodded, stabbing its staff towards it, grunting and chanting in a language the Beastlord did not understand, although he felt its dark power in the depths of his bones. Powerful winds of magic were stirred and the Beastlord could feel the gathering energy being channelled into the shaman with each passing second.

Another group of creatures stamped forward as the Beastlord again waved its massive axe: thickset centaurs with iron-clawed hooves, hard skins of vermillion and elongated shaggy rumps like powerful dray horses. The reek of powerful spirits was upon them and their snarling faces were flushed with its consumption. Each carried a long, stabbing spear and thick, goring horns curled from their fearsome skulls.

The shaman nodded and the Beastlord ordered them forwards, the bellowing centaurs rearing in wild abandon before thundering towards the trees. As the centaurs charged, the shaman hauled its twisted bulk to its feet and pointed its writhing staff at the barrier of thorns and branches.

Glittering blue flames leapt from the staff and the shaman braced its malformed legs to control the spurting fires. Smoke billowed from the edge of the forest as the magical flames consumed the woodland. White light flared as the magic of the waystone fought the raw power of the god's breath. The barrier swiftly disintegrated under the relentless assault and the roaring centaurs leapt through the gap the shaman's magic had created.

Six of the powerful beasts made it through the barrier of thorns before the shaman's spell was exhausted and it reared up once more. The other beasts turned back as the tearing wall of branches and thorns snatched at them. The forest dragged one down before it could halt its charge, ripping its belly open, breaking its legs and wrenching its limbs off before grinding its ravaged carcass to powder beneath the grasping roots of the trees.

The shaman shook its thick, horned skull and pointed at the base of the waystone, snarling and grunting in pleasure. The Beastlord saw that the grasses surrounding the waystone were blackened and withered, twisting into new and unnatural forms – the influence of the Shadow-Gave reaching from its lair in the mountains...

Once again the Beastlord pictured the waystone as it would soon be – toppled and dragged into the mountains to become the greatest herd-stone of all the beasts of Chaos.

CHAPTER FIVE

Cairbre was waiting for Kyarno when he rode up to the hall where the prophetess had sequestered the human. The aged warrior wore an expression of faint disapproval, and his stance was guarded. As ever, he was ready to fight in an instant. Kyarno saw that he carried the Blades of Midnight unsheathed, and held the reins of a heavily muscled, human-bred horse with a wide chest and thick limbs.

'Expecting trouble?' asked Kyarno, nodding towards the white-bladed spear as he vaulted from Eiderath's back.

'Where have you been?' said Cairbre, ignoring Kyarno's question. 'You were to be here at dawn.'

'Good morning to you too, uncle,' replied Kyarno, giving the huge, snorting horse a wide berth. There was a crudity to the animal that no amount of grooming could erase, its bulk powerful, but vulgar. Trust a human to ride something like this, he thought. Curious spites flickered around the beast. The horse's eyes were wide and its ears were pressed flat against its skull.

'That beast is very you,' he said.

'I said you were to be–'

'I heard what you said, Cairbre. I came as soon as Tarean Stormcrow came for me. What more do you want?'

Cairbre nodded stiffly, biting back a response, and said, 'The human is inside. The prophetess asks for him to be taken to the Crystal Mere and for him to be allowed to bathe. Once he is clean enough to be presented to Lord Aldaeld, bring him back.'

'Yes, Tarean told me this,' said Kyarno. 'Is that all?'

'Yes, that's all,' said Cairbre. 'Do you think you can manage that without any trouble?'

'I think so, yes,' snapped Kyarno, tilting his head back to look up into the crisp sunlight as it speared through the autumnal canopy high above. 'It is a fine morning to take a filthy human to the healing waters of the Crystal Mere. I wonder if he will appreciate how privileged he is to see such a sight?'

'I would doubt it.'

'Then why show him, uncle?' asked Kyarno. 'He will only speak of it if he is returned to his lands. And what he speaks of will draw others of his kind here like blights to the dying.'

Cairbre nodded. 'I know, but it is Naieth's wish that he be taken there.'

'Has she seen something?'

Cairbre shrugged, obviously reluctant to speak. 'I do not know. Perhaps.'

'She has been wrong before,' hissed Kyarno. 'Have you forgotten?'

'No, damn you, I have not,' said Cairbre, his pale features ashen. 'And I do not need you to remind me! I see it every day I look at you.'

Kyarno swallowed hard. 'And I see it every time I close my eyes, uncle. Tell me again whose burden is the greater.'

Cairbre was silent for long seconds before he said, 'If I could change things I would, lad. I loved your mother and father, you know that.'

'But you can't change things, can you?' said Kyarno. 'For all your skill at arms, you couldn't save them, could you?'

'I lost a brother that day,' whispered Cairbre.

'No,' said Kyarno. 'You lost a lot more than that.'

Naieth listened with growing sadness to the harsh words spoken between the Hound of Winter and Kyarno. The youngster would never understand the choices she had had to make, the awful truths that woke her weeping in the night with visions of death and ruin. He would never understand that she had needed him to suffer in order to mould him into the weapon she required.

He would never understand and he would never forgive her if he knew.

She closed her eyes, seeing again the wooded glade, the stream that ran red with elven blood, the flames that burned, the guttural brays of the twisted beastkin and the agonised screams that haunted her every nightmare.

What she had told Leofric was the truth: this world *was* a dangerous place and the asrai had enemies all around. Every rhyme sung to elven youngsters taught them this cold, hard fact.

The forest realm of Athel Loren was one of the last bastions of pure magic in the world, and she would do whatever was necessary to protect it.

Even though the price was sometimes almost too high to bear.

Dressed in fresh clothes – a fine silken shirt of pale cream, downy britches of auburn leather and soft boots that fitted as though they had been made specially for him – Leofric felt almost human again. The air here had a crisp, invigorating quality and, as much as he kept reminding himself that he was in the lair of the enemy, he found himself strangely energised. The ache of loss was still lodged in his heart like a splinter of ice, but he forced himself to maintain a composed exterior in the face of the elves.

It chafed him not to have his armour and sword, but he supposed that if one of the elves had been held prisoner in the oubliettes of Castle Carrard, he would not have allowed it a weapon either.

Though he knew it was autumn, with the season on the cusp of changing to winter, the climate here was mild, far milder than it had any right to be, as though a moment in time of summer had been somehow slowed.

The elf-witch had left an hour ago, though it was difficult to judge time in this place, and the two elf-maids who had earlier brought him food returned with the clothes he now wore. Atop the neatly folded clothes was Helene's silken blue scarf, and Leofric wept once more as he picked up her favour. He had tucked the folded scarf into a pocket of the overshirt while one expressionless maid delicately sewed the wound on his hip. He had thanked them, but they had once again proven to be uncommunicative. Upon leaving, they stared at him blankly as Leofric had bowed graciously, his chivalric code demanding no less a courtesy to ladies, even though these ladies were elves.

The pain in his hip was lessened and the injuries to his chest and head had diminished to a dull throbbing ache. He paced the room, catching fleeting glimpses of the world beyond his confinement – laughter, music and arching voices that spoke of great meaning just beyond his comprehension. His earlier companions, the flitting, winged creatures of light had returned, buzzing around him like irritating insects. He had long since given up trying to dissuade them from annoying him, such attempts only spurring them to greater heights of nuisance.

As far as confinement went, this place was far more salubrious than anything Castle Carrard had to offer, its arched timber walls curved and sweet smelling. Gently waving branches formed the ceiling, the bright sunlight diffusing softly through the canopy of wide green leaves. Nowhere was there anything that appeared to have had the hand of a craftsman upon it, no carved furniture, no hand-blown glass, no skilfully moulded ceramic – everything had a natural, almost... grown quality to it.

But as natural and harmonious as everything was, to his human eyes there was a subtle wrongness to the surroundings. He felt no kinship with his environment, though there was a familiarity to it: walls, floor, ceiling, clothes. Everything was familiar, yet at the same time disturbingly different, giving him a caged, impatient feeling.

Just as he was thinking of making his own way from this place once more, an elf clad in simple, practical garb entered. His manner was immediately hostile and his youthful features were fixed in an expression that told Leofric that he would much rather be anywhere else than here.

The elf wore the natural colours of the forest, brown leggings and a pale grey overshirt with embroidered gold stitching along its collar. A feathered cloak of deep blue covered one arm and hung to his calves from his shoulders. A worn, shagreen scabbard housed an elegant, plain-handled sword and across his back hung a long, gracefully curved bow.

Despite its craftsmanship, the bow was still a lowborn peasant's weapon to Leofric's way of thinking, and he wondered whether this was some subtle insult. Had the elves sent a peasant to be his gaoler?

'Who are you?' asked Leofric.

The elf did not reply immediately, sizing him up with his wide, green eyes and pursing his lips together. By any human standards, the elf was darkly handsome, with narrow, sardonic features and long, straw-coloured hair that spilled around his shoulders in a fringe of tightly braided locks. Feathers and beads were woven into his hair and Leofric sensed a recklessness in this elf like that of many a knight errant.

'Are you Kyarno?' asked Leofric, raising his voice and speaking more slowly. 'I am Leofric Carrard of Quenelles, knight of the realm of Bretonnia and loyal subject of King Louen Leoncoeur.'

The elf's face twisted in a grimace as he spoke and Leofric wondered if he had somehow insulted him.

'By Kurnous, your voice is ugly and you mangle my name such that I do not recognise it,' said the elf at last, his tone betraying his impatience to be done with this business. 'I know who you are, and yes, I am Kyarno Daelanu. I am to take you to the Crystal Mere.'

'So I am told. What is it?'

'Somewhere you would not be seeing if I had my way,' answered Kyarno.

Leofric nodded in resignation and said, 'Very well, I see we are going to get along like brothers in arms.'

Kyarno ignored the comment and smoothly turned on his heels, heading for the arched exit to the chamber. 'Come. If we do not leave now it will be nightfall before we return, and night is no time for one like you to be abroad in Athel Loren.'

Leofric sighed and set off after the truculent Kyarno, following him through the archway and into a passageway of gently curving branches that swayed in an unfelt breeze. Though Kyarno spoke human language flawlessly, there was a stiltedness to his speech that Leofric had noticed in all the elves. Their own language was spoken with a lyrical fluidity, but they voiced the human tongue as though it were unfamiliar and distasteful to them.

The scent of outdoors came to him and he felt a warm gust as his sprightly companions flitted past his head.

Kyarno turned a corner and Leofric, without seeming to pass any boundary that marked the structure he had been in, suddenly found himself outside in a leafy glade, the scent of wood and sap strong in his nostrils and the sounds of life coming from all around him.

He spun, confused and dismayed to find that he could see no sign of any doorway they might have emerged from. Saplings and the towering trunks of mighty trees were all that he could see of the shimmering clearing, and he was seized anew with a fear of this faerie magic.

What manner of race could beguile the senses so?

A familiar and heartily welcome whinny shook him from his discomfort and he smiled as he saw the reassuring form of his horse, Taschen. The horse looked frightened and was without his yellow caparison, his reins held by Cairbre, the warrior elf with the two-bladed spear. Leofric saw that the elven warrior had the reins unwisely wrapped around his wrist like a novice groom. If the horse bolted suddenly, it would wrench Cairbre's shoulder from its socket.

Kyarno stood nearby, beckoning a pale, saffron-maned steed of elvish stock towards him. The beast's neck was clad in a shimmering fabric, its tail and mane braided and woven with colourful garlands, and Leofric was struck by the wonderful impracticality of such a mount. Too narrow chested and slender limbed to carry an armoured warrior into battle, the beast was nevertheless a magnificent specimen of equine beauty and poise.

Cairbre led Taschen towards him, his face a mask of open hostility, and Leofric wondered what he had done to offend these elves so deeply. Was his very presence here an affront to them?

'Thank you,' he said as Cairbre gingerly handed Leofric the reins and Kyarno swung onto the back of his own steed.

'Where is the caparison?' asked Leofric, stroking his horse's mane.

'I removed it,' said Cairbre. 'It was too conspicuous and it is unwise to attract too much attention to yourself, human.'

'Too conspicuous?' replied Leofric, indicating Kyarno's steed. 'That beast is hardly the most subtle of creatures! It could be seen for miles in open country.'

'But it is ridden by one of the asrai, and you are in Athel Loren,' said Cairbre before turning and marching away. Leofric put the missing caparison from his mind and set his boot in the stirrup, hauling himself onto Taschen's back, relishing the power and security of being back in the saddle.

As he settled himself on his mount's back, Leofric saw that Kyarno's steed had no tack whatsoever, no bridle, no saddle or any other piece of riding equipment. Now he understood Cairbre's careless handling of Taschen's reins.

It felt strange – and, Leofric had to admit, strangely liberating – being on horseback without a suit of heavy plate armour and the sense of weight that it brought. He looked over at Kyarno, who, despite having no saddle or reins, rode his steed as though it were a natural extension of his body.

'That is a magnificent steed,' said Leofric.

'He is indeed,' agreed Kyarno. 'Yours is… strong.'

Leofric patted Taschen's neck. 'He is indeed, he comes from the king's own stables and is said to be have been sired from the line of Tamasin.'

'Who is that?'

'Tamasin was the noble destrier that carried King Charlen into battle against the orcs at the Battle of Blood River in the land of the Border Princes,' said Leofric proudly. 'Thrice was the great steed wounded by foul orcish archery, but ne'er once did he falter in service of his master, bearing him through blood and battle to carry the day. After the battle, King Charlen decreed that his faithful steed had served his master enough, and put him out to stud in the royal stables until the day came when his mighty heart beat no more.'

'At least he ended his days well,' said Kyarno. 'Given the chance to fornicate day and night with all the younger, feisty mares in the comfort of a warm stable. Better than being shot at by greenskins.'

'I suppose so,' agreed Leofric, annoyed that such a fine example of Bretonnian horse had been dismissed so flippantly.

Without seeming to guide his horse in any way, Kyarno rode away from him, beckoning lazily for Leofric to follow.

His irritation at this surly elf growing by the second, Leofric dug his heels into Taschen's sides and followed Kyarno into the depths of Coeth-Mara.

And Athel Loren opened up before him.

Awe. Wonderment. Enchantment. Fear.

Emotions whirled in Leofric's head as Kyarno led him through the realm of wonders and rapture that was Athel Loren. The land of the wood elves had been described in dark faerie tales throughout Bretonnia for centuries, telling of magic and spells that wove their domain from dreams. Minstrels and tellers of tales spoke of places where the elves gathered that were not of this world, where the seasons never changed and the inhabitants of the forest could live forever.

As he rode through the place Kyarno had called Coeth-Mara, followed by his darting companions of light, Leofric now knew that those taletellers understood but a fraction of the truth.

Athel Loren was a realm of magic and light, soaring trees as tall as the tallest tower of Castle Carrard with great gnarled trunks of incredible girth. Laughing elves on horseback rode through the trees, followed by more of the darting balls of light. The very air seemed alive with possibility, as though rich with restless motion. This was a place of life, vitality and fecundity – everything he saw, from forest animals to gliding hawks and the elves themselves, had a fierce vigour, the like of which he had never seen.

The peasantry of Bretonnia certainly never displayed such vigour in their daily tasks, never went about their business as though the pleasure in completing a duty was its own reward. They were wretched, hunched specimens and Leofric found himself wondering what manner of beings these elves were to live in such joy.

The heady aroma of sweet sap and pungent blossoms made Leofric feel giddy and light-headed and he had to force himself not to take such deep breaths. As they rode onwards, he saw he was attracting suspicious looks from every elf they passed – first there would be surprise and then either outright hostility or faint curiosity. Nor, he saw, was he the only one attracting suspicious glances. Kyarno drew his own fair share of scornful stares, but if the elf was aware of it he gave no sign.

'Why is everyone staring at me?' asked Leofric.

'Most of them have never seen a human before,' answered Kyarno without turning.

'Really?'

'Why would they have? We have no interest in contact with your kind.'

Leofric bit back an angry retort and said, 'What are they all doing out here in the middle of the forest?'

'What do you mean? This is Coeth-Mara, this is where they live.'

Leofric looked around for dwellings of any sort, but all he could see were the towering trees, verdant greenery and the abundance of forest creatures. A more picturesque scene he could scarce imagine, but he saw nowhere that might be considered a dwelling.

'If this is Coeth-Mara, then where do your people live? I see no homes or dwellings.'

'No,' agreed Kyarno. 'You won't, not unless the forest consents to let you. You ride through one of the greatest halls in Athel Loren, yet you see it not.'

Leofric wasn't sure whether or not Kyarno was making fun of him, and looked harder for any signs of habitation, but try as he might he could see nothing to indicate that anyone or anything lived here. Eventually he gave up, content just to watch the magical beauty unfold around him.

Trees shaped into gently rounded archways formed roofless processionals, like the nave of the great cathedral of Quenelles, and the golds and reds of autumn mingled with the greens of summer in their high branches.

Springs bubbled up through rocky cracks in the ground, gurgling along shaped channels of curved wood and into crystal pools lined with wondrous wooden sculptures that looked as though they had grown there rather than having been crafted. Leofric watched amazed as each of the sculptures began moving as though with an inner life of its own, the wood reshaping itself in newer and more graceful forms.

A soft glow appeared in the centre of one and a dazzling light emerged from the living wood, trilling, musical laughter emanating from it as it zipped towards another of the sculptures. It vanished into the depths of the wood and almost immediately the sculpture writhed with life as the joyous spirits shaped it in new and pleasing ways.

More of the dancing lights capered in the canopy above and Leofric turned in his saddle to see if his will-o'-the-wisp companions were still with him. They bobbed behind him, three impish lights with wings and tiny bodies that Leofric swore were shaped like miniature knights.

'What are these things?' asked Leofric, pointing behind him and then up at the shoal of lights above them.

'Spites,' said Kyarno. 'Magical spirits of the forest that are as much a part of Athel Loren as the trees themselves.'

'Can you make them go away?'

'Not if they've taken a liking to you, no. They are mischievous creatures, but mostly harmless.'

'*Mostly* harmless?'

'Yes, mostly. Like the birds of the air and the beasts of the earth, there are many kinds of spite. Some are harmless, some are not.'

'What about these ones?' asked Leofric, pointing at the spites bobbing after him.

'Mostly harmless,' repeated Kyarno. Leofric glanced warily behind him as they rode through a woven arch of leaves and branches, hung with gem-encrusted belts of gold and silver. Beyond the archway, Leofric immediately sensed a shift in the temperature.

The air here was as invigorating as that he had breathed earlier, but there was a raw, threatening quality to it, as though it possessed a wilder, more energetic essence.

Kyarno had ridden ahead and Leofric quickly dug his heels into Taschen's flanks to catch up with his guide, not wanting to become separated in this darker part of the forest.

The forest itself seemed more alive here, and Leofric shivered, sensing a darker presence lurking in the depths of the wood, a brooding sentience that looked upon him with eyes that were far from friendly.

Kyarno rode along a wide but overgrown path that Leofric would never have noticed had he not been following the elf, its subtle outline blending perfectly with the forest. Leofric began to see how skilfully the forest's shifting patterns could mislead a person, and remembered tales of those who claimed to have become hopelessly lost within the forest despite many a distinctive landmark. Nothing in this place was as it seemed and Leofric knew he would need to be on his guard lest the glamours of the forest beguile him once more with their confusions.

'You still haven't told me where we are going,' said Leofric as he rode up alongside Kyarno. 'What is the Crystal Mere?'

Kyarno brushed a strand of hair from his face and said, 'It is a pool of the clearest water at the foot of a waterfall on the river you know as the Brienne. The water there is so clear and refreshing it is as though it is wept from the eyes of Isha herself.'

'And who is Isha?'

'You humans are ignorant creatures,' said Kyarno, shaking his head. 'No wonder all you can do is take axes to the trees and clear your lands of all that is green and living, grubbing in muddy fields with your bare hands.'

'Why must you always attempt to antagonise me so?' asked Leofric. 'If you wish to fight then give me a weapon and I will fight you in an honourable duel.'

'Fight you?' said Kyarno. 'No, human, I cannot fight you. Lord Aldaeld has placed you in my care and I will see to your protection, but understand this – you are my enemy.'

'Very well,' said Leofric angrily, 'though tell me why I should be your enemy. I have done you no wrong.'

Kyarno rounded on Leofric and said, 'We are enemies because your kind would take what I hold dear and tear it down if you could. Throughout the centuries we have fought to protect our realm from humans, dwarfs, orcs and beastmen who come with axes and fires to slaughter my kin!'

'No…' said Leofric. 'We do not–'

'Yes,' interrupted Kyarno, visibly struggling with his anger. 'You do. You fear us, yet secretly you envy us, and because you fear us you would destroy us.'

Leofric fought for calm and hissed, 'Perhaps there is truth in what you say, Kyarno, but it was your forest that took my wife. It was your forest that snatched away my ancestor all those years ago. I have as much reason to hate your kind as anyone!'

'The forest took your wife?' asked Kyarno, halting his steed with a whispered word.

'Aye,' said Leofric, masking his sorrow with anger. 'Creatures of branch and thorn, with faces of wicked crones, attacked us and took her from me.'

Kyarno turned his steed until he was facing Leofric directly, a measure of understanding now in his eyes. He bowed his head briefly and said, 'The dryads of winter. They are capricious beings and often take great offence where none is intended. Spiteful things they are, and best avoided. I am sorry for your loss, but it changes nothing.'

'Then let us not speak of it,' said Leofric sadly, changing the subject. 'Tell me of this Isha.'

At first, Leofric thought that Kyarno wasn't going to answer as he turned his steed and carried on riding, but eventually the elf said, 'Why should I speak of her? You humans could never understand what she is to my people.'

'Because I want to know,' said Leofric. 'Perhaps if we understand one another better we might not be enemies.'

'I do not think so, human, but I will indulge you for now,' said Kyarno, adopting a tone Leofric recognised as that of a taleteller. 'Isha is the ancestral goddess of the asrai, the mother of the earth and source of all things. The spirit of Isha pervades the soil of the earth and brings forth the water welling up from the ground. She provides the bounty and life upon which we all depend. She is the breath of warmth on the last of the winter winds and the sigh of life in the first shoots of spring.'

'And she is the god of the elves?'

'One of them,' nodded Kyarno. 'Together with Kurnous and Loec, we honour the gods of earth and life above all others. This forest is sacred to Isha and is potent with her magic.'

Leofric stared with rapt fascination at the forest around him, its fierce beauty beyond anything he had ever seen before, easily able to imagine that the power of an ancient elven goddess gave it such splendour.

'Does Isha have a temple?' asked Leofric. 'It must be a place of some magnificence.'

Kyarno laughed and said, 'How like a human.'

'What is?' sighed Leofric, awaiting Kyarno's next barb.

'Imagining that you would build a temple of walls to enclose a goddess whose very soul is in the wilderness and yearns for the passions of nature,' said Kyarno, raising his hands and spreading them to the heavens. 'Human, you are within her temple even now. The trees and grasses are her places of worship, the ground we ride upon sacred to her.'

'Oh,' said Leofric, looking down at the ground with new eyes.

In truth, the notion of sacred earth was not alien to Leofric, who had seen several groves and pools where the Lady of the Lake had appeared to courageous knights, and which those knights who had supped from the grail were pledged to defend with their lives. Such places were holy indeed and Leofric had felt a sensation akin to what he felt in this forest of unearthly beauty.

They rode in silence for what seemed like an hour or so. The wild wood around Leofric was alive with whispers and sounds of faraway voices. The temperature remained chill and the knight shivered, wishing he had a cloak of some kind to warm him. Kyarno appeared unwilling to talk and Leofric had no real desire to break the silence, weary of the elf's antagonism.

Though the forest around him had become a darker, gloomier place, there was still the touch of magic on the breeze and Leofric could feel it in every breath he took. What might the magic of the forest do to him were he to spend much more time here? What changes might be wrought upon him by this place, which was plainly steeped in the fey power of enchantment?

As he considered this, he became aware of a prickling sensation on the back of his neck, an instinctive warning of danger. He shook himself from his reverie and looked around, alert for possible danger.

He saw that Kyarno was similarly alert and asked, 'What is it?'

Kyarno silenced him with a gesture, placing his finger against his lips and shaking his head. Leofric's warrior instinct spoke to him of approaching danger and his hand unconsciously strayed to his side before he realised he was unarmed.

He scanned the undergrowth, gripping Taschen's reins tightly and letting his eyes drift over the forest. Dimly he could hear a rustling, thumping sound that he recognised as hoof beats and he looked to Kyarno, who circled his horse and gripped the hilt of his own sword.

A nameless dread settled upon Leofric, though he could still see nothing of the approaching horsemen. Hot fear settled in his gut and he fought the urge to rake back his heels and ride from this place. He remembered the last time he had felt such fear, watching the thunderous charge of the Swords of Chaos coming towards him with the Lord of the End Times at their head.

The sound of approaching riders grew louder and Leofric rubbed Taschen's neck, whispering soothing words as the beast pranced nervously, also sensing the palpable tension in the air.

Leofric saw shapes moving in the periphery of his vision, catching fleeting glimpses of dark riders atop great elven steeds. A single, rising note of a hunting horn sounded, wild and exultant, and Taschen whinnied in fear.

Leofric shared that fear, feeling as helpless as a cornered stag awaiting the hunter's lance.

'Do nothing,' warned Kyarno. 'Say nothing.'

'Who are they?'

'The Wild Riders of Kurnous…' said Kyarno as the riders emerged from the trees like ghosts, a pall of fear travelling before them like a shadow.

Tall they were, and strong: six elves mounted on powerful steeds cloaked with hoar frost, with eyes that shone with an inner fire. Each rider wore a shaggy bearskin cloak the colour of the blood-red sun, and their bare flesh was tattooed and scarred with spirals and blood. Bleached skulls hung from their belts and torques of dark metal banded their arms. Tall helms of bronze with engraved cheek plates and long, curling horns like a stag's covered most of their faces, but Leofric could see pale eyes, as cold as chips of ice, but afire with something magical and terrible. They carried tall spears of silver, looped with coils of thorns and feathers, and tipped with lethally sharp iron blades.

Barbaric and feral, these elves looked more akin to the savage Norse than any of the elves Leofric had thus far seen. A savage death-lust radiated from every one.

'You bring a human into Athel Loren?' said one of the riders, his voice cold, threatening and unnatural.

'We could smell him for miles around,' added another.

'We will kill him,' said a third, drawing a long dagger from a leather sheath at his hip. Leofric looked at Kyarno and was surprised by the tension he saw in the youthful elf's face. He returned his gaze to the wild riders, the power and presence of these elves sending a thrill of fear coursing through his veins.

Another of the wild riders walked his horse forwards, lowering his spear as he spoke. 'It is not permitted for you to be here, human. You travel near the King's Glade.'

As one, the remaining wild riders lowered their spears and closed in on Leofric.

'No,' said Kyarno, sidestepping his horse to put himself between Leofric and the wild riders.

'No?' hissed one of the wild riders. 'You defy us?'

'To defy the wishes of those who serve the King of the Wood is to die,' said the wild rider who had first spoken. Looking at him, Leofric sensed a fearsome, ancient power. The rider's features were cold and emotionless, and he knew that these elves would kill him without a second thought.

'This human is under my protection,' shouted Kyarno, whipping his bow from his back and nocking an arrow in one swift motion.

The wild rider looked quizzically at the arrow in Kyarno's bow and said, 'You cannot fight the wild riders of Kurnous. My warriors would kill you in a heartbeat.'

'Maybe,' agreed Kyarno, 'but I'd put this arrow through your eye before that happened.'

'Why would you raise arms against the servants of Orion for a human?'

Kyarno did not answer immediately, and Leofric wondered if the elf was now going to give him up to these savage elves, whose spear tips were getting uncomfortably close to his unarmoured body.

'I am Kyarno Daelanu and I have been entrusted with his care. I have sworn an oath that this human will come to no harm.'

'An oath to whom?' demanded the wild rider. 'What kinband do you serve?'

'That of Aldaeld Éadaoin, Lord of a Hundred Battles and steward of this domain.'

'And he wishes this human to live?'

'For now,' nodded Kyarno in a tone that reassured Leofric not at all.

'Where do you take him?'

'To the Crystal Mere,' explained Kyarno. 'To wash as much of the filth from his body as the waters are able.'

The wild rider nodded, putting up his spear. 'The forest warns us of danger, the touch of evil is upon it.'

'Mayhap this human is not the cause of it after all,' said another.

The leader of the wild riders nodded, though his eyes of cold fire never left Leofric.

'A taint is on the land, darkness comes and the king is gone from us until the vernal equinox. There is evil abroad in the forest this day, Kyarno Daelanu of the Éadaoin kinband. Keep your bow and sword ready, Athel Loren may have need of it 'ere the sun sets.'

'I will,' promised Kyarno, lowering his bow and easing the string.

The wild rider turned his horse and without a word being spoken, the rest of the riders set off after him, disappearing into the forest in eerie silence.

Leofric let out a huge shuddering breath as the dread presence of the wild riders faded into memory. Kyarno slung his bow, leaning over his horse's neck and patting it softly as he too let out a breath of pent-up fear.

When he was sure the riders had passed beyond earshot, Leofric asked, 'What were they? I have never seen the like.'

'They are the king's guard,' said Kyarno. 'The wild huntsmen who ride alongside Kurnous when he awakens in spring and who guard his sacred places while he slumbers.'

'The wild hunt...' breathed Leofric, remembering nights when the horn of the hunter echoed through his lands and the exultant howls and cries of the terrifying charge of the wild hunt tore through the countryside.

Nights when only the foolhardy or desperate dared venture out, and both peasant and nobleman offered prayers to the Lady that the wild hunt would pass them by.

These were fearful times of dread, when the long watches of the night echoed to the howls of hunting beasts and the timbers and roofs of the towns shook to the thunder of flaming hooves that beat on the storm-wracked skies. Come the morn, a trail of devastation marked its passage, bodies gathered into the storm of the hunt, torn to shreds and let fly to drop many miles from where they had been taken.

'Yes,' agreed Kyarno, and Leofric was surprised to hear a tremor of fear in his voice. He had not considered the possibility that the elves of the forest might fear the awakening of their king as much as the human inhabitants of the lands nearby.

'Come,' said Kyarno, 'we should be on our way before they change their mind and return for you.'

'Might they do that?'

'Indeed they might. You heard what their leader said. There is something evil abroad in the forest this day and if they do not find it soon, their lust for battle may bring them back to you.'

Leofric nodded, casting nervous glances around him for fear that the wild riders might already be surrounding them. He had no wish to lay eyes on these savage warriors again and knew that, but for Kyarno's words, he would now be spitted on a spear point, his blood soaking the grass at his feet.

'Thank you for speaking for me,' said Leofric. 'I think I would be dead now but for your words.'

'I did not speak for you, human,' said Kyarno. 'I spoke for me. Lord Aldaeld would have my head on a lance if I had let the wild riders slay you.'

'Well, I thank you anyway,' said Leofric. 'You saved my life and I will not forget that.'

Kyarno nodded curtly and urged his mount onwards, Leofric following swiftly behind him, and they rode at a swifter pace through the unseen paths of the forest towards their destination.

Eventually, Leofric could hear the sound of rushing water from ahead and felt a curious lightness touch him, as though even drawing near the Crystal Mere placed a soothing balm upon his soul. The roar of the falling water had a musical quality to it, like the chime of an exquisite crystal goblet.

The trees thinned ahead and he could make out a fine white spray, the rippling reflections of light fracturing on a large body of water.

'The Crystal Mere,' said Kyarno proudly.

Leofric rode into the glade and his breath was snatched away by the ethereal beauty laid out before him.

CHAPTER SIX

Kyarno had described the Crystal Mere as something natural, in terms Leofric would understand, but he saw now that the description did not do this incredible place justice. A rock-sided pool filled the wide glade, with a gracefully curved beach of pure white sand opposite a tumbling waterfall of water so pure its sheen was like that of a mirror.

The elf had compared the falls to the tears of Isha and though Leofric had only the vaguest understanding of this elven god, he knew that her sorrow must be sublime indeed to weep such wondrous tears. White water foamed at the base of the waterfall, tumbling a hundred feet or more from the rocky, moss-covered slabs above. Water plummeted in billowing clouds to strike a knife-edged wedge of rock that hurled it back into the air, diffusing multiple rainbows of dazzling colour throughout the glade.

The sun was almost directly overhead, dappling the soft, sweet-scented grass in velvet light and the chill Leofric had felt in the dark of the forest vanished, the fine mist of water imbuing the air with a pleasant coolness.

Wild and vivid flowers of red and yellow blossomed at the edge of the glade, filling it with an incredible perfume that soothed Leofric's troubled heart and gave him a sense of tranquillity that was beyond words. Brightly plumed birds nested in the trees and the ever-present spites darted swiftly between the trunks, chasing each other in the shallows of the pool or cavorting in the waterfall's spume.

'It's incredible…' breathed Leofric, drinking in the unearthly beauty of the scene.

'It's pretty, yes,' agreed Kyarno, gracefully dismounting, while Leofric clambered from his saddle.

'Pretty? This place is beyond such a poor word,' said Leofric, dropping to his knees and clasping his hands to his face in prayer. 'Its beauty makes my heart ache.'

Kyarno released his horse, slapping its rump and setting it loose in the wondrous glade. The elf bounded atop a low collection of rocks at the water's edge and said, 'It's just a glade. A pretty one to be sure, but just a glade.'

Leofric shook his head, unable to comprehend how Kyarno could so blithely dismiss such incredible beauty and wonder. The clearing seethed with life and richness of colour, so much so that Leofric felt tears of joy coursing down his cheeks as he wandered like a blind man who had suddenly regained his sight.

Fruits of incredible colours hung from the branches of the nearest trees and Leofric suddenly realised how hungry he was as he caught their intoxicating scent – bitter and rich, but with a strangely sweet aroma.

'What are these?' asked Leofric.

'They are called aoilym fruit,' replied Kyarno with a smile, reclining back onto the rocks and rolling onto his side. 'Try one, they are deliciously sweet.'

Leofric reached out to pluck a scarlet, pear-like fruit, but pulled his hand back at the last second, remembering tales of faerie food and its effects on humans. From the earliest age, children of Quenelles and Carcassonne were taught never to accept food or wine from fey strangers. Bretonnian lore was replete with ballads of those unfortunates who had drunk faerie wines or eaten faerie food and been driven mad with all manner of bizarre and hallucinogenic experiences.

Leofric withdrew his hand from the pungent fruit and said, 'No, I don't think I will after all.'

'Your loss,' said Kyarno, lying back on the rock and pillowing his head on his arms. 'It is a feast beyond anything you will have tasted before, human.'

'Perhaps,' said Leofric, returning to the edge of the water. 'But that is a chance I am willing to take.'

'Well, go on then,' said Kyarno, as Leofric continued to stare in wonderment around the glade.

'What?' asked Leofric, startled from his reverie.

'You were brought here to get cleaned up,' said Kyarno, pointing to the sparkling waters of the Crystal Mere, 'so get cleaned up.'

Leofric nodded, eager to bathe in the water. An ache flared in his heart as he thought of how much Helene would have been enchanted by this place, though, shamefully, the ache was more bearable than it had previously been.

As Kyarno lounged on the rocks with a bored expression on his face,

Leofric stripped off his shirt, britches and boots, leaving them folded on the soft grass at the edge of the pale beach. Normally, Leofric would have felt incredibly self-conscious stripping naked before a stranger, but such notions of modesty seemed ridiculous in this place.

He descended to the beach, letting out a sigh of pleasure as the soft sand eased between his toes, like the deepest, most luxuriant rug. He wiggled his toes in the sand, smiling as a warm, relaxing sensation eased its way up his legs.

Leofric stared at the pool before him, able to see its sandy bottom, and already wet from the foaming water misting the air from the waterfall. The crystalline waters rippled with life and light, looping sprays of sparkling water spites playing in the shallows.

'Is it safe to bathe with those spites in there?' asked Leofric.

'They won't bite. Nip, maybe, but this is a place of healing and rest,' sighed Kyarno. 'You are safe here.'

Though the forest tore at them and flocks of black-winged birds swooped and dived above them, the roaring centaur creatures did not slow their charge. Powerful muscles, swollen by the breath of the gods, drove them onwards and kept them strong, the intoxicating brew in their wineskins keeping their courage high in the face of the creatures that assailed them.

Branches whipped them, fanged, darting lights befuddled their senses, but ever onwards they charged, guided by an image that burned with an all-consuming clarity in their minds.

One beast was brought low, slashing roots scything its legs out from under it in a flurry of leaves and mud. It crashed down with a mighty roar, its legs flailing as it skidded to a halt. The beast bellowed in pain, the gleam of bone jutting from torn flesh where its back legs had been broken. Ravening spites swarmed from the undergrowth, ripping and tearing and biting as the monster's blood ran in thick rivulets into the ground.

Its companions did not stop to come to its aid or even acknowledge that it had had been caught by the vengeful spirits of the forest. Thrashing bursts of light obscured its form and its roars of pain were muffled and gurgling as it died.

The remaining beasts continued onwards, leaping grasping roots and lashing branches as the forest fought to halt the progress of these bestial intruders, carrying words of warning through the root networks of the trees, the leaves that waved in the air and in the cries of the beasts and spirits of Athel Loren.

The forest closed in around them, pathways shifting and reshaping themselves, but such was the speed of the charge that the monsters outpaced the forest's enchantments and hurtled onwards.

Their nostrils burned with the scent of the choicest meat.

Human flesh.

* * *

The water was chill, having its origin high in the Grey Mountains, and as he waded deeper into the Crystal Mere its touch felt like cold silk wrapping around his limbs. As the water rose, Leofric felt a pleasant lethargy suffuse his limbs and took a deep, cleansing breath as he lowered himself.

'This water is incredible,' he whispered as it slipped and slid around his flesh, flowing like a living thing, the glittering spites that flitted like underwater fireflies spinning around him with ticklish bursts of speed.

Immediately the pain in his hip lessened and the ache in his head vanished like morning mist as the water rose to his neck. He spread his arms, enjoying the bracing cold of the water and the susurration of spites around his flesh, strangely untroubled by the darting creatures below the surface. Holding his breath, Leofric ducked his head under the water, and swam towards the churning mass of foaming water that marked the base of the waterfall.

The floor of the pool was of the same pale sand that marked the beach, shaped like a gentle bowl and dotted with gently waving fronds. Glittering crystals drifted across the base of the pool and sparkled in the streaks of sunbeams. Sand and water foamed ahead and Leofric swam with powerful strokes towards the mass of bubbles, feeling fresh vigour course through his body with every second.

He surfaced within the deafening torrent of falling water, closing his eyes against the thunderous spray. Water hammered his shoulders, massaging the tension from his body and easing his muscles with its power.

Leofric lowered his head, taking a fleeting breath as the sound of musical laughter drifted through the air, hazy and indistinct over the roaring water. Within the crystal waterfall Leofric could hear little but the impact of the falling water, and had only the vaguest impression of shifting white shapes as they slid gracefully through his field of vision.

He leaned his head back, relishing the incredibly invigorating sensation as he felt years fall from him and the waters cleansed away the dirt and pain of the last few days. Leofric felt a detached quality descend upon him, the rhythmic sound of the waterfall lulling him into a fugue-like state.

He pictured Helene's face, the image of her blonde hair and soft eyes leaping unbidden to his mind, and he smiled as he remembered her sweet laughter, feeling her loss as something less harsh. Instead of the ache that filled his soul with despair, a sense of warmth and gratitude swept through him as he knew he was incredibly lucky to have had any time with Helene at all. This world stood on the brink of falling to Chaos and to have snatched any such happiness was a victory.

He smiled as he heard her laughter in the sound of the waterfall, seeing her pale face in the patterns formed in the spray, a nimbus of soft light playing about her almond eyes and blonde tresses. A dreamlike smile touched him as he realised she had come back to him, her love for him reaching beyond the veil of death.

Nor had she come alone, he saw, as a host of similarly beautiful women ghosted through the misting water, naked and with expressions of faint amusement. He wanted to feel the touch of Helene's ivory skin and reached out to her, trailing his eyes along the soft curves of her shoulders and the fullness of her breasts.

'Helene...' he whispered, but the woman before him shook her head, and Leofric saw that Helene's companions had spread out to surround him. Their slender arms reached out and touched his broad shoulders and muscled arms, stroking them with an unfamiliar hesitancy.

Their touch was light, but intense, as though his every nerve ending were suddenly drawn to the surface of his skin. Hands stroked his chest, running along the nape of his neck and through his dark, soaking hair. Laughter filled the air and he laughed along with it, the magical sensation of her nearness filling him with light and joy.

The woman before him drew nearer, gliding through the foaming spray of the waterfall without a single lock of her hair displaced by the torrent. She smiled and Leofric's heart broke as he finally saw that this was not Helene at all, but some sylvan nymph with eyes of gold and ringlets of hair the colour of ripened corn. Her features were beautiful, ethereal and haunting beyond anything Leofric had ever imagined. The water played over her alabaster skin, the rivulets speckled with light as they trickled down her naked body.

The others were as varied as any other group of elves he had seen, with hair colours varying from flame-red to midnight-black and features with a subtlety of difference that was beguiling and unearthly at the same time.

'Who are you?' he managed at last.

They laughed at him and though he sensed an edge of condescension to it, a wave of desire washed through him.

As they circled him they sang in the silken tones of their native tongue, musical language spinning through his head and enchanting him with its beauty.

He felt their hands upon him, touching, stroking and though he knew it was wrong, he did not want it to stop, the idea of betrayal pushed from his mind by the exquisiteness of sensation coursing through him at the touch of these beautiful women.

All was peace and beauty in Leofric's mind when a discordant, jagged sound intruded on his bliss – a shouting voice and splashes of noise. The women scattered with squeals of false terror and Leofric's eyes suddenly snapped back into focus as an armoured gauntlet reached through the falling water and grabbed him by the scruff of the neck.

'What–' was all he could manage before he was hauled unceremoniously from beneath the waterfall. A powerful grip had him fast, and as he shook off the last of the dreamlike fatigue that had enveloped him,

Leofric looked up to see the furious face of Cairbre as he was frogmarched from the water.

The women swam in gracefully lazy circles around them, their hair like great coloured slicks on the surface of the clear water as they pointed and laughed at him.

'Wait!' shouted Leofric, between mouthfuls of water.

Cairbre unleashed a torrent of elvish at him, which, though he knew not what was being said, left him in no doubt as to the mood of the cold-eyed warrior. He splashed and stumbled into the shallows of the pool, suddenly very conscious of his nakedness as the elven women continued to laugh and gawp at him like buyers at a horse fair.

Shame and anger burned hot in Leofric's breast as he saw that these women looked upon him as nothing more than a plaything for their amusement or some sort of savage curio. Cairbre shoved him forward to land in an ungainly heap on the pale sand of the beach.

He heard the whinny of horses and turned to see six grey-cloaked elven riders, their armour and twin-bladed spears brilliant in the sunshine. Thankfully, these were not the wild riders he and Kyarno had encountered earlier that day, but appeared to be the same as those he had seen in Coeth-Mara when he had first awoken. One rider carried a silver banner set with gemstones and fluttering azure blossoms. Kyarno's steed nuzzled one of the newcomers' horses, while Leofric's horse grazed on the rich grass at the edge of the glade.

'Get up!' stormed Cairbre. 'You dare to molest the handmaidens of Lady Morvhen Éadaoin! You are nothing but a base animal, human.'

'Molest? What? No!' coughed Leofric, rolling onto his back and spitting water.

'Then what was it you were doing in there?' shouted Cairbre. 'And get some clothes on! Your hairy body is unsightly to me.'

Leofric pushed himself to his knees and said, 'I was doing what was asked of me. Kyarno brought me here to bathe and clean myself. That's what I was doing when these women came to me. Then you dragged me out here.'

'Morvhen…' said Cairbre angrily, his eyes scanning the glade for something or someone he could not see. 'He must have sent word to her somehow. I knew it.'

'Knew what?' asked Leofric as he reached over to lift his clothes, feeling the warm sunlight swiftly drying his skin. Cairbre marched onto the grassy bank surrounding the waters of the Crystal Mere, his anger a terrible thing to behold.

'Loec's spite! A curse upon that boy!' snapped Cairbre, rounding on Leofric, and unsheathing his twin-bladed spear. 'Where is my nephew?'

'Who?' asked Leofric, nonplussed.

'Kyarno!' roared Cairbre. 'Where is Kyarno?'

Leofric looked around the glade for his surly travelling companion.

But Kyarno was nowhere to be seen.

'Eternal Guard!' shouted Cairbre. 'With me!'

Kyarno laughed as he and Morvhen ran hand in hand through the twilight beneath the trees, overjoyed that she had received his message to meet him here. Her dress billowed like a great crimson sail, though Kyarno had only ever imagined what an ocean-going vessel might look like.

Her face was alive with the illicit thrill of this tryst and Kyarno felt fierce joy as she let out an exultant, whooping yell like a battle cry.

He was sure to be disciplined by Lord Aldaeld for this, but did not much care any more. He had suffered too many punishments at the hands of Morvhen's father for one more to matter.

And looking at Morvhen's finely sculpted features, the sweeping cheekbones, the chestnut hair, the sparkling eyes and the seductive mouth, Kyarno knew she was worth all the torments that Lord Aldaeld might heap upon him.

Eventually they stopped running, chests heaving and breath hot in their lungs as they circled one another with lustful eyes.

'You got my message then?' chuckled Kyarno.

'Indeed I did,' smiled Morvhen, glancing over her shoulder for any signs of pursuit from the Eternal Guard. 'You are a bad influence on me, Kyarno Daelanu.'

'I know,' nodded Kyarno. 'But that is why you like me.'

'True, but I cannot tarry long. Cairbre will notice I am gone soon and he was suspicious enough on the way here.'

'How did you get away from him?'

Morvhen giggled with wicked glee and said, 'I sent my handmaids into the water to cavort with the human. Cairbre and the others were so mortified that they did not notice me slip into the woods. I can be quite stealthy when the mood suits me, you know.'

'You let your handmaids get into the water with a human?' said Kyarno, aghast.

'Of course! I think they quite enjoyed the opportunity to have a look at one up close,' replied Morvhen. 'For all their graceless thickness of limb, there is a certain savage vitality to humans.'

'They are brutish oafs with all the poise of a wounded bear.'

'A particularly clumsy bear,' added Morvhen, leaning back on the tilted bole of a weeping willow and beckoning Kyarno to come closer with an impish smile.

'A wounded, clumsy and blind bear,' finished Kyarno, leaning in and kissing her as her arms slid around his neck and pulled him into her.

Leofric pulled up his britches, averting his gaze from the beautiful elf maids swimming leisurely in the Crystal Mere and trying to shut out their beautiful, but mocking laughter. The warriors on horseback showed no such compunction, openly watching the naked women as though it were the most natural thing in the world. Perhaps for them it was, mused Leofric, wondering again at the alien ways of these woodland folk.

Though he knew he had been little more than a plaything to the women, he felt soothed, as though their touch had imparted some serene acceptance to him.

He saw again Helene's face, but this time the sense of love and wonder she had given him far outweighed the pain of her loss. More than ever he was resolved to leave this place, though how that might be achieved was sure to be problematic. Those held in the realm of the elves did not return unchanged, if they were able to return at all.

Leofric remembered the tale of Duke Melmon, a knight who ruled the Dukedom of Quenelles in the year three hundred and fifty-eight, who was said to have vanished on a night when the wild hunt stormed the skies. The mystery of his disappearance was never solved, though Leofric remembered when he was but a child, the stooped elders of Quenelles once speaking of a knight who was said to have emerged from Athel Loren in the time of their great grandfathers, who presented himself at the doors of the duke's castle. This knight had been brought before the court of the current duke where he had claimed to be none other than Duke Melmon himself, lost these last thousand years.

Of course, the court had scoffed at such a claim, but upon finishing his tale the knight had supposedly crumbled to naught but dust and ashes before their very eyes. Leofric had never really believed the tale of Duke Melmon, thinking it to be no more than the fanciful tale spun by old men who wanted to scare a little boy.

Now, he wasn't so sure, but he had a son to raise, lands to defend and a king to serve – and a knight of Bretonnia did not shirk such duties while he still drew breath and his sword arm was strong.

He ran his hands through his dark hair, feeling more refreshed than he had done for as long as he could remember. The rigours of war and a life of dedication to land and king was a demanding one and took its toll, but here, Leofric felt as though he could defeat almost any foe.

Almost any foe, he reminded himself, again seeing the horror of the battle against the Swords of Chaos and the daemons of the northern tribes. Could anything stand against such warriors, he wondered? When the power of the Dark Gods waxed strong the lands of men were ravaged by war and blood, and each time brought the final victory of Chaos closer.

Trying to banish such melancholy thoughts, he took another breath of the honeysuckle-scented air and awaited the return of Cairbre.

The warrior had ridden off into the forest to search for Kyarno with two of his warriors – the Eternal Guard, presumed Leofric – leaving the remaining four to watch over the elven maids. Elven curses that were no less vile for the beauty of the language had spat from his mouth as he damned his nephew.

Leofric had not noticed the familial resemblance before, but once revealed, it was patently obvious: both elves shared the same confident poise and had the same cruel, warrior features.

Leofric pulled on his overshirt and removed the silk scarf from the pocket, twining the smooth material around his fingers as he knelt on the moist grass.

He closed his eyes and offered a short prayer to the Lady of the Lake, entreating her to guide the spirit of his wife to its final rest. Tears coursed down his cheeks, but they were not shed in bitterness, but fond remembrance.

'Why do you weep?' asked a lilting female voice as he finished his prayers.

Leofric started in surprise, not having heard the elven woman approach. He tucked Helene's scarf back into his pocket and turned to address her, blushing as he saw she was completely naked, water running from her willowy body in glistening droplets.

'I... uh... that is,' stammered Leofric, turning away as the elf circled around to stand before him once again, her head tilted coquettishly to one side and a curious, confused look in her eye.

'Why do you not look at me?' asked the elf. 'Am I not beautiful?'

'Yes, yes you are,' confirmed Leofric, keeping his eyes cast down. 'You are indeed beautiful, but it would be wrong of me to see you like this.'

'Like what?' said the elf, reaching out and lifting his head.

'Without clothes,' finished Leofric, drinking in the vision of grace and beauty before him.

The elven woman tilted her head, puzzled by his answer and spun gracefully before him, 'What is wrong with that? Beauty is a precious thing and should be savoured at all times. You should not deny yourself that pleasure.'

Her body was slender and artfully shaped, though her waist was waspish and too narrow for his tastes. Thick hair the colour of flame hung wetly around her long neck and arched shoulders and her skin was smooth and pale like virgin snow. As she completed her pirouette, oval eyes of a red-gold colour examined him with curious amusement, but no malice, and he kept his gaze firmly locked with hers, lest his eyes stray lower and catch a glimpse of something more libidinous.

'Be that as it may,' said Leofric with embarrassment. 'But it is against my chivalric code to see you thus.'

'You humans are a strange race,' said the elf, shaking her head and sweeping up a diaphanous white gown of a strange, shimmering fabric that slid over her body with the barest shrug of effort. 'Bloodshed and death are second nature to your people, yet the sight of naked flesh leaves you tongue-tied. Baffling.'

Leofric shrugged. 'Yes, it is odd I suppose.'

'Do you have a name, human?'

'Of course I do,' replied Leofric with a deep bow. 'I am Leofric Carrard of Quenelles.'

The elf bowed back to him. 'I am Tiphaine of the Éadaoin kinband, handmaid to Lady Morvhen Éadaoin.'

'It is an honour and a privilege to make your acquaintance,' said Leofric, bowing once more. 'Tell me, is Lady Éadaoin the wife of Lord Aldaeld?'

Tiphaine shook her head. 'No, she is his daughter. A wonderful child, but wilful and drawn to troublemakers.'

'Like Kyarno?' ventured Leofric, nodding towards the reduced numbers of the Eternal Guard.

'Indeed,' agreed Tiphaine. 'Cairbre will not be happy when he finds the lovers.'

Leofric blushed at such frankness, though it explained Cairbre's anger at finding that Kyarno and Morvhen were missing from the glade of the Crystal Mere.

'Is she betrothed to another?' asked Leofric.

'Morvhen? No, she is not, but a wild one like Kyarno does not please her father, who fears he will lead her to ruin.'

'I can see why,' agreed Leofric.

'Truly it is a shame that love choses you rather than the other way round. I knew she was planning to meet with Kyarno and had thought I had dissuaded her, but love is deaf as well as blind it seems.'

'She does not obey the wishes of her father?'

'Sometimes, but she can be capricious and I am only surprised she has not yet sought you out to speak to at length.'

'Me?'

Tiphaine nodded, moving to sit on the rocks at the edge of the pool and stirring it with a languidly circling finger as her fellow handmaids continued to swim and bathe in the spite-rippled water.

'Oh yes, I should imagine she will have many questions for you. Morvhen has an unhealthy thirst for knowledge of that which lies beyond our borders, foolish child.'

'Is it customary for the servants of your lords and ladies to be so forthright about their faults and foibles?' asked Leofric, knowing that he would have had his servants whipped for speaking in such a fashion.

'I say nothing to you that I have not said to her many times before.'

'Oh…' said Leofric, sitting a discreet distance from the beautiful elf woman, watching the warriors of the Eternal Guard glare disapprovingly at him. The sun shone on Tiphaine's hair, making it glow as though afire and the shimmering fabric of her dress did little to conceal her pale flesh.

He looked away as Tiphaine said, 'You still have not told me why you weep in this place of beauty.'

Leofric was silent for long moments, wondering whether to answer or not, but Tiphaine had shown him a kindness he had not experienced thus far in Athel Loren and he was strangely compelled to speak truly.

'My wife is lost to me,' he said at last. 'The spirits of the forest took her. Winter dryads I think they were called, I'm not sure.'

'Ah... now I understand your tears,' said Tiphaine with a wistful smile. 'Well, this is a good place to bring such sorrows, the waters are said to ease the pain of loss and remind us of the wonder of what was once ours. I came here when my brother was killed.'

'I am truly sorry for your loss, my lady.'

Tiphaine nodded in polite acceptance of Leofric's sentiment. 'I thank you, but it was many decades ago and the pain is lessened now by time and the waters of the Crystal Mere.'

'The waters take away the pain?' asked Leofric.

Tiphaine shook her head. 'No, never that, for the pain reminds us of what we have lost and without that, the blessings of the life that has passed are forgotten. And that is the saddest thing of all, Leofric, to forget the joy of life.'

'I feel that more now, though the pain is still there,' said Leofric.

Tiphaine nodded. 'Then your time in Athel Loren has not been misspent.'

Leofric was about to reply when the smile fell from Tiphaine's face and a rustle of thickly-leaved branches shook the treetops, making the brightly patterned birds take to the air with a shrill caw of warning.

Though the sun still filled the glade with its golden light, a shadow passed through it, an elemental cry of warning as the spites in the water flickered into the air with primal hisses of rage.

'What is it?' said Leofric, rising to his feet as the handmaids began swimming to the edge of the pool and the riders of the Eternal Guard readied their spears with angry yells. Tiphaine sprang nimbly to her feet and called to her fellow handmaids as spites spun angrily through the air, flitting into the trees to the south and changing from shapeless glows to jagged, clawed imps with wings of light.

The Eternal Guard rode to the edge of the pool and began shouting in frantic elvish to the women in the water. Leofric's warrior instincts now spoke to him of imminent danger and he shouted over to the Eternal Guard. 'Give me a weapon! I can fight.'

If they understood him, they gave no sign, but continued to hurry the elven women from the water. Leofric felt utterly helpless and ran over to where Tiphaine helped her fellow handmaids from the waters.

He heard a sudden thunder of hoof beats and looked up in time to see one of the Eternal Guard punched from his saddle by a long, crudely-crafted spear hurled from the edge of the glade.

The elf cried out in pain and landed with a splash in the shallows of the pool.

Leofric spun to face the direction from which the spear had come.

Emerging from the trees were five hideous monsters, their brazen roars and twisted, mutated bodies marking them out as creatures of Chaos. Centaur creatures, they were red-furred and horned, their hideous bodies massively muscled and terrible.

With a terrifying, bestial roar, the monsters charged.

CHAPTER SEVEN

The tracks of their passing were easy to follow, the lovers not even bothering to conceal their flight into the forest. Cairbre's anger and frustration grew as he rode deeper into the forest, as did his fear that something terrible was going to happen. The forest had an ill-favoured sense to it this day and his warrior soul responded to its unease.

'Spread out,' he ordered, 'and watch for them circling behind us. I don't want to be away from the Crystal Mere any longer than need be.'

The two mounted warriors that accompanied him nodded and peeled away, eyes scanning the forest for sign of Kyarno and Morvhen, their spears held lightly at their sides.

Cairbre followed tracks that led him a merry dance through the thickly gathered trunks of the trees, his route taking him further and further from the Crystal Mere. Branches and fronds brushed him as he rode, their touch speaking to him of their unease and fear. Something was amiss, and to be abroad in the depths of the forest at such a time was both foolish and dangerous.

He still found it difficult to believe that Kyarno and Morvhen had defied the will of their lord and master once more. Such things were simply unthinkable – to defy the leader of a kinband was to break faith with those appointed guardianship of the forest, and such a thought gave Cairbre cold shivers.

But beyond even that, he was angry with himself for allowing this to happen. He was Lord Aldaeld's champion, the Hound of Winter, and to allow his charges to come to harm would be the gravest failure imaginable. The long centuries hung heavily on Cairbre and the twilight of his life was upon him more than ever.

This would not have happened even a century ago, when the summer sun cast its last rays upon his youth and vigour. He was slowing and knew it. His skill with a blade was unmatched by any save the deadly wardancers, but his strength and stamina were a shadow of what they had once been.

The Hound of Winter would soon no longer be the hunting beast of his master, but the aged companion that lives out its days in comfort by the fire. That time was not yet come, and until it did, Cairbre would serve Lord Aldaeld with all his devotion and love.

And if that meant that he had to throw Kyarno from Coeth-Mara?

The youth had had his fair share of chances and though none could doubt the tragedy that had befallen him as a youngster, there was no excuse for his continued reckless disobedience and disrespect.

The trees thinned and Cairbre halted his horse as he came to a leafy glade with white blossoms and shifting branches. Cackling faces creaked in the depths of the gnarled wood and the desperately alluring scent of honey drifted on the light breeze. He turned his horse away as the thorn bushes crackled and moved, dark shapes within them shaking the branches in frustration as he rode away.

Cairbre knew the lovers would not have come this way, the malicious spites of this part of the forest serving to divert them from such a course. Leaving the treacherously scented glade, he rode back along the overgrown path, now seeing the carefully disguised tracks that looped back on the ones he had been following.

So their flight had not been as frantic and reckless as they would have him believe...

Kyarno might be wild, but he had a fine grasp of the hunter's skills.

But the Hound of Winter had hunted the enemies of the asrai long before Kyarno had been born and, though he may be getting long in the tooth, he had lost none of the fearsome skills that had seen him honoured as Lord Aldaeld's champion.

And his title of the Hound of Winter was well earned.

He rode swiftly but silently through the woods, weaving between the trees and closing on a gathering of gently bobbing spites that circled in the high branches of the trees in the distance. Spites were curious, flighty spirits and were easily attracted to new things, and Cairbre hoped that they might yet lead him to Kyarno and Morvhen.

Laughter drifted to him and his jaw clenched as he recognised his nephew's voice. Morvhen's voice joined Kyarno's, and there was no mistaking the tone as that reserved for lovers and those who had shared their bodies with one another.

Cairbre slid from the back of his steed and spun the Blades of Midnight in a tight circle, loosening the muscles of his shoulders and forearms as he closed on the sounds of the voices.

He reached the edge of another glade, moving as silently and stealthily as he was able, glancing up at the voyeuristic spites to make sure they would not give his approach away. Through the grass and obscuring branches he could see Kyarno and Morvhen lying naked on a bed of leaves and grass, enfolded in one another's arms. He looked away, relieved that they were safe, but angry at the wilful defiance they had both shown.

Parting the branches with the Blades of Midnight, Cairbre strode into the clearing and said, 'Get dressed, both of you. We are going back to the Crystal Mere.'

Kyarno leapt to his feet, reaching for his bow, but relaxed as he saw who had discovered them.

'Uncle,' said Kyarno. 'You appear with monotonous regularity when I least wish you to.'

Cairbre said nothing, simply stepping forward and backhanding his nephew hard enough across the jaw to draw blood.

'You are a disgrace to your kin, Kyarno,' hissed Cairbre. 'You insult your lord, you dishonour me and you dishonour yourself.'

Kyarno wiped the trickle of red from his chin and spat a mouthful of blood, his eyes full of controlled anger. Without a word, he set aside his bow and turned to pull on his clothes. Cairbre turned to Morvhen, his eyes averted as she too slipped into her clothing.

'My lady, I am disappointed with you,' he said. 'I suspected you might try and see my nephew, but I had hoped you held me in enough regard not to.'

'I hold you in the highest regard, Hound of Winter, you know that,' said Morvhen.

'Then why do you try me so?' shouted Cairbre, taking hold of her arm and marching her towards his horse. 'I am sworn to protect you, yet you behave like a spoilt child. You dishonour your father with such behaviour.'

'Take your hand from her,' said Kyarno.

Cairbre heard the note of warning in his nephew's tone a fraction too late and turned in time to have Kyarno's fist thunder against his cheek. He stumbled, but quickly righted himself, swinging the haft of the Blades of Midnight around and slamming it into Kyarno's midriff.

His nephew doubled over, winded, and Cairbre brought the haft up sharply, cracking it against his jaw and sending him spinning backwards.

'Know your place, Kyarno,' said Cairbre, turning away.

Morvhen looked fearfully at him and he pulled her towards his horse, anxious to return to his warriors. He heard a cry of anger behind him and spun in time to block a hooking right cross with the haft of his weapon as Kyarno came at him again. He spun the Blades of Midnight, twisting

Kyarno's arm away, and stabbed the blade into the ground between his feet.

Cairbre leapt into the air, twisting around the haft to hammer his boots into Kyarno's chest and fling him across the clearing. He landed lightly as Kyarno rolled to his feet and shouted in frustration, drawing his sword and preparing to charge. Cairbre spread his stance, bringing the Blades of Midnight around to aim at his nephew's heart.

He took a step towards Kyarno then jumped in shock as a long, blue-fletched arrow slashed through the air and hammered into the trunk of a tree, an inch from his head. Another shaft buried itself in the wood beside Kyarno's head and the two combatants were suddenly brought up short.

Morvhen stood beside her lover's steed with Kyarno's recurved bow held horizontally before her, a fresh pair of arrows nocked to the bowstring.

'Both of you put up your weapons!' she yelled. 'Or do I have to put arrows in you to get you to stop this madness?'

'Morvhen, put that bow down,' said Cairbre slowly, seeing the hurt in her eyes.

'Put up your weapons, both of you,' repeated Morvhen and Cairbre could see she meant every word. Slowly he extended a hand towards her, palm-up, and raised the Blades of Midnight until the weapon was upright beside him. Kyarno did the same, taking deep, calming breaths and sheathing his sword once more.

'Morvhen, be careful with that bow,' said Kyarno.

'Yes,' agreed Cairbre. 'Please.'

'Be quiet, both of you!' snapped Morvhen. 'By all the gods of the asrai, I am heartsick of this constant battle between you. Why must you fight? You are kin!'

'He struck me!' shouted Kyarno.

'You struck me first,' pointed out Cairbre.

'Shut up! Isha's mercy, can't you hear yourselves? You are like children squabbling over a bowstave.'

Both Kyarno and Cairbre opened their mouths to argue, but the creak of the tautening bowstring silenced them both.

Morvhen wept bitter tears as she spoke again, 'I hate this constant bickering between you. You pretend to all the world that you are enemies when everyone can see the love and kinship between you. You are bonded by blood and nothing can break that. As much as you might try to.'

Cairbre plucked the arrow from the tree next to his head and said, 'You are right, Morvhen, but that does not alter anything. I have a duty to my lord and must fulfil it. You need to put down that bow and come with me back to the Crystal Mere. You understand that, yes?'

'I want to hear you say that you will stop this incessant feuding,' said

Morvhen, aiming her words as well as her arrows at both Cairbre and Kyarno.

Kyarno nodded and Cairbre could see that, with the surge of anger drained from him, his nephew was deathly worried at what had just happened. True, there was a bond of blood between them, but Kyarno had struck the champion of Lord Aldaeld, and there could be only one punishment for such a blatant attack on the honour of an elven lord.

Cairbre sighed, his duty and honour warring with the call of kith and kin, and he turned from Morvhen to say, 'Kyarno, you are my nephew and I love you dearly, however much you may not want to believe that. You have struck the champion of Lord Aldaeld and you know the penalty for such an attack.'

'Cairbre, no!' cried Morvhen.

'You would take my head with the Blades of Midnight, uncle?' asked Kyarno, trying to sound defiant, but Cairbre could sense the fear of his realisation.

'You know what you have done, Kyarno and were you anyone else, then yes, you would already be dead,' nodded Cairbre, looking beyond Morvhen to see his two Eternal Guard warriors approaching through the forest.

'It is time to leave, Morvhen. Lower the bow.'

Morvhen glanced over her shoulder at the approaching horsemen and nodded, easing the string on the bow and dropping to one knee to slip the arrows back into Kyarno's quiver.

Cairbre turned his back on the Eternal Guard and said, 'Only we three know of this and I see no reason to change that. Clean the blood from your face, Kyarno, and we will say nothing more about this for now.'

'You would do that?' asked Kyarno, obviously surprised.

'I would, but we have much yet to resolve, you and I, so let this be a lesson to you, eh?'

Kyarno nodded warily and retrieved his bow from Morvhen, swiftly cleaning the blood from his face as the two Eternal Guard rode into the clearing.

'I found them,' Cairbre told them needlessly. 'Let's get back to–'

Cairbre's words trailed off as he felt the forest around him cry out in warning, the impending sense of doom he had felt earlier now filling him with dread.

Branch and leaf, earth and water cried out in loathing and Cairbre felt the soul of the land shudder at the touch of something terrible.

Now the growing unease he had felt earlier in the day became clear as the magic of the forest spoke to him of the intruders in its midst.

The creatures of Chaos were upon Athel Loren.

And Cairbre knew exactly where they were going.

Roars and war-cries filled the glade of the Crystal Mere as the beasts charged. Their brazen hooves threw up great clods of earth and grass and the forest itself trembled in rage at such gross trespassers. Leofric felt his limbs as lead weights, unable to move at the sight of such vile, terrible creatures of Chaos.

Memories of the fateful charge into the diabolical ranks of the daemon lord and the horrifying moments of blood and death against the Lord of the End Times flooded him, momentarily rooting him to the spot.

He heard a cry of warning, recognising it as that of Tiphaine, and shook off the torpor that seized him, running to the fallen elf with the beast's spear wedged through his chest. Lady Morvhen's handmaids ran from the water as one of the Eternal Guard began shepherding them towards the edge of the glade and away from the creatures of Chaos. Leofric saw Taschen at the edge of the glade, the beast's eyes wide at the sight and scent of the beasts, but its spirit held it fast and prevented it from fleeing.

With feral, whooping battle cries, the remaining two warriors of the Eternal Guard leaned forward over their horses' necks and charged the thundering, red-skinned monsters. Leofric had seen such beasts before and knew that they would tear the elves from their steeds and feast on their flesh unless the odds were evened.

Leofric splashed into the shallows of the Crystal Mere, through the thickening cloud of blood that fanned from the floating corpse, and reached for the elf's weapon, a long, twin-bladed spear. The weapon was light in his hands and unfamiliar, the fighting style required to wield it effectively unknown to him. He dropped the spear and dragged out the elf's sword, a fine and beautifully forged blade, confident he could spill some enemy blood with this weapon.

'Leofric!' shouted Tiphaine and he turned to see what she was shouting at.

The Eternal Guard and the beastmen smashed into one another, elf-forged iron and jagged-edged obsidian clashing in a flurry of sparks. A flock of ravening spites flew from the forest, transformed from harmless specks of light to snapping, biting imps. One centaur creature fell to the blades of the Eternal Guard, its chest cloven by a blindingly quick slash, its bellow of pain deafening in the once-peaceful glade.

An elven steed reared and lashed out at one of the beastmen, its hooves slashing for its horned head, but instead of quailing before such an attack, the monster lowered its head and lunged forward, hammering its long, curling horns into the steed's belly.

'No!' cried Leofric, loath to see such a fine equine specimen defiled by these monsters. But his denial was in vain as the white steed fell, its innards flooding from its torn flesh. Its rider leapt clear, only to be impaled in mid air by another beast's horns and tossed into the air like a limp and bloody rag.

Leofric staggered from the water and ran towards the handmaids as two of the bellowing creatures broke from the battle with the surviving Eternal Guard. They thundered towards the handmaids and Leofric ran to intercept their course. He could not allow these women to come to any harm; his chivalric code would not permit such an affront. Taschen stamped the ground beside them, the scent of blood provoking his desire to fight, yet needing his rider to enter the fray.

Leofric pushed himself harder as he heard galloping hoof beats behind him. The warrior who guarded the women spun his long spear as his horse reared in defiant challenge to the creatures of Chaos. Leofric continued towards the women, watching in surprise as they retrieved bows from the edge of the clearing. With barely a breath of pause, they pulled on the bowstrings and loosed a hail of arrows towards him.

He cried out as the arrows slashed past him, hearing the hiss of air as some came within a fingerbreadth of him. Grunts and bellows of pain told him that some of the arrows had found homes in the flesh of the beastmen and he spun as he heard the thud of something hitting the earth.

One of the bestial creatures was on its knees, a trio of grey-fletched arrows protruding from its body. Its hideous face, so like a man's, yet so different, was twisted in animal rage as it plucked the feathered shafts from its body. He heard the clash of weapons to one side and knew that battle was joined between the Eternal Guard with the women and the other beastmen. The wounded creature began to pick itself up. He could see the two beastmen behind it trample the body of another elven warrior to death. Spites flickered around the monsters, biting them with spirit fangs and blinding them with glittering magicks. The beasts roared and swatted at their tiny attackers, distracted for the moment, and Leofric knew he had seconds at best.

Trusting the defence of the women to the Eternal Guard, Leofric yelled, 'For Quenelles, the king and the Lady!' and charged the wounded monster with his borrowed sword raised high. It saw him coming and its terrible face twisted in a savage grin, holding its spear before it.

'You die, manskin!' it shouted, and Leofric's surprise almost cost him his life. The beast's spear stabbed towards his belly, but Leofric frantically threw himself out of the way, rolling to his feet and slashing for the beast's neck with his blade.

The monster lowered its head and his sword impacted against one of its horns, hacking clean through the thick, brass-tipped bone. The roaring beastman rocked backwards under the force of the blow and Leofric didn't give it a chance to recover, spinning on his heel and ramming the sword deep into its chest.

He twisted the blade as he drove it hilt-deep into its body, dark blood pumping from the wound as the creature died.

His breath came in hard gulps, the thick reek of strong liquor from the beast making him gag as he wrenched his blade free. He heard more screams and the hiss of arrows, spinning to see the last warrior of the Eternal Guard dragged from his steed and gored repeatedly by the beastman's wickedly sharp horns. Arrows jutted from its shaggy-furred back, but it seemed not to care, hurling the corpse of the warrior it had just killed to the ground and roaring in triumph as the two surviving creatures turned to join it for the kill.

Leofric ran from the dead beastman towards his horse, knowing that he needed to be mounted to fight most effectively. His steed ran towards him and Leofric gripped the saddle and vaulted onto Taschen's back with a wild yell.

Another flurry of arrows slashed towards the nearest beastman, but its thick hide was proof against the elven archery. It roared and Leofric saw the muscles of its back legs bunch as it prepared to wreak bloody havoc amongst the handmaids.

Leofric dug his heels into Taschen's sides and the horse surged forward. 'For the Lady!' shouted Leofric as he surged towards the beast. Its charge altered direction and man and beast thundered towards each other. The centaur creature raised its spear to plunge down into his chest, but Leofric was a veteran of many a joust on the tilting field and swayed aside from its thrust, slashing his sword across its shoulder.

Vile blood sprayed from the wound and the beast roared in anger as the spear dropped from its useless arm and the two combatants rode past one another. Leofric wheeled his horse quickly and struck again at the monster, opening a deep gash across its thickly furred back.

The remaining two beasts charged towards him through a hail of arrows loosed by the handmaids, though they appeared to be largely untroubled by such hurts. Leofric yelled in challenge as the bloodied beast turned to face him once more, lowering its thick horns to gore him.

Leofric raised his sword above him and shouted, 'Come on then, you bastard! Come on and die!'

But before the bestial creature could move, a pair of blue-fletched arrows slashed from the trees and skewered its skull, the barbed arrow-heads bursting from its eyes with a wet thud. With little more than a brutish exhalation, the creature toppled, dead before it hit the ground.

Amazed, Leofric saw Cairbre and two more of the Eternal Guard ride from the trees, the Hound of Winter's twin-bladed spear tucked under one arm as he galloped from the forest. At his heels came Kyarno and a young elven woman with chestnut hair wearing a tight-fitting dress of crimson. His heart lurched at the sight, remembering his last sight of Helene in such a dress. She carried a bow that Leofric recognised as belonging to Kyarno and sent another, wickedly-aimed shaft towards the charging beastmen.

The Eternal Guard rode after their leader as Cairbre charged past Leofric, the Hound of Winter letting loose a feral, ululating yell as his spear came up to spin around his head. The elf rose to stand on the back of his horse, holding his spear two-handed above his head and Leofric yanked on Taschen's reins as he charged after the howling elf.

He shouted wildly, caught up in the thrill of the charge. Cairbre twisted the grip of his spear and Leofric saw the shaft of the weapon split apart to become two long-handled swords.

The venerable elf rode between the two charging centaur beasts, a flurry of screeching spites flying from the folds of his cloak and swarming over his enemies. Cairbre crouched low atop the back of his horse and his flashing blades were streaking blurs of white steel. One centaur crashed to the ground in a pile of thrashing limbs, its head spinning through the air, while the other halted its charge in a spray of earth and grass as it sought to turn to face this new foe and fight off the firefly creatures that clawed its flesh.

Its flanks were exposed and Leofric held his sword out before him, riding hard and slashing its edge through the beast's flesh. It roared and twisted free of the weapon in a froth of blood, its spear stabbing towards him. Leofric brought his sword up to block its powerful thrust, rolling his wrists and stabbing for the beast's throat.

Leofric's blade missed its target as Cairbre leapt from his horse onto the beast's back and it reared wildly in an attempt to throw him.

But incredibly, the Hound of Winter easily kept his balance, ramming his twin swords into the beastman's back. White blades flashed once more and an arcing spray of blood filled the air as Cairbre's swords slashed the monster's throat open. Clawed hands frantically tried to stem the spray of blood, but nothing could halt its demise and the beast collapsed with gurgling grunts of pain.

Cairbre vaulted lightly from the dying beast's body and landed on the back of his own steed, which circled the fallen creature warily. Leofric reined in Taschen and turned to make sure the other monsters were dead.

Relief flooded him as he saw that the handmaids were all safe, their expressions defiant. Tiphaine smiled in gratitude at him and he lowered his sword. The elven woman with the bow ran towards them and Leofric could only assume that this was the Lady Morvhen, seeing the regal cast to her features.

A fierce shout of anger tore the air and Leofric readied his sword once more. He wheeled his horse to face the sound, lowering the weapon as he saw Kyarno hacking at the fallen corpse of the beast Leofric had killed. Kyarno's sword rose and fell, sending blood arcing high into the air as he chopped the foul monster into gory chunks.

The young elf wept as he hacked at the beast's corpse, tears and blood streaking his face as he dropped to his knees. Morvhen ran towards him and he collapsed in her arms, weeping like a newborn babe.

Leofric made to walk his horse towards Kyarno, but a hand gripped the reins and he turned to face Cairbre, who shook his head slowly.

'No,' said the Hound of Winter. 'Leave him be.'

'What is wrong with him?' asked Leofric.

'Nothing that need concern you, human,' replied Cairbre, turning his steed away and riding towards the elven steeds that sadly nuzzled their fallen riders.

'Cairbre!' called Leofric after the Hound of Winter's retreating back.

The champion of the Eternal Guard halted his horse and looked back over his shoulder. 'What?'

'You fight… like no one I have ever seen before.'

Cairbre's expression softened for a moment and he nodded, accepting the compliment, saying, 'You also fought well, human. I will ensure that Lord Aldaeld hears of your bravery defending his daughter's handmaids.'

Leofric said, 'Thank you,' watching as Morvhen helped Kyarno to his feet and led him towards his horse. Singing lilting songs of lament, her handmaids moved slowly through the glade, gathering up the weapons and bodies of the fallen Eternal Guard, lifting them and gently laying them across the backs of their steeds.

Cairbre himself took up the body of the warrior whose steed had been killed and, with eyes cast down, the sad procession left the glade of the Crystal Mere and began the journey back to Coeth-Mara.

BOOK TWO
WINTER'S GREY DESPAIR

'Four came over,
Without boat or ship,
One yellow and white,
One brown abounding with twigs,
One to handle the flail,
And one to strip the trees.'

CHAPTER EIGHT

Coming back to her body was always the hardest part. The reunion of flesh and spirit after travelling the secret paths that linked the realms beyond the senses and the beating heart of the forest was becoming more difficult and dangerous for her each time. Naieth felt a momentary claustrophobia as her spirit fought the confinement of her body, eager to be flying on the currents of magic that saturated Athel Loren.

She recited the names of the elven gods one by one, the ancient primal ones of the land and the newer idols of civilisation and culture embraced by the distant kin of the asrai across the water, forcing her spirit to settle.

As always after journeying through the lines of power that threaded the forest she knew she would be weak, and so lay still, keeping her eyes open to reassure herself that she was indeed back in her body. A hooting caw nearby made her smile and she rolled her head on the soft pillow of leaves.

'I know, Othu,' she said, addressing a grey-feathered owl that perched on a low branch beside her. 'I am getting too old to travel the forest's secret paths.'

The owl hooted again, rolling its eyes and turning its head from her.

'Easy for you to say,' said Naieth, sitting upright with a low moan. 'But I had to see. I had to know for sure.'

Afternoon sunlight dappled this place of branches, gathering in golden pools in the low hollows of the chambers Lord Aldaeld had appointed to her and she smiled at this simple beauty. She enjoyed the sense of peace she felt in Coeth-Mara and felt closer to being at home here than she did anywhere else in Athel Loren. The smile fell from her face as she remembered that she was something of an unwelcome guest, that her skill of divination and her power to pierce the veil of time was both sought after and dreaded.

Naieth sat up, reached over to an artfully shaped wooden bowl and cupped her hands to lift out some water, rubbing the refreshingly cool liquid into her face. As she leaned over the bowl, she saw her reflection staring back at her, the long chin, melancholy mouth and the sad, accusing eyes. Droplets rippled the water in the bowl and she looked deep into her wavering reflection for a moment longer before averting her eyes, unwilling to meet her own gaze.

She had seen much too blood shed in her long life and as she looked at her hands, long, thin and worn, she knew that much of that blood was down to her. For too many centuries she had guided the asrai along their path, and none of those years had been easy. She thought of Kyarno and told herself once again that it had been for the best, that it would...

That it would what?

Naieth scooped a handful of water from the bowl, shattering her reflection, and drank the gloriously fresh liquid, feeling strength return to her body and a reassuring solidity come upon her limbs. Travelling in the realm of the spirit was incredibly liberating, but returning to flesh grew harder and harder each time.

Her companion, Othu the owl, hooted once more and she said, 'I know I look tired. I *feel* tired and don't need you to remind me!'

The bird hopped from its perch, flying into the higher branches of the tree and Naieth closed her eyes. She took a deep, calming breath, already angry at snapping at Othu. After all, he was right. She *did* look tired.

The owl hooted again and she looked up to see his beak bobbing in the direction of the main hall of Coeth-Mara, now hearing soft footfalls approaching. She closed her eyes and took another deep breath, opening her mind to the souls of those who came to her.

Two of them – one proud and regal and with a will of oak, the other young and courageous, but with the heart of a poet.

She smiled as she recognised them as Lord Aldaeld Éadaoin and Tarean Stormcrow, feeling their suspicion of her like a red ripple in the magical air of Athel Loren.

When she had arrived at Coeth-Mara a week ago and asked for permission to enter, Lord Aldaeld had offered her the hospitality of his halls, but she had seen the wary look in his eyes as he had done so.

Plainly he did not wish her here, but knew better than to offend a spellweaver by refusing her entry. All the asrai knew that the mages of Athel Loren travelled nowhere without good reason and were wary of them, even amongst their own kind

Though many kinbands called Athel Loren home, there was often little contact between them, and any dealings were fraught with suspicion. She turned and lifted her arm, apologising to Othu with a nod of her head as he dropped from above to land on her wrist.

She bowed as Lord Aldaeld and his herald entered, both elves moving with the supple grace of warriors. The Lord of Coeth-Mara wore a long cape of restless leaves and feathers, glowing spites rippling the fabric as they slipped around him. Naieth felt a thickening of the air and smiled inwardly as she realised Aldaeld had somehow persuaded a cluster of radiants to gather about him, tiny imps, little more than colourful lights that sapped the winds of magical energy.

Clearly Aldaeld was taking no chances that she might attempt to cloud his mind with her spells. His tattooed chest was crossed with two thin-bladed daggers and his hand gripped the glowing green pommel of his longsword.

Tarean Stormcrow was clad as he had been when her spirit had watched him speak to Kyarno this morning, his easy smile and confident manner radiating calm.

'Something has happened,' stated Aldaeld, without wasting any words on a welcome. 'The forest is angry and speaks of blood spilled.'

'Yes,' agreed Naieth. 'Blood has been spilled. At the Crystal Mere.'

'You have seen it?' asked Tarean Stormcrow.

'I saw it, yes,' said Naieth.

'Well?' snapped Aldaeld, taking a step towards her when she did not continue. Naieth flinched, the radiants making her skin crawl, and feeling her connection to the consciousness of Athel Loren fade at their nearness.

'Your daughter is safe, Lord Aldaeld. No harm has come to her.'

The elven lord's shoulders sagged a fraction in relief, then straightened as his eyes narrowed and he asked, 'Then whose blood was shed?'

'Four of the Hound of Winter's warriors are dead.'

'Four! Blood of Kurnous! What happened?'

Naieth backed away from Lord Aldaeld, saying, 'Beasts of Chaos penetrated the forest and attacked them.'

'Chaos,' spat Aldaeld. 'How in Isha's name did they reach so far into Athel Loren?'

'And how is it you did not know of them?' added Tarean Stormcrow.

'You know well that beyond the Crystal Mere, Athel Loren is dangerous,' said Naieth. 'The dark fey of the wood dwell in that region of the forest and there is often a sense of danger lurking there, mayhap the beasts knew to approach within its cloaking shadow.'

Neither of her visitors looked convinced and Aldaeld said, 'They are base creatures, mere beasts. How could they possibly know such a thing?'

Naieth shrugged as Othu flapped his wings and flew to land upon the shoulder of Tarean Stormcrow.

'He likes you,' smiled Naieth. 'It is a sign of good favour that he does so.'

Lord Aldaeld frowned at this change of subject and said, 'I do not like this, prophetess. Beasts of darkness reach deep into Athel Loren, the forest grows restless as winter comes and you bring a human into my halls. I tell you, I do not like it. A barbarian human! You know he should be dead already.'

'Leofric is just one human, you should not trouble yourself with him.'

'I do not have that luxury, prophetess,' spat Lord Aldaeld, waving his arm towards the south and dislodging several of the jostling radiants that gathered in the folds of his cloak. 'We dwell within reach of unnumbered enemies who bend their every effort to destroying everything I hold dear and have sworn to protect.'

'I know that, Lord Aldaeld, and–'

'I am not sure that you do, prophetess,' cut in Tarean Stormcrow. 'Winter is upon the forest and the King of the Wood prepares to go to his pyre. If we be not vigilant against such threats, then who?'

'There are many threats to this realm, Tarean Stormcrow, and know that I have seen them all. I have fought the secret war since before the seasons of your father, and I have seen a time beyond this where the restless dead rise from their tombs once more and red-skinned daemons of the Dark Gods stalk the lands where men once dwelt.'

'And what has that to do with this human?'

Naieth hesitated briefly before saying, 'In this time of blood and war we will have need of this human.'

'Humans live short, brutal lives, prophetess, surely he will be long dead by then?' said Aldaeld. 'And in any case, since when do the asrai need the help of a human?'

'Without this human, the handmaids of your daughter would now be dead,' pointed out Naieth. 'He fought alongside the Hound of Winter and slew one of the creatures of Chaos in single combat.'

Tarean Stormcrow moved to stand at the edge of her chambers, looking beyond the woven branches and said, 'I still find it strange that you were not aware of these creatures. You speak of things far distant from us, but see not what is to pass within days. How can that be?'

Othu flapped and flew from the chamber, hooting loudly as Tarean Stormcrow spoke. Aldaeld's herald watched the bird go, turning his eyes back to Naieth as the owl vanished from sight.

'The future is not a straight path, Tarean Stormcrow, it weaves and misleads like a befuddlement of mischiefs, twisting and teasing with half-truths and shadows. There are none who can see where it leads with certainty.'

'And yet you would have us hold this human here as though you see it with the surest certainty?' asked Aldaeld.

'Yes, I would,' agreed Naieth, lifting her wrist as Othu flew back into the chamber to land on her arm. 'In all the futures I see Leofric standing beside the asrai in defence of Athel Loren. Trust me Aldaeld, put your hatred of them aside, for more is at stake than the fate of one human.'

'Tell me of it,' demanded Aldaeld.

'I cannot,' said Naieth, shaking her head. 'To speak of the future is to change it.'

Othu hooted at her ear, a trilling series of clicks and whistles, and Naieth smiled.

'What does he say?' asked Lord Aldaeld.

'He brings word of another visitor to your halls,' said Naieth. 'One I bade come.'

Before Aldaeld could ask more, a grey-cloaked warrior of the Eternal Guard appeared at the entrance to the chamber with an anxious expression. Tarean Stormcrow nodded towards the warrior and Lord Aldaeld turned to face him.

'What news?' he asked, wary of the answer.

'The Red Wolf is come to Coeth-Mara,' said the warrior.

'Cu-Sith?' hissed Aldaeld, turning to Naieth, his face a mask of anger and not a little fear. 'Why would you bring the Red Wolf here?'

Naieth lifted her staff and said, 'He and his wardancers will perform the Dance of the Seasons at the Winter Feast. It is a great honour he does you by consenting to come here.'

'Indeed,' snapped Lord Aldaeld, turning to march from her chambers. 'Be careful that you do not heap too many honours upon me, prophetess. I do not think I would be thankful for any more.'

Leaving the Crystal Mere, Leofric was both saddened and relieved to bid farewell to such a vista of incredible beauty. Its wonder was something he knew he would never forget, but it had been sullied for him by Chaos. Much as everything in this world, he mused.

All that was good in the world would eventually be tainted by Chaos, no matter how remote or seemingly untouchable. Even this place of beauty and magic, hundreds of miles from the northern steppes and protected by faerie magic, could not protect itself from the predations of the Dark Gods. Every victory won, every invasion defeated, was but a respite – a pause in the inevitable doom of this world.

Any fool could see that...

He had helped drag the bodies of the beastmen into the forest where Leofric had assumed they would be burned, but Cairbre had shaken his head, saying, 'Leave them. The forest will claim them and they will return to the earth.'

The Hound of Winter had then extended his hand and said, 'That weapon you carry is an elven blade and does not belong to you.'

Briefly Leofric considered refusing to return the weapon, but knew that Cairbre could take it from him without even trying. Though he was loath to render himself unarmed once more, he reversed the blade and handed the sword, hilt first, to the Hound of Winter.

Cairbre had nodded and said no more, riding off at the head of their column back to Coeth-Mara. Once they had set off, Leofric had offered his mount to Tiphaine, uncomfortable with the idea of riding while a woman walked, but she had politely refused, walking hand in hand with one of her fellow handmaids.

Kyarno rode in silence, his head hung low over his chest and his braided hair cloaking his face in shadow. The chestnut-haired elven woman in the red dress who had loosed the deadly accurate shafts rode alongside him, speaking soft words of comfort.

As their journey back to the elven halls continued, Leofric found himself glancing warily into the darkness of the forest, wondering what fey creatures might dwell in the depths of Athel Loren, as a soft chorus of plaintive voices drifted from the trees.

Were the wild riders of Kurnous still out there? Might they come for him again?

His pack of spites still followed him, all now changed to resemble bobbing unicorns of light, the sight of them now mildly alarming after he had seen the fury with which they had attacked the beastmen.

It seemed as though there were low whispers coming from beyond the trees, hissing, sibilant tones like branches and leaves rustling in a chorus of wondrous ancient voices. As he listened, the sound filled his head with magic, lilting words like songs and beguiling tones like symphonies of joyful nuance. Leofric had thought that the language of the elves was like sweet music, but this was greater still, like the language of the soul made real. Leofric tugged on Taschen's reins, eager to hear more of this incredible sound, but a light hand reached out and gripped his wrist.

'Don't,' said the Lady Morvhen. 'You are human and the forest is not kind to humans.'

'What is it?' asked Leofric. 'It sounds like the forest is speaking.'

'It is.'

'What is it saying?' asked Leofric.

'It is the ancient language of the world, spoken only by the tree-kin and ancients of the wood,' said Morvhen. 'None but the spirits of the forest may speak it.'

'It's beautiful,' said Leofric.

Morvhen nodded and said, 'Yes, it is. There are only two places left in the world where it can be heard. Here and the Forest of Avelorn.'

'Avelorn? I have not heard of such a place.'

'It is far away on the island of Ulthuan, the birthplace of the asrai.'

'What is it like there?'

Morvhen shook her head. 'I do not know, I have never seen it. Our people left this land many thousands of years ago to return to Ulthuan, but my kin remained behind in Athel Loren.'

'Why?'

She smiled, looking around at the wild beauty of the forest around her. 'Could you leave this place? No, our forebears had made their home here and, though it broke their hearts never to see the land of their birth again, they could not bear to leave the forest to the beasts and…'

Morvhen's voice trailed off and Leofric said, 'Humans.'

'Yes,' she said, 'humans. By the time the Phoenix King called his subjects home our kin had become part of the forest, their souls and fates entwined forever. We could not abandon the forest to the axes of the lesser races.'

'I understand,' nodded Leofric, wanting to rise to the defence of his race, but knowing that Morvhen was right.

'I am the Lady Morvhen Éadaoin, daughter of Lord Aldaeld Éadaoin,' said Morvhen. 'I think you know that already, but it is only proper that I introduce myself.'

'Yes, I know who you are, my lady,' replied Leofric, seeing Cairbre keeping a close eye on him as they spoke. 'Is Éadaoin your family name?'

'It is,' said Morvhen. 'In your language it means Fleetmane.'

'I am Leofric Carrard, but then I am sure *you* know that already.'

Morvhen laughed, a wonderful, enchanting sound, and said, 'There are few in the forest who do not. The trees have carried word of your presence to all the corners of Athel Loren. Hence it might be wise for you not to go into the woods on your own. As I said, the forest is a dangerous place for humans.'

'I know,' said Leofric bitterly. 'It took my wife.'

'Yes,' said Morvhen. 'I know and I am truly sorry for your loss, but the waters of the Crystal Mere helped, yes?'

Leofric nodded, 'Aye, they did, and, Lady forgive me, I feel Helene's loss less keenly now.'

Morvhen frowned at his tone and said, 'But that is a good thing, surely?'

'Is it?' snapped Leofric, waving an arm at the forest around him. 'This place is eroding what I have of her, taking away the pain of my grief.'

'Why should you wish to hold onto grief?'

'Because it is *my* grief,' said Leofric. 'I desire to carry the pain of her loss, I do not want it taken away by faerie magic. I will grieve for my lost love in my own way, not yours!'

'Yours is a strange race, Leofric,' said Morvhen, echoing Tiphaine's earlier sentiment. 'You suffer when you do not need to.'

'Perhaps,' agreed Leofric, already ashamed at giving vent to such passion in front of a lady, 'but it is what I wish for. Leave me my grief. I will remember Helene in my own way.'

'As you wish, Leofric,' shrugged Morvhen, as Cairbre turned his horse and dropped back along the column of riders towards them, lowering her voice to a conspiratorial whisper. 'But when we return to Coeth-Mara may I speak with you some more? I would know of your adventures, the strange things you have seen and the far-off lands you have visited.'

Leofric shook his head. 'Regretfully, I must decline, my lady, for I shall be leaving Athel Loren upon returning you safely to your father. I have lands to rule in the name of my king and a son to raise without his mother. I cannot stay here.'

The crestfallen look on Morvhen's face cut Leofric deeply. He was unused to declining a lady's request, but there was little she could do to persuade him to stay in Athel Loren when he had responsibilities back in Bretonnia.

'Surely you can stay a little longer?' said Morvhen, and Leofric detected a note of petulance in her tone.

'No, my lady, I cannot, and please do not ask me again, for it ill becomes a knight to refuse a lady twice.'

'Very well,' said Morvhen sharply as Cairbre rode alongside them.

'My lady,' he said, 'you should not be talking to the human. You know what your father would say.'

'No matter, Hound of Winter,' said Morvhen, turning her horse to ride back to Kyarno. 'He does not wish to speak anyway.'

As she rode away, Cairbre said, 'If I were you, I would stay away from the Lady Morvhen.'

'Is that a threat?' asked Leofric, unable to take his eyes from the dead warrior laid across the rump of Cairbre's steed.

'No,' said the Hound of Winter. 'A warning between warriors.'

'How so?'

'She is the daughter of Lord Aldaeld and he holds your life in his hands. It would not please him to know that she was associating with a human.'

'I understand,' nodded Leofric. 'Then I thank you for your words. Tell me, why do they call you the Hound of Winter?'

At first, Leofric thought Cairbre wasn't going to answer, but the venerable elf smiled and said, 'I am Lord Aldaeld's champion, a warrior of the Eternal Guard, and I hunt down the enemies of my kinband. None who have earned the wrath of Lord Éadaoin have escaped my hunt and none ever shall.'

Leofric nodded. In any other warrior, such a boast would have been arrogant, but having seen the Hound of Winter's deadly skills in battle, Leofric had no trouble believing Cairbre's words.

'The Eternal Guard, is that the name given to the army of Athel Loren?' he asked, pointing at the body behind Cairbre.

'Army?' said Cairbre, 'We have no need of such a thing, human. Every member of a kinband has a duty to guard the domain entrusted to their lord, and every elf of the forest has great skill with a bow. No, the Eternal Guard is no army of Athel Loren. We are its guardians through the long dark of winter, when branch and tree slumber. It is our duty and privilege to defend the sacred places of the forest and the lords and ladies that dwell within.'

'A heavy duty indeed,' said Leofric. 'But a welcome one, I should think.'

'It is a great honour to be chosen by the Eternal Guard, an honour earned through skill at arms. To meet death in the service of something so noble as Athel Loren is more than any warrior can ask for,' said Cairbre. 'But I see that you are a human who understands such things.'

'I do indeed,' agreed Leofric. 'Only by such feats of arms may a knight rise to become a knight of the realm. The king desires only warriors of courage and honour to defend his realm and there are none greater in all the lands of men than the knights of Bretonnia.'

'You are a great warrior in your lands?'

'A warrior, yes,' nodded Leofric. 'I have some skill with lance and blade, but modesty forbids me from vulgar boasts of prowess.'

'Spoken like a true warrior,' said Cairbre with a wry grin. 'One who lets his deeds attest to his mettle.'

Despite himself, Leofric found himself warming to Cairbre. The elf had the easy confidence of a warrior born, coupled with a manner that spoke of a life of great experience and wisdom. As he looked at the regal profile of the Hound of Winter, he found it increasingly difficult to reconcile this softly spoken, yet powerful warrior as being kin to the brash, argumentative Kyarno.

'Perhaps we are not so different after all,' said Leofric.

Cairbre shook his head. 'Do not mistake a warrior's respect for anything other than that. You are human and I am elf, and we will always be different. Though we can speak in the same language and live mortal lives, your kind will never understand mine.'

'That is a shame,' said Leofric. 'We could learn much from each other.'

'I do not believe so,' replied Cairbre, his cold-eyed expression settling upon his features once more. 'You humans have nothing we wish to know, and we do not wish to be part of your world. Let us leave it at that.'

'As you wish,' said Leofric as Cairbre rode off to the head of the column.

Alone once more, he glanced over to where Kyarno rode with Morvhen, catching the eye of Tiphaine and smiling at the scarlet-haired handmaid. Leofric saw that Kyarno had roused himself from his melancholic reverie, talking in a low voice with Morvhen and casting wary glances his way.

He did not know what had driven the young elf into such a bloody frenzy back in the glade of the Crystal Mere, nor did he have any reason to believe that Cairbre would be more forthcoming than he had been earlier.

Such matters were none of his business and since he had resolved to leave Athel Loren tonight – Naieth's wishes be damned – there was no need for him to pry further.

Whatever inner torments plagued Kyarno would remain his own to face.

He returned his attention to the path before him, allowing the gentle rhythm of the forest's song to carry him onwards.

To Coeth-Mara and then home.

CHAPTER NINE

Riding back into Coeth-Mara through the same woven arch of leaves and branches, Leofric felt a familiar warmth enfold him, like the homely sensation he had every time he rode through the arched gateway of Castle Carrard upon his return from campaign. It felt like coming home, as though he was somehow welcome now...

The hanging belts of jewels and gold tinkled musically as they passed beneath them, sad and mournful at the dead they brought with them. The sense of things moving in the dark of the forest receded and Leofric again felt the strange sensation of feeling like he had moved from one season to another.

Cairbre's normally stony exterior softened as they entered the realm of his kinband and even Kyarno's face lit up with relief and pleasure at his return home. He saw the same expressions on every face – Morvhen's, Tiphaine's and all the handmaids. He could not deny that the uplifting feeling was palpable and fought against its lulling qualities.

He was not long for this woodland realm and could not fall prey to its faerie magicks now. Leofric rode through the golden splendour of Coeth-Mara, remembering the words that had passed between him and Kyarno only this morning as he saw subtle hints of archways and pillars, suggestions of roof and beam and the barest outlines of passages and doorways. Where once he had seen nothing but tree and branch, forest and bush, he now saw signs of habitation, of life and living.

Here he saw a mother and child shaping a bowstave, there an elf skinning a brace of coneys. Leofric smiled as he passed many such domestic vignettes, amazed that he had not seen them before. Had he simply been ignorant of what to look for or was the forest now allowing him to see its gracefully shaped structures? Or was there something more sinister at work? Was the magic of the forest even now altering him in ways he could not fathom, reshaping what his human senses could perceive?

Such a worrying notion only heightened his desire to leave Athel Loren and, once night fell, he decided he would make his way from this place before he was lost to its fey power forever. He had no wish to suffer the same fate as the vanished Duke Melmon and knew that the longer he stayed here, the more likely such an end became.

The handmaids of Morvhen seemed to glide past him, each one offering him a shy smile and a bow of gratitude as they did so and Leofric felt a great humility at their recognition. As she passed him, Tiphaine whispered, 'They want me to tell you that they are sorry for teasing you at the Crystal Mere and to thank you for rising to their defence against the monsters.'

Leofric shivered as he remembered how close the arrows loosed by the handmaids had come to his head and said, 'I am not sure they really needed my help, but I am glad to have been of service.'

Tiphaine smiled, reaching up to touch his arm, and Leofric felt a soothing warmth to her touch. 'Take care, Leofric Carrard. I wish you well.'

'Thank you, my lady,' said Leofric as she moved away. 'I hope I may one day be of service to you again.'

Looking over her shoulder as she joined Morvhen and the rest of her handmaids, Tiphaine smiled and said, 'As do I.'

Leofric watched as Morvhen and her handmaids gently relieved Cairbre of the body carried on the back of his horse and led the elven steeds bearing the other dead warriors of the Eternal Guard into the winding paths of Coeth-Mara. Soft laments sighed from their lips as they vanished and Leofric found himself sad to see Tiphaine go, but shook such thoughts from his mind as Kyarno rode alongside him.

'Where are they taking the fallen?' asked Leofric.

Kyarno looked up and Leofric saw that the young elf's earlier manner had reasserted itself in his suspicious stare.

'They are being taken to be cleansed before being laid to rest in the forest,' said Kyarno, 'but it is not fitting for a human to speak of elven dead.'

'I am sorry,' said Leofric. 'I meant no offence.'

'No,' replied Kyarno slowly, 'it is I who am sorry.'

Leofric could see the difficulty Kyarno had in making such an admission as he spoke again. 'You fought to defend my kin when all I have offered you is anger and hostility. For that I thank you.'

'No thanks are necessary. They were creatures of Chaos and though, in the end it is fruitless, evil must be fought at all times.'

'Fighting Chaos is never fruitless... Leofric. May I call you that?'

Leofric bowed his head and said, 'Yes, you may. But I have seen the face of evil, Kyarno. I rode with my king down the east causeway of Middenheim to face the lord of daemons and though we fought like Gilles and the Companions, we could not defeat it. The best and the bravest of Bretonnia, and still we could not defeat it.'

'Perhaps you were not strong enough?' said Kyarno without malice.

'On the charge, there are no mightier warriors than the knights of Bretonnia,' said Leofric proudly. 'Or at least... at least I thought so... until...'

Leofric's eyes misted over and the gold and greens of Athel Loren faded from sight as he saw again the mud-and corpse-choked wasteland around the great northern city of Middenheim. The Ulricsberg towered over the group of knights, its tall spires wreathed in smoke and flames as the shamans of the Dark Gods hurled their vile magicks at its walls and terrifying dragons and other nameless, winged horrors breathed gouts of fire.

Smoke and a thick, cloying mist hung over the battlefield, the twisted corpses of slaughtered beastmen lying strewn about amid the hacked apart bodies of men in various liveries of the Empire's provinces. The red and white of Talabheim mingled with the gold and yellow of Nuln and the blue and red of Altdorf. Shattered breastplates, discarded halberds and dented sallet helmets rusted in the open air. Leofric remembered the stench of death, the rotten aroma of opened bowels and decomposing flesh.

The knights had walked their horses through the battlefield, scattering carrion birds as they feasted on eyes and tongues, as well as foxes and dogs fighting over the contents of ruptured bellies. Here and there, looters of the dead scurried from corpse to corpse, slitting open purses for coin and pilfering gold teeth or trinkets.

Where they came upon such animals they killed those they could and drove away others, though Leofric knew it was a hopeless task, for as soon as they moved on, the scavengers, both human and animal, would return.

It had begun slowly, as a soft drumming noise like far away thunder.

Then it had grown to a rumbling storm of slow hoof beats and the knights had circled their horses and twisted in the saddle to pinpoint its direction, for none now could doubt that the sound was approaching cavalry. And in the forests around Middenheim, it could only be that of the enemy.

The hateful mist had conspired to confound their efforts to locate the approaching foe and Leofric had felt the tension rise as the noise grew louder and louder. Some of the younger knights cried that the mist was unnatural, that it was the result of an enemy spell. Older, wiser heads scoffed at such protestations, but Leofric had heard the unease in their denials as the mist closed in.

The maddeningly slow drumbeat of hooves grew louder with every passing second, and though it seemed their foe must surely be upon them, there was still no sign of them.

None could now doubt the sorcerous nature of the mist as it thickened and coiled about them, acrid and unpleasant, and dulling the sound of the approaching riders. A carnyx horn sounded in the mist and Leofric could hear the galloping jingle of trace and the metallic scrape of swords being drawn.

The knights lowered their lances, but by now it was already too late as the mist suddenly rose and the thunderous charge of the riders of Chaos struck them. A single dread rune blazed with power on a banner carried by one of the knights and Leofric's heart trembled as he recognised to which warlord the rune belonged.

Riding at the head of the terrifying knights of Chaos was Archaon himself, seated astride his monstrous steed of the apocalypse, swollen by dark magicks to many times the size of even the mightiest Bretonnian steed. Its eyes were burning coals, its breath that of a furnace.

The Lord of the End Times was vast and awesome in his evil, clad in armour forged of brazen iron and a horned helmet blazing with fell energies. A great bearskin cloak flared out behind him and he carried a terrible, flaming sword, its blade screaming with a soul-destroying roar.

Knights fell, both they and their mounts hewn in twain by each swing of Archaon's colossal blade. Bloody arcs clove the air as Chaos-forged blades shattered armour and weapons alike, killing men and beasts without pity or remorse. Leofric's shield was smashed from his arm, his body numbed by the force of the blow. The knights fought bravely, but against such brute ferocity there could be no victory.

Though it shamed every knight among them, they had turned their horses and fled from the battle, the raucous cries of the chosen warriors of Chaos ringing in their ears as they rode on to find more prey.

The shame of that rout had not lessened, and though the king had honoured each and every one of them after the final victory, they had all left the Empire with the guilt of fleeing before the enemy festering in their hearts. Men who Leofric had fought alongside for years would no longer meet his eye, the shared guilt making each man loath to seek out the company of his fellows.

It had been a black day for honour and the memory of it had all but unmanned him. Leofric had seen the raw power of Chaos that day and it had settled like a shroud upon him, filling him with dread for the day when the Dark Gods finally took the world for their own.

Filled with such gloomy thoughts, all he could picture was Helene's face, wishing he could have spent the last days of this world's life by her side. Such selfish thoughts did not become a knight of Bretonnia, but faced with the inevitability of the fall of nations, he knew he was but a man, with a man's desires.

And yet, amid such darkness was life. The image of his son's face, smiling and full of innocence leapt unbidden to his mind. Beren's green eyes were the image of his own, his laugh like an angel's. There was no malice or guile to his son, only a child's unquestioning love and purity. While such things existed in the world, there was something worth fighting for, even if only to preserve it for a little longer.

Leofric smiled ruefully, the darkness of his thoughts retreating in the face of the love he felt for his son. The battlefields and horrors of the Storm of Chaos faded and he saw that he was once again in Athel Loren, its enchanted boughs of red and brown leaves like a fire above him, its beauty almost painful against such horrors as he had just relived.

The sweet scent of wood sap and leavening bread caught in his nostrils and Leofric felt a strange peace settle upon him, as though such homely, domestic scents had somehow brought his soul back to him.

He saw Kyarno looking strangely at him and said, 'Athel Loren is a place of wonders and miracles, but I can never forget that, for my kind, it is also a place of fear and death. I think that if I were to remain here I would soon have a surcease of sorrow, but that is not for me and I must go before I forget my duties.'

'Leave?' said Kyarno. 'You still do not understand, human. You cannot leave.'

'No?' replied Leofric coldly.

'No, you are deep in Athel Loren and without the leave of Lord Aldaeld and the forest you would be dead before you were out of sight of Coeth-Mara.'

'Be that as it may, I have to try.'

'I wouldn't if I were you,' shrugged Kyarno, 'but then who am I to give advice on what to do?'

'Then tell me where I may find this Lord Aldaeld,' said Leofric. 'If I must secure his leave to travel through his lands, then so be it.'

'It looks like he has come to find you,' said Kyarno, pointing towards a group of horsemen that approached along the main thoroughfare of Coeth-Mara.

Leofric followed Kyarno's gaze and saw Cairbre riding out to meet a group of elves led by a powerful-looking elven warrior atop a golden-coloured horse with a pale mane and tail. The elf's bare chest was adorned with numerous tattoos of twisting, knotted thorns and wild beasts, his long cloak of leaves and feathers rippling with motion.

The warrior carried a long, green-hilted sword across his back and wore a crown of woven branches and leaves atop his patrician features. His oval eyes were utterly dark, seemingly without pupils, and Leofric sensed a power to this elf beyond anything he had felt from any other – even Cairbre or Naieth.

This elf was empowered with the magic of the forest and Leofric knew that this must be none other than Lord Aldaeld Fleetmane, lord of

Coeth-Mara and protector of this domain of the forest.

He saw an unmistakable hostility and disdain in Lord Aldaeld's eyes, and knew that if his fate truly lay in this elf's hands, then it was doubtful that it would be a happy one. Accompanying Lord Aldaeld was Naieth, clad in a long dress of green velvet with a grey-feathered owl sitting on her shoulder, and a golden haired elf in clothing similar to Kyarno's but of exquisitely tailored reds and blues. A trio of the Eternal Guard followed behind their lord on foot, their twin-bladed spears held at their sides.

Cairbre dismounted and stood before the elven lord, the Blades of Midnight held across his body in a defensive posture. Turning back to Leofric, he said, 'You are required to dismount.'

Leofric nodded and climbed down from Taschen's saddle, holding himself tall and proud before this elf. Aldaeld may be lord of this place, but Leofric was a knight of Bretonnia and bowed to no king but his own.

The elven lord spoke to the richly dressed elf riding alongside him who bore a longsword and carried a short, recurved bow slung over one shoulder. His hair was long and golden, held in place by a silver circlet, and Leofric saw a softness to his features that he had not seen in other elven warriors.

The elf nodded and said, 'I am Tarean Stormcrow, and I am herald to Aldaeld Éadaoin, guardian of the forest realm of Athel Loren and Lord of Coeth-Mara. Lord Aldaeld welcomes you to his hall.'

Leofric switched his gaze from the herald to Aldaeld himself, seeing no hint of that welcome in his patrician features. Behind the elven lord, Leofric saw Naieth's owl hoot nervously and had the distinct impression it was talking to her. The faerie legends spoke of elf sorcerers who could speak to the beasts of the forest, and it appeared that Naieth was one of them.

Leofric ignored Aldaeld's herald and addressed the elven lord directly. 'Do you not speak for yourself? Must you hide behind another?'

'Lord Aldaeld does not lower himself to speak the tongues of men,' explained the elf named Stormcrow. 'You will address me and, through me, Lord Aldaeld may consent to speak to you.'

Leofric folded his arms across his chest as Aldaeld spoke again to Stormcrow, who shook his head and said, 'Lord Aldaeld asks why you insult him by speaking to him directly. Do you not accord honour to other kings besides your own?'

'I do,' acknowledged Leofric, 'when I am their guest or supplicant. But not when I am their prisoner.'

'Ah...' said Stormcrow, spreading his arms wide and smiling broadly. The elf's smile was contagious and Leofric found himself smiling as well. 'You think you are a prisoner here?'

'Am I not?'

'No,' replied Stormcrow, shaking his head. 'You are a guest in Athel

Loren, though, for your own safety, it would be wise not to enter the forest without the consent of Lord Aldaeld or the trees themselves.'

'A prison may be called many things, but if one is not free to leave, then it amounts to the same thing does it not?'

'There is truth in what you say,' nodded Tarean Stormcrow, looking over Leofric's shoulder at Kyarno, 'but Coeth-Mara truly is not a prison, save for those who choose it to be so.'

Lord Aldaeld spoke a swift burst of elvish and his herald took a step towards Leofric, saying, 'The lord of Coeth-Mara wishes it known that he is grateful for the aid you gave to his daughter's handmaids. To have fought the beasts of Chaos took great courage for a human and he is pleased that you survived.'

'The Lady Tiphaine has thanked me on their behalf, and the gratitude of a lady is its own reward.'

Tarean Stormcrow bowed slightly to Leofric and said, 'You are a human who knows the value of honour. Nevertheless, Lord Aldaeld is indebted to you and extends to you the hospitality of his halls for so long as you remain within them.'

Leofric glanced at Naieth, wondering how much of Lord Aldaeld's hospitality was as a result of her and how much of it was resented. Even he could sense the frostiness between Aldaeld and Naieth.

'In addition to this great honour, he bids you to attend upon his kin at the Winter Feast, when the Wardancers of the Red Wolf will perform the Dance of the Seasons.'

Though nothing was said, Leofric could sense a sudden shift in mood and felt a shiver of fear work its way up his spine at the mention of this Red Wolf.

He shook off his momentary unease and said, 'Convey my thanks to Lord Aldaeld and inform him that I accept his gracious offer of hospitality for as long as I shall remain here.'

Tarean Stormcrow smiled broadly, nodding slightly to Lord Aldaeld, who wheeled his horse and rode away without another word. The herald swung onto the back of his own horse and he, Cairbre and the Eternal Guard, followed their master as he departed.

As they left, Naieth rode forwards, the owl flying off towards the treetops above, a strange, sad expression on her face as she spoke to Kyarno in the gentle cadences of her native tongue.

Kyarno shook his head at whatever she said and spat some harsh elven words back to her before riding off, leaving Naieth and Leofric alone together in the forest.

'What did you say to him?' asked Leofric.

'Nothing,' said Naieth. 'It is not important.'

Leofric turned from the elf witch and climbed back into his saddle, running a hand through his unruly hair and brushing grass and dirt from his clothes.

'Well, it seems as though your idea of sending me to the Crystal Mere was not entirely successful,' said Leofric.

'I wouldn't be so sure, Leofric,' said Naieth, her voice taking on a distant, ethereal quality… as though she looked straight *through* him. 'I think perhaps it achieved exactly what was intended.'

'What does that mean?'

'It means that there are often many things that need to happen for the present to choose the right path into the future,' said Naieth, and Leofric was unsure as to whether she was talking to him or herself.

The chamber of branches was clearer to him now than when he had first awoken here, the distinct outlines of shaped wood and curved bough now obvious. Where first he had seen nothing but the riotousness of nature, he now saw the guiding hand of artifice, though nowhere did he see anything as crude as a straight line.

Late evening sunlight streaked the branches of the trees, the distant sounds of melodic voices and the warm smells of summer mingling with the crispness of autumn and the bite of winter, and Leofric had a sense of time slipping away from him.

'Time to be away from this place,' he whispered to himself as he dismounted and unbuckled the girth. He looked for somewhere to hitch his steed's reins, but saw nothing that would serve. He turned back to the horse and watched with amazement as the glowing spites – that seemed now to be his constant companions – flitted past his head and vanished into the low, twisting branches of the tree. The wood writhed and swelled, growing and reshaping itself into a knotted branch at just the right height to form a hitching rail.

Leofric chuckled, already becoming more used to the strange creatures of the forest, and said, 'Thank you, little ones,' as he hitched Taschen's reins to the newly formed branch. The glowing spites emerged from the wood and resumed their bobbing pattern above his head as he began stripping the tack from his horse.

With a grunt, he hauled off the saddle and dropped it onto the hitching rail then began rubbing down the flanks of his weary horse. In this place of magic and mystery, there was a reassuring sense of reality in this simple task that, ordinarily, he would have ordered his squire attend to.

Having seen to the needs of his mount, who now began feeding on the long grass, he entered the chambers Naieth had escorted him to. She had left him to his own devices, saying, 'Rest well, Leofric, we will talk again soon.'

He had merely nodded, seeing no reason to speak to her of his plans to depart Athel Loren this very night. As he had watched her depart he felt no guilt at this deception, merely a desire to be away and to be reunited with his son.

Inside, the trees and branches of his chambers smelled of warm jasmine and were filled with light, softly glowing traceries as though the sap within ran like liquid amber. He saw the same bed of leaves where he had awoken and, beside it, a deep wooden bowl of water and another set of fresh clothes, identical to the ones he wore.

But beside them – and a much more welcome sight – was a tall, intertwined arrangement of branches upon which was hung his armour, polished to a mirror sheen, and his scabbard. The hilt of the Carrard sword glittered in the fading light and he marched across the chamber to grasp its soft, leather-wound hilt.

Drawing the sword, he cut the air with its silvered blade, running through a series of martial exercises designed to loosen the muscles of his shoulder. He frowned as he swung the blade, twisting its length through the air in a series of dazzling thrusts, ripostes and cuts. Though he performed each move flawlessly, the sword's weight felt strangely different, and it took Leofric several moments to realise why.

Next to the elven blade he had wielded in battle earlier, this sword felt clumsy and inelegant, heavy and ponderous, though he knew the blessing of the Lady was upon it and it was many times lighter than any similar blade.

Disturbed, he sheathed the sword and placed his palm against the breastplate of his armour. The surface was smooth to the touch and the gold chasing along its edges and the unicorn in its centre shone like fire with the touch of the setting sun.

Leofric turned from his armour and stripped off the bloodstained clothes he wore, washing himself with water from the bowl and using the bunched garments as a cloth. When he was as clean as he could make himself, he dressed quickly in the fresh attire, noting that the scar on his hip from the forest spirit's attack had completely vanished. Leofric was a fast healer, but he knew that such speed was unnatural – there was not even a blemish to mark its passing.

Perhaps the waters of the Crystal Mere had healing properties beyond those of easing the torments of the bereaved?

Putting the vanished wound from his mind, Leofric lifted his greaves from the frame of branches, buckling them onto his shins. Normally he would be wearing quilted hose beneath his armour, but there was no sign of the ones he had been wearing upon entering Athel Loren, so he had to content himself with buckling the armour on tighter than normal.

Piece by piece, Leofric donned his armour, shrugging into his heavy mail shirt and coif and wincing as the links bit into his skin through the thin shirt he wore. Silver moonlight streamed into the chamber as he lifted the breastplate and fitted it across his chest, smiling at the familiar feel of armour again.

Only then did he realise how difficult putting it on was going to be without his squire to help him.

With some difficulty, and not a little distraction from the curious spites that circled him, he was able to get one strap buckled and reached around in vain for the next.

'Instead of just watching me, it would be useful if you could help,' snapped Leofric as a spite shaped like a tiny dragon circled his flailing hands as he tried to grasp the next buckle.

No sooner had he spoken than he felt the buckle pressed into his palm and looked down to see a tiny glowing figure, no larger than his hand floating beside him. Like a miniature elf, the small, red-capped figure smiled with a wicked grin and nodded towards the next buckle.

'Now then, what are you, my little friend?' asked Leofric, but the diminutive creature didn't answer, content merely to hover in the air beside him. Despite himself, Leofric couldn't help but smile at this absurd little creature. Here, in this place, he supposed he should not be surprised at anything any more.

'Thank you,' he said, pleased that the little spites appeared to have taken a liking to him. 'Your help is most welcome.'

The glowing spite giggled, the sound like the chiming of glass, and Leofric buckled the strap of his armour and moved onto the next, not surprised when it was also pressed into his hand.

'I may make you my squire...' said Leofric, the smile falling from his face as he suddenly pictured Baudel, his guts spilling over the forest floor as he was disembowelled by one of the deadly forest spirits. Without speaking again, he finished donning his armour and turned to put on his sword belt.

He felt better now that he was armed and armoured once again, as though the mere act of putting on the apparel of a knight of Bretonnia had reminded him of his duty, a duty the magic of this forest seemed keen to erode the memory of.

He drew his sword once more and dropped to his knees, holding the sword by the hilt with its point resting on the soft floor of the chamber. Taking Helene's favour, he wrapped the scarf around the hilt and quillons of the weapon, entwining it with his fingers as he knelt in prayer.

Closing his eyes and resting his forehead on the pommel of his sword, Leofric softly recited the vow of the knight: 'Lady, I am your servant and in this time of trial I once again offer you my blade and service. When the clarion call is sounded, I will ride out and fight in the name of liege and Lady. Whilst I draw breath the lands bequeathed unto me shall remain untainted by evil. Honour is all, chivalry is all. Such is my vow.'

With each word spoken came a feeling of peace and tranquillity and Leofric knew that his prayer had been answered.

He stood and sheathed his sword in one smooth motion, lifting the last of his armour from the frame. He slid his helm over his head and snapped shut the angled visor, before turning and marching from the chamber.

The Lady herself had come to him, easing his troubled mind, and he knew that the time was now right for him to leave Athel Loren.

CHAPTER TEN

Even at night, Coeth-Mara was a place of light and magic, the boughs and branches of the forest garlanded with moonlight and starfire. Snow was falling, carpeting the ground in white and the sense of hostility Leofric had felt before was much lessened now, though he knew that the forest would never be a safe place for a human.

His armour chafed against his skin and clanked loudly with every step, but Leofric knew there was no sense in trying to be stealthy – such a thing was next to impossible in a suit of heavy plate armour anyway. He left the chamber of branches and passed through the blurred boundary between his dwelling and the forest itself, seeing Taschen still feeding on the grasses of Athel Loren. The horse had eaten its way through a wide swathe of grass and Leofric rubbed his mount's neck, saying, 'Elven grass obviously agrees with you, my friend. I wonder, would you prefer it to grain?'

Taschen ignored him as he threw his saddle blanket over the horse's back then lifted his saddle from the spite-formed hitching rail. It had been many years since Leofric had saddled a horse himself and the process took longer than he remembered it taking Baudel. Nevertheless, it was a skill that, once learned, was never forgotten, and soon he had his steed saddled and ready to ride.

Leofric climbed into the saddle, settling himself and adjusting his scabbard before grasping the reins and spurring his horse onwards into the night.

In the veiled twilight of darkness, the forest was perhaps even more spectacular than during the day, though there was a chill to the air that felt to Leofric like the depths of winter rather than its onset. The sense of time slipping away from him felt more acute at night, as though the moons above him were circling the world differently.

He angled his horse along a trunk-lined processional, the leafy arches shining with reflected light from the glittering snowflakes on the wide leaves and drooping foliage. As spectacular as it was, there was also something infinitely sad and fearful to the forest, a sense of things dying and never to be seen again. Leofric felt a sense of ancient melancholy as he rode through the leaf-strewn paths of Coeth-Mara, the sounds of faraway voices and tree-song filling him with an unexpected wistfulness.

'I will remember this,' whispered Leofric. 'For good and ill, I will remember this.'

Whether it was the moonlight shadows or his apparent acceptance by the forest, he did not know, but he could now clearly see the softly lit outlines of tall columns of trees and gently curving roofs of branches and leaves. He had noticed the same thing upon his return to Coeth-Mara, but only now in the moonlight were the song-woven structures of the elven halls truly visible. Only a day before he would have ridden through here and seen nothing of Lord Aldaeld's domain and Leofric's would have been the loss.

But for all its beauty, it was still a place of shadows and fear. It was still the forest that had taken his wife and though the pain of her death was still fresh, it felt like a lifetime had passed since the spirits of the wood had taken her. He could feel the pain of her loss diminishing, as though the forest itself sought to heal his hurt, and knew he had to leave before he forgot her completely.

He could feel many eyes upon him, though he saw not a single soul. The eyes of Athel Loren were ever watchful and he knew that his departure from Coeth-Mara would already be known. He gripped the hilt of his sword, hoping that he would not need to draw it, but knowing that such a hope was ultimately doomed.

A red-furred wolf padded softly from the trees, its coat gleaming like copper in the moonlight and its eyes a glistening red. A golden hawk with a curious expression sat on its back and examined him carefully. Leofric tensed, wondering if the wolf would attack as it turned to face him and bared its fangs.

But before the wolf could advance, a hunting hound with fur the colour of snow ghosted from the shadows, a low, threatening growl building in its throat.

Leofric slowly drew his sword, holding it close to his side as the hound leaned forwards and barked in the wolf's ear. The wolf ignored the hound and took slow, stalking steps through the snow towards him, never once taking its eyes from his. Leofric rubbed Taschen's neck as the animal approached.

He raised his sword and pulled on his horse's reins to better angle himself to meet the wolf's attack.

As he drew back his sword arm, a gentle voice whispered, 'I wouldn't if I were you...'

Leofric risked a glance over his shoulder, seeing Morvhen Éadaoin atop a glorious roan mare with a mane the colour of snow on the mountains. She had changed from her red dress into more practical attire of buckskin trews and a feather-laced jerkin with strips of gold woven into the fabric. Her long, chestnut hair was teased up into a high, feather-woven cascade of silver pins, leaves and braids. Her long, delicate features were curious and unafraid, her wide eyes dark in the shadowy night.

'What are they?' asked Leofric.

'Spirits of the wild,' said Morvhen. 'The spirits and beasts of the forest have a strange relationship and not even we really understand it.'

'Are they dangerous?'

'That depends on whether you mean them harm,' said Morvhen. 'Do you?'

Leofric shook his head and sheathed his sword as the hound again barked at the wolf. The wolf stopped in its tracks and held his gaze for a second more before bobbing its head towards Morvhen and turning to pad back the way it had come, crossing the path and disappearing into the forest across from them. Satisfied that the wolf had gone, the hound also bowed its head to Morvhen and ran off into the forest after its red-furred companion.

Leofric let out a deep breath, shaking his head at such strangeness.

'Where are you going?' asked Morvhen. 'Are you leaving my father's halls?'

'I have to,' said Leofric, raking his spurs back and riding onwards. 'I have to return to my son and my lands.'

'Yes, you said that before,' said Morvhen, riding to catch up. 'I didn't think you really meant it.'

'Why would you think that?'

'I don't know,' shrugged Morvhen, pointing at the glowing spites that followed Leofric. 'It doesn't look like they want you to leave and my father says that you humans change your minds all the time. I just thought that once Coeth-Mara welcomed you, you might want to stay for a time.'

'What do you mean by that?'

'That once you'd seen how beautiful Athel Loren was, you'd want to see more of it and speak more with me. I told you, I want to hear all about your adventures.'

'No,' said Leofric, halting his horse. 'I meant what you said about humans changing their minds. What do you mean?'

Morvhen pulled ahead of him, riding her horse in a tight circle, and Leofric could see that she was armed. An elven bow was slung from the flank of her steed and she wore a narrow, short-bladed sword across her back. Had she come here to stop him leaving?

Cunning of them to send a woman, knowing he would not harm her.

'Well, he says that you make war on each other all the time and that a human's word is like summer mist. My father fought in a land called the Empire before I was born in the time when they had three emperors. He said that the leaders of the humans couldn't decide on who was to rule them and that they fought bitter wars with one another with alliances like shifting sands.'

Leofric cast his mind back to Maixent's history lessons in the draughty garrets of Castle Carrard, trying to recall his teachings of the land of Sigmar to the north of Bretonnia. Since the time of Magnus the Pious, a single Emperor had led the Empire, though there had been a time…

'But that was over five hundred years ago,' said Leofric. 'How could your father have fought in the Empire then?'

'He was young then,' admitted Morvhen. 'But we elves have a greater span of years than you humans. Didn't you know that?'

'There are stories that say you are immortal, but I had taken them for flights of fancy. I never believed you were so long-lived.'

Morvhen laughed. 'We are not immortal, Leofric. Nor is it that we are long-lived. It is just that your kind exists so fleetingly that all others appear to be immortal. It is no wonder your people live such rushing, desperate lives. To have such a limited time to experience the joys that life has to offer must be terrible indeed. How do you cope with it?'

Leofric tugged on Taschen's reins and rode around Morvhen, saying, 'You have never ventured beyond the borders of Athel Loren, have you?'

'No. What has that to do with anything?' replied Morvhen, riding to catch up with him once more.

'It means that you have no idea what you are talking about,' snapped Leofric. 'Try living in the world beyond your cosy forest paradise and then ask me about the joy of living, little girl! I have been a warrior for most of my adult life. I have killed men and I have killed monsters. I have seen good men slaughtered by warriors of the Dark Gods and seen my wife murdered by the creatures of this damned forest. So don't you dare talk to me about living! I have done my share of living in the brief span allowed to me by the gods and I am going home to spend the rest of it with my son.'

Morvhen's jaw dropped open and Leofric could see that she had clearly never been spoken to in such a manner. No sooner had her shock faded than her regal blood flushed her face and she said, 'I forbid you to go. I want you to stay and tell me of faraway lands, of monsters you have slain and wars you have fought.'

'You want to know about the wars I have fought?' demanded Leofric.

'Yes,' said Morvhen. 'I do.'

'Very well, Lady Éadaoin. Shall I tell you of men screaming for their mothers as their guts spill from their bellies, of boys carried from the field of battle with their legs no more than a bloody pulp because they tried to stop a rolling cannonball? Is that what you want to hear? Or maybe I should tell you of the women beaten and raped by passing soldiers and left to die by the roadside, of the children dragged off to a life of slavery by the northmen, or the field hospitals that stink of gangrene from wounds that have become infected because injured men lay in a bloody field for days before being found by their fellows?'

Morvhen's face twisted in disgust at such things, and though Leofric regretted such a breach of his chivalric code, he was in no mood to humour this spoilt little girl. He took a deep breath to try and calm himself, softly reciting the vow of the knight under his breath.

'You speak as though I am innocent of war,' spat Morvhen. 'I am not. Athel Loren is forever threatened. We have enemies all around and I have lived a hundred years and shed my share of blood in its defence. I too have known the loss of friends and loved ones.'

Morvhen wheeled her horse and Leofric could see a cold hardness to her eyes and a defiant strength he had not noticed before.

'Those who died at the Crystal Mere?' she said. 'They were not strangers to me.'

He opened his mouth to speak, but Morvhen dug her heels into the mare's flanks and rode off in the direction of Coeth-Mara.

Leofric cursed and watched her ride away, sorry for hurting her, but unwilling to be diverted from his course. The spites following behind him hung motionless in the air and he could sense their disapproval of him.

'Don't say a word,' he cautioned them, before realising he was talking to glowing balls of light. Surprised at his own foolishness, he turned from them and rode onwards.

The forest flashed past her in a blur, emotions raging within her head at the human's words. Though part of her knew there was some truth to what he had said, her pride would not yet allow her anger to diminish. Morvhen pushed the mare hard, releasing that anger through the speed of her horse. She was not worried about Ithoraine stumbling or plunging her leg into a rabbit hole or root. The horse knew the forest well enough to gallop headlong in the darkness without fear of such things.

She rode hard through the overgrown paths of the forest, feeling branches and leaves pull themselves from her path as her mad gallop continued. The human thought her ignorant of the harsh realities of life, that she knew nothing of loss and pain.

Well, he would soon know of loss and pain if he rode further into the forest without her father's blessing. The dryads of winter were far from welcoming to outsiders and though he rode *from* Coeth-Mara, they would offer no mercy to a human in their forest.

The thought gave her pause and she leaned over Ithoraine's neck and whispered to her, entwining her fingers in the horse's mane. Her steed circled, coming to a halt with a neigh of disappointment that their wild ride was over.

As she rode back into Coeth-Mara, the reality of the human's fate sank in and her anger vanished as she knew who would bear the full wrath of her father should he be killed by the forest spirits.

Kyarno.

With a whooping yell, she rode to warn her lover.

With Morvhen gone, the forest took on a darker aspect, the moonlight now imparting a sinister, spectral glow instead of the silver sheen it had once provided. Where before there had been a strange warmth to the inky blackness between the trees, there was now only the chill of the grave.

'Foolish,' Leofric muttered, 'very foolish.'

Had the forest sensed the anger of the words that had passed between him and the elven princess? Was it even now withdrawing the welcome it had offered him at Coeth-Mara? If so, he would need to hurry.

Clouds covered the moon and as he rode deeper into the woods, the snow fell more heavily, and it became increasingly difficult to see the path before him. Rustling in the undergrowth and a high pitched whispering that sounded as though it came from all around him set his nerves on edge.

Leofric kept one hand loose on Taschen's reins, the other tight upon the hilt of his sword. An owl hooted nearby and he saw the grey-feathered bird perched on a snow-laden branch, watching him intently with its saucer eyes. He ignored the bird and kept his eyes flitting from shadow to shadow as they danced before him.

The sounds of the forest were magnified by his isolation – every creak of a wind blown branch or rustle of leaves made him jump, ever fearful of the creatures that had killed his men-at-arms. A clammy, creeping mist snaked through the trees and coiled around their tall trunks.

'I am a knight of Bretonnia and servant of the Lady, no harm can come to me.'

Taschen whinnied in fear and Leofric could feel a shadow steal across his soul, a dark pall of fear that he could not name or pinpoint. Unseen things rustled in the depths of the wood and a hundred whispering voices seemed to hiss from the depths of the unnatural mist.

A branch caught his armour and his sword flashed from its scabbard before he realised that he was not under attack. He rode on, not sheathing his weapon, but keeping the blade bared.

'I am a knight of Bretonnia and servant of the Lady, no harm can come to me,' he repeated, willing the simple prayer to work in the face of this darkness.

Taschen's progress through the undergrowth became slower and slower, branches, roots and bushes growing thicker with every yard gained. Leofric pushed aside low branches and twisted in the saddle as grasping thorns and briars snagged on his armour. Though he kept his sword at the ready he was unwilling yet to use its edge to clear a path, his instincts warning him of the danger of such action.

The hoot of an owl sounded again and Leofric turned to see the bird close by once more.

'You are said to be wise, friend. Do you know an easier way out of this damned forest?' he called up to it.

The owl did not reply and Leofric found himself surprised that it did not, having seen stranger things than talking animals in Athel Loren. The bird turned its head to the left and then to the right and Leofric had the distinct impression that it was shaking its head at him.

Despite his growing unease, he laughed and said, 'Perhaps you are wise after all.'

The owl bobbed its head up and down and Leofric's laughter died in his throat as it continued to watch him struggle through the gathering forest. He turned from the bird and continued onwards.

The moon emerged from behind the clouds and a deathly chill seized his heart, the light like ice-water pouring from the skies and filling his veins with the touch of death. Shadows gathered at the edge of his vision as he felt the approach of something of terrible power through the silver-streaked mist.

Leaves snatched at his helm, branches caught on his armour and roots twisted around the legs of his steed. Though his determination was still strong, he began to question the sense of his current course. Should he continue or retreat?

The hiss of something dreadful in the depths of the rising mist told him that he had long since passed the point where such a choice could be made. Shapes moved all around him, shadowy and sinuous, like ghosts in the mist, and he heard a cackling laughter. There was no humour or warmth in it though, only malice and a spiteful glee at his predicament.

His breathing came hard and fast, his heart hammering fit to break his chest, and he shouted, 'The Lady of the Lake protects me, so if you come seeking death then come out and face me!'

No sooner had the words left his mouth than the mist retreated and a blinding radiance emerged from the trees.

Leofric cried out and shielded his eyes against the glare as its shining brilliance turned the forest from night into day.

Kyarno pushed Eiderath hard, galloping into the dark, moonlit paths of the forest with terrible urgency. The foolish human was going to get himself killed and Kyarno knew that he would be the one to suffer for Leofric's stupidity. The snow was falling in earnest as he reached the edge of Coeth-Mara and though he barely felt the cold, he shivered in fearful anticipation.

He plunged headlong into the trees, taking the secret ways that only the asrai knew of, travelling in a manner beyond the purely physical. Eiderath's speed was great, the horse having been raised from a foal for a swiftness and agility that no thick-limbed human beast could ever match, but Kyarno only hoped that he could reach the human in time.

Morvhen had come to him, breathless and afraid, and as he sought to discover the source of her distress, he had felt the ancient soul of Athel Loren rise up somewhere deep within the forest.

She had told him what had passed between her and the human and unless Kyarno reached him soon, the forest would deal with him as it dealt with all intruders.

'Come, my friend,' he yelled to Eiderath as they rode. 'Tonight I need you to fly as never before!'

Leofric squinted through the halo of white light, seeing a shimmering figure emerge from the trees, and he raised his sword. The growing nimbus of light that surrounded the approaching figure began to dim, and where Leofric expected to see more of the hag creatures of branch and tree, he instead saw something far more astonishing.

Beauteous and divine, a woman of unearthly grace stood revealed in the new sunlight, unseen winds swirling around her and rippling her pale green robes. Artists would weep to see her face, knowing that they could never capture such beauty, and her eyes pierced Leofric with their kindness and wisdom. Her body shone with an inner radiance, like captured moonlight, and her arms reached out to him, trailing streamers of glittering stardust.

Leofric wept to see such splendour and felt his sword tumble from his hand, the very thought of raising arms against this goddess abhorrent to him. Helene's favour trailed from the hilt of the falling sword, blue and stark against the brilliant glow of this wonderful apparition.

'My Lady...' he whispered, his soul crying out with the rapture of this vision before him. She smiled and his heart sang with joy to be blessed so.

Leofric dismounted and dropped to his knees, clasping his hands to his breast and averting his eyes. Magical zephyrs spun her robes around her, billowing around her back like pale, gossamer wings.

Leofric...

He raised his gaze to the Lady of the Lake, for it could surely be none other, and cried out in wonder at her giving voice to his name. Leofric struggled to find words to say, but who could ever express what it was to be in the presence of a goddess?

Every knight of Bretonnia longed and dreamed for this, to be judged virtuous and valorous enough to be granted a vision of the Lady of the Lake. That such a vision should come to him here, in this place of magic and terror, was surely a sign that he had earned her favour.

Whither goest thou?

Though he was loath to defile such a divine moment with his own crude words, Leofric said, 'I return to your lands, my Lady. To your service and to my son and heir.'

You would abandon me so soon?

'No! Never!' cried Leofric.

Then why do you leave this place?

Confused, Leofric stared into the liquid pools of the Lady's eyes, awed by the power and compassion he saw there and feeling all the hurt and sorrow of the last few days rise up inside him in an unstoppable wave.

'My wife is dead!' he cried. 'This place took her from me and now I am lost!'

Leofric fell forwards onto his elbows in the snow, weeping as the full force of his grief poured from him in great, wracking sobs. The light of the Lady surrounded him and he felt her healing warmth enfold him, like a mother's comfort or a lover's embrace.

No, she is not gone from you. She is with me.

Soothing, wordless song came to him and he saw Helene standing beside the Lady, smiling and with her ringleted hair caught in the same impossible winds that stirred the Lady's robes.

'Helene...' he cried, reaching out to her.

She dwells at my side and awaits the day when you will come to her.

Leofric pushed himself to his knees and watched as the vision of Helene faded, his last sight of her a wistful smile on her lips and a playful glint in her eye. Though his heart broke to see her go, he felt a great weight lift from his shoulders at the thought of her at peace with the Lady.

'Tell me what I must do,' said Leofric. 'I am yours to command.'

There was a time when the knights of Bretonnia and the folk of this realm stood together as brothers. That day must come again. You must return.

'Return? To Coeth-Mara?' asked Leofric. 'But what of my son?'

Those around him will love him and he will grow to be a fine man.

'Will I ever see him again?'

You shall, but not now. You and Helene may yet raise him to manhood.

'I don't understand, my lady... Helene and I? How is that possible?'

Time is a winding river beneath the boughs of Athel Loren, Leofric, and many things are possible here that some would think hopeless. Paths once trod may be trod again and their ends woven anew.

Leofric fought to follow the Lady's words as they echoed within his head, their beauty and meaning slipping through his grasp like water.

Times of war and blood are coming and you must be ready, Leofric.

'I will be,' he promised.

* * *

The very air was alive with magic. Kyarno could feel it in every breath and see it in the luminescence that filled every tree with light. The song of the trees grew stronger, a rousing chorus of wondrous power that leapt from branch to branch as it spread outwards from somewhere ahead. Ghostly mists conspired to mislead and befuddle him, but Kyarno had ridden the wilder parts of the forest for decades – the groves of the dark fey and the chasm glades of Beithir-Seun – and was too clever to be taken in by such petty diversions.

Eiderath was as surefooted as ever, weaving in and out of the close-pressed trees like liquid, with barely a motion from him. Like all riders in Lord Aldaeld's kindred of Glade Riders, Kyarno had a bond with his steed nurtured from birth, and rider and mount were in perfect synchrony.

There was power afoot in the forest this night and Leofric was riding blindly into it. This was no orc-infested wood, this was Athel Loren and a thousand times more dangerous.

Apparitions moved in the mist, the cackling faces of crones and thorn-clawed harridans of winter, but Kyarno ignored them all, riding towards a brilliant glow and potent sense of magic that filled the forest ahead.

'This human will be the death of me,' he whispered as the full force of the magic rushed towards him. His skin prickled and he felt the power of Athel Loren reach deep inside him, its warmth and love coursing through his veins like an elixir.

Kyarno gasped as the power sought out all his hurts and pain, soothing them and filling him with peace. He whispered to Eiderath and the horse pulled up, stamping the ground and wishing to be at the gallop again.

The light from ahead was eclipsed as a rider emerged from the glow and Kyarno cried out as it began to fade, the wonderful light retreating into the depths of the forest. He wanted to follow, to bathe in its radiance again, but a warning voice in his head told him that such would not be permitted.

He looked up at the rider, amazed to see Leofric alive and well.

Better than that in fact. The glow that had bathed the forest in its light seemed to have left some lingering radiance on the human, his flesh and armour rippled with luminescence and elven magic. Leofric's armour shone like new and his face was alight with purpose and life.

'What happened?' managed Kyarno.

'The Lady came to me,' said Leofric, his voice awed and humbled.

'She came to you?' he asked as the knight rode past him, amazed that she would deign to take an interest in the fate of one human.

'Yes.'

'Where are you going?' asked Kyarno, turning his horse and following.

'Back to Coeth-Mara.'

'Why? I thought you wanted to leave?'

'I will leave, Kyarno, but the Lady has charged me with a quest and I am sworn to its completion.'

'A quest?' asked Kyarno. 'What quest?'

Leofric smiled and said, 'To save Athel Loren.'

CHAPTER ELEVEN

Winter reached its zenith the following morning, layering the forest in a crisp white blanket and dropping the temperature quicker than Leofric could ever remember. Snow lay thick on the ground, snapping branches from the trees with its weight and robbing the forest of its life and vitality.

But what the forest lost in life, it gained in magical beauty. Long spears of ice drooped from the branched archways, glittering in the cold sun like vast chandeliers, and snowflakes glimmered and shone like shimmering rose petals as they floated through the air. Coeth-Mara still breathed with life, but it was a still, silent life as its inhabitants awaited the first breath of spring.

The elven halls became a new home to Leofric, this dwelling of branch and leaf never cold despite the biting chill of winter beyond its confines. Whether magic or his ever-present spites kept it warm, he didn't know, but each passing day made him feel more comfortable.

Though few of the elven halls' inhabitants spoke to him, he could sense a lessening of the hostility towards him as word spread of his encounter in the woods. How the elves of the forest could understand the rapture of the Lady of the Lake was beyond Leofric's comprehension, but it was further proof that the course he had chosen was the correct one.

Weeks of winter passed, with Leofric and Kyarno often riding out into the silent forest to explore the twisting paths that lay hidden beyond the trees. Such ventures beneath the icy, snow-wreathed boughs of Athel Loren further thawed their dealings with one another, as though the shared experience in the forest that night had allowed human and elf to find some common ground, though the hostility that had characterised their previous meetings had not entirely vanished.

This was brought home to Leofric one afternoon when Kyarno had offered to teach him how to use a bow.

'No, Kyarno,' Leofric said. 'Such a weapon is fit only for peasants and those of low birth. As a warrior who follows the rules of honour I cannot countenance using such a weapon for battle.'

Leofric had seen the anger in Kyarno's face and though he now regretted his harsh words, he could not change his belief. A hurled weapon had slain Gilles le Breton, first king of Bretonnia, and, since that day, no knight had ever loosed an arrow or hurled a spear in battle.

Sometimes Morvhen would join them, chaperoned always by the Hound of Winter, and Leofric found himself looking forward to their arrival, as it invariably meant that Tiphaine and some of her handmaids would be present.

Though they never spoke, Leofric would sometimes catch Tiphaine stealing a glance towards him, and though he often wished to converse with her, he felt it would somehow sully their courtly relationship were he to thank her for the gift he was sure had come from her.

Upon waking one morning, Leofric had found fresh clothes awaiting him as he always did, but atop them was an exquisitely fashioned quilted jerkin of tan leather and silky fabric, together with soft buckskin hose. Twisting patterns of leaves and thorns were embroidered along the jerkin's sleeves and a rearing unicorn was picked out in gold thread above the heart. The garments were extraordinary, comfortable and warm, and fitted him better than anything he had ever worn before.

He had worn the jerkin beneath his armour and it had felt as natural as any armour ever had, the links of his mail shirt soft against his skin instead of biting into his flesh. He had said nothing, but Tiphaine smiled slyly when she had seen him wear it, and he resolved to do her honour by wearing her gift in whatever battles were yet to come.

Kyarno ran a hand through his long hair, the beads and jewels woven there jingling as he walked below the branches that twisted above him and marked the entrance to Lord Aldaeld's halls. The Eternal Guard stood to attention further down the leaf-strewn nave of the glittering hall. The spell-sung walls rippled with inner life and movement and Kyarno could feel the magic of the spites moving beneath the surface.

He ignored them and the sculptures of wood they formed as they played, moving through the curving paths of the inner halls towards his destination. Dressed in his finest attire, a soft green tunic embroidered with silver thread and woven with intricate patterns of leaf and tree, he hoped he looked less like Kyarno the troublemaker and more like Kyarno the peacemaker.

He sensed the stares of the Eternal Guard and those who served Lord Aldaeld upon him, their wary eyes ever vigilant for him causing some mischief. He felt his anger growing with every suspicious glance that came his way and fought to control it, casting his mind back to the divine presence he had witnessed in the forest.

Though he knew what it was he had seen, that knowledge made it no less miraculous, and he held to the peace and love he had felt at that moment, calming his simmering emotions with the memory.

He saw Cairbre across the hall, but kept his head down and walked on, not yet ready to face his uncle and the issues they had between them. Until he understood more about himself and the newly unlocked feelings within him, he knew that his anger would only get the better of him, and he didn't want that.

Kyarno found who he was looking for in a snowy glade, open to the skies and utterly silent, no sounds of bird or beast to disturb the peaceful solitude. A lone horseman galloped around the circumference of the glade, bare-chested and with an unsheathed sword.

Tarean Stormcrow swung from the back of his horse and slashed his sword at an imaginary enemy before pulling himself back up and bounding smoothly to stand on the beast's back. He drew another blade and threw himself forward in a twisting pirouette, his swords flashing left and right like silver darts. The golden-haired elf landed lightly on the back of his steed, directing it in a zigzag course through the glade with gentle pressure of his knees.

Kyarno let Tarean finish his basic exercises, watching the consummate ease with which elf and steed worked together. Tarean Stormcrow was a fine rider, though Kyarno knew that in a kindred of Glade Riders, there were others of much greater skill.

'You are leaning too far to your left, Tarean Stormcrow,' called out Kyarno as Lord Aldaeld's herald finished his exercises. 'A right-handed enemy with a longer reach would kill you first.'

Tarean leapt lightly from his horse, a light sheen of sweat coating his lean, tattooed body, and sheathed his twin swords. He nodded in recognition as he saw who observed him, and pulled his hair back to settle his circlet upon his brow as Kyarno walked towards him.

'Thank you for the advice, Kyarno, I will remember it.'

'Your next battle would have reminded you soon enough.'

Tarean nodded, sensing that Kyarno was not here to argue or berate him for some real or imagined slight, and slapped his shoulder, saying, 'To what do I owe the pleasure of this visit, my friend? You didn't just come here to advise me on my swordplay.'

'You do not miss anything, Tarean, do you?'

'You are not hard to read, my friend.'

Kyarno smiled weakly. 'I suppose not. But you're right, I did come here for more than that, though Isha knows you need it,' he said, reaching up to pat the bay gelding Tarean had been riding. The beast was magnificent, easily one of the finest steeds of the Éadaoin kinband, its flaxen coat smooth and shining. 'I came to apologise to you, Tarean.'

'Apologise to me?' said Tarean, wiping the sweat from his face with a fine cloth.

'Yes,' nodded Kyarno. 'You once said that you offered me friendship. I threw it back in your face, and for that I am sorry.'

'No apology is necessary, my friend,' said Tarean, offering his hand to Kyarno.

'Does your offer still stand?'

Tarean nodded. 'Of course it does, Kyarno. I do not make such offers just to retract them later.'

'Good,' replied Kyarno and reached out to grip Tarean's hand. 'I think that you and I could be friends and am willing to see if such a thing is possible.'

Tarean walked to a tree where his overshirt hung and pulled it over his head, settling it over his shoulders and straightening his sword belt.

'I am glad you think so, Kyarno, but tell me, what brought about this change of heart?'

'I'm not sure,' admitted Kyarno, unwilling yet to share what had happened in the forest. 'I think that I carried a great bitterness and it poisoned me to those who loved me. I shut myself off from them and my heart became like one of the humans' hateful fortresses of stone.'

Kyarno paced as he spoke, having to force every word and finding each one both difficult and cathartic to say.

'When my parents were killed... I... I...'

'You blamed Cairbre,' finished Tarean. 'I know. He rescued you from the beastmen attack and carried you to safety. You blamed him for not reaching you in time to save your parents.'

'No,' said Kyarno, shaking his head. 'That's not it.'

'No?'

'No,' repeated Kyarno. 'I blamed him for not letting me die with them.'

Tarean said nothing, plainly surprised at his admission, but the well was undammed now and Kyarno's words would not stop.

'But then I learned that it wasn't his fault that he hadn't got to us in time. It was Naieth. She was to blame.'

'Why do you think this?'

'Cairbre told me years later that she had come to Lord Aldaeld with a vision of beastmen raiding the Meadow Glades in the south. Cairbre's Eternal Guard and the Waywatchers had been sent to destroy them.'

'I remember now,' whispered Tarean. 'But she was wrong, wasn't she? They were not in the Meadow Glades at all.'

'No, they were not,' said Kyarno. 'The creatures of Chaos had penetrated deep into Athel Loren and came upon the halls of my father. They came with burning brands and bloody axes and killed everyone they found. My mother, my father and my sisters... all of them died that day.'

Tarean laid his hand on Kyarno's arm, and he could feel the pain of those memories rise up in a suffocating wave. 'I was just a child, but I remember it all, the flames, the fear and the blood... so much blood. I can see it even now, clear as a winter's morning. Cairbre must have heard the forest cry out in anger or felt his brother's fear for his kin, I don't know, but he and the Eternal Guard swiftly travelled the secret paths of the forest and destroyed the monsters. But it was too late, I was the only one left alive.'

The two elves sat in silence for some time, Kyarno lost in the pain of a time long passed and Tarean sitting patiently with a fellow elf and letting him speak in his own time.

'Cairbre saved you,' said Tarean at last. 'You should be thankful for that.'

'I know,' agreed Kyarno, 'but I was young and foolish. I screamed and cursed him for not coming sooner, for deserting his kin and letting them die. Isha alone knows why I said the things I did, for they must have cut him deeply. But I did say them and when I finally accepted that it wasn't even his fault, it was too late, we had erected impenetrable walls between us.'

'No wall is impenetrable, Kyarno,' said Tarean. 'Remember that.'

The breath of the gods blew strong, the power of the shaman growing with each passing heartbeat. The presence of the Shadow-Gave in the mountains aided its magic, empowering the shaman as one chosen by the Dark Gods. The rain continued to fall around it, black and noxious, and the ground turned to a stinking quagmire beneath its hoofs.

The wind blew cold and hard, flapping the tattered and rotted robes around its twisted and hunched body of shaggy fur. Its horns dripped with black moisture and its magically attuned eyes were filled with the crackling lines of magic that flared from the waystone before it.

The lethal wall of thorn and branch still stood, though the shaman could see the tips of the furthest growths were blackened and twisted, dying as the power of Chaos touched it. Time had ceased to have meaning for the herd, days and nights blurring into one continual span, though the shaman was dimly aware of enemy magic at work, some unknown force sweeping them up in its wake. Snow froze them, rain lashed them and the sun baked the mud on their backs to hard clay, all within the space of a passing of the sun.

But for each faerie trick unleashed by the forest, the shaman had an answer, his greater power causing black veins of necrotic energy to leech their way up the length of the waystone. The enchantments woven into the living rock were strong, forged when the world was young, but the breath of the gods was eternal and unyielding.

The shaman's staff crackled with energy, bruised arcs of light flaring from its gnarled tip and the stink of raw, dangerous magic.

The Beastlord paced like a caged thing, its impatience to be about its bloody work palpable, and the shaman knew that if it did not bring the waystone down soon then its life was forfeit.

Soon the waystone's magic would be all but spent and it would fall, unable to bend the dark forest around it to its will.

And then the Beastlord's herd would hunt.

As the winter locked Coeth-Mara in its enveloping crystalline grip, the days passed with funereal slowness, each short span of daylight gratefully seized by the inhabitants of Lord Aldaeld's halls. Leofric spent his days riding into the forest with Kyarno and learning more of the culture he now found himself immersed in.

Though he and Kyarno often spoke of the asrai, their history and their society, he never felt any real connection to them, as though there was a barrier between man and elf that no amount of conversation could ever erode. He and Kyarno, and, to a lesser extent, Morvhen, had become friendly enough, but Leofric would not count them as friends. In every word that passed between them, he always sensed a faint air of condescension, as though the elves were somehow lessening themselves by talking to him.

Of Naieth he saw almost nothing, save for a chance encounter at the spite-wrought sculpture pools where Leofric performed his ablutions each morning. The day was crisp and clear, though not cold, and Leofric had taken off the jerkin Tiphaine had fashioned for him and was in the process of trying to shave when Naieth had silently come up behind him. The sudden appearance of her reflection behind him made him jump and his razor nicked his cheek.

A drop of blood fell into the pool and the water instantly foamed as though boiling, a trio of water-formed tendrils leaping up from the water, a dazzling core of light in each one. Leofric dropped his razor and stumbled back from the pool as the tendrils angrily reached for him.

Before they could touch him, his own spites sped forward and interposed themselves between the water spites, shifting to become angry red balls of light with fanged mouths and gleaming stag horns of light. Both groups of spites hissed and spat at one another until Naieth's lyrical elven tones sang out and the three tendrils of water retreated back into the pool, mollified by whatever she had said.

'Greetings, Leofric,' said Naieth. 'You are well?'

'Well enough,' nodded Leofric, rubbing his cheek where his blade had cut his skin. 'What happened there?'

'The water spites don't like human blood,' explained Naieth, sitting on the edge of the pool and waving to something high in the snowy treetops. 'They feel it is impure and should not be mixed with the waters of Athel Loren.'

'That suits me, I would prefer for my blood not to be shed,' said Leofric as a familiar looking, grey-feathered owl dropped from the trees and landed on Naieth's shoulder. It hooted once and bobbed its head in Leofric's direction.

'Is that your owl?' asked Leofric, recovering his razor and warily rinsing his face in the pool.

'Yes, his name is Othu.'

'I saw him,' said Leofric. 'In the forest.'

The owl hooted again and made a sound that Leofric could only interpret as laughter.

'Indeed you did,' smiled Naieth. 'Othu asks if you have recovered from your journey?'

Leofric nodded as he gathered up the rest of his clothes, pulling his dark hair back and tying it at the base of his neck with a leather cord. He was becoming unkempt here without his servants to keep him presentable and he knew his appearance was becoming closer to the elves than a knight of Bretonnia.

'Tell him I have, thank you very much.'

'Tell him yourself, he is right here.'

Leofric looked at the owl and said, 'I feel foolish talking to an owl.'

'Then imagine how *he* feels,' sniffed Naieth, rising from the pool and walking away. As she departed, the owl turned its head and shifted its feathers in a manner that looked for all the world like a weary shrug.

Gathering up his things, Leofric left the pool and made his way back through the leafy paths and hollows of Coeth-Mara, intending to change into his armour and practise his swordplay. He might be far from home, but that was no excuse to let his skills become rusty.

As he made his way through the silent forest of ice, he felt he might as well be walking alone, such was his sense of peaceful solitude and tranquillity. His heart still ached to see his son again and he missed Helene's soft company, but each day the hurt was lessened and his will to serve the quest entrusted to him by the Lady of the Lake grew stronger.

He smiled as he again pictured the Lady's wondrous, aquiline features, her hair of gold and overwhelming powers of healing and renewal. Such visions were a thing of beauty and rarity and he wanted to remember every detail flawlessly.

So caught up in his reverie was he that he didn't hear the first shrill yell as it echoed through the forest. It took a second, high-pitched shriek to intrude on Leofric's senses before he realised that he was not alone any more.

Fast-moving figures spun from the trees around him, leaping from branch to branch and corkscrewing madly through the air. Elves, that much was obvious, but these were of a kind he had not seen before. How many there were, he couldn't say, their speed was too great to make any kind of guess.

They circled him with whooping yells and bared blades, and as the noose closed tighter about him, Leofric dropped his towel and shaving razor and gripped the hilt of his sword. One of the figures stopped moving long enough for him to take a proper look at his new companions.

The elf was tall and slender-limbed, though the taut, corded muscles of his chest, stomach and arms belied his frailty. Despite the snow and ice that lay over the forest, the elf was nearly naked, a thin loincloth and golden torques on his upper arms the only concession to attire. His body was covered almost entirely in tattoos, weaving thorns and briars, and a snarling blood-red wolf decorated his chest.

His hair was a wild coxcomb of red, raised in jagged points, and his face was as tattooed as his body, with looping spirals of thorns decorating each cheek and sharpened jawbones and teeth adorning the skin around his own jaw. The elf wore a thin necklace of gold and bronze, his wild eyes alight with savage mischief.

Leofric tore his gaze from this barbaric-looking elf as the others closed in, their wild cries and yells disorientating as they leapt and bounded around him.

Each one carried twin blades and their swords snaked around their bodies like liquid trails of silver, their every movement lithe and supple. One leapt from the ground and seemed to run up the side of a mighty oak before bounding to perch, bird-like, atop a thin branch that was surely too slender to bear his weight. Another spun through the air, her swords like striking snakes as they danced and she pirouetted to land before him with her blades aimed at his heart.

Each one performed impossible feats of acrobatics, leaping and twisting through the air in defiance of gravity before landing in aggressive stances around him, not one looking even slightly out of breath.

Leofric looked beyond the warlike elves, but saw no one that might come to his aid anywhere near. The elf who had stopped moving first spat something in elvish and the others took a perfectly choreographed step towards him, their swords cutting the air with a slow, purposeful grace. The leader, if such he was, looked at him with naked hostility, his perfect features curled in contempt and disgust. As he approached, Leofric saw that the tattoo of the wolf on his chest rippled with life, its fangs baring and its eyes narrowing in feral anticipation.

Looking at the tattoo he realised the identity of the elf he stood before.

'The Red Wolf...' said Leofric.

Quicker than he would have believed anyone could move, even an elf, a tattooed hand snatched out and gripped his throat, the tip of a long knife an inch from his eye.

'You dare speak of Cu-Sith?' hissed the elf. 'Cu-Sith should kill you now. Loec? What say you, shall Cu-Sith kill him?'

'No!' gagged Leofric, hoping whichever of these elves was Loec could hear him.

'Let us perform the Dance of a Hundred Wounds,' said another of the elves as they slowly began circling Leofric like stalking cats. A sword slashed out, cutting a lock of hair from Leofric's head.

'No, the Masque of the Red Rain,' said another, leaping into the air and stabbing his swords either side of Leofric's head, a fingerbreadth from his ears.

'The Tarantella of the Wailing Death!' cried a third, her blades flicking out and kissing the underside of his jaw. Leofric's heart pounded in fear of these wild elves, fighting to keep his panic in check as more blades licked out and wove a tapestry of silver steel around him. He knew that if he moved so much as a muscle he was a dead man, though the Red Wolf was clearly untroubled by the storm of blades flashing around them.

'Enough!' said the Red Wolf, cocking his head to one side. 'Loec tells Cu-Sith that we need something special for this one!'

Leofric took a great, gulping breath of air as the iron grip around his throat was released and the Red Wolf took a step back. With the flashing blades no longer weaving around him, Leofric felt his heartbeat begin to slow, and he watched as the elves began circling him again. Each one was practically naked, but for golden torques and thin harnesses of leather. Their skin was daubed with chalk and lime and heavily painted with vivid dyes, and they wore their resin-stiffened hair in wild, elaborate styles. They watched him with predatory eyes, but moved like the most graceful dancers and Leofric realised he looked upon the Red Wolf's troupe of wardancers.

'I am a guest of Lord Aldaeld,' said Leofric, massaging his bruised throat.

The Red Wolf lunged forward, baring his teeth like the wolf on his chest. 'You think Cu-Sith doesn't know that? Cu-Sith knows everything Loec does!'

'Loec...' said Leofric, now remembering Kyarno mentioning the name. 'Wait, isn't he one of your gods?'

'That he is,' nodded the Red Wolf, reaching up to dab his finger in the blood on Leofric's cheek. 'And a close friend of Cu-Sith, human.'

'I see,' nodded Leofric.

'Kill him and garland the trees with his entrails!' shouted one of the wardancers.

'No, present them to Lord Aldaeld!'

'Silence!' shouted the Red Wolf, somersaulting backwards onto the bough above Leofric. 'Cu-Sith likes this one. Didn't flinch during the sword dance. Sensible. Might keep him as a pet.'

'Pet! Pet! Pet!' chanted the circling wardancers.

'Are you Cu-Sith?' asked Leofric, as the Red Wolf swung from the branch to land lightly in a crouch before him. The leader of the wardancers nodded, rolling forwards and twirling a pair of swords as he rose to his feet with a grace no human dancer could ever hope to match.

'Cu-Sith heard that a human was kept in Lord Aldaeld's halls, but did not believe it. Now Cu-Sith sees him and wonders why he is not dead,' said the wardancer, the eyes of his wolf tattoo following Leofric as Cu-Sith circled him in the opposite direction to his troupe.

'Tell me, human, why are you not dead and why should Cu-Sith not make it so?'

Leofric tried to stay calm as the snarling, hissing elf stopped behind him, sniffing his neck and shoulders like a wild animal.

'I... I was spared from the forest spirits by Naieth,' said Leofric.

'The prophetess?'

'Yes, yes, the prophetess.'

Cu-Sith circled back around, leaning in close and turning Leofric's head with the flat of his blade. 'She wants you alive? Why?'

'I don't know for certain,' said Leofric, the words tumbling from him in a frantic rush. 'She says there are times of war coming and that I am to fight alongside the elves of Athel Loren.'

'You?' spat Cu-Sith, spinning his blades and sheathing them before catching another pair hurled towards him without his asking. 'Cu-Sith does not believe you. What about you, Loec?'

The leader of the wardancers closed his eyes and cocked his head to one side, as though listening to a voice only he could hear. The other wardancers looked on in awe as their leader nodded and laughed to himself at some unheard jest. Suddenly Cu-Sith's eyes snapped open and he brought his new swords up in a cross-wise slash, each blade slicing the skin of Leofric's cheeks.

Leofric flinched from the thin cuts, more in surprise than pain, as Cu-Sith spoke again. 'Loec says for Cu-Sith to let you go, but you are marked now, human. Cu-Sith's pet you are now!'

The wardancers laughed and spun faster and faster around him, peeling off one by one and disappearing into the forest in bounding somersaults and incredible leaps from tree to tree.

The Red Wolf remained before him for a second longer before giving out a manic laugh and flipping up into the high branches above. Leofric tried to follow his progress as he leapt higher and higher into the branches, but was forced to look away as dislodged powdery snow fell into his eyes.

And when he looked again, Cu-Sith was nowhere to be seen.

Leofric made his way back down into the more populated halls of Coeth-Mara, shaken to the core by his brush with the wardancers. Cu-Sith had terrified him with his fearsome display of lunacy, the leader of the wardancers clearly insane to believe that he spoke directly to a god.

There had been a wild madness to the Red Wolf and its sheer

unpredictability scared him more than anything else. Who knew what such an individual might do?

As he descended into Coeth-Mara, he dabbed the cuts on his cheeks, wondering if he actually was Cu-Sith's pet in the eyes of the elves, or whether it was just another indication of his madness.

Now Leofric understood the wariness and unease he had sensed when Tarean Stormcrow had first mentioned the leader of the wardancers.

Leofric shivered, feeling a tremor of unease pass through the boughs and branches around him and a sudden chill pierced him. He looked around him for the source of his unease, but could see nothing specific.

Elves moved through the snow-wreathed paths of Coeth-Mara, but there was an urgency to their movements now, a suspicious fear in their glances as they retreated to their halls.

Ahead, Leofric could see a group of riders coming towards him and stood aside as the Lord of Coeth-Mara and his daughter rode past, accompanied by Tarean Stormcrow, Naieth, the Hound of Winter and a dozen of his warriors. Both Aldaeld and Morvhen were regal and magnificent in pale robes of cream silk and embroidered gold. Lord Aldaeld wore a crown of antlers and carried his green-hilted longsword belted at his side, while Morvhen was unarmed.

Neither gave him a second glance as they passed.

Naieth gave him the briefest of acknowledgements, her robes of gold shining in the morning sun and her staff of woven branches shimmering with dew. Tarean Stormcrow, dressed in an elaborate tunic of sky blue silk and silver, and carrying a long, hardwood spear, peeled away from the procession to stop before Leofric.

'What happened to you?' he asked, noticing the cuts on his face.

Leofric glanced over his shoulder and said, 'I met the Red Wolf.'

'Cu-Sith!' hissed Tarean. 'You encountered his wardancers?'

'Yes,' nodded Leofric. 'It was… a memorably frightening experience.'

'I should imagine it was,' agreed Tarean. 'I am surprised he let you live. Cu-Sith has no love for those of your race.'

'So I saw,' said Leofric, dabbing at the cuts once more.

'Be that as it may, Leofric, you must return to your chambers and prepare yourself. Clean the blood from your face, put on your finest clothes, polish your armour then await my summons.'

'Why? What is happening?'

Tarean nodded in the direction of the group of Lord Aldaeld's riders as they disappeared into the trees.

'The Laithu kinband has arrived for the Winter Feast,' he said.

CHAPTER TWELVE

Two score of them there were. Each was richly attired, outlandishly so, thought Caelas Shadowfoot as he watched the procession of riders from his vantage point in the heights of a hoary old willow tree. The easily recognisable figure of Valas Laithu rode at the head of the column, his cloak of red a bad omen in these times of trouble, knew Caelas.

A human in Coeth-Mara and the Red Wolf attending the Winter Feast. No good could come of it. Where the Red Wolf danced, trouble followed.

He watched Valas turn to say something to a young, sharp-featured elf beside him, the youth nodding curtly, as though he had heard these words many times before. Caelas recognised the stripling as Sirda, son of Valas, and felt a shiver travel up his spine that had nothing to do with the frost that coated the gnarled bark of the tree he clung to.

Both Valas and his offspring were known to the Eadaoin kinband, as was their reputation for deviousness and cruelty. Where other kinbands might kill intruders to Athel Loren or send them back the way they had come in equal measure, the Laithu kinband would see all such trespassers dead, their bones left at the forest's edge as a grim warning to others.

Even from hundreds of feet up, Caelas could see the cruel lines on Valas Laithu's pale face and did not envy Lord Aldaeld the coming gathering. Sirda was no better, having inherited the worst of his father's traits as well as developing some bad ones of his own.

Caelas edged around the bole of the tree, leaning out onto a snow-covered branch and signalling that the Laithu kinband drew near to one of the Éadaoin kinband's waywatchers nearer to Coeth-Mara. Though, truth be told, none needed warning, as the riders below had made no attempt to disguise their approach. A single scout had travelled before them, Caelas and his waywatchers having tracked him for the past week, oft times passing within a few paces of his position to test his skills – but not once had the Laithu scout observed them.

Caelas was disappointed in the lack of caution shown by the Laithu kinband. Everything he had heard of them had led him to believe they were warriors of skill and cunning, though what he had seen over the last week did not bear such a reputation out. He and his waywatchers could have ambushed the Laithu kinband a dozen times or more, slaughtering them in a hail of arrows before their prey had even known they were there.

But such were not their orders. These visitors to Coeth-Mara were to be allowed to approach unmolested. As he watched them draw away from him in the direction of Lord Aldaeld's halls, Caelas briefly considered following them and returning to the place where he had been born. It had been many years since he had seen his kin, but the thought of being amongst others sat uncomfortably with him.

He loved his kin and kinband, but only here, in the magnificent wilds of the forest, did he feel truly at home. Indeed, it had been months since he had laid eyes on any of his fellow waywatchers, content to read their signs in the wild and communicate through the secret language of the forest known only to them.

Caelas ran along the tall branches of the willow and leapt across the gap between it and a white-leaved chestnut, swinging around its thin trunk and looping his way down the tree. Even before he landed, his bow was drawn and an arrow nocked as he scanned the undergrowth for signs of life. He already knew there was nothing around here for hundreds of yards that he was not already aware of, but a waywatcher did not live to be as old as Caelas by relaxing his guard.

He risked a glance around the chestnut's trunk, watching the last signs of the Laithu kinband vanish from sight. Something sat ill with him and the decades spent alone in the wilderness had taught him to trust his instincts.

Caelas ghosted from tree to tree, invisible in his grey cloak and stealthy movements, examining the trail left by the riders. He shook his head as he silently gauged the depths of their tracks, seeing that they had taken no care to cover their back trail or ride in single file to better disguise their numbers.

No, something sat ill indeed and Caelas was not one to let such things lie.

The waywatcher set off into the forest, determined to find the truth of what was going on.

* * *

'Blood of Kurnous,' whispered Lord Aldaeld as he watched Valas Laithu and his retinue come into view over the snow-covered rise ahead. 'This will be a trial indeed.'

'My lord?' said Tarean Stormcrow, adjusting his cloak and tunic so that it sat perfectly. Tarean altered his grip on the spear he held, brushing a melting snowflake from his shoulder. The rituals of elven greetings were highly formalised and were Tarean to fail in his duty as herald, the dishonour would pass to Aldaeld himself.

Aldaeld and his most trusted kin, his herald, his daughter, his champion and a dozen of his loyal Eternal Guard, had come for this rare meeting of elves from across the forest. The prophetess had insisted on accompanying him too, and while he had only grudgingly offered her the hospitality of his halls, he was glad of her presence here now. Lord Valas was known to be a dabbler in the mystic arts and Naieth's presence was, this time, a welcome one.

The tension in this leaf-strewn archway of ice and snow was palpable, none able to deny the apprehension that Lord Valas's visit had brought.

'I will be glad when this snake is far from my halls,' said Aldaeld.

'I understand, my lord, but custom demands that we make him welcome,' pointed out Tarean Stormcrow.

'I know that,' snapped Aldaeld, gripping the hilt of his sword tightly. 'It does not mean I have to like it.'

'Perhaps you should not hold your sword thusly,' suggested his daughter.

He looked down, startled that he had not even noticed he was gripping the hilt so tightly. Aldaeld smiled at his daughter and said, 'Yes, you are probably right, my dear.'

She was beautiful, thought Aldaeld, regal and every inch the daughter of an elven lord and, were circumstances different, he had hoped Morvhen would have plighted her troth to Tarean Stormcrow by now. Alas, her heart had gone to the ne'er-do-well, Kyarno, and as much as he had tried to keep her from Cairbre's nephew, his every attempt had served only to bring them closer.

Thinking of the miscreant Kyarno brought a scowl to his rugged, ancient features. His every instinct was to throw Kyarno to Valas Laithu, but both Tarean Stormcrow and the Hound of Winter had recently spoken to him of their belief that Kyarno was not yet a hopeless case. Aldaeld was still to see proof of that and this visitation by the Laithu kinband was yet another reason for Aldaeld to wish him gone from his halls.

'Do not worry, father, this will be over with soon,' promised Morvhen.

'I fear it will not be over soon enough, daughter,' said Aldaeld. 'Valas will want his pound of flesh for your lover's mischief before this is out and I only hope his foolishness does not cost us all too dearly.'

'Father–' began Morvhen.

'You should not think to defend him, Morvhen,' interrupted Aldaeld.

'He would not thank you for it and he does not deserve it. Do not think me ignorant of all that passes in my domain, daughter. I know what happened in the forest between Kyarno and the Hound of Winter before the creatures of Chaos attacked.'

Morvhen flushed and looked away and even Cairbre had the good grace to look embarrassed at Aldaeld's words. Seeing the hurt in his daughter's eyes, Aldaeld's expression softened and he reached out to touch her shoulder.

'Neither am I blind to the desires of your heart towards Kyarno, but I must put the welfare of this kinband before anyone's feelings. Even yours. Kyarno has a good soul, I see it, truly I do, but until he *learns* his place in my kinband, there is no place for him in it.'

'My lord,' said Tarean Stormcrow. 'Perhaps this is a conversation best had another time? Lord Valas approaches.'

Aldaeld kept his eyes on his daughter for a few seconds more before turning to face Lord Valas and his warriors, his stern, patrician demeanour reasserting itself once more.

Lord Valas was tall, thin and pale-skinned, even for an elf, his slender frame clad in rich robes of heavy furs and soft tan leather. The hood of his spite-rippled cloak of red leaves was pulled back and his long, dark hair was swept into a tight ponytail with a circlet of gold across his brow. His tapered ears were hung with beads of gold and his eyes were a brilliant shade of blue.

Valas nodded to Aldaeld and bowed his head a fraction. Aldaeld echoed the gesture as Tarean edged his horse forward, a precise bowstave-length away from the newcomers. His herald lifted the long spear he carried. Its shaft was etched with spiral grooves and tipped with a patterned copper blade engraved with eyes that were said to seek out and defeat an enemy's blows.

'Lord Valas,' began Tarean, holding the spear by the hardwood haft and offering it to the lord of the Laithu kinband. 'Aldaeld, Lord of a Hundred Battles, bids me welcome you to Coeth-Mara and offers you this gift as a token of our kinbands' fellowship. Fashioned at Vaul's Anvil by Daith, master craftsman of the Ash Groves, it is potent with the magic of Athel Loren and was wielded in battle by the great eagle-rider Thalandor.'

Valas Laithu reached out and plucked the spear from Tarean's hand, examining the magnificent weapon without apparent interest. He nodded briefly and handed the weapon to his son, who gave the spear a much more thorough examination.

Sirda was the image of his father, saw Aldaeld, sharp-featured and without the grace of the asrai who dwelt in harmony and balance with the forest. Sirda seemed furtive, always looking beyond the Éadaoin Eternal Guard, and Aldaeld could guess who he was looking for. The Laithu were a harsh kinband, merciless to those not their own, even other elves, and unlike his father, Sirda was armed, bearing a pair of elegant swords and a long, ornamented bow across his back.

'Lord Aldaeld's gift is most welcome,' said Valas Laithu. 'I thank him for it and bid him greetings from my kin. Will he permit us to enter his halls freely?'

Tarean Stormcrow turned back to Aldaeld and the elven lord held the moment before saying, 'I will indeed. I offer you the freedom of Coeth-Mara and bid you join my kin for the Winter Feast.'

'You honour me,' said Valas. 'Rightly is it said that even the lowest that arrive at Lord Aldaeld's hall will receive his charity.'

Aldaeld bristled at Valas's words. Obviously Valas knew of the human in Coeth-Mara and was keen to show his disapproval.

He nodded and said, 'All are welcome within my halls, even those who would normally be turned away.'

Valas smiled, though there was no warmth to it, and said, 'Happily we are all in accord here. Is that not so?'

'It is indeed,' said Tarean Stormcrow quickly. 'Lord Aldaeld has spoken of little else but your visit to his halls.'

'I'm sure,' laughed Valas and Aldaeld fought to control his temper as he saw Sirda Laithu cast secretive, lascivious glances towards Morvhen. Catching Aldaeld's eye, Sirda gave a guilty smile and returned to surveying the forest behind them.

'He is not here, Sirda,' said Aldaeld, now sure of the object of the young elf's search.

'Who?' replied Sirda, feigning ignorance.

'You know who I mean, boy. Kyarno.'

'I am not a boy,' snarled Sirda. His face flushed and he reached for his sword. His father's hand snatched out and gripped his son's wrist.

'Ah, yes, the outlaw,' said Valas, easing his son's hand from his sword hilt. 'His theft of our steeds was an act of great skill and cunning. I much desire to meet him. He still resides within your halls, Lord Aldaeld?'

'For now,' nodded Aldaeld.

'Then bid him attend the Winter Feast,' said Valas. 'I wish to meet this elf who can evade my waywatchers and steal away with our most beloved steeds.'

'Kyarno let them loose as soon as he stole them!' snapped Morvhen. 'They must have returned to their stable glades soon after.'

'Daughter!' barked Aldaeld. 'Know your place here! Be silent!'

Aldaeld could see the amusement in the faces of the Laithu kinband and knew he had to end this farce of a welcome.

'Come,' he said, turning his steed. 'The Winter Feast awaits!'

Leofric thought he had already seen the full majesty of Coeth-Mara, but as he sat in the inner halls of Lord Aldaeld, he realised that what he had seen thus far had been but a taster for this miraculous sight.

The abiding impression he would take to his grave was that of light.

Though winter had laid its velvet blanket of night upon the forest and the darkness crept back into the world almost as soon as it had left, the feast hall of Coeth-Mara was lit with dazzling brightness and colour.

'Close your mouth,' said Kyarno. 'A spite will fly in and then you'll be sorry.'

Leofric snapped his mouth shut, having not realised it had fallen open again at the awe-inspiring sight of such incredible beauty. He and Kyarno sat at a gracefully curved table that grew from the soft earthen floor of the hall, alongside laughing elves who told lyrical tales and sang heartbreakingly beautiful ballads in their wonderfully musical language.

'Sorry,' he mumbled, taking another drink of water.

The spell-sung walls were tall and majestic, twisting, looping spirals of pale branches weaving in intricate, natural patterns towards an arched ceiling of great, needle-pointed icicles. Each one was home to a spite of some sort, the ice glittering with the golden light of the creatures at play within.

Tresses of branch and flower garlanded every wall and a tall fire of dead wood burned in the centre of the hall, surrounded by tables and benches shaped from the roots of the mighty trees that enclosed Lord Aldaeld's hall.

Warmth and life filled the hall as the elves of Coeth-Mara gathered for feasting and song, perhaps a hundred souls come to make merry with their fellows. Attending to the elves of Coeth-Mara were youngsters who bore platters of meats and fruit and jugs of wine throughout the hall. None looked older than ten summers and the sight of them reminded Leofric of his own son's face once more. The boys each wore a simple tunic of pale green, upon which was embroidered a white stag, and the sight of these youths sent a pang of aching sadness through Leofric.

Through previous discourse with Kyarno, he had learned that winter was a time of sadness within Athel Loren as the forest slept away the long watches of darkness before the joyous coming of the spring.

But even amidst this time of darkness it seemed there was life and joy to be had, the darkness tempered by the sure and certain knowledge of the forest's rebirth.

Such was the purpose of the Winter Feast, a celebration of life amid death.

The scent of new blooming flowers was incongruous, but welcome, and the sense of shared kinship and love amongst Lord Aldaeld's people was contagious, even though Leofric knew he was not truly a part of this celebration.

Leofric wondered if perhaps it was that very detachment that allowed him to better see the tension lurking behind the smiling faces of the revellers, for he could sense an underlying current of wariness among Lord Aldaeld's people. Whether that wariness was due to the surly presence of the newly-arrived warriors of the Laithu kinband or Cu-Sith and his prowling wardancers, who stalked through the hall like predatory cats, Leofric did not know, but he had felt it the moment he had entered.

Leofric wasn't even sure why he was here, Tarean having sent for him as the pale light of afternoon turned to the soft purple of dusk. True to his word, Leofric had cleaned himself up as best he could – though his beard and hair were beginning to get the better of him – put on Tiphaine's jerkin and hose, polished his armour and awaited his summons. More used to the stiff formality of the court feasts at Quenelles, Leofric had been pleasantly surprised by the informality he saw here.

Though even in such apparent informality he saw there was a hierarchy at work. Seated at the far end of the hall, on a raised dais of pale wood, were Lord Aldaeld and his closest kin. Naieth and Morvhen sat beside the lord of Coeth-Mara, together with Tarean Stormcrow, while behind them stood the warriors of the Eternal Guard.

'What manner of weapon does Cairbre wield?' asked Leofric as he watched the Hound of Winter complete another circuit of the hall with his long twin-bladed spear held beside him.

'It is called a *Saearath*, which means "spear-stave" in your tongue,' explained Kyarno, procuring himself a plate of aoilym fruit and another jug of wine, 'though the weapon Cairbre carries is unique. He is the bearer of the Blades of Midnight.'

'Unique? Is it magical?'

'It is said so,' nodded Kyarno, 'but none but the bearer may know its powers.'

'Why is that?'

'I don't know,' shrugged Kyarno, obviously unwilling to be drawn further. Leofric decided to change the subject and looked over to the end of the hall at the guests of Lord Aldaeld, saying, 'Is that the leader of the Laithu kinband with Lord Aldaeld? He looks quite different from the elves I have seen in Coeth-Mara.'

'As well he ought,' nodded Kyarno, taking a bite from the red-skinned fruit, the bittersweet aroma filling the air and making Leofric's mouth water. He longed to taste the strange fruit, but the dire consequences that would result from partaking of magical faerie food and wine had been drummed into him from boyhood.

He shook his head clear of the desire to eat the elven fruit as Kyarno spoke again of the Laithu kinband. 'They hail from the Vaults of Winter, a gloomy place of permanent darkness and cold, where the season never changes and the glow of the moons is the only light to touch their skins.'

'That sounds like a terrible place,' said Leofric. 'Why do they stay there?'

'It is their home,' replied Kyarno, as though the answer should be obvious. 'In your tongue, the name Laithu means Moonblade, and it is said they work their finest enchantments with the light of the stars.'

'And why are they here?'

'Ah…' said Kyarno, wiping the aoilym fruit's juice from his chin and taking a long drink of wine from the jug. 'That might have something to do with me...'

'What do you mean?'

'During the summer I crept into their stable glades and took some of their steeds.'

'You stole from them?'

'Only for a while,' protested Kyarno. 'I let the horses go once I was clear of their domain. The steeds would have returned to the stable glades soon after.'

'If you let them go then why did you steal them in the first place?' asked Leofric.

'It was a bit of harmless fun,' sighed Kyarno. 'Isha's tears, you are starting to sound like Cairbre! I took them to show that I could. Haven't you ever tried something impossible just to prove that it could be done?'

Leofric started to shake his head, then stopped as a memory surfaced. Kyarno saw his realisation and said, 'You have, haven't you? Come on, tell me of it.'

'No, it's not the same.'

'Come on, tell me!' laughed Kyarno, relishing Leofric's discomfort and drinking more wine.

Leofric spread his hands and said, 'All right, all right. You have to understand though, that I was but a knight errant at the time and young and foolish.'

'You're stalling. Come on, tell me what you did,' urged Kyarno.

'Very well,' said Leofric. 'To be worthy of the chance to court Helene, I rashly challenged Duke Chilfroy of Artois to a joust on the tilting fields of Couronne. He was the best and bravest knight in Bretonnia, skilled beyond all others with a lance, and no man had ever unhorsed him. We faced each other down the length of the field and though I was shaking fit to soil my armour, I knew... somehow I just knew that I could best him.'

'How?'

'I don't know, I just knew,' shrugged Leofric. 'It was as though the Lady had whispered it as a certainty in my ear.'

'And did you beat him?' asked Kyarno, finishing the last of the wine.

'Yes,' nodded Leofric proudly. 'My lance took him clean in the centre of his chest and sent him flying from the back of his horse. I do not think I have ever had as sweet a memory as that.'

'You see?' said Kyarno, putting down the empty wine jug and rising unsteadily to his feet. 'Don't pretend you don't understand what I did. It's the urge to achieve what can't be achieved, the drive to succeed in the impossible task that makes us feel really alive! You felt it as you challenged the knight and I felt it when I stole the Laithu kinband's steeds. And I'd do it again!'

'Really? Even after the trouble it's caused you?'

'Are you saying you wouldn't challenge that knight again?'

Leofric shook his head. 'I am older and wiser now, Kyarno. I have become a knight of the realm and I recognise the difference between valour and impetuosity.'

'That's no answer!' cried Kyarno. 'And anyway, I need some more wine.'

Kyarno's voice was getting louder and louder, and Leofric could see he was attracting some unwelcome stares, but before he could say anything, Kyarno set off in the direction of the serving tables in search of fresh wine.

Leofric let him go, watching the smooth grace of the wardancers as they circled the tables and firepit with unhurried dances. The inhabitants of Coeth-Mara were deferential to the painted elves, but Leofric could see that none were entirely comfortable being near them. Cu-Sith himself leapt and tumbled through the high arches of the hall, moving as though free of the constraints of gravity.

Leofric remembered the performance of the companion of the troubadour, Tristran, when he had performed for Duke Tancred in Quenelles, dazzling the assembled court with his wonderful acrobatics and somersaulting. But even the most graceful human acrobats moved like a pregnant sow when compared to the savage grace of Cu-Sith.

He reached for the water jug, only to discover it was empty. He was about to search for more when a small voice beside Leofric asked, 'Would my lord wish more water or fruit?'

Leofric looked down to see one of the green-liveried serving boys standing behind him, a brimming jug of water held in one hand and a platter of fruit in the other. Leofric nodded, holding out his goblet to be filled, noticing that the boy's face had a ruddy, healthy glow, quite unlike the alabaster skin of the elves.

The boy poured some water into Leofric's goblet and asked, 'Does my lord require anything else?'

'No, thank you,' said Leofric. 'That will be–'

His words trailed off as he looked closer and saw that the boy was not what he had first taken him to be.

'You are human...'

Leofric put down his goblet and turned to face the boy, now seeing the more rounded face, the darker skin and the ears of a human being. The boy turned to leave, but Leofric gripped his tunic and held him fast.

'You are human,' repeated Leofric.

'My lord?' said the boy, a puzzled look in his eyes. Leofric kept hold of him and cast his gaze throughout the hall, looking at the rest of the serving boys. Confronted with the truth, it was now obvious that all the children who served the elves of Coeth-Mara were human.

'Can I go now, my lord?' asked the boy.

'No,' said Leofric, still struggling with the humanity of the child. 'Not yet. What is your name, boy?'

'My name?'

'Yes, what do they call you?'

'Aidan, my lord.'

'A good Bretonnian name,' said Leofric. 'Tell me, Aidan, why are you here?'

'I am here to serve at the Winter Feast.'

'No, I mean here in Athel Loren. How did you come to be here?'

'This is where I have always been,' said Aidan with a puzzled expression.

'Always? How long have you been here?' asked Leofric, a terrible suspicion forming in his mind.

'Since... I don't know, my lord. Always.'

'Very well, Aidan. Tell me which king sits upon the throne of Bretonnia?'

'The king?' said Aidan, pulling his face in the grimace of concentration common to all small boys. 'I think his name was Baudoin. I remember they called him the Dragonslayer.'

Leofric sat back, releasing his grip on the boy's tunic, feeling as though he'd been punched in the gut. King Baudoin had indeed been known as the Dragonslayer after he had slain the great wyrm, Mergaste – a great fresco in the cathedral of Bastonne commemorated the heroic deed.

'How could that be?' said Leofric. 'King Baudoin slew the dragon more than a thousand years ago.'

'Really? It seems like only yesterday. I don't remember much about it. My mother told me the tale.'

'And where is your mother? Where do you come from?'

'I don't remember,' shrugged the boy. 'I come from Athel Loren, my lord.'

'But you are not elven, you are human. You must have come from somewhere.'

'I don't know, my lord,' said Aidan. 'I have always been here.'

'Stop calling me "my lord", boy,' snapped Leofric, his exasperation growing with every obtuse answer.

'What should I call you then?'

'Call me Sir Carrard,' snapped Leofric. 'Now tell me–'

'Carrard?' exclaimed the boy. 'There is another here called that. Shall I fetch him for you?'

Leofric felt a sudden chill seize him at these words and the colour drained from his face. If the boy spoke the truth and he had served the elves of Coeth-Mara since ancient times... might then this Carrard boy be his...

Looking closely at the boy, Leofric saw a ghostly luminescence to his skin, an ageless quality that spoke of a moment frozen in time. The boy's eyes were differently coloured – one blue, one green – and Leofric knew that such fey children of Bretonnia often received a visitation from the prophetesses of the Lady before being spirited off to the Otherworld.

Though it was a great honour for a child to be chosen, families mourned their sons and daughters as lost, believing they were going to a better place to serve the Lady of the Lake. Sometimes the girl-children returned to Bretonnia many years later as damsels of the Lady, but of the boy-children's fate, nothing was known.

Was this what befell them? Doomed to live here in Athel Loren, ageless and unchanging, forever...

'My lord?' asked the boy. 'Are you unwell?'

'What?' whispered Leofric. 'No... no, I am well, Aidan, but I wish you to go now.'

The boy nodded and bowed to Leofric, returning to his duties in the hall.

Leofric watched him go, a mix of emotions vying for supremacy in his heart. The life of most children in Bretonnia was one of misery, pain and poverty, but the thought of a child denied the potential of his natural span of years horrified him.

Who was to say that this life was better or worse?

Kyarno threaded his way through the thronged hall, smiling at folk he knew and enjoying the warmth he now felt in Coeth-Mara. Was this how it felt to belong to something? All his life, he had felt like an outsider, but now he felt accepted and welcome. Perhaps he was ready now to take his place within the Éadaoin kinband.

He knew the wine was making him mellow, but didn't care. Not even the hostile stares of the Laithu kinband could dampen his spirits. Yes, he decided, he would do honour to his kin by accepting his place within the kinband and thus secure Lord Aldaeld's blessing to wed his daughter. He chuckled to himself at the thought, knowing that the wine put such spring fantasies into his head, but he could not deny he desired them.

Kyarno paused to join a group of elves watching a female wardancer give a display of incredible martial acrobatics, the near-naked girl leaping and twirling in the air while slashing a long, two-handed sword around her body. The blade swept around her like silver wire, its edge cutting the air no more than an inch from her painted flesh.

Though the presence of wardancers had put everyone on edge, not least because it was the troupe of the Red Wolf, there was much to admire in the incredible skills they had. Though he had seen the Dance of the Seasons before, Kyarno looked forward to witnessing it performed by Cu-Sith and his warriors, for it was certain to be something spectacular.

The wardancer's display ended as she landed in a crouch, the sword angled upwards behind her body, and Kyarno joined her audience's rapturous applause. The wardancer stood, her every movement fluid and graceful, and stalked away without acknowledgement, joining her kindred warriors as they gathered around the fire at some unheard summons of Cu-Sith. The Red Wolf stood with his arms upraised, holding a long spear garlanded with leaves in a spiral pattern in both hands. The taut muscles on his chest rippled with the motion of the great wolf tattoo while his wardancers adorned his flesh with chalk, lime and fresh talismanic paint.

Kyarno looked for one of the human serving boys and made his way towards him, looking for more wine. He saw Morvhen weaving her way through the crowd and forgot about wine, angling his course towards her. She saw him and smiled, and Kyarno felt the sun on his face to be in love with a sylph of such beauty. Attired in a regal gown of cream silk and gold, she looked every inch the daughter of an elven lord, the fabric clinging wonderfully to the curves of her lithe body.

'Morvhen,' he said. 'It is a glorious night is it not?'

She nodded, 'It is, though I'll be happier when Valas and Sirda are gone from here.'

'As will I,' said Kyarno, slipping his hand into hers. 'Has Laneir not come with his father and brother?'

'No,' said Morvhen, 'and for that I am glad. Sirda is bad enough, but his brother carries more ill-will than a blight of terrors.'

'True,' agreed Kyarno. 'His absence here will not be mourned. Least of all by me.'

Kyarno leaned down and gave Morvhen a quick kiss, slipping his arm around her shoulder.

'Walk with me,' he said.

'Where to?'

'Nowhere, just walk,' he said. 'For I am happy to see you.'

'And I you, but we must talk. My father knows what passed between you and your uncle in the forest. He knows you struck him.'

Kyarno nodded in understanding and said, 'That doesn't matter any more.'

'No? Why not?'

'Because I think I am ready to become truly a part of this kinband now. I am ready to pledge myself to Lord Aldaeld and take my place within the halls of Coeth-Mara.'

Morvhen stopped and gave him a piercing look, as though searching for any sign of mockery. 'Truly?'

'Yes,' he smiled. 'I love you, Morvhen, and I know that I am nothing without you. Your father will not countenance our union while I am an outsider, so, yes, I am ready.'

Morvhen put her hand to her mouth and said, 'I have waited so long for you to say these words, Kyarno.'

'Then you will have me?'

'Of course I will, my love,' she cried, throwing herself into his arms. 'I thought I would lose you, that you would never come back to us.'

'For you, Morvhen, always,' said Kyarno, kissing her and holding her tight.

'How very touching,' hissed a voice behind them and the lovers broke apart, turning to see the mocking features of Sirda Laithu. The son of Lord Valas was dressed in thick furs and a black and silver tunic with rich embroidery at the cuffs and seams; a pair of swords was sheathed across his back. Kyarno could see the tension and aggression in Sirda's eyes, the knuckles of his right hand white where he gripped his sword hilt.

Sirda cast an appreciative eye over Morvhen's body and said, 'I had thought the daughter of Lord Aldaeld would have known better than to associate with a common reaver.'

'Sirda,' said Kyarno with a forced smile. 'You are welcome in Coeth-Mara.'

'Such welcome is not yours to give, outlaw,' snarled Sirda.

'Perhaps not, but I offer it anyway,' said Kyarno.

'I should cut you down where you stand,' said Sirda, stepping close to him.

'Why are you so angry, Sirda?' snapped Kyarno. 'Your steeds returned to their stable glades. No harm was done.'

Sirda laughed, a high, almost hysterical quality to it, and said, 'No harm was done, he says. You are a bigger fool than even I took you for!'

Kyarno fought to quell his rising anger, saying, 'Sirda, this is not the place for this. If you must have a reckoning with me, then it can wait until tomorrow, yes?'

'Oh, there will be a reckoning, outlaw, sooner than you think!'

'What in the name of Kurnous does that mean?' asked Kyarno, taking his arm from Morvhen and sliding his hand towards the hilt of his own sword. Sirda altered the grip on his weapon and Kyarno saw that he was itching to plunge the blade into his body.

'Sirda!' said Morvhen, stepping between them. 'You are a guest in my father's halls, remember that. Do not bring shame to your kinband by your behaviour.'

'It is too late for that,' snapped Sirda, taking a deep breath, and Kyarno could see bitter tears in his eyes. 'There is blood between us and only in blood will it be settled.'

Kyarno slowed his breathing, knowing that whatever was driving Sirda's aggression would not be calmed by any of Morvhen's words.

But before either he or Sirda could draw their weapons, the fire in the centre of the hall erupted in a great blazing pillar. The wardancers leapt and spun through the flickering flames, whooping and yelling songs of war and death.

Cu-Sith stood before the roaring fire, his face savage and daemonic in the red glow. The wolf on his chest howled in time with the cries of his wardancers, its eyes alight with feral anticipation.

Throughout the hall, elves stood transfixed as the Red Wolf lowered the spear he carried and let loose a piercing cry that echoed through the branches of the trees and touched the primal heart of every elf with a fierce longing.

The Red Wolf turned and bowed to Lord Aldaeld, saying, 'Coeth-Mara is fortunate. Cu-Sith and his wardancers shall perform the Dragon Dance.'

CHAPTER THIRTEEN

The hall fell silent at Cu-Sith's pronouncement. The Dragon Dance was performed but rarely. Only the greatest wardancers of Athel Loren were able to perform such a dangerous, intricate dance. The pillar of flames that reared from the centre of the hall dropped in a flurry of sparks, the fire reduced to its natural state, and the elves of Coeth-Mara swiftly returned to their tables as the wardancers took up their positions around the fire.

A hush descended on the hall and without another word spoken, the dance began.

Leofric watched the wardancers hurl themselves around the fire, not truly understanding what was happening, but content to watch the spectacle unfold before him. The paint on the wardancers' bodies blurred with the speed of their movements, a weaving pattern of colours as they danced with fierce, savage abandon. Cu-Sith stood motionless behind the fire as his troupe danced faster and faster, a singing sensation of loss, pain and joy spreading outwards from the dancers in the centre of the hall.

The dancers became wilder, their passions stronger and their joys more extreme, more menacing. They leapt, cartwheeled and somersaulted through the flames, coming together like a whirlpool and breaking apart as Cu-Sith landed in the centre of the fire.

Leofric gasped as sparks and embers were thrown up by Cu-Sith's landing, but the leader of the wardancers seemed untroubled by the flames licking around him. He bounded from the firepit with a wild yell, his spear trailing fire behind him.

The wardancers leapt towards him with wild howls of exultation, but with a cry, he flew above their heads, tumbling in flight to land facing them. As they tumbled, he leapt again, the weapons of the troupe clawing empty air as he passed between them.

Cu-Sith laughed maniacally as he leaped and spun, evading the darting swords and spears with ease. A soft wind tugged at Leofric's hair as the dance grew wilder and wilder, he could hardly believe that any being could move so swiftly or so gracefully. The beat of a pounding drumbeat filled the hall, thumping in time with his rising heartbeat and Leofric could not tell whether he truly heard the rhythmic music or if it resounded deep in his soul.

Almost too fast to follow, the wardancers broke apart from the centre of the hall, spinning and twisting through the air to land amid the stunned onlookers.

As one, their blades flashed quicker and quicker, spear and sword spinning in silver blurs of steel that whipped the air into frantic motion. The wind built and filled the hall, rising from a soft zephyr to a sighing breeze and finally to a howling gale.

Leaves spun from the ground, fluttering round the hall as the wind carried them upwards and within moments, the air was thick with gold and red. The beauty of the sight took Leofric's breath away as the leaves spun around the hall with ever increasing speed.

The shrieking wardancers closed on the firepit once more, their flashing blades spinning and keeping the tornado of leaves afloat with their movements. Cu-Sith spun like a dervish through the gathering spiral of flying leaves, his blade carving looping spiral patterns through them as he bounded from table to table.

Slowly the tornado of leaves shifted in its movements, its course angling until each one passed through the roaring fire at the heart of the hall. Each leaf burst into flames, blazing like a firefly as it spun through the air.

Leofric watched amazed as the blazing leaves, thousands of them surely, looped upwards as the wardancers spun around the column of fire, their swords and spears spinning and moulding it into some new and magnificent form. The dance spoke to him on some deep, instinctual level and his flesh answered with fierce exultation, his soul soaring at the magic he was seeing.

Slowly at first, but with greater speed as the shape took form, Leofric saw the sinuous form of a great beast emerge from the burning leaves. A great body of light was shaped, then a long tail and massive flaring wings of fire emerged from the wardancers' creation. Finally, a vast, draconic head was fashioned from the blazing leaves, its jaws wide and powerful.

Scarce able to believe his overwhelmed senses, Leofric saw the great dragon of fire twist and spin through the air, the leaping wardancers sustaining it with their deadly dance and flashing blades. It swooped and dived, the roar of the flames giving the dragon a mighty voice.

A lone figure stood before the might and majesty of the fiery dragon. Cu-Sith stood unmoving with his spear held before him, and laughing with wild abandon. The dragon leapt towards him, its blazing jaws spread wide to swallow him whole and Leofric had to fight the urge to draw his sword and fight the monster.

Cu-Sith leapt from the path of the dragon, somersaulting over its long neck and slashing with his weapon. The dragon came at him again and again, directed by the energies of the wardancers, but each time it bit thin air as Cu-Sith expertly evaded its attacks, turning to strike back each time.

The confrontation went on and on, the dragon snapping and biting, and Cu-Sith cartwheeling and leaping around it. Leofric was lost in admiration for the incredible beauty of the sight before him and the unbelievable skill of Cu-Sith. The memory of Cu-Sith's blades at his throat was swept away as the wild exultation that had seized every elf in the hall reached deep inside him and stirred his primal heart.

Unable to stop himself, he beat his palm against the table in time to the drumming beat of the unheard music, swept up in exultation by the phenomenal exhibition.

Instantly, the dragon of fiery leaves dropped from the air, its mighty form extinguished as the wardancers abruptly stopped their dance.

Every eye in the hall turned upon him and Leofric knew he had made a terrible mistake.

A blur of colour and movement exploded beside him and the breath was knocked from his body as he was hurled to the ground. A blur of silver steel flashed before him and he found himself looking into the crazed eyes of Cu-Sith.

'You interrupted Cu-Sith's dance,' said the wardancer, hauling him to his feet and pushing him back towards the table.

The Red Wolf spun in the air, his foot lashing out to strike Leofric square in the chest and hurl him onto his back on the table. Fast as quicksilver, Cu-Sith was upon him and Leofric felt the touch of cold steel at his groin.

'You should keep your animals on a leash, Lord Aldaeld!' yelled the wardancer.

'I'm sorry,' gasped Leofric, fearful of moving lest Cu-sith's blade unman him.

'Sorry?' hissed Cu-Sith. 'The Red Wolf will geld his pet and then you will know your place, human!'

'No!' shouted Leofric as he felt the tip of Cu-Sith's blade pierce his flesh.

* * *

Though darkness had closed in and the snowfall had grown heavier, Caelas Shadowfoot could follow the trail of the Laithu kinband without difficulty. Their tracks were easily visible through the powdered snow that fell, and the more he saw of them, the more uneasy he became.

Elves did not travel the paths of Athel Loren so recklessly. Something was amiss, and it sat ill with him that he did not yet see what.

Kneeling beside the deep tracks of a horse, he knew there was little point in following the back trail anymore and turned to head back towards Coeth-Mara. The moonlight pooled in the glade, filling it with a silver glow and long, angled shadows.

He slung his bow, pulling his green scarf over his face and setting the hood of his cloak over his head.

And then he saw it.

Sudden fear seized him as he ran lightly across the snow and dropped to his belly beside the tracks. Caelas drew his long knife and reached gently into one of the tracks with the blade, an angled shadow within showing a subtle difference in the shade of snow. He cursed as he realised what he was looking at, the fresh fall of snow having hidden it from his keen eyes.

He had thought the new snow accounted for the deepness of the tracks, but as he looked closer, he saw that the original prints were deeper than would normally be expected of a single rider. He leapt to his feet, caution forgotten in the wash of fear that chilled him worse than the weather.

Swiftly, he checked the tracks of the other riders, finding the same depth of tracks.

These horses had carried more than one rider.

Somewhere between here and the time he had seen the Laithu kinband, these horses had shed a rider. Which meant that somewhere between here and Coeth-Mara were at least forty warriors hidden in the wilds.

Caelas had no idea why Valas Laithu would want to have warriors stealthily approach Coeth-Mara, but such concerns were irrelevant just now.

Warning had to be taken back to Lord Aldaeld of the threat to his domain.

Now he understood the Laithu kinband's apparent lack of caution, and he cursed himself for assuming that they had rode blindly into Coeth-Mara, allowing his disdain for their skills to blind him to their true wiles.

He cleaned the snow from his knife and, as he prepared to sheath it, the briefest reflection ghosted across its mirror sheen. Without thought, Caelas threw himself forward as a trio of arrows slashed through the air above him.

Caelas dropped his knife and rolled, his bow drawn and an arrow nocked as he rose to one knee. He loosed a shaft to where the arrows had come from and was rewarded with a cry of pain and the sound of a falling body.

He dived to one side as two more arrows flew from the undergrowth, one passing within a finger's breadth of his shoulder. But the second archer had anticipated his move and the arrow thudded home in his chest. Caelas grunted and tore it from his body, feeling warm blood wet his cloak. He scrambled painfully into the cover of a stately birch tree as another pair of arrows thunked into its trunk.

His breathing came hard and fast. By now at least one of his unseen foes would be circling him, aiming for a clear shot while the other kept him pinned behind the tree.

There was no way out and his eyes darted from tree to tree as he tried to guess where the next attack would come from. He could see four places where an enemy might loose a killing arrow, but there was no way to tell which one his attackers would head for.

But then Loec smiled upon him as a stray moonbeam glittered from something in the undergrowth over to his right. Caelas nocked a fresh arrow and waited. Once he was sure the second archer would have reached his new position, he stepped out from behind the birch, his arrow aimed to the left.

No sooner had he moved than an archer rose from the undergrowth where the reflection had come from and Caelas spun, dropping to one knee and sending his arrow through the throat of the cloaked figure before he could fire.

He dropped his bow and dived forwards as a second arrow flashed towards him from a cleft in a boulder before him. The arrow sliced across his shoulder, but Caelas continued his roll, scooping up his fallen knife and hurling it towards the shadowy outline of the hidden archer. A strangled scream told him he had struck his target and Caelas fell to his knees as blood bubbled up in his throat.

He knew his lung had been punctured and he was losing blood rapidly, but before he tended to his wound, he slipped silently around the boulder to discover the identity of his attackers.

An elf in furred winter garb in the colours of the forest lay dead with Caelas's knife buried in his throat. He knelt and pulled open the elf's cloak, nodding to himself as he saw the Laithu kinband's rune of moonlight.

A waywatcher of Valas Laithu.

Dizzy from blood loss, Caelas wrenched his knife clear of the body, wiping the blade clean on the corpse's tunic then taking the arrows from its quiver. He cut the dead waywatcher's cloak into strips to fashion an impromptu bandage, plugging the sucking hole in his chest, then pulled himself to his feet.

His senses tingled and his warrior instinct warned him that these three would not be alone. Time was of the essence, knew Caelas, and though it was doubtful that he would survive to make it back to Coeth-Mara and warn Lord Aldaeld, he had to try.

Leofric gasped as the razor-edged steel of Cu-Sith's blade touched the skin of his inner thigh and tried in vain to pull free of the wardancer's grip. His efforts were to no avail as he was held fast by the wild elf. The tattoo of the red wolf on Cu-Sith's chest snarled at him, relishing the prospect of spilled blood.

'Cu-Sith does not suffer interruptions to his dance, human,' snarled the wardancer. The tip of the blade broke the skin and Leofric felt a trickle of warm blood run down his thigh.

'I am sorry,' cried Leofric. 'The music! It roused my soul with its magnificence.'

'Cu-Sith needs no human's appreciation. Cu-Sith already knows he is the greatest wardancer of Athel Loren. No enemy has ever laid a blade upon Cu-Sith, nor does he bear scar or bruise.'

Leofric twisted his head from side to side, hoping that someone would come to his aid, but all he could see was a tightening circle of angry wardancers, their weapons drawn and once exultant features now curled in anger.

'Cu-Sith!' shouted a voice, and Leofric recognised it as Naieth's. 'Wait!'

The wardancer looked up as the prophetess moved through the circle of wardancers, their whooping cries angry and hostile as they parted before her. They spat insults at her, leaping close and slashing around her with their blades, but she did not react to their taunts.

'You speak for this human?' asked Cu-Sith. 'Loec is listening.'

'I ask you to release him.'

'Why should Cu-Sith do such a thing? Cu-Sith has already marked him and may do with him as he pleases.'

'It would displease Loec were you to kill him now,' said Naieth.

The wardancer leapt from the table and landed lightly before the gold-robed Naieth, circling her with a wary look in his eyes. Leofric sat up, hyperventilating at the thought of Cu-Sith's promised castration. The Red Wolf's spear spun in a glittering circle as he leaned close to Naieth and looked straight in her eyes.

'Loec speaks to you as he does Cu-Sith?'

'Yes,' agreed Naieth, 'and this is not his will.'

'No? Cu-Sith will ask him!' yelled the wardancer, leaping in a backwards somersault to land astride Leofric once more, placing his blade at his throat.

'Loec! Does this base human deserve to live?' he yelled into the air.

The wind that had built when the wardancers had performed the Dragon Dance gusted once more, a flurry of blackened leaves taking to the air in a miniature spiralling whirlwind. Cu-Sith laughed and bent down until his face was inches from Leofric's.

'You are lucky, human,' hissed the wardancer, dragging Leofric to his feet. 'Loec says you get to keep your manhood today.'

Leofric was barely able to stand, his legs unsteady beneath him. Cu-Sith hurled him from the table and vaulted away, shouting, 'Loec smiles upon you, human. Don't waste that fortune!'

He felt hands at his shoulders and looked up to see a pale-faced Kyarno above him. The elf hauled him to his feet and dragged him away from the wardancers who followed their leader, bounding and leaping towards the fire.

'Even for a human, that was stupid,' said Kyarno, watching as the wardancers gathered around the fire to drink.

Leofric did not reply, his heart was hammering in his chest and his limbs were shaking in fear. He reached out and grabbed the nearest goblet, desperate for a drink to calm his shredded nerves.

He lifted the goblet to his lips and drank gulping mouthful after gulping mouthful of its contents. The sweet, honeyed scent of the elven wine flooded his senses and the warm nectar of its taste was beyond anything he had ever drunk before.

Leofric put down the empty goblet, only now realising what he had just done.

'Oh no...' he heard Kyarno say, before his world exploded in golden light.

Light and colour filled his senses and he gasped as the sky changed hue as though the branches of the trees had caught fire. Brilliant lights and colours filled the air, rising in clouds of vermilion, azure and jade smoke. The fire in the centre blazed a vivid blue and Leofric could see the threads of golden life that saturated every living thing in Coeth-Mara.

His normal sight began to fade until he saw nothing mundane, neither flesh nor fabric of his perception of reality. He laughed as he saw the golden haloes of life everywhere, touching and connecting everything in the hall, the colours of movement and emotion writ large in the auras of those around him.

'I can see...' slurred Leofric as he slid from his chair, his mind over-loading with sensation. As he toppled to the ground the colours spiralled and spun, blending together in a blur of vital essence. He could see the answers to everything – they were encapsulated in the hues, if only he could find the words to express them.

'Isha's tears,' hissed Kyarno, pulling him to his feet. Leofric smiled dreamily as the elven wine coursed through his newly refined and ele-vated senses. He giggled drunkenly, waving his hands before him and laughing at the colours that rippled around them as they moved. He saw no flesh or bone, just the pulsing yellow light of his life as it thundered around his body.

'What is wrong with him?' asked a woman's voice. Naieth's, thought Leofric.

'He drank some wine when I wasn't looking,' replied Kyarno.

'Elven wine is not for humans!' snapped Naieth. 'We'll be lucky if he ever comes back! Take him outside and get him some air. Keep talking to him, give him a connection to this world.'

Leofric wanted to speak, but felt that the words would choke him, clamping his hands across his mouth as Kyarno dragged him through the hall. Sparks and swirls of light followed him and Leofric gagged as a vertiginous nausea seized him. His legs buckled and but for Kyarno's support he would have fallen.

Sudden cold hit him and he gasped, feeling his stomach clench agonisingly. Embers of fire fell around him, spinning in a sickening web of gold.

'Come on, Leofric,' urged Kyarno. 'Remember who you are. You are a knight of Bretonnia. Stay with that!'

Leofric barely heard the voice, feeling as though he was falling into a dark pit without bottom, spinning and tumbling end over end into a swirling maelstrom of vibrant colours.

The voice grew fainter and fainter, echoing within his skull as though coming from along a faraway corridor. Something within his crude flesh came loose and with a start, Leofric's sight spun from his body out into the forest.

He saw trees as columns of fire, their leaves as bright spots against the dark of the night. Sap ran in molten rivers through the trees, flowing into the ground and spreading through the forest in an interconnected web that linked all things.

Everything was connected by life and the realisation was so profound and clear that he was amazed no one had seen it before.

All life was one and everything was a circle.

All he had to do was hold on to that realisation and everything would be all right. He heard a voice again, but ignored it, revelling in his new-found freedom as he soared through Athel Loren, his spirit no longer shackled to his flesh.

Was this what it was like to be divine? Journeying through realms hidden from the sight of mortals, able to see and hear the beating heart of the world as it seethed with all its myriad fecundities. Everywhere was life…

No… not everywhere, he saw.

In the depths of the forest, Leofric saw pain. Hot, searing and deathly. His spirit form flashed through the golden fires of the trees towards it, eager to soothe the pain he felt.

An elf, his life-light weak and flickering, stumbled from tree to tree, desperation flaring from him in bright red waves as he fought a losing battle to outdistance three pursuers. Leofric could see the goodness of his failing heart and the thought of this noble elf dying at the hands of these villains pierced Leofric's heart with sorrow.

* * *

Caelas Shadowfoot fell against a tree trunk, blood pouring from the sucking wound in his chest, and knew that he could not run any further. He had run as fast as he was able to bring them to this place, but now the game was over. He turned to face his hunters as they emerged from the trees, their bowstrings pulled taut and gleaming arrowheads aimed at his head.

'You have great skill, old man,' said one.

'It took you long enough to catch me,' hissed Caelas, drawing his knife.

'You think to fight us?' said another. 'Don't. It will be less painful for you.'

'I'll fight you if I have to,' wheezed Caelas.

'No need,' said the third, sadly. 'You will be dead in minutes anyway.'

Caelas pushed himself painfully from the tree, intending to gut one of these Laithu swine before they finished him. They lowered their bows, but as the first stepped towards him, Caelas felt the fury of the forest rise up around him. Something powerful rippled through the forest and even as he felt it, the hunters realised the trap he had led them into.

Branches and roots ripped from the snow as the dark fey of this haunted glade arose, smashing the nearest of his pursuers to splintered bone and pulverised meat. Thorned barbs slashed from the undergrowth, whipping the second to the ground where heaving, groaning roots crushed his trapped body. The third waywatcher turned and fled into the forest, but cracking branches and screams told Caelas that he didn't get far.

The rippling branches and grasping thorns turned towards him and Caelas knew he had to get out of this glade before they killed him too, but a wave of dizziness swamped him and his vision began to grey at the edges. He dropped to the ground as the last of his strength left him, seeing a shimmering, ghostly image hovering in the air above him.

He felt its compassion and knew that he had been offered one final chance. Caelas tried to form words of warning, but blood burst from his mouth and he toppled to the snow as his life faded.

With his last breath he fought to speak, tears of frustration freezing on his cheeks at his inability to communicate, but the spirit being nodded and he knew that it understood.

Caelas Shadowfoot died knowing he had fulfilled his duty to his kinband.

Leofric's spirit watched the elf's life-light fade, immense sadness smothering his soul as the brave warrior before him died. The blood of the elves the forest had slain was like molten gold against the snow and Leofric felt the wrench of reality strike him with great hammerblows.

Without warning, the scene before him sped away as he rushed back through the forest, the irresistible pull of flesh wrenching him back to his body. He screamed as his spirit form plunged into his frame of meat and bone, rolling onto his side and vomiting explosively onto the snow.

His stomach heaved as he expelled the last of the elven wine, his senses feeling dull and deadened without the freedom of the spirit. The acrid taste of vomit burned his throat and he heard Kyarno say, 'Maybe that will teach you not to drink our wine.'

He struggled to stand, his body feeling leaden and clumsy after his flight through the forest.

'No...' he gasped. 'No, no, no...'

'No, what?' asked Kyarno. 'Are you sure you're all right?'

'They're coming,' cried Leofric. 'They're coming to kill you all.'

'What? Who are?'

'Warriors of the Laithu kinband,' said Leofric stumbling like a drunk as he fought for balance. 'He found them.'

'Who did? What are you talking about?' asked Kyarno.

'Shadowfoot he was called,' wept Leofric. 'Caelas Shadowfoot. He found them and died to bring warning to Coeth-Mara.'

'Shadowfoot?' demanded Kyarno. 'You saw Caelas Shadowfoot?'

'Yes... They're coming!' pleaded Leofric. 'You have to warn them!'

Kyarno dropped Leofric and ran for Lord Aldaeld's hall.

'This is what happens when you bring humans into Athel Loren,' said Lord Valas, shaking his head and sipping his wine. 'Your halls have become the refuge of outlaws, vagabonds and animals, Aldaeld.'

Lord Aldaeld struggled to keep his temper in the face of this latest insult. Throughout the feast, the tension had been almost unbearable as Valas kept up a steady stream of jibes and veiled threats. Watching Kyarno drag the human from Coeth-Mara was but the latest barb for Valas to prick him with.

But as Valas was his guest, Aldaeld could do little but grit his teeth.

'These are strange times, Valas,' replied Aldaeld. 'There is much that displeases me about the human's presence, but he has a crude form of courage and fought beside the Hound of Winter against the creatures of Chaos.'

'Pah!' sneered Valas. 'Is the Hound of Winter now so old that he needs the aid of a human to triumph? Truly this is a sad day for the asrai.'

Aldaeld glanced over his shoulder towards Cairbre, but his champion made no indication that he had heard the jibe.

'The Hound of Winter's fangs are as deadly as ever, Valas.'

'We shall see,' muttered Valas. 'But it matters little any more.'

'What do you mean by that?'

'I mean that it is time for you to make good to me the dishonour done to my kinband, Aldaeld,' said Valas.

Aldaeld kept his tone even as he said, 'Valas, there is no need for us to be enemies. Your steeds were taken, that is true, but I have punished Kyarno for his recklessness.'

'There is a blood debt between us, Aldaeld, and only in blood will it ᵉ settled.'

'I don't understand,' said Aldaeld warily. 'What blood is there between us?'

'The blood of my son, Laneir,' hissed Valas. 'As he gave chase to the reaver who thieved our steeds his course took him through the wild glades of the forest and the dark fey arose and claimed his life.'

Aldaeld felt his blood chill at Valas's words, his instinct for danger screaming that something was very, very wrong.

He struggled to keep his expression neutral as he said, 'I did not know that, Valas. My heart is saddened at your loss and whatever is in my power to grant is yours.'

'Really, Lord Aldaeld? Are your powers now so great as the Lady Ariel's as to be able to bring the dead back to life?'

'No, of course not, but–'

'Can you bring my son back, Aldaeld?' asked Valas with cold fury, reaching inside his furred cloak. 'Can you restore my son to me?'

Aldaeld heard the sound of frantic shouting from the entrance to the hall and tore his gaze from the anguished Lord Valas.

He saw Kyarno fighting his way through the crowds of his people, shouting and yelling at the top of his voice.

Lord Aldaeld turned back to Valas in horror as he heard what Kyarno was shouting and the Hound of Winter gave a cry of warning.

'Only in blood will it be settled!' shouted Valas as he surged from his seat and plunged a curved dagger into Lord Aldaeld's heart.

CHAPTER FOURTEEN

Kyarno saw Valas Laithu lunge from his seat and thrust a curved blade between Lord Aldaeld's ribs. He screamed in warning, but could only watch helplessly as bright blood burst from the wound and the lord of the Éadaoin kinband slumped in his throne. The Blades of Midnight stabbed for the throat of Aldaeld's attacker, but a copper-headed spear leapt to Valas Laithu's hand and the blow was intercepted.

Kyarno's sword was in his hand as the hall of Coeth-Mara erupted in yells of outrage and anger at this terrible, treacherous attack. He saw Morvhen run towards her father and followed her, shouting, 'To arms! To arms! We are betrayed!'

Warriors of the Laithu kinband threw off their fur cloaks and drew their weapons, but the Éadaoin kinband was not as helpless as they had expected. Arrows flashed through the air and elves of Valas Laithu fell, their throats pierced by deadly accurate shafts. Swords and spears were readied as elves clashed, leaping across the tables of the hall to do battle with one another.

Kyarno leapt a fallen warrior, sprinting towards the raised dais where Lord Valas expertly parried Cairbre's blows with a long, spiral-patterned spear. The Hound of Winter attacked with all the grim, brutal ferocity he was famed for, but nothing could penetrate Valas's defences.

Morvhen knelt beside her father with Naieth, fighting without success to stem the bleeding from the grievous wound in his chest.

Morvhen looked up through her tears and shouted, 'Kyarno! Look out!'

He risked a glance to his left, throwing himself flat as he saw Sirda Laithu loose an arrow towards him. He hit the ground and rolled, putting the fire between himself and Sirda.

The air was thick with arrows and cries of pain. Kyarno edged around the fire as the clash of steel on steel rang from the walls of Coeth-Mara. Denied complete surprise, the Laithu kinband knew they had a fight on their hands. A shape moved through the flickering flames and he dropped as another arrow flew through the fire, thudding into a root-formed table a handspan from his head, its goose-feathered fletching aflame.

'Nowhere to run, outlaw!' shouted Sirda as he circled the fire, looking to deliver the killing shot. Kyarno circled with him, keeping the fire between them.

'I told you there was blood between us, outlaw! Your death for my brother's!'

'Your brother is dead?' shouted back Kyarno. 'What has that to do with me?'

'Laneir died chasing you from our stable glades!'

'I didn't kill him,' cried Kyarno. 'I swear by all the gods I did not!'

'It doesn't matter, you're going to die anyway,' said Sirda.

He could not go on like this. Unless he could close the gap – or get Sirda to close it – there could only be one outcome between a swordsman and a bowman.

'Your brother was a treacherous cur!' shouted Kyarno. 'Just like you, Sirda.'

He heard Sirda give a strangled cry of rage and hurled himself backwards as another arrow struck the table between his legs. He rolled over the table in a clatter of plates and goblets as Sirda leapt around the fire and drew another arrow.

A spinning platter struck Sirda square in the face and the elf tumbled to the floor, dropping his bow and clutching his head. Kyarno vaulted the table, and sprang towards the fallen Sirda with his sword raised.

His foe rose quickly to his feet, his swords flashing in his hands as he shook his head free of the impact of Kyarno's makeshift missile.

Kyarno's sword struck for Sirda's heart, but the twin swords of the Laithu swordsman swept up and blocked the blow. A streaking riposte tore a gash along Kyarno's left arm and he dodged away from a low cut intended to gut him. Sirda followed up his counterattack with a blistering series of cuts and thrusts, Kyarno just barely managing to block them.

He parried a blisteringly quick lunge and had a moment of sick realisation that Sirda was a far better swordsman than he.

Sirda saw the awful knowledge in his eyes and grinned.

'You are going to die, outlaw,' he promised.

'We'll see,' said Kyarno as the battle raged around them.

* * *

Cairbre sent another lethal blow arcing towards Valas Laithu's head, the white blade slashing in to behead the traitorous vermin that had attacked his lord and killed three of his warriors. Once again the copper spearhead caught his blow and turned it aside at the last moment. The haft spun and jabbed at his head, and Cairbre barely evaded the blow.

Beside him, Tarean Stormcrow attacked with his golden sword, his blows parried by the magical spear.

'You cannot defeat me,' said Valas Laithu. 'So why try? Your lord is dead, but neither of you need to die. You can serve me.'

'Serve the murderer who betrayed the hospitality offered him? Never,' swore Tarean, nodding towards the furious battle between the elven kin-bands that filled the hall with blood and violence. 'You bring dishonour on us all.'

Cairbre slashed the Blades of Midnight towards Valas once more, but again the magical spear thwarted his attempts to gut Aldaeld's killer, turning aside his blow with unnatural ease.

'Aldaeld was weak,' sneered Valas. 'He gave shelter to base humans and welcomed them into his hall! Where will it end, Cairbre? I know you, Hound of Winter – it must have sat ill with you that a human dwelt in Coeth-Mara.'

'It is not for me to question my lord's decisions,' gasped Cairbre as the Spear of Daith laid his bicep open to the bone. His hand spasmed and he lost his grip on his weapon, the Blades of Midnight dropping to the floor of the dais.

Valas Laithu darted in, thrusting the spear at his stomach, but Cairbre dodged aside and gripped the haft with his good hand, spinning inside his foe's guard and hammering his elbow against his temple.

The lord of the Laithu kinband staggered, dropping to one knee and dragging the spear back, slashing Cairbre's palm open. But before either Cairbre or Tarean could take advantage of Valas's stumble, a flurry of black, bat-like malevolents erupted from his cloak, spitting darts and chittering cries as the vicious little spites swarmed them.

They fell back before their onslaught, feeling needle-like claws and teeth tear and cut them. The spites were small, but they were numerous. Cairbre shook them clear, swatting them away with his uninjured arm, seeing Tarean Stormcrow launch another attack at Valas.

Tarean was brave and a swordsman of great skill, but the Spear of Daith had been fashioned with some of the most powerful magic of Athel Loren and his blow was easily intercepted. Cairbre saw Valas aim the weapon at the herald's stomach, the engraved eyes on the leaf-shaped blade glowing with bright magic as they sought out the swiftest route to his vitals. The spear lanced towards Tarean, the herald swiftly bringing his sword down to block, but quicker than Cairbre would have believed possible, the weapon altered direction.

'No!' shouted Cairbre as the spear rammed up into Tarean's chest, the

tip erupting from his back in a bloody shower. Lord Aldaeld's herald
shuddered and cried out in agony as the spear spitted him like a wild
boar. The blade was wrenched clear and Tarean fell to the dais, his eyes
glazing over as he died.

Leofric stumbled towards his horse, his senses only just recovering their
equilibrium after his inebriation with the elven wine. Before he had run
into the hall, Kyarno had alerted the Glade Guard still on duty of the
threat to Coeth-Mara and within moments, sixty riders had assembled
on snorting steeds, their blades bared and ready for battle.

He had briefly considered following Kyarno, but knew that he could
fight best from the back of a horse. Cries of alarm and shouts of anger
echoed from the starlit avenues and processionals beyond Lord Aldaeld's
hall as the riders circled in the moonlight, ready to take the fight to their
enemies.

Leofric found Taschen hitched to the rail in front of his abode and
climbed into the saddle, unsheathing his sword and galloping back to
Lord Aldaeld's riders as a hail of arrows flashed from the treeline.

Against an unprepared foe, such a volley would have been deadly,
but the Glade Riders of the Éadaoin kinband had been waiting for this
moment and surged forwards to meet their attackers. A handful of warriors fell to the enemy arrows, but the skill of the Glade Riders was so
great that the majority were able to evade the deadly shafts.

An arrow ricocheted from the solid plate of Leofric's armour, but a
knight cared not for such things, and he urged his steed onwards as the
faster mounts of the Glade Guard pulled away.

More arrows slashed out and more riders were punched from their
steeds by the enemy bowfire. An arrow thudded into Leofric's breastplate, the point slowed, but not stopped by his armour. He felt its point
break the skin and wrenched it clear as he thundered onwards.

Then they were through the treeline and Leofric saw the archers of the
Laithu kinband running for fresh cover as the Glade Riders rode them
down without mercy. Leofric angled his horse towards a fleeing, grey-
cloaked archer, raking his spurs viciously into Taschen's flanks.

The elf dodged nimbly, but Leofric was in his element, having ridden
down broken enemies in countless battles, riding just ahead of his prey
and slashing his sword back into his foe's face.

The elf screamed horribly, his skull split open, and Leofric set off in
pursuit once more. Arrows flashed through the air, but in ones and twos
rather than the concentrated volleys of before.

Scattered and disorganised, the Laithu warriors were easy prey for
the Glade Riders, amongst the finest mounted warriors in Athel Loren.
Leofric felt the blood surge through his veins as he slew another enemy
warrior, remembering the savage joy of bloody combat and the thrill of
riding down a defeated enemy.

Whooping riders rode hither and thither through the trees, hunting down their enemies with savage fury. None of the Glade Riders were in any mood to offer mercy towards the Laithu kinband and the snow-bound forest echoed to the sounds of their screams.

He watched as an enemy archer took refuge behind the thick bole of an ancient oak, drawing and loosing a shaft in one swift motion. The Glade Rider next to Leofric tumbled from the saddle of his flame-maned elven steed and Leofric hauled Taschen's reins in the direction of his killer. No sooner had he done so than the elven archer loosed a shaft towards him.

But instead of aiming high, the archer sent his arrow low, the lethally sharp missile plunging so deeply into Taschen's chest that only the fletching was visible. Another arrow followed the first and the horse collapsed beneath him, foaming blood erupting from its screaming mouth.

Leofric kicked his feet from the stirrups as his horse died, leaping clear as it slammed into the snow in a tangle of broken limbs. He hit the ground hard, rolling and losing his grip on his sword as the breath was driven from him.

He shook his helmet free of snow as he pushed himself to one knee, and saw the archer who had felled his steed draw his bowstring back to send a shaft through his helmet's visor.

A blur of white leapt over Leofric and the flame-maned elven steed landed in front of the archer, its hooves smashing him from his feet. Leofric gathered up his sword and scrambled back towards his wounded mount.

Incredibly, Taschen still lived, but his every breath foamed red with blood and Leofric knew the horse was beyond saving. The horse's front legs were broken where it had fallen and it was in agony.

'You were a faithful steed, my friend,' said Leofric, drawing his blade across the horse's throat. Warm blood gushed from the wound and Taschen's eyes rolled back in their sockets as he died.

He would mourn the loss of the fine Bretonnian warhorse later, but for now there were still foes to hunt. He turned from the dead beast, seeing the elven steed that had saved his life sadly nuzzling its fallen rider. It looked up at him and Leofric was struck by the fierce intelligence he saw in the creature's eyes.

'What say you and I finish these murderers off?' said Leofric.

The horse seemed to consider his proposal for a moment then bobbed its head, reluctantly leaving its dead rider and cantering across to him. As it approached him, he sensed the steed's strength and loyalty in its every movement.

Clearly there would be no master in this arrangement, only two warriors fighting together. Just as Leofric was wondering how he was going to climb onto the back of a steed with no saddle, the horse dropped to its knees.

'I can see we are going to get along famously,' said Leofric as he climbed on and the horse rose up, seemingly unhindered by the weight of an armoured warrior on its back.

He gripped its coppery mane as the pale horse reared and with a wild, exultant yell, they rode off into the forest after the remaining enemy warriors.

Kyarno bled from a score of shallow cuts, his endurance fading in the face of Sirda's overwhelming superiority with a blade. His every attack was batted aside with contemptuous ease, his every defence countered and defeated. He backed away through the press of combat that filled the hall, unable to tell which kinband held the upper hand.

'This is it, Kyarno,' laughed Sirda, twisting one of his blades around Kyarno's and sending it spinning through the air. 'Now you are going to die.'

Kyarno staggered back, desperate to put some distance between himself and Sirda, but each time his escape was blocked by his more nimble foe. He stumbled and fell back against a table, exhausted and defeated as Sirda closed in with a predatory smile.

Sirda raised his sword and shouted, 'This is for my brother!'

Kyarno closed his eyes and yelled defiantly as the sword slashed towards his throat.

But with a clash of steel and sparks, the blow never landed.

The frozen moment stretched and Kyarno looked up to see Cu-Sith standing on the table above him, the haft of his spear an inch before his neck where it had intercepted Sirda's blow.

'Red Wolf,' cried Sirda. 'This is not your concern. You swore to stay your hand.'

'Cu-Sith decides what is Cu-Sith's concern, and you should know better than to try and make deals with followers of the Trickster God,' said the wardancer, sweeping his spear up and effortlessly twisting Sirda's blade from his grip. Kyarno cried out in relief as the wardancer somersaulted backwards, the heel of his foot lashing out, catching Sirda under his chin and hurling him into the firepit.

The last son of Valas Laithu fell into the fire, the flames hungrily seizing his furs and tunic and he screamed as his hair and clothes caught light. Sirda rolled from the fire, ablaze from head to foot, his screams terrible to hear as his flesh began to burn.

Kyarno watched Sirda climb to his feet and stumble like a drunk as the flames devoured him, the sickening stench of cooked flesh filling the hall.

Gasps of horror at the fate of Sirda Laithu spread from his smoking corpse, but Kyarno felt no pity for him. In the lull of battle, Kyarno pulled himself to his feet and turned to Cu-Sith.

'Why?'

'Loec told me that he did not like that one,' said Cu-Sith, turning away.

'That's it?' asked Kyarno, retrieving his fallen sword. 'Loec didn't like him?'

'What more do you want?' shrugged Cu-Sith. 'You are alive are you not? Be thankful Loec likes you very much. Now begone, for Cu-Sith will dance the dance of war and it would be wise of you not to get too close.'

Kyarno nodded and staggered towards the dais as Cu-Sith shouted, 'Wardancers! Begin the storm of blades!'

Naieth tried to shut out the sounds of battle as she reached deep inside herself for the power needed to do what must be done. Her elven soul cried out to unleash the terrible energies of the forest against the betrayers, but she had foreseen this moment and knew she needed all her power for one thing.

She had not used magic this powerful in many decades and the thought of tapping into the vital heart of the forest both excited and terrified her.

Naieth knelt beside Lord Aldaeld, his chest a soaking mess of blood where Valas Laithu's dagger had pierced his heart. The elven lord's skin was ashen and his eyes unseeing, but she could sense that death had not yet claimed him, though its shadow hovered near.

Watching the unequal struggle unfold between Valas Laithu and the Hound of Winter, tears blurred her eyes as the blow she knew would end Tarean Stormcrow's life finally landed. Behind her, the battle in the hall raged with undiminished violence, vengeance driving the Laithu and betrayed fury filling the hearts of the Éadaoin.

'Please,' begged Morvhen, her hands stained with her father's blood. 'Save him!'

'I will try,' said Naieth, 'but it will be difficult. Take my hand, child.'

Morvhen reached over and Naieth took her slippery hand, placing it on the wound that still weakly pumped blood down Lord Aldaeld's robes. The heart had not yet stopped beating, which meant there was still a chance to save him.

'Focus all your thoughts on your love for your father, child,' ordered Naieth, pressing her own hand atop Morvhen's. 'Picture him in his prime, as a warrior of brave heart and noble aspect. Can you do that?'

'I will,' cried Morvhen. 'Just please save him.'

Naieth nodded and began speaking the words of power, feeling the ancient strength of Athel Loren's magic rush to fill her, breathing deeply and opening herself to the magic of the forest. She gasped as its power poured into her, the rampant need of the forest to grow and spread tempered by her desire to preserve the natural balance of the world.

She let the power flow from her, surging though her fingertips, through Morvhen and into the flesh of Lord Aldaeld. Her eyes shone with golden fire as she saw the terrible damage wreaked within his chest. She shaped the healing powers to her will, reknitting the torn muscle of his heart

Graham McNeill

and forcing the sliced arteries to regrow.

Naieth felt the power of the Queen of the Forest working through her, warmth and healing compassion pouring from her in a wave of incredible strength. The flesh around Aldaeld's wound changed from angry red to pink, the skin sealing up over the wound and the bruising around it fading to nothing.

The power flowed through Aldaeld and into his throne, the wood cracking and splitting as new life and new ambition for growth seized it. Budding branches writhed from the back of the throne, bursting to verdant life and blossoming with snow-white flowers that curled and grew higher and higher. The throne writhed with power, growing into a tall tree with spreading branches and an intoxicating scent.

Aldaeld gasped and cried out as his chest hiked convulsively, his eyes snapping open in shock at the power within him.

Morvhen cried out in elation as her father's eyes opened and he gave vent to a cry of terrible rage.

Kyarno leapt to the dais as a ferocious, ululating yell built from the throats of the wardancers and their battle dance began. Cu-Sith led his spinning, leaping warriors as they bounded through the hall, swords and spears stabbing and slashing at their foes as they wove through the battle with lethal grace. Screams and cries of pain followed in their wake as shrieking, laughing wardancers struck down warriors of the Laithu kinband and left those of the Éadaoin unscathed.

Valas Laithu and Cairbre fought behind Lord Aldaeld's strange, new throne, the Hound of Winter bleeding from deep wounds to his arm and leg. He fought with the Blades of Midnight clutched in one hand, his wounded arm held tight to his chest.

'Valas Laithu!' shouted Kyarno, leaping forward with his sword aimed at his foe's heart.

The lord of the Laithu kinband spun, smiling with malicious anticipation as he saw Kyarno coming. The Spear of Daith whipped around, deflecting Kyarno's attack, the haft coming round and thudding into Kyarno's stomach.

Kyarno doubled up, swaying aside as the spear point stabbed for his chest. The blade scored across his side and he leapt back as the magical weapon's return stroke slashed at his head.

'I will enjoy killing you, outlaw!' snarled Valas Laithu as he closed in.

Kyarno parried a thrust of the spear and circled left as the Hound of Winter flanked Valas from the right. The sounds of battle began to fade from the hall, the clash of weapons and the battle cries of the wardancers replaced with the moans of the injured and the weeping for the dead.

'It's over, Valas,' said Cairbre, pointing to the terrible aftermath of the battle for Coeth-Mara. 'Your warriors are defeated. Put up your weapon.'

Valas backed away from the Hound of Winter, his face ashen as he saw the blackened, burned form of Sirda lying sprawled across a table, the lust for battle draining from him in an instant.

'I cannot,' said Valas sadly. 'I am set upon this course and have sworn the oath of vengeance with the Kindred of Talu.'

Kyarno's blood chilled at the mention of the Talu, a dark and dangerous kindred of elves sworn to fulfil oaths of retribution for terrible wrongs done to them.

'You are a Mourn-singer?' asked Kyarno, lowering his weapon. 'Then there is no peace for you until you die or you slay me.'

'Even so,' agreed Valas Laithu as Lord Aldaeld climbed from his throne of blossoming life with Morvhen and Naieth's help to stand before him. Kyarno saw the anguished relief on Cairbre's face as he saw that his lord still lived, which was quickly replaced by simmering anger as he turned back to Valas Laithu.

'You will not leave this hall alive, Lord Valas,' promised the Hound of Winter.

'I know,' replied Valas, the imminence of his death granting him a dignity he had not possessed in life. 'What is left to me now anyway? The outlaw has seen to it that my sons are no more and that my line will vanish from the forest like the wythel trees. Death is all I have left.'

'It did not have to be this way, Valas,' said Lord Aldaeld, his palm pressed to his chest where he had been stabbed.

'No? What would you have done if he had been responsible for your daughter's death?' asked Valas, pointing at Kyarno. 'Could you have forgiven him?'

Lord Aldaeld shook his head and said, 'I suppose not, but it changes nothing, Valas. I cannot let you live.'

'No, you cannot,' agreed Valas. 'I would ask a boon of you before I die though.'

'Name it.'

'Allow those of my warriors who still live to return to their homes. They took no oath and have followed my lead in all things with honour and love. Let them live to bear my body back to the Vaults of Winter that it may lie beneath the moonlight.'

Aldaeld nodded and said, 'It shall be so, Valas, I swear by Isha's mercy that they will live.'

'Thank you,' said Valas, placing the Spear of Daith on the ground as Kyarno heard the sound of an armoured warrior approaching the dais.

He turned to see Leofric enter the hall, leading a pale, blood spattered elven steed with a coppery mane. A broken arrow jutted from the metal of his armour and his sword was blooded.

Aldaeld also faced Leofric, and said, 'Human, is my domain safe?'

Leofric looked surprised that Lord Aldaeld had deigned to speak to him, but nodded and said, 'It is, Lord Aldaeld. The enemy warriors have been driven off.'

'Very well,' said Aldaeld, turning and nodding to the Hound of Winter.

Cairbre brought the Blades of Midnight up and faced Valas Laithu.

'I will make it swift,' he promised.

'I am glad it is you, Hound of Winter,' said Valas.

Cairbre nodded and Kyarno winced as the Hound of Winter rammed the long blade of his spear into Valas Laithu's body. The powerful strike tore through his lungs and up into his heart, killing the lord of the Laithu kinband instantly. Valas sighed as his last breath left him and sagged against Cairbre, who gently lowered the elf lord to the floor.

Surprisingly, Kyarno felt nothing but immense sadness at Valas Laithu's death, his honourable end contrary to everything he had known of him. Only then did he see the lifeless body of Tarean Stormcrow. Giving a cry of loss, he dropped his sword and ran to Lord Aldaeld's fallen herald.

Blood pooled in a vast lake around Tarean's body and as he placed his palm against his chest, Kyarno knew that the Stormcrow had passed from Athel Loren. He felt a splinter of ice lodge in his heart at this great loss to Coeth-Mara, tears blinding him as he wept openly for Tarean Stormcrow, a friend he had never taken the time to know.

He heard footsteps behind him and looked up to see Lord Aldaeld's cold, unforgiving eyes staring down at him.

'Much blood has been shed this day and it is upon your hands, boy.'

'You think I don't know that?' wept Kyarno.

'I hope that you do,' said Aldaeld. 'For the knowledge of what you have brought upon my halls shall be your only companion henceforth.'

'Father–' began Morvhen, but Aldaeld cut her off with a look of cold fury.

'No. I will hear no more of this, my decision is made. A line of the asrai is gone from the world and it is Kyarno's folly that has given rise to this dark day. It is time for him to face the consequences of his actions.'

Kyarno stood, facing the lord of the Éadaoin kinband, ready to face Aldaeld's judgement upon him.

'Leave,' said Aldaeld simply. 'You are a ghost in Coeth-Mara.'

BOOK THREE
SPRING'S RED HARVEST

'A little madness in the spring,
is wholesome even for the King.'

CHAPTER FIFTEEN

The Battle for Coeth-Mara had been won, but the first rays of morning revealed how terrible had been the cost. Twenty-one elves of the Éadaoin kinband were carried from the hall of battle and forty-nine of the Laithu kinband were dead.

Those followers of Valas Laithu that had not sworn vengeance oaths were allowed to leave Coeth-Mara with Lord Aldaeld's blessing, mournfully bearing the body of their lord and his son back to the Vaults of Winter.

As dusk fell the following day, Leofric joined the end of a torch-bearing procession of green-cloaked elves who marched solemnly through Coeth-Mara following the bodies of their dead. Each body was borne upon the shoulders of their kin and loved ones, wrapped in shrouds of leaves as they prepared to take their last journey.

Leofric had cleaned his armour of blood, but he was no smith and the holes punctured by enemy arrows remained. Now that the battle was won, a brooding melancholy settled upon him. Though it had begun as a prison, a hateful place that had taken Helene from him, he had come to regard Athel Loren and Coeth-Mara with a fondness he had not expected. Its golden light of autumn and crystalline splendour of winter were visions of unspoiled beauty, but now even they were tainted with blood.

Truly there was nowhere left in the world that the grim darkness of war and death could not reach. But looking around him as the funeral procession made its way along the snow-lined avenue of trees, Leofric knew that there were some things worth fighting for. Surrounded by such beauty, Leofric could understand the insular nature of the elves and their fierce desire to protect their forest kingdom.

With such a wondrous land of raptures to dwell within, who would not defend it as vigorously?

The procession passed through a dripping archway, the melting snow and ice falling on those who passed beneath it, as though the forest itself wept to see such bloodshed unleashed beneath its boughs. Leofric tilted his head back as he walked through the arch, the cold meltwater chilling him to the bone as it covered his face.

Naieth led the procession, Lord Aldaeld and the Hound of Winter following behind her carrying the body of Tarean Stormcrow. Morvhen walked beside her father with her head held high, Tiphaine bearing the long train of her dress. The Eternal Guard followed their master with their dead warriors borne upon their shoulders. The grey-feathered owl that was Naieth's companion flew overhead, even its hoots managing to convey boundless grief.

Kyarno was not part of the funeral procession, already gone from Coeth-Mara as if he had never existed. After his banishment by Lord Aldaeld, he had sheathed his sword before slowly marching from the hall and no one had seen him since. Morvhen had made to follow him, but Cairbre had held her back, knowing that her protestations would do no good. The lord of Coeth-Mara had spoken and no one but he could change his will.

The sad procession marched into the woods, passing through silent glades and along cold pathways, the trees sighing with soft songs of grief. The frozen bracken and thorny bushes parted for the elves, the forest mourning along with the elves who dwelt within it.

At length, the procession reached a wide glade of simple beauty, tall trees ringing its circumference like watchful sentinels and thin shoots of green pushing through the snow. Leofric saw that the glade was open to the heavens, the dusky sky shot through with vivid purples and reds. He did not know Tarean Stormcrow well, but had instinctively warmed to him upon their meeting and felt sure that he would have chosen something like this for his final resting place.

The procession circled the glade, now giving voice to a song of aching sadness that touched Leofric's heart, and he found himself unable to hold back tears at its sorrowful lament. He wanted to join in, but knew that his poor human voice would only do the dead a disservice.

As the column became a circle, Naieth walked into the centre of the glade and Leofric found himself standing next to Tiphaine and Morvhen. Cairbre and Aldaeld stood near and Leofric saw that the lord of the Éadaoin kinband looked tired and worn, still holding a hand to his heart. The normally stoic Cairbre looked ancient, even amongst a race for whom time passed much more slowly. Morvhen's features were regal and strong, though even she bore the hallmarks of great sorrow.

Naieth, slender and noble in a long gown of silver feathers, raised her staff of woven branches as her owl fluttered down to perch on her shoulder. Gemstones glittered on her belt of woven leaves and her golden tresses were woven with briar leaves. Her features were more careworn than he had ever seen them before.

Death ages people, realised Leofric, even the asrai.

Having borne his share of sorrow, he wondered how his own features appeared.

The elves who bore the dead on their shoulders lifted them down and took a step forward in perfect unison, laying their kin gently onto the snow. At a signal from Naieth, they retreated, leaving the ring of the dead in the centre of the glade.

Naieth began to speak, her words hauntingly beautiful even though Leofric could not understand them, sounding more like song than speech. He felt a presence near him and turned to face Tiphaine, her smooth, oval face expressionless, yet also infinitely sad.

'The prophetess asks the forest to welcome the dead,' she whispered, answering Leofric's unasked question. He nodded as Naieth's song wove new heights of loss and the elves of Coeth-Mara joined her, adding their own words of loss to the song. The grief-song continued until the purple sky darkened to the black of night, the orange glow of flickering torches giving the glade a comforting warmth as night fell.

Her song concluded, Naieth walked from the centre of the glade, the circle of elves parting to allow her to leave. Lord Aldaeld and Cairbre followed her and the rest of his people slowly peeled from the circle and disappeared into the forest.

Leofric watched them go, wondering who would come to bury the dead, when Tiphaine said, 'Come, the duty to the dead is done and we must allow them their time beneath the stars.'

'They are to be left like this?'

'Of course,' said Tiphaine. 'What else would we do?'

'Bury them?' suggested Leofric. 'Erect grave markers to their memory? Something to ensure that they will not be forgotten.'

Tiphaine shook her head. 'No, Athel Loren claims back its own. They will become part of our woodland realm and live forever as they give life to the forest. The continued beauty of the forest is their legacy, and what better remembrance to a life is there than in the immortal soul of the forest?'

'I suppose,' said Leofric. 'What will become of them?'

'Let us not speak of it,' said Tiphaine, turning and gliding from the star-lit glade. 'It is not seemly to discuss matters of the dead in their presence.'

Leofric followed her and said, 'It just feels wrong leaving them out in the open.'

'You would have us entomb the dead within a prison of stone as the dwarfs are wont to?' asked Tiphaine. 'No, to confine a soul thus is to deny it its final journey.'

'Journey?'

'To the immortality of memory. Those that loved them will remember them in song and tale, and they will pass these to their kin that come after them. In this way they will never die. Will you not remember your wife, Leofric? Will you not tell your son of her beauty and grace?'

'If I see him again, I will,' nodded Leofric sadly.

Tiphaine reached up and stroked Leofric's cheek with a smile of faint amusement creasing the corner of her mouth, the touch of her fingers light and smooth.

'You think you will not?'

'I don't know, I hope so. I don't even know if such a thing is possible.'

'This is Athel Loren,' Tiphaine reminded him. 'All things are possible.'

The cold days following the funeral procession blurred into weeks, winter's grey despair reaching its peak then falling away as the world turned its face to the sun once more. Leofric passed much of his time resting to recover from his wounds or in prayer, strangely missing the company of Kyarno now that he had been banished from Coeth-Mara. The young elf – though Leofric knew that such a term was absurd in relation to a human – had become, if not a friend, then someone he could at least talk to.

Denied such distractions for the mind, the dark days passed slowly, and Leofric was now forced to endure the loneliness of a stranger in a strange land. The impish figures of his ever-present spites followed his every movement, and though he was glad of their presence, they were no substitute for real companionship. The halls of Lord Aldaeld were beautiful and majestic, but Leofric missed the warmth of human company, the energy of his race that, for all their beauty and grace, the elves could not match.

Most of all he missed Helene and Beren. Without the diversion of people around him he brooded more on her loss and his continued absence from his son. He dreamed of them more and more often, waking with a smile on his lips until he remembered that they were lost to him.

He wondered what Beren would know of his disappearance. Would those men-at-arms who fled the edge of the forest return to Castle Carrard or would the shame of their desertion cause them to flee to other lands?

Might his family and retainers not even be aware of the fate of their lord and lady?

Days passed, then weeks, and Leofric dared to spend more time in the forest around Coeth-Mara on the elven steed he had ridden into battle against the Laithu kinband. After the battle, he had attempted to return the horse to the riders of the Glade Guard, but their leader had shaken his head, saying, 'He is called Aeneor and he has chosen you, human. You are blooded together and bound to one another now.'

Pleased to have been so chosen, he and his new mount spent the last weeks of winter becoming used to one another. The beast was fast and bore his armoured weight without complaint, and though it had not the stamina or mass of a Bretonnian warhorse, its speed and agility were beyond compare.

The passing days also gave him time to think on the fate of the young boy-children taken by the elves and his decision not to seek out the one who may very well have been one of his ancestors. What would he say to him? What *could* he say to him?

As much as he wanted to see him with his own eyes, he feared to reopen old wounds and knew that there was nothing he could offer the boy. He could not take him from Athel Loren for fear he suffer a similar fate to the vanished Duke Melmon and, in truth, he did not believe the boy would want to leave.

Aidan had seemed content enough in Coeth-Mara, but was that true contentment or was it the result of the enchantments of Athel Loren? He had spoken briefly to Naieth of the children, but she had said simply, 'Would he have been happier back in your lands? Here they are happy. Here they will live forever.'

He had had no answer for her, knowing that the life of such fey children was the life of a pariah, shunned and feared for being different. Even so, he also knew that there was a terrible cruelty in denying a child whatever life they might have forged for themselves, to keep them forever young with no hope of ever attaining anything beyond service to the elves.

Of the rest of the inhabitants of Coeth-Mara, he saw little – Morvhen now directed her energies in ministering to her father, who, despite the prophetess's healing magic, was still much in need of care.

The wardancers of Cu-Sith remained in the forest around Coeth-Mara, much to Lord Aldaeld's annoyance, but there was little that could be done about their presence and so they were left to prowl the woodland in peace.

Often Leofric would think of both Naieth and the Lady's warning that days of blood and death were coming, wondering from whence the danger would come.

But the sun lingered a little longer each day and patches of green and colour appeared throughout the woodland as the tremors of coming spring rippled through the forest, and such dangers seemed far away.

Leofric rode carefully through the depths of the forest, the air crisp and the day clear. The snow was now in retreat from spring's advance, though the forest retained much of its white cloak. He felt a curious excitement, the same awareness of possibility that he sensed in the elves of Coeth-Mara as the thaw came. Perhaps the budding sense of anticipation that lingered on the air was being communicated to him with his every breath?

Whatever the reason, he was glad to be outside on this new day of sunlight, travelling the paths of the forest to find Kyarno.

Morvhen had come to his chambers the previous evening, entreating him to travel into the forest to find her lost lover. Since the attack of the Laithu kinband, the Hound of Winter had increased his watchfulness of her and there was no way she could go to him, but she had passed a leaf-wrapped scroll to Leofric.

'Talk to him,' urged Morvhen.

'I would not know where to find him,' said Leofric.

Morvhen smiled. 'He will remain close to Coeth-Mara for a time. Seek him out at the Crystal Mere, for it is there that he knew peace.'

As a tolerated guest of Lord Aldaeld, Leofric knew he ought to refuse Morvhen's request, but the guilt of having berated her in the forest before his vision of the Lady of the Lake still lingered in his memory.

'Very well, my lady,' said Leofric, taking the scroll.

'He loves me,' said Morvhen sadly.

'That is a good thing, surely?' said Leofric, seeing the sorrow on her face.

'Is it? Not for me.'

'Why not? Love is a gift that should be treasured.'

'Only if you can have it,' said Morvhen bitterly. 'Only if you can have it. He can never come back to Coeth-Mara. Not now. Our foolishness has cost me the one thing I wanted most in the world.'

'Lord Aldaeld may change his mind,' said Leofric. 'You told me Kyarno has been cast from his halls before.'

'By the Hound of Winter, yes, but never by my father. Isha's tears, I almost wish Cairbre had never brought him back to Coeth-Mara after his family was killed. Then I would never have known this pain for I would have known nothing of Kyarno Daelanu.'

Leofric wanted to reach out to Morvhen, to place a comforting hand on her shoulder, but felt that such a gesture would be inappropriate and that she would resent the pity of a human.

'I do not believe you mean that, Morvhen,' he said. 'It is always good to know love, even if it cannot be yours.'

'You really believe that?'

'I do,' replied Leofric, feeling the magic of Athel Loren flowing through him as he spoke. 'I loved Helene with all my heart and when she was taken from me I thought I would die. The pain of her loss is great... almost too great, but even if I could change things so that I had never met her and was spared this hurt, I would not.'

'You would not?' asked Morvhen.

'No,' said Leofric, shaking his head. 'I miss her so much, but I remember the golden time we shared and the son we conceived. If nothing else came of our union, then that is worth all the pain I suffer.'

'What will become of your son?'

'I don't know,' said Leofric. 'He will grow to be a fine man, of that I am sure. He will make me proud.'

'Will he become a knight like you?'

Leofric smiled. 'I hope so. Maixent, my chamberlain, will tutor him in the ways of a knight of Bretonnia and he will make his way in the world with courage and nobility.'

'I think that he shall,' agreed Morvhen.

Leofric had ridden out at first light, trusting that Aeneor could locate the Crystal Mere without running into the Wild Riders or anything else that might wish him harm.

The journey to the blessed pool was one of joy to Leofric, the scent of sweet sap heavy in his nostrils and the cold sunlight refreshing his skin as it dappled through the fractured canopy above him. Though the path he rode was unknown to him, he had a sudden skewed sense of déjà vu, as though he had come this way before... *or would come this way again...*

He shrugged off the unsettling sensation, seeing the sunlit glade through the trees ahead and hearing the growing thunder of the waterfall. The undergrowth and trees thinned and once more Leofric rode into the glade, its breathtaking beauty still with the power to render him speechless. He had thought its magic would have been spoiled for him by the touch of the creatures of Chaos, but as with all things natural, it had healed itself and the wonder of its magnificence was undimmed.

Sure enough, Kyarno was here, lounging atop the same rock from which he had watched Leofric when he had brought him here to bathe, his steed grazing at the edge of the glade. Dressed in the same clothes he had been wearing the last time Leofric had seen him, Kyarno looked sad and tired, his pale, narrow face turned towards the thundering waterfall.

Leofric sat for a moment to allow the calming presence of the glade's air to fill him, smiling and pleased to be back.

'Why are you here, Leofric?' asked Kyarno without turning.

Leofric did not reply immediately, sliding from the back of his horse and setting him loose in the glade to join Kyarno's.

'I came to see you.'

'Why?'

'To tell you that you are missed.'

Kyarno snorted in disbelief. 'By whom? Who misses the elf who leaves so many dead in his foolish wake? I do not deserve to be missed.'

'Morvhen misses you,' said Leofric, holding out the leaf-wrapped scroll.

Kyarno finally turned to face him and smiled wistfully. 'And she sent you to find me? No doubt because the Hound of Winter watches her like a hawk now.'

Leofric nodded. 'Yes, he does, and I should not have come here.'

'So why did you?'

'You should know by now it is never wise to refuse the requests of a woman.'

'There is truth in that,' agreed Kyarno, slipping from the rock and approaching Leofric to take the scroll.

Leofric turned to give Kyarno privacy to read Morvhen's words and walked to the edge of the crystal waters of the wide pool. Lights darted beneath the surface and glittering gems winked on the sandy bottom.

Kyarno joined him at the water's edge, a faraway look on his face as he watched the tumbling waterfall foam the water white.

'Thank you. I know you did not have to do this,' said Kyarno.

'You are welcome,' nodded Leofric, squatting down on his haunches and running a hand through the waters.

Kyarno tucked the message into his shirt and sat on the grass beside him, and both man and elf shared a companionable silence, listening to the crash of the water and the sighing song of the trees.

'Tell me of your lands,' said Kyarno suddenly.

'I thought elves had no interest in what lay beyond Athel Loren?'

'Normally we do not, but I wish to hear you speak of them.'

Leofric thought of the world he knew, surprised to find that his memories of it were dim and hollow. He struggled to recall what he knew of the world, finding it difficult to think of the kingdoms beyond the forest.

'Bretonnia is a fine land, of honour and virtue,' said Leofric eventually, 'but it suffers as do all in these dark times. Orcs and undead raiders from across the seas attack our coasts, and our people live in squalor and poverty. For those lucky enough to be born to a noble family, it can be a fine place, but for all others it is a grim land.'

'And beyond Bretonnia?' asked Kyarno.

'To the north, across the Grey Mountains, lies the Empire, a grim and fearful place of sprawling, dark forests that are home to all manner of foul creatures – goblins, beastmen and worse. It is hardly a nation at all, riven with discord and its ruler barely able to keep his lands in order. Further east is the cold northern realm of Kislev, a land said to be locked in ice and snow.'

'Have you ever been there?'

'No,' said Leofric, 'I have never seen it, and nor do I wish to. It is a savage land, peopled by harsh men and women who fight a constant battle for survival against the northern tribes of the Dark Gods. It breeds them tough, but it breeds them dour. The closest I have come to Kislev is Middenheim, city of the White Wolf.'

'White Wolf? Who is that?'

'The city is named for the god of battles and winter, Ulric, and is a magnificent-looking place that sits atop a great crag of rock that rises from the forest like a mountain.'

'Why did you travel there?'

Leofric sighed, remembering the fierce battles fought around the northern city of the Empire, the death, the blood and, most of all, the hateful memory of their rout at the hands of the Swords of Chaos.

'The hordes of Chaos had poured southwards from the steppes, led by a powerful warlord named Archaon, burning and destroying everything in their path as they clove through Kislev towards the Empire. Though great victories were won at Mazhorod and Urszebya, nothing could halt the advance of the horde and they invaded the Empire in their thousands. They sought to destroy the city of the White Wolf and thence the world. My king declared an errantry war against Archaon and the knights of Bretonnia rode out to do battle.'

'I see by your eyes that it was a battle not easily won.'

'No,' said Leofric. 'It was not. We were victorious, but the cost was high. We fought to save the world and, though, in the end it is fruitless, Chaos must be fought at all times.'

'You have said that before,' said Kyarno. 'Why do you say that it is fruitless?'

Leofric hesitated before speaking again, unsure why he had made such a frank confession to Kyarno. Were the healing waters of the Crystal Mere working their enchantments on him once more? The thought of his sorrows being eased by the magic of the glade did not trouble him anymore. *This* pain he would be happy to be rid of.

'Each time the warriors of Chaos come, they come in greater numbers and reach further into the domains of men. In their wake comes death, famine, sickness and suffering. How long will it be until there is nothing left for them to destroy, until their armies reach the deserts of the far south?'

'But each time you have turned back the darkness,' pointed out Kyarno.

'We hold them back each time, but each time we are lessened.'

Kyarno shook his head. 'No, each time you hurl the forces of Chaos back you are strengthened. There is nothing fruitless about fighting Chaos, Leofric, nothing. Chaos *must* be opposed, for it is that fight that makes us strong. I have heard you speak of the lands of your race and one thing is clear.'

'And what is that?'

'That against all the odds they endure,' said Kyarno. 'For thousands of years – through plague, warriors of the north, dusty revenants of the southern deserts or foul orcs – these realms have survived.'

'For now,' said Leofric. 'It is only a matter of time before they are swept away in blood and war.'

'True, many kingdoms have arisen that their rulers thought would last forever, but are now nothing more than dust and legend, but they fought to preserve them for as long as they could.'

'What is the point if they are just going to fail?'

'I know you don't really believe that,' said Kyarno. 'You would not have become a warrior if you did.'

'What do you mean?'

'You know what I mean,' said Kyarno. 'A true warrior fights not because he wants to, but because he has to. To defend those who cannot defend themselves. To give hope to those around him who look to him to do what is right and to fight because that is what must be done.'

Kyarno's words spoke to Leofric of the last time he had entered the waters of the Crystal Mere, desperately scrambling for a weapon to fight the beasts of Chaos.

Though victory had seemed impossible he had fought anyway.

'Perhaps you are right, Kyarno,' said Leofric, rising to his feet and running his wet hands through his hair. 'I will think on what you have said.'

'You are returning to Coeth-Mara?' asked Kyarno with a disappointed sigh.

'Yes, is there a message you wish me to take to Morvhen?'

Kyarno said nothing, and Leofric saw the elf's attention was fixed on something over his shoulder. He turned to see the object of Kyarno's stare and his mouth fell open at the magnificent sight before him.

A great hart grazed with the horses at the edge of the glade, its furred hide a glorious, unblemished white, its mighty antlers curling above its head in a wide fan of bone. Leofric had hunted deer throughout his lands for years, but had never set eyes on a creature so fine and regal as this.

It stood amid a burst of yellow primrose, the scent of which was suddenly strong and intoxicating. The hart lifted its mighty head, as if sensing their scrutiny, and as its eyes met his, Leofric was humbled by the ancient wisdom and intelligence he saw there.

As he watched the wonderful animal feed, a tremor rippled through the earth, sending the imps that capered in the water scurrying into the undergrowth with wild squeals. A surging, powerful energy rose from the very ground and Leofric felt his heartbeat race with a nameless exhilaration. A breathless shiver of anticipation rushed along his spine, a primal energy filling his muscles with a wild urge to run, to fight and to hunt. He turned to ask Kyarno what was happening, the words dying in his throat as he saw golden wychfires blazing in the elf's eyes.

'Primrose…' breathed Kyarno, an ancient longing suffusing his voice as the echoing blast of a mighty hunting horn sounded from far away.

'What about them?' asked Leofric nervously, the distant skirl of the horn chilling him with its promise of blood.

'…the first flower of spring,' finished Kyarno.

CHAPTER SIXTEEN

Deep in Athel Loren, in a secret glade sacred to both forest and elf, a mighty oak tree trembled, its ancient surface gnarled and pitted with age. Five thousand and more summers had it seen, its roots stretching deep into the rock of the world. Known as the Oak of Ages, yellow blooming primrose flowered amid its thick, twisting roots and green, verdant grass bent and swayed in the gathering breeze.

A crack split the trunk from roots to branches and a gust of wind, like the first breath of the world, billowed from within. The deafening blast of a hunting horn echoed from deep inside the tree, as though a vast hall lay beneath the ground; the baying of hounds and the raucous cries of birds stirred from their eyries rising from the forest to accompany the exultant echo of the horn.

Sweet-smelling sap ran from the crack in the oak tree and the thunder of mighty hooves beat on the air as something ancient, terrifying and primal stirred from its slumbers and spread through the forest once more.

The sound of the hunting horn came again, Leofric could feel its power in the very depths of his soul. He trembled at its might, a fear deep in his bones screaming that he was this hunter's prey. His every sense told him to run, that nothing good could come of this sound.

He remembered a similar sensation when he had first ridden through the forest, when the wild riders of Kurnous had surrounded them. Kyarno had said that those warriors were the wild huntsmen who rode alongside the King of the Wood when he awoke in spring...

Leofric looked back towards the edge of the glade, seeing that the white hart had vanished into the forest at the sound of the horn and that the yellow of the flowers seemed much more vivid.

'We have to get out of here,' said Leofric.

'Yes,' agreed Kyarno, the gold fire still glittering in his wide eyes. 'We are in serious danger. The King of the Wood has awoken and is on the hunt...'

Every tale Leofric knew of the dangerous king of the faerie forest ended in blood. The same fear he had felt when confronted by the warriors who served him arose, but this was much worse: the paralysing dread felt by all hunted things.

Leofric and Kyarno ran for their steeds, climbing onto their backs and riding hard into the trees. As they plunged into the forest, Leofric saw that the bright feeling of vitality had vanished utterly, the beauty and grace changed to something far darker.

Where the sunlight had warmed his face, now it cast fearful shadows. Where the curve of branches had artfully shaped pleasant bowers, now they grasped for him and tore at his clothes as they rode headlong for Coeth-Mara.

Leofric saw the true face of the forest, ancient and powerful, its need to grow and spread manifest in the impossibly fecund hearts of the trees. Stark against the skies, the tall, clawed branches reached out for him as they rode and he cried out in terror as the rising hornblast came again, louder and more powerful than before.

Kyarno rode beside him, his eyes alight with savage lust as the forest came alive around them. Shadows rushed alongside them, darting shapes and capering creatures with wings and branch-like limbs.

Faces leered from the trunks of gnarled trees and a shimmering mist gathered between them as the distant howls of hunting packs drew closer. Though it had been morning when he had set out for the Crystal Mere, the sky above swiftly changed from pale blue to an angry, bruised purple, dark clouds forming above the treetops and the first rumbles of thunder building.

'Kyarno!' shouted Leofric. 'What's happening?'

'The wild hunt is abroad! Hurry!'

Leofric urged his mount to greater speed as lightning split the sky and a rolling thunder tolled from the clouds. Ghostly shapes loomed in the mist, clawed hands of twigs reaching out to him with spiteful laughter. The horn came again and Leofric cried out, the wild blast sounding as though it came from right beside him.

Thunder came again and this time he realised that the sound came not from the clouds above, but was the hammering of hooves. He heard branches snapping aside, the barking of hounds and the caw of dark birds.

He looked up to see the sky alive with thousands of shapes, murders of ravens and crows swirling in huge numbers above as something massive thundered through the forest towards them. Rain, heavy spring rain, now fell from the skies as the full fury of the storm broke.

Dark light flared in the forest around him and he saw shrieking shapes in the mist either side of him, riders on dark steeds with eyes of golden fire. Whooping yells of fierce joy echoed from the forest and Leofric saw that cloaked riders surrounded them.

They rode with wild abandon, leaping and weaving in and out of the mist, brandishing long, thorn-looped spears above their heads. Skulls bounced from their belts and torques as they rode, and they had the look of a devil about them, their aspect no longer truly elven, but something far older and more powerful.

The wild riders of Kurnous unleashed…

Snapping hounds bounded alongside them, howling in praise of their king. Leofric gave his horse its head, knowing that it could better evade these riders and hounds than he. Something massive drew near from behind. He could hear the crash of its thunderous approach even over the booming storm that raged above, and Leofric felt a suffocating fear arise in his breast at the thought of laying eyes on this terrible, bloody king.

'Leofric!' shouted Kyarno. 'This way!'

He needed no further urging and yelled as his steed broke towards Kyarno. The beasts of the wild hunt howled and cried, the snapping crash of their king deafening as he charged towards them.

Leofric plunged after Kyarno, crouched over Aeneor's neck, his heart hammering in his chest as the undergrowth around them grew thinner. He heard Kyarno shouting something in the magical tongue of the elves and felt the forest shift in response to his words. Branches whipped past them, one laying open his cheek across the scar given to him by Cu-Sith, but Leofric ignored the stinging pain, too intent on the hunting packs behind them.

A sudden sense of vertigo seized him and the forest around him became blurred and ghostly, as though he looked at it through a fogged window. Lights streaked his vision and he fought to stay on the back of his horse as a wave of dizziness swamped him.

Sounds became muted and his every breath was like the bellowing of an angry god in his ears. He clapped his hands to his head in pain, tumbling from the back of his horse and landing heavily on the forest floor.

He lay still for several moments before he realised that the sounds of pursuit were no longer behind them and that the forest was no longer as hostile in appearance or deed. Kyarno lay across his horse's neck, his breathing shallow and his skin even paler than normal.

'What happened?' gasped Leofric, fighting to calm his rampant heartbeat as he climbed to his feet using the trunk of a nearby tree. 'Are we safe?'

'For the moment,' wheezed Kyarno. 'We have a brief respite. But we will need to ride again soon.'

'What did you do?'

'I spoke to the trees and asked them if we might pass along the secret paths that travel between worlds and link some of the glades of the forest. I told them of your service to the Éadaoin kinband and they were gracious enough to allow you to travel with me. We are some miles yet from Coeth-Mara, but if the Lady Ariel is with us we can still make it.'

Leofric rubbed his side where he had hit the ground, looking up into the sky where the thunder and lightning still seethed. Ghostly lights flickered above them and he knew that they were not yet safe.

'Coeth-Mara?' asked Leofric. 'Will you find welcome there?'

Kyarno shrugged. 'Let us worry about that if we get there. Can you ride?'

'I can,' said Leofric, climbing back onto his horse as he heard the far-off sound of the hunting horn once more.

'Then let us be away before the wild hunt catches up to us once again!'

Like a rotten tooth expelled from a diseased gum, the waystone heaved from the blackened ground, its vast granite bulk swaying gently for a moment before it toppled to the earth with an almighty crash. The beastherd roared and bellowed in triumph as the stone fell, stamping the ground and locking horns with one another.

The shaman held himself upright with his staff. Its battle with the magic of the waystone had exhausted it to the point of collapse. The power of the gods had given it the strength it needed to drag the waystone down, but had left it precious little to sustain its life, and it knew that its last breath was upon it.

The Beastlord beat its chest with the flat of its mighty axe, the weapon ringing from its brazen hide as it sent the massive forms of its largest followers forward to gather up the waystone. A pack of hulking trolls, their massive muscles swollen by dark energies, grunted and roared as they lifted the enormous stone onto their backs.

Even the smallest of the trolls was twice the size of the Beastlord, their leathery skin a mottled green and brown. Their thick skulls and stupid features marked them as creatures of Chaos, but the shaman knew that they were not the chosen children of the Dark Gods. Such a vaunted position was that of the beastmen.

The shaman turned a milky, distended eye back to the forest, grunting in satisfaction as it saw the raw wound in the ground where the waystone had once stood. The forest writhed as though in pain, roots and rapidly growing shoots of greenery bursting from the ground.

As though spilling outwards, the edge of the forest appeared to be drawing nearer, expanding beyond its previous boundary. The shaman slid down its staff as its life force faded, looking up as a wild horn blast echoed over the treetops.

The trolls bearing the waystone lurched back towards the mountains, their steps slow and ponderous, but they were easily outpacing the encroachments of the forest. Dark shapes moved within the forest's edge, wild, monstrous things, and the shaman shuddered in fear as the horn blast sounded again and the breath of something impossibly ancient roared from the trees.

Like the last breath of winter, the wind gusted over the assembled beastmen, carrying with it the promise of death, blood and the huntsman's spear. A low bray of fear rose from the herd at the sound and sent many fleeing for the mountains.

The shaman's last sight was of the Beastlord standing firm against the power of the forest's magic, roaring its defiance and mastery. It had taken one of the fabled waystones of Athel Loren and no mere wind was going to frighten it.

It had taken what it had come for and with the waystone well on its way towards the mountains, the Beastlord led its herd from Athel Loren.

Leofric and Kyarno rode off into the forest once more, willing their horses to greater speed as the charge of the wild hunt drew nearer with each passing second.

Leofric could feel the hot breath of the hunting hounds on his neck, the claws of the battle raven on his flesh and the gaze of the mighty King of the Wood upon his soul, but told himself they were but fearful illusions. They galloped a weaving course between the trees, the ghostly mists clawing from the trees once more as Leofric began to recognise parts of the forest from the times he had spent riding around Coeth-Mara.

Though in that recognition was strangeness, a sense that even though individual parts of the forest were familiar, they were gathered oddly, as though different parts of the forest had shifted and moved.

Nor were they challenged as they rode beneath the woven arch of leaves, branches and gem-encrusted belts of gold and silver that marked the edge of Lord Aldaeld's halls.

'Come on!' shouted Kyarno as Leofric heard the crash of something huge emerging from the trees and felt a lustful wave of aggression and power wash over him. Ahead he saw Kyarno stiffen in the grip of this power, his eyes alight with its energies.

He risked a glance over his shoulder and cried out in fear as he saw something huge and muscular, its antlered flesh green hued and daubed with runic symbols. Fiery-eyed riders surrounded it, whooping and yelling as scores of baying hounds loped through the thoroughfares and tree-lined avenues of Coeth Mara.

Branches and leaves obscured Leofric's sight of the massive King of the Wood as he and Kyarno altered course and rode into the hall of Lord Aldaeld, passing into a high, vaulted chamber filled with the inhabitants of Coeth-Mara, their faces fearful and wary.

Shouts and cries of alarm followed them as they entered, warriors with spears and swords rushing to surround them. Leofric slumped across the neck of his horse, laughing and crying in relief to have escaped the charge of the wild hunt as it thundered past.

'You dare return in defiance of your banishment?' shouted a voice.

'Lord Aldaeld will have your head for this!' said another, and Leofric looked up to see grey-cloaked warriors of the Eternal Guard drag Kyarno from his horse.

'Wait!' he shouted. 'No! Kyarno saved us both in the forest.'

The elven warriors ignored him and Leofric felt his fury build at them. Kyarno had saved his life. He dropped from Aeneor's back, lurching towards the struggling elves. A crowd gathered to watch the unfolding drama in their midst, grateful for the chance to take their minds from the danger beyond the hall.

'Release him!' shouted Leofric, his voice laden with anger and authority.

None of the Eternal Guard bothered to take notice of him, and he ran towards them, gripping the cloak of the nearest one and hauling him off Kyarno. Leofric hurled the warrior aside and reached for the next, but the fallen warrior was upon him a second later and, within moments, both he and Kyarno were held fast.

'Get off me!' yelled Leofric.

'Be silent!' shouted the Hound of Winter, emerging from the press of bodies surrounding them. Cairbre carried the Blades of Midnight in one hand and his helm in the other. Behind him came Lord Aldaeld, Morvhen and Naieth.

Cairbre marched towards them, his face an unreadable mask, though Leofric could see a flicker of emotion cross his stoic features as he spoke to Kyarno.

'You know you are forbidden to return to Coeth-Mara,' he said.

'I know,' replied his nephew.

'Then why are you here?'

'He saved my life!' shouted Leofric. 'Without Kyarno, the wild hunt would have caught me. He risked his own life to save mine. That is why he is here.'

Cairbre turned from Kyarno as Lord Aldaeld approached, his power and strength undeniable, though Leofric saw he still bore a faint white scar where Valas Laithu's dagger had pierced his heart. His cloak of leaves and his tattoos writhed with motion, and his face spoke of great anger, but also great regret.

'Is this true, Kyarno?' asked Lord Aldaeld.

Kyarno nodded, shrugging off the restraining arms of the Eternal Guard. Leofric felt the grip of the warriors holding him relax and threw them off angrily. In the silence that followed, he could clearly hear the howling hounds and the crash of the wild hunt as it passed through Coeth-Mara.

Behind Aldaeld, Morvhen looked on fearfully and Leofric's heart went out to her. Her lost love stood before her, yet she could not reach out and touch him for fear of her father's banishment, and the absurdity of this roused Leofric to speak out.

'Lord Aldaeld,' he said. 'May I speak?'

'I don't need you to speak for me,' snapped Kyarno.

'I do not speak for you, Kyarno,' said Leofric. 'I speak for the Lady Morvhen.'

Lord Aldaeld spun at the mention of Morvhen's name and his eyes narrowed. 'You speak for Morvhen? Why would you speak for her?'

'Because no one else will speak for her or Kyarno,' answered Leofric. 'She loves Kyarno, and he loves her. Why will you not allow them to be together?'

'Because he will lead her to ruin,' growled Aldaeld. 'Kyarno has had every chance to prove himself to me and each time he has thrown it away. I will tolerate him no more.'

'Then you are a fool!' said Leofric to a gasp of shock. 'For you do not see what you throw away for the sake of spite.'

Lord Aldaeld's face twisted in anger and his sword flashed into his hand as he stepped close to Leofric. 'I should kill you where you stand, human! You think to speak to me thus in my own halls!'

'I apologise for such harsh words, Lord Aldaeld, but I speak from the heart.'

'Your kind always thinks it knows better than any other,' sneered Aldaeld. 'You meddle and you throw your might around like children, heedless of the cultures of others, always thinking in your blinkered way that only you can know the will of the world.'

'What you say has truth to it, but give me a chance. That's all I ask.'

'Say what it is you want to say, but my course is set.'

Leofric stood before the lord of Coeth-Mara, but addressed his words to the assembled throng, raising his voice so that all could hear him over the howling and thunder of hooves from beyond the hall.

'I come from the land that borders Athel Loren. It is called Bretonnia and I am a knight of that realm. I serve my king and defend his lands when he calls me. I am a warrior and my path to earn my knighthood has been long and arduous.

'I began as a young man, what we Bretonnians call a knight errant. I was young, impetuous and ready to fight the world if it would mean I could become a knight of the realm. There are many young men of my land who aspire to this great height, but only a few who reach it. A knight errant is the very image of bravado – arrogant and haughty, brave to the point of recklessness. In battle they charge heedlessly towards the enemy, earning either great glory or a heroic death.'

'What has this to do with anything?' demanded Lord Aldaeld.

'Bear with me,' cautioned Leofric. 'Most of these knights errant do not survive and many a mother of Bretonnia has mourned a son before her time.'

'Then they are fools,' said Aldaeld. 'Recklessness has no place on the battlefield.'

'You are of course correct, Lord Aldaeld, but think on this – those who survive know that. While reckless bravery has its place, courage is at its best when tempered with duty. This is the lesson they learn.'

'You would throw the lives of your young away for this lesson?'

'To do otherwise would be to deny a young knight his destiny,' said Leofric. 'And by such means are the knights of Bretonnia kept mighty, for those who have not experienced such passions cannot truly understand the nobility of courage.'

'So what are you saying?'

'That Kyarno is young and has made many foolish choices, but that he is alive and he is brave. I believe he has learned the lesson of courage and duty and is fit to take his place within your halls.'

Aldaeld shook his head. 'His actions caused the death of many of my people. I have a responsibility to my kinband and I cannot trust him.'

'I know that, and so does he,' said Leofric. 'He will carry the knowledge of what he has done to his dying day, and no punishment of yours can make that any worse. All you will do is break your daughter's heart.'

'Do not think to manipulate me by recourse to my daughter,' warned Aldaeld.

'I do not, I swear. I am a knight of Bretonnia and I never lie. I speak only what I know to be true.'

Aldaeld did not reply, switching his gaze from Kyarno to Morvhen before turning to Cairbre and asking, 'What say you, Hound of Winter? Can your nephew be trusted?'

Cairbre took a step towards Kyarno and looked him square in the eye, daring him to look away. They stared deep into one another for long moments before Cairbre said, 'His heart is true, my lord. I have known that since he was born.'

'But can he be trusted?'

'I do not know, my lord,' confessed Cairbre. 'I want to believe he can, but I do not know for sure.'

'You have your answer, sir knight,' said Aldaeld, turning away from Leofric. 'Kyarno can stay until the wild hunt passes. Then I want him gone again.'

'No!' said Leofric. 'Did you hear nothing of what I said?'

'I heard, human,' snapped Aldaeld, turning and marching back towards him, 'but it changes nothing. I am lord of this domain, not you or your king, and I do what is necessary to protect it. I do not care for the traditions of your lands, for they are not mine. Did you think to come into my halls, make a pretty speech and return everything to normal? You should know your place, human, for life is not that simple in Athel

Loren. For your kind it might be, but you are not among your kind now. Do not ever forget that.'

In the sudden silence that followed, Leofric became aware that the thunderous noise beyond the hall had vanished.

'Prophetess…' hissed Aldaeld, realising the same thing. 'The wild hunt… what has become of it?'

Naieth closed her eyes and Leofric watched as a dim glow built behind her eyelids, feeling the prickling sensation of magic nearby.

'It moves on,' said Naieth, her voice taking on the dreamlike quality of a sleepwalker.

'Where does it go?' demanded Aldaeld.

'It goes beyond,' cried Naieth, gasping and dropping to her knees. Cairbre rushed to help her and she sagged against him, opening her eyes and staring directly at Leofric.

'It goes beyond,' she repeated, tears streaming down her face. 'The way-stones are breached!'

'Breached?' cried Aldaeld. 'How?'

'I do not know,' wept Naieth. 'I did not see. I did not see…'

'You said the wild hunt had gone beyond,' said Leofric, fearful of what the prophetess might say. 'Where do you mean?'

'I am so sorry…' whispered Naieth. 'It rides for your lands now.'

Satisfied that his animals were bedded down for the night, Varus Martel closed the latch on the gate that separated the byre where he kept his three pigs from where he and his family slept. He circled the low-burning fire to reach his threadbare jerkin where it lay beside the simple pallet bed he shared with his wife and two children.

The hard-packed mud floor of their hovel was damp and cold, the thin soles of his boots keeping in not a shred of warmth. He lifted his jerkin from beside the fire, pulling out a carved wooden pipe from within, and began tamping what little weed he had left into the bowl. He jammed the pipe between his teeth and pulled on his leather skullcap, tying the thin cords beneath his chin before leaning in towards the fire and lifting out a lighted taper.

Varus lit the pipe and took a hefty drag before making his way outside.

The night was chill, but not cold, the winter having done its worst already. It had been hard on the villagers of Chabaon, many of the local families suffering sad losses amongst their children or elderly. Varus himself had lost a prime sow to the cold, and while it had meant they had had enough to eat for a few weeks, there would be no more piglets until he could afford to buy another at market.

The thought depressed him and he tried not to think about the future as he heard a distant rumble, like approaching thunder. He looked up into the sky, his brow wrinkling in puzzlement as he saw nothing but the pale face of Mannslieb as it shone down upon the little village.

The rumble grew louder and he saw several other doors open and inquisitive faces appear.

'Varus,' shouted Ballard from the hovel across the way. 'What d'you think that is?'

'Don't rightly know,' said Varus. 'Ain't likely thunder. Not a cloud in the sky.'

'Peculiar is what it is,' said Ballard, nodding sagely at his own pronouncement and taking out a pipe of his own.

'Aye, peculiar right enough,' agreed Varus, blowing a ragged smoke ring. He scanned the horizon, looking for any sign of horsemen, for the noise sounded a lot like riders. Lots of them too. The only riders round these parts were knights and suchlike from Castle Carrard and that was a good many miles away. Not like riders to be out this late so far from home…

Then he realised that the noise wasn't coming from the north, but the east. He looked up at the sky once more, the pipe falling from his hand as he saw spectral clouds slip across the face of the moon and heard an echoing horn blast carried on the wind.

'Oh no…' he whispered. 'Oh no, no, no…'

He saw the same realisation strike Ballard and hauled open the door to his hovel with a cry of alarm.

'Up! Up!' he cried. 'For the love of the Lady, up!'

His wife sat bolt upright, already frightened by his tone, his children still groggy with sleep. He shut the door behind him and threw the locking bar into place, hoping that it would be enough.

'What's the matter, Varus?' screamed his wife as he dropped to his knees before the badly painted statuette of the Lady that sat in a small alcove in the wall.

'Lady, please save us from the wrath of the faerie folk!' shouted Varus as the mounting wind rattled the ill-fitting door in its frame. The rumble of hooves beat the air, growing louder each second, and the first peal of thunder shook the hovel with its booming violence.

His children screamed as a terrible, bloodcurdling horn echoed across the cold landscape. A shuddering tremor shook the hovel and the howls of wild hounds drifted across the bleak moorland. Plates and cups fell to the floor and the squeals of his pigs added to the din.

Varus rushed over to his family, holding them tightly as the terrible sound of the wild hunt closed in on the village of Chabaon. They huddled on the bed, weeping in terror at the sound of their approaching doom, praying to the Lady of the Lake that it would pass them by.

Howling winds tore through the village and Varus screamed as the roof of the hovel was ripped off, the lightning-streaked sky thick with shrieking ravens and ghostly riders on pale horses. Wild laughter and horns followed the charging huntsmen of the sky and thunder boomed in the wake of their charge.

The walls of his hovel blew inwards, but Varus Martel and his family had already been carried up into the sky by the wild hunt as it laid waste to the village of Chabaon.

CHAPTER SEVENTEEN

Ancient ancestral fear clutched at Leofric as he heard Naieth tell him that the wild hunt now wreaked havoc in Bretonnia. The dread of the howling gale of destruction and the terrible carnage it left in its wake surged through his body and he felt hollow, as though he had been winded by a fall from a horse.

'Are you sure?' he asked.

Naieth nodded sadly. 'Yes, I am sure. The King of the Wood has tasted blood already and he will not stop until much more has been shed.'

'Is there anything we can do?'

'No, Leofric, there is not. With the waystone barrier breached, the power of the king is free to reach beyond the borders of Athel Loren.'

'Then we must restore the barrier!' he cried. 'How can we do that?'

'Only by restoring the waystone to its former position, Leofric.'

Leofric turned to Lord Aldaeld and said, 'Please, my people are dying. Help me.'

'Help you?' said Aldaeld. 'What is it you think I can do?'

'I don't know,' said Leofric helplessly. 'Whatever you can.'

Aldaeld shook his head. 'The lives of humans are not worth the effort and risk to elven lives. The wild hunt will return to the forest once the king's lust for battle and destruction is sated. When he returns to Athel Loren, we will recover the waystone.'

'But my people are dying!' shouted Leofric. 'Your king is killing the people of Bretonnia and you will stand by while that happens?'

Aldaeld nodded and hissed, 'I would stand by while he wiped humans from the face of the world if that were his course. You bring nothing into this world and it is certain you will take nothing out of it. Why should I mourn your kind?'

Leofric stood speechless, shocked at this candid admission by Lord Aldaeld, who turned from him to address Naieth.

'How is it that the barrier has failed?' demanded the elven lord. 'Has the power of the enchantments wrought upon the waystone faded?'

'No,' whispered Naieth, closing her eyes once more and allowing her spirit to travel the mystic paths of the forest. 'The power of such ancient magic does not fade easily, some other power is at work here.'

'What other power? What could overcome the power of the elder magic?'

Suddenly Naieth cried out in horror and pain, and but for the support of the Hound of Winter, would have fallen. Blood ran from her nose and she wept tears of pain.

'No!' she wept, and Leofric was surprised to hear the venom of hatred in the prophetess's tone. 'It is the beast. It is Cyanathair! It has returned.'

A ripple of horror spread through the halls at the mention of this name, though Leofric did not understand what it meant. Swiftly the horror turned to anger and the mood of the hall changed to one of vengeful aggression. He saw the same golden fire he had seen in Kyarno's eyes at the waking of the King of the Wood reflected in every elf within the hall, a wild anger and lust for killing that sent a chill along his spine.

The elves of Coeth-Mara milled like caged wolves, the threat of violence in every face and every gesture as they clutched at sword hilts or gripped the hafts of spears.

Was this part of the King of the Wood's power? Did part of his anger and destructive nature pass to his people upon his waking?

'Who is this Cyanathair?' asked Leofric warily.

'Do not speak its name again!' gasped Naieth.

'It is the Corruptor,' said Cairbre. 'It is the enemy.'

'Your race knows it as the Shadow-Gave,' said Naieth. 'It is the bane of all things living, an abomination. It is the thing that should not be.'

The Shadow-Gave...

Legends spoke of such a creature, a fell monster too terrible to imagine, that had ripped its way into the world in a village near the Forest of Arden. A bestial creature of Chaos that warped everything around it into horrific new forms, it was a tale to frighten young children with. The myth of the creature was recorded in the Bretonnian lay 'Requiem', a tragic poem that spoke of men who crawled in the mud like beasts and animals that walked on their hind legs and babbled nonsensical doggerel as they feasted on one another.

'Surely such a creature must be dead?' said Leofric. 'Beastmen are no longer lived than humans. It must have died many hundreds of years ago.'

'How little you know, Leofric,' said Naieth, not unkindly. 'If only it were so. No, the Corruptor is a creature of Chaos Eternal. It has been slain many times in the secret war, but each time it is reborn anew to continue its destructive quest amongst the races of this world. The Lady Ariel seeks always to defeat it, but the power of the Dark Gods is strong and the beast lives still.'

Leofric struggled to understand Naieth's words, grasping at their meaning as a drowning man clutches for a lifeline. But amid the words of the prophetess, something stood out above all others.

'Who is the Lady Ariel?' asked Leofric.

'She is the voice and will of Isha,' said Naieth carefully and Leofric knew that she was not telling him the whole truth. He suspected he might not want to know the true answer to his question and decided to let Naieth's evasion go for the moment, the more pressing concern of his people uppermost in his mind.

'Well, human,' said Aldaeld. 'The Corruptor is a foe to all races, so it seems we will aid your people after all.'

'I welcome your help, Lord Aldaeld, however it is given,' said Leofric.

Lord Aldaeld shrugged and said, 'Circumstance makes strange bedfellows of us all,' as the elves of Coeth-Mara scattered throughout the hall, gathering up weapons and girding themselves for war.

Kyarno sidled close to him and whispered, 'Thank you for your words, even though they carried no weight with Aldaeld.'

Morvhen approached and Leofric said, 'My lady. I apologise if I spoke out of turn earlier, but I meant no disrespect in speaking for you.'

Lord Aldaeld's daughter smiled and gave Leofric a chaste kiss on the cheek. 'I was glad of your words, Leofric. They came from the heart and I felt that, even if my father did not.'

The Hound of Winter appeared at Morvhen's shoulder and said, 'Kyarno, I am sorry that I could not vouch for you.'

'It does not matter, uncle,' said Kyarno. 'I know your loyalty must be to your lord. It is as it should be. You would not be Lord Aldaeld's champion were it otherwise.'

'Will you fight alongside us against the Corruptor?'

'If Lord Aldaeld will allow me to, then yes, I shall,' nodded Kyarno, glancing in Leofric's direction. 'A true warrior fights not because he wants to, but because he has to.'

'He will be fortunate to have your blade,' said Cairbre, his eyes cast down.

'Uncle,' said Kyarno, gripping the Hound of Winter's sleeve. 'The bad blood between us is no more. The light of the Lady Ariel touched me and... well, I feel cleansed of the bitterness I carried. I tried to tell Tarean Stormcrow of this and I believe he and I might have been friends, but alas, that was not to be. I foolishly missed the chance to know his friendship, but I will not make that mistake again with my kin.'

Cairbre smiled and Leofric now saw the resemblance between the two elves as the barriers between them began to come down.

The reconciliation between uncle and nephew was interrupted by the raised voice of Lord Aldaeld as he shouted, 'To arms! The host of Lord Aldaeld Éadaoin goes to war! I will send word to the kindreds of the forest that Cyanathair has returned, and the blades of battle shall be wetted in blood, the fires of war fanned by hatred of the children of Chaos.'

Warlike cheering greeted Aldaeld's words, the wild exultation of the hall infectious as the elves of Coeth-Mara roared with the lust for battle. Leofric felt his heart quicken, caught up by the thought of taking the fight to the monsters of Chaos.

Kyarno was right: it was the fight that mattered, not the outcome. It did not matter whether they won or lost in the long war, it was that they fought at all that was the victory. So long as warriors of courage stood against the dark powers, evil could not triumph. So long as one blade was raised against evil then it could never win.

A flurry of swords, like a forest of glittering stars, flashed into the air as all the warriors in Coeth-Mara shouted their allegiance to their lord.

As the cheering died down, the Hound of Winter asked, 'If we take the fight to the Corruptor, how then are we to bring the waystone back to its home in the earth?'

Stony silence greeted his words, as the practicality of them sank in.

No one said anything until Kyarno hesitantly ventured, 'Beithir-Seun could do it.'

Morvhen said, 'No, he is surely gone from the world, is he not?'

Naieth took a step forward and said, 'No, he is not, but his chasm glade has been lost amidst the mountains for centuries. None now live who know of it.'

'I know of it,' said Kyarno slowly. 'I have walked in his glade and spied upon his mighty form. He lives still and if anyone could carry the waystone, then it is he.'

'Who is Beithir-Seun?' asked Leofric.

Naieth led the way, following her owl companion through a part of the forest Leofric had not seen during his time in Athel Loren. The trees grew thickly here and a potent sensation of magic seeped into Leofric through the soles of his boots. Winged imps buzzed through the air, their bodies alight with faerie fire and the song of the trees was a gentle lilt on the air.

Despite the pastoral scene, Leofric was acutely aware of the ancient power behind this part of the forest's benign appearance. He followed Cairbre and Kyarno along the overgrown path, grateful for the chance to strike back at the creatures of Chaos that had unleashed the wild hunt on the world. Leofric still had no idea who this Beithir-Seun was, and no one seemed inclined to tell him.

Lord Aldaeld had reluctantly agreed that Kyarno should lead the

Hound of Winter to the chasm glades of Beithir-Seun and entreat him to aid the recovery of the waystone.

'You have a chance to show me your worth, Kyarno,' Aldaeld had said. 'Live up to this human's faith in you.'

'I will not fail you, Lord Aldaeld. You will yet see my worth,' promised Kyarno.

Leofric had stepped forward, his sword drawn and said, 'I too will accompany you. For it is my people who are dying and the Shadow-Gave threatens us all.'

'Very well, human. May the blessing of Isha go with you all.'

Now the three of them followed the prophetess deep into the secret glades of the forest, though if what he understood of the chasm glades was true, then they were in for a long journey.

'Am I to understand the chasm glades are in the Grey Mountains?' asked Leofric.

'They are,' agreed Cairbre. 'If what Kyarno says is correct, then the cleft Beithir-Seun dwells within is in the Grey Mountains north of the river you call the Grismerie.'

'But that is what, two hundred miles away? Are we to walk all the way?'

Kyarno turned and said, 'Have you learned nothing from your time in Athel Loren, Leofric? There are many secret paths through the forest and time and distance may mean different things along different paths.'

The answer only served to confuse Leofric even more and he asked no further questions as they made their way deeper and deeper into the forest.

The trees grew thicker and darker the further they went, branches overhanging like creepers and the sounds of life and song growing fainter and fainter until they travelled in silence, the only noise the snap of twigs and the rustle of leaves beneath Leofric's feet.

Leofric's instinct for danger raised the hackles on the back of his neck as the light from above dimmed, obscured by the thickly growing branches of the leering hag trees. The scars on his cheek tingled and he reached up to touch one, his finger coming away bloody. He stopped in surprise and touched his other cheek, finding that it too wept a trickle of red.

The others had not waited for him and he quickened his pace, not wanting to be left alone in this dark part of the forest. He heard voices from ahead and emerged into a gloomy glade of mist and cold. Kyarno and Cairbre stood warily beside one another while the prophetess spoke to someone or something he could not yet see.

He moved to stand beside Kyarno and his heart skipped a beat as he saw Cu-Sith sitting cross-legged in the centre of the glade with Naieth's owl on his shoulder. The Red Wolf was just as Leofric had last seen him, his flesh painted in vivid colours, the tattoo on his chest regarding him with a terrible hunger. The wardancer held a pair of swords crossed on his lap and as Leofric entered, he rose smoothly to his feet.

'Cu-Sith wondered who would come,' he said.

'Why are you here, Cu-Sith?' asked Cairbre.

'Loec told me to come here,' answered the wardancer. 'Why are *you* here?'

'We travel the hidden path to the chasm glades.'

The wardancer nodded, moving gracefully towards Leofric, and he felt a tightening in his groin at the memory of Cu-Sith's blade at his manhood. The wardancer raised his eyebrows and smiled crookedly at him.

'You bring Cu-Sith's pet with you,' he said, reaching up to dab his fingers in the blood on Leofric's cheek. 'His flesh remembers its place, even if he does not.'

'Why did Loec tell you to come here?' asked Cairbre.

'You should ask the prophetess. She told Cu-Sith that Loec speaks to her. Was that a lie?'

'No,' said Naieth, 'He does. But he does not tell me everything.'

The Red Wolf laughed, 'That is ever the Trickster's way. Cu-Sith cares not anyway, he is here and Loec tells him to offer you his blades and dances of war.'

'You are here to help us?' asked Kyarno.

Cu-Sith slid over to Kyarno and circled him with a nodding smile. 'Yes, Loec likes you very much, Kyarno of the Éadaoin kinband. You please him with your nature. Too bad for you.'

Leofric released a tense breath, glad that the Red Wolf did not appear to be here to kill or otherwise maim him.

'Why should we need your help, Cu-Sith?' asked Naieth. 'I can open the paths that lead through the secret heart of the forest myself. I need no help for that.'

'No, but such paths can be dangerous. Does your band of heroes know the way?'

'We will find a way,' growled Cairbre.

'Spoken like a true warrior,' said Cu-Sith. 'Brave, but stupid. The paths between worlds are not to be travelled lightly, warrior. The dark fey and the spirit guardians of the forest do not take kindly to mortals entering their domain.'

'And you can show us the way?' asked Kyarno.

'Cu-Sith can show you the way,' agreed the wardancer.

Naieth said, 'Then you shall do so, Cu-Sith. Now stand back while I open the doorway to the path you must travel.'

The four warriors retreated from the prophetess as Othu flew from Cu-Sith's shoulder to return to Naieth. The prophetess raised her staff of woven branches and began a musical chant that spoke to Leofric's heart of yearning and powerful magic. The song of the trees echoed from the mists as though in answer to Naieth's, and Leofric heard a crack and creak of twisting wood.

He watched as the thick, gnarled trunk of a blackened tree at the edge of the glade groaned and twisted, its roots clawing the dark earth and reshaping itself into some new, unknown form.

Its bark split and the sweet smell of sap wafted out, together with a cold so intense, Leofric shivered as though pierced by a spear of ice. The tree twisted in the grip of its transformation, swelling and growing until a glowing, mist-wreathed portal was revealed. Hissing voices, spiteful laughter and wicked cries of malice gusted from within and Leofric wanted nothing more than to turn from this frightful thing, but knew with heavy heart that this was exactly where they had to go.

'The gateway is open,' breathed Naieth, 'but I cannot maintain it for long. Hurry.'

Leofric exchanged worried glances with Kyarno and Cairbre. They could all feel the malicious presences beyond the gateway and each felt some deep part of themselves recoil from them in terror.

Cu-Sith leapt towards the portal, grinning wildly. 'Come. Follow Cu-Sith's lead and do not stray from the silver path. The dark fey will try to beguile you, terrify you and attempt to claim you for their own. But believe them not, for they are lies designed to ensnare you in their world forever. You understand?'

'Yes,' said Cairbre, impatiently, 'we do.'

'They all say that,' laughed Cu-Sith, 'then they die. Do as Cu-Sith does and you will live. Do it not and every one of you will die.'

'We understand,' said Kyarno.

'We will see,' shrugged Cu-Sith, stepping into the glowing mist of the gateway and disappearing.

Cairbre followed him without another word and Kyarno stepped carefully after his uncle, both elves vanishing in the light.

'Go, Leofric,' said Naieth. 'I will see you on your return. And remember the words of the Red Wolf.'

Leofric nodded and, taking a deep breath, plunged into the gateway.

Light blinded him and he cried out as his body told him that he was falling. He felt solid ground beneath his feet and dropped to his knees as the falling sensation seized him again. He opened his eyes, slowly seeing the soft earth beneath him, veins of silver light threading the ground and casting a soft glow about him.

Leofric's breath came in short, panicked heaves, his body unable to shake the sensation of falling despite the evidence of his eyes. He tried to climb to his feet, but his terrified instinct for self-preservation kept him rooted to the spot.

'What is wrong with him?' he heard Kyarno ask.

'Humans were never meant to walk between worlds,' said Cu-Sith.

Leofric's resentment at Cu-Sith's easy condescension fanned a flame in his heart and he angrily climbed to his feet, fighting the nauseous vertigo his body felt.

'Maybe not,' he hissed, 'but I will be damned if I will be left behind.'

Cu-Sith bounded over to him and wrapped his hand around the back of his neck and pulled him close until their eyes were inches apart. 'You have spirit, human. It looks like Cu-Sith was right to let you keep your balls.'

The wardancer released him and set off along the silver-veined pathway. Leofric fought to calm his breathing and adjust to his surroundings.

The sky above was a ghostly grey colour, bleached of all life, and the landscape around them was one of glittering mist and twisted, dark trees as far as the eye could see. Laughter, cruel and hurtful, drifted from within the mists and a multitude of whispering voices chattered on the wind.

'Where are we?' asked Leofric.

'We can talk later,' warned Cairbre. 'Cu-Sith leads the way and we cannot linger here.'

Leofric nodded and followed the Hound of Winter as he and Kyarno set off after the wardancer. His senses rebelled against the enchantments of this place and though Cu-Sith's words had angered Leofric, he knew that the wardancer was right: humans were not meant to see such things.

Their course followed the ribbon of silver light as it wound a path through the dark forest. Blurred shapes shadowed their every movement and Leofric kept his gaze fixed on a point between Kyarno's shoulder blades for fear of the terrible things he might see if he allowed himself to look anywhere else. Whispered voices drifted to him, taunts and promises of wealth, flesh and peace, but he forced them from his head as he concentrated on putting one foot in front of the other.

He heard a cry of pain, a woman's, and his ingrained chivalric code turned his head before his body's warning could prevent him.

Leofric cried out as the mists parted and he saw Helene on her knees, wearing the same red dress she had worn the day the forest had taken her. She wept and pleaded with cackling creatures of branch and root, their whipping, thorny limbs and bark-formed faces mocking her helplessness. Was this where Helene had been taken? Had she been brought to this damnable otherworld to be tormented by these maniacal spirits for all eternity?

His hatred of these beasts knew no bounds and he drew his sword, the blade shining with silver fire, running towards her and shouting, 'Helene!'

No sooner had his feet left the silver pathway than the scene before him dissolved into a whirling blur of light and mist, and he heard a host of wickedly gleeful laughs surround him. Sinuous shadows flitted towards him from the darkness between the claw-branched trees and Leofric's heart chilled to see such primal, elemental spirits of the forest as they slipped through the air like liquid.

But he was a knight of Bretonnia and his courage was greater than his fear of these things. Leofric brought his sword to bear, its silver blade a shining beacon in the darkness as the shadows circled him like sharks with the taste of blood.

He backed away, casting darting glances around him as he sought the silver path once more, but all was darkness and shadow, the path lost to him.

'Lady protect me,' he whispered as a dark shadow darted towards him. He swung his sword, the blade passing clean through it without effect. Black, clawed arms slashed for him and slid through his armour without effort, reaching into his flesh with the chill of the grave.

Leofric cried out as the deathly touch of the spirit creature filled him with pain. He dropped to his knees as aching cold spread agonisingly through his body. His heart beat wildly in his chest as he fought the glacial chill. More of the shadow creatures slipped from the trees, their eyes pinpricks of yellow against the dark of their ghostly forms, and Leofric knew he was undone.

Then a howling shape spun through the air and a painted figure with twin swords of golden light landed before him.

Cu-Sith spun his swords before him in a dazzling circle and said, 'You cannot have him. This human belongs to Cu-Sith.'

The shadow beasts circled the wardancer, wary of his bright swords, and hissed in anger at his interruption of their hunt.

'Human,' shouted Cu-Sith. 'Get up! Fight their touch!'

Leofric gritted his teeth, biting the inside of his cheek hard enough to draw blood, the warm liquid and pain forcing the chill of the shadow's touch from his flesh. As the dark touch left him, his strength returned and he stood beside the wardancer, silver and gold blades keeping the spirits at bay for the moment.

'Follow Cu-Sith,' said the wardancer. 'Walk where he walks.'

Leofric nodded as he once again saw Helene beyond the shadows, naked and bloody as the branch-creatures whipped the flesh from her bones.

'It is not real, human,' warned Cu-Sith. 'Whoever she is, she is not real.'

Leofric forced himself to look away, following the careful steps of the wardancer as they backed away from the dark fey of the forest. Sadness welled in his heart at the sight of Helene's tortured body, but he held to Cu-Sith's assertion that it was but an illusion.

Then there was silver light beneath his feet once more and the hissing curses that had followed them faded to a faint susurration.

'Foolish human!' snapped the wardancer. 'Did you hear nothing of Cu-Sith's warning? Cu Sith told you to stay on the path.'

'I saw Helene!' shouted Leofric. 'I saw my wife.'

'Your wife is dead,' said Cu-Sith. 'That was not her. Now come, there is a long way to go yet.'

Leofric fought past the grief at having seen Helene so close once more and nodded, looking down at his shining sword.

'Why does my sword glow?' asked Leofric.

'The weapon is touched by magic,' said Cu-Sith. 'It fades, but there is still some power left to it.'

'Yes,' said Leofric proudly. 'It was blessed by the Lady of the Lake herself.'

Cu-Sith winked and turned away, but before Leofric could ask more, he saw the Hound of Winter emerge from the mist bearing a weeping Kyarno back onto the path.

Like Leofric's sword, the Blades of Midnight shone with a nimbus of light.

'I saw them,' cried Kyarno. 'My mother! My father! We have to go back.'

Cairbre dropped his nephew to the path and Leofric saw that the Hound of Winter's body was cut and bruised. He took a great breath as Cu-Sith shook his head and met Cairbre's gaze.

'Foolish youths,' said the wardancer and Cairbre nodded in agreement.

Kyarno blinked and let out a shuddering breath as the power of the dark fey faded from his mind. Leofric helped him up and the four warriors set off once again down the silver path.

Dreams and nightmares assailed them from every turn, scenes of horror and bliss paraded before them in equal measure. But their hearts were hardened to the glamours of the dark fey and though each blandishment was more outlandish or horrific than the one before, nothing could now tempt them from the path.

'We are here,' said Cu-Sith at last, and Leofric looked up to see a shining, mist-wreathed gateway hovering before them. Through it he could see craggy mountaintops and a pale sky of clear blue. Nothing had ever looked so welcoming and they hurried towards the gateway, stepping through with none of the reticence they had felt when entering this dark domain of the spirit.

Leofric's heart sang to be back in the real world, the rocks and trees and earth having a reassuring, familiar solidity to them that he had not realised was so necessary an anchor for the human soul. Stepping through the shimmering gateway, he had stepped onto bare rock high in the mountains, the air wondrously clear and refreshing.

He stood on the edge of the mountain, drawing great lungfuls of crisp air into his body and tilting his face towards the sun as it warmed his flesh. After the journey through the secret paths of the forest, to feel the sun on his skin was the most incredible sensation Leofric could remember.

'By the Lady, I never want to have to do that again,' he said.

'Nor I,' agreed Cairbre, shuddering at the memory of whatever visions had come to him within the spirit realm.

To have travelled so far in so short a time amazed Leofric. Such a journey would normally have taken well over a week, but, by the position of the sun, they had reached the mountains in a matter of hours.

Jagged crags of grey stone reared above them, cloaked in shawls of white and patches of fragrant pine, the highest peaks of the Grey Mountains lost in the clouds. Below them, the forest stretched out across the landscape, a massive swathe of green and red and gold and brown.

He could not see all the forest, wisps of cloud far below them conspiring to conceal some areas and shimmering heat hazes rippling the image of the far distant treetops. The sight of the forest laid out like this was truly magnificent and Leofric took a moment to drink in its savage beauty.

'What is that?' he asked, pointing to a cluster of distant golden spires that rose above the forest canopy.

'It is the Waterfall Palace of the Naiad Court,' replied Cairbre. 'It is a place of wonders and raptures.'

'Who lives there?'

'The naiads, beautiful nymphs of lakes, rivers, springs and fountains. They make their court amid a torrent of a hundred waterfalls. I have visited their court once before and it was... most pleasurable.'

Leofric raised an eyebrow, surprised at Cairbre – if he understood the Hound of Winter correctly. He was spared asking more by the arrival of Kyarno and Cu-Sith, who beckoned them over to the sheer cliff face behind them.

A thin, snaking crack split the cliff, barely wide enough for an elf, let alone a human in armour, and Kyarno nodded, saying, 'This is it, this is the way.'

'You are sure?' asked Cairbre, doubtfully.

'Yes, uncle, I'm sure,' said Kyarno. 'Remember I have been here before.'

Cairbre shrugged and followed Kyarno as he disappeared into the mountain. Cu-Sith indicated that Leofric should go next and he squeezed himself into the fissure with some difficulty as the wardancer slipped effortlessly between the rocks behind him.

After a while, the crack widened a little. Not by much, but enough so that every step was not an effort. Nor was it a simple path, branching off many times into a maze of thin cracks in the rock and low passages. Each path divided over and over again, and Leofric wondered how they were going to navigate their way back.

Their course carried them deep into the mountain, sheer rock rising on all sides and thickly growing pines fringing the top of the chasm. Oft times their route carried them along narrow paths with drops of thousands of feet to one side or over narrow bridges of rock that crossed yawning rents in the earth. A pungent, animal aroma permeated the chasms and the further they went, the easier their passing became as the chasm finally widened into a tall, steep sided valley.

Tall trees dotted the valley, the vertical sides of the chasm rearing hundreds of feet above them. A craggy cave entrance opened into the mountain on one side of the chasm, the ground before it strewn with boulders and the white gleam of bone.

'What manner of creature would live in such a remote place?' asked Leofric, seeing human skulls amongst the piles of bone. 'The only way you could get in without difficulty is…'

Leofric's words trailed off as a great shadow enveloped their group and a powerful downdraught of air threw up clouds of blinding dust with a deafening boom. The odour Leofric had smelled in the chasms was much stronger now. He shielded his eyes from the dust and heard something take a powerful intake of breath that echoed from the rocks.

He squinted through the slowly settling dust and saw a great form silhouetted against the sky, a massive, sinuous body with a long, muscular neck and a pair of slowly folding wings.

Leofric blinked away the last of the dust and gasped at the monstrous creature that perched on the rocks above them.

A dragon.

CHAPTER EIGHTEEN

A dragon. It was a dragon. Leofric was looking at a dragon. It took several seconds for the reality of the sight to sink in, but when it did, his hand instinctively reached for his sword. As his hand grasped the hilt, Cairbre gripped his arm and shook his head.

A dragon... creatures of terrible aspect and fearsome reputation, it was the stuff of every knight's dream to slay a dragon. Of such things were the legends and tales of Bretonnia built.

The mighty creature regarded them quizzically, its huge, horned head leaning down into the chasm glade and its huge jaws opening to reveal row upon row of saw-like fangs. Its breath reeked of noxious gases, the blades of its teeth longer than Leofric's forearm.

It climbed head first down the vertical sides of the glade, its great claws gripping the rock as it descended to the dusty valley floor, its scaled green body rippling with massive slabs of muscle. Its huge, leathery wings were folded across its spined back, frills of tissue stretched between the sharp spines.

'A dragon...' breathed Leofric, straining to draw his sword despite Cairbre's restraining hand. 'It's a dragon.'

'I know,' hissed Cairbre. 'This is Beithir-Seun. This is who we have come to see.'

Leofric looked incredulously at the Hound of Winter. This terrifying beast was who they had risked travelling through the realm of the dark fey to find?

'Are you insane? It is a monster. It has to die!'

'Be silent!' warned Cairbre. 'Beithir-Seun is an ancient denizen of the forest and we are here for his help. Do not anger him.'

Leofric looked across to Kyarno and Cu-Sith to see if they were as deluded as the Hound of Winter in believing that this creature was anything other than a monster to be destroyed.

He saw tension on their features, even those of Cu-Sith, but nothing to show that they shared his intent. Slowly he released his grip on his sword hilt and though his knightly traditions screamed at him to charge the beast, he forced himself to wait.

The dragon approached them, towering above them as it reared up on its hind legs and let out a terrible roar that shook rocks from the sides of the glade. Leofric flinched, but followed the example of the elves and remained motionless. The creature sniffed the air, its jaws drawing open again to reveal its razor-sharp fangs, and lowered its head towards them. One of the dragon's eyes was a mass of poorly-healed scar tissue, the other a fierce yellow and slitted like a cat's. Leofric saw an ancient intelligence within that eye and knew that this was a creature not to be trifled with.

'I smell human,' snarled the dragon, its rumbling voice deep and laden with authority.

Leofric fought to control his mounting panic in the face of the dragon's pronouncement. The great wyrm's eyes narrowed and it cocked its vast head to one side, its breath sounding like the bellows of some mighty, piston-driven engine of the dwarfs.

'Beithir-Seun,' began Cairbre. 'We come as emissaries from–'

'I smell human,' repeated the dragon, thrusting its jaws towards Leofric. Its head was the size of a coach and though its enormous fangs were inches from his body, he held himself immobile before the monster's scrutiny.

'I know your kind,' said the dragon. 'Humans in armour slay my kind. Brave heroes out to make a name for themselves. Is that it, human, have you come to slay me?'

Leofric said nothing until nudged in the ribs by Kyarno, who gestured urgently that he should reply.

'Uh... no,' said Leofric. 'No. We... that is... no.'

'It is as well for you,' rumbled the dragon, 'for you would die if you tried. Beithir-Seun has eaten humans in armour before and one more would be of no consequence. The bones of a hundred men lie strewn before my cave. Yours may join them yet.'

The dragon drew back its head and Leofric let out the breath he had been holding. The creature scraped deep furrows in the rock with its claws and said, 'I smell elf as well as human. It has been long centuries since Beithir-Seun awoke and yet longer since he tasted warm flesh bitten from the bone.'

Its long tongue slid from its jaws and Leofric had a terrifying mental image of their bodies sliding down its throat to be digested in its stomach.

'Blood and meat,' hissed the dragon, taking a long step towards them. 'Yes... blood and meat and bone.'

'Beithir-Seun,' said Cairbre again. 'We come to you for help.'

'Help?' roared Beithir-Seun. 'What help can elves want from me?'

'We come with tidings from Aldaeld, Lord of a Hundred Battles and guardian of Coeth-Mara. He sends you greetings from the asrai and bids you take heed of our words.'

'Beithir-Seun knows of Coeth-Mara,' nodded the dragon. 'A grove of saplings in the south of the forest.'

'It has grown since last you awoke, Beithir-Seun. Now it is a mighty hall of the asrai and its beauty is beloved by all the forest kin.'

'Now I see why you bring armoured humans to my glade,' said the dragon, its mouth splitting in a grin of monstrous appetite. 'It is an offering to me to secure my aid. One of the armoured humans that put out my eye with a lance brought to me for a meal of flesh and bone.'

'No,' said Leofric. 'I am a friend to the asrai. I have fought alongside the warriors of Coeth-Mara and do so again to save both our peoples.'

'A human fights with the asrai?' asked Beithir-Seun.

'He does,' said Kyarno. 'He is a warrior of courage and has slain creatures of Chaos.'

'Mention not that word,' spat the dragon. 'For Beithir-Seun has feasted upon the flesh of the unclean and still I taste their rankness. If this human be not an offering to me, then what do you bring?'

'We bring only the chance to once again defend Athel Loren,' said Cairbre. 'For Cyanathair has returned to the forest.'

Beithir-Seun let out a terrible, echoing roar at the mention of the Corruptor, its bellow full of anger and loathing.

'Cyanathair walks the earth once more?'

'It does,' said Cairbre. 'Its minions have managed to topple one of the sacred waystones and we need your help to retrieve it, for we cannot bear it back to Athel Loren without your mighty strength.'

'Flatter me not, elf,' cautioned the dragon. 'Centuries have I slumbered in this deep mountain and many are the creatures of evil I have destroyed.'

Beithir-Seun shook its horned head and said, 'A human fights alongside the asrai and the Corruptor walks the earth. Truly it is well that the forest wakes me that I might see such strange times.'

'Then you will aid us?'

The dragon nodded and bared its fangs. 'Yes, I will aid you, for I see that your cause is that of Athel Loren. Too long is it since Beithir-Seun slaughtered the children of Chaos.'

Leofric watched as the great dragon spread its wings, the enormous pinions almost scraping the sides of the valley as it reared up to its full height.

'Come!' bellowed Beithir-Seun. 'Climb upon my back and we will away. The call to war is upon us!'

Leofric's stomach lurched at the dragon's words and he grabbed Kyarno's arm as the young elf took a step towards the mighty creature.

'What does it mean?'

'By what?'

'By "climb upon my back".'

'Exactly what he says,' said Kyarno, looking oddly at Leofric and then chuckling to himself as he clapped Leofric on the shoulder. 'How did you think we were going to get back to Coeth-Mara?'

'I'm not sure,' said Leofric. 'I assumed the same way we got here.'

'You would rather travel the paths of the dark fey once more?'

'No,' said Leofric, 'But this…'

'You should relish this,' laughed Kyarno. 'After all, how many humans get the chance to soar through the sky on the back of a dragon?'

'Oh yes,' said Leofric sourly, 'I feel so privileged.'

Rushing wind whipped past Leofric's head, but he kept his eyes tightly shut for fear of seeing what lay below him. Or, more accurately, what did not lie below him. He gripped the spine on the dragon's back as tight as he could, his arms wrapped around it and his fingers digging into a frill of skin with all his strength.

They had lifted from the chasm glade of Beithir-Seun in the beat of powerful wings nearly an hour ago, and Leofric had barely opened his eyes the entire time. To be carried on the back of a horse was the way for a knight to travel, not like this.

Man was not meant to fly, and though the king oft rode to battle on the back of his hippogryph, Beaquis, and some of the richer knights of Bretonnia boasted a trained battle pegasus, the saddle of a warhorse was as far as Leofric wanted to get from the ground.

He could feel the great creature's powerful heartbeat through its tough scales, a deep and slow thudding boom, and the motion of its muscles lifted him up and down as they bunched and relaxed to keep its wings moving.

'You are missing a spectacular view,' shouted Kyarno.

Leofric looked up to see Kyarno standing at the dragon's shoulders next to Cairbre, the wind rushing through his braided hair as he called back to Leofric. Behind them, all he could see was sky, brilliant blue and cloudy.

'Do you have to do that?' asked Leofric. 'You are making me feel sick.'

Cu-Sith sat astride Beithir-Seun's neck, but Leofric kept his eyes focussed on the hard, scaled back of the dragon. The elves seemed completely at ease, their stance shifting in response to the creature's movements, looking for all the world like they were having the time of their lives.

The dragon dipped one of its wings, curling round in a slow bank and Leofric saw the green canopy of the forest speeding past, thousands of feet below him, and cried out, clutching onto the spine even tighter.

Far below he could see the snaking course of the Grismerie as it meandered through the forest, sparkling and clear as it flowed from the mountains towards Parravon, one of the frontier towns of Bretonnia, with its deep chasms, high walls and many towers.

Though it was a great distance away, Leofric could see a slender bridge crossing the river, a graceful structure of wood and crystal. Thousands of birds of many colours flocked around the bridge, the sound of their trilling song reaching Leofric even up here.

Soon the bridge was lost to sight, but hundreds of the birds flew up from their circling to join them, crying out in welcome to the dragon as though it were a long lost friend unexpectedly returned. The dragon slowed its flight to allow the birds to keep up with it, roaring in answer to their cries.

Leofric began anew his prayers to the Lady of the Lake as the tremors of the dragon's roars reached him, entreating her to keep him safe until he had solid ground beneath his feet.

'Lady watch over your humble servant,' whispered Leofric as the long flight continued. 'Keep my grip strong. And keep this beast from moving too suddenly!'

Soon Beithir-Seun angled his course to the west and as a thin line of green came into view above the blades of his muscular shoulders, Leofric could tell they were descending. He began to relax a little at the thought of being on the ground once more, opening his eyes and watching as the forest canopy rushed up to meet them.

Birds surrounded them, hundreds, if not thousands of them, and though he was utterly terrified to be travelling in this manner, he could not deny the magnificence of the sight.

The motion of the dragon's wings ceased as they flared outwards to slow his flight, the left wing dipping, and once again Beithir-Seun banked sharply as he descended in ever-tighter circles towards the ground. Leofric saw the River Brienne and realised they must be approaching Coeth-Mara.

'Hold on, Leofric!' shouted Kyarno from the dragon's shoulders. 'We will be on the ground in a moment!'

'Not a moment too soon!' shouted back Leofric as Beithir-Seun folded his wings in close to his body and dropped towards the forest floor. Leofric screamed in sudden alarm, fearing that some calamity had befallen the mighty creature, but at the last moment, the dragon's wings shot out and gave a powerful beat to flare outwards and control his descent into the elven halls.

Leofric felt the dragon's claws settle on the ground and let out a heartfelt sigh of relief as he released his death-grip on its spine. He slid down the dragon's haunches, landing on unsteady legs, supporting himself on the trunk of a silver-barked birch. Hundreds of birds fluttered and flapped through Coeth-Mara – white plumed doves, colourful finches, robins and sparrows, and their song filled the air with music.

Kyarno landed lightly beside him, his face alight with amusement, and Cairbre soon followed him, a youthful vigour creasing his features with a boyish grin. The Red Wolf somersaulted to the ground in front of Leofric and he could see that quite a crowd had gathered to greet them.

Elves stared at Beithir-Seun in fascination, thrilled to have one of the most ancient guardians of the forest in their midst. They came forward in great number, eager to meet this defender of Athel Loren, and the lack of fear they showed towards the powerful creature amazed Leofric.

As he regained his equilibrium, he saw that Coeth-Mara was thronged with elves, more than he had ever seen before. Elves of all different appearance and garb clustered around the dragon and Leofric saw a wide variety of runic symbols on furs, tunics, robes and cloaks, realising that these elves must belong to different kinbands.

The kindreds of Athel Loren had answered Lord Aldaeld's call.

Night was drawing in and the torches had been lit by the time the last of the warrior kindreds that had answered Lord Aldaeld's summons arrived in Coeth-Mara. Not all had come, and many had not even acknowledged his call. But enough had come and at first light, the elves of Athel Loren would take the fight to the mountains and the children of Chaos.

Kyarno sat with his back to an ancient willow, feeling its connection to the earth in the rhythmic pulsing of its sap. He had hoped Morvhen would have been waiting for him upon their triumphant return on the back of Beithir-Seun, but she was nowhere to be seen, no doubt Aldaeld was keeping her safely ensconced from his attentions.

The forest was alive with elves of many kinbands, warhawk riders, waywatchers, glade riders, Eternal Guard and the wardancers of Cu-Sith. Tomorrow they would fight and Kyarno would go with them. What awaited him, he did not know, but it had to be better than the life of solitude that was his lot from now on.

What was left to him now? Was he to travel the lands of humans as an itinerant adventurer, forced to seek his fortune by grubbing through ancient ruins and dungeons for treasure?

He traced the rune of Vaul in the forest floor with a twig, pondering on his uncertain future, when he heard soft footfalls behind him. He recognised the tread and said, 'You grow no stealthier with age, uncle.'

'No,' agreed Cairbre. 'I was never cut out to be a waywatcher, was I?'

Kyarno shook his head. 'No, you always were noisy. It's the one thing I remember of you from when I was a child.'

'You must remember more than that, surely?'

'Yes, uncle, I do,' whispered Kyarno. 'I remember the flames and blood when the beastmen killed my mother and father. I remember you carrying me clear of the burning ruin of our halls. But most of all I remember the loneliness.'

'I know, boy, I know,' said Cairbre, sitting on the other side of the willow trunk with his back to Kyarno. 'There's not a day goes by I don't wish I could have reached you sooner.'

Kyarno smiled, staring up at the pale glow of the moon. Flocks of birds still circled Coeth-Mara and he said, 'I never hated you, uncle. I want you to know that before tomorrow.'

'I never thought you did, Kyarno,' sighed Cairbre. 'And I always loved you and wanted the best for you.'

'Strange how such thoughts often come on the eve of battle,' said Kyarno.

'Yes,' agreed Cairbre. 'War makes philosophers of us all. I suppose the nearness of death brings home to us what matters most.'

'And what is that?'

'Kin,' said Cairbre simply.

The next day dawned bright and clear, the spring sun bathing the central glade of Coeth-Mara in warmth and light. Everywhere was bustling activity as the elves readied themselves for battle. Leofric watched as solitary individuals in hooded cloaks disappeared into the forest surrounding the elven halls to protect its borders, while others took the fight to the mountains.

Warriors checked the keenness of blades and archers gauged the line of their arrows, smoothing the fletching and sharpening the points.

But of all those gathered beneath the boughs of Coeth-Mara, the most pleasing to Leofric's eyes were the giant hawks with long tails, hooked bills, strong talons and broad wings that would carry them into battle. He had hunted with falcons many times, and appreciated the grace and deadly beauty of such birds, but these were magnificent and regal, quite unlike anything he had seen before. The warhawk riders shared many similarities with their mounts, slender-limbed and agile, with quick, lethal-looking movements.

Though not nearly as huge as Beithir-Seun, who growled impatiently at the edge of the glade, Leofric had a more obvious connection to the warhawks than a beast he would normally have tried to slay. The flight on the dragon had been terrifying, but Leofric strangely relished the idea of riding into battle on a warhawk. The prospect filled him with a mixture of terror and excitement. Though saddened not to be able to ride into battle on Aeneor, there was no way a steed, even an elven one, could match the speed of the warhawks.

Leofric had tended to his sword and armour as best he could, and though the impish spites that followed him around Coeth-Mara were helpful when it came to putting the armour on, without an actual squire to clean them properly, they looked far from their best.

He saw Kyarno and the Hound of Winter approaching, Kyarno with his sword strapped at his side and his bow slung over one shoulder, and Cairbre with the Blades of Midnight carried lightly in his right hand.

'Good morning,' said Leofric. 'It is a fine sight indeed to see so many magnificent warriors gathered together.'

Cairbre nodded and placed his hand on Kyarno's shoulder.

'Isha watch over you, boy,' said the Hound of Winter, 'and may Kurnous guide your hand this day.'

The two elves embraced one another, the gesture looking forced and awkward to Leofric's eyes. Cairbre and Kyarno may have made their peace, but there were still barriers between them. Eventually, the Hound of Winter released his nephew and, without another word spoken between them, turned and walked away.

'Ready?' asked Kyarno.

'Yes,' said Leofric. 'I am. It is time to hold back the darkness one more time. For we are warriors are we not?'

'That we are,' agreed Kyarno, as Leofric held out his hand to him.

Kyarno took the proffered hand and said, 'There is much I do not understand about humans, too much I think for us ever to be friends, but you and I may yet be brothers in battle.'

'That would sit well with me, Kyarno,' said Leofric. 'And who knows what the future holds. Perhaps one day our races may become friends.'

'I would not count on it, but it is a noble dream,' said Kyarno.

'Tell me one thing though,' said Leofric.

'What?'

'I know Éadaoin means Fleetmane in my language, but what does Daelanu mean?'

'It means Silvermorn, the promise of the new sun after the long night.'

'It is a good name,' said Leofric. 'I wanted to know so I could speak of you when I leave Athel Loren.'

'When you leave?'

'Yes,' said Leofric. 'If we win this day it will be to save the lives of the people of my lands. I will return to them soon, I can feel it.'

'I feel it too,' said Kyarno, falling silent as Lord Aldaeld and his warriors made their way to the centre of Coeth-Mara. Naieth walked with Lord Aldaeld, dressed as Leofric had first seen her, in a robe of gold and elven runes, her copper hair teased into braided tresses above her tapered ears with silver pins and garlanded with feathers and gemstones.

She carried her long staff of woven twigs with a carved eye at its top and Leofric saw she wore a secret smile, one of pride and love for those around her.

Lord Aldaeld wore a scarlet cloak of feathers and his body was adorned with many fresh tattoos and painted designs. Gleaming torques of gold and silver banded his arms and he wore a golden helm with the curling horns of a stag. His sword was scabbarded at his hip and he carried a silver lance with a spiral pattern carved on its blade.

Behind him came Morvhen, clad in simple brown leathers and furs, with a powerful recurved bow carried at her side and a pair of crossed quivers across her back. Leofric straightened as he saw that Tiphaine accompanied Morvhen.

Aldaeld crossed the glade towards Leofric and Kyarno, stopping just before them and fixing them with a stern gaze.

'Lord Aldaeld,' said Kyarno, giving a respectful nod to the lord of the Éadaoin kinband. Leofric followed suit, unsure as to why Lord Aldaeld felt the need to speak to them this morning of all mornings.

'Kyarno,' began Aldaeld. 'You have done my kinband a great service by bringing us the great Beithir-Seun. I thank you for that.'

'I was happy to do it,' said Kyarno. 'I may not be part of your kinband now, but I am glad to fight alongside it.'

For a moment neither said anything until Lord Aldaeld finally said, 'The Hound of Winter speaks highly of you, Kyarno Daelanu, and my daughter seems taken with you, though Isha alone knows why. I can see just by looking at you that you are no longer Kyarno the troublemaker. Only time will tell what you have become, but should you live through this day, we shall speak again.'

Kyarno struggled for words, but settled on saying, 'Thank you, Lord Aldaeld.'

Aldaeld nodded and turned away, moving to stand in the centre of the glade. As he left, Morvhen approached Kyarno and spoke softly to him in elvish as Tiphaine drew near Leofric.

She nodded in greeting, her almond eyes sad.

'Hello, Leofric,' she said, holding her hand out to him, and Leofric saw she offered him a beautiful, faultless crystal, its surface smooth and unblemished.

'I cannot,' said Leofric. 'It is too beautiful.'

'I desire you to have it,' insisted Tiphaine. 'It is a moonstone from the Crystal Mere, like the one gifted to the warrior hero Naithal by a naiad of the Waterfall Court. It has great power and will protect you from harm.'

'It is beautiful,' said Leofric, pulling the blue silken scarf of Helene's favour from his gauntlet and wrapping the gemstone within. He returned the favours to his gauntlet and started to say more, but Tiphaine stopped him, placing her finger on his lips.

'I do not know if I will ever see you again, Leofric Carrard,' she said, 'so think on all we have spoken of and your time in our forest realm will have been well spent.'

'I will,' promised Leofric. 'For you have inspired me to great deeds and have always spoken to me with courtesy and grace. For that I thank you, my lady.'

Tiphaine did not reply, but stepped away from him, all activity in Coeth-Mara coming to a halt as Lord Aldaeld cast his head back and raised his lance to the sky. The sunlight reflected dazzlingly on the silver blade, the power of its magic clear for all to see.

For a moment all was silence until Leofric heard the faint beat of wings and looked up to see a gigantic eagle circling to land before the elven lord. A gasp of astonishment swept the glade as the powerful bird landed gracefully before Aldaeld, its feathers golden and its bearing both noble and fierce.

The magnificent creature took Leofric's breath away, his admiration for the warhawks swept away by the regal countenance of this noble bird of prey. From the looks of awed admiration of the assembled elves, it was clearly a sign of great favour to have such a beast consent to carry an elven lord into battle.

Aldaeld climbed swiftly onto the great eagle's back, the elves following his example and climbing to the backs of their warhawks. Leofric, Kyarno and Morvhen ran for the warhawks chosen to carry them as passengers and climbed onto their backs behind the elven riders.

The great eagle spread its graceful wings and leapt into the air, carrying Lord Aldaeld into the sky. The eagle gave a piercing cry and the warhawks also took flight, following the golden form of Lord Aldaeld's eagle.

Beithir-Seun took to the air immediately after, his bulk slower to gather speed, but soon catching up to his smaller, more nimble brethren.

Leofric felt a wild exhilaration as he was carried higher and higher above the trees, his earlier fear of the skies forgotten in the rush of adrenaline that surged around his body at the thought of battle.

He watched as the aerial armada climbed into the air, privileged to be in the company of these magnificent warriors. Scores of warhawks filled the sky, with Lord Aldaeld at their head atop his eagle and the terrible form of the great dragon, Beithir-Seun, flying above them.

Once again, hundreds of brightly coloured birds flew alongside them, their cries sounding as sweet as the call for battle from the silver trumpet of a Bretonnian clarion.

CHAPTER NINETEEN

With its high walls of red stone, wide barbican and many towers, the strength of Castle Carrard never failed to impress Teoderic Lendast of Quenelles. Though ill-fortune had dogged the line of its lords, it remained a formidable bastion against any foe.

He rode his snorting steed through its thick gateway, hung with a banner of gold depicting a scarlet unicorn rampant below a bejewelled crown. Teoderic straightened his cloak over the rump of his horse then checked that his sword hung correctly at his side. A muster of levies and peasant men-at-arms were gathered outside the castle and a knight of Bretonnia did not appear before the lowborn looking less than his best. Behind him came Clovis and Theudegar, brothers-in-arms and virtuous knights of the realm both. Three score knights followed behind, resplendent in surcoats of many colours with guidons snapping from the ends of their lances and banners raised high.

Passing from the gateway and thumping across the wooden drawbridge, Teoderic watched as the peasants stood to attention at the sight of him, displaying the proper reverence to a knight of the realm such as he. He lifted the visor of his helmet and stared up into the darkening sky. Though the sun was barely past its zenith, the day was dim and had the purple cast of twilight. Dark thunderheads gathered on the eastern horizon, though Teoderic knew that they preceded no natural storm.

A shiver of anticipation ran down his spine at the thought of facing the might of the forest spirits. What did such creatures know of honour or chivalry? Was there glory to be earned in their destruction or would he feel no more than a woodsman might feel in hewing a tree?

'How many more men arrived this morning?' he asked, turning in the saddle to address the knights who rode after him.

'A goodly number,' answered Clovis, raising his visor and surveying the assembled peasantry. 'Perhaps a thousand men now muster at Castle Carrard in answer to their lord's summons: archers, yeomanry from nearby villages and the men-at-arms we brought with us.'

'Indeed,' said Theudegar, 'as well there might be. For it is their lands that are ravaged by the faerie king. It is only right and proper that they fight.'

Teoderic nodded his agreement, though he knew that to defeat the force arrayed against them, they would need a lot more. Fear was already rife in the peasants and he saw no need to add more with any pessimistic opinions just yet. He watched as a group of tired-looking peasants hammered sharpened stakes into the hillside before the river and others dragged a cart of boulders and rubble inside the castle for the trebuchet mounted on the walls. Teoderic disliked such weapons, but could nevertheless appreciate the strategic value of being able to drop large blocks of masonry on an enemy from far away.

'They say another village was destroyed last night,' added Theudegar. 'Orberese, I think. Not a soul lives there now, carried away to their deaths by the wild hunt.'

'Orberese?' said Clovis. 'That's a damn shame, they bred a fine pig there. Made some good sausage as I recall.'

'How many is that then?' asked Teoderic.

'Nine this past two weeks alone,' answered Clovis. 'The eastern parts of Quenelles and Carcassonne are virtually deserted. All have fled to the castles of their liege lords.'

Teoderic saw desperation on every face they passed, knowing that peasants expected the knights to save them and end the threat of the Green King. Mounted yeomen had brought word that the rampant forest creatures were heading towards Castle Carrard, covering all the land in a swathe of violent life. Battle was soon to be joined.

For nearly fourteen nights, the King of the Forest and his wild hunt had rampaged through the southern dukedoms of Bretonnia, destroying all those in their path, and now they rode out to stop them. It would be some time before a larger muster of knights could be gathered, and though Teoderic knew that it was folly to meet this threat with so few warriors, they had a duty to their people to protect them in times of trouble.

Teoderic relished the chance to ride out and face the enemy on the field of battle as much as the next knight, but knew that, if the scouts' reports were to be believed, they were likely to be outnumbered nearly four to one. Better that the enemy come to them and then the creatures of the wood would break themselves against walls of stone.

But as he turned to look at the silver-haired lord of Castle Carrard, who stood on the crenellated battlements of the tallest tower, Teoderic knew that nothing less than the glory of a bloody charge would satisfy the venerable lord's lust for vengeance.

The forest swept by beneath them as the warhawks carried them swiftly through the sky, the wind whipping past in a blur of cold air. Leofric clutched the bird's feathers tightly, gripping its body with his thighs as its powerful wings bore him and its elven rider towards the mountains.

The mighty bird carrying Kyarno flew alongside him, with Cairbre and Naieth carried on the backs of birds just behind Lord Aldaeld's great eagle. Morvhen rode atop a warhawk of her own, balancing easily on its back with her long hair cascading darkly behind her. Cu-Sith and his wardancers made their own way towards the Shadow-Gave, easily able to keep pace with the warhawks through secret paths of the forest that they alone knew or dared to travel.

The site of the breach in the waystone barrier was clearly visible from the air, a spreading patch of darkest green that spilled out from the forest's edge. Who knew how many had died in Bretonnia already and how many were yet to die? It seemed as though the undulating green swathe moved even as he watched, the speed of its growth swifter than he would have believed possible.

The mountains ahead reared up like grim, grey sentinels, towering peaks that marked the southern boundaries of Bretonnia and Athel Loren, and, beyond which lay the mercenary city-states of Tilea.

Their ultimate destination was easily visible, the corruption unleashed by the Shadow-Gave impossible to miss from the air, a spreading dark stain on the mountain that pulsed like a wound in the rock itself. A huge fire burned at the centre of the darkness that smothered the mountainside, circled by scores of howling beastmen. The host of monstrous, baying abominations waved spears and axes towards the massive form of the missing waystone, perched on a rocky plateau below a wide cave mouth.

Dark pinioned shapes wheeled in the air above the fire, their piercing cries carried on the cold wind and sending a jolt of loathing through Leofric.

'What are they?' he shouted, pointing to the shapes.

'Creatures of Chaos!' cried Kyarno in answer. 'Beasts of the air warped by the Corruptor's foulness and drawn to its fell powers.'

Leofric watched as the monstrous birds began climbing higher into the air, angling their flight towards them, and gripped the warhawk's flanks tighter as its rider coaxed it into a rapid descent. The elf looked over his shoulder at Leofric and said, 'I will need to set you down, human. I cannot carry you and fight.'

Leofric nodded as the warhawk riders that carried passengers dropped from the aerial armada, heading quickly for the ground to deposit their burdens before rejoining their comrades for battle.

The ground rushed up to meet Leofric as the warhawk rapidly lost altitude, dropping through the air until it was skimming the rocks, no more than a few feet above the mountainside.

He saw Kyarno and the Eternal Guard leap from the backs of the warhawks, landing easily on the jagged rocks as though such a feat of acrobatics was the most natural thing in the world.

Fortunately, he did not have to try and imitate the natural grace of the elves, as the warhawk he rode upon spread its wings and landed atop a flat slab of rock above them. Leofric slid from the back of the mighty bird and started to thank the rider for bearing him this far, but no sooner was he down than the bird leapt back into the sky to rejoin its fellows.

The ground underfoot was black and slick, as though the fabric of the rock itself softened and attempted to reshape itself under the malign influence of the Shadow-Gave. Leofric heard wild howls and brays from above and knew that the creatures of Chaos were ready for them now.

Behind him, he saw Kyarno and Cairbre, both with their weapons at the ready, bounding from rock to rock, heading uphill towards the Corruptor. Morvhen still rode upon the back of a warhawk, an arrow nocked to her bow, the dark shapes of the warped creatures of the air closing rapidly with her, and Leofric wished her safe in the battle she would fight.

Leofric drew his sword and began making his way uphill, unable to match the grace of the elves, but making up for it with sheer determination.

The route uphill was steep and treacherous, winding through a copse of dark trees whose branches twisted towards the sky as though clawing at the clouds in agony at the foul transformation wrought upon them.

Further on, the ground levelled off onto the rock-strewn plateau and Leofric saw the silhouettes of dozens upon dozens of bestial creatures appear at its edge.

With an echoing bellow, the monstrous creatures loped down the mountainside towards the mutated trees and Leofric felt his fury at such abominations spill out in a cry of purest rage.

'For Quenelles, the king and the Lady!' he cried as he ran towards the charging beastmen with the warriors of the asrai beside him.

Like harpies of their dark kin, the winged beasts of Chaos sped through the air towards them, their ungainly flight a crude mockery of the graceful movements of the warhawks and their riders. As the gap between the foes closed, Morvhen saw how badly they were outnumbered as yet more rose from dark eyries in the mountains.

She took aim at a creature with the head of a slavering wolf and the leathery wings of a bat. Its eyes were red and slitted, its mouth filled with long fangs. Her warhawk banked, instinctively swinging into a position that gave her a better shot. Between breaths she loosed her arrow, the shaft arcing through the air to pierce its skull and the monster tumbled from the air, clawing at its face.

A flurry of arrows flew from the warhawk riders and a dozen or more beasts fell from the sky, their foul flesh home to blue-fletched arrows. Morvhen bent her knees, leaning into the sharp turn of her bird as it banked again.

Then all semblance of formation was lost as the flying monsters were among them, the sky awash with spinning birds and creatures as each manoeuvred for position. She saw Beithir-Seun tear a Chaos beast in two with his claws as he bit another in half. Morvhen loosed a trio of arrows, one after another, as the white underbelly of a beast flashed overhead, swiftly drawing another arrow as she saw another beast slash at one of the warhawk riders and tear him from his mount's back.

'No!' she screamed as the elf fell from the warhawk. She spitted his killer on an arrow, ducking as long, yellowed claws snatched at her head. Her bird spun around and she sent an arrow into her attacker, a monstrous black-winged creature with the twisted body of a snarling lion, but the shaft passed through the thin membrane of its wing. It screeched in pain and looped around, turning with its clawed rear legs reaching for her.

She dropped to her knees, gripping her mount's feathers as it rolled to avoid the beast's claws, but as fast as it reacted, it wasn't quite quick enough and she felt the mighty bird shudder as the beast's jaws snapped and tore open its belly. Her warhawk screamed in pain and broke from the combat, desperately heading for the ground to save its rider before it expired, but Morvhen knew they were too high for such a manoeuvre.

Morvhen heard a screech of triumph behind her and risked a glance over her shoulder to see the same leonine beast closing for the kill. She slung her bow over her shoulder and leaned in close to the warhawk's head.

'Farewell, great heart, I will avenge you,' she said to the dying bird as she rose to her feet and leapt towards the diving monster.

It roared in anger, snapping at her as she flew towards it, but her unexpected jump had caught it by surprise and its wide jaws snapped empty air as she looped one arm around its neck and swung herself onto its furred back.

The creature bit and clawed at her, but could not reach her. It rolled and lowered itself into a dive, attempting to shake her from its back, but she wound her fingers into its mane and held on tightly. Morvhen's sword hissed from its sheath and she plunged the blade deep into the beast's back, pulling it clear and stabbing it in again and again. Blood gushed from the mortal wounds and the monster let out a piercing roar of agony as the elven blade ripped through its body.

Morvhen looked up as she heard the shrill cry of a warhawk and yelled in relief as she saw a riderless bird flying alongside her. Abandoning the dying monster, she leapt from its plummeting corpse, the ground rushing towards her until the warhawk slotted itself between her and the rocks and pulled into a shallow dive before climbing back to the battle.

'My thanks,' shouted Morvhen as she sheathed her sword and slung her bow from her shoulders. Climbing towards the furious aerial battle, she saw warhawk riders jink and roll in a deadly ballet with the black-winged creatures of Chaos. Many of the warhawks fought alone, too many of her fellows having been torn from the backs of their mounts by the flying beasts.

Above her, her father slew beast after beast with his unerringly accurate lance strikes, skewering their vile bodies upon the blade of his magical weapon while his noble eagle tore at them with claw and beak. Beithir-Seun roared and fought with all the fury and might of his kind, his jaws snapping at his enemies and his claws tearing them limb from limb as they swarmed him. Deadly accurate bowfire picked off the beasts that were able to evade his huge jaws and land on his massive body, but the dragon still bled from a score of wounds where his thick, scaled hide had been torn open by bestial claws.

The battle was far from over, the sky filled with spinning, looping combatants, arrows flashing through the air, claws and beaks tearing at flesh and screaming bodies falling to their doom.

She nocked another arrow to her bow and angled her bird's course back into the thick of the fighting.

A booming peal of thunder sounded, though no rain fell and no storm broke upon the fields. A wild, exultant horn echoed from the mist that gathered on the darkened eastern horizon, and the distant howls of hunting packs drifted on the cold wind. Despite himself, Teoderic Lendast shivered at the sound of the horn, its skirl promising blood and death. He gripped his lance and cast an eye along the thousand men that awaited the wild hunt on the slopes before Castle Carrard.

Nervous bowmen were arrayed behind lines of defensive stakes and trembling men-at-arms stood ready with long, hooked polearms. The lord of this host, though Teoderic knew that to call such a paltry gathering of force a host was a joke, rode at the head of a group of twenty knights in the centre, his scarlet and gold banner snapping in the strong wind.

Teoderic commanded a score of knights, banners and lances held upright and ready for the charge, and at the far end of their battle line, Theudegar led another twenty armoured warriors. Clovis sat on his whinnying steed beside Teoderic, struggling to calm his mount as yet another blast of the horn sounded, much closer this time.

'Damn, but I loathe the sound of that horn,' swore Clovis. 'It chills my blood to hear it.'

'I know what you mean,' agreed Teoderic, rubbing his gauntlet over his own mount's neck as it stamped in fear at the sound.

'Never fear, though,' he said, with a confidence he did not feel. 'We'll soon put these things to flight and it will sound naught but their retreat.'

Clovis nodded, but Teoderic could see his eyes through the visor of his helmet and remained fearful. Teoderic did not blame him, Clovis had but recently been elevated to a knight of the realm and knew full well the bloodshed that awaited them in battle.

'Look!' cried Clovis, pointing to the eastern horizon. 'The mist parts!'

Teoderic followed Clovis's pointing finger and saw that he spoke true. The mist thinned as the crack and snap of branches sounded from within and the rustle of leaves, like malicious laughter, came to the assembled Bretonnians.

'Stand firm!' shouted the lord of the host as a ripple of fear passed through the men. 'Not one man shall take a backward step or he shall have me to answer to!'

Teoderic heard that damnable horn again, accompanied by the wild baying of hounds and the shrieks of ravens and crows. The ground before the mist rippled with life and growth as shoots of plant and flower erupted from the ground and shifting forms of green light emerged.

Like packs of capering maidens of briar and thorn, the forest creatures threw off their concealing cloak of mist and stood revealed in all their terrible glory. Cries of alarm and fear sounded from the Bretonnian lines, yeomen and those of more stout heart steadying the ranks with clubs and stern words.

Packs of hunting hounds swarmed over the ridge, weaving in and out of the wraiths of branch and root as they flocked downhill in a tide of razor thorns and spiteful shrieks. Billowing clouds of black birds thronged the air and ghostly clouds spread across the face of the moons as a peal of thunder and a sheet of actinic lightning split the sky.

The terrible, brazen note of the hunting horn sounded once more and Teoderic felt a primal fear seize him as he saw the enormous horn blower emerge from the mist, tall and mighty, with a crown of antlers and a cloak of leaves and clutching a terrifying, many bladed spear. Crackling magical energies wreathed the awesome figure and there could be no doubt as to this mighty being's identity.

The King of the Forest…

Snapping hounds and fiery-eyed riders atop rearing black horses and bucks that snorted in fury surrounded the king, whose burning gaze swept across the pitiful army arrayed against the might of the forest.

Teoderic lowered his lance as the woodland king's booming laughter echoed in time with another rumble of thunder, nodding to Clovis as the giant figure unleashed another deafening blast of his hunting horn and led his wild riders in a furious charge towards them.

* * *

The haunted copse of dark trees beneath the plateau was a bloodbath as elf and man and beast clashed in furious combat. Leofric hacked his sword through a thickly furred limb and deflected an axe strike away from his body, turning and slashing his silver sword across his foe's back. A spear thudded into his breastplate, spinning him around, and he backed into a tree as a bestial horror with monstrously wide jaws and a frill of reptilian skin around its neck lunged for him.

He roared and thrust his sword into its mouth, stabbing the point up into its brain. The monster bellowed in pain, its jaw snapping shut on the blade. Leofric wrenched it clear and beheaded the creature as Kyarno moved to stand beside him, firing arrow after arrow into the mass of beastmen.

The young elf was unbelievably swift with his bow, nocking and firing almost without pause and sending shafts into the eyes and vitals of every beast he shot at. The two forged a path through the beastmen, Kyarno loosing deadly accurate arrows and Leofric hacking them down with his brutal swordwork.

Cairbre fought like no one Leofric had ever seen before, twisting, stabbing and cutting with a skill unmatched by any other. He fought to protect Naieth, a wild wind of bright power weaving around her as she smote the beastmen with her magic. Though twisted into new and vile shapes, the trees of the copse arose to her bidding, a storm of razor-sharp missiles of jagged wood engulfing any beastmen who drew near her.

The venerable Cairbre was always in motion, never stopping or slowing as he slew the foul children of Chaos, the Blades of Midnight cleaving through unclean flesh with ease as he fought to protect the prophetess.

The elves of Coeth-Mara fought side by side, swords and spears cutting down beastmen by the score, but always there were more howling monstrosities to take their place. Bestial and elven blood mingled on the rocky ground as elf after elf was torn down by the brute savagery of the beasts, and Leofric knew that such losses could not be maintained.

Even as he thought this, Leofric chopped his sword through the face of a baying monster with myriad eyes and mouths as a snapping, red-furred hound with two heads leapt upon him, its claws scraping down his pauldron and ripping it from his armour.

The hound bore him to the ground, one set of its bloody fangs closing on his visor and crushing it in its powerful jaws as the other sought his throat. Leofric cried out and slammed his armoured head into one of the hound's faces, rolling as he struggled to remove his helmet. A squeal of pain came from the hound and as he tore off his ruined helmet, he saw two of Kyarno's arrows buried in its ribs.

He clambered to his feet and drove his sword into its flank to finish it off as he heard a great clamour from the ridge above him and yet more beastmen came charging towards them.

'Kyarno!' he yelled. 'There are more!'

'I see them!' called back the elf as he retrieved arrows from the corpses of the dead.

'We must get past them,' said Cairbre, panting and out of breath from the exertions of the battle. The white blades of his spear were streaked with black blood and he bled from a number of minor wounds, but the Hound of Winter's courage was undimmed.

The charge of the monsters was almost upon them when Leofric saw a spectral mist of sparkling lights form around his feet. It oozed from the bark of the trees, a whisper of things unseen rustling nearby, and as he readied his weapon to fight once more, he shook his head to clear it of the ghostly apparitions he thought he saw. Had the two-headed monster's attack stunned him more seriously than he had thought?

An ululating war cry, wild and passionate, burst from the trees and, with a wild howl, the ghostly apparitions suddenly resolved themselves into solidity as Cu-Sith and his wardancers appeared from the mist.

The Red Wolf leapt amongst the beastmen, a sword and short-hafted spear cutting and stabbing. The painted wardancers smashed into the beastmen with weapons spinning around them in blindingly swift cuts – beheading, disembowelling and cleaving them with a speed and viciousness that was breathtaking.

No matter where the bestial monsters attacked, the wardancers evaded them, somersaulting and bounding aside from their clumsy attacks before darting in with a graceful pirouette to ram a blade into an exposed throat or eye socket.

While the monsters reeled from this unexpected attack, Leofric, Cairbre and Kyarno pushed on towards the plateau.

But before they could do more than gather their wits, they heard a monstrous bellow of rage and power that sent a wave of terror through every one of them.

Leofric looked up through the leaping wardancers to the plateau and saw the monolithic form of the waystone towering above them. Crude symbols had been daubed upon it, blotting out the elven runes carved there. Before it stood a beastman of colossal proportions, its hide dark with blood and scaled in bronze. Its horned head was scarred and burned, but its flickering, multi-coloured eyes burned with purpose and power.

Thick, hooked chains looped across its chest and it wore spiked shoulder guards crudely fashioned from beaten breastplates. It carried a massive, double-headed axe, its blades rusted, but with a potent magical aura surrounding them.

In front of it thrashed a diabolical creature that defied any recognisable shape or form, its limbs a slashing web of thorned pseudopods, its fluid form shifting and roiling in constant motion. A cadre of similarly gigantic monsters surrounded the waystone, hulking bull-headed monsters, slavering wolf creatures and drooling, slack-jawed trolls with tough, warty hides and great stone clubs.

Naieth cried out in anger as some unseen force drained her skin of colour, and she cried, 'The Corruptor... it is here!'

'Where?' asked Cairbre, rushing to her side.

'Upon the mountain!' gasped Naieth, pointing to the cave mouth.

Leofric looked into the darkness of the cave, feeling an instinctual dread of the dark claw its way up his spine as he saw something lurch from the depths. A powerful beast with a dark miasma of power swirling around it like black mist emerged into the sunlight, though a shadow crept with it, as though unwilling to allow such an abomination to bask in its light. Gibbering, screeching wails accompanied the monster, skulls woven within its fur and horns screaming in anguish.

Leofric dropped to his knees in pain as a powerful nausea clamped his gut. All around him elves fell to the ground, assaulted by the dark forces surrounding this monster.

Naieth reached up to grip Cairbre's wrist and shouted, 'Quickly, now is your time! The white hound, the red wolf and the hawk, I see it now!'

'Prophetess,' said Cairbre. 'What–'

'No time!' cried Naieth. 'If the Corruptor reaches the waystone then all will have been for naught, the magic will be perverted to serve the Dark Gods and it will be lost to us. Go now! Destroy the beast!'

CHAPTER TWENTY

Cairbre ran from the tearful prophetess and made his way uphill, gritting his teeth against the rising pain and dark energies he felt assail him. Behind him the elves of Coeth-Mara began climbing to their feet as they fought against the power of the Corruptor, but their advance was slower and more painful than his.

He felt his flesh answering the dark call of the Corruptor's foulness and exerted every last ounce of his will to resist its vile imprecations. Before him, the wardancers carved apart the last of the beasts between them and the waystone, but rather than continue their bloody rampage up the mountainside, they gathered around their painted leader, the wolf tattoo on his chest writhing and snapping beneath his skin as it revelled in the bloodshed.

The corpses of beastmen surrounded the bloodied troupe, but their victory had not been won without loss, fully half of their number lay gored on the dark rocks. Cu-Sith met Cairbre's stare and the wardancer nodded, 'It is our time then? The white hound and the red wolf?'

The Hound of Winter frowned at the Red Wolf's familiar turn of phrase and nodded, saying, 'Yes, the prophetess–'

'Cu-Sith knows,' interrupted the wardancer with a wild grin of feral anticipation on his gory features. 'Loec knows all and Loec tells Cu-Sith what he must do.'

'But how did–'

'No time!' said Cu-Sith as more packs of wild beastmen charged towards them from the plateau above. Cairbre nodded again, glancing into the sky at the vicious battle being fought above them as winged monsters clashed with the warhawk riders and the mighty Beithir-Seun.

Arrows slashed past the Hound and the Wolf as the elves of Coeth-Mara and the human fought through the Corruptor's power to make for the waystone. The odds had been evened by Cu-Sith's arrival, but there were still many scores of beastmen to slay before victory could be won.

The Red Wolf set off up the mountain, his sword and spear spinning in his grip, but Cairbre could see that even the mighty Cu-Sith was in great pain from the touch of the Corruptor's dark magic.

Once again the beasts of Chaos and the asrai clashed in the shadow of the waystone, but Cairbre did not stop to fight them, cutting himself a path through their motley ranks to follow the Red Wolf towards the terrible beast that advanced from the mouth of the cave towards the waystone.

Leofric could barely hold off the agonising pain wracking him as he fought to climb uphill. His flesh seethed with rebellion, and it took all his rage and anger to hold himself true to his form. He slew beasts without mercy, channelling all his emotion into each blow.

Axes struck him and his own blood ran from his body, but he cared not, striking down his foes with each sweep of his gleaming sword. Beside him Kyarno screamed with each arrow loosed, his movements supple and swift despite the battle he fought against his own unquiet flesh.

They fought their way alongside a score of elves, their blades and bows reaping a fearsome tally of their bestial foes. But each yard gained was paid for in blood and the dead were left to fall in their wake. Only victory would grant them eternal life in the funeral glades of the forest, and Leofric just hoped they could give them such a memory.

At last, awash with blood and death, they reached the plateau and the waystone.

Cairbre and Cu-Sith had already broken through the beastmen and were working their way up the steep rocks towards the cave mouth above them. Leofric wished them the blessing of the Lady, but could ill afford to spare them more than a glance as he took in the scale of the foes before them.

Surely this massive, bull-headed monster must be the leader of this herd, its terrible bulk greater than any beast they had slain thus far. As they stood before it, the monster gave out a deafening bellow and raised its massive axe in a defiant challenge.

An arrow from Kyarno's bow slashed towards it, but it batted it aside with its axe blade, the weapon moving impossibly swiftly for its bulk. Another arrow slashed towards the Beastlord – this time from above – thudding into the meat of its shoulder and Leofric looked up to see

Morvhen circling above them, bloodied and riding a ragged, scarred warhawk.

Brutish trolls lumbered forward with the Beastlord and with another fearsome bellow, it released the chained spawn creature towards them. Faster than Leofric would have believed such a malformed abomination could move, it slithered and lurched towards them, howling and screeching in blind, lunatic hunger.

Its thorned limbs ended in snapping mouths of razored fangs and bladed hooks, and ripping claws seethed in its riotous flesh. Arrows hammered into the soft meat of its body, but if it felt any pain from them, it gave no sign.

Leofric charged to meet the beast headlong, his sword cleaving into its rippling body. The blade parted the skin easily, slicing through warped muscle and bone, but before he could bring his sword back for another blow, a fanged jaw surged from the spawn's flesh and snapped shut on his vambrace. He cried out as the metal compressed on his arm, stabbing his sword into the mouth and ripping his arm free as a club-like limb smashed him from his feet. A clutch of stabbing, blade-like appendages writhed from its body and reached for his face.

Another blade slashed above him and the creature screeched as Kyarno dragged him back, his sword stabbing at each of the beast's grasping limbs as they snatched at them. More arrows thudded into its flesh as the elves overcame their horror at the vile beast and rushed to aid them.

Leofric and Kyarno attacked together, their swords hacking great lumps of greasy fat and gristle from the heaving spawn's body. Its struggles grew weaker and weaker, but still it would not die until its flesh was carved to bloody chunks.

But by then it had served its purpose as the Beastlord and its monstrous acolytes smashed into the elves. Three were killed instantly as it clove its axe through their bodies with one mighty blow, another two smashed to bloody ruin by the return stroke.

It bellowed as it slew, red-flecked spittle flying from its jaws and a dark light flaring in its eyes. Yet another arrow thunked into the great, bull-headed monster, but it ignored the wound as it turned to face Leofric and Kyarno.

Perhaps a dozen elves still stood with them, and each loosed a shaft towards the mighty beastman as it hacked yet more of their number down in a welter of blood and bone. Leofric raised his sword and darted in to slash it across the Beastlord's side, his blade biting an inch before sliding clear.

Kyarno rolled beneath a scything blow of its axe and drove his sword into its gut with all his might. The blade penetrated a handspan before snapping off in his hand and Kyarno threw himself back as the huge axe swept towards him, the edge of the blade coming within an inch of gutting him.

Leofric took advantage of the Beastlord's distraction to chop at his foe's arm, his sword slicing into the meat and rebounding from the bone beneath. The Beastlord roared and its wounded arm slashed down to break him in two.

But instead of tearing him to pieces, a dazzling white light erupted from Leofric's gauntlet and the Beastlord's claws simply carved a series of parallel grooves diagonally down his breastplate and hurled him back across the rocks. The terrible creature's blood splashed his vambrace and cuirass, burning through them like engraver's acid.

He rolled to his knees as fragments of white crystal fell from his gauntlet, and he silently thanked Tiphaine for her favour, knowing it had just saved his life.

Despite their courage and Morvhen's arrows, Leofric saw that while the Beastlord lived, this fight could have but one outcome. The creatures were killing them one by one and every elf slain brought them closer to defeat. The wardancers had joined the fight, cutting down the trolls with deadly grace, but it was slow, brutal work, their enemies able to withstand even the most terrible wounds before finally succumbing.

But such things did not matter any more. They had to fight and if that meant they had to die, then so be it. They fought because Chaos had to be opposed wherever it was found.

Leofric rose to his feet once more and charged back into the fray.

Cairbre struggled to keep up with Cu-Sith as the more nimble wardancer bounded from rock to rock, climbing the slope towards the Corruptor as it closed on the waystone. He heard wild howls below him and saw that around forty of the more agile creatures were following them, rushing to defend their despicable leader.

Every step and every breath was pain, the dark power of the monstrous beastman above him threatening to change him into something vile and terrible. Only his indomitable will kept his form constant, though he knew that should he falter for an instant he would be lost.

'Come on!' shouted Cu-Sith from above as he vaulted onto the ledge in front of the cave mouth. Cairbre bit back an angry retort and forced himself to climb faster as the yelping howls of the creatures behind him intensified.

His breath came in sharp bursts, his muscles burning with fatigue and their continued resistance to the power at work on this mountain. His hand closed on the rock of the ledge and he hauled himself upwards, but as he pulled, the rock melted beneath his fingers and he felt himself falling backwards.

A hand shot out and gripped his wrist, pulling him onto the ledge as claws snatched at him from below. He had no time to thank Cu-Sith as a horned head appeared at the lip of the ledge and roared in fury at him. The Blades of Midnight flashed and the headless beastman spun through the air to dash itself on the rocks below.

Cairbre ran after the Red Wolf, glancing up to see more of the black-winged creatures dropping through the air to come to the defence of the Corruptor, which now halted its advance upon the waystone to face this new threat.

The terrifying creature turned its burning gaze upon them and both elves groaned in pain as they fought the full force of its corrupting powers. It threw back its head and let loose an ear-splitting roar of hate and bloodlust, the twisting staff it held rippling with smoky magic.

'Loec says they will talk of this battle for centuries,' said Cu-Sith, giving Cairbre a sly wink.

'I look forward to hearing it,' answered Cairbre, as they hurled themselves towards the howling beastman. Wardancer and Eternal Guard attacked the Corruptor from either side, flashing swords and spears stabbing for its unclean flesh. But for all its lumpen appearance, the Corruptor was a terrifyingly powerful beast and fought with all the ferocity and cunning its kind were famed for.

Its thick hide turned aside their every blow, its deadly staff turning in midair to intercept their attacks without apparent effort. Its claws smashed Cairbre from his feet, sending him skidding to the very lip of the ledge. The Hound of Winter grunted in pain and clutched his chest where he knew at least one rib was broken and his flesh burned with the touch of the beast.

He climbed painfully to his feet, seeing that they were now cut off from the rest of the elves, a mass of chanting, bellowing beastmen surrounding their struggle on the ledge. They knew better than to approach the Corruptor too closely and seemed content to let their master fight this battle alone.

Cairbre watched as Cu-Sith leapt and spun around the vile beastman, his sword and spear batted aside at every turn. No matter where his blades struck, its dark staff blocked his every attack. A shadow flashed overhead and Cairbre looked up to see one of the winged beastmen slash through the air towards the Red Wolf.

Cu-Sith swayed aside from its attack, hacking its head from its shoulders as it writhed with rampant mutation at its proximity to the Corruptor. But the momentary distraction was all the opening the beastman lord needed, its mighty staff hammering into Cu-Sith's temple and driving him to his knees.

The great wolf tattoo on his chest howled in anger and the wardancer looked in amazement at the red liquid pouring from his head.

'You made Cu-Sith bleed his own blood...' he said in shock.

Cairbre pushed himself forward, but he already knew he would be too late as the Corruptor's staff swung back around and smashed the Red Wolf's skull to splinters.

* * *

Leofric sliced his sword across the Beastlord's side, drawing a spray of dark blood, but not slowing the beast at all. Elves were dying every second, the monstrous beast's axe slaying them with an unnatural savagery. Dark magic pulsed in the blades and Leofric knew that with such power, even their skill and courage could not triumph.

Kyarno jumped back, barely avoiding a deadly stroke of the creature's axe as yet another arrow loosed by Morvhen thudded into its flesh. There seemed to be no stopping the monster, but Leofric attacked again regardless. Kyarno stumbled, his left leg bloody where it had been gashed from hip to knee by one of the Beastlord's followers.

Only Leofric stood before the terrifying creature, his silver sword glowing with a faint light as he faced the Beastlord. Its blood hissed and spat where it dripped from its body onto the rocks and its mighty chest heaved with exertion. It may have nearly defeated them, but it had not been an easy battle.

The two combatants circled one another as he heard a scream of rage from the ledge above, but Leofric dared not risk tearing his gaze from the monster before him. It growled and its chest hiked, giving voice to a low, growling bray. Leofric was confused for a moment before he realised that the creature was laughing at him. Laughing at him for daring to stand against such a monstrously powerful avatar of the Dark Gods.

Leofric's fury lent his tired limbs strength and he charged the monster with a cry of rage, 'Lady guide my hand!'

He swung his sword towards the beast's midriff, feeling the hilt of his weapon grow hot as the blade leapt with silver fire, outshining the sun with its brilliance. The Beastlord's axe came round to block the blow and the two weapons met in a shower of dazzling sparks and fire.

The gigantic axe exploded into fragments of dark iron and wood, a flaring after-image of some malevolent shadow erupting from the shattered weapon. Leofric fell back, reeling and numb from the impact, blinking to clear his vision from the glaring after-images of the explosion.

He dropped to one knee, still clutching his glowing sword, amazed and thankful for its hidden power when a shadow swept over him and a powerful voice shouted, 'Human! Down!'

Leofric threw himself flat as the golden form of Lord Aldaeld atop his magnificent eagle swooped low across the battlefield and streaked towards the stunned Beastlord. He looked up in time to see Lord Aldaeld ram the blade of his silver lance into the creature's chest, the shaft plunging deep into its body and ripping out through its back in a fountain of blood and fragmented bone. Lord Aldaeld angled the flight of his eagle back into the air and, skewered like an insect on the needle of an academic, the Beastlord was carried high above the battle.

It fought to drag the weapon from its body, its flesh smoking where the faerie lance of Athel Loren seared it with its purity, but it could not escape as Lord Aldaeld lifted it higher and higher.

Only when both figures were little more than dots of black against the sky, did Lord Aldaeld finally allow the creature to slide from his lance, the tumbling figure of the Beastlord falling thousands of feet to smash on the jagged rocks of the mountains.

Leofric bowed his head and gave thanks to the Lady of the Lake as clouds of dust were blown skyward and another huge shadow enveloped the plateau. He squinted through the clouds of swirling dust, seeing the mighty form of Beithir-Seun hovering just above the plateau, his green, scaled flesh torn and bloody, but triumphant. Warhawk riders circled him, their faces alight with the savage joy of victory.

The great dragon reached down with his claws and ripped the waystone from the pile of skulls, weapons and armour that surrounded it and slowly began to climb into the sky. Riderless warhawks set down on the bloody field of battle to collect the few surviving warriors of Coeth-Mara.

Kyarno limped over to a scarred bird and said, 'Come on. We have the stone, now let's get Cairbre and Cu-Sith and get out of here.'

Leofric nodded and breathlessly staggered over to Kyarno, climbing onto the back of the mighty bird.

'We won,' he said, hardly able to believe it.

'Oh, no...' gasped Kyarno, looking at something above them.

Leofric turned on the warhawk's back in time to see a battle he would remember to his dying day.

The Corruptor's staff again thwarted Cairbre's every attempt to breach his defences and the Hound of Winter knew that he could not defeat this monster alone. The Red Wolf was dead, and as he watched Beithir-Seun lift into the sky with the waystone clutched in its claws, he smiled as he realised they had succeeded.

Blood ran from his mouth and his breath rasped in his throat. But he was the Hound of Winter and he never gave up, never stopped fighting and never took a backwards step in the face of the enemy.

'Come on then, you monster,' he snarled. 'Time for you to die.'

He lunged forward, the Blades of Midnight spinning in a whirling arc of white blades. Though pain stabbed through him with every movement, he shut himself off from it, focussing all his thoughts on slaying the monster before him.

The skulls woven into the fur of its back and horns screamed at him, promising death in all manner of uncounted ways, the dark miasma of change that surrounded the Corruptor straining at the bounds of his will to rupture his flesh with mutation.

'You shall not have me!' shouted Cairbre, swaying aside from a scything blow and spinning close to the stinking, shaggy monster. His left blade slashed across the beast's stomach, a spray of black blood gushing from the wound and ripping a bellowing roar of pain from its jaws.

Its writhing staff slashed down, hooking under Caibre's legs and sending him flying backwards to land atop the corpse of Cu-Sith. He rolled from the body of the Red Wolf and felt a fresh vigour course through him.

Loec is not done with Cu-Sith...

Cairbre cried out in amazement as the voice of the wardancer echoed in his head and he looked down to see that the great, snarling tattoo of the Red Wolf now adorned *his* chest, its fangs slavering for blood and vengeance.

He heard a bestial roar and looked up in time to see the Corruptor's staff arcing towards his head. He leapt into the air, somersaulting over its head with a maniacal laugh that was not his own.

As he leapt through the air, he twisted the haft of the Blades of Midnight, separating them into his twin swords and drove them straight down into the shoulders of the Corruptor.

The terrible beast shook the mountains with its roar of agony, its unclean flesh seething at the touch of faerie magic. Cairbre landed behind the beast, dropping lightly on the balls of his feet and pulled his swords clear with a wild yell of fierce anger. The Corruptor spun, its flesh burned, and its insane gaze settled on Cairbre once more.

The Hound of Winter felt his new found strength wither before its gaze, dropping to his knees as agonising pain returned to swamp him.

The Corruptor staggered away from him, blood flooding from its body and the dark, smoky trails of its vile, magical essence pouring into the air. It let out a howl of outrage and pain, before turning and limping back into its cave to recover its strength before the power that sustained it was undone forever.

Cairbre watched it go with a mixture of regret and exultation. Regret that he had not rid the world of its foulness, and exultation in the atavistic glory of victory.

He looked down and smiled weakly as the snarling tattoo of the red wolf on his chest began to fade and nodded in thanks to the departed Cu-Sith as the wardancer's voice echoed in his head one last time.

Not bad for an old man and a wild one, eh, Hound?

'No,' agreed Cairbre, watching as the vengeful followers of the Corruptor closed in on him now that the mutating influence of their master had withdrawn. 'Not bad at all.'

He counted at least forty, and while, in his prime, he could have taken them on with some chance of success, he was far from in his prime. Slotting the Blades of Midnight together again to form the twin-bladed spear, the Hound of Winter painfully pushed himself to his feet, watching as the warhawks took to the air alongside Beithir–Seun.

He smiled as he saw that Kyarno still lived, his nephew's bird racing towards him in a futile attempt to save him. No, the Hound of Winter's season had passed and with it his stewardship of the Blades of Midnight.

As the creatures of Chaos closed on him with axes and swords raised to cut him down, he shouted Kyarno's name, drew back his arm and hurled his spear into the clear blue of the sky.

'Cairbre, no!' screamed Kyarno as he saw what his uncle intended. But Cairbre's course was set and the white-bladed spear streaked into the air like a glittering comet. Its arcing course cut the air above them and Kyarno leapt onto the warhawk's back to catch the spinning spear as it began to curve downwards.

'Go back!' shouted Kyarno as the warhawk began to turn away from the mountain and back to Athel Loren, but the bird could see the outcome of the battle below, even if he would not.

Both he and Leofric could only watch helplessly as the beastmen surrounded Cairbre, clubbing him and stabbing him with their crude weapons. Though he fought bravely, killing over a dozen with a short sword taken from a dead foe, he could not defeat them all, and soon his body was lost to sight beneath a mound of thrashing, stabbing beasts.

Kyarno sobbed in loss as his uncle was finally overwhelmed, unable to believe that so mighty a warrior as the Hound of Winter could have been bested.

The warhawk dipped its wings in sadness at the passing of a great warrior, and beneath the shadow of mourning they flew back to Athel Loren.

CHAPTER TWENTY-ONE

Saddened but victorious, the warriors of Coeth-Mara descended towards the forest in the wake of Beithir-Seun, welcomed home by the same host of birds that had seen them on their way. Too many had died and too much had been lost for there to be any kind of celebration at this battle's end, but it would be remembered in song and tale for centuries to come as one of the great battles against Cyanathair.

The waystone had been saved by the might and strength of the Hound of Winter and the Red Wolf, and their names would live forever in the glory of the forest, remembered by all the asrai in their dreams and their songs.

The mighty dragon hovered above the ground, weeds and thorny branches reaching up to try and snag its limbs as it gently lowered the waystone back into its rightful place. Leofric and the survivors of the battle watched the dragon return the waystone to the ground from a rocky hillock, an island of grey amid a seething carpet of verdant greenery.

Leofric had taken it for beautiful from the air, but upon landing, he saw it for the wild, savage glory of nature unbound that it truly was. Everywhere the greenery smothered all other life, destroying it and replacing it with its own. Kyarno stood next to him, still clutching the Blades of Midnight, with Morvhen's arm around his shoulders as they wept for the lost Cairbre. Leofric had shed no tears for the old elf. After all, they were

not friends, but even so, he was saddened to see such a noble warrior fall
to such base creatures as beastmen.

Lord Aldaeld and Naieth stood before them, knee deep in the swaying
undergrowth that swirled around them with questing fronds and curious
flowers. The greenery parted before Naieth, her staff held before her and
her owl once again perched on her shoulder now that she had returned
to the forest.

'What are they doing?' asked Leofric. 'Is it over? Is the wild hunt over?'

'Not yet, no,' said Morvhen. 'Terrible violence was done here, dark
magicks have been unleashed, and it has tainted the forest.'

'Tainted it?' said Leofric, horrified at the thought of all they had fought
and bled for being snatched away and that his people might still be
dying. 'No, that cannot be.'

He took a faltering step from the hillock, stepping through the rising greenery and calling out to Naieth. 'Prophetess! The waystone is
returned. Why does the wild hunt still lay waste to my lands?'

Aldaeld and Naieth turned to face Leofric as the waving strands of
growth slithered around him, curious and hostile to this human within
their domain. As he drew nearer to them, his armoured boot crunched
bone and he looked down to see the leather-wrapped skeleton of a
beastman, its bony hands clutching a staff of dark wood. Not a scrap of
flesh remained on its bones, but whether they had been picked clean by
insects or the ravages of time and the elements, Leofric could not say.

'The healing magic will take time to undo the damage done here, Leofric,' said Naieth. 'You must be patient.'

'Patient?' he yelled, turning his attention to the lord of Coeth-Mara.
'My people may be dying even now! I beseech you, allow me to travel
upon one of these mighty birds to my lands. I have fought beside your
kinband and I ask this boon of you as one warrior to another.'

Lord Aldaeld nodded and said, 'So be it... Leofric. We have much to
work against here, the foulness of the children of Chaos runs deep and I
know what it is to lose those under your care. If there is a warhawk willing to bear you back to your lands, then you may go with my blessing.'

'Thank you, Lord Aldaeld,' said Leofric, bowing deeply before the
elven lord.

'Go in peace, Leofric Carrard,' nodded Aldaeld slowly. He turned back
to Naieth then said. 'You will be welcome in Coeth-Mara again, human.'

Leofric said, 'I would be glad to visit here again some day,' and turned
back to the rocky hillock he had come from.

'I will come with you,' said Kyarno. 'I wish to see this land you call
home.'

Leofric smiled, 'And I would be glad to show it to you.'

'I will come too,' added Morvhen. 'I may never have another chance.'

Leofric and Kyarno climbed atop the warhawk that had borne them
from the battle, its proud head held high as they settled upon its back.

Morvhen mounted the bird that had saved her life upon leaping from the winged beast she had killed, and together they leapt into the sky, both warhawks climbing rapidly into the west as they flew towards Bretonnia.

Naieth watched the birds rise into the sky with a great sense of sadness for the armoured form carried on the back of the second warhawk. As they vanished over the treetops, Lord Aldaeld asked, 'Does he know?'

'No,' said Naieth quietly, 'but he will soon enough.'

'Do you have any regrets?'

'Regrets? No. I did what I had to do to guide my people, Aldaeld. You of all people should understand that.'

'I do,' nodded Aldaeld, 'but I thought that you had perhaps developed an affection for the human. Am I wrong?'

'No,' admitted Naieth. 'He has many admirable qualities, but in the end, he is still only human.'

'Very well,' said Aldaeld. 'I will accept that for now. But next time there is a threat to Athel Loren, speak to me of it first.'

'You know I could not,' cautioned Naieth as a shimmering white light built from within the trees and the waystone finally groaned into place.

She smiled in welcome and both she and Aldaeld dropped to their knees before the radiance of the goddess before them, her beauteous form indistinct in the haze of brilliant sunlight that enveloped her.

As the light spread before her, the dark greenery that reached beyond the forest's edge lightened, becoming thinner and more lush, the darkened branches and malignant mosses vanishing before the incredible power of her compassion and love.

Everywhere her light touched, the dark sorcery of the enemies of Athel Loren was undone, the foulness and corruption that had touched the land leeched from the ground in a dark mist that dissipated in the face of such radiance.

Naieth and Aldaeld watched in wonder as the balance of the world was restored and the beauty of the forest surged in their blood.

The light of Isha flowed through the Lady Ariel and both elves felt their hearts lifted as they heard her soft words in their heads.

The healing of Athel Loren must begin anew...

Blood and screams filled the air. Men-at-arms fell like wheat before the scythe, unable to stand against the primal ferocity of the forest king. Arrows peppered his flesh and lances shattered upon his great muscles, but his mighty form was impervious to such things.

Teoderic raised his lance as his knights circled back to the fray after yet another desperate charge and shouted, 'Once more for the Lady! Once more for honour!'

Barely a handful of his knights still lived, the charge of the wild hunt crashing into their numbers like a thunderbolt. Each charge of the knights had smashed deep into the enemy lines, creatures of branch and thorn splintering and crumbling beneath their might. But each time the momentum of the charge had faltered, they had risen up once more, stinking of sap and fresh-cut wood as they tore warriors from the saddle.

Clovis still fought beside him, his lance splintered and useless, his sword clutched in his bloody gauntlet. Theudegar fought on the left flank, his knights surrounded by the whooping riders on the dark steeds who hung the skulls of those they had slain from their belts.

The forest king stood in the centre of the field, bellowing in fury and blowing deafening blasts of his hunting horn. Those who came near him died, and everywhere his long spear reached, blood was shed. There was no shape to the battle now, simply wild charges and furious combats as the muster of Bretonnia fought for honour.

Honour was all they had left, for victory was surely beyond their grasp now.

But the impossibility of victory was no reason for a knight of Bretonnia to give up and Teoderic punched the air as he saw the scarlet and gold banner of Castle Carrard's lord raised high in the gloom and charge towards the green-fleshed King of the Forest.

'With me!' he yelled, raking back his spurs and riding towards their commander's banner. Nine brave knights followed him as a thunderous impact slammed into the ground barely a dozen yards from his horse. A huge piece of rock, hurled from the trebuchet mounted on the walls of Castle Carrard, crashed through the encroaching forest creatures, smashing them to splinters and scattering them once more.

Teoderic lowered his lance as he saw Theudegar angle his charge towards the centre of the battlefield, having also seen the gold and scarlet unicorn banner raised high.

His charge thundered through the snapping hounds of the forest king, his thick-limbed steed trampling the howling animals beneath his iron-shod hooves as he closed on the faerie king.

Truly was he a terrifying sight, taller even than an ogre and with a fearsome aura of great power surrounding him. His cloak of leaves billowed in the storm winds and his curling antlers sprang directly from the brow of his savagely regal countenance. His giant spear dripped with blood and his eyes blazed with unimaginable power.

Theudegar reached the forest king first, his lance shattering on his iron-hard emerald flesh. Teoderic cried out as the immense spear slashed around and clove through Theudegar's breastplate, punching him from the back of his horse. The king swung his spear and hurled the brave knight's body across the battlefield before lunging towards the rest of Theudegar's warriors and slaughtering them in a frenzy.

Teoderic and the knights of the master of Castle Carrard charged at the same time, cries of vengeance spilling from their lips as they hit home. Teoderic was hurled from his horse by the thunderous impact, blood and screams of pain surrounding him as he fell. The shattered haft of his lance was all that was left of his weapon, and as he picked himself up, he threw aside the splintered wood and unsheathed his sword.

The lord of Castle Carrard stood before his enemy, his lance having pierced the forest king's flesh. White sap spilled from the wound and Teoderic quailed before the great and terrible anger of this monstrous god.

Man and god faced one another and, for a second, Teoderic felt the world hold its breath as a sudden sense of incredible peace fell upon the battlefield. The fury of battle fled from his body and he felt a wave of – something wonderful – pass through the land.

The forest king bellowed in anger and ripped the lance from his body, looming over the knight before him. His bloody spear was poised to strike, but for some unknown reason, the forest king held his blow.

Teoderic rose unsteadily to his feet and quickly moved to stand beside the lord of Castle Carrard, his sword held before him, though he knew it was scant defence against such a mighty being as towered above him. Clovis limped towards him, and the knights who still lived rallied to their commander's banner that fluttered in the breeze.

Shafts of sunlight broke through the clouds above and Teoderic saw that the forest king's army was melting away, the wild riders gathering to their liege lord while the creatures of branch and wood froze into immobility. The ghostly forms of withering hags faded like morning mist in the gathering sunlight and Teoderic watched as the spectral clouds dissipated into the brightening sky.

Deathly silence filled the field before the castle, broken only by the cries of dying men and the whinny of horses. The forest king put up his spear and hooked his mighty hunting horn to his belt of skulls.

'What's happening?' asked Teoderic of no one in particular.

No one answered, their eyes turned to the heavens as a pair of great, winged creatures swooped towards the motionless tableau in the centre of the battlefield.

As they drew near, Teoderic saw they were giant birds, hawks by the look of them, but hawks that carried riders. They circled the battlefield before landing some twenty yards away, one depositing an elf woman of startling grace and beauty, the other a male elf and a human warrior in the armour of a Bretonnian knight.

Teoderic thought there was something familiar about the knight, but could not say for sure what. But before he could question these new arrivals, the forest king leaned down to address the assembled knights.

'In all things must there be balance,' he said, his powerful voice redolent with age. 'My queen calls me home and the realm of the asrai is restored. The world is now as it should be. But do not forget this lesson, for I will hunt again.'

And with that, the forest king turned away and thundered over the eastern horizon with his wild riders back towards the realm of Athel Loren.

* * *

Leofric watched the King of the Wood go and felt a great surge of pride in the warriors who had so gallantly stood against him. Though the battlefield was littered with the bodies of the fallen, he knew a great victory had been won here. A low mist, the bodies of dead hounds and flocks of circling ravens were all that remained of the wild hunt, and Leofric smiled as he realised that he now set foot upon the soil of Bretonnia once more.

Sunlight filled the sky, the warmth of spring upon the air, and he looked up at the welcoming sight of Castle Carrard, its many towers and red stone walls a wondrously familiar and welcome sight to him after so long.

Kyarno and Morvhen stood behind him, wary and unsure of this new and unsettling place. Leofric pointed at the castle high upon the hill above the glittering waters of the Brienne.

'This is my castle,' he said with a wide smile. 'This is my domain. I am home.'

He turned as he heard the sound of armoured warriors approaching and saw a pair of blood-spattered knights. One wore a surcoat with heraldry he did not recognise, while the other…

The other…

The other knight wore heraldry that depicted a scarlet unicorn rampant beneath a jewelled crown against a golden field. Leofric started as he recognised the heraldry as his own and began to speak when the knight removed his helmet.

His hair was the colour of silver, his features regal and sculpted, with green eyes set in a face lined with sorrow. Leofric's skin crawled as he saw a dreadful familiarity in them.

'I would have your name, sir,' demanded the silver-haired knight. 'Who are you and what is your business in Carrard lands?'

'Carrard lands…' said Leofric, looking up at his castle and now seeing towers and hoardings where none had been before.

'Sir, I require an answer,' said the knight, a trace of recognition in his voice. 'And are these elves you consort with?'

'My name is… unimportant,' said Leofric, 'and, yes, these are elves. Kyarno Silvermorn and Morvhen Fleetmane of Coeth-Mara. Are you lord of these lands?'

'I am,' said the knight. 'I am Leofric Carrard, servant of the king and the Lady of the Lake.'

'Leofric Carrard…' said Leofric. 'How came you by that name?'

'It was my great grandfather's,' answered the knight. 'He was taken by the forest a hundred years ago and never seen again.'

Leofric dropped to his knees as the full weight of the knight's words sank in.

All that had passed within the forest had been but the turn of three seasons to him, but beyond the forest… a hundred years had gone by.

Could it be true? Could this Leofric Carrard who stood before him truly be his descendant?

'Your grandfather,' said Leofric. 'He was called Beren?'

'He was,' nodded the silver-haired Leofric. 'A great and noble warrior.'

Leofric smiled at such an accolade given to the son he had never had the chance to know.

All that he knew had passed away and all that remained was... what?

He looked up at the castle on the hill once more as a strange lightness came upon him, a fugue-like dreaminess filling his mind with thoughts of faraway lands. The sun shone from behind the red towers of the fastness, blinding in its intensity. As he watched, the glow spread until it filled his vision and he saw again the same glorious brilliance he had seen in the forest many months ago.

At its centre he saw a slender pair of delicate hands cupping a silver chalice that overflowed with dazzling light, a light that spilled over the towers and walls of the castle and washed it away in a tide of wondrous radiance.

His eyes lit up as he recognised the chalice of the Lady of the Lake.

The grail itself...

He rose to his feet as the vision faded from his sight, the knights around him seeing the rapture in his eyes as he smiled at them. He drew his sword and knelt before his namesake.

'This belongs to you, Leofric Carrard,' he said, offering him the blade, hilt first.

The knight reached out hesitantly and took the sword, holding it before him as though it were the most ancient of relics.

'The Carrard blade!' breathed Leofric. 'Lost this last century!'

'Indeed it is. Do it honour, for it is yours to bear now.'

The knight nodded, stepping back as Leofric rose and turned back to Morvhen and Kyarno, not surprised to see the prophetess standing beside them. How she had come to be here, he did not know, but her presence was the final piece of the puzzle before him.

'You knew this would happen?' he asked her.

'Yes, Leofric, I did,' agreed Naieth. 'I am sorry I could not tell you before, but there was much at stake.'

'For you,' snapped Leofric. 'What is there left to me?'

'You heard the words of the Lady,' said Naieth. 'You know what is left to you.'

Leofric wanted to feel anger towards Naieth, but the vision of the grail had purged him of such petty considerations. The Lady had indeed told him what was left to him and he nodded, dropping to one knee and pulling Helene's favour from his gauntlet. He wrapped the blue silk scarf around his hands as he recited a vow he had learned from childhood and had hoped always to some day pledge.

'I set down my lance, symbol of duty. I spurn those whom I love. I relinquish all, and take up the tools of my quest. No obstacle will stand before me. No plea for help shall find me wanting. No moon will look upon me twice lest I be judged idle. I give my body, heart and soul to the Lady whom I seek...'

He rose as Kyarno stood before him.

'What do those words mean?' asked Kyarno.

'That I am sworn to the quest for the grail,' said Leofric, bending to pick up a fallen helmet. Its shape was of a design unfamiliar to him, but it was not displeasing to the eye and he placed it over his head, raising the visor as he saw a flame-maned elven steed come galloping over the eastern horizon.

'Aeneor,' he said, recognising the beast as it cantered towards him.

'Would I be right in thinking that these are dangerous lands?' asked Kyarno.

'All lands are dangerous, Kyarno, you should know that.'

'Then you will need a weapon,' said the elf, twisting the haft of the Blades of Midnight and separating them into a pair of white-bladed swords. He offered one of the weapons to Leofric, who smiled and took up the weapon.

'It is light,' he said, spinning the blade.

'I believe the Hound of Winter would not have been displeased to know you bear it,' said Kyarno. 'May it keep you safe in your quest.'

'I will return it to Coeth-Mara when it is at an end,' swore Leofric.

Leofric turned back to Naieth and asked, 'I will return to these lands?'

'You shall, Leofric,' nodded Naieth. 'Many times.'

'Good,' said Leofric, nodding towards the assembled knights who watched their discourse fearfully, 'then I will say no goodbyes.'

Leofric climbed onto the back of his elven steed and snapped down the visor as he considered what lay before him. He was now sworn to the quest for the grail and his entire body sang with the glory and yearning of such a venture. Leofric took a last look at the castle that had once been his as his namesake approached him, the Carrard blade held before him.

'You never told me your name,' said the knight.

'These are your lands now,' replied Leofric. 'I charge you to keep them safe in the name of the king and the Lady.'

'Please, sir knight, I beg of you,' said the silver-haired knight. 'Your name?'

'You know my name,' said Leofric, before turning and riding into the west in search of the grail.

'There was a knight came riding by,
in early spring when the roads were dry,
And he heard that Lady sing at the noon,
Two red roses across the moon.'

SEASON OF THE KNIGHT

Leofric Carrard travelled far and wide on his quest for the grail, journeying to lost lands and encountering many strange and wondrous things before its completion. In distant Cathay, he slew the Jade Dragon of the Emerald River and saved the wives of Emperor Zhang-Jimou from decapitation by the Executioner Cult of the Jade Pearl.

The mysteries of far-off Ind were laid before him as he quested for the grail in the Caves of Fire and learned the secrets of the ancient stylites who dwelt there.

His quest drove him ever onwards until, at last, in the darkest place of the world, Leofric discovered the grail and supped from its radiant waters as a hunter's moon arose over the forest of the asrai.

Leofric was to return to Athel Loren many times over the years, each time travelling its secret paths and hoping to reach a young knight searching for his lost wife before it was too late.

...time is a winding river beneath the boughs of Athel Loren, and many things are possible there that some would think hopeless. Paths once trod may be trod again and their ends woven anew...

FREEDOM'S HOME
OR GLORY'S GRAVE

Shadows leapt like dancers around the tall garrets of the crumbling towers and Leofric Carrard was starting to think that it had been a bad idea to agree to Lord d'Epee's request to venture into the abandoned depths of his castle.

The blade of Leofric's sword shone with a milky glow in the moonlight, its edge like a razor despite him never having taken a whetstone to it. The Blade of Midnight was elven and Leofric hoped that whatever enchantments had been woven in its forging would be proof against the monster they were hunting, a creature of the netherworld, neither alive nor dead.

The ruined inner walls of the gatehouse reared above Leofric, the ramparts empty and dusty, and the merlons broken and saw-toothed. The gateway before him sagged on rusted iron hinges, the timbers splintered and yawning like an open mouth. Beyond the gateway, he could see one of the inner keeps, its solid immensity a brooding black shape against the sky.

'Do you see anything, Havelock?' he called to his squire.

'No, sir,' whispered the squire, his voice sounding scared, and Leofric hoped that this venture would not see Havelock meet as grisly a fate as his previous squire, Baudel. Leofric still saw the bloody image of Baudel in his nightmares, his belly ripped open by the forest creatures of Athel Loren.

'Very well,' he said, keeping his voice even. 'Let's keep on.'

Leofric advanced cautiously through the gateway, keeping his head moving from left to right in search of anything out of place. It saddened and angered Leofric to see such a fine castle left to such neglect. In its day, this would have been an almost impregnable fastness, but its glory days had long since passed and its current lord, the lunatic Lord d'Epee was in no fit state to restore it. Where would the local peasants find shelter in times of war? Every lord and noble of Bretonnia had a sacred duty to preserve the natural order of things in his lands, and that could not happen were he to allow the peasants of his lands to be butchered by orcs or beastmen because they had nowhere to run to.

True, Aquitaine was a largely peaceful dukedom – aside from the fractious populace – but that was no excuse for a noble lord to let his castle fall into disrepair. When Leofric had commanded a castle of his own, back in Quenelles, he had spent a goodly sum from his coffers to ensure the castle remained defensible at all times.

But there was more than simple neglect at the heart of Castle d'Epee's abandonment. The lord and his family dwelled in the outermost gatehouse, fearful of the darkness and the creatures of evil that had taken the inner reaches of their ancestral home, and unwilling to risk their own lives to recover the treasures and heirlooms that lay there.

One such heirloom was the object of Leofric and Havelock's quest, a stuffed stag's head said to be hung within the great hall of the third keep. Privately, Leofric thought it a frivolous use of his knightly skills to retrieve such a folly, but the twitching Lord d'Epee had offered Leofric and Havelock shelter on their journey in search of the Grail, and his code of honour bound him to accede to his host's request for aid.

Beyond the gate, Leofric found himself in a cobbled courtyard with ruined outbuildings leaning against the walls, their roofs collapsed and open to the sky. Rotted straw was strewn across the cobbles and the derelict keep loomed like an enormous black cliff before him. Moonlight pooled in the courtyard and glittered from the silver of his plate armour, but the keep remained resolutely dark and threatening, its casement windows invisible against its darkness and its crumbling towers like spikes of black rock.

Havelock moved to stand beside him, the man's presence reassuring even though his skill with the bow he carried would be negligible in the darkness. His rough peasant clothes were dull and blended with the gloom so that only the light reflecting from his eyes stood out.

'I don't like this place,' said Havelock. 'I can see why they abandoned it.'

'It's a grim place, right enough,' agreed Leofric. 'Someone should come here in force and reclaim it. It's not right that a castle this strong should be left like this.'

Havelock nodded and started to reply, but Leofric raised his hand to silence him as he caught sight of something moving at the base of the keep, a darting shadow that had nothing to do with those cast by the moon and drifting clouds above.

Leofric pointed to where he had seen the movement and set off towards the shadow, hoping to discover some way of entering the keep or a foe he could defeat.

He drew closer to the keep and with every step he took, it seemed to him that he could smell the aroma of roasting meat and hear the sounds of revelry. He turned to Havelock and saw that his squire's senses were similarly intrigued.

'Sounds like a feast,' whispered Havelock.

Leofric nodded and returned his attention to the keep as he saw a soft light emanating from beneath a door of thick wood and banded black iron. He heard a woman's laughter and felt an ache of loss as it summoned unbidden memories of his lost wife, Helene. He reached to his gorget, beneath which he wore the blue, silken scarf she had given him on the tilting fields outside Couronne after he had unhorsed Duke Chilfroy of Artois.

He could not feel the soft material through the metal of his gauntlets, but just knowing it was there was enough to warn him of the falsehood of the woman's laughter. Even as they drew near, a warm and friendly glow built from the windows of the keep, spilling like warm honey into the courtyard. The sound of voices grew louder, laughter and ribald jokes echoing from the walls around them. Though he knew it was but an illusion, his heart ached to go to these revellers and join their carousing, to throw off the shackles of discipline enforced upon him by his quest for the Grail.

Havelock took a step towards the keep, the bowstring going slack as he lowered the weapon. 'My lord… should we ask the people within whether they've seen the stag's head? Maybe we can stop for a while, rest and get some food?'

Leofric shook his head and reached out to pull Havelock back. He felt resistance and pulled harder, stopping the squire in his tracks. The man twisted in his grip, sudden hostility flashing in his eyes.

'Let me go!' hissed Havelock. 'I want some food and wine!'

Leofric's palm snapped out and cracked against Havelock's jaw. The squire staggered and Leofric said, 'Use your head, man. There *is* no food or wine, it is all an illusion to ensnare us.'

Havelock spat blood and shook his head in contrition as he saw that Leofric spoke the truth. He pulled his bowstring taut once more. 'Sorry, my lord.'

'Remember,' said Leofric. 'Lord d'Epee said the creature would attempt to make us lower our guard by promising us a warm welcome and attempting to confuse our senses with friendly images. We must not let that happen.'

'No, my lord,' said Havelock.

Satisfied his squire understood the threat before them, Leofric once again advanced on the door. Light streamed from the windows and at the threshold, but it was a dead light now, bereft of warmth or sustenance. He could feel it calling to him, bidding him enter with promises of comfort and an easement of burdens, but knowing it for the lie it was, the illusory light had no power over him.

He reached out to grip the black ring that opened the door, and was not surprised when it turned easily beneath his hand. Cold, glittering light enveloped him as the door swung open with a grinding squeal of rusted hinges and he felt its attraction grow in power as he saw what lay within the keep.

Where he had expected emptiness and desolation, instead there was life and people. The great hall stretched out before him, its tables groaning with wild meats and fruit of all descriptions. Earthenware jugs overflowed with wine and a colourful jester capered madly in the centre of the chamber, juggling squawking chickens. Children played 'smell the gauntlet', a game banned in Bretonnia after it had incited a peasant revolt, and a laughing nobleman clapped enthusiastically to a badly played lute. Above the nobleman, Leofric saw a stuffed stag's head, its antlers drooping and sad, and shook his head at the idea of risking his and Havelock's life for such a tawdry prize.

Leofric took a step inside, wary at the sight of so many apparitions and forced himself to remember that they were not real. Lord d'Epee had only mentioned one creature, calling it a Dereliche, a spectral horror that sucked the very life from a person with its deathly touch. He had said nothing about a host of creatures…

The revellers appeared to ignore him, but having attended the court of the king and been on the receiving end of courtly snobbery, Leofric recognised their studied disinterest as false. Whoever or whatever these ghostly people were, they *knew* he was there.

'Lord d'Epee didn't say nothing about a party,' whispered Havelock.

'No,' said Leofric grimly, 'he didn't.'

Each of the revellers glimmered with a sheen of silken frost and Leofric approached the nearest, a man dressed in the garb of a minor noble, his clothes bright and well cut, though of a fashion even Leofric knew had passed out of favour many hundreds of years ago.

Leofric slowly extended his sword arm towards the apparition, the blade white in the reflected light of the hall. The tip of the sword passed into the outline of the man, and it had penetrated barely a fingerbreadth when the man hissed and leapt away, the guise of humanity falling from his features in a heartbeat.

Instantly, the gaudy banquet vanished and Leofric was plunged into utter darkness. A low moaning soughed on the cold, dry air and he felt the hairs on the back of his neck rise at the sound. He heard Havelock cry out in fear and spun around, trying to pinpoint the sound of the moaning voice.

'Havelock!' commanded Leofric. 'Where are you?'

'Right here, my lord!' shouted Havelock, though Leofric could see nothing in the blackness.

'Find a wall and get to the door, I don't want to hit you by mistake!'

'Yes, my lord,' replied Havelock.

Leofric blinked and rubbed a hand across his eyes as he attempted to penetrate the gloom. He turned quickly on the spot, keeping his sword extended before him until his eyes could adjust. He heard a hissing behind him and spun to face it, but another sound came to him from behind and he realised he was surrounded by a host of creatures that were as insubstantial as mist.

He cried out as something cold brushed against the skin of his back, flinching in sudden pain and surprise. His flesh burned as though with frostbite, but he could tell his armour was still whole. Whatever powers these creatures possessed was such that his armour was useless and he cursed d'Epee for sending them on this fool's errand. He remembered the same deathly chill touch when shadow creatures of the dark fay had attacked him when he had journeyed to the lair of the dragon, Beithir-Seun. Cu-Sith had saved him then, but the Wardancer was long dead and Leofric was on his own now.

Another cold touch stole into his flesh from the side, but he was ready this time and swept his sword down, the white blade cutting through something wispy and soft like wadded cheesecloth. A sparkle of light fell to the stone floor like a rain of diamond dust and Leofric heard a shriek torn from what sounded like a dozen throats simultaneously.

'So you can be hurt?' taunted Leofric as he heard a chorus of hisses drawing nearer.

'Yes, we can,' said a sibilant voice that came from many places, 'but your flesh is ours, your spirit is ours...'

He could see the faint outlines of perhaps a dozen figures drifting towards him, their outlines blurred and indistinct, but that was enough. Ever since his time in Athel Loren, his sight had been keener and he had been sensitive to the proximity of magic in the air. He narrowed his eyes, letting his awareness of the approaching creatures steal over him like a warm blanket.

'Come on... ' he whispered as he saw they all moved in perfect concert, as though they were but fragments of a whole... as though orchestrated by a single will.

He could see that the apparitions were unaware that he could see them in the darkness and continued turning blindly to maintain the deception.

You're not the only ones who have the power of illusion, he thought.

When the nearest creature was an arm's length from him, Leofric lunged, spearing it with the point of his sword. The multitude cried out in pain as it vanished in a puff of light, but by then Leofric was amongst them, his sword slashing left and right and destroying each creature it cut into. Shrieks and wails of pain filled the hall and Leofric saw the apparitions whip through the air like smoke in a storm.

'Now, Havelock!' shouted Leofric.

Once again the rusted hinges squealed as Havelock threw open the door to the banqueting hall and bright moonlight streamed inside. Further illuminated by the light of the night sky, the apparition was bathed in white, its spectral outline limned in glittering light as its ghostly avatars returned to it and became part of the whole once more.

So this was a Dereliche, thought Leofric. Its features were twisted in hatred as its form grew in power, though Leofric knew he must have hurt it with those he had destroyed.

With a shriek of rage, the Dereliche hurled itself forward, its arms extended and ending in ghostly talons that reached for his heart. Its speed was astonishing, but Leofric had been expecting its attack and twisted out of its reach and swung his sword for its head.

His blade cut into the monster and he felt its rage as the Blade of Midnight burned its ethereal body with its keen edge. The Dereliche spun behind him and its claws raked deep into his side as it passed, and Leofric cried out in pain as he felt his strength flow from his body and into his foe.

'Your strength fills me, knight!' laughed the Dereliche. 'I will feast well on you.'

Manic laughter followed him as Leofric spun to face his foe once more, launching a deadly riposte to its body. The sword sailed past the creature and it darted in again with a predatory hiss of hunger.

The Blade of Midnight snapped up and Leofric shouted, 'Lady guide my arm!' as he leapt towards the Dereliche and felt the blade pierce its unnatural flesh.

It shrieked in agony as the magical blade of the elves dealt it a dreadful wound, the powerful enchantments breaking its hold on the mortal realm. Even as it wailed and spat in its dissolution, Leofric spun his sword until it was held, point down, before him. He dropped to one knee and whispered his thanks to the Lady of the Lake.

'She will not save you!' hissed the Dereliche. 'You are already marked for death, Leofric Carrard.'

Leofric's eyes snapped open and he saw the fading form of the Dereliche as it sank slowly to the stone floor of the chamber, its form wavering and fading with each passing second.

'How do you know my name?' demanded Leofric.

The Dereliche gave a gurgling chuckle and said, 'The Red Duke will rise again in Châlons and his blade will drink deeply of your blood. The realm of the dead already knows your name.'

Leofric rose to his feet and advanced on the creature, but before he could demand further explanation, its form faded completely until only a dimming shower of sparkling light remained.

With the Dereliche's destruction, the last vestiges of the hall's illusion fell away and Leofric saw it for the faded, forgotten place it truly was. Neglect and despair hung over everything and the wan moonlight only served to highlight the melancholic air of decay.

He looked up and saw that the stag's head was still there, looking even more pathetic than it had before, its fur fallen out in clumps and one antler broken. Havelock moved to stand beside him and followed his gaze.

'Looks like he's seen better days, my lord.'

'Haven't we all?' said Leofric, sheathing his sword and turning from the stag, his thoughts dark and filled with foreboding.

A light rain fell and Leofric shivered beneath his armour as he rode along the muddy, rutted road north-east from Castle d'Epee towards the squat brutal mountains of the Massif Orcal. He rode a magnificent elven steed, its flanks as white as virgin snow on a mountain top and a mane like fiery copper. Aeneor had consented to be his steed after a great battle in the heart of Athel Loren when his original rider had been killed and Leofric had ridden him into battle to defend the elves of Coeth-Mara.

Bretonnian steeds were widely regarded as the finest mounts of the Old World, but even the mightiest horse in the king's stables would be humbled by Aeneor's beauty and power.

Havelock rode behind him on a considerably less imposing beast, grumbling and miserable as the rain soaked through his oiled leather cape.

Castle d'Epee was many miles behind them and Leofric was glad to see the back of it. Upon presenting the mouldering stag's head to Lord d'Epee, the man had hurled it to the floor and screamed at the pair of them that they had brought him the wrong one.

Manners forbade Leofric from responding, but even had the vow he had sworn upon embarking on his quest for the Grail not forbidden him to rest more than a single night in any one place, he would not have remained for fear of his temper causing an unforgivable breach of etiquette.

He and Havelock had ridden from the castle as soon as the sun rose over the World's Edge Mountains, a distant smudge of dark rock on the eastern horizon. Castle d'Epee was now several days behind them, and they had made good time until the rains from the coast had closed in, turning Bretonnian roads to thick, cloying mud. The grim weather suited Leofric's mood perfectly and he had brooded long over the last words the Dereliche had said to him.

Normally he would give no credence to the utterances of a creature of evil, but it had known his name and spoken of the Red Duke, and such things were not to be taken lightly.

As they had made camp on their first night away from Castle d'Epee,

Havelock had started a fire and begun polishing Leofric's armour. Leofric himself had found a nearby spring and offered prayers of thanks to the Lady for protecting them from the foul Dereliche.

The sky above was dark by the time Havelock had prepared a thin stew for him and as he sat on his riding blanket, Havelock said, 'This Red Duke, who's he then? Someone you crossed before?'

Leofric shook his head, blowing to cool the hot stew. 'No, Havelock, he's not. He's something far worse. I'm surprised you haven't heard of him. He was quite the terror of Aquitaine in his day.'

'Maybe he was, but I'm from Gisoreux and we got enough troubles enough of our own to bother with them quarrelsome types from Aquitaine.'

'And you've never heard the Lay of the Red Duke?' asked Leofric.

Havelock shook his head. 'Can't says I have, my lord. Me and mine, well, we worked the land, didn't we? All we had was a red horse and a black pig. Didn't have no time for fancy stories like that.'

Leofric hadn't known exactly what the reference to coloured farm animals meant, but assumed it was some Gisoren expression for poverty. Havelock was of peasant stock and Leofric had to remind himself that his squire was unlikely to have been exposed to any culture or heard any courtly tales.

'So who was he then, my lord?' asked Havelock.

'The Red Duke was a monster,' began Leofric, wishing he remembered more of the flowery passages of the lay. 'One of the blood drinkers. A vampire knight. No one really remembers where he came from, but he terrorised this land over a thousand years ago, murdering hundreds of innocents and slaying any who dared to stand against him, then raising them up to join his army of the dead.'

'Sounds like a right bad sort,' said Havelock, making the sign of the horns to ward off any evil spirits that might be attracted by such tales of dark creatures of the night.

'He was,' agreed Leofric. 'His blood-drenched debaucheries are said to have shamed the Dark Gods themselves.'

'So what became of him?'

'Like all creatures of evil, he was eventually defeated,' said Leofric. 'The noble knights of the day fought the great battle of Ceren Field and the king himself skewered the fiend on the end of his lance.'

'So he's dead and gone then?' asked Havelock, scooping up the last of his stew with his fingers and wiping his mouth with his sleeve.

'So they say,' said Leofric, grimacing at Havelock's lack of manners. Uncouth and peasant born he most certainly was, but he was a fine squire and was the only other human that Aeneor allowed near him. 'It's said that he rose again nearly five hundred years later, but he was defeated once again, though the Duke of Aquitaine was killed in the battle on the edge of the Forest of Châlons. Accounts of the battle differ, but some say that the Red Duke's spirit escaped the battle and fled into the depths of the forest, where it remains to this day.'

'And that ghost thing you killed says he's going to rise again? That don't sound good.'

'No, it does not, and as a knight sworn to the quest it is my duty to see if there is any truth to what it said. And if evil is rising there, I must defeat it.'

Fine words, remembered Leofric as a droplet of rain fell into his eye and roused him from the memory of his recounting of the Red Duke's infamy. The Forest of Châlons was still some days distant and there were more uncomfortable days ahead. Leofric had no clear idea of where to seek the Red Duke, but the Barrows of Cuileux lay crumbling and forgotten in the south-western skirts of the mountain forests, and such a place was as good as any to seek the undead.

A low mist hugged the ground as the rain eased off and Leofric caught a scent of woodsmoke carried on the evening's breeze. The landscape around him was undulating, but mostly flat and devoid of landmarks to help him find his bearings.

'Havelock?' said Leofric, turning in the saddle. 'Do you know where we are? What villages are around here?'

His squire stood high in the saddle, cupping his hand over his eyes as he surveyed the bleak landscape around him.

'I'm not rightly sure, my lord,' apologised Havelock. 'I don't know this part of the country, but I think this road, more or less, follows the border between Aquitaine and Quenelles.'

Leofric felt homesick as he looked eastwards towards the realm of his birth, the lands that had once been his, and the heartbreaking memory of his family.

'So that means there's maybe a few villages a few miles north of here, round the edges of the Forest of Châlons. Maybe even…' said Havelock, his voice trailing off.

Leofric heard the faint longing in Havelock's voice and said, 'Maybe even what?'

'Nothing, my lord,' said his squire, staring at the mud.

'Don't lie to me, Havelock,' warned Leofric.

'It's nothing, my lord, just something the servants at Castle d'Epee were talking about.'

'And what might that be?' demanded Leofric, tiring of Havelock's reticence. 'Out with it, man!'

'A village they talked about,' said Havelock. 'A place they called Derrevin Libre.'

The name rang a bell for Leofric, but he couldn't place it until he remembered the long, rambling discourses of Lord d'Epee. The man had mentioned something about the place, but his ravings had been too nonsensical to take much of it in. Clearly the servants had been talking about it too, and probably with more sense.

'Well, what did they say about it?'

Havelock was clearly uncomfortable talking about what he'd heard and Leofric supposed some peasant code of honour kept his tongue in check.

He wheeled Aeneor to face his squire and said, 'Tell me.'

They made camp for the evening and after finishing a meal of black bread and cheese, Havelock told him what he'd heard in the sculleries of Castle d'Epee. Derrevin Libre, it turned out, was indeed a village on the southern edge of the Forest of Châlons, but it was a most remarkable village. Some six months ago, Havelock said, the peasants there had risen up in revolt and overthrown their rightful lord and master before killing him. Once over his initial hesitation, his squire had relished the chance to tell the tale of the peasant revolt, embellishing his tale with lurid details of how truly repellent the local lord had been, even going so far as to link the man with the dark gods of the north.

Leofric sighed as Havelock continued with yet more details of the lord's vileness in an attempt to justify the overthrow of the natural order of things.

'So why didn't the local lords just ride in and crush the rebellion?' interrupted Leofric. 'Why aren't those peasants strung up by their necks from the top of the Lace Tower?'

'They would have been, you see,' said Havelock, wagging his finger at Leofric, before a stern glance warned him not to continue doing so. 'Aye, they would have been, except that the local lords was in the middle of not one, not two, but three different feuds! You know how these Aquitaine folks are, they don't have to fight for their land so they fight each other.'

That at least was true, reflected Leofric. The nobles of Aquitaine were ever in the grip of some internal feud or war, and no sooner would one die down than a new one would flare up.

'So the peasants were just left to rule the village themselves?' said Leofric, horrified at the idea of such a thing. Were word of this to travel beyond the borders of Aquitaine, who knew what might happen if peasants were allowed to get the idea that their noble masters could be overthrown at will...

'More or less,' agreed Havelock. 'Though Lord d'Epee's scullion told me that they'd managed to attract the attention of a few bands of Herrimaults to help them fight to keep their freedom.'

'Herrimaults?' snapped Leofric, spitting into the fire. 'I might have known. Criminals and revolutionaries, the lot of them.'

'But sir,' said Havelock. 'They's good men, the Herrimaults. They only rob from them's as can afford the loss and give what they take to feed the poor. They's good men.'

Leofric could see the admiration in Havelock's eyes, and shook his head.

'No, Havelock, they are nothing more than bandits who no doubt perpetuate the stories of their code of honour and reputation as underdog heroes to gullible people like you in order to secure their help in keeping them beyond the reach of the law. Honestly, Havelock, if a dwarf asked you to invest in the Loren Logging Company you'd say yes.'

The smile fell from Havelock's face at Leofric's dressing down, but Leofric could still see the spark of defiance there, fuelled by the romantic notion of peasants casting off their noble masters, and knew he had to crush it.

'Very well, Havelock,' said Leofric. 'I have no issue with people wishing a better life for themselves, but there is a natural order to things that cannot be upset or the land will descend into anarchy. If every peasant wanted to rule his village who would till the fields, gather the crops or rear the animals? Nobles rule and peasants work the land, *that's* the proper order of things.'

'But, that's not–'

Leofric held up his hand to stifle Havelock's protests and said, 'Let me tell you of the last time a peasant tried to rise above his station. He was a young man of Gisoreux, and though you say you never had time for fancy stories, I think you'll know it.'

'You're talking about Huebald, my lord?' said Havelock.

'I am indeed. Yes, he was a brave and handsome young man who saved the Duke of Gisoreux's bride from the terrible beasts of the forest, but the thanks of the fair Lady Ariadne should have been enough for him. Instead he used his friendship with the lady to have her go begging to her husband to dub him a knight of the realm. A peasant becoming a knight, I mean whoever heard of such a thing?'

'I don't think that's quite what happened,' said Havelock, clearly hesitant about contradicting a questing knight.

'Of course it is,' said Leofric, 'This Huebald, despite the armour, weapons and squire he was gifted with by the duke, was still a peasant at heart and his true nature was what was to undo him when he sought to move in higher circles. With the noble knights of Gisoreux, he rode into battle against a horde of beasts and was slain as he fled the field of battle.'

'My lord, with respect, I do know this story, and if I might be so bold as to say so, I think you might have heard a different version from mine.'

'Oh?' said Leofric. 'And what happens in your version?'

'The way I heard it,' said Havelock, 'was that Huebald was shot in the back by his squire as he charged the monsters.'

'Shot by his squire?' exclaimed Leofric. 'Why in the world would a squire shoot his knight?'

'Rumour has it the nobles paid him to do it,' shrugged Havelock. 'Gave him a gold coin, more wealth than anyone like him would see in five lifetimes, to do it. The nobles didn't want some uppity peasant thinking he could be as good as them and they put him back down in the mud with the rest of us.'

'I had not heard that version of the story,' said Leofric.

'Well you wouldn't have, would you, my lord,' said Havelock, absently stirring the embers of the fire. 'You nobles hear your version 'cause it puts us peasants in our place, and we hear our version and it gives us something to hope for. Something better than grubbing in the mud and shit, which is what we normally do.'

'So which version do you think is true?' asked Leofric.

Havelock shrugged, 'Honestly? I don't know, probably somewhere in the middle, but that doesn't matter, does it? All that matters is we each have our own version that keeps us happy I suppose.'

Leofric said nothing, staring at Havelock with a little more respect than he had done before. When Havelock had come to him and begged to be his squire, Leofric had initially refused, for a questing knight traditionally travelled alone, but something in Havelock's demeanour had changed his mind. Perhaps it was his newly acquired sense for things yet to pass that had made him change his mind, a disquieting gift, he presumed, of his time spent beneath the boughs of Athel Loren. Whatever the reason, he had allowed Havelock to accompany him and, thus far, had no cause to regret the decision.

'Maybe you're right, Havelock,' said Leofric. 'I suppose each strata of society perceives past events through its own filters and hears what it wants or needs to.'

His squire looked blankly at him and Leofric cursed for expressing himself in ways beyond the ken of a peasant. He smiled and said, 'I'm agreeing with you.'

Havelock smiled back and said. 'Oh. Good.'

'Don't get used to it,' said Leofric and stretched, looking up into the darkness of the night sky. The Forest of Châlons was still some days off and as he watched a shooting star streak across the heavens, he wondered whether it was a good omen or not.

The Forest of Châlons stretched out before Leofric in a wide swathe of emerald green that lay in the shadow of the rearing crags of the Massif Orcal. The outer trees were stripped of their leaves on their lower reaches by a technique Havelock informed him was known as pollarding, and the dawn light didn't make the forest look any more appealing than it had when they had arrived last night.

Dawn was only an hour old and there was no point in wasting the light, so Leofric pressed his heels to Aeneor's flanks. He disdained the use of spurs, for to use such things on an animal as wondrous as an elven steed would be grossly insulting to it.

'Come on,' said Leofric, as Havelock's horse displayed more reluctance to approach the forest before them. 'We have to make as much progress as possible before night falls.'

'I know, my lord, but there's not a man alive who wouldn't be a bit wary of entering a place like this. We're heading towards barrows, ain't we? A man oughtn't to mess with the resting places of the dead.'

'That might be difficult if we're to hunt down a vampire knight, Havelock,' said Leofric, though he understood his squire's reticence The forests of Bretonnia were notorious havens for orcs, brigands and the mutated beasts of Chaos, their dark depths unknown by men for hundreds of years. Many a brave, if foolhardy, duke had attempted to clear out the deep forests of his lands only to fail miserably and lose many of his knights in the process. The depths of the forests were the domains of evil and none dared walk beneath their tangled branches or follow their forgotten pathways without good reason.

Leofric was no stranger to mysterious forests, having spent a span of time with the asrai of Athel Loren, but even he had to admit that the darkness within the Forest of Châlons was unnerving, as though the forest itself looked back at him with hungry eyes.

He shook off the sensation and guided Aeneor between the tall, thin trees on the outer edges of the forest. The undergrowth was thin and wiry, the forest floor hard packed and well trodden, as though many people had come this way recently, and Leofric fancied he could see hoof prints in the soil.

They rode for several hours before stopping for some food and water, though Leofric had quite lost track of time in the gloomy half-light of the forest. Havelock walked the horses before feeding them grain that had cost Leofric more than most peasants would see in a month.

'I don't like this place,' said Havelock, as he always did. 'Feels like someone's watching me all the time.'

Leofric looked up from the blue scarf wrapped around the hilt of his sword and cast his eyes around the clearing they had stopped in. The trees in this part of the forest were larger than those at the fringes, older and gnarled with age. They grew thicker here too, blocking the light and wreathing the forest in a perpetual twilight that blurred the passage of time and hung a pall of wretchedness upon the soul.

But Havelock was right. As much as Leofric tried to dismiss his concerns as that of a superstitious peasant, he knew enough to know that in places like this, someone – or some*thing* – might very well be watching them. Since they had left the sunlight behind them at the edge of the forest, his warrior's instinct had been screaming at him that they were not alone in this dark place.

'I don't like it much, either, Havelock,' agreed Leofric, 'but for some reason, creatures of evil never make their lairs in beautiful groves or in the middle of golden corn fields. It's always a haunted forest or deserted castle atop a forbidding crag of black rock.'

Havelock laughed, 'Yes, not very original are they?'

'No, but there's a certain evil tradition to uphold I suppose,' said Leofric, rising from the log he sat upon to climb onto the back of his horse once more.

The barrows were at least another day's ride away and Leofric had no wish to stay within the forest any longer than was absolutely necessary.

For the rest of the day and much of the next, Leofric and Havelock rode deeper into the Forest of Châlons, their passage growing slower with each mile as though the trees themselves sought to impede their progress. The sensation of being watched remained with them the whole way and Havelock's nervousness was not helped when they came upon the first of the barrows.

The burial mound had long since been ransacked, its stone door lying splintered and mossy beside its overgrown entrance. Mouldering bones lay scattered around, not even the animals of the forest wishing to gnaw on the dead of this place. A broken sword blade of corroded bronze lay wedged in the dark earth and Leofric guessed that this tomb had been open to the elements for hundreds of years.

They passed on, lest some wild beast had made its lair within the barrow, but the forlorn sight of the plundered barrow depressed Leofric. What hope was there for an honourable warrior if his grave was certain to be robbed by greedy delvers? A warrior should be allowed his rest when he finally made the journey through Morr's gates, not disturbed by thieves seeking gold or treasures of ancient magic.

He and Havelock said little as they passed onwards, seeing more and more of the gloomy barrows the further they travelled. Bleached bones, grinning skulls and rusted weaponry littered the forest floor and though they heard the sounds of animals and beasts through the trees, they saw nothing of the forest's fauna.

As dusk approached on the second day of their travels, Leofric felt a subtle shift in the forest around them, as though the very air and landscape had suddenly become less hostile to their presence. He could see patches of purpling sky above him and the scent of honeysuckle came to him, where before he had smelled only death and desolation.

He raised his hand to halt their progress as he saw a gleam of low sunlight catching on something ahead. From here he could not yet see what had reflected the light, but its pale gleam was like a beacon through the darkness of the tree canopy.

'There's something ahead,' said Leofric, his hand sliding towards the hilt of his sword.

Havelock did not reply, his mood too gloomy after the monotonous ride through the forest, though he raised his head to look. As he caught sight of the reflected light, Leofric saw his spirits rise, as though the sight of something bright was enough to rouse him from the melancholy the darkness of the forest had laid upon him.

'What do you think it is?' he asked.

'I don't know,' replied Leofric. 'This deep in the forest, it could be anything.'

He eased Aeneor forward, the undergrowth and trees growing thinner and more scattered the closer they came. Yet more bones and ancient shards of rusted armour lay strewn around, too many to simply be the result of despicable grave robbers, though Leofric saw that these were no ordinary bones or weapons.

'Was there a battle fought here?' asked Havelock.

Leofric had been wondering the same thing, though if there had been a battle, it had not been fought by men, for the fleshless cadavers and the accoutrements of war that lay here were those of elves and orcs. Graceful, leaf-shaped swords and snapped bowstaves lay strewn all about, and long kite-shields were splintered by monstrously toothed cleavers that would take two strong men to lift.

Narrow elven skulls of porcelain white mingled with thickly ridged and fanged skulls of orcs and it was clear that no quarter had been asked or given in whatever battle had been fought here.

And this was no ordinary battlefield either, saw Leofric as they emerged into a wide, overgrown space of undulating barrows and ruined structures. The remains of a tall tower stood upon a rugged spur of silver rock, its once noble battlements cast down and forgotten. Fashioned from a stone of pale blue, it was clear that no human hand had been part of its construction, for its curves and smooth facing was beyond the skill of even the most gifted stonemasons.

'It's beautiful…' breathed Havelock, his gaze sweeping around the cluster of overgrown buildings.

'These are elven,' said Leofric, riding into the centre of what must once have been an outpost of the asrai in the Forest of Châlons, forgotten and abandoned hundreds of years ago or more. Weeds and grass grew up through the remains of stone roads and each of the fine buildings that once gathered around the foot of the tower had been smashed and burned in the fighting. The setting sun threw a golden light over the scene and Leofric thought it almost unbearably sad to see such beauty destroyed.

'Do you think your Red Duke is here?' asked Havelock nervously and Leofric shook himself from his contemplation of the ruined elven outpost.

'Perhaps,' he said. 'We should explore this place and see what we can find.'

'Yes, my lord,' said Havelock, looking into the dusky sky, 'but shouldn't we do that with the sun at our backs? Don't seem like sense to go delving into a place like this in darkness.'

Leofric nodded, wheeling his horse to face his squire. 'Yes, you're right.

We'll make camp a few miles distant and return at first light.'

He saw the relief on his squire's face and chuckled, 'I may be a knight sworn to destroy evil wherever I find it, Havelock, but I'm not going to go charging off into a ruined tower as night falls looking for the undead. I learned my lessons as a Knight Errant.'

The smile fell from his face as he heard a dry crack, like that of a snapping branch. His sword flashed into his hand and Leofric was amazed to see a cold fire slithering along the length of the blade. The liquid flames gave off no heat, and Leofric could feel the powerful magic surging within the enchanted blade.

'What's happening?' cried Havelock, as Leofric heard more dusty cracks and the scrape of metal on metal. He spun his mount to identify the source of the noises, seeing that the sun was now almost vanished beneath the western treetops.

Before Leofric could answer, the source of the noises was revealed as a host of shambling warriors emerged from the collapsed and greenery-draped buildings. Their skeletal forms marched with a horrid animation, for each of the warriors was a dead thing, a revenant clad in the armour of forgotten times and bearing a rusted sword or spear. They rose from the undergrowth with the powdery crack of bone and their empty eye sockets were pools of darkness that burned with ancient malice.

'The living dead!' shouted Leofric, his revulsion and fury at these abominations rising in his gorge like a sickness. Havelock's mount reared in terror, its ears pressed flat against its skull. His squire had drawn his bow and, without a firm grip on the reins, he tumbled from the saddle as the horse bolted from the clearing. Leofric cursed and angled Aeneor towards the fallen Havelock as more of the skeletal warriors picked themselves up from the ground or emerged from the ruined structures.

He held out his hand and Havelock took hold of his forearm, swinging up onto Aeneor's back as Leofric caught sight of two figures emerge from the tower that stood above them. The first was a warrior in gold and silver armour, and where there was a mindless malevolence to the warriors that rose around them, Leofric saw a black will and dark purpose at the heart of this creature. Though the flesh had long since rotted from its bones, it was clear that it had once been a mighty warrior, its thin skull and gleaming hauberk marking it out as one of the asrai. The creature bore two ancient longswords and a high helm of tarnished silver reflected the last dying rays of the sun.

The second was a hunched man robed in black who bore a long, skull-topped staff and whose face was gaunt to the point of emaciation. Leofric saw the skeins of powerful magic playing over his pallid flesh.

'Let's go, my lord!' begged Havelock, his primal terror of the undead making his voice shrill as the skeletal warriors closed the noose of bone around them.

Leofric dug his heels into Aeneor's flanks, knowing that speed was more important than manners now. The horse leapt forwards, smashing the nearest of the dead warriors to the ground. Leofric's white blade clove the skull of another and he cut left and right as the armoured skeletons pressed in around them.

The fire of his blade surged with every blow and Leofric felt the hatred of the weapon as a potent force that guided his arm and struck the head from his every opponent with a deadly grace. Clawed hands tore at Aeneor and the horse lashed out with his back legs, its hoofs caving in brittle ribcages and shattering rusted shields.

Havelock loosed arrows from the back of the horse, though most of his shots flew wide of the mark. Leofric chopped with brutal efficiency at the grimly silent horde of undead, battling to get enough space to fight with all the skill he possessed.

But the long dead warriors were too numerous and even Aeneor's strength was insufficient to forge them a path.

'Lady protect us!' shouted Leofric, smashing his sword through a skeleton warrior's chest and dropping it to the ground as another slashed a spear across Aeneor's chest. The steed screamed foully, rearing up and almost toppling them from its back. The spear was knocked from the dead warrior's grip and Aeneor's hooves crushed his attacker as they came back down to earth.

Leofric cried out as he saw the blood spray from the wound and kicked the skull from another warrior's shoulders as he saw that they were pulling back, forming an unbreakable ring of blades and bone around them. He heard Aeneor's breath heave and saw blood-flecked foam gather at the corner of his mouth.

'What are they doing?' asked Havelock, his survival instincts overcoming his fear for the moment.

'They are waiting for that,' said Leofric, as he saw the armoured warrior that had emerged from the ruined tower striding towards him with grim purpose and murderous intent.

Clearly this was one of the champions of the undead, an ancient warrior bound to the mortal plane by evil magic. It would not attack mindlessly, but with malice and all the skill it had possessed in life. Closer, Leofric could see the skill wrought in every link of its armour and the fine workmanship of its weapons. An obsidian charm hung around the champion's neck, gleaming and polished to a mirror finish.

Leofric risked a glance towards the tower, seeing the robed figure extend his hand towards the silent horde, now understanding that he was surely a practitioner of the dark arts of necromancy. The will of this necromancer was what held the dead warriors at bay while his champion took the glory of the kill. Did such a creature even understand the concept of glory or honour?

The armoured champion stopped and spun his swords in an elaborate pattern of swirling blades that Leofric recognised as elven. He had seen the Hound of Winter perform similarly intricate blade weaving and fervently hoped that this warrior was not as skilled as the venerable champion of Lord Aldaeld had been.

'You will fight me,' said the creature, its voice dusty and lifeless. 'And you will die.'

Leofric did not deign to reply, he had no wish to trade words with this creature of darkness. A dark pall of fear sought to envelop him at the unnatural horror of this dead warrior, but he fought against it, raising his sword as a talisman against such weakness.

The undead champion raised its swords and dropped into a fighting crouch. 'You *will* fight me. The Red Duke will have need of warriors like you and I when he rises.'

'The Red Duke...' said Leofric, suddenly understanding. 'He has not risen.'

'No,' agreed the champion, 'he bides his time, but you have been brought here to die like many before you to swell the ranks of his army for when that day comes.'

Leofric cursed his impetuous decision to ride towards Châlons from Castle d'Epee in such haste. How many other knights had fallen into this trap and been slain only to rise again as one of the living dead? For all his smug words to Havelock earlier, he knew that he was not as far from his days as a Knight Errant as he had thought.

Further words were useless and he gave a cry of rage as he charged towards the undead champion. His sword speared towards its chest, but a black-bladed sword intercepted the blow and the champion slashed high towards Leofric's neck. The edge clanged on the metal gorget of Leofric's armour, but with the force of the blow he almost fell. He swayed in the saddle as Aeneor turned nimbly on the spot as the champion came at them again.

With Havelock behind him, Leofric was nowhere near as mobile as he would normally be, but he could not simply push him from the horse. Twin longswords stabbed for him, but the Blade of Midnight moved like a snake, blocking each blow and sending blistering ripostes towards the champion's head.

The dark warrior circled Leofric and he thought he could sense its dark amusement at their plight. He felt his anger rise and quashed it savagely, knowing that such anger would lead him to make a fatal error. He felt Aeneor's chest heave with exertion and hoped his faithful mount could bear them away from this evil place.

Once again, he charged towards the warrior, using the mass of his steed to drive his sword home. The Blade of Midnight smashed aside the first of the warrior's longswords and plunged towards his chest. Leofric yelled in triumph, then cried out in pain as a shock of numbing cold flared up his sword arm and his sword slid clear without having caused any harm to the undead warrior.

He circled around, gritting his teeth against the pain and stared, uncomprehending, at his foe. His strike had been a good one, he was certain of it. The monster should even now be cloven in twain upon the ground, yet it stood unharmed before him, the amulet on its chest burning with afterimages of dark fire.

The sun had now dropped behind the horizon and Leofric felt a cold weight settle in his belly as he realised that this warrior was protected from harm by powerful dark magic.

'My lord,' begged Havelock from behind him. 'We must flee. Please, I don't want to die here.'

'No, I will not run from this evil. I will defeat it,' said Leofric with a confidence he did not feel. Before the pall of fear that still sought to crush his courage could take hold, he attacked once more, a cry for aid from the Lady of the Lake bursting from his lips. Once again, Leofric's white blade and the warrior's black swords traded blows. The champion's skill was great, but so too was Leofric's and he bore the enchanted blade of the Hound of Winter.

They fought within the circle of the undead warriors, Leofric finding his attacks thwarted time and time again by the skill of his foe and the unnatural magic that protected it.

When the end came it was sudden, Leofric raising his sword to block a lightning riposte a fraction of a second too late. The black blade glittered with evil runes and Leofric cried out in agony as it smashed through the waist lames of his breastplate. Numbing cold and pain spread from the wound, the hurt increased tenfold by the spiteful runes inscribed onto the champion's blade. Leofric swayed in the saddle as his vision greyed and only Havelock's grip and Aeneor's sure footing kept him from falling.

Aching cold spread from where the champion's blow had landed, blood streaming down the buckled strips of laminated plate that had protected his midriff.

'You have great skill for a mortal,' hissed the undead warrior. 'You will make a fine addition to the Red Duke's army.'

'No...' whispered Leofric, attempting to lift his sword, but his arm was leaden and useless.

'Yes,' promised the champion, its grinning skull face alight with triumph as it drew back its arm to deliver the deathblow. Leofric felt the fear that had threatened to seize him earlier rise in a suffocating wave at the thought of rising to become one of the living dead.

But before the undead warrior could strike Havelock cried, 'Aeneor! Ride! Carry us away!'

The elven steed reared once more, his lashing hooves forcing the champion back, before turning and galloping towards the ring of skeletal warriors who stood sentinel around the duel. Havelock held Leofric tightly as the steed thundered onwards and closed his eyes as he felt the horse surge into the air.

Aeneor smashed through the ranks of the dead with the clang of metal and the snap of bone as he crushed those he landed upon and scattered the others with the power of his charge. Swords and spears stabbed, but none could touch the fast moving steed as it battered its way clear of its rider's enemies.

Then they were clear and Leofric felt a measure of his senses returning as they rode clear of the dark fear that filled the air around the undead.

He raised his head and said, 'We have to go back and fight!'

'With all due respect,' wheezed Havelock, 'don't be a fool! Don't listen to him, Aeneor, keep going!'

Leofric wanted to protest, but his strength was gone. He gripped his sword hilt tightly and looked down at his wound, where blood pumped weakly down his leg. He had suffered worse in his time as a knight, but the real damage had been done – and was *still* being done – by the evil magic worked into the champion's blade.

He heard the mournful howl of wolves echoing from the furthest reaches of the forest and knew that the minions of the Red Duke were not about to let him escape that easily.

'Havelock...' gasped Leofric.

'My lord?' said his squire.

'Get me clear of this place...'

'That's what I'm doing, my lord,' confirmed Havelock as the elven steed thundered through the forest and away from the domain of the undead. 'Though I think Aeneor's doing a better job of it than I am.'

Leofric nodded weakly as the cold spread to his chest and he felt the pain deep in his heart. 'We have to warn the lord of Aquitaine...'

Aeneor galloped onwards.

How long they had ridden for, Leofric could not say, his only memories blurred and pain-filled. Deathly cold filled his limbs and his every movement felt like it would be his last. He was dimly aware of the forest flashing past him and the howling of wolves in the night. The passage of time became meaningless to him as the pain of his wound threatened to overwhelm him.

Waking dreams plagued him in which he saw Helene once more, alive and wrapped in her favourite red dress as she danced for him and held his son, Beren, out before her. He wept to see such visions and though they showed him wondrous memories, he cast them from his thoughts as he knew they were the vanguard of the journey to Morr's embrace.

In moments of lucidity, he tried to converse with Havelock and ask of the health of Aeneor, but each time he tried to speak, he found his words slurred and unintelligible.

An eternity or a heartbeat passed in silent, cold agony and it was with a start Leofric opened his eyes to see that they were no longer beneath the oppressive branches of the forest. Golden fields of corn stretched away for miles in all directions and warm sunlight streamed from the sky.

He smiled as he wondered if this was what it was like to die. He had heard that Morr's realm was cold, but he felt the warmth of the sun on his skin as a sweet nepenthe.

Thin columns of smoke rose from a pleasant looking walled hamlet in the distance and he wondered what fine fellows dwelled within. He realised that he was still riding a horse, feeling the grip of another holding him upright and with that realisation came the pain again.

He groaned, remembering the battle in the forest and the dire warning they had to bring to the knights of Aquitaine.

'Havelock...' he gasped, seeing a handful of hooded peasants walking towards them from the direction of the hamlet.

'I see them,' said Havelock.

Leofric squinted through the bright sunshine and his heart sank as he saw that the men were all carrying longbows fashioned from yew.

And as his consciousness finally slipped away, he saw that every arrowhead was aimed unerringly towards him.

When next Leofric opened his eyes, he saw woven straw bound by twine above him and the animal stench of livestock was thick in his nostrils. He blinked, his eyes gummed by sleep and his mouth felt unbearably dry. His head rested on a pillow of wadded hessian and he saw that a thin blanket covered his body.

He lay still for several moments, piecing together the events of the last few... days?

How long had he lain here?

And where *was* here?

Leofric rolled his head to the side, seeing that he lay in a small room with a floor of hard-packed earth and walls formed from wattle and daub. His armour lay neatly stacked in the corner of the room and the Blade of Midnight stood propped against one wall.

He tried to rise, but a wave of nausea rose and threatened to make him vomit, so he lay back down and marshalled his strength as memories began to return to him. He remembered the fight against the undead warrior and reached below the blanket to where he recalled the monster's diabolical sword had cut him.

He could feel the wound was stitched, and that it was no more than a couple of days old. Of the flight from the undead, he remembered almost nothing, save a frantic ride through the dark groves of the forest towards what he supposed was safety.

'So where in the name of the Lady am I?' he whispered.

From the look of the room, he surmised he was in a peasant village somewhere near the edge of the Forest of Châlons, but which one he had no idea. Perhaps Havelock would know...

Havelock!

What had become of his squire? Leofric was overcome by a sudden horror that Havelock had met the same fate as Baudel, and vowed that never again would he ride into danger with a squire.

Even as the thought formed, a shadow moved at the entrance to the room and the blanket that covered the door and afforded him a little privacy moved aside and Havelock entered, carrying a steaming bowl that smelled delicious.

'Havelock!' cried Leofric. 'You're alive!'

'Well, begging your pardon, my lord, of course I am,' replied Havelock. 'It's you that almost didn't make it out of the forest in one piece.'

Leofric smiled to see his squire alive and well, pushing himself slowly upright. He winced at the numb stiffness in his side, but could already feel that it was a fading hurt. Havelock sat at the end of the cot bed and handed him the bowl, together with a hunk of hard bread. He saw the bowl was filled with a thin soup and dipped the bread in to moisten it before chewing it slowly.

He said nothing for a while, content just to wolf down the soup and bread, feeling stronger already as it reached his stomach. At last he put aside the bowl and said, 'How long have I lain here?'

'Two days,' replied Havelock. 'You were unconscious before I brought you in.'

'I was badly hurt,' said Leofric, again touching the stitches in his side.

'Aye, my lord,' nodded Havelock. 'That you were. I stitched the wound easy enough, but there was something about that wound that I couldn't fix.'

'The undead warrior,' said Leofric. 'He carried a blade of dark magic. I should be dead. Why am I not dead?'

'Always looking for the cloud around every silver lining, eh?' smiled Havelock. 'There's a woman here, knows her herbs and a thing or two about the human body. More than a thing or two in her younger years, if you take my meaning.'

'What?' said Leofric, utterly nonplussed.

Havelock sighed. 'Sometimes I swear trying to get the nobles to understand something simple's like duelling an avalanche.'

'What are you talking about, Havelock?'

'I'm saying that there's a grandmother here with more than a touch of the fay about her,' whispered Havelock conspiratorially. 'Her eyes are different colours and she's as quick on her feet as a Bordeleaux tavern wench.'

'What about her?' asked Leofric. 'What did she do?'

'Well I don't know,' shrugged Havelock. 'You don't go asking about those with the fay upon them, you just accept it and hope they don't turn you into a frog. She dug up some herbs from the edge of the forest and made you some kind of poultice. Rubbed it on your wound and mumbled some mumbo-jumbo I never ever heard before. Fair put the wind up me.'

'Put the wind up you?'

'Aye, my lord,' nodded Havelock, appearing more reluctant to continue. 'Once she'd finished, you was raving for the whole night, shouting about Morr's gate and... well.... how you had to get back to Athel Loren to save her... '

Leofric lay back down on the bed, well able to imagine how his ravings must have appeared to one who knew that his wife was dead.

'But anyway,' continued Havelock. 'Whatever it was she did seems to have worked, eh?'

'So it would appear,' agreed Leofric, sitting upright again as another thought occurred to him. 'Two days? The undead? Is there any sign of them?'

'No,' said Havelock. 'We got away from them. I think Aeneor would have outrun Glorfinial himself.'

'Aeneor!' cried Leofric.

Havelock held up a hand and said, 'He's fine. I took care of him myself. He's a tough old beast that one, the hard muscles of his chest kept the spear from going too deep. He'll have a nasty scar to show off, but he'll live.'

Relieved beyond words, Leofric swung his legs from the bed and said, 'My thanks, Havelock, you have done me proud. I'll not forget this. Nor the kindness of the peasants of... actually, where are we?'

'Ah...' said Havelock. 'Funny you should ask that.'

'Funny?' said Leofric. 'Funny how?'

Havelock was spared from answering by the arrival of another man at the door, his build powerful and his bearing martial. Dressed in the rough clothing of a huntsman, he carried a quiver of arrows over his shoulder and had a long bladed sword partially concealed beneath his hooded cloak. Beneath his peaked and feathered hunter's cap, his face was rakishly handsome and Leofric saw a glint of mischief there that he instantly disliked.

'Who are you?' asked Leofric. 'And where am I?'

The man smiled. 'My name is Carlomax and you are in the Free Peasant Republic of Derrevin Libre.'

Leofric sat on the wall on the edge of the village, his breath coming in shallow gasps as he walked the circumference of the village to regain his strength. He wore his armour, for a knight of Bretonnia had to be able to fight in his armour as though it weighed nothing at all, though he felt very far from such fitness.

The blade of the undead champion had wounded him grievously, and despite the healing power of this village's fay woman, it was going to take time for his strength to fully return. He set off again, feeling stronger with each step and casting an eye around the village of Derrevin Libre.

Two score buildings of a reddish orange wattle and daub comprised the village, though at its centre stood a largely dismantled stone building that must once have belonged to the noble lord of this village. Only the nobles of Bretonnia were permitted to use stone in their dwellings, but such laws obviously held no sway in this place as Leofric watched gangs of peasants chipping away the mortar and ferrying the stone to the ground via a complicated series of block and tackle.

A tall palisade wall of logs with sharpened tops formed a defensive wall around the village and Leofric knew that this was higher and stronger than most villages could hope for. Having climbed to the top of the wall earlier, he had seen a bare swathe of the forest where the logs had come from and knew that the revolting peasants had put their brief time of freedom to good use in preparing for the inevitable counter-attack. Hooded Herrimaults with longbows patrolled the walls and land beyond the village, alert and ready for the attack from the local lords that must surely come soon.

The village was thronged with laughing peasants and Leofric found the effect quite unsettling. Men and women worked in the fields beyond the walls and children played in the earthen streets, chasing hoops of cane or teasing the local dogs. The villages Leofric remembered from Quenelles were a far cry from Derrevin Libre, their peasants surly and hunched with their faces to the soil.

The sun was hot and he could feel his skin reddening, though he had refused Havelock's offer of a hooded Herrimault cloak, seeing it as an acceptance of what had happened here. The few people he encountered in his slow circuit of the village were amiable, if wary of him, as they had good right to be. For Leofric represented exactly what they had rebelled against six months ago.

Leofric still found it hard to believe that a peasant revolt had managed to survive this long, but if there was anywhere it could do so, it was the fractious dukedom of Aquitaine. He did not know the names of the local lords, but knew it was only a matter of time until they came with fire and sword and put an end to this futile dream of freedom. Strangely, the thought of the status quo being restored here did not give him as much comfort as he expected it would. People would die and the ringleader of this revolution would be hanged.

Speaking of the ringleaders, he saw Carlomax, the charismatic Herrimault who appeared to be the self-appointed leader of this revolt walking towards him, a longbow clutched in one hand, while his other hand gripped the hilt of his sword.

'Mind if I walk with you?' asked Carlomax.

'Do I have a choice?' asked Leofric.

'This is Derrevin Libre,' smiled Carlomax. 'Everyone has a choice.'

'Did the local lord have a choice before your little revolution killed him?'

Carlomax's lips pursed and Leofric saw him bite back a retort before his easy composure reasserted itself. 'You are angry with me, yet I have done nothing to you, sir knight.'

'You are a revolutionary, that is enough to make me angry.'

'A revolutionary?' said Carlomax. 'Yes, I suppose I am. But if I am, then I fight for honour and justice, that is the true revolution here.'

'Honour and justice now includes murder does it?' spat Leofric.

Again Carlomax struggled to stay calm, and said, 'If you'll allow me to show you something, I think you might change your mind.'

'Show me what?'

'Come,' said Carlomax, indicating that Leofric should follow him. 'It's easier if you see it first.'

The ice room of the former lord of Derrevin Libre was dug deep into the earth, far below ground level, and as Leofric descended the stairs he relished the drop in temperature after the heat of the day. A compact room of rough-hewn stone blocks, there was of course no ice left, but it was still nevertheless pleasantly cool, though the shelves were empty of meat and vegetables as he might have expected.

In fact the room was empty save for the bloated shape of the corpse concealed beneath a large blanket. Despite the cool air, the stench was appalling and Leofric was forced to cover his nose and mouth to keep it at bay.

'You kept the body?' said Leofric, aghast. 'Why?'

'You'll see,' promised Carlomax. 'Take a look.'

Against his better judgement Leofric approached the covered body, keeping one hand pressed over his mouth as Carlomax took hold of the blanket and pulled it back to reveal the dead body beneath.

Leofric dropped to his knees at the horror that was revealed, his stomach turning in loops as he fought to prevent himself from vomiting. The body was that of a man, but a man so bloated and repellent that Leofric could barely believe such a thing was human. Sagging folds of flab hung slackly from the man's frame, his skin discoloured and ruptured in numerous places, each long gash encrusted with filth and dried pustules. The man had clearly been diseased and he backed away lest some contagion remained in the rotted flesh.

'You need to burn this,' said Leofric. 'It has become rank with corruption.'

'No,' said Carlomax. 'The body has not changed since we killed him.'

Leofric looked back at the repulsive corpse and said, 'Impossible. The body has rotted from within.'

'I swear to you, Leofric, that this is exactly how this… thing was put here. Look at his arms, he was a worshipper of the Dark Gods.'

Leofric was loath to look again at the horrendous sight, but bent once again to the body. His eyes roamed the purulent, flabby arms, at last seeing what Carlomax was referring to. All along the length of the man's arms were a regular series of blisters, each formed in a triangular pattern of three adjoining circles. Each cluster was arranged in the same pattern.

'I have seen this before,' said Leofric.

'You have? Where?'

'I fought alongside the king at the great battle against the northern tribes at the foot of the Ulricsberg. I saw this symbol painted on the banners and carved into the flesh of the warriors who worshipped the Dark God of pestilence and decay.'

Carlomax made the sign of the protective horns as Leofric saw that many of the open wounds on the man's body had more than a hint of mouth to them, some even having twisted vestigial teeth and gums protruding from the grey meat of the body.

'The man was an altered,' said Carlomax. 'He deserved to die.'

Leofric nodded. The mutating power of Chaos had warped the dead man's flesh into this morbidly repulsive form for some unguessable purpose and the horror of it sickened him.

The power of Chaos was a foulness that infected the minds of the weak with promises of easy power and immortality, but it inevitably led to corruption and death, though such a fate never seemed to deter others from believing they could master it.

'I've seen enough,' he said, turning and marching up the stairs. He needed to be out of that foetid darkness and away from the disgusting vision of the mutated corpse. He emerged into the sunlight, taking a deep breath of fresh air and feeling his head clear almost instantly as he moved away from the building.

'You see now why this happened?' asked Carlomax, following Leofric back into the daylight above.

Leofric nodded, but said, 'It won't make any difference though.'

Carlomax shook his head. 'It has to. When people see what happened here and why, justice will prevail.'

'Justice?'

'Yes, justice,' snapped Carlomax. 'That is the code of the Herrimaults, to uphold justice where the law has failed and to reject the dark gods and to fight against them at all times.'

'The Herrimaults truly have a code of honour?'

'We do,' said Carlomax defiantly.

'Tell me of it,' said Leofric.

As the last rays of sunlight faded from the sky, Leofric sat on the edge of the palisade wall looking out over the surrounding lands, his thoughts confused and uncertain. When he had first heard of Derrevin Libre, he had been horrified at the upsetting of the natural order of things and branded the Herrimaults as little better than brigands, but the day spent with Carlomax had disabused him of that notion.

The man's brother had been hung for smiling at a noble's daughter and his mother crippled by a beating for weeping at the execution. Small wonder he had turned to the life of an outlaw.

Carlomax had told him how he had later abducted the noble's daughter, intending to rape and torture her, but had found that he had not the stomach for such vileness, and had released her unharmed.

How much of that story was true, he didn't know for sure, but Carlomax had an integrity to him that Leofric had quickly recognised and despite his initial misgivings, he found he believed the man. The code of the Herrimaults had impressed him, its tenets not unfamiliar to a knight such as he: to protect the innocent, to uphold justice, to be true to your fellows and to fight the powers of Chaos wherever they are found.

Following such a code, Carlomax might himself have been a knight were it not for his low birth. And from what Leofric had seen around Derrevin Libre, he couldn't argue that Carlomax had created a functioning society for its people that was superior to the lot of the majority of Bretonnian peasants.

The night's darkness was absolute and Leofric knew that come the morning he and Havelock would ride to the city of Aquitaine itself to warn the duke of the threat gathering in the north of his lands.

Filled with such gloomy thoughts, Leofric did not hear Havelock approach, his squire appearing absurdly cheerful, though he was not surprised. To another peasant, Derrevin Libre must seem like paradise and Leofric found that he could not find it in himself to disagree.

'You should get some sleep, it's going to be a long day tomorrow and you still haven't got your strength back yet... my lord,' said Havelock, and Leofric couldn't help but notice the tiniest hesitation before he had added 'my lord'.

'I know,' said Leofric.

Havelock nodded, suddenly awkward and Leofric said, 'Do you want to stay here, Havelock? In the village, I mean?'

His squire frowned and shook his head. 'No, my lord. Why would I want to do such a thing?'

Leofric was surprised and said, 'I thought you admired the Herrimaults?'

'I do, my lord,' agreed Havelock. 'But I swore an oath to you and I plan on honouring that. It's nice here, don't get me wrong, but...'

'But what?'

'But it won't last,' whispered Havelock sadly. 'You know it and I know it. When the local lords finally get over whatever feuds are keeping them busy, they'll come in force and burn this place to the ground. Can't have the peasants believing that there might be other ways of life than the one they're born to, eh? Tell me I'm wrong.'

Leofric shook his head. 'No, you're not wrong. I just wish the notions that underpin the knightly code and the Herrimaults' code could be put into practice beyond the conduct of a single knight or outlaw.'

'Well, it's a noble dream, my lord, but we live in the real world, don't we?'

Leofric said, 'That we do, Havelock, that we do. Here, help me up.'

Havelock pulled Leofric to his feet, the pair of them freezing as a chorus of wolf howls echoed through the darkness.

Leofric's gaze was drawn to the edge of the forest as he heard new sounds beyond that of the howling wolves, the tramp of feet and the crack of snapping branches as armed warriors marched through the trees.

'Oh no… ' whispered Leofric as he saw scores of armoured skeletons emerge from the treeline, packs of snapping wolves at their heels.

Standing in the centre of the battle line, dimly illuminated by the flickering glow of the torches set on the palisade walls of Derrevin Libre, was the gold and silver armoured champion of the dead and the hooded necromancer. The champion rode the monstrous carcass of the blackest horse, its eyes afire with the flames of the damned.

'Run, Havelock!' shouted Leofric. 'Get Carlomax! Tell him to get every man who can hold a sword to the walls. We're under attack!'

Within moments, a hundred men were at the wall, some armed with longbows, but most with peasant weapons: axes, spears and scythes. The army of undead had not moved since Leofric's warning, their utter stillness draining the courage of the men at the walls with every passing second.

'Where have they come from?' asked Carlomax, standing beside Leofric with his bow at the ready and a quiver full of arrows.

'From deep in the forest,' said Leofric. 'They are the heralds of the Red Duke.'

'The Red Duke!' hissed Carlomax, his handsome features twisted in the fear that such a name carried for the people of Aquitaine. 'He rises again?'

Leofric nodded. 'I believe he will soon. Havelock and I were riding for the duke's lands bearing warning when we came upon your village.'

'Can we hold them?' asked Carlomax. 'There are quite a lot of them…'

'We'll hold them,' promised Leofric, casting his gaze along the length of the palisade wall. 'By my honour, we will hold them.'

Like a wind driven before a storm, the fear of these dreadful creatures reached outwards, and Leofric could see that each man's heart was icy with the chill of the grave at the very unnaturalness of the risen dead.

Though the men on the walls were clearly brave, Leofric knew that their courage balanced on a knife-edge and that they needed some fire in their bellies if they weren't to flee in terror from the first charge.

Leofric marched along the length of the wall facing the undead, lifting his white bladed sword high so that every man could see its purity in the face of such evil.

'Men of Bretonnia!' he shouted. 'You will hold these walls!'

'Why should we listen to you?' cried a voice in the darkness.

'If you want to live, you will listen to him!' returned Carlomax.

Leofric nodded his thanks and continued. He had thought to appeal to their duty to the king, but had thought the better of it when he saw the number of Herrimault cloaks among the villagers. As much as he had considered them little more than bandits before today, he was savvy enough to know that their skill with a bow would be useful in the coming fight.

'You are right to question me, but I say this not as an order, but as a statement of fact. You *have* to hold these walls, for if you do not, your families will die and your homes will become your graves. At least until fell sorcery brings your spirit back to your dead flesh and you are denied eternal rest.'

He could see the horror of such a thought writ large on every face, knowing that the fear of such a fate would rouse each man to great deeds.

'Your courage and strength will decide if you live or die tonight, so if you fight not for the king or your lord, fight for that. No grand gestures or lordly ambitions will be satisfied by this battle, only survival. I have fought things like this before and I tell you now they *can* be defeated. Cut them down as you would an orc or beast, but be wary of them rising again. Destroy the head if you can or smash the ribcage. Though these things have no hearts that beat as ours do, a mortal blow will still destroy them. Fight hard and may the Lady guide your arms!'

'Derrevin!' shouted Carlomax, seeing that Leofric had finished.

'Libre!' cheered the men of the village in response.

'Nice speech, my lord,' said Havelock, nocking an arrow to his bow, 'but I think his was punchier.'

'Evidently,' agreed Leofric as the chant of 'Libre! Libre! Libre!' echoed through the darkness.

Leofric gripped his sword a little tighter as he saw that the time for speeches and waiting was over as the army of undead began its advance on the village. Marching in ordered squares a general of the Empire would have been proud of, the dead warriors tramped in silence towards the walls, the only sound the clink and scrape of rusted chainmail on bone.

'Steady!' shouted Carlomax, nocking an arrow and pulling his bowstring tight. For a moment Leofric wished he had a bow, but then shook his head at such foolishness... a knight with a bow! He chuckled at the idea and knew he had spent too much time in Derrevin Libre if its revolutionary ideals were starting to put such thoughts in his head.

'Loose!' shouted Carlomax and a flurry of arrows slashed towards the marching warriors.

As Leofric had said, the undead could indeed be brought down, and a dozen skeletons collapsed into jumbled piles of bone as the magic binding their form together was undone. The remainder paid these losses no heed and came on, uncaring of the volleys of shafts that punched through skulls or severed spines.

Though dozens fell with each volley, there were hundreds more and Leofric knew that within moments the enemy would be at the walls. Dark fear spread like a bow wave before the undead and Leofric could see many shafts loosed in haste from shaking hands thud harmlessly into the ground.

'Bretonnia!' he shouted. 'The spirit of Gilles le Breton is in each of you! Do not give in to the fear! Remember that your loved ones depend on your courage!'

Further words were wasted as the undead warriors slammed into the wall and Leofric felt the logs sway as the implacable will of the Necromancer gave the undead strength. Ancient sword blades hacked into the timbers and skeletal hands dug into the gnarled bark as dead warriors hauled themselves towards the parapet.

A leering skull encased in a fluted helmet of bronze appeared before Leofric and he swept his sword through the neck, sending the body tumbling to the earth. No sooner had it vanished than yet more appeared. The Blade of Midnight smote them down, but armoured skeletons clambered over the sharpened logs all along the length of the wall.

The villagers of Derrevin Libre hacked at them with axes and stabbed them from the walls with their spears, but for some the horror of the living dead was too much and they broke and ran from the battle. Havelock sent shaft after shaft into the horde at the bottom of the wall as they chopped at the logs or slithered over the bones of the fallen.

Screams of fear and pain filled the air as ancient blades and clawed hands tore at warm flesh and Leofric hacked his way through the dead to where the fighting was thickest, bellowing cries to the Lady and the King as he smashed the undead from the walls.

Carlomax held a section of wall above the gate, his sword battering skeletons from the walls with every stroke. Leofric could see that the man was reasonably skilled with a sword, and what he lacked in elegance, he made up for in ferocity.

The night rang to the clash of iron on bronze, the battle fought in the flickering glow of torches set on the wall. Leofric heard wailing screams and turned to see the men on the wall to his right shrieking like banshees and clawing at their flesh in agony. Age-withered flesh slid from their muscles and wasted organs blistered as they ruptured and turned to dust.

'No!' shouted Leofric, tasting the rank odour of dark magic on the air. He risked a glance to the hillside where the undead champion and the necromancer watched the battle below. Leaping scads of power swirled around the dread sorcerer.

Even as he returned his gaze to the battle, he saw it was hopeless. Skeletal warriors had footholds along the wall and the men of Derrevin Libre who had fallen were even now climbing to their feet to hurl themselves at their former comrades with monstrous hunger.

'Carlomax! Havelock!' shouted Leofric. 'The sorcerer!'

He had no way of knowing whether or not his words had been heard as he fought his way along the wall, hacking a path through the living dead. He saw Havelock pinned against the inner face of the wall by a skeleton attempting to throttle the life from him, while Carlomax battled a trio of armoured skeletons. Leofric killed the first and kicked the second over the wall as Carlomax despatched the last.

He hacked his sword through the spine of the skeleton attacking Havelock and, together with Carlomax, the three of them formed a fighting wedge above the gate.

'My thanks,' breathed Carlomax. 'I don't think I could have taken them all.'

Leofric nodded and said, 'We can't hold them like this.'

'No,' agreed Carlomax. 'What do you suggest?'

'Something more direct,' said Leofric, pointing to the two dark figures that observed the battle from their vantage point at the treeline. 'I need to get them down here!'

'What?' said Carlomax. 'Are you mad?'

A thunderous crash and crack of shorn timbers sounded from below and Havelock shouted, 'The gate!' as a white blur galloped through the village towards the wall.

'Be ready for my shout!' yelled Leofric as he dropped from the parapet and onto the back of Aeneor. Leofric yelled an oath to the Lady, and rode into the gateway, where a dozen skeletons pushed through with spears lowered. He smashed their blades aside and bludgeoned them to splinters with the weight of his charge and the brutality of his sword blows.

Aeneor reared in the gateway before the advancing horde of the dead, Leofric's Blade of Midnight throwing off loops of white fire that reflected from the insides of the skulls of the warriors before him.

'Come on then, you dead bastards!' he shouted. 'I'll kill you for good this time!'

A shadow loomed beyond the gateway and he urged Aeneor onwards, leaping the splintered ruin of the gate and scattering the skeletal warriors before him. His sword cut skulls from necks and arms from shoulders as he cut a deadly swathe through the enemy, but beyond the press of bone and bronze at the gateway, he saw what he had been hoping for.

Mounted on his dark steed, the undead champion awaited him, the necromancer hunched in his shadow and dark coils of magic leaping from his wizened fingers.

'Carlomax! Havelock!' called Leofric. 'Now! Shoot!'

A pair of arrows leapt from the walls and hammered into the champion's breastplate, but the dead warrior appeared not to notice them.

'Not him!' shouted Leofric, but further words were impossible as the champion charged towards him, the eyes of his terrifying black steed burning with dreadful malice. Leofric knew his strength was not the equal of this warrior, but he was no man's inferior on horseback. He had toppled Chilfroy of Artois and would be damned if this creature of darkness was going to be the death of him.

The distance between the two warriors closed rapidly and Leofric swayed aside at the last possible second as the champion's sword struck to deal him a mortal blow. The Blade of Midnight turned aside the blow and Leofric lunged, the tip of the blade spearing the heart of the champion's obsidian amulet and splitting it apart with a hideous crack of thunder.

The champion gave a cry of fury as Aeneor turned on the spot and Leofric swept his sword out in a wide arc as a pair of arrows slashed through the air above him.

Even amid the clamour of battle and the screams of the dying, Leofric heard the thud of arrows striking flesh and the hollow clang as his sword smashed the undead champion's helmet and skull to shards.

The dark steed rode on for a moment before its substance began to unravel and it finally collapsed into a clattering pile of dead flesh and bones. The fallen champion was pitched from the saddle, his own form coming apart as the will that held him to the mortal world fled his ruined shell.

Leofric lifted his sword in victory as he saw the necromancer struggle to pull Carlomax and Havelock's arrows from his chest, but it was a futile gesture and Leofric watched as dissolution rendered his flesh down to naught but dust.

The sounds of battle began to fade and Leofric saw the undead horde begin to collapse before the walls of Derrevin Libre as the dark magic that empowered them faded from their long-dead bones.

He sighed in relief and felt his spirits rise as he realised that the night's horror was over.

The Battle for Derrevin Libre had been won.

'So what will you tell the duke of us, Leofric?' asked Carlomax as Leofric and Havelock prepared to ride from the village the following morning. Havelock's horse had been lost in the depths of the forest, but he had been furnished with one of the previous master of the village's prize steeds.

With the defeat of the undead, Leofric felt that the sky was clearer and he could smell the scent of wild flowers carried on the back of a delightfully crisp breeze.

Leofric considered the question for a moment before answering. 'I will tell him the truth.'

'And what is that?'

'That Derrevin Libre has no lord,' said Leofric. 'And that it might be better were it to be allowed to go on without one for a while.'

Carlomax nodded. 'Thank you, that is more than I would have asked for.'

'It won't change anything though,' warned Leofric. 'They *will* come with bared swords.'

'I know,' agreed Carlomax. 'But now we have a few battles under our belts and even if they do kill us all, what we achieved here will be spoken of for years. Even the mightiest forest fire begins with but a single spark…'

Leofric shook his head. 'Then Derrevin Libre will be freedom's home or glory's grave.'

He turned Aeneor for the southern horizon and said, 'And I do not know which one I fear the most.'

ABOUT THE AUTHOR

Graham McNeill has written more than twenty novels for Black Library. His Horus Heresy novel, *A Thousand Sons*, was a New York Times bestseller and his Time of Legends novel, *Empire*, won the 2010 David Gemmell Legend Award. Originally hailing from Scotland, Graham now lives and works in Nottingham.

WARHAMMER

DAN ABNETT

GILEAD'S
CURSE

NIK VINCENT

An extract from Gilead's Curse
by Dan Abnett and Nik Vincent

On sale now

Within a matter of weeks, as the days began to lengthen into a tired, pale form of spring, Gilead started to know who the enemy was and where he could be found. Whoever, whatever it was, clearly lacked Gilead's skills. It did not avoid detection by tracking. It appeared to return to the same haunts over and over again, approaching the town from the same direction, being spotted, or imagined in a small area close to where Gilead had entered the town for the first time. The best, most reliable of the rumours all came from the same road into Bortz.

The spectre was humanoid, although its dimensions were exaggerated by the hysteria that had grown up around it. Had it been another elf, Gilead would have felt its presence. It had to be human, or some humanoid monster.

There were reports of it drifting away at twilight. It was said to be pale, deathly and ethereal, while being a strong fighter, and there were rumours of an impressive steed of the kind a warrior might ride.

Gilead spent two days in the woods tracking the creature. Its prints were clearly made by feet that were long and slender, large for a human man, but certainly not inhuman. Gilead tracked the horse, too, more often ridden than led, although, in the heaviest, most overgrown acres of the wood, two tracks wove side by side between the trees. The ground was otherwise undisturbed; there was no digging for roots to eat. Gilead found only the pale, scrawny carcasses of meatless rodents, bloodless and papery.

It was night when Gilead knew that he was close. It was the smell. It was like the smell of humans, but older and more decayed. There was a smell of dry graves, sepulchral almost. There was a mingled scent of horse sweat, warm leather and grease. The earth smelt of a fire that had been lit and extinguished more than once, but which had cooked nothing, and of blankets used too often between laundering. Gilead almost mistook the whole for the smell of death, but human death did not smell like this, nor animal death, either. This was the antithesis of the death-smell.

Gilead ducked between the lowest branches of the trees that surrounded the tight, narrow area from which the smell emanated. He saw the horse first, tethered to a tree, its head at full stretch trying to reach fresh sources of grass to chew on. The horse looked up for the briefest of moments, and then bowed again to its purpose.

Confident the horse would raise no alarm, Gilead looked through the darkness beyond it to the curl of grey smoke that rose a foot or two above the tiny fire pit that shed the only light for miles. A figure sat bent before the fire, its back to Gilead, its silhouetted elbow working small circles as its hands performed some monotonous task.

Gilead drew the shorter of his blades. There was little enough room to fight hand to hand, and none to wield a sword. He wondered for a moment whether a fight was necessary. Could he not simply kill the man, quietly, while his back was turned? It was not the elf way. Gilead would stand face to face with any foe, believing that his greater skill and longer practice would lead to the defeat of any opponent he met in mortal combat.

He ducked under the last of the branches overhanging the space in the wood that hardly qualified as a glade, making no effort to quiet his footsteps. Gilead noticed the gleam of metal in the dim firelight. The creature was polishing a large piece of armour, a cuisse or a pauldron. A helmet, adorned with a battered plume, sat on one side of the figure, and he appeared to be wearing a mail headpiece, although his chest and back were covered in nothing more than a loose shirt.

As Gilead took another step, the war steed's head came up, and its ears flicked forwards. The figure sitting at the fireside turned towards Gilead, stepping swiftly to its feet. It dropped the polishing cloth, and bent slightly at the knees to lower to the ground the section of armour that it had been polishing, keeping its gaze on Gilead.

Their eyes locked, and Gilead knew, at last, that this man had transcended human mortality. It had been a man once, but was no longer constrained by the passage of time or the decaying of the mind or body. This sham of a man, this facsimile of a noble knight, had faced death and been reborn. It was, perhaps, as long-lived as Gilead, and might live longer than any elf, unless Gilead could put an end to it.

The first blow came fast and cruel as the knight turned, swinging one foot high and wide to connect with Gilead's shoulder. The knight had not removed his boots and a gleaming spur left a tight row of pinprick holes in the flesh of Gilead's arm. The elf had expected to land the first blow, but he was quick to react, and blocked the knight's kick just above the knee with his own foot, before too much damage was inflicted.

The knight was caught off-balance when the side of Gilead's foot landed squarely against the inside of his thigh, and he had to wheel sharply to bring himself squarely in front of Gilead for another attack. Gilead brought his knife up, and wove quick movements into his assailant's chest. The knight ducked and backed away from two of the passes, but a third made contact with the mail coif covering his head and neck, but for which, the blade would have sliced a convenient artery in the knight's neck.

The knight was strong and agile, and faster than any human,

and it had been some time since Gilead had done serious battle. He had spent a considerable amount of time fighting humans, but always from a defensive stance, never intending to mark or maim, let alone kill.

Gilead caught the knight's wrist as it propelled a roundhouse punch in his direction, but the knight was too quick, and twisted his fist, loosening the elf's grip. Then the knight turned his back so that Gilead was behind him, at close quarters, and drove an elbow up hard under the elf's ribs.

If Gilead had been human, that blow would have winded him and probably left him badly bruised with a couple of cracked ribs, but Gilead was not human.

Order the novel or download the eBook
from *blacklibrary.com*
Also available from

GAMES
WORKSHOP®

and all good bookstores